EX LIBRIS

VINTAGE CLASSICS

War and Peace

LEO TOLSTOY

War and Peace

TRANSLATED, ANNOTATED AND INTRODUCED BY
Richard Pevear and
Larissa Volokhonsky

VINTAGE BOOKS
London

Published by Vintage 2007

2 4 6 8 10 9 7 5 3 1

This translation of *War and Peace* has been made from the text in volumes 4–7 of the
Collected Works in Twenty Volumes by Leo Tolstoy, published by Goslitizdat
(Moscow, 1962)

Portions of this book originally appeared in *The Hudson Review*

First published in the United States by Alfred A. Knopf in 2007

First published in Great Britain by Vintage in 2007

Vintage
Random House, 20 Vauxhall Bridge Road,
London SW1V 2SA

www.vintage-classics.info

Addresses for companies within The Random House Group Limited can be found at:
www.randomhouse.co.uk/offices.htm

The Random House Group Limited Reg. No. 954009

A CIP catalogue record for this book
is available from the British Library

ISBN 9780099512233

The Random House Group Limited makes every effort to ensure that the papers used in
its books are made from trees that have been legally sourced from well-managed and
credibly certified forests. Our paper procurement policy can be found at:
www.randomhouse.co.uk/paper.htm

Printed and bound in Great Britain by
Clays Ltd, St Ives Plc

CONTENTS

INTRODUCTION

If the world could write by itself, it would write like Tolstoy.

— ISAAC BABEL

War and Peace is the most famous and at the same time the most daunting of Russian novels, as vast as Russia itself and as long to cross from one end to the other. Yet if one makes the journey, the sights seen and the people met on the way mark one's life for ever. The book is set in the period of the Napoleonic wars (1805–12) and tells of the interweaving of historical events with the private lives of two very different families of the Russian nobility—the severe Bolkonskys and the easygoing Rostovs—and of a singular man, reminiscent of the author himself—Count Pierre Bezukhov. It embodies the national myth of "Russia's glorious period," as Tolstoy himself called it, in the confrontation of the emperor Napoleon and Field Marshal Kutuzov, and at the same time it challenges that myth and all such myths through the vivid portrayal of the fates of countless ordinary people of the period, men and women, young and old, French as well as Russian, and through the author's own passionate questioning of the truth of history.

Tolstoy wrote that he "spent five years of ceaseless and exclusive labour, under the best conditions of life," working on *War and Peace*. Those were the years from 1863 to 1868. He was thirty-five when he began. The year before, he had married Sofya Behrs, the daughter of a Moscow doctor, who was eighteen, and they had moved permanently to his estate at Yasnaya Polyana, in Tula province, a hundred and twenty miles south of Moscow. She bore him four children while he worked on the book, was his first reader (or listener), and was in part the model for his heroine, Natasha Rostov.

The orderliness and routine of family life and estate management were not only the best conditions for work, they were also new conditions for Tolstoy. His mother had died when he was two. His father had moved to Moscow with the children in 1830, but died himself seven years later, and the children were eventually taken to Kazan by their aunt. Tolstoy entered Kazan University in 1844 but never graduated; his later attempts to pass examinations at Petersburg University also led to nothing. In 1851, after several years of idle and dissipated life in Moscow and Petersburg, he visited the Caucasus with his brother Nikolai, who was in the army, and there took part in a raid on a Chechen village, which he described a year later in a story entitled "The Raid," his first attempt to capture the actuality of warfare in words. His experiences in the Caucasus were also reflected in his novel *The Cossacks*, which he began writing in 1853 but finished only nine years later, and in his very last piece of fiction, the superb short novel *Hadji Murad*, completed in 1904 but published only posthumously.

In 1852, he joined the army as a noncommissioned officer and served in Wallachia. Two years later he was promoted to ensign and was transferred at his own request to the Crimea, where he fought in the Crimean War and was present at the siege of Sevastopol. His *Sevastopol Sketches*, which were published in 1855, made him famous in Petersburg social and literary circles. They were a second and fuller attempt at a true depiction of war.

During his army years, Tolstoy lived like a typical young Russian officer, drinking, gambling, and womanizing. In 1854 he lost the family house in Yasnaya Polyana at cards, and it was dismantled and moved some twenty miles away, leaving only a foundation stone on which Tolstoy later had carved: HERE STOOD THE HOUSE IN WHICH L. N. TOLSTOY WAS BORN. In 1856 he was promoted to lieutenant but resigned his commission and returned to the estate, where he lived in one of the surviving wings of the house and began to occupy himself with management and the education of the peasant children. By then, besides the works I have already mentioned, he had also published the semi-fictional trilogy *Childhood*, *Boyhood*, and *Youth*.

The years from 1857 to 1862 were a time of restlessness and seeking for Tolstoy. He had left Petersburg, disgusted by the literary life there. He made two trips abroad. During the first, in 1857, he forced himself to witness a public execution in Paris, and the sight shook him so deeply that he vowed he would never again serve any government. At the beginning of the second trip, in September 1860, he visited his beloved brother Nikolai, who was dying of tuberculosis in the southern French town of Hyères. The death and burial of his brother were, he said, "the strongest impression in my life." In 1861 he returned to Yasnaya Polyana, where he began work on a novel about the Decembrists, a group of young aristocrats and officers who, at the death of the emperor Alexander I in December 1825, rose up in the name of constitutional monarchy, were arrested and either executed or sent to Siberia. This novel would eventually become *War and Peace*.

Tolstoy himself later described the process of its transformation. At first he had wanted to write about a Decembrist on his return from Siberia in 1856, when the exiles were pardoned by Alexander II. In preparation for that, he went back to 1825, the year of the uprising itself, and from there to the childhood and youth of his hero and the others who took part in it. That brought him to the war of 1812, with which he became fascinated, and since those events were directly linked to events of 1805, it was there that he decided to begin. The original title, in the serial publication of the book, was *The Year*

1805; it was only in 1867 that he changed it to *War and Peace,* which he may
have borrowed from a work by the French socialist thinker Pierre-Joseph
Proudhon, whom he had met in Brussels during his second trip abroad.
All that remains of the Decembrists in the final version are some slight hints
about the futures of Pierre Bezukhov and of Prince Andrei Bolkonsky's son
Nikolenka.

The book grew organically as Tolstoy worked on it. In 1865, partly under
the influence of Stendhal's *Charterhouse of Parma,* he revised the battle scenes
he had already written and added new ones, including one of the most important, the description of the battle of Schöngraben. Coming across a collection
of Masonic texts in the library of the Rumyantsev Museum, he became interested and decided to make Pierre Bezukhov a Mason. He studied the people of
Moscow at the theatres, in the clubs, in the streets, looking for the types he
needed. A great many of his fictional characters, if not all of them, had real-life
models. The old Prince Bolkonsky and the old Count Rostov were drawn from
Tolstoy's grandfathers, Nikolai Rostov and Princess Marya from his parents,
Sonya from one of his aunts. The Rostov estate, Otradnoe, is a reflection of
Yasnaya Polyana. Tolstoy spent two days on the battlefield of Borodino and
made his own map of the disposition of forces, correcting the maps of the historians. He collected a whole library of materials on the Napoleonic wars,
many bits of which also found their way into the fabric of the book. His memory for historical minutiae was prodigious. But above all, there is the profusion
and precision of sensual detail that brings the world of *War and Peace* so
vividly to life. In his autobiographical sketch, *People and Situations* (1956),
Pasternak wrote of Tolstoy:

> All his life, at every moment, he possessed the faculty of seeing phenom-
> ena in the detached finality of each separate instant, in perfectly distinct
> outline, as we see only on rare occasions, in childhood, or on the crest of
> an all-renewing happiness, or in the triumph of a great spiritual victory.
>
> To see things like that, our eye must be directed by passion. For it is pas-
> sion that by its flash illuminates an object, intensifying its appearance.
>
> Such passion, the passion of creative contemplation, Tolstoy constantly
> carried within him. It was precisely in its light that he saw everything in its
> pristine freshness, in a new way, as if for the first time. The authenticity of
> what he saw differs so much from what we are used to that it may appear
> strange to us. But Tolstoy was not seeking that strangeness, was not pur-
> suing it as a goal, still less did he apply it to his works as a literary method.

I was struck, while working on the translation of *War and Peace,* by the
impression that I was translating two books at the same time. Not two books
in alternation, as one might expect from the title, but two books simultaneously. One is a very deliberate and self-conscious work, expressive of the out-

size personality of its author, who is everywhere present, selecting and manipulating events, and making his own absolute pronouncements on them: "On the twelfth of June, the forces of Western Europe crossed the borders of Russia, and war began—that is, an event took place contrary to human reason and to the whole of human nature." It is a work full of provocation and irony, and written in what might be called Tolstoy's signature style, with broad and elaborately developed rhetorical devices—periodic structure, emphatic repetitions, epic similes. The other is an account of all that is most real and ordinary in life, all that is most fragile and therefore most precious, all that eludes formulation, that is not subject to absolute pronouncements, that is so mercurial that it can hardly be reflected upon, and can be grasped only by a rare quality of attention and self-effacement. And it is written in a style that reaches the expressive minimum of a sentence like *Kápli kápali*, "Drops dripped"—which makes silence itself audible. It seems to me that the incomparable experience of reading *War and Peace* comes from the shining of the one work through the other—an effect achieved by artistic means of an unusual sort.

The first thing a reader today must overcome is the notion of *War and Peace* as a classic, the greatest of novels, and the model of what a novel should be. In 1954, Bertolt Brecht wrote a note on "Classical Status as an Inhibiting Factor" that puts the question nicely. "What gets lost," he says of the bestowing of classical status on a work (he is speaking of works for the theatre), "is the classic's original freshness, the element of surprise . . . of newness, of productive stimulus that is the hallmark of such works. The passionate quality of a great masterpiece is replaced by stage temperament, and where the classics are full of fighting spirit, here the lessons taught the audience are tame and cozy and fail to grip."

The first readers of *War and Peace* were certainly surprised, but often also bewildered and even dismayed by the book. They found it hard to identify the main characters, to discover anything like a plot, to see any connection between episodes, to understand the sudden leaps from fiction to history, from narration to philosophizing. There seemed to be no focus, no artistic unity to the work, no real beginning, and no resolution. It was as if the sheer mass of detail overwhelmed any design Tolstoy might have tried to impose on it. Such observations were made by Russian critics, including Tolstoy's great admirer, Ivan Turgenev, and when the book became known in translation, they were repeated by Flaubert and by Henry James, who famously described *War and Peace* as a "large loose baggy monster."

Another cause of surprise for its first readers was the language of *War and Peace*. The book opens in French—not with a few words of French (as in those English versions that do not eliminate the French altogether), but with a whole paragraph of French, with only a few phrases of Russian at the end. This mixing of French and Russian goes on for another five chapters or more, and occurs frequently throughout the rest of the book. There are also some long letters entirely in French, as well as official dispatches, and quotations from the French historian Adolphe Thiers. There are passages in German as well. For all of them Tolstoy supplied his own translations in footnotes, as we do. But that made the question still more problematic, because Tolstoy's translations are occasionally inaccurate, perhaps deliberately so. The amount of French in the text is smaller than some early critics asserted—not a third, but only about two per cent. But there is also a great deal of gallicized Russian, either implying that the speaker is speaking in French, or showing that upper-class ladies like Julie Karagin are unable to write correctly in their own language. And there are other heterogeneous elements in the composition: Tolstoy's map and commentary on the battlefield of Borodino, and his own interpolated essays, which repeatedly disrupt the fictional continuum.

The formal structure of *War and Peace* and the texture of its prose are indeed strange. Those who did not simply declare the book a failure, dismissing the newness, the "passionate quality" and "fighting spirit" of what Tolstoy was doing as artistic helplessness and naïveté, often said that it succeeded in spite of its artistic flaws. But that is a false distinction. *War and Peace* is a work of art, and if it succeeds, it cannot be in spite of its formal deficiencies, but only because Tolstoy created a new form that was adequate to his vision.

It is equally mistaken to go to the other extreme and declare, as more recent critics have done, that, far from being a magnificent failure, *War and Peace* is a masterpiece of nineteenth-century realism, simple and artless, a direct transcription of life. Tolstoy was well aware of the perplexities his book caused and addressed them in an article (included here as an appendix) entitled "A Few Words Apropos of the Book *War and Peace*," published in the magazine *Russian Archive* in 1868, before the final parts of the book had appeared in print. "What is *War and Peace*?" he asked.

> It is not a novel, still less an epic poem, still less a historical chronicle. *War and Peace* is what the author wanted and was able to express, in the form in which it is expressed. Such a declaration of the author's disregard of the conventional forms of artistic prose works might seem presumptuous, if it were premeditated and if it had no previous examples. The history of Russian literature since Pushkin's time not only provides many examples of such departure from European forms, but does not offer even one example to the contrary. From Gogol's *Dead Souls* to Dostoevsky's *Dead House,* there is not a single work of artistic prose of the modern period of Russian literature, rising slightly above mediocrity, that would fit perfectly into the form of the novel, the epic, or the story.

Two things in this passage are especially characteristic of Tolstoy: first, the negative definition of the genre; and second, the assertion that his departure from artistic convention was not premeditated. Both might be taken as disingenuous, but I do not think they are. Tolstoy was trying to express something which, to his mind, had never been expressed before, and which therefore required a new form that could only define itself as he worked. By excluding the known forms of extended narrative, he leaves an empty place in which an as yet unknown form, indefinable and unnameable, may appear. (He uses the same negative method throughout *War and Peace* itself.) But this procedure was not premeditated—that is, as Pasternak rightly said, it was not a literary method, not a play with form for its own sake in the modernist sense. He found it necessary for the task he had set himself.

What was that task? What was it that Tolstoy "wanted to express" in his book, which he deliberately does not call a novel? Boris de Schloezer, a fine critic and philosopher, wrote in the preface to his French translation of *War and Peace* (1960) that Tolstoy's one aim, from the beginning, was "to speak the truth" as perceived by his eye and his conscience. "All the forces of his imagination, his power of evocation and expression, converge on that one single goal. Outside any other religious or moral considerations, Tolstoy when he writes obeys one imperative, which is the foundation of what one might call his literary ethic. That imperative is not imposed on the artist by the moralist, it is the voice of the artist himself." As early as the sketch "Sevastopol in May" of 1855, Tolstoy had asserted, "My hero is truth." In *War and Peace* he wanted to speak the truth about a certain period of Russian life—the period of the Napoleonic wars of 1805 to 1812. He wanted to say, not how that period could be made to appear in a beautiful lie, an entertaining or instructive story, a historical narrative, but how it was. He wanted to capture in words what happened the way it happened. But how does happening happen? How can words express it without falsifying it? How can one capture the past once it is past? These were questions that Tolstoy constantly brooded on. He had already posed them for himself in 1851, in his very first literary work, the fragment "A History of Yesterday." The composition of *War and Peace* was his fullest response to them.

Poète et non honnête homme, wrote Pascal, meaning that a poet cannot be an honest man. Tolstoy fully agreed with Pascal; he tried all his life to be *honnête homme et non poète.* Nabokov, in his lecture notes on *Anna Karenina,* speaks of "Tolstoy's style with its readiness to admit any robust awkwardness if that is the shortest way to sense." Yet Tolstoy found that the truth could not be approached directly, that every attempt at direct expression became a simplification and therefore a lie, and that the "shortest way to sense" was rather long and indirect. He was acutely aware of the inadequacy of all human means of speaking the truth, but his artistic intuition told him that those means might be composed in such a way as to allow the truth to appear. Against his will, he found that to be an honest man he had to be a poet.

In the fifth section of "A Few Words," Tolstoy freely embraces that role, discussing the differences between the historian and the artist. "A historian and an artist, describing a historical epoch, have two completely different objects . . . For a historian, considering the contribution rendered by some person towards a certain goal, there are heroes; for the artist, considering the correspondence of this person to all sides of life, there cannot and should not be any heroes, but there should be people." And further on: "A historian has to do with the results of an event, the artist with the fact of the event." And again: "The difference between the results obtained is explained by the sources from which the two draw their information. For the historian (we continue the example of a battle), the main source is the reports of individual commanders and the commander in chief. The artist can draw nothing from such sources, they tell him nothing, explain nothing. Moreover, the artist turns away from them, finding in them a necessary falsehood." Neither here nor elsewhere, however, does Tolstoy say what sources the artist does draw from. To compound the problem, he says at the end of the same section: "But the artist should not forget that the notion of historical figures and events formed among people is based not on fantasy, but on historical documents, insofar as historians have been able to amass them; and therefore, while understanding and presenting these figures and events differently, the artist ought to be guided, like the historian, by historical materials." The difference lies not in the figures and events that are seen, but in the way of seeing them: the artist sees not heroes but people, not results but facts, and considers a person not in terms of a goal, but "in correspondence to all sides of life"—with what Pasternak calls "the passion of creative contemplation," which Tolstoy wisely avoids defining.

This leads to a crucial if paradoxical reversal: the most real and even, in Tolstoy's sense, historical figures in *War and Peace* turn out to be the fictional ones; and the most unreal, the most insubstantial and futile, the historical ones.* Tolstoy undermines the idea of significant action, though it was the foundation of virtually all narrative before him. He does not say that all action is insignificant, but that the only significant actions are the insignificant ones, whose meaning lies elsewhere, not in the public space but in absolute solitude. For Prince Andrei there *is* something in the infinite sky above him, but it is not a general idea, and he is unable to communicate it to anyone else. In her comparison of Homer and Tolstoy (*On the Iliad*, translated by Mary McCarthy, New York, 1947), Rachel Bespaloff wrote: "Great common truths are disclosed to man only when he is alone: they are the revelation made by solitude in the thick of collective action." Tolstoy grants this intimate but immense reality to each of his major characters, and to many of the minor ones (who then

---

*The great exception to this rule is Field Marshal Kutuzov, who for Tolstoy is "historical" in both senses of the word and thus becomes a touchstone figure in the book.

cease to be minor). Yet there is nothing very remarkable about these characters. Turgenev complained that they were all mediocrities, and in a sense he
was right. They are ordinary men and women. Tolstoy was aware of that; it
was what he intended. As Rachel Bespaloff observed: "Tolstoy's universe, like
Homer's, is what our own is from moment to moment. We don't step into it;
we are there."

*   *   *

A few words about translation and this translation.

It is often said that a good translation is one that "does not feel like a translation," one that reads "smoothly" in "idiomatic" English. But who determines the standard of the idiomatic, and why should it be applied to something
so idiolectic as a great work of literature? Is Melville idiomatic? Is Faulkner? Is
Beckett? Those who raise the question of the "idiomatic" in translation do not
seem to realize that they are imposing their own, often very narrow, limits on
the original. A translator who turns a great original into a patchwork of ready-
made "contemporary" phrases, with no regard for its particular tone, rhythm,
or character, and claims that that is "how Tolstoy would have written today in
English," betrays both English and Tolstoy. Translation is not the transfer of a
detachable "meaning" from one language to another, for the simple reason
that in literature there is no meaning detachable from the words that express it.
Translation is a dialogue between two languages. It occurs in a space between
two languages, and most often between two historical moments. Much of the
real value of translation as an art comes from that unique situation. It is not
exclusively the language of arrival or the time of the translator and reader that
should be privileged. We all know, in the case of *War and Peace,* that we are
reading a nineteenth-century Russian novel. That fact allows the twenty-first-
century translator a different range of possibilities than may exist for a twenty-
first-century writer. It allows for the enrichment of the translator's own language, rather than the imposition of his language on the original.

To move from that fertile ground towards either extreme—that is, towards
interlinear literalness or total accommodation to the new language—is to lose
the possibilities that exist only in the space between two times and languages.
Tolstoy's prose has been much praised and much criticized. He scorned fine
writers, calling them "hairdressers," yet we know from the many drafts he preserved that he constantly worked over his texts, revising and refining them,
bringing them closer to what he wanted to express. Tolstoy's prose is an artistic medium; it is all of a piece; it is not good or bad Russian prose, it is Tol-
stoyan prose. What the translator should seek in his own language is the
equivalent of that specific artistic medium. He must have the freedom in his
own language to be faithful to the original.

In *Tolstoy: A Critical Introduction* (Cambridge, 1969), R. H. Christian says: "From the point of view of language and style, Tolstoy has been better served by his translators than many of his fellow-countrymen. Nevertheless, standards fall a long way short of perfection. Clumsiness and *simplesse* apart, no English version of *War and Peace* has succeeded in conveying the power, balance, rhythm and above all the repetitiveness of the original. Perhaps it is repetition which is the most characteristic single feature of Tolstoy's prose style." He illustrates his point with two passages, the second of which, in our translation, reads as follows (italics added):

> . . . thought Prince Andrei, waiting among many significant and insignificant persons in Count Arakcheev's *anteroom.*
>
> During his service, mostly as an adjutant, Prince Andrei had seen many *anterooms* of significant persons, and the differing characters of these *anterooms* were very clear to him. Count Arakcheev's *anteroom* had a completely special character. The insignificant persons waiting in line for an audience in Count Arakcheev's *anteroom* . . .

Without mentioning the parallel play on "significant and insignificant persons," Christian notes that the Russian word *priémnaya* ("anteroom") recurs five times in as many lines, and that the Maude translation (1927) glosses over that fact by omitting the word once and using three different words for the rest. I will add that in Ann Dunnigan's translation (1968) the repetitions are treated in exactly the same way as in the Maudes'; that Anthony Briggs, in his 2005 version, omits the repeated word twice and varies it twice; while Constance Garnett (1904) omits it once, but otherwise keeps the repetitions. This passage is a fairly restrained example of what I have called Tolstoy's "signature style," but it does illustrate how the balance and rhythm of his prose depend on repetition. These qualities are lost when the general principle of avoiding repetitions is mechanically applied to it. Tolstoy also had a fondness for larger rhetorical structures based on repeated triads of nouns, verbs, adjectives, and so on. We have made it a point to keep his repetitions, as well as other devices of formal rhetoric (for instance, chiasmus) that Tolstoy consciously used and that his translators have often ignored. Tolstoy once boasted that in writing *War and Peace* he had used every rhetorical device of the old Latin grammarians, which means they are not there by chance.

The other extreme of Tolstoy's style is exemplified by the short sentence (the shortest in *War and Peace*) that I have already quoted: "Drops dripped." It is the first sentence of a paragraph made up of four brief, staccato sentences, four quite ordinary observations, which acquire a lyrical intensity owing solely to the sound and rhythm of the words: *Kápli kápali. Shyól tíkhii góvor. Lóshadi zarzháli i podrális. Khrapél któ-to.* "Drops dripped. Quiet talk went on. Horses neighed and scuffled. Someone snored." It is a night scene, and one of the most haunting moments in the book. Other English versions translate the first sentence as "The branches dripped," "The trees were dripping," or, closer to the Russian, "Raindrops dripped." They all state a fact instead of rendering a sound, which (by a stroke of translator's luck) comes out almost the same in English as in Russian.

Here is another example of the same stylistic compactness, this time expressing a psychological insight rather than a sense impression. It describes the moment when Natasha, who has almost cut herself off from all life, suddenly has to take care of her grief-stricken mother. Tolstoy says simply: *Prosnúlas lyubóv, i prosnúlas zhízn.* "Love awoke, and life awoke." All that Tolstoy leaves unsaid about Natasha's inner life in these few words is implied by their very matter-of-factness, expressed in the exact rhetorical balance of the phrasing. Other English versions read: "Love was awakened, and life waked with it," "Love awoke, and so did life," or "When love reawakened, life reawakened." They convey the same general meaning, but hardly the same sense as the original.

A final example. Tolstoy describes children playing in their room when their mother comes in: *Dyéti na stúlyakh yékhali v Moskvú i priglasíli yeyó s sobóyu.* "The children were riding to Moscow on chairs and invited her to go with them." To translate the first phrase as "The children were sitting on chairs playing at driving to Moscow," or "The children were playing at 'going to Moscow' in a carriage made of chairs," or "The children were perched on chairs playing at driving to Moscow," as has been done, is to miss both the rhythm and the point. The charm of Tolstoy's sentence comes from the fact that he does not explain in an adult way what the children are doing; he enters into the spirit of their game by the phrasing he uses to describe it, and the whole atmosphere of the moment is suddenly there, naïve, natural, and alive.

I do not mean to suggest that Tolstoy calculated these effects. They are not "effects" at all, they are what he saw and felt, as he wanted and was able to express it. But to translate what he saw and felt, one must also translate, as far as possible, the way it is expressed. These examples will give at least an idea of how we have gone about that task. We have kept all the French and German as Tolstoy had it, as well as the mixed voicings, the Gallicisms, Germanisms and implied foreign accents, as they play throughout the book. We have tried to be true to Tolstoy's rhetorical power, his sharp irony, and his astonishing delicacy.

— RICHARD PEVEAR

PRINCIPAL CHARACTERS

Russian names are composed of first name, patronymic (from the father's first name), and family name. Formal address requires the use of first name and patronymic; diminutives are commonly used among family and friends and are for the most part endearing, though in a certain blunt form (Katka for Katerina, Mitka for Dmitri) they can be rude or dismissive; the family name alone can also be used familiarly or casually, and on occasion only the patronymic is used, usually among the lower classes. In speech, the patronymic can also take a shortened form: Andreich instead of Andreevich, or Kirilych instead of Kirillovich. The accented syllables of Russian names are long, the others very short. We also give the French forms of first names as Tolstoy uses them.

BEZÚKHOV, COUNT KIRÍLL VLADÍMIROVICH
   COUNT PYÓTR KIRÍLLOVICH or KIRÍLYCH (Pierre), his son
   PRINCESS KATERÍNA SEMYÓNOVNA (Catiche), his niece

BOLKÓNSKY, PRINCE NIKOLÁI ANDRÉEVICH or ANDRÉICH
   PRINCE ANDRÉI NIKOLÁEVICH (Andryúsha, André), his son
   PRINCESS MÁRYA NIKOLÁEVNA (Másha, Máshenka, Marie), his
     daughter
   PRINCESS ELIZAVÉTA KÁRLOVNA, née Meinen (Líza, Lizavéta, Lise), the
     "little princess," Prince Andrei's wife
   PRINCE NIKOLÁI ANDRÉEVICH (Nikólushka, Nikólenka, Coco),
     their son

ROSTÓV, COUNT ILYÁ ANDRÉEVICH or ANDRÉICH (Élie)
   COUNTESS NATÁLYA (no patronymic) (Natalie), his wife
   COUNTESS VÉRA ILYÍNICHNA (Verúshka, Vérochka), their elder
     daughter
   COUNT NIKOLÁI ILYÍCH (Nikólushka, Nikólenka, Nikoláshka, Kólya,
     Nicolas, Coco), their elder son
   COUNTESS NATÁLYA ILYÍNICHNA (Natásha, Natalie), their younger
     daughter
   COUNT PYÓTR ILYÍCH (Pétya, Petrúsha), their younger son
   SÓFYA ALEXÁNDROVNA (no family name) (Sónya, Sophie), orphaned
     cousin of the younger Rostovs

KURÁGIN, PRINCE VASSÍLY SERGÉEVICH
  PRINCE ANATÓLE VASSÍLIEVICH, his elder son
  PRINCE IPPOLÍT VASSÍLIEVICH (Hippolyte), his younger son
  PRINCESS ELÉNA VASSÍLIEVNA (Lélya, Hélène), his daughter

DRUBETSKÓY, PRINCESS ÁNNA MIKHÁILOVNA
  PRINCE BORÍS (no patronymic) (Bórya, Bórenka), her son

AKHROSÍMOV, MÁRYA DMÍTRIEVNA, Moscow society matron

ALPÁTYCH, YÁKOV (no family name), steward of the Bolkonsky estates

BAZDÉEV, ÓSIP (IÓSIF) ALEXÉEVICH, an important figure in the Masons

BERG, ALPHÓNSE KÁRLOVICH or KÁRLYCH (later called Adólf), a young
  Russian officer

BOURIÉNNE, AMÁLIA EVGÉNIEVNA (Amélie, Bourriénka), Princess
  Marya's French companion

DENÍSOV, VASSÍLY DMÍTRICH (Váska), a hussar officer, friend of Nikolai
  Rostov

DÓLOKHOV, FYÓDOR IVÁNOVICH (Fédya), a Russian officer

KARÁGIN, JULIE (no Russian first name or patronymic), a wealthy heiress

KARATÁEV, PLATÓN, peasant foot soldier befriended by Pierre Bezukhov

LAVRÚSHKA (no patronymic or family name), Denisov's and later Nikolai
  Rostov's orderly

SCHÉRER, ÁNNA PÁVLOVNA (Annette), hostess of an aristocratic salon in
  Petersburg

TÍKHON (no patronymic or family name) (Tíshka), old Prince Bolkonsky's
  personal manservant

TÚSHIN (no first name or patronymic), captain of Russian artillery at the
  battle of Schöngraben

WILLÁRSKI (no first name or patronymic), Polish count and Mason

VOLUME I

Part One

I

"Eh bien, mon prince, Gênes et Lucques ne sont plus que des apanages, des estates, *de la famille Buonaparte.*[1] *Non, je vous préviens, que si vous ne me dites pas que nous avons la guerre, si vous vous permettez encore de pallier toutes les infamies, toutes les atrocités de cet Antichrist (ma parole, j'y crois)—je ne vous connais plus, vous n'êtes plus mon ami, vous n'êtes plus* my faithful slave, *comme vous dites.* Well, good evening, good evening. *Je vois que je vous fais peur,* sit down and tell me about it."*

So spoke, in July 1805, the renowned Anna Pavlovna Scherer, maid of honour and intimate of the empress Maria Feodorovna, greeting the important and high-ranking Prince Vassily, the first to arrive at her soirée. Anna Pavlovna had been coughing for several days. She had the *grippe,* as she put it (*grippe* was a new word then, used only by rare people). Little notes had been sent out that morning with a red-liveried footman, and on all of them without distinction there was written:

Si vous n'avez rien de mieux à faire, Monsieur le comte (or mon prince), et si la perspective de passer la soirée chez une pauvre malade ne vous effraye pas trop, je serai charmée de vous voir chez moi entre 7 et 10 heures.[†]

Annette Scherer.

"Dieu, quelle virulente sortie!"[‡] the entering prince replied, not ruffled in the least by such a reception. He was wearing an embroidered court uniform, stockings, shoes, and stars, and had a bright expression on his flat face.

He spoke that refined French in which our grandparents not only spoke but thought, and with those quiet, patronizing intonations which are proper to a significant man who has grown old in society and at court. He went over to

---

*Well, my prince, Genoa and Lucca are now no more than possessions, *estates,* of the Buonaparte family. No, I warn you, if you do not tell me we are at war, if you still allow yourself to palliate all the infamies, all the atrocities of that Antichrist (upon my word, I believe it)—I no longer know you, you are no longer my friend, you are no longer . . . as you say . . . I see that I'm frightening you . . .

†If you have nothing better to do, Monsieur the Count (*or* My Prince), and if the prospect of spending the evening with a poor sick woman does not frighten you too much, I shall be delighted to see you here between 7 and 10 o'clock.

‡God, what a virulent outburst!

Anna Pavlovna, kissed her hand, presenting her with his perfumed and shining bald pate, and settled comfortably on the sofa.

"*Avant tout dites-moi, comment vous allez, chère amie.** Set me at ease," he said, without changing his voice and in a tone in which, through propriety and sympathy, one could discern indifference and even mockery.

"How can one be well . . . when one suffers morally? Is it possible to remain at ease in our time, if one has any feeling?" said Anna Pavlovna. "You'll stay the whole evening, I hope?"

"And the fête at the British ambassador's? Today is Wednesday. I must put in an appearance," said the prince. "My daughter will come to fetch me and take me there."

"I thought today's fête was cancelled. *Je vous avoue que toutes ces fêtes et tous ces feux d'artifice commencent à devenir insipides.*"†

"If they had known that you wished it, the fête would have been cancelled," said the prince, uttering out of habit, like a wound-up clock, things that he did not even wish people to believe.

"*Ne me tourmentez pas. Eh bien, qu'a-t-on décidé par rapport à la dépêche de Novosilzoff?*² *Vous savez tout.*"‡

"What can I tell you?" said the prince, in a cold, bored tone. "*Qu'a-t-on décidé? On a décidé que Buonaparte a brûlé ses vaisseaux, et je crois que nous sommes en train de brûler les nôtres.*"§

Prince Vassily always spoke lazily, the way an actor speaks a role in an old play. Anna Pavlovna Scherer, on the contrary, despite her forty years, was brimming with animation and impulses.

Being an enthusiast had become her social position, and she sometimes became enthusiastic even when she had no wish to, so as not to deceive the expectations of people who knew her. The restrained smile that constantly played on Anna Pavlovna's face, though it did not suit her outworn features, expressed, as it does in spoiled children, a constant awareness of her dear shortcoming, which she did not wish, could not, and found no need to correct.

In the midst of a conversation about political doings, Anna Pavlovna waxed vehement.

"Ah, don't speak to me of Austria! Maybe I don't understand anything, but Austria does not want and has never wanted war. She's betraying us.³ Russia alone must be the saviour of Europe. Our benefactor knows his lofty calling and will be faithful to it. That is the one thing I trust in. Our kind and wonderful

---

*Before all, tell me how you are doing, my dear friend.

†I confess to you that all these fêtes and all these fireworks are beginning to become insipid.

‡Don't torment me. Well, what has been decided in connection with Novosiltsov's dispatch? You know everything.

§What has been decided? It has been decided that Bonaparte has burned his boats, and I believe that we are in the process of burning ours.

sovereign is faced with the greatest role in the world, and he is so virtuous and good that God will not abandon him, and he will fulfil his calling to crush the hydra of revolution, which has now become still more terrible in the person of this murderer and villain. We alone must redeem the blood of the righteous one.[4] In whom can we trust, I ask you? . . . England with her commercial spirit will not and cannot understand all the loftiness of the emperor Alexander's soul. She refused to evacuate Malta.[5] She wants to see, she searches for ulterior motives in our acts. What did they say to Novosiltsov? Nothing. They did not, they could not understand the self-denial of our emperor, who wants nothing for himself and everything for the good of the world. And what have they promised? Nothing. And what they did promise will not be done! Prussia has already declared that Bonaparte is invincible and that all Europe can do nothing against him . . . And I don't believe a single word of Hardenberg or of Haugwitz.[6] *Cette fameuse neutralité prussienne, ce n'est qu'un piège.** I trust only in God and in the lofty destiny of our dear emperor. He will save Europe! . . ." She suddenly stopped with a mocking smile at her own vehemence.

"I think," the prince said, smiling, "that if they sent you instead of our dear Wintzingerode, you would take the Prussian king's consent by storm.[7] You're so eloquent! Will you give me tea?"

"At once. *À propos*," she added, calming down again, "I'll have two very interesting men here tonight, *le vicomte de Mortemart, il est allié aux Montmorency par les Rohan,†* one of the best French families. He's one of the good émigrés,[8] one of the real ones. And then *l'abbé Morio‡*—do you know that profound mind? He's been received by the sovereign. Do you know him?"

"Ah! I'll be very glad," said the prince. "Tell me," he added, as if just recalling something and with special casualness, though what he asked about was the main purpose of his visit, "is it true that *l'impératrice-mère§* wants Baron Funke to be named first secretary in Vienna? *C'est un pauvre sire, ce baron, à ce qu'il paraît.*#" Prince Vassily wanted his son to be appointed to this post, which, through the empress Maria Feodorovna, had been solicited for the baron.

Anna Pavlovna all but closed her eyes as a sign that neither she nor anyone else could judge of the empress's good pleasure or liking.

"*Monsieur le baron de Funke a été recommandé à l'impératrice-mère par sa soeur,*"** she merely said in a sad, dry tone. The moment Anna Pavlovna mentioned the empress, her face suddenly presented a profound and sincere

---

*This famous Prussian neutrality is nothing but a trap.
†The viscount of Mortemart, he is allied to the Montmorency family through the Rohans.
‡The abbot Morio.
§The dowager empress.
#He's a poor fellow, this baron, so it seems.
**Monsieur the baron of Funke was recommended to the dowager empress by her sister.

expression of devotion and respect, combined with sadness, which happened each time she referred to her exalted patroness in conversation. She said that her majesty had deigned to show Baron Funke *beaucoup d'estime,** and her eyes again clouded over with sadness.

The prince lapsed into indifferent silence. Anna Pavlovna, with her courtly and feminine adroitness and ready tact, wanted both to swat the prince for daring to make such a pronouncement about a person recommended to the empress, and at the same time to comfort him.

"*Mais à propos de votre famille,*" she said, "do you know that your daughter, since her coming out, *fait les délices de tout le monde? On la trouve belle, comme le jour.*"†

The prince bowed in a sign of respect and gratitude.

"I often think," Anna Pavlovna went on after a moment's silence, moving closer to the prince and smiling tenderly at him, as if to show thereby that the political and social conversations were at an end and a heart-to-heart one was beginning, "I often think how unfairly life's good fortune is sometimes distributed. Why has fate given you two such nice children (excluding Anatole, your youngest, I don't like him)," she put in peremptorily, raising her eyebrows, "such lovely children? And you really value them less than anyone and are therefore unworthy of them."

And she smiled her rapturous smile.

"*Que voulez-vous? Lavater aurait dit que je n'ai pas la bosse de la paternité,*"‡ said the prince.

"Stop joking. I wanted to talk seriously with you. You know, I'm displeased with your younger son. Just between us," her face acquired a sad look, "there was talk about him at her majesty's, and you were pitied . . ."

The prince did not reply, but she fell silent, looking at him significantly, waiting for a reply. Prince Vassily winced.

"What am I to do?" he said finally. "You know, I did all a father could for their upbringing, and they both turned out *des imbéciles.* Ippolit is at least an untroublesome fool, but Anatole is a troublesome one. That's the only difference," he said, smiling more unnaturally and animatedly than usual, and with that showing especially clearly in the wrinkles that formed around his mouth something unexpectedly coarse and disagreeable.

"Ah, why do such people as you have children? If you weren't a father, I'd have nothing to reproach you for," said Anna Pavlovna, raising her eyes pensively.

"*Je suis votre* faithful slave, *et à vous seule je puis l'avouer.* My children—

---

*Much respect.
†But apropos of your family . . . has been the delight of everyone. They find her beautiful as the day.
‡What do you want? Lavater would have said that I lack the bump of paternity.

*ce sont les entraves de mon existence.** That's my cross. I explain it that way to myself. *Que voulez-vous? . . .*" He paused, expressing with a gesture his submission to cruel fate.

Anna Pavlovna fell to thinking.

"Have you never thought of getting your prodigal son Anatole married? They say," she observed, "that old maids *ont la manie des marriages.*† I don't feel I have that weakness yet, but I know one *petite personne* who is very unhappy with her father, *une parente à nous, une princesse* Bolkonsky."‡ Prince Vassily did not reply, though, with the quickness of grasp and memory characteristic of society people, he showed by a nod of the head that he had taken this information into account.

"No, you know, this Anatole costs me forty thousand a year," he said, obviously unable to restrain the melancholy course of his thoughts. He paused.

"How will it be in five years, if it goes on like this? *Voilà l'avantage d'être père.*§ Is she rich, this princess of yours?"

"Her father is very rich and stingy. He lives in the country. You know, it's the famous Prince Bolkonsky,⁹ already retired under the late emperor and nicknamed 'the King of Prussia.' He's a very intelligent man, but an odd and difficult one. *La pauvre petite est malheureuse comme les pierres.*# She has a brother, Kutuzov's adjutant, the one who recently married Lise Meinen. He'll come tonight."

"*Écoutez, chère Annette,*" said the prince, suddenly taking his interlocutor by the hand and pulling it down for some reason. "*Arrangez-moi cette affaire et je suis votre* faithful slave *à tout jamais* (slafe—*comme mon* village headman *écrit des* reports: *f* instead of *v*).** She's from a good family and rich. That's all I need."

And with those free and familiarly graceful movements which distinguished him, he took the maid of honour's hand, kissed it, and, having kissed it, waved the maid-of-honourly hand a little, sprawled himself in an armchair, and looked away.

"*Attendez,*" Anna Pavlovna said, pondering. "Tonight I'll discuss it with Lise *(la femme du jeune* Bolkonsky*)*. And maybe something can be settled. *Ce sera dans votre famille que je ferai mon apprentissage de vielle fille.*"††

---

*I am your . . . and to you alone can I confess it . . . they are the fetters of my existence.
†Have a mania for marriages.
‡Little person . . . a relation of ours, a princess *Bolkonsky.*
§There's the advantage of being a father.
#The poor little thing is as unhappy as can be.
**Listen, dear Annette . . . Arrange this business for me and I am your . . . for ever (. . . as my . . . writes me in . . .).
††Wait . . . Liza (the wife of young *Bolkonsky*) . . . It will be in your family that I serve my apprenticeship as an old maid.

II

Anna Pavlovna's drawing room gradually began to fill up. The high nobility of Petersburg came, people quite diverse in age and character, but alike in the society they lived in. Prince Vassily's daughter, the beautiful Hélène, came to fetch her father and go with him to the fête at the ambassador's. She was wearing a ball gown with a monogram.[10] The young little princess Bolkonsky, known as *la femme la plus séduisante de Pétersbourg*,* also came; married the previous winter, she did not go into *high* society now for reason of her pregnancy, but did still go to small soirées. Prince Ippolit, Prince Vassily's son, came with Mortemart, whom he introduced; the abbé Morio also came, and many others.

"Have you seen yet" or "have you made the acquaintance of *ma tante?*"† Anna Pavlovna said to the arriving guests, and led them quite seriously to a little old lady in high ribbons, who had come sailing out of the next room as soon as the guests began to arrive, called them by name, slowly shifting her gaze from the guest to *ma tante*, and then walked away.

All the guests performed the ritual of greeting the totally unknown, totally uninteresting and unnecessary aunt. With sad, solemn sympathy, Anna Pavlovna followed their greetings, silently approving of them. To each of them *ma tante* spoke in the same expressions about his health, her own health, and the health of her majesty, which, thank God, was better that day. All those who went up to her, showing no haste for propriety's sake, left the little old lady with a feeling of relief after the fulfilment of a heavy obligation, never to approach her again all evening.

The young princess Bolkonsky came with handwork in a gold-embroidered velvet bag. Her pretty upper lip with its barely visible black moustache was too short for her teeth, but the more sweetly did it open and still more sweetly did it sometimes stretch and close on the lower one. As happens with perfectly attractive women, her flaw—a short lip and half-opened mouth—seemed her special, personal beauty. Everyone felt cheerful looking at this pretty future mother full of health and liveliness, who bore her condition so easily. To old men and to bored, morose young ones it seemed that they themselves came to resemble her, having been with her and spoken with her for a time. Anyone who talked with her and saw her bright little smile at every word and her gleaming white teeth, which showed constantly, thought himself especially amiable that day. And that is what each of them thought.

*The most seductive woman of Petersburg.
†My aunt.

The little princess, waddling, went round the table with small, quick steps, her bag of handwork hanging on her arm, and, cheerfully straightening her dress, sat down on the sofa near the silver samovar, looking as though everything she did was a *partie de plaisir** for her and for everyone around her.

"*J'ai apporté mon ouvrage,*"† she said, unclasping her reticule and addressing them all together.

"Look, Annette, *ne me jouez pas un mauvais tour,*" she turned to the hostess. "*Vouz m'avez écrit que c'était une toute petite soirée; voyez comme je suis attifée.*"‡

And she spread her arms to show her elegant grey, lace-trimmed dress, tied slightly below the breasts with a broad ribbon.

"*Soyez tranquille, Lise, vous serez toujours la plus jolie,*"§ Anna Pavlovna replied.

"*Vous savez, mon mari m'abandonne,*" she went on in the same tone, turning to a general, "*il va se faire tuer. Dites moi, pourquoi cette vilaine guerre?*"# she said to Prince Vassily and, not waiting for an answer, turned to Prince Vassily's daughter, the beautiful Hélène.

"*Quelle délicieuse personne, que cette petite princesse!*"** Prince Vassily said to Anna Pavlovna.

Soon after the little princess came a massive, fat young man with a cropped head, in spectacles, light-coloured trousers of the latest fashion, a high jabot, and a brown tailcoat. This fat young man was the illegitimate son of a famous courtier from Catherine's time, Count Bezukhov, who was now dying in Moscow. He did not serve anywhere yet, he had only just arrived from abroad, where he had been educated, and this was his first time in society. Anna Pavlovna greeted him with a nod reserved for people of the lowest hierarchy in her salon. But, despite this greeting of the lowest sort, at the sight of the entering Pierre uneasiness and fear showed in Anna Pavlovna's face, like that expressed at the sight of something all too enormous and unsuited to the place. Though Pierre was indeed somewhat larger than the other men in the room, this fear could have referred only to the intelligent and at the same time shy, observant, and natural gaze which distinguished him from everyone else in that drawing room.

"*C'est bien aimable à vous, monsieur Pierre, d'être venu voir une pauvre*

---

*Pleasure party.
†I've brought my work.
‡Don't play a dirty trick on me . . . You wrote me that it was a very small soirée; look how I'm got up.
§Don't worry, Liza, you'll always be the prettiest.
#You know, my husband is leaving me . . . he's going to get himself killed. Tell me, why this nasty war?
**What a delightful person this little princess is!

malade," Anna Pavlovna said to him, exchanging fearful looks with the aunt, to whom she was bringing him. Pierre burbled something incomprehensible and went on searching for something with his eyes. He smiled joyfully, merrily, bowed to the little princess as to a close acquaintance, and went up to the aunt. Anna Pavlovna's fear was not in vain, because Pierre, without hearing out the aunt's talk about her majesty's health, walked away from her. The frightened Anna Pavlovna stopped him with the words:

"You don't know the abbé Morio? He's a very interesting man . . ." she said.

"Yes, I've heard about his plan for eternal peace,[11] and it's very interesting, but hardly possible . . ."

"You think so? . . ." said Anna Pavlovna, in order to say something, and again turned to her duties as mistress of the house, but Pierre committed the reverse discourtesy. Earlier he had walked away without hearing out a lady who was talking to him; now he held with his conversation a lady who needed to leave him. Lowering his head and spreading his big feet, he began to explain to Anna Pavlovna why he thought that the abbé's plan was a chimera.

"We'll talk later," Anna Pavlovna said, smiling.

And, ridding herself of the young man who did not know how to live, she returned to her duties as mistress of the house and went on listening and looking out, ready to come to the rescue at any point where the conversation lagged. As the owner of a spinning mill, having put his workers in their places, strolls about the establishment, watching out for an idle spindle or the odd one squealing much too loudly, and hastens to go and slow it down or start it up at the proper speed—so Anna Pavlovna strolled about her drawing room, going up to a circle that had fallen silent or was too talkative, and with one word or rearrangement set the conversation machine running evenly and properly again. But amidst all these cares there could still be seen in her a special fear for Pierre. She glanced at him concernedly when he went over to listen to what was being talked about around Mortemart and went on to another circle where the abbé was talking. For Pierre, brought up abroad, this soirée of Anna Pavlovna's was the first he had seen in Russia. He knew that all the intelligentsia of Petersburg was gathered there, and, like a child in a toy shop, he looked everywhere at once. He kept fearing to miss intelligent conversations that he might have listened to. Looking at the self-assured and elegant expressions on the faces gathered here, he kept expecting something especially intelligent. Finally he went up to Morio. The conversation seemed interesting to him, and he stopped, waiting for a chance to voice his thoughts, as young people like to do.

---

*It's very nice of you, Monsieur Pierre, to have come to see a poor sick woman.

III

Anna Pavlovna's soirée got going. The spindles on all sides hummed evenly and ceaselessly. Besides *ma tante,* next to whom sat only one elderly lady with a thin, weepy face, somewhat alien to this brilliant company, the company had broken up into three circles. In one, mostly masculine, the centre was the abbé; in another, of young people, it was the beautiful Princess Hélène, Prince Vassily's daughter, and the pretty, red-cheeked little princess Bolkonsky, too plump for her age. In the third, it was Mortemart and Anna Pavlovna.

The viscount was a nice-looking young man, with soft features and manners, obviously regarded himself as a celebrity, but, from good breeding, modestly allowed himself to be made use of by the company in which he found himself. Anna Pavlovna was obviously treating her guests to him. As a good maître d'hôtel presents, as something supernaturally excellent, a piece of beef one would not want to eat if one saw it in the dirty kitchen, so that evening Anna Pavlovna served up to her guests first the viscount, then the abbé, as something supernaturally refined. In Mortemart's circle the conversation turned at once to the murder of the duc d'Enghien.[12] The viscount said that the duc d'Enghien had perished from his own magnanimity and that there were special reasons for Bonaparte's viciousness.

"*Ah, voyons. Contez-nous cela, vicomte,*"* said Anna Pavlovna, joyfully sensing that something à la Louis XV echoed in this phrase, "*contez-nous cela, vicomte.*"

The viscount bowed as a sign of submission and smiled politely. Anna Pavlovna circled around the viscount and invited everyone to listen to his story.

"*Le vicomte a été personellement connu de monseigneur,*" Anna Pavlovna whispered to one. "*Le vicomte est un parfait conteur,*" she said to another. "*Comme on voit l'homme de la bonne compagnie,*"† she said to a third; and the viscount was presented to the company in a most refined and advantageous light, like a roast beef on a hot platter sprinkled with herbs.

The viscount was just about to begin his story and smiled subtly.

"Come over here, *chère* Hélène," Anna Pavlovna said to the beautiful princess, who was sitting some way off, forming the centre of another circle.

Princess Hélène was smiling; she got up with the same unchanging smile of a perfectly beautiful woman with which she had entered the drawing room. Lightly rustling her white ball gown trimmed with ivy and moss, her white

---

*Ah, there now. Tell us about that, Viscount.

†The viscount was known personally to my lord . . . The viscount is a perfect storyteller . . . How one can tell a man of good company.

shoulders gleaming, her hair and diamonds shining, she walked straight on between the parted men, not looking at anyone, but smiling to everyone, and as if kindly granting each of them the right to admire the beauty of her figure, her full shoulders, her very exposed bosom and back, as the fashion then was, and, as if bringing with her the brilliance of a ball, approached Anna Pavlovna. Hélène was so good-looking that there was not only not a trace of coquetry to be seen in her, but, on the contrary, it was as if she was embarrassed by her unquestionable and all too strongly and triumphantly effective beauty. It was as if she wished but was unable to diminish the effect of her beauty.

"*Quelle belle personne!*"* said everyone who saw her. As if struck by something extraordinary, the viscount shrugged his shoulders and lowered his eyes while she was seating herself before him and shining upon him that same unchanging smile.

"*Madame, je crains pour mes moyens devant un pareil auditoire,*"† he said, inclining his head with a smile.

The princess rested the elbow of her bare, rounded arm on a little table and did not find it necessary to say anything. She waited, smiling. Throughout the story she sat erect, glancing occasionally now at her rounded, beautiful arm lying lightly on the table, now at the still more beautiful bosom on which she straightened a diamond necklace; she also straightened the folds of her gown several times, and, when the story produced an impression, turned to look at Anna Pavlovna and at once assumed the same expression as on the maid of honour's face, and then settled back into a radiant smile. After Hélène, the little princess also came over from the tea table.

"*Attendez-moi, je vais prendre mon ouvrage,*" she said. "*Voyons, à quoi pensez-vous?*" she turned to Prince Ippolit. "*Apportez-moi mon reticule.*"‡

The princess, smiling and talking with everyone, suddenly effected the transposition, and, taking a seat, cheerily settled herself.

"Now I feel good," she said several times, and, asking them to begin, started to work.

Prince Ippolit fetched her reticule, came after her, and, moving his chair towards her, sat down close by.

Le charmant Hippolyte was striking in his extraordinary resemblance to his beautiful sister, and still more in being strikingly unattractive, despite that resemblance. The features of his face were the same as his sister's, but in her everything was lit up by her joyous, self-contented, young, unchanging smile

*What a beautiful person!
†Madame, I fear for my powers before such an audience.
‡Wait for me, I'm going to bring my handwork . . . Come, what are you thinking of? . . . Bring me my reticule.

and the extraordinary classical beauty of her body. In her brother, on the contrary, the same face was clouded by idiocy and invariably expressed a self-assured peevishness, and his body was skinny and weak. His eyes, nose, and mouth all seemed to shrink into an indefinite and dull grimace, and his arms and legs always assumed an unnatural position.

"*Ce n'est pas une histoire des revenants?*"* he said, sitting down near the princess and hastily affixing a lorgnette to his eyes, as if he was unable to start talking without this instrument.

"*Mais non, mon cher,*"† the surprised storyteller said, shrugging his shoulders.

"*C'est que je déteste les histoires des revenants,*"‡ said Prince Ippolit in such a tone that it was clear he had said these words and only then understood what they meant.

Because of the self-assurance with which he spoke, no one could make out whether what he had said was very clever or very stupid. He was wearing a dark green tailcoat, trousers the colour of *cuisse de nymphe effrayée,*§ as he said himself, stockings and shoes.

The *vicomte* told very nicely the then current anecdote that the duc d'Enghien had secretly gone to Paris to meet with Mlle George, and that there he had met Bonaparte, who also enjoyed the famous actress's favours, and that there, having met the duke, Napoleon happened to fall into one of those faints he was prone to and found himself in the duke's power, which the duke did not take advantage of, and that Bonaparte afterwards revenged himself for this magnanimity with the duke's death.

The story was very nice and interesting, especially the moment when the rivals suddenly recognized each other, and the ladies, it seemed, were stirred.

"*Charmant,*" said Anna Pavlovna, looking questioningly at the little princess.

"*Charmant,*" whispered the little princess, sticking the needle into her work as if to signify that the interest and charm of the story kept her from going on working.

The viscount appreciated this silent praise and, smiling gratefully, began to go on; but at that moment Anna Pavlovna, who kept glancing at the young man she found so frightening, noticed that his conversation with the abbé was much too loud and vehement, and she rushed to the rescue at the place of danger. Indeed, Pierre had managed to strike up a conversation with the abbé about political balance, and the abbé, obviously intrigued by the young man's simple-hearted vehemence, was developing his favourite idea before him. The

---

*It's not a ghost story?
†No, my dear.
‡Because I detest ghost stories.
§Thigh of frightened nymph.

two men listened and talked too animatedly and naturally, and it was this that Anna Pavlovna did not like.

"The means are European balance and the *droit des gens*,"* the abbé was saying. "Let a powerful state like Russia, famous for its barbarism, stand disinterestedly at the head of a union having as its purpose the balance of Europe—and it will save the world!"

"How are you going to find such balance?" Pierre began; but just then Anna Pavlovna came over and, with a stern glance at Pierre, asked the Italian how he was taking the local climate. The Italian's face suddenly changed and acquired an insultingly false sweetness of expression, which was probably habitual with him in conversations with women.

"I'm so enchanted with the charms of the intelligence and cultivation of society, especially the women's, where I have had the happiness to be received, that I have not yet had time to think about the climate," he said.

Not letting go of the abbé and Pierre, Anna Pavlovna, the better to keep an eye on them, joined them to the general circle.

Just then a new person entered the drawing room. This new person was the young Prince Andrei Bolkonsky, the little princess's husband. Prince Bolkonsky was of medium height, a rather handsome young man with well-defined and dry features. Everything in his figure, from his weary, bored gaze to his quiet, measured gait, presented the sharpest contrast with his small, lively wife. Obviously, he not only knew everyone in the drawing room, but was also so sick of them that it was very boring for him to look at them and listen to them. Of all the faces he found so boring, the face of his pretty wife seemed to be the one he was most sick of. With a grimace that spoiled his handsome face, he turned away from her. He kissed Anna Pavlovna's hand and, narrowing his eyes, looked around at the whole company.

"*Vous vous enrôlez pour la guerre, mon prince?*"† said Anna Pavlovna.

"*Le général Koutouzoff,*" said Bolkonsky, emphasizing the last syllable, *zoff*, like a Frenchman, "*a bien voulu de moi pour aide-de-camp . . .*"‡

"*Et Lise, votre femme?*"§

"She'll go to the country."

"Shame on you to deprive us of your lovely wife."

"André," said his wife, addressing her husband in the same coquettish tone in which she addressed others, "what a story the viscount told us about *mademoiselle* George and Bonaparte!"

Prince Andrei closed his eyes and turned away. Pierre, who had not taken his

---

*The right of nations.
†You're enlisting for the war, my prince?
‡General Kutuzov wanted me for his adjutant.
§And Liza, your wife?

joyful, friendly eyes off Prince Andrei since he entered the drawing room, went up to him and took his arm. Prince Andrei, without turning round, wrinkled his face into a grimace, expressing vexation at whoever had taken his arm, but, seeing Pierre's smiling face, suddenly smiled an unexpectedly kind and pleasant smile.

"Well, well! . . . So you, too, are in high society!" he said to Pierre.

"I knew you'd be here," Pierre replied. "I'll come to you for supper," he added softly, so as not to interfere with the viscount, who was going on with his story. "May I?"

"No, you may not," Prince Andrei said, laughing, letting Pierre know by the pressure of his hand that there was no need to ask. He was about to say more, but just then Prince Vassily and his daughter rose, and the men stood up to let them pass.

"You will excuse me, my dear viscount," Prince Vassily said to the Frenchman, gently pulling him down on his chair by the sleeve, so that he would not stand up. "This unfortunate fête at the ambassador's deprives me of my pleasure and interrupts you. I'm very sorry to leave your delightful soirée," he said to Anna Pavlovna.

His daughter, Princess Hélène, lightly holding the folds of her gown, walked between the chairs, and the smile shone still more brightly on her beautiful face. Pierre looked with enraptured, almost frightened eyes at this beauty as she walked past him.

"Very good-looking," said Prince Andrei.

"Very," said Pierre.

Passing by, Prince Vassily seized Pierre by the hand and turned to Anna Pavlovna.

"Educate this bear for me," he said. "He's been living with me for a month, and this is the first time I've seen him in society. Nothing is so necessary for a young man as the company of intelligent women."

IV

Anna Pavlovna smiled and promised to occupy herself with Pierre, who she knew was related to Prince Vassily through his father. The elderly lady who had so far been sitting with *ma tante* hastily got up and overtook Prince Vassily in the front hall. All the former sham interest disappeared from her face. Her kind, weepy face expressed only anxiety and fear.

"What can you tell me, Prince, about my Boris?" she said, overtaking him in the front hall. (She pronounced the name Boris with a special emphasis on the *o*.) "I cannot remain in Petersburg any longer. Tell me, what news can I bring my poor boy?"

Though Prince Vassily listened to the elderly lady reluctantly and almost impolitely, and even showed impatience, she smiled at him gently and touchingly, and even took him by the arm to keep him from walking away.

"It won't cost you anything to say a word to the sovereign, and he'll be transferred straight away to the guards," she pleaded.

"Believe me, Princess, I'll do all I can," replied Prince Vassily, "but it's hard for me to ask the sovereign. I'd advise you to turn to Rumyantsev through Prince Golitsyn—that would be smarter."

The elderly lady bore the name of Princess Drubetskoy, one of the best families of Russia, but she was poor, had long since left society, and had lost her former connections. She had come now to solicit an appointment to the guards for her only son. She had invited herself and come to Anna Pavlovna's soirée only in order to see Prince Vassily, only for that had she listened to the viscount's story. Prince Vassily's words frightened her; her once beautiful face showed spite, but that lasted no more than a moment. She smiled again and took a slightly stronger grip on Prince Vassily's arm.

"Listen, Prince," she said, "I've never asked you for anything, and never will, I've never reminded you of my father's friendship for you. But now, I adjure you in God's name, do this for my son, and I will consider you my benefactor," she added hastily. "No, don't be angry, but promise me. I asked Golitsyn and he refused. *Soyez le bon enfant que vous avez été,*"* she said, trying to smile, though there were tears in her eyes.

"Papá, we'll be late," said Princess Hélène, who was waiting at the door, turning her beautiful head on her classical shoulders.

But influence in society is a capital that must be used sparingly, lest it disappear. Prince Vassily knew that and, having once realized that if he were to solicit for everyone who solicited from him, it would soon become impossible for him to solicit for himself, he rarely used his influence. In Princess Drubetskoy's case, however, after her new appeal, he felt something like a pang of conscience. She had reminded him of the truth: he owed his first steps in the service to her father. Besides, he could see from the way she behaved that she was one of those women, especially mothers, who, once they take something into their heads, will not leave off until their desire is fulfilled, and are otherwise prepared to pester you every day and every minute, and even to make scenes. This last consideration gave him pause.

"*Chère* Anna Mikhailovna," he said, with his usual tone of familiarity and boredom, "it is almost impossible for me to do what you want; but to prove to you how much I love you and honour the memory of your late father, I will do the impossible: your son will be transferred to the guards, here is my hand on it. Are you satisfied?"

*Be the good boy you used to be.

"My dear, you are our benefactor! I expected nothing else from you; I knew how kind you are."

He was about to leave.

"Wait, two more words. *Une fois passé aux gardes . . .*"* She faltered. "You're on good terms with Mikhail Ilarionovich Kutuzov, recommend Boris as his adjutant. Then I'll be at peace and . . ."

Prince Vassily smiled.

"That I will not promise you. You know how besieged Kutuzov has been since he was appointed commander in chief.[13] He told me himself that all the Moscow ladies are conspiring to send their children to be his adjutants."

"No, you must promise, I won't let you go, my dear benefactor."

"Papá," the beauty repeated in the same tone, "we'll be late."

"Well, *au revoir*, goodbye, you see . . ."

"So you'll speak to the sovereign tomorrow?"

"Without fail, but to Kutuzov I don't promise."

"No, do promise, do promise, Basile," Anna Mikhailovna said behind him, with the smile of a young coquette, which must have suited her very well once, but now did not go with her emaciated face.

She evidently forgot her age and employed, out of habit, all her old feminine resources. But as soon as he left, her face again acquired the same cold, sham expression it had had before. She went back to the circle, where the viscount was going on with his story, and again pretended to listen, waiting for the moment to leave, since her business was done.

"But how do you find all this latest comedy *du sacre de Milan*,"[14] asked Anna Pavlovna. "*Et la nouvelle comédie des peuples de Gênes et de Lucques, qui viennent présenter leurs voeux à M. Buonaparte. M. Buonaparte assis sur un trône, et exauçant les voeux des nations! Adorable! Non, mais c'est à en devenir folle! On dirait, que le monde entier a perdu la tête.*"†

Prince Andrei grinned, looking straight into Anna Pavlovna's face.

" '*Dieu me la donne, gare à qui la touche,*' " he said (Bonaparte's words, spoken as the crown was placed on him). "*On dit qu'il a été très beau en prononçant ces paroles,*"‡ he added, and repeated the words once more in Italian: " '*Dio mi la dona, guai a chi la tocca.*' "

"*J'espère enfin,*" Anna Pavlovna continued, "*que ça a été la goutte d'eau*

*Once he's transferred to the guards . . .

†. . . of the coronation in Milan . . . And the new comedy of the people of Genoa and Lucca, who come to present their best wishes to M. Buonaparte. M. Buonaparte seated on a throne and granting the wishes of the nations! Adorable! No, but it could make you crazy! You'd think the whole world has lost its mind!

‡"God gives it to me, woe to him who touches it" . . . They say he was very handsome as he spoke those words.

qui fera déborder le verre. Les souverains ne peuvent plus supporter cet homme, qui menace tout." *

"*Les souverains? Je ne parle pas de la Russie,*" the viscount said courteously and hopelessly. "*Les souverains, madame? Qu'ont-ils fait pour Louis XVI, pour la reine, pour madame Elisabeth?*[15] *Rien,*" he continued, growing animated. "*Et croyez-moi, ils subissent la punition pour leur trahison de la cause des Bourbons. Les souverains? Ils envoient des ambassadeurs complimenter l'usurpateur."* †

And with a contemptuous sigh, he again changed position. At these words, Prince Ippolit, who had long been gazing at the viscount through his lorgnette, suddenly turned his whole body to the little princess and, asking her for a needle, began showing her the coat of arms of the Condés,[16] drawing with the needle on the table. He explained this coat of arms to her with a significant air, as if the princess had asked him about it.

"*Baton de gueules, engrêlé de gueules d'azur—maison Condé,*" ‡ he said.

The princess listened, smiling.

"If Bonaparte remains on the throne of France for another year," the viscount continued the new conversation, with the air of a man who does not listen to others, but, in matters known better to him than to anyone else, follows only the train of his own thoughts, "things will go too far. Intrigues, coercion, banishments, executions will for ever destroy French society—I mean good society—and then . . ."

He shrugged his shoulders and spread his arms. Pierre was about to say something: the conversation interested him, but Anna Pavlovna, who was keeping watch on him, interrupted.

"The emperor Alexander," she said, with the sadness that always accompanied her talk about the imperial family, "declared that he would leave it to the French themselves to choose their form of government. And I think there's no doubt that the whole nation, freed of the usurper, will throw itself into the arms of the lawful king," Anna Pavlovna said, trying to be amiable to the émigré and royalist.

"That's doubtful," said Prince Andrei. "*Monsieur le vicomte* quite rightly supposes that things have already gone too far. I think it would be hard to return to the old ways."

---

*I hope, finally . . . that this was the drop of water that will make the glass overflow. The sovereigns can no longer put up with this man who threatens everything.

†The sovereigns? I'm not speaking of Russia . . . The sovereigns, madame! What did they do for Louis XVI, for the queen, for Madame Elizabeth? Nothing . . . And believe me, they are being punished for their betrayal of the cause of the Bourbons. The sovereigns? They send ambassadors to compliment the usurper.

‡Bar of gules, engrailed with gules of azure—house of Condé.

"From what I've heard," Pierre, blushing, again mixed into the conversation, "almost all the nobility have already gone over to Bonaparte's side."

"It's the Bonapartists who say that," said the viscount, not looking at Pierre. "Right now it's hard to know public opinion in France."

"*Bonaparte l'a dit,*"* Prince Andrei said with a grin. (It was evident that he did not like the viscount and that, though he was not looking at him, his talk was directed against him.)

" '*Je leur ai montré le chemin de la gloire,*' " he said after a short silence, again repeating the words of Napoleon, " '*ils n'en ont pas voulu; je leur ai ouvert mes antichambres, ils se sont précipités en foule . . .*' *Je ne sais pas à quel point il a eu le droit de le dire.*"†

"*Aucun,*" the viscount retorted. "After the duke's murder, even the most partial people ceased to see a hero in him. *Si même ça a été un héros pour certains gens,*" the viscount said, turning to Anna Pavlovna, "*depuis l'assassinat du duc il y a un martyr de plus dans le ciel, un héros de moins sur la terre.*"‡

Before Anna Pavlovna and the others had time to smile appreciatively at these words of the viscount's, Pierre again burst into the conversation, and Anna Pavlovna, though she anticipated that he would say something improper, could no longer stop him.

"The execution of the duc d'Enghien," said Pierre, "was a necessity of state; and I precisely see greatness of soul in the fact that Napoleon was not afraid to take upon himself alone the responsibility for this act."

"*Dieu! mon dieu!*"§ Anna Pavlovna whispered in a frightened whisper.

"*Comment, monsieur Pierre, vous trouvez que l'assassinat est grandeur d'âme?*"# said the little princess, smiling and drawing her work towards her.

"Ah! Oh!" said various voices.

"Capital!" Prince Ippolit said in English and began slapping his knee with his palm. The viscount merely shrugged.

Pierre gazed triumphantly at his listeners over his spectacles.

"I say that," he went on desperately, "because the Bourbons fled from the revolution, abandoning the people to anarchy; and Napoleon alone was able to understand the revolution, to defeat it, and therefore, for the sake of the common good, he could not stop short at the life of a single man."

"Wouldn't you like to move to that table?" asked Anna Pavlovna. But Pierre, not answering, went on with his speech.

---

*Bonaparte has said that.

†"I showed them the path to glory . . . they did not want it; I opened my antechambers to them, they rushed there in a mob." I don't know to what extent he had the right to say it.

‡None . . . Even if that had been a hero for certain people . . . since the assassination of the duke there is one more martyr in heaven, one less hero on earth.

§God! my God!

#What, Monsieur Pierre, you find that assassination is greatness of soul?

"No," he said, growing more and more inspired, "Napoleon is great, because he stood above the revolution, put an end to its abuses, and kept all that was good—the equality of citizens and freedom of speech and of the press—and that is the only reason why he gained power."

"Yes, if he had taken that power and, without using it for murder, given it to the lawful king," said the viscount, "then I would call him a great man."

"He couldn't do that. The people gave him power only so that he could deliver them from the Bourbons, and because the people saw a great man in him. The revolution was a great thing," M'sieur Pierre went on, showing by this desperate and provocative parenthetical phrase his great youth and desire to speak everything out all the sooner.

"Revolution and regicide a great thing? . . . After that . . . wouldn't you like to move to that table?" Anna Pavlovna repeated.

"*Contrat social,*"*[17] the viscount said with a meek smile.

"I'm not talking about regicide. I'm talking about ideas."

"Yes, the ideas of pillage, murder, and regicide," an ironic voice interrupted again.

"Those were extremes, to be sure, but the whole meaning wasn't in them, the meaning was in the rights of man, emancipation from prejudice, the equality of citizens; and Napoleon kept all these ideas in all their force."

"Liberty and equality," the viscount said scornfully, as if finally deciding to prove seriously to this young man all the stupidity of his talk, "these are resounding words that have long been compromised. Who doesn't love liberty and equality? Our Saviour already preached liberty and equality. Did people become happier after the revolution? On the contrary. We wanted liberty, but Bonaparte destroyed it."

Prince Andrei kept glancing with a smile now at Pierre, now at the viscount, now at the hostess. For the first moment of Pierre's outburst, Anna Pavlovna was horrified, accustomed though she was to society; but when she saw that despite the blasphemous speeches uttered by Pierre, the viscount did not lose his temper, and when she became certain that it was now impossible to suppress these speeches, she gathered her forces and, joining the viscount, attacked the orator.

"*Mais, mon cher monsieur Pierre,*" said Anna Pavlovna, "how do you explain a great man who could execute a duke, or, finally, any simple man, without a trial and without guilt?"

"I'd like to ask," said the viscount, "how *monsieur* explains the eighteenth Brumaire.[18] Was that not a deception? *C'est un escamotage, qui ne ressemble nullement à la manière d'agir d'un grand homme.*"†

---

*Social contract.
†It is a conjuring trick which in no way resembles the way a great man acts.

"And the prisoners he killed in Africa?"[19] said the little princess. "It's terrible!" And she shrugged her shoulders.

"*C'est un roturier, vous aurez beau dire,*"* said Prince Ippolit.

M'sieur Pierre did not know whom to answer, looked around at them all, and smiled. His smile was not like that of other people, blending into a non-smile. With him, on the contrary, when a smile came, his serious and even somewhat sullen face vanished suddenly, instantly, and another appeared—childish, kind, even slightly stupid, and as if apologetic.

To the viscount, who was meeting him for the first time, it was clear that this Jacobin was not at all as frightening as his words. Everyone fell silent.

"Do you want him to answer everybody at once?" asked Prince Andrei. "Besides, in the acts of a statesman one must distinguish among the acts of the private person, the military leader, and the emperor. So it seems to me."

"Yes, yes, of course," Pierre picked up, gladdened by the arrival of unexpected help.

"It's impossible not to admit," Prince Andrei went on, "that Napoleon was a great man on the bridge of Arcole, and in the Jaffa hospital, when he shook hands with the plague victims,[20] but . . . there are other acts which are hard to justify."

Prince Andrei, who evidently wanted to soften the awkwardness of Pierre's speech, got up, intending to leave and making a sign to his wife.

Suddenly Prince Ippolit rose and, gesturing for everyone to stay and sit down, began to speak:

"*Ah! aujourd'hui on m'a raconté une anecdote moscovite, charmante: il faut que je vous en régale. Vous m'excusez, vicomte, il faut que je raconte en russe. Autrement on ne sentira pas le sel de l'histoire.*"†

And Prince Ippolit began to speak in Russian, with a pronunciation such as Frenchmen have after spending a year in Russia. Everyone stayed: so animatedly, so insistently did Prince Ippolit call for attention to his story.

"In *Moscou* there is a ladee, *une dame.* And she is very stingee. She must 'ave two *valets de pied*‡ behind the carriage. And of very grand height. That was in her taste. Now, she 'ad *une femme de chambre,*§ also of grand height. She said . . ."

Here Prince Ippolit fell to thinking, evidently having a hard time working it out.

*He's a commoner, you may as well say.
†Ah! today someone told me a charming Muscovite anecdote: I must treat you to it. Excuse me, Viscount, I must tell it in Russian. Otherwise the salt of the story won't be felt.
‡Footmen.
§A chambermaid.

"She said . . . yes, she said: 'Girl' (to the *femme de chambre*), 'put on a *livrée* and come with me, behind the carriage, *faire des visites.*' "*

Here Prince Ippolit snorted and guffawed, far in advance of his listeners, which produced an impression unfavourable to the narrator. Many smiled, however, the elderly lady and Anna Pavlovna among them.

"So she went. Suddenly there was a strong wind. The girl lost her hat, and her long hairs came undone . . ."

Here he could no longer control himself and began laughing fitfully, saying through his laughter:

"And the whole world found out . . ."

With that the anecdote ended. Though it was not clear why he had told it, and why it absolutely had to be told in Russian, all the same Anna Pavlovna and the others appreciated Prince Ippolit's social grace, in thus pleasantly putting an end to M'sieur Pierre's unpleasant and ungracious outburst. After the anecdote, the conversation broke up into small, insignificant commentaries on past and future balls, on performances, and on who would see whom when and where.

V

Having thanked Anna Pavlovna for her *charmante soirée,* the guests began to leave.

Pierre was clumsy. Fat, unusually tall, broad, with enormous red hands, he did not, as they say, know how to enter a salon, and still less did he know how to leave one, that is, by saying something especially pleasant at the door. Besides that, he was absent-minded. Getting up, he took a three-cornered hat with a general's plumage instead of his own and held on to it, plucking at the feathers, until the general asked him to give it back. But all his absent-mindedness and inability to enter a salon and speak in it were redeemed by his expression of good nature, simplicity, and modesty. Anna Pavlovna turned to him and, with a Christian meekness expressing forgiveness for his outburst, nodded to him and said:

"I hope to see you again, but I also hope that you will change your opinions, my dear M'sieur Pierre," she said.

When she said this to him, he made no reply, but only bowed and once more showed everyone his smile, which said nothing except perhaps this: "Opinions are opinions, but you see what a good and nice fellow I am." And everyone, including Anna Pavlovna, involuntarily felt it.

Prince Andrei went out to the front hall and, offering his shoulders to the footman, who was putting his cloak on him, listened indifferently to his wife's

---

*. . . livery . . . to make visits.

chatter with Prince Ippolit, who also came out to the front hall. Prince Ippolit stood beside the pretty, pregnant princess and looked at her directly and intently through his lorgnette.

"Go in, Annette, you'll catch cold," said the little princess, taking leave of Anna Pavlovna. *"C'est arrêté,"** she added softly.

Anna Pavlovna had already managed to speak with Liza about the match she was contriving between Anatole and the little princess's sister-in-law.

"I'm relying on you, my dear friend," Anna Pavlovna said, also softly, "you'll write to her and tell me *comment le père envisagera la chose. Au revoir.*"† And she left the front hall.

Prince Ippolit went over to the little princess and, bringing his face down close to hers, began saying something to her in a half whisper. Two footmen, one the princess's, the other his, waiting for them to finish talking, stood with shawl and redingote and listened to their French talk, which they could not understand, with such faces as if they understood what was being said but did not want to show it. The princess, as usual, talked smilingly and listened laughingly.

"I'm very glad I didn't go to the ambassador's," said Prince Ippolit, "it's boring . . . A wonderful evening. Wonderful, isn't it so?"

"They say the ball will be very nice," replied the princess, her slightly moustached lip pulling upwards. "All the beautiful society women will be there."

"Not all, since you won't be there; not all," said Prince Ippolit, laughing joyfully, and, snatching the shawl from the footman, even shoving him, he began putting it on the princess. Either from awkwardness or intentionally (no one would have been able to tell), he was a long while lowering his arms, even when the shawl was already put on, and it was as if he was embracing the young woman.

Graciously, but still smiling, she withdrew, turned, and looked at her husband. Prince Andrei's eyes were shut, which made him look tired and sleepy.

"Are you ready, madame?" he asked his wife, looking past her.

Prince Ippolit hastily put on his redingote, which, in the new style, hung lower than his heels, and, tangling himself in it, ran to the porch after the princess, whom the footman was helping into the carriage.

"Princesse, au revoir," he cried, his tongue getting as tangled as his feet.

The princess, picking up her dress, was settling herself in the darkness of the carriage; her husband was straightening his sword; Prince Ippolit, on the pretext of being of service, got in everyone's way.

"Ex-cuse me, sir," Prince Andrei, with dry unpleasantness, addressed himself in Russian to Prince Ippolit, who was standing in his way.

*It's agreed.
†How the father will look upon it. Goodbye.

"I'll be waiting for you, Pierre," the same voice of Prince Andrei said gently and tenderly.

The postilion touched up the horses, and the wheels of the carriage rumbled. Prince Ippolit laughed fitfully, standing on the porch and waiting for the viscount, whom he had promised to take home.

"*Eh, bien, mon cher, votre petite princesse est très bien, très bien,*" said the viscount, getting into the carriage with Ippolit. "*Mais très bien.*" He kissed the tips of his fingers. "*Et tout-à-fait française.*"*

Ippolit laughed with a snort.

"*Et savez-vous que vous êtes terrible avec votre petit air innocent,*" the viscount continued. "*Je plains le pauvre mari, ce petit officier, qui se donne des airs de prince régnant.*"†

Ippolit snorted again and said through his laughter:

"*Et vous disiez, que les dames russes ne valaient pas les dames françaises. Il faut savoir s'y prendre.*"‡

Pierre, arriving first, went to Prince Andrei's study, being a familiar of the house, and, as was his habit, at once lay down on the sofa, took the first book that caught his eye from the shelf (it was Caesar's *Commentaries*),²¹ and, leaning on his elbow, began reading it from the middle.

"What have you done to *mademoiselle* Scherer? She'll be quite ill now," said Prince Andrei, coming into his study and rubbing his small white hands.

Pierre swung his whole body so that the sofa creaked, turned his animated face to Prince Andrei, smiled, and waved his hand.

"No, that abbé is very interesting, only he has the wrong notion of things . . . In my opinion, eternal peace is possible, but I don't know how to say it . . . Only it's not through political balance . . ."

Prince Andrei was obviously not interested in these abstract conversations.

"*Mon cher*, you can't go saying what you think everywhere. Well, so, have you finally decided on anything? Are you going to be a horse guard or a diplomat?" Prince Andrei asked after a moment's silence.

Pierre sat up on the sofa with both legs tucked under him.

"Can you imagine, I still don't know. I don't like either of them."

---

*Well, my dear, your little princess is very nice, very nice . . . Very nice indeed . . . And completely French.

†And you know, you're terrible with your innocent little air . . . I pity the poor husband, that little officer who gives himself the airs of a reigning prince.

‡And you were saying that Russian ladies were not as good as French ladies. You just have to know how to handle them.

"But you must decide on something. Your father's waiting."

At the age of ten, Pierre had been sent abroad with an abbé-tutor and had remained there until he was twenty. When he returned to Moscow, his father dismissed the abbé and said to the young man: "Go to Petersburg now, look around, and choose. I'll agree to anything. Here's a letter to Prince Vassily, and here's some money. Write to me about everything, I'll help you in everything." Pierre had been choosing a career for three months already and had done nothing. This was the choice that Prince Andrei was talking about with him. Pierre rubbed his forehead.

"But he must be a Mason,"[22] he said, meaning the abbé he had seen at the soirée.

"That's all rubbish," Prince Andrei stopped him again, "better let's talk about business. Have you been to the horse guards? . . ."

"No, I haven't, but here's what's come into my head and I wanted to tell you. There's war now against Napoleon. If it were a war for freedom, I could understand it, I'd be the first to go into military service; but to help England and Austria against the greatest man in the world . . . is not right."

Prince Andrei merely shrugged his shoulders at Pierre's childish talk. He made it look as though he could not reply to such stupidity; but in fact it was hard to reply to this naïve question in any other way than Prince Andrei had done.

"If everyone made war only according to his own convictions, there would be no war," he said.

"And that would be excellent," said Pierre.

Prince Andrei smiled.

"It might very well be excellent, but it will never happen . . ."

"Well, what makes you go to war?" asked Pierre.

"What makes me? I don't know. I have to. Besides, I'm going . . ." He paused. "I'm going because this life I lead here, this life—is not for me!"

VI

There was the rustle of a woman's dress in the next room. Prince Andrei shook himself as if coming to his senses, and his face took on the same expression it had had in Anna Pavlovna's drawing room. Pierre lowered his legs from the sofa. The princess came in. She had already changed to a house dress, but one just as elegant and fresh. Prince Andrei stood up, politely moving an armchair for her.

"Why is it, I often wonder," she began, in French as always, hurriedly and fussily sitting down in the armchair, "why is it that Annette has never married? How stupid you all are, *messieurs,* not to have married her. Forgive me, but you understand nothing about women. You're such an arguer, M'sieur Pierre."

"I also keep arguing with your husband. I don't understand why he wants to go to the war," said Pierre, without any constraint (so usual in the relations of a young man with a young woman), turning to the princess.

The princess gave a flutter. Evidently Pierre's words had touched her to the quick.

"Ah, that's just what I say!" she said. "I don't understand, I decidedly do not understand, why men can't live without war. Why is it that we women want none of it and have no need of it? Well, you be the judge. I keep telling him: here he's his uncle's adjutant, a most brilliant position. He's so well-known, so appreciated by everyone. The other day at the Apraksins' I heard a lady ask: '*C'est ça le fameux prince André?' Ma parole d'honneur!*"* she laughed. "He's so well received everywhere. He could easily become an imperial adjutant. You know, the sovereign spoke to him very graciously. Annette and I were saying that it could easily be arranged. What do you think?"

Pierre looked at Prince Andrei and, noticing that his friend did not like this conversation, made no reply.

"When do you go?" he asked.

"*Ah! ne me parlez pas de ce départ, ne m'en parlez pas. Je ne veux pas en entendre parler,*"† the princess said in the same capriciously playful tone in which she had spoken with Ippolit in the drawing room and which was so obviously unsuited to the family circle, where Pierre was like a member. "Today, when I thought how I'd have to break off all these dear relations . . . And then, you know, André?" She winked meaningfully at her husband. "*J'ai peur, j'ai peur!*"‡ she whispered, her back shuddering.

Her husband looked at her as if he was surprised to notice there was someone else in the room besides himself and Pierre. However, with cold politeness he enquiringly addressed his wife:

"What are you afraid of, Liza? I cannot understand," he said.

"See what egoists all men are; all, all egoists! For the sake of his whims, God knows why, he abandons me, he locks me up in the country alone."

"With my father and sister, don't forget," Prince Andrei said quietly.

"Alone all the same, without *my* friends . . . And he wants me not to be afraid."

Her tone was querulous now, her little lip rose, giving her face not a joyful but an animalish, squirrel-like expression. She fell silent, as if finding it inde-

---

* "So that's the famous Prince Andrei?" My word of honour.
† Ah! do not speak to me of this departure, do not speak to me of it. I do not want to hear it spoken of.
‡ I'm afraid, I'm afraid!

cent to speak of her pregnancy in front of Pierre, though that was where the essence of the matter lay.

"I still haven't understood *de quoi vous avez peur,*"* Prince Andrei said slowly, not taking his eyes off his wife.

The princess blushed and waved her hands desperately.

"Non, André, je dis que vous avez tellement, tellement changé . . ."†

"Your doctor tells you to go to bed earlier," said Prince Andrei. "You should get some sleep."

The princess said nothing, and her short lip with its little moustache suddenly trembled. Prince Andrei, getting up and shrugging his shoulders, began to pace the room.

Pierre gazed wonderingly and naïvely through his spectacles now at him, now at the princess, and stirred as if he also wanted to get up, but changed his mind again.

"What do I care if M'sieur Pierre is here," the little princess said suddenly, and her pretty face suddenly spread into a tearful grimace. "I've long wanted to say to you, André: why have you changed so much towards me? What have I done to you? You're going into the army, you have no pity for me. Why is it?"

"Lise!" was all Prince Andrei said; but in this word there was an entreaty, and a threat, and above all the conviction that she herself would regret her words; but she hurriedly went on:

"You treat me like a sick person or a child. I see it all. You weren't like this six months ago."

"Lise, I beg you to stop," Prince Andrei said still more expressively.

Pierre, who was becoming more and more agitated during this conversation, got up and went over to the princess. He seemed unable to bear the sight of tears and was about to start crying himself.

"Calm yourself, Princess. It seems so to you, because, I assure you, I myself have experienced . . . why . . . because . . . No, excuse me, an outsider is in the way here . . . No, calm yourself . . . Goodbye . . ."

Prince Andrei caught him by the arm.

"No, wait, Pierre. The princess is so good that she will not want to deprive me of the pleasure of spending an evening with you."

"No, he thinks only of himself," said the princess, not holding back her angry tears.

"Lise," Prince Andrei said drily, raising his tone to a degree which showed that his patience had run out.

Suddenly the angry, squirrel-like expression on the princess's beautiful little face changed to an attractive and compassion-provoking expression of fear;

*. . . what you are afraid of.
†No, Andrei, I say you've changed so much, so much . . .

her pretty eyes glanced from under her eyebrows at her husband, and her face acquired the timid and admissive look of a dog rapidly but weakly wagging its drooping tail.

"*Mon dieu, mon dieu!*" said the princess, and taking up a fold of her dress in one hand, she went over to her husband and kissed him on the forehead.

"*Bonsoir, Lise,*"* said Prince Andrei, standing up and kissing her hand politely, as if she were a stranger.

The friends were silent. Neither of them would begin talking. Pierre kept glancing at Prince Andrei; Prince Andrei was rubbing his forehead with his small hand.

"Let's go and have supper," he said with a sigh, getting up and heading for the door.

They went into the elegantly, newly, richly decorated dining room. Everything from the napkins to the silverware, china, and crystal bore that special stamp of newness that is found in the households of the recently married. In the middle of supper, the prince leaned his elbow on the table and, with an expression of nervous irritation such as Pierre had never seen in his friend before, began to talk, like a man who has long had something on his heart and suddenly decides to speak it out:

"Never, never marry, my friend. Here's my advice to you: don't marry until you can tell yourself that you've done all you could, and until you've stopped loving the woman you've chosen, until you see her clearly, otherwise you'll be cruelly and irremediably mistaken. Marry when you're old and good for nothing . . . Otherwise all that's good and lofty in you will be lost. It will all go on trifles. Yes, yes, yes! Don't look at me with such astonishment. If you expect something from yourself in the future, then at every step you'll feel that it's all over for you, it's all closed, except the drawing room, where you'll stand on the same level as a court flunkey and an idiot . . . Ah, well! . . ."

He waved his hand energetically.

Pierre took off his spectacles, which made his face change, expressing still more kindness, and looked at his friend in astonishment.

"My wife," Prince Andrei went on, "is a wonderful woman. She's one of those rare women with whom one can be at ease regarding one's own honour; but, my God, what wouldn't I give now not to be married! You're the first and only one I'm saying this to, because I love you."

Prince Andrei, in saying this, was less than ever like that Bolkonsky who sat sprawled in Anna Pavlovna's armchair and, narrowing his eyes, uttered French phrases through his teeth. His dry face was all aquiver with the nervous

---

* Good night, Liza.

animation of every muscle; his eyes, in which the fire of life had seemed extinguished, now shone with a bright, radiant brilliance. One could see that, the more lifeless he seemed in ordinary times, the more energetic he was in moments of irritation.

"You don't understand why I'm saying this," he went on. "Yet it's a whole life's story. You talk of Bonaparte and his career," he said, though Pierre had not talked of Bonaparte. "You talk of Bonaparte; but Bonaparte, when he was working, went step by step towards his goal, he was free, he had nothing except his goal—and he reached it. But bind yourself to a woman—and, like a prisoner in irons, you lose all freedom. And whatever hope and strength you have in you, it all only burdens and torments you with remorse. Drawing rooms, gossip, balls, vanity, triviality—that is the vicious circle I can't get out of. I'm now going to the war, to the greatest war that has ever been, yet I know nothing and am good for nothing. *Je suis très aimable et très caustique,*"* Prince Andrei went on, "and they listen to me at Anna Pavlovna's. And this stupid society, without which my wife cannot live, and these women . . . If you only knew what *toutes les femmes distinguées*† and women in general really are! My father is right. Egoism, vanity, dull-wittedness, triviality in everything—that's women, when they show themselves as they are. Looking at them in society, it seems there's something there, but there's nothing, nothing, nothing! No, don't marry, dear heart, don't marry," Prince Andrei concluded.

"I find it funny," said Pierre, "that *you, you yourself,* consider that you have no ability and that your life is a ruined life. You have everything, everything ahead of you. And you . . ."

He did not say *you what,* but his tone already showed how highly he valued his friend and how much he expected from him in the future.

"How can he say that!" thought Pierre. Pierre considered Prince Andrei the model of all perfections, precisely because Prince Andrei united in the highest degree all those qualities which Pierre did not possess and which could be most nearly expressed by the notion of strength of will. Pierre always marvelled at Prince Andrei's ability to deal calmly with all sorts of people, at his extraordinary memory, his erudition (he had read everything, knew everything, had notions about everything), and most of all at his ability to work and learn. If Pierre had often been struck by Andrei's lack of ability for dreamy philosophizing (for which Pierre had a particular inclination), he saw it not as a defect, but as a strength.

In the best, the friendliest and simplest relations, flattery or praise is necessary, just as grease is necessary to keep wheels turning.

---

*I am very amiable and very caustic.
† . . . all refined women.

"*Je suis un homme fini,*"* said Prince Andrei. "Why talk about me? Let's talk about you," he said, pausing and smiling at his comforting thoughts. This smile was instantly reflected on Pierre's face.

"But what is there to say about me?" asked Pierre, spreading his mouth into a carefree, merry smile. "What am I? *Je suis un bâtard!*" And he suddenly flushed crimson. One could see that it had cost him great effort to say that. "*Sans nom, sans fortune*† . . . And what, really . . ." But he did not say *what really.* "I'm free so far, and I feel fine. Only I have no idea where to make my start. I seriously wanted to ask your advice."

Prince Andrei looked at him with kindly eyes. But in his friendly, gentle gaze a consciousness of his own superiority still showed.

"You're dear to me especially because you're the only live person in our whole society. That's fine for you. Choose whatever you like; it's all the same. You'll be fine anywhere, but there's one thing: stop going to those Kuragins and leading that sort of life. It simply doesn't suit you: all this carousing with hussars, and all . . ."

"*Que voulez-vous, mon cher,*" said Pierre, shrugging his shoulders, "*les femmes, mon cher, les femmes!*"‡

"I don't understand," replied Andrei. "*Les femmes comme il faut* are another matter; but *les femmes* of Kuragin, *les femmes et le vin,*§ I don't understand!"

Pierre lived at Prince Vassily Kuragin's and took part in the dissolute life of his son Anatole, the same one they planned to marry to Prince Andrei's sister in order to reform him.

"You know what?" said Pierre, as if a lucky thought had unexpectedly occurred to him. "Seriously, I've been thinking that for a long time. With this life I can't decide or even consider anything. I have a headache and no money. He invited me tonight, but I won't go."

"Give me your word of honour that you won't go any more?"

"Word of honour!"

It was already past one o'clock when Pierre left his friend's house. It was a duskless Petersburg June night. Pierre got into a hired carriage with the intention of going home. But the closer he came, the more he felt the impossibility of falling asleep on that night, which more resembled an evening or a morning. One could see far down the empty streets. On the way, Pierre recalled that

*I'm a finished man.
†I'm a bastard . . . With no name, no fortune . . .
‡What do you want, my dear . . . women, my dear, women!
§Proper women . . . women . . . women and wine.

the usual gambling company was to gather at Anatole Kuragin's that evening, after which there was usually drinking, ending with one of Pierre's favourite amusements.

"It would be nice to go to Kuragin's," he thought. But at once he remembered the word of honour he had given Prince Andrei not to visit Kuragin.

But at once, as happens with so-called characterless people, he desired so passionately to experience again that dissolute life so familiar to him, that he decided to go. And at once the thought occurred to him that the word he had given meant nothing, because before giving his word to Prince Andrei, he had also given Prince Anatole his word that he would be there; finally he thought that all these words of honour were mere conventions, with no definite meaning, especially if you considered that you might die the next day, or something so extraordinary might happen to you that there would no longer be either honour or dishonour. That sort of reasoning often came to Pierre, destroying all his decisions and suppositions. He went to Kuragin's.

Driving up to the porch of a large house near the horse guards' barracks, in which Anatole lived, he went up the lighted porch, the stairs, and entered an open door. There was no one in the front hall; empty bottles, capes, galoshes were lying about; there was a smell of wine, the noise of distant talking and shouting.

Cards and supper were over, but the guests had not dispersed yet. Pierre threw off his cape and went into the first room, where the remains of supper lay and one lackey, thinking no one could see him, was finishing on the sly what was left of the wine in the glasses. From the third room came a racket, guffawing, the shouting of familiar voices, and the roaring of a bear. Some eight young men were crowded busily by an open window. Three were romping with a young bear, one of them dragging it by a chain, trying to frighten the others.

"I stake a hundred on Stevens!" shouted one.

"Make sure there's no holding on!" shouted another.

"I'm for Dolokhov!" cried a third. "Break the grip, Kuragin."[23]

"Let Bruin be, we're making a bet."

"At one go, otherwise you lose," shouted a fourth.

"Yakov! Let's have a bottle, Yakov!" shouted the host himself, a tall, handsome man, who was standing in the midst of the crowd in nothing but a fine shirt open on his chest. "Wait, gentlemen. Here's Petrusha, my dear friend," he turned to Pierre.

Another voice, that of a not very tall man with clear blue eyes, especially striking amidst all these drunken voices by its sober expression, shouted from the window: "Come here—break the grip!" This was Dolokhov, an officer of the Semyonovsky regiment, a notorious gambler and duellist, who lived with Anatole. Pierre smiled, looking around merrily.

"I don't understand a thing. What's up?" he asked.

"Wait, he's not drunk. Give me a bottle," said Anatole, and taking a glass from the table, he went up to Pierre.

"First of all, drink."

Pierre started drinking glass after glass, looking from under his brows at the drunken guests, who again crowded by the window, and listening to their talk. Anatole poured the wine for him and told him that Dolokhov was making a bet with the Englishman Stevens, a sailor who was there, that he, Dolokhov, could drink a bottle of rum sitting in the third-floor window with his legs hanging out.

"Well, drink it all," said Anatole, handing Pierre the last glass, "otherwise I won't let you go!"

"No, I don't want to," said Pierre, pushing Anatole away, and he went over to the window.

Dolokhov was holding the Englishman by the hand and clearly, distinctly articulating the terms of the bet, mainly addressing Anatole and Pierre.

Dolokhov was a man of medium height, curly-haired and with light blue eyes. He was about twenty-five. Like all infantry officers, he wore no moustache, and his mouth, the most striking feature of his face, was entirely visible. The lines of his mouth were remarkably finely curved. In the middle, the upper lip came down energetically on the sturdy lower lip in a sharp wedge, and at the corners something like two smiles were constantly formed, one on each side; and all of that together, especially combined with a firm, insolent, intelligent gaze, made up such an expression that it was impossible not to notice this face. Dolokhov was not a rich man and had no connections. And though Anatole ran through tens of thousands, Dolokhov lived with him and managed to place himself so that Anatole and all those who knew them respected Dolokhov more than Anatole. Dolokhov gambled at all games and almost always won. No matter how much he drank, he never lost his clear-headedness. Kuragin and Dolokhov were both celebrities at that time in the world of Petersburg scapegraces and carousers.

A bottle of rum was brought. Two lackeys were tearing out the frame that prevented one from sitting on the outer ledge of the window; they were obviously hurrying and intimidated by the orders and shouts of the surrounding gentlemen.

Anatole went up to the window with his victorious look. He wanted to break something. He pushed the lackeys away and pulled at the frame, but the frame did not yield. He smashed a pane.

"You next, strongman," he turned to Pierre.

Pierre took hold of the crosspieces, pulled, and, with a crash, here broke and there ripped out the oak frame.

"Away with all of it, otherwise they'll think I'm holding on," said Dolokhov.

"The Englishman's boasting . . . eh? . . . all right? . . ." said Anatole.

"All right," said Pierre, looking at Dolokhov, who, holding the bottle of rum in his hand, was approaching the window, through which the light of the sky could be seen and the glow of morning and evening merging in it.

Dolokhov jumped up into the window with the bottle of rum in his hand.

"Listen!" he shouted, standing on the windowsill and turning to the room. Everyone fell silent.

"I put down" (he spoke in French so that the Englishman would understand him, and he did not speak the language all that well), "I put down fifty imperials—want to make it a hundred?" he added, addressing the Englishman.

"No, fifty," said the Englishman.

"Very well, fifty imperials, that I will drink a whole bottle of rum, without taking it from my lips, drink it sitting outside the window, on this place" (he bent down and indicated the sloping ledge outside the window), "and without holding on to anything . . . Right? . . ."

"Very good," said the Englishman.

Anatole turned to the Englishman and, taking him by the button of his tail-coat and looking at him from above (the Englishman was short), began repeating the terms of the bet to him in English.

"Wait," cried Dolokhov, tapping the bottle against the window to attract attention. "Wait, Kuragin; listen. If anybody else does the same, I'll pay him a hundred imperials. Understood?"

The Englishman nodded his head, in no way making clear whether he did or did not accept this new bet. Anatole did not let go of the Englishman, and though he had nodded to show he had understood everything, Anatole translated Dolokhov's words into English for him. A young, lean boy, a life-hussar, who had gambled away everything that evening, climbed up on the window, stuck his head out, and looked down.

"Oooh!" he said, looking out of the window at the stone of the pavement.

"Attention!" cried Dolokhov and pulled the officer from the window. Getting tangled in his spurs, the boy jumped down awkwardly into the room.

After placing the bottle on the windowsill to have it conveniently at hand, Dolokhov slowly and carefully climbed into the window. Lowering his legs and spreading both hands against the sides of the window, he tried his position, settled himself, let go with his hands, shifted a little to the right, to the left, and took the bottle. Anatole brought two candles and set them on the windowsill, though it was already quite light. Dolokhov's back in its white shirt and his curly head were lit up from both sides. Everyone crowded by the window. The Englishman stood in front. Pierre smiled and said nothing. One of those present, older than the others, with a frightened and angry face, suddenly moved forward and was about to seize Dolokhov by the shirt.

"Gentlemen, this is stupid; he'll kill himself," said this more reasonable man.

Anatole stopped him.

"Don't touch, you'll frighten him, and he'll be killed. Eh? . . . What then? . . .
Eh? . . ."

Dolokhov turned, adjusting his position, and again spreading his hands.

"If anybody else tries to get at me," he said, slowly forcing the words
through his compressed and thin lips, "I'll chuck him down from here right
now. So! . . ."

Having said "So!" he turned back again, let go with his hands, took the bottle and put it to his lips, threw his head back, and thrust his free arm up for balance. One of the lackeys, who had begun picking up the glass, stopped in a
bent position, not taking his eyes from the window and Dolokhov's back. Anatole stood erect, his eyes gaping. The Englishman, his lips thrust out, watched
from the side. The man who had tried to stop them rushed to the corner of the
room and lay down on a sofa, face to the wall. Pierre covered his face, and a
faint smile remained forgotten on it, though it now expressed terror and fear.
Everyone was silent. Pierre took his hands away from his eyes. Dolokhov was
sitting in the same position, only his head was thrown far back, so that the
curly hair of his nape touched the collar of his shirt, and the hand holding the
bottle rose higher and higher, trembling and making an effort. The bottle was
apparently emptying and rising at the same time, pushing the head back. "Why
is it taking so long?" thought Pierre. It seemed to him that more than half an
hour had gone by. Suddenly Dolokhov made a backward movement, and his
arm trembled nervously; this shudder was enough to shift his whole body,
which was sitting on the sloping ledge. He shifted completely, and his arm and
head trembled still more from the effort. One arm rose to take hold of the
windowsill, but lowered itself again. Pierre again shut his eyes and said to himself that he was never going to open them. Suddenly he felt everything around
him stirring. He looked: Dolokhov was standing on the windowsill, his face
pale and merry.

"Empty!"

He tossed the bottle to the Englishman, who deftly caught it. Dolokhov
jumped down from the window. He smelled strongly of rum.

"Excellent! Good boy! There's a bet for you! Devil take you all!" they cried
on all sides.

The Englishman, having produced his purse, counted out the money. Dolokhov frowned and said nothing. Pierre climbed into the window.

"Gentlemen! Who wants to make a bet with me? I'll do the same thing," he
suddenly shouted. "And there's no need for a bet, that's what. Tell them to
bring a bottle. I'll do it . . . tell them."

"Let him, let him!" said Dolokhov, smiling.

"What, have you lost your mind? Who'd let you? You get dizzy on the stairs," came from various sides.

"I'll drink it, give me a bottle of rum!" Pierre cried, pounding the table with a determined and drunken gesture, and he climbed into the window.

They seized him by the arms; but he was so strong that he pushed those who came near him far away.

"No, you won't get anywhere with him that way," said Anatole. "Wait, I'll trick him. Listen, I'll make a bet with you, but tomorrow, and now let's all go to the * * *."

"Let's go," cried Pierre, "let's go! . . . And we'll take Bruin with us . . ."

And he seized the bear and, hugging him and lifting him up, began waltzing around the room with him.

VII

Prince Vassily fulfilled the promise he had given at Anna Pavlovna's soirée to Princess Drubetskoy, who had solicited him for her only son Boris. A report on him was made to the sovereign, and, unlike others, he was transferred to the Semyonovsky guards regiment as an ensign. But Boris was not to be appointed adjutant or attaché to Kutuzov, despite all Anna Mikhailovna's soliciting and scheming. Soon after Anna Pavlovna's soirée, Anna Mikhailovna returned to Moscow, straight to her rich relations, the Rostovs, with whom she stayed in Moscow, and with whom her adored Borenka, just made an ensign in the army and transferred to the guards, had been brought up and had lived for years. The guards had already left Petersburg on the tenth of August, and her son, who had remained in Moscow to equip himself, was to catch up with them on the way to Radzivilov.

At the Rostovs' it was the name day of the Natalyas, mother and younger daughter.[24] Since morning, coach-and-sixes had constantly been driving up and leaving, bringing people with congratulations to the big house of the countess Rostov on Povarskaya Street, which was known to all Moscow. The countess with her beautiful older daughter and the guests, who constantly replaced each other, were sitting in the drawing room.

The countess was a woman with a thin, Oriental type of face, forty-five years old, evidently worn out by children, of whom she had had twelve. The slowness of her movements and speech, caused by weakness, gave her an air of importance that inspired respect. Princess Anna Mikhailovna Drubetskoy, as a member of the household, sat right there, helping with the business of receiving the guests and occupying them with conversation. The young people were in the back rooms, finding it unnecessary to take part in receiving visits. The count met the guests and saw them off, inviting them all to dinner.

"Much obliged to you, *ma chère* or *mon cher*" (he said *ma chère* or *mon cher* to everyone without exception and without the slightest nuance, whether they were of higher or lower standing than himself), "for myself and the dear name-day ladies. See that you come for dinner. You'll offend me if you don't, *mon cher*. I cordially invite you on behalf of the whole family, *ma chère*." These words he said with the same expression on his full, cheerful, and clean-shaven face, with the same strong handshake and repeated short bows, to everyone without exception or variation. Having seen off a guest, the count would return to the gentleman or lady who was still in the drawing room; moving up an armchair, and with the look of a man who loves life and knows how to live it, spreading his legs dashingly and putting his hands on his knees, he would sway significantly, offer his surmises about the weather, discuss health, sometimes in Russian, sometimes in very poor but self-confident French, and again, with the look of a man weary but firm in the fulfilment of his duty, would go to see people off, smoothing the thin grey hair over his bald spot, and again invite them to dinner. Occasionally, on returning from the front hall, he would pass through the conservatory and the servants' room to a big marble hall, where a table of eighty settings was being laid, and, looking at the servants carrying silver and china, opening out tables, and spreading damask tablecloths, he would call Dmitri Vassilievich, a nobleman who managed all his affairs, and say:

"Well, well, Mitenka, see that it's all nice. Right, right," he would say, looking over the enormous, opened-out table. "The main thing's the setout. So, so . . ." And, sighing self-contentedly, he would go back to the drawing room.

"Marya Lvovna Karagin with daughter!" the countess's enormous footman announced in a bass voice, coming to the door of the drawing room. The countess pondered and took a pinch from a gold snuffbox with her husband's portrait on it.

"I'm worn out with these visits," she said. "Well, she'll be the last I receive. She's so prim. Ask her in," she said to the footman in a sad voice, as if to say: "Well, so finish me off."

A tall, stout, proud-looking lady and her round-faced, smiling daughter came into the room, rustling their skirts.

"*Chère comtesse, il y a si longtemps . . . elle a été alitée, la pauvre enfant . . . au bal des Razoumowsky . . . et la comtesse Apraksine . . . j'ai été si heureuse . . .*"* women's voices were heard, interrupting each other and merging with the rustling of skirts and the moving of chairs. That sort of conversation began which is designed to last just long enough so that one can get

---

*Dear countess, it's been so long . . . she was bedridden, the poor child . . . at the Razumovskys' ball . . . and the countess Apraksin . . . I was so happy . . .

up at the first pause, with a rustling of skirts, say, *"Je suis bien charmée; la santé de maman . . . et la comtesse Apraksine,"* * and again, with a rustling of skirts, go back to the front hall, put on a fur coat or a cloak, and drive off. The conversation turned to the main news of the town at that time—the illness of the rich and famous beau of Catherine's time, old Count Bezukhov, and his illegitimate son Pierre, who had behaved so improperly at Anna Pavlovna Scherer's soirée.

"I'm very sorry for the poor count," said the guest. "He was in poor health to begin with, and now this distress on account of his son. It will kill him!"

"What do you mean?" asked the countess, as if she did not know what the guest was talking about, though she had already heard the cause of Count Bezukhov's distress a good fifteen times.

"It's modern upbringing! While still abroad," the guest went on, "this young man was left to himself, and now in Petersburg, they say, he did such awful things that he's been banished by the police."

"You don't say!" said the countess.

"He chose his acquaintances poorly," Princess Anna Mikhailovna mixed in. "Prince Vassily's son, he and a certain Dolokhov, they say, were up to God knows what. And they've both suffered for it. Dolokhov has been broken to the ranks, and Bezukhov's son has been banished to Moscow. As for Anatole Kuragin—his father somehow hushed it up. But they did banish him from Petersburg."

"Why, what on earth did they do?" asked the countess.

"They're perfect ruffians, especially Dolokhov," said the guest. "He's the son of Marya Ivanovna Dolokhov, such a respectable lady, and what then? Can you imagine: the three of them found a bear somewhere, put it in the carriage with them, and went to the actresses. The police came running to quiet them down. They took a policeman and tied him back to back with the bear, and threw the bear into the Moika. So the bear goes swimming about with the policeman on him."

"A fine figure the policeman must have cut, *ma chère*," cried the count, dying with laughter.

"Ah, how terrible! What is there to laugh at, Count?"

But the ladies could not help laughing themselves.

"They barely managed to save the poor fellow," the guest went on. "That's how intelligently the son of Count Kirill Vladimirovich Bezukhov amuses himself!" she added. "And I heard he was so well-bred and intelligent. There's what all this foreign upbringing leads to. I hope no one receives him here, despite his wealth. They wanted to introduce him to me. I decidedly refused: I have daughters."

*I'm quite delighted; mama's health . . . and the countess Apraksin.

"What makes you say this young man is so wealthy?" asked the countess, leaning away from the girls, who at once pretended they were not listening. "The man has only illegitimate children. It seems . . . Pierre, too, is illegitimate."

The guest waved her hand.

"He has a score of them, I should think."

Princess Anna Mikhailovna mixed into the conversation, clearly wishing to show her connections and her knowledge of all the circumstances of society.

"The thing is this," she said significantly and also in a half whisper. "Count Kirill Vladimirovich's reputation is well-known . . . He's lost count of his children, but this Pierre was his favourite ."

"How good-looking the old man was," said the countess, "even last year! I've never seen a handsomer man."

"He's quite changed now," said Anna Mikhailovna. "So, as I was about to say," she went on, "Prince Vassily is the direct heir to the whole fortune through his wife, but the father loved Pierre very much, concerned himself with his upbringing, and wrote to the sovereign . . . so that when he dies (he's so poorly that they expect it any moment, and Lorrain has come from Petersburg), no one knows who will get this enormous fortune, Pierre or Prince Vassily. Forty thousand souls,[25] and millions of roubles. I know it very well, because Prince Vassily told me himself. And Kirill Vladimirovich is my uncle twice removed through my mother. And he's Borya's godfather," she added, as if ascribing no importance to this circumstance.

"Prince Vassily came to Moscow yesterday. He's going to do some inspecting, I'm told," said the guest.

"Yes, but *entre nous*,"* said the countess, "it's a pretext. He's come, essentially, to see Count Kirill Vladimirovich, having learned that he was so poorly."

"However, *ma chère*, that was a nice stunt," said the count and, noticing that the elder guest was not listening, he turned to the young ladies. "A fine figure that policeman cut, I imagine."

And, picturing how the policeman waved his arms, he again burst into resounding, bass-voiced laughter, which shook his whole stout body, as people laugh who always eat, and especially drink, very well. "So please do come for dinner," he said.

VIII

Silence ensued. The countess looked at the guest with a pleasant smile, without concealing, however, that she would not be upset in the least now if the guest

*Between us.

got up and left. The guest's daughter was already smoothing her dress, looking questioningly at her mother, when suddenly from the neighbouring room came the sound of several men's and women's feet running to the door, the crash of a tripped-over and fallen chair, and a thirteen-year-old girl ran in, bundling something in her short muslin skirt, and stopped in the middle of the room. It was obvious that she had run so far inadvertently, miscalculating the distance. At the same moment a student in a raspberry-coloured collar,[26] an officer of the guards, a fifteen-year-old girl, and a fat, red-cheeked boy in a child's jacket appeared in the doorway.

The count jumped up and, swaying, spread his arms wide around the running girl.

"Ah, here she is!" he shouted, laughing. "The name-day girl! *Ma chère* name-day girl!"

"*Ma chère, il y a un temps pour tout,*"* said the countess, feigning sternness. "You always spoil her, *Élie,*" she added to her husband.

"*Bonjour, ma chère, je vous félicite,*" said the guest. "*Quelle délicieuse enfant!*"† she added, turning to the mother.

The dark-eyed, big-mouthed, not beautiful, but lively girl, with her child's bare shoulders popping out of her bodice from running fast, with her black ringlets all thrown back, her thin, bare arms, her little legs in lace-trimmed knickers and low shoes, was at that sweet age when a girl is no longer a child, but the child is not yet a young lady. Wriggling out of her father's arms, she ran to her mother and, paying no attention to her stern remark, buried her flushed face in her mother's lace mantilla and laughed. She laughed at something, talking fitfully about the doll she took out from under her skirt.

"You see? . . . My doll . . . Mimi . . . You see . . ."

And Natasha could say no more (everything seemed funny to her). She fell on her mother and burst into such loud and ringing laughter that everyone else, even the prim guest, laughed involuntarily.

"Well, off you go, off you go, you and that ugly thing!" said the mother, pushing her daughter away with feigned gruffness. "This is my younger one," she turned to her guest.

Natasha, tearing her face momentarily from her mother's lace wrap, looked up at her through tears of laughter and hid her face again.

The guest, forced to admire the family scene, found it necessary to take some part in it.

"Tell me, my dear," she said, addressing Natasha, "what is this Mimi to you? Your daughter, it must be?"

*My dear, there's a time for everything.
†Hello, my dear, I congratulate you . . . What a delightful child!

Natasha did not like the tone of condescension to childish talk in which the guest addressed her. She made no reply and gave the guest a serious look.

Meanwhile all this younger generation—Boris, the officer, son of Princess Anna Mikhailovna; Nikolai, the student, the count's eldest son; Sonya, the count's fifteen-year-old niece; and little Petrusha, the youngest son—all settled themselves in the drawing room and obviously tried to keep within the limits of propriety the animation and gaiety which their every feature still breathed. It was clear that there in the back rooms, from which they had all come running so precipitously, the talk was merrier than the talk here about town gossip, the weather, and the *comtesse Apraksine*. They glanced at each other from time to time and could barely hold back their laughter.

The two young men, the student and the officer, friends from childhood, were of the same age and both handsome, but they did not resemble each other. Boris was a tall, blond youth with the regular, fine features of a calm and handsome face. Nikolai was a curly-haired young man, not very tall, and with an open expression of the face. On his upper lip a little black hair had already appeared, and his whole face expressed impetuousness and rapturousness. Nikolai blushed as soon as he came into the drawing room. One could see that he was searching for something to say and could not find it. Boris, on the other hand, got his bearings at once and told calmly, jokingly, how he had known this Mimi, the doll, when she was still a young girl, with an unspoiled nose, how she had grown old in the five years he remembered, and how her head had got cracked across the entire skull. Having said this, he glanced at Natasha. Natasha turned away from him, glanced at her younger brother, who, with his eyes shut tight, was shaking with soundless laughter, and, unable to hold herself back any longer, jumped down and ran out of the room as fast as her quick feet would carry her. Boris did not laugh.

"I believe you also wanted to go, *maman*? Do you need a carriage?" he said, turning to his mother with a smile.

"Yes, go, go, tell them to make ready," she said, smiling.

Boris quietly went to the door and followed Natasha out; the fat boy angrily ran after them, as if vexed at the disturbance that had interfered with his pursuits.

IX

Of the young people, not including the countess's elder daughter (who was four years older than her sister and already behaved like an adult), and the young lady guest, only Nikolai and the niece Sonya remained in the drawing room. Sonya was a slender, diminutive brunette with a soft gaze shaded by long eyelashes, a thick black braid wound twice round her head, and a sallow tinge to the skin of her face and especially of her bared, lean, but gracefully muscular arms and neck. In the smoothness of her movements, the softness and suppleness of her small limbs, and her somewhat sly and reserved manner, she resembled a pretty but not yet fully formed kitten, which would one day be a lovely little cat. She evidently considered it the proper thing to show by a smile her interest in the general conversation; but, against her will, her eyes under their long, thick lashes kept looking with such passionate girlish adoration at her cousin, who was leaving for the army, that her smile could not deceive anyone for a moment, and it was clear that the little cat crouched down only in order to leap up more energetically and play with her cousin as soon as they, like Boris and Natasha, could get out of this drawing room.

"Yes, *ma chère*," said the old count, addressing the guest and pointing to his Nikolai. "Here his friend Boris has just been made an officer, and out of friendship he doesn't want to lag behind; he's leaving both the university and his old father: he's going into the army, *ma chère*. And a post had already been prepared for him in the archives and all.²⁷ Isn't that friendship?" the count said questioningly.

"Yes, they say war has been declared," said the guest.

"They've been saying it for a long time," said the count. "Again they'll talk and talk and leave it at that. *Ma chère*, that's friendship!" he repeated. "He's joining the hussars."

The guest, not knowing what to say, shook her head.

"Not at all out of friendship," replied Nikolai, blushing and protesting, as if it was a shameful calumny. "It's not friendship, I simply feel a calling for military service."

He shot a glance at his cousin and the young lady guest: they both looked at him with a smile of approval.

"Tonight Schubert will be dining with us, a colonel in the Pavlogradsky hussar regiment. He's been on leave here and is taking him along. What to do?" said the count, shrugging his shoulders and speaking jokingly about a matter that obviously cost him much grief.

"I've already told you, papa," said his son, "that if you don't want to let me go, I'll stay. But I know I'm not good for anything but military service; I'm not a diplomat, not a functionary, I'm unable to hide my feelings," he said, glancing all the while with the coquetry of a handsome youth at Sonya and the young lady guest.

The little cat fixed her eyes on him and seemed ready at any instant to begin playing and show all her cat nature.

"Well, well, all right!" said the old count. "He keeps getting heated up. It's this Bonaparte who's turned all their heads; they all wonder how it is that from the lieutenants he landed among the emperors. Well, God grant it," he added, not noticing the guest's mocking smile.

The adults began talking about Bonaparte. Julie, Mme Karagin's daughter, turned to the young Rostov:

"What a pity you weren't at the Arkharovs' on Thursday. I was bored without you," she said, smiling tenderly at him.

The flattered young man, with the coquettish smile of youth, sat closer to her and got into a separate conversation with the smiling Julie, completely unaware that his involuntary smile cut the heart of the blushing and falsely smiling Sonya with the knife of jealousy. In the middle of the conversation, he turned to look at her. Sonya gave him a passionately angry look and, barely holding back the tears in her eyes, with a false smile on her lips, got up and left the room. All of Nikolai's animation vanished. He waited for the first lull in the conversaton and with an upset face left the room to look for Sonya.

"How crystal clear all these young ones' secrets are!" said Anna Mikhailovna, pointing to Nikolai as he left. "*Cousinage dangereux voisinage*,"* she added.

"Yes," said the countess, when the ray of sunlight that had penetrated the room with the young generation vanished, and as if answering a question no one had asked her, but which constantly preoccupied her. "So much suffering, so much anxiety endured so as to rejoice in them now! And now, too, there's really more fear than joy. One is afraid, always afraid! It's precisely the age when there are so many dangers both for girls and for boys."

"Everything depends on upbringing," said the guest.

"Yes, true for you," the countess went on. "Up to now, thank God, I've been a friend to my children and have enjoyed their full trust," said the countess, repeating the error of many parents who suppose that their children have no secrets from them. "I know that I'll always be my daughters' first *confidente* and that if Nikolenka, with his fiery character, gets up to some mischief (boys can't do without it), it still won't be the same as with these Petersburg gentlemen."

"Yes, nice, nice children," agreed the count, who always resolved all tangled questions by finding everything nice. "Just look at him! Decided to be a hussar! Well, what do you want, *ma chère*!"

"What a sweet creature your younger one is!" said the guest. "A ball of fire!"

"Yes, a ball of fire," said the count. "She takes after me! And what a voice! Though she's my daughter, I'll tell you the truth: she'll be a singer, another Salomoni. We've hired an Italian to teach her."

"Isn't it too early? They say it harms the voice to study at that age."

"Oh, no, not too early at all!" said the count. "How is it, then, that our mothers got married when they were twelve or thirteen?"

*Cousinhood is a dangerous neighbourhood.

"She's already in love with Boris now! What a one!" said the countess, smiling quietly, looking at Boris's mother, and, evidently responding to the thought that always preoccupied her, she went on: "Well, so you see, if I were strict with her, if I forbade her . . . God knows what they'd do on the sly" (the countess meant they would be kissing), "but now I know her every word. She'll come running to me herself in the evening and tell me everything. I may be spoiling her, but it really seems better. I was strict with the elder one."

"Yes, I was brought up quite differently," said the elder one, the beautiful Countess Vera, smiling.

But the smile did not embellish Vera's face, as usually happens; on the contrary, her face became unnatural and therefore unpleasant. The elder one, Vera, was good-looking, far from stupid, an excellent student, well-brought-up, had a pleasant voice, and what she said was correct and appropriate; but, strangely, everyone, both the guest and the countess, turned to look at her, as if wondering why she had said it, and they felt awkward.

"One is always too clever with the older children, wanting to do something extraordinary," said the guest.

"There's no use denying it, *ma chère*! The dear countess was too clever with Vera," said the count. "Well, so what! She still turned out nice," he added, winking at Vera approvingly.

The guests got up and left, promising to come for dinner.

"What manners! They sat and sat!" said the countess, after seeing the guests off.

X

When Natasha left the drawing room and ran off, she ran no further than the conservatory. In that room she stopped, listening to the talk in the drawing room and waiting for Boris to come out. She was already growing impatient and, stamping her little foot, was about to cry because he did not come at once, when she heard the neither slow nor quick, but proper footsteps of the young man. Natasha quickly darted among the tubs of plants and hid herself.

Boris stopped in the middle of the room, looking around, brushed some specks of dust off the sleeve of his uniform with his hand, and went up to a mirror, studying his handsome face. Natasha kept still, peeking from her ambush, waiting to see what he would do. He stood for some time before the mirror, smiled, and walked to the other door. Natasha was about to call him, but then changed her mind.

"Let him search," she said to herself. As soon as Boris left, the flushed Sonya came from the other door, whispering something spitefully through her tears. Natasha restrained her first impulse to rush out to her and remained in her ambush, as if under the cap of invisibility, observing what went on in the world. She experienced a special new pleasure. Sonya was whispering something and kept looking back at the door of the drawing room. Nikolai came out of that door.

"Sonya! what's wrong? how can you?" said Nikolai, rushing to her.

"Never mind, never mind, leave me alone!" Sonya burst into sobs.

"No, I know what it is."

"So you know, and that's wonderful, and so go to her."

"So-o-onya! One word! How can you torment me and yourself so because of a fantasy?" said Nikolai, taking her hand.

Sonya did not pull her hand away and stopped crying.

Natasha, motionless and breathless, with shining eyes, watched from behind her ambush. "What will happen now?" she thought.

"Sonya! The whole world is no use to me! You alone are everything," said Nikolai. "I'll prove it to you."

"I don't like it when you talk like that."

"Well, then I won't, well, forgive me, Sonya!" He drew her to him and kissed her.

"Ah, how nice!" thought Natasha, and when Sonya and Nikolai left the room, she went out after them and called Boris.

"Boris, come here," she said with a significant and sly air. "There's something I must tell you. Here, here," she said and led him to the conservatory, to the place between the tubs where she had been hiding. Boris, smiling, followed her.

"What is this *something*?" he asked.

She became embarrassed, looked around, and, seeing her doll abandoned on a tub, took it in her hands.

"Kiss the doll," she said.

Boris looked into her animated face with attentive, gentle eyes and said nothing.

"You don't want to? Well, come here, then," she said and went deeper among the plants and dropped her doll. "Closer, closer!" she whispered. She caught the officer by the cuffs with both hands, and her flushed face showed solemnity and fear.

"And do you want to kiss me?" she whispered barely audibly, looking at him from under her eyebrows, smiling and almost weeping with excitement.

Boris blushed.

"You're so funny!" he said, bending down to her, blushing still more, but not undertaking anything and waiting.

She suddenly jumped up onto a tub, becoming taller than he, embraced him with her thin, bare arms, which bent higher than his neck, and, tossing her hair back with a movement of the head, kissed him right on the lips.

She slipped between the pots to the other side of the plants and stopped, her head lowered.

"Natasha," he said, "you know I love you, but . . ."

"You're in love with me?" Natasha interrupted.

"Yes, I am, but, please, let's not do like just now . . . Another four years . . . Then I'll ask for your hand."

Natasha reflected.

"Thirteen, fourteen, fifteen, sixteen . . ." she said, counting on her thin little fingers. "All right! So it's settled?"

And a smile of joy and reassurance lit up her animated face.

"Settled!" said Boris.

"For ever?" said the girl. "Till death?"

And, taking him under the arm, with a happy face she slowly walked beside him to the sitting room.

XI

The countess was so tired out from the visits that she ordered no one else to be received, and the porter was told simply to be sure to invite for dinner everyone who came by with congratulations. The countess wanted to talk personally with her childhood friend, Princess Anna Mikhailovna, whom she had not seen properly since her return from Petersburg. Anna Mikhailovna, with her weepy and pleasant face, moved closer to the countess's armchair.

"I'll be perfectly frank with you," said Anna Mikhailovna. "There are few of us old friends left! That's why I cherish your friendship so much."

Anna Mikhailovna looked at Vera and stopped. The countess pressed her friend's hand.

"Vera," said the countess, turning to her older daughter, obviously not her favourite. "How is it you have no notion of anything? Can't you feel that you're not needed here? Go to your sisters, or . . ."

The beautiful Vera smiled disdainfully, apparently not feeling the slightest offence.

"If you had told me long ago, mama, I would have left at once," she said and went to her room. But, passing through the sitting room, she noticed two couples sitting symmetrically by the two windows. She stopped and smiled disdainfully. Sonya was sitting close to Nikolai, who was writing out some verses for her, the first he had ever written. Boris and Natasha were sitting by the other window and fell silent when Vera came in. Sonya and Natasha looked at Vera with guilty and happy faces.

It was amusing and touching to look at these enamoured girls, but the sight of them evidently did not arouse any pleasant feelings in Vera.

"How many times have I asked you not to take my things," she said. "You have a room of your own." She took the inkstand from Nikolai.

"Just a moment," he said, dipping his pen.

"You manage to do everything at the wrong time," said Vera. "The way you came running into the drawing room just now, everyone was ashamed of you."

In spite of, or precisely because of, the fact that what she said was perfectly correct, no one answered her, and the four only exchanged glances with each other. She lingered in the room, with the inkstand in her hand.

"And what secrets can there be at your age between Natasha and Boris and between you two? It's all silliness!"

"Well, what does it matter to you, Vera?" Natasha said pleadingly in a quiet little voice.

Clearly, that day she was being kinder and more affectionate with everyone than ever.

"Very silly," said Vera. "I'm ashamed of you. Why secrets?"

"We all have our secrets. We don't bother you and Berg," Natasha said, flaring up.

"Of course you don't," said Vera, "because there can never be anything bad in my actions. But I shall tell mama how you behave with Boris."

"Natalya Ilyinichna behaves very well with me," said Boris. "I can't complain," he said.

"Stop it, Boris, you're such a diplomat" (the word *diplomat* was much in vogue among children in that special sense they endowed it with); "it's even boring," Natasha said in an offended, trembling voice. "Why is she pestering me?"

"You'll never understand it," she said, turning to Vera, "because you've never loved anybody, you have no heart, you're just a Madame de Genlis" (this nickname, considered very offensive, had been given to Vera by Nikolai), "and your highest pleasure is to do unpleasant things to others. Go and flirt with Berg as much as you like," she said quickly.

"I certainly won't go running after a young man in front of guests . . ."

"Well, she's done it," Nikolai mixed in, "she's said unpleasant things to everybody and upset everybody. Let's go to the nursery."

All four, like a frightened flock of birds, got up and left.

"They said unpleasant things to *me*, but I said nothing to anybody," said Vera.

"Madame de Genlis, Madame de Genlis!" laughing voices said behind the door.

The beautiful Vera, who had such an irritating, unpleasant effect on everyone, smiled and, apparently untouched by what had been said to her, went up to the mirror and straightened her scarf and hair. Looking at her beautiful face, she appeared to become even colder and calmer.

. . .

In the drawing room the conversation was still going on.

"*Ah! chère,*" said the countess, "in my life, too, *tout n'est pas rose.* Don't I see that, *du train que nous allons,** our fortune won't last long! It's all his club and his kindness. Our life in the country—is that any respite? Theatre, hunting, God knows what. Ah, why talk about me! Well, how did you arrange it all? I often marvel at you, Annette, how at your age you can gallop off in a carriage, by yourself, to Moscow, to Petersburg, to all the ministers, to all the nobility, and you know how to deal with them all—I marvel at it! Well, how did it get arranged? I don't know how to do any of it."

"Ah, my dear heart!" Princess Anna Mikhailovna replied. "God forbid that you ever learn how hard it is to be left a widow without support and with a son whom you love to distraction. One learns everything," she went on with a certain pride. "My lawsuit has taught me. If I need to see one of these trumps, I write a note: '*Princesse une telle*† wishes to see so and so'—and I go in person, in a hired cab two, even three times, even four—until I get what I want. It's all the same to me what they think of me."

"Well, whom did you solicit for Borenka?" asked the countess. "Here your son is an officer in the guards, and Nikolushka is going as a junker.[28] There's no one to solicit. Who did you ask?"

"Prince Vassily. He was very nice. He agreed at once to do everything and reported to the emperor," Princess Anna Mikhailovna said with rapture, forgetting entirely about all the humiliation she had gone through to achieve her goal.

"And what, has he aged, Prince Vassily?" asked the countess. "I haven't seen him since our theatre performances at the Rumyantsevs'. And I suppose he's forgotten me. *Il me faisait la cour,*"‡ the countess remembered with a smile.

"He's the same as ever," replied Anna Mikhailovna, "amiable, overflowing. *Les grandeurs ne lui ont pas tourné la tête de tout.*§ 'I'm sorry I can do so little for you, dear Princess,' he says to me, 'I'm yours to command.' No, he's a nice man, and excellent family. But you know my love for my son, Nathalie. I don't know what I wouldn't do for his happiness. And my circumstances are so bad," Anna Mikhailovna went on sadly, lowering her voice, "so bad that I'm now in a most terrible position. My wretched lawsuit eats up all I have and doesn't get anywhere. Can you imagine, I don't have even ten kopecks *à la lettre,*# and I don't know how I'll pay to equip Boris." She took out a handkerchief and began to cry. "I need five hundred roubles, and all I have is one

---

*. . . all is not rosy . . . at the rate we're going . . .
†Princess So-and-So.
‡He once courted me.
§Grandeurs haven't turned his head at all.
#Literally.

twenty-five-rouble note. I'm in such a position . . . My only hope now rests with Count Kirill Alexandrovich Bezukhov. If he doesn't care to support his godson—he's Borya's godfather—and lay out something for his maintenance, all my troubles will have been in vain, I won't have the money to equip him."

The countess also waxed tearful and silently pondered something.

"I often think—maybe it's sinful," said the princess, "but I often think: here Count Kirill Vladimirovich Bezukhov lives alone . . . this enormous fortune . . . and what does he live for? Life's a burden to him, and Borya is only beginning to live."

"He'll surely leave Boris something," said the countess.

"God knows, *chère amie*! These rich courtiers are such egoists. But even so I'll go to him now with Boris and tell him outright what it's about. Let them think whatever they like of me, it really makes no difference to me, when my son's destiny depends on it." The princess got up. "It's now two o'clock, and you dine at four. I have time to go."

And with the air of a practical Petersburg lady who knows how to make use of her time, Anna Mikhailovna sent for her son and went out with him to the front hall.

"Goodbye, dear heart," she said to the countess, who came to see her to the door; "wish me success," she added in a whisper, so that her son would not hear.

"Are you going to see Count Kirill Vladimirovich, *ma chère*?" the count asked from the dining room, also coming out to the front hall. "If he's better, invite Pierre to dine with us. He used to come here, danced with the children. Invite him without fail, *ma chère*. Well, we'll see how Taras distinguishes himself today. He says that Count Orlov had no such dinners as we're going to have."

XII

"*Mon cher Boris*," Princess Anna Mikhailovna said to her son when Countess Rostov's carriage, in which they were sitting, drove down the straw-laid street[29] and into the wide courtyard of Count Kirill Vladimirovich Bezukhov. "*Mon cher Boris*," said the mother, freeing her hand from under her old mantle and placing it with a timid and caressing movement on her son's hand, "be gentle, be attentive. Count Kirill Vladimirovich is, after all, your godfather, and your future fate depends on him. Remember that, *mon cher*, be nice, as you know how to be . . ."

"If I knew anything would come of it besides humiliation . . ." her son replied coldly. "But I've promised you, and I'm doing it for you."

Despite the fact that someone's carriage was standing at the entrance, the porter, having looked over the mother and son (who, without asking to be announced, had walked directly through the glass entryway between two rows of statues in niches), with a significant glance at the old mantle, asked whom they wanted to see, the princesses or the count, and, on learning that it was the count, said that his excellency was feeling worse that day, and that his excellency was not receiving anyone.

"We can leave," the son said in French.

"*Mon ami!*" the mother said in a pleading voice, again touching her son's hand as if this touch could calm or encourage him.

Boris fell silent and, without taking off his overcoat, looked questioningly at his mother.

"Dearest," Anna Mikhailovna said in a tender little voice, turning to the porter, "I know Count Kirill Vladimirovich is very ill . . . that's why I've come . . . I'm a relation . . . I won't trouble anyone, dearest . . . All I need is to see Prince Vassily Sergeevich: he is staying here, I believe. Announce us, please."

The porter sullenly pulled the bell rope that rang upstairs and turned away.

"Princess Drubetskoy to see Prince Vassily Sergeevich," he called out to the servant in stockings, shoes, and a tailcoat, who had come running down and was now peering from the turn of the stairway.

The mother smoothed the folds of her re-dyed silk dress, looked in a full-length Venetian mirror on the wall, and, in her down-at-heel shoes, went briskly up the carpet of the stairs.

"*Mon cher, vous m'avez promis,*"* she addressed her son again, touching his hand to encourage him.

The son, lowering his eyes, calmly followed after her.

They entered a large room, in which one door led to the apartment assigned to Prince Vassily.

As the mother and son reached the middle of the room, intending to ask their way from an old servant who had jumped up when they came in, the bronze handle of one of the doors turned, and Prince Vassily, in an informal velvet house jacket, with one star, came out, accompanying a handsome dark-haired man. This man was the famous Petersburg doctor, Lorrain.

"*C'est donc positif?*"† the prince was saying.

"*Mon prince, 'errare humanum est,' mais . . .*"‡ the doctor replied, swallowing his *r*s and pronouncing the Latin words with a French accent.

"*C'est bien, c'est bien . . .*"§

---

*My dear, you promised me.
†So it's positive?
‡My prince, "to err is human," but . . .
§Very well, very well.

Noticing Anna Mikhailovna and her son, Prince Vassily dismissed the doctor with a bow and silently, but with a questioning look, came over to them. The son noticed how deep grief suddenly appeared in his mother's eyes and smiled slightly.

"Yes, Prince, we meet here under such sad circumstances . . . Well, how is our dear patient?" she said, as if oblivious of the cold, insulting gaze directed at her.

Prince Vassily looked questioningly, to the point of bewilderment, at her, then at Boris. Boris bowed courteously. Prince Vassily, without responding to the bow, turned to Anna Mikhailovna and replied to her question with a movement of the head and lips signifying the worst hopes for the patient.

"Can it be?" exclaimed Anna Mikhailovna. "Ah, it's terrible! I'm afraid to think . . . This is my son," she added, pointing to Boris. "He wanted to thank you himself."

Boris once more bowed courteously.

"Believe me, Prince, a mother's heart will never forget what you have done for us."

"I'm glad that I could give you pleasure, my dearest Anna Mikhailovna," said Prince Vassily, straightening his jabot and in his gesture and voice displaying here, in Moscow, before the patronized Anna Mikhailovna, far greater importance than in Petersburg, at Annette Scherer's soirée.

"Try to serve well and be worthy," he added, sternly addressing Boris. "I'm glad . . . You're here on leave?" he dictated in his passionless tone.

"Awaiting orders, Your Excellency, to be dispatched to my new assignment," replied Boris, showing neither vexation at the prince's abrupt tone, nor the wish to get into conversation, but so calmly and deferentially that the prince looked at him intently.

"You live with your mother?"

"I live at the countess Rostov's," said Boris, again adding, "Your Excellency."

"It's that Ilya Rostov who married Nathalie Shinshin," said Anna Mikhailovna.

"I know, I know," said Prince Vassily in his monotone voice. "*Je n'ai jamais pu concevoir comment Natalie s'est décidée à épouser cet ours mal-léché! Un personnage complètement stupide et ridicule. Et joueur à ce qu'on dit.*"*

"*Mais très brave homme, mon prince,*"† observed Anna Mikhailovna, smiling touchingly, as though she, too, knew that Count Rostov deserved such an opinion, but begged for pity on the poor old man.

*I've never been able to conceive how Nathalie decided to marry that unkempt bear! A completely stupid and ridiculous personage. And a gambler from what they say.
†But a very nice man, my prince.

"What do the doctors say?" the princess asked after a brief pause and again showing great sorrow on her weepy face.

"There's little hope," said the prince.

"And I wished so much to thank *Uncle* for all his benefactions to me and to Borya. *C'est son filleul*,"* she added in such a tone, as though this news was to make Prince Vassily extremely glad.

Prince Vassily pondered and winced. Anna Mikhailovna understood that he feared to find in her a rival over Count Bezukhov's will. She hastened to reassure him.

"If it weren't for my true love and devotion to *Uncle*," she said, uttering this word with special assurance and casualness, "I know his character, noble, direct, but there are just the princesses around him . . . They're still young . . ." She inclined her head and added in a whisper: "Has he fulfilled his last duty,[30] Prince? How precious these last moments are! It cannot get any worse; he must be prepared, if he's so poorly. We women," she smiled tenderly, "always know how to say these things, Prince. I must see him. However hard it is for me, by now I'm used to suffering."

The prince apparently realized, as at Annette Scherer's soirée, that it was difficult to get rid of Anna Mikhailovna.

"This meeting might be hard on him, *chère* Anna Mikhailovna," he said. "Let's wait till evening; the doctors have predicted a crisis."

"But we cannot wait, Prince, at such a moment. *Pensez, il y va du salut de son âme . . . Ah! c'est terrible, les devoirs d'un chrétien . . .*"†

The door to the inner rooms opened and one of the young princesses—the count's nieces—came out, with a cold and sullen face and a long waist strikingly out of proportion with her legs.

Prince Vassily turned to her.

"Well, how is he?"

"The same. And, like it or not, this noise . . ." said the princess, looking Anna Mikhailovna over like a stranger.

"*Ah, chère, je ne vous reconnaissais pas,*" Anna Mikhailovna said with a happy smile, approaching the count's niece at a light amble. "*Je viens d'arriver et je suis à vous pour vous aider à soigner* mon oncle. *J'imagine combien vous avez souffert,*"‡ she added, rolling up her eyes sympathetically.

The princess made no reply, did not even smile, and left at once. Anna Mikhailovna took off her gloves and settled into a hard-won position in an armchair, inviting Prince Vassily to sit down beside her.

---

*He's his godson.

†Think, it's a question of the salvation of his soul . . . Ah! it's terrible, the duties of a Christian . . .

‡Ah, dear, I didn't recognize you . . . I've just come and I'm at your service to help you look after *my uncle*. I can imagine how much you've suffered.

"Boris!" she said to her son and smiled. "I'll go to the count, my uncle, and meanwhile you go to Pierre, *mon ami,* and don't forget to convey to him the invitation from the Rostovs. They're inviting him to dinner. He won't go, I suppose?" she turned to the prince.

"On the contrary," said the prince, now plainly out of sorts. "*Je serais très content si vous me débarassez de ce jeune homme . . .** He just sits here. The count has never once asked about him."

He shrugged his shoulders. The servant led the young man down and up another stairway to Pyotr Kirillovich.

XIII

Pierre had not managed to choose a career for himself in Petersburg, and had indeed been banished to Moscow for riotous behaviour. The story told at Count Rostov's was true. Pierre had taken part in tying the policeman to the bear. He had arrived several days ago and was staying, as usual, at his father's house. Though he supposed that his story was already known in Moscow, and that the ladies who surrounded his father, always ill-disposed towards him, would have used this chance to rile the count, he nevertheless went to his father's part of the house the day he arrived. On entering the drawing room, where the princesses were usually to be found, he greeted the ladies, who were sitting over their embroidery and a book, which one of them was reading aloud. There were three of them. The eldest, a neat, long-waisted, stern young lady, the one who had come out to Anna Mikhailovna, was reading; the younger ones, both red-cheeked and pretty, differing from each other only in that one had a mole above her lip, which was very becoming to her, were doing embroidery. Pierre was met like a dead man or a leper. The eldest princess interrupted her reading and silently stared at him with frightened eyes; the younger one, without the mole, assumed exactly the same expression; the youngest, with the mole, of a merry, laughter-prone character, bent over her embroidery frame to hide a smile, probably evoked by the forthcoming scene, which she foresaw would be amusing. She drew the woollen thread through and bent down as if studying the design, barely able to keep from laughing.

"*Bonjour, ma cousine,*" said Pierre. "*Vous ne me reconnaissez pas?*"†

"I recognize you only too well, only too well."

"How is the count's health? May I see him?" Pierre asked awkwardly, as usual, but without embarrassment.

---

*I would be very happy if you would rid me of this young man . . .
†Hello, cousin. Don't you recognize me?

"The count is suffering both physically and morally, and it seems you have taken care to cause him as much moral suffering as possible."

"May I see the count?" Pierre repeated.

"Hm! . . . If you want to kill him, to kill him outright, you may see him. Olga, go and see whether uncle's bouillon is ready, it's soon time," she added, thereby showing Pierre that they were busy, and busy comforting his father, while he was obviously only busy upsetting him.

Olga went out. Pierre stood looking at the sisters for a while and, bowing, said:

"I'll go to my room, then. Tell me when I can see him."

He went out, and the ringing, though not loud, laughter of the sister with the mole could be heard behind him.

The next day Prince Vassily came and settled in the count's house. He summoned Pierre and said to him:

"*Mon cher, si vous vous conduisez ici, comme à Pétersburg, vous finirez très mal; c'est tout ce je vous dis.** The count is very, very ill: you must not see him at all."

Since then Pierre had not been disturbed, and he spent whole days alone upstairs in his room.

When Boris came in, Pierre was pacing his room, stopping now and then in the corners, making threatening gestures to the wall, as if piercing the invisible enemy with a sword, and looking sternly over his spectacles, and then starting his promenade again, uttering vague words, shrugging his shoulders, and spreading his arms.

"*L'Angleterre a vécu,*" he said, frowning and pointing his finger at someone. "*Monsieur Pitt comme traître à la nation et au droit des gens est condamné à . . .*"†—he did not have time to finish Pitt's sentence, imagining at that moment that he was Napoleon himself and with his hero had already carried out the dangerous crossing of the Pas de Calais and conquered London, before he saw a young, trim, and handsome officer come into his room. He stopped. Pierre had left Boris a fourteen-year-old boy and had decidedly no recollection of him; but, despite that, with the quick and cordial manner proper to him, he took his hand and smiled amiably.

"Do you remember me?" Boris said quietly, with a pleasant smile. "I've come to see the count with my mother, but it seems he's not entirely well."

"Yes, it seems he's unwell. They keep disturbing him," Pierre replied, trying to recall who this young man was.

---

*My dear, if you behave yourself here as you did in Petersburg, you will end very badly; that is all I can say to you.

†England has had its day . . . Mister Pitt, as a traitor to the nation and to the right of nations, is condemned to . . .

Boris felt that Pierre did not recognize him, but he did not consider it necessary to give his name, and, not feeling the least embarrassed, looked him straight in the eye.

"Count Rostov invites you to dinner today," he said after a rather long silence, which was awkward for Pierre.

"Ah! Count Rostov!" Pierre began joyfully. "So you're his son Ilya? Can you imagine, I didn't recognize you at first. Remember, we used to go to the Sparrow Hills with Madame Jacquot . . . long ago."

"You are mistaken," Boris said unhurriedly, with a bold and slightly mocking smile. "I am Boris, the son of Princess Anna Mikhailovna Drubetskoy. The Rostov father is called Ilya, the son is Nikolai. And I never knew any Madame Jacquot."

Pierre waved his hands and head, as if he was being attacked by mosquitoes or bees.

"Ah, well, how about that! I got everything confused. There are so many relations in Moscow! You're Boris . . . yes. So we've finally straightened it out. Well, what do you think of the Boulogne expedition? Won't the English be in trouble if Napoleon crosses the channel? I think the expedition is very important. If only Villeneuve doesn't botch it!"[31]

Boris knew nothing about the Boulogne expedition; he did not read the newspapers, and was hearing about Villeneuve for the first time.

"Here in Moscow we're more taken up with dinners and gossip than with politics," he said in his calm, mocking tone. "I neither know nor think about any of it. Moscow is taken up with gossip most of all," he went on. "Now the talk is about you and the count."

Pierre smiled his kindly smile, as if fearing that his interlocutor might say something he would then regret. But Boris spoke distinctly, clearly, drily, looking Pierre straight in the eye.

"Moscow has nothing else to do but gossip," he went on. "Everyone's concerned about whom the count will leave his fortune to, though maybe he'll outlive us all, which is my heartfelt wish . . ."

"Yes, it's all very painful," Pierre picked up, "very painful." Pierre kept fearing that this officer would accidentally fall into a conversation awkward for himself.

"And it must seem to you," Boris said, blushing slightly, but without changing his voice or pose, "it must seem to you that all everyone is concerned with is getting something out of the rich man."

"Here we go," thought Pierre.

"But I precisely wish to tell you, so as to avoid misunderstandings, that you are greatly mistaken if you count my mother and me among those people. We're very poor, but I can speak for myself at least: precisely because your father is rich, I don't consider myself his relation, and neither I nor my mother will ever ask for or accept anything from him."

Pierre could not understand for a long time, but when he did, he jumped up from the sofa, seized Boris's arm from below with his peculiar quickness and awkwardness, and, turning much more red than Boris, began speaking with a mixed feeling of shame and vexation:

"How strange! Did I ever . . . and who could think . . . I know very well . . ."

But Boris interrupted him again:

"I'm glad I've spoken it all out. Maybe it's unpleasant for you, you must excuse me," he said, reassuring Pierre instead of being reassured by him, "but I hope I haven't offended you. I make it a rule to say everything directly . . . What shall I tell them, then? Will you come to the Rostovs' for dinner?"

And Boris, obviously relieving himself of a painful duty, getting out of an awkward situation himself, and putting another man in one, again became perfectly pleasant.

"No, listen," said Pierre, calming down. "You're a surprising man. What you just said is good, very good. Of course, you don't know me. We haven't met for so long . . . since we were children . . . You may suppose that I . . . I understand you, understand you very well. I wouldn't have done it, I wouldn't have courage enough, but it's beautiful. I'm very glad to have made your acquaintance. It's strange," he added, after a pause, and smiling, "what you supposed of me!" He laughed. "Well, so what? We'll become better acquainted. If you please." He shook Boris's hand. "You know, I haven't once been to see the count. He hasn't sent for me . . . I pity him as a human being . . . But what to do?"

"And you think Napoleon will manage to send the army across?" Boris asked, smiling.

Pierre understood that Boris wanted to change the subject, and, agreeing with him, began to explain the advantages and disadvantages of the Boulogne undertaking.

A lackey came to summon Boris to the princess. The princess was leaving. Pierre promised to come for dinner, in order to become closer with Boris, pressed his hand hard, looked him affectionately in the eye through his spectacles . . . After his departure, Pierre spent a long time pacing the room, no longer piercing the invisible enemy with his sword, but smiling at the memory of this nice, intelligent, and firm young man.

As happens in early youth, and especially when one is alone, he felt a gratuitous tenderness for this young man and promised himself to be sure to become friends with him.

Prince Vassily was seeing the princess off. The princess was holding a handkerchief to her eyes, and her face was all in tears.

"It's terrible! terrible!" she was saying. "But whatever it costs me, I will fulfil my duty. I will come to spend the night. He can't be left like that. Every minute is precious. I don't understand why the princesses keep delaying. Maybe

God will help me find the means to prepare him . . . *Adieu, mon prince, que le bon Dieu vous soutienne . . .*"*

"*Adieu, ma bonne,*"† Prince Vassily replied, turning away from her.

"Ah, he's in a terrible state," the mother said to the son, as they were getting back into the carriage. "He hardly recognizes anyone."

"I don't understand, mama, what is his attitude towards Pierre?" asked the son.

"It will all be spelled out in the will; our fate, too, depends on it . . ."

"But why do you think he'll leave us anything?"

"Ah, my friend! He's so rich, and we're so poor!"

"Well, that's still not enough of a reason, mama."

"Ah, my God! my God! he's so ill!" the mother exclaimed.

XIV

When Anna Mikhailovna and her son left for Count Kirill Vladimirovich Bezukhov's, Countess Rostov sat for a long time alone, putting her handkerchief to her eyes. Finally she rang.

"What's wrong, dear," she said crossly to the girl, who made her wait a few minutes. "You don't want to serve me? Then I'll find another place for you, miss."

The countess was upset by her friend's woes and humiliating poverty, and was therefore out of sorts, which always expressed itself in her calling the maid "dear" and "miss."

"Beg pardon, ma'am," said the maid.

"Ask the count to come to me."

The count, waddling, approached his wife with a somewhat guilty look, as he always did.

"Well, my little countess! what a *sauté au madère* of hazel grouse we'll have, *ma chère!* I sampled it. Not for nothing did I pay a thousand roubles for Taraska. He's worth it!"

He sat down by his wife, resting his elbows dashingly on his knees and ruffling his grey hair.

"What are your orders, little countess!"

"The thing is, my friend—what's this stain you've got there?" she said, pointing to his waistcoat. "Must be the *sauté,*" she added, smiling. "The thing is, Count, that I need money."

Her face grew sad.

*Goodbye, my prince, may the good Lord sustain you . . .
†Goodbye, my good one.

"Ah, little countess! . . ." And the count began fussing, pulling out his wallet.

"I need a lot, Count, I need five hundred roubles." And, taking out a cambric handkerchief, she began rubbing her husband's waistcoat.

"Just a moment. Hey, you there!" he cried in a voice such as people use who are sure that those they call will come rushing to them. "Send Mitenka to me!"

Mitenka, that nobleman's son, brought up by the count, who now managed all his affairs, came into the room with quiet steps.

"The thing is, my dear . . ." the count said to the deferential young man as he came in. "Bring me . . ." He pondered. "Yes, yes, seven hundred roubles. And see that you don't bring torn and dirty ones like the other time, but nice ones, for the countess."

"Yes, Mitenka, please, be sure they're clean," said the countess, sighing sadly.

"When shall I bring it, Your Excellency?" asked Mitenka. "Allow me to tell you that . . . However, please don't worry," he added, noticing that the count was beginning to breathe heavily and quickly, which was always a sign of incipient wrath. "I almost forgot . . . Shall I deliver it this minute?"

"Yes, yes, right, bring it. Give it to the countess."

"He's pure gold, my Mitenka," the count added, smiling, when the young man went out. "Nothing's ever impossible. I can't stand that. Everything's possible."

"Ah, money, Count, money—there's so much grief in the world because of it!" said the countess. "But I need this money very badly."

"You, my dear countess, are a notorious spendthrift," said the count, and, kissing his wife's hand, he went back to his study.

When Anna Mikhailovna came back from Bezukhov's, the money was already lying before the countess, all in new notes, under a handkerchief on a little table, and Anna Mikhailovna noticed that something was troubling the countess.

"Well, my friend?" asked the countess.

"Ah, he's in such a terrible state! You wouldn't recognize him, he's so poorly, so poorly; I stayed only a minute and didn't say two words . . ."

"Annette, for God's sake, don't refuse me," the countess said suddenly, blushing, which was quite strange with her thin, dignified, and no longer young face, and taking the money from under the handkerchief.

Anna Mikhailovna instantly realized what it was about and bent forward so as to embrace the countess adroitly at the right moment.

"This is for Boris from me, to have his uniform made . . ."

Anna Mikhailovna was already embracing her and weeping. The countess was also weeping. They wept because they were friends; and because they were kind; and because they, who had been friends since childhood, were concerned with such a mean subject—money; and because their youth was gone . . . But for both of them they were pleasant tears . . .

XV

Countess Rostov, with her daughters and an already large number of guests, was sitting in the drawing room. The count led the male guests to his study, to offer them his prize collection of Turkish pipes. From time to time he came out and asked whether *she* had come yet. They were expecting Marya Dmitrievna Akhrosimov, known in society as *le terrible dragon*, a lady famous neither for her wealth nor for her rank, but for her directness of mind and frank simplicity of manners. Marya Dmitrievna was known to the tsar's family, was known to all Moscow and all Petersburg, and both cities, astonished at her, chuckled secretly at her rudeness and told anecdotes about her; nevertheless, everyone without exception respected and feared her.

In the smoke-filled study the conversation turned to the war, which had been declared in the manifesto, and to recruitment.[32] No one had read the manifesto yet, but everyone knew of its appearance. The count sat on an ottoman between two smoking and talking neighbours. The count himself neither smoked nor talked, but, inclining his head now to one side, now to the other, looked with obvious pleasure at the smokers and listened to the conversation of his two neighbours, whom he had set on each other.

One of the talkers was a civilian with a wrinkled, bilious, gaunt, and clean-shaven face, a man approaching old age, though dressed like a most fashionable young man; he sat with his feet on the ottoman, looking like a familiar of the house, the amber bit deep in the side of his mouth, impetuously sucking in smoke and squinting. This was the old bachelor Shinshin, the countess's cousin, a wicked tongue, as the talk went in Moscow drawing rooms. He seemed to be condescending to his interlocutor. The other, a fresh, pink officer of the guards, impeccably scrubbed, combed, and buttoned-up, held the amber bit in the middle of his mouth and drew the smoke in lightly with his pink lips, letting it out of his handsome mouth in rings. This was that Lieutenant Berg, an officer of the Semyonovsky regiment, with whom Boris was going off to join the regiment, and whom Natasha, teasing Vera, her older sister, called her fiancé. The count sat between them and listened attentively. For the count, the most agreeable occupation, apart from the game of Boston, which he liked very much, was the position of listener, especially when he managed to set two garrulous interlocutors on each other.

"Well, what then, old boy, *mon très honorable* Alphonse Karlych," said Shinshin, chuckling and combining (which was a peculiarity of his speech) the simplest popular Russian expressions with refined French phrases. "*Vous comptez vous faire des rentes sur l'état,** you want to get a little something from your company?"

"No, Pyotr Nikolaevich, I merely wish to prove, sir, that the cavalry is much less profitable than the infantry. Now look, Pyotr Nikolaevich, just consider my position."

Berg always spoke very precisely, calmly, and courteously. His conversation was always concerned with himself alone; he always kept calmly silent when the talk was about something that had no direct relation to himself. And he could be silent like that for several hours, without experiencing in himself or causing in others the slightest embarrassment. But as soon as the conversation concerned him personally, he began to speak expansively and with obvious pleasure.

"Consider my position, Pyotr Nikolaich: if I were in the cavalry, I'd get no more than two hundred roubles every four months, even with the rank of sub-lieutenant; while now I get two hundred and thirty," he said with a joyful, pleasant smile, looking at Shinshin and the count as though it was obvious to him that his success would always constitute the chief goal of everyone else's desires.

"Besides that, Pyotr Nikolaevich, in transferring to the guards, I am in view," Berg went on, "and vacancies in the foot guards are much more frequent. Then, consider for yourself how I'm able to get along on two hundred and thirty roubles. Yet I save some and also send some to my father," he went on, letting out a smoke ring.

"*La balance y est* . . . A German can make cheese from chalk, *comme dit le proverbe,*"† said Shinshin, shifting the amber to the other side of his mouth, and he winked at the count.

The count burst out laughing. Other guests, seeing that Shinshin was conducting a conversation, came over to listen. Berg, oblivious of both the mockery and the indifference, went on to tell how he, by being transferred to the guards, was already one rank ahead of his comrades in the corps, how in wartime the company commander might be killed, and he, remaining the senior in the company, could very easily become the commander, and how everyone in the regiment liked him, and how his papa was pleased with him. Berg apparently enjoyed telling about it all and seemed not to suspect that other people might also have their interests. But everything he told about was so nice, so earnest, the naïveté of his youthful egoism was so obvious, that his listeners were disarmed.

"Well, old boy, infantry or cavalry, you'll make it anywhere; that I prophesy

---

*You are counting on getting an income from the state.
†There you have it . . . as the proverb says.

to you," said Shinshin, patting him on the shoulder and lowering his feet from the ottoman.

Berg smiled joyfully. The count, and his guests after him, went to the drawing room.

It was that time before a formal dinner when the assembled guests refrain from beginning a long conversation, expecting to be called to the hors d'oeuvres, but at the same time consider it necessary to move about and not be silent, in order to show that they are not at all impatient to sit down at the table. The hosts keep glancing at the door and occasionally exchange glances with each other. The guests try to guess from these glances who or what they are still waiting for: an important belated relation or a dish that is not ready yet.

Pierre arrived just before dinner and sat awkwardly in the middle of the drawing room, in the first armchair he happened upon, getting in everyone's way. The countess wanted to get him to talk, but he looked around naïvely through his spectacles, as if searching for someone, and gave monosyllabic answers to all the countess's questions. He was an inconvenience and was the only one not to notice it. The majority of the guests, knowing his story with the bear, looked curiously at this big, fat, and placid man, wondering how such a clumsy and shy fellow could perform such a stunt with a policeman.

"Did you arrive recently?" the countess asked him.

"*Oui, madame,*" he replied, looking around.

"Have you seen my husband?"

"*Non, madame.*" He smiled quite inappropriately.

"It seems you were recently in Paris? I suppose it was very interesting."

"Very interesting."

The countess exchanged glances with Anna Mikhailovna. Anna Mikhailovna understood that she was being asked to take up this young man, and sitting beside him, she began speaking of his father; but, as with the countess, he gave her nothing but monosyllabic answers. The guests were all taken up with each other.

"*Les Razoumovsky . . . Ça a été charmant . . . Vous êtes bien bonne . . . La comtesse Apraksine . . .*"* was heard on all sides. The countess got up and went to the reception room.

"Marya Dmitrievna?" her voice was heard from there.

"Herself," a rough female voice was heard in reply, after which Marya Dmitrievna came into the room.

All the girls and even the ladies, except for the oldest ones, rose. Marya

---

*The Razumovskys . . . That was charming . . . You are very kind . . . The countess Apraksin . . .

Dmitrievna stood in the doorway and, from the height of her corpulent body, her fifty-year-old head with its grey curled hair held high, looked over the guests, and unhurriedly straightened the wide sleeves of her dress, as if pushing them up. Marya Dmitrievna always spoke in Russian.

"Congratulations to the dear name-day lady and her children," she said in her loud, dense voice, which overwhelmed all other noises. "And you, you old sinner," she turned to the count, who was kissing her hand, "I bet you're bored in Moscow? No chasing about with dogs here? Nothing to be done, old boy, look how these birdies are growing up." She pointed to the girls. "Like it or not, you'll have to hunt for suitors."

"Well, how's my Cossack?" (Marya Dmitrievna called Natasha a Cossack), she said, caressing Natasha, who came up to kiss her hand fearlessly and merrily. "I know she's a wicked girl, but I love her."

She took from her enormous reticule a pair of pear-shaped ruby earrings and, having given them to the festively radiant and red-cheeked Natasha, turned away at once and addressed Pierre.

"E-eh! my gallant! come here to me!" she said in a falsely quiet and high voice. "Come here to me, my gallant . . ."

And she menacingly pushed her sleeves up still higher.

Pierre approached, gazing at her naïvely through his spectacles.

"Come on, come on, my gallant! I was the only one to tell your father the truth when chance smiled on him,³³ and to you, too, God willing."

She paused. Everyone fell silent, waiting for what would happen and feeling that this was only the preface.

"A fine one, to say the least! a fine lad! . . . His father's lying on his deathbed, and he's having fun, sitting a policeman on the back of a bear! Shame on you, old boy, shame on you! You'd do better to go to the war."

She turned away and offered her arm to the count, who could barely keep from laughing.

"Well, so, I suppose it's to table?" said Marya Dmitrievna.

The count went first with Marya Dmitrievna; then came the countess, led by a hussar colonel, a useful man, with whom Nikolai was to overtake his regiment, and Anna Mikhailovna with Shinshin. Berg offered his arm to Vera. The smiling Julie Karagin went to the table with Nikolai. After them came other couples, stretching the whole length of the room, and behind them all the children, tutors, and governesses came singly. Servants bustled about, chairs scraped, music began playing in the gallery, and the guests seated themselves. The sounds of the count's household music were replaced by the sounds of knives and forks, the talk of the guests, the soft footsteps of the servants. At the head of the table on one end sat the countess. To her right Marya Dmitrievna, to her left Anna Mikhailovna and the other ladies. At the other end sat the count, to his left the hussar colonel, to his right Shinshin and the other male guests. One side of the long table was occupied by the older young people: Vera sat next to Berg, Pierre next to Boris; on the other side were the children, tutors, and governesses. From behind the crystal, the bottles, and the bowls of fruit, the count kept glancing at his wife and her tall cap with blue ribbons, and diligently poured wine for his neighbours, not forgetting himself. The countess, too, from behind the pineapples, never forgetting her duties as hostess, cast meaningful glances at her husband, the redness of whose face and bald head, it seemed to her, contrasted sharply with his grey hair. At the ladies' end a steady chatter went on; at the men's, louder and louder voices could be heard, especially that of the hussar colonel, who ate and drank so much, growing redder and redder, that the count now set him as an example to the other guests. Berg was saying to Vera, with a tender smile, that love was a heavenly, not an earthly, feeling. Boris was naming the guests at the table for his new friend Pierre, while exchanging glances with Natasha, who was sitting across from him. Pierre spoke little, looked at the new faces, and ate a lot. Starting with the two soups, of which he chose *à la tortue,** and the savoury pie, and right up to the hazel grouse, he did not skip a single dish or a single wine, which the butler mysteriously displayed for him behind his neighbour's shoulder, the bottle wrapped in a napkin, murmuring: "dry Madeira," or "Hungarian," or "Rhine wine." Of the four crystal glasses with the count's monogram that stood before each place, he would hold out the first he happened upon and drank with enjoyment, glancing around at the guests with a more and more pleasant air. Natasha, who was sitting across from him, gazed at Boris as a thirteen-year-old girl gazes at a boy she has just kissed for the first time and is in love with. She occasionally turned this same gaze to Pierre, and, under the gaze of this funny, lively girl, he wanted to laugh himself, without knowing why.

Nikolai sat far away from Sonya, next to Julie Karagin, and again was saying something to her with an involuntary smile. Sonya smiled formally, but was clearly suffering from jealousy: she turned pale, then red, and tried as hard as she could to hear what Nikolai and Julie were saying to each other. The governess looked around anxiously, as if preparing to resist, if anyone took it into his head to offend the children. The German tutor tried to memorize all the kinds of dishes, desserts, and wines, in order to describe everything in detail in his letter to his family in Germany, and was quite offended that the butler with the napkin-wrapped bottle bypassed him. The German frowned, trying to show by his look that he did not even wish to have this wine, but was offended because no one wanted to understand that the wine was necessary for him, not in order to quench his thirst, nor out of greed, but out of a conscientious love of knowledge.

*Turtle.

XVI

At the men's end of the table, the conversation was becoming more and more animated. The colonel said that the manifesto with the declaration of war had already been published in Petersburg, and that a copy, which he had seen himself, had been delivered today by messenger to the commander in chief.

"And what the deuce makes us go to war with Bonaparte?" said Shinshin. "*Il a déjà rabattu le caquet à l'Autriche. Je crains que cette fois ce ne soit notre tour.*"*

The colonel was a tall, stout, and sanguine German, obviously a seasoned soldier and a patriot. He took offence at Shinshin's words.

"Pecause, my tear sir," he said, pronouncing the *b* as a *p* and the *d* as a *t*, "pecause the emperor knows that. He said in the manifesto that he cannot look mit intifference at the tangers that threaten Russia, and that the security of the empire, its tignity, and the sacretness of its *alliances* . . ." he said, for some reason giving special emphasis to the word *alliances,* as if this was the essence of the matter.

And with that impeccable official memory peculiar to him, he repeated the introductory words of the manifesto: ". . . and the desire, which constitutes the sole and absolute aim of the sovereign, to establish peace in Europe on firm foundations, led to his present decision to move part of the army abroad and to make further efforts towards the achievement of that intention."[34]

"It's pecause of that, my tear sir," he concluded didactically, drinking a glass of wine and looking to the count for encouragement.

"*Connaissez-vous le proverbe:* 'Jerome, Jerome, stay close to home, keep your shovel in the loam'?" asked Shinshin, wincing and smiling. "*Cela nous convient à merveille.* Take Suvorov[35]—even he got beaten *à plate couture,* and where are our Suvorovs now? *Je vous demande un peu,*"† he said, constantly switching from Russian to French.

"Ve must fight to the last trop of plood," said the colonel, pounding the table, "und ti-i-ie for our emperor, and then all vill be vell. And reason as little as po-o-ossible" (he especially drew out the word *possible*), "as little as po-o-ossible," he concluded, again addressing the count. "So ve old hussars see it, anyvay. And how to you, a young man and a young hussar, see it?" he added, turning to Nikolai, who, hearing that things had got on to the war, had abandoned his interlocutrice and was looking all eyes and listening all ears to the colonel.

*He has already stopped Austria's cackling. I'm afraid this time it will be our turn.
†Do you know the proverb . . . That suits us perfectly . . . flat as a pancake . . . I ask you kindly.

"I agree with you completely," replied Nikolai, blushing all over, turning his plate and rearranging the glasses, and with such a determined and desperate air as though he was exposed right then to great danger. "I'm convinced that the Russians must either die or conquer," he said, aware himself, as the others were, once the word had been spoken, that it was too rapturous and pompous for the present occasion and therefore awkward.

"*C'est bien beau ce que vous venez de dire,*"* Julie, who was sitting next to him, said with a sigh. Sonya trembled all over and blushed to her ears, behind her ears, and down her neck and shoulders, as Nikolai was speaking. Pierre listened to what the colonel said and nodded approvingly.

"That's very nice," he said.

"A real hussar, young man," cried the colonel, pounding the table again.

"What's this noise about?" Marya Dmitrievna's bass voice was suddenly heard all down the table. "What are you pounding the table for?" she addressed the hussar. "Why are you getting excited? Maybe you think the French are here in front of you?"

"I'm speakink the truth," the hussar said, smiling.

"It's all about the war," the count shouted down the table. "My son's going, Marya Dmitrievna, my son."

"I've got four sons in the army, and I'm not grieving. It's all God's will: you can die in your sleep, and God can spare you in battle," the dense voice of Marya Dmitrievna rang out effortlessly from the other end of the table.

"That's so."

And the conversation again became concentrated, the ladies' at their end of the table, the men's at theirs.

"You don't dare ask," said Natasha's little brother, "you don't dare ask!"

"Yes, I do," replied Natasha.

Her face suddenly flushed, expressing a desperate and merry resolve. She stood up, her eyes inviting Pierre, who sat across from her, to listen, and addressed her mother.

"Mama!" her throaty child's voice rang out for the whole table to hear.

"What is it?" the countess asked fearfully, but, seeing from her daughter's face that it was a prank, she sternly waved her hand at her, making a threatening and negative gesture with her head.

The conversation hushed.

"Mama! what's for dessert?" Natasha's little voice rang out still more resolutely, without faltering.

The countess wanted to frown, but could not. Marya Dmitrievna shook her fat finger.

"Cossack!" she said menacingly.

*That's very beautiful, what you just said.

Most of the guests looked at the parents, not knowing how to take this escapade.

"You're going to get it!" said the countess.

"Mama! what's for dessert?" cried Natasha, boldly now and with capricious merriment, certain beforehand that her escapade would be taken well.

Sonya and fat Petya hid their faces with laughter.

"So I dared," Natasha whispered to her little brother and to Pierre, at whom she glanced again.

"Ice cream, only you won't get any," said Marya Dmitrievna.

Natasha saw there was nothing to fear, so she was not afraid of Marya Dmitrievna either.

"What kind of ice cream, Marya Dmitrievna? I don't like vanilla."

"Carrot."

"No, what kind, Marya Dmitrievna, what kind?" she nearly shouted. "I want to know!"

Marya Dmitrievna and the countess laughed, and all the guests followed suit. Everyone laughed not at Marya Dmitrievna's reply, but at the inconceivable boldness and adroitness of this girl, who was both smart and pert enough to treat Marya Dmitrievna that way.

Natasha left off only when they told her there would be pineapple ice cream. Before the ice cream, champagne was served. The music struck up again, the count kissed his dear countess, and the guests, rising, wished the countess a happy name day, and clinked glasses across the table with the count, the children, and each other. Again the waiters scurried about, chairs scraped, and the guests, in the same order but with redder faces, returned to the drawing room and the count's study.

XVII

Tables were set up for boston, parties were chosen, and the count's guests settled themselves in the two drawing rooms, the sitting room, and the library.

The count, his cards spread in a fan, refrained with difficulty from his usual after-dinner nap and laughed at everything. The young people, at the countess's urging, gathered around the clavichord and the harp. Julie was the first, at everybody's request, to play a piece with variations for the harp, and, along with the other girls, began asking Natasha and Nikolai, known for their musicality, to sing something. Natasha, who was addressed like a grown-up, was obviously very proud of it, but at the same time timid.

"What shall we sing?" she asked.

" 'The Spring,' "[36] replied Nikolai.

"Well, let's be quick about it. Boris, come here," said Natasha. "But where's Sonya?"

She looked around and, seeing that her friend was not in the room, ran to look for her.

Running into Sonya's room and not finding her friend there, Natasha ran to the nursery—Sonya was not there either. Natasha realized that Sonya was in the corridor on the chest. The chest in the corridor was the place of sorrows for the young female generation of the Rostov house. Indeed, Sonya, in her airy pink dress, crushing it, was lying face down on the nanny's dirty striped feather-bed, on the chest, and, covering her face with her fingers, was sobbing, her bare little shoulders twitching. Natasha's face, animated and festive all day, suddenly changed: her eyes stared, then her broad neck shuddered, and the corners of her mouth drooped.

"Sonya! what is it? . . . What, what's the matter with you? Wa-a-a! . . ."

And Natasha, spreading her big mouth and looking perfectly ugly, started howling like a baby, not knowing the reason why, only because Sonya was crying. Sonya wanted to raise her head and reply, but could not and buried herself still more. Natasha wept, sitting on the blue featherbed and embracing her friend. Gathering her forces, Sonya sat up and began wiping away her tears and telling her story.

"Nikolenka's leaving in a week, his . . . papers . . . are ready . . . he told me himself . . . But all the same I wouldn't be crying" (she held up the paper she had in her hand: it was verses written by Nikolai) ". . . all the same I wouldn't be crying, but you can't . . . nobody can understand . . . what a soul he has."

And again she began to cry, because his soul was so good.

"It's all right for you . . . I'm not envious . . . I love you, and Boris, too," she said, gathering her forces a little, "he's nice . . . there are no obstacles for you. But Nikolai's my cousin . . . we need . . . the metropolitan himself[37] . . . even then it's impossible. And then, if mama" (Sonya considered and called the countess her mother) ". . . she'll say that I'm ruining Nikolai's career, that I have no heart, that I'm ungrateful, and really . . . I swear to God" (she crossed herself) ". . . I love her and all of you so much, only Vera . . . Why? What have I done to her? I'm so grateful to you that I'd be glad to sacrifice everything I have, but I don't have anything . . ."

Sonya could not speak any more and again hid her head in her hands and in the featherbed. Natasha began to calm down, but it was clear from her face that she realized all the importance of her friend's grief.

"Sonya!" she said suddenly, as if guessing the real reason for her cousin's distress. "Vera must have talked with you after dinner? Did she?"

"Yes, Nikolai himself wrote out these verses, and I wrote down some others; she found them on my desk and said she'd show them to mama, and she also said I was ungrateful, that mama would never let him marry me, and that he'd marry Julie. You see how he's been with her the whole day . . . Natasha! Why? . . ."

And again she burst out crying more bitterly than before. Natasha pulled her up, hugged her, and, smiling through her tears, began to reassure her.

"Sonya, don't believe her, dear heart, don't believe her. Remember how we and Nikolenka, the three of us, talked in the sitting room—remember, after supper? We decided how everything was going to be. I don't remember how any more, but remember how good and possible it all was? Why, Uncle Shinshin's brother married his first cousin, and we're just second cousins. And Boris said it was very possible. You know, I told him everything. And he's so intelligent and so nice," Natasha went on saying ". . . so don't cry, Sonya, dearest, darling Sonya." And she kissed her, laughing. "Vera's wicked, God help her! But everything will be all right, and she won't tell mama; Nikolenka will tell her himself, and he never gave a thought to Julie."

And she kissed her on the head. Sonya got up, the kitten revived, its eyes sparkled, and it seemed ready to raise its tail any moment, spring up on its soft paws, and play with a ball of yarn, as a kitten ought to do.

"Do you think so? Really? Swear to God?" she said, quickly straightening her dress and hair.

"Really! Swear to God!" replied Natasha, straightening a strand of stiff hair that had come loose from her friend's braid.

And the two girls laughed.

"So, let's go and sing 'The Spring.' "

"Yes, let's."

"You know, that fat Pierre, who sat across from me, is so funny!" Natasha said suddenly, stopping. "I feel so merry!"

And Natasha went running down the corridor.

Sonya, brushing off feathers, and hiding the verses in her bosom, near her neck with its protruding collarbones, her face flushed, went running after Natasha with light, merry steps down the corridor to the sitting room. At the request of the guests, the young people sang the quartet "The Spring," which everyone liked very much. Then Nikolai sang a song he had just learned:[38]

> On a pleasant night beneath the moon
> How happy is the reverie
> *That in this world there still is one*
> *Whose thoughts do ever turn to thee!*
> And as her lovely hand, which she
> Lets wander o'er the harp's bright strings,
> Plays in impassioned harmony,
> So she to thee her summons sings!

One day, two days, then paradise . . .
But ah! thy friend is cold as ice!

And he had not finished singing the last words before the young people in the ballroom began preparing to dance, and the musicians began stamping their feet and coughing in the gallery.

Pierre was sitting in the drawing room, where Shinshin, knowing he had come from abroad, had started a boring political conversation with him, in which other people joined. When the music began to play, Natasha came into the drawing room and, going straight up to Pierre, blushing and with laughing eyes, said:

"Mama told me to ask you to dance."

"I'm afraid I'll confuse the figures," said Pierre, "but if you'd like to be my teacher . . ."

And, lowering his fat arm, he offered it to the slender girl.

While the couples were being placed and the musicians were tuning up, Pierre sat with his little partner. Natasha was perfectly happy: she was dancing with a *grown-up* who had come *from abroad*. She sat in full view of everyone and talked to him like a grown-up. In her hand was a fan which a young lady had given her to hold. And, assuming a most worldly pose (God knows where and when she had learned it), fanning herself and smiling through the fan, she talked with her partner.

"Look at her! Just look at her!" said the old countess, walking through the room and pointing at Natasha.

Natasha blushed and laughed.

"Well, what is it, mama? What are you getting at? What's so surprising?"

In the middle of the third *écossaise*, chairs began moving in the drawing room where the count and Marya Dmitrievna were playing, and the greater part of the honoured guests and old folk, stretching after sitting so long and putting their wallets and purses in their pockets, came to the door of the ballroom. At their head came Marya Dmitrievna and the count—both with merry faces. The count, with jocular politeness, somehow in a ballet-like fashion, offered his rounded arm to Marya Dmitrievna. He drew himself up and his face brightened with a special dashingly sly smile, and as soon as the last figures of the *écossaise* came to an end, he clapped his hands and called out to the musicians in the gallery, addressing the first fiddle:

"Semyon! Do you know 'Daniel Cooper'?"

That was the count's favourite dance, which he used to dance while still in his youth. ("Daniel Cooper" was in fact one of the figures of the *anglaise*.)

"Look at papa," Natasha shouted to the whole ballroom (completely forgetting that she was dancing with a grown-up), bending her curly head to her knees and dissolving into her ringing laughter for the whole ballroom to hear.

Indeed, all who were in the ballroom looked with smiles of joy at the merry old man, who, beside his stately partner, Marya Dmitrievna, who was taller than he, rounded his arms, shook them in time to the music, squared his shoulders, flexed his legs, stamped slightly, and, the smile widening more and more on his round face, prepared the spectators for what was to come. As soon as the merry, provocative sounds of "Daniel Cooper," resembling a rollicking *trepak*,[39] rang out, all the doors of the ballroom suddenly filled with the smiling faces of the servants—the men on one side, the women on the other—who came to watch their master's merrymaking.

"Look at the old dear! An eagle!" the nanny said loudly from one door.

The count danced well and knew it, but his partner could not and would not dance well at all. Her enormous body stood straight, her powerful arms hung down (she had given her reticule to the countess); only her stern but handsome face danced. What was expressed in the whole round figure of the count, in Marya Dmitrievna was expressed in her ever more smiling face and ever more thrust-up nose. On the other hand, if the count, who got himself going more and more, fascinated his spectators by his unexpectedly deft capers and the light leaps of his supple legs, Marya Dmitrievna, by the slightest exertion in moving her shoulders or rounding her arms while turning or stamping, produced no less of an impression by its merit, which everyone appreciated in view of her corpulence and perpetual severity. The dance became more and more lively. The other couples could not draw attention to themselves for a minute and did not even try to. All were taken up with the count and Marya Dmitrievna. Natasha pulled everyone present by the sleeve or the dress, demanding that they look at papa, though even without that they never took their eyes off the dancers. The count, during the pauses in the dance, panted heavily, waved and shouted to the musicians to play faster. More and more quickly, more and more dashingly the count deployed himself, now on tiptoe, now on his heels, racing around Marya Dmitrievna, and finally, returning his partner to her seat, he performed the last step, raising his supple leg behind him, bending down his sweating head with its smiling face, and waving his rounded right arm amidst the thunder of applause and laughter, especially from Natasha. The two dancers stopped, breathing heavily and wiping their faces with cambric handkerchiefs.

"That's how people danced in our time, *ma chère*," said the count.

"Ah, what a Daniel Cooper!" said Marya Dmitrievna, letting out a long, deep breath and pushing up her sleeves.

XVIII

Just as the sixth *anglaise* was being danced in the Rostovs' ballroom to the sounds of the weary, out-of-tune musicians and the weary servants and cooks were preparing supper, Count Bezukhov had his sixth stroke. The doctors declared that there was no hope of recovery; the sick man was given a blank confession⁴⁰ and communion; preparations for extreme unction were made, and the house was filled with the bustle and anxiety of expectation usual at such moments. Outside the house, beyond the gate, avoiding the carriages that drove up, undertakers crowded in anticipation of a rich order for the count's funeral. The commander in chief of Moscow, who had constantly been sending adjutants to ask after the count's health, came in person that evening to take leave of Catherine's celebrated courtier, Count Bezukhov.

The magnificent reception room was filled. Everyone rose deferentially when the commander in chief, having spent about half an hour alone with the sick man, came out, responding slightly to the bows and trying to go quickly past the looks that doctors, clergymen, and relations directed at him. Prince Vassily, grown thin and pale during those days, accompanied the commander in chief and quietly repeated something to him several times.

Having seen the commander in chief off, Prince Vassily sat by himself on a chair in the hall, his legs crossed high up, his elbow resting on his knee, his hand over his eyes. Having sat like that for some time, he got up and, with unhabitually hurried steps, looking around with frightened eyes, went down the long corridor to the rear half of the house, to the eldest princess.

Those who were in the dimly lit room talked together in broken whispers, and fell silent each time, turning with eyes full of enquiry and expectation to the door which led to the dying man's room and which made a faint noise whenever someone went in or came out.

"A limit has been set," said a little old man, a clerical person, to a lady who sat down beside him and listened to him naïvely, "a limit has been set to human life, which cannot be overstepped."

"I wonder if it's not too late to give extreme unction?" the lady asked, adding his clerical title, as if she had no opinion on the subject.

"It is a great sacrament, my dear," the clerical person replied, passing his hand over his bald head, which had several strands of half-grey hair combed over it.

"Who was that? The commander in chief himself?" someone asked at the other end of the room. "What a youthful man! . . ."

"He's in his sixties! Well, so they say the count no longer recognizes anyone? Do they mean to give him extreme unction?"

"I knew a man who received extreme unction seven times."

The second princess came out of the sick man's room with tearful eyes and sat down next to Dr. Lorrain, who was sitting in a graceful pose under a portrait of Catherine, leaning his elbow on a table.

"*Très beau,*" the doctor said in reply to a question about the weather, "*très beau, princesse, et puis, à Moscou on se croit à la campagne.*"*

"*N'est-ce-pas?*"† said the princess, sighing. "So he's allowed to drink?"

Lorrain pondered.

"Has he taken his medicine?"

"Yes."

The doctor looked at his Breguet.⁴¹

"Take a glass of boiled water and put in *une pincée*" (with his slender fingers he showed what *une pincée* meant) "*de cremortartari . . .*"‡

"Dere hass been no occasion," a German doctor said to an adjutant, "dat one remains alife after a second shtroke."

"And he was such a fresh man!" said the adjutant. "And to whom will all that wealth go?" he added in a whisper.

"Dere vill be no lack of seekers," the German said, smiling.

Everyone looked at the door again: it creaked, and the second princess, having prepared the drink prescribed by Lorrain, carried it to the sick man. The German doctor went over to Lorrain.

"He may still last until tomorrow morning?" the German asked in poorly pronounced French.

Lorrain, compressing his lips, wagged his finger sternly and negatively in front of his nose.

"Tonight, no later," he said softly, with a decent smile of self-satisfaction at being able to clearly understand and explain the patient's condition, and walked away.

Meanwhile, Prince Vassily had opened the door to the princess's room.

The room was in semi-darkness, only two icon lamps burned before the icons, and there was a good smell of incense and flowers. The whole room was filled with small furniture: little chiffoniers, cupboards, tables. Behind a screen the white covers of a high featherbed could be seen. A little dog barked.

"Ah, it's you, *mon cousin?*"

She got up and straightened her hair, which was always, even now, so extraordinarily smooth that it seemed varnished and of one piece with her head.

*Very fine . . . very fine, Princess, and then, in Moscow one thinks one is in the country.
†Isn't it so?
‡A pinch . . . of *cremortartari.*

"What, has something happened?" she asked. "I'm so frightened."

"Nothing, it's all the same; I have only come to have a talk with you, Catiche, about business," said the prince, sitting with an air of fatigue in the armchair from which she had got up. "How warm you keep it, though," he said. "Well, sit down here, *causons.*"*

"I thought something had happened," said the princess, and with her unchanging, stern and stony expression, she sat down opposite the prince and prepared to listen.

"I wanted to get some sleep, *mon cousin,* but I can't."

"Well, and so, my dear?" said Prince Vassily, taking the princess's hand and pulling it down, as was his habit.

It was clear that this "and so" referred to many things they both understood without naming them.

The princess, with her dry and straight waist, incongruously long for her legs, looked straight and passionlessly at the prince with her prominent grey eyes. She shook her head and, sighing, turned to look at the icons. Her gesture could have been interpreted either as an expression of sorrow and devotion, or as an expression of weariness and hope for a speedy repose. Prince Vassily interpreted this gesture as an expression of weariness.

"And do you think it's any easier for me?" he said. "*Je suis éreinté comme un cheval de poste;*† but all the same I must talk with you, Catiche, and very seriously."

Prince Vassily fell silent, and his cheeks began to twitch nervously now on one side, now on the other, giving his face an unpleasant expression which never appeared on Prince Vassily's face when he was in a drawing room. His eyes were also not the same as usual: now they looked with insolent jocularity, now they glanced around fearfully.

The princess, holding the dog on her lap with her dry, thin hands, looked attentively into Prince Vassily's eyes; but it was evident that she would not break the silence with a question, even if she had to remain silent till morning.

"So you see, my dear princess and cousin, Katerina Semyonovna," Prince Vassily continued, evidently getting himself to continue his talk only after an inner struggle, "at moments like this, it is necessary to think of everything. It is necessary to think of the future, of you . . . I love you all like my own children, you know that."

The princess went on looking at him just as dully and fixedly.

"Finally, it is necessary to think of my family, too," Prince Vassily continued, angrily pushing a little table away and without looking at her. "You know, Catiche, that you three Mamontov sisters, and my wife as well—we are the

---

*Let's talk.
†I'm as exhausted as a post-horse.

count's only direct heirs. I know, I know how hard it is for you to speak and think about such things. It's no easier for me; but I'm over fifty, my friend, I must be ready for anything. Do you know that I have sent for Pierre, and that the count, pointing directly at his portrait, demanded that he come?"

Prince Vassily looked questioningly at the princess, but could not tell whether she was considering what he had said to her, or was simply staring at him . . .

"There's one thing for which I never cease praying to God, *mon cousin*," she replied, "that He have mercy on him and grant that his beautiful soul peacefully depart this . . ."

"Yes, that's right," Prince Vassily went on impatiently, rubbing his bald head and angrily seizing the little table he had pushed away and moving it towards him again, "but, finally . . . finally, the thing is, as you know yourself, that last winter the count wrote a will according to which, passing over his direct heirs and us, he bequeathed all his property to Pierre."

"He has written all sorts of wills," the princess said calmly, "but he cannot bequeath anything to Pierre! Pierre is illegitimate."

"But, *ma chère*," Prince Vassily said suddenly, clutching the little table to him, becoming animated, and beginning to speak more quickly, "what if a letter had been written to the sovereign and the count had asked to adopt Pierre? You understand, given the count's merits, his request would be granted . . ."

The princess smiled as people smile who think they know more about a matter than those they are talking with.

"I'll tell you more," Prince Vassily went on, gripping her hand. "The letter has been written, though not sent, and the sovereign knows of it. The only question is whether it has been destroyed or not. If not, then as soon as it's *all over*," Prince Vassily sighed, letting it be understood *what* he meant by the words *all over*, "and the count's papers are opened, the will and the letter will be sent to the sovereign, and his request will most likely be granted. As a legitimate son, Pierre will get everything."

"And our share?" asked the princess, smiling ironically, as if anything but that could happen.

"*Mais, ma pauvre Catiche, c'est clair comme le jour.** He alone is then the legitimate heir to everything, and you won't get even this much. You must know, my dear, whether the will and the letter were written, and whether they have been destroyed. And if they've been overlooked for some reason, you must know where they are and must find them, because . . ."

"That's all we need!" the princess interrupted, smiling sardonically and without changing the expression of her eyes. "I'm a woman; in your opinion,

---

*But, my poor Catiche, it's clear as day.

we're all stupid; but I know enough to be sure that an illegitimate son cannot inherit . . . *Un bâtard,*" she added, supposing that this translation would definitively prove to the prince his groundlessness.

"How is it you don't understand, finally, Catiche? You're so intelligent, how is it you don't understand: if the count wrote a letter to the sovereign, in which he asked that his son be recognized as legitimate, it means that Pierre will no longer be Pierre, but Count Bezukhov, and then according to the will he'll get everything. And if the will and the letter have not been destroyed, there will be nothing left for you except the consolation that you have been virtuous *et tout ce qui s'en suit.** That is certain."

"I know that the will has been written; but I also know that it is not valid, and you seem to consider me a perfect fool, *mon cousin,*" said the princess, with that expression with which women speak when they suppose they have said something witty and insulting.

"My dear Princess Katerina Semyonovna!" Prince Vassily began speaking impatiently. "I have come to you not in order to exchange barbs, but in order to talk with you, as with a kinswoman, a good, kind, true kinswoman, about your own interests. I tell you for the tenth time that if the letter to the sovereign and the will favouring Pierre are among the count's papers, then, my darling, you and your sisters do not inherit. If you don't believe me, believe people who know: I've just spoken with Dmitri Onufrich" (this was the family lawyer), "and he says the same thing."

Evidently something suddenly changed in the princess's mind; her thin lips turned pale (her eyes remained the same), and her voice, when she began to speak, kept breaking into such tremors as she evidently did not expect herself.

"That would be just fine," she said. "I don't want anything and never did."

She threw the dog off her lap and straightened the folds of her dress.

"There's gratitude, there's thankfulness to people who have sacrificed everything for him," she said. "Wonderful! Very fine! I need nothing, Prince."

"Yes, but you're not alone, you have sisters," replied Prince Vassily.

But the princess was not listening to him.

"Yes, I've long known, but I had forgotten, that apart from baseness, deceit, envy, intrigue, apart from ingratitude, the blackest ingratitude, I could expect nothing in this house . . ."

"Do you or do you not know where the will is?" Prince Vassily asked, his cheeks twitching still more than before.

"Yes, I was stupid, I still believed in people, and loved them, and sacrificed myself. But only those who are mean and vile succeed. I know whose intrigue this is."

---

*And all that follows from it.

The princess was about to get up, but the prince held her by the arm. The princess had the air of someone who has suddenly become disappointed in the whole human race; she looked spitefully at her interlocutor.

"There's still time, my friend. Remember, Catiche, it was all done inadvertently, in a moment of wrath, illness, and then forgotten. Our duty, my dear, is to correct his mistake, to alleviate his last moments by not allowing him to do this injustice, by not letting him die thinking he has made unhappy those people who . . ."

"Those people who sacrificed everything for him," the princess picked up, again trying to rise, but the prince did not let her, "something he was never able to appreciate. No, *mon cousin*," she added with a sigh, "I shall remember that one can expect no reward in this world, that in this world there is neither honour nor justice. One must be cunning and wicked in this world."

"Well, *voyons,** calm down; I know your excellent heart."

"No, I have a wicked heart."

"I know your heart," the prince repeated, "I value your friendship, and I wish you were of the same opinion about me. Calm down and *parlons raison,*† while there's time—maybe a day, maybe an hour. Tell me all you know about the will, and above all, where it is: you must know. We'll take it right now and show it to the count. He has surely forgotten about it by now and will want it destroyed. You understand that my only desire is to fulfil his wishes religiously; that is the only reason I've come here. I am here only to help him and you."

"Now I've understood everything. I know whose intrigue it is. I know," said the princess.

"That's not the point, dear heart."

"It's your protégée, your dear Anna Mikhailovna, whom I wouldn't have as a housemaid—that vile, loathsome woman."

"*Ne perdons point de temps.*"‡

"Ah, don't speak to me! Last winter she wormed her way in here and told the count a whole heap of such vile, such nasty things about us all, especially Sophie—I can't repeat it—that the count became ill and didn't want to see us for two weeks. I know it was then that he wrote that nasty, loathsome document; but I thought the document meant nothing."

"*Nous y voilà,*§ why didn't you tell me anything before?"

"It's in the inlaid portfolio he keeps under his pillow. Now I know," said the princess, not replying. "Yes, if I have a sin, a great sin, it's my hatred of that loathsome woman," the princess nearly shouted, changing into a completely

*Come now.
†Let's talk reason.
‡Let's not waste time.
§There we are.

different person. "And why is she worming her way in here? But I'll have it out with her, I'll have it all out. The time will come!"

XIX

While such conversations were going on in the reception room and the princess's apartments, the carriage bringing Pierre (who had been sent for) and Anna Mikhailovna (who found it necessary to go with him) was driving into Count Bezukhov's courtyard. As the wheels of the carriage rumbled softly over the straw spread under the windows, Anna Mikhailovna, turning to her companion with words of comfort, discovered that he was asleep in the corner of the carriage, and woke him up. Coming to his senses, Pierre followed Anna Mikhailovna out of the carriage and only then thought about the meeting with his dying father that lay ahead of him. He noticed that they had driven up not to the front, but to the back entrance. Just as he was stepping out, two men in tradesman's clothes hastily ran away from the entrance into the shadow of the wall. Having stopped, Pierre made out several more men of the same sort in the shadow of the house on both sides. But neither Anna Mikhailovna, nor the footman, nor the coachman, who could not help seeing these men, paid any attention to them. So that is how it has to be, Pierre decided to himself and went after Anna Mikhailovna. Anna Mikhailovna went up the dimly lit, narrow stone stairs with hasty steps, calling to Pierre, who lagged behind her, and who, though he did not understand why in general he had to go to the count, and still less why he had to go by the back stairs, decided to himself, judging by Anna Mikhailovna's assurance and haste, that this had necessarily to be so. Halfway up the stairs, they were nearly knocked off their feet by some people with buckets who came running down the stairs, stamping with their boots. These people pressed themselves to the wall to let Pierre and Anna Mikhailovna pass and did not show the least surprise when they saw them.

"Is this the way to the princesses' apartments?" Anna Mikhailovna asked one of them.

"Yes," the lackey answered in a bold, loud voice, as though everything was permitted now, "the door on the left, good lady."

"Maybe the count didn't send for me," said Pierre, when he came to the landing. "I'll just go to my own rooms."

Anna Mikhailovna stopped so that Pierre could catch up with her.

"*Ah, mon ami!*" she said, with the same gesture as in the morning, when she touched her son's arm, "*croyez que je souffre autant que vous, mais soyez homme.*"*

---

*Ah, my friend! . . . believe me, I'm suffering as much as you, but be a man.

"Really, why don't I go?" asked Pierre, looking at Anna Mikhailovna affectionately through his spectacles.

"Ah, mon ami, oubliez les torts qu'on a pu avoir envers vous, pensez que c'est votre père . . . peut-être à l'agonie." She sighed. *"Je vous ai tout de suite aimé comme mon fils. Fiez à moi, Pierre. Je n'oublierais pas vos intérêts."**

Pierre understood none of it; he had a still stronger impression that this was how it had to be, and he obediently followed Anna Mikhailovna, who was already opening the door.

The door led to the backstairs hallway. In the corner sat the princesses' old servant knitting a sock. Pierre had never been in this part of the house; he had not even suspected the existence of these rooms. Anna Mikhailovna asked a girl who walked past them with a carafe on a tray (calling her dear and sweetheart) about the princesses' health, and drew Pierre further down the stone corridor. The first room to the left from the corridor led to the princesses' living quarters. The maid with the carafe, in her haste (everything was being done in haste just then in this house), did not close the door, and as they were passing by, Pierre and Anna Mikhailovna involuntarily glanced into the room where the eldest princess and Prince Vassily were sitting close together, talking. Seeing them pass by, Prince Vassily made an impatient movement and drew back; the princess jumped up and, in a desperate gesture, slammed the door shut with all her might.

This gesture was so unlike the princess's usual calm, the fear that showed on Prince Vassily's face was so inconsistent with his augustness, that Pierre stopped and looked at his guide questioningly through his spectacles. Anna Mikhailovna expressed no surprise, she only smiled slightly and sighed, as if to show that she had expected it all.

"Soyez homme, mon ami, c'est moi qui veillerai à vos intérêts,"† she said in response to his look and went still more quickly down the corridor.

Pierre did not understand what it was all about, and still less what *veiller à vos intérêts* meant, but he understood that it all had to be so. From the corridor they went into the half-lit salon adjoining the count's anteroom. It was one of those cold and luxurious rooms which Pierre knew only from the front porch. But in this room, too, in the middle of it, stood an empty tub, and water had been spilled on the carpet. They encountered a servant and an acolyte with a censer, who were walking on tiptoe and paid no attention to them. They went into the anteroom, so familiar to Pierre, with its two Italian windows opening on the winter garden, a big bust, and a full-length portrait of

---

*Ah, my friend, forget the wrongs that may have been done you, think that this is your father . . . perhaps in his death agony . . . I loved you at once like my own son. Trust me, Pierre. I won't forget your interests.

†Be a man, my friend, it is I who will watch over your interests.

Catherine. The same people, in almost the same positions, were sitting in the anteroom, exchanging whispers. They all fell silent and turned to look at the entering Anna Mikhailovna, with her pale, weepy face, and the big, fat Pierre, who, with his head hanging, obediently followed her.

Anna Mikhailovna's face expressed an awareness that the decisive moment had come; with the manner of a businesslike Petersburg lady, she entered the room still more boldly than in the morning, not letting Pierre stray from her. She felt that, since she was bringing with her the person whom the dying man wished to see, her reception was assured. With a quick glance around, taking in everyone who was in the room and noticing the count's father confessor, not really bending down, but suddenly making herself smaller, at a quick amble, she glided over to the father confessor and respectfully received a blessing first from the one, then from the other clerical person.

"Thank God we're in time," she said to the clerical person. "We, his relations, were all so afraid. This young man is the count's son," she added in a lower voice. "A terrible moment!"

Having spoken these words, she went over to the doctor.

"Cher docteur," she said to him, *"ce jeune homme est le fils du comte . . . y a-t-il de l'espoir?"* *

The doctor was silent, raising his eyes and shoulders with a quick movement. Anna Mikhailovna, with exactly the same movement, raised her shoulders and eyes, almost closing them, sighed, and walked away from the doctor towards Pierre. She addressed Pierre with special respectfulness and tender sorrow.

"Ayez confiance en sa miséricorde!" † she said to him and, pointing to a little settee on which he could sit and wait for her, made inaudibly for the door that everyone was looking at, and, following the barely audible noise of that door, disappeared behind it.

Pierre, having decided to obey his guide in all things, made for the little settee she had pointed out to him. As soon as Anna Mikhailovna disappeared, he noticed that the eyes of everyone in the room turned to him with something more than curiosity and sympathy. He noticed that they all exchanged whispers, indicating him with their eyes, as if with fear and even obsequiousness. He was being shown a respect no one had ever shown him before: a lady unknown to him, who had been talking with the clerical persons, got up from her place and offered him a seat; the adjutant picked up a glove Pierre had dropped and handed it to him; the doctors fell deferentially silent when he walked past them and stepped aside to make way for him. Pierre first wanted to sit somewhere else, so as not to inconvenience the lady, wanted to pick up the glove himself, and to bypass the doctors, who were not standing in his way;

---

*Dear doctor . . . this young man is the count's son . . . is there any hope?
†Trust in His mercy!

but he suddenly felt that that would be improper, he felt that that night he was the person responsible for performing some terrible rite which everyone expected, and that he therefore had to accept services from them all. He silently accepted the glove from the adjutant, sat down in the lady's place, putting his big hands on his symmetrically displayed knees in the naïve pose of an Egyptian statue, and decided to himself that this was precisely as it had to be and that that evening, so as not to lose his head and do something foolish, he ought not to act according to his own reasoning, but give himself up entirely to the will of those who were guiding him.

Two minutes had not gone by before Prince Vassily, in his kaftan with three stars, holding his head high, majestically entered the room. He seemed to have grown thinner since morning; his eyes were larger than usual as he looked around and saw Pierre. He went over to him, took his hand (something he had never done before), and pulled it down, as if testing whether it was well attached.

"*Courage, courage, mon ami. Il a demandé de vous voir. C'est bien . . .*"*
And he was about to leave.

But Pierre considered it necessary to ask:

"How is the health of . . ." He hesitated, not knowing whether it was proper to call the dying man "count"; yet he was embarrassed to call him "father."

"*Il a eu encore un coup, il y a une demi-heure.*† Yet another stroke. *Courage, mon ami . . .*"

Pierre was in such a state of mental confusion that, at the word "stroke," he pictured some sort of blow to the body. He looked at Prince Vassily in perplexity, and only then realized that "stroke" referred to an illness. Prince Vassily spoke several words to Lorrain in passing and went through the door on tiptoe. He did not know how to walk on tiptoe, and his whole body bobbed up and down awkwardly. The elder princess went in after him, then the clerical persons and the acolytes went in, then the servants also went through the door. Behind the door movement was heard, and finally, with the same face, pale but firm in the fulfilment of her duty, Anna Mikhailovna rushed out and, touching Pierre's arm, said:

"*La bonté divine est inépuisable. C'est la cérémonie de l'extrême onction qui va commencer. Venez.*"‡

Pierre went through the door, stepping on the soft carpet, and noticed that the adjutant and the unknown lady, and some other servants—all came in after him, as if there was no longer any need to ask permission to enter that room.

---

*He has asked to see you. That's good . . .
†He had another stroke half an hour ago.
‡The divine goodness is inexhaustible. The ceremony of extreme unction is about to begin. Come.

XX

Pierre knew well that big room, divided by columns and an archway, all hung with Persian carpets. The part of the room behind the columns, where on one side stood a high mahogany bed under a silk canopy and on the other an enormous stand with icons, was brightly lit with red light, as is usual in churches during evening services. Under the shining casings of the icons stood a long Voltaire armchair, and on the chair, its upper part spread with snow-white, unrumpled, apparently just-changed pillows, covered to the waist with a bright green coverlet, lay the majestic figure, so familiar to Pierre, of his father, Count Bezukhov, with the same mane of grey hair, reminiscent of a lion's, above his broad forehead, and the same characteristically noble, deep furrows on his handsome reddish-yellow face. He lay directly under the icons; his two large, fat arms were freed of the coverlet and lay on top of it. In his right hand, which lay palm down, a wax candle had been placed between the thumb and the index finger, held in place by an old servant who reached from behind the armchair. Over the armchair stood the clerical persons in their majestic, shining vestments, their long hair spread loose on them, lighted candles in their hands, performing the service with slow solemnity. A little behind them stood the two younger princesses, holding handkerchiefs to their eyes, and in front of them the elder princess, Catiche, with a spiteful and resolute air, not taking her eyes off the icons for a moment, as if telling everyone that she would not answer for herself if she glanced back. Anna Mikhailovna, meek sorrow and all-forgiveness on her face, and the unknown lady stood by the door. Prince Vassily stood on the other side of the door, close to the armchair, behind a velvet-upholstered chair with its carved back turned to him, resting his elbow on it, holding a candle in his left hand, crossing himself with the right, raising his eyes each time he put the fingers to his forehead. His face expressed calm piety and submission to the will of God. "If you don't understand these feelings, the worse for you," his face seemed to say.

Behind him stood the adjutant, the doctors, and the male servants; the men and women were separated as in church. All were silent, crossing themselves, only the church reading could be heard, the restrained bass singing, and, in moments of silence, sighing and the shuffling of feet. Anna Mikhailovna, with a significant air which showed that she knew what she was doing, went all the way across the room to give Pierre a candle. He lit it and, diverted by observing the others, began to cross himself with the same hand in which he was holding the candle.

The youngest, the red-cheeked and laughter-prone Princess Sophie, with the little mole, looked at him. She smiled, hid her face in her handkerchief, and did not uncover it for a long time; but, looking at Pierre, she laughed again. She evidently felt herself unable to look at him without laughing, but could not keep from looking at him, and, to avoid temptation, slowly moved behind a column. Midway through the service, the voices of the clergy suddenly fell silent; the clerical persons said something to each other in a whisper; the old servant who was holding the count's hand straightened up and turned to the ladies. Anna Mikhailovna stepped forward and, bending over the sick man, beckoned behind her back for Lorrain to come. The French doctor—who stood without a lighted candle, leaning on a column, in the respectful pose of a foreigner, which showed that, despite differences of belief, he understood all the importance of the rite being performed and even approved of it—went over to the sick man with the inaudible steps of a man in the prime of life, took up his free hand from the green coverlet in his white, slender fingers, and, turning away, began taking his pulse and pondering. The sick man was given something to drink, there was stirring around him, then everyone went to their places and the service resumed. During this interruption, Pierre noticed that Prince Vassily came from behind the back of his chair and with that same look which showed that he knew what he was doing, and so much the worse for the others if they did not understand him, did not go up to the sick man, but passing by him, joined the eldest princess and together with her made for the depths of the bedroom, to the high bed under the silk canopy. From the bed, both prince and princess disappeared through a rear door, but before the end of the service they came back to their places one after the other. Pierre paid no more attention to this circumstance than to all the others, having decided in his mind once and for all that everything taking place before him that evening had necessarily to be so.

The sound of the church singing ceased, and the voice of the clerical person was heard deferentially congratulating the sick man with having received the sacrament. The sick man went on lying in the same way, lifelessly and motionlessly. Around him everyone stirred, footsteps and whispers were heard, among which the whisper of Anna Mikhailovna stood out more sharply than the rest.

Pierre heard her say:

"He must be transferred to his bed, here it will be quite impossible . . ."

The sick man was so surrounded by doctors, princesses, and servants that Pierre could no longer see the reddish-yellow head with its grey mane, which, though he did see other faces, had never once left his sight during the whole service. By the cautious movements of the people standing around the armchair, Pierre guessed that the dying man was being lifted up and transferred.

"Hold on to my arm, otherwise you'll drop him," the frightened whisper of one of the servants reached him, "from below . . . one more," voices said, and the heavy breathing and the tread of people's feet quickened, as if the load they were carrying was beyond their strength.

The carriers, who also included Anna Mikhailovna, came even with the young man, and for a moment, over people's backs and necks, he saw the high, fleshy, bared chest and massive shoulders of the sick man, raised up by the people who held him under the arms, and his curly, grey leonine head. That head, with its extraordinarily wide brow and cheekbones, handsome sensual mouth, and majestic, cold gaze, was not disfigured by the proximity of death. It was the same as Pierre had known it three months earlier, when the count had seen him off to Petersburg. But this head swayed helplessly from the uneven steps of the carriers, and the cold, indifferent gaze did not know where to rest.

Several minutes were spent bustling around the high bed; the people who had carried the sick man dispersed. Anna Mikhailovna touched Pierre's arm and said: "*Venez.*"* Together with her, Pierre went up to the bed, on which the sick man had been laid in a stately pose, evidently having to do with the just-received sacrament. He lay with his head resting on the highly propped pillows. His hands were symmetrically laid out, palms down, on the green silk coverlet. When Pierre went up, the count looked straight at him, but looked with a gaze the meaning and significance of which no man could possibly understand. Either this gaze said nothing at all, except that as long as one has eyes one must look somewhere, or it said all too much. Pierre stood there not knowing what to do, and looked questioningly at his guide, Anna Mikhailovna. Anna Mikhailovna made a hasty gesture with her eyes, indicating the sick man's hand and sending it an airborne kiss with her lips. Pierre, diligently stretching his neck so as not to snag the coverlet, followed her advice and put his lips to the wide-boned and fleshy hand. Neither the hand nor a single muscle of the count's face stirred. Pierre again looked questioningly at Anna Mikhailovna, asking what he was to do now. Anna Mikhailovna pointed him with her eyes to an armchair that stood by the bed. Pierre obediently began to sit down in the chair, his eyes still asking whether he was doing the right thing. Anna Mikhailovna nodded her head approvingly. Pierre again assumed the symmetrically naïve pose of an Egyptian statue, evidently regretting that his clumsy and fat body took up so much space, and applying all his inner forces to making himself seem as small as possible. He looked at the count. The count looked at the same place where Pierre's face had been when he was standing. Anna Mikhailovna's face expressed an awareness of the touching importance of this last-minute meeting of father and son. This went on for two minutes, which seemed like an hour to Pierre. Suddenly a shuddering came over the big muscles and furrows of the count's face. The shuddering increased, the hand-

*Come.

some mouth became contorted (only here did Pierre realize how close to death his father was), a vague, hoarse sound came from the contorted mouth. Anna Mikhailovna diligently looked into the sick man's eyes, trying to guess what he wanted, pointed to Pierre, then to the drink, then in a questioning whisper named Prince Vassily, then pointed to the coverlet. The sick man's eyes and face showed impatience. He made an effort to look at the servant who never left his post at the head of the bed.

"He would like to be turned on that side," whispered the servant, and he got up to turn the count's heavy body face to the wall.

Pierre stood up to help the servant.

As the count was being turned, one of his arms was left hanging helplessly, and he made a vain attempt to drag it over. Either the count noticed the horror with which Pierre looked at this lifeless arm, or some other thought flashed in his dying head at that moment, but he looked at the disobedient arm, at the expression of horror on Pierre's face, at the arm again, and on his face there appeared—so incongruous with his features—a faint, suffering smile, as if expressing mockery at his own strengthlessness. Unexpectedly, at the sight of this smile, Pierre felt a shuddering in his breast, a tickling in his nose, and tears blurred his vision. The sick man was turned on his side to the wall. He sighed.

"*Il est assoupi,*" said Anna Mikhailovna, noticing the princess coming to replace them. "*Allons.*"*

Pierre went out.

XXI

There was no one in the reception room now except Prince Vassily and the elder princess, who were sitting under the portrait of Catherine having a lively talk. As soon as they saw Pierre with his guide, they fell silent. The princess hid something, as it seemed to Pierre, and whispered:

"I can't bear that woman."

"*Catiche a fait donner du thé dans le petit salon,*" Prince Vassily said to Anna Mikhailovna. "*Allez, ma pauvre Anna Mikhailovna, prenez quelque chose, autrement vous ne suffirez pas.*"†

He said nothing to Pierre, only squeezed his upper arm feelingly. Pierre and Anna Mikhailovna moved on to the small drawing room.

"*Il n'y a rien qui restaure, comme une tasse de cet excellent thé Russe après une nuit blanche,*"‡ said Lorrain, with an expression of restrained ani-

---

*He has dozed off . . . Let's go.
†Catiche has had tea served in the small drawing room. Go, my poor *Anna Mikhailovna*, have something, otherwise you won't hold out.
‡There's nothing so restorative as a cup of this excellent Russian tea after a sleepless night.

mation, sipping from a fine china cup without a handle, standing in the small, round drawing room in front of a table on which a tea service and a cold supper had been laid. Everyone who was in Count Bezukhov's house that night gathered around the table to fortify themselves. Pierre remembered very well this small, round drawing room with its mirrors and little tables. During balls at the count's house, Pierre, who danced poorly, liked to sit in this little room of mirrors and watch how ladies in ball gowns, with diamonds and pearls on their bare shoulders, passing through this room, looked at themselves in the brightly lit mirrors, which repeated their reflections several times. Now the same room was barely lit with two candles, and in the middle of the night a tea service and some dishes lay in disorder on one of the little tables, and various non-festive people, exchanging whispers, were sitting in it, showing with each movement, each word, that none of them had forgotten what was going on and was yet to be consummated in the bedroom. Pierre did not eat, though he very much wanted to. He glanced questioningly at his guide and saw her going out on tiptoe, back to the reception room, where Prince Vassily had remained with the elder princess. Pierre supposed that it had to be so, lingered a little, and followed her. Anna Mikhailovna was standing by the princess, and the two women were speaking simultaneously in agitated whispers.

"Allow me, Princess, to know what is and what is not necessary," the younger woman was saying, evidently in the same agitated state she had been in when she had slammed the door to her room.

"But, my dear princess," Anna Mikhailovna was saying meekly and persuasively, barring the way to the bedroom and preventing the princess from going in, "won't it be too hard on poor, dear uncle at such a moment, when he needs rest? To talk about worldly things at such a moment, when his soul is already prepared . . ."

Prince Vassily was sitting in an armchair, in his casual pose, one leg crossed high up over the other. His cheeks were twitching badly, and, when they slackened, seemed fatter below; but he had the look of a man who was little taken up with the conversation of the two ladies.

"*Voyons, ma bonne* Anna Mikhailovna, *laissez faire Catiche.* * You know how the count loves her."

"I don't even know what's in this document," said the princess, turning to Prince Vassily and pointing to the inlaid portfolio she was holding in her hands. "I only know that the real will is in his desk, and this is a forgotten document . . ." She tried to go around Anna Mikhailovna, but Anna Mikhailovna sprang over and again barred her way.

"I know, dear, good princess," said Anna Mikhailovna, seizing the portfolio with her hand and so firmly that it was clear she would not soon let go

*Come, my good *Anna Mikhailovna*, let Catiche do as she likes.

of it. "Dear princess, I beg you, I beseech you, have pity on him. *Je vous en conjure . . .**

The princess said nothing. All that could be heard were the sounds of the efforts of the struggle over the portfolio. It was clear that if she did start to talk, it would not be flattering for Anna Mikhailovna. Anna Mikhailovna held on tight, but in spite of that her voice retained all its sweet, drawling softness.

"Pierre, come here, my friend. I think he won't be out of place in the family council—isn't that so, Prince?"

"Why are you silent, *mon cousin?*" the princess suddenly shouted so loudly that the people in the drawing room heard and were frightened by her voice. "Why are you silent, when here God knows who allows herself to interfere and make scenes on a dying's man's threshold? Intriguer!" she whispered spitefully and tugged at the portfolio with all her might, but Anna Mikhailovna went a few steps so as not to let go of the portfolio, and shifted her grip.

"Oh!" Prince Vassily said with reproach and astonishment. He got up. "*C'est ridicule. Voyons*, let go, I tell you."

The princess let go.

"You, too!"

Anna Mikhailovna did not obey him.

"Let go, I tell you. I take it all upon myself. I'll go and ask him. I . . . let that be enough for you."

"*Mais, mon prince*," said Anna Mikhailovna, "give him a moment's rest after such a great sacrament. Here, Pierre, tell us your opinion," she turned to the young man who, coming up close to them, looked with astonishment at the princess's spiteful face, which had lost all decency, and at the twitching cheeks of Prince Vassily.

"Remember that you will answer for all the consequences," Prince Vassily said sternly. "You don't know what you're doing."

"Loathsome woman!" the princess cried, suddenly falling upon Anna Mikhailovna and tearing the portfolio from her.

Prince Vassily hung his head and spread his hands.

At that moment the door, that awful door at which Pierre had stared for so long and which had opened so softly, now opened noisily, banging against the wall, and the younger princess ran out clasping her hands.

"What are you doing!" she said desperately. "*Il s'en va et vous me laissez seule.*"†

The elder princess dropped the portfolio. Anna Mikhailovna quickly bent down and, picking up the disputed object, ran to the bedroom. The elder princess and Prince Vassily came to their senses and followed her. A few min-

---

*I entreat you . . .
†He's going and you leave me alone.

utes later, the elder princess was the first to come out, with a pale and dry face, biting her lower lip. At the sight of Pierre, her face showed irrepressible spite.

"Yes, rejoice now," she said, "you've been waiting for this."

And, bursting into sobs, she covered her face with a handkerchief and ran out of the room.

After the princess, Prince Vassily came out. Staggering, he reached the sofa on which Pierre was sitting and collapsed on it, covering his eyes with his hand. Pierre noted that he was pale and his lower jaw was twitching and shaking as in a fever.

"Ah, my friend!" he said, taking Pierre by the elbow; and in his voice there was sincerity and weakness, such as Pierre had never noticed in him before. "We sin so much, we deceive so much, and all for what? I'm over fifty, my friend . . . I'll . . . Everything ends in death, everything. Death is terrible." He wept.

Anna Mikhailovna was the last to come out. She went to Pierre with quiet, slow steps.

"Pierre! . . ." she said.

Pierre looked at her questioningly. She kissed the young man on the forehead, wetting it with tears. She paused.

"*Il n'est plus . . .*"*

Pierre looked at her through his spectacles.

"*Allons, je vous reconduirai. Tâchez de pleurer. Rien ne soulage comme les larmes.*"†

She led him to the dark drawing room, and Pierre was glad that nobody could see his face. Anna Mikhailovna left him, and when she came back, he was sound asleep, his head resting on his arm.

The next morning Anna Mikhailovna said to Pierre:

"*Oui, mon cher, c'est une grande perte pour nous tous. Je ne parle pas de vous. Mais Dieu vous soutiendra, vous êtes jeune et vous voilà à la tête d'une immense fortune, je l'espère. Le testament n'a pas été encore ouvert. Je vous connais assez pour savoir que cela ne vous tournera pas la tête, mais cela vous impose des devoirs, et il faut être homme.*"‡

Pierre was silent.

"*Peut-être plus tard je vous dirai, mon cher, que si je n'avais pas été là, Dieu sait ce que serait arrivé. Vous savez mon oncle avant-hier encore me*

*He's no more.
†Come, I'll see you out. Try to weep. Nothing relieves one like tears.
‡Yes, my dear, it is a great loss for us all. To say nothing of you. But God will sustain you, you are young, and here you are at the head of an immense fortune, I hope. The will has not yet been opened. I know you well enough to know that this will not turn your head, but it does impose duties on you, and one must be a man.

promettait de ne pas oublier Boris. Mais il n'a pas eu le temps. J'espère, mon cher ami, que vous remplirez le désir de votre père."*

Pierre understood nothing and silently gazed at Anna Mikhailovna, blushing shyly. Having talked with Pierre, Anna Mikhailovna drove off to the Rostovs' and went to bed. She woke up in the morning and told the Rostovs and all her acquaintances the details of Count Bezukhov's death. She said that the count had died as she would like to die, that his end had been not only touching, but also instructive; and the last meeting of the father and son had been so touching that she could not recall it without tears, and that she did not know who had behaved better in those terrible moments: the father, who remembered everything and everyone so well in the last minutes and said such touching things to the son; or Pierre, who was a pity to see, he was so crushed, but who nevertheless tried to hide his sorrow, so as not to upset his dying father. *"C'est pénible, mais cela fait du bien; ça élève l'âme de voir des hommes comme le vieux comte et son digne fils,"*† she said. She also told disapprovingly about the actions of the princess and Prince Vassily, but as a great secret and in a whisper.

XXII

At Bald Hills, the estate of Prince Nikolai Andreevich Bolkonsky, the arrival of the young Prince Andrei and the princess was expected any day; but that expectation did not disrupt the harmonious order in which life went on in the old prince's house. General in Chief Prince Nikolai Andreevich, known in society as *le roi de Prusse*,‡ had been banished to his country estate under Paul, and had lived uninterruptedly at Bald Hills ever since, with his daughter, Princess Marya, and her companion, Mlle Bourienne. And under the new reign, though he was permitted entry to the capitals,[42] he went on living uninterruptedly in the country, saying that anyone who needed him could travel the hundred miles from Moscow to Bald Hills, but that he himself needed no one and nothing. He used to say that there were only two sources of human vice: idleness and superstition; and that there were only two virtues: activity and intelligence. He occupied himself personally with his daughter's upbringing, and to develop the two chief virtues in her, gave her lessons in algebra and geometry and portioned out her whole life among constant studies. He himself

---

*Perhaps later on I'll tell you, my dear, that if I hadn't been there, God knows what would have happened. You know my uncle just the day before yesterday promised me not to forget Boris. But he had no time. I hope, my dear friend, that you will fulfil your father's wish.
†It's painful, but it does one good; it elevates the soul to see men like the old count and his worthy son.
‡The king of Prussia.

was constantly occupied, now with writing his memoirs, now with higher mathematical calculations, now with turning snuffboxes on a lathe, now with working in the garden and supervising the construction work that never ceased on his estate. As the main condition for activity was order, so the order in his way of life was brought to the utmost degree of precision. His coming to the table was performed under the same invariable conditions, and not only at the same hour, but at the same minute. With the people around him, from his daughter to the servants, the prince was brusque and invariably demanding, and thus, without being cruel, inspired a fear and respect for himself such as the cruellest of men would not find it easy to obtain. Though he was retired and now had no importance in state affairs, every governor of the province in which the prince's estate lay considered it his duty to call on him and, like the architect, the gardener, or Princess Marya, to wait at the appointed hour for the prince to come out to the high-ceilinged waiting room. And each person in the waiting room experienced the same feeling of respect and even fear at the moment when the immensely high door to the study opened and revealed the small figure of the old man, in a powdered wig, with small dry hands and grey beetling brows, which sometimes, when he frowned, hid the brightness of his intelligent and youthfully bright eyes.

On the day of the young couple's arrival, in the morning, as usual, Princess Marya went into the waiting room at the appointed hour for the morning greeting and fearfully crossed herself and inwardly recited a prayer. Every day she went in and every day she prayed that this daily meeting would go well.

A powdered old servant who was sitting in the waiting room got up with a quiet movement and in a whisper announced: "If you please."

From behind the door came the regular sounds of a lathe. The princess timidly pulled the easily and smoothly opening door and stopped in the doorway. The prince was working at the lathe and, having glanced at her, went on with what he was doing.

The immense study was filled with things obviously in constant use. The big table with books and plans lying on it, the tall bookcases with keys in their glass doors, the tall table for writing in a standing position, on which lay an open notebook, the lathe with tools laid out and wood shavings strewn around it—everything spoke of constant, diverse, and orderly activity. By the movements of the small foot shod in a silver-embroidered Tartar boot, by the firm pressure of the sinewy, lean hand, one could see in the prince the still persistent and much-enduring strength of fresh old age. Having made a few more turns, he took his foot from the pedal of the lathe, wiped the chisel, dropped it into a leather pouch attached to the lathe, and, going to the table, called his daughter over. He never blessed his children, but, offering her his bristly, as yet unshaven cheek and giving her a stern and at the same time attentively tender look, merely said:

"Are you well? . . . Sit down, then!"

He took the geometry notebook, written in his own hand, and moved a chair over with his foot.

"For tomorrow!" he said, quickly finding the page and marking it paragraph by paragraph with his hard fingernail.

The princess bent to the table over the notebook.

"Wait, there's a letter for you," the old man said suddenly, taking an envelope with a woman's handwriting on it from a pouch attached to the table and dropping it in front of her.

At the sight of the letter, the princess's face became covered with red blotches. She hastily took it and bent over it.

"From Héloïse?"[43] asked the prince, baring his still strong and yellowish teeth in a cold smile.

"Yes, from Julie," said the princess, glancing up timidly and smiling timidly.

"I'll skip two letters and read the third," the prince said sternly. "I'm afraid you write a lot of nonsense. I'll read the third."

"You can read this one, *mon père*," the princess replied, blushing still more and handing him the letter.

"The third, I said, the third," the prince shouted curtly, pushing the letter away, and, leaning his elbow on the table, he drew the notebook with geometric drawings towards him.

"Well, ma'am," the old man began, bending close to his daughter over the notebook and putting one arm on the back of the chair in which the princess was sitting, so that the princess felt herself surrounded on all sides by her father's smell of tobacco and pungent old age, which she had known so long. "Well, ma'am, these triangles are similar; kindly look, the angle ABC..."

The princess glanced fearfully at her father's bright eyes, so near to her; red blotches came over her face, and it was obvious that she understood nothing, and was so afraid that fear would prevent her from understanding all of her father's further explanations, however clear they were. Whether it was the teacher or the pupil who was at fault, the same thing repeated itself each day: the princess felt giddy, saw nothing, heard nothing, but only felt the lean face of her stern father near her, felt his breathing and his smell, and thought only of how to get out of the study as quickly as possible and work out the problem in the freedom of her own room. The old man would get beside himself: he would noisily move the chair he was sitting in back and forth, try hard to keep himself from flying into a rage, and almost always flew into a rage, poured out abuse, and sometimes flung the notebook away.

The princess gave the wrong answer.

"Well, aren't you a fool!" shouted the prince, shoving the notebook away, but he got up at once, paced about, touched the princess's hair with his hands, and sat down again.

He moved closer and continued his explanations.

"It won't do, Princess, it won't do," he said, when the princess, having taken and closed the notebook with the next day's lesson, was getting ready to leave. "Mathematics is a great thing, my lady. And I don't want you to be like our stupid women here. Much patience, much pleasure." He patted her on the cheek. "It will knock the foolishness out of your head."

She was about to leave, but he gestured for her to stop and took a new, uncut book from the tall table.

"Here's some *Key to the Mystery*[44] your Héloïse sends you. Religious. But I don't interfere with anyone's beliefs . . . I've looked through it. Take it. Well, off with you, off with you!"

He patted her on the shoulder and locked the door behind her himself.

Princess Marya went back to her room with the sad, frightened expression which rarely left her and made her unattractive, sickly face still more unattractive, and sat down at her desk, covered with miniature portraits and heaped with books and notebooks. The princess was as disorderly as her father was orderly. She put down her geometry notebook and impatiently unsealed the letter. The letter was from the princess's closest childhood friend; this friend was that same Julie Karagin who had been at the Rostovs' name-day party.

Julie wrote:

Chère et excellente amie, quelle chose terrible et effrayante que l'absence! J'ai beau me dire que la moitié de mon existence et de mon bonheur est en vous, que malgré la distance qui nous sépare, nos coeurs sont unis par des liens indissolubles; le mien se révolte contre la destinée, et je ne puis, malgré les plaisirs et les distractions qui m'entourent, vaincre une certaine tristesse cachée que je ressens au fond du coeur depuis notre séparation. Pourquoi ne sommes-nous pas réunies, comme cette été dans votre grand cabinet sur le canapé bleu, le canapé à confidences? Pourquoi ne puis-je, comme il y a trois mois, puiser de nouvelles forces morales dans votre regard si doux, si calme et si pénétrant, regard que j'aimais tant et que je crois voir devant moi, quand je vous écris?*

Having read that far, Princess Marya sighed and glanced into the pier glass that stood to the right of her. The mirror reflected an unattractive, weak body

---

*Dear and excellent friend, what a terrible and frightening thing is absence! Though I tell myself that half of my existence and of my happiness is in you, that despite the distance which separates us, our hearts are united by indissoluble bonds, my own heart revolts against destiny, and despite the pleasures and distractions that surround me, I am unable to overcome a certain hidden sadness which I feel at the bottom of my heart since our separation. Why are we not reunited, as this summer in your big study on the blue couch, the couch of confidences? Why can I not, as three months ago, draw new moral strength from your look, so gentle, so calm, so penetrating, that look I loved so much and that I think I see before me as I write to you?

and a thin face. Her eyes, always sad, now looked into the mirror with particular hopelessness. "She's flattering me," thought the princess, and she turned away and went on reading. Julie, however, was not flattering her friend: indeed, the princess's eyes, large, deep, and luminous (sometimes it was as if rays of warm light came from them in sheaves), were so beautiful that very often, despite the unattractiveness of the whole face, those eyes were more attractive than beauty. But the princess had never seen the good expression of those eyes, the expression they had in moments when she was not thinking of herself. As with all people, the moment she looked in the mirror, her face assumed a strained, unnatural, bad expression. She went on reading:

Tout Moscou ne parle que guerre. L'un de mes deux frères est déjà a l'étranger, l'autre est avec la garde, qui se met en marche vers la frontière. Notre cher empereur a quitté Pétersbourg et, à ce qu'on prétend, compte lui-même exposer sa précieuse existence aux chances de la guerre. Dieu veuille que le monstre corsicain, qui détruit le repos de l'Europe, soit terrassé par l'ange que le tout-puissant, dans sa miséricorde, nous a donné pour souverain. Sans parler de mes frères, cette guerre m'a privée d'une relation des plus chères à mon coeur. Je parle du jeune Nicolas Rostoff, qui avec son enthousiasme n'a pu supporter l'inaction et a quitté l'université pour aller s'enrôler dans l'armée. Eh bien, chère Marie, je vous avouerai, que, malgré son extrême jeunesse, son départ pour l'armée a été un grand chagrin pour moi. Le jeune homme, dont je vous parlais cet été, a tant de noblesse, de veritable jeunesse qu'on rencontre si rarement dans le siècle où nous vivons parmi nos viellards de vingt ans. Il a surtout tant de franchise et de coeur. Il est tellement pur et poétique, que mes relations avec lui, quelques passagères qu'elles fussent, ont été l'une des plus douces jouissances de mon pauvre coeur, qui a déjà tant souffert. Je vous raconterai un jour nos adieux et tout ce qui s'est dit en partant. Tout cela est encore trop frais. Ah! chère amie,*

---

*All Moscow talks only of war. One of my two brothers is already abroad, the other is with the guards, who are starting on the march to the frontier. Our dear emperor has left Petersburg and, they claim, is intending to expose his own precious existence to the hazards of war. God grant that the Corsican monster, who is destroying the peace of Europe, be overthrown by the angel whom the Almighty, in His mercy, has given us for a sovereign. Not to mention my brothers, this war has deprived me of a relation that is one of the dearest to my heart. I am speaking of young Nikolai Rostov, who with his enthusiasm could not bear inaction and has left the university to go and enlist in the army. Well, dear Marie, I'll admit to you that, despite his extreme youth, his leaving for the army has been a great sadness for me. The young man, of whom I spoke to you this summer, has so much nobility, so much true youthfulness, which one encounters so rarely in the age we live in among our old men of twenty. Above all he has so much candour and heart. He is so pure and poetical that my relations with him, ephemeral as they were, have been one of the sweetest joys of my poor heart, which has already suffered so much. One day I'll tell you about our farewells and all that got said in parting. It's all still too fresh. Ah! dear friend, you are fortunate not to know these

vous êtes heureuse de ne pas connaître ces jouissances et ces peines si poignantes. Vous êtes heureuse, puisque les dernières—sont ordinairement les plus fortes! Je sais fort bien que le comte Nicolas est trop jeune pour pouvoir jamais devenir pour moi quelque chose de plus qu'un ami, mais cette douce amitié, ces relations si poétiques et si pures ont été un besoin pour mon coeur. Mais n'en parlons plus. La grande nouvelle du jour qui occupe tout Moscou est la mort du vieux comte Bezukhov *et son héritage. Figurez-vous que les trois princesses n'ont reçu que très peu de chose, le prince Basile rien, et que c'est M. Pierre qui a tout hérité, et qui par-dessus le marché a été reconnu pour fils légitime, par conséquant comte* Bezukhov *et possesseur de la plus belle fortune de la Russie. On prétend que le prince Basile a joué un très vilain rôle dans toute cette histoire et qu'il est reparti tout penaud pour Pétersbourg.*

Je vous avoue, que je comprends très peu toutes ces affaires de legs et de testament; ce que je sais, c'est que depuis que le jeune homme que nous connaissions tous sous le nom de M. Pierre tout court est devenu comte Bezukhov *et possesseur de l'une des plus grandes fortunes de la Russie, je m'amuse fort à observer les changements de ton et des manières des mamans accablées de filles à marier et des demoiselles elles-mêmes à l'égard de cet individu, qui, par parenthèse, m'a paru toujours être un pauvre sire. Comme on s'amuse depuis deux ans à me donner des promis que je ne connais pas le plus souvent, la chronique matrimoniale de Moscou me fait comtesse* Bezukhov. *Mais vous sentez bien que je ne me soucie nullement de le devenir. A propos de mariage, savez-vous que tout dernièrement la "tante en générale"* Anna Mikhailovna *m'a confié sous le sceau du plus grand secret*

---

so poignant joys and sorrows. You are fortunate, because the latter—are usually the stronger! I know very well that Count Nikolai is too young ever to be able to be anything more than a friend to me, but this sweet friendship, these relations, so poetical and so pure, have been a need of my heart. But let us speak no more of that. The big news of the day, with which all Moscow is taken up, is the death of old Count *Bezukhov* and his inheritance. Imagine, the three princesses got very little, Prince Vassily nothing, and it is M. Pierre who has inherited everything, and who on top of that has been recognized as a legitimate son, consequently as Count *Bezukhov* and possessor of the handsomest fortune in Russia. They claim that Prince Vassily played a very nasty role in this whole story and that he has gone back quite sheepishly to Petersburg.

I confess to you that I understand very little of all these matters of legacies and wills; what I do know is that since the young man we knew simply under the name of M. Pierre has become Count *Bezukhov* and possessor of one of the largest fortunes in Russia, I have been much amused to observe the changes of tone and manners of mamas burdened with marriageable daughters and of the young ladies themselves with regard to this individual, who, parenthetically, has always seemed a poor sort to me. Since people have amused themselves for the past two years by making matches for me that I mostly knew nothing about, the matrimonial chronicle of Moscow is now making me Countess *Bezukhov*. But you can feel very well that I do not care at all to become that. Speaking of marriage, do you know that the "aunt in general" *Anna Mikhailovna*, under the seal of the greatest secrecy, has confided to me a plan to get you married? It is no more nor less than the son of Prince Vassily, Anatole, whom they would like to set up by marrying him to a rich and distin-

un projet de mariage pour vous. Ce n'est ni plus ni moins, que le fils du prince Basile, Anatole, qu'on voudrait ranger en le mariant à une personne riche et distinguée, et c'est sur vous qu'est tombé le choix des parents. Je ne sais comment vous envisagerez la chose, mais j'ai cru de mon devoir de vous en avertir. On le dit très beau et très mauvais sujet; c'est tout ce que j'ai pu savoir sur son compte.

Mais assez de bavardage comme cela. Je finis mon second feuillet, et maman me fait chercher pour aller dîner chez les Apraksines. Lisez le livre mystique que je vous envoie et qui fait fureur chez nous. Quoiqu'il y ait des choses dans ce livre difficiles à atteindre avec la faible conception humaine, c'est un livre admirable dont la lecture calme et élève l'âme. Adieu. Mes respects à monsieur votre père et mes compliments à mlle Bourienne. Je vous embrasse comme je vous aime.

Julie.

P.S. Donnez-moi des nouvelles de votre frère et de sa charmante petite femme.

The princess pondered, smiled pensively (at which her face, lit up by her luminous eyes, was completely transformed) and, suddenly getting up, went with her heavy step to the desk. She took out some paper, and her hand quickly began moving across it. This is what she wrote in reply:

*Chère et excellente amie.** Votre lettre du 13 m'a causé une grande joie. Vous m'aimez donc toujours, ma poétique Julie. L'absence, dont vous dites tant de mal, n'a donc pas eu son influence habituelle sur vous. Vous vous plaignez de l'absence—que devrai-je dire moi si j'osais me plaindre, privée de tous ceux qui me sont chers? Ah! si nous n'avions pas la religion pour nous consoler, la vie serait bien triste. Pourquoi me supposez-vous un regard sévère, quand vous me parlez de votre affection pour le jeune homme? Sous*

---

guished person, and the choice of the parents has fallen on you. I do not know how you would look at it, but I thought it my duty to warn you of it. He's said to be very handsome and a very bad boy; that is all I have been able to learn about him.

But enough of this chattering. I am finishing my second sheet, and mama has sent for me to go to dinner at the Apraksins. Read the mystical book I am sending you and that is causing a furore here. Though there are things in this book that are hard to grasp with weak human understanding, it is an admirable book, the reading of which calms and elevates the soul. Farewell. My respects to your father and my compliments to Mlle Bourienne. I embrace you as I love you. Julie. P.S. Give me news of your brother and his charming little wife.

*Dear and excellent friend. Your letter of the 13th gave me great joy. So you still love me, my poetical Julie. Absence, of which you say such bad things, has thus not had its usual influence on you. You complain about absence—what would I have to say if I *dared* to complain, deprived of all those who are dear to me? Ah! if we did not have religion to console us, life would be quite sad. Why do you suppose me to have a stern look when you speak to me of your affection for the young man? In that connection I am strict only with myself. I understand these feelings in others and if I cannot approve of them, never having felt them, I do not condemn them. It only seems to me that

ce rapport je ne suis rigide que pour moi. Je comprends ces sentiments chez les autres et si je ne puis approuver ne les ayant jamais ressentis, je ne les condamne pas. Il me parait seulement que l'amour chrétien, l'amour du prochain, l'amour pour ses ennemis est plus méritoire, plus doux et plus beau, que ne le sont les sentiments que peuvent inspirer les beaux yeux d'un jeune homme à une jeune fille poétique et aimante comme vous.

La nouvelle de la mort du comte Bezukhov *nous est parvenue avant votre lettre, et mon père en a été très affecté. Il dit que c'était l'avant-dernier représentant du grand siècle, et qu'a présent c'est son tour; mais qu'il fera son possible pour que son tour vienne le plus tard possible. Que Dieu nous garde de ce terrible malheur! Je ne puis partager votre opinion sur Pierre que j'ai connu enfant. Il me paraissait toujours avoir un coeur excellent, et c'est la qualité que j'estime le plus dans les gens. Quant à son héritage et au rôle qu'y a joué le prince Basile, c'est bien triste pour tous les deux. Ah! chère amie, la parole de notre divin Sauveur qu'il est plus aisé à un chameau de passer par le trou d'une aiguille, qu'il ne l'est à un riche d'entrer dans le royaume de Dieu, cette parole est terriblement vraie; je plains le prince Basile et je regrette encore davantage Pierre. Si jeune et accablé de cette richesse, que de tentations n'aura-t-il pas a subir! Si on me demandait ce que je désirerais le plus au monde, ce serait d'être plus pauvre que le plus pauvre des mendiants. Mille grâces, chère amie, pour l'ouvrage que vous m'envoyez, et qui fait si grande fureur chez vous. Cependant, puisque vous me dites qu'au milieu de plusieurs bonnes choses il y en a d'autres que la faible conception humaine ne peut atteindre, il me paraît assez inutile de s'occuper d'une lecture inintelligible; qui par là même, ne pourrait être d'aucun fruit. Je n'ai jamais pu comprendre la passion qu'ont certaines personnes de s'em-*

Christian love, the love of one's neighbour, the love for one's enemies, is more meritorious, sweeter, and more beautiful than are the feelings that the beautiful eyes of a young man can inspire in a poetical and loving young girl like you.

The news of the death of Count *Bezukhov* reached us before your letter, and my father was much affected by it. He says that he was the next-to-last representative of the grand century, and that now it is his turn; but that he will do his best to put his turn off as long as possible. God keeps us from that terrible misfortune! I cannot share your opinion of Pierre, whom I knew as a child. He always seemed to me to have an excellent heart, and that is the quality I esteem the most in people. As for his inheritance and the role Prince Vassily played in it, it is a sad thing for them both. Ah! dear friend, the word of our divine Saviour, that it is easier for a camel to pass through the eye of a needle than for a rich man to enter the kingdom of God, that word is terribly true; I pity Prince Vassily and I feel even sorrier for Pierre. So young and burdened with such wealth, what temptations he will have to endure! If I were asked what I would like most in the world, it would be to be poorer than the poorest beggar. A thousand thanks, dear friend, for the work you have sent me, and which is causing such a furore there. However, since you tell me that amidst several good things there are others that weak human understanding cannot grasp, it would seem to me rather useless to occupy myself with unintelligible reading matter; which by that very fact cannot be of any fruit. I have never been able to understand the passion certain persons have for muddling their wits by fastening upon mystical books, which only awaken doubts in their minds, excite their imagination,

brouiller l'entendement, en s'attachant à des livres mystiques, qui n'élèvent que des doutes dans leurs esprits, exaltent leur imagination et leur donnent un charactère d'exagération tout-à-fait contraire à la simplicité Chrétienne. Lisons les Apôtres et l'Évangile. Ne cherchons pas à pénétrer ce que ceux-là renferment de mystérieux, car, comment oserions-nous, misérable pécheurs que nous sommes, prétendre à nous initier dans les secrets terribles et sacrés de la Providence, tant que nous portons cette dépouille charnelle, qui élève entre nous et l'éternel un voile impénétrable? Bornons-nous donc à étudier les principes sublimes que notre divin Sauveur nous a laissé pour notre conduite ici-bas; cherchons à nous y conformer et à les suivre, persuadons-nous que moins nous donnons d'essor à notre faible esprit humain et plus il est agréable à Dieu, qui rejette toute science ne venant pas de lui; que moins nous cherchons à approfondir ce qu'il lui a plu de dérober à notre connaissance, et plutôt il nous en accordera la découverte par son divin esprit.

Mon père ne m'a pas parlé du prétendant, mais il m'a dit seulement qu'il a reçu une lettre et attendait une visite du prince Basile. Pour ce qui est du projet de mariage qui me regarde, je vous dirai, chère et excellente amie, que le mariage, selon moi, est une institution divine à laquelle il faut se conformer. Quelque pénible que cela soit pour moi, si le Tout-puissant m'impose jamais les devoirs d'épouse et de mère, je tâcherai de les remplir aussi fidèlement que je le pourrai, sans m'inquieter de l'examen de mes sentiments à l'égard de celui qu'il me donnera pour époux.

J'ai reçu une lettre de mon frère, qui m'annonce son arrivée à Bald Hills *avec sa femme. Ce sera une joie de courte durée, puisqu'il nous quitte pour prendre part à cette malheureuse guerre, à laquelle nous sommes entraînés*

---

and give them an exaggerated character totally contrary to Christian simplicity. Let us read the Apostles and the Gospel. Let us not seek to penetrate what they contain of the mysterious, for how should we dare aspire, miserable sinners that we are, to initiate ourselves into the terrible and sacred secrets of Providence, so long as we wear this fleshly husk, which raises an impenetrable veil between us and the eternal? Let us limit ourselves, then, to studying the sublime principles that our divine Saviour has left us for our conduct here below; let us seek to conform ourselves to them and to follow them, let us persuade ourselves that the less flight we give to our weak human spirit, the more pleasing it is to God, who rejects all science that does not come from Him; that the less we seek to delve into what He has been pleased to conceal from our knowledge, the sooner He will grant us the discovery of it through His divine spirit.

My father did not speak to me of the suitor, he only told me that he had received a letter and was awaiting a visit from Prince Vassily. As for the marriage plan regarding me, I shall tell you, dear and excellent friend, that for me marriage is a divine institution to which one must conform oneself. However painful it may be for me, if the Almighty ever imposes upon me the duties of a wife and mother, I shall try to fulfil them as faithfully as I can, without troubling myself with the examination of my feelings regarding him whom He will give me for a husband.

I have received a letter from my brother, who announces his arrival at *Bald Hills* with his wife. This will be a short-lived joy, since he is leaving us to take part in this wretched war, into which we are being dragged God knows how or why. Not just with you there in the centre of affairs and of

Dieu sait comment et pourquoi. Non seulement chez vous au centre des affaires et du monde on ne parle que de guerre, mais ici, au milieu de ces travaux champêtres et de ce calme de la nature que les citadins se représentent ordinairement à la campagne, les bruits de la guerre se font entendre et sentir péniblement. Mon père ne parle que marche et contremarche, choses auxquelles je ne comprends rien; et avant hier en faisant ma promenade habituelle dans la rue du village, je fus témoin d'une scène déchirante . . . C'était un convoi des recrues enrôlées chez nous et expédiées pour l'armée . . . Il fallait voir l'état dans lequel se trouvaient les mères, les femmes, les enfants des hommes qui partaient et entendre les sanglots des uns et des autres! On dirait que l'humanité a oublié les lois de son divin Sauveur, qui prêchait l'amour et le pardon des offenses, et qu'elle fait consister son plus grand mérite dans l'art de s'entretuer.

Adieu, chère et bonne amie, que notre divin Sauveur et sa très sainte Mère vous aient en leur sainte et puissante garde.

Marie.

*"Ah, vous expédiez le courrier, princesse, moi j'ai déjà expedié le mien. J'ai écris à ma pauvre mère,"** the smiling Mlle Bourienne spoke in a quick, pleasant, juicy little voice, swallowing her *r*s and bringing with her into the concentrated, sad, and dreary atmosphere of Princess Marya a completely different, frivolously gay and self-contented world.

"Princesse, il faut que je vous prévienne," she added, lowering her voice, *"le prince a eu une altercation,"* she said, deliberately swallowing her *r*s and listening to herself with pleasure, *"une altercation avec Michel Ivanoff. Il est de très mauvaise humeur, très morose. Soyez prévenue, vous savez . . ."*†

"Ah, chère amie," answered Princess Marya, *"je vous ai priée de ne jamais me prévenir de l'humeur dans laquelle se trouve mon père. Je ne me permets pas de le juger, et je ne voudrais pas que les autres le fassent."*‡

The princess glanced at her watch and noticing that she was already five

---

the world is there talk only of war, but here, in the midst of these rural labours and this calm of nature which city dwellers usually picture to themselves in the country, the noise of war makes itself heard and felt painfully. My father speaks of nothing but marches and countermarches, things of which I have no understanding; and the day before yesterday, while going for my usual stroll along the village street, I was witness to a heartrending scene . . . It was a convoy of recruits enlisted from our estate and being sent off to the army . . . You should have seen the state that the mothers, the wives, the children of these departing men were in, and heard the sobs on both sides! You would think that humanity has forgotten the laws of its divine Saviour, who preached love and the forgiveness of transgressions, and that it finds its greatest merit in the art of mutual killing.

Farewell, dear and good friend. May our divine Saviour and His most holy Mother keep you in their holy and powerful care. Marie.

*Ah, you're sending a letter, Princess; I've already sent mine. I wrote to my poor mother.

†Princess, I must warn you . . . the prince has had an altercation . . . an altercation with Mikhail Ivanov. He's in a very bad humour, very morose. Be warned, you know . . .

‡Ah! dear friend . . . I've begged you never to warn me of the humour my father happens to be in. I do not allow myself to judge him, and I would prefer that others not do so.

minutes late for playing the clavichord, went with a frightened face to the sitting room. According to the established order of the day, between noon and two o'clock the prince rested and the princess played the clavichord.

XXIII

The grey-haired valet sat dozing and listening to the prince's snoring in the immense study. From the far side of the house, from behind a closed door, came the sounds of a Dusek sonata,[45] the difficult passages repeated twenty times.

Just then a carriage and a britzka drove up to the porch, and from the carriage stepped Prince Andrei, who helped his little wife out and allowed her to go ahead. Grey-haired Tikhon, in a wig, stuck himself out of the door of the waiting room, said in a whisper that the prince was sleeping, and hastily closed the door. Tikhon knew that neither the son's arrival nor any sort of extraordinary event was to interrupt the order of the day. Prince Andrei evidently knew it as well as Tikhon; he looked at his watch, as if to check whether his father's habits had changed during the time he had not seen him, and, verifying that they had not, turned to his wife.

"He'll get up in twenty minutes. Let's go to Princess Marya," he said.

The little princess had filled out during this time, but her eyes and her short lip with its little moustache and smile rose as gaily and sweetly as ever when she began to speak.

"*Mais c'est un palais,*" she said to her husband, looking around with the expression of someone paying compliments to the host at a ball. "*Allons, vite, vite! . . .*"* Looking about, she smiled at Tikhon, and at her husband, and at the servant who accompanied them.

"*C'est Marie qui s'exerce? Allons doucement, il faut la surprendre.*"†
Prince Andrei walked behind her with a polite and sad expression.

"You've aged, Tikhon," he said to the old man, who kissed his hand as he passed.

Before the room from which the sounds of the clavichord came, a pretty blonde Frenchwoman popped out of a side door. Mlle Bourienne seemed wildly ecstatic.

"*Ah! quel bonheur pour la princesse,*" she said. "*Enfin! Il faut que je la prévienne.*"‡

"*Non, non, de grâce . . . Vous êtes Mlle Bourienne, je vous connais déjà par l'amitié que vous porte ma belle-soeur,*" said the princess, kissing her. "*Elle ne nous attend pas!*"§

*Why, it's a palace . . . Let's go, quickly, quickly! . . .
†Is that Marie practising? Let's go quietly, we must surprise her.
‡Ah! what happiness for the princess . . . At last! I must inform her.
§No, no, please . . . You are Mlle Bourienne, I know you already by the friendship my sister-in-law feels for you . . . She's not expecting us!

They went up to the door of the sitting room, through which came the sounds of the same passage repeated again and again. Prince Andrei stopped and winced, as if expecting something unpleasant.

The princess went in. The passage broke off in the middle; a cry was heard, then the heavy footsteps of Princess Marya and the sounds of kissing. When Prince Andrei went in, the two princesses, who had seen each other only once for a short time at Prince Andrei's wedding, were standing with their arms round each other, their lips pressed hard to whatever place they had happened upon in the first moment. Mlle Bourienne was standing beside them, her hands pressed to her heart, smiling piously, apparently as ready to weep as to laugh. Prince Andrei shrugged his shoulders and winced, as music lovers wince when they hear a false note. The two women let go of each other, then again, as if fearing it would be too late, seized each other by the hands, began kissing, tore their hands away, and then again began kissing each other on the face, and, quite unexpectedly for Prince Andrei, they both wept and began to kiss again. Mlle Bourienne also wept. Prince Andrei obviously felt awkward; but for the two women it seemed natural to weep; it seemed it had never occurred to them that their meeting could be otherwise.

"*Ah! chère! . . . Ah! Marie! . . .*" the two women suddenly began to speak and then laughed. "*J'ai revé cette nuit . . .*" "*Vous ne nous attendiez donc pas? . . .*" "*Ah, Marie, vous avez maigri . . .*" "*Et vous avez repris . . .*"*

"*J'ai tout de suite reconnu madame la princesse,*"† Mlle Bourienne put in.

"*Et moi qui ne me doutais pas! . . .*" exclaimed Princess Marya. "*Ah! André, je ne vous voyais pas.*"‡

Prince Andrei and his sister kissed each other's hands, and he told her she was the same *pleurnicheuse*§ she had always been. Princess Marya turned to her brother, and through her tears the loving, warm, and meek gaze of her big, luminous eyes, very beautiful at that moment, rested on Prince Andrei's face.

The little princess talked non-stop. Her short upper lip with its moustache would momentarily flit down, touching, where it had to, the rosy lower lip, and open up again in a smile of gleaming teeth and eyes. She told about an incident that had happened to her on Spasskoe Hill, which was dangerous for her in her condition, and just after that said she had left all her dresses in Petersburg and would go about here in God knows what, and that Andrei was quite changed, and that Kitty Ordyntsev had married an old man, and that there was

---

*Ah! dear! . . . Ah! Marie! . . . I dreamed last night . . . So you weren't expecting us? . . . Ah, Marie, you've grown thinner . . . And you have put on weight . . .

†And I recognized madame the princess at once.

‡And I had no idea! . . . Ah! André, I didn't see you.

§Crybaby.

a suitor for Princess Marya *pour tout de bon,** but we'll talk about that later. Princess Marya went on silently looking at her brother, and there was love and sadness in her beautiful eyes. It was clear that she had established her own train of thought, independent of her sister-in-law's talk. In the middle of her story about the last fête in Petersburg, she addressed her brother.

"And you're decidedly going to the war, André?" she said, sighing.

Lise also sighed.

"Tomorrow even," her brother answered.

"Il m'abondonne ici et Dieu sait pourquoi, quand il aurait pu avoir de l'avancement . . ."†

Princess Marya did not finish listening and, continuing with the thread of her thoughts, turned to her sister-in-law, her gentle eyes indicating her stomach.

"Is it certain?" she asked.

The princess's face changed. She sighed.

"Yes, certain," she said. "Ah! It's very frightening . . ."

Liza's little lip lowered. She brought her face close to her sister-in-law's face and again wept unexpectedly.

"She needs rest," said Prince Andrei, wincing. "Isn't it so, Liza? Take her to your rooms, and I'll go to father. How is he, the same?"

"The same, yes, the same; I don't know whether in your eyes," the princess replied joyfully.

"The same hours, and the strolls in the avenues? The lathe?" asked Prince Andrei with a barely perceptible smile, which showed that, despite all his love and respect for his father, he was aware of his weaknesses.

"The same hours, and the lathe, also mathematics, and my geometry lessons," Princess Marya replied joyfully, as though her lessons in geometry were one of the most joyful impressions of her life.

When they had waited out the twenty minutes until it was time for the old prince to get up, Tikhon came to summon the young prince to his father. In honour of his son's arrival, the old man had made an exception in his way of life: he gave orders to allow him into his part of the house while he was still dressing for dinner. The prince held to the old fashion of wearing a kaftan and powdering his hair. And at the moment when Prince Andrei (not with that peevish expression and manner he assumed in drawing rooms, but with the same animated face he had when he talked with Pierre) came to his father's, the old man was sitting in his dressing room, on a wide morocco-upholstered armchair, in a powdering mantle, entrusting his head to Tikhon's hands.

"Ah! The warrior! So you want to defeat Bonaparte?" said the old man, shaking his powdered head as much as the braided queue, which was in Tikhon's hands, would let him. "At least give him a good drubbing, or pretty

*In all reality.
†He's abandoning me here and God knows why, when he could have had a promotion . . .

soon he'll be writing us down, too, as his subjects. Greetings!" And he offered his cheek.

The old man was in high spirits following his before-dinner nap. (He used to say that an after-dinner nap was silver, but a before-dinner nap was gold.) He joyfully cast sidelong glances at his son from under his thick, beetling brows. Prince Andrei went up and kissed his father on the place indicated to him. He did not respond to his father's favourite subject—poking fun at the present-day military, and especially at Bonaparte.

"Yes, I've come to see you, papa, and with a pregnant wife," said Prince Andrei, his animated and respectful eyes following the movement of every feature of his father's face. "How is your health?"

"Only fools and profligates can be unwell, my boy, and you know me: I'm busy from morning till evening, I'm temperate, and so I'm well."

"Thank God," his son said, smiling.

"God has nothing to do with it. Well, tell me," he went on, getting back on his hobbyhorse, "how have the Germans taught you to fight Bonaparte by this new science of yours known as strategy?"

Prince Andrei smiled.

"Let me collect my wits, papa," he said, with a smile which showed that his father's weaknesses did not prevent him from loving and respecting him. "I haven't even settled in."

"Nonsense, nonsense," cried the old man, shaking his queue to see whether it was tightly braided and seizing his son's arm. "The house is ready for your wife. Princess Marya will take her around and show her and babble three cart-loads. That's their womanish business. I'm glad of her. Sit down, tell me. Mi-khelson's army I understand, and Tolstoy's . . . a simultaneous landing . . . What's the southern army going to do? Prussia, neutrality . . . that I know. What about Austria?" he said, getting up from his chair and pacing the room, with Tikhon running after him and handing him pieces of clothing. "What about Sweden? How will they cross Pomerania?"[46]

Seeing his father's insistent demand, Prince Andrei, reluctantly at first, but then with more and more animation, and inadvertently switching from Russian to French, out of habit, in the middle of his discourse, began to explain the plan of operations for the proposed campaign. He told how a ninety-thousand-man army was to threaten Prussia, so as to draw her out of neutrality and involve her in the war, how part of that army was to unite with the Swedish army in Strahlsund, how two hundred and twenty thousand Austrians, united with a hundred thousand Russians, were to go into action in Italy and on the Rhine, and how fifty thousand Russians and fifty thousand English would land at Naples, and how in all a five-hundred-thousand-strong army was to attack the French from different sides. The old prince showed not the slightest interest during the telling, as though he was not listening, and, continuing to dress as he paced, interrupted him three times unexpectedly. Once he stopped him and shouted:

"The white one! the white one!"

This meant that Tikhon had not handed him the waistcoat he wanted. Another time he stopped, asked:

"And how soon will she give birth?" and, shaking his head reproachfully, said: "Not good! Go on, go on."

The third time, as Prince Andrei was finishing his description, the old man sang in an old man's off-key voice: "*Malbroug s'en va-t-en guerre. Dieu sait quand reviendra.*"*47

His son merely smiled.

"I'm not saying that this is a plan I approve of," the son said, "I've only told you what's in it. Napoleon has already put together a plan no worse than this one."

"Well, you haven't told me anything new." And the old man muttered pensively to himself in a quick patter: "*Dieu sait quand reviendra.* Go to the dining room."

XXIV

At the appointed hour, powdered and clean-shaven, the prince came out to the dining room, where he was awaited by his daughter-in-law, Princess Marya, Mlle Bourienne, and the prince's architect, who by the prince's strange caprice was admitted to the table, though by his insignificant position the man could in no way count on such an honour. The prince, who in his life kept firmly to social distinctions and rarely admitted even important provincial officials to the table, suddenly decided to demonstrate by means of the architect Mikhail Ivanovich, who used to blow his nose in the corner on a checkered handkerchief, that all men are equal, and more than once impressed it upon his daughter that Mikhail Ivanovich was no worse than you or I. At table the prince most often addressed himself to the wordless Mikhail Ivanovich.

In the dining room, immensely high like all the rooms in the house, the prince's entrance was awaited by the domestics and servants standing behind each chair; the butler, a napkin over his arm, examined the place settings, winking to the lackeys and constantly shifting his anxious gaze from the wall clock to the door from which the prince was to appear. Prince Andrei was looking at a huge gilded frame, new to him, with a picture of the family tree of the princes Bolkonsky, which hung across the room from an equally huge frame with a poorly painted portrait (obviously from the hand of a household

---

*Malbroug [Marlborough] is going to war. God knows when he'll come back.

artist) of a sovereign prince in a crown, who was supposed to be a descendant of Rurik and the first ancestor of the Bolkonsky family. Prince Andrei looked at this genealogical tree, shaking his head and chuckling with the air of someone looking at a portrait that is a ridiculously good likeness.

"That's him all over!" he said to Prince Marya, who came up to him.

Princess Marya looked at her brother in surprise. She did not understand what made him smile. Everything her father did evoked an awe in her which was not subject to discussion.

"Every man has his Achilles' heel," Prince Andrei went on. "With *his* enormous intelligence, *donner dans ce ridicule!*"*

Princess Marya could not understand her brother's bold opinions and was getting ready to object to him when the awaited footsteps were heard from the study: the prince came in quickly, gaily, as he always did, as if deliberately contrasting his hasty manners to the strict order of the house. At the same moment, the big clock struck two and another in the drawing room responded in a high voice. The prince stopped; from under his thick, beetling brows, his lively, bright, stern eyes looked around at everyone and rested on the young princess. The young princess experienced at that moment the feeling courtiers experience at the appearance of the tsar, that feeling of fear and respect which this old man evoked in all those around him. He stroked the princess's head and then, with an awkward gesture, patted her on the back of the neck.

"Delighted, delighted," he said and, looking her intently in the eye once again, quickly stepped away and sat down in his place. "Sit down, sit down! Mikhail Ivanovich, sit down."

He pointed his daughter-in-law to the place next to him. A servant pulled out the chair for her.

"Ho, ho!" said the old man, looking at her rounded waist. "Rushing things; that's not good!"

He laughed drily, coldly, unpleasantly, as he always laughed—only with his mouth, not with his eyes.

"You must walk, walk as much as possible, as much as possible," he said.

The little princess either did not hear or did not want to hear his words. She was silent and seemed embarrassed. The prince asked about her father, and the princess began to speak and smiled. He asked her about mutual acquaintances: the princess became still more animated and started talking away, giving the prince greetings and town gossip.

"*La comtesse Apraksine, la pauvre, a perdu son mari et elle a pleuré les larmes de ses yeux,*"† she said, becoming more and more animated.

As her animation increased, the prince looked at her more and more sternly,

*To take to such ridiculousness.
†Countess Apraksin, poor woman, lost her husband and wept her eyes out.

and suddenly, as if he had studied her enough and arrived at a clear idea of her, turned away and addressed Mikhail Ivanovich.

"Well, now, Mikhail Ivanovich, things are going badly for our friend Buonaparte. Prince Andrei" (he always referred to his son in the third person like this) "has just been telling me what forces are being prepared against him! But you and I always considered him an empty man."

Mikhail Ivanovich, who had no idea when this *you and I* had spoken such words about Bonaparte, but who understood that he was needed in order to launch into the favourite subject, looked at the young prince in surprise, not knowing what would come of it.

"We have a great tactician here!" the prince said to his son, pointing to the architect.

And the conversation turned again to the war, to Bonaparte, and to today's generals and statesmen. The old prince seemed to be convinced not only that all present-day men of action were mere boys, who did not even understand the ABCs of military and state affairs, and that Bonaparte was a worthless little Frenchman who was successful only because there were no Potemkins and Suvorovs to oppose him; but he was also convinced that there were no political difficulties in Europe, nor was there a war, but only some sort of marionette comedy that today's people played at, pretending they meant business. Prince Andrei cheerfully endured his father's mockery of the new people, and provoked his father to talk and listened to him with obvious delight.

"All that there was before seems good," he said, "but wasn't it that same Suvorov who fell into the trap set for him by Moreau and was unable to get out of it?"[48]

"Who told you that? Who told you?" cried the prince. "Suvorov!" And he flung away his plate, which was deftly caught by Tikhon. "Suvorov! . . . Think a little, Prince Andrei. Two men: Friedrich and Suvorov . . . Moreau! Moreau would have been captured if Suvorov had had a free hand; but he had the Hofs-kriegs-wurst-schnapps-rath[49] on his hands. Even the devil wouldn't be glad of that. But go, and you'll learn about these Hofs-kriegs-wurst-schnapps-raths! Suvorov couldn't get on with them, how is Mikhail Kutuzov going to do it?! No, my friend," he went on, "you and your generals won't get around Bonaparte; you need to get hold of a Frenchman, so that their own don't know their own, and their own beat their own.[50] They sent the German Pahlen to New York, to America, to fetch the Frenchman Moreau,"[51] he said, alluding to the invitation made to Moreau that year to enter the Russian service. "Wonders!! What, were the Potemkins, the Suvorovs, the Orlovs Germans? No, brother, either you've all lost your wits there, or mine have burnt out. God help you, but we'll see. They take Bonaparte for a great general! Hm! . . ."

"I'm by no means saying that all the plans are good," said Prince Andrei, "only I can't understand how you can make such a judgement about Bonaparte. Laugh all you like, but Bonaparte is still a great general!"

"Mikhail Ivanovich!" the old prince cried to the architect, who, being busy with the roast, had hoped to be forgotten. "Didn't I tell you Bonaparte was a great tactician? Well, he says so, too."

"Sure thing, Your Excellency," replied the architect.

The prince again laughed his cold laugh.

"Bonaparte was born lucky. He has excellent soldiers. And the Germans were the first he attacked. You'd have to be a do-nothing not to beat the Germans. Ever since the world began, everybody's beaten the Germans. And they've beaten nobody. Except each other. It was on them he earned his glory."

And the prince began to analyse all the mistakes which, to his way of thinking, Bonaparte had made in all his wars and even in state affairs. His son did not object, but it was clear that, whatever the arguments presented to him, he was as little able to change his opinion as the old prince was. Prince Andrei listened, holding back his objections, and involuntarily amazed at how this old man, who had sat alone in the country uninterruptedly for so many years, could know and discuss, in such detail and with such subtlety, all the military and political circumstances of Europe in recent years.

"You think I'm an old man and don't understand the real state of affairs," he concluded. "But I have it all up here! I don't sleep nights. So, where has this great general of yours shown himself?"

"That would be a long story," said his son.

"Off with you to your Buonaparte, then. *Mademoiselle Bourienne, voilà encore un admirateur de votre goujat d'empereur!*"* he shouted in excellent French.

"*Vous savez que je ne suis pas bonapartiste, mon prince.*"†

"*Dieu sait quand reviendra . . .*" the prince sang off-key, laughed still more off-key, and left the table.

All through the argument and the rest of dinner, the little princess was silent and kept glancing fearfully now at Princess Marya, now at her father-in-law. When they left the table, she took her sister-in-law by the arm and led her to another room.

"*Comme c'est un homme d'esprit, votre père,*" she said, "*c'est à cause de cela peut-être qu'il me fait peur.*"‡

"Ah, he's so kind!" said the princess.

---

*Mademoiselle Bourienne, here's another admirer of your boor of an emperor!
†You know I am not a Bonapartist, my prince.
‡What a witty man your father is . . . maybe that's why he scares me.

XXV

Prince Andrei was leaving the next evening. The old prince, not abandoning his order, went to his rooms after dinner. The little princess was with her sister-in-law. Prince Andrei, dressed in a travelling frock coat without epaulettes, was packing with his valet in the rooms assigned to him. He personally saw to the carriage and the loading of the trunks, and ordered the horses harnessed up. All that remained in the room were the objects Prince Andrei always carried with him: a strongbox, a big silver cellaret, two Turkish pistols, and a sabre — a present from his father, brought back from Ochakov. All these travelling accessories Prince Andrei kept in great order: everything was new, clean, in broadcloth covers, carefully tied with tapes.

At moments of departure and a change of life, people capable of reflecting on their actions usually get into a serious state of mind. At these moments they usually take stock of the past and make plans for the future. Prince Andrei's face was very thoughtful and tender. His hands behind his back, he paced rapidly up and down the room, looking straight ahead and thoughtfully shaking his head. Was he afraid of going to the war, was he sad to be leaving his wife — perhaps both, but, evidently not wishing to be seen in such a state, when he heard footsteps in the hallway, he quickly unclasped his hands, stopped by the table, pretending to tie the tapes on the strongbox cover, and assumed his usual calm and impenetrable expression. They were the heavy footsteps of Princess Marya.

"They told me you gave orders to harness up," she said breathlessly (she had obviously come running), "and I wanted so much to talk more with you alone. God knows for how long we're parting again. You're not angry that I've come? You've changed very much, Andryusha," she added, as if to explain her question.

She smiled as she pronounced the name *Andryusha*. It must have been strange to her to think that this stern, handsome man was that same Andryusha, a thin, frolicsome boy, her childhood companion.

"And where is Lise?" he asked, only smiling in answer to her question.

"She was so tired that she fell asleep in my room on the sofa. *Ah, André! Quel trésor de femme vous avez*,"* she said, sitting down on the sofa opposite her brother. "She's a perfect child, such a dear, merry child. I've come to love her so."

Prince Andrei was silent, but the princess noticed the ironic and scornful expression that appeared on his face.

*Ah, Andrei! What a treasure of a wife you have.

"But one must be indulgent towards little weaknesses—who doesn't have them, André! Don't forget that she grew up and was formed in society. And then, her position now isn't very rosy. One must enter into each person's position. *Tout comprendre, c'est tout pardonner.** Just think how it is for the poor dear, in her condition, after the life she's used to, to part with her husband and remain alone in the country? It's very hard."

Prince Andrei smiled, looking at his sister, as we smile listening to people whom we think we can see through.

"You live in the country, and you don't find this life so terrible," he said.

"I'm another matter. Why talk of me! I do not and cannot wish for any other life, because I don't know any other life. But think, André, for a young and worldly woman, in the best years of her life, to be buried in the country, alone, because papa's always busy, and I . . . you know me . . . how poor I am *en ressources,* for a woman accustomed to the best society. Mademoiselle Bourienne alone . . ."

"I dislike her very much, your Bourienne," said Prince Andrei.

"Oh, no! She's a very dear and kind, and, above all, a pitiful girl. She has nobody, nobody. To tell the truth, she's not only unnecessary to me, she's even an inconvenience. You know, I've always been a wild creature, and now more than ever. I like being alone . . . *Mon père* likes her very much. She and Mikhail Ivanovich are the two persons with whom he's always gentle and kind, because he's their benefactor. As Sterne[52] says: 'We love people not so much for the good they've done us, as for the good we've done them.' *Mon père* took her as an orphan *sur le pavé,*† and she's very kind. And *mon père* likes her way of reading. She reads aloud to him in the evenings. She reads beautifully."

"Well, but in truth, Marie, I wonder if father's character isn't sometimes hard on you?" Prince Andrei asked suddenly.

Princess Marya was first surprised, then frightened by this question.

"On me? . . . On me?! Hard on me?!" she said.

"He's always been tough, but now I think he's becoming difficult," said Prince Andrei, probably speaking so lightly of their father on purpose, to puzzle or test his sister.

"You're good in every way, André, but you have a sort of mental pride," the princess said, following her own train of thought more than the course of the conversation, "and that is a great sin. Is it possible to judge one's father? And even if it were possible, what other feeling than *vénération* can a man like *mon père* evoke? And I am so content and happy with him. I only wish everyone could be as happy as I am."

Her brother shook his head mistrustfully.

"The one thing that's hard for me—to tell you the truth, André—is father's

---

*To understand all is to forgive all.
†From the street.

way of thinking in the religious respect. I don't understand how a man with such an enormous intellect cannot see what is clear as day and can be so deluded. That constitutes my one unhappiness. But here, too, I've seen a shade of improvement recently. His mockery recently hasn't been so biting, and there's a monk whom he received and with whom he spoke for a long time."

"Well, my friend, I'm afraid you and this monk are wasting your powder," Prince Andrei said mockingly but affectionately.

"Ah, *mon ami.* I only pray to God and hope He will hear me. André," she said timidly, after a moment's silence, "I have a big request to make of you."

"What is it, my friend?"

"No, promise me you won't refuse. It won't be any trouble for you, and there won't be anything in it that's unworthy of you. Only you'll comfort me. Promise, Andryusha," she said, putting her hand into her reticule and taking hold of something in it, but not showing it yet, as if what she was holding constituted the object of her request, and before she got his promise to fulfil her request, she could not take this *something* out of her reticule.

She looked at her brother with a timid, pleading gaze.

"Even if it was a great deal of trouble for me . . ." Prince Andrei said, as if guessing what it was about.

"You can think what you like! I know you're the same as *mon père.* Think what you like, but do it for me. Do it, please! Father's father, our grandfather, wore it through all the wars . . ." She still would not take what she was holding out of the reticule. "So promise me? . . ."

"Of course, what is it?"

"André, I'm going to bless you with an icon, and you promise me never to take it off . . . Do you promise?"

"Of course, if it doesn't weigh a hundred pounds and pull my neck down . . . To give you pleasure . . ." said Prince Andrei, but that same second, noticing the distressed look that came to his sister's face at this joke, he instantly repented. "I'm very glad, truly, very glad, my friend," he added.

"Against your will He will save you and have mercy on you and turn you to Him, because in Him alone there is truth and peace," she said in a voice trembling from emotion, with a solemn gesture holding up in both hands before her brother an old oval icon of the Saviour with a blackened face, in a silver setting, on a finely wrought silver chain.

She crossed herself, kissed the icon, and gave it to Andrei.

"Please, André, for me . . ."

From her big eyes shone rays of a kindly and timid light. These eyes lit up her whole thin, sickly face and made it beautiful. Her brother wanted to take the icon, but she stopped him. Andrei understood, made the sign of the cross, and kissed the icon. His face was at the same time tender (he was touched) and mocking.

"*Merci, mon ami.*"

She kissed him on the forehead and sat down again on the sofa. They were silent.

"So as I was saying to you, André, be kind and magnanimous, as you've always been. Don't judge Lise too severely," she began. "She's so dear, so kind, and her position is very hard now."

"I don't believe I've said anything to you, Masha, about reproaching my wife for anything or being displeased with her. Why are you saying all this to me?"

Princess Marya broke out in red blotches and said nothing, as if she felt guilty.

"I haven't said anything to you, but it has already *been said* to you. And that makes me sad."

The red blotches stood out still more on Princess Marya's forehead, neck, and cheeks. She wanted to say something, but could not bring it out. Her brother had guessed right: the little princess had wept after dinner, had said she had a foreboding of a bad delivery, was afraid of it, and had complained about her life, her father-in-law, and her husband. After her tears, she had fallen asleep. Prince Andrei felt sorry for his sister.

"Know one thing, Masha, I cannot, have not, and never will reproach *my wife* for anything, nor can I reproach myself for anything in relation to her; and that will always be so, whatever circumstances I find myself in. But if you want to know the truth . . . if you want to know whether I'm happy? No. Is she happy? No. Why is that? I don't know . . ."

As he was saying this, he got up, went over to his sister, and, bending down, kissed her on the forehead. His fine eyes shone with an intelligent and kindly, unhabitual light, but he was looking not at his sister but into the darkness of the open doorway, over her head.

"Let's go to her, I must say goodbye! Or you go alone, wake her up, and I'll come presently. Petrushka!" he called to his valet. "Come here, take these things out. This goes under the seat, this to the right-hand side."

Princess Marya got up and went to the door. She paused.

"*André, si vous avez la foi, vous vous seriez adressé à Dieu, pour qu'il vous donne l'amour que vous ne sentez pas, et votre prière aurait été exaucée.*"*

"Yes—there's always that!" said Prince Andrei. "Go, Masha, I'll come presently."

On the way to his sister's room, in the gallery that connected one house to the other, Prince Andrei met the sweetly smiling Mlle Bourienne, who three times that day had already run into him with her rapturous and naïve smile in secluded passages.

---

*Andrei, if you had faith, you would have turned to God, asking that He give you the love you do not feel, and your prayer would have been answered.

"*Ah! je vous croyais chez vous,*"* she said, blushing and lowering her eyes for some reason.

Prince Andrei looked at her sternly. A spiteful look suddenly came to Prince Andrei's face. He said nothing to her, but, avoiding her eyes, looked at her forehead and hair with such scorn that the Frenchwoman blushed and left without saying anything. When he approached his sister's room, the princess was already awake, and her merry little voice could be heard through the open door hurriedly sending out one word after another. She was talking as if, after a long abstinence, she wanted to make up for lost time.

"*Non, mais figurez-vous, la vieille comtesse Zouboff avec des fausses boucles et la bouche pleine de fausses dents, comme si elle voulait défier les années . . .*† Ha, ha, ha, Marie!"

Five times already, with other people, Prince Andrei had heard exactly the same phrase about the countess Zubov and the same laughter from his wife. He quietly went into the room. The princess, round, rosy, with her work in her hands, was sitting in an armchair and talking non-stop, telling over her Petersburg memories and even phrases. Prince Andrei went to her, stroked her head, and asked whether she had rested from the journey. She made a reply and went on with the same talk.

The coach-and-six was standing at the porch. Outside it was a dark autumn night. The coachman could not see the shafts of the carriage. On the porch people with lanterns bustled about. Lights shone through the big windows of the immense house. The domestic servants crowded in the front hall, wishing to say goodbye to the young prince; in the reception room stood the whole household: Mikhail Ivanovich, Mlle Bourienne, Princess Marya, and the little princess. Prince Andrei had been summoned to his father's study, where the old prince wanted to say goodbye to him man to man. Everyone was waiting for them to emerge.

When Prince Andrei went into the study, the old prince, in his old man's spectacles and his white smock, in which he received no one except his son, was sitting at the table and writing. He looked up.

"You're leaving?" And he started writing again.

"I've come to say goodbye."

"Kiss me here," he pointed to his cheek. "Thank you, thank you!"

"What are you thanking me for?"

"For not overstaying and clinging to a woman's skirt. Service before all. Thank you, thank you!" And he went on writing, so that spatters flew from his scratching pen. "If you want to say something, speak. I can do the two things at once," he added.

"About my wife . . . I'm so ashamed to be leaving her on your hands . . ."

---

*Ah! I thought you were in your room.

†No, but picture it, the old countess Zubov with false curls and a mouth full of false teeth, as if she wanted to defy the years . . .

"What's this drivel? Say what you want."

"When it's time for my wife to give birth, send to Moscow for an *accoucheur** ... So that he'll be here."

The old prince stopped and, as if unable to understand, stared with stern eyes at his son.

"I know no one can help if nature doesn't help," Prince Andrei said, visibly embarrassed. "I agree that only one case in a million ends badly, but it's her and my fantasy. People have said things to her, she's had dreams, and she's afraid."

"Hm ... hm ..." the old prince said to himself, still writing. "I'll do it."

He signed with a flourish, suddenly turned quickly to his son, and laughed.

"A bad business, eh?"

"What is, papa?"

"A wife!" the old prince said curtly and significantly.

"I don't understand," said Prince Andrei.

"Nothing to be done, my friend," said the prince, "they're all like that, no use unmarrying. Don't be afraid; I won't tell anybody; but you know it yourself."

He seized his hand in his bony little fist, shook it, looked straight into his son's face with his quick eyes that seemed to see through a person, and again laughed his cold laugh.

The son sighed, admitting by this sigh that his father had understood him. The old man, continuing to fold and seal letters with his habitual dexterity, kept snatching up and throwing down wax, seal, and paper.

"What can you do? She's beautiful! I'll do everything. You can rest easy," he said brusquely while sealing a letter.

Andrei said nothing: he was both pleased and displeased that his father understood him. The old man got up and handed the letter to his son.

"Listen," he said, "don't worry about your wife: whatever can be done, will be done. Now listen: give this letter to Mikhail Ilarionovich. I write that he should use you in good posts and not keep you long as an adjutant: nasty duty! Tell him I remember him and love him. And write and tell me how he receives you. If he's all right, serve him. Nikolai Andreevich Bolkonsky's son won't serve anyone on charity. Well, now come here."

He spoke so quickly that half the words remained unfinished, but his son was used to understanding him. He led his son to the desk, opened the lid, pulled out a drawer, and took from it a notebook filled with his bold, tall, compact handwriting.

"I'm sure to die before you. Know that these are my journals, to be given to the sovereign after my death. Now here is a Lombard note[53] and a letter: it's a prize for whoever writes the history of Suvorov's campaigns. To be sent to the Academy. Here are my jottings, read them for yourself when I'm gone, you'll find useful things."

---

*Male midwife.

Andrei did not tell his father that he would probably live for a long time yet. He understood that there was no need to say it.

"I'll do it all, father," he said.

"Well, and now goodbye!" He gave his son his hand to kiss and embraced him. "Remember one thing, Prince Andrei: if you're killed, I, your old father will be pained . . ." He unexpectedly fell silent and suddenly went on in a shrill voice: "But if I learn that you have not behaved like Nikolai Bolkonsky's son, I will be ashamed!" he shrieked.

"That you might not have told me, father," the son said, smiling.

The old man fell silent.

"I also wanted to ask you," Prince Andrei continued, "if I'm killed, and if I should have a son, don't let him leave you, as I told you yesterday; he should grow up here with you . . . please."

"Not give him to your wife?" the old man said and laughed.

They stood silently facing each other. The old man's quick eyes were aimed straight into his son's eyes. Something twitched in the lower part of the old prince's face.

"We've said our goodbyes . . . off with you!" he said suddenly. "Off with you!" he shouted in a loud and angry voice, opening the door of the study.

"What is it? What's wrong?" asked both princesses, seeing Prince Andrei and the momentarily emerging figure of the old man in a white smock, wigless, and in an old man's spectacles, shouting in an angry voice.

Prince Andrei sighed and said nothing.

"Well," he said, turning to his wife, and this "well" sounded like cold mockery, as if he had said: "Now perform your tricks."

"*André, déjà?*"* the little princess said, turning pale and looking at her husband in fear.

He embraced her. She cried out and fell unconscious on his shoulder.

He cautiously withdrew the shoulder she was lying on, looked into her face, and carefully seated her in an armchair.

"*Adieu, Marie,*" he said softly to his sister, they kissed each other's hands, and with quick steps he walked out of the room.

The princess lay in the armchair, and Mlle Bourienne rubbed her temples. Princess Marya, supporting her sister-in-law, went on looking with her beautiful, tear-filled eyes at the door through which Prince Andrei had gone and making signs of the cross at him. From the study, like gunshots, came the oft-repeated angry sounds of the old man blowing his nose. As soon as Prince Andrei left, the door to the study quickly opened, and the old man's stern figure appeared in its white smock.

"Gone? Well, that's good!" he said, gave the unconscious little princess an angry look, shook his head reproachfully, and slammed the door.

*Already?

Part Two

I

In October 1805 Russian troops were occupying villages and towns in the archduchy of Austria, and more new regiments kept arriving from Russia to be stationed by the fortress of Braunau, burdening the local inhabitants with their billeting. In Braunau the commander in chief, Kutuzov, had his headquarters.

On the eleventh of October, 1805, one of the infantry regiments just arrived in Braunau had halted half a mile from the town, waiting to be reviewed by the commander in chief. Despite the non-Russian locality and surroundings—orchards, stone walls, tile roofs, mountains visible in the distance—and the non-Russian folk gazing with curiosity at the soldiers, the regiment looked exactly the same as any Russian regiment waiting for review somewhere in central Russia.

In the evening of the latest march an order had been received that the commander in chief would review the regiment on the march. Though the wording of the order seemed unclear to the regimental commander and the question arose of how to take the wording of the order—in marching uniform or not?—in the council of battalion commanders it was decided to present the regiment for review in parade uniform, on the grounds that it is always better to bow too much than not to bow enough. And so the soldiers, after a twenty-mile march, without a wink of sleep, spent the whole night mending and cleaning; the adjutants and company commanders calculated and counted off; and by morning the regiment, instead of the straggling, disorderly crowd it had been the day before, during the latest march, was a well-ordered mass of two thousand men, each of whom knew his place, his duty, each of whose buttons and straps was in its place and sparkling clean. Not only were the externals in good order, but if it should please the commander in chief to look under the uniform, he would see on each man the same clean shirt, and in each pack he would find the prescribed number of things, "the whole kit and caboodle," as soldiers say. There was only one circumstance with regard to which no one could be at ease. This was footgear. More than half the men had their boots falling to pieces. But this shortcoming was not the regimental commander's fault, since, despite his repeated requests, the Austrian department had not released a supply, and the regiment had walked seven hundred miles.

The regimental commander was an elderly, sanguine general with grizzled eyebrows and side-whiskers, stocky and broader from chest to back than from shoulder to shoulder. He was wearing a brand-new uniform with creases from being packed away, and thick gold epaulettes which seemed not to weigh down but to lift up his massive shoulders. The regimental commander had the look of a man happily performing one of the most solemn duties in life. He strolled about before the front line, bouncing at each step as he strolled, and arching his back slightly. It was clear that the regimental commander admired his regiment, was happy with it, and that all his inner forces were taken up only with the regiment; but, in spite of that, his bouncing gait seemed to say that, besides military interests, no small part of his soul was taken up by the interests of social life and the female sex.

"Well, Mikhailo Mitrich, old boy," he addressed one of the battalion commanders (the battalion commander, smiling, moved forward; it was clear that both men were happy), "we were hard put to it last night. However, it seems the regiment's not such a bad one . . . Eh?"

The battalion commander understood the merry irony and laughed.

"Wouldn't even be driven off the Tsaritsyn Field."[1]

"What?"

Just then two horsemen appeared on the road from town along which signalmen had been posted. They were an adjutant with a Cossack riding behind him.

The adjutant had been sent from headquarters to confirm to the regimental commander what had been said unclearly in the previous day's order, namely, that the commander in chief wished to see the regiment in exactly the same condition it had been in on the march—in greatcoats, in dustcovers, and without any preparations.

The day before, a member of the Hofkriegsrath from Vienna had come to Kutuzov with proposals and demands that he go as quickly as possible to join with the army of the archduke Ferdinand and Mack, and Kutuzov, who did not consider that juncture advantageous, intended, among other arguments in favour of his opinion, to show the Austrian general the sorry condition in which his troops arrived from Russia. It was with that purpose that he wanted to come and meet the regiment, so that the worse the condition of the regiment was, the more pleasing it would be to the commander in chief. Though the adjutant did not know these details, he conveyed to the regimental commander the absolute demand of the commander in chief that his people be in greatcoats and dustcovers, and that in the contrary case the commander in chief would be displeased.

Having listened to these words, the regimental commander hung his head, silently heaved his shoulders, and spread his arms in a sanguine gesture.

"Now we've done it!" he said. "See, I told you, Mikhailo Mitrich, if it's on the march, then it's greatcoats," he turned reproachfully to the battalion commander. "Ah, my God!" he added and resolutely stepped forward. "Company commanders!" he cried in a voice accustomed to command. "Sergeant majors! . . . How soon will he come?" he turned to the adjutant with an expression of deferential politeness which evidently related to the person of whom he was speaking.

"In an hour, I think."

"Do we have time to change?"

"I don't know, General . . ."

The regimental commander approached the ranks himself and gave orders to change back into overcoats. The company commanders ran to their companies, the sergeant majors began bustling about (the overcoats were not in good order), and that same instant the previously orderly, silent rectangles heaved, stretched, and began humming with talk. Soldiers ran back and forth on all sides, tossed their packs off one shoulder and pulled them over their heads, took their overcoats out, and raised their arms high, putting them into the sleeves.

Half an hour later everything was back in its former order, only the rectangles had become grey instead of black. The regimental commander again stepped before the regiment with his bouncing gait and looked it over from a distance.

"What's this now? what's this?" he shouted, stopping. "Commander of the third company! . . ."

"Commander of the third company to the general! commander to the general, third company to the commander! . . ." voices were heard in the ranks, and an adjutant ran to look for the belated officer.

When the sounds of the zealous voices, distorting the message and now shouting "the general to the third company," reached their destination, the summoned officer emerged from the back of the ranks and, though already an elderly man and not accustomed to running, cantered, clumsily tripping over his toes, towards the general. The captain's face expressed the anxiety of a schoolboy who is asked to recite a lesson he had not learned. Blotches appeared on his red (evidently from intemperance) face, and his mouth would not stay put. The regimental commander looked the captain up and down as he approached, puffing, slackening his pace the nearer he came.

"Soon you'll have your people dressed in sarafans! What is that?" shouted the regimental commander, thrusting his lower jaw out and pointing to a soldier in the ranks of the third company who was wearing a greatcoat of blue factory broadcloth, different from the other greatcoats. "Where have you been? We're expecting the commander in chief, and you leave your post? Eh? . . . I'll teach you to dress your people in gaudy colours for a review! . . . Eh! . . ."

The company commander, not taking his eyes off his superior officer, pressed his two fingers more and more firmly to his visor, as if he now saw salvation only in this pressing.

"Well, why are you silent? Who have you got there dressed up like a Hungarian?" the regimental commander joked sternly.

"Your Excellency . . ."

"Well, 'Your Excellency' what? Your Excellency! Your Excellency! But Your Excellency what—nobody knows."

"Your Excellency, it's Dolokhov, who was reduced . . ." the captain said softly.

"What, he's been reduced to a field marshal, is it, or to a common soldier? If it's a common soldier, then he should be dressed in the proper uniform like everybody else."

"Your Excellency, you yourself gave him permission for the march."

"Permission? Permission? You young people are always that way," said the regimental commander, cooling down a little. "Permission? Say something to you, and you . . ." The regimental commander paused. "Say something to you, and you . . . What?" he said, getting irritated again. "Kindly dress your men properly . . ."

And, having glanced at the adjutant, the regimental commander walked with his bouncing gait towards the regiment. It was clear that he liked his own irritation and that he wanted to walk the length of the regiment and find more pretexts for his wrath. Having snapped at one officer for an unpolished insignia, and another for an unevenness in one rank, he came to the third company.

"Ho-o-ow's that you're standing? Where's your leg? Where's your leg?" the regimental commander shouted with an expression of suffering in his voice, still five men away from Dolokhov, who was wearing a bluish greatcoat.

Dolokhov slowly straightened his bent leg and looked the general directly in the face with his light and insolent gaze.

"Why a blue greatcoat? Away! . . . Sergeant major! Have him changed . . . the dir . . ." He did not have time to finish.

"General, I am duty-bound to obey orders, but I am not duty-bound to put up with . . ." Dolokhov said hastily.

"No talking at attention! . . . No talking, no talking! . . ."

"Not duty-bound to put up with insults," Dolokhov finished loudly and resoundingly.

The eyes of the general and the soldier met. The general said nothing, angrily pulling down on his tight sash.

"Kindly change, I ask you," he said, walking away.

II

"He's coming!" the signalman shouted just then.

The regimental commander, turning red, ran to his horse, took the stirrup in his trembling hands, threw his body over, straightened up, drew his sword, and, with a happy, resolute face, opening his mouth askew, prepared to shout. The regiment fluttered up briefly, like a bird preening itself, and grew still.

"Te-n-n-n-HUT!" shouted the regimental commander in a soul-shattering voice, overjoyed for himself, strict in regard to the regiment, and welcoming in regard to his approaching superior.

Down the wide, tree-lined, unpaved main road, rumbling slightly on its springs, a high, light-blue Viennese coach-and-six came driving at a quick canter. Behind the coach galloped the suite and a convoy of Croats. Beside Kutuzov sat an Austrian general in a white uniform, strange amidst the black Russian ones. The coach drew up by the regiment. Kutuzov and the Austrian general conversed quietly about something, and Kutuzov smiled slightly, at the same time stepping down heavily from the footboard, as if these two thousand men staring at him and at the regimental commander with bated breath did not exist.

A shout of command rang out, and again the regiment quivered, jingling, as it presented arms. In the dead silence, the weak voice of the commander in chief was heard. The regiment barked: "Long live Your Excellen-cellen-cellency!" And again everything grew still. At first Kutuzov stood in place while the regiment moved; then Kutuzov, with the white general beside him, on foot, followed by his suite, started walking along the ranks.

By the way the regimental commander saluted the commander in chief, fastening his eyes on him, stretching and drawing himself up; by the way he walked along the ranks behind the generals, his body leaning forward, barely controlling his bouncing movement; by the way he jumped at each word and movement of the commander in chief—one could see that he fulfilled his duties as a subordinate with still greater pleasure than his duties as a superior. Owing to the regimental commander's strictness and zeal, the regiment was in excellent condition compared with others that had come to Braunau at the same time. The stragglers and sick amounted to only two hundred and seventeen men. And everything was in order, except the footgear.

Kutuzov walked along the ranks, stopping every once in a while and saying a few affectionate words to the officers he knew from the Turkish war, and sometimes to soldiers as well. Looking at the footgear, he several times shook his head sadly and pointed it out to the Austrian general with such an expression as though, while not blaming anyone for it, he could not help seeing how bad it was. The regimental commander ran ahead each time, afraid to miss a word of what the commander in chief said about the regiment. Behind Kutuzov, at a distance from which every faintly uttered word could be heard, walked some twenty men of his suite. The gentlemen of the suite talked among themselves and occasionally laughed. Closest behind the commander in chief walked a handsome officer. This was Prince Bolkonsky. Beside him walked his comrade Nesvitsky, a tall staff officer, extremely fat, with a kind, smiling, handsome face and moist eyes. Nesvitsky could barely hold back his laughter, provoked by a swarthy hussar officer who was walking near him. The hussar officer, without smiling, without changing the expression of his fixed gaze, was staring with a serious face at the regimental commander's back and mimicking his every movement. Each time the regimental commander bounced and leaned forward, the hussar officer bounced and leaned forward in the same, in exactly the same way. Nesvitsky laughed and nudged the others, urging them to look at the funnyman.

Kutuzov walked slowly and indolently past the thousands of eyes that were popping from their sockets, following the superior. Coming up to the third company, he suddenly stopped. His suite, not foreseeing this stop, inadvertently ran into him.

"Ah, Timokhin!" said the commander in chief, recognizing the red-nosed captain who had suffered on account of the blue greatcoat.

It would seem impossible to draw oneself up more than Timokhin had drawn himself up when the regimental commander reprimanded him. But the moment the commander in chief addressed him, the captain drew himself up so much that it seemed, if the commander in chief were to look at him a little longer, the captain would be unable to stand it; and therefore Kutuzov, evidently understanding his situation, and wishing the captain, on the contrary, nothing but good, hastened to turn away. A barely noticeable smile passed over Kutuzov's puffy face, disfigured by a wound.

"Another Izmail comrade,"[2] he said. "A brave officer! Are you pleased with him?" Kutuzov asked the regimental commander.

And the regimental commander, reflected as in a mirror, invisibly to himself, in the hussar officer, bounced, came forward, and replied:

"Very pleased, Your Excellency."

"We all have our weaknesses," said Kutuzov, smiling and moving away from him. "His was a devotion to Bacchus."

The regimental commander was afraid that he might be blamed for that and made no reply. Just then the officer noticed the face of the captain with the red nose and drawn-in stomach and mimicked his face and pose so perfectly that Nesvitsky could not keep from laughing. Kutuzov turned round. It was clear that the officer could control his face at will: the moment Kutuzov turned round, the officer managed to make a scowl and then assume a most serious, deferential, and innocent expression.

The third company was the last, and Kutuzov fell to thinking, evidently recalling something. Prince Andrei stepped from among the suite and said quietly in French:

"You asked me to remind you about the demoted officer Dolokhov in this regiment."

"Where's this Dolokhov?" asked Kutuzov.

Dolokhov, now changed into a grey soldier's greatcoat, did not wait to be called out. The trim figure of the fair-haired soldier with clear blue eyes stepped from the line. He went up to the commander in chief and presented arms.

"A grievance?" Kutuzov asked, frowning slightly.

"This is Dolokhov," said Prince Andrei.

"Ah!" said Kutuzov. "I hope this lesson will set you straight. Serve well. Our sovereign is merciful. And I won't forget you, if you prove worthy."

The blue, clear eyes looked at the commander in chief just as boldly as at the regimental commander, as if tearing by their expression the curtain of convention that had so widely separated the commander in chief from the soldier.

"I ask only one thing, Your Excellency," he said in his firm, sonorous, unhurried voice. "I ask to be given a chance to wipe out my guilt and prove my devotion to the sovereign and to Russia."

Kutuzov turned away. The same smile of the eyes flashed over his face as when he had turned away from Captain Timokhin. He turned away and winced, as if wishing to express thereby that all that Dolokhov had said to him and all that he could say had long, long been known to him, that it all bored him, and that it was all by no means what was needed. He turned away and made for the coach.

The regiment broke up into companies and dispersed to their assigned quarters not far from Braunau, where they hoped to find footgear, mend their clothes, and get some rest after their hard marching.

"Don't hold it against me, Prokhor Ignatych!" said the regimental commander, circling around the third company, which was moving to its quarters, and riding up to Captain Timokhin, who was walking at the head of it. The face of the regimental commander, after the happily passed-off review, expressed irrepressible joy. "The tsar's service . . . impossible . . . sometimes one gets snappish on parade . . . I'm the first to apologize, you know me . . . He was very grateful!" And he held out his hand to the company commander.

"Mercy, General, I wouldn't be so bold!" replied the captain, his nose reddening, smiling and revealing with his smile the absence of his two front teeth, knocked out by a rifle butt at Izmail.

"And tell Mr. Dolokhov that I won't forget him, he should rest easy. And tell me, please, I keep forgetting to ask, how is he, how does he behave? And all . . ."

"He's very correct in his service, Your Excellency . . . but his charickter . . ." said Timokhin.

"What, what about his character?" asked the regimental commander.

"It comes over him, Your Excellency, some days," said the captain. "He's clever, and learned, and kind. And then he's a beast. In Poland he all but killed a Jew, if you want to know . . ."

"Well, yes, yes," said the regimental commander, "still one must pity the young fellow in his misfortune. Big connections . . . So you just . . ."

"Right, Your Excellency," said Timokhin, his smile letting it be felt that he understood his superior's wishes.

"Well, yes, yes."

The regimental commander sought out Dolokhov in the ranks and reined in his horse.

"With the first action—epaulettes," he said to him.

Dolokhov looked, said nothing, and did not change the expression of his mockingly smiling mouth.

"Well, that's fine," the regimental commander went on. "The men get a glass of vodka each from me," he added loudly, so that the soldiers could hear. "I'm grateful to you all! Thank God!" And, going ahead of the company, he rode to the next one.

"Why, he's really a good man, you can serve with him," Timokhin said to a subaltern officer who was walking beside him.

"All heart, in a word! . . ." the subaltern officer said, laughing (the regimental commander's nickname was "the King of Hearts").

The happy state of mind of the officers after the review passed itself on to the soldiers. The company walked along merrily. On all sides soldiers' voices exchanged remarks.

"How come they said Kutuzov was blind in one eye?"

"Hell he's not! Stone blind . . ."

"Naw . . . brother, he's sharper-eyed than you—the boots and the foot cloths, he took it all in . . ."

"The way he looked my feet over, dear brother mine . . . Well! I think . . ."

"And that other one, the Austriak with him, it's like he's all smeared with chalk. White as flour! I s'pose they clean him like ammunition!"

"What about it, Fedeshou! . . . Did he say when the fighting would begin? You were standing closer. They all said Boonapart himself was stationed in Brunovo."

"Boonapart stationed there! Lies, you fool! What do you know! It's the Prussky's up in arms now. The Austriak's pacifying him. Soon as they make peace, the war with Boonapart will open up. And he says Boonapart's in Brunovo! It's plain you're a fool, no point listening to you."

"Devilish billeters! The fifth company's already tucked into the village, see, they'll have their kasha boiled, and we've still got no place."

"Give us a biscuit, you devil."

"And did you give me tobacco yesterday? So there, brother. Well, here, take it, God help you."

"They could at least call a halt, or else we'll slog on for three more miles unfed."

"It was a pretty thing the way the Germans sent us carriages.[3] You go riding along, you know: it's grand!"

"But here, brother, the folk have gone clean wild. There it was all some kind of Poles, all under the Russian crown, but now, brother, it's gone solid German."

"Singers, up front!" the captain's shout was heard.

And some twenty men from various ranks ran to the front of the company. The drummer and lead singer turned to face the singers, waved his arm, and struck up a drawn-out soldiers' song that began: "It was dawn, the sun was rising . . ." and ended with the words: "And that, brothers, will our glory be with old man Kamensky . . ." The song had been composed in Turkey, and was now being sung in Austria, only with one change, that instead of "old man Kamensky," they put in "old man Kutuzov."

Having snapped out these last words in soldierly fashion and waved his arms as if throwing something on the ground, the drummer, a lean and handsome soldier of about forty, sternly looked the soldier-singers over and narrowed his eyes. Then, making sure that all eyes were aimed at him, he raised his arms as if carefully lifting some invisible precious object over his head, held it there for a few seconds, and all at once desperately threw it down:

Ah, my porch, my new porch!

"Ah, my new porch . . ." twenty voices picked up, and a spoon player, despite the weight of his ammunition, nimbly leaped out in front and walked backwards facing the company, moving his shoulders and threatening someone with his spoons. The soldiers swung their arms in time with the song, striding freely along and involuntarily keeping in step. From behind the company came the sound of wheels, the creaking springs, and the tramping of horses. Kutuzov and his suite were returning to town. The commander in chief gave a sign for the men to go on marching freely, and his face and all the faces of his suite expressed pleasure at the sounds of the song, at the sight of the dancing soldier and the merrily and briskly marching soldiers. In the second row of the right flank, where the coach overtook the company, the eye was involuntarily struck by the blue-eyed soldier Dolokhov, who marched especially briskly and gracefully in time with the song and looked at the faces of people passing by with such an expression as if he pitied all those who were not then marching with the company. The hussar cornet from Kutuzov's suite, who had been mimicking the regimental commander, dropped behind the coach and rode over to Dolokhov.

The hussar cornet Zherkov had belonged for some time to the rowdy company headed by Dolokhov in Petersburg. Abroad, Zherkov had encountered Dolokhov as a soldier, but had found it unnecessary to recognize him. Now, after Kutuzov had talked with the demoted man, he addressed him with the joy of an old friend.

"Friend of my heart, how are you?" he said to the sounds of the song, adjusting the pace of his horse to the pace of the company.

"How am I?" Dolokhov replied coldly. "As you see."

The brisk song gave a special meaning to the tone of casual merriment with which Zherkov spoke, and to the intentional coldness of Dolokhov's replies.

"Well, how are you getting along with your superiors?" asked Zherkov.

"Well enough, they're good people. How did you manage to turn up on the staff?"

"By appointment. I'm on duty."

They fell silent.

"She let the falcon go, from her right sleeve let it go," said the song, involuntarily arousing a cheerful, merry feeling. Their conversation would probably have been different, if they had not been talking to the sounds of the song.

"So, is it true the Austrians have been beaten?" asked Dolokhov.

"Devil knows, they say so."

"I'm glad," Dolokhov replied briefly and clearly, as the song required.

"So, then, come over some evening, we'll set up a game of faro," said Zherkov.

"What, have you got a lot of money?"

"Come over."

"Impossible. I've sworn off it. No drinking and no gambling, until I've been promoted."

"So, then, till the first action . . ."

"We'll see . . ."

They again fell silent.

"Just come, if you need something, the staff can always be helpful . . ." said Zherkov.

Dolokhov grinned.

"You'd best not worry. If I need anything, I won't ask, I'll take it myself."

"So, then, I just . . ."

"Well, and I, too, just . . ."

"Goodbye."

"Be well . . ."

> . . . And high and far he flew
> To his own native land . . .

Zherkov touched his horse with his spurs; it shifted its footing three times excitedly, not knowing which leg to start with, worked it out, and galloped off, going ahead of the company and catching up with the coach, also in time with the song.

III

On returning from the review, Kutuzov, accompanied by the Austrian general, went to his office and, calling his adjutant, told him to bring him certain papers pertaining to the condition of the arriving troops and letters from Archduke Ferdinand, who was heading the army of the vanguard. Prince Andrei Bolkonsky came into the commander in chief's office with the requested papers. Kutuzov and the Austrian member of the Hofkriegsrath were sitting over a map spread out on the table.

"Ah . . ." said Kutuzov, glancing at Bolkonsky, as if with this word he was inviting the adjutant to wait, and went on with the conversation begun in French.

"I'm saying only one thing, General," Kutuzov said with a pleasant graciousness of expression and intonation, which made one listen well to every unhurriedly uttered word. It could be seen that Kutuzov, too, listened to himself with pleasure. "I'm only saying one thing, General, that if the matter depended on my own personal wish, the will of his majesty the emperor Franz would have been fulfilled long ago. I would long ago have joined the archduke. And believe me on my honour, for me personally to hand over the supreme command of the army to a more knowledgeable and skilful general, such as Austria abounds in, and to lay down all this heavy responsibility, for me personally it would be a delight. But circumstances are sometimes stronger than we are, General."

And Kutuzov smiled with such an expression as if he was saying: "You have every right not to believe me, and I'm even quite indifferent to whether you believe me or not, but you have no cause for telling me so. And that's the whole point."

The Austrian general had a displeased look, but he had no choice but to answer Kutuzov in the same tone.

"On the contrary," he said in a peevish and angry tone, quite contradictory to the flattering meaning of the words he spoke, "on the contrary, Your Excellency's participation in the common cause is highly appreciated by his majesty; but we think that the present delay is depriving the valiant Russian army and its commanders of the laurels they are accustomed to reap in battle," he finished an obviously prepared phrase.

Kutuzov bowed with an unchanging smile.

"But I am convinced and, basing myself on the last letter with which his highness Archduke Ferdinand has honoured me, I suppose that the Austrian troops under the command of so skilful a leader as General Mack, have now gained a decisive victory and are no longer in need of our help," said Kutuzov.

The general frowned. Though there was no positive news about the defeat of the Austrians, there were far too many circumstances confirming the general unfavourable rumours; and therefore Kutuzov's supposition about an Austrian victory looked very much like mockery. But Kutuzov was smiling meekly, with the same expression which said that he had the right to suppose so. In fact, the last letter he had had from Mack's army had informed him of the victory and of the most advantageous strategic position of the army.

"Give me that letter," said Kutuzov, turning to Prince Andrei. "Take a look, if you please," and Kutuzov, with a mocking smile at the corners of his lips, read in German for the Austrian general the following passage from the letter of Archduke Ferdinand:

Wir haben vollkommen zusammengehaltene Kräfte, nahe an 70,000 Mann, um den Feind, wenn er den Lech passierte, angreifen und schlagen zu können. Wir können, da wir Meister von Ulm sind, den Vorteil, auch von beiden Ufern der Donau Meister zu bleiben, nicht verlieren; mithin auch jeden Augenblick, wenn der Feind den Lech nicht passierte, die Donau übersetzen, uns auf seine Kommunications-Linie werfen, die Donau unterhalb repassieren und dem Feinde, wenn er sich gegen unsere treue Alliierte mit ganzer Macht wenden wollte, seine Absicht alsbald vereiteln. Wir werden auf solche Weise dem Zeitpunkt, wo die Kaiserlich-Russische Armée ausgerüstet sein wird, mutig entgegenharren, und sodann leicht gemeinschaftlich die Möglichkeit finden, dem Feinde das Schicksal zuzubereiten, so er verdient.[4]

Kutuzov sighed deeply as he finished this paragraph and looked at the member of the Hofkriegsrath attentively and benignly.

"But Your Excellency knows the wise rule which prescribes that one should assume the worst," said the Austrian general, evidently wishing to put an end to the joking and get down to business.

He glanced with displeasure at the adjutant.

"Excuse me, General," Kutuzov interrupted him and also turned to Prince Andrei. "I tell you what, my gentle, you get all the reports our scouts have

---

*We have a fully massed force of about 70,000 men, and can attack and crush the enemy if he crosses the Lech. Since we are already the masters of Ulm, we cannot lose the advantage of being masters of both banks of the Danube; so that, if the enemy does not cross the Lech, we can at any moment cross the Danube, fall upon his lines of communication, cross back lower down the Danube, and prevent the enemy, if he decides to turn all his forces against our faithful allies, from fulfilling his intention. Thus we shall cheerfully await the time when the Russian imperial army is in full readiness, and then together we shall easily find the means of preparing for the enemy the fate he deserves.

received from Kozlovsky. Here are two letters from Count Nostitz, here is the letter from his highness Archduke Ferdinand, here are some others," he said, handing him several papers. "And from all this compose a clear memorandum, in French, presenting all the news we've had about the actions of the Austrian army. Well, do that, and give it to his excellency."

Prince Andrei inclined his head to indicate that he had understood from the first word not only what had been said, but also what Kutuzov had wished to tell him. He gathered up the papers and, making a general bow, stepping softly over the carpet, went out to the waiting room.

Though not much time had passed since Prince Andrei left Russia, he had changed much during that time. In the expression of his face, in his movements, in his gait there was almost no trace of the former affectation, fatigue, and laziness; he had the look of a man who had no time to think of the impression he made on others and who was occupied with pleasant and interesting things. His face expressed more satisfaction with himself and those around him; his smile and glance were more cheerful and attractive.

Kutuzov, whom he had overtaken still in Poland, had received him very affectionately, promised not to forget him, distinguished him from the other adjutants, taken him along to Vienna, charged him with more serious missions. From Vienna Kutuzov wrote to his old comrade, Prince Andrei's father.

"Your son," he wrote, "promises to become an outstanding officer, by his knowledge, firmness, and industry. I consider myself fortunate to have such a subordinate at hand."

On Kutuzov's staff, among his comrades and colleagues, and in the army in general, as in Petersburg society, Prince Andrei had two completely opposite reputations. Some, the smaller part, considered Prince Andrei to be something distinct from themselves and from all others, expected great success from him, listened to him, admired him, and imitated him; and with these people Prince Andrei was simple and pleasant. Others, the majority, did not like Prince Andrei, considering him a pompous, cold, and unpleasant man. But with these people Prince Andrei was able to behave in such a way as to be respected and even feared.

Coming out to the waiting room from Kutuzov's office, Prince Andrei, holding the papers, went up to his colleague on duty, the adjutant Kozlovsky, who was sitting by the window with a book.

"Well, what is it, Prince?" asked Kozlovsky.

"I've been ordered to compose a memorandum explaining why we are not moving forward."

"And why is it?"

Prince Andrei shrugged his shoulders.

"Any news from Mack?" asked Kozlovsky.

"No."

"If it were true that he's been defeated, the news would have come."

"Probably," said Prince Andrei and headed for the front door; but just then the door slammed and a tall Austrian general, evidently just arrived, in a frock coat, his head bound in a black bandage and the order of Maria Theresa on his neck, quickly entered the waiting room. Prince Andrei stopped.

"General in Chief Kutuzov?" the just-arrived general spoke quickly, with a strong German accent, glancing to both sides and going to the door of the office without pausing.

"The general in chief is busy," said Kozlovsky, hastily going up to the unknown general and barring his way to the door. "How shall I announce you?"

The unknown general looked down scornfully at the short Kozlovsky, as if surprised that there could be people who did not know him.

"The general in chief is busy," Kozlovsky calmly repeated.

The general's face frowned, his lips twitched and trembled. He took out a notebook, quickly jotted something with a pencil, tore out the page, handed it over, went with quick steps to the window, dropped his body into a chair, and looked around at those who were in the room, as if asking why they were looking at him. Then the general raised his head, stretched his neck, as if intending to say something, but at once, as if casually beginning to hum to himself, produced a strange sound, which at once broke off. The door to the office opened, and Kutuzov appeared on the threshold. The general with the bandaged head, leaning forward as if fleeing from danger, went up to Kutuzov with long, rapid strides of his thin legs.

"*Vous voyez le malheureux Mack,*"* he uttered in a breaking voice.

The face of Kutuzov, who was standing in the doorway of his office, remained perfectly immobile for a few moments. Then a wrinkle passed like a wave over his face, his brow became smooth again, he inclined his head deferentially, closed his eyes, silently allowed Mack to pass, followed him in, and closed the door behind him.

The rumour that had already spread earlier about the defeat of the Austrians and the surrender of the entire army at Ulm turned out to be true. Within half an hour adjutants had been sent out in various directions with orders demonstrating that the Russian troops, so far inactive, would soon also have to meet the enemy.

Prince Andrei was one of the rare officers on the staff who placed his main interest in the general course of military operations. Seeing Mack and hearing the details of his ruin, he understood that half the campaign was lost, understood all the difficulty of the Russian troops' position, and vividly pictured to himself what awaited the army, and the role he was to play in it. Involuntarily, he experienced an excited, joyful feeling at the thought of the disgrace of self-

---

*You are looking at the unfortunate Mack.

confident Austria and of the fact that in a week, perhaps, he would have to see and take part in the encounter of the Russians with the French, the first since Suvorov. But he feared the genius of Bonaparte, which might prove stronger than all the courage of the Russian troops, and at the same time he could not allow for the disgrace of his hero.

Excited and irritated by these thoughts, Prince Andrei went to his room to write to his father, to whom he wrote every day. In the corridor he met his roommate Nesvitsky and the joker Zherkov; they were laughing at something, as usual.

"Why so glum?" asked Nesvitsky, noticing Prince Andrei's pale face with its glittering eyes.

"There's nothing to be merry about," replied Bolkonsky.

Just as Prince Andrei met Nesvitsky and Zherkov, the Austrian general Strauch, attached to Kutuzov's staff to oversee the supplying of the Russian army, came from the other end of the corridor, along with the member of the Hofkriegsrath who had arrived the day before. The corridor was wide enough for the generals to pass the three officers unhindered, but Zherkov, pushing Nesvitsky aside with his hand, said in a breathless voice:

"They're coming! . . . they're coming! . . . step aside, make way, make way, please."

The generals came on, looking as if they could do without embarrassing honours. The face of the joker Zherkov suddenly showed a stupid smile of joy, which he seemed unable to suppress.

"Your Excellency," he said in German, stepping forward and addressing the Austrian general, "I have the honour to congratulate you."

He bowed his head and began scraping with one foot, then the other, awkwardly, like children who are learning to dance.

The general who was a member of the Hofkriegsrath looked at him sternly; but, noticing the seriousness of the stupid smile, could not refuse it a moment's attention. He narrowed his eyes, showing that he was listening.

"I have the honour to congratulate you: General Mack has arrived in good health, except for a slight wound here," he added with a beaming smile, pointing to his head.

The general frowned, turned away, and walked on.

"*Gott, wie naiv!*"* he said angrily after going a few steps.

Nesvitsky, guffawing, put his arm around Prince Andrei, but Bolkonsky, turning still more pale, with an angry expression on his face, pushed him away and turned to Zherkov. The nervous irritation he had felt at the sight of Mack, the news of his defeat, and the thought of what awaited the Russian army now found its outlet in his anger at Zherkov's inappropriate joke.

*God, how naïve!

"If you, my dear sir," he began in a shrill voice, with a slight trembling of the lower jaw, "wish to be a *buffoon,* I cannot prevent you from being one; but I announce to you that the next time you *dare* to clown in my presence, I will teach you how to behave."

Nesvitsky and Zherkov were so astounded by this outburst that they silently stared wide-eyed at Bolkonsky.

"Why, I only congratulated him," said Zherkov.

"I am not joking with you, kindly keep silent!" shouted Bolkonsky, and, taking Nesvitsky by the arm, he walked away from Zherkov, who was at a loss how to reply.

"Well, what's with you, brother?" Nesvitsky said peaceably.

"What's with me?" said Prince Andrei, stopping in agitation. "Understand that we're either officers serving our tsar and fatherland, and rejoice in our common successes and grieve over our common failures, or we're lackeys, who have nothing to do with their masters' doings. *Quarante mille hommes massacrés et l'armée de nos alliés détruite, et vous trouvez là le mot pour rire,*" he said, as if clinching his opinion by this French phrase. "*C'est bien pour un garçon de rien, comme cette individu, dont vous avez fait un ami, mais pas pour vous, pas pour vous.* * Only *schoolboys* can have fun like that," Prince Andrei added in Russian, pronouncing the word with a French accent, noticing that Zherkov was still within earshot.

He waited for the cornet to make some reply. But the cornet turned and left the corridor.

IV

The Pavlogradsky hussar regiment was stationed two miles from Braunau. The squadron in which Nikolai Rostov served as a junker had settled in the German village of Salzeneck. The squadron commander, Captain Denisov, known to the whole cavalry division as Vaska Denisov, was assigned the best quarters in the village. Junker Rostov had been living with the squadron commander ever since he caught up with his regiment in Poland.

On the eighth of October, the day when at headquarters all were brought to their feet by the news of Mack's defeat, in the squadron staff life quietly went on as before. Denisov, who had spent the whole night playing cards, was still not home when Rostov, on horseback, came back from foraging early in the morning. Rostov, in his junker's uniform, rode up to the porch, nudged his horse

---

*Forty thousand men massacred and the army of our allies destroyed, and you find that an excuse for laughing . . . It's all right for a worthless fellow, like that individual you have made friends with, but not for you, not for you.

round, swung his leg over him in a supple, youthful movement, stood in the stirrup as if not wishing to part with his horse, finally jumped down, and shouted for the orderly.

"Ah, Bondarenko, friend of my heart," he said to the hussar who came rushing for his horse. "Give him a cooling down, my friend," he said with that merry brotherly tenderness with which all fine young men treat everyone when they are happy.

"Yes, Your Excellency," the Ukrainian replied, merrily shaking his head.

"See that you give him a cooling down!"

Another hussar also rushed to the horse, but Bondarenko had already thrown the reins over the horse's head. One could see that the junker gave good tips and it was profitable to be of service to him. Rostov stroked the horse's neck, then his croup, and stopped on the porch.

"Very nice! What a horse he'll be!" he said to himself and, smiling and holding his sabre, ran up the steps, his spurs jingling. The German landlord, in a vest and a cap, holding the fork he was using to clear away dung, peeked out of the cowshed. As soon as he saw Rostov, the German's face suddenly brightened. He smiled merrily and winked: *"Schön, gut Morgen! Schön, gut Morgen!"** he repeated, obviously taking pleasure in greeting the young man.

"Schon fleissig!"† said Rostov, still with the same joyful, brotherly smile, which never left his animated face. *"Hoch Oestreicher! Hoch Russen! Kaiser Alexander hoch!"‡* he addressed the German, repeating words often spoken by the landlord.

The German laughed, came all the way out of the cowshed door, pulled off his cap, and, waving it above his head, cried:

"Und die ganze Welt hoch!"§

Rostov himself, like the German, waved his peaked cap above his head and, laughing, shouted: *"Und vivat die ganze Welt!"* Though there was no particular reason for rejoicing either for the German, who was cleaning his cowshed, or for Rostov, who had gone for hay with his section, the two men looked at each other with happy delight and brotherly love, shook their heads as a sign of mutual love, and, smiling, went their way—the German to the cowshed, and Rostov to the cottage he occupied with Denisov.

"How's the master?" he asked Lavrushka, Denisov's lackey, a rogue known to the whole regiment.

"Hasn't been back since evening. Must've lost," replied Lavrushka. "I know

---

*Good morning! Good morning!
†Already busy!
‡Long live the Austrians! Long live the Russians! Long live Tsar Alexander!
§And long live the whole world!

for sure, if he wins, he comes early so as to boast, but if he stays away till morning, it means he blew it—and he'll come angry. Shall I serve coffee?"

"Go on, go on."

Ten minutes later Lavrushka brought coffee.

"He's coming," he said. "Now for trouble."

Rostov looked out of the window and saw Denisov coming home. Denisov was a small man with a red face, shining black eyes, and dishevelled black moustaches and hair. He was wearing an unbuttoned dolman, wide pleated trousers ballooning over his boots, and a crumpled hussar cap perched on the back of his head. He was approaching the porch gloomily, his head hanging.

"Lavghrushka," he shouted loudly and crossly. "Well, take it off, blockhead!"

"I am taking it off," Lavrushka's voice replied.

"Ah! you're up alghready," said Denisov, going into the room.

"Long ago," said Rostov. "I already went for hay and saw Fräulein Mathilde."

"Ah, ghreally! And I blew eveghrything last night, bghrother, like a son of a bitch!" shouted Denisov, swallowing his *r*s. "Such bad luck! Such bad luck! . . . As soon as you left, it staghrted. Hey, tea!"

Denisov, wincing as if he was smiling and baring his short, strong teeth, began tousling his forest-thick, tangled, bushy black hair with both short-fingered hands.

"The devil pghrompted me to go to that ghrat" (the officer's nickname was "the Rat"), he said, rubbing his forehead and face with both hands. "Can you imagine, not a single good caghrd, not one."

Denisov took the lighted pipe served to him, clutched it in his fist, banged it on the floor, spraying sparks, and went on shouting:

"He gives you the simple, and beats it with the paghroli; gives you the simple, and beats it with the paghroli."

He spilled the fire, smashed the pipe, and threw it away. Then he paused and suddenly glanced merrily at Rostov with his shining black eyes.

"If only there were some women. But here, except for dghrinking, there's nothing to do. If only we'd staghrt fighting soon . . . Hey, who's there?" he turned to the door, hearing the tread of heavy boots with jingling spurs come to a stop and then a respectful cough.

"The sergeant major!" said Lavrushka.

Denisov winced still more.

"Ghrotten luck," he said, throwing down a purse with a few gold pieces. "Ghrostov, dear heaghrt, count up what's left and put it under the pillow," he said and went out to the sergeant major.

Rostov took the money and, mechanically sorting the old and new coins into separate piles, began counting it.

"Ah! Telyanin! Ghreetings! I blew eveghrything last night," Denisov's voice came from the other room.

"Where? At Bykov's, at the Rat's? . . . I knew it," said a high-pitched voice, and after that Lieutenant Telyanin, a small officer from the same squadron, came in.

Rostov threw the purse under the pillow and shook the small, moist hand that was held out to him. Telyanin had for some reason been transferred from the guards just before the campaign. He behaved very well in the regiment; but he was not liked, and Rostov especially could neither overcome nor conceal his causeless loathing for the man.

"Well, so, young cavalryman, how's my Little Rook serving you?" he asked. (Little Rook was a saddle horse, recently broken, that Telyanin had sold to Rostov.)

The lieutenant never looked the person he was talking to in the eye; his eyes constantly shifted from one object to another.

"I saw you ride by today . . ."

"He's all right, a good horse," replied Rostov, although the horse, which he had bought for seven hundred roubles, was not worth even half that price. "He's begun to favour the left foreleg . . ." he added.

"The hoof's cracked! It's nothing. I'll teach you, I'll show you what sort of clinch nail to put on it."

"Yes, please show me," said Rostov.

"I will, I will, it's no secret. And you'll be thankful for the horse."

"I'll have the horse brought, then," said Rostov, wishing to be rid of Telyanin, and he went to give orders for the horse to be brought.

In the front hall, Denisov, crouching on the threshold with his pipe, sat facing the sergeant major, who was reporting something. Seeing Rostov, Denisov winced and pointed over his shoulder with his thumb to the room where Telyanin was sitting, winced again, and shuddered with loathing.

"Ach, I dislike the fellow," he said, unembarrassed by the sergeant major's presence.

Rostov shrugged his shoulders, as if to say, "So do I, but what to do!" and, having given orders, went back to Telyanin.

Telyanin was sitting in the same indolent pose in which Rostov had left him, rubbing his small white hands.

"There are such repulsive faces in the world," thought Rostov, going into the room.

"So, did you order the horse brought?" asked Telyanin, getting up and glancing around casually.

"I did."

"Well, come on then. I only stopped to ask Denisov about yesterday's orders. Did you receive them, Denisov?"

"Not yet. And where are you going?"

"I want to teach the young man how to shoe a horse."

They went out to the porch and to the stable. The lieutenant showed him how to do a clinch nail, and went home.

When Rostov came back, there was a bottle of vodka and some sausage on the table. Denisov was sitting at the table scratching on a piece of paper with his quill. He glanced darkly at Rostov's face.

"I'm writing to her," he said.

He leaned his elbow on the table, the quill in his hand, and, obviously glad of the chance to quickly speak out everything he wanted to write, began reciting his letter to Rostov.

"You see, fghriend," he said, "we're asleep until we love. We're childgrhen of dust . . . but fall in love—and you're God, you're pure as on the fighrst day of cghreation . . . Who's that now? Send him to the devil. No time!" he shouted to Lavrushka, who came up to him without the slightest timidity.

"Who is it? You gave the order yourself. The sergeant major's come for money."

Denisov winced, was about to shout something, but kept silent.

"Ghrotten business," he said to himself. "How much money was left in the pughrse?" he asked Rostov.

"Seven new and three old."

"Ah, ghrot! Well, what are you standing there for, scarecghrow, off to the sergeant major," Denisov shouted at Lavrushka.

"Please, Denisov, take money from me, I've got it," Rostov said, blushing.

"I don't like getting fghriends involved, no, I don't," Denisov muttered.

"If you won't take money from me as a friend, you'll offend me. I really have got it," Rostov repeated.

"No, no, I won't."

And Denisov went to the bed to take his purse from under the pillow.

"Where'd you put it, Ghrostov?"

"Under the bottom pillow."

"It's not there."

Denisov threw both pillows on the floor. The purse was not there.

"That's odd!"

"Wait, maybe you dropped it?" said Rostov, picking up first one pillow, then the other, and shaking them.

He tore off the blanket and shook it. The purse was not there.

"Maybe I forgot? No, I thought then that it was as if you were hiding a treasure under your head," said Rostov. "I put the purse there. Where is it?" he turned to Lavrushka.

"I didn't come in. It should be wherever you put it."

"But it's not."

"It's always that way, you toss something somewhere and then forget. Look in your pockets."

"No, maybe if I hadn't thought about the treasure," said Rostov, "but I remember putting it there."

Lavrushka rummaged through the whole bed, looked under it, looked under the table, rummaged about everywhere, and stopped in the middle of the room. Denisov silently followed Lavrushka's movements, and when Lavrushka spread his arms in surprise, saying it was not to be found anywhere, he looked at Rostov.

"Ghrostov, you're not a pghrankst . . ."

Rostov felt Denisov's gaze on him, raised his eyes, and instantly lowered them. All the blood he had locked up somewhere under his throat rushed to his face and eyes. He could scarcely breathe.

"There was nobody in the room except the lieutenant and you. It's here somewhere," said Lavrushka.

"Ah, you devil's puppet, stir your stumps, get looking," Denisov shouted suddenly, turning purple and hurling himself at the lackey with a menacing gesture. "There'll be a pughrse, or I'll flog you to death. I'll flog you all to death!"

Rostov, avoiding Denisov's eyes, began to button his jacket, buckled on his sabre, and put on his peaked cap.

"I tell you, there'll be a pughrse," Denisov shouted, shaking the orderly by the shoulder and pushing him against the wall.

"Denisov, leave him alone; I know who took it," said Rostov, approaching the door and not raising his eyes.

Denisov paused, reflected, and, evidently realizing what Rostov was alluding to, seized his arm.

"Ghrubbish!" he shouted so that the veins swelled like ropes on his neck and forehead. "You've lost your mind, I tell you, I won't stand for it. The pughrse is here; I'll skin this scoundghrel alive, and it will be here."

"I know who took it," Rostov repeated in a trembling voice, going to the door.

"And I tell you, don't you dare do that," cried Denisov, rushing at the junker to hold him back.

But Rostov tore his arm free and, with as much spite as if Denisov was his greatest enemy, directly and firmly fixed his eyes on him.

"Do you realize what you're saying?" he said in a trembling voice. "Besides me, there was no one else in the room. Which means, if that's not it, then . . ."

He was unable to finish and ran out of the room.

"Ah, the devil take you and all the ghrest of them" were the last words Rostov heard.

Rostov went to Telyanin's quarters.

"The master's not at home, he's gone to the staff," Telyanin's orderly told him. "Has something happened?" the orderly added, surprised to see the junker's upset face.

"No, nothing."

"You just missed him," said the orderly.

The staff was quartered two miles from Salzeneck. Without stopping at home, Rostov took his horse and rode to the staff. In the village occupied by the staff there was a tavern frequented by the officers. Rostov rode to the tavern; near the porch he saw Telyanin's horse.

The lieutenant was sitting in the second room of the tavern over a plate of sausage and a bottle of wine.

"Ah, you've come, too, young man," he said, smiling and raising his eyebrows high.

"Yes," said Rostov, as if it cost him great effort to utter this word, and sat at the next table.

Both were silent; there were two Germans in the room and a Russian officer. Everyone was silent, and only the clank of knives against plates was heard and the lieutenant's chomping. When Telyanin finished his lunch, he took a double purse from his pocket, opened the clasp with his small, white, upturned fingers, took out a gold coin and, raising his eyebrows, gave it to the waiter.

"Make it quick, please," he said.

The coin was a new one. Rostov got up and went over to Telyanin.

"May I look at your purse?" he said in a low, barely audible voice.

With shifty eyes, but still raising his eyebrows, Telyanin handed him the purse.

"Yes, a pretty purse . . . Yes . . . yes . . ." he said and suddenly turned pale. "Have a look, young man," he added.

Rostov took the purse in his hands and looked at it, and at the money that was in it, and at Telyanin. The lieutenant glanced about, as was his habit, and suddenly seemed to become very merry.

"If we get to Vienna, I'll leave it all there, but there's nothing to do with it in these trashy little towns," he said. "Well, young man, give it to me, I'm leaving."

Rostov was silent.

"And why are you here? Also to have lunch? The food's quite good," Telyanin went on. "Give it to me."

He reached out and put his hand on the purse. Rostov let go of it. Telyanin took the purse and began to lower it into the pocket of his riding breeches, his eyebrows raised casually, and his mouth slightly open, as if he was saying: "Yes, yes, I'm putting my purse in my pocket, and it's quite simple, and it's nobody's business."

"Well, then, young man?" he said, sighing and looking into Rostov's eyes from under his raised eyebrows. Some sort of light, quick as an electric spark, passed from Telyanin's eyes to the eyes of Rostov and back, and forth and back again, all in an instant.

"Come here," said Rostov, seizing Telyanin by the arm. He almost dragged him to the window. "That's Denisov's money, you took it . . ." he whispered in his ear.

"What? . . . What? . . . How dare you? What? . . ." said Telyanin.

But these words sounded like a pitiful, desperate cry and a plea for forgiveness. As soon as Rostov heard the sound of that voice, a huge burden of doubt fell from his soul. He felt joy and in the same instant also pity for the wretched man standing before him; but he had to bring the matter he had begun to a conclusion.

"God knows what the people here may think," Telyanin murmured, seizing his peaked cap and going into a small empty room, "we must have a talk . . ."

"I know it and I'll prove it," said Rostov.

"I . . ."

Every muscle in Telyanin's frightened, pale face began to quiver; his eyes shifted as before, but somewhere low down, not rising to Rostov's face, and there was a sound of sobbing.

"Count! . . . don't ruin . . . a young man . . . here's this wretched . . . money, take it . . ." He threw it on the table. "I have an old father, a mother! . . ."

Rostov took the money, avoiding Telyanin's eyes, and, not saying a word, started out of the room. But at the door he stopped and came back.

"My God," he said, with tears in his eyes, "how could you have done it?"

"Count . . ." said Telyanin, going up to the junker.

"Don't touch me," said Rostov, drawing back. "If you need the money, take it." He flung the purse at him and ran out of the tavern.

V

On the evening of the same day, an animated conversation was going on among the squadron officers in Denisov's quarters.

"And I tell you, Rostov, that you've got to apologize to the regimental commander," said a tall staff captain with grizzled hair, enormous moustaches, and a large-featured, wrinkled face, to the crimson-faced, excited Rostov.

Staff Captain Kirsten had twice been broken to the ranks for affairs of honour and had twice won back his commission.

"I won't allow anyone to call me a liar!" cried Rostov. "He called me a liar, and I called him a liar. Let it remain at that. He can assign me to duty every day, or put me under arrest, but no one will make me apologize, because if he, as the regimental commander, considers it beneath him to give me satisfaction, then . . ."

"Wait a minute, my dear boy, listen to me," the staff captain interrupted in his bass voice, calmly stroking his long moustache. "You tell the regimental commander, in front of other officers, that an officer has stolen . . ."

"It's not my fault that the conversation started in front of other officers. Maybe I shouldn't have spoken in front of them, but I'm no diplomat. I joined the hussars because I thought there was no need for subtleties here, but he calls me a liar . . . so let him give me satisfaction . . ."

"That's all well and good, nobody thinks you're a coward, but that's not the point. Ask Denisov what it looks like if a junker demands satisfaction from a regimental commander."

Denisov, chewing his moustache, was listening to the conversation with a gloomy air, apparently unwilling to enter into it. To the staff captain's question he shook his head negatively.

"You tell the regimental commander about this muck in front of officers," the staff captain went on. "Bogdanych" (the regimental commander was known as Bogdanych) "brings you up short."

"He didn't bring me up short, he said I wasn't telling the truth."

"Well, yes, and you said a heap of foolish things to him, and you've got to apologize."

"Not for anything!" cried Rostov.

"I wouldn't have thought it of you," the staff captain said gravely and sternly. "You don't want to apologize, but you, my dear boy, are to blame all round, not only before him, but before the whole regiment, before us all. And here's how: you might have reflected and taken advice on how to handle this matter, but you blurted it right out, and in front of officers. What's the regimental commander to do now? Should he prosecute the officer and besmirch the whole regiment? Disgrace the whole regiment because of one scoundrel? Is that your view of it? Well, it's not ours. And Bogdanych is a fine fellow for saying you weren't telling the truth. It's unpleasant, but what's to be done, my dear boy, you asked for it. And now, when the affair should be hushed up, out of some sort of cockiness you refuse to apologize, but want to have it all out. It offends you that you have to go on duty, but what is it for you to apologize to an old and honourable officer! Whatever Bogdanych may have done, he is, after all, an honourable and brave old colonel—and yet you're offended, and to besmirch the whole regiment is nothing to you!" The staff captain's voice began to tremble. "You, my dear boy, have been with the regiment next to no time; here today, tomorrow somewhere else as a little adjutant; you couldn't care less if people say: 'There are thieves among the Pavlogradsky officers!' But it's not all the same to us. Isn't that right, Denisov? It's not all the same?"

Denisov still kept silent and did not stir, glancing at Rostov from time to time with his shining black eyes.

"Your cockiness is dear to you, you don't feel like apologizing," the staff captain went on, "but for us old-timers, since we've grown up and, God willing, will die serving in the regiment, the honour of the regiment is dear to us, and Bogdanych knows it. Oh, how dear it is! And this is not good, not good. Whether it offends you or not, I always speak the plain truth. It's not good!"

And the staff captain got up and turned away from Rostov.

"Tghrue, devil take it!" shouted Denisov, jumping up. "Well, so, Ghrostov!"

Rostov, blushing and paling, looked now at the one, now at the other officer.

"No, gentlemen, no . . . don't think . . . I understand very well, you're wrong to think it of me . . . I . . . for me . . . for the honour of the regiment . . . well, so? I'll show it by my deeds, and for me the honour of the flag . . . Well, anyhow, it's true, I'm to blame! . . ." Tears welled up in his eyes. "I'm to blame, I'm to blame all round! Well, what more do you want? . . ."

"That's the way, Count!" the staff captain cried, turning and slapping him on the shoulder with his big hand.

"It's tghrue what I told you," shouted Denisov, "he's a good lad!"

"That's better, Count!" the staff captain repeated, as if beginning to call him by his title on account of his acknowledgement. "Go and apologize, Your Excellency, yes, sir."

"Gentlemen, I'll do anything, nobody will hear a word from me," Rostov said in a pleading voice, "but apologize I cannot, by God, I cannot, do what you will! How am I going to apologize, like a little boy asking forgiveness?"

Denisov laughed.

"So much the worse for you. Bogdanych is rancorous, you'll pay for your stubbornness," said Kirsten.

"By God, it's not stubbornness! I can't describe the feeling to you, I can't . . ."

"Well, as you will," said the staff captain. "So, what's become of the blackguard now?" he asked Denisov.

"He's ghreported himself sick, as of tomoghrrow he's been ordered stghruck off," said Denisov.

"It's a sickness, there's no other explanation," said the staff captain.

"Sickness or no sickness, he'd better not show his face to me—I'll kill him!" Denisov shouted out bloodthirstily.

Zherkov came into the room.

"What brings you here?" the officers suddenly addressed the newcomer.

"On the march, gentlemen. Mack has surrendered and his whole army with him."

"No!"

"I saw him myself."

"What? Saw Mack alive? with all his arms and legs?"

"On the march! On the march! Give him a bottle for such news. How did you wind up here?"

"I've been sent back to the regiment again on account of this devil, this

Mack. An Austrian general made a complaint. I congratulated him on Mack's arrival . . . What's with you, Rostov, come straight from the bathhouse?"

"We've had a mess brewing here, brother, for two days now."

A regimental adjutant came in and confirmed the news brought by Zherkov. The orders were to set out the next day.

"On the march, gentlemen!"

"Well, thank God, we've sat enough."

VI

Kutuzov fell back towards Vienna, destroying behind him the bridges over the rivers Inn (in Braunau) and Traun (in Linz). On the twenty-third of October, the Russian troops were crossing the river Enns. At midday Russian transport, artillery, and troop columns were strung out through the town of Enns, on both sides of the bridge.

The day was warm, autumnal, and rainy. The vast prospect that opened out from the height where the Russian batteries stood, defending the bridge, was now suddenly covered by a muslin curtain of slanting rain, then suddenly widened out, and in the sunlight objects became visible and clear in the distance, as if freshly varnished. At one's feet one could see the little town with its white houses and red roofs, the cathedral, and the bridge, on both sides of which streamed crowding masses of Russian troops. At the bend of the Danube one could see boats and an island, and a castle with a park, surrounded by the waters of the Enns falling into the Danube; one could see the left bank of the Danube, rocky and covered with pine forest, with a mysterious distance of green treetops and bluish gorges. One could see the towers of a convent looming up from the pine forest with its wild and untouched look, and far away on a hilltop, on the other side of the Enns, one could see the mounted patrols of the enemy.

Amidst the cannons on the height, the general in charge of the rear guard stood out in front with an officer of the suite, examining the area through a spyglass. Slightly behind him on the trail of a cannon sat Nesvitsky, sent to the rear guard by the commander in chief. The Cossack who accompanied Nesvitsky handed him a bag and a flask, and Nesvitsky treated the officers to savoury little pies and real *Doppelkümmel*. The officers joyfully surrounded him, some kneeling, some sitting Turkish fashion on the wet grass.

"Yes, the Austrian prince who built a castle here was no fool. A fine place. Why aren't you eating, gentlemen?" said Nesvitsky.

"I humbly thank you, Prince," replied one of the officers, taking pleasure in conversing with such an important staff official. "An excellent place. We passed just by the park, saw two deer, and such a wonderful house!"

"Look, Prince," said another, who very much wanted to take one more little pie, but was embarrassed, and who therefore pretended to be surveying the area, "look, our infantrymen have already got in there. Over there in the little meadow beyond the village, three of them are dragging something. They'll ransack that castle," he said with obvious approval.

"They will, they will," said Nesvitsky. "No, but what I'd like," he added, chewing a little pie with his handsome, moist mouth, "is to climb in there."

He pointed to the convent with its towers, visible on the hilltop. He smiled, his eyes narrowed and lit up.

"Wouldn't that be nice, gentlemen?"

The officers laughed.

"At least to put a fright into those little nuns. There are some Italian girls, young ones, they say. Really, I'd give five years of my life!"

"They must be bored, too," an officer, a bolder one, said laughing.

Meanwhile, the officer of the suite, who was standing in front, was pointing something out to the general; the general was looking through the glass.

"Well, that's it, that's it," the general said angrily, taking the glass from his eye and shrugging his shoulders, "that's it, they're going to fire on the crossing. And what are they dawdling for?"

On the other side the naked eye could make out the enemy and his battery, from which a puff of milk-white smoke appeared. The smoke was followed by the sound of a distant shot, and it could be seen how our troops speeded up at the crossing.

Nesvitsky, huffing, got up and, smiling, went over to the general.

"Wouldn't Your Excellency like a bite to eat?" he said.

"A bad business," said the general, not answering him, "our men have been dawdling."

"Shouldn't I ride over, Your Excellency?" said Nesvitsky.

"Yes, please do," said the general, repeating what had already been ordered in detail, "and tell the hussars that they are to cross last and set fire to the bridge as I said, and inspect the flammable material while still on the bridge."

"Very good, sir," replied Nesvitsky.

He called the Cossack with the horse, told him to put the bag and flask away, and lightly swung his heavy body into the saddle.

"I'll stop by those nuns, really," he said to the officers, who were looking at him smilingly, and rode down the hill along a winding path.

"Well, let's give it a try, Captain, see how far it will carry!" said the general, turning to the artillerist. "Have some fun out of boredom."

"Crew, to your pieces!" the officer commanded, and in a minute the artillery crew ran merrily from their campfires and loaded up.

"One!" came the command.

Number one leaped back briskly. A deafening metallic sound rang out, and a shell flew whistling over the heads of all our men at the foot of the hill and, falling far short of the enemy, showed by a puff of smoke the place where it hit and burst.

The faces of the soldiers and officers cheered up at this sound; everybody stood up and began watching the movements of our troops below, visible as on the palm of the hand, and further away the movements of the advancing enemy. Just then the sun came all the way out from behind the clouds, and the beautiful sound of the solitary shot and the shining of the bright sun merged into one cheerful and merry impression.

VII

Two enemy cannonballs had already gone flying over the bridge, and there was a crush on the bridge itself. In the middle of the bridge, dismounted from his horse, his fat body pressed to the railing, stood Prince Nesvitsky. He looked back laughingly at his Cossack, who stood a few paces behind him holding the two horses by the bridle. The moment Prince Nesvitsky tried to move on, soldiers and carts pushed him back and pressed him to the railing again, and there was nothing left for him but to smile.

"You there, brother!" the Cossack said to a supply soldier with a cart, who was pushing through the infantrymen crowded right against his wheels and horses, "you there! As if you can't wait: look, the general needs to pass."

But the supply soldier, paying no heed the denomination of general, shouted at the soldiers who blocked his way:

"Hey, countrymen! keep to the left, hold up!"

But the countrymen, pressed shoulder to shoulder, catching on their bayonets and never pausing, moved across the bridge in a solid mass. Looking down over the railing, Prince Nesvitsky saw the swift, noisy, low waves of the Enns, which, merging, rippling, and swirling around the pilings of the bridge, drove on one after the other. Looking at the bridge, he saw the same monotonous living waves of soldiers, shoulder braids, shakos with dustcovers, packs, bayonets, long muskets, and under the shakos faces with wide cheekbones, sunken cheeks, and carefree, weary faces, and feet moving over the sticky mud that covered the planks of the bridge. Occasionally, amidst the monotonous waves of soldiers, like a spray of white foam on the waves of the Enns, an officer pushed his way through, in a cape, with his physiognomy distinct from the soldiers'; occasionally, like a chip of wood swirled along by the river, a dismounted hussar, an orderly, or a local inhabitant was borne across the bridge by the waves of infantry; occasionally, like a log floating down the river, a company's or an officer's cart floated across the bridge, surrounded on all sides, loaded to the top, and covered with leather.

"Look at 'em, it's like a dam burst," the Cossack said, stopping hopelessly. "Are there many of you there?"

"One shy of a million," a merry soldier in a torn greatcoat, passing close by, said with a wink and vanished; after him came another old soldier.

"Once *he*" (*he* was the enemy) "starts peppering the bridge," the old soldier said gloomily, addressing his comrade, "you'll forget about scratching yourself."

And the soldier passed by. After him came another soldier on a cart.

"Where the devil did you stuff those foot cloths?" said an orderly, running behind the cart and rummaging in the back.

And this one passed by with the cart.

After him came some merry and apparently tipsy soldiers.

"He just gave it to him, the dear fellow, right in the teeth with his musket butt . . ." one soldier in a high-tucked greatcoat said joyfully, swinging his arm widely.

"That's it, the sweet taste of ham," replied another with a guffaw.

And they passed by, so that Nesvitsky never learned who got it in the teeth and what the ham referred to.

"Look at 'em scurrying! *He* fires off a cold one, and you'd think they were all getting killed," a warrant officer said angrily and reproachfully.

"When that cannonball went flying by me, uncle," a young soldier with a huge mouth said, barely holding back his laughter, "I just went dead. By God, I got scared really bad!" the soldier said, as if boasting that he was scared.

And that one passed by. After him came a cart unlike all those that had driven by so far. It was a German *Vorspann* and pair, loaded with what seemed like a whole household; behind the *Vorspann*, led by a German, was tied a beautiful spotted cow with a huge udder. A woman with a nursing baby, an old woman, and a young, healthy German girl with purple-red cheeks were sitting on featherbeds. It was clear that these were local people, who had been allowed to move by special permission. The eyes of all the soldiers turned to the women, and as the cart went by, moving step by step, all the soldiers' remarks were addressed only to these two women. All the soldiers' faces bore virtually one and the same smile of indecent thoughts about these women.

"Look, the sausage is also taking off!"

"Sell me the little lady," another soldier said, with a stress on the last syllable, addressing the German, who, lowering his eyes, walked on with big strides, angry and frightened.

"Look how dressed up she is! The devils!"

"Nice to get billeted on them, Fedotov!"

"I should live so long, brother!"

"Where are you going?" asked an infantry officer, eating an apple, also with a half smile and looking at the beautiful girl.

The German shut his eyes to show that he did not understand.

"If you want it, take it," said the officer, handing the apple to the girl.

The girl smiled and took it. Like everyone else on the bridge, Nesvitsky never took his eyes off the women until they had passed. Once they had passed, there again came the same soldiers, with the same talk, and finally everybody stopped. As often happens, the horses pulling the company cart balked at the exit from the bridge, and the whole crowd had to wait.

"What did they stop for? There's no order!" said the soldiers. "What's this shoving ahead? Devil take it! There's such a thing as waiting. It'll be worse if *he* sets fire to the bridge. See, even the officer got shoved aside," the halted crowds were saying on different sides, looking at each other, and still pressing forward towards the exit.

Having looked under the bridge at the waters of the Enns, Nesvitsky suddenly heard a sound still new to him, the swift approach of . . . something big, and something splashed into the water.

"See what he's fixing on!" a soldier standing nearby said sternly, turning towards the sound.

"He's hustling us so we'll cross quicker," another said uneasily.

The crowd started moving again. Nesvitsky realized that it was a cannonball.

"Hey, Cossack, my horse!" he said. "Hey, you! Aside, step aside! make way!"

With great effort he reached his horse. Shouting constantly, he began to move ahead. The soldiers pressed back to let him pass, then pressed together again so hard that his leg was squashed, and those closest to him were not to blame, for they were pressed still harder.

"Nesvitsky! Nesvitsky! You ghrascal!" a hoarse voice came from behind just then.

Nesvitsky turned and saw, fifteen paces away, separated from him by the living mass of moving infantry, red, black, dishevelled, his peaked cap pushed back, his dolman thrown dashingly over his shoulder—Vaska Denisov.

"Tell these damned devils to clear the ghroad!" shouted Denisov, obviously in a fit of temper, his coal-black eyes with bloodshot whites rolling and shining, and waving his sheathed sabre, which he held in a small, bare hand as red as his face.

"Hey! Vasya!" Nesvitsky replied joyfully. "What's the matter?"

"The squadghron can't pass," shouted Vaska Denisov, angrily baring his white teeth, spurring his handsome raven-black Bedouin, who, twitching his ears from running into bayonets, snorting, spraying foam around him from his bit, jingling, stamped his hooves on the planks of the bridge and seemed ready to jump over the railing if his rider would let him.

"What is this? like sheep! just like sheep! Away! . . . clear the ghroad! Wait, you there! you with the caghrt, you devil! I'll take my swoghrd to you!" he shouted, actually drawing his sabre and beginning to wave it.

The soldiers pressed close together with frightened faces, and Denisov joined Nesvitsky.

"How is it you're not drunk today?" Nesvitsky said to Denisov, when he rode up to him.

"They don't even give us time to dghrink!" replied Vaska Denisov. "They dghrag the ghregiment here and there all day. If it's fighting, it's fighting. Or else devil knows what it is!"

"What a dandy you are today!" said Nesvitsky, looking over his new dolman and saddlecloth.

Denisov smiled, took from his pouch a handkerchief that gave off a smell of scent, and put it to Nesvitsky's nose.

"Have to be, I'm going into action! Shaved, bghrushed my teeth, and doused myself with scent."

The stately figure of Nesvitsky, accompanied by the Cossack, and the resoluteness of Denisov, waving his sabre and shouting desperately, had such an effect that they pushed through to the other end of the bridge and stopped the infantry. At the exit Nesvitsky found the colonel to whom he was to give the order, and, having fulfilled his mission, rode back again.

Having cleared the road, Denisov stopped at the entrance to the bridge. Casually holding back his stallion, who was straining towards his fellows and stamping his foot, he looked at the squadron that was moving towards him. The transparent sounds of hooves rang out on the planks of the bridge, as if several horses were galloping, and the squadron, with officers in front, four men abreast, stretched across the bridge and began to come out on the other side.

The halted infantry soldiers, crowding in the trampled mud by the bridge, gazed at the clean, foppish hussars going past them in order, with that special feeling of ill will, alienation, and mockery with which different branches of the military usually meet each other.

"Spruced-up lads! Fit for the fairground!"

"What's the good of them! They're only led around for show!" said another.

"Don't raise dust, you footsloggers!" joked a hussar, whose horse, prancing, splashed mud at the infantryman.

"Make a couple of marches with a pack on your back, your fancy trim will turn shabby," the infantryman said, wiping the mud from his face with his sleeve, "or maybe it's not a man but a bird perched up there!"

"Wouldn't you be a nimble one, Zikin, if they set you on a horse," a corporal joked to a thin little soldier bent under a heavy pack.

"Put a stick between your legs, that'll do you for a horse," rejoined the hussar.

VIII

The rest of the infantry hurriedly crossed the bridge, squeezing into a funnel at the entrance. Finally all the carts passed over, the crush eased up, and the last battalion entered the bridge. Only the hussars of Denisov's squadron remained on the other side of the bridge facing the enemy. The enemy, visible in the distance from the opposite hill, were not yet visible from the bridge below, because, from the bottom where the river flowed, the horizon was bounded by the opposite heights less than half a mile away. Ahead was a deserted space over which clusters of our Cossack patrols moved here and there. Suddenly on the road going up the opposite heights appeared troops in blue coats and artillery. It was the French. A Cossack patrol moved down the hill at a trot. All the officers and men of Denisov's squadron, though they tried to talk about unrelated things and look elsewhere, constantly thought only about what was there on the hill, and kept peering at the spots that appeared on the horizon, which they recognized as enemy troops. After midday the weather cleared again, the sun shone brightly, going down over the Danube and the dark hills around it. It was still, and once in a while from that hill floated the sounds of bugles and the shouts of the enemy. Between the squadron and the enemy there was now nothing but some small patrols. They were separated by an empty space of about six hundred yards. The enemy stopped shooting, and that strict, menacing, inaccessible, and elusive line that separates two enemy armies became all the more clearly felt.

"One step beyond that line, reminiscent of the line separating the living from the dead, and it's the unknown, suffering, and death. And what is there? who is there? there, beyond this field, and the tree, and the roof lit by the sun? No one knows, and you would like to know; and you're afraid to cross that line, and would like to cross it; and you know that sooner or later you will have to cross it and find out what is there on the other side of the line, as you will inevitably find out what is there on the other side of death. And you're strong, healthy, cheerful, and excited, and surrounded by people just as strong and excitedly animated." So, if he does not think it, every man feels who finds himself within sight of an enemy, and this feeling gives a particular brilliance and joyful sharpness of impression to everything that happens in those moments.

On a knoll occupied by the enemy, the smoke of a shot appeared, and a cannonball flew whistling over the heads of the hussar squadron. The officers, who were standing together, rode to their posts. The hussars assiduously began lining up their horses. Everything became hushed in the squadron. Everyone kept looking ahead at the enemy and at the squadron commander, awaiting a command. Another cannonball flew over, then a third. Obviously, the shots were aimed at the hussars; but the cannonballs, with a rapid, steady whistling, kept flying over the hussars' heads and hitting somewhere behind them. The hussars did not look back, but with each sound of a flying cannonball, the whole squadron, as if on command, with all their similarly dissimilar faces, holding their breath while the cannonball flew over, rose in their stirrups, then lowered themselves again. Without turning their heads, the soldiers looked sideways at each other, curious to spy out a comrade's impressions. On each face, from Denisov's down to the bugler's, there appeared around the lips and chin one common trait of a struggle between irritation and excitement. The sergeant major frowned, looking the soldiers over as if threatening them with punishment. Junker Mironov ducked down each time a cannonball flew by. Rostov, standing on the left flank, on his slightly lame but imposing Little Rook, had the happy air of a schoolboy called up before a large public at an examination in which he is sure he will distinguish himself. He looked around at them all serenely and brightly, as if asking them to pay attention to how calmly he stood under fire. But on his face, too, that same trait of something new and stern appeared, against his will, around the mouth.

"Who's that bowing there? Junker Mighronov! Not ghright, look at me!" shouted Denisov, who could not stay still and fidgeted on his horse in front of the squadron.

Vaska Denisov's pug-nosed and black-haired face, and his whole small, compact figure with his sinewy hand (the short fingers covered with hair), in which he gripped the hilt of his bared sabre, was the same as ever, especially towards evening, after drinking a couple of bottles. Only he was more red than usual and, throwing his shaggy head back, the way birds do when they drink, and mercilessly digging the spurs on his small feet into the sides of the good Bedouin, he galloped off, as if falling backwards, to the other flank of the squadron and shouted in a hoarse voice that they should inspect their pistols. He rode up to Kirsten. The staff captain, on his broad and sedate mare, rode slowly to meet Denisov. The staff captain, with his long moustaches, was as serious as ever, only his eyes shone more than usual.

"Well, what?" he said to Denisov. "It won't come to a fight. You'll see, we'll withdraw."

"Devil knows what they're up to!" Denisov grumbled. "Ah! Ghrostov!" he cried to the junker, noticing his cheerful face. "Well, you're done waiting!"

And he smiled approvingly, obviously glad for the junker. Rostov felt himself perfectly happy. Just then the commander appeared on the bridge. Denisov galloped towards him.

"Your Excellency! allow us to attack! I'll cghrush them!"

"Attack, indeed!" the colonel said in a bored voice, wincing as if a fly was pestering him. "And why are you standing here? You can see the flanks are retreating. Bring the squadron back across."

The squadron crossed the bridge and moved out of the range of fire without losing a single man. After them the second squadron, forming a line, also crossed, and the last Cossacks cleared off from that side.

Having crossed the bridge, the two squadrons of the Pavlogradsky hussars went back up the hill one after the other. The regimental commander, Karl Bogdanovich Schubert, rode over to Denisov's squadron and fell in step with them not far from Rostov, paying no attention to him, though this was the first time they had seen each other since their confrontation over Telyanin. Rostov, feeling himself at the front and in the power of a man before whom he now considered himself guilty, fixed his eyes on the athletic back, blond nape, and red neck of the regimental commander. At first it seemed to Rostov that Bogdanych was only pretending to be inattentive and that his whole goal now consisted in testing the junker's courage, and he sat up straight and looked around cheerfully. Then it seemed to him that Bogdanych was deliberately riding close to him in order to show Rostov his own courage. Then he thought that his enemy would now deliberately send the squadron into a desperate attack in order to punish him, Rostov. Then he thought that, after the attack, he would come to him as he lay wounded and magnanimously offer him a conciliatory hand.

Zherkov, with his shoulders raised high, a familiar figure to the Pavlogradsky hussars (he had recently quit their regiment), rode up to the regimental commander. After his expulsion from the head staff, Zherkov had not remained with the regiment, saying that he was no fool to drudge away at the front when he could get more decorations while doing nothing on the staff, and he had managed to set himself up as an orderly officer for Prince Bagration. He came to his former superior with an order from the commander of the rear guard.

"Colonel," he said with his gloomy earnestness, addressing Rostov's enemy and looking around at his comrades, "there is an order to stop and set fire to the bridge."

"An order of who?" the colonel asked sullenly.

"I don't know *of who,* Colonel," the cornet replied earnestly, "only the prince told me: 'Go and tell the colonel that the hussars must turn back quickly and set fire to the bridge.' "

After Zherkov, an officer of the suite rode up to the hussar colonel with the same order. After the officer of the suite, on a Cossack horse that was barely able to gallop under him, fat Nesvitsky rode up.

"What is this, Colonel?" he cried while still riding. "I told you to set fire to the bridge, and somebody got it wrong; everybody's going crazy there, they can't figure it out."

The colonel unhurriedly halted his regiment and turned to Nesvitsky.

"You spoke to me about flammable material," he said, "but you said nothing to me about setting *feuer* to it."

"What do you mean, my dear man?" Nesvitsky said, stopping, taking off his cap, and smoothing his sweat-dampened hair with a plump hand. "What do you mean I didn't tell you to set fire to the bridge, since you put flammable material there?"

"I am not 'dear man' to you, Mister Staff Officer, and you did not tell me to set *feuer* to the bridge! I know the serfiss, and I am habituated to strictly fulfilling orders. You said the bridge vas to be set on *feuer,* but who vould set it on *feuer* I cannot know by the Holy Spirit . . ."

"It's always like that," Nesvitsky said, waving his hand. "What are you doing here?" he turned to Zherkov.

"The same as you. You're soaking wet, though, let me wring you out."

"You said, Mister Staff Officer . . ." the colonel went on in an offended tone.

"Colonel," the officer of the suite interrupted, "you must hurry, otherwise the enemy will move up his canister guns."

The colonel looked silently at the officer of the suite, at the fat staff officer, at Zherkov, and frowned.

"I vill set *feuer* to the bridge," he said in a solemn tone, as if to show that, despite all the unpleasantness done to him, he would still do what he had to do.

Striking his horse with his long, muscular legs, as if it was all the horse's fault, the colonel moved forward and commanded the second squadron, the one in which Rostov served under Denisov, to go back to the bridge.

"Well, that's it," thought Rostov, "he wants to test me!" His heart contracted and the blood rushed to his face. "Let him see whether I'm a coward," he thought.

Again there appeared on all the cheerful faces of the men of the squadron that serious trait that had been there when they were under fire. Rostov, never taking his eyes away, kept looking at his enemy, the regimental commander, wishing to find on his face a confirmation of his surmises; but the colonel never once glanced at Rostov, but, as always at the front, looked stern and solemn. The command was heard.

"Step lively! Step lively!" several voices said near him.

Their sabres catching in their bridles, their spurs jingling, the hussars hurriedly dismounted, not knowing themselves what they were going to do. The hussars crossed themselves. Rostov no longer looked at the regimental commander—he had no time. He was afraid, with a sinking heart he was afraid to lag behind the hussars. His hand shook as he turned his horse over to the handler, and he felt the blood throbbing as it rose to his heart. Denisov, lurching backwards and shouting something, rode past him. Rostov saw nothing but the hussars running around him, their spurs catching and their sabres clanking.

"Stretcher!" someone's voice shouted behind.

Rostov did not think of what the call for a stretcher meant; he ran on, trying only to be ahead of everyone else; but just by the bridge, not looking under his feet, he got into the slimy, trampled mud, stumbled, and fell on his hands. Others ran past him.

"On *bote* sides, Captain," he heard the voice of the regimental commander, who, having ridden ahead, stood mounted near the bridge with a triumphant and merry face.

Rostov, wiping his muddy hands on his breeches, looked at his enemy and wanted to run further, supposing that the further ahead he got, the better it would be. But Bogdanych, though he neither looked at nor recognized Rostov, shouted at him.

"Who's that running in the middle of the bridge? Keep to the right! Back, junker!" he cried out angrily and turned to Denisov, who, flaunting his courage, rode out onto the planks of the bridge.

"*Vy riskiert*, Captain! Better dismount," said the colonel.

"Eh! it'll find the one it's meant for," replied Denisov, turning on his saddle.

Meanwhile, Nesvitsky, Zherkov, and the officer of the suite stood together out of the range of fire and looking at this small bunch of men in yellow shakos, dark green jackets embroidered with cord, and blue breeches, pottering about by the bridge and, on the other side, at blue coats and groups with horses, which could easily be identified as artillery, approaching in the distance.

"Will they set fire to it or won't they? Who'll be first? Will they run and set fire to the bridge, or will the French come within canister-shot range and kill them all?" These questions were involuntarily asked with sinking heart by each man of that large mass of troops which stood above the bridge and in the bright evening light looked at the bridge and the hussars and, on the other side, at the advancing blue coats with bayonets and guns.

"Ah! the hussars are going to get it!" said Nesvitsky. "It's close enough for canister shot now."

"He shouldn't have taken so many men," said the officer of the suite.

"Indeed not," said Nesvitsky. "If he'd sent two brave lads, it would be the same."

"Ah, Your Excellency," Zherkov mixed in, not taking his eyes from the hussars, but still with his naïve manner, which made it impossible to tell whether he was speaking seriously or not. "Ah, Your Excellency! What a way to reason! Send two men, and who's going to give us a Vladimir with a bow?[5] This way they may get beaten, but the squadron will be distinguished, and he'll get a bow. Our Bogdanych knows the system."

"Well," said the officer of the suite, "there's the canisters!"

He pointed to the French guns, which were being taken from their limbers and hurriedly deployed.

On the French side, among those groups where the guns were, a puff of smoke appeared, a second, a third almost simultaneously, and just as the sound of the first shot reached them, a fourth appeared. Two sounds one after another, and a third.

"Oh, oh!" gasped Nesvitsky, as if from burning pain, seizing the officer of the suite by the arm. "Look, he's fallen, one of them has fallen, fallen!"

"Two of them, I believe?"

"If I were the tsar, I'd never go to war," Nesvitsky said, turning away.

The French guns were being hurriedly reloaded. The infantry in blue coats moved towards the bridge at a run. Again puffs of smoke appeared at various intervals, and canister shot went crackling and rattling over the bridge. But this time Nesvitsky could not see what was happening on the bridge. Thick smoke rose from it. The hussars had managed to set fire to the bridge, and the French batteries were now shooting not in order to hinder them, but because the guns had been aimed and there were people to shoot at.

The French managed to fire three rounds of canister shot before the hussars got back to the horse-tenders. Two of the rounds were poorly aimed and all the shot went overhead, but the last round landed in the middle of a bunch of hussars and brought down three of them.

Rostov, preoccupied by his relations with Bogdanych, stopped on the bridge, not knowing what to do with himself. There was no one to cut down (as he had always pictured battle to himself), nor could he help set fire to the bridge, because, unlike the other soldiers, he had not brought a plait of straw with him. He was standing and looking about, when suddenly there was a rattling on the bridge, as if someone had spilled nuts, and one of the hussars, the one nearest him, fell on the railing with a groan. Rostov ran to him with the others. Again someone cried: "Stretcher!" Four men took hold of the hussar and began to lift him up.

"Oooh! Leave me alone, for Christ's sake," the wounded man cried; but all the same they lifted him up and laid him on the stretcher.

Nikolai Rostov turned away, and, as if searching for something, began looking at the distance, at the waters of the Danube, at the sky, at the sun! How good the sky seemed, how blue, calm, and deep! How bright and solemn the setting sun! How tenderly and lustrously glistened the waters of the distant Danube! And better still were the distant blue hills beyond the Danube, the convent, the mysterious gorges, the pine forests bathed in mist to their tops . . . there was peace, happiness . . . "There's nothing, nothing I would wish for, there's nothing I would wish for, if only I were there," thought Rostov. "In me alone and in this sun there is so much happiness, but here . . . groans, suffering, fear, and this obscurity, this hurry . . . Again they're shouting something, and again everybody's run back somewhere, and I'm running with them, and here it is, here it is, death, above me, around me . . . An instant, and I'll never again see this sun, this water, this gorge . . ."

Just then the sun began to hide itself behind the clouds. Ahead of Rostov, another stretcher appeared. And his fear of death and the stretcher, and his love of the sun and life—all merged into one painfully disturbing impression.

"Lord God! the one there in this sky, save, forgive, and protect me!" Rostov whispered to himself.

The hussars ran up to the handlers, the voices became louder and calmer, the stretchers disappeared from sight.

"What, bghrother, got a whiff of powder?" Denisov's voice shouted by his ear.

"It's all over, but I'm a coward, yes, I'm a coward," thought Rostov and, sighing deeply, he took his lame Little Rook from the handler and began to mount.

"What was it, canister shot?" he asked Denisov.

"And then some!" shouted Denisov. "Good work, lads! And it was a ghrotten job! Attacking's a lovely thing, cut 'em to pieces, but here, devil knows, it's more like target pghractice."

And Denisov rode off to a group that had stopped not far from Rostov: the regimental commander, Nesvitsky, Zherkov, and the officer of the suite.

"However, it seems nobody noticed," Rostov thought to himself. And indeed no one had noticed anything, because they were all familiar with the feeling a junker experiences when he is under fire for the first time.

"There'll be a report in it for you," said Zherkov. "Just see if I don't get promoted sub-lieutenant."

"Inform the prince that I haf set *feuer* to the bridge," the colonel said triumphantly and cheerfully.

"And what if he asks about the losses?"

"Trifles!" the colonel boomed. "Two hussars wounded and one *killed on the spot*," he said with obvious joy, unable to hold back a happy smile, sonorously rapping out the beautiful phrase *killed on the spot*.

IX

Pursued by the hundred-thousand-man French army under the leadership of Bonaparte, encountering a hostile local populace, no longer trusting their allies, suffering from a shortness of supplies, and forced to act outside all foreseeable conditions of war, the thirty-five-thousand-man Russian army, under the leadership of Kutuzov, hastily retreated down the Danube, stopping whenever the enemy caught up with it and fighting rear-guard actions, only insofar as it was necessary in order to retreat without loss of heavy equipment. There was action at Lambach, Amstetten, and Mölk;[6] but despite the courage and steadfastness, acknowledged by the enemy themselves, with which the Russians fought, the result of these actions was only a still speedier retreat. The

Austrian troops that had escaped capture at Ulm and joined Kutuzov at Braunau now separated from the Russian army, and Kutuzov was left with nothing
but his own weak, exhausted forces. To defend Vienna was no longer thinkable. Instead of the offensive war, profoundly thought out according to the
laws of the new science of strategy, the plan of which had been given to Kutuzov while in Vienna by the Austrian Hofkriegsrath, the sole, almost unattainable goal now remaining for Kutuzov was to unite with the troops coming
from Russia without losing his own army, as Mack had done at Ulm.

On the twenty-eighth of October, Kutuzov crossed with his army to the left
bank of the Danube and halted for the first time, having put the Danube
between himself and the main forces of the French. On the thirtieth he attacked
Mortier's division, which was on the left bank of the Danube, and crushed it.
In this action trophies were taken for the first time: a banner, cannon, and two
enemy generals. For the first time, after a two-week retreat, the Russian troops
halted and after the fighting not only held the field of battle but drove the
French away. Despite the fact that the troops were ill-clad, worn-out, weakened by a third with the stragglers, the wounded, the dead, and the sick;
despite the fact that the sick and the wounded had been left on the other side of
the Danube with a letter from Kutuzov entrusting them to the humaneness
of the enemy; despite the fact that the big hospitals and the houses in Krems
that had been turned into infirmaries could no longer accommodate all the
sick and wounded—despite all that, the halt at Krems and the victory over
Mortier raised the spirits of the troops significantly. Throughout the army and
in headquarters joyful, though incorrect, rumours were rife about the imaginary approach of columns from Russia, about some victory won by the Austrians, and about the retreat of the frightened Bonaparte.

At the time of the battle, Prince Andrei was attached to the Austrian general
Schmidt, killed in that action. His horse had been shot from under him, and his
arm had been slightly grazed by a bullet. As a sign of special favour, the commander in chief had sent him with news of the victory to the Austrian court, no
longer in Vienna, which was threatened by the French, but in Brünn. On the
night of the battle, Prince Andrei, agitated but not tired (despite his apparently
slight build, Prince Andrei could endure physical fatigue far better than the
strongest people), having come on horseback with a message from Dokhturov
to Kutuzov in Krems, was sent that same night as a courier to Brünn. Being
sent as a courier, apart from its rewards, also signified an important step
towards promotion.

The night was dark, starry; the road lay black amidst the white snow that
had fallen that day, the day of the battle. Now going over his impressions of the
past battle, now joyfully imagining the impression he would make with his
news of the victory, recalling his leave-taking from the commander in chief and
his comrades, Prince Andrei galloped along in a post britzka, experiencing the

feeling of a man who has long been awaiting and has finally achieved the beginning of the happiness he desired. As soon as he closed his eyes, the firing of muskets and cannon resounded in his ears, merging with the rattle of the carriage and the impression of the victory. Now he would begin to imagine that the Russians were fleeing, that he himself had been killed; but then he would hurriedly wake up and happily learn as if for the first time that none of it had happened and that, on the contrary, the French had fled. He would recall once more all the details of the victory, his calm manliness during the battle, and, reassured, would doze off . . . After the dark starry night came a bright, cheerful morning. The snow melted in the sun, the horses galloped swiftly, and to right and left alike passed new and various forests, fields, villages.

At one of the posting stations he overtook a convoy carrying Russian wounded. The Russian officer who was leading the transport, sprawled in the front cart, shouted something, abusing a soldier in rude terms. Six or more pale, bandaged, and dirty wounded went jolting down the rocky road in each of the long German *Vorspanns*. Some of them were talking (he heard Russian speech), others were eating bread, the most seriously wounded gazed at the courier galloping past them silently, with a meek and sickly childish interest.

Prince Andrei ordered the driver to stop and asked the soldiers what action they had been wounded in.

"Two days ago on the Danube," a soldier replied. Prince Andrei took out a purse and gave the soldier three gold pieces.

"For all of you," he added, addressing the approaching officer. "Get well, lads," he said to the soldiers, "there's still a lot to be done."

"Well, Mister Adjutant, what news?" asked the officer, obviously wishing to strike up a conversation.

"Good news! . . . Drive on," he cried to the coachman and galloped on his way.

It was already quite dark when Prince Andrei drove into Brünn and saw himself surrounded by tall buildings, lighted shops, windows, street lamps, fine carriages noisily driving over the pavement, and all the atmosphere of a big, lively town, which is always so attractive for a military man after camp life. Prince Andrei, despite the quick driving and the sleepless night, felt himself still more animated than the day before as he pulled up to the palace. Only his eyes shone with a feverish gleam and his thoughts followed one another with extraordinary speed and clarity. He vividly pictured again all the details of the battle, not vaguely now, but in the well-defined, concise account which, in his imagination, he was giving to the emperor Franz. He vividly pictured the casual questions that might be put to him and the answers he would give to them. He supposed that he would be presented to the emperor at once. But at the main entrance to the palace, an official came running out to him and, recognizing that he was a courier, led him to another entrance.

"To the right from the corridor; there, *Euer Hochgeboren,** you will find the imperial adjutant on duty," said the official. "He will take you to the minister of war."

The imperial adjutant on duty, meeting Prince Andrei, asked him to wait and went to the minister of war. Five minutes later the imperial adjutant returned and, inclining with particular courtesy and letting Prince Andrei go ahead of him, led him down the corridor to the office where the minister of war worked. The imperial adjutant seemed to want to protect himself from any attempts at familiarity from the Russian adjutant. Prince Andrei's joyful feeling weakened significantly as he approached the doors of the minister of war's office. He felt offended, and the feeling of offence turned that same instant, without his noticing it, into a feeling of totally groundless scorn. His resourceful mind suggested to him that same instant the point of view from which he had the right to scorn both the adjutant and the minister of war. "To him it must seem very easy to win a victory, having never had a whiff of powder!" he thought. His eyes narrowed scornfully; he entered the minister of war's office especially slowly. This feeling increased still more when he saw the minister of war sitting at the big desk and for the first two minutes paying no attention to the one who had entered. The minister of war had lowered his bald head with grey temples between two wax candles and was reading some papers, making notes with a pencil. He went on reading to the end, without raising his head, when the door opened and footsteps were heard.

"Take this and deliver it," the minister of war said to his adjutant, handing him the papers and still paying no attention to the courier.

Prince Andrei felt that either, of all the matters that occupied the minister of war, the actions of Kutuzov's army must interest him the least, or that he had to give the Russian courier that feeling. "But it's all quite the same to me," he thought. The minister of war put the rest of the papers together, stacked them evenly, and raised his head. He had an intelligent and characteristic head. But the moment he turned to Prince Andrei, the intelligent and firm expression on the minister of war's face changed, evidently habitually and consciously: there remained on his face the stupid, feigned smile, which did not conceal its feigning, of a man who receives many petitioners one after the other.

"From General Field Marshal Kutuzov?" he asked. "With good news, I hope? There was an encounter with Mortier? A victory? About time!"

He took the dispatch, which was addressed to him, and began reading it with a sorrowful expression.

"Ah, my God! My God! Schmidt!" he said in German. "What a misfortune! What a misfortune!"

*Your Excellency.

Having looked through the dispatch, he put it on the table and glanced at Prince Andrei, clearly weighing something.

"Ah, what a misfortune! You say it was a decisive action? Mortier wasn't taken, however." (He reflected.) "I'm very glad you've come with good news, though Schmidt's death is a high price for a victory. His Majesty will certainly wish to see you, but not today. Thank you, get some rest. Be at the levee tomorrow after the parade. I'll let you know, however."

The stupid smile that had disappeared during the conversation reappeared on the minister of war's face.

"Goodbye, thank you very much. The sovereign emperor will probably wish to see you," he repeated and inclined his head.

When Prince Andrei left the palace, he felt that all the interest and happiness afforded him by the victory had now left him and been given over into the indifferent hands of the minister of war and the courteous adjutant. His whole way of thinking changed instantly: the battle appeared to him now as a long-past, far-off memory.

X

Prince Andrei stayed in Brünn with his acquaintance, the Russian diplomat Bilibin.

"Ah, dear prince, there's no guest more welcome," said Bilibin, coming out to meet Prince Andrei. "Franz, take the prince's things to my bedroom!" he turned to the servant who accompanied Bolkonsky. "What, are you a herald of victory? Excellent. And I'm sitting here sick, as you see."

Prince Andrei, having washed and dressed, came out to the diplomat's luxurious study and sat down to the prepared dinner. Bilibin settled comfortably by the fireplace.

Not only after his trip, but after the whole campaign, during which he had been deprived of all the comforts of cleanliness and the refinements of life, Prince Andrei experienced the pleasant feeling of repose amidst the luxurious conditions of life to which he had been accustomed since childhood. Besides, it was pleasant for him, after his Austrian reception, to speak, if not Russian (they spoke French), at least with a Russian man, who, he supposed, shared the general Russian aversion (now especially sharply felt) to the Austrians.

Bilibin was a man of about thirty-five, a bachelor, of the same society as Prince Andrei. They had been acquainted back in Petersburg, but had become more closely acquainted during Prince Andrei's visit to Vienna with Kutuzov. As Prince Andrei was a young man who promised to go far in his military career, so, and still more, was Bilibin promising in the diplomacy. He was still a young man, but no longer a young diplomat, since he had begun to serve at the age of sixteen, had been in Paris, in Copenhagen, and now occupied a rather important post in Vienna. Both the chancellor and our ambassador in Vienna[7] knew him and valued him. He did not belong to that large number of diplomats whose duty it is to have only negative merits, to not do certain things, and to speak French so as to be very good diplomats; he was one of those diplomats who like and know how to work, and, despite his laziness, he occasionally spent nights at his desk. He worked equally well whatever the essence of the work consisted of. He was interested not in the question "Why?" but in the question "How?" What the diplomatic business consisted of made no difference to him; but to compose a circular, a memorandum, a report artfully, aptly, and elegantly—in that he took great pleasure. Bilibin's merits were valued, apart from his written work, also for his skill at moving and speaking in higher spheres.

Bilibin liked conversation, just as he liked work, only when the conversation could be elegantly witty. In society he constantly waited for the opportunity to say something remarkable and entered into conversation not otherwise than on that condition. Bilibin's conversation was constantly sprinkled with wittily original and well-turned phrases of general interest. These phrases were manufactured in Bilibin's inner laboratory, as if intentionally of a portable nature, so that society nonentities could readily remember them and pass them on from drawing room to drawing room. And indeed, *les mots de Bilibine se colportaient dans les salons de Vienne*,* as they say, and often had an influence on so-called important affairs.

His thin, drawn, yellowish face was all covered with deep wrinkles, which always looked as neatly and thoroughly washed as one's fingertips after a bath. The movements of these wrinkles constituted the main play of his physiognomy. Now his forehead would wrinkle into wide folds as his eyebrows rose, then his eyebrows would descend and deep wrinkles would form on his cheeks. His small, deep-set eyes always looked out directly and merrily.

"Well, now tell us about your exploits," he said.

In a most modest way, not once mentioning himself, Bolkonsky told about the action and his reception by the minister of war.

"*Ils m'ont reçu avec ma nouvelle comme un chien dans un jeu de quilles*,"† he concluded.

Bilibin smiled and released the folds of his skin.

"*Cependant, mon cher*," he said, studying his fingernail from a distance and gathering up the skin over his left eye, "*malgré la haute estime que je professe*

---

*Bilibin's sayings were peddled in all the drawing rooms of Vienna.
†They received me with my news like a dog in a game of ninepins [i.e., like a bull in a china shop].

pour le Orthodox Russian armed forces,[8] *j'avoue que votre victoire n'est pas des plus victorieuses."**

He went on in the same way, in French, pronouncing in Russian only those words he wanted to underscore contemptuously.

"How, then? With all your mass you fell upon the unfortunate Mortier with his one division, and this Mortier slips between your fingers? Where's the victory?"

"All the same, seriously speaking," replied Prince Andrei, "we can still say without boasting that this is a bit better than Ulm . . ."

"Why didn't you capture us at least one, at least one marshal?"

"Because not everything goes as it's supposed to, and with such regularity as on parade. We planned, as I told you, to attack their rear by seven in the morning, but we didn't even get there by five in the afternoon."

"But why didn't you get there at seven in the morning? You had to get there at seven in the morning," Bilibin said, smiling, "you had to get there at seven in the morning."

"And why didn't you convince Bonaparte through diplomatic channels that he'd better leave Genoa?" Prince Andrei said in the same tone.

"I know," Bilibin interrupted, "you think it's very easy to capture marshals while sitting on a sofa in front of a fireplace. That's true, but even so, why didn't you capture him? And don't be surprised if not only the minister of war, but the most august emperor and king Franz is not made very happy by your victory; nor do I, a miserable secretary of the Russian embassy, feel any particular joy . . ."

He looked straight at Prince Andrei and suddenly relaxed all the skin gathered on his forehead.

"Now it's my turn to ask you 'why,' my dear," said Bolkonsky. "I confess to you that I don't understand, maybe there are diplomatic subtleties here that are beyond my feeble mind, but I don't understand: Mack loses a whole army, the archduke Ferdinand and the archduke Karl give no signs of life and make blunder after blunder, Kutuzov alone finally gains a real victory, destroys the *charme*† of the French, and the minister of war isn't even interested in learning the details!"

"Precisely for that reason, my dear. *Voyez-vous, mon cher:* hurrah for the tsar, for Rus, for the faith! *Tout ça est bel et bon,*‡ but what do we—I mean the Austrian court—care about your victories? Bring us some nice little news about a victory of the archduke Karl or Ferdinand—*un archiduc vaut l'autre,*§

*Nevertheless, my dear . . . despite the high esteem I profess for the *Orthodox Russian armed forces,* I own that your victory is not of the most victorious.
†Magic spell.
‡You see, my dear . . . That is all well and good . . .
§One archduke is as good as another.

as you know—even over a fire brigade of Bonaparte's, and that will be a different story, we'll shoot off all our cannons. Whereas this, as if on purpose, can only exasperate us. The archduke Karl does nothing, the archduke Ferdinand covers himself in shame. You abandon Vienna, you no longer protect it, *comme si vous disiez:** God is with us, and God help you and your capital. There was one general we all loved: Schmidt. You put him in the path of a bullet and congratulate us with your victory! . . . You must agree that to think up more exasperating news than what you've brought would be impossible. *C'est comme un fait exprés, comme un fait exprés.*† Besides that, well, if you were to gain a truly brilliant victory, if the archduke Karl were even to gain a victory, what would it change in the general course of affairs? It's too late now, since Vienna's occupied by French troops."

"Occupied? Vienna occupied?"

"Not only occupied, but Bonaparte is in Schönbrunn, and the count, our dear Count Vrbna, is going to him for orders."[9]

After the fatigues and impressions of the journey, the reception, and especially after dinner, Bolkonsky felt that he did not quite understand the full significance of the words he had heard.

"This morning Count Lichtenfels was here," Bilibin went on, "and he showed me a letter which described in detail the parade of the French in Vienna. *Le prince Murat et tout le tremblement . . .*‡ You see that your victory doesn't bring much joy and that you can't be received as a saviour . . ."

"Really, it's all the same to me, all quite the same!" said Prince Andrei, beginning to realize that his news about the battle at Krems was indeed of little importance in view of such events as the occupation of the capital of Austria. "How is it that Vienna's been taken? What about the bridge? And the famous *tête de pont,*§ and Prince Auersperg? There was a rumour among us that Prince Auersperg was defending Vienna," he said.

"Prince Auersperg is standing on this side, our side, and defending us; I suppose he's defending us very poorly, but still he's defending us. But Vienna is on the other side. No, the bridge has not yet been taken and, I hope, will not be taken, because it's mined and there's an order to blow it up. Otherwise we'd have been in the mountains of Bohemia long ago, and you and your army would have spent a bad quarter of an hour between two fires."

"That still doesn't mean the campaign is over," said Prince Andrei.

"But I think it's over. And the bigwigs here think so, too, though they don't dare say it. It will turn out as I said at the beginning of the campaign, that the

*As if you were saying.
†It's like a deliberate thing, a deliberate thing.
‡Prince Murat and all the tumult . . .
§Bridgehead.

matter won't be decided by your *échauffourée de Dürenstein,** nor by gun-powder, but by those who invented gunpowder," said Bilibin, repeating one of his *mots,*[†10] releasing the skin on his forehead, and pausing. "The only ques-tion is what the meeting in Berlin between the emperor Alexander and the king of Prussia will tell us. If Prussia enters the alliance, *on forcera la main à l'Autriche,‡* and there will be war. If not, it will only be a matter of arranging where to draw up the preliminary articles for a new Campo Formio."[11]

"But what an extraordinary genius!" Prince Andrei cried suddenly, clench-ing his small fist and pounding it on the table. "And what luck the man has!"

"Buonaparte?" Bilibin said questioningly, wrinkling his forehead and with that letting it be felt that a *mot* was coming. "Buonaparte?" he said with spe-cial emphasis on the *u.* "I think, however, that now that he's prescribing laws for Austria from Schönbrunn, *il faut lui faire grâce de l'*u. I decidedly make an innovation and call him Bonaparte *tout court.*"[§]

"No, joking aside," said Prince Andrei, "do you really think the campaign is over?"

"Here's what I think. Austria's been played for a fool, and she's not used to it. And she'll pay it back. She's been played for a fool because, first, the provinces are devastated (*on dit, le* Orthodox army *est terrible pour le pil-lage*), her army is destroyed, her capital has been taken, and all that *pour les beaux yeux du* his Sardinian majesty. And therefore—*entre nous, mon cher*[#]—I feel instinctively that we're being deceived, I feel instinctively that communi-cations with France and plans for peace, a secret peace, are being concluded separately."[12]

"That can't be!" said Prince Andrei. "It would be too vile."

"*Qui vivra verra,*"[**] said Bilibin, again releasing his skin as a sign that the conversation was over.

When Prince Andrei went to the room prepared for him and lay down on the featherbed and fragrant, warmed-up pillows in clean linen—he felt that the battle, the news of which he had brought, was far, far away from him. The Prussian alliance, the treachery of Austria, the new triumph of Bonaparte, the levee, and the parade, and his reception by the emperor Franz the next day pre-occupied him.

He closed his eyes, but at that same instant in his ears there crackled a can-nonade, gunfire, the rattle of carriage wheels, and now again the stretched-out line of musketeers goes down the hill, and the French are shooting, and he feels

*Skirmish at Dürenstein.
†Phrases.
‡It will force Austria's hand.
§We must spare him the *u* . . . simply *Bonaparte.*
#They say the *Orthodox army* is a terrible pillager . . . just for the sake of . . . between us, my dear.
**Time will tell.

his heart thrill, and he is riding in front next to Schmidt, and bullets are whistling merrily around him, and he experiences that feeling of the tenfold joy of life, such as he has not experienced since childhood.

He woke up . . .

"Yes, all that happened! . . ." he said, smiling happily to himself like a child, and he fell into a sound, youthful sleep.

XI

The next day he woke up late. Going over his recent impressions, he remembered first of all that he had to present himself to the emperor Franz that day, remembered the minister of war, the courteous Austrian imperial adjutant, Bilibin, and the conversation yesterday evening. Putting on his full dress uniform, which he had not worn in a long time, for his trip to the palace, fresh, animated, and handsome, with his arm in a sling, he went into Bilibin's study. In the study there were four gentlemen from the diplomatic corps. Bolkonsky was acquainted with Prince Ippolit Kuragin, who was a secretary at the embassy; Bilibin introduced him to the others.

The gentlemen who frequented Bilibin, young, rich, and merry society people, constituted here, as in Vienna, a separate circle, which Bilibin, who was the head of it, called "ours"—*les nôtres*. This circle, made up almost exclusively of diplomats, clearly had its own high-society interests, which had nothing in common with war and politics, interests in relations with certain women and in the administrative side of their service. These gentlemen received Prince Andrei into their circle with apparent eagerness, as "theirs" (an honour they accorded to few). Out of courtesy and as a subject for getting into conversation, he was asked several questions about the army and the battle, and the conversation again broke up into inconsequentially merry jokes and gossip.

"But it was especially nice," one said, telling about a fellow diplomat's failure, "it was especially nice that the chancellor told him straight out that his appointment to London was a promotion and that he should look at it as such. Can you picture his face when he heard that? . . ."

"But what's worst of all, gentlemen—I'm betraying Kuragin to you—is that the man is in misfortune, and this Don Juan, this terrible fellow, is taking advantage of it!"

Prince Ippolit was lying in a Voltaire armchair, his legs thrown over the armrest. He laughed.

"*Parlez-moi de ça,*"* he said.

* Just tell me about it.

"Oh, you Don Juan! Oh, you serpent!" said various voices.

"You don't know, Bolkonsky," Bilibin turned to Prince Andrei, "that all the horrors of the French army (I almost said the Russian army) are nothing compared to what this man has been doing among the women."

"*La femme est la compagne de l'homme,*"* uttered Prince Ippolit, and he began examining his raised feet through his lorgnette.

Bilibin and "ours" burst out laughing, looking Ippolit in the eye. Prince Andrei saw that this Ippolit, of whom he (it had to be admitted) had almost been jealous over his wife, was the buffoon of the company.

"No, I must treat you to Kuragin," Bilibin said softly to Bolkonsky. "He's charming when he argues about politics, you should see such gravity."

He sat beside Ippolit and, gathering the folds of his forehead, began a conversation about politics with him. Prince Andrei and the others stood around them.

"*Le cabinet de Berlin ne peut pas exprimer un sentiment d'alliance,*" Ippolit began, looking around significantly at them all, "*sans exprimer . . . comme dans sa dernière note . . . vous comprenez . . . vous comprenez . . . et puis si sa Majesté l'Empereur ne déroge pas au principe de notre alliance . . .*

"*Attendez, je n'ai pas fini . . .*" he said to Prince Andrei, seizing him by the arm. "*Je suppose que l'intervention sera plus forte que la non-intervention. Et . . .*" He paused. "*On ne pourra pas imputer à la fin de nonrecevoir notre dépêche du 28 novembre. Voilà comment tout cela finira.*"†

And he let go of Bolkonsky's arm, thus indicating that he was quite finished.

"*Démosthène, je te reconnais au caillou que tu as caché dans ta bouche d'or!*"‡[13] said Bilibin, whose shock of hair moved on his head with pleasure.

They all laughed. Ippolit laughed more than anyone else. He obviously suffered, choked, but was unable to hold back the wild laughter that distended his ever immobile face.

"Well, I tell you what, gentlemen," said Bilibin, "Bolkonsky is a guest in my house and here in Brünn, and I want to treat him, as far as I can, to all the joys of life here. If we were in Vienna, that would be easy; but here, *dans ce vilain trou morave* it's harder, and I ask you all to help. *Il faut lui faire les honneurs*

---

*Woman is man's helpmeet.
†The Berlin cabinet cannot express a feeling of alliance . . . without expressing . . . as in its last note . . . you understand . . . you understand . . . and then if his majesty the emperor does not derogate from the principle of our alliance . . . Wait, I haven't finished . . . I suppose that intervention will be stronger than non-intervention. And . . . One cannot impute our dispatch of 28 November to point-blank refusal. That is how all this will end up.
‡Demosthenes, I recognize you by the pebble you've hidden in your golden mouth!

de Brünn.* You'll take the theatre upon yourselves, I'll take society, and you, Ippolit, naturally, the women."

"We must show him Amélie—charming!" said one of "ours," kissing the tips of his fingers.

"Generally, this bloodthirsty soldier," said Bilibin, "needs to be converted to more humane views."

"It's unlikely that I'll take advantage of your hospitality, gentlemen, and it's now time for me to go," Bolkonsky said, glancing at his watch.

"Where?"

"To the emperor."

"Oh! oh! oh!"

"Well, goodbye, Bolkonsky! Goodbye, Prince; come early to dinner," said several voices. "We'll take good care of you."

"Try to praise the order for the delivery of provisions and the itineraries as much as possible to the emperor," said Bilibin, seeing Bolkonsky off to the front hall.

"I wish I could, but I can't, as far as I know," Bolkonsky replied, smiling.

"Well, generally, talk as much as possible. Audiences are his passion; but he neither likes nor is able to talk himself, as you'll see."

XII

At the levee, the emperor Franz merely looked intently into the face of Prince Andrei, who was standing in the place assigned to him among the Austrian officers, and nodded his long head at him. But after the levee, yesterday's imperial adjutant courteously conveyed to Bolkonsky the emperor's wish to grant him an audience. The emperor Franz received him standing in the middle of the room. Before the conversation began, it struck Prince Andrei that the emperor was as if confused, did not know what to say, and blushed.

"Tell me, when did the battle begin?" he asked hastily.

Prince Andrei replied. After that question, other equally simple questions followed: "Was Kutuzov in good health? How long ago had he left Krems?" and so on. The emperor spoke with such an expression as if his whole goal consisted in asking a certain number of questions. The replies to these questions, as was only too clear, were of no interest to him.

"At what time did the battle begin?" asked the emperor.

"I am unable to tell Your Majesty at what time the battle at the front began, but in Dürenstein, where I was, the troops went into attack between five and six o'clock in the evening," said Bolkonsky, livening up and supposing on this

---

*In this wretched Moravian hole . . . We must do him the honours of Brünn.

occasion that he would be able to present the truthful description already prepared in his head of all he knew and had seen.

But the emperor smiled and interrupted him:

"How many miles?"

"From where to where, Your Majesty?"

"From Dürenstein to Krems."

"Three and a half miles, Your Majesty."

"Have the French abandoned the left bank?"

"According to the scouts' reports, the last of them crossed at night on rafts."

"Is there enough forage in Krems?"

"Forage was not delivered in the quantities . . ."

The emperor interrupted him:

"At what time was General Schmidt killed?"

"At seven o'clock, I believe."

"At seven o'clock? Very sad! Very sad!"

The emperor said that he thanked him and inclined his head. Prince Andrei went out and was at once surrounded on all sides by courtiers. On all sides affectionate eyes looked at him and affectionate words came to him. Yesterday's imperial adjutant reproached him for not staying in the palace, and offered him his own house. The minister of war came up to congratulate him on the Order of Maria Theresa of the third degree, which the emperor was to bestow on him. The empress's chamberlain invited him to her majesty. The archduchess also wanted to see him. He did not know whom to answer and needed a few seconds to collect his wits. The Russian ambassador took him by the shoulder, led him to the window, and started talking to him.

Contrary to what Bilibin had said, the news he brought was received joyfully. A thanksgiving prayer service was ordered. Kutuzov was awarded a Maria Theresa with large cross, and the whole army received rewards. Bolkonsky received invitations from all sides and had to spend the whole morning paying visits to the high dignitaries of Austria. Having finished his visits past four in the afternoon, mentally composing a letter to his father about the battle and his journey to Brünn, Prince Andrei was returning home to Bilibin's. Before going to Bilibin's, Prince Andrei had gone to a bookstore to stock up on books for the campaign and had spent a long time there. By the porch of the house occupied by Bilibin stood a britzka half filled with things, and Franz, Bilibin's servant, dragging a trunk with difficulty, came out of the door.

"What's this?" asked Bolkonsky.

"*Ach, Erlaucht!*" said Franz, loading the trunk into the britzka with difficulty. "*Wir ziehen noch weiter. Der Bösewicht ist schon wieder hinter uns her!*"*

---

*Ah, Your Excellency! . . . We are moving further on. The villain is just behind us!

"What is it? What?" Prince Andrei kept asking.

Bilibin came out to meet Bolkonsky. The usually calm face of Bilibin was troubled.

"*Non, non, avouez que c'est charmant,*" he was saying, "*cette histoire du pont de Tabor*" (a bridge in Vienna). "*Ils l'ont passé sans coup férir.*"*

Prince Andrei understood nothing.

"But where are you coming from that you don't know what every coachman in town already knows?"

"I'm coming from the archduchess. I didn't hear anything there."

"And you didn't see people packing up everywhere?"

"No, I didn't . . . But what's it all about?" Prince Andrei asked impatiently.

"What's it all about? It's about the French having crossed the bridge defended by Auersperg, and the bridge wasn't blown up, so Murat is now racing down the road to Brünn, and they'll be here today or tomorrow."

"What do you mean, here? How is it they didn't blow up the bridge, since it's mined?"

"That's what I'm asking. Nobody knows, not even Bonaparte himself."

Bolkonsky shrugged his shoulders.

"But if the bridge has been crossed, that means the army is lost: it will be cut off," he said.

"That's just the thing," answered Bilibin. "Listen. The French enter Vienna, as I said. Everything's fine. The next day, that is, yesterday, the gentlemen marshals, Murat, Lannes, and Belliard, get on their horses and set out for the bridge. (Note that all three are Gascons.) 'Gentlemen,' says one, 'you know that the bridge of Tabor has been mined and countermined, and that in front of it is a terrible *tête de pont* and fifteen thousand troops, who have been ordered to blow up the bridge and not let us onto it. But it will be pleasing to our sovereign emperor Napoleon if we take this bridge. Let's go the three of us and take the bridge.' 'Let's go,' say the others; and they go and take the bridge, cross it, and are now on this side of the Danube with their whole army, coming against us, against you and your communications."

"Enough joking," Prince Andrei said sadly and seriously.

This news was grievous and at the same time pleasant for Prince Andrei. As soon as he learned that the Russian army was in such a hopeless situation, it occurred to him that it was precisely he who was destined to lead the Russian army out of that situation, that here was that Toulon[14] which would take him out of the ranks of unknown officers and open for him the first path to glory! Listening to Bilibin, he was already considering how, on coming to the army, he would submit an opinion at the military council which

---

*No, no, admit that it's charming . . . this story of the bridge of Tabor . . . They crossed it without opposition.

alone would save the army, and how he alone would be charged with carrying out this plan.

"Enough joking," he said.

"I'm not joking," Bilibin went on, "nothing is more true or sad. These gentlemen come to the bridge by themselves and wave white handkerchiefs; assure them all that a truce has been called and that they, the marshals, are coming to negotiate with Prince Auersperg. The officer on duty lets them into the *tête de pont.* They tell him a thousand Gascon absurdities: that the war is over, that the emperor Franz has fixed a meeting with Bonaparte, that they wish to see Prince Auersperg, and so on. The officer sends for Auersperg; these gentlemen embrace the officers, joke, sit on the cannons, and meanwhile a French battalion gets onto the bridge unnoticed, throws the sacks of flammable material into the water, and approaches the *tête de pont.* Finally, the lieutenant general himself comes, our dear Prince Auersperg von Mautern. 'Our dear enemy! Flower of the Austrian military, hero of the Turkish wars! The hostilities are over, we can shake hands with each other . . . The emperor Napoleon is burning with desire to meet Prince Auersperg.' In short, these men aren't Gascons for nothing, they so shower Auersperg with beautiful words, he's so charmed by his quickly established intimacy with the French marshals, so dazzled by the sight of Murat's mantle and ostrich feathers, *qu'il n'y voit que du feu, et oublie celui qu'il devait faire, faire sur l'ennemi.*"* (Despite the animation of his speech, Bilibin did not forget to pause after this *mot,* to allow time for it to be appreciated.) "The French battalion rushes into the *tête de pont,* spikes the cannons, and the bridge is taken. No, but the best thing of all," he went on, his excitement with his own charming story subsiding, "is that the sergeant in charge of the cannon that was to give the signal to ignite the mines and blow up the bridge, this sergeant, seeing that French troops were running onto the bridge, was about to fire, but Lannes pushed his hand away. The sergeant, who was clearly smarter than his general, goes up to Auersperg and says: 'Prince, you are deceived, the French are here!' Murat sees that the game is up if the sergeant is allowed to speak. With feigned astonishment (a real Gascon), he turns to Auersperg: 'Where is that Austrian discipline the world praises so much,' he says, 'if you allow the lower ranks to speak to you like that.' *C'est génial. Le prince Auersperg se pique d'honneur et fait mettre le sergeant aux arrêts. Non, mais avouez que c'est charmant toute cette histoire du pont de Tabor. Ce n'est ni bêtise, ni lâcheté . . .*"†[15]

---

*That he only sees fire [i.e., is dazzled], and forgets that he ought to fire on the enemy.

†It's ingenious. Prince Auersperg's honour is pricked, and he has the sergeant put under arrest. No, but admit that it's charming, this whole story about the bridge of Tabor. It's neither stupidity, nor cowardice . . .

"*C'est trahison peut-être,*"* said Prince Andrei, vividly imagining grey great-coats, wounds, gunsmoke, the sounds of shooting, and the glory that awaited him . . .

"*Non plus. Cela met la cour dans de trop mauvais draps,*" Bilibin went on. "*Ce n'est ni trahison, ni lâcheté, ni bêtise; c'est comme à Ulm . . .*" It was as if he fell to pondering, searching for a phrase: "*C'est . . . c'est du Mack. Nous sommes mackés,*"† he concluded, feeling that he had uttered a *mot*, and a fresh *mot*, a *mot* that would be repeated.

The folds on his forehead, gathered till then, quickly released themselves as a sign of satisfaction, and, smiling slightly, he began to examine his nails.

"Where are you going?" he said suddenly, turning to Prince Andrei, who got up and made for his room.

"I'm leaving."

"For where?"

"The army."

"Why, didn't you want to stay another two days?"

"But now I'm leaving at once."

And Prince Andrei, having given orders for his departure, left for his room.

"You know what, my dear," said Bilibin, coming into his room, "I've been thinking about you. Why should you go?"

And in proof of the irrefutability of his argument, all the folds fled his face.

Prince Andrei looked at his interlocutor questioningly and said nothing.

"Why should you go? I know, you think it's your duty to gallop off to the army, now that the army is in danger. I understand that, *mon cher, c'est de l'héroisme.*"

"Not in the least," said Prince Andrei.

"But you are *un philosophe,* so be one fully, look at things from another angle, and you'll see that your duty is, on the contrary, to protect yourself. Let others, who are good for nothing else, do that . . . You weren't told to come back, and you haven't been dismissed from here; therefore you can stay and come with us wherever our sorry fate takes us. They say they're going to Olmütz. Now, Olmütz is a very nice town. And you and I can calmly drive there together in my carriage."

"Stop joking, Bilibin," said Bolkonsky.

"I'm saying it to you sincerely as a friend. Consider. Where will you go now, and what for, when you can stay here? One of two things awaits you" (he gathered the skin over his left temple): "either peace will be concluded before you

---

*It may be treason.
†Not that either. It puts the court in too bad a fix . . . It's neither treason, nor cowardice, nor stupidity; it's like at Ulm . . . It's . . . it's like Mack. We've been macked.

reach the army, or it will be defeat and disgrace along with the whole of Kutuzov's army."

And Bilibin released the skin, feeling that his dilemma was irrefutable.

"I cannot consider that," Prince Andrei said coldly, and thought: "I'm going
in order to save the army."

"*Mon cher, vous êtes un héros,*" said Bilibin.

XIII

That same night, having repectfully taken leave of the minister of war, Bolkonsky rode off to the army, not knowing himself where he would find it and fearing to be intercepted by the French on his way to Krems.

In Brünn all the court population was packing, and the heavy baggage had
already been sent to Olmütz. Near Etzelsdorf Prince Andrei came out on the
road along which the Russian army was moving with the greatest haste and in
the greatest disorder. The road was so choked with wagons that it was impossible to drive in a carriage. Having taken a horse and a Cossack from the chief
of the Cossacks, Prince Andrei, hungry and tired, got ahead of the baggage
train, going in search of the commander in chief and his own wagon. The most
sinister rumours about the army's situation had reached him on the way, and
the sight of the feverishly fleeing army confirmed those rumours.

"*Cette armée Russe que l'or de l'Angleterre a transportée des extrémités
de l'univers, nous allons lui faire éprouver le même sort (le sort de l'armée
d'Ulm)*" *—he recalled the words of Napoleon's order to his army before the
start of the campaign, and these words aroused in him at once an astonishment
at the genius of the hero, a feeling of offended pride, and a hope of glory. "And
what if there's nothing left but to die?" he thought. "Why not, if need be! I'll
do it no worse than others."

Prince Andrei looked with scorn at these countless mixed-up detachments,
wagons, caissons, artillery, and again wagons, wagons of all possible sorts, trying to get ahead of each other and choking the muddy road three or four
abreast. On all sides, behind and before, as far as hearing could reach, there
was the noise of wheels, the rumbling of flatbeds, carts, and gun carriages, the
thud of hooves, the crack of whips, the shouts of drivers, the cursing of soldiers, orderlies, and officers. On the roadsides one constantly saw now dead
horses, skinned or unskinned, now broken-down wagons, near which solitary
soldiers sat waiting for something, now soldiers who separated from their
detachments and went in groups to the neighbouring villages or came from the

---

*We shall make this Russian army, which the gold of England has brought from the ends of the
universe, experience the same fate (the fate of the army of Ulm).

villages dragging chickens, sheep, hay, or sacks filled with something. On the ascents and descents the crowds became thicker, and there was a ceaseless moan of cries. Soldiers, sunk in mud up to their knees, carried cannon and wagons with their hands; whips lashed, hooves slipped, traces snapped, and chests strained with shouting. The officers in charge of the movement rode up and down among the trains. Their voices were faintly heard amidst the general hubbub, and one could see from their faces that they despaired of the possibility of stopping this disorder.

"*Voilà le cher* Orthodox armed forces,"* thought Bolkonsky, recalling Bilibin's words.

Wishing to ask someone among these people where the commander in chief was, he rode up to the baggage train. Directly in front of him rolled a strange one-horse vehicle, evidently constructed by soldiers using homegrown means, something between a cart, a cabriolet, and a carriage. The driver of the vehicle was a soldier, and in it, under a leather top and apron, sat a woman all wrapped in shawls. Prince Andrei rode up and was about to address the soldier with his question when his attention was attracted by the desperate cries of the woman sitting in the little kibitka. The officer in charge of the baggage train was beating the soldier who sat on the box of this little carriage for trying to get ahead of the others, and his lash struck the apron of the vehicle. The woman cried out piercingly. Seeing Prince Andrei, she thrust her head out from under the apron and, waving her thin arms freed from the ruglike shawl, cried:

"Adjutant! Mister Adjutant! . . . For God's sake . . . protect us . . . What's it all about? . . . I'm the wife of the doctor of the seventh chasseurs . . . they won't let us pass; we couldn't keep up, lost our people . . ."

"I'll flatten you like a pancake—turn back!" the officer shouted angrily at the soldier. "Turn back with your trollop!"

"Mister Adjutant, protect us. What is it?" cried the doctor's wife.

"Kindly let this wagon pass. Don't you see it's a woman?" said Prince Andrei, riding up to the officer.

The officer glanced at him and, without replying, turned back to the soldier:

"I'll teach you to go ahead . . . Back!"

"Let them pass, I tell you," Prince Andrei repeated, pressing his lips.

"And who do you think *you* are?" the officer addressed him with drunken rage. "Who do you think *you* are? Are *you*" (he especially emphasized the word *you*) "a superior officer, or what? I'm the superior here, not *you*. And you, back!" he repeated, "or I'll flatten you like a pancake."

The officer obviously liked the expression.

"He told that little adjutant off grandly," a voice came from behind.

Prince Andrei could see that the officer was in the sort of drunken fit of

*There's our dear *Orthodox armed forces*.

senseless rage when people do not know what they are saying. He could see that his intercession for the doctor's wife in the kibitka was replete with what he feared most in the world, with what is known as *ridicule*.* But his instinct told him otherwise. Before the officer had time to finish his last words, Prince Andrei, his face disfigured with rage, rode up to him and raised his whip:

"Kind-ly-let-them-pass!"

The officer waved his hand and hastily rode off.

"It's all from them, these staff officers, all this disorder," he grumbled. "Do it your way."

Prince Andrei, without raising his eyes, hastily rode away from the doctor's wife, who was calling him her saviour, and, recalling with disgust the minutest details of this humiliating scene, rode on towards the village where he had been told the commander in chief was.

On entering the village, he got off his horse and went to the first house, intending to rest for at least a moment, eat something, and bring clarity to all these insulting, tormenting thoughts. "These are not troops, they're a mob of ruffians," he was thinking as he went to the window of the first house, when a familiar voice called his name.

He turned round. Nesvitsky's handsome face was looking out of a small window. Nesvitsky, chewing something with his juicy mouth and waving his arms, was calling to him.

"Bolkonsky, Bolkonsky! Are you deaf, or what? Come quickly," he shouted.

Going into the house, Prince Andrei saw Nesvitsky and another adjutant having something to eat. They hastily turned to Bolkonsky with the question whether he had any fresh news. On their familiar faces Prince Andrei read the expression of alarm and anxiety. This expression was especially noticeable on the always laughing face of Nesvitsky.

"Where's the commander in chief?" asked Bolkonsky.

"Here, in that house," the adjutant replied.

"Well, so, is it true there's peace and capitulation?" asked Nesvitsky.

"I was going to ask you. I know nothing except that I had a hard time getting to you."

"And what's going on with us, brother! Terrible! I confess, brother, we laughed at Mack, and yet it's going much worse for us," said Nesvitsky. "But sit down, eat something."

"Now, Prince, you'll find no wagons, nothing, and God knows where your Pyotr is," said the other adjutant.

"Where are headquarters?"

"We'll spend the night in Znaim."

"What I did was repack everything I need onto two horses," said Nesvitsky,

*Ridiculousness.

"and I had excellent packs made for me. I could skip off over the Bohemian Mountains now. It's bad, brother. But you're surely unwell, the way you're shivering?" asked Nesvitsky, noticing how Prince Andrei twitched as if he had touched a Leiden jar.[16]

"It's nothing," replied Prince Andrei.

He had just recalled his recent encounter with the doctor's wife and the convoy officer.

"What is the commander in chief doing here?" he asked.

"I understand nothing," said Nesvitsky.

"I understand one thing, that it's all vile, vile, vile," said Prince Andrei, and he went to the house where the commander in chief was staying.

Going past Kutuzov's carriage, the winded riding horses of the suite, and the Cossacks talking loudly among themselves, Prince Andrei came to the entryway. Kutuzov himself, as Prince Andrei was told, was inside the cottage with Prince Bagration and Weyrother. Weyrother was an Austrian general who had replaced the slain Schmidt. In the entryway, little Kozlovsky was crouching in front of a scribe. The scribe, the cuffs of his tunic turned up, was writing hurriedly on an overturned tub. Kozlovsky's face looked exhausted—obviously he also had not slept that night. He glanced at Prince Andrei and did not even nod to him.

"Second line . . . Have you written that?" he went on dictating to the scribe. "The Kievsky grenadiers, the Podolsky . . ."

"Don't rush, Your Honour," the scribe replied disrespectfully and crossly, looking up at Kozlovsky.

From behind the door just then came the animated and displeased voice of Kutuzov, interrupted by another, unknown voice. From the sound of that voice, from the inattention with which Kozlovsky had glanced at him, from the disrespectfulness of the exhausted scribe, from the fact that the scribe and Kozlovsky were sitting so close to the commander in chief on the floor by the tub, and from the fact that the Cossacks who tended the horses were laughing loudly outside the window—from all that Prince Andrei could feel that something grave and unfortunate must be happening.

Prince Andrei plied Kozlovsky with insistent questions.

"One moment, Prince," said Kozlovsky. "A disposition for Bagration."

"And capitulation?"

"Nothing of the sort; orders have been issued for battle."

Prince Andrei went to the door, behind which voices could be heard. But just as he was about to open the door, the voices in the room fell silent, the door opened by itself, and Kutuzov, with his eagle's beak on his plump face, appeared in the doorway. Prince Andrei was standing directly in front of Kutuzov; but from the expression in the commander in chief's one good eye, it was clear that his thoughts and concerns occupied him so greatly that it was as if they interfered with his vision. He looked directly at his adjutant's face and did not recognize him.

"Well, what, are you finished?" he addressed Kozlovsky.

"This second, Your Excellency."

Bagration, of medium height, with a firm and immobile face of the Oriental type, dry, not yet an old man, came out after the commander in chief.

"I have the honour of reporting to you," Prince Andrei repeated quite loudly, handing him an envelope.

"Ah, from Vienna? Very well. Later, later!"

Kutuzov and Bagration stepped out to the porch.

"Well, goodbye, Prince," he said to Bagration. "Christ be with you. I bless you for a great deed."

Kutuzov's face suddenly softened, and tears welled up in his eyes. He pulled Bagration to him with his left hand, and with his right, which had a ring on it, making an obviously habitual gesture, crossed him and offered him his plump cheek, instead of which Bagration kissed him on the neck.

"Christ be with you!" Kutuzov repeated and went to his carriage. "Get in with me," he said to Bolkonsky.

"Your Excellency, I should like to be of use here. Allow me to stay in Prince Bagration's detachment."

"Get in," said Kutuzov, and noticing that Bolkonsky hung back, said: "I need good officers myself."

They got into the carriage and rode for several minutes in silence.

"There is still much before us, much of everything," he said, with an old man's perceptive expression, as though he understood everything that was going on in Bolkonsky's soul. "If one tenth of his detachment comes back tomorrow, I'll thank God," Kutuzov added, as if speaking to himself.

Prince Andrei looked at Kutuzov and his eyes were involuntarily struck by the carefully washed creases of the scar on Kutuzov's temple, a foot away from him, where the Izmail bullet had pierced his head and put out his eye. "Yes, he has the right to speak so calmly about the deaths of these people!" thought Bolkonsky.

"That is why I am asking you to send me to that detachment," he said.

Kutuzov did not reply. He seemed to have forgotten what he had said, and sat deep in thought. After five minutes, rocking smoothly on the soft springs of the carriage, Kutuzov turned to Prince Andrei. There was no trace of emotion on his face. With fine irony he questioned the prince about the details of his meeting with the emperor, about the opinions he had heard at court concerning the action at Krems, and about several women of their mutual acquaintance.

XIV

On the first of November Kutuzov received information through one of his scouts that placed the army he commanded in an almost hopeless position. The scout had reported that the French in enormous force, having crossed the bridge in Vienna, were heading towards Kutuzov's line of communications with the troops coming from Russia. If Kutuzov decided to stay in Krems, the one-hundred-and-fifty-thousand-man army of Napoleon would cut him off from all communications, surround his exhausted forty-thousand-man army, and he would find himself in the position of Mack at Ulm. If Kutuzov decided to abandon the road leading to communications with the troops from Russia, he would have to enter with no road into the unknown territory of the Bohemian Mountains, defending himself from the superior numbers of the enemy, and abandoning any hope of communications with Buxhöwden. If Kutuzov decided to retreat down the road from Krems to Olmütz to unite with the troops from Russia, he would risk being forestalled on that road by the French, who had crossed the bridge in Vienna, and thus being forced to accept battle on the march, with all his heavy baggage and transport, and to deal with an enemy that outnumbered him three to one and surrounded him on both sides.

Kutuzov chose this last course.

The French, as the scout reported, had crossed the bridge in Vienna and by forced marches were making for Znaim, which lay on the path of Kutuzov's retreat, more than sixty miles ahead of him. To reach Znaim before the French meant to gain great hope of saving the army; to let the French forestall them in Znaim meant certainly to subject the whole army to a disgrace similar to that at Ulm, or to total destruction. To forestall the French with his entire army was impossible. The road from Vienna to Znaim was shorter and better than the Russians' road from Krems to Znaim.

The night he received this information, Kutuzov sent Bagration's four-thousand-man vanguard to the right over the hills from the Krems–Znaim to the Vienna–Znaim road. Bagration was to make this march without resting, to stop with his face to Vienna and his back to Znaim, and, if he managed to forestall the French, to detain them there as long as he could. Kutuzov himself started out for Znaim with all the heavy baggage.

Having gone thirty miles across the hills with hungry, ill-shod soldiers, with no road, on a stormy night, losing a third of his men as stragglers, Bagration came out in Hollabrunn, on the Vienna–Znaim road, several hours ahead of the French, who were approaching Hollabrunn from Vienna. Kutuzov still needed to go a whole twenty-four hours with his baggage train to reach Znaim, and therefore, to save the army. Bagration, with four thousand hungry, exhausted soldiers, had to hold off for twenty-four hours the entire enemy army coming to meet him at Hollabrunn, which was obviously impossible. But a freak of fate made the impossible possible. The success of the trick which gave the Vienna bridge into the hands of the French without a fight prompted Murat to try to trick Kutuzov in the same way. Murat, meeting Bagration's weak detachment on the Znaim road, thought it was the whole of Kutuzov's army. In order to crush this army indubitably, he awaited the troops that lagged behind on the road from Vienna, and with that aim suggested a three-day truce, on condition that neither army change its position or stir from its place. Murat assured them that peace negotiations were already under way and that therefore, to avoid useless bloodshed, he was suggesting a truce. The Austrian general, Count Nostitz, who occupied the advance posts, believed the words of Murat's envoy and fell back, exposing Bagration's detachment. Another envoy rode to the Russian line to announce the same news of peace negotiations and offer the Russian army a three-day truce. Bagration replied that he could neither accept nor reject a truce and sent his adjutant to Kutuzov with a report of the offer made to him.

For Kutuzov the truce was the sole means of gaining time, giving Bagration's exhausted detachment some rest, and allowing the train and heavy baggage (whose movement was concealed from the French) to make at least one extra march towards Znaim. The offer of a truce gave the sole and unexpected possibility of saving the army. On receiving this news, Kutuzov immediately sent the adjutant general Wintzingerode, who was attached to him, to the enemy camp. Wintzingerode was not only to accept the truce, but also to offer conditions for capitulation, and meanwhile Kutuzov sent his adjutants back to speed up as much as possible the movement of the whole army's baggage trains along the Krems–Znaim road. Bagration's exhausted, hungry detachment, covering this movement of the baggage trains and the whole army, had alone to remain unmoving before an enemy eight times its strength.

Kutuzov's expectations came true both with regard to the fact that the offer of capitulation, without committing them to anything, might gain time for some portion of the baggage train to pass, and with regard to the fact that Murat's mistake was bound to be discovered very quickly. As soon as Bonaparte, who was in Schönbrunn, some fifteen miles from Hollabrunn, received Murat's communication with the project of a truce and capitulation, he saw through the deception and wrote the following letter to Murat.

> *Au Prince Murat.*
> *Schoenbrunn, 25 brumaire en 1805*
> *à huit heures du matin.*

Il m'est impossible de trouver des termes pour vous exprimer mon mécontentement. Vous ne commandez que mon avant-garde et vous n'avez pas le droit de faire d'armistice sans mon ordre. Vous me faites perdre le fruit d'une campagne. Rompez l'armistice sur-le-champ et marchez à l'ennemi. Vous lui ferez déclarer, que le général qui a signé cette capitulation, n'avait pas le droit de le faire, qu'il n'y a que l'Empereur de Russie qui ait ce droit.

Toutes les fois cependant que l'Empereur de Russie ratifierait la dite convention, je la ratifierai; mais ce n'est q'une ruse. Marchez, détruisez l'armée russe . . . vous êtes en position de prendre son bagage et son artillerie.

L'aide-de-camp de l'Empereur de Russie est un . . . Les officiers ne sont rien quand ils n'ont pas de pouvoirs: celui-ci n'en avait point . . . Les Autrichiens se sont laissé jouer pour le passage du pont de Vienne, vous vous laissez jouer par un aide-de-camp de l'Empereur.

*Napoléon.**[17]

Bonaparte's adjutant galloped off at full speed with this threatening letter to Murat. Bonaparte himself, not trusting his generals, moved with all his guards to the field of battle, fearing to let the ready victim slip, while Bagration's four-thousand-man division cheerfully lit campfires, dried out, warmed up, cooked kasha for the first time in three days, and not one man in the division knew or thought about what lay ahead of him.

XV

It was past three o'clock in the afternoon when Prince Andrei, who had persuaded Kutuzov to grant his request, arrived in Grunt and went to Bagration. Bonaparte's adjutant had not yet reached Murat's division, and the battle had not yet begun. In Bagration's division, nothing was known about the general course of affairs; they talked of peace, but did not believe in its possibility. They talked of battle and also did not believe in the nearness of battle.

Bagration, knowing Bolkonsky to be a favourite and trusted adjutant, received him with a superior officer's special distinction and indulgence, explained to

---

*To Prince Murat. Schönbrunn, 25 Brumaire [15 November] 1805, at eight o'clock a.m. It is impossible for me to find words to express to you my displeasure. You command only my vanguard and you do not have the right to make an armistice without my order. You are making me lose the fruits of a campaign. Break the armistice on the spot and march to the enemy. Declare to him that the general who signed this capitulation did not have the right to make it, that only the Emperor of Russia has that right.

Any time, however, that the Emperor of Russia will ratify the said convention, I will ratify it; but it is only a trick. March, destroy the Russian army . . . you are in a position to take their baggage and artillery.

The adjutant of the Emperor of Russia is a . . . Officers are nothing when they have no power: this one has none . . . The Austrians let themselves be fooled in the crossing of the bridge of Vienna, you are letting yourself be fooled by one of the Emperor's adjutants. Napoleon.

him that there would probably be a battle that day or the next, and allowed him full freedom to stay by him during the battle or to supervise the order of retreat in the rear guard, "which was also very important."

"However, there will probably be no action today," said Bagration, as if to soothe Prince Andrei.

"If he's one of those ordinary staff dandies sent to earn himself a little cross, he can earn it just as well in the rear guard, but if he wants to be with me, let him . . . he'll be useful, if he's a brave officer," thought Bagration. Prince Andrei, having said nothing, asked permission to go around the lines and learn the disposition of the forces, so as to know where to go in case of an errand. The officer on duty in the detachment, a handsome man, foppishly dressed and with a diamond ring on his index finger, who spoke French poorly but eagerly, volunteered to accompany Prince Andrei.

On all sides one saw wet, sad-faced officers, who seemed to be looking for something, and soldiers, who were dragging doors, benches, and fences from the village.

"You see, Prince, we can't rid ourselves of these folk," said the staff officer, pointing to them. "The commanders neglect discipline. And here," he pointed to a sutler's tent, "they crowd in and sit. This morning I drove them all out: look, it's full again. We must ride over, Prince, and scare them away. For a moment."

"Let's go in. I'll have some bread and cheese," said Prince Andrei, who had not yet had time to eat.

"Why didn't you tell me, Prince? I'd have offered you my hospitality."

They dismounted and went into the sutler's tent. Several officers with flushed and languorous faces were sitting at tables eating and drinking.

"Well, what is this, gentlemen?" the staff officer said in a tone of reproach, like a man who has already repeated the same thing several times. "You can't absent yourselves like this. The prince ordered that nobody should be found here. Well, take you, Mister Staff Captain," he addressed a small, dirty, thin artillery officer, who was standing bootless before the entering men (he had given his boots to the sutler to dry), just in his stockings, smiling not quite naturally.

"Well, Captain Tushin, aren't you ashamed?" the staff officer went on. "It would seem that you, as an artillerist, ought to set an example, and here you are bootless. They'll sound the alarm, and a fine one you'll be with no boots on." (The staff officer smiled.) "Kindly go back to your posts, gentlemen—all, all of you," he added in a superior's tone.

Prince Andrei smiled involuntarily, looking at Captain Tushin. Silent and smiling, Tushin shifted from one bare foot to the other, and looked questioningly with his large, intelligent and kindly eyes first at Prince Andrei, then at the staff officer.

"Soldiers say it's nimbler barefoot," said Captain Tushin with a timorous smile, evidently wishing to turn his awkward position into a joke.

But before he finished, he felt that his joke was unsuccessful and had not gone over. He became embarrassed.

"Kindly go," said the staff officer, trying to maintain his seriousness.

Prince Andrei looked once more at the little figure of the artillerist. There was something special in it, totally unmilitary, slightly comical, but extremely attractive.

The staff officer and Prince Andrei got on their horses and rode further.

Having left the village, constantly meeting and going ahead of walking soldiers, officers of various detachments, they saw to their left the reddish, fresh, newly dug clay of the fortification under construction. Several battalions of soldiers in nothing but their shirts, despite the cold wind, were swarming like white ants over this fortification; someone invisible kept shovelling out red clay from behind the rampart. They rode up to the fortification, examined it, and rode on. Just behind the fortification they ran into several dozen soldiers, constantly replacing each other, running down the rampart. They had to hold their noses and set their horses at a trot to get away from that poisoned atmosphere.

"*Voilà l'agrément des camps, monsieur le prince,*"* said the staff officer on duty.

They rode to the opposite hill. From this hill they could already see the French. Prince Andrei stopped and began to examine.

"Here's where our battery stands," said the staff officer, indicating the highest point, "the one of that odd bird who was sitting there without boots. You can see everything from there: let's go, Prince."

"I humbly thank you, I'll go by myself now," said Prince Andrei, wishing to rid himself of the staff officer, "don't trouble yourself, please."

The staff officer stayed behind, and Prince Andrei rode on alone.

The further ahead he moved, the closer to the enemy, the more orderly and cheerful the troops looked. The greatest disorder and despondency had been in that baggage train before Znaim, which Prince Andrei had circled round in the morning, and which was some seven miles away from the French. In Grunt there was also a feeling of a certain alarm and fear of something. But the closer Prince Andrei rode to the French line, the more self-assured our troops looked. Lined up in ranks, the soldiers stood in their greatcoats, and a sergeant major and a company commander counted heads, jabbing a finger towards the last soldier in the row and ordering him to raise his hand; scattered all over the area, soldiers were carrying firewood and brushwood and building little lean-tos, laughing merrily and talking among themselves; some sat by the campfires, dressed or naked, drying their shirts and foot cloths, or mending boots and

*That's the pleasure of camp life, Prince.

greatcoats, crowding around the cauldrons and cooks. In one company, dinner was ready, and the soldiers looked greedily at the steaming cauldrons, waiting until an officer who was sitting on a log facing his lean-to had tried the kasha brought to him in a wooden bowl by a quartermaster sergeant.

In another, more fortunate company, since not all of them had vodka, soldiers crowded around a pockmarked, broad-shouldered sergeant major, who, tipping a keg, poured into the canteen caps that the soldiers held out in turn. The soldiers, with pious faces, brought the caps to their mouths, upended them, and, rinsing their mouths and wiping them on their greatcoat sleeves, walked away from the sergeant major with cheered faces. All the faces were as calm as though everything was happening not in view of the enemy, prior to an action in which at least half the division would be left on the field, but somewhere in their home country, in expectation of a peaceful stay. Having passed the regiment of chasseurs, and through the lines of the Kievsky grenadiers—brave folk, occupied with the same peaceful affairs—Prince Andrei drew near the tall lean-to, unlike the others, of the regimental commander, and came out to a lined-up platoon of grenadiers before whom lay a stripped man. Two soldiers were holding him, and two, swinging supple switches, were beating him rhythmically on his stripped back. The punished man was crying out unnaturally. A fat major walked in front of the line and, paying no attention to the cries, ceaselessly repeated:

"It is a disgrace for a soldier to steal, a soldier should be honest, noble, and brave; and if one steals from his comrade, there is no honour in him, he is a scoundrel. More, more!"

Again there came the supple strokes and a desperate but feigned cry.

"More, more," repeated the major.

A young officer, with an expression of perplexity and suffering on his face, walked away from the punished man, looking questioningly at the passing adjutant.

Prince Andrei, having reached the front line, rode along it. Our line and the enemy's stood far from each other on the left and right flanks, but in the centre, where the envoys had passed that morning, the lines came so close that the men could see each other's faces and talk to each other. Besides the soldiers who occupied the line at that place, many of the curious stood on both sides and gazed, laughing, at their strange and foreign-looking enemies.

Since early morning, though it was forbidden to go near the line, the officers had been unable to ward off the curious. The soldiers stationed on the line, like people displaying something rare, no longer looked at the French, but made their observations to those who came and, languishing, waited to be relieved. Prince Andrei stopped to examine the French.

"Look, look," one soldier said to his comrade, pointing to a Russian musketeer who had gone up to the line along with an officer and was speaking rapidly and heatedly with a French grenadier. "See how clever he patters away. Even the Khrenchman can't keep up with him. Now you, Sidorov . . ."

"Wait, listen. That's really clever!" replied Sidorov, who was considered an expert at speaking French.

The soldier at whom the laughing men were pointing was Dolokhov. Prince Andrei recognized him and listened to what he was saying. Dolokhov and his company commander had come to the line from the left flank, where their regiment was stationed.

"Go on, more, more!" the company commander egged him on, leaning forward and trying not to miss a single incomprehensible word. "Thicker and faster! What's he saying?"

Dolokhov did not answer his company commander; he was involved in a heated argument with the French grenadier. They were talking, as they could only have been, about the campaign. The Frenchman, confusing the Austrians with the Russians, insisted that the Russians had surrendered and fled all the way from Ulm. Dolokhov insisted that the Russians had not surrendered, but had beaten the French.

"We have orders to drive you away, and that's what we're going to do," said Dolokhov.

"Only try hard not to get captured with all your Cossacks," said the French grenadier.

The French onlookers and listeners laughed.

"We'll make you dance, as you danced for Suvorov" *(on vous fera danser)*, said Dolokhov.

*"Qu'est-ce qu'il chante?"** said one Frenchman.

"De l'histoire ancienne," said a third, realizing that the talk was about former wars. *"L'Empereur va lui faire voir à votre Souvara, comme les autres . . ."*†

"Bonaparte . . ." Dolokhov began, but the Frenchman interrupted him.

"There is no Bonaparte. There is the Emperor! *Sacré nom . . .*"‡ he cried angrily.

"Devil take your emperor!"

And Dolokhov produced a rude soldier's curse and, shouldering his gun, walked off.

"Come on, Ivan Lukich," he said to the company commander.

"That's the Khrench for you," the soldiers started talking in the line. "Now you, Sidorov!"

Sidorov winked and, turning to the French, began pouring out a thick patter of incomprehensible words:

---

*What's he singing?
†Ancient history . . . The Emperor will show your Souvara, just like the others . . .
‡In God's name . . .

"Kari, mala, tafa, safi, muter, kaskà," he pattered, trying to give his voice expressive intonations.

"Ho, ho, ho! Ha, ha, ha, ha! Hoo, hoo!" Peals of such healthy and merry guffawing came from among the soldiers that it crossed the line and involuntarily infected the French, after which it seemed they ought quickly to unload their guns, blow up their munitions, and all quickly go back home.

But the guns remained loaded, the loopholes in the houses and fortifications looked out just as menacingly, and the unlimbered cannon remained turned against each other just as before.

XVI

Having ridden all along the line of troops from the right flank to the left, Prince Andrei went up to the battery, from which, according to the staff officer's words, one could see the whole field. Here he got off his horse and stopped by the last of the four unlimbered cannon. In front of the cannon paced an artillery sentry, who snapped to attention before the officer, but at a sign from him renewed his measured, tedious pacing. Behind the cannon stood their limbers, further behind a hitching rail and the campfires of the artillerists. To the left, not far from the last cannon, there was a newly plaited lean-to from which came the animated voices of the officers.

Indeed, from the battery a view opened out of almost the entire disposition of the Russian troops and the greater part of the enemy's. Directly facing the battery, on the crest of the knoll opposite, one could see the village of Schöngraben; to left and right it was possible to make out in three places amidst the smoke of their campfires the masses of the French troops, of whom the greater part were evidently in the village itself and behind the hill. To the left of the village, in the smoke, appeared something resembling a battery, but it was impossible to see it well with the naked eye. Our right flank was disposed on a rather steep elevation, which dominated the positions of the French. On it our infantry was disposed, and at the very end one could see the dragoons. In the centre, where Tushin's battery stood, from where Prince Andrei was surveying the position, there was a gently sloping and direct descent and ascent to the stream that separated us from Schöngraben. To the left our troops adjoined a woods, where smoked the campfires of our infantry, who were cutting firewood. The French line was wider than ours, and it was obvious that the French could easily encircle us from both sides. Behind our position was a steep and deep ravine, through which it would be hard for artillery and cavalry to retreat. Prince Andrei, leaning his elbow on the cannon and taking out his notebook, drew a plan of the disposition of the troops for himself. In two places he pencilled some notes, intending to tell Bagration about them. He proposed, first, to concentrate all the artillery in the centre; second, to transfer the cavalry back to the other side of the ravine. Prince Andrei had been constantly at the commander in chief's side, had followed the movements of masses and the general orders, and had constantly been taken up with historical descriptions of battles, and in this forthcoming action involuntarily considered the future course of the military operations only in general terms. He pictured only major occurrences of the following kind: "If the enemy mounts an attack on the right flank," he said to himself, "the Kievsky grenadiers and the Podolsky chasseurs will have to hold their positions until reserves from the centre reach them. In that case, the dragoons can strike at the flank and overthrow them. In case of an attack on the centre, we can deploy the central battery on this elevation, and under its cover pull back the left flank and retreat into the ravine by echelons," he reasoned to himself . . .

All the while he was in the battery by the cannon, as often happens, he had never stopped hearing the sounds of the officers' voices, talking in the lean-to, but had not understood a single word of what they were saying. Suddenly the sound of voices from the lean-to struck him with such soul-felt tones that he involuntarily began to listen.

"No, dear heart," spoke a pleasant voice, which seemed familiar to Prince Andrei, "I say that if it were possible to know what there will be after death, none of us would be afraid of death. That's so, dear heart."

Another, younger voice interrupted him:

"Afraid or not, all the same you can't avoid it."

"But you're still afraid! Eh, you learned people," said a third, manly voice, interrupting the two others. "That's why you artillerists are so learned, because you can tote everything along with you, both vodka and grub."

And the owner of the manly voice, probably an infantry officer, laughed.

"But you're still afraid," the first, familiar voice went on. "Afraid of the unknown, that's what. However much we say that the soul will go to heaven . . . we know that there is no heaven, but only atmosphere."[18]

Again the manly voice interrupted the artillerist.

"Well, let's have some of your herb liqueur, Tushin," it said.

"Ah, it's that same captain who stood without boots in the canteen," thought Prince Andrei, glad to have identified the pleasant, philosophizing voice.

"Herb liqueur's possible," said Tushin, "but even so, to understand the future life . . ." He did not finish.

Just then a whistling was heard in the air; closer, closer, faster and louder, louder and faster, and a cannonball, as if not finishing all it had to say, crashed to the ground with inhuman force not far from the lean-to, throwing up a spray of dirt. The earth seemed to gasp from the terrible blow.

At that same moment little Tushin came running out of the lean-to ahead of everyone else, his pipe askew in his teeth; his kindly, intelligent face was slightly pale. After him the owner of the manly voice came out, a dashing infantry officer, and ran to his company, buttoning himself up as he ran.

XVII

Prince Andrei, mounted up, stayed at the battery, looking at the smoke of the cannon from which the cannonball had come flying. His eyes ran over the vast space. He saw only that the previously immobile masses of the French began to sway, and that there was indeed a battery to the left. The smoke there had not yet dispersed. Two French horsemen, probably adjutants, were galloping over the hill. A small column of the enemy, clearly visible, was moving down the hillside, probably to reinforce the line. The smoke of the first shot had not scattered when another puff appeared, followed by a report. The battle had begun. Prince Andrei turned his horse and rode back to Grunt to look for Prince Bagration. Behind him he heard the cannonade growing louder and heavier. Evidently ours had begun to respond. Below, in the place where the envoys had passed, musket fire was heard.

Lemarrois had just come galloping to Murat with the menacing letter from Bonaparte, and the shamed Murat, wishing to smooth over his mistake, at once moved his troops up to the centre and round both flanks, hoping before evening and the emperor's arrival to crush the insignificant detachment that stood facing him.

"It's begun! Here it is!" thought Prince Andrei, feeling the blood beginning to rush more quickly to his heart. "But where, then? How will my Toulon declare itself?" he thought.

Riding among the same companies that had been eating kasha and drinking vodka a quarter of an hour ago, he saw everywhere the same quick movements of soldiers lining up and taking their muskets, and on all faces he recognized the feeling of animation that was in his heart. "It's begun! Here it is! Fearful and merry!" spoke the face of every soldier and officer.

Before he reached the still-unfinished fortification, he saw horsemen moving towards him in the evening light of the grey, autumnal day. The foremost, in a felt cloak and peaked astrakhan cap, was riding a white horse. It was Prince Bagration. Prince Andrei stopped to wait for him. Prince Bagration reined in his horse and, recognizing Prince Andrei, nodded to him. He went on looking ahead all the while Prince Andrei was telling him what he had seen.

The expression "It's begun! Here it is!" was even on the firm, swarthy face of Prince Bagration, with its half-closed eyes, lacklustre as if from want of sleep. Prince Andrei peered into that immobile face with anxious curiosity, and wished to know whether this man thought and felt, and what he thought and felt, at that moment. "Is there anything there behind that immobile face?" Prince Andrei asked himself, looking at him. Prince Bagration inclined his head as a sign of assent to Prince Andrei's words, and said "Very good" with such an expression as if everything that was taking place and that had been reported to him was precisely what he had already foreseen. Prince Andrei, breathless from fast riding, spoke quickly. Prince Bagration pronounced words especially slowly with his Oriental accent, as if to suggest that they were not hurrying anywhere. Nevertheless, he started his horse at a trot towards Tushin's battery. Prince Andrei and the suite followed behind him. Behind Prince Bagration rode an officer of the suite, the prince's personal adjutant, Zherkov, an orderly officer, the staff officer on duty, on a handsome bobtailed horse, and a state councillor, an auditor, who had asked to come to the battle out of curiosity. The auditor, a plump man with a plump face and a naïve smile of joy, looked around him, jolting along on his horse, and made a strange sight in his camlet coat, on a government issue saddle, among the hussars, Cossacks, and adjutants.

"See, he wants to have a look at a battle," Zherkov said to Bolkonsky, pointing to the auditor, "but he's got a knot in the pit of his stomach."

"Well, enough from you," the auditor said with a beaming smile, naïve and at the same time sly, as if he was flattered to be the butt of Zherkov's jokes, and as if he was deliberately trying to seem stupider than he really was.

"*Très drôle, mon monsieur prince,*"* said the staff officer on duty. (He remembered that there was some special way of addressing a prince in French, but was unable to get it right.)

Just then they were all approaching Tushin's battery, and a cannonball landed in front of them.

"What fell?" the auditor asked, smiling naïvely.

"French pancakes," said Zherkov.

"So that's what they hit you with?" asked the auditor. "How frightful!"

And he seemed to melt all over with satisfaction. He had barely finished speaking when there again came an unexpected, dreadful whistle, suddenly ending in a thud against something liquid, and f-f-flop—a Cossack, riding a little to the right and behind the auditor, crashed to the ground with his horse. Zherkov and the staff officer on duty crouched low to their saddles and turned their horses away. The auditor stopped in front of the Cossack, examining him with attentive curiosity. The Cossack was dead, the horse was still thrashing.

Prince Bagration, narrowing his eyes, turned to look and, seeing the cause of the confusion, looked away indifferently, as if saying: "Is it worth bothering with such stupidities?" He stopped his horse the way a good rider does, bent over a little, and straightened his sword, which had caught in his felt cloak. The

---

*Very funny, my Mister Prince.

sword was an old one, not the kind men wore now. Prince Andrei recalled the story of how Suvorov had made a gift of his sword to Bagration in Italy, and this recollection was especially pleasing to him at that moment. They rode up to the battery near which Bolkonsky had stood when he examined the battlefield.

"Whose company?" Prince Bagration asked a fireworker standing by the caissons.

He asked, "Whose company?" but essentially he was asking, "You're not scared here, are you?" And the fireworker understood that.

"Captain Tushin's, Your Excellency," the red-haired, freckle-faced fireworker cried out in a merry voice, snapping to attention.

"So, so," said Bagration, calculating something, and he rode past the limbers to the end cannon.

While he was on his way there, a shot rang out from that cannon, deafening him and his suite, and in the smoke that suddenly surrounded the cannon one could see the artillerists seize hold of it and, straining hurriedly, pull it back to its former place. The broad-shouldered, enormous soldier number one, with a swab in his hand, his legs spread wide, jumped over to the wheel. Number two was loading a charge into the muzzle with a trembling hand. A small, stooping man, the officer Tushin, stumbling over the trail, ran forward, not noticing the general and peering from under his small hand.

"Add two more notches and it'll be just right," he shouted in a high-pitched voice, trying to give it a dashing sound, which did not go with his little figure. "Number two," he squeaked. "Smash 'em, Medvedev!"

Bagration called to the officer, and Tushin went over to the general, putting three fingers to his visor in a timid and awkward movement, not as military men salute, but as priests bless. Though Tushin's guns were meant to be shooting into the hollow, he was sending fireballs at the village of Schöngraben visible straight ahead, before which large masses of French were moving forward.

No one had given Tushin any orders about where to shoot or with what, and, having consulted his sergeant major Zakharchenko, for whom he had great respect, he had decided that it would be good to set fire to the village. "Very good!" Bagration said to the officer's report, and he began to survey the whole battlefield opened out before him, as if calculating something. On the right side the French had come nearest of all. Below the elevation on which the Kievsky regiment stood, in the river hollow, the soul-wrenching roll and crackle of musket fire could be heard, and much further to the right, beyond the dragoons, the officer of the suite pointed out to the prince a column of the French turning our flank. To the left the horizon was limited by the neighbouring woods. Prince Bagration ordered two battalions from the centre to go as reinforcements to the right. The officer of the suite ventured to observe to the prince that, with those two battalions gone, the cannon would remain exposed. Prince Bagration turned to the officer of the suite and looked at him silently with his lacklustre eyes. It seemed to Prince Andrei that the officer of the suite's observation was correct and there was indeed nothing to say. But just then an adjutant came galloping from the regimental commander who was in the hollow with a report that huge masses of the French were coming from below, that the regiment was in disarray and was falling back towards the Kievsky grenadiers. Prince Bagration inclined his head as a sign of assent and approval. He rode to the right at a walk and sent an adjutant to the dragoons with an order to attack the French. But the adjutant sent there came back half an hour later with the report that the regimental commander of the dragoons had already pulled back beyond the ravine, because heavy fire had been directed at him and he had been losing men uselessly, and therefore he had dismounted his riflemen in the woods.

"Very good!" said Bagration.

As he was riding away from the battery, shots were also heard to the left, in the woods, and as it was too far from the left flank for him to get there in time himself, Prince Bagration sent Zherkov there to tell the senior general, the one who had presented the regiment to Kutuzov in Braunau, to pull back beyond the ravine as quickly as possible, because the right flank would probably be unable to hold the enemy for long. Tushin and the battalion covering him were forgotten. Prince Andrei listened carefully to Prince Bagration's exchanges with the commanders and to the orders he gave, and noticed, to his surprise, that no orders were given, and that Prince Bagration only tried to pretend that all that was done by necessity, chance, or the will of a particular commander, that it was all done, if not on his orders, then in accord with his intentions. Owing to the tact shown by Prince Bagration, Prince Andrei noticed that, in spite of the chance character of events and their independence of the commander's will, his presence accomplished a very great deal. Commanders who rode up to Prince Bagration with troubled faces became calm, soldiers and officers greeted him merrily and became more animated in his presence, and obviously showed off their courage before him.

XVIII

Prince Bagration, having ridden to the highest point on our right flank, started down to where rolling gunfire could be heard and nothing could be seen through the powder smoke. The further they descended into the hollow, the less they could see, but the more they could sense the nearness of the actual battlefield. They began to meet the wounded. One with a bloodied head, hatless, was being dragged under the arms by two soldiers. He gurgled and spat. The bullet seemed to have hit him in the mouth or the throat. Another came towards them, walking briskly by himself, without his musket, groaning loudly and waving his arm from the fresh pain, while blood poured over his greatcoat as if from a flask. His face showed more fear than suffering. He had been wounded a moment before. Crossing the road, they began a steep descent and on the slope saw several men who were lying down; they met a crowd of soldiers, some of whom were not wounded. The soldiers were walking up the hill, breathing heavily and, though they saw the general, were talking loudly and waving their arms. Ahead, in the smoke, lines of grey greatcoats could now be seen, and an officer, catching sight of Bagration, ran shouting after the soldiers walking in a crowd, demanding that they turn back. Bagration rode up to the lines, along which there was here and there a rapid crackle of gunfire, drowning out talk and shouts of command. The air was completely saturated with powder smoke. The soldiers' faces were all smudged with powder and animated. Some tamped down with ramrods, others primed the pans and took shot from their pouches, still others fired. But who they were firing at could not be seen owing to the smoke, which there was no wind to scatter. Pleasant buzzing and whistling noises were heard rather often. "What's that?" thought Prince Andrei, riding up to the crowd of soldiers. "It can't be a line, because they're in a bunch! It can't be an attack, because they're not moving; it can't be a square: they're not standing right."

A lean, weak-looking old man, a regimental commander, with a pleasant smile, with eyelids that more than half covered his old man's eyes, giving him a meek look, rode up to Prince Bagration and received him as a host receives a welcome guest. He reported to Prince Bagration that the French had mounted a cavalry attack against his regiment, and that, while the attack had been beaten off, the regiment had lost more than half its men. The regimental commander said that the attack had been beaten off, coming up with this military term to describe what had happened in his regiment; but in reality he did not know himself what had happened in that half hour among the troops entrusted to him, and he could not say for certain whether the attack had been beaten off or his regiment had been crushed by the attack. At the start of the action he knew only that cannonballs and shells began flying all over his regiment and hitting people, that someone then shouted, "Cavalry!" and our men began to fire. And they were still firing, no longer at the cavalry, who had disappeared, but at the French infantry who had appeared in the hollow and were shooting at our men. Prince Bagration inclined his head as a sign that this was all exactly as he had wished and supposed. Turning to the adjutant, he ordered him to bring down from the hill two battalions of the sixth chasseurs, which they had just ridden past. Prince Andrei was struck at that moment by the change that came over Prince Bagration's face. His face expressed that concentrated and happy resolve which occurs in a man who is about to throw himself into the water on a hot day and is making a running start. Neither the sleepy, lacklustre eyes nor the falsely profound look was there: his round, firm, hawk's eyes looked straight ahead with rapture and a certain disdain, apparently not resting on anything, though his movements were as slow and measured as before.

The regimental commander turned to Prince Bagration, entreating him to ride back, because here it was too dangerous. "Please, Your Excellency, for God's sake!" he repeated, glancing for confirmation at the officer of the suite, who turned away from him. "There, kindly see!" He drew attention to the bullets that constantly shrieked, sang, and whistled around them. He spoke in the same tone of entreaty and reproach in which a carpenter speaks to a gentleman who has picked up an axe: "We're used to it, but you'll get blisters on your hands." He spoke as if he himself could not be killed by these bullets, and his half-closed eyes gave his words a still more persuasive expression. The staff officer joined in the regimental commander's admonitions; but Prince Bagration did not respond to them and merely ordered the men to stop shooting and line up so as to make room for the two expected battalions. While he was speaking, the rising wind, as with an invisible hand, drew from right to left the curtain of smoke that had concealed the hollow, and the hill opposite, with the French moving over it, opened out before them. All eyes were involuntarily turned to this French column that was moving towards them, winding down the terraces of the slope. The soldiers' shaggy hats were already visible; one could already distinguish the officers from the men; one could see their standard fluttering against its staff.

"Nice marching," said someone in Bagration's suite.

The head of the column was already down in the hollow. The confrontation was to take place on this side of the slope . . .

The remnants of our regiment which had been in action, lining up hastily, moved to the right; from behind them, scattering the stragglers, came the two battalions of the sixth chasseurs in good order. They had not yet reached Bagration, but one could already hear the heavy, weighty tread of a whole mass of men marching in step. On the left flank, closest of all to Bagration, marched a company commander, a round-faced, stately man with a stupid, happy expression on his face, the same one who had come running from the lean-to. He was obviously thinking of nothing at that moment but the fine figure he would cut as he marched past his superior.

With a parade-like self-satisfaction, he marched lightly on his muscular legs, as if floating, holding himself straight without the least effort, and distinguishing himself by this lightness from the heavy tread of the soldiers who marched in step with him. He carried by his leg an unsheathed, thin, and narrow sword (a curved little sword, not resembling a weapon), and he lithely turned his whole strong body, looking now at his superior, now behind him, without losing step. It seemed that all the forces of his soul were aimed at marching past his superior in the best possible way, and, feeling that he was doing it well, he was happy. "Left . . . left . . . left . . ." he seemed to be saying to himself at every other step, and the wall of soldiers' figures, burdened by packs and muskets, with variously stern faces, moved to this rhythm, as if each of those hundreds of soldiers was mentally saying: "Left . . . left . . . left . . ." at every other step. A fat major, puffing and breaking the step, turned round a bush that was in his way; a lagging soldier, breathless, with a frightened face because of his negligence, trotted to catch up with his company; a cannonball, pushing through the air, flew over the heads of Prince Bagration and his suite, and to the rhythm of "Left . . . left . . . left!" struck the column. "Close ranks!" came the dashing voice of the company commander. The soldiers curved round something at the spot where the cannonball had landed, and a decorated old soldier, a sergeant on the flank, after lingering by the dead men, caught up with his line, skipped to change feet, fell into step, and looked back angrily. "Left . . . left . . . left . . ." seemed to be heard through the ominous silence and the monotonous sound of feet simultaneously tramping the ground.

"Bravo, lads!" said Prince Bagration.

"Glad to be of . . . Your Ex-ex-ex-ex-ex! . . ." rolled through the ranks. A sullen soldier, marching on the left, turned his eyes to Bagration as he shouted, with an expression that seemed to say: "We know it ourselves"; another, without looking and as if fearing to be distracted, opened his mouth wide, shouted, and passed by.

They were ordered to stop and remove their packs.

Bagration rode round the ranks that had gone past him and dismounted. He handed the reins to a Cossack, removed and handed over his felt cloak, stretched his legs, and straightened his peaked cap. The head of the French column, with officers in the fore, appeared from the bottom of the hill.

"God be with us!" Bagration said in a firm, audible voice, turned for a moment to the front line, and, swinging his arms slightly, with the awkward gait of a cavalryman, as if working at it, he went forward over the uneven field. Prince Andrei felt that some invincible force was drawing him forward, and he experienced great happiness.*

The French were already close; walking beside Bagration, Prince Andrei could already make out clearly the bandoliers, the red epaulettes, even the faces of the French. (He clearly saw one old French officer walking uphill with difficulty on splayed feet in gaiters, holding on to bushes.) Prince Bagration

---

*At this point an attack took place of which Thiers says: *"Les russes se conduisirent vaillament, et chose rare à la guerre, on vit deux masses d'infanterie marcher resolument l'une contre l'autre sans qu'aucune des deux céda avant d'être abordée"* (The Russians behaved valiantly and, a rare thing in war, one saw two masses of infantry marching resolutely against each other with neither of them giving way before they met). And Napoleon on the island of St. Helena[19] said: *"Quelques bataillons russes montrèrent de l'intrépidité"* (Some Russian battalions showed dauntlessness). (Tolstoy's note.)

gave no new order and went on walking silently in front of the ranks. Suddenly from among the French came the crack of a shot, a second, a third . . . and all across the disordered enemy ranks spread smoke and the crackle of gunfire. Several of our men fell, among them the round-faced officer who had marched so cheerfully and diligently. But just as the first shot rang out, Bagration turned round and shouted, "Hurrah!"

"Hurra-a-ah!" the prolonged cry spread throughout our line, and, outstripping Prince Bagration and each other, in a disorderly but cheerful and lively crowd, our men ran down the hill after the disordered French.

XIX

The attack of the sixth chasseurs secured the retreat of the right flank. In the centre, the action of Tushin's forgotten battery, which managed to set fire to Schöngraben, stayed the movement of the French. The French were putting out the fire, which was spread by the wind, and allowing time for retreat. The retreat of the centre across the ravine was hasty and noisy; however, the troops, in retreating, did not mix up their detachments. But the left flank, which was simultaneously being attacked and encircled by the superior forces of the French under Lannes, and which consisted of the Azovsky and Podolsky infantry regiments and the Pavlogradsky hussar regiment, was in disorder. Bagration sent Zherkov to the general of the left flank with an order to retreat immediately.

Zherkov, not taking his hand from his cap, briskly started his horse and galloped off. But as soon as he left Bagration, his strength failed him. An insurmountable fear came over him, and he was unable to go where there was danger.

Having reached the troops of the left flank, he did not ride forward, where the shooting was, but went looking for the general and the officers where they could not be, and therefore did not deliver the order.

The command of the left flank belonged, in order of superiority, to the commander of the same regiment that had been presented to Kutuzov at Braunau and in which Dolokhov served as a private. But the command of the extreme left flank was given to the commander of the Pavlogradsky regiment, in which Rostov served, owing to which a misunderstanding arose. The two officers were greatly vexed with each other, and at a time when action had long since started on the right flank, and the French had already begun their offensive, the two officers were taken up with an exchange which had the aim of insulting each other. The regiments, cavalry as well as infantry, were very little prepared for the forthcoming action. The men of the regiments, from private to general, were not expecting a battle and were calmly occupied with peaceful matters: feeding horses in the cavalry, gathering firewood in the infantry.

"If he, however, is senior to mine in the ranking," the German hussar colonel said, turning red and addressing an adjutant who had ridden up, "leave him to do as he wants. I my hussars cannot sacrifice. Bugler! Sound the retreat!"

But things were becoming urgent. Cannonades and gunfire, blending, rumbled on the right and in the centre, and the French greatcoats of Lannes's riflemen were already passing the mill dam and forming up on this side, two musket shots away. The infantry general went up to a horse with his bouncing gait, mounted it, becoming very straight and tall, and rode to the Pavlogradsky commander. The regimental commanders came together with polite bows and with concealed spite in their hearts.

"Once again, Colonel," the general said, "I cannot in any case leave half my men in the woods. I *beg* you, I *beg* you," he repeated, "to take up your *position* and prepare for the attack."

"And I beg you not to interfieren in vat is not your business," the colonel replied hotly. "If you vere a cavalryman . . ."

"I am not a cavalryman, Colonel, but I am a Russian general, and if that is not known to you . . ."

"Very much known, Your Excellency," the colonel suddenly cried, starting his horse and turning a reddish purple. "Be so kind please to go to the front, and you vill see that this position is good *für* nothing. I do not vant to destroy my regiment *für* your pleasure."

"You forget yourself, Colonel. I am not concerned with my own pleasure, and I will not allow you to say so."

The general, accepting the colonel's invitation to a tournament of courage, drew himself up and, frowning, rode with him in the direction of the front, as if all their differences had to be resolved there, at the front, amidst the bullets. They reached the front, several bullets flew over them, and they stopped in silence. There was nothing to look at there, because even from the place where they had been standing before, it had been clear that cavalry could not operate in the bushes and ravines, and that the French were turning their left wing. The general and the colonel stared sternly and significantly at each other, like two cocks preparing to fight, vainly waiting for signs of cowardice. Both passed the examination. Since there was nothing to say, and neither of them wanted to give the other a pretext for claiming he had been the first to run away from the bullets, they would have stood there for a long time, testing each other's courage, if at that moment, in the woods, almost behind them, there had not come a crackle of musket fire and a muffled, merging cry. The French had attacked the soldiers who had gone there for firewood. The hussars could no longer retreat together with the infantry. They were cut off from the path of retreat to the left by the French line. Now, however inconvenient the terrain was, it was necessary to attack in order to cut a path for themselves.

The squadron in which Rostov served had just had time to mount its horses when it was halted facing the enemy. Again, as on the Enns bridge, there was no one between the squadron and the enemy, and there lay between them, separating them, that same terrible line of the unknown and of fear, like the line separating the living from the dead. All the men sensed that line, and the question of whether they would or would not cross that line, and how they would cross it, troubled them.

The colonel rode up to the front, angrily gave some answer to the officers' questions, and, like a man desperately insisting on having his own way, gave some order. No one said anything definite, but the rumour of an attack swept through the squadron. The command to form up was heard, then sabres shrieked as they were drawn from their scabbards. But still no one moved. The troops of the left flank, both infantry and hussars, sensed that their superiors themselves did not know what to do, and the indecisiveness of the superiors communicated itself to the troops.

"Hurry up, hurry up," thought Rostov, sensing that the time had come at last to experience the delight of an attack, of which he had heard so much from his hussar comrades.

"God be with us, lads," Denisov's voice rang out. "At a tghrot, maghrch!"

The croups of the horses in the front row moved. Little Rook pulled at the reins and started off himself.

To the right Rostov saw the first rows of his hussars, and still further ahead he could see a dark strip, which he could not make out but thought to be the enemy. Shots were fired, but in the distance.

"Quicken the tghrot," came the command, and Rostov felt his Little Rook kick up his rump, switching to a canter.

He guessed his movements ahead of time, and felt merrier and merrier. He noticed a solitary tree ahead. This tree was first ahead of him, in the middle of the line that seemed so terrible. But then they crossed that line, and not only was there nothing frightening, but everything became merrier and livelier. "Oh, how I'm going to slash at him," thought Rostov, gripping the hilt of his sabre.

"Hur-r-ra-a-ah!" voices droned.

"Well, now let anybody at all come along," thought Rostov, spurring Little Rook and, outstripping the others, sending him into a full gallop. The enemy could already be seen ahead. Suddenly something lashed at the squadron as if with a broad besom. Rostov raised his sword, preparing to strike, but just then the soldier Nikitenko galloped past, leaving him behind, and Rostov felt, as in a dream, that he was still racing on with unnatural speed and at the same time was staying in place. The familiar hussar Bandarchuk galloped towards him from behind and looked at him angrily. Bandarchuk's horse shied, and he swerved round him.

"What is it? I'm not moving ahead? I've fallen, I've been killed . . ." Rostov asked and answered in the same instant. He was alone now in the middle of the field. Instead of moving horses and hussar backs, he saw the immobile earth and stubble around him. There was warm blood under him. "No, I'm wounded, and my horse has been killed." Little Rook tried to get up on his forelegs, but fell back, pinning his rider's leg. Blood flowed from the horse's head. The horse thrashed and could not get up. Rostov went to get up and also fell: his pouch caught on the saddle. Where ours were, where the French were— he did not know. There was no one around.

Having freed his leg, he got up. "Where, on which side now was that line which had so sharply separated the two armies?" he asked himself, and could not answer. "Has something bad happened to me? There are such cases, and what must be done in such cases?" he asked himself, standing up; and just then he felt that something superfluous was hanging from his numb left arm. His hand was like someone else's. He examined the hand, vainly looking for blood on it. "Well, here are some people," he thought joyfully, seeing several men running towards him. "They'll help me!" In front of these people ran one in a strange shako and a blue greatcoat, dark, tanned, with a hooked nose. Two more and then many came running behind him. One of them said something strange, non-Russian. Among the men in the back, wearing the same shakos, stood a Russian hussar. He was being held by the arms; behind him they were holding his horse.

"He must be one of ours taken prisoner . . . Yes. Can it be they'll take me, too? What men are these?" Rostov kept thinking, not believing his eyes. "Can they be Frenchmen?" He looked at the approaching Frenchmen and, though a moment before he had been galloping only in order to meet these Frenchmen and cut them to pieces, their closeness now seemed so terrible to him that he could not believe his eyes. "Who are they? Why are they running? Can it be they're running to me? Can it be? And why? To kill me? *Me,* whom everybody loves so?" He remembered his mother's love for him, his family's, his friends', and the enemy's intention to kill him seemed impossible. "But maybe even—to kill me!" He stood for more than ten seconds without moving from the spot or understanding his situation. The first Frenchman with the hooked nose came so close that the expression on his face could already be seen. And the flushed alien physiognomy of this man who, with lowered bayonet, holding his breath, was running lightly towards him, frightened Rostov. He seized his pistol and, instead of firing it, threw it at the Frenchman, and ran for the bushes as fast as he could. He ran not with the feeling of doubt and conflict with which he had gone to the Enns bridge, but with the feeling of a hare escaping from hounds. One undivided feeling of fear for his young, happy life possessed his entire being. Quickly leaping over the hedges, with that swiftness with which he had run playing tag, he flew across the field, turning his pale, kind young face back from time to time, and a chill of terror ran down his spine. "No, it's better not to look," he thought, but, running up to the bushes, he turned once more. The Frenchmen lagged behind, and even as he looked back, the front one had just changed his trot to a walk and, turning round, shouted something loudly to his comrade behind him. Rostov stopped. "Something must be wrong," he thought, "it's impossible that they should want to kill me." And meanwhile his left arm was as heavy as though a twenty-pound weight was hanging from it. He could not run any further. The Frenchman also stopped and took aim. Rostov closed his eyes and crouched down. One, two bullets flew whistling past him. He gathered his last strength, held on to his left arm with his right hand, and ran to the bushes. In the bushes there were Russian riflemen.

XX

The infantry regiments, caught unawares in the woods, ran out of the woods, and, companies mixing with other companies, retreated in disordered crowds. One soldier uttered in fear the words: "Cut off!"—senseless and terrible in time of war—and the words, together with the fear, communicated themselves to the whole mass.

"We're surrounded! Cut off! Lost!" cried the voices of running men.

The regimental commander, the moment he heard shooting and cries behind him, knew that something terrible had happened to his regiment, and the thought that he, an exemplary officer, with many years of service, to blame for nothing, might be blamed before his superiors for negligence or inefficiency, struck him so much that, at that same moment, forgetting both the disobedient cavalry colonel and his own dignity as a general, and above all totally forgetting danger and the sense of self-preservation, he gripped the pommel, spurred his horse, and galloped off to his regiment under a hail of bullets that poured down on but luckily missed him. He wanted one thing: to find out what was going on, and help to rectify at all costs any error, if there was one, on his part, so that he, an exemplary officer, with twenty-two years of service, and never reprimanded for anything, would not be blamed for it.

Having galloped luckily through the French, he came to the field beyond the woods through which our men were running and, disobeying commands, heading down the hill. That moment of moral hesitation came which decides the fate of battles: would these disorderly crowds of soldiers heed the voice of their commander, or look at him and go on running? Despite the desperate shouts of the regimental commander, formerly so terrible for the soldiers, despite the furious, crimson face of the regimental commander, who no longer resembled himself, and the waving of his sword, the soldiers went on running, talking, firing into the air, and not listening to his commands. The moral hesitation that decides the fate of battles was obviously being resolved in favour of fear.

The general began to choke from shouting and powder smoke, and stopped in despair. All seemed lost, but at that moment the French, who had been advancing upon our men, suddenly, for no visible reason, ran back, disappeared from the edge of the woods, and in the woods Russian riflemen appeared. This was Timokhin's company, which alone had kept its order in the woods and, having hidden in a ditch nearby, had unexpectedly attacked the French. Timokhin had fallen upon the French with such a desperate cry and such insane and drunken determination, running at the enemy with nothing but a little sword, that the French, having no time to recover, threw down their arms and fled. Dolokhov, who was running beside Timokhin, killed one Frenchman point-blank and was the first to take a surrendering officer by the collar. The fleeing men returned, the battalions formed up, and the French, who had divided the troops of the left flank in two, were momentarily pressed back. The reserve units had time to join in, and the fleeing soldiers stopped. The regimental commander was standing by the bridge with Major Ekonomov, letting the retreating companies pass by him, when a soldier came up to him, took hold of his stirrup, and almost leaned against him. The soldier was wearing a greatcoat of bluish factory broadcloth, he had no pack or shako, his head was bandaged, and there was a French ammunition pouch slung over his shoulder. In his hand he was holding an officer's sword. The soldier was pale, his blue eyes looked insolently into the regimental commander's face, and his mouth smiled. Though the regimental commander was busy giving orders to Major Ekonomov, he could not help paying attention to this soldier.

"Your Excellency, here are two trophies," said Dolokhov, pointing to the French sword and pouch. "I captured an officer. I stopped the company." Dolokhov was breathing heavily from fatigue; he spoke with pauses. "The whole company can testify. I ask you to remember, Your Excellency!"

"Very well, very well," said the regimental commander, and he turned to Major Ekonomov.

But Dolokhov did not go away; he untied the handkerchief, pulled it off, and showed the clotted blood on his head.

"A bayonet wound. I stayed at the front. Remember, Your Excellency."

Tushin's battery was forgotten, and only at the very end of the action did Prince Bagration, still hearing cannon fire from the centre, send the staff officer on duty there and then Prince Andrei, to order the battery to retreat as quickly as possible. The covering troops stationed next to Tushin's cannon had left on somebody's order in the middle of the action; but the battery went on firing and was not taken by the French only because the enemy could not suppose that such bold firing was coming from four unprotected cannon. On the contrary, from the energetic operation of the battery, they supposed that the main Russian forces were concentrated there in the centre, and they tried twice to attack that point, and were driven off both times by the canister fire of the four cannon standing solitarily on the elevation.

Soon after Prince Bagration's departure, Tushin managed to set fire to Schöngraben.

"Look, they're scurrying around! It's burning! Look at the smoke! Fine work! Grand! What smoke, what smoke!" said the crews, growing animated.

Without any order, all the cannon were turned in the direction of the fire. As if egging it on, the soldiers kept crying at each shot: "Fine work! That's the way! Just look . . . Grand!" The fire, borne by the wind, spread quickly. The French columns that had moved out of the village went back, but, as if in punishment for this failure, the enemy set up ten guns to the right of the village and began firing them at Tushin.

Owing to the childlike joy aroused by the fire, and the excitement of their successful shooting at the French, our artillerists noticed this battery only when two cannonballs and then four more landed among the guns, and one brought down two horses and another tore the leg off a caisson master. The animation, once established, did not weaken, however, but only changed in mood. The horses were replaced by others from spare carriages, the wounded were removed, and the four guns were turned against the ten-cannon battery. An officer, Tushin's comrade, had been killed at the beginning of the action, and in the course of an hour seventeen out of the forty men of the gun crews had been eliminated, yet the artillerists were still just as merry and animated. Twice they noticed that the French had appeared below, close to them, and then they fired on them with canister shot.

The small man with weak, awkward movements constantly asked his orderly to give him *another little pipeful for that,* as he put it, and spilling fire from it, ran forward and looked at the French from under his small hand.

"Smash 'em, lads!" he kept saying and would seize the guns by the wheel and unscrew the screws himself.

Amidst the smoke, deafened by the ceaseless firing, which made him jump each time, Tushin, without relinquishing his nose-warmer, ran from one gun to the other, now taking aim, now counting the charges, now ordering the dead and wounded horses to be changed and reharnessed, and shouting all the while in his weak, high, irresolute voice. His face was growing more and more animated. Only when people were killed or wounded, he winced and, turning away from the dead man, shouted angrily at his crew, who, as always, were slow to pick up a wounded man or a body. His soldiers, for the most part fine, handsome fellows (two heads taller and twice as broad as their officer, as always in a battery company), all looked to their commander, like children in a difficult situation, and the expression on his face was inevitably mirrored on theirs.

As a result of the dreadful rumbling, the noise, the necessity for attention and activity, Tushin did not experience the slightest unpleasant feeling of fear, and the thought that he could be killed or painfully wounded did not occur to him. On the contrary, he felt ever merrier and merrier. It seemed to him that the moment when he saw the enemy and fired the first shot was already very long ago, maybe even yesterday, and that the spot on the field where he stood was a long-familiar and dear place to him. Though he remembered everything, considered everything, did everything the best officer could do in his position, he was in a state similar to feverish delirium or to that of a drunken man.

From the deafening noise of his guns on all sides, from the whistling and thud of the enemy's shells, from the sight of the sweaty, flushed crews hustling about the guns, from the sight of the blood of men and horses, from the sight of the little puffs of smoke on the enemy's side (after each of which a cannon-ball came flying and hit the ground, a man, a cannon, or a horse)—owing to the sight of all these things, there was established in his head a fantastic world of his own, which made up his pleasure at that moment. In his imagination, the enemy's cannon were not cannon but pipes, from which an invisible smoker released an occasional puff of smoke.

"Look, he's puffing away again," Tushin said to himself in a whisper, as a puff of smoke leaped from the hillside and was borne leftwards in a strip by the wind, "now wait for the ball—and send it back."

"What orders, Your Honour?" asked the fireworker, who was standing close to him and heard him mutter something.

"Nothing . . . a shell . . ." he replied.

"Now for our Matvevna," he said to himself. In his imagination, Matvevna was the big cannon at the end, of ancient casting. The French looked like ants around their guns. A handsome man and a drunkard, the number one at the second gun was known in his world as *uncle;* Tushin looked at him more often than at the others and rejoiced at his every movement. The sound of musket fire at the foot of the hill, now dying down, now intensifying again, seemed to him like someone's breathing. He listened to the fading and flaring up of these sounds.

"Hah, breathing again, breathing," he said to himself.

He pictured himself as of enormous size, a mighty man, flinging cannonballs at the French with both hands.

"Well, Matvevna, old girl, don't let us down!" he said, moving away from the gun, when a strange, unfamiliar voice rang out over his head.

"Captain Tushin! Captain!"

Tushin turned round, frightened. It was the same staff officer who had driven him out of Grunt. He was shouting at him in a breathless voice:

"What, have you lost your mind? You've been ordered twice to retreat, but you . . ."

"Well, what are they getting at me for? . . ." Tushin thought to himself, looking fearfully at his superior.

"I . . . nothing . . ." he said, putting two fingers to his visor. "I . . ."

But the colonel did not finish everything he wanted to say. A cannonball flew close to him and made him duck and crouch down on his horse. He fell silent and was about to say something more when another cannonball stopped him. He turned his horse and galloped away.

"Retreat! Everybody retreat!" he called from the distance.

The soldiers laughed. A moment later an adjutant arrived with the same order.

This was Prince Andrei. The first thing he saw on riding out into the space occupied by Tushin's cannon was an unharnessed horse with a shattered leg that was whinnying near the harnessed horses. Blood was pouring from its leg as from a spout. Among the limbers several men lay dead. One cannonball after another flew over him as he rode on, and he felt a nervous shiver run down his spine. But the thought alone that he was afraid picked him up again. "I can't be afraid," he thought and slowly dismounted among the cannon. He delivered the order and did not leave the battlefield. He decided that the guns would leave the position and be taken away in his presence. Together with Tushin, stepping over the bodies and under the dreadful fire of the French, he got busy with removing the guns.

"Another superior just came, and he turned tail quickly," the fireworker said to Prince Andrei, "not like Your Honour."

Prince Andrei said nothing to Tushin. The two men were so busy that they seemed not even to see each other. Having limbered up the two remaining guns of the four (one smashed cannon and a unicorn[20] were abandoned), Prince Andrei rode up to Tushin.

"Well, goodbye," said Prince Andrei, offering his hand to Tushin.

"Goodbye, dear heart," said Tushin, "you good soul! Goodbye, dear heart," Tushin said with tears, which for some reason suddenly came to his eyes.

XXI

The wind grew still, black clouds hung low over the place of battle, merging on the horizon with powder smoke. It was getting dark, and the glow of the fire showed more clearly in two places. The cannonade became weaker, but the crackle of gunfire behind and to the right was heard more often and close. As soon as Tushin with his guns, driving round or over the wounded, came out from under fire and descended into the ravine, he met the superiors and adjutants, among whom were the staff officer and Zherkov, who had been sent twice and had twice failed to reach Tushin's battery. All of them, interrupting each other, gave and conveyed orders of how and where to go, and reproached and reprimanded him. Tushin had no orders to give and rode silently behind them on his artillery nag, fearing to speak, because he was ready at every word to burst into tears, not knowing why himself. Though the order was to abandon the wounded, many of them dragged after the troops, asking to be put on the guns. The dashing infantry officer who had run out of Tushin's lean-to before the battle was put on Matvevna's carriage, a bullet in his stomach. At the foot of the hill a pale hussar junker, holding one arm with his other hand, came up to Tushin and asked for a seat.

"Captain, for God's sake, I've bruised my arm," he said timidly. "For God's sake, I can't walk. For God's sake!"

It was clear that this junker had already asked for a seat more than once elsewhere and everywhere had been refused. He asked in an irresolute and pitiful voice.

"Tell them to give me a seat, for God's sake."

"Give him a seat, give him a seat," said Tushin. "You, uncle, spread a greatcoat under him," he turned to his favourite soldier. "And where's the wounded officer?"

"We unloaded him, he died," someone answered.

"Give this one a seat. Sit down, my dear, sit down. Spread the greatcoat under him, Antonov."

The junker was Rostov. He was holding one arm with the other hand, was pale, and his lower jaw was trembling feverishly. He was seated on Matvevna, the same cannon from which they had unloaded the dead officer. The greatcoat spread under him had blood on it, which stained Rostov's breeches and hands.

"What, are you wounded, dear heart?" asked Tushin, coming to the cannon on which Rostov was sitting.

"No, bruised."

"Why is there blood on the side plate?" asked Tushin.

"That officer bloodied it, Your Honour," the artillerist replied, wiping the blood with the sleeve of his greatcoat and as if apologizing for the unclean state the gun was in.

They were barely able, with the help of the infantry, to get the guns up the hill, and having reached the village of Guntersdorf, they halted. It grew so dark that it was impossible to make out the soldiers' uniforms from ten paces away, and the crossfire began to die down. Suddenly, close by on the right-hand side, shouts and gunfire were heard again. Shots flashed in the darkness. This was the last attack of the French, which was being fought off by soldiers sheltering in the village houses. All rushed out of the village again, but Tushin's guns could not move, and the artillerists, Tushin, and the junker silently looked at each other, awaiting their fate. The crossfire began to die down, and soldiers, talking animatedly, poured out of a side street.

"Unhurt, Petrov?" asked one.

"We roasted 'em, brother. They won't try that again," said another.

"Couldn't see a thing. What a roasting they gave their own! Couldn't see, it's so dark, brother. Got anything to drink?"

The French had been beaten off for the last time. And again, in total darkness, Tushin's guns, as if framed by the humming infantry, moved on somewhere.

It was as if an invisible, gloomy river were flowing in the darkness, all in one direction, with a hum of whispers, talk, and the sounds of hooves and wheels. In the general hum, the groans and voices of the wounded sounded most clearly of all in the gloom of the night. Their groans seemed to fill all the gloom surrounding the troops. Their groans and the gloom of that night were one and the same. After some time there was a stir in the moving crowd. Someone with a suite rode by on a white horse and said something as he rode by.

"What did he say? Where to now? A halt, or what? Did he thank us, or what?" eager questions came from all sides, and the entire moving mass began to push upon itself (evidently those in front had stopped), and a rumour spread that there was an order to halt. They all halted where they were, in the middle of the muddy road.

Fires were lit and the talk became more audible. Captain Tushin, having given orders to his company, sent one of the soldiers to look for a dressing station or a doctor for the junker and sat down by the fire the soldiers had started on the road. Rostov also dragged himself to the fire. A feverish trembling from pain, cold, and dampness shook his whole body. Sleep was coming over him irresistibly, yet he could not fall asleep from the tormenting pain in his arm, which ached and found no comfortable position. Now he closed his eyes, then he gazed at the fire, which seemed a hot red to him, then at the stooping, weak little figure of Tushin, who was sitting next to him Turkish fashion. Tushin's large, kind, and intelligent eyes were directed at him with compassion and commiseration. He saw that Tushin wanted with all his heart to help him in some way and could not.

On all sides one could hear the footsteps and talk of the infantry walking, driving, and settling themselves around. The sounds of voices, footsteps, and horses' hooves treading in the mud, the crackling of firewood far and near merged into one rippling hum.

Now it was not, as before, an invisible river flowing in the darkness, but like a gloomy sea subsiding and quivering after a storm. Rostov mindlessly watched and listened to what was happening before him and around him. An infantryman came up to the fire, squatted down, put his hands to the fire, and turned his face away.

"You don't mind, Your Honour?" he said, turning questioningly to Tushin.

"I've strayed from my company, Your Honour; I don't know where myself. Worse luck!"

Along with the soldier, an infantry officer with a bound cheek came up to the campfire and addressed Tushin, asking him to move the guns a little bit to let his wagon pass. After the company commander, two soldiers ran to the campfire. They fought and cursed terribly, pulling some boot from each other.

"Sure you picked it up! What a quick-fingers!" one cried in a hoarse voice.

Then came a thin, pale soldier, his neck bandaged with a bloody foot cloth, and in an angry voice demanded water from the artillerists.

"What, is a man to die like a dog?" he said.

Tushin ordered them to give him water. Then a merry soldier ran up, asking for a little fire for the infantry.

"Some hot little fire for the infantry! Keep well, dear countrymen, thanks for the fire, we'll pay it back with interest," he said, carrying the burning brand somewhere into the darkness.

After this soldier, four soldiers carrying something heavy on a greatcoat passed by the campfire. One of them tripped.

"The devils left firewood on the road," he growled.

"He's dead, why carry him around?" asked one of them.

"Eh, you!"

And they disappeared into the darkness with their burden.

"What? it hurts?" Tushin asked Rostov in a whisper.

"Yes."

"The general wants you, Your Honour. He's staying in a cottage here," said the fireworker, coming up to Tushin.

"At once, dear heart."

Tushin got up and, buttoning his greatcoat and smoothing himself out, left the campfire . . .

Not far from the artillerists' campfire, in a cottage prepared for him, Prince Bagration was sitting over dinner, talking with some commanders of branches who had gathered with him. There was the little old man with half-closed eyes, greedily gnawing on a lamb bone, and the twenty-two-year irreproachable general, flushed from a glass of vodka and dinner, and the staff officer with the signet ring, and Zherkov, looking around uneasily at them all, and Prince Andrei, pale, with compressed lips and feverishly shining eyes.

In the corner of the cottage stood a captured French standard, and the auditor with the naïve face fingered the fabric of the standard and shook his head in perplexity, perhaps because he was indeed interested in the look of the standard, or perhaps because it was hard for him, hungry as he was, to look at the table where there was no place set for him. In the cottage next door was a French colonel, taken prisoner by the dragoons. Our officers clustered around him, studying him. Prince Bagration thanked particular superiors and asked for details about the action and the losses. The regimental commander who had been reviewed at Braunau reported to the prince that, as soon as the action began, he withdrew from the woods, gathered the woodcutters and, letting them pass by him, started a bayonet attack with two battalions and overwhelmed the French.

"As soon as I saw that the first battalion was in disorder, Your Excellency, I stood there on the road and thought: 'I'll let them pass and then meet them with ranged fire,' and that's what I did."

The regimental commander had so wanted to do that, he had been so sorry that he had had no time to do it, that it seemed to him that all this was exactly so. And perhaps it really was so? As if one could make out in that confusion what was and was not so?

"With that I must observe, Your Excellency," he went on, remembering Dolokhov's conversation with Kutuzov and his own last encounter with the demoted soldier, "that the demoted private Dolokhov, before my eyes, took a French officer prisoner and particularly distinguished himself."

"And I also saw the attack of the Pavlogradsky hussars, Your Excellency," interrupted Zherkov, looking around uneasily, though he had not seen any hussars that day, but had only heard about them from an infantry officer. "They broke two squares, Your Excellency."

Some smiled at Zherkov's words, expecting a joke from him as usual; but, noticing that what he said also contributed to the glory of our arms and of that day, they assumed serious expressions, though many knew very well that what Zherkov had said was a lie, with no foundation at all. Prince Bagration turned to the little old colonel.

"I thank you all, gentlemen, all the branches acted heroically: infantry, cavalry, and artillery. How is it that two guns in the centre were abandoned?" he asked, seeking someone with his eyes. (Prince Bagration did not ask about the guns of the left flank; he already knew that all the cannon there had been abandoned at the very beginning.) "I asked you to go, I believe," he turned to the staff officer on duty.

"One was knocked out," the staff officer replied, "but I cannot understand about the other. I was there myself all the while and giving orders, and I had only just left . . . It was hot, to tell the truth," he added modestly.

Someone said that Captain Tushin was there near the village and had already been sent for.

"You were there, too," said Prince Bagration, turning to Prince Andrei.

"Of course, we nearly ran into each other," said the staff officer on duty, smiling pleasantly at Bolkonsky.

"I did not have the pleasure of seeing you," Prince Andrei said coldly and abruptly. They all fell silent.

Tushin appeared in the doorway, timidly making his way from behind the generals' backs. Going round the generals in the crowded cottage, embarrassed as usual at the sight of his superiors, Tushin did not see the staff of the standard and stumbled over it. Several voices laughed.

"How is it that a gun was abandoned?" asked Bagration, frowning not so much at the captain as at those who laughed, among whom Zherkov's voice sounded louder than the others.

Only now, at the sight of his dread superiors, did Tushin realize in all its horror his guilt and disgrace at having remained alive while losing two guns. He had been so agitated that until that moment he had not managed to think of it. The laughter of the officers threw him off still more. He stood before Bagration with a trembling lower jaw and was barely able to say:

"I don't know . . . Your Excellency . . . I had no men, Your Excellency."

"You could have taken some of the covering troops!"

Tushin did not tell him that there were no covering troops, though that was the plain truth. He was afraid to *let down* another officer that way and silently, with fixed eyes, looked straight into Bagration's face, as a confused student looks into his examiner's eyes.

The silence was rather prolonged. Prince Bagration, probably unwilling to be severe, could not find what to say; the rest did not dare mix into the conversation. Prince Andrei looked at Tushin from under his eyebrows, and his fingers twitched nervously.

"Your Excellency," Prince Andrei broke the silence with his sharp voice, "you were pleased to send me to Captain Tushin's battery. I was there and found two-thirds of the men and horses killed, two guns crippled, and no cover at all."

Prince Bagration and Tushin now looked with the same intentness at Bolkonsky, who was speaking with restraint and agitation.

"And if Your Excellency will allow me to voice my opinion," he went on, "we owe the success of the day most of all to the operation of this battery and the heroic endurance of Captain Tushin and his company," said Prince Andrei and, without waiting for a reply, he got up at once and stepped away from the table.

Prince Bagration looked at Tushin and, obviously not wishing to show any mistrust of Bolkonsky's sharp judgement, and at the same time feeling himself unable to believe him fully, inclined his head and told Tushin he could go. Prince Andrei went out after him.

"Thank you, dear heart, you rescued me," Tushin said to him.

Prince Andrei looked at Tushin and, saying nothing, walked away. Prince Andrei felt sad and downhearted. All this was so strange, so unlike what he had hoped for.

. . .

"Who are they? Why are they here? What do they want? And when will it all end?" thought Rostov, looking at the shifting shadows before him. The pain in his arm was becoming more and more tormenting. Sleep drew him irresistibly, red circles danced before his eyes, and the impressions of those voices and those faces and a feeling of loneliness merged with the feeling of pain. It was they, these soldiers, wounded and not wounded—it was they who crushed and weighed down and twisted the sinews and burned the flesh of his racked arm and shoulder. To get rid of them, he closed his eyes.

He became oblivious for a moment, but in that brief interval of oblivion he saw a numberless multitude of things in a dream: he saw his mother and her large white hand, saw Sonya's thin little shoulders, Natasha's eyes and laughter, and Denisov with his voice and moustache, and Telyanin, and his whole story with Telyanin and Bogdanych. That whole story was the same as this soldier with the sharp voice, and that whole story and this soldier were what held, crushed, and pulled his arm to one side so painfully and relentlessly. He tried to get away from them, but they would not let go of his shoulder for a moment, for a split second. It would not hurt, it would be well, if they were not pulling on it; but there was no getting rid of them.

He opened his eyes and looked up. The black canopy of the night hung three feet above the light from the coals. A dust of falling snow flew through that light. Tushin did not return, the doctor did not come. He was alone, only some little soldier now sat naked on the other side of the fire, warming his thin, yellow body.

"Nobody needs me!" thought Rostov. "There's nobody to help me or pity me. And once I was at home, strong, cheerful, loved." He sighed and involuntarily groaned as he sighed.

"Ouch, it hurts, eh?" the little soldier asked, waving his shirt over the fire and, not waiting for a reply, he grunted and said: "Quite a few folk got damaged today—awful!"

Rostov was not listening to the soldier. He looked at the snowflakes dancing above the fire and remembered the Russian winter with a warm, bright house, a fluffy fur coat, swift sleighs, a healthy body, and all the love and care of a family. "And why did I come here?" he wondered.

The next day the French did not renew the attack, and the remnant of Bagration's detachment joined Kutuzov's army.

Part Three

I

Prince Vassily did not think out his plans. Still less did he think of doing people harm in order to profit from it. He was simply a man of the world, who succeeded in the world and made a habit of that success. According to his circumstances and his intimacy with people, he constantly formed various plans and schemes which he himself was not quite aware of, but which constituted all the interest of his life. He would have not one or two of these plans and schemes going, but dozens, of which some were only beginning to take shape for him, while others were coming to completion, and still others were abolished. He did not say to himself, for instance: "Here is a man who is now in power, I must gain his trust and friendship and through him arrange for myself the payment of a one-time subsidy," nor did he say to himself: "Here Pierre is rich, I must entice him to marry my daughter and borrow the forty thousand that I need from him"; but let him meet a man in power, and in the same moment his instinct would tell him that the man might be useful, and Prince Vassily would become intimate with him and at the first opportunity, without any preparation, instinctively, would flatter him, behave familiarly, talk about what was needed.

He had Pierre at hand in Moscow, and Prince Vassily arranged for him an appointment as gentleman of the bedchamber, which was then equal to the rank of state councillor, and insisted that the young man should go with him to Petersburg and stay in his house. As if absent-mindedly and at the same time with an indubitable assurance that it had to be so, Prince Vassily did everything necessary to have Pierre marry his daughter. If Prince Vassily had thought out his plans beforehand, he would not have had such naturalness in his dealings and such simplicity and familiarity in his relations with all people, whether of higher or lower station than himself. Something constantly drew him to people more powerful or richer than he, and he was endowed with the rare art of seizing the precise moment when he should and could make use of people.

Pierre, on unexpectedly becoming a rich man and Count Bezukhov, felt himself, after his recent solitary and carefree life, so surrounded, so taken up, that it was only in bed that he managed to remain alone with himself. He had to sign papers, communicate with government offices of whose significance he had no clear notion, ask his chief steward about something, go to his estate near Moscow, and receive a host of persons who formerly did not even care to know of his existence, but who now would be hurt and chagrined if he did not wish to see them. All these various persons—business connections, relations, acquaintances—were equally well and benignly disposed towards the young heir; they were all obviously and indubitably convinced of Pierre's high merits. He so constantly heard the words: "With your extraordinary kindness," or "With your excellent heart," or "You yourself, Count, are so pure . . . ," or "If he were as intelligent as you are," and so on, that he was sincerely beginning to believe in his extraordinary kindness and his extraordinary intelligence, the more so because, deep in his heart, it had always seemed to him that he really was very kind and very intelligent. Even people who had formerly been wicked and obviously hostile became affectionate and loving with him. The angry older princess with the long waist and hair slicked down like a doll's, came to Pierre's room after the funeral. Lowering her eyes and blushing constantly, she told him that she was very sorry about the past misunderstandings between them and that she now felt she had no right to ask for anything, except permission, after the blow she had suffered, to stay on for a few weeks in the house in which she had loved so much and sacrificed so much. She could not help herself and wept at these words. Touched to see that this statue-like princess could change so much, Pierre took her by the hand and apologized, not knowing for what himself. Since that day, the princess had begun to knit a striped scarf for Pierre and was totally changed towards him.

"Do it for her, *mon cher;* after all, she suffered much from the deceased," Prince Vassily said to him, handing him some paper to sign for the princess's benefit.

Prince Vassily had decided that they had to throw this bone, a promissory note for thirty thousand, to the poor princess, so that she would not take it into her head to talk about Prince Vassily's part in the affair of the inlaid portfolio. Pierre had signed the promissory note, and since then the princess had become still kinder. The younger sisters also became affectionate with him, especially the youngest, the pretty one with the little mole, who often confused Pierre with her smiles and her own confusion on seeing him.

It seemed so natural to Pierre that everyone should love him, it would have seemed so unnatural if someone did not love him, that he could not help believing in the sincerity of the people around him. Besides, he had no time to ask himself about the sincerity or insincerity of these people. He was constantly busy, he constantly felt himself in a state of mild and merry intoxication. He felt himself the centre of some important general movement; felt that something was constantly expected of him; that if he were to fail to do this or that, he would upset many people and deprive them of what they expected, but if he were to do this or that, all would be well—and he did what was demanded of him, but this "well" always remained ahead of him.

More than anyone else during this first time, it was Prince Vassily who took possession both of Pierre's affairs and of Pierre himself. Since the death of Count Bezukhov, he never let Pierre out of his hands. Prince Vassily had the look of a man burdened by affairs, weary, exhausted, but finally unable, out of compassion, to leave to the mercies of fate and of swindlers this helpless youth, his friend's son, *après tout,* and with such an immense fortune. In those few days he spent in Moscow after Count Bezukhov's death, he summoned Pierre to him or went to him himself and prescribed for him what was to be done, in such a tone of weariness and assurance as if he were adding each time:

*"Vous savez, que je suis accablé d'affaires et que ce n'est pas que par pure charité, que je m'occupe de vous, et puis vous savez bien que ce que je vous propose est la seule chose faisable."**

"Well, my friend, tomorrow we're off at last," he said to him one day, closing his eyes, fingering Pierre's elbow, and in such a tone as if what he said had been decided between them long, long ago and could not have been decided otherwise.

"Tomorrow we're off, I'm giving you a place in my carriage. I'm very glad. We've finished everything that matters here. I should have left long ago. I have received this from the chancellor. I solicited him on your behalf, and you've been enrolled in the diplomatic corps and made a gentleman of the bedchamber. Now the diplomatic path is open to you."

Despite all the force of the weary and assured tone in which these words were uttered, Pierre, who had been thinking for so long about his career, was about to object. But Prince Vassily interrupted him in that cooing, bass-voiced tone which precluded the possibility of interrupting his speech and which he made use of in cases requiring extreme persuasiveness.

"Mais, mon cher, I did it for myself, for my conscience, and there's nothing to thank me for. No one ever complained about being loved too much; and besides, you're free, you can drop it tomorrow. You'll see everything for yourself in Petersburg. And it's long since time that you distanced yourself from these terrible memories." Prince Vassily sighed. "Yes, yes, dear heart. And let my valet ride in your carriage. Ah, I nearly forgot," Prince Vassily added, "you know, *mon cher,* I had some accounts with the deceased, so I'll keep what I received from Ryazan: you don't need it. We'll work it out later."

What Prince Vassily referred to as "received from Ryazan" was several thousand in quitrent, which Prince Vassily kept for himself.

In Petersburg, just as in Moscow, an atmosphere of affectionate, loving people surrounded Pierre. He could not refuse the post or, rather, the rank

---

*You know that I am overburdened with business and that it is only out of pure charity that I concern myself with you, and then, too, you know very well that what I am proposing to you is the only feasible thing.

(because he did nothing) that Prince Vassily had provided him with, and the acquaintances, invitations, social occupations were so many that Pierre experienced, even more than in Moscow, a feeling of fogginess, hurriedness, and some ever approaching but never attained good.

Of his former bachelor company, many were not in Petersburg. The guards had left on campaign, Dolokhov had been demoted, Anatole was in the army in the provinces, Prince Andrei was abroad, and therefore Pierre had no chance either to spend the nights as he had liked to spend them before, or to ease his heart in a friendly conversation with an older, respected friend. All his time was spent on dinners, balls, and mostly at Prince Vassily's—in the company of the old, fat princess, his wife, and the beautiful Hélène.

Anna Pavlovna Scherer, like the others, manifested to Pierre the change that had occurred in society's view of him.

Formerly, in Anna Pavlovna's presence, Pierre had constantly felt that what he said was improper, tactless, out of place; that his remarks, which seemed clever to him while he was preparing them in his imagination, became stupid as soon as he spoke them aloud, and that, on the contrary, the dullest remarks of Ippolit came out as clever and pleasing. Now everything he said came out as *charmant*. Even if Anna Pavlovna did not say it, he could see that she wanted to say it and only restrained herself out of respect for his modesty.

In the beginning of the winter of 1805–6, Pierre received the customary pink note from Anna Pavlovna with an invitation, to which was added: "*Vous trouverez chez moi la belle Hélène, qu'on ne se lasse jamais voir.*"*

Reading this passage, Pierre felt for the first time that between him and Hélène some sort of connection had been formed, recognized by other people, and this thought at the same time frightened him, as if an obligation had been laid upon him which he could not fulfil, and also pleased him as an amusing supposition.

The soirée at Anna Pavlovna's was the same as the first, only the novelty that Anna Pavlovna was now treating her guests to was not Mortemart, but a diplomat who had come from Berlin and brought the freshest details about the emperor Alexander's visit to Potsdam and the two august friends swearing an indissoluble union in defending the right cause against the enemy of the human race.[1] Pierre was received by Anna Pavlovna with a tinge of sorrow which obviously referred to the fresh loss that had befallen the young man, the death of Count Bezukhov (everyone constantly considered it their duty to convince Pierre that he was very grieved by the death of a father he had hardly known)—and the sorrow was of the same sort as that supreme sorrow which was expressed at the mention of the august empress Maria Feodorovna. Pierre felt flattered by it. Anna Pavlovna arranged the circles in her drawing room with

---

*You will find with me the beautiful Hélène, whom one never tires of seeing.

her usual artfulness. The large circle where Prince Vassily and the generals were had use of the diplomat. Another circle was formed by the tea table. Pierre wanted to join the first, but Anna Pavlovna, who was in the excited state of a commander on the battlefield, when thousands of brilliant new thoughts come along which one scarcely has time to bring to fulfilment—Anna Pavlovna, seeing Pierre, touched his sleeve with her finger:

"*Attendez, j'ai des vues sur vous pour ce soir.*"* She glanced at Hélène and smiled at her.

"*Ma bonne Hélène, il faut que vous soyez charitable pour ma pauvre tante, qui a une adoration pour vous. Allez lui tenir companie pour dix minutes.*† And so that it won't be too boring for you, here you have the dear count, who will not refuse to follow you."

The beauty went to the aunt, but Anna Pavlovna kept Pierre by her, making it look as though she had to give some last necessary instructions.

"She's ravishing, isn't she?" she said to Pierre, pointing to the majestic beauty as she sailed off. "*Et quelle tenue!*‡ What tact for such a young girl, and what a masterly ability to behave! It comes from the heart. Happy the one to whom she will belong! With her even the most unworldly husband will involuntarily and effortlessly occupy a brilliant place in society. Isn't that so? I only wanted to know your opinion." And Anna Pavlovna let Pierre go.

Pierre was sincere in answering affirmatively Anna Pavlovna's question about the artfulness of Hélène's behaviour. If he ever thought about Hélène, he thought precisely about her beauty and that extraordinary, calm ability of hers to be silently dignified in society.

The aunt received the two young people in her corner, but, it seemed, wished to hide her adoration of Hélène and rather wished to show her fear before Anna Pavlovna. She glanced at her niece as if asking what she was to do with these people. As she was leaving them, Anna Pavlovna again touched Pierre's sleeve with her finger and said:

"*J'espère, que vous ne direz plus qu'on s'ennui chez moi*"§—and she glanced at Hélène.

Hélène smiled with an air that said she did not allow the possibility that anyone could see her and not feel admiration. The aunt cleared her throat, swallowed her saliva, and said in French that she was very glad to see Hélène; then she turned to Pierre with the same greeting and the same mien. In the middle of the boring and faltering conversation, Hélène glanced at Pierre and smiled at him that serene, beautiful smile which she smiled at everyone. Pierre was

---

*Wait, I have plans for you this evening.
†My good Hélène, you must be charitable towards my poor aunt, who adores you. Go and keep her company for ten minutes.
‡And what bearing!
§I hope you won't go on saying that it's boring in my house.

so used to that smile, it said so little to him, that he did not pay any attention to it. The aunt was talking just then about a collection of snuffboxes that had belonged to Pierre's late father, Count Bezukhov, and she showed her own snuff-box. Princess Hélène asked to see the portrait of the aunt's husband, which was painted on this snuffbox.

"It must be the work of Vinesse,"[2] said Pierre, naming a famous miniaturist, leaning towards the table in order to take the snuffbox in his hands, and listening to the conversation at the other table.

He got up, wishing to go around, but the aunt handed him the snuffbox right over Hélène, behind her back. Hélène leaned forward so as to make room and, smiling, glanced around. As always at soirées, she was wearing a gown in the fashion of the time, quite open in front and back. Her bust, which had always looked like marble to Pierre, was now such a short distance from him that he could involuntarily make out with his near-sighted eyes the living love-liness of her shoulders and neck, and so close to his lips that he had only to lean forward a little to touch her. He sensed the warmth of her body, the smell of her perfume, and the creaking of her corset as she breathed. He saw not her marble beauty, which made one with her gown, he saw and sensed all the loveliness of her body, which was merely covered by clothes. And once he had seen it, he could not see otherwise, as we cannot return to a once-exposed deception.

She turned, looked straight at him with her shining dark eyes, and smiled.

"So you never noticed before how beautiful I am?" Hélène seemed to say. "You never noticed that I am a woman? Yes, I am a woman who could belong to anyone, even you," said her gaze. And at that moment Pierre felt that Hélène not only could, but must be his wife, that it could not be otherwise.

He knew it at that moment as certainly as he would have known it standing at the altar with her. How it would be and when, he did not know; he did not even know whether it would be good (he even felt that it was not good for some reason), but he knew that it would be.

Pierre lowered his eyes, raised them again, and wanted to see her once more as a distant, alien beauty, the way he had seen her every day before then; but he could no longer do that. Could not, just as a man who once looked at a stalk of tall grass in the mist and saw it as a tree, can look at the stalk of grass itself and once more see it as a tree. She was terribly close to him. She already had power over him. And there were no longer any obstructions between them, except for the obstruction of his own will.

"*Bon, je vous laisse dans votre petit coin. Je vois que vous y êtes très bien,*"* said the voice of Anna Pavlovna.

And Pierre, trying fearfully to recall whether he had done anything repre-

---

*Good, I'll leave you in your little corner. I see you're doing very well there.

hensible, blushed and looked around him. It seemed to him that everyone knew what had happened to him as well as he did.

A short time later, when he went up to the large circle, Anna Pavlovna said to him:

"*On dit que vous embellissez votre maison de Pétersbourg.*"*

(That was true: the architect had said it was needed, and Pierre, not knowing why himself, was redecorating his enormous house in Petersburg.)

"*C'est bien, mais ne déménagez pas de chez le prince Basile. Il est bon d'avoir un ami comme le prince,*" she said, smiling at Prince Vassily. "*J'en sais quelque chose. N'est-ce pas?*† And you're still so young. You need advice. You're not angry with me for exercising an old woman's rights?" She paused, as women always pause and wait for something after referring to their age. "If you get married, that's another matter." And she united them in a single glance. Pierre did not look at Hélène, nor she at him. But she was still just as terribly close to him. He mumbled something and blushed.

On returning home, Pierre could not fall asleep for a long time, thinking about what had happened to him. And what had happened to him? Nothing. He had simply realized that a woman he had known as a child, of whom he used to say distractedly, "Yes, good-looking," when told that Hélène was a beauty—he had realized that this woman could belong to him.

"But she's stupid, I've said myself that she's stupid," he thought. "This isn't love. On the contrary, there's something vile in the feeling she aroused in me, something forbidden. I've been told that her brother Anatole was in love with her and she with him, and there was a whole story, and that's why Anatole was sent away. Ippolit is her brother. Prince Vassily is her father. It's not good," he thought; but while he was arguing like that (these arguments were left unfinished), he caught himself smiling and was aware that a whole series of arguments had floated up from behind the others, that he was at the same time thinking about her worthlessness and dreaming of how she would be his wife, how she might come to love him, how she might be quite different, and how everything he had thought and heard about her might be untrue. And again he saw her not as some daughter of Prince Vassily, but saw her whole body, merely covered by a grey dress. "But no, why did this thought not occur to me before?" And again he said to himself that it was impossible, that there would be something vile, unnatural, as it seemed to him, and dishonest in this marriage. He recalled her former words and looks, and the words and looks of those who had seen them together. He recalled the words and looks of Anna Pavlovna when she spoke to him about his house, recalled hundreds of similar

---

*They say you're redecorating your house in Petersburg.
†That's good, but don't move out of Prince Vassily's. It's good to have a friend like the prince . . . I know something about it. Isn't that so?

hints from Prince Vassily and others, and terror came over him at the thought that he might already have bound himself in some way to go through with something which was obviously not good and which he ought not to do. But while he expressed this realization to himself, on the other side of his soul her image floated up in all its feminine beauty.

II

In November of 1805 Prince Vassily was to go to inspect four provinces. He arranged this assignment for himself so as to visit his disordered estates at the same time and, having picked up his son Anatole (where his regiment was stationed), to go with him to see Prince Nikolai Andreevich Bolkonsky, in order to marry his son to the daughter of this rich old man. But before his departure and these new affairs, Prince Vassily had to decide things with Pierre, who of late had indeed been spending whole days at home, that is, at Prince Vassily's, where he lived, and who was ridiculous, agitated, and stupid (as a man in love ought to be) in Hélène's presence, but had still not made a proposal.

*"Tout ça est bel et bon, mais il faut que ça finisse,"** Prince Vassily said to himself one morning with a sad sigh, conscious that Pierre, who owed so much to him (well, Christ be with him!), was not quite acting properly in this matter. "Youth . . . frivolity . . . well, God be with him," thought Prince Vassily, pleasantly aware of his kindness, *"mais il faut que ça finisse.* The day after tomorrow is Lelya's name day. I'll invite people, and if he doesn't understand what he ought to do, then it will be my business. Yes, my business. I'm a father!"

In the month and a half since Anna Pavlovna's soirée, followed by the sleepless, agitated night in which he decided that marriage to Hélène would be a misfortune and that he must avoid her and go away, Pierre, after this decision, did not move out of Prince Vassily's house, and felt with horror that in people's eyes he was becoming more and more bound to her every day, that he simply could not go back to his former view of her, nor could he tear himself away from her, that it would be terrible, but that he would have to bind his fate to hers. He might perhaps have refrained, but not a day passed without Prince Vassily (who rarely held receptions) having a soirée at which Pierre had to be present, if he did not want to spoil the general pleasure and disappoint everyone's expectations. Prince Vassily, in those rare moments when he was at home, would pass by Pierre, pull his hand downwards, distractedly offer him his clean-shaven, wrinkled cheek to kiss, and say either "See you tomorrow," or "At dinner, otherwise I won't see you," or "I'm staying for your sake," and so on. But despite the fact that, when Prince Vassily stayed for Pierre's sake (as

*This is all well and good, but it must come to an end.

he put it), he did not say two words to him, Pierre did not feel himself capable of disappointing his expectations. Every day he said one and the same thing to himself: "I must finally understand her, and find out for myself who she is. Was I mistaken before, or am I mistaken now? No, she's not stupid; no, she's a wonderful girl!" he sometimes said to himself. "She's never mistaken in anything, she never says anything stupid. She speaks little, but what she says is always simple and clear. So she's not stupid. She's never been embarrassed and is not embarrassed now. So she's not a bad woman!" It often happened when he was with her that he would begin to argue, to think aloud, and she responded to that each time either by a brief but appropriate remark, showing that it did not interest her, or by a silent smile and glance, which showed Pierre her superiority most palpably. She was right in considering all arguments as nonsense compared with that smile.

She always addressed him with a joyful, trusting smile, meant for him alone, in which there was something more significant than what was in the general smile that always adorned her face. Pierre knew that everyone was only waiting for him finally to say one word, to cross a certain line, and he knew that sooner or later he would cross it; but some incomprehensible terror seized him at the mere thought of that frightful step. A thousand times in the course of that month and a half, all the while feeling himself drawn more and more into that frightening abyss, Pierre had said to himself: "But what is it? I need resolve. Don't I have any?"

He wanted to resolve it, but felt with terror that in this case he lacked the resolve that he knew he had and that indeed was in him. Pierre was one of those people who are strong only when they feel themselves perfectly pure. And since the day when he had been possessed by that feeling of desire which he had experienced over the snuffbox at Anna Pavlovna's, an unconscious feeling of guilt on account of that attraction had paralysed his resolve.

On Hélène's name day a small company of friends and relations—the closest people, as the princess put it—had supper at Prince Vassily's. All these friends and relations had been given the feeling that the name-day girl's lot was to be decided that day. The guests were sitting over supper. Princess Kuragin, a massive, once-beautiful, imposing woman, presided as mistress of the house. On either side of her sat the guests of honour—an old general, his wife, and Anna Pavlovna Scherer; at the end of the table sat the less old and honoured guests, and there also, as part of the household, sat Pierre and Hélène—next to each other. Prince Vassily did not eat: he strolled around the table in a merry state of mind, sitting down now with one, now with another of the guests. To each he spoke a casual and agreeable word, except for Pierre and Hélène, whose presence he seemed not to notice. Prince Vassily enlivened everyone. The wax candles burned brightly, the silver and crystal, the ladies' gowns, and the gold and silver epaulettes shone; servants in red kaftans scurried around the table; the sounds of knives, glasses, plates were heard, and the sounds of animated talk in several conversations around that table. An old chamberlain was heard at one end assuring a little old baroness of his ardent love for her, and so, too, was her laughter; at the other end, the story of the unsuccess of some Marya Viktorovna. At the middle of the table Prince Vassily concentrated listeners around himself. He was telling the ladies, with a jocular smile on his lips, about the latest session—on Wednesday—of the state council, at which Sergei Kuzmich Vyazmitinov, the new military governor general of Petersburg, had received and read the then-famous rescript of the sovereign Alexander Pavlovich from the army, in which the sovereign, addressing Sergei Kuzmich, said that he had received declarations of the people's devotion from all sides, and that the declaration from Petersburg was especially pleasing to him, that he was proud of the honour of being the head of such a nation and would try to prove worthy of it. The rescript began with the words: "Sergei Kuzmich! From all sides rumours reach me," and so on.

"So it never went further than 'Sergei Kuzmich'?" one lady asked.

"No, no, not a hair's breadth," Prince Vassily replied, laughing. "'Sergei Kuzmich . . . from all sides. From all sides, Sergei Kuzmich.' Poor Vyazmitinov just couldn't get any further. He took up the letter several more times, but as soon as he said 'Sergei' . . . sobs . . . 'Ku . . . zmi . . . ch'—tears . . . and 'from all sides' was drowned in weeping, and he couldn't go on. And again his handkerchief, and again 'Sergei Kuzmich, from all sides,' and tears . . . so that they finally asked someone else to read it."

"'Kuzmich . . . from all sides . . .' and tears," someone repeated, laughing.

"Don't be wicked," Anna Pavlovna said from the other end of the table, shaking her finger, "c'est un si brave et excellent homme notre bon Viasmitinoff . . ."*

Everyone laughed a lot. At the upper, honoured end of the table, everyone seemed to be merry and under the influence of the most varied, lively moods; only Pierre and Hélène silently sat next to each other almost at the lowest end of the table; on both their faces there was a restrained, radiant smile that had nothing to do with Sergei Kuzmich—a smile of bashfulness about their own feelings. Whatever the others said, however they laughed and joked together, whatever the appetite with which they savoured the Rhein wine, the sauté, the ice cream, however they avoided glancing at this couple, however indifferent or inattentive to them they seemed, the feeling for some reason was, from the occasional glances cast at them, that the anecdote about Sergei Kuzmich, and the laughter, and the food were all a pretence, and all the power of attention of the entire company was directed only at this couple—Pierre and Hélène. Prince Vassily imitated Sergei Kuzmich's sobbing, and at the same time shot a

---

*He's such a fine and excellent man, our good Vyazmitinov.

glance at his daughter; and all the while he laughed, the expression on his face said: "Yes, yes, it's all going well; tonight it will all be decided." Anna Pavlovna shook her finger at him for *notre bon Viasmitinoff,* but in her eyes, which flashed momentarily at Pierre, Prince Vassily read congratulations on his future son-in-law and his daughter's happiness. The old princess, offering wine with a sad sigh to the lady next to her and glancing angrily at her daughter, seemed to be saying with that sigh: "Yes, now you and I have nothing left but to drink sweet wine, my dear; now it's time for these young ones to be so boldly and defiantly happy." "And what stupidity all this that I'm going on about is, as if it interests me," thought the diplomat, glancing at the happy faces of the lovers. "That is happiness!"

Amidst the insignificant trifles, the artificial interests, that bound this company together, there turned up the simple feeling of attraction of a handsome and healthy young man and woman for each other. And this human feeling overwhelmed everything and soared above all this artifical babble. The jokes were not funny, the news was not interesting, the animation was obviously feigned. Not only they, but the footmen serving at the table seemed to feel the same and forgot the order of the service, gazing at the beauty Hélène with her radiant face, and at the red, fat, happy, and uneasy face of Pierre. It seemed that even the light of the candles was concentrated only on those two happy faces.

Pierre felt that he was the centre of everything, and this position delighted and embarrassed him. He found himself in the state of a man immersed in some occupation. He neither saw, nor understood, nor heard anything clearly. Only rarely, unexpectedly, did fragmentary thoughts and impressions of reality flash in his soul.

"So it's all over!" he thought. "And how did it all happen? So quickly! Now I know that, not for her alone, not for me alone, but for all of them, *this* inevitably had to come about. They all expect *this* so much, they're so certain it will be, that I simply cannot disappoint them. But how will it be? I don't know; but it will be, it will be without fail!" thought Pierre, glancing at those shoulders gleaming just near his eyes.

Then he suddenly became ashamed of something. He felt embarrassed that he alone was taking up everyone's attention, that he was a lucky fellow in the eyes of others—he, with his unattractive face, some sort of Paris taking possession of Helen. "But surely it always happens that way and must be so," he comforted himself. "And, anyhow, what did I do for it? When did it begin? I left Moscow along with Prince Vassily. There wasn't anything yet. And then, why shouldn't I have stayed with him? Then I played cards with her, picked up her reticule, went for a ride with her. When did it begin, when did it all happen?" And here he is sitting next to her, a fiancé; he hears, sees, feels her closeness, her breathing, her movements, her beauty. Now it suddenly seems to him that it is not she but he himself who is so extraordinarily beautiful, that that is why they are looking at him that way, and he, happy in the general astonishment, draws himself up, raises his head, and rejoices at his happiness. Suddenly some voice, someone's familiar voice, is heard and says something to him yet again. But Pierre is so taken up that he does not understand what is said to him.

"I'm asking you when you got a letter from Bolkonsky," Prince Vassily repeats for the third time. "You're so distracted, my dear."

Prince Vassily smiles, and Pierre sees that everyone, everyone is smiling at him and at Hélène. "Well, so what if you all know," Pierre says to himself. "Well, so what? it's true," and he smiles his meek, childlike smile, and Hélène smiles, too.

"When did you get it? From Olmütz?" Prince Vassily repeats, as if he needs to know in order to settle an argument.

"Can one really speak and think about such trifles?" thinks Pierre.

"Yes, from Olmütz," he answers with a sigh.

After supper Pierre led his lady after the others to the drawing room. The guests began to depart, and some left without saying goodbye to Hélène. As if not wishing to tear her away from her serious occupation, some approached for a moment and left quickly, forbidding her to see them off. The diplomat was sadly silent as he left the drawing room. He was thinking about all the vanity of his diplomatic career compared with Pierre's happiness. The old general grumbled angrily at his wife when she asked him how his foot was. "Ah, you old fool," he thought. "Elena Sergeevna, now, she'll be the same beauty even when she's fifty."

"It seems I can congratulate you," Anna Pavlovna whispered to the princess and kissed her warmly. "If it weren't for my migraine, I would have stayed."

The princess said nothing in reply; she was tormented by envy of her daughter's happiness.

While the guests were taking their leave, Pierre remained alone with Hélène for a long time in the small drawing room where they were sitting. Often before, during the last month and a half, he had remained alone with Hélène, but he had never spoken to her of love. Now he felt that this was necessary, but he simply could not resolve upon this last step. He was ashamed; it seemed to him that here, beside Hélène, he was occupying someone else's place. "This happiness is not for you," some inner voice was telling him. "This happiness is for those who do not have what you have." But he had to say something, and so he began to speak. He asked her whether she was pleased with tonight's soirée. She answered with her usual simplicity that this name day had been one of the most pleasant for her.

Some of the nearest relations were still there. They were sitting in the big drawing room. Prince Vassily walked lazily over to Pierre. Pierre stood up and said it was already late. Prince Vassily gave him a sternly questioning look, as if what he had said was so strange that he could not even hear it well. But then the expression of sternness changed, and Prince Vassily pulled Pierre's arm down, seated him, and smiled gently.

"Well, Lelya?" he at once addressed his daughter in that careless tone of habitual tenderness which is adopted by parents who have been affectionate with their children since childhood, but which Prince Vassily only approximated by means of imitating other parents.

And again he turned to Pierre.

" 'Sergei Kuzmich, from all sides,' " he said, undoing the top button of his waistcoat.

Pierre smiled, but it was clear from his smile that he realized it was not the anecdote about Sergei Kuzmich that interested Prince Vassily just then; and Prince Vassily realized that Pierre realized it. Prince Vassily suddenly burbled something and left. To Pierre it looked as if even Prince Vassily was embarrassed. The sight of this worldly old man's embarrassment touched Pierre; he glanced at Hélène—she, too, seemed embarrassed, and her glance said: "Well, it's your own fault."

"I must inevitably cross it, but I can't, I can't," thought Pierre, and again he began talking about unrelated things, about Sergei Kuzmich, asking what the anecdote was, because he had not heard it well. Hélène replied with a smile that she did not know either.

When Prince Vassily came into the drawing room, the princess was talking softly with an elderly lady about Pierre.

"Of course, *c'est un parti très brilliant, mais le bonheur, ma chère . . .*"*

"*Les marriages se font dans les cieux,*"† the elderly lady replied.

Prince Vassily, as if not listening to the ladies, went to the far corner and sat on the sofa. He closed his eyes and seemed to be dozing. His head began to nod, and he woke up.

"*Aline,*" he said to his wife, "*allez voir ce qu'ils font.*"‡

The princess went to the door, passed by it with a significant, indifferent look, and peeked into the drawing room. Pierre and Hélène were sitting and talking in the same way.

"All the same!" she said to her husband.

Prince Vassily frowned, his mouth twisted to one side, his cheeks twitched with an unpleasant, coarse expression peculiar to him; he roused himself, got up, threw his head back, and with a resolute stride walked past the ladies into the small drawing room. He strode quickly, joyfully up to Pierre. The prince's expression was so extraordinarily joyful that Pierre stood up, frightened, when he saw him.

---

*Of course, it's a brilliant match, but happiness, my dear . . .
†Marriages are made in heaven.
‡Aline . . . go and see what they're doing.

"Thank God!" he said. "My wife has told me everything." He embraced Pierre with one arm, his daughter with the other. "Lelya, my friend! I'm very, very glad." His voice quavered. "I loved your father . . . and she will be a good wife to you . . . God bless you! . . ."

He embraced his daughter, then Pierre again, and kissed him with his old man's mouth. Tears actually wet his cheeks.

"Princess, come here," he called.

The princess came in and also wept. The elderly lady also dabbed herself with her handkerchief. They kissed Pierre, and he kissed the beautiful Hélène's hand several times. After a while, they were left alone again.

"All this had to be so and could not be otherwise," thought Pierre, "therefore there's no point in asking whether it's good or bad. It's good because it's definite, and there's no more of the old tormenting doubt." Pierre silently held his fiancée's hand and looked at her beautiful breast rising and falling.

"Hélène!" he said aloud and stopped.

"Something special is said on these occasions," he thought, but he simply could not remember precisely what was said on these occasions. He looked at her face. She moved closer to him. Her face blushed.

"Oh, take off those . . . whatever they're . . ." She was pointing to his spectacles.

Pierre took off his spectacles, and his eyes, on top of the general strangeness of people's eyes when they take off their spectacles, had a frightened and questioning look. He was about to bend down to her hand and kiss it; but she, with a quick and crude movement of her head, intercepted his lips and brought them together with her own. Her face struck Pierre by its altered, unpleasantly perplexed expression.

"It's too late now, it's all over; and anyway I love her," thought Pierre.

"*Je vous aime!*" he said, having remembered what needed to be said on these occasions; but the words sounded so meagre that he felt ashamed of himself.

A month and a half later he was married and settled down, as they say, the happy possessor of a beautiful wife and millions of roubles, in the big, newly done-over house of the counts Bezukhov in Petersburg.

III

Old Prince Nikolai Andreich Bolkonsky received a letter from Prince Vassily in December 1805, informing him of his arrival together with his son. ("I am going to an inspection, and, of course, for me seventy miles is no detour if I can visit you, my much-esteemed benefactor," he wrote, "and my Anatole is keeping me company on his way to the army; and I hope you will allow him personally to express the deep respect which he, in imitation of his father, has for you.")

"So Marie doesn't have to be taken out: suitors are coming to us them-selves," the little princess said indiscreetly on hearing of it.

Prince Nikolai Andreich winced and said nothing.

Two weeks after the receipt of the letter, in the evening, Prince Vassily's people arrived in advance of him, and the next day he himself arrived with his son.

Old Bolkonsky had always had a rather low opinion of Prince Vassily's char-acter, and the more so in recent times, when Prince Vassily, under the new reigns of Paul and Alexander, had gone far in rank and honours. Now, from the hints in the letter and from the little princess, he understood what the mat-ter was, and the low opinion of Prince Vassily in Prince Nikolai Andreich's soul turned into a feeling of hostile disdain. He snorted constantly when he spoke of him. On the day of Prince Vassily's arrival, Prince Nikolai Andreich was especially displeased and ill-humoured. Whether he was ill-humoured because Prince Vassily was coming, or he was especially displeased with Prince Vassily's coming because he was ill-humoured, in any case he was ill-humoured, and already in the morning Tikhon had advised the architect against going to the prince with a report.

"Do you hear how his honour is walking?" Tikhon said, drawing the archi-tect's attention to the sound of the prince's footsteps. "Stepping full on his heels—we know about that . . ."

However, as usual, after eight o'clock the prince went out for a walk in his velvet coat with the sable collar and matching hat. It had snowed the day before. The path on which Prince Nikolai Andreich always walked to the con-servatory had been cleared, the traces of the broom could be seen on the swept snow, and a shovel was stuck in one of the loosely heaped-up snowbanks that lined both sides of the path. The prince walked through the conservatory, the servants' quarters and outbuildings, frowning and silent.

"But can one get through in a sleigh?" he asked the steward, who accompa-nied him back to the house, a respectable man, in face and manner resembling his master.

"The snow is deep, Your Excellency. I've already ordered it cleared on the avenue."

The prince inclined his head and went up to the porch. "Thank God," thought the steward, "the cloud has passed!"

"It would have been hard to get through, Your Excellency," the steward added. "So we've heard, Your Excellency, that a minister is going to be visiting Your Excellency?"

The prince turned to the steward and fixed him with a frowning gaze.

"What? A minister? What minister? Who ordered it?" he began speaking in his piercingly harsh voice. "You didn't clear it for the princess, my daughter, but for a minister! I have no ministers!"

"Your Excellency, I assumed . . ."

"You assumed!" cried the prince, articulating the words still more hastily and incoherently. "You assumed . . . Brigands! Knaves! . . . I'll teach you to assume." And, raising his stick, he swung it at Alpatych, and would have hit him, if the steward had not instinctively avoided the blow. "Assumed! . . . Knaves! . . ." he shouted hurriedly. But even though Alpatych, frightened by his own boldness in avoiding the blow, approached the prince with his bald head obediently bowed, or perhaps precisely because of it, the prince, while shouting, "Knaves! . . . Cover the road!"—did not raise his stick again and ran inside.

Before dinner the young princess and Mlle Bourienne, knowing that the prince was ill-humoured, stood waiting for him, Mlle Bourienne with a beaming face which said: "I know nothing, I'm the same as ever," and Princess Marya, pale, frightened, with lowered eyes. The hardest thing of all for Princess Marya was that she knew that on these occasions she ought to behave like Mlle Bourienne, but could not do it. She imagined: "If I make as if I don't notice, he'll think I have no compassion for him; if I make as if I myself am dull and ill-humoured, he'll say (as has happened) that I'm moping," and so on.

The prince looked at his daughter's frightened face and snorted.

"Tra . . . or a dimwit! . . ." he said.

"And the other one's not here! They've already spread the gossip," he thought about the little princess, who was not in the dining room.

"And where is the princess?" he asked. "Hiding? . . ."

"She's not quite well," Mlle Bourienne replied with a cheerful smile, "she won't be coming out. It's so understandable in her condition."

"Hem! hem! huff! huff!" said the prince and sat down at the table.

His plate did not seem clean to him; he pointed to a spot and flung it aside. Tikhon caught it and handed it to the butler. The little princess was not unwell; but her fear of the prince was so insuperable that, on learning that he was ill-humoured, she decided not to come out.

"I'm afraid for the baby," she said to Mlle Bourienne, "God knows what fright may do."

In general, the little princess lived at Bald Hills under a constant feeling of fear and antipathy for the old prince, though she was not aware of the antipathy, because the fear was so predominant that she could not feel it. On the prince's side there was also antipathy, but it was smothered by contempt. The princess, having made herself at home at Bald Hills, had especially grown to love Mlle Bourienne, spent whole days with her, invited her to sleep in her room, and often talked with her about her father-in-law, criticizing him.

"*Il nous arrive du monde, mon prince,*" said Mlle Bourienne, unfolding a white napkin with her pink little hands. "*Son excellence le prince Kouragine avec son fils, à ce que j'ai entendu dire?*"* she said questioningly.

"Hm! this *excellence* is a little brat . . . I solicited his post for him in the ministry," the prince said peevishly. "And why the son, I cannot comprehend. Princess Lizaveta Karlovna and Princess Marya may know, but I don't know why they're bringing this son here. I have no need of him." And he looked at his blushing daughter.

"Unwell, are you? Afraid of the minister, as that blockhead Alpatych said today?"

"No, *mon père.*"

Unfortunate as Mlle Bourienne's choice of subject had been, she did not stop and babbled about the conservatory, about the beauty of a newly opened flower, and after the soup the prince relented.

After dinner he went to see his daughter-in-law. The little princess was sitting at a small table chatting with the maid Masha. She turned pale when she saw her father-in-law.

The little princess was much changed. She was rather more bad- than good-looking now. Her cheeks sagged, her lip rose up, her eyes were drawn down.

"Yes, a sort of heaviness," she replied to the prince's question of how she felt.

"Do you need anything?"

"No, *merci, mon père.*"

"Well, all right, all right."

He left and went to the servants' room. Alpatych, his head bowed, was standing in the servants' room.

"Has the road been covered?"

"It has, Your Excellency; forgive me, for God's sake, it was only my stupidity."

The prince cut him short and laughed his unnatural laugh.

"Well, all right, all right."

He offered his hand for Alpatych to kiss and went to his study.

---

*There are people coming to see us, my prince . . . His excellency Prince Kuragin and his son, I've heard?

In the evening Prince Vassily arrived. He was met on the "avenue" (as they called the front drive) by the coachmen and servants, who with shouts dragged his carts and sleigh to the wing over the road that had been deliberately covered with snow.

Prince Vassily and Anatole were given separate rooms.

Anatole, having taken off his tunic, sat with arms akimbo before a table, at a corner of which, smiling, he directed fixedly and distractedly his beautiful big eyes. He looked upon his whole life as a ceaseless entertainment, which somebody for some reason had taken it upon himself to arrange for him. Now, too, he looked in this way upon his journey to the wicked old man and the rich, ugly heiress. All this, as he supposed, might turn out very nice and amusing. "And why shouldn't I marry her, if she's very rich? That never hurts," thought Anatole.

He shaved, scented himself with a thoroughness and foppishness that had become habitual to him, and with his innately good-humoured and triumphant expression, carrying his handsome head high, went into his father's room. Two valets were bustling around Prince Vassily, dressing him; he himself looked around animatedly and nodded cheerfully to his entering son, as if to say: "Right, that's how I need you to look!"

"No, without joking, father, is she very ugly? Eh?" he asked in French, as if continuing a conversation they had had more than once during the journey.

"Enough nonsense! Above all, try to be respectful and sensible with the old prince."

"If he starts being abusive, I'll leave," said Anatole. "I can't stand these old men. Eh?"

"Remember, for you everything depends on this."

By that time in the maids' quarters not only was everything known about the arrival of the minister and his son, but their external appearance had already been described in detail. Princess Marya sat alone in her room, vainly trying to overcome her inner excitement.

"Why did they write, why did Liza tell me about it all? It just can't be!" she kept saying to herself, looking in the mirror. "How will I come out to the drawing room? Even if I liked him, I couldn't be myself with him now." The mere thought of her father's gaze terrified her.

The little princess and Mlle Bourienne had already received all the necessary information from the maid Masha about what a ruddy, dark-browed, handsome fellow the minister's son was, and how his papa could barely drag his feet up the stairs, while he, like an eagle, ran up after him taking three steps at a time. On receiving this information, the little princess and Mlle Bourienne, their animatedly chattering voices heard already from the corridor, came into Princess Marya's room.

"*Ils sont arrivés, Marie,** do you know?" said the little princess, waddling in with her belly and lowering herself heavily into an armchair.

She was no longer in the smock she had on that morning, but was wearing one of her best gowns; her hair was carefully done, and in her face there was animation, which, however, did not conceal the sagging and deadened contours of her face. In a costume she used to wear in Petersburg society, it was still more noticeable how far she had lost her good looks. Mlle Bourienne's costume had also undergone some sort of inconspicuous improvement, which made her fresh, pretty face still more attractive.

"*Et bien, et vous restez comme vous êtes, chère princesse?*" she said. "*On va venir annoncer que ces messieurs sont au salon; il faudra descendre, et vous ne faites pas un petit brin de toilette!*"†

The little princess got up from the armchair, rang for the maid, and began hurriedly and cheerfully devising a costume for Princess Marya and carrying it out. Princess Marya felt insulted in her sense of her own dignity, because the arrival of the promised suitor excited her, and she was still more insulted that her two friends did not suppose it could be otherwise. To tell them how ashamed she was of herself and of them would mean to betray her excitement; besides, to refuse the dressing-up they suggested would lead to prolonged bantering and insistence. She flushed, her beautiful eyes faded, her face became covered with blotches, and, with that unattractive expression of a victim which most often lingered on her face, she gave herself into the power of Mlle Bourienne and Liza. The two women concerned themselves *in all sincerity* with making her beautiful. She was so plain that the thought of rivalry with her did not occur to either of them; they therefore undertook to dress her up in all sincerity, with that naïve and firm conviction of women that clothes can make a face beautiful.

"No, really, *ma bonne amie*, this dress won't do," Liza said, looking sideways at the princess from a distance, "have them bring the maroon one you've got there! Really! Why, this may just be the deciding of your fate in life. And this is too light, it won't do, no, it won't do!"

What would not do was not the dress, but the face and the whole figure of the princess, but neither Mlle Bourienne nor the little princess sensed that; it seemed to them that if a blue ribbon was put in the hair, done up high, and a blue scarf hung down on the brown dress, and so on, all would be well. They forgot that the frightened face and figure could not be changed, and therefore, no matter how they changed the frame and decoration of that face, the face itself remained pitiful and unattractive. After two or three changes, to which

---

*They've come, Marie.

†Well, and are you staying as you are, dear princess? ... They'll come to announce that these gentlemen are in the drawing room; we'll have to go down, and you're not doing the least bit to dress!

Princess Marya submitted obediently, when her hair had been done up high (a style that totally changed and spoiled her face), and she was wearing the blue scarf and fancy maroon gown, the little princess walked round her twice, straightened a fold here, pulled at the scarf there with her little hand, and, inclining her head, looked now from this side, now from that.

"No, it's impossible," she said resolutely, clasping her hands. "*Non, Marie, décidément, ça ne vous va pas. Je vous aime mieux dans votre petite robe grise de tout les jours. Non, de grâce, faites cela pour moi.** Katya," she said to the maid, "bring the princess her little grey dress, and watch, Mlle Bourienne, how I'm going to arrange it," she said, with a smiling foretaste of artistic delight.

But when Katya brought the dress requested, Princess Marya was still sitting motionless before the mirror, looking at her face, and saw in the mirror that tears had welled up in her eyes and her mouth was trembling, getting ready to weep.

"*Voyons, chère princesse,*" said Mlle Bourienne, "*encore un petit effort.*"†

The little princess, taking the dress from the maid's hands, was approaching Princess Marya.

"No, now we'll make it simple and sweet," she said.

Her voice, Mlle Bourienne's, and Katya's, who was laughing about something, blended into a merry warbling which resembled the song of birds.

"*Non, laissez-moi,*"‡ said the princess.

And there was so much seriousness and suffering in her voice that the birds' warbling immediately ceased. They looked at her big, beautiful eyes, filled with tears and thought, looking at them clearly and pleadingly, and understood that to insist would be useless and even cruel.

"*Au moins changez la coiffure,*" said the little princess. "*Je vous disais,*" she said with reproach, turning to Mlle Bourienne, "*Marie a une de ces figures, auxquelles ce genre de coiffure ne vas pas du tout. Mais du tout, du tout. Changez de grâce.*"§

"*Laissez-moi, laissez-moi, tout ça m'est parfaitement égal,*"# answered a voice barely holding back its tears.

Mlle Bourienne and the little princess had to confess to themselves that as she was Princess Marya looked very bad, worse than ever; but it was already late. She looked at them with that expression they knew, an expression of

*No, Marie, this decidedly doesn't suit you. I like you better in your little grey everyday dress. No, for pity's sake, do it for me.
†Come, dear princess . . . one more little effort.
‡No, leave me alone.
§At least change your hairstyle . . . I told you . . . Marya has one of those faces which this sort of hairstyle does not suit at all. Not at all, not at all. Change it, for pity's sake.
#Leave me alone, leave me alone, all this is perfectly the same to me.

thought and sadness. This expression did not inspire any fear of Princess Marya in them. (She never inspired that feeling in anyone.) But they knew that when that expression appeared on her face, she became silent and unshakeable in her decisions.

"*Vous changerez, n'est-ce pas?*"* said Liza, and when Princess Marya made no reply, Liza left the room.

Princess Marya remained alone. She did not carry out Liza's wish, and not only did not change her hairstyle, but did not even look at herself in the mirror. Strengthlessly lowering her eyes and arms, she sat silently and thought. She imagined a husband, a man, a strong, dominating, and incomprehensibly attractive being, suddenly carrying her off into his own completely different, happy world. *Her own* baby, like the one she had seen yesterday at her nurse's daughter's—she imagined at her own breast. The husband stands and looks tenderly at her and the baby. "But no, it's impossible, I'm too plain," she thought.

"Please come to tea. The prince will come out shortly," said the maid's voice outside the door.

She roused herself and was horrified at what she had been thinking. And before going downstairs, she stood up, went to her icon room, and, fixing her eyes on the dark lamp-lit face of a large icon of the Saviour, stood before it with clasped hands for several minutes. There was tormenting doubt in Princess Marya's soul. Was the joy of love, of earthly love for a man, possible for her? Thinking of marriage, Princess Marya dreamed of family happiness and children, but her chiefest, strongest, and most secret dream was of earthly love. This feeling was all the stronger, the more she tried to conceal it from others and even from herself. "My God," she said, "how can I suppress these devil's thoughts in my heart? How can I renounce evil imaginings for ever, so as peacefully to do Thy will?" And she had barely asked this question, when God answered her in her own heart: "Desire nothing for yourself; do not seek, do not worry, do not envy. The future of people and your own fate must be unknown to you; but live so as to be ready for anything. If God should see fit to test you in the duties of marriage, be ready to fulfil His will." With this reassuring thought (but still with a hope that her forbidden earthly dream would be fulfilled), Princess Marya sighed, crossed herself, and went downstairs without thinking about her dress, or her hairstyle, or how she would walk in, or what she would say. What could all that mean in comparison with the predestination of God, without whose will not one hair falls from man's head.

*You'll change, won't you?

IV

When Princess Marya came in, Prince Vassily and his son were already in the drawing room, talking with the little princess and Mlle Bourienne. When she came in with her heavy step, planting her heels, the men and Mlle Bourienne rose, and the little princess, pointing to her, said, *"Voilà Marie!"* Princess Marya saw them all, and saw them in detail. She saw the face of Prince Vassily, momentarily freezing in a serious expression at the sight of the princess, and the face of the little princess, curiously reading on the faces of the guests the impression Marie made. She also saw Mlle Bourienne with her ribbon, and her beautiful face, and her gaze—lively as never before—directed at *him;* but she could not see *him,* she saw only something big, bright, and beautiful, which moved towards her as she came into the room. Prince Vassily went up to her first, and she kissed the bald head that bowed over her hand, and to his words replied that, on the contrary, she remembered him very well. Then Anatole came up to her. She still did not see him. She only felt a gentle hand firmly take hold of her hand, and barely touched the white forehead with beautiful, pomaded blond hair above it. When she looked at him, his beauty struck her. Anatole, the thumb of his right hand placed behind a fastened button of his uniform, chest thrust out, shoulders back, swinging his free leg slightly, and inclining his head a little, gazed silently and cheerfully at the princess, obviously without thinking of her at all. Anatole was not resourceful, not quick and eloquent in conversation, but he had instead a capacity, precious in society, for composure and unalterable assurance. When an insecure man is silent at first acquaintance and shows an awareness of the impropriety of this silence and a wish to find something to say, it comes out badly; but Anatole was silent, swung his leg, and cheerfully observed the princess's hairstyle. It was clear that he could calmly remain silent like that for a very long time. "If anyone feels awkward because of this silence, speak up, but I don't care to," his look seemed to say. Besides that, in Anatole's behaviour with women there was a manner which more than any other awakens women's curiosity, fear, and even love—a manner of contemptuous awareness of his own superiority. As if he were saying to them with his look: "I know you, I know, but why should I bother with you? And you'd be glad if I did!" Perhaps he did not think that when he met women (and it is even probable that he did not, because he generally thought little), but such was his look and manner. The princess felt it, and, as if wishing to show him that she dared not even think of interesting him, turned to the old prince. The conversation was general and lively, thanks to the little princess's voice and the lip with its little moustache which kept rising up over her white teeth. She met Prince Vassily in that jocular mode often made use of by garrulously merry people, which consists in the fact that, between the person thus addressed and oneself, there are supposed to exist some long-established jokes and merry, amusing reminiscences, not known to everyone, when in fact there are no such reminiscences, as there were none between the little princess and Prince Vassily. Prince Vassily readily yielded to this tone; the little princess also involved Anatole, whom she barely knew, in this reminiscence of never-existing funny incidents. Mlle Bourienne also shared in these common reminiscences, and even Princess Marya enjoyed feeling herself drawn into this merry reminiscence.

"So at least we can make full use of you now, dear Prince," the little princess said, in French, of course, to Prince Vassily. "It won't be as at our soirées at Annette's, where you always run away. Remember *cette chère Annette!*"

"Ah, but you won't *go talking* politics with me, like Annette!"

"And our little tea table?"

"Oh, yes!"

"Why did you never come to Annette's?" the little princess asked Anatole. "Ah! I know, I know," she said, winking, "your brother Ippolit has told me about your affairs. Oh!" she shook her finger at him. "I even know your Parisian pranks!"

"But he, Ippolit, didn't he tell you?" said Prince Vassily, turning to his son and seizing the princess by the hand as if she was about to run away and he had barely managed to hold her back, "didn't he tell you how he himself, Ippolit, pined for the dear princess and how she *le mettait à la porte? Oh! C'est la perle des femmes, princesse!*"* he said, turning to Princess Marya.

For her part, Mlle Bourienne did not miss her chance, at the word *Paris,* to enter as well into the general conversation of reminiscences.

She permitted herself to ask whether Anatole had left Paris long ago and how he liked the city. Anatole answered the Frenchwoman quite willingly and, gazing at her with a smile, conversed with her about her fatherland. Seeing the pretty Bourienne, Anatole decided that even here, at Bald Hills, it would not be boring. "Not bad at all!" he thought, looking her over. "She's not bad at all, this *demoiselle de compagnie.* I hope she'll bring her along when she marries me," he thought, "*la petite est gentille.*"†

The old prince was dressing unhurriedly in his study, frowning and thinking over what he was going to do. The arrival of these guests angered him. "What are Prince Vassily and his boy to me? Prince Vassily's an empty babbler, so the son must also be a fine one," he grumbled to himself. He was angry because the arrival of these guests raised in his soul an unresolved, constantly stifled question—a question in regard to which the old prince always deceived him-

---

*Showed him the door? Oh! She's a pearl among women, Princess!
†Lady's companion . . . She's a sweet little thing.

self. The question was whether he could ever resolve to part with Princess Marya and give her to a husband. The prince had never ventured to ask himself this question directly, knowing beforehand that he would answer it in all fairness, and fairness contradicted more than feeling, it contradicted the whole possibility of his life. For Prince Nikolai Andreich, life without Princess Marya, despite the fact that he seemed to value her little, was unthinkable. "And why should she marry?" he thought. "She's sure to be unhappy. Liza's married to Andrei (a better husband would seem hard to find these days), but is she pleased with her fate? And who's going to take her out of love? She's plain, awkward. She'll be taken for her connections, for her wealth. Don't girls live unmarried? And all the happier!" So thought Prince Nikolai Andreich as he dressed, but at the same time the ever-deferred question called for immediate resolution. Prince Vassily had obviously brought his son with the intention of making a proposal, and would probably ask for a direct answer today or tomorrow. His name, his position in society were decent. "Well, I'm not against it," the prince said to himself, "but he must be worthy of her. We'll see about that."

"We'll see about that," he said aloud. "We'll see about that."

And with brisk steps, as usual, he entered the drawing room, took everyone in with a quick glance, noticed the little princess's change of dress, the ribbon on Bourienne, and Princess Marya's ugly hairstyle, and the smiles of Bourienne and Anatole, and his daughter's solitude amidst the general conversation. "Got herself up like a fool!" he thought, looking spitefully at his daughter. "No shame! And he doesn't even want to know her!"

He went over to Prince Vassily.

"Well, greetings, greetings; glad to see you."

"For a dear friend, no detour's too long," Prince Vassily began, as usual, quickly, self-confidently, and familiarly. "Here is my second one, I recommend him to your loving kindness."

Prince Nikolai Andreevich looked Anatole over.

"A fine boy, a fine boy!" he said. "Well, come and kiss me." And he offered him his cheek.

Anatole kissed the old man, then looked at him curiously and with perfect calm, expecting him to come out with something eccentric, as his father had promised.

Prince Nikolai Andreevich sat in his usual place at the end of the sofa, moved a chair for Prince Vassily towards him, pointed to it, and began asking questions about political matters and the latest news. He listened as if with attention to Prince Vassily's account, but kept glancing at Princess Marya.

"So they're already writing from Potsdam?" he repeated Prince Vassily's last words, suddenly stood up, and went over to his daughter.

"So you've spruced yourself up like that for the guests, eh?" he said. "Fine, very fine. You do your hair up in some new way for the guests, but I say to you in front of the guests that in future you dare not change anything without my permission."

"*Mon père,* it's my fault," the little princess intervened, blushing.

"That's entirely as you will, ma'am," said Prince Nikolai Andreevich, bowing and scraping before his daughter-in-law, "but she needn't make herself ugly—she's plain enough as it is."

And he sat down in his place again, paying no further attention to the daughter he had driven to tears.

"On the contrary, this hairstyle is very becoming to the princess," said Prince Vassily.

"Well, my good fellow, young prince what's your name?" said Prince Nikolai Andreevich, turning to Anatole, "come here, let's talk, let's get acquainted."

"Now the fun begins," thought Anatole and, smiling, he took a seat nearer to the old prince.

"Well, now, they say, my dear, that you were educated abroad. Not like your father and me, who were taught to read by the beadle. Tell me, my dear, you're now serving in the horse guards?" the old man asked, studying Anatole closely and intently.

"No, I've been transferred to the infantry," replied Anatole, barely able to keep from laughing.

"Ah! a good thing. So, my dear, you want to serve your tsar and country? It's wartime. Such a fine fellow must serve, must serve. So, off to the front?"

"No, Prince. Our regiment is already on the march. But I'm enlisted—what am I enlisted in, papa?" Anatole turned with a laugh to his father.

"Nice service, very nice. What am I enlisted in! Ha, ha, ha!" Prince Nikolai Andreevich laughed.

And Anatole laughed still louder. Suddenly Prince Nikolai Andreevich frowned.

"Well, go," he said to Anatole.

Anatole, with a smile, went back to the ladies.

"So you did educate them abroad, Prince Vassily? Eh?" The old prince turned to Prince Vassily.

"I did what I could; and I'll tell you, the education there is much better than ours."

"Yes, everything's different nowadays, everything's the new way. A fine lad, though! A fine lad! Well, come with me."

He took Prince Vassily under the arm and led him to his study.

Prince Vassily, finding himself alone with the prince, at once declared to him his wishes and hopes.

"And what do you think," the old prince said gruffly, "that I'm holding on to her, that I can't part with her? People imagine things!" he pronounced gruffly.

"She can marry tomorrow! Only I'll tell you, I'd like to know my son-in-law better. You know my rules: everything's in the open! I'll ask her tomorrow in your presence: if she wants, let him stay a while. Let him stay, and I'll see." The prince snorted. "Let her marry him, it's all the same to me," he shrieked in the same shrill voice in which he had shouted on taking leave of his son.

"I'll tell you straight out," said Prince Vassily, in the tone of a cunning man convinced that it is unnecessary to use cunning in view of his interlocutor's perceptiveness. "You see through people. Anatole is no genius, but he's an honest, good lad, an excellent son, and one of us."

"Well, well, all right, we'll see."

As always happens with lonely women who have long lived without the society of men, on Anatole's appearance all three women in Prince Nikolai Andreevich's house felt equally that their life had not been life until that moment. The power of thought, feeling, observation instantly increased tenfold in them, as if their life, going on in darkness till then, was suddenly lit up by a new light filled with meaning.

Princess Marya did not think at all or even remember about her face and hairstyle. The handsome, open face of the man who would perhaps be her husband absorbed all her attention. To her he seemed kind, brave, resolute, manly, and magnanimous. She was convinced of it. Thousands of fancies of her future family life kept emerging in her imagination. She drove them away and tried to hide them.

"But am I not too cold with him?" thought Princess Marya. "I'm trying to restrain myself, because deep in my soul I feel myself already too close to him; but he doesn't know all that I'm thinking about him and may imagine that I find him disagreeable."

And Princess Marya tried and was unable to be cordial with the new guest.

"*La pauvre fille! Elle est diablement laide,*"* thought Anatole.

Mlle Bourienne, whom Anatole's arrival had also brought to a high level of excitement, was thinking along different lines. Of course, the beautiful young woman, with no definite position in the world, with no family or friends or even country, did not intend to devote her life to serving Prince Nikolai Andreevich, reading books to him, or being friends with Princess Marya. Mlle Bourienne had long been waiting for a Russian prince who would at once be able to appreciate her superiority over the plain, badly dressed, awkward Russian princesses, would fall in love with her and carry her off; and this Russian prince had finally come. Mlle Bourienne had a story, heard from her aunt, completed by herself, which she liked to tell over in her imagination. It was a

*The poor girl. She's devilishly ugly.

story about a seduced girl, whose poor mother, *sa pauvre mère,* appeared to her in a vision and reproached her for giving herself to a man outside wedlock. Mlle Bourienne often brought herself to tears, telling *him,* the seducer, this story in her imagination. Now *he,* this real Russian prince, had come. He will carry her off, then *ma pauvre mère* will appear, and he will marry her. Thus the whole future story of Mlle Bourienne had taken shape in her head while she was talking with him about Paris. Mlle Bourienne was not guided by calculation (she did not spend a moment thinking of what she was to do), but it had all been long prepared in her and now merely arranged itself around the visiting Anatole, whom she wished and strove to please as much as she could.

The little princess, like an old warhorse hearing the sound of trumpets, was preparing herself, unconsciously and forgetting her condition, for her habitual coquettish gallop, without any second thoughts or struggles, but with naïve, light-minded merriment.

Although Anatole, in women's company, usually placed himself in the position of a man who is sick of having women running after him, he took a vain pleasure in seeing his effect on these three women. Besides, he was beginning to experience for the pretty and provocative Bourienne that passionate, animal feeling which came over him with extraordinary quickness and urged him towards the most coarse and bold actions.

After tea the company went to the sitting room, and the princess was asked to play on the clavichord. Anatole leaned on his elbow before her next to Mlle Bourienne, and his eyes, laughing and joyful, looked at Princess Marya. Princess Marya felt his gaze upon her with tormenting and joyful excitement. Her favourite sonata transported her into her innermost poetic world, and the gaze she felt upon her endowed that world with still greater poetry. Anatole's gaze, though directed at her, referred not to her but to the movements of Mlle Bourienne's little foot, which he touched just then with his own foot under the pianoforte. Mlle Bourienne was also looking at the princess, and in her beautiful eyes there was an expression of frightened joy and hope which was also new for Princess Marya.

"How she loves me!" thought Princess Marya. "How happy I am now, and how happy I may be with such a friend and such a husband! Can it be—a husband?" she thought, not daring to look up at his face, still feeling that same gaze directed at her.

In the evening, when they all began to disperse after supper, Anatole kissed Princess Marya's hand. She did not know herself how she had boldness enough, but she glanced straight at the beautiful face as it approached her near-sighted eyes. After the princess, he went to kiss Mlle Bourienne's hand (this was improper, but he did everything so confidently and simply), and Mlle Bourienne blushed and glanced fearfully at the princess.

"*Quelle délicatesse!*"* thought the princess. "Can Amélie" (that was Mlle Bourienne's name) "really think I could be jealous of her and not appreciate her pure affection for and devotion to me?" She went over to Mlle Bourienne and kissed her warmly. Anatole went to kiss the little princess's hand.

"*Non, non, non! Quand votre père m'écrira, que vous vous conduisez bien, je vous donnerai ma main à baiser. Pas avant.*"†

And, raising her finger and smiling, she left the room.

V

They all dispersed and, except for Anatole, who fell asleep as soon as he lay down, it was long before anyone slept that night.

"Can it be that he's my husband, precisely this stranger, this handsome, kind man—above all, kind," thought Princess Marya, and fear, which hardly ever came to her, came over her now. She was afraid to look around; she fancied someone was standing there behind the screen, in the dark corner. And that someone was he—the devil—and he was this man with the white forehead, black eyebrows, and red mouth.

She rang for the maid and asked her to sleep in her room.

Mlle Bourienne spent a long time that evening walking in the winter garden, vainly waiting for someone and now smiling at someone, now waxing tearful, touched in her imagination by the words of *sa pauvre mère* reproaching her for her fall.

The little princess grumbled at her maid because the bed was not right. It was impossible for her to lie either on her side or on her front. Everything was heavy and awkward. Her belly got in her way. It got in her way more than ever precisely today, because Anatole's presence transported her more vividly into another time, when it was not there, and everything was light and merry for her. She sat in an armchair in her bed jacket and nightcap. Katya, sleepy and with her braid tangled, plumped up and turned the heavy featherbed for the third time, muttering something.

"I told you, it's all bumps and hollows," the little princess repeated. "I'd be glad to fall asleep myself, so it's not my fault." And her voice quavered, like the voice of a child who is about to cry.

The old prince was also awake. Tikhon, through his sleep, heard him pacing about angrily and snorting through his nose. It seemed to the old prince that he was offended for his daughter. The offence was most painful because it con-

---

*What delicacy!
†No, no, no. When your father writes me that you are behaving well, I will give you my hand to kiss. Not before.

cerned not himself but another, his daughter, whom he loved more than himself. He told himself that he would think over the whole matter again and find what was fair and ought to be done, but instead he only irritated himself more.

"The first comer turns up—and her father and everything's forgotten, and she runs, does her hair up, and wags her tail, and isn't like herself at all! Glad to abandon her father! She knew I'd notice. Snort . . . snort . . . snort . . . As if I don't see that this fool is only looking at Bourrienka (she must be thrown out)! And how can she not have enough pride to realize it! If she has no pride for herself, at least she could have it for me. She must be shown that that blockhead doesn't even give her a thought, but is only looking at Bourienne. She has no pride, but I'll show her that she . . ."

By telling his daughter that she was mistaken, that Anatole intended to pay court to Bourienne, the old prince knew he would rouse Princess Marya's *amour propre,* and his cause (the wish not to part with his daughter) would be won, and that calmed him down. He called Tikhon and began to undress.

"The devil brought them here!" he thought, as Tikhon slipped a nightgown over his dry old man's body, the chest overgrown with grey hair. "I didn't invite them. They've come to upset my life. And there's not much left of it."

"Devil take them!" he said, while the shirt still covered his head.

Tikhon knew the prince's habit of sometimes expressing his thoughts aloud, and therefore with an unchanged face met the irately questioning gaze of the face that emerged from the shirt.

"Gone to bed?" asked the prince.

Tikhon, like all good valets, instinctively knew his master's train of thought. He guessed that he was being asked about Prince Vassily and his son.

"They've gone to bed and put out the lights, if you please, Your Excellency."

"No need, no need . . ." the prince said quickly and, putting his feet into his slippers and his arms through the sleeves of his dressing gown, he went to the sofa on which he slept.

Though nothing had yet been said between Anatole and Mlle Bourienne, they understood each other perfectly in regard to the first part of the romance, before the appearance of the *pauvre mère,* understood that they had much to tell each other in secret, and therefore in the morning they both sought an occasion to see each other alone. When Princess Marya went at the usual hour to see her father, Mlle Bourienne met with Anatole in the winter garden.

Princess Marya came to her father's door that day with particular trepidation. It seemed to her not only that everyone knew her fate was to be decided that day, but that they also knew what she thought about it. She read that expression on the face of Tikhon, and on the face of Prince Vassily's valet, who met her in the corridor while carrying hot water and bowed low to her.

The old prince was extremely gentle and painstaking in dealing with his daughter that morning. Princess Marya knew this painstaking expression of her father's very well. It was the expression he had on his face in the moments when his dry hands clenched into fists from vexation at Princess Marya's not understanding a problem in arithmetic, and, getting up, he would step away from her and in a soft voice repeat the same words several times.

He got down to business straightaway and began the conversation in a formal tone.

"A proposal has been made to me concerning you, miss," he said, smiling unnaturally. "You have guessed, I believe," he went on, "that Prince Vassily came here and brought with him his pupil" (for some reason Prince Nikolai Andreich called Anatole a pupil), "not just for my good pleasure. A proposal was made to me yesterday concerning you. And since you know my rules, I am referring it to you."

"How am I to understand you, *mon père?*" said the princess, turning pale, then red.

"How understand!" her father cried irately. "Prince Vassily finds you to his taste as his daughter-in-law and proposes to you on behalf of his pupil. That's how! How understand?! And I am asking you."

"I don't know, *mon père,* how you . . ." the princess said in a whisper.

"I? I? What have I got to do with it? Leave me out of it. It's not I who am getting married. What about *you,* miss? That's what it's desirable to know."

The princess saw that her father looked unfavourably on this matter, but at the same moment it occurred to her that her fate in life would be decided now or never. She lowered her eyes so as not to see his gaze, under the influence of which she felt she could not think but only obey out of habit, and said:

"I desire only one thing—to do your will," she said, "but if my desire must needs be expressed . . ."

She did not have time to finish. The prince interrupted her.

"Splendid!" he cried. "He'll get you and your dowry and incidentally take along Mlle Bourienne. She'll be his wife, and you . . ."

The prince stopped. He noticed the impression these words made on his daughter. She hung her head and was about to cry.

"Well, well, I'm joking, I'm joking," he said. "Remember one thing, Princess: I hold to the rule that a girl has the full right to choose. And I give you freedom. Remember one thing: the happiness of your life depends on your decision. There's no point in talking about me."

"But I don't know . . . *mon père.*"

"There's no point in talking! They'll tell him, and he'll marry not only you but anyone else as well; but you're free to choose . . . Go to your room, think it over, and in an hour come to me and say in his presence: yes or no. I know you'll be praying. Well, pray then. Only you'd better think. Now go."

"Yes or no, yes or no, yes or no!" he went on shouting, once the princess, reeling as if in a fog, had left his study.

Her fate was decided and decided happily. But what her father had said about Mlle Bourienne—that was a terrible hint. Untrue, let us suppose, but all the same it was terrible, she could not help thinking about it. She was walking straight ahead through the winter garden without seeing or hearing anything, when suddenly the familiar whispering of Mlle Bourienne roused her. She looked up and saw Anatole two steps away from her, embracing the French-woman and whispering something to her. Anatole, with a frightful expression on his handsome face, turned to look at Princess Marya, and for the first second did not let go of the waist of Mlle Bourienne, who did not see her.

"Who's there? Why? Wait!" Anatole's face seemed to say. Princess Marya was looking at them silently. She could not understand it. Finally Mlle Bourienne gave a little cry and ran away. Anatole, with a merry smile, bowed to Princess Marya, as if inviting her to laugh at this odd incident, and, shrugging his shoulders, went to the door that led to his part of the house.

An hour later Tikhon came to summon Princess Marya. He summoned her to the prince and added that Prince Vassily Sergeich was also there. When Tikhon came, the princess was sitting on the sofa in her room, holding the weeping Mlle Bourienne in her arms. Princess Marya was gently stroking her head. Her beautiful eyes, with all their former calm and luminosity, looked at the pretty face of Mlle Bourienne with tender love and pity.

"*Non, princesse, je suis perdue pour toujours dans votre coeur,*"* said Mlle Bourienne.

"*Pourquoi? Je vous aime plus que jamais,*" said Princess Marya, "*et je tâcherai de faire tout ce qui est en mon pouvoir pour votre bonheur.*"†

"*Mais vous me méprisez, vous si pure, vous ne comprendrez jamais cet égarement de la passion. Ah, ce n'est que ma pauvre mère . . .*"‡

"*Je comprends tout,*"§ Princess Marya answered with a sad smile. "Calm down, my friend. I'll go to my father," she said and went out.

Prince Vassily, one leg crossed high up on the other, a snuffbox in his hand, as if moved to the utmost, and as if regretting and laughing at his sentimentality himself, was sitting with a smile of tender emotion on his face. When Princess Marya came in, he quickly brought a pinch of snuff to his nose.

"*Ah, ma bonne, ma bonne,*" he said, rising and taking her by both hands. He sighed and added: "*Le sort de mon fils est en vos mains. Décidez, ma bonne, ma chère, ma douce Marie, qui j'ai toujours aimé comme ma fille.*"#

---

*No, Princess, I am lost for ever in your heart.
†Why? I love you more than ever . . . and I shall try to do everything in my power for your happiness.
‡But you despise me, you who are so pure, you will never understand this fit of passion. Ah, only my poor mother . . .
§I understand everything.
#Ah, my good one, my good one . . . My son's fate is in your hands. Decide, my good, my dear, my sweet Marie, whom I have always loved like my own daughter.

He stepped aside. An actual tear came to his eye.

"Snort . . . snort . . ." snorted Prince Nikolai Andreich.

"The prince, on behalf of his pupil . . . son, is proposing to you. Do you or do you not want to be the wife of Prince Anatole Kuragin? Say yes or no!" he shouted, "and then I retain my right to give my opinion as well. Yes, my opinion and only my opinion," added Prince Nikolai Andreich, turning to Prince Vassily and replying to his pleading expression. "Yes or no? Well?"

"My wish, *mon père*, is never to leave you, never to separate my life from yours. I do not want to marry," she said resolutely, her beautiful eyes looking at Prince Vassily and her father.

"Rot! Foolishness! Rot, rot, rot!" shouted Prince Nikolai Andreich, frowning, and taking his daughter by the hand, he pulled her to him and did not kiss her, but, leaning his forehead to her forehead, touched it, and squeezed her hand, which he was holding, so hard that she winced and cried out.

Prince Vassily rose.

"*Ma chère, je vous dirai, que c'est un moment que je n'oublierai jamais, jamais; mais, ma bonne, est-ce que vous ne nous donnerez pas un peu d'espérance de toucher ce coeur si bon, si généreux? Dites, que peut-être . . . L'avenir est si grand. Dites: peut-être.*"*

"Prince, what I said is all that is in my heart. I thank you for the honour, but I shall never be your son's wife."

"Well, that ends that, my dear. Very glad to see you, very glad to see you. Go to your room, Princess, go," said the old prince. "Very, very glad to see you," he repeated, putting his arm round Prince Vassily.

"My calling is different," Princess Marya thought to herself, "my calling is to be happy with a different happiness, the happiness of love and self-sacrifice. And whatever the cost, I shall make for poor Amélie's happiness. She loves him so passionately. She repents so passionately. I shall do everything to arrange her marriage to him. If he is not rich, I shall give her means. I shall ask father, and ask Andrei. I shall be so happy when she is his wife. She is so unhappy, a stranger, lonely, helpless! And, my God, how passionately she loves him, if she could so forget herself. I might have done the same! . . ." thought Princess Marya.

---

*My dear, I shall tell you that this is a moment I shall never, never forget; but, my good one, will you not give us a little hope of touching so good, so generous a heart? Say that perhaps . . . The future is so large. Say: perhaps.

VI

For a long time the Rostovs had no news of Nikolushka; only in midwinter was the count handed a letter addressed in what he recognized as his son's handwriting. On receiving the letter, the count fearfully and hastily, trying not to be noticed, ran on tiptoe to his study, shut himself in, and began to read. Anna Mikhailovna, learning (as she knew everything that went on in the house) of the letter that had come, went into the count's study with soft steps, and found him with the letter in his hands, sobbing and laughing at the same time.

Anna Mikhailovna, though her affairs had improved, went on living with the Rostovs.

"*Mon bon ami?*" Anna Mikhailovna uttered with questioning sadness and a readiness for all sorts of sympathy.

The count sobbed still louder.

"Nikolushka . . . a letter . . . wounded . . . wa . . . was . . . *ma chère* . . . wounded . . . my darling boy . . . my little countess . . . promoted to officer . . . thank God . . . How shall I tell my little countess? . . ."

Anna Mikhailovna sat down beside him, took her handkerchief, wiped the tears from his eyes, the letter stained by them, and her own tears, read the letter, reassured the count, and decided that she would prepare the countess over dinner and before tea, and after tea would announce everything, with God's help.

All through dinner, Anna Mikhailovna talked about rumours of the war, about Nikolushka; she asked twice when the last letter had come from him, though she already knew, and observed that a letter could very easily come that day. Each time these hints made the countess begin to worry and look anxiously now at the count, now at Anna Mikhailovna, Anna Mikhailovna quite imperceptibly turned the conversation to insignificant subjects. Natasha, the best endowed of all the family with the ability to detect the nuances of intonations, glances, and facial expressions, had pricked up her ears since the beginning of dinner, and knew that there was something between her father and Anna Mikhailovna, and something concerning her brother, and that Anna Mikhailovna was making preparations. In spite of all her boldness (Natasha knew how sensitive her mother was to everything that had to do with news of Nikolushka), she did not venture to ask any questions during dinner, and ate nothing from anxiousness, and fidgeted on her chair, not listening to her governess's reproaches. After dinner, she rushed headlong after Anna Mikhailovna and threw herself on her neck at full speed in the sitting room.

"Auntie, darling, tell me, what is it?"

"Nothing, my friend."

"No, my darling, my dear heart, my honey, my peach, I won't let go, I know you know something."

Anna Mikhailovna shook her head.

"*Vous êtes une fine mouche, mon enfant,*"* she said.

"A letter from Nikolenka? Surely!" cried Natasha, reading the affirmative answer in Anna Mikhailovna's face.

"But for God's sake be more careful: you know what a shock it may give your *maman.*"

"I will, I will be, but tell me. You won't? Then I'll go and tell her now."

Anna Mikhailovna briefly recounted to Natasha the contents of the letter, on condition that she not tell anyone.

"My noble word of honour," said Natasha, crossing herself, "I won't tell anyone"—and she immediately ran to Sonya.

"Nikolenka . . . wounded . . . a letter . . ." she said solemnly and joyfully.

"Nicolas!" Sonya merely said, instantly turning pale.

Seeing the impression the news of her brother's wound made on Sonya, Natasha felt for the first time the whole grievous side of this news.

She rushed to Sonya, embraced her, and wept.

"Slightly wounded, but promoted to officer; he's recovered now, he wrote himself," she said through her tears.

"It's obvious all you women are crybabies," said Petya, pacing the room in big, resolute strides. "I'm very glad, really very glad, that my brother has distinguished himself. You're all blubberers! You understand nothing."

Natasha smiled through her tears.

"You haven't read the letter?" asked Sonya.

"No, I haven't, but she said it's all over and he's already an officer . . ."

"Thank God," said Sonya, crossing herself. "But maybe she deceived you? Let's go to *maman.*"

Petya silently paced the room.

"If I were in Nikolushka's place, I'd have killed even more of those Frenchmen," he said, "they're so disgusting! I'd have cut down so many, there'd be a whole pile," Petya went on.

"Shut up, Petya, what a fool you are! . . ."

"I'm not a fool, the fools are the ones who cry over trifles," said Petya.

"Do you remember him?" Natasha suddenly asked, after a moment's silence. Sonya smiled.

"Do I remember Nicolas?"

"No, Sonya, do you remember him so as to remember everything, remember

*You're a sharp one, my child.

really well," said Natasha, with an assiduous gesture, evidently wishing to give her words the most serious meaning. "I remember Nikolenka, too, I do," she said. "But not Boris. I don't remember him at all."

"What? You don't remember Boris?" Sonya asked in surprise.

"It's not that I don't remember him—I know how he is, but I don't remember him the way I do Nikolenka. I close my eyes, and I remember him, but Boris I don't" (she closed her eyes), "no—nothing!"

"Ah, Natasha!" Sonya said rapturously and seriously, without looking at her friend, as if she considered her unworthy of what she intended to say, and as if she was saying it to someone else, with whom it was impossible to joke. "I've fallen in love with your brother once and for all, and whatever happens to him, or to me, *I* will never stop loving him—all my life."

Natasha looked at Sonya with astonished, curious eyes and said nothing. She felt that what Sonya had said was true, that there was such love as Sonya was talking about; but Natasha had never experienced anything like that. She believed it could be, but did not understand it.

"Will you write to him?" she asked.

Sonya fell to thinking. The question of how to write to Nicolas, and whether she should write to him, was a question that tormented her. Now that he was already an officer and a wounded hero, would it be right on her part to remind him of herself and, as it were, of the commitment he had taken upon himself in her regard.

"I don't know; I think, since he writes, I'll write, too," she said, blushing.

"And you won't be ashamed to write to him?"

Sonya smiled.

"No."

"But I'd be ashamed to write to Boris, so I won't."

"Ashamed of what?"

"Just so, I don't know. Awkward, ashamed."

"But I know why she'd be ashamed," said Petya, offended by Natasha's first remark, "because she was in love with that fat one in spectacles" (so Petya described his namesake, the new Count Bezukhov); "now she's in love with this singer" (Petya was referring to Natasha's Italian singing teacher): "so she's ashamed."

"Petya, you're stupid," said Natasha.

"No stupider than you, old girl," said the nine-year-old Petya, as if he was an old brigadier.

The countess had been prepared during dinner by Anna Mikhailovna's hints. Going to her room, she sat in an armchair, not taking her eyes from the miniature portrait of her son on a snuffbox, and tears welled up in her eyes. Anna Mikhailovna came to the countess's room on tiptoe with the letter and paused.

"Don't come in," she said to the old count, who was following her, "later," she said, and closed the door behind her.

The count put his ear to the keyhole and began to listen.

At first he heard the sounds of indifferent talk, then only the sound of Anna Mikhailovna's voice making a long speech, then a cry, then silence, then both voices again, speaking together with joyful intonations, and then footsteps, and then Anna Mikhailovna opened the door to him. Anna Mikhailovna's face bore the proud expression of a surgeon who has completed a difficult amputation and admits the public so that it can appreciate his art.

"*C'est fait!*"* she said to the count, pointing with a solemn gesture to the countess, who was holding the snuffbox with the portrait in one hand and the letter in the other, and pressing her lips first to the one, then to the other.

Seeing the count, she held her arms out to him, embraced his bald head, and again, over his bald head, looked at the letter and the portrait, and again pushed the bald head slightly away so as to press her lips to them. Vera, Natasha, Sonya, and Petya came into the room, and the reading began. In the letter Nikolushka gave a brief description of the march, the two battles in which he had taken part, and his promotion to officer, and said that he kissed the hands of *maman* and *papa*, asking their blessing, and kissed Vera, Natasha, and Petya. Besides that, he sent his greetings to M. Schelling, and Mme Schoss, and the nanny, and besides that he asked them to kiss his dear Sonya, whom he loved as ever and remembered as ever. Hearing that, Sonya blushed so much that tears came to her eyes. And, unable to bear the gazes turned to her, she rushed to the ballroom, made a run, twirled, and, her dress ballooning, all flushed and smiling, sat down on the floor. The countess was crying.

"What are you crying for, *maman?*" said Vera. "From all that he writes, you should rejoice and not cry."

That was perfectly correct, but the count, and the countess, and Natasha— everyone looked at her with reproach. "Who does she take after?" thought the countess.

Nikolushka's letter was read a hundred times, and those who were deemed worthy of listening to it had to come to the countess, who never let it out of her hands. Tutors, nannies, Mitenka, some acquaintances came, and the countess reread the letter each time with new delight and each time, through this letter, discovered new virtues in her Nikolushka. How strange, extraordinary, joyful it was that her son—that son who twenty years ago had moved his tiny limbs barely perceptibly inside her, that son over whom she had quarrelled with the too-indulgent count, that son who had first learned to say "brush," and then "mama," that this son was now there, in a foreign land, in foreign surroundings, a manly warrior, alone, with no help or guidance, and doing there some

---

*It's done!

manly business of his own. All the worldwide, age-old experience showing that children grow in an imperceptible way from the cradle to manhood, did not exist for the countess. Her son's maturing had been at every point as extraordinary for her as if there had not been millions upon millions of men who had matured in just the same way. As it was hard to believe twenty years ago that the little being who lived somewhere under her heart would start crying, and suck her breast, and begin to talk, so now it was hard to believe that this same being could be the strong, brave man, an example to sons and people, that he was now, judging by this letter.

"What *shtil*, how nicely he describes things!" she said, reading the descriptive part of the letter. "And what soul! Nothing about himself . . . nothing! About some Denisov, but he himself is probably braver than all of them. He writes nothing about his sufferings. And what heart! It's so like him! And how he remembered everyone! He didn't forget anybody. I always, always said, when he was only so high, I always said . . ."

For more than a week the whole house prepared, wrote drafts, and rewrote clean copies of letters to Nikolushka; under the countess's supervision and the count's solicitude the necessary things and money were gathered to outfit the newly promoted officer and provide for his needs. Anna Mikhailovna, a practical woman, had been able to arrange patronage for herself and her son in the army even for purposes of correspondence. She could send her letters to the grand duke Konstantin Pavlovich, who commanded the guards. The Rostovs assumed that the address *Russian Guards Abroad* was a perfectly definite address, and that, if the letter reached the grand duke who was in command of the guards, there was no reason to think it would not reach the Pavlogradsky regiment, which should be in the vicinity; and therefore it was decided to send the letters and money through the grand duke's courier to Boris, and Boris would have to deliver them to Nikolushka. There were letters from the old count, from the countess, from Petya, from Vera, from Natasha, and from Sonya, and, finally, 6,000 roubles for outfitting, as well as various things the count sent to his son.

VII

On the twelfth of November, Kutuzov's active army, camped near Olmütz, was preparing to be reviewed the next day by two emperors—Russian and Austrian. The guards, just arrived from Russia, were spending the night some ten miles from Olmütz, and the next day would come straight to the review, entering the field at Olmütz by ten o'clock in the morning.

Nikolai Rostov received a note from Boris that day, informing him that the Izmailovsky regiment was spending the night ten miles from Olmütz, and that

Boris was waiting for him, so as to give him a letter and money. Rostov especially needed money now, since the troops, having returned from the campaign, were stationed near Olmütz, where well-stocked sutlers and Austrian Jews filled the camp, offering all sorts of temptations. The Pavlogradsky hussars had one feast after another, celebrating the rewards they had received for the campaign, and made trips to Olmütz to visit the newly arrived Karolina the Hungarian, who had opened a tavern there with female waiters. Rostov had recently celebrated his promotion to cornet, had bought Bedouin, Denisov's horse, and was in debt all around to comrades and sutlers. On receiving Boris's note, Rostov rode to Olmütz with a comrade, had dinner there, drank a bottle of wine, and rode on alone to the guards' camp to look for his childhood friend. Rostov had not yet had time to outfit himself. He was in a much-worn junker's jacket with a soldier's cross, the same sort of riding breeches with a shabby leather seat, and an officer's sabre with a sword knot; he was riding a Don horse that he had bought from a Cossack while on campaign; his crumpled hussar's cap was dashingly pushed back and cocked. Riding up to the camp of the Izmailovsky regiment, he was thinking about how he would impress Boris and all his comrades in the guards by his look of a battle-seasoned hussar.

The guards had made the whole march as if on a promenade, showing off their cleanness and discipline. The stages were short, their packs were transported in wagons, the Austrian authorities prepared excellent dinners for the officers all along the way. The regiments entered and left towns to music, and for the whole march (something the guards took pride in), on the order of the grand duke, the men had walked in step, the officers on foot at their posts. All during the march, Boris had walked and quartered with Berg, who was now already a company commander. Berg, who had obtained the company during the march, had managed by his efficiency and neatness to earn the confidence of his superiors, and had arranged his financial affairs rather profitably; Boris had made many acquaintances during the march with people who could be useful to him, and, through a letter of recommendation brought to him from Pierre, had become acquainted with Prince Andrei Bolkonsky, through whom he hoped to get a post on the commander in chief's staff. Berg and Boris, cleanly and neatly dressed, having rested after the day's march, were sitting at a round table in the clean apartment assigned to them and playing checkers. Berg was holding a smoking little pipe between his knees. Boris, with his particular neatness, had piled the pieces in a pyramid with his slender white hands, waiting for Berg's move and watching his partner's face, obviously thinking about the game, as he always thought only about what he was engaged in.

"Well, how are you going to get out of that?" he said.

"We'll try," replied Berg, touching a piece and taking his hand away again.

Just then the door opened.

"Ah, here he is at last!" cried Rostov. "And Berg's here, too! Ah, you *petis-enfan, allay cushay dormir!*"* he cried, repeating the words of their nanny, at whom he and Boris used to laugh together.

"Good heavens! how you've changed!" Boris rose to meet Rostov, but in rising did not forget to pick up the fallen chessmen and put them in place, and was about to embrace his friend, but Nikolai drew back from him. With that feeling peculiar to youth, which fears beaten paths and wants, not to imitate others, but to express its feelings in a new, personal way, only not in the often feigned way its elders do, Nikolai wanted to do something special on meeting his friend: he wanted somehow to pinch or push Boris, only not to kiss him as everybody does. Boris, on the contrary, calmly and amicably embraced Rostov and kissed him three times.

They had not seen each other for nearly half a year; and at their age, when young men take their first steps on life's path, they both found enormous changes in each other, totally new reflections of the society in which they had taken their first steps in life. Both had changed greatly since their last meeting, and both wanted the sooner to show each other the changes that had taken place in them.

"Ah, you cursed floor-scrubbers! Clean, fresh, as if from a promenade, not like us sinful army folk," Rostov said, with baritone sounds in his voice and an army manner that were new for Boris, pointing to his mud-splashed breeches.

The German landlady stuck her head through the door, hearing Rostov's loud voice.

"A pretty little thing, eh?" he said, winking.

"Why are you shouting so? You'll frighten them," said Boris. "I wasn't expecting you today," he added. "I sent you a note just yesterday through an acquaintance, Kutuzov's adjutant—Bolkonsky. I didn't think he'd deliver it to you so soon . . . Well, how are you? Already been under fire?" asked Boris.

Rostov, without answering, shook the soldier's Cross of St. George that hung on the cords of his uniform and, pointing to his arm in a sling, looked smiling at Berg.

"As you see," he said.

"Well, there, yes, yes!" Boris said, smiling. "And we also had a nice march. You know, the grand duke constantly rode with our regiment, and so we had all the conveniences and advantages. The receptions we had in Poland, the dinners, the balls—I can't tell you! And the grand duke was very gracious to all our officers."

And the two friends began telling each other—the one about his hussar carousing and life at the front, the other about the pleasures and advantages of serving under the command of highly placed persons, and so on.

*Little children, go lie down to sleep! [Transliterated French.]

"Oh, you guards!" said Rostov. "But listen, send for some wine."

Boris winced.

"If you're sure you want it," he said.

And going to his bed, he took a purse from under the clean pillows and ordered wine brought.

"Yes, and I have to give you your money and letter," he added.

Rostov took the letter and, throwing the money on the sofa, leaned both elbows on the table and began to read. He read a few lines and glanced angrily at Berg. Having met his eyes, Rostov covered his face with the letter.

"They sent you a decent sum of money, though," said Berg, looking at the heavy purse pressing down on the sofa. "And we just get by on our pay, Count. I'll tell you about myself . . ."

"The thing is this, Berg, my dear," said Rostov. "If you received a letter from home and met one of your people, whom you'd like to question about everything, and I happened to be there—I'd leave at once, so as not to interfere with you. Listen, please go away, somewhere, anywhere . . . to the devil!" he cried, and taking him by the shoulder at once and looking amiably into his face, obviously trying to soften the rudeness of his words, he added: "You know, don't be angry, my dear, kind fellow, I'm speaking from the heart, as to our old acquaintance."

"Ah, for pity's sake, Count, I understand very well," said Berg, getting up and speaking to himelf in a guttural voice.

"Go across to the landlords: they invited you," added Boris.

Berg put on the cleanest of frock coats, with not a spot or speck on it, fluffed up his whiskers in front of the mirror, as Alexander Pavlovich wore them, and, assuring himself from Rostov's glance that his frock coat had been noticed, left the room with a pleasant smile.

"Ah, what a beast I am, though!" said Rostov, reading the letter.

"What's wrong?"

"Ah, what a swine I am, though, that I didn't write even once and frightened them so. Ah, what a swine I am!" he repeated, suddenly blushing. "So send Gavrilo for wine! Let's have a drink!" he said.

Among the letters from his family there was also a letter of recommendation to Prince Bagration, which the old countess had obtained through acquaintances, on the advice of Anna Mikhailovna, and sent on to her son, asking him to take it to its destination and make use of it.

"What stupidity! As if I need it," said Rostov, throwing the letter under the table.

"Why did you throw it on the floor?" asked Boris.

"It's some sort of letter of recommendation, what the devil is a letter to me!"

"How do you mean, what the devil is a letter?" said Boris, picking it up and reading the address. "You need this letter very much."

"I don't need anything, and I won't go and be anybody's adjutant."

"Why not?" asked Boris.

"It's a lackey's job."

"You're still the same dreamer, I see," said Boris, shaking his head.

"And you're the same diplomat. Well, but that's not the point . . . Well, how are you?" asked Rostov.

"As you see. So far everything's fine; but I confess, my wish, and it's a great one, is to become an adjutant and not stay at the front."

"Why?"

"Because once you've set out on a career in military service, you should try to do all you can to make it a brilliant career."

"Ah, so that's it!" said Rostov, evidently thinking about something else.

He looked intently and questioningly into his friend's eyes, evidently searching in vain for the answer to some question.

Old Gavrilo brought the wine.

"Shouldn't we send for Alphonse Karlych now?" asked Boris. "He'll drink with you. I can't."

"Send for him, send for him! Well, and what's this German like?" Rostov asked with a scornful smile.

"He's a very good, honest, and agreeable man," said Boris.

Rostov once again looked intently into Boris's eyes and sighed. Berg returned, and over a bottle of wine the conversation of these three officers became animated. The two guardsmen told Rostov about their march, about how they were honoured in Russia, Poland, and abroad. They told about the words and deeds of their commander, the grand duke, anecdotes about his kindness and hot temper. Berg, as usual, kept silent when things did not concern him personally, but on the occasion of anecdotes about the grand duke's hot temper, he told with delight how in Galicia he had managed to talk with the grand duke, when he was making the rounds of the regiments and waxed wroth at the incorrectness of a manoeuvre. With a pleasant smile on his face, he told how the grand duke, in great wrath, had ridden up to him and shouted: "Arnauti!"[3] (*Arnauti* was his highness's favourite word when he was wrathful), and summoned the regimental commander.

"Would you believe it, Count, I wasn't afraid at all, because I knew I was right. You know, Count, I can say without boasting that I know the regimental orders by heart, and I also know the regulations like the *Our Father in Heaven*. That's why there's no negligence in my company, Count. So my conscience was at ease. I presented myself." (Berg stood up and impersonated how he had presented himself with his hand to his visor. Indeed, it would be hard to impersonate any greater deference and self-satisfaction.) "He roasted me, as they say, roasted, roasted; roasted me not to the quick, but to death, as they say: 'Arnauti,' and 'devils,' and 'to Siberia,' " Berg said, smiling shrewdly. "I know I'm right, so I say nothing, isn't that the way, Count? 'Are you mute, or what?' he shouts. I still say nothing. And what do you think, Count? The next day there was nothing in the orders; that's what it means not to get flustered! There you are, Count," said Berg, lighting his pipe and letting out little smoke rings.

"Yes, very nice," said Rostov, smiling.

But Boris, noticing that Rostov was preparing to make fun of Berg, artfully diverted the conversation. He asked Rostov to tell them how and where he had received his wound. This pleased Rostov, and he began telling the story, growing more and more animated as it went on. He told them about his Schöngraben action in just the way that those who take part in battles usually tell about them, that is, in the way they would like it to have been, the way they have heard others tell it, the way it could be told more beautifully, but not at all the way it had been. Rostov was a truthful young man, not for anything would he have deliberately told an untruth. He began telling the story with the intention of telling it exactly as it had been, but imperceptibly, involuntarily, and inevitably for himself, he went over into untruth. If he had told the truth to these listeners, who, like himself, had already heard accounts of attacks numerous times and had formed for themselves a definite notion of what an attack was, and were expecting exactly the same sort of account—they either would not have believed him or, worse still, would have thought it was Rostov's own fault that what usually happens in stories of cavalry attacks had not happened with him. He could not simply tell them that they all set out at a trot, he fell off his horse, dislocated his arm, and ran to the woods as fast as he could to escape a Frenchman. Besides, in order to tell everything as it had been, one would have to make an effort with oneself so as to tell only what had been. To tell the truth is very difficult, and young men are rarely capable of it. They were expecting an account of how he got all fired up, forgetting himself, how he flew like a storm at the square; how he cut his way into it, hacking right and left; how his sabre tasted flesh, how he fell exhausted, and so on. And he told them all that.

In the middle of his story, just as he was saying: "You can't imagine what a strange feeling of fury one experiences during an attack," Prince Andrei Bolkonsky, whom Boris was expecting, came in. Prince Andrei, who liked to patronize young men, who was flattered to be turned to for a favour, and was well-disposed towards Boris, who had managed to please him the day before, wished to fulfil the young man's wish. Sent by Kutuzov with papers for the grand duke, he stopped to see the young man, hoping to find him alone. Coming into the room and seeing a frontline hussar telling about his military adventures (the sort of people Prince Andrei could not stand), he smiled affectionately to Boris, winced, narrowed his eyes at Rostov, and, bowing slightly, sat down wearily and lazily on the sofa. He was not pleased to have landed among bad company. Rostov blushed, understanding that. But it was all the same to him: the man was an outsider. But, glancing at Boris, he saw that he, too, seemed ashamed of the front-line hussar. In spite of Prince Andrei's unpleasant, mocking tone, in spite of the general disdain which Rostov, from his fighting army point of view, had for all these staff adjutants, to whom the newcomer obviously belonged, Rostov felt embarrassed, turned red, and fell silent. Boris asked what was the news at the staff and what, without being indiscreet, was rumoured about our dispositions.

"They'll probably advance," Bolkonsky replied, clearly not wishing to say more in front of strangers.

Berg used the opportunity to ask with particular courtesy whether, as rumour had it, company commanders were now to draw a double allotment for forage. To which Prince Andrei replied with a smile that he was unable to opine about such important government instructions, and Berg laughed joyfully.

"About your affair," Prince Andrei turned to Boris again, "we'll speak later," and he glanced at Rostov. "Come to me after the review, we'll do all that's possible."

And, glancing around the room, he turned to Rostov, whose state of uncontrollable childish embarrassment, turning into spite, he did not deign to notice, and said:

"It seems you were telling about the Schöngraben action? Were you there?"

"*I* was there," Rostov said spitefully, as if wishing to insult the adjutant by it.

Bolkonsky noticed the hussar's state and found it amusing. He gave a slightly contemptuous smile.

"Yes! many stories are told now about that action."

"Yes, stories!" Rostov began speaking loudly, glancing now at Boris, now at Bolkonsky, with eyes suddenly grown furious. "Yes, many stories are told, but our stories—the stories of those who were there, right under enemy fire—our stories have weight, not the stories of those fellows on the staff, who get rewards for doing nothing."

"To whom you suppose that I belong?" Prince Andrei said calmly and with an especially pleasant smile.

A strange feeling of spite and along with that of respect for the calmness of this figure came together at that moment in Rostov's soul.

"I'm not talking about you," he said, "I don't know you, and, I confess, I don't wish to. I'm talking about the staff in general."

"And I will tell you this," Prince Andrei interrupted him with calm power in his voice. "You want to insult me, and I am ready to agree with you that it is very easy to do so, if you lack sufficient respect for yourself; but you must agree that the time and place have been rather poorly chosen for that. One of these days we'll all take part in a big, more serious duel, and besides that, Drubetskoy, who says he's your old friend, is not at all to blame for the fact that my physiognomy has the misfortune not to please you. However," he said, getting up, "you know my name and where to find me; but don't forget," he added, "that I consider neither myself nor you insulted in the least, and my advice, as an older man, is to let this matter go without consequences. So I'll be waiting for you on Friday after the review, Drubetskoy. Goodbye," Prince Andrei concluded and left, after bowing to them both.

Rostov remembered what reply he should have given only when the man was already gone. And he was the more angry because he had forgotten to say it. Rostov ordered his horse brought at once, and having drily taken leave of Boris, rode home. Should he go to headquarters tomorrow and challenge this mincing adjutant, or indeed let the affair go at that? This was the question that tormented him all the way. Now he thought spitefully of what a pleasure it would be to see this small, weak, and proud man's fear in the face of his pistol, then he was surprised to feel that, of all the people he knew, there was no one he so wished to have for a friend as this hateful little adjutant.

VIII

On the day after the meeting of Boris and Rostov, there was a review of the Russian and Austrian troops, the fresh ones come from Russia, as well as those returned from campaigning with Kutuzov. Both emperors, the Russian with his heir the grand duke, and the Austrian with the archduke, made this review of the combined eighty-thousand-man army.

Since early morning, the trim and smartly polished troops had been on the move, lining up in the field in front of the fortress. Now thousands of feet and bayonets moved with flying standards and, at the officers' command, halted, turned, and lined up at intervals, circling around other similar masses of infantry in different uniforms; now there came the sounds of the measured thudding and clanking of the dressed-up cavalry, in blue, red, and green embroidered uniforms, with embroidered musicians in front, on black, chestnut, or grey horses; now, stretching out with the brazen noise of polished, shining cannon shaking on their carriages, and with their smell of linstocks, the artillery crawled between the infantry and cavalry and settled in their appointed places. Not only the generals in full parade dress, their waists, fat or slender, tightened to the utmost, their necks reddened by high-propped collars, wearing sashes and all their decorations; not only the pomaded, spruced-up officers, but every soldier, his face freshly scrubbed and shaven, his equipment polished to the highest shine possible, and every horse, groomed so that its hide gleamed like satin, its wetted mane lying hair by hair—they all felt that what was taking place was earnest, significant, and solemn. Every general and soldier sensed his own nullity, aware of being a grain of sand in this sea of people, and at the same time sensed his strength, aware of being part of this enormous whole.

From early morning strenuous bustling and efforts had begun, and by ten o'clock everything had reached the required order. The ranks were drawn up on the enormous field. The entire army was stretched out in three lines. In the front, the cavalry; behind them, the artillery; further behind, the infantry.

Between each kind of troops was a sort of street. The three parts of this army could be clearly distinguished from each other: Kutuzov's fighting force (in which the Pavlogradsky regiment stood on the right flank in the front line), the infantry and guards regiments come from Russia, and the Austrian troops. But they all stood in one line, under one command, and in the same order.

Like wind in the leaves, an excited whisper passed: "They're coming! they're coming!" Frightened voices were heard, and the bustle of final preparations rippled through the troops.

Before them, coming from Olmütz, a moving group appeared. And at the same time, though it was a windless day, a light current of wind ran through the army and barely stirred the lance pennants and slack standards, which began to flutter against their staffs. It seemed the army itself, by this slight movement, was expressing its joy at the approaching sovereigns. A single voice was heard: "Attention!" Then, like cocks at dawn, voices repeated it from all ends. And everything became still.

In the deathly silence only the thud of hooves could be heard. This was the emperors' suite. The sovereigns rode up to the flanks, and the trumpets of the first cavalry regiment rang out, playing the general march. It seemed it was not the trumpeters playing, but the army itself, rejoicing at the sovereigns' approach, that naturally produced these sounds. Through these sounds the one young, gentle voice of the emperor Alexander was distinctly heard. He uttered a greeting, and the first regiment bawled out such a deafening, prolonged, and joyful "Hurrah!" that the men themselves were awestruck at the multitude and strength of the huge bulk they made up.

Rostov, standing in the front ranks of Kutuzov's army, which the sovereign rode up to first, had the same feeling that was experienced by every man in that army—a feeling of self-forgetfulness, a proud awareness of strength, and a passionate attraction to him who was the cause of this solemnity.

He felt that it would take only one word from this man for that whole mass (and he himself bound up with it—an insignificant speck) to go through fire and water, to crime, to death, or to the greatest heroism, and therefore he could not but tremble and thrill at the sight of that approaching word.

"Hurrah! Hurrah! Hurrah!" thundered on all sides, and one regiment after another received the sovereign to the strains of the general march; then "Hurrah!" and the general march, and again "Hurrah!" and "Hurrah!"—which, ever growing and swelling, merged into a deafening roar.

Before the approach of the sovereign, each regiment, in its speechlessness and immobility, seemed a lifeless body; but as soon as the sovereign drew level with it, the regiment came alive and thundered, joining the roar of the entire line which the sovereign had already passed. To the terrible, deafening sound of these voices, amidst the masses of troops, motionless, as if petrified in their rectangles, the hundreds of horsemen of the suite moved casually, asymmetrically, and, above all, freely, and in front of them two men—the emperors. Upon them was concentrated the restrainedly passionate, undivided attention of this entire mass of men.

The handsome young emperor Alexander, in the uniform of the horse guards, in a triangular hat, worn brim first, with his pleasant face and sonorous but not loud voice, attracted the full force of attention.

Rostov stood not far from the trumpeters, and with his keen-sighted eyes he recognized the sovereign from afar and followed his approach. When the sovereign had approached to within twenty paces, and Nikolai could make out clearly, in all its details, the handsome, young, and happy face of the emperor, he experienced a feeling of tenderness and rapture such as he had never experienced before. Every feature, every movement of the sovereign seemed lovely to him.

Having stopped facing the Pavlogradsky regiment, the sovereign said something in French to the Austrian emperor and smiled.

Seeing that smile, Rostov involuntarily began to smile himself and felt a still stronger surge of love for his sovereign. He wanted to show his love for the sovereign in some way. He knew that this was impossible and wanted to cry. The sovereign summoned the regimental commander and said a few words to him.

"My God! what would happen to me if the sovereign addressed me!" thought Rostov. "I'd die of happiness."

The sovereign also addressed the officers.

"I thank you all, gentlemen" (every word Rostov heard was like a sound from heaven), "with all my heart."

How happy Rostov would be if he could die now for his sovereign!

"You have merited the St. George standards and will be worthy of them."

"Just to die, to die for him!" thought Rostov.

The sovereign said something more which Rostov did not hear, and the soldiers, straining their chests, shouted: "Hurrah!"

Rostov also shouted with all his might, leaning towards his saddle, wishing to hurt himself with this cry, only so as to express fully his rapture for the sovereign.

The sovereign stood for a few seconds facing the hussars, as if undecided.

"How can a sovereign be undecided?" thought Rostov, and then even this indecision seemed majestic and enchanting to Rostov, like everything the sovereign did.

The sovereign's indecision lasted only a moment. The sovereign's foot, in the narrow, sharp toe of its boot, as they wore them then, touched the belly of the bobtailed bay mare he was riding; the sovereign's hand in its white glove picked up the reins, and he set off, accompanied by a disorderly swaying sea of adjutants. He rode further and further, stopping by other regiments, and at last Rostov could only see his white plumes beyond the suite that surrounded the emperors.

Among the gentlemen of the suite, Rostov noticed Bolkonsky, sitting his horse lazily and casually. Rostov remembered his quarrel with him yesterday, and the question arose whether he should or should not challenge him. "Of course not," Rostov thought now . . . "And is it worth thinking and talking about it at a moment like this? At a moment of such a feeling of love, rapture, and self-denial—what are all our quarrels and offences?! I love everybody, I forgive everybody now," thought Rostov.

When the sovereign had ridden by almost all the regiments, the troops began a ceremonial march past him, and Rostov, on Bedouin, newly purchased from Denisov, rode at the tail end of his squadron—that is, alone and in full view of the sovereign.

Before he reached the sovereign, Rostov, an excellent horseman, twice put the spurs to his Bedouin and happily brought him to that furious-paced trot which Bedouin was prone to when excited. Lowering his foaming muzzle to his chest, his tail extended, and as if flying through the air without touching the ground, gracefully lifting his legs high as he shifted them, Bedouin, who also felt the sovereign's gaze upon him, passed by superbly.

Rostov himself, flinging his legs back, drawing his stomach in, and feeling himself one piece with his horse, with a frowning but blissful face, like the "veghry devil," as Denisov used to say, rode past the sovereign.

"Bravo, Pavlogradskies!" said the sovereign.

"My God! How happy I'd be if he ordered me right now to throw myself into the fire," thought Rostov.

When the review was over, the officers, both the newly arrived and Kutuzov's, began to gather in groups, and talk sprang up about rewards, about the Austrians and their uniforms, about their front, about Bonaparte and how bad things were going to be for him now, especially when the corps from Essen also arrives and Prussia takes our side.

But most of all, in all circles, they talked about the sovereign Alexander, repeating his every word and movement and admiring him.

They all wished for only one thing: to go quickly against the enemy under the sovereign's leadership. Under the command of the sovereign himself, it would be impossible not to defeat anyone whatever—so thought Rostov and most of the officers.

After the review, there was greater assurance of victory than there might have been after two victorious battles.

IX

The day after the review, Boris, putting on his best uniform and with parting wishes of success from his comrade Berg, rode to see Bolkonsky in Olmütz, wishing to avail himself of his friendliness and arrange the best position for himself, in particular the position of adjutant to an important person, which seemed to him particularly attractive in the army. "It's all right for Rostov, whose father sends him ten thousand roubles at a time, to talk about how he doesn't want to bow to anybody or be anybody's lackey; but I, who have nothing except my own head, must make my career and not let chances slip, but avail myself of them."

He did not find Prince Andrei in Olmütz that day. But the sight of Olmütz, where the headquarters and the diplomatic corps were stationed and both emperors lived with their suites of courtiers and attendants, increased still more his desire to belong to that supreme world.

He knew nobody, and, despite his dashing guardsman's uniform, all these higher people going up and down the streets in dashing carriages, plumes, ribbons and decorations, courtiers and military, seemed to stand so immeasurably higher than he, a little officer of the guards, that they not only did not want to, but even could not recognize his existence. In the quarters of the commander in chief Kutuzov, where he asked for Bolkonsky, all these adjutants and even orderlies looked at him as if wishing to impress upon him that quite a few officers such as he hung around there, and that they were all quite sick of it. Despite that, or rather, because of it, the next day, the fifteenth, after dinner he went to Olmütz again, and, going into the house occupied by Kutuzov, asked for Bolkonsky. Prince Andrei was at home, and Boris was taken to a large hall, which probably had once been used for dancing, and now was filled with five beds and various furnishings: tables, chairs, and a pianoforte. One adjutant, closer to the door, in a Persian dressing gown, was sitting at a table and writing. A second, the red, fat Nesvitsky, was lying on a bed with his hands behind his head and laughing along with another officer who was sitting with him. A third was playing a Viennese waltz on the pianoforte, a fourth was lying on the pianoforte and singing along. Bolkonsky was not there. None of these gentlemen changed his position on noticing Boris. The one who was writing and whom Boris addressed, turned to him vexedly and told him that Bolkonsky was on duty, and that if he wanted to see him, he should go through the door on the left, to the reception room. Boris thanked him and went into the reception room. In the reception room there were some ten officers and generals.

Just as Boris came in, Prince Andrei, narrowing his eyes disdainfully (with that particular air of polite weariness which says clearly that, were it not my duty, I would not talk with you for a minute), was listening to an old Russian general with decorations, who, drawn up almost on tiptoe, with an obsequious soldierly expression on his purple face, was reporting something to him.

"Very well, be so good as to wait," he said to the general in Russian, with that French pronunciation which he used when he wanted to speak disdainfully, and, noticing Boris and no longer addressing the general (who pleadingly ran after him asking to be heard out), Prince Andrei turned to Boris with a cheerful smile, nodding to him.

Boris clearly understood at that moment what he had foreseen earlier, namely, that in the army, besides the subordination and discipline that were written in the regulations and known to the regiment, and which he knew, there was another more essential subordination, which made this tightly girded, purple-faced general wait deferentially while the captain Prince Andrei, for his own pleasure, found it preferable to talk with the ensign Drubetskoy. Boris resolved more than ever to serve in the future according to this unwritten subordination, not the one written in the regulations. He now felt that, merely as the result of his having been recommended to Prince Andrei, he had at once become higher than the general, who, on other occasions, at the front, could annihilate an ensign of the guards like him. Prince Andrei went up to him and took his hand.

"Very sorry you didn't find me in yesterday. I spent the whole day fussing about with the Germans. Went to see Weyrother to check the disposition. When Germans start being accurate, there's no end to it!"

Boris smiled as if he understood what Prince Andrei was hinting at as common knowledge. But it was the first time he had heard the name of Weyrother and even the word *disposition*.

"Well, what is it, my friend, do you still want to be an adjutant? I've been thinking about you meanwhile."

"Yes," said Boris, blushing involuntarily for some reason, "I thought of asking the commander in chief; he received a letter about me from Prince Kuragin; I wanted to ask," he added, as if apologizing, "because I'm afraid the guards won't see action."

"Very good, very good! We'll discuss it all," said Prince Andrei. "Just let me report about this gentleman, and then I'm yours."

While Prince Andrei went to report about the purple general, that general, who obviously did not share Boris's notions about the advantages of the unwritten subordination, so fixed his eyes on the insolent ensign who had prevented him from finishing his talk with the adjutant that Boris felt awkward. He turned away and waited impatiently for Prince Andrei to come back from the commander in chief's office.

"You see, my friend, I've been thinking about you," said Prince Andrei, when they came to the big room with the pianoforte. "There's no point in your going to the commander in chief," said Prince Andrei. "He'll tell you a heap of nice things, ask you to dinner" ("That wouldn't be so bad for service by the other subordination," thought Boris), "but nothing further will come of it. There will soon be a battalion of us adjutants and orderly officers. But here's what we'll do: I have a good friend, an adjutant general and a wonderful man, Prince Dolgorukov; and though you couldn't know this, the thing is that Kutuzov and his staff and all of us mean precisely nothing: everything is now concentrated on the sovereign. So let's go to Dolgorukov, I have to go to him anyway, and I've already spoken to him about you; so we'll see whether he can't find it possible to set you up with him or somewhere else closer to the sun."

Prince Andrei always became especially animated when he had to guide a young man and help him towards worldly success. Under the pretext of this help for another, which out of pride he would never accept for himself, he found himself close to the milieu which conferred success and which attracted him. He took up Boris quite willingly and went with him to Prince Dolgorukov.

It was already late in the evening when they entered the Olmütz palace, which was occupied by the emperors and their retinues.

On that same day there had been a council of war in which all the members of the Hofkriegsrath and both emperors took part. At the council, in opposition to the opinion of the old men—Kutuzov and Prince Schwarzenberg—it was decided to go on the offensive immediately and give general battle to Bonaparte. The council of war had just ended when Prince Andrei, accompanied by Boris, came to the palace to look for Prince Dolgorukov. The headquarters personnel were all still under the charm of that day's council of war, which had been victorious for the younger party. The voices of the foot-draggers, who advised waiting for something else and not going on the offensive, had been so unanimously stifled and their arguments refuted by the indubitable proofs of the advantages of an offensive, that what was talked about at the council—the future battle and undoubted victory—seemed no longer future but past. All the advantages were on our side. Enormous forces, undoubtedly superior to Napoleon's, were massed in one place; the troops were inspired by the presence of the emperors and straining for action; the strategic point at which they were to act was known in the smallest detail to the Austrian general Weyrother, who was leading the army (as if by a lucky chance, the Austrian troops had been on manoeuvres a year before precisely on the fields where they were now to fight the French); the lay of the land was known and mapped in the smallest detail; and Bonaparte, obviously weakened, was undertaking nothing.

Dolgorukov, one of the most fervent advocates of the offensive, had just come back from the council, weary, exhausted, but animated and proud of the victory won. Prince Andrei introduced the officer he was patronizing, but Prince Dolgorukov, giving him a polite and firm handshake, said nothing to Boris and, obviously unable to keep from speaking out the thoughts that occupied him most at that moment, addressed Prince Andrei in French.

"Well, my friend, what a battle we went through! God only grant that the one that results from it is as victorious. However, my dear," he spoke haltingly and animatedly, "I must confess my guilt before the Austrians and especially before Weyrother. What precision, what detail, what knowledge of the terrain, what foresight of all possibilities, all conditions, all the smallest details! No, my dear, more advantageous conditions than those we find ourselves in could not be purposely invented. The combination of Austrian clarity with Russian courage—what more do you want?"

"So the offensive is definitely decided upon?" asked Bolkonsky.

"And you know, my friend, it seems to me that Bonaparte has decidedly lost his Latin.⁴ You know, a letter to the emperor came from him today." Dolgorukov smiled significantly.

"Well, now! What does he write?" asked Bolkonsky.

"What can he write? Fal-di-diddle-da and the like, all only with the purpose of gaining time. I tell you, he's in our hands, that's certain. But the most amusing thing," he said, suddenly laughing good-naturedly, "is that we simply couldn't decide how to address the reply! If not as consul, and naturally not as emperor, then as General Buonaparte, it seemed to me."

"But there's a difference between not acknowledging him as emperor and calling him General Buonaparte," said Bolkonsky.

"That's just it," Dolgorukov interrupted, laughing and speaking quickly. "You know Bilibin, he's a very intelligent man, he suggested addressing him as 'Usurper and Enemy of the Human Race.' "

Dolgorukov burst into merry laughter.

"No more than that?" remarked Bolkonsky.

"But anyhow Bilibin found a serious title of address. A witty and intelligent man . . ."

"What is it?"

" 'To the head of the French Government, *Au chef du gouvernement français,*' " Dolgorukov said seriously and with satisfaction. "It's good, isn't it?"

"It's good, but he'll dislike it very much," remarked Bolkonsky.

"Oh, very much! My brother knows him: he dined with him, the present emperor, more than once in Paris, and he told me that he never saw a more subtle and clever diplomat—you know, a combination of French adroitness and Italian play-acting. Do you know the anecdotes about him and Count Markóv? Count Markóv was the only one who knew how to handle him. Do you know the story of the handkerchief? It's charming!"

And the loquacious Dolgorukov, turning now to Boris, now to Prince Andrei, told how Bonaparte, wishing to test Markóv, our ambassador, purposely dropped his handkerchief in front of him and stood there looking at him, probably expecting a service from Markóv, and how Markóv at once dropped his own handkerchief next to it and picked it up, without picking up Bonaparte's handkerchief.

"*Charmant,*" said Bolkonsky. "But the thing is, Prince, that I've come to solicit you for this young man. You see . . ."

But before Prince Andrei finished, an adjutant came into the room to summon Prince Dolgorukov to the emperor.

"Ah, how vexing!" said Dolgorukov, hurriedly getting up and shaking hands with Prince Andrei and Boris. "You know, I'll be very glad to do everything in my power both for you and for this nice young man." He shook Boris's hand once more with an expression of good-natured, sincere, and animated light-mindedness. "But you see—till next time!"

Boris was excited by the thought of the closeness to supreme power in which he felt himself to be at that moment. He was conscious of himself being in touch with the springs that controlled all those huge mass movements, of which he, in his regiment, felt himself a small, submissive, and insignificant part. They followed Prince Dolgorukov to the corridor and met, coming out of the door to the sovereign's room by which Dolgorukov went in, a short man in civilian clothes, with an intelligent face and a distinctive, sharply protruding jaw, which, without spoiling his looks, endowed him with a particular liveliness and shiftiness of expression. This short man gave the nod of a close acquaintance to Dolgorukov, and began peering at Prince Andrei with an intently cold gaze, walking straight at him, and clearly expecting Prince Andrei to greet him or give way to him. Prince Andrei did neither; his face expressed spite, and the young man, turning away, went down the side of the corridor.

"Who's that?" asked Boris.

"That is one of the most remarkable, and for me most unpleasant, of men. That is the minister of foreign affairs, Prince Adam Czartoryski. It's these people," Bolkonsky said with a sigh which he could not suppress, as they were leaving the palace, "it's these people who decide the fates of nations."

The next day the troops set out on the march, and Boris had no time up to the battle of Austerlitz itself to visit either Bolkonsky or Dolgorukov and remained for a time with the Izmailovsky regiment.

X

At dawn on the sixteenth, Denisov's squadron, in which Nikolai Rostov served and which was in Bagration's detachment, moved from its night lodgings into action, as they said, and having gone about half a mile behind other columns, halted on the high road. Rostov saw the Cossacks go past him, the first and second squadrons of hussars, the infantry battalions with the artillery, and then Generals Bagration and Dolgorukov rode past with their adjutants. All the fear which, as previously, he experienced before action, all the inner struggle by means of which he overcame that fear, all his dreams of how he would distinguish himself as a fine hussar in this action—went for naught. Their squadron was kept in reserve, and Nikolai Rostov spent that day feeling bored and melancholy. Between eight and nine in the morning, he heard gunfire ahead of him, shouts of "Hurrah," saw some wounded brought back (they were not many), and finally saw a whole detachment of French cavalry led along in the midst of a Cossack hundred. Obviously the action was over, and the action had obviously been not big, but successful. The soldiers and officers coming back told of a brilliant victory, of the taking of the town of Wischau and the capture of a whole French squadron. The day was clear, sunny, after a heavy night frost, and the cheerful brightness of the autumn day coincided with the news of the victory, which was reported not only by those who took part in it, but also by the joyful expression on the faces of the soldiers, officers, generals, and adjutants who went there and came back past Rostov. The more wrung was Rostov's heart, who had uselessly suffered all the fear that precedes a battle, and had spent this cheerful day in inaction.

"Ghrostov, come here, let's dghrink fghrom ghrief!" shouted Denisov, sitting down by the edge of the road in front of a flask and some food.

The officers gathered in a circle, eating and talking, around Denisov's mess kit.

"Here they come with another one!" said one of the officers, pointing to a captured French dragoon whom two Cossacks were leading along on foot.

One of them was leading by the bridle the captive's tall and beautiful French horse.

"Sell me the hoghrse!" Denisov shouted to the Cossack.

"If you like, Your Honour . . ."

The officers stood up and surrounded the Cossacks and the captured Frenchman. The French dragoon was a young fellow, an Alsatian, who spoke French with a German accent. He was breathless with agitation, his face was red, and, hearing some words of French, he began speaking quickly to the officers, addressing now one, now another. He said that he would not have been taken, that it was not his fault that he was taken, but that of *le caporal* who had sent him to fetch the horse-cloths, that he had told him the Russians were already there. And to everything he said, he added: *"mais qu'on ne fasse pas de mal à mon petit cheval,"** and caressed his horse. It was clear that he did not quite understand where he was. He now apologized for being taken, now, supposing he was facing his superiors, displayed his soldierly punctiliousness and zeal for service. He brought with him to our rear guard all the freshness of atmosphere of the French troops, which was so foreign to us.

The Cossacks let the horse go for two gold pieces, and Rostov, who now, having received money, was the richest of the officers, bought it.

"Mais qu'on ne fasse pas de mal à mon petit cheval," the Alsatian said good-naturedly to Rostov, when the horse was handed over to the hussar.

Rostov, smiling, reassured the dragoon and gave him some money.

"Allee, allee!" said the Cossack, touching the prisoner's arm to urge him on.

"The sovereign! The sovereign!" was suddenly heard among the hussars.

Everyone began running, hurrying, and Rostov saw behind him on the road several horsemen with white plumes in their hats riding up. In a single moment, everyone was in his place and waiting.

Rostov did not remember and did not feel how he ran to his place and mounted his horse. His regret over his non-participation in the action, his humdrum mood in the circle of usual faces, instantly went away, and all thought of himself instantly vanished: he was wholly consumed by the feeling of happiness that came from the nearness of the sovereign. He felt himself rewarded by this nearness alone for the loss of that day. He was as happy as a lover who has obtained a hoped-for rendezvous. Not daring to turn to look while in line, and not looking, his rapturous senses felt *his* approach. And he felt it not only from the hoofbeats of the approaching cavalcade, but felt it because as it approached everything around him became brighter, more joyful, more significant, and more festive. This sun moved ever nearer and nearer to Rostov, spreading around itself rays of mild and majestic light, and he already feels himself caught up in those rays, he hears his voice—that gentle, calm, majestic, and at the same time so simple voice. As it had to be, according to Rostov's feeling, a deathly silence ensued, and in that silence the sounds of the sovereign's voice rang out.

"Les hussards de Pavlograd?" he said questioningly.

"La réserve, sire!" someone's voice replied, so human after the non-human voice that had said: *"Les hussards de Pavlograd?"*

The sovereign drew even with Rostov and stopped. Alexander's face was still more beautiful than three days before at the review. It shone with such cheer and youth, such innocent youth that it reminded one of a boyish

*But don't hurt my little horse.

fourteen-year-old friskiness, and at the same time it was still the face of a majestic emperor. Looking the squadron over at random, the sovereign's eyes met the eyes of Rostov and rested on them for no more than two seconds. The sovereign may or may not have understood everything that was going on in Rostov's soul (it seemed to Rostov that he had understood everything), but for about two seconds he looked with his pale blue eyes into Rostov's face. (A soft, mild light poured from them.) Then he suddenly raised his eyebrows, spurred his horse with a sharp movement of his left foot, and rode on at a gallop.

On hearing gunfire in the vanguard, the young emperor could not restrain his desire to be present at the battle, and, despite all the remonstrations of his courtiers, at noon, having separated from the third column with which he was proceeding, he rode to the vanguard. Before he reached the hussars, several adjutants met him with news of the successful outcome of the action.

The battle, which consisted merely in the capture of a French squadron, was presented as a brilliant victory over the French, and therefore the sovereign and the whole army, especially while the powder smoke still hung over the battle-field, believed that the French were defeated and were retreating against their will. A few minutes after the sovereign rode by, the Pavlogradsky division was ordered to advance. In Wischau itself, a small German town, Rostov saw the sovereign once more. On the town square, where a rather intense exchange of gunfire had taken place before the sovereign's arrival, lay several dead and wounded men, whom there had been no time to pick up. The sovereign, sur-rounded by his suite of military and non-military men, was on a bobtailed chestnut mare, already different from the one at the review, and, leaning to one side, holding a gold lorgnette to his eyes with a graceful gesture, was looking through it at a soldier who lay face down, without his shako, his head bloody. The wounded soldier was so dirty, coarse, and vile that Rostov was offended by his nearness to the sovereign. Rostov saw how the sovereign's stooping shoulders shuddered as if a chill ran through them, and how his left foot con-vulsively began to spur the horse's side. The well-trained horse looked about indifferently and did not stir from its place. Getting off their horses, some adju-tants took the soldier under the arms and began laying him on a stretcher which had just appeared. The soldier groaned.

"Gently, gently, can't you do it gently?" said the sovereign, clearly suffering more than the dying soldier, and he rode off.

Rostov saw the tears that filled the sovereign's eyes, and heard him say in French to Czartoryski, as he rode off:

"What a terrible thing war is, what a terrible thing! *Quel terrible chose que la guerre!*"

The troops of the vanguard were positioned before Wischau within sight of the enemy line, which yielded ground to us throughout the day at the least exchange of fire. The sovereign's gratitude was announced to the vanguard, with a promise of rewards, and the men were given a double ration of vodka. The bivouac fires crackled and the soldiers' songs rang out still more merrily than the previous night. Denisov celebrated his promotion to major that night, and Rostov, who had already drunk quite a bit, proposed a toast at the end of the party to the health of the sovereign, "but not of the sovereign emperor, as they say at official dinners," he said, "but to the health of the sovereign, that kind, enchanting, and great man. We drink to his health and to certain victory over the French!"

"If we fought before," he said, "and gave no quarter to the French, as at Schöngraben, how will it be now when he himself is at our head? We'll all die, we'll gladly die for him. Right, gentlemen? Maybe I'm not speaking well, I've drunk a lot; but that's how I feel, and so do you. To the health of Alexander the First! Hurrah!"

"Hurrah!" rang out the enthusiastic voices of the officers.

And old Captain Kirsten shouted enthusiastically and no less sincerely than the twenty-year-old Rostov.

When the officers drank up and smashed their glasses, Kirsten filled others, and, in nothing but his shirt and breeches, with the glass in his hand, went up to the soldiers' campfires, struck a majestic pose, with his long grey moustache, his white chest showing through his unbuttoned shirt, stood in the firelight, and swung his arm up.

"Lads, to the health of the sovereign emperor, to victory over our foes, hurrah!" he cried in his dashing old hussar's baritone.

The hussars clustered around him and responded all together in a loud shout.

Late that night, when everyone had dispersed, Denisov, with his short hand, patted his favourite, Rostov, on the shoulder.

"There's nobody to fall in love with on campaign, so he's fallen in love with the tsaghr," he said.

"Don't joke about that, Denisov," cried Rostov, "this is such a lofty, such a beautiful feeling, such a . . ."

"I believe it, my fghriend, I believe it, and I share it and appghrove . . ."

"No, you don't understand!"

And Rostov got up and began wandering among the campfires, dreaming of what happiness it would be to die, not saving the life (he dared not even dream of that), but simply to die before the eyes of the sovereign. He was indeed in love with the tsar, and with the glory of Russian arms, and with the hope of the future triumph. And he was not the only one who experienced that feeling in those memorable days preceding the battle of Austerlitz: nine tenths of the men in the Russian army were then in love, though less rapturously, with their tsar and with the glory of Russian arms.

XI

The next day the sovereign stayed at Wischau. The court physician Villiers was summoned to him several times. In headquarters and among the nearby troops the news spread that the sovereign was unwell. He had eaten nothing and slept poorly that night, as people close to him said. The cause of it was the strong impression made on the sovereign's sensitive soul by the sight of the wounded and dead.

At dawn on the seventeenth, a French officer was sent to Wischau from our outposts, who had come under a flag of truce, asking for a meeting with the Russian emperor. This officer was Savary. The sovereign had only just fallen asleep, and therefore Savary had to wait. At noon he was admitted to the sovereign, and an hour later he rode with Prince Dolgorukov to the outposts of the French army.

As rumour had it, the purpose of sending Savary was to propose peace and to propose a meeting between the emperor Alexander and Napoleon. A personal meeting, to the joy and pride of the whole army, was refused, and instead of the sovereign, Prince Dolgorukov, the victor at Wischau, was sent with Savary to negotiate with Napoleon, on the chance that these negotiations, contrary to expectation, had as their purpose a real desire for peace.

In the evening Dolgorukov came back, went straight to the sovereign, and spent a long time alone with him.

On the eighteenth and nineteenth of November, the troops made two more marches forward, and the enemy's outposts retreated after brief exchanges of fire. In the highest spheres of the army, an intense, bustlingly agitated movement began from noon of the nineteenth, continuing until the morning of the next day, the twentieth of November, when the memorable battle of Austerlitz took place.

Until noon on the nineteenth, the movement, animated conversation, running, and sending of adjutants were limited to the emperors' headquarters; after noon of the same day the movement spread to the headquarters of Kutuzov and the staffs of the leaders of columns. By evening this movement had spread through adjutants to all ends and parts of the army, and during the night of the nineteenth to the twentieth, rising up from its night camp, humming with talk, the eighty-thousand-man mass of the allied army undulated and set off in a huge six-mile sheet.

The concentrated movement which began that morning in the emperors' headquarters and gave a push to all subsequent movement was like the first movement of the central wheel in a big tower clock. Slowly one wheel started, another turned, a third, and the wheels, pulleys, and gears were set turning more and more quickly, chimes began to ring, figures popped out, and the clock hands started their measured advance, showing the result of that movement.

As in the mechanism of a clock, so also in the mechanism of military action, the movement once given is just as irrepressible until the final results, and just as indifferently motionless are the parts of the mechanism not yet involved in the action even a moment before movement is transmitted to them. Wheels whizz on their axles, cogs catch, fast-spinning pulleys whirr, yet the neighbouring wheel is as calm and immobile as though it was ready to stand for a hundred years in that immobility; but a moment comes—the lever catches, and, obedient to its movement, the wheel creaks, turning, and merges into one movement with the whole, the result and purpose of which are incomprehensible to it.

As in a clock the result of the complex movement of numberless wheels and pulleys is merely the slow and measured movement of the hands pointing to the time, so also the result of all the complex human movements of these hundred and sixty thousand Russians and French—all the passions, desires, regrets, humiliations, sufferings, bursts of pride, fear, rapture—was merely the loss of the battle of Austerlitz, the so-called battle of the three emperors, that is, a slow movement of the world-historical hand on the clockface of human history.

Prince Andrei was on duty that day and constantly by the commander in chief.

After five in the evening, Kutuzov came to the emperors' headquarters and, having spent a short time with the sovereign, went to see the grand marshal of the court, Count Tolstoy.

Bolkonsky made use of this time to go to Dolgorukov and find out the details of the action. Prince Andrei sensed that Kutuzov was upset and displeased about something, and that there was displeasure with him at headquarters, and that all the persons of the imperial headquarters used with him the tone of people who knew something that others did not, and therefore he wanted to talk with Dolgorukov.

"Well, greetings, *mon cher,*" said Dolgorukov, who was having tea with Bilibin. "The fête is tomorrow. How's your old man? In a bad humour?"

"I wouldn't say he's in a bad humour, but it seems he'd like to be heard."

"He was heard at the council of war and will be heard when he talks to the point; but to drag our feet and wait for something now, when Bonaparte is afraid of a general battle more than anything—is impossible."

"So you saw him?" asked Prince Andrei. "Well, what is Bonaparte like? What impression did he make on you?"

"Yes, I saw him and became convinced that he is afraid of a general battle more than anything in the world," Dolgorukov repeated, obviously cherishing this overall conclusion which he had come to after his meeting with Napoleon. "If he wasn't afraid of a battle, what would make him ask for this meeting, conduct negotiations, and, above all, retreat, when retreat is so contrary to his whole method of conducting war? Believe me, he's afraid, afraid of a general battle, his hour has come. That I can tell you."

"But tell me, how is he, what's he like?" Prince Andrei asked again.

"He's a man in a grey frock coat, who wished very much that I would say 'Your Majesty' to him, but, to his regret, did not receive any titles from me. That's what he's like, and nothing more," Dolgorukov replied, glancing at Bilibin with a smile.

"Despite my full respect for old Kutuzov," he went on, "what good ones we'd all be, waiting for something and giving him a chance to escape or trick us, whereas now he's certainly in our hands. No, we mustn't forget Suvorov and his rules: don't put yourself in a position to be attacked, but attack yourself. Believe me, in war the energy of young men often points to a surer way than all the experience of the old cunctators."[5]

"But in what position are we going to attack him? I was at the outposts today, and it's impossible to tell precisely where he's camped with his main forces," said Prince Andrei.

He wanted to explain to Dolgorukov the plan of attack he had worked out for himself.

"Oh, that makes no difference at all," Dolgorukov began speaking quickly, getting up and unfolding a map on the table. "All the possibilities have been foreseen: if he's camped by Brünn . . ."

And Prince Dolgorukov quickly and vaguely recounted Weyrother's plan for a flanking movement.

Prince Andrei started to object and demonstrate his own plan, which might have been just as good as Weyrother's, but had the shortcoming that Weyrother's had already been approved. As soon as Prince Andrei began to demonstrate the disadvantages of the latter and the advantages of his own, Prince Dolgorukov stopped listening to him, and gazed absent-mindedly not at the map, but at Prince Andrei's face.

"Anyhow, there'll be a council of war at Kutuzov's today: you can speak all this out there," said Dolgorukov.

"I'll do just that," said Prince Andrei, stepping away from the map.

"What are you worrying about, gentlemen?" asked Bilibin, who up to then had been listening to their conversation with a merry smile and was now obviously going to come out with a quip. "Whether there's victory or defeat tomorrow, the glory of Russian arms is assured. Besides your Kutuzov, there's not a single Russian leader of a column. The leaders are: *Herr General Wimpfen, le comte de Langeron, le prince de Liechtenstein, le prince de Hohenloe, et enfin Prsch . . . Prsch . . . et ainsi de suite, comme tous les noms polonais.*"*[6]

---

*And finally Prsch . . . Prsch . . . and so on, like all Polish names.

"*Taisez-vous, mauvaise langue,*"* said Dolgorukov. "It's not true, there are now two Russians: Miloradovich and Dokhturov, and there would have been a third, Count Arakcheev, but he has weak nerves."

"However, I think Mikhail Ilarionovich has come out," said Prince Andrei. "I wish you luck and success, gentlemen," he added and left, after shaking hands with Dolgorukov and Bilibin.

On the way home, Prince Andrei could not help asking Kutuzov, who was sitting silently next to him, what he thought about the next day's battle.

Kutuzov looked sternly at his adjutant, paused, and said:

"I think the battle will be lost, and I said so to Count Tolstoy and asked him to convey it to the sovereign. And what do you think he replied? *Eh, mon cher général, je me mêle de riz et des côtelettes, mêlez-vous des affaires de la guerre.*† Yes . . . That was the answer I got!"

XII

After nine in the evening, Weyrother moved with his plans to Kutuzov's quarters, where a council of war was called. All the leaders of columns were summoned to the commander in chief, and, apart from Bagration, who refused to come, they all arrived at the appointed time.

Weyrother, who was fully in charge of the forthcoming battle, presented, in his liveliness and briskness, a sharp contrast with the displeased and drowsy Kutuzov, who reluctantly played the role of chairman and leader of the council of war. Weyrother obviously felt himself at the head of the movement which had now become irrepressible. He was like a horse harnessed to a wagon and running downhill. Whether he was pulling or being pushed, he did not know; but he was racing with all possible speed, having no time left to discuss what this movement would lead to. That evening Weyrother had gone twice to inspect the enemy lines in person and twice to the emperors, Russian and Austrian, to report and explain, and then to his office, where he had dictated the German disposition. Exhausted, he now arrived at Kutuzov's.

He was clearly so preoccupied that he even forgot to be respectful with the commander in chief: he interrupted him, spoke quickly, unclearly, not looking into his interlocutor's eyes, not answering the questions put to him, was covered with mud, and looked pitiful, exhausted, disconcerted, and at the same time presumptuous and proud.

Kutuzov occupied a modest nobleman's castle near Ostralitz. In the big draw-

*Quiet, wicked tongue.
†Ah, my dear general, I'm involved in rice and cutlets, involve yourself in matters of war.

ing room, turned into the commander in chief's office, were gathered: Kutuzov himself, Weyrother, and the members of the council of war. They were having tea. They were only waiting for Prince Bagration in order to begin the council of war. Finally, after seven o'clock Prince Bagration's orderly officer arrived with the news that the prince could not be there. Prince Andrei came in to report that to the commander in chief, and, availing himself of the permission given him earlier by Kutuzov to be present at the council, remained in the room.

"Since Prince Bagration won't be coming, we can begin," said Weyrother, hurriedly getting up from his place and approaching the table, on which an enormous map of the environs of Brünn was spread.

Kutuzov, in an unbuttoned uniform, from which his fat neck, as if released, poured out over the collar, was sitting in a Voltaire armchair, his pudgy old man's hands placed symmetrically on the two armrests, and was almost asleep. At the sound of Weyrother's voice, he opened his one eye with effort.

"Yes, yes, please, or it will get late," he said, and, nodding his head, lowered it and again closed his eye.

If the members of the council at first thought Kutuzov was pretending to sleep, the sounds his nose produced during the reading that followed proved that for the commander in chief at that moment the point of the matter was something far more important than a wish to show his contempt for the disposition or for anything at all: the point of the matter was to satisfy the irresistible human need for sleep. He was indeed asleep. Weyrother, with the gesture of a man who is too busy to waste even a moment of his time, glanced at Kutuzov and, assuring himself that he was asleep, took up the paper and began to read the disposition for the future battle in a loud, monotonous tone, under the title, which he also read:

"Disposition for the attack on the enemy's position behind Kobelnitz and Sokolnitz, 20 November 1805."

The disposition was very complex and difficult. The original began:

Da der Feind mit seinem linken Flügel an die mit Wald bedeckten Berge lehnt und sich mit seinem rechten Flügel längs Kobelnitz und Sokolnitz hinter die dort befindlichen Teiche zieht, wir im Gegenteil mit unserem linken Flügel seinen rechten sehr debordieren, so ist es vorteilhaft letzteren Flügel des Feindes zu attakieren, besonders wenn wir die Dörfer Sokolnitz und Kobelnitz im Besitze haben, wodurch wir dem Feind zugleich in die Flanke fallen und ihn auf der Fläche zwischen Schlapanitz und dem Thuerassa-Walde verfolgen können, indem wir dem Defileen von Schlapanitz und Bellowitz ausweichen, welche die feindliche Front decken. Zu diesem Endzwecke ist es nötig . . . die erste Kolonne marschiert . . . die zweite Kolonne marschiert . . . die dritte Kolonne mar-

*schiert . . ."** and so on, read Weyrother. The generals seemed to listen reluctantly to the difficult disposition. The tall, fair-haired General Buxhöwden stood leaning his back against the wall, and, resting his eyes on the burning candle, seemed not to be listening and even not to want it to be thought that he was listening. Directly opposite Weyrother, fixing his shining, wide-open eyes on him, in a martial pose, hands on his knees, elbows turned out, sat ruddy Miloradovich, with raised-up moustache and shoulders. He was obstinately silent, staring into Weyrother's face, and took his eyes off him only when the Austrian chief of staff fell silent. Then Miloradovich looked around significantly at the other generals. But by the significance of this significant gaze it was impossible to tell whether he agreed or disagreed, was satisfied or dissatisfied with the disposition. Closest of all to Weyrother, Count Langeron sat and, with a subtle smile on his southern French face, which did not abandon him throughout the reading, gazed at his slender fingers, quickly twirling by the corners a golden snuffbox with a portrait. In the middle of one of the longest periods, he stopped the spinning movement of the snuffbox, raised his head, and, with an unpleasant politeness at the very corners of his thin lips, interrupted Weyrother and wanted to say something; but the Austrian general, without breaking off his reading, frowned angrily and waved his elbows, as if to say: later, later you can tell me your thoughts, but now kindly look at the map and listen. Langeron looked up with an expression of perplexity, glanced at Miloradovich as if seeking an explanation, but, meeting Miloradovich's significant gaze, which signified nothing, he sadly lowered his eyes and again began twirling the snuffbox.

"*Une leçon de géographie,*" he said, as if to himself, but loudly enough to be heard.

Przebyszewski, with deferential but dignified politeness, put his hand to his ear towards Weyrother, having the air of a man whose attention is absorbed. The short Dokhturov sat directly opposite Weyrother with a diligent and modest look, and, bending over the spread-out map, conscientiously studied the disposition and the unfamiliar terrain. He asked Weyrother several times to repeat words he had not heard properly and the difficult names of the villages. Weyrother did as he asked, and Dokhturov wrote them down.

When the reading, which lasted more than an hour, was over, Langeron again stopped the snuffbox and, without looking at Weyrother or anyone in particular, began speaking about the difficulty of following such a disposition,

* As the enemy's left wing lies on the wood-covered hills, and the right extends along Kobelnitz and Sokolnitz behind the ponds that are there, while we, on the contrary, far outflank his left wing with our right, it is advantageous for us to attack that wing of the enemy, especially if we have taken the villages of Sokolnitz and Kobelnitz, which will enable us both to fall upon the enemy's flank and to pursue him across the plain between Schlapanitz and the Thuerassa forest, avoiding the defiles of Schlapanitz and Bellowitz, which are covered by the enemy's front. To this end it is necessary . . . the first column marches . . . the second column marches . . . the third column marches . . .

in which the position of the enemy is assumed to be known, when that position may not be known to us, since the enemy is on the move. Langeron's objections were well-founded, but it was obvious that the purpose of those objections consisted primarily in bringing it home to General Weyrother, who had read his disposition with such self-assurance, as if to schoolboys, that he had to do not with mere fools, but with people who could give him lessons in military matters. When the monotonous sound of Weyrother's voice fell silent, Kutuzov opened his eyes, like a miller who wakes up at an interruption of the soporific sound of the mill wheels, listened to what Langeron was saying, and—as if to say, "Ah, you're still going on about these stupidities!"—quickly closed his eyes and lowered his head still more.

Trying to offend Weyrother as stingingly as he could in his amour propre as a military author, Langeron demonstrated that Bonaparte could easily attack, instead of being attacked, and thereby make this disposition totally useless. Weyrother responded to all his objections with a firm, contemptuous smile, obviously prepared beforehand for every objection, regardless of what might be said to him.

"If he could attack us, he would have done so today," he said.

"You think, then, that he is powerless?" asked Langeron.

"He has forty thousand men, if that," Weyrother replied, with the smile of a doctor being told by a wise woman how to treat a patient.

"In that case he's going to his destruction by waiting for our attack," Langeron said with a subtle, ironic smile, again glancing for support to Miloradovich, who was nearest to him.

But at that moment Miloradovich was obviously thinking least of all of what the generals were arguing about.

"*Ma foi,*" he said, "tomorrow we'll see it all on the battlefield."

Weyrother again smiled that same ironic smile, which said that *to him* it was ridiculous and strange to meet objections from Russian generals and prove that of which he was not only all too well assured himself, but of which he had assured the two emperors.

"The enemy has put out his fires, and a continual noise is heard from his camp," he said. "What does that mean? Either he is retreating, which is the one thing we should fear, or he is changing his position" (he smiled). "But even if he takes up a position in Thuerassa, he is only saving us a great deal of trouble, and all orders, to the smallest detail, remain the same."

"But how is that? . . ." said Prince Andrei, who had already been waiting a long time for a chance to express his doubts.

Kutuzov woke up, cleared his throat loudly, and glanced around at the generals.

"Gentlemen, the disposition for tomorrow, for today even (because it's already past twelve), cannot be changed," he said. "You have heard it, and we

will all do our duty. And there's nothing more important before a battle . . ."
(he paused) "than a good night's sleep."

He made as if to rise. The generals bowed and withdrew. It was already past
midnight. Prince Andrei left.

The council of war, at which Prince Andrei had not managed to speak out his
opinion as he had hoped to, left in him a vague and disturbing impression.
Who was right—Dolgorukov and Weyrother, or Kutuzov and Langeron and
the others who did not approve the plan of attack—he did not know. "But
was it really impossible for Kutuzov to speak his mind directly to the sovereign? Can it really not be done otherwise? Can it really be that, for court and
personal considerations, tens of thousands of lives must be risked—and my
own, *my life*?" he thought.

"Yes, I may very well be killed tomorrow," he thought. And suddenly, with
that thought of death, a whole series of the most remote and most soul-felt
memories arose in his imagination; he remembered his last farewell from his
father and his wife; he remembered the first time of his love for her; remembered her pregnancy and felt sorry for her and for himself; and in an emotionally softened and troubled state, he left the cottage in which he was billeted
with Nesvitsky and began pacing in front of the house.

The night was misty, and through the mist moonlight shone mysteriously.
"Yes, tomorrow, tomorrow!" he thought. "Tomorrow maybe everything will
be over for me, all these memories will be no more, all these memories will simply have no more sense for me. Tomorrow maybe—even certainly, I have a
presentiment of it—for the first time I'll finally have to show all I can do." And
he imagined the battle, its loss, the concentration of the fighting at one point,
and the bewilderment of all the superiors. And here that happy moment, that
Toulon he has so long awaited, finally presents itself to him. He voices his opinion firmly and clearly to Kutuzov and Weyrother, and to the emperors. All are
struck by the correctness of his thinking, but no one undertakes to carry it out,
and here he takes a regiment, a division, negotiates the condition that no one
interfere with his instructions, and leads his division to the decisive point, and
alone wins the victory. "And death and suffering?" says another voice. But
Prince Andrei does not respond to that voice and goes on with his successes.
The disposition for the next battle he does alone. He bears the title of an officer
on duty in Kutuzov's army, but he does everything alone. He alone wins the
next battle. Kutuzov is replaced, he is appointed . . . "Well, and then?" the
other voice says again. "And then, if you're not wounded, killed, or deceived
ten times over—well, then what?" "Well, then . . ." Prince Andrei answers
himself, "I don't know what will happen then, I don't want to know and I can't
know; but if I want this, want glory, want to be known to people, want to be

loved by them, it's not my fault that I want it, that it's the only thing I want, the only thing I live for. Yes, the only thing! I'll never tell it to anyone, but my God! what am I to do if I love nothing except glory, except people's love? Death, wounds, loss of family, nothing frightens me. And however near and dear many people are to me—my father, my sister, my wife—the dearest people to me—but, however terrible and unnatural it seems, I'd give them all now for a moment of glory, of triumph over people, for love from people I don't know and will never know, for the love of these people here," he thought, listening to the talk in Kutuzov's yard. From Kutuzov's yard came the voices of orderlies preparing to sleep; one voice, probably of a coachman who was teasing Kutuzov's old cook, whom Prince Andrei knew and whose name was Titus, said: "Titus, hey, Titus?"

"Well?" replied the old man.

"Titus, don't bite us," said the joker.

"Pah, go to the devil," a voice cried, drowned out by the guffawing of the orderlies and servants.

"And still the only thing I love and cherish is triumph over all of them, I cherish that mysterious power and glory hovering over me here in this mist!"

XIII

That night Rostov was on the picket line with his platoon forward of Bagration's detachment. His hussars were scattered in pairs along the line; he himself rode the line on horseback, trying to fight off the sleep that was irresistibly overcoming him. Behind him could be seen the immense expanse of our army's campfires burning dimly in the mist; ahead of him was misty darkness. However much Rostov peered into this misty distance, he saw nothing: now some greyish, some blackish shape seemed to appear; now it was as if lights flickered where the enemy ought to be; now it seemed only some glimmer in his own eyes. His eyes kept closing, and in his imagination the sovereign appeared, then Denisov, then Moscow memories, and he hurriedly opened his eyes again and saw close in front of him the head and ears of the horse he was riding, sometimes the black figures of hussars, when he came within six paces of them, and in the distance the same misty darkness. "Why not? It might well be," thought Rostov, "that the sovereign, meeting me, gives me some assignment, saying as to any officer: 'Go and find out what's there.' There are many stories about how he got to know some officer quite by chance and attached him to himself. What if he attached me to himself? Oh, how I'd protect him, how I'd tell him the whole truth, how I'd expose the deceivers!" And so as to picture vividly to himself his love and devotion for the sovereign, he pictured to himself an enemy or a deceitful German, whom he delighted not only in killing, but in slapping in the face before the sovereign's eyes. Suddenly a distant cry aroused Rostov. He gave a start and opened his eyes.

"Where am I? Ah, yes, in the line; watchword and password—'shaft,' 'Olmütz.' How vexing that our squadron will be in reserve tomorrow . . ." he thought. "I'll ask to be sent into action. That may be the only chance I'll get to see the sovereign. Yes, it's not long now till we're relieved. I'll make another round, and as soon as I get back, I'll go to the general and ask him." He righted himself in the saddle and touched up his horse, in order to make one more round of his hussars. He thought it was getting lighter. To the left he could see a sloping, lit-up hillside and across from it a black knoll that seemed steep as a wall. On this knoll was a white spot that Rostov could not make sense of: was it a moonlit clearing in the woods, or some leftover snow, or some white houses? It even seemed to him that something was moving on that white spot. "It must be snow—this spot; a spot—*une tache*," thought Rostov. "*Tache* or no *tache* . . ."

"Natasha, my sister, dark eyes. Na . . . tashka . . . (She'll be so surprised when I tell her how I saw the sovereign!) Natashka . . . take the . . . tashka . . ." "Keep to the right, Your Honour, there's bushes here," said the voice of a hussar whom Rostov, falling asleep, was riding past. Rostov suddenly raised his head, which had already dropped to his horse's mane, and stopped beside the hussar. A young, childish sleep was irresistibly coming over him. "But what was I thinking? I mustn't forget. How am I going to speak with the sovereign? No, not that—that's for tomorrow. Yes, yes! Na-tashka . . . at-tack a . . . attack who? Hussars. Whose hussars? The hussar you saw ride down the boulevard, remember, just across from Guryev house . . . Old man Guryev . . . Eh, nice fellow, Denisov! But that's all trifles. The main thing now is that the sovereign's here. How he looked at me, and he wanted to say something, but he didn't dare . . . No, it was I who didn't dare. But that's all trifles, the main thing is not to forget that I was thinking of something important, yes. Na-tashka, at-tack a . . . yes, yes, yes. That's good." And again his head dropped to his horse's neck. Suddenly it seemed to him that he was being shot at. "What? What? . . . Cut them down! What? . . ." said Rostov, coming to his senses. The moment he opened his eyes, Rostov heard ahead of him, where the enemy was, the drawn-out cries of thousands of voices. His horse and the hussar's who was standing next to him pricked up their ears at these cries. In the place where the cries came from, a little fire flared up and went out, then another, then all along the line of French troops on the hill fires flared up and the cries grew louder and louder. Rostov heard the sounds of French words but could not make them out. Too many voices were shouting. All that was heard was: *aaaa!* and *rrrr!*

"What is it? What do you think?" Rostov turned to the hussar standing beside him. "Is it from the enemy?"

The hussar did not reply.

"What, don't you hear it?" Rostov asked again, after waiting some time for a reply.

"Who knows, Your Honour," the hussar replied reluctantly.

"By the place, it should be the enemy," Rostov repeated.

"Maybe him, or maybe just so," the hussar said, "a night thing. Easy, now!" he cried to his horse, who was stirring under him.

Rostov's horse was also restive, stamping its hoof on the frozen ground, listening to the sounds and looking at the fires. The cries of the voices grew louder and louder and merged in a general clamour that only an army of several thousand could produce. The lights spread more and more, probably along the line of the French camp. Rostov was no longer sleepy. The cheerful, triumphant cries from the enemy army had an exhilarating effect on him. Rostov could now hear clearly: *Vive l'empereur, l'empereur!*

"It's nearby—must be across the stream," he said to the hussar standing beside him.

The hussar only sighed, making no reply, and cleared his throat angrily. Down the line of hussars the hoofbeats of a trotting horse were heard, and suddenly out of the night mist, looking like a huge elephant, emerged the figure of a hussar sergeant.

"The generals, Your Honour!" said the sergeant, riding up to Rostov.

Rostov, still looking towards the fires and cries, rode with the sergeant to meet several horsemen who were riding along the line. One was on a white horse. Prince Bagration and Prince Dolgorukov, with their adjutants, had ridden out to look at the strange phenomenon of the fires and cries in the enemy army. Rostov, riding up to Bagration, reported to him and joined the adjutants, trying to hear what the generals were saying.

"Believe me," said Prince Dolgorukov, addressing Bagration, "this is nothing but a ruse: he has retreated and has ordered the rear guard to light fires and make noise in order to deceive us."

"Hardly," said Bagration. "I saw them on that knoll this evening; if they had left, they would have pulled out from there as well. Officer," Prince Bagration turned to Rostov, "are his pickets still posted there?"

"This evening they were. But now I can't tell, Your Excellency. Give the order, and I'll go there with my hussars," said Rostov.

Bagration stopped and, without replying, tried to make out Rostov's face in the mist.

"Go, then," he said, after a brief silence.

"Yes, sir."

Rostov spurred his horse, called Sergeant Fedchenko and two more hussars, told them to follow him, and rode at a trot down the hill in the direction of the continuing cries. Rostov felt both frightened and elated to be riding alone with three hussars into that mysterious and dangerous misty distance, where no one had been before him. Bagration shouted to him from above not to go beyond the brook, but Rostov pretended not to hear his words, and, without stopping, rode further and further on, constantly making mistakes, taking bushes for trees and hollows for people, and constantly explaining his mistakes to himself. Having trotted down the hill, he no longer saw either our own or the enemy's fires, but he heard the cries of the French more loudly and clearly. In the bottom he saw before him something like a stream, but when he reached it, he recognized it as a trodden road. Coming out onto the road, he reined in his horse, undecided whether to follow it or to cross and ride over the black field up the hillside. To ride along the road, which stood out lighter in the mist, was less dangerous, because he could see people better. "Follow me!" he said, crossed the road, and began to gallop up the hill to the place where French pickets had been posted in the evening.

"There he is, Your Honour!" one of the hussars said behind him.

And before Rostov had time to make out something that loomed up black in the mist, a flash gleamed, a shot cracked, and a bullet, as if complaining about something, whined high up in the mist and flew out of earshot. A second musket misfired, but there was a flash in the pan. Rostov turned his horse and galloped back. Four more shots rang out at various intervals, and bullets went singing in various tones somewhere in the mist. Rostov reined in his horse, who was elated like himself by the shooting, and rode on slowly. "More now, more now!" a cheerful voice was saying in his soul. But there was no more_ shooting.

Only as he approached Bagration, Rostov sent his horse into a gallop again and, with his hand to his visor, rode up to him.

Dolgorukov was still insisting on his opinion that the French had retreated and lit fires only to deceive us.

"What does that prove?" he was saying as Rostov rode up to them. "They could retreat and leave pickets."

"Clearly they have not all left, Prince," said Bagration. "Till tomorrow morning, tomorrow we'll find out everything."

"There are pickets on the hill, Your Excellency, in the same place as this evening," Rostov reported, bending forward, holding his hand to his visor, and unable to repress a cheerful smile, called up in him by his ride and above all by the whine of the bullets.

"Very good, very good," said Bagration, "thank you, Lieutenant."

"Your Excellency," said Rostov, "allow me to make a request."

"What is it?"

"Tomorrow our squadron is assigned to the reserves. Allow me to request that you attach me to the first squadron."

"What is your name?"

"Count Rostov."

"Ah, very well. Stay with me as an orderly officer."

"Are you Ilya Andreich's son?" asked Dolgorukov.

But Rostov did not reply.

"So I'll be counting on it, Your Excellency."

"I will give the order."

"Tomorrow," thought Rostov, "I may very well be sent on some sort of mission to the sovereign. Thank God!"

The cries and fires in the enemy army came from the fact that, while Napoleon's orders were being read to the troops, the emperor himself rode around his bivouacs. The soldiers, seeing the emperor, set fire to bundles of straw and ran after him, shouting, *"Vive l'empereur!"* Napoleon's orders were the following:

Soldiers! The Russian army is marching against us in order to avenge the Austrian army of Ulm. These are the same battalions that you crushed at Hollabrunn[7] and have since been pursuing constantly as far as this place. The positions we occupy are strong, and while they move to surround me on the right, they will expose their flank to me! Soldiers! I myself will direct your battalions. I will stay out of fire if you, with your usual courage, bring disorder and confusion to the enemy's ranks; but if victory should be doubtful even for a moment, you will see your emperor subjecting himself to the first blows of the enemy, because there can be no hesitations about victory, especially on this day when what is at stake is the honour of the French infantry, which is so necessary to the honour of our nation.

Do not break ranks on the pretext of removing the wounded! Let each of you be fully pervaded by the thought that we must defeat these mercenaries of England, inspired by such hatred of our nation. This victory will end our campaign, and we will be able to return to our winter quarters, where new French troops, now being raised in France, will find us; and then the peace which I will conclude will be worthy of my people, you, and myself.

Napoleon.

XIV

At five o'clock in the morning it was still quite dark. The troops of the centre, the reserves, and Bagration's right flank still stood motionless, but on the left flank the columns of infantry, cavalry, and artillery which were to be the first to descend from the heights in order to attack the French right flank and drive them back to the Bohemian Mountains, according to the disposition, had already begun to stir and get up from their night camp. The smoke of the bon-fires, onto which everything superfluous was thrown, stung the eyes. It was cold and dark. Officers hastily drank tea and ate breakfast, soldiers chewed on biscuits, beat their feet to warm them up, and streamed towards the bonfires, throwing onto them the remains of their lean-tos, chairs, tables, wheels, bar-rels, everything superfluous which it was impossible to take with them. Aus-trian column leaders shuttled among the Russian troops and served as heralds of the departure. As soon as an Austrian officer appeared at a regimental com-mander's camp, the regiment began to stir: soldiers ran from the bonfires, stuffed pipes into boot tops, bags into wagons, took their muskets and fell in. Officers buttoned their coats, buckled on their swords and pouches, and strode along the ranks, calling out; carters and orderlies harnessed, packed, and tied down the wagons. Adjutants, battalion and regimental commanders mounted up, crossed themselves, gave final orders, instructions, and commissions to those who were staying with the train, and the monotonous tramp of thou-sands of feet began. Columns started to move, not knowing where and, owing to the surrounding people, the smoke, and the thickening fog, seeing neither the place they were leaving nor the place they were going to.

A soldier in movement is as hemmed in, limited, and borne along by his regi-ment as a sailor by his ship. However far he may go, whatever strange, unknown, and dangerous latitudes he gets into, around him—as for the sailor always and everywhere there are the same decks, masts, and rigging of his ship—always and everywhere there are the same comrades, the same ranks, the same sergeant major Ivan Mitrich, the same company dog Zhuchka, the same superiors. A soldier rarely wishes to know what latitudes his whole ship has got to; but on the day of battle, God knows how and from where, a stern note is heard in the moral world of the troops, the same for everyone, which sounds the approach of something decisive and solemn and arouses in them an unaccustomed curiosity. On days of battle, soldiers excitedly try to get beyond the interests of their regiment, listen intently, look about, and greedily enquire into what is going on around them.

The fog was so thick that, though day was breaking, one could not see ten paces ahead. Bushes looked like enormous trees, level places like cliffs and slopes. Everywhere, on all sides, one might run into an enemy invisible ten paces away. But the columns marched for a long time through the same fog, going down and up hills, past gardens and fences, over new, incomprehensible terrain, without coming across the enemy anywhere. On the contrary, the sol-diers realized that ahead, behind, on all sides, our Russian columns were mov-ing in the same direction. Every soldier felt pleased at heart, knowing that many, many more Russian soldiers were going where he was going, that is, no one knew where.

"See there, the Kursky lads just marched by," came from one of the ranks.

"It's scary, brother, the troops we've gathered! Last night I looked, when they lit the fires, there was no end of them. Moscow—in short!"

Though none of the column leaders rode up to the ranks and spoke to the soldiers (the column leaders, as we saw at the council of war, were ill-humoured and displeased with the action undertaken and therefore were only following orders and did not bother cheering up the soldiers), despite that, the soldiers marched on cheerily, as always when going into action, especially on the offensive. But, having gone for about an hour in the thick fog, the major part of the troops were forced to halt, and an unpleasant awareness of disorder and muddle-headedness passed through the ranks. How such awareness is conveyed is quite difficult to define; but it is unquestionable that it is conveyed with extraordinary sureness, and flows swiftly, imperceptibly and irresistibly, like water through a glen. If the Russian army had been alone, without allies, much time might still have passed before this awareness of disorder became a general conviction; but now, ascribing the cause of the disorder with particular pleasure and naturalness to the muddle-headed Germans, everyone became convinced that the harmful confusion taking place was the doing of the sausage makers.

"What's the hold-up? Is the way blocked? Or have we already run into the French?"

"No, doesn't sound like it. Otherwise they'd have started shooting."

"So they were in a hurry to get started, but once they got started—here we stand witless in the middle of a field—it's all these cursed Germans confusing things. What muddle-headed devils!"

"So I'd have let them take the lead. But no, they huddle in the rear. And now we stand here on empty stomachs."

"Well, how long will it be? They say the cavalry's blocked the road," said an officer.

"Eh, the cursed Germans, they don't know their own country!" said another.

"What division are you?" an adjutant shouted, riding up.

"The eighteenth."

"Then what are you doing here? You should have gone ahead long ago; now you won't get through till evening. Such stupid orders; they don't know what they're doing themselves," the officer said and rode off.

Then a general rode by and angrily shouted something not in Russian.

"Tafa-lafa, and there's no telling what he's mumbling," a soldier said, mimicking the general as he rode off. "I'd shoot the scoundrels!"

"We were ordered to be in place before nine, but we're not halfway there. What orders!" was repeated from different sides.

And the feeling of energy with which the troops had set out for action began to turn into vexation and anger at the muddle-headed orders and the Germans.

The reason for the confusion was that, while the Austrian cavalry was moving on the left flank, the superior officers decided that our centre was too far from the right flank, and the entire cavalry was ordered to cross over to the right. Several thousand cavalry were advancing ahead of the infantry, and the infantry was forced to wait.

At the head, a confrontation took place between an Austrian column leader and a Russian general. The Russian general shouted, demanding that the cavalry be stopped; the Austrian insisted that the fault lay not with him but with the superior officers. The troops meanwhile stood there, bored and losing heart. After an hour's delay, the troops finally moved on and began to descend the hill. The fog, which was lifting on the hilltop, only grew thicker in the bottom where the troops were descending. At the head, in the fog, a shot rang out, then another, at first irregularly, at various intervals: trata . . . tat, then more regularly and rapidly, and the action at the Goldbach stream began.

Not counting on meeting the enemy below, by the stream, and coming upon them by chance in the fog, hearing not a word of encouragement from the superior officers, with the awareness spread among the troops that they were late, and, above all, seeing nothing ahead or around them in the thick fog, the Russians lazily and slowly exchanged fire with the enemy, moved forward and again halted, not receiving timely orders from the officers and adjutants, who wandered through the fog over the unfamiliar terrain, unable to find their units. Thus the action began for the first, second, and third columns, which had descended the hill. The fourth column, with which Kutuzov himself was, occupied the Pratzen heights.

In the bottom, where the action began, the fog was still thick; up above it had cleared, but nothing of what was happening ahead could be seen. Whether all the enemy forces were six miles away from us, as we supposed, or were there in that fog, no one knew until past eight o'clock.

It was nine o'clock in the morning. An unbroken sea of fog spread below, but at the village of Schlapanitz, on the heights, where Napoleon stood, surrounded by his marshals, it was perfectly light. Over him was the clear blue sky, and the enormous ball of the sun, like an enormous, hollow, crimson float, bobbed on the surface of the milky sea of fog. The whole French army, including Napoleon himself and his staff, not only were not on the far side of the streams and bottomland of the villages of Sokolnitz and Schlapanitz, where we intended to take up a position and begin the action, but were on the near side, so close to our troops that Napoleon with his naked eye could distinguish between our troops on horseback and on foot. Napoleon sat a little in front of his marshals on a small grey Arabian horse, in his dark blue greatcoat, the same in which he had made the Italian campaign. He peered silently at the hills, which seemed to rise up from the sea of fog, and over which Russian troops were moving in the distance, and he listened to the sounds of gunfire in the hollow. On his face, still lean at that time, not a muscle stirred; his glistening eyes were fixed motionlessly on one place. His conjectures turned out to be correct. Part of the Russian army had already descended into the hollow towards the ponds and lakes, part was still clearing off from the Pratzen heights, which he intended to attack and considered the key to the position. He saw amidst the fog, in the depression between two hills near the village of Pratz, Russian columns, their bayonets glittering, moving all in one direction towards the hollows, and disappearing one after another into the sea of fog. From the information he had received in the evening, from the sounds of wheels and footsteps heard during the night at the outposts, from the disorderly movement of the Russian columns, from all his conjectures, he saw clearly that the allies considered him to be far ahead of them, that the columns moving near Pratz constituted the centre of the Russian army, and that the centre was already sufficiently weakened for him to attack it successfully. But he still did not begin the action.

That day was a solemn day for him—the anniversary of his coronation. Before morning he had dozed off for a few hours and, healthy, cheerful, fresh, in that happy state of mind in which everything seems possible and everything succeeds, he mounted his horse and rode out into the field. He stood motionless, gazing at the heights appearing from the fog, and on his cold face there was that particular tinge of self-confident, well-deserved happiness that can be seen on the face of a boy who has happily fallen in love. His marshals stood behind him, not daring to distract his attention. He looked now at the Pratzen heights, now at the sun floating out of the fog.

When the sun had fully emerged from the fog and its dazzling brilliance sprayed over the fields and the fog (it was as if he had only been waiting for that to begin the action), he took the glove from his beautiful white hand, made a sign to the marshals, and gave the order for the action to begin. The marshals, accompanied by adjutants, galloped off in various directions, and a few minutes later the main forces of the French army were moving swiftly towards those same Pratzen heights from which the Russian troops had cleared off more and more, descending to the left into the hollow.

XV

At eight o'clock Kutuzov rode to Pratz at the head of Miloradovich's fourth column, the one which was to take the place of the columns of Przebyszewski and Langeron, which had already gone down. He greeted the men of the head regiment and gave the order to move, thus showing that he intended to lead the column himself. Having ridden to the village of Pratz, he halted. Prince Andrei, one of the enormous number of persons constituting the commander in chief's suite, stood behind him. Prince Andrei felt excited, irritated, and at the same time restrainedly calm, as a man usually is when a long-desired moment comes. He was firmly convinced that this was the day of his Toulon or his bridge of Arcole.[8] How it would happen, he did not know, but he was firmly convinced that it would be so. The locality and position of our troops were known to him, as far as they could be known to anyone in our army. His own strategic plan, which there obviously could be no thought of carrying out now, was forgotten. Now, entering into Weyrother's plan, Prince Andrei pondered the possible happenstances and came up with new considerations, such as might call for his swiftness of reflection and decisiveness.

To the left below, in the fog, exchanges of fire between unseen troops could be heard. There, it seemed to Prince Andrei, the battle would concentrate, there an obstacle would be encountered, and "it's there that I'll be sent with a brigade or division, and there, with a standard in my hand, I'll go forward and crush everything ahead of me."

Prince Andrei could not look with indifference at the standards of the battalions going past him. Looking at a standard, he thought: maybe it is that very standard with which I'll have to march at the head of the troops.

By morning the night's fog had left only hoarfrost turning into dew on the heights, but in the hollows the fog still spread its milk-white sea. Nothing could be seen in that hollow to the left, into which our troops had descended and from which came the sounds of gunfire. Over the heights was a dark, clear sky, and to the right—the enormous ball of the sun. Far ahead, on the other shore of the sea of fog, one could make out the jutting, wooded hills on which the enemy army was supposed to be, and something was discernible. To the right the guards were entering the region of the fog, with a sound of tramping and wheels and an occasional gleam of bayonets; to the left, beyond the village, similar masses of cavalry approached and disappeared into the sea of fog. In front and behind moved the infantry. The commander in chief stood on the road out of the village, letting the troops pass by him. Kutuzov seemed exhausted and irritable that morning. The infantry going past him halted without any command, apparently because something ahead held them up.

"But tell them, finally, to form into battalions and go round the village," Kutuzov said angrily to a general who rode up. "Don't you understand, Your Excellency, my dear sir, that to stretch out in a defile through village streets is impossible when we're marching against an enemy?"

"I intended to form them up outside the village, Your Excellency," said the general.

Kutuzov laughed biliously.

"A fine sight you'd be, lining up in view of the enemy, a very fine sight!"

"The enemy's still far off, Your Excellency. According to the disposition . . ."

"The disposition!" Kutuzov exclaimed biliously. "Who told you that? . . . Kindly do as you're ordered."

"Yes, sir!"

"*Mon cher,*" Nesvitsky said to Prince Andrei in a whisper, "*le vieux est d'une humeur de chien.*"*

An Austrian officer in a white uniform with green plumes on his hat rode up to Kutuzov and asked on behalf of the emperor whether the fourth column had started into action.

Kutuzov turned away without answering him, and his gaze chanced to rest on Prince Andrei, who was standing close by. Seeing Bolkonsky, Kutuzov softened the angry and caustic expression of his gaze, as if aware that his adjutant was not to blame for what was going on. And, without answering the Austrian adjutant, he addressed Bolkonsky:

"*Allez voir, mon cher, si la troisième division a dépassé le village. Dites-lui de s'arrêter et d'attendre mes ordres.*"†

Prince Andrei had only just started when he stopped him.

"*Et demandez-lui si les tirailleurs sont postés,*" he added. "*Ce qu'ils font, ce qu'ils font!*"‡ he said to himself, still not answering the Austrian.

Prince Andrei galloped off to carry out his mission.

Overtaking all the advancing battalions, he stopped the third division and ascertained that there was in fact no line of riflemen in front of our columns. The regimental commander of the front regiment was very surprised by the order conveyed to him from the commander in chief to send out riflemen. The regimental commander stood there in the full conviction that there were more troops ahead of him, and that the enemy was no less than six miles away. In fact, nothing could be seen ahead but empty terrain sloping away and covered with thick fog. Having ordered on behalf of the commander in chief that the omission be rectified, Prince Andrei galloped back. Kutuzov still stood in the same place and, his corpulent body sagging over the saddle in old man's fashion, yawned deeply, closing his eyes. The troops were no longer moving, but stood at parade rest.

"Very good, very good," he said to Prince Andrei and turned to a general who stood there with a watch in his hand, saying it was time to move on, because all the columns of the left flank had already descended.

"We still have time, Your Excellency," Kutuzov said through a yawn. "We have time!" he repeated.

Just then, from well behind Kutuzov, came shouts of regimental greetings, and these voices began to approach quickly along the whole extended line of the advancing Russian columns. It was clear that the one being greeted was riding quickly. When the soldiers of the regiment Kutuzov was standing in front

---

*My dear . . . the old man's in a foul humour.
†Go and see, my dear, if the third division has passed the village. Tell him to stop and wait for my orders.
‡And ask him if the riflemen are posted . . . What they're doing, what they're doing!

of began to shout, he rode slightly to one side and, wincing, turned to look. Down the road from Pratz galloped what looked like a squadron of vari-coloured horsemen. Two of them rode side by side at a great gallop ahead of the rest. One, in a black uniform with white plumes, rode a bobtailed chestnut horse, the other, in a white uniform, rode a black horse. These were the two emperors with their suite. Kutuzov, with the affectation of a front-line veteran, ordered his standing troops to "attention" and, saluting, rode up to the emperor. His whole figure and manner suddenly changed. He acquired the look of a sub-ordinate, unthinking man. With affected deference, which obviously struck the emperor Alexander unpleasantly, he rode up and saluted him.

The unpleasant impression, like the remains of fog in a clear sky, passed over the emperor's young and happy face and disappeared. He was somewhat thin-ner that day, after his illness, than on the field of Olmütz, where Bolkonsky had seen him for the first time abroad, but there was the same enchanting combina-tion of majesty and mildness in his beautiful grey eyes, and the fine lips had the same possibility of various expressions, with a prevalent expression of good-natured, innocent youth.

At the Olmütz review he was more majestic; here he was more cheerful and energetic. He was slightly flushed after galloping two miles and, reining in his horse, gave a sigh of relief and looked around at the faces of his suite, as young, as animated as his own. Czartoryski and Novosiltsev, and Prince Volkonsky and Stroganov, and the others, all richly clad, cheerful young men on splendid, pampered, fresh, only slightly sweaty horses, talking and smiling, stopped behind the sovereign. The emperor Franz, a ruddy, long-faced young man, sat extremely straight on his handsome black stallion and looked around him with a preoccupied, unhurried air. He called up one of his white adjutants and asked something. "Most likely what time they started," thought Prince Andrei, observing his old aquaintance, and recalling his audience with a smile he was unable to repress. In the emperors' suite there were picked fine young orderly officers, Russian and Austrian, from the guards and infantry regiments. Among them were grooms leading the handsome spare horses of the royalty in embroi-dered cloths.

As fresh air from the fields suddenly breathes through an open window into a stuffy room, so youth, energy, and certainty of success breathed upon Kutu-zov's cheerless staff as these brilliant young men galloped up.

"Why don't you begin, Mikhail Larionovich?" the emperor Alexander hur-riedly addressed Kutuzov, at the same time glancing courteously at the emperor Franz.

"I am waiting, Your Majesty," answered Kutuzov, inclining deferentially.

The emperor cupped his ear, frowning slightly and showing that he had not heard properly.

"I'm waiting, Your Majesty," Kutuzov repeated (Prince Andrei noticed that

Kutuzov's upper lip twitched unnaturally as he said this "waiting"). "Not all the columns are assembled, Your Majesty."

The sovereign heard, but this reply clearly did not please him; he shrugged his slightly stooping shoulders, glanced at Novosiltsev, who stood nearby, as if complaining of Kutuzov by this glance.

"We're not on the Tsaritsyn Field,⁹ Mikhail Larionovich, where you don't start a parade until all the regiments are assembled," said the sovereign, again glancing into the eyes of the emperor Franz, as though inviting him, if not to take part, at least to listen to what he was saying; but the emperor Franz went on looking around and did not listen.

"That is just why I do not begin, Sire," Kutuzov said in a ringing voice, as if to forestall the possibility of not being heard, and again something twitched in his face. "I do not begin, Sire, because we are not on parade and not on the Tsaritsyn Field," he uttered clearly and distinctly.

All the faces in the sovereign's suite instantly exchanged glances with each other, expressing murmur and reproach. "Old as he may be, he should not, he simply should not speak that way," these faces expressed.

The sovereign looked fixedly and attentively into Kutuzov's eyes, waiting to see if he would say something more. But Kutuzov, for his part, bowed his head deferentially and also seemed to be waiting. The silence lasted for about a minute.

"However, if you order it, Your Majesty," said Kutuzov, raising his head and again changing his tone to that of a dull, unthinking, but obedient general.

He touched up his horse and, calling to him the column leader Miloradovich, gave him the order to advance.

The troops stirred again, and two battalions of the Novgorodsky regiment and a battalion of the Apsheronsky regiment moved on past the sovereign.

While this Apsheronsky battalion was marching by, ruddy-faced Miloradovich, with no greatcoat, in his uniform tunic and decorations and a hat with enormous plumes, worn at an angle and brim first, galloped ahead hup-two, and with a dashing salute, reined in his horse before the sovereign.

"God be with you, General," said the sovereign.

"*Ma foi, sire, nous ferons ce que qui sera dans notre possibilité, sire!*"* he replied merrily, nevertheless calling up mocking smiles among the gentlemen of the suite with his bad French.

Miloradovich turned his horse sharply and placed himself slightly behind the sovereign. The Apsherontsy, excited by the presence of the sovereign, marched past the emperors and their suite at a dashingly brisk pace, beating their feet.

"Lads!" cried Miloradovich in a loud, self-assured, and merry voice, obvi-

*By my faith, Sire, we will do that what which will be within our possibility, Sire!

ously so excited by the sounds of gunfire, the anticipation of battle, and the sight of his gallant Apsherontsy—his companions from Suvorov's time— marching briskly past the emperors, that he forgot the sovereign's presence. "Lads, it won't be the first village you've taken!" he shouted.

"We do our best, sir!" the soldiers shouted out.

The sovereign's horse shied at the sudden shout. This horse, who had carried the sovereign at reviews while still in Russia, also carried her rider here, on the field of Austerlitz, enduring the distracted nudges of his left foot, pricked up her ears at the sound of gunshots just as she did on the Field of Mars, under-standing neither the meaning of the shots she heard, nor the presence of the emperor Franz's black stallion, nor anything of what her rider said, thought, or felt that day.

The sovereign turned with a smile to one of his retinue, pointing to the gal-lant Apsherontsy, and said something to him.

XVI

Kutuzov, accompanied by his adjutants, rode at a walk behind the carabineers.

Having gone less than half a mile at the tail of the column, he stopped by a solitary, deserted house (probably a former tavern), where the road forked. Both roads went down the hill, and troops were marching along both.

The fog began to lift, and enemy troops could be dimly seen about a mile and a half away on the heights opposite. To the left below, the gunfire was growing louder. Kutuzov stopped, talking with an Austrian general. Prince Andrei, standing slightly behind him, peered at the enemy and turned to an adjutant, wishing to borrow a field glass from him.

"Look, look," said this adjutant, looking not at the distant troops, but down the hill in front of him. "It's the French!"

The two generals and the adjutants began snatching at the field glass, pulling it away from each other. All their faces suddenly changed, and on all of them horror appeared. The French were supposed to be a mile and a half from us, and they suddenly turned up right in front of us.

"Is it the enemy? . . . No! . . . Yes, look, he's . . . for certain . . . What is this?" voices said.

With his naked eye, Prince Andrei saw below, to the right, a dense column of French coming up to meet the Apsherontsy, no further than five hundred paces from where Kutuzov was standing.

"Here it is, the decisive moment has come! Now it's my turn," thought Prince Andrei, and, spurring his horse, he rode up to Kutuzov.

"The Apsherontsy must be stopped, Your Excellency!" he cried.

But at that same moment everything became covered with smoke, there was the sound of gunfire nearby, and a naïvely frightened voice two steps from Prince Andrei cried: "Well, brothers, that's it for us!" And it was as if this voice was a command. At this voice everyone began to run.

Confused, ever increasing crowds came running back to the place where, five minutes before, the troops had marched past the emperors. Not only was it difficult to stop this crowd, but it was impossible not to yield and move back with it. Bolkonsky tried only not to be separated from Kutuzov and looked around in perplexity, unable to understand what was happening in front of him. Nesvitsky, looking angry, red, and not like himself, shouted to Kutuzov that if he did not leave at once, he would certainly be taken prisoner. Kutuzov stood in the same place and, without responding, took out his handkerchief. Blood was flowing from his cheek. Prince Andrei forced his way to him.

"Are you wounded?" he asked, barely able to control the trembling of his lower jaw.

"The wound isn't here, it's there!" said Kutuzov, pressing the handkerchief to his wounded cheek and pointing to the fleeing men.

"Stop them!" he cried, and at the same time, probably realizing that it was impossible to stop them, spurred his horse and rode to the right.

A fresh crowd of fleeing men streamed past, caught him up, and carried him backwards.

The troops were fleeing in such a dense crowd that, once one landed in the middle of it, it was difficult to get out. Someone shouted, "Keep going, don't drag your feet!" Another, turning round, fired into the air; someone else struck the horse on which Kutuzov himself was riding. Extricating themselves with the greatest effort from the flow of the crowd to the left, Kutuzov and his suite, diminished by more than half, rode towards the sounds of nearby cannon fire. Extricating himself from the crowd of fleeing men, Prince Andrei, trying to keep up with Kutuzov, saw on the slope of the hill, amidst the smoke, a Russian battery still firing, and the French running up to it. Slightly higher stood Russian infantry, neither moving ahead to aid the battery, nor back-wards in the direction of the fugitives. A general on horseback separated him-self from the infantry and rode up to Kutuzov. There were only four men left in Kutuzov's suite. They were all pale and exchanged glances silently.

"Stop those villains!" Kutuzov said breathlessly to the regimental commander, pointing to the fleeing men; but at the same moment, as if in punishment for those words, bullets, like a flock of birds, flew whistling at the regiment and Kutuzov's suite.

The French had attacked the battery and, seeing Kutuzov, were shooting at him. With this volley, the regimental commander seized his leg; several soldiers fell, and an ensign holding a standard let it drop from his hands; the standard wavered and fell, stopped momentarily by the bayonets of the soldiers around it. The soldiers began firing without any orders.

"Oooh!" Kutuzov moaned with an expression of despair and looked around. "Bolkonsky," he whispered in a voice trembling with awareness of his old man's strengthlessness. "Bolkonsky," he whispered, pointing to the disordered battalion and the enemy, "what's going on?"

But before he finished saying it, Prince Andrei, feeling sobs of shame and anger rising in his throat, was already jumping off his horse and running towards the standard.

"Forward, lads!" he cried in a childishly shrill voice.

"Here it is!" thought Prince Andrei, seizing the staff of the standard and hearing with delight the whistle of bullets, evidently aimed precisely at him. Several soldiers fell.

"Hurrah!" cried Prince Andrei, barely able to hold up the heavy standard, and he ran forward with unquestioning assurance that the entire battalion would run after him.

And indeed he ran only a few steps alone. One soldier started out, another, and the whole battalion, with a shout of "Hurrah!" rushed forward and overtook him. A sergeant of the battalion ran up, took the standard that was wavering in Prince Andrei's hands because of its weight, but was killed at once. Prince Andrei again seized the standard and, dragging it by the staff, ran with the battalion. Ahead of him he saw our artillerists, some of whom were fighting, while others abandoned the cannon and came running in his direction; he also saw French infantrymen, who had seized the artillery horses and were turning the cannon. Prince Andrei and his battalion were now twenty paces from the cannon. Above him he heard the unceasing whistle of bullets, and soldiers ceaselessly gasped and fell to right and left of him. But he did not look at them; he looked fixedly only at what was happening ahead of him—at the battery. He clearly saw the figure of a red-haired gunner, his shako knocked askew, pulling a swab from one side, while a French soldier pulled it towards him from the other side. Prince Andrei saw clearly the bewildered and at the same time angry expression on the faces of the two men, who evidently did not understand what they were doing.

"What are they doing?" Prince Andrei wondered, looking at them. "Why doesn't the red-haired artillerist run away, since he has no weapon? Why doesn't the Frenchman stab him? Before he runs away, the Frenchman will remember his musket and bayonet him."

In fact, another Frenchman with his musket atilt ran up to the fighting men, and the lot of the red-haired artillerist, who still did not understand what awaited him and triumphantly pulled the swab from the French soldier's hands, was about to be decided. But Prince Andrei did not see how it ended. It seemed to him as though one of the nearest soldiers, with the full swing of a stout stick, hit him on the head. It was slightly painful and above all unpleasant, because the pain distracted him and kept him from seeing what he had been looking at.

"What is it? am I falling? are my legs giving way under me?" he thought, and fell on his back. He opened his eyes, hoping to see how the fight between the French and the artillerists ended, and wishing to know whether or not the red-haired artillerist had been killed, whether the cannon had been taken or saved. But he did not see anything. There was nothing over him now except the sky—the lofty sky, not clear, but still immeasurably lofty, with grey clouds slowly creeping across it. "How quiet, calm, and solemn, not at all like when I was running," thought Prince Andrei, "not like when we were running, shouting, and fighting; not at all like when the Frenchman and the artillerist, with angry and frightened faces, were pulling at the swab—it's quite different the way the clouds creep across this lofty, infinite sky. How is it I haven't seen this lofty sky before? And how happy I am that I've finally come to know it. Yes! everything is empty, everything is a deception, except this infinite sky. There is nothing, nothing except that. But there is not even that, there is nothing except silence, tranquillity. And thank God! . . ."

XVII

At nine o'clock, the action had not yet begun for Bagration on the right flank. Not wishing to agree to Dolgorukov's request to begin action, and wishing to avert responsibility from himself, Prince Bagration suggested to Dolgorukov that he send to ask the commander in chief. Bagration knew that, with a stretch of nearly six miles separating one flank from the other, if the messenger was not killed (which was very probable), and even if he found the commander in chief, which would be quite difficult, he would not come back before evening.

Bagration looked over his suite with his big, expressionless, sleepy eyes, and Rostov's childlike face, involuntarily transfixed with excitement and hope, was the first thing that struck his eye. He sent him.

"And if I should meet His Majesty before the commander in chief, Your Excellency?" asked Rostov, holding his hand to his visor.

"You can give the message to His Majesty," said Dolgorukov, hastily cutting off Bagration.

After being relieved from the picket line, Rostov had managed to sleep for a few hours before morning, and he felt cheerful, bold, resolute, with that suppleness of movement, assurance of his good luck, and in that state of mind in which everything seems easy, cheerful, and possible.

All his wishes were being fulfilled that morning: general battle was to be given, he was to take part in it; moreover, he was an orderly officer of the bravest of generals; moreover, he was going with a message to Kutuzov and maybe to the sovereign himself. The morning was bright, the horse under him was good. He felt joyful and happy. On receiving the order, he started his horse and rode along the line. First he rode along the line of Bagration's troops, who had not yet gone into action and stood motionless; then he rode into the space occupied by Uvarov's cavalry, and here he noticed movement and signs of preparation for action; having passed Uvarov's cavalry, he clearly heard the sounds of cannon and gunfire ahead of him. The fire kept intensifying.

In the fresh morning air, the shooting was no longer as before—at irregular intervals, two or three gunshots, then one or two cannon shots—now on the slopes of the hills before Pratz one could hear rolling salvos of musket fire, interrupted by such rapid cannon fire that at times the separate shots could not be distinguished from each other, but merged into a general roar.

One could see the puffs of gunsmoke as if running and chasing each other on the slopes, and the smoke of the cannon swirling, spreading, and merging together. One could see, from the gleam of bayonets amidst the smoke, the moving masses of infantry and the narrow strips of artillery with green caissons.

Rostov stopped his horse for a minute on a knoll, so as to see what was going on; but no matter how he strained his attention, he could neither understand nor make out what was going on: some sort of men were moving about in the smoke; some sort of sheets of troops were moving in front and behind; but why? who? where?—it was impossible to grasp. The sights and sounds not only did not arouse any sort of dejected or timid feelings in him, but, on the contrary, gave him energy and determination.

"More, more, step it up!" he addressed these sounds mentally, and again started riding along the line, penetrating further and further into the area of the troops already going into action.

"How it's going to be, I don't know, but all will be well!" thought Rostov.

Having ridden past some Austrian troops, Rostov noticed that the next part of the line (this was the guards) had already gone into action.

"So much the better! I'll see it close-up," he thought.

He was riding almost along the front line. Several horsemen came riding in his direction. They were our life uhlans, who were returning from an attack in disorderly ranks. Rostov passed by them, involuntarily noticing that one of them was covered with blood, and rode on.

"It's none of my business!" he thought. He had not managed to go a few hundred paces after that when to the left of him, cutting across, there appeared along the whole width of the field an enormous mass of cavalrymen on black horses, in white gleaming uniforms, coming straight at him at a canter. Rostov sent his horse into a full gallop to get out of the way of these cavalrymen, and he would have got away from them if they had continued at the same speed, but they kept increasing their pace, so that some of the horses were already galloping. Rostov heard their hoofbeats and the clanging of their weapons growing louder and louder, and saw their horses, their figures, and even their faces more and more clearly. These were our horse guards going into attack against the French cavalry, which was coming towards them.

The horse guards galloped, but still holding back their horses. Rostov could now see their faces and heard the command "Forward, forward!" uttered by an officer, letting his thoroughbred go at full speed. Rostov, afraid of being trampled or swept into the attack on the French, galloped along the front as hard as his horse could go, and still did not manage to avoid them.

The last horse guard, a pockmarked man of enormous height, frowned angrily, seeing Rostov in front of him, where he would inevitably run into him. This horse guard would certainly have knocked Rostov and his Bedouin down (Rostov felt himself so small and weak compared to these enormous men and horses), if it had not occurred to him to swing his whip at the eyes of the guardsman's horse. The heavy, black, twenty-hand horse shied, laying back his ears; but the pockmarked horse guard spurred him as hard as he could with his huge spurs, and the horse, tossing his tail and stretching his neck, raced on still faster. The horse guards had barely gone past Rostov, when he heard their shout of "Hurrah!" and, turning, saw their front ranks mingling with other, probably French, horsemen with red epaulettes. Beyond that nothing could be seen, because just after that cannon began firing from somewhere and everything was covered in smoke.

At the moment when the horse guards, going past him, disappeared into the smoke, Rostov hesitated whether to gallop after them or ride where he was supposed to. This was that brilliant attack of the horse guards which astonished the French themselves. Rostov was horrified to hear later that, of all that mass of enormous, handsome men, of all those brilliant, rich men, youths, officers, and junkers, who had ridden past him on thousand-rouble horses, only eighteen were left after the attack.

"Why should I envy them, mine won't go away, and now maybe I'll see the sovereign!" thought Rostov, and he rode on.

Having drawn even with the infantry guards, he noticed that cannonballs were flying over and around them, not so much because he heard the sound of the cannon, but because he saw uneasiness on the soldiers' faces, and on the officers' an unnatural military solemnity.

Riding behind one of the lines of the infantry guard regiments, he heard a voice call him by name.

"Rostov!"

"What?" he replied, not recognizing Boris.

"Imagine, we got into the front line! Our regiment went into an attack!" said Boris, smiling that happy smile which occurs in young men who have been under fire for the first time.

Rostov stopped.

"Really!" he said. "And what then?"

"We beat them back," Boris said animatedly, becoming talkative. "Can you imagine?"

And Boris began telling how the guards, taking up their position and seeing troops in front of them, took them for Austrians, and suddenly, from the cannonballs fired from those troops, realized that they were in the front line and had unexpectedly to go into action. Rostov, not hearing Boris out, touched up his horse.

"Where are you going?" asked Boris.

"To His Majesty with a message."

"There he is!" said Boris, who thought he heard Rostov say "his highness" instead of "his majesty."

And he pointed him to the grand duke, who, a hundred paces from them, in a helmet and a horse guard's tunic, with his raised shoulders and frowning brows, was shouting something to a white and pale-faced Austrian officer.

"But that's the grand duke, and I need the commander in chief or the sovereign," said Rostov, and he touched up his horse.

"Count, Count!" cried Berg, as animated as Boris, running up to him from the other side. "Count, I'm wounded in the right hand," he said, showing his hand, bloody and bandaged with a handkerchief, "and I stayed in the line. I hold the sword in my left hand, Count: our race, the von Bergs, Count, were all knights."

Berg was still saying something, but Rostov did not listen any further and rode on.

Having gone past the guards and an empty space, Rostov, to avoid getting into the front line again, as he had during the attack of the horse guards, followed the line of the reserves, making a wide circle round the place where the hottest shooting and cannon fire were heard. Suddenly, ahead of him and behind our troops, in a place where he could never have supposed the enemy to be, he heard nearby musket fire.

"What can that be?" thought Rostov. "The enemy in the rear of our troops? It can't be," thought Rostov, and the terror of fear for himself and for the outcome of the whole battle suddenly came over him. "Whatever it may be, however," he thought, "there's no point now in going round. I must look for the commander in chief here, and if all is lost, then it's my business to perish along with everybody."

The bad presentiment that suddenly came over Rostov was confirmed more and more the further he rode into the space beyond the village of Pratz, occupied by crowds of different troops.

"What is this? What is this? Who's being shot at? Who's shooting?" asked Rostov, drawing even with Russian and Austrian soldiers running in mixed crowds across his path.

"Devil knows about them! He's beaten everybody! Perish them all!"

answers came in Russian, German, and Czech from the crowds of fleeing men who, like himself, did not understand what was going on there.

"Shoot the Germans!" cried one.

"Devil take them—the traitors!"

"Zum Henker diese Russen! . . ."* a German grumbled.

Several wounded soldiers were walking down the road. Oaths, shouts, groans merged into one general clamour. The shooting died down, and, as Rostov learned later, it had been Russian and Austrian soldiers shooting at each other.

"My God! What is it?" thought Rostov. "Here, where the sovereign may see them at any moment! . . . But no, it must be just a few scoundrels. It will pass, that's not it, it can't be," he thought. "Just ride past them quickly, quickly!"

The thought of defeat and flight could not enter Rostov's head. Though he saw French guns and troops precisely on the Pratzen heights, in the very place where he had been told to look for the commander in chief, he could not and would not believe it.

XVIII

Rostov had been told to look for Kutuzov and the sovereign near the village of Pratz. But not only were they not there, but there was not a single superior officer, there were only various crowds of disorderly troops. He urged on his already tired horse so as to get quickly past these crowds, but the further he went, the more disorderly the crowds became. The high road he came out on was crowded with carriages, vehicles of all kinds, Russian and Austrian soldiers of all arms, wounded and not wounded. All this droned and swarmed confusedly, under the grim sound of cannonballs flying from the French batteries set up on the Pratzen heights.

"Where is the sovereign? Where is Kutuzov?" Rostov asked everyone he could stop, and he got no answer from any of them.

At last, seizing a soldier by the collar, he made him answer.

"Eh, brother! They all ran off ahead there long ago!" the soldier said to Rostov, laughing at something and trying to free himself.

Abandoning that soldier, who was obviously drunk, Rostov stopped the horse of an orderly or groom of some important person and began questioning him. The orderly announced to Rostov that the sovereign had been driven away at top speed in a carriage an hour earlier and that he was dangerously wounded.

"It can't be," said Rostov, "it must have been somebody else."

"I saw him myself," said the orderly with a self-assured grin. "I ought to

*To the devil with these Russians! . . .

know the sovereign by now: seems I saw him lots of times in Petersburg this close. He was sitting in the carriage pale as can be. Four black horses, saints alive, how they went rattling past us: seems I ought to know the tsar's horses and Ilya Ivanych by now; seems Ilya the coachman drives nobody but the tsar."

Rostov let go of his horse and wanted to ride on. Passing by, a wounded officer addressed him.

"Who do you want?" asked the officer. "The commander in chief? He was killed by a cannonball, hit in the chest in front of our regiment."

"Not killed, wounded," another officer corrected.

"Who? Kutuzov?" asked Rostov.

"Not Kutuzov, but what's his name—well, it makes no difference, there weren't many left alive. Go over there, to that village, all the superiors are assembled there," said this officer, pointing to the village of Hostieradek, and he passed by.

Rostov rode at a walk, not knowing why and to whom he was going now. The sovereign was wounded, the battle lost. It was impossible not to believe it now. Rostov rode in the direction indicated to him and in which he could see a tower and a church in the distance. Why should he hurry? What was he to say now to the sovereign or to Kutuzov, even if they were alive and not wounded?

"Go that way, Your Honour, here you'll get killed straight off," a soldier cried to him. "Killed straight off!"

"Ah! What are you saying!" said another. "Where are you sending him? This way's closer."

Rostov pondered and went precisely in the direction in which he was told he would be killed.

"It makes no difference now! If even the sovereign is wounded, why should I look out for myself?" he thought. He rode into that space in which the most men fleeing from Pratz had been killed. The French had not yet taken this space, but the Russians—those who were alive or wounded—had abandoned it long ago. Over the field, like sheaves on good wheatland, lay dead or wounded men, ten to fifteen to an acre. The wounded crept together by twos and threes, and one could hear their unpleasant cries and moans, sometimes feigned, as it seemed to Rostov. He sent his horse into a canter, so as not to see all these suffering men, and he felt frightened. He was afraid, not for his life, but for the courage he needed and which, he knew, could not bear the sight of these wretches.

The French, who had stopped firing on this field strewn with dead and wounded because there was nothing left alive on it, seeing an adjutant riding across it, aimed a cannon and fired several shots. The sensation of these whistling, fearsome sounds and the surrounding dead merged for Rostov into a single impression of terror and pity for himself. He recalled his mother's last letter. "What would she feel," he wondered, "if she saw me here now, on this field, with cannon aimed at me?"

In the village of Hostieradek, he found Russian troops, confused, but heading away from the battlefield in greater order. The French cannon fire did not carry that far, and the sounds of shooting seemed a long way off. Here everyone already clearly saw and said that the battle was lost. No matter who Rostov turned to, no one could tell him where the sovereign was, or where Kutuzov was. Some said that the rumour of the sovereign's wound was correct, others said it was not and explained the spread of this false rumour by the fact that the grand marshal of the court, Count Tolstoy, who had ridden to the battlefield with others in the emperor's suite, had indeed galloped away from the battlefield, pale and frightened, in the sovereign's carriage. One officer told Rostov that he had seen someone from the high command to the left beyond the village, and Rostov went there, no longer hoping to find anyone, but only to keep his own conscience clear. Having ridden two miles and left behind the last of the Russian troops, Rostov saw two horsemen standing near a kitchen garden surrounded by a ditch. They were facing this ditch. One, with white plumes on his hat, seemed familiar to Rostov for some reason; the other, an unfamiliar horseman on a beautiful chestnut horse (the horse seemed familiar to Rostov), rode up to the ditch, spurred his horse and, releasing the reins, lightly jumped over the garden ditch. Only a little soil crumbled down the bank from the horse's hind hoofs. Turning his horse sharply, he leaped back over the ditch and courteously addressed the horseman with the white plumage, evidently suggesting that he do the same. The horseman whose figure seemed familiar to Rostov and for some reason involuntarily riveted his attention, made a negative gesture with his head and hand, and by this gesture Rostov instantly recognized his lamented, adored sovereign.

"But that can't be him, alone in the middle of this empty field," thought Rostov. Just then Alexander turned his head, and Rostov saw the beloved features so vividly imprinted on his memory. The sovereign was pale, his cheeks were hollow, his eyes sunken; but there was all the more loveliness and mildness in his features. Rostov was happy now to be assured that the rumour of the sovereign's wound was incorrect. He was happy to see him. He knew that he could, even must, address him directly and convey to him what Dolgorukov had ordered him to convey.

But as a young man in love trembles and thrills, not daring to utter what he dreams of by night, and looks about fearfully, seeking help or the possibility of delay and flight, when the desired moment comes and he stands alone with her, so now Rostov, having attained what he desired more than anything in the world, did not know how to approach the sovereign and presented thousands of considerations to himself for why it was unsuitable, improper, and impossible.

"What! It's as if I was glad to take advantage of his being alone and dejected. It may be unpleasant and difficult for him to meet an unknown person at this moment of sorrow, and then, what can I say to him now, when at the mere sight of him my heart stops and my mouth goes dry?" Not one of the countless speeches to the sovereign that he had composed in his imagination came to his head now. Those speeches were for the most part held under quite different conditions; they were spoken for the most part in moments of victory and triumph, and predominantly on his deathbed from the wounds he had received, while the sovereign thanked him for his heroic deeds, and he, dying, voiced the love confirmed by his acts.

"And then, what am I to ask the sovereign about his orders for the right flank, when it is now past three in the afternoon and the battle is lost? No, decidedly, I should not approach him, should not disturb his thoughts. Better to die a thousand times than to get a bad look or a bad opinion from him," Rostov decided and rode away with sorrow and despair in his heart, constantly turning to look at the sovereign, still standing in the same attitude of indecision.

While Rostov was making these considerations and sorrowfully riding away from the sovereign, Captain von Toll happened to arrive in the same place and, seeing the sovereign, rode straight up to him, offered him his services, and helped him to cross the ditch on foot. The sovereign, wishing to rest and feeling unwell, sat down under an apple tree, and Toll stopped beside him. Rostov, from a distance, with envy and regret, saw von Toll say something to the sovereign at length and with ardour, and saw the sovereign, probably weeping, cover his eyes with his hand and press Toll's hand.

"And I could be in his place!" Rostov thought to himself and, barely holding back tears of pity over the sovereign's fate, rode on in complete despair, not knowing where he was going now or why.

His despair was the stronger in that he felt his own weakness was the cause of his grief.

He could . . . not only could, but should have ridden up to the sovereign. And that was a unique chance to show the sovereign his devotion. And he had not made use of it . . . "What have I done?" he thought. And he turned his horse and rode back to the place where he had seen the emperor; but there was no one now on the other side of the ditch. Only wagons and carriages drove along. From one cart driver he learned that Kutuzov's staff was in a nearby village, where the train was going. Rostov followed them.

Ahead of him walked Kutuzov's groom, leading horses covered with cloths. Behind the groom came a wagon, and behind the wagon an old house serf in a peaked cap, a short coat, and with bandy legs.

"Titus, hey, Titus!" said the groom.

"What?" the old man asked distractedly.

"Titus! Don't bite us!"

"Eh, you fool! Pah!" the old man said and spat angrily. Some time passed in silent movement, and the same joke was repeated again.

. . .

By five o'clock in the afternoon, the battle had been lost at all points. More than a hundred cannon had already been captured by the French.

Przebyszewski and his corps laid down their arms. Other columns, having lost about half their men, were retreating in disorderly, confused crowds.

The remains of Langeron's and Dokhturov's troops, mixed together, crowded around the dams and banks of the ponds near the village of Augesd.

After five o'clock it was only at the dam of Augesd that the hot cannon fire of the French alone could be heard, from numerous batteries lined up on the slopes of the Pratzen heights and firing at our retreating troops.

In the rear guard, Dokhturov and others, drawing up some battalions, fired back at the French cavalry who were pursuing our troops. It was beginning to get dark. On the narrow dam of Augesd, on which for so many years an old miller in a cap used to sit peacefully with his fishing rods, while his grandson, his shirtsleeves rolled up, fingered the silvery, trembling fish in the watering can; on this dam over which, for so many years, Moravians in shaggy hats and blue jackets had peacefully driven in their two-horse carts laden with wheat and had driven back over the same dam all dusty with flour, their carts white—now, on this narrow dam, between wagons and cannon, under horses and between wheels, crowded men disfigured by the fear of death, crushing each other, dying, stepping over the dying, and killing each other, only to go a few steps and be killed themselves just the same.

Every ten seconds, pushing through the air, a cannonball smacked or a shell exploded in the midst of this dense crowd, killing and spattering with blood those who stood near. Dolokhov, wounded in the arm, on foot, with a dozen soldiers of his company (he was already an officer), and his regimental commander, on horseback, represented the remainder of the entire regiment. Drawn by the crowd, they pressed into the entrance to the dam and, hemmed in on all sides, stopped, because ahead of them a horse had fallen under a cannon and the crowd was pulling it out. One cannonball killed someone behind them, another landed in front and spattered Dolokhov with blood. The crowd pushed on desperately, shrank back, went a few steps, and stopped again.

"Get through these hundred steps and I'm saved for sure; stand here another two minutes and I'm sure to be dead," each man was thinking.

Dolokhov, who was standing in the middle of the crowd, tore his way to the edge of the dam, knocking two soldiers off their feet, and ran down onto the slippery ice that covered the pond.

"Turn off!" he cried, skipping over the ice, which cracked under him; "turn off!" he cried to the ordnance. "It holds! . . ."

The ice held him, but it sagged and cracked, and it was obvious that it would give way, not only under a cannon or a crowd, but under him alone. People looked at him and pressed to the bank, not yet daring to step onto the ice. The regimental commander, standing on horseback at the entrance, raised his arm and opened his mouth, addressing Dolokhov. Suddenly one of the cannonballs came whistling so low over the crowd that everybody ducked. There was a wet smack, and the general and his horse fell in a pool of blood. No one looked at the general, still less thought of picking him up.

"Go onto the ice! Go onto the ice! Go! Turn off! Don't you hear? Go!" cried countless voices after the cannonball hit the general, themselves not knowing what and why they were shouting.

One of the rearmost cannon going onto the dam turned off onto the ice. Crowds of soldiers started running down off the dam onto the frozen pond. The ice cracked under one of the foremost soldiers and one foot went into the water; he tried to right himself and fell through to the waist. The nearest soldiers hesitated, the cannon driver stopped his horse, but shouts were still heard from behind: "Go onto the ice, don't stop, go! go!" And cries of terror were heard in the crowd. The soldiers around the gun waved at the horses and beat them to make them turn and move on. The horses set out from the bank. The ice that had held the foot soldiers gave way in one huge piece, and about forty of them rushed, some back, some forward, drowning each other.

The cannonballs went on regularly whistling and smacking into the ice, into the water, and most often into the crowd that covered the dam, the ponds, and the bank.

XIX

On the Pratzen hill, in the same place where he fell with the staff of the standard in his hands, Prince Andrei Bolkonsky lay bleeding profusely and, unbeknownst to himself, letting out soft, pitiful, and childlike moans.

Towards evening he stopped moaning and became completely still. He did not know how long he was unconscious. Suddenly he felt himself alive again and suffering from a burning and rending pain in the head.

"Where is it, that lofty sky, which I never knew till now and saw today?" was his first thought. "And I never knew this suffering either," he thought. "Yes, I knew nothing, nothing till now. But where am I?"

He began to listen, and heard the sounds of approaching hoofbeats and the sound of voices speaking French. He opened his eyes. Over him again was that same lofty sky with floating clouds rising still higher, through which showed the blue of infinity. He did not turn his head and did not see those who, judging by the sounds of hoofs and voices, had ridden up to him and stopped.

The horsemen who had ridden up were Napoleon accompanied by two adjutants. Bonaparte, riding over the battlefield, had given final orders about the reinforcement of the batteries firing at the dam of Augesd and was looking at the dead and wounded who were left on the battlefield.

"*De beaux hommes!*"* said Napoleon, looking at a dead Russian grenadier who, his face buried in the ground and his nape blackened, lay on his stomach, one of his already stiff arms flung far out.

"*Les munitions des pièces de positions sont épuisées, sire!*"† an adjutant said just then, having come from the batteries that were firing on Augesd.

"*Faites avancer celles de la réserve,*"‡ said Napoleon, and, riding on a few paces, he stopped over Prince Andrei, who lay on his back, the staff of the standard fallen beside him (the standard had already been taken as a trophy by the French).

"*Voilà une belle mort,*"§ said Napoleon, looking at Bolkonsky.

Prince Andrei understood that it had been said about him, and that it was Napoleon speaking. He heard the man who had said these words being addressed as *sire*. But he heard these words as if he was hearing the buzzing of a fly. He not only was not interested, he did not even notice, and at once forgot them. He had a burning in his head; he felt that he was losing blood, and he saw above him that distant, lofty, and eternal sky. He knew that it was Napoleon—his hero—but at that moment, Napoleon seemed to him such a small, insignificant man compared with what was now happening between his soul and this lofty, infinite sky with clouds racing across it. To him it was all completely the same at that moment who was standing over him or what he said about him; he was only glad that people had stopped over him and only wished that those people would help him and bring him back to life, which seemed so beautiful to him, because he now understood it so differently. He gathered all his strength in order to stir and produce some sound. He stirred his leg weakly and produced a weak, painful moan that moved even him to pity.

"Ah! he's alive," said Napoleon. "Lift up this young man, *ce jeune homme,* and take him to the first-aid station!"

Having said that, Napoleon rode on further to meet Marshal Lannes, who was riding up to the emperor, taking off his hat and congratulating him on the victory.

Prince Andrei remembered nothing more: he lost consciousness from the terrible pain of being put on the stretcher, the jolting while he was being carried, and the probing of his wound at the first-aid station. He came to only at the end of the day, when he, along with other Russian wounded and captured offi-

---

*Fine men!
†The ammunition for the guns in position is exhausted, Sire!
‡Bring up more from the reserves.
§There's a fine death.

cers, was taken to the hospital. During this transfer, he felt somewhat fresher and could look around and even speak.

The first words he heard when he came to were the words of the French convoy officer, who was saying hurriedly:

"We must stop here. The emperor will ride by now; it will give him pleasure to see all these gentlemen prisoners."

"There are so many prisoners today, almost the whole Russian army, that he must be bored with it," said another officer.

"Well, really! This, they say, is the commander of all the emperor Alexander's guards," said the first, pointing to a wounded Russian officer in the white uniform of the horse guards.

Bolkonsky recognized Prince Repnin, whom he used to meet in Petersburg society. Next to him stood another wounded officer of the horse guards, a nineteen-year-old boy.

Bonaparte, riding up at a gallop, stopped his horse.

"Who's the senior man?"

They named the colonel, Prince Repnin.

"Are you the commander of the emperor Alexander's regiment of horse guards?" asked Napoleon.

"I commanded a squadron," replied Repnin.

"Your regiment fulfilled its duty honourably," said Napoleon.

"The praise of a great general is a soldier's best reward," said Repnin.

"I bestow it on you with pleasure," said Napoleon. "Who is this young man next to you?"

Prince Repnin named Lieutenant Sukhtelen.

Napoleon looked at him and said, smiling:

"*Il est venu bien jeune se frotter à nous.*"*

"Youth is no impediment to bravery," Sukhtelen said in a halting voice.

"A fine answer," said Napoleon. "You'll go far, young man!"

Prince Andrei, who, to complete the trophy of prisoners, was also brought out before the eyes of the emperor, could not fail to attract his attention. Napoleon evidently remembered seeing him on the battlefield, and, turning to him, used the same appellation of young man, *jeune homme,* under which Bolkonsky had been imprinted on his memory the first time.

"*Et vous, jeune homme?* And you, young man?" he addressed him. "How do you feel, *mon brave?*"

Though five minutes earlier Prince Andrei had been able to say a few words to the soldiers transporting him, now, with his eyes fixed directly on Napoleon, he was silent . . . To him at that moment all the interests that occupied Napoleon seemed so insignificant, his hero himself seemed so petty to him,

*He's young to go crossing swords with us.

with his petty vanity and joy in victory, compared with that lofty, just, and kindly sky, which he had seen and understood, that he was unable to answer him.

Then, too, everything seemed so useless and insignificant compared with that stern and majestic way of thinking called up in him by weakness from loss of blood, suffering, and the expectation of imminent death. Looking into Napoleon's eyes, Prince Andrei thought about the insignficance of grandeur, about the insignificance of life, the meaning of which no one could understand, and about the still greater insignificance of death, the meaning of which no one among the living could understand or explain.

The emperor, receiving no answer, turned away and, as he rode off, addressed one of the officers:

"Have these gentlemen looked after and taken to my bivouac; have my doctor Larrey examine their wounds. Goodbye, Prince Repnin." And, touching up his horse, he galloped on.

On his face was the radiance of self-satisfaction and happiness.

The soldiers who had carried Prince Andrei and had taken from him the little golden icon hung on her brother by Princess Marya, seeing the kindness with which the emperor treated the prisoners, hastened to return the icon.

Prince Andrei did not see how or by whom it was put back on him, but suddenly, on his chest over the uniform, a little icon on a fine gold chain turned up.

"It would be good," thought Prince Andrei, looking at this icon which his sister had hung on him with such feeling and reverence, "it would be good if everything was as clear and simple as it seems to Princess Marya. How good it would be to know where to look for help in this life and what to expect after it, there, beyond the grave! How happy and calm I'd be, if I could say now: Lord, have mercy on me! . . . But to whom shall I say it? Either it is an indefinable, unfathomable power, which I not only cannot address, but which I cannot express in words—the great all or nothing," he said to himself, "or it is that God whom Princess Marya has sewn in here, in this amulet? Nothing, nothing is certain, except the insignificance of everything I can comprehend and the grandeur of something incomprehensible but most important!"

The stretchers began to move. At every jolt he again felt unbearable pain; his feverish state worsened, and he became delirious. Those reveries of his father, wife, sister, and future son, and the tenderness he had experienced on the night before the battle, the figure of the little, insignificant Napoleon, and the lofty sky over it all, constituted the main basis for his feverish imaginings.

He imagined a quiet life and peaceful family happiness at Bald Hills. He was already enjoying this happiness, when suddenly little Napoleon appeared with his indifferent, limited gaze, happy in the unhappiness of others, and doubts and torments set in, and only the sky promised tranquillity. Towards morning all his reveries became confused and merged into the chaos and darkness of unconsciousness and oblivion, which, in the opinion of Larrey himself, Napoleon's doctor, would most likely end in death rather than recovery.

"*C'est un sujet nerveux et bilieux,*" said Larrey, "*il n'en réchappera pas.*"*

Prince Andrei, among other hopeless wounded, was handed over to the care of the local inhabitants.

---

*He's the nervous and bilious sort . . . he won't pull through.

VOLUME II

I

At the beginning of 1806, Nikolai Rostov came home on leave. Denisov also went home to Voronezh, and Rostov persuaded him to come with him as far as Moscow and stay in their house. At the next to last posting station, Denisov met a friend, drank three bottles of wine with him, and, despite the bumps of the road, did not wake up all the way, lying on the bottom of the horse-drawn sleigh beside Rostov, who became more and more impatient the closer they came to Moscow.

"Soon now? Soon now? Oh, these unbearable streets, shops, bakeries, street lamps, cabbies!" thought Rostov, when they had already registered their leaves at the city gates and entered Moscow.

"Denisov, we're here!—he's asleep," he said, leaning his whole body forward, as if hoping by this posture to speed up the movement of the sleigh. Denisov did not respond.

"Here's the intersection where the cabby Zakhar stands; here's Zakhar, and still the same horse! Here's the grocery where we used to buy gingerbread. Soon now? Come on!"

"Which house is it?" asked the driver.

"The one at the end, the big one, don't you see? It's our house," said Rostov, "it's our house! Denisov! Denisov! We're nearly there."

Denisov raised his head, cleared his throat, and made no reply.

"Dmitri," Rostov said to the servant on the box. "Aren't those lights in our house?"

"Exactly so, sir, and there's light in your papa's study."

"So they're not in bed yet? Eh? What do you think?"

"See that you don't forget to take out my new Hungarian jacket for me at once," Rostov added, feeling his new moustache. "Well, on with you," he cried to the driver. "Wake up now, Vasya," he turned to Denisov, who was lowering his head again. "Well, on with you, three roubles for vodka, on with you!" shouted Rostov, when the sleigh was three houses away from their entrance. It seemed to him the horses were not moving. At last the sleigh pulled to the right at the entrance; over his head Rostov saw the familiar cornice with its chipped stucco, the porch, the hitching post. He jumped out of the sleigh while it was still moving and ran into the front hall. The house stood as immobile, unwelcoming, as if it cared nothing for the one who had arrived. There was no one in the hall. "My God! is everything all right?" thought Rostov, stopping for a moment with a sinking heart, and at once set off running down the hall and up the familiar slanting steps. The same door handle, the dirtiness of which always angered the countess, turned as slackly as ever. One tallow candle was burning in the front room.

Old Mikhailo was sleeping on a trunk. The footman Prokofy, the one who was so strong he could lift a carriage by the back rail, was sitting and plaiting slippers out of cloth trimmings. He glanced at the opening door, and his indifferent, sleepy expression suddenly transformed into a rapturously alarmed one.

"Saints alive! The young count!" he cried, recognizing his young master. "What is this? My dear heart!" And Prokofy, trembling with excitement, rushed for the door to the living room, probably to announce him, but clearly thought again, came back, and pressed himself to the young master's shoulder.

"Everyone well?" asked Rostov, pulling his arm away.

"Thank God! All of them, thank God! They've just finished eating! Let me look at you, Your Excellency!"

"Everything's quite all right?"

"Thank God! Thank God!"

Rostov, forgetting all about Denisov, not wishing anyone to announce him beforehand, threw off his fur coat and ran on tiptoe to the big, dark reception room. Everything was the same—the same card tables, the same chandelier in its cover; but someone had already seen the young master, and before he reached the drawing room, something flew out of a side door precipitously, like a storm, and embraced and began kissing him. A second, then a third such being sprang from a second, a third door; more embraces, more kisses, more shouts, tears of joy. He could not make out where and who was his papa, who was Natasha, who was Petya. Everybody wept, talked, and kissed him at the same time. Only his mother was not among them—he noticed that.

"And I didn't know . . . Nikolushka . . . Kolya, my friend."

"Here he is . . . our boy. So changed! No! Candles! Tea!"

"Give me a kiss!"

"Darling . . . and me, too."

Sonya, Natasha, Petya, Anna Mikhailovna, Vera, the old count embraced him; servants and maids filled the room, talking and ah-ing.

Petya clung to his legs.

"And me, too!" he cried.

Natasha pulled him down to her and kissed his face all over, then jumped back and, holding the skirt of his Hungarian jacket, hopped up and down in one place like a little goat and shrieked piercingly.

On all sides there were loving eyes, glistening with tears of joy, there were lips that wanted to kiss him.

Sonya, bright red, also held him by the hand, all beaming in the blissful gaze she directed at his eyes, which she had been waiting for. Sonya had already turned sixteen, and she was very beautiful, especially in this moment of happy, rapturous animation. She looked at him, not taking her eyes away, smiling and holding her breath. He glanced at her gratefully, but was still waiting and looking for someone. The old countess had not come out yet. And then footsteps were heard at the door. The footsteps were so quick that they could not have been his mother's.

But it was she, in a new dress, unfamiliar to him, which must have been made in his absence. Everyone let him go, and he ran to her. When they came together, she fell on his breast, weeping. She could not lift her face, and only pressed it to the cold cords of his Hungarian jacket. Denisov, unnoticed by anyone, came into the room, stood there, and rubbed his eyes looking at them.

"Vassily Denisov, fghriend of your son," he said, introducing himself to the old count, who was looking at him questioningly.

"I bid you welcome. I know, I know," said the count, kissing and embracing Denisov. "Nikolushka wrote to us . . . Natasha, Vera, here's Denisov."

The same happy, rapturous faces turned to Denisov's shaggy little figure with its black moustaches and surrounded him.

"Darling Denisov!" shrieked Natasha, beside herself with rapture, and she ran to him, embraced and kissed him. Everyone was embarrassed by Natasha's behaviour. Denisov also blushed, but smiled, and, taking Natasha's hand, kissed it.

Denisov was taken to the room prepared for him, and all the Rostovs gathered in the sitting room around Nikolushka.

The old countess, never letting go of his hand, which she kissed every other moment, sat next to him; the rest clustered around them, catching his every movement, word, gaze, and not taking their rapturously loving eyes off him. His brother and sisters argued, and snatched the places nearest to him from each other, and fought over who was going to bring him tea, a handkerchief, a pipe.

Rostov was very happy in the love that was shown him, but the first moment of their meeting had been so blissful that his present happiness seemed too little to him, and he kept waiting for more, and more, and more.

The next morning the new arrivals slept till past nine.

In the adjoining room, sabres, bags, pouches, open suitcases, dirty boots lay about. Two pairs of polished boots with spurs had just been put near the wall. The servants brought washbasins and hot water for shaving, and brushed their clothes. There was a smell of tobacco and men.

"Hey, Ghrishka, my pipe!" cried Vaska Denisov's hoarse voice. "Get up, Ghrostov!"

Rostov, rubbing his glued-together eyes, raised his dishevelled head from the hot pillow.

"What, is it late?"

"Yes. It's past nine," Natasha's voice replied, and in the next room the rustle of starched skirts, whispers, and the laughter of girls' voices were heard, and through the slightly open door flashed something light blue, ribbons, dark hair, and merry faces. This was Natasha, with Sonya and Petya, who had come to see whether he had got up.

"Nikolenka, get up!" Natasha's voice was again heard at the door.

"Right away!"

Just then Petya, glimpsing the sabres in the adjoining room, and seizing them with the feeling of rapture which boys experience at the sight of a military older brother, and forgetting that it was improper for his sisters to see undressed men, opened the door.

"Is this your sabre?" he shouted. The girls jumped away. Denisov, with frightened eyes, hid his shaggy legs under the blanket, glancing at his friend for help. The door admitted Petya and closed again. Behind the door there was laughter.

"Nikolenka, come out in your dressing gown," said Natasha's voice.

"Is this your sabre?" asked Petya. "Or is it yours?" he turned to the moustached, black Denisov with obsequious respect.

Rostov hastily put on his shoes, his dressing gown, and went out. Natasha had put on one spurred boot and was getting into the other. Sonya was twirling and was just about to balloon her dress and crouch down when he came in. The two girls, in identical new light blue dresses, were fresh, red-cheeked, merry. Sonya ran away, but Natasha, taking her brother under the arm, led him to the sitting room, and started talking with him. They hastened to ask and answer each other about a thousand little things that could interest only them. Natasha laughed at every word he said and she said—not because what they were saying was funny, but because she felt merry and was unable to hold back her joy, which expressed itself in laughter.

"Ah, how good, excellent!" she added after every word. Rostov felt how his face and soul expanded under the influence of these hot rays of Natasha's love, for the first time in a year and a half, into that childish and pure smile which he had not once smiled since he left home.

"No, listen," she said, "you're quite a man now. I'm terribly glad you're my brother." She touched his moustache. "I'd like to know how you men are. Are you like us?"

"No. Why did Sonya run away?" Rostov asked.

"Ah, that's a whole other story! How are you going to address Sonya, as 'Miss' or not?"

"However it happens," said Rostov.

"Address her as 'Miss,' please, I'll tell you later."

"But what?"

"Well, then I'll tell you now. You know that Sonya's my friend, such a friend that I'd burn my arm for her. Look here." She pushed up her muslin sleeve and showed a red mark on her long, thin, and delicate arm, below the shoulder but far above the elbow (where it is covered even by ball gowns).

"I burned it to show her my love. I just heated a ruler in the fire and pressed it there."

Sitting in his former schoolroom, on the sofa with padded armrests, and looking into Natasha's desperately lively eyes, Rostov again entered that world of his family and childhood, which had no meaning for anyone but him, but which had provided him with one of the best enjoyments in life; and the burning of the arm with a ruler to show love did not seem nonsense to him; he understood and was not surprised at it.

"So what, then?" he merely asked.

"Well, we're such friends, such friends! This is just silliness—the ruler; but we're friends for ever. If she loves someone, it's for ever. I don't understand it. I forget at once."

"Well, so what?"

"Well, so she loves me and you." Natasha suddenly blushed. "Well, you remember, before you left . . . So she says you should forget it all . . . She said: 'I'll always love him, but let him be free.' That's excellent, excellent and noble, isn't it? Right, right? very noble? right?" Natasha asked so earnestly and excitedly that it was clear that what she was saying now, she had said before through tears. Rostov pondered.

"I don't take back my word in anything," he said. "And besides, Sonya is so lovely—what fool would renounce his happiness?"

"No, no," cried Natasha. "She and I already talked about it. We knew you'd say that. But it's impossible, because, you see, if you say that—if you consider yourself bound by your word, it comes out as if she'd said it on purpose. It comes out as if you're forced to marry her, and doesn't come out right at all."

Rostov saw that they had thought it out very well. Sonya had already struck him with her beauty yesterday. Today, having glimpsed her fleetingly, he thought her better still. She was a lovely sixteen-year-old girl, obviously passionately in love with him (he did not doubt it for a moment). Why shouldn't he love her and even marry her? thought Rostov; but not now. Now there were so many other joys and things to do! "Yes, they've thought it out splendidly," he thought. "I should remain free."

"Well, that's splendid," he said, "we'll talk later. Ah, I'm so glad to see you!" he added. "Well, and what about you, you haven't betrayed Boris?" asked her brother.

"What silliness!" cried Natasha, laughing. "I don't want to think or know about him or anybody else."

"Well, now! So what's with you?"

"Me?" Natasha repeated, and a happy smile lit up her face. "Have you seen Duport?"

"No."

"The famous Duport, the ballet master—you haven't seen him? Then you won't understand. Here's what I am." Natasha rounded her arms, took up her skirt as if to dance, ran a few steps, turned, made an entrechat, tapped her foot against her ankle, and went a few steps on the very tips of her toes. "See me standing? So there!" she said; but she could not hold it. "That's what I am! I'll never marry anyone, I'll become a dancer. Only don't tell anybody."

Rostov laughed so loudly and merrily that Denisov felt envious in his room, and Natasha, unable to help herself, laughed with him. "No, but it's nice, isn't it?" she kept saying.

"Very nice. So you no longer want to marry Boris?"

Natasha blushed.

"I don't want to marry anybody. I'll tell him the same when I see him."

"Well, now!" said Rostov.

"Oh, yes, that's all trifles," Natasha went on babbling. "And what, is Denisov nice?" she asked.

"Yes."

"Well, goodbye, go and get dressed. Is he scary, Denisov?"

"Why scary?" asked Nicolas. "No, Vaska's a sweet man."

"You call him Vaska? . . . Strange. And what, is he very nice?"

"Very nice."

"Well, come quickly and have tea. All of us together."

And Natasha got up on tiptoe and walked out of the room as ballet dancers do, but smiling as only happy fifteen-year-old girls do. Meeting Sonya in the drawing room, Rostov blushed. He did not know how to treat her. Yesterday they had kissed each other in the first moment of the joy of meeting, but today he felt he could not do so; he felt that all of them, his mother and sisters, were looking at him questioningly, waiting to see how he behaved with her. He kissed her hand and addressed her as Miss Sonya. But their eyes met without any formality and gave each other a tender kiss. Her look asked forgiveness for daring, through Natasha's embassy, to remind him of his promise, and thanked him for his love. His look thanked her for the offer of freedom, and said that, one way or another, he would never stop loving her, because it was impossible not to love her.

"How strange it is, though," said Vera, finding a moment of general silence, "that Sonya and Nikolenka now treat each other like strangers, on formal terms." Vera's observation was correct, as were all her observations; but, like most of her observations, this one made everyone feel awkward, and not only Sonya, Nikolai, and Natasha, but even the old countess, who feared that her son's love for Sonya might deprive him of a brilliant match, blushed like a girl.

To Rostov's surprise, Denisov, in a new uniform, pomaded and perfumed, appeared in the drawing room looking as dashing as he did in battle, and more of an amiable ladies' man than Rostov had ever expected to see him.

II

Having returned to Moscow from the army, Nikolai Rostov was received by all the family as the best of sons, a hero, and their darling Nikolushka; by relations as a nice, agreeable, and courteous young man; by acquaintances as a handsome hussar lieutenant, an adroit dancer, and one of the best suitors in Moscow.

All Moscow was acquainted with the Rostovs. The old count had enough money that year, because all the estates had been remortgaged, and therefore Nikolushka, having acquired his own trotter and the most fashionable riding breeches, special ones such as no one in Moscow yet had, and the most fashionable boots, with the most pointed toes and small silver spurs, spent his time very gaily. Rostov, on returning home, experienced a pleasant feeling, after measuring himself for a certain time against the old conditions of life. It seemed to him that he had grown and matured greatly. Despair over a failed examination in catechism, borrowing money from Gavrilo for a cab, secret kisses with Sonya—he remembered it all as childishness, from which he was immeasurably far removed now. Now he was a lieutenant of the hussars, in a silver-trimmed dolman, with his soldier's St. George, preparing his trotter for a race together with well-known, older, respectable fanciers. He had a lady acquaintance on the boulevard, whom he visited in the evenings. He led the mazurka at the Arkharovs' ball, talked about the war with Field Marshal Kamensky, visited the English Club,[1] and was on familiar terms with a forty-year-old colonel whose acquaintance he had made through Denisov.

His passion for the sovereign weakened somewhat in Moscow, since he did not see him during that time. But all the same he often told about the sovereign, about his love for him, letting it be felt that he was not telling all, that there was something else in his feeling for the sovereign that not everyone could understand; and he shared with all his soul the general feeling at that time in Moscow of adoration for the emperor Alexander Pavlovich, who in Moscow at that time was given the nickname of "Angel in the Flesh."

During Rostov's short stay in Moscow before leaving for the army, he did not become closer but, on the contrary, drew away from Sonya. She was very pretty, sweet, and obviously passionately in love with him; but he was in that season of youth when one seems to have so much to do that there is *no time* for that, and a young man is afraid of being tied down—he cherishes his freedom, which he needs for many other things. When he thought about Sonya during his stay in Moscow, he said to himself: "Ah, there will be and there are many, many like her, somewhere, whom I don't know yet. I'll still have time, when I want, to occupy myself with love, but right now I'm busy." Besides, it seemed to him that there was something humiliating to his manliness in women's society. He went to balls and into women's society pretending that he was doing so against his will. The races, the English Club, carousing with Denisov, going *there*—that was another matter: it was suitable to a dashing hussar.

At the beginning of March, the old count Ilya Andreevich Rostov was taken up with arranging a dinner at the English Club in honour of Prince Bagration.

The count walked about the reception hall in his dressing gown, giving orders to the club manager and to the famous Feoktist, the head chef of the English Club, about asparagus, fresh cucumbers, strawberries, veal, and fish for Prince Bagration's dinner. The count had been a member and trustee of the club since the day it was founded. He had been charged by the club with arranging the celebration for Bagration, because few men could arrange a feast with such largesse and hospitality, and especially because few men could and would supply their own money, if it was needed to arrange the feast. The chef and the club manager listened to the count's orders with cheerful faces, because they knew that with him as with no one else could they profit so well from a dinner costing several thousand.

"So, mind you, cock's-combs, put cock's-combs in the *tortue,** you know!"

"Three cold sauces, then? . . ." the chef asked.

The count pondered.

"Not less than three . . . mayonnaise, for one," he said, counting off on his fingers . . .

"So your orders are to take the big sterlet?" asked the manager.

"No help for it, take the big ones, since that's what they've got. Ah, dear me, I almost forgot! We must have one more entrée on the table. Oh, mercy!" He clutched his head. "Who's going to bring flowers? Mitenka! Hey, Mitenka! Gallop to the Moscow estate, Mitenka," he said to the steward, who came in on hearing his call, "gallop to the Moscow estate and tell Maximka the gardener to prepare the corvée now. Tell him to bring the whole conservatory here, wrapped in felt. Two hundred pots must be here by Friday."

Having given more and more orders of various kinds, he was on his way to rest with his little countess, but remembered another necessary thing, came back himself, brought the chef and the manager back, and again began giving orders. A light male footstep was heard at the door, a jingle of spurs, and the young count came in, handsome, ruddy, with a black little moustache, obviously rested and pampered by his peaceful life in Moscow.

*Turtle [sauce].

"Ah, my dear fellow! My head is spinning," said the old man, smiling to his son, as if embarrassed. "You might at least help me! We need singers. I have musicians, but shall we invite some Gypsies? You military folk like that."

"Really, papa, I think Prince Bagration made less fuss preparing for the battle of Schöngraben than you're doing now," the son said, smiling.

The old count pretended to be angry.

"Yes, talk, go ahead!"

And the count turned to the chef, who, with an intelligent and respectful face, glanced at the father and son observantly and affectionately.

"How about these young ones, eh, Feoktist?" he said, "laughing at us old folk."

"Why, Your Excellency, all they want is to eat well, but putting it all together and serving it is none of their business."

"Right, right!" cried the count, and, merrily seizing his son by both hands, he cried: "I've caught you now! Here's what to do, take the sleigh and pair and go to Bezukhov, and tell him that the count, Ilya Andreich, sends to ask you for some strawberries and fresh pineapples. One can't get them from anybody else. If he's not there himself, go and tell the princesses, and from there go to Razgulyai—Ipatka, the coachman, knows where it is—find Ilyushka the Gypsy² there, the one who used to dance at Prince Orlov's, remember, in a white little kaftan, and drag him here to me."

"Shall I have him bring Gypsy girls?" Nikolai asked, laughing.

"Well, well! . . ."

Just then Anna Mikhailovna stepped inaudibly into the room, with the businesslike, preoccupied, and at the same time meek Christian look that never left her. Though Anna Mikhailovna found the count in his dressing gown every day, he became embarrassed each time and apologized for his costume. He did so now as well.

"Never mind, my dear Count," she said, closing her eyes meekly. "And I'll go to Bezukhov's myself," she said. "Young Bezukhov has arrived, and we'll now get everything from his conservatory. I have to see him anyway. He has sent me a letter from Boris. Thank God, Boris is with the staff now."

The count was delighted that Anna Mikhailovna was taking on part of his errands, and he ordered the smaller carriage readied for her.

"Tell Bezukhov to come. I'll put his name down. Is he with his wife?" he asked.

Anna Mikhailovna raised her eyes, and her face expressed deep sorrow . . .

"Ah, my friend, he's very unfortunate," she said. "If what we've heard is true, it's terrible. And could we have thought of it when we rejoiced over his happiness? And such a lofty, heavenly soul, this young Bezukhov! Yes, I pity him with all my soul, and I'll try to give him comfort, as far as it depends on me."

"But what is it?" asked both Rostovs, old and young.

Anna Mikhailovna sighed deeply.

"Dolokhov, Marya Ivanovna's son," she said in a mysterious whisper, "they say he has totally compromised her. He introduced him, invited him to his house in Petersburg, and now . . . She has come here, and that daredevil after her," said Anna Mikhailovna, wishing to express her sympathy for Pierre, but by involuntary intonations and a half smile expressing her sympathy for the daredevil, as she called Dolokhov. "They say Pierre is totally crushed by his grief."

"Well, all the same, tell him to come to the club—it will distract him. There'll be a sumptuous feast."

The next day, the third of March, between one and two in the afternoon, the two hundred and fifty members of the English Club and fifty guests were awaiting at dinner the dear guest and hero of the Austrian campaign, Prince Bagration. At first, when news of the battle of Austerlitz was received, Moscow was thrown into perplexity. At that time the Russians were so used to victories that, on receiving news of the defeat, some simply did not believe it, others sought to explain such a strange occurrence by some extraordinary causes. In the English Club, where all that was elite, had accurate information, and carried weight used to gather, nothing was said in December, when news began to come in about the war and the last battle, as if there was a general agreement to keep silent about it. People who guided conversation, such as Count Rastopchin, Prince Yuri Vladimirovich Dolgoruky, Valuev, Count Markov, and Prince Vyazemsky did not appear at the club, but gathered in people's houses, in their intimate circles, and those Muscovites who spoke with the voices of others (to whom Count Ilya Andreevich Rostov also belonged), were left for a short time without any definite opinion on the matter of the war and without guidance. The Muscovites felt that something was wrong, and that to discuss this bad news was difficult, and therefore it was better to be silent. But after a while, just as the jurors emerge from the conference room, so the aces appeared again, creating opinion in the club, and all began speaking clearly and definitely. The causes had been found for that unbelievable, unheard-of, and impossible event of a Russian defeat, and everything became clear, and in all corners of Moscow the same things were said. These causes were: the treachery of the Austrians, the bad provisioning of the troops, the treachery of the Pole Przebyszewski and the Frenchman Langeron,[3] the inability of Kutuzov, and (in a low voice) the youth and inexperience of the sovereign, who had trusted bad and worthless people. But the troops, the Russian troops, everyone said, were extraordinary and had performed miracles of courage. The soldiers, the officers, and the generals were heroes. But the hero of heroes was Prince Bagration, who won fame for his action at Schöngraben and for the retreat from Austerlitz, in which he alone had led his column in order and for a whole day had beaten back a twice-stronger enemy. What contributed to the choice of Bagration as hero in Moscow was that he had no Moscow connections and was an outsider. In his person, honour was paid to the simple Russian fighting soldier, without connections or intrigues, and still associated through memories of the Italian campaign with the name of Suvorov.[4] Besides, rendering him such honours was the best way of showing dislike and disapproval of Kutuzov.

"If there were no Bagration, *il faudrait l'inventer,*"* said the joker Shinshin, parodying the words of Voltaire.[5] No one spoke of Kutuzov, and some denounced him in whispers, calling him a court weathercock and an old satyr.

All over Moscow they repeated the words of Prince Dolgorukov: "Paste, paste, and you get pasted"—comforting himself for our defeat with the memory of previous victories, and repeated the words of Rastopchin, that French soldiers had to be urged into battle by high-flown phrases, that with Germans you had to reason logically, persuading them that it was more dangerous to run away than to go forward, but that Russian soldiers only had to be held back and begged to slow down. On all sides more and more new stories were heard about particular examples of courage shown by soldiers and officers at Austerlitz. This one had saved a standard, that one had killed five Frenchmen, that one had loaded five cannons single-handed. It was even said of Berg, by those who did not know him, that, wounded in the right hand, he had taken his sword in his left and forged ahead. Of Bolkonsky nothing was said, and only those who knew him closely regretted that he had died early, leaving his pregnant wife with his eccentric father.

III

On the third of March, the drone of talking voices hung in all the rooms of the English Club and, like bees in spring, the members and guests of the club shuttled back and forth, sat, stood, came together and dispersed again, in uniforms, tailcoats, and some even in powdered wigs and kaftans.[6] Powdered, liveried servants in stockings and buckled shoes stood by every door and strained to catch every movement of the guests and members of the club, in order to offer their services. The majority of those present were venerable old people with broad, self-confident faces, fat fingers, firm movements and voices. This sort of guests and members sat in their known, habitual places, and met together in known, habitual circles. A small part of those present consisted of chance guests—mostly young men, among whom were Denisov, Rostov, and Dolokhov, who had again become an officer of the Semyonovsky regiment. On the faces of the young men, especially the military, there was an expression of that

*He would have to be invented.

feeling of disdainful deference towards the old men which seemed to say to the older generation: "We're prepared to respect and honour you, but remember all the same that the future is ours."

Nesvitsky was there as an old member of the club. Pierre, who, on his wife's orders, had let his hair grow long and removed his spectacles, was fashionably dressed, but walked about the rooms with a sad and dejected air. As everywhere, he was surrounded by an atmosphere of people who bowed before his wealth, and he treated them with a habitual lordliness and absent-minded disdain.

By his age he should have been with the young people, but by his wealth and connections he was a member of the circle of old, venerable guests, and therefore he kept going from one circle to another. The most distinguished old men were at the centres of the circles, deferentially surrounded even by strangers, who came to listen to the well-known people. Big circles formed around Count Rastopchin, Valuev, and Naryshkin. Rastopchin was telling about how the Russians had been overrun by the fleeing Austrians and had had to use bayonets to make their way through the fugitives.

Valuev told confidentially that Uvarov had been sent from Petersburg to find out the opinion of the Muscovites about Austerlitz.

In the third circle, Naryshkin was talking about the meeting of the Austrian council of war in which Suvorov had crowed like a cock in response to some Austrian general's stupidity.[7] Shinshin, who was standing there, was about to make a joke, saying that Kutuzov had been unable to learn even that simple skill—of crowing like a cock—from Suvorov; but the old men gave the joker a stern look, letting him feel that there and on that day it was improper to speak like that about Kutuzov.

Count Ilya Andreich Rostov, hurried, preoccupied, paced in his soft boots from dining room to drawing room, greeting in a hasty and perfectly identical manner both important and unimportant persons, all of whom he knew, and, occasionally seeking out his trim, dashing son with his eyes, joyfully rested his gaze on him and winked to him. Young Rostov was standing by the window with Dolokhov, with whom he had recently become acquainted, and whose acquaintance he valued. The old count came up to him and shook Dolokhov's hand.

"Be so good as to call on us, since you know my fine lad . . . you're together there . . . two heroes . . . Ah, Vassily Ignatyich . . . greetings, old boy," he addressed a little old man who was passing by, but before he finished the greeting everything stirred, and a servant came running with a frightened face and announced: "He's here!"

There was a ringing of bells; the club stewards rushed forward; scattered through different rooms, the guests, like rye shaken in a shovel, came together in one heap and stopped in the big drawing room by the door to the reception hall.

In the doorway of the anteroom Bagration appeared, without his hat and sword, which, as was customary at the club, he had left with the doorman. He was not in an Astrakhan peaked cap, with a whip over his shoulder, as Rostov had seen him on the eve of the battle of Austerlitz, but in a trim new uniform with Russian and foreign decorations and the star of St. George on his left breast. He had evidently had his hair and side-whiskers trimmed just before the dinner, which changed his physiognomy to its disadvantage. On his face there was something naïvely festive, which, in combination with his firm, manly features, even gave his face a somewhat comical expression. Bekleshov and Fyodor Petrovich Uvarov, who came with him, stopped in the doorway, wishing him, as the main guest, to go ahead of them. Bagration was embarrassed, not wishing to take advantage of their courtesy; a pause in the doorway ensued, and Bagration finally did go ahead of them. He walked over the parquet of the reception hall bashfully and awkwardly, not knowing what to do with his hands; it was easier and more usual for him to walk under bullets over a ploughed field, as he had walked ahead of the Kursky regiment at Schöngraben. The stewards met him at the first door, spoke a few words to him about the joy of seeing such a dear guest, and, not waiting for him to reply, and as if taking possession of him, surrounded him and led him to the drawing room. It was impossible to go through the door of the drawing room because of the thronging members and guests, who pressed against each other, trying to get a glimpse of Bagration, as of a rare animal, over each other's shoulders. Count Ilya Andreich—more energetically than anyone, laughing and repeating, "Allow me, *mon cher*, allow me, allow me!"—pushed through the crowd, led the guests to the drawing room, and seated them on the middle sofa. The aces, the club's most respected members, stood around the new arrivals. Count Ilya Andreich, again pushing through the crowd, left the drawing room and came back a moment later with another steward, carrying a large silver platter, which he offered to Prince Bagration. On the platter lay verses composed and printed in honour of the hero. Seeing the platter, Bagration glanced fearfully around, as if looking for help. But all eyes were demanding that he submit. Feeling himself in their power, Bagration resolutely took the platter in both hands and looked angrily and reproachfully at the count who had offered it to him. Someone obligingly took the platter from Bagration's hands (otherwise he seemed prepared to hold it that way till evening and go to the table with it), and drew his attention to the verses. "Well, so I'll read them," Bagration seemed to say, and, fixing his weary eyes on the paper, he began to read with a concentrated and serious look. The author himself took the verses from him and began to read. Prince Bagration inclined his head and listened.

> Glorify, then, the age of Alexander
> And keep our noble Titus on the throne,
> Be both a good man and a fierce commander,

Caesar in battle, Ripheus at home.
And fortunate Napoleon,
Taught by experience of Bagration,
The Russian Alcides dares no more to scorn . . .[8]

But before he finished the verses, the loud-voiced butler announced: "Dinner is served!" The door opened, from the dining room thundered the polonaise: "Thunder of victory resound, be of good cheer, O valiant Russ . . ."—and Count Ilya Andreich, glancing angrily at the author, who went on reading his verses, bowed before Bagration. They all stood up, feeling that dinner was more important than verses, and again Bagration went ahead of everyone to the table. He was seated in the first place, between two Alexanders— Bekleshov and Naryshkin—which also made reference to the sovereign's name. Three hundred people were then seated in the dining room by rank and importance, the more important closer to the guest of honour, as naturally as water flows deeper where the terrain is lower.

Just before dinner, Count Ilya Andreich introduced his son to the prince. Bagration, recognizing him, spoke a few incoherent, awkward words, like all the words he spoke that day. While Bagration was talking with his son, Count Ilya Andreich looked everyone over joyfully and proudly.

Nikolai Rostov, with Denisov and his new acquaintance, Dolokhov, sat together almost at the middle of the table. Opposite them sat Pierre, beside Prince Nesvitsky. Count Ilya Andreich sat opposite Bagration, together with the other stewards, and did the honours for Prince Bagration, personifying Moscow hospitality in himself.

His labours had not gone in vain. The dinners—both lenten and non-lenten[9]— were splendid, but even so he could not be perfectly at ease until dinner was over. He winked to the barman, whispered orders to the servants, and waited not without anxiety for each familiar dish. Everything was excellent. With the second course, along with a giant sterlet (seeing which Ilya Andreich blushed from joy and bashfulness), the servants began to pop corks and pour champagne. After the fish, which produced a certain impression, Count Ilya Andreich exchanged glances with the other stewards. "There'll be many toasts, it's time to begin!" he whispered, and, taking a glass in his hand, he arose. Everyone fell silent and waited for what he would say.

"To the health of our sovereign emperor!" he cried, and at the same moment his kindly eyes grew moist with tears of joy and rapture. At that same moment, the "Thunder of victory resound" was played. They all rose from their seats and shouted "Hurrah!" Bagration, too, shouted "Hurrah!" in the same voice in which he had shouted on the field of Schöngraben. Young Rostov's rapturous voice could be heard above the other three hundred voices. He was almost weeping.

"To the health of the sovereign emperor!" he cried. "Hurrah!" Emptying his glass at one gulp, he flung it on the floor. Many followed his example. And the loud shouts continued for a long time. When the voices died down, the servants cleared away the broken glass, and everybody began to take their seats, smiling at their own shouts and talking among themselves. Count Ilya Andreevich rose again, glanced at the little note that lay next to his plate, and pronounced a toast to the health of the hero of our latest campaign, Prince Pyotr Ivanovich Bagration, and again the count's blue eyes grew moist with tears. "Hurrah!" the voices of the three hundred guests shouted again, and, instead of music, a choir was heard, singing a cantata composed by Pavel Ivanovich Kutuzov:[10]

> Vain are all barriers to Russians,
> In us victory and valour meet,
> We have our Bagrations,
> All enemies will be at our feet . . . etc.

As soon as the choir finished, more and more new toasts followed, at which Count Ilya Andreevich grew more and more sentimental, and more glasses were smashed, and more shouts were heard. They drank to the health of Bekleshov, Naryshkin, Uvarov, Dolgorukov, Apraksin, Valuev, to the health of the stewards, to the health of the manager, to the health of all the members of the club, to the health of all the guests of the club, and finally, separately, to the health of the dinner's host, Count Ilya Andreevich. At this toast, the count took out his handkerchief, covered his face, and burst completely into tears.

IV

Pierre was sitting across from Dolokhov and Nikolai Rostov. He ate a lot and greedily, and drank a lot, as usual. But those who knew him intimately could see that some great change had taken place in him that day. He was silent all through dinner and, squinting and wincing, looked around him or, fixing his eyes with a completely absent-minded air, rubbed the bridge of his nose with his finger. His face was dejected and gloomy. He seemed to see and hear nothing of what was going on around him and to be thinking of some one painful and unresolved thing.

This unresolved question that tormented him came from the hints of the young princess in Moscow at Dolokhov's intimacy with his wife, and from an anonymous letter he had received that morning, which said, with the mean jocularity of all anonymous letters, that he saw poorly through his spectacles and that his wife's liaison with Dolokhov was a secret to no one but him. Pierre decidedly did not believe either the princess's hints or the letter, but it was scary for him now to look at Dolokhov, who was sitting in front of him. Each time his gaze chanced to meet Dolokhov's handsome, insolent eyes, Pierre felt something terrible and ugly rise up in his soul, and he quickly turned away. Involuntarily recalling all his wife's past and her relations with Dolokhov, Pierre saw clearly that what was said in the letter might be true, might at least seem true, if it had not concerned *his wife*. Pierre involuntarily recalled how Dolokhov, to whom everything had been restored after the campaign, had returned to Petersburg and come to see him. Using his relations of carousing friendship with Pierre, Dolokhov had come straight to his house, and Pierre had put him up and lent him money. Pierre recalled how Hélène, smiling, had expressed her displeasure at Dolokhov's living in their house, and how Dolokhov had cynically praised his wife's beauty to him, and how from then until they came to Moscow, he had not parted from them for a minute.

"Yes, he's very handsome," thought Pierre, "I know him. For him there would be a special charm in disgracing my name and laughing at me, precisely because I solicited for him, took him in, and helped him. I know, I understand what salt it would give his deceit in his own eyes, if it were true. Yes, if it were true; but I don't believe it, I have no right to and cannot believe it." He recalled the expression Dolokhov's face assumed in moments when cruelty came over him, as when he tied the policeman to the bear and threw him into the water, or when he challenged a man to a duel for no reason, or killed a cabby's horse with a pistol. That expression was often on Dolokhov's face when he looked at him. "Yes, he's a duellist," thought Pierre, "to kill a man is nothing to him, he must think everybody's afraid of him, it must make him feel good. He must think I'm also afraid of him. And, in fact, I am afraid of him," thought Pierre, and again, at these thoughts, he felt something frightful and ugly rise up in his soul. Dolokhov, Denisov, and Rostov now sat facing Pierre and seemed very merry. Rostov talked merrily with his two friends, one of whom was a dashing hussar, the other a notorious duellist and scapegrace, and from time to time glanced mockingly at Pierre, who stood out at this dinner because of his concentrated, absent-minded, massive figure. Rostov looked at Pierre unkindly, first, because in his hussar's eyes Pierre was a rich civilian, the husband of a beauty, and generally an old woman; second, because Pierre, in his concentrated and absent-minded mood, had not recognized Rostov and had not responded to his bow. When they drank to the sovereign's health, Pierre, being deep in thought, did not rise or take his glass.

"What's with you?" Rostov shouted, looking at him with rapturously spiteful eyes. "Don't you hear: to the health of the sovereign emperor!" Pierre sighed, rose obediently, drank his glass, and, waiting for everyone to sit down, turned to Rostov with his kindly smile.

"And I just didn't recognize you," he said. But Rostov could not be bothered, he was shouting "Hurrah!"

"Why don't you renew your acquaintance?" Dolokhov said to Rostov.

"He's a fool, God help him," said Rostov.

"We must cheghrish the husbands of pghretty women," said Denisov.

Pierre did not hear what they were saying, but he knew it was about him. He blushed and turned away.

"Well, now to the health of beautiful women," said Dolokhov, and with a serious expression, but with a smile at the corners of his mouth, he turned to Pierre, glass in hand. "To the health of beautiful women, Petrusha, and of their lovers," he said.

Pierre, his eyes lowered, drank from his glass without looking at Dolokhov or answering him. The servant who was handing out Kutuzov's cantata laid a sheet before Pierre, as one of the more honoured guests. Pierre was about to pick it up, but Dolokhov leaned across, snatched it from his hand, and began to read it. Pierre looked at Dolokhov, the pupils of his eyes sank: the something terrible and ugly that had sickened him during dinner rose up and took possession of him. He leaned his entire corpulent body across the table.

"Don't you dare take it!" he cried.

Hearing this cry and seeing to whom it was addressed, Nesvitsky and Pierre's neighbour on the right turned fearfully and hastily to Bezukhov.

"Enough, enough, what's wrong?" frightened voices whispered. Dolokhov looked at Pierre with his light, merry, cruel eyes, and with the same smile, as if saying: "Ah, this is what I like."

"I won't give it to you," he said distinctly.

Pale, his lip trembling, Pierre tore at the page.

"You . . . you . . . are a scoundrel! . . . I challenge you!" he said and, having moved his chair back, he got up from the table. The very second he did so and uttered those words, he felt that the question of his wife's guilt, which had tormented him all that past day, was definitively and indubitably resolved in the affirmative. He hated her and was severed from her for ever. In spite of Denisov's pleas that Rostov not get involved in the affair, Rostov agreed to be Dolokhov's second, and after dinner talked over the conditions of the duel with Nesvitsky, Bezukhov's second. Pierre went home, and Rostov sat in the club with Dolokhov and Denisov till late in the evening, listening to the Gypsies and the singers.

"So, till tomorrow in Sokolniki," said Dolokhov, taking leave of Rostov on the porch of the club.

"And you're calm?" asked Rostov.

Dolokhov stopped.

"Look, I'll reveal to you in two words the whole secret of a duel. If you're going to a duel, and you write your will and tender letters to your parents, if you think you may be killed, you're a fool and are certainly lost; you should go with the firm intention of killing him as quickly and certainly as possible; then everything's in good order, as our bear hunter in Kostroma used to say. 'How can you not be afraid of a bear?' he'd say. 'But once you see him, your fear goes away, except of letting him escape!' Well, that's how I am. *À demain, mon cher.*" *

The next day, at eight o'clock in the morning, Pierre and Nesvitsky arrived at the Sokolniki woods and found Dolokhov, Denisov, and Rostov already there. Pierre had the look of a man occupied with some considerations of no concern to the present affair. His pinched face was yellow. He obviously had not slept that night. He looked around absent-mindedly and winced as if from the bright sun. Two considerations occupied him exclusively: the guilt of his wife, of which, after the sleepless night, not the least doubt remained; and the innocence of Dolokhov, who had no reason whatever to preserve the honour of a man who was a stranger to him. "Maybe I would have done the same thing in his place," thought Pierre. "I even certainly would have done the same thing. Why this duel, this murder? Either I'll kill him, or he'll hit me in the head, in the elbow, in the knee. Leave here, run away, bury myself some-where," came to his head. But precisely in the moments when such thoughts came to him, he, with that especially calm and absent-minded air, which inspired respect in those who looked at him, would ask: "Will it be soon, are we ready?"

When everything was ready, the swords stuck in the snow to mark the bar-rier to which they had to walk, and the pistols loaded, Nesvitsky came over to Pierre.

"I would not be fulfilling my duty, Count," he said in a timid voice, "and would not justify the trust and honour you have shown me by choosing me as your second, if I did not tell you the whole truth at this important, this very important, moment. I think this affair has no sufficient grounds and is not worth shedding blood over . . . You were wrong, you lost your temper . . ."

"Ah, yes, terribly stupid . . ." said Pierre.

"Then allow me to convey your regrets, and I'm certain that our adversaries will agree to accept your apology," said Nesvitsky (like the other partici-pants in the affair, and like everyone in similar affairs, not believing that things would go so far as an actual duel). "You know, Count, it's much more noble to acknowledge your mistake than to bring the matter to a point beyond repair . . . There was no offence on either side. Allow me to talk it over . . ."

"No, what is there to talk about!" said Pierre. "It makes no difference . . . So, are we ready?" he added. "Only tell me, where am I to go and where am I to shoot?" he said with an unnaturally meek smile. He took the pistol in his hands and began asking how to pull the trigger, because until then he had never

---

* Till tomorrow, my dear.

handled a pistol, something he did not want to admit. "Ah, yes, like that, I know, I just forgot," he said.

"No apologies, decidedly nothing," Dolokhov replied to Denisov, who for his part also made an attempt at reconciliation, and he also walked to the designated place.

The place chosen for the duel was some eighty paces off the road, where the sleighs had been left, in a small clearing in the pine woods, covered with snow wet from the thaw that had set in over the last few days. The adversaries stood some forty paces from each other, at the edges of the clearing. Nesvitsky and Denisov, measuring out the paces, left tracks imprinted in the deep, wet snow from the places where they were standing to their swords, marking the barrier and stuck into the ground ten paces apart. The thaw and the fog persisted; at a distance of forty paces they could not see each other clearly. In three minutes all was ready, and still they were slow to begin. Everyone was silent.

V

"Well, begin!" said Dolokhov.

"Let's," said Pierre, with the same smile.

It was becoming frightening. It was obvious that the affair, having begun so lightly, could no longer be prevented by anything, that it was going on by itself, independently of men's will, and would be accomplished. Denisov first went to the barrier and announced:

"Since the adversaghries have ghrefused a ghreconciliation, kindly begin: take your pistols and at the word thghree start walking towards each other."

"O-one! Two! Thghree! . . ." Denisov cried out angrily and stepped aside. The two men began walking over the imprinted tracks, getting closer and closer, and recognizing each other in the fog. The adversaries had the right to fire at any time while coming to the barrier. Dolokhov walked slowly, without raising his pistol, his light, shining blue eyes peering into his adversary's face. On his mouth there was, as usual, the semblance of a smile.

At the word *three*, Pierre walked forward with quick steps, getting off the beaten track and stepping into the untouched snow. Pierre stretched his arm out and held the pistol as if he was afraid of killing himself with it. He carefully put his left hand behind him, because he would have liked to support his right hand with it, and he knew that was not allowed. Having gone some six paces and veered off the track into the snow, Pierre looked down at his feet, again gave a quick glance at Dolokhov, and, pulling his finger as he had been taught, fired. Never expecting such a loud noise, Pierre gave a start, then smiled at his own impression and stood still. The smoke, especially thick because of the fog, at first prevented him from seeing anything; but the other shot he was expecting did not follow. All he could hear were Dolokhov's hurrying steps; then his figure appeared through the smoke. He was holding one hand to his left side, the other clutched his lowered pistol. His face was pale. Rostov ran over and said something to him.

"N-no," Dolokhov said through his teeth, "no, it's not over," and, taking several more dipping, hobbling steps to the sword, he fell on the snow beside it. His left hand was bloody; he wiped it on his coat and propped himself up with it. His face was pale, frowning, and trembled.

"Kind . . ." Dolokhov began but could not get the word out, "kindly," he finished with effort. Pierre, barely holding back his sobs, ran towards Dolokhov and was about to cross the space separating the barriers when Dolokhov cried: "To the barrier!" And Pierre, realizing what it was about, stopped at his sword. Only ten paces separated them. Dolokhov lowered his head to the snow, bit at it greedily, raised his head again, pulled himself together, tucked his legs under, and sat up, trying to find a steady point of balance. He filled his mouth with cold snow and sucked on it; his lips trembled, but went on smiling; his eyes glittered with the effort and the anger of a last summoning of strength. He raised his pistol and began to take aim.

"Turn, cover yourself with the pistol," said Nesvitsky.

"Cover youghrself!" even Denisov could not help crying to his adversary.

Pierre, with a meek smile of pity and regret, his legs and arms spread helplessly, his broad chest exposed, stood before Dolokhov and looked at him sorrowfully. Denisov, Rostov, and Nesvitsky closed their eyes. The shot and Dolokhov's angry cry came simultaneously.

"Missed!" cried Dolokhov, and, strengthless, he sprawled face down on the snow. Pierre clutched his head and, turning round, walked off towards the woods, treading on the untouched snow and mouthing incoherent words aloud.

"Stupid . . . stupid! Death . . . lies . . . ," he repeated, wincing. Nesvitsky stopped him and took him home.

Rostov and Denisov drove off with the wounded Dolokhov.

Dolokhov, silent, his eyes closed, lay in the sleigh and did not answer a word to the questions they put to him; but as they entered Moscow, he suddenly came to and, raising his head with difficulty, took the hand of Rostov, who was sitting next to him. Rostov was struck by the totally altered, unexpectedly and rapturously tender expression on Dolokhov's face.

"Well, so? how do you feel?" asked Rostov.

"Rotten! but that's not the point. My friend," said Dolokhov in a halting voice, "where are we? We're in Moscow, I know. Never mind me, but I've killed her, killed . . . She won't survive it. She won't survive . . ."

"Who?" asked Rostov.

"My mother. My mother, my angel, my adored angel, my mother." And

Dolokhov wept, pressing Rostov's hand. When he had calmed down a little, he explained to Rostov that he lived with his mother, that if his mother saw him dying, she wouldn't survive it. He begged Rostov to go and prepare her.

Rostov went on ahead to carry out his errand, and, to his great surprise, discovered that Dolokhov, this rowdy duellist, lived in Moscow with his old mother and hunchbacked sister, and was a most affectionate son and brother.

VI

Of late Pierre had rarely seen his wife alone. Both in Petersburg and in Moscow, their house was constantly full of guests. The night after the duel, he did not go to his bedroom, but remained, as he often did, in his father's enormous study, the same in which old Count Bezukhov had died. Tormenting as the inner work of the previous sleepless night had been, still more tormenting work was beginning now.

He lay down on the sofa and wanted to fall asleep in order to forget all that had happened to him, but he could not do it. Such a storm of feelings, thoughts, and memories suddenly arose in his soul that he not only could not sleep, but could not stay in place and had to jump up from the sofa and pace the room with quick steps. Now he pictured her in the initial time of their marriage, with bared shoulders and weary, passionate eyes, and at once beside her he pictured Dolokhov's handsome, insolent, and firmly mocking face, as it had been at the dinner, and the same face of Dolokhov, pale, trembling, and suffering, as it had been when he turned and fell on the snow.

"What has happened?" he asked himself. "I killed a *lover,* yes, I killed my wife's lover. Yes, it happened. Why? How did I come to that?" "Because you married her," an inner voice answered.

"But what am I to blame for?" he asked. "For having married her without loving her, for deceiving both myself and her," and he vividly pictured that moment after supper at Prince Vassily's, when he had spoken those words: *"Je vous aime,"* which had refused to come out of him. "It's all because of that! I felt then, too," he thought, "I felt then that it was wrong, that I had no right to it. And so it turned out." He recalled their honeymoon and blushed at the recollection. Especially vivid, insulting, and shameful for him was the recollection of how once, soon after his marriage, he had come from his bedroom to his study, before noon, wearing a silk dressing gown, and in his study had found his head steward, who bowed respectfully, looked at Pierre's face, at his dressing gown, and smiled slightly, as if expressing with this smile a respectful sympathy for his employer's happiness.

"And how many times I felt proud of her," he thought, "proud of her majestic beauty, her worldly tact; proud of my house, in which she received all

Petersburg, proud of her inaccessibility and beauty. So this is what I was proud of?! I thought then that I didn't understand her. How often, pondering her character, I said to myself that I was to blame, that I didn't understand her, didn't understand that eternal calm, contentment, and lack of any predilections and desires, and the whole answer was in this terrible word, that she is a depraved woman: I said this terrible word to myself, and everything became clear!

"Anatole would come to borrow money from her and would kiss her bare shoulders. She didn't give him the money, but allowed him to kiss her. Her father, joking, tried to arouse her jealousy; she said with a calm smile that she was not so stupid as to be jealous: he can do as he likes, she said of me. I asked her once whether she felt any signs of pregnancy. She laughed scornfully and said she was not such a fool as to want to have children, and that she would not have children from *me*."

Then he recalled the clarity and coarseness of thought and the vulgarity of expression typical of her, despite her upbringing in high aristocratic circles. "I'm not such a fool . . . go and give it a try . . . *allez vous promener*"* she used to say. Often, looking at her success in the eyes of old and young men and women, Pierre could not understand why he did not love her. "And I never loved her," Pierre said to himself. "I knew she was a depraved woman," he repeated, "but I didn't dare admit it to myself."

"And now Dolokhov—sitting on the snow, with a forced smile, maybe dying, and responding to my regret with some sort of swagger!"

Pierre was one of those people who, despite their ostensible weakness of character, as it is called, do not seek to confide their grief. He worked over his grief alone with himself.

"She, she alone is to blame for everything, everything," he said to himself. "But what of it? Why did I bind myself to her, why did I say that *'Je vous aime'* to her, which was a lie, and still worse than a lie," he said to himself. "I'm to blame and I must bear . . . But what? The disgrace to my name, the unhappiness of my life? Eh, it's all nonsense," he thought, "the disgrace to my name and honour—it's all a convention, it's all independent of me."

"Louis XVI was executed for being, as *they* said, dishonest and criminal," came into Pierre's head, "and they were right from their point of view, and equally right were those who died a martyr's death for him and counted him among the saints. Then Robespierre[11] was executed because he was a despot. Who's right, and who's wrong? No one. You're alive—so live: tomorrow you'll die, just as I could have died an hour ago. And is it worth suffering, when there's only a second left to live compared with eternity?" But the moment he considered himself comforted by this sort of reasoning, he suddenly pictured

---

*Get lost.

her in those moments when he had shown her his insincere love most intensely, and he felt the blood rush to his heart, and he had to get up again and move about, and break and tear things that happened to be within his reach. "Why did I say '*Je vous aime*' to her?" he kept repeating to himself. And, having repeated this question for the tenth time, Moliere's *mais que diable allait-il faire dans cette galère?*[*12] came to his head, and he laughed at himself.

In the night he called his valet and told him to pack up to go to Petersburg. He could not remain under the same roof with her. He could not imagine how he was going to speak to her now. He decided that he would go the next day and leave her a letter in which he would announce his intention to part with her for ever.

In the morning, when the valet came into his study bringing coffee, Pierre was lying asleep on the sofa with an open book in his hand.

He woke up and looked around fearfully for a long time, unable to understand where he was.

"The countess told me to ask whether Your Excellency is at home," said the valet.

But before Pierre decided on what answer he would give, the countess herself, in a white satin dressing gown embroidered with silver, and with her hair done up simply (two enormous braids wound twice round her lovely head *en diadème*), came into the room calmly and majestically; only there was a wrinkle of wrath on her marble and slightly prominent forehead. With her all-enduring calm, she refrained from speaking in front of the valet. She knew about the duel and had come to talk about it. She waited until the valet set down the coffee and went out. Pierre looked at her timidly through his spectacles and, as a hare surrounded by hounds presses its ears back and goes on sitting in full view of its enemies, so he attempted to go on reading; but he felt that it was senseless and impossible, and again glanced at her timidly. She did not sit down and looked at him with a contemptuous smile, waiting for the valet to leave.

"What is this? What have you done, I ask you?" she said sternly.

"I? . . . what? I . . ." said Pierre.

"What a brave fellow we've got here! Well, answer, what is this duel? What did you want to prove by it? What, I ask you." Pierre shifted heavily on the sofa, opened his mouth, but could not answer.

"Since you don't answer, I'll tell you . . ." Hélène went on. "You believe everything you're told. You were told . . ." Hélène laughed, "that Dolokhov is my lover," she said in French, with her coarse precision of speech, pronouncing the word *lover* like any other word, "and you believed it! But what did you prove by it? What did you prove by this duel? That you're a fool, *que vous êtes*

*But what the devil was he going to do in that galley [i.e., did he get into that mess for]?

un sot; everybody knew that anyway. What will it lead to? That I will become the laughing-stock of all Moscow; that everyone will say that you, in a drunken state, forgetting yourself, challenged to a duel a man of whom you were groundlessly jealous," Hélène raised her voice and became more and more inspired, "and who is better than you in all respects . . ."

"Hm . . . hm . . ." Pierre grunted, without looking at her or stirring any limb of his body.

"And why should you believe that he is my lover? . . . Why? Because I like his company? If you were more intelligent and agreeable, I'd prefer yours."

"Don't speak to me . . . I beg you," Pierre whispered hoarsely.

"Why shouldn't I speak! I can speak, and I'll say boldly that there are few wives who wouldn't take lovers *(des amants)* with a husband like you, but I didn't do that," she said. Pierre wanted to say something, gave her a strange look, the expression of which she did not understand, and lay back again. He was suffering physically at that moment: there was a tightness in his chest, and he could not breathe. He knew he had to do something to stop this suffering, but what he wanted to do was too terrible.

"It's better for us to part," he said haltingly.

"We'll part, if you please, but only if you give me a fortune," said Hélène . . . "To part—how scary!"

Pierre jumped up from the sofa and, staggering, rushed at her.

"I'll kill you!" he shouted, and with a strength as yet unknown to him, he seized the marble slab from a table, took a step towards her, and swung.

Hélène's face became frightful; she shrieked and sprang away from him. His father's blood told in him. Pierre felt the enthusiasm and enchantment of rage. He threw down the slab, broke it, and, approaching Hélène with widespread arms, shouted "Out!" in such a frightful voice that everybody in the house was terrified on hearing this shout. God knows what Pierre would have done at that moment if Hélène had not run out of the room.

A week later Pierre gave his wife power of attorney for the management of all his estates in Great Russia,[13] which formed the major part of his fortune, and left alone for Petersburg.

VII

Two months had gone by since the news of the battle of Austerlitz and the loss of Prince Andrei was received at Bald Hills. And, despite all the letters sent through the embassy, despite all the searches, his body had not been found, nor was he among the prisoners. Worst of all for his family was that there still remained a hope that he had been picked up by the local populace on the battlefield and might be lying somewhere recovering or dying alone, among strangers, unable to send news of himself. In the newspapers, from which the old prince had first learned of the defeat at Austerlitz, it was written, as usual, quite briefly and indefinitely, that, after brilliant battles, the Russians had been forced to retreat, and that the retreat had been carried out in perfect order. From this official report the old prince understood that the Russians had been defeated. A week after the newspapers brought news of the battle of Austerlitz came a letter from Kutuzov, which informed the prince of the fate that had befallen his son.

"Before my eyes," wrote Kutuzov, "your son, with a standard in his hands, at the head of a regiment, fell as a hero worthy of his father and his fatherland. To the general regret of myself and the entire army, it is still unknown whether he is alive or not. I flatter myself and you with the hope that your son is alive, for otherwise he would be among the officers found on the battlefield and his name would be on the list given me by the peace envoys."

Having received this news late in the evening, when he was alone in his study, the old prince did not say anything to anyone. As usual, the next day he went for his morning walk; but he was silent with the steward, the gardener, and the architect, and though he looked angry, he said nothing to anyone.

When Princess Marya came into his study at the usual time, he was standing and working at his lathe, but, as usual, did not turn to her.

"Ah! Princess Marya!" he suddenly said unnaturally and threw down his chisel. (The wheel went on turning by inertia. Princess Marya long remembered the dying creak of the wheel, which merged for her with what followed after.)

Princess Marya moved towards him, saw his face, and something suddenly sank inside her. Her eyes ceased to see clearly. By her father's face, not sad, not crushed, but angry and working itself unnaturally, she could see that there, there above her, hanging over her and crushing her, was a terrible misfortune, the worst misfortune in life, one she had not yet experienced, an irreparable, inconceivable misfortune—the death of a loved one.

"*Mon père—André?*" said the graceless, awkward princess, with such an inexpressible loveliness of sorrow and self-forgetfulness that her father could not endure her gaze and, sobbing, turned away.

"I've received news. He's not among the prisoners, and not among the dead. Kutuzov writes," he cried shrilly, as if wishing to drive the princess away with this cry, "he's been killed!"

The princess did not fall, did not feel faint. She had been pale to begin with, but when she heard these words, her face changed and something lit up in her luminous, beautiful eyes. It was as if joy, the supreme joy, independent of the sorrows and joys of this world, poured over the deep sorrow that was in her. She forgot all her fear of her father, went up to him, took him by the hand, pulled him to her, and embraced his dry, sinewy neck.

"*Mon père,*" she said. "Don't turn away from me, let's weep together."

"Villains! Scoundrels!" cried the old man, pulling his face away from her. "To destroy an army, to destroy men! Why? Go, go and tell Liza."

The princess sank strengthlessly into the armchair next to her father and wept. She now saw her brother at the moment when he had taken leave of her and Liza, with his tender and at the same time arrogant air, saw him at the moment when, tenderly and mockingly, he had put on the little icon. "Did he believe? Did he repent of his unbelief? Was he now there? There, in the place of eternal rest and bliss?" she wondered.

"*Mon père,* tell me how it happened?" she asked through her tears.

"Go, go; he was killed in a battle, into which they led the best of Russian men and Russian glory to be killed. Go, Princess Marya. Go and tell Liza. I'll come."

When Princess Marya came back from her father, the little princess was sitting over her work, and she looked at Princess Marya with that special expression of an inward and happily serene gaze that only pregnant women have. It was clear that she did not see Princess Marya, but was looking deep inside herself—into something happy and mysterious that was being accomplished in her.

"Marie," she said, leaving the embroidery frame and throwing herself backwards, "give me your hand." She took the princess's hand and placed it on her belly.

Her eyes were smiling in expectation, her little lip with its moustache rose and remained raised in a childishly happy way.

Princess Marya knelt before her and hid her face in the folds of her sister-in-law's dress.

"There, there—do you feel it? It's so strange. And you know, Marie, I'll love him very much," said Liza, looking at her sister-in-law with shining, happy eyes. Princess Marya could not raise her head: she was weeping.

"What's the matter, Masha?"

"Never mind . . . I just feel sad . . . sad about Andrei," she said, wiping her tears on her sister-in-law's knees. Several times in the course of the morning Princess Marya began to prepare her sister-in-law, and each time she began to weep. These tears, the reason for which the little princess did not understand, alarmed her, though she was little attentive. She did not say anything, but glanced around anxiously, as if looking for something. Before dinner the old prince, whom she had always been afraid of, came into her room, now with an especially uneasy, angry face, and left without saying a word. She looked at Princess Marya, then became thoughtful, with that expression of inward attention that pregnant women have, and suddenly began to cry.

"Have you received something from Andrei?" she asked.

"No, you know it's still too early for any news, but *mon père* worries, and I'm frightened."

"So there's nothing?"

"Nothing," said Princess Marya, looking firmly at her sister-in-law with her luminous eyes. She had decided not to tell her and persuaded her father to conceal the terrible news from her sister-in-law until her delivery, which was expected any day. Princess Marya and the old prince, in their own ways, bore with the grief and concealed it. The old prince did not want to hope: he decided that Prince Andrei had been killed, and though he sent an official to Austria to look for his son's traces, he ordered a gravestone for him in Moscow, which he intended to put in his garden, and told everyone that his son had been killed. He tried to go on with his old way of life unchanged, but his strength failed him: he walked less, ate less, slept less, and grew weaker every day. Princess Marya went on hoping. She prayed for her brother as for one of the living,[14] and expected news of his return any moment.

VIII

"*Ma bonne amie,*" the little princess said on the morning of the nineteenth of March, and her moustached little lip rose by old habit; but as, ever since the day the terrible news had been received, there had been sorrow not only in the smiles, but in the sounds of talk, even in the footsteps in that house, so now the smile of the little princess, who had succumbed to the general mood—though she did not know its cause—was such that it was all the more a reminder of the general sorrow.

"*Ma bonne amie, je crains que le fruschtique (comme dit* Foka, the cook) *de ce matin ne m'aie pas fait du mal.*"*

"What's the matter, darling? You're pale. Ah, you're very pale," Princess Marya said fearfully, rushing to her sister-in-law with her heavy, soft steps.

"Your Excellency, shouldn't we send for Marya Bogdanovna?" asked one of the maids. (Marya Bogdanovna was a midwife from the provincial capital, who had already been living at Bald Hills for over a week.)

"Indeed," Princess Marya picked up, "you may be right. I'll go. *Courage, mon ange!*"† She kissed Liza and was about to leave the room.

"Ah, no, no!"—and besides the paleness, the face of the little princess showed a childish fear of unavoidable physical suffering.

---

*My good friend, I'm afraid this morning's fruschtique (as *Foka the cook* says [breakfast]) may have made me sick.
†Courage, my angel!

"Non, c'est l'estomac . . . dites que c'est l'estomac, dites, Marie, dites . . ."*
And the princess wept with a capricious child's suffering, even shamming
somewhat, wringing her little hands. The princess ran out of the room to fetch
Marya Bogdanovna.

"Oh! Mon dieu! Mon dieu!" she heard behind her.

The midwife was already coming to meet her, with a significantly calm face,
rubbing her small, plump, white hands.

"Marya Bogdanovna! It seems it's begun," said Princess Marya, looking at
the midwife with frightened, wide-open eyes.

"Well, thank God, Princess," Marya Bogdanovna said, without quickening
her pace. "You young girls oughtn't to know about these things."

"But the doctor hasn't come from Moscow yet," said the princess. (At the
wishes of Liza and Prince Andrei, they had sent to Moscow in due time for an
accoucheur, and he was expected at any moment.)

"Never mind, Princess, don't worry," said Marya Bogdanovna, "everything
will be fine without the doctor."

Five minutes later, in her rooms, the princess heard something heavy being
carried. She peeked out—the servants were for some reason carrying a leather
sofa that had been in Prince Andrei's study. There was something solemn and
quiet in the carriers' faces.

Princess Marya sat alone in her room, listening to the noises in the house,
opening her door from time to time when someone passed by, and watching
over what was happening in the corridor. Several women passed back and
forth there with soft steps, glanced at the princess, and turned away from her.
She did not dare ask anything, closed her door, returned to her room, and now
sat in her armchair, now took her prayer book, now knelt before the icons.
Unfortunately, and to her astonishment, she felt that prayer did not calm her
agitation. Suddenly the door to her room opened quietly, and her old nanny
Praskovya Savishna, who hardly ever came to her room, because the old prince
forbade it, appeared in the doorway, her head bound with a kerchief.

"I've come to sit with you, Mashenka," said the nanny, "and here I've
brought the prince's wedding candles[15] to light before the saint, my angel," she
said, sighing.

"Ah, I'm so glad, nanny."

"God is merciful, dear heart." The nanny lit the gold-decorated candles in
front of the icon stand and sat down by the door with her knitting. Princess
Marya took a book and began to read. Only when steps or voices were heard,
they looked at each other, the princess fearfully, questioningly, and the nanny
soothingly. The same feeling that Princess Marya was experiencing as she sat in
her room came over everyone and spread to all ends of the house. Following

*No, it's my stomach . . . tell her it's my stomach, tell her, Marya, tell her . . .

the belief that the less people know about the suffering of a woman in labour, the less she suffers, everyone tried to pretend they knew nothing; no one spoke of it, but, apart from the usual staidness and respectfulness of good manners that prevailed in the prince's house, one could see a sort of general concern, a softness of heart, and the awareness of something great, inconceivable, that was being accomplished at that moment.

No laughter was heard in the big maids' room. In the footmen's quarters the men all sat silently, ready for something. The caretakers did not sleep and had splinters and candles burning. The old prince paced his study, stepping on his heels, and sent Tikhon to Marya Bogdanovna to ask what news.

"Just say the prince told me to ask what news. And come and tell me what she says."

"Tell the prince that labour has begun," said Marya Bogdanovna, glancing significantly at the messenger. Tikhon went and told him.

"Very well," said the prince, closing the door behind him, and Tikhon did not hear the least sound from the study after that. A little later, Tikhon went into the study as if to tend to the candles. Seeing the prince lying on the sofa, Tikhon looked at him, at his upset face, shook his head, silently went over to him, kissed him on the shoulder, and went out without tending to the candles or saying why he had come. The mystery, the most solemn in the world, continued to be accomplished. Evening passed, night came. And the feeling of expectation and of the heart's softness before the inconceivable did not diminish, but heightened. No one slept.

It was one of those March nights when it is as if winter wants to claim its own back and with desperate malice pours out its last snows and storms. The German doctor from Moscow was expected any moment, a carriage had been sent for him to the turning from the highway to the country road, and mounted men with lanterns went to lead him along the bumpy and muddy road.

Princess Marya had long ago abandoned her book: she was sitting silently, her luminous eyes fixed on her nanny's wrinkled face, familiar to her in the smallest detail: on the lock of grey hair that strayed from under her kerchief, at the little pouch of skin that hung under her chin.

The nanny Savishna, holding her knitting, was telling in a low voice, herself not hearing or understanding the words, the story she had told a hundred times, about how the late princess had given birth to Princess Marya in Kishinev, with a Moldavian peasant woman instead of a midwife.

"With God's mercy, there's no need for any dokhturs," she said. Suddenly a gust of wind blew open the poorly latched window (at the prince's behest, with the coming of the larks, one frame of the double windows was removed in each room), sent the heavy silk curtain fluttering, blew in cold and snow, and put out the candle. Princess Marya shuddered; the nanny set her knitting down, went to the window, leaned out, and began snatching at the open window frame. Cold wind blew about the ends of her kerchief and her stray locks of grey hair.

"Princess, dearest, somebody's driving down the avenue!" she said, holding the frame and not closing it. "With lanterns. Must be the dokhtur."

"Ah, my God! Thank God!" said Princess Marya. "I must go and meet him; he doesn't know Russian."

Princess Marya threw on her shawl and ran to meet the arrivals. As she went down the hall, she saw through the window a carriage with lanterns standing by the porch. She went out to the stairs. A tallow candle stood on a baluster, melting in the wind. The servant Filipp, with an alarmed face and holding another candle, stood below on the first landing of the stairs. Still lower, around the turning of the stairs, footsteps in warm boots could be heard. And a voice that seemed familiar to Princess Marya was saying something.

"Thank God!" said the voice. "And father?"

"Gone to bed," replied the voice of the butler Demyan, who was already downstairs.

Then the voice said something else, Demyan made some reply, and the footsteps in warm boots began to approach more quickly the invisible turning of the stairs. "It's Andrei!" thought Princess Marya. "No, it can't be, it would be too extraordinary," she thought, and the moment she thought it, the face and figure of Prince Andrei, in a fur coat with a snow-sprinkled collar, appeared on the landing where the servant stood with a candle. Yes, it was he, but pale and thin, with a changed, strangely softened, but anxious expression on his face. He came up the stairs and embraced his sister.

"You didn't get my letter?" he asked, and, not waiting for an answer, which he would not have received, because the princess was unable to speak, he went back and, together with the accoucheur, who came in behind him (they had met at the last posting station), came upstairs again with quick steps, and again embraced his sister.

"What fate!" he said. "Masha, dear!" And, throwing off his fur coat and boots, he went to his wife's rooms.

IX

The little princess lay propped on pillows, in a white cap (her suffering had just eased), locks of her black hair curled round her inflamed, sweaty cheeks; her rosy, lovely little mouth with its little lip covered with fine black hair was open, and she was smiling joyfully. Prince Andrei came into the room and stopped before her, at the foot of the sofa on which she was lying. Her glittering eyes, looking childishly frightened and anxious, rested on him without changing expression. "I love you all, I did no harm to anyone, why am I suffering? Help me," her expression said. She saw her husband, but did not understand the meaning of his appearance before her. Prince Andrei went round the sofa and kissed her on the forehead.

"My darling!" he spoke words he had never said to her before. "God is merciful . . ." She looked at him questioningly with childlike reproach.

"I expected help from you, and there's nothing, nothing—you, too!" said her eyes. She was not surprised that he had come; she did not understand that he had come. His coming had no relation to her suffering and its relief. The pain started again, and Marya Bogdanovna advised Prince Andrei to leave the room.

The accoucheur came in. Prince Andrei left, and, meeting Princess Marya, went up to her again. They spoke in whispers, but the conversation stopped every other minute. They waited and listened.

"*Allez, mon ami,*"* said Princess Marya. Prince Andrei went to his wife again and sat in the next room waiting. Some woman came out of the room with a frightened face and became embarrassed on seeing Prince Andrei. He covered his face with his hands and sat that way for several minutes. Pitiful, helplessly animal moans came from behind the door. Prince Andrei got up, went to the door, and wanted to open it. Someone was holding the door.

"You mustn't, you mustn't!" a frightened voice said from inside. He started pacing the room. The cries ceased, another few seconds went by. Suddenly a terrible cry—not her cry, she could not cry like that—came from the next room. Prince Andrei rushed to the door; the cry ceased, but another cry was heard, a baby's cry.

"Why did they bring a baby there?" was Prince Andrei's first thought. "A baby? What baby? . . . Why is he there? Or has a baby been born?"

When he suddenly realized all the joyful meaning of that cry, tears choked him and, leaning both elbows on the windowsill, he wept, sobbing, as children weep. The door opened. The doctor, his shirtsleeves rolled up, without his frock coat, pale, his jaw trembling, came out of the room. Prince Andrei turned to him, but the doctor gave him a bewildered look and passed by without saying a word. A woman ran out, and, seeing Prince Andrei, hesitated in the doorway. He went into his wife's room. She lay dead in the same position in which he had seen her five minutes before, and, despite her still eyes and pale cheeks, there was the same expression on that lovely, timid, childish face, with its lip covered with fine black hair.

"I loved you all and did nothing bad to anybody, and what have you done to me? Ah, what have you done to me?" said her lovely, pitiful, dead face. In the

*Go, my friend.

corner, something small and red snorted and squealed in Marya Bogdanovna's white, trembling hands.

Two hours after that, Prince Andrei went into his father's study with quiet steps. The old man already knew everything. He was standing just by the door, and as soon as it opened, the old man silently embraced his son's neck with his old, tough arms, as in a vise, and burst into sobs like a child.

Three days later the funeral service was held for the little princess, and, in bidding farewell to her, Prince Andrei went up the steps to the coffin. She had the same face in the coffin, though her eyes were closed. "Ah, what have you done to me?" it kept saying, and Prince Andrei felt that something snapped in his soul, that he was to blame for something he could neither set aright nor forget. He was unable to weep. The old man also came and kissed her waxen little hand, which lay calmly over the other hand, and to him her face also said: "Ah, what is it that you have done to me and why?" And the old man turned angrily away on seeing that face.

After another five days, the young prince Nikolai Andreich was baptized. The foster mother held the swaddling clothes up with her chin, while the priest anointed the boy's wrinkled red palms and feet with a goose feather.

The godfather—his grandfather—in fear of dropping him, shook as he carried the infant round the dented tin baptismal font, and then handed him to his godmother, Princess Marya. Prince Andrei, his heart sinking for fear they would drown the baby, sat in another room, waiting for the sacrament to be over. He looked joyfully at the baby when the nanny brought him out to him and nodded approvingly when the nanny told him that, when thrown into the font, the piece of wax with the baby's hair had not sunk, but had floated in the font.[16]

X

Rostov's participation in the duel between Dolokhov and Bezukhov was hushed up through the efforts of the old count, and Rostov, instead of being demoted, as he expected, was appointed adjutant to the governor general of Moscow. As a result of that, he could not go to the country with the whole family, but remained in Moscow all summer with his new duties. Dolokhov recovered, and Rostov became especially close to him during the time of his convalescence. Dolokhov lay ill at his mother's, who loved him passionately and tenderly. Old Marya Ivanovna came to love Rostov for his friendship with Fedya, and often spoke with him about her son.

"Yes, Count," she used to say, "he's too noble and pure-hearted for the depraved world of our time. No one loves virtue, it's a sty in everyone's eye. Now tell me, Count, was it fair, was it honest on Bezukhov's part? Yet Fedya, in his nobility, loved him and never says anything bad about him even now. All that mischief with the policeman in Petersburg, some sort of fools' play, didn't they do it together? Why, nothing happened to Bezukhov, and Fedya had to bear it all on his shoulders! He's had to bear so much! Suppose they did restore him, but how could they not? I don't think there were so many brave sons of the fatherland like him there. And now—this duel. Do these people have any feeling, any honour? To challenge him to a duel, knowing he's an only son, and shoot straight at him! It's a good thing God was merciful to us. And for what? Who in our time doesn't have love affairs? Why, if he was so jealous—I can understand—then he should have let him feel it sooner, but no, it lasted a whole year. And so he challenged him to a duel, assuming that Fedya wouldn't fight because he owed him money. How mean! How vile! I know you've understood Fedya, my dear Count, that's why I love you from the heart, believe me. Few people understand him. He's such a lofty, heavenly soul . . ."

Dolokhov himself, during his convalescence, often spoke such words to Rostov as he could never have expected from him.

"People consider me a wicked man, I know," he used to say, "and let them. I don't care about anyone except those I love; but those I love, I love so much that I'd give my life for them, and the rest I'd crush if they stood in my way. I have an adored, a priceless mother, two or three friends, you among them, and to the rest I pay attention only insofar as they're useful or harmful. And almost all of them are harmful, especially women. Yes, my dear heart," he went on, "I have met loving, noble, lofty men; but I have never yet met any women who weren't bought—whether countesses or kitchen maids. I have never yet met that heavenly purity and faithfulness that I seek in a woman. If I had ever found such a woman, I would have given my life for her. But these! . . ." He made a gesture of contempt. "And believe me, if I still value my life, it's only because I still hope to meet the heavenly being who will resurrect, purify, and elevate me. But you don't understand that."

"No, I understand very well," replied Rostov, who was under the influence of his new friend.

In the autumn the Rostov family returned to Moscow. At the beginning of winter, Denisov also returned and stayed with the Rostovs. This early wintertime of 1806 that Nikolai Rostov spent in Moscow was one of the happiest and merriest for him and his whole family. Nikolai attracted many young men to his parents' house. Vera was a beautiful twenty-year-old girl; Sonya a sixteen-year-old, with all the loveliness of a just-opened flower; Natasha, half young lady, half child, now childishly funny, now girlishly bewitching.

At that time there was a special atmosphere of amorousness in the Rostovs' house, as happens in a house where there are very nice and very young girls. Every young man who came to the Rostovs' house, looking at these young, susceptible girlish faces, always smiling at something (probably their own happiness), at this lively rushing about, listening to this young female babble, incoherent, but affectionate towards everyone, ready for anything, filled with hope, listening to these incoherent noises, now of singing, now of music, experienced the same feeling of readiness for love and expectation of happiness that these young people of the Rostovs' house themselves experienced.

Among the young men introduced by Rostov, one of the first was Dolokhov, whom everyone in the house liked with the exception of Natasha. She almost quarrelled with her brother over Dolokhov. She insisted that he was a wicked man, that, in his duel with Bezukhov, Pierre had been right and Dolokhov wrong, that he was unpleasant and unnatural.

"There's nothing for me to understand!" Natasha cried with stubborn wilfulness. "He's wicked and unfeeling. I do like your Denisov, and he's a carouser and all that, but even so I like him, which means I understand. I don't know how to tell you; he has it all calculated, and I don't like that. But Denisov . . ."

"Well, Denisov's something else," replied Nikolai, making it clear that, compared with Dolokhov, even Denisov was nothing, "you should understand what a soul Dolokhov has, you should see him with his mother, he has such a heart!"

"Well, that I don't know, but I feel awkward with him. And do you know that he's in love with Sonya?"

"What silliness . . ."

"I'm certain, you'll see."

Natasha's prediction was proving true. Dolokhov, who did not like the society of women, began to frequent their house, and the question of whom he was doing it for was soon resolved (though no one spoke of it), in the sense that he was doing it for Sonya. And Sonya knew it, though she would never have dared to say it, and she flushed crimson every time Dolokhov appeared.

Dolokhov dined frequently with the Rostovs, never missed a play when they went, and attended the balls for *adolescentes** at Iogel's, where the Rostovs always went. He paid most attention to Sonya and looked at her with such eyes that not only was she unable to endure that gaze without turning red, but even the old countess and Natasha blushed when they noticed it.

---

*Adolescent girls.

It was clear that this strong, strange man was under the irresistible influence produced on him by this dark-haired, graceful girl who loved another.

Rostov noticed something new between Dolokhov and Sonya; but he did not define for himself what these new relations were. "They're all in love with somebody," he thought about Sonya and Natasha. But he now felt less at ease with Sonya and Dolokhov, and he began to stay away from home more often.

With the autumn of 1806, everyone again began talking about war with Napoleon,[17] with still greater ardour than the previous year. A recruitment was announced, not only of ten recruits, but of another nine fighting men per thousand. Bonapartius was anathematized everywhere, and around Moscow the only talk was of the impending war. For the Rostov family, all the interest of these preparations for war consisted only in the fact that Nikolushka absolutely refused to remain in Moscow and was simply waiting for the end of Denisov's leave in order to go with him to their regiment after the holidays. The impending departure not only did not hinder his merrymaking, but even encouraged it. He spent most of the time away from home, at dinners, evening parties, and balls.

XI

On the third day of Christmas, Nikolai dined at home, which had rarely happened with him recently. This was an official farewell dinner, because he and Denisov would be leaving for their regiment after Epiphany.[18] There were some twenty guests at dinner, Dolokhov and Denisov among them.

Never had the amorous air in the Rostovs' house, the atmosphere of being in love, manifested itself so strongly as during these festive days. "Seize the moments of happiness, make them love you, fall in love yourself! That is the only real thing in this world—the rest is all nonsense. And that is the one thing we're taken up with here," said this atmosphere.

Nikolai, as always, having exhausted two pairs of horses and still not having managed to get to all the places he had to go and to which he had been invited, came home just before dinner. As soon as he came in, he noticed and felt the intensity of the amorous atmosphere in the house; but besides that, he noticed a strange perplexity prevailing among certain members of the company. Sonya, Dolokhov, and the old countess were especially perplexed, and Natasha somewhat. Nikolai realized that something must have happened before dinner between Sonya and Dolokhov, and with a sensitivity of heart all his own, he treated them both very delicately and carefully during dinner. That same evening of the third day of the feast one of those balls was to take place that Iogel (a dancing master) gave during the holidays for all his pupils, boys and girls.

"Will you go to Iogel's, Nikolenka? Please do," Natasha said to him, "he has asked you specially, and Vassily Dmitrich (that is, Denisov) is going."

"I'll go anywhere the countess oghrders me to!" said Denisov, who had jokingly placed himself on the footing of Natasha's knight in the Rostovs' house. "I'm ghready to dance the *pas de châle*."*

"If I have time! I promised to be at the Arkharovs' soirée," said Nikolai. "And you? . . ." he turned to Dolokhov. And as soon as he asked it, he noticed that he should not have asked.

"Yes, perhaps . . ." Dolokhov answered coldly and angrily, glancing at Sonya, and, frowning, he glanced at Nikolai exactly as he had looked at Pierre during the club dinner.

"There's something here," thought Nikolai and, still more convinced of his conjecture by Dolokhov's departure right after dinner, he called Natasha out and asked what it was.

"And I've been looking for you," said Natasha, running out to him. "I kept saying it, and you refused to believe me," she said triumphantly. "He proposed to Sonya."

Little as Nikolai had been occupied with Sonya during that time, it was as if something snapped in him when he heard it. Dolokhov was a decent and in some respects a brilliant match for the dowerless orphan Sonya. From the point of view of the old countess and of society, it was impossible to refuse him. And therefore Nikolai's first feeling when he heard it was anger at Sonya. He was preparing to say: "Splendid, and of course she must forget her childish promises and accept the proposal"; but before he had time to say it . . .

"Can you imagine! She refused him, refused him altogether!" said Natasha. "She said she loved another," she added after a brief pause.

"Yes, my Sonya couldn't have acted otherwise!" thought Nikolai.

"No matter how much mama begged her, she refused, and I know she won't change once she's said something . . ."

"And mama begged her!" Nikolai said with reproach.

"Yes," said Natasha. "You see, Nikolenka, don't be angry, but I know you won't marry her. I know, God knows how, but I know for certain that you won't marry her."

"Well, that you really can't know," said Nikolai, "but I must speak with her. What a delight this Sonya is!" he added, smiling.

"She is a delight! I'll send her to you." And Natasha, having kissed her brother, ran off.

A moment later, Sonya came in, frightened, bewildered, and guilty. Nikolai went up to her and kissed her hand. It was the first time during his visit that they spoke alone and about their love.

*Shawl dance.

"Sophie," he said, timidly at first, then more and more boldly, "if you want to refuse not only a brilliant but an advantageous match; but he's a wonderful, noble man . . . he's my friend . . ."

Sonya interrupted him.

"I've already refused," she said hurriedly.

"If you've refused for my sake, I'm afraid I . . ."

Sonya interrupted him again. She looked at him with a pleading, frightened gaze.

"Nicolas, don't say that to me," she said.

"No, I must. Maybe it's *suffisance** on my part, but it's still better to say everything. If you refused for my sake, I must tell you the whole truth. I love you, I think, more than anyone . . ."

"That's enough for me," Sonya said, blushing.

"No, but I have fallen in love and will fall in love a thousand times, though I have no such feeling of friendship, trust, and love for anyone but you. Besides, I'm young. *Maman* doesn't want it. Well, simply, I don't promise anything. And I ask you to think about Dolokhov's proposal," he said, speaking his friend's name with difficulty.

"Don't say that to me. I don't want anything. I love you as a brother, and will love you always, and I need nothing more."

"You're an angel, I'm not worthy of you, only I'm afraid to deceive you." And Nikolai kissed her hand once more.

XII

The balls at Iogel's were the merriest in Moscow. Mothers said so, looking at their *adolescentes* performing their just-learned *pas;* the *adolescentes* and *adolescents* said so themselves, dancing until they dropped; grown-up girls and young men said so, who came to these balls thinking they were condescending and found the best of merriment in them. That year two matches were made at these balls. The two pretty Gorchakov princesses found fiancés and got married, and this added still more to the reputation of these balls. The particularity of these balls was that there was no host or hostess; there was the good-natured Iogel, scraping the parquet by all the rules of art, flitting about like a bit of down, receiving tickets for lessons from his pupils;[19] another thing was that only those came to these balls who wanted to dance and be merry, the way thirteen- and fourteen-year-old girls do, who put on long gowns for the first time. All of them, with rare exceptions, were or seemed pretty: so rapturously they smiled, so lit-up were their eyes. Sometimes the best girl pupils even

*Presumptuousness.

danced the *pas de châle*, and the best of them was Natasha, distinguished by her gracefulness; but at this last ball only the *écossaise* and the *anglaise* were danced, and the mazurka, which was just coming into fashion. Iogel rented the ballroom in Bezukhov's house, and the ball was very successful, as everyone said. There were many pretty girls, and the Rostov girls were among the best. They were both especially happy and gay that evening. Sonya, proud of Dolokhov's proposal, of her refusal, and of the talk with Nikolai, started twirling while she was still at home, not letting her maid do up her braids, and now she shone all through with impetuous joy.

Natasha, no less proud of wearing a long gown for the first time, at a real ball, was still happier. The two girls wore white muslin gowns with pink ribbons.

Natasha fell in love from the moment she entered the ballroom. She was not in love with anyone in particular, but with everyone. She fell in love with whomever she looked at, the moment she looked at him.

"Ah, how nice!" she kept saying, running to Sonya.

Nikolai and Denisov walked around the rooms, looking at the dancers benignly and patronizingly.

"How pghretty she is, she'll be a beauty," said Denisov.

"Who?"

"Countess Natasha," replied Denisov. "And how well she dances, what ghrace!" he said again, after some silence.

"Who are you talking about?"

"Your sister," Denisov cried angrily.

Rostov smiled.

"*Mon cher comte, vous êtes l'un de mes meilleurs écoliers, il faut que vous dansiez,*" said little Iogel, coming over to Nikolai. "*Voyez combien de jolies demoiselles.*"* He turned with the same request to Denisov, who was also his former pupil.

"*Non, mon cher, je ferai tapisserie,*"† said Denisov. "Don't you remember what poor use I made of your lessons?"

"Oh, no!" Iogel hastened to reassure him. "You were merely inattentive, but you had the ability, yes, you had the ability."

They began to play the newly fashionable mazurka. Nikolai could not refuse Iogel and asked Sonya to dance. Denisov sat down with the old ladies, and, his elbow propped on his sabre, his foot beating time, told some merry story and made the old ladies laugh, while glancing at the dancing young people. Iogel danced in the lead couple with Natasha, his pride and his best pupil. Moving

---

*My dear Count, you are one of my best pupils. You should be dancing . . . Look at all the pretty young ladies.

†No, my dear, I'll sit it out.

his feet softly, delicately, in his little boots, Iogel flew down the ballroom with Natasha, who timidly but carefully performed her *pas*. Denisov's eyes were fixed on her, and he beat time with an air which said clearly that he was not dancing himself only because he did not want to, not because he could not. In the middle of a figure, he called out to Rostov, who was just passing by.

"That's not it at all," he said. "Is that a Polish mazughrka? But she dances splendidly."

Knowing that Denisov was famous even in Poland for his skill in dancing the Polish mazurka, Nikolai ran over to Natasha.

"Go and choose Denisov. You should see him dance! It's a wonder!" he said.

When Natasha's turn came again, she got up and, stepping quickly in her beribboned little shoes, she timidly ran alone across the room to the corner where Denisov was sitting. She saw that everyone was looking at her and waiting. Nikolai saw that Denisov and Natasha were having a smiling argument, and that Denisov was protesting but smiling joyfully. He ran over.

"Please, Vassily Dmitrich," Natasha said, "please do."

"No, ghreally. Spaghre me, Countess," said Denisov.

"Enough, now, Vasya," said Nikolai.

"He talks to me like Vaska the cat," Denisov said jokingly.

"I'll sing for you all evening," said Natasha.

"The sorceghress, she does whatever she likes with me!" said Denisov, and he unbuckled his sabre. He came out from behind the chairs, took his lady firmly by the hand, threw back his head, and advanced his foot, waiting for the downbeat. Only on horseback and in the mazurka did Denisov's small stature not show, and he looked like the fine fellow he felt himself to be. On the downbeat, he gave his lady a victorious and jocular sidelong look, unexpectedly stamped his foot, bounced off the floor springily, like a ball, and flew along in a circle, drawing his lady after him. He flew inaudibly across half the room on one leg, and, seeming not to see the chairs that stood before him, raced straight for them; but suddenly, clanking his spurs and spreading his legs, he stopped on his heels, paused like that for a second, tapped his feet in place with a clanking of spurs, spun quickly, then, tapping his right ankle with his left foot, again flew along in a circle. Natasha intuitively guessed what he was about to do and, not knowing how herself, followed him—giving herself to him. Now he twirled her on his right arm, now on his left, now he fell on his knees and led her round him, then jumped up and sped on as precipitously as if he intended to run through all the rooms without pausing for breath; now he suddenly stopped again and performed a new and unexpected caper. When he swiftly twirled his lady in front of her seat and jingled his spurs before her as he bowed, Natasha did not even curtsy to him. She fixed her eyes on him in perplexity, smiling as though she did not recognize him.

"What on earth is this?" she said.

Even though Iogel did not acknowledge this mazurka as authentic, everyone admired Denisov's skill, began choosing him constantly, and the old men, smiling, began to talk about Poland and the good old days. Denisov, flushed from the mazurka and wiping himself with a handkerchief, sat down by Natasha and did not leave her for the whole ball.

XIII

For two days after that, Rostov did not see Dolokhov at his house and could not find him at home; on the third day, he received a note from him.

"Since I do not intend to frequent your house any more, for reasons known to you, and am leaving for the army, tonight I am giving a farewell party for my friends—come to the English Hotel." That evening, after nine o'clock, Rostov went to the English Hotel from the theatre, where he had been with his family and Denisov. He was brought at once to the best rooms of the hotel, taken for the night by Dolokhov.

Some twenty men crowded around the table at which Dolokhov sat between two candles. On the table lay gold and banknotes, and Dolokhov kept the bank. Nikolai had not seen Dolokhov since his proposal and Sonya's refusal, and he felt embarrassed at the thought of how they would meet.

Dolokhov's light, cold gaze met Rostov at the door, as if he had long been waiting for him.

"We haven't seen each other for a long time," he said. "Thank you for coming. Let me just finish the game, and Ilyushka will come with the chorus."

"I called at your place," Rostov said, blushing.

Dolokhov did not reply.

"You can stake," he said.

Rostov remembered at that moment a strange conversation he had once had with Dolokhov. "Only fools can gamble on luck," Dolokhov had said then.

"Or are you afraid to play with me?" Dolokhov said now, as if guessing Rostov's thought, and he smiled. Behind his smile, Rostov saw in him that mood he had been in during the dinner at the club and generally at those times when, bored with everyday life, Dolokhov felt the necessity of getting out of it by some strange, most often cruel, act.

Rostov felt awkward; he sought and could not find in his mind a joke which would reply to Dolokhov's words. But, before he managed to do it, Dolokhov, looking straight in Rostov's face, said to him, slowly and measuredly, so that everyone could hear:

"Remember, we talked once about gambling . . . he's a fool who wants to gamble on luck; gambling needs certainty, but I want to try it."

"Try gambling on luck or on certainty?" Rostov wondered.

"But you'd better not gamble," Dolokhov added, and, flexing a newly opened deck, he said: "Bank, gentlemen!"

Moving money forward, Dolokhov prepared to keep the bank. Rostov sat beside him and at first did not play. Dolokhov kept glancing at him.

"Why aren't you playing?" said Dolokhov. And, strangely, Nikolai felt the need to take a card, stake an insignificant sum on it, and begin to play.

"I have no money with me," said Rostov.

"I'll trust you!"

Rostov staked five roubles and lost, staked once more and lost again. Dolokhov "killed"—that is, won—ten cards in a row from Rostov.

"Gentlemen," he said, after keeping the bank for a while, "I ask you to put your money on your cards, otherwise I may get confused in the accounting."

One of the players said he had hoped he could be trusted.

"That I can do, but I'm afraid to get confused; I ask you to put money on the cards," replied Dolokhov. "And don't you be shy, we'll settle our accounts," he added, turning to Rostov.

The game went on; a servant constantly went around with champagne.

All of Rostov's cards were beaten, and eight hundred roubles were already scored against him. He wrote eight hundred roubles on a card, but, while champagne was served to him, he changed his mind and again wrote an ordinary stake, twenty roubles.

"Leave it," said Dolokhov, though it seemed he was not even looking at Rostov, "you'll win it back the sooner. I let the others win, but you I beat. Or are you afraid of me?" he repeated.

Rostov obeyed, left the eight hundred as written and laid down a seven of hearts with a torn corner that he had picked up from the floor. He remembered it very well afterwards. He laid down the seven of hearts and wrote eight hundred above it with a piece of chalk in round, straight figures; drank the glass of now warm champagne that had been served him, smiled at Dolokhov's words, and, waiting with sinking heart for a seven, began watching Dolokhov's hands which held the deck. The winning or losing of this seven meant a lot to Rostov. Last Sunday, Count Ilya Andreich had given his son two thousand roubles, and he, who never liked to talk about money problems, had told him that this money was the last until May and that he therefore asked his son to be more economical this time. Nikolai had said that it was even too much for him and on his word of honour he would not ask for more money until spring. He now had twelve hundred roubles of that money left. Therefore the seven of hearts meant not only the loss of sixteen hundred roubles, but the necessity of breaking his word. With sinking heart he watched Dolokhov's hands and thought: "Well, be quick, deal me the card, and I'll take my cap and go home to have supper with Denisov, Natasha, and Sonya, and will certainly never touch cards again." At that moment his life at home—jokes with Petya, talks with Sonya, duets with Natasha, piquet with his father, and even his quiet bed in the house on Povarskaya—presented itself to him with such force, clarity, and delight, as though it were all a long past, lost, and unappreciated happiness. He could not imagine that stupid chance, making the seven fall to the right rather than the left, could deprive him of all this newly understood, newly illumined happiness and cast him into an abyss of as yet unexperienced and undefined misfortune. It could not be, but even so he waited with sinking heart for the movement of Dolokhov's hands. Those broad-boned, reddish hands, with hair showing from under the cuffs, set down the deck of cards and took the glass and pipe that had been served him.

"So you're not afraid to gamble with me?" Dolokhov repeated, and, as if in order to tell a merry story, he set the cards down, leaned back in his chair, and, with a smile, slowly began to speak:

"Yes, gentlemen, I've been told there's a rumour going around Moscow that I'm a cardsharper, so I advise you to be more careful with me."

"Well, deal then!" said Rostov.

"Ah, these Moscow gossips!" said Dolokhov, and he picked up the cards with a smile.

"Ahh!" Rostov nearly cried, seizing his hair with both hands. The seven he needed was lying on top, the first card in the deck. He had lost more than he could pay.

"Don't overdo it, though," said Dolokhov, with a fleeting glance at Rostov, and he went on dealing.

XIV

An hour and a half later, most of the players looked upon their own game as a joke.

The whole game was concentrated on Rostov alone. Instead of sixteen hundred roubles, he had a long column of figures scored against him, which he had reckoned up to ten thousand, but which by now, as he dimly supposed, had already risen to fifteen thousand. In fact, the score already exceeded twenty thousand roubles. Dolokhov no longer listened or told stories; he watched every movement of Rostov's hands and from time to time glanced quickly through his score. He had decided to continue playing until the score grew to forty-three thousand. He had chosen this number because forty-three made up the sum of his age plus Sonya's. Rostov, his head propped in both hands, sat at the written-on, wine-stained, card-strewn table. One tormenting impression would not leave him: those broad-boned, reddish hands, with hair showing from under the cuffs, those hands which he loved and hated, and which held him in their power.

"Six hundred roubles, ace, corner, nine . . . I can't win it all back! . . . And how cheerful it would be at home . . . A jack, ah, no . . . it can't be! . . . And why is he doing this to me? . . ." Rostov thought and tried to recall. Occasionally he staked a large sum, but Dolokhov refused to play and set the stake himself. Nikolai obeyed him, and first he prayed to God as he had prayed during the battle on the Amstetten bridge; then he decided that the first card that came to hand from the pile of bent cards under the table would be the one to save him; then he counted the cords on his jacket and chose the card with the same number to stake against his entire loss; then he looked at the other players for help; then he peered into the now cold face of Dolokhov and tried to figure out what was going on in him.

"He does know what this loss means to me," he said to himself. "Can he really wish for my ruin? He used to be my friend. I loved him . . . But it's not his fault either; what can he do if he's in luck? Nor is it my fault," he said to himself. "I've done nothing wrong. Did I kill anyone, insult or wish evil to anyone? Why, then, such a terrible misfortune? And when did it start? Just now, when I came to this table, wishing to win a hundred roubles to buy that sewing box for mama's birthday and go home, I was so happy, so free, so cheerful! And I didn't realize then how happy I was! When did it end, and when did this new, terrible condition begin? What marked the change? I kept sitting in the same way in this place, at this table, choosing cards and playing them, and watching those broad-boned, deft hands. When did it happen, and what has happened? I'm healthy, strong, I'm the same and in the same place. No, it can't be! Surely it will all come to nothing."

He was red, all in a sweat, though it was not hot in the room. And his face was frightful and pitiful, especially in its impotent desire to seem calm.

The score reached the fateful number of forty-three thousand. Rostov prepared a card which was to go corners on the three thousand just given him, when Dolokhov tapped the deck on the table, set it aside, and, taking the chalk, quickly began in his clear, strong hand, breaking the piece of chalk, to add up Rostov's score.

"Supper, time for supper! The Gypsies are here!" Indeed, some dark-haired men and women, saying something with a Gypsy accent, were already coming in from the cold. Nikolai knew it was all over, but he said in an indifferent voice:

"So you won't go on? And I had a nice card ready." As if he was most interested in the amusement of the game itself.

"It's all over, I'm lost!" he thought. "A bullet in the head is all that's left to me," and at the same time he said in a cheerful voice:

"Well, one more little card."

"All right," said Dolokhov, having finished reckoning, "all right! I'll go twenty-one roubles," he said, pointing to the difference of twenty-one roubles over the exact sum of forty-three thousand, and, taking the deck, prepared to deal. Rostov obediently unbent the corner and, instead of the six thousand he had prepared, carefully wrote twenty-one.

"It's all the same to me," he said. "I'm just curious to know whether you'll kill this ten or let me win it."

Dolokhov gravely began to deal. Oh, how Rostov hated at that moment those reddish hands, with their short fingers and the hair sticking out from the cuffs, which had him in their power . . . He won the ten.

"You owe me forty-three thousand, Count," said Dolokhov, and he stood up from the table and stretched. "It's tiring, though, to sit so long," he said.

"Yes, I'm tired, too," said Rostov.

Dolokhov, as if to remind him that it was unsuitable for him to joke, interrupted him:

"When will I get the money, Count, if you please?"

Rostov flushed and invited Dolokhov to another room.

"I can't pay it all, I suppose you'll accept a promissory note," he said.

"Listen, Rostov," said Dolokhov, smiling brightly and looking into Nikolai's eyes, "you know the saying, 'Lucky in love, unlucky at cards.' Your cousin's in love with you. I know it."

"Oh! it's terrible to feel myself so much in this man's power," thought Rostov. Rostov knew what a blow he would deal to his father, to his mother, in announcing this loss; he knew what happiness it would be to be delivered of it all, and he realized that Dolokhov knew he could deliver him from this shame and grief, but still wanted to play with him as a cat plays with a mouse.

"Your cousin . . ." Dolokhov tried to begin; but Nikolai interrupted him.

"My cousin has nothing to do with it, and there is no point in talking about her!" he cried in a rage.

"So when will I get it?" asked Dolokhov.

"Tomorrow," Rostov said and left the room.

XV

To say "tomorrow" and keep up the tone of propriety was not difficult, but to come home alone, to see his sisters, brother, mother, father, to confess and ask for money to which he had no right after giving his word of honour, was terrible.

At home no one was asleep. The young people of the Rostovs' house, having come back from the theatre and had supper, were sitting by the clavichord. As soon as Nikolai came into the reception room, he was enveloped by that amorous, poetic atmosphere which had prevailed in their house that winter and which now, after Dolokhov's proposal and Iogel's ball, seemed to thicken still more, like the air before a thunderstorm, over Sonya and Natasha. Sonya and Natasha, in the light blue dresses they had worn to the theatre, pretty and knowing it, happy, smiling, stood by the clavichord. Vera and Shinshin were playing chess in the drawing room. The old countess, waiting for her son and husband, was playing patience with an old gentlewoman who lived in their house. Denisov, eyes shining and hair dishevelled, was sitting, his leg thrust back, at the clavichord, banging out chords on it with his stubby fingers and, his eyes rolling, was singing in his small, hoarse, but true voice some verses of his own composition, "The Sorceress," which he was trying to set to music.

> Sorceress, tell me by what art
> Thou drawest me to abandoned strings;
> What fire has thou instilled in my heart,
> What rapture through my fingers sings!

he sang in a passionate voice, his agate-black eyes flashing at the frightened and happy Natasha.

"Splendid! Excellent!" cried Natasha. "Another stanza," she said, not noticing Nikolai.

"For them everything's the same," thought Nikolai, peeking into the drawing room, where he saw Vera and his mother with the little old lady.

"Ah! here's Nikolenka!" Natasha ran over to him.

"Is papa at home?" he asked.

"I'm so glad you've come!" Natasha said without replying. "We're having such fun! Vassily Dmitrich is staying one more day for my sake, you know!"

"No, papa hasn't come yet," said Sonya.

"Coco, you're home, come here to me, my dearest," the countess's voice came from the drawing room. Nikolai went over to his mother, kissed her hand, silently sat down at her table, and began watching her hands, which were laying out cards. From the reception room came laughter and merry voices persuading Natasha.

"Well, all ghright, all ghright," cried Denisov, "now there's no getting out of it, you owe us a *baghrcarolle*, I beg you."

The countess glanced at her silent son.

"What's the matter?" the mother asked Nikolai.

"Oh, nothing," he said, as if he was already sick of this one and the same question. "Will papa come soon?"

"I think so."

"For them everything's the same. They don't know anything! What am I to do with myself?" thought Nikolai, and he went back to the reception room, where the clavichord stood.

Sonya was sitting at the clavichord and playing the prelude to the *barcarolle* that Denisov especially liked. Natasha was preparing to sing. Denisov was looking at her with rapturous eyes.

Nikolai began pacing up and down the room.

"Why on earth make her sing! What can she sing? There's no fun in it at all," thought Nikolai.

Sonya played the first chord of the prelude.

"My God, I'm a dishonest, lost man. A bullet in the head is all that's left for me, not singing," he thought. "Go away? but where? Never mind, let them sing!"

Nikolai, continuing to pace the room, glanced gloomily at Denisov and the girls, avoiding their eyes.

"Nikolenka, what's the matter with you?" asked Sonya's eyes, turned to him. She saw at once that something had happened to him.

Nikolai turned away from her. Natasha, with her sensitivity, also instantly noticed her brother's state. She noticed it, but she felt so merry herself at that moment, she was so far from grief, sorrow, reproach, that she purposely deceived herself (as often happens with young people). "No, I'm too merry now to spoil my merriment by sympathy for someone else's grief," she felt and said to herself: "No, I'm surely mistaken, he must be as merry as I am."

"Well, Sonya," she said, and went out to the very middle of the reception room, where, in her opinion, the resonance was best. Raising her head, lowering her lifelessly hanging arms as dancers do, Natasha made a few energetic steps from heel to toe in the middle of the room and stopped.

"Here I am!" she seemed to be saying, responding to the rapturous gaze of Denisov, who was watching her.

"What's she so glad about!" thought Nikolai, looking at his sister. "How is it she's not bored and ashamed!" Natasha took the first note, her throat expanded, her chest straightened, her eyes acquired a serious expression. She did not think of anyone or anything at that moment, and from her lips composed into a smile sounds poured forth, sounds that anyone can produce for the same lengths of time, at the same intervals, but which leave one cold a thousand times, then for the thousand and first time make one tremble and weep.

That winter Natasha had begun to sing seriously for the first time, especially because Denisov admired her singing. She no longer sang like a child, there was none of that comic, childish assiduousness in her singing which had been in it before; but her singing was not good yet, as all the critical connoisseurs said who had heard her sing. "Her voice has no polish, it's beautiful, but it needs polish," they all said. But they usually said it long after her voice had fallen silent. While this unpolished voice with its wrong breathing and strained transitions was singing, even the critical connoisseurs said nothing and merely enjoyed this unpolished voice, merely wanted to hear it again. Her voice had that virgin, intact quality, that unawareness of its strength, that unpolished velvetiness, which were so combined with a deficiency in the art of singing that it seemed impossible to change anything in this voice without spoiling it.

"What on earth is this?" thought Nikolai, hearing her voice and opening his eyes wide. "What's happened with her? How she sings today!" he thought. And suddenly the whole world became concentrated for him on the expectation of the next note, the next phrase, and everything in the world became divided into three beats: "*Oh mio crudele affetto . . .** One, two, three . . . one, two . . . three . . . one . . . *Oh mio crudele affetto* . . . One, two, three . . . one. Ah, our foolish life!" thought Nikolai. "All this misfortune, and money, and Dolokhov, and spite, and honour—it's all nonsense . . . and here is—the real thing . . . Ah, Natasha, ah, darling! ah, dearest! . . . How is she going to take this B . . . She did it? Thank God!" And without noticing it, he himself was singing, so as to strengthen that B, taking the second voice a third below the high note. "My God! how beautiful! Did I sing that? What happiness!" he thought.

Oh, how that third had vibrated, and how touched was something that was best in Rostov's soul. And that something was independent of anything in the world and higher than anything in the world. What are gambling losses, and Dolokhovs, and words of honour! . . . It's all nonsense! One can kill, and steal, and still be happy . . .

XVI

It was long since Rostov had experienced such enjoyment from music as on that day. But as soon as Natasha finished her *barcarolle,* reality again reminded him of itself. Saying nothing, he left and went downstairs to his room. A quarter of an hour later, the old count, merry and content, came home from the club. Nikolai, hearing him come, went to him.

"Well, did you have a good time?" asked Ilya Andreich, smiling joyfully and proudly at his son. Nikolai wanted to say "yes," but could not: he all but burst into sobs. The count was lighting his pipe and did not notice his son's state.

"Eh, it's inevitable!" Nikolai thought for the first and last time. And suddenly, in the most casual tone, which made him seem vile to himself, as if he was asking for a carriage in order to go to town, he said to his father:

"Papa, I've come on business. I nearly forgot. I need money."

"Well, now," said his father, who was in an especially cheerful mood. "I told you it wouldn't be enough. How much?"

"Very much," said Nikolai, blushing and with a stupid, casual smile for

*Oh my cruel affliction . . .

which he could not forgive himself for a long time afterwards. "I've lost a bit at cards, that is, a good deal, even a very great deal, forty-three thousand."

"What? To whom? . . . You're joking!" the count cried, his neck and nape suddenly turning an apoplectic red, as happens with old people.

"I promised to pay tomorrow," said Nikolai.

"Well! . . ." said the old count, spreading his arms and sinking strengthlessly onto the sofa.

"No help for it! It happens to everybody," his son said in a careless, brazen tone, while in his soul he considered himself a villain, a scoundrel, whose whole life would not be enough to redeem his crime. He would have liked to kiss his father's hands, to go to his knees and ask forgiveness, yet he said in a careless and even rude tone that it happened to everybody.

Hearing his son's words, Count Ilya Andreich lowered his eyes and began fussing about, as if looking for something.

"Yes, yes," he said, "it's hard, I'm afraid it's hard to find . . . it happens! Yes, it happens to everybody . . ." And, giving his son a fleeting look, the count started out of the room . . . Nikolai had been prepared for a rebuff, but he had never expected this . . .

"Papa! Pa . . . pa!" he cried out after him, sobbing, "forgive me!" And, seizing his father's hand, he pressed his lips to it and wept.

While father and son were having a talk, a no less important talk was going on between mother and daughter. Natasha, excited, had come running to her mother.

"Mama! . . . Mama! . . . He . . ."

"He what?"

"He, he proposed to me. Mama! Mama!" she cried.

The countess could not believe her ears. Denisov had proposed. To whom? To this tiny little girl, Natasha, who still recently was playing with dolls and was having lessons even now.

"Natasha, enough of this silliness!" she said, still hoping it was a joke.

"Well, there—silliness! I'm telling you a real thing," Natasha said crossly. "I come to ask you what to do, and you say 'silliness' . . ."

The countess shrugged her shoulders.

"If it's true that Monsieur Denisov has proposed to you, ridiculous as it is, tell him he's a fool, that's all."

"No, he's not a fool," Natasha said in an offended and serious tone.

"Well, what do you want, then? You're all in love these days. Well, if you're in love, marry him," the countess said, laughing crossly. "God help you!"

"No, mama, I'm not in love with him, it must be I'm not in love with him."

"Well, then tell him so."

"Mama, are you cross? Don't be cross, dearest, is it my fault?"

"No, but what then, my dear? Would you like me to go and tell him?" the countess said, smiling.

"No, I'll do it, only teach me how. Everything's so easy for you," she added, responding to her smile. "If you'd seen how he said it to me! Oh, I know he didn't want to say it, but just said it by accident."

"Well, even so you must refuse him."

"No, I mustn't. I'm so sorry for him! He's so nice."

"Well, then accept his proposal. It's really time you were married," her mother said crossly and mockingly.

"No, mama, I'm so sorry for him. I don't know how to tell him."

"There's no need for you to tell him, I'll tell him myself," said the countess, indignant that someone had dared to consider her little Natasha a grown-up.

"No, not for anything, I'll do it, and you go and listen at the door." And Natasha ran across the drawing room to the reception room, where Denisov was sitting on the same chair at the clavichord, covering his face with his hands. At the sound of her light footsteps, he jumped up.

"Natalie," he said, going to her with quick steps, "decide my fate. It is in your hands!"

"Vassily Dmitrich, I'm so sorry for you! . . . No, but you're so nice . . . but you mustn't . . . that . . . but I'll always love you like this."

Denisov bent over her hand, and she heard strange, incomprehensible sounds. She kissed him on his black, tousled, curly head. At that moment there was a hasty rustle of the countess's skirts. She went up to them.

"Vassily Dmitrich, I thank you for the honour," the countess said in an embarrassed tone, which seemed stern to Denisov, "but my daughter is so young, and I thought that you, as my son's friend, would have addressed me first. In that case, you would not have brought me to the necessity of a refusal."

"Countess . . ." said Denisov, with lowered eyes and a guilty look, and he was about to say something more, but faltered.

Natasha could not calmly see him so pitiful. She began to sob loudly.

"Countess, I am to blame before you," Denisov went on in a halting voice. "But know that I adore your daughter and your whole family so much that I would give two lives . . ." He looked at the countess and, noticing her stern face . . . "Goodbye, Countess," he said, kissed her hand, and, without looking at Natasha, with quick, resolute steps, left the room.

The next day Rostov saw off Denisov, who did not want to remain in Moscow a day longer. All Denisov's Moscow friends were seeing him off at the Gypsies', and he did not remember how he was put in the sleigh and driven the first three posting stations.

After Denisov's departure, Rostov, waiting for the money, which the old count could not raise all at once, spent two more weeks in Moscow without leaving the house, mostly in the young ladies' room.

Sonya was more devoted and tender to him than ever. It was as if she wanted to show him that his loss at cards was a feat which made her love him still more; but Nikolai now considered himself unworthy of her.

He covered the girls' albums with verses and music, and, without taking leave of any of his acquaintances, having finally sent off the entire forty-three thousand and received Dolokhov's receipt, left at the end of November to catch up with his regiment, which was already in Poland.

Part Two

I

After his talk with his wife, Pierre went to Petersburg. At the Torzhok posting station there were no horses, or else the postmaster did not want to give them to him. Pierre had to wait. Without undressing, he lay down on a leather sofa in front of a round table, put his big feet in their warm boots on the table, and lapsed into thought.

"Would you like to have the suitcases brought in? Would you like to have the bed made, or tea served?" asked his valet.

Pierre did not reply, because he heard and saw nothing. He had lapsed into thought at the previous station and went on thinking about the same thing—so important that he paid no attention to what was happening around him. He not only was not interested in whether he would get to Petersburg sooner or later, or whether he would or would not find a place to rest in this station, but, compared with the thoughts that occupied him then, it was all the same to him whether he spent a few hours or his whole life in this station.

The postmaster, his wife, the valet, a peasant woman with Torzhok embroidery kept coming into the room, offering their services. Pierre, not changing the position of his raised legs, looked at them through his spectacles without understanding what they could possibly want or how they could possibly live without resolving the questions that occupied him. And he had been occupied with the same questions ever since the day when he came back from Sokolniki after the duel and spent the first tormenting, sleepless night; only now, in the solitude of the journey, they came over him with particular force. Whatever he started thinking about, he came back to the same questions, which he could not resolve and could not stop asking himself. It was as if the main screw in his head, which held his whole life together, had become *stripped*. The screw would not go in, would not come out, but turned in the same groove without catching hold, and it was impossible to stop turning it.

The postmaster came in and humbly began asking his excellency to wait only two little hours, after which (come what might) he would give his excellency post-horses. The postmaster was obviously lying and only wanted to get extra money from the traveller. "Is that bad, or is it good?" Pierre asked himself. "For me it's good, for some other traveller it would be bad, and for the postmaster it's inevitable, because he has nothing to eat: he says an officer gave

him a thrashing on account of that. The officer gave him a thrashing because
he had to leave soon. And I shot at Dolokhov because I considered myself
insulted. And Louis XVI was executed because he was considered a criminal,
and a year later those who executed him were also killed for something. What
is bad? What is good? What should one love, what hate? Why live, and what
am I? What is life, what is death? What power rules over everything?" he asked
himself. And there was no answer to any of these questions except one, which
was not logical and was not at all an answer to these questions. This answer was:
"You will die—and everything will end. You will die and learn everything—
or stop asking." But to die was also frightening.

The Torzhok pedlar woman offered him her wares in a shrill voice,
especially a pair of goatskin shoes. "I have hundreds of roubles that I
don't know what to do with, and she stands there in a tattered coat and
looks at me timidly," thought Pierre. "And what does she need the money
for? As if this money can add one hair's breadth to her happiness, her peace
of mind? Can anything in the world make her or me less subject to evil and
death? Death, which will end everything and which must come today or
tomorrow—in a moment, anyhow, compared with eternity." And he again
put pressure on the stripped screw, and the screw kept turning in one and the
same place.

His servant handed him a book cut as far as the middle, an epistolary novel
by Mme Souza.[1] He started reading about the sufferings and virtuous struggle
of some Amélie de Mansfield. "And why did she struggle against her seducer,"
he wondered, "if she loved him? God could not have put into her soul a yearning that was contrary to His will. My former wife didn't struggle, and maybe
she was right. Nothing has been discovered," Pierre again said to himself,
"nothing has been invented. We can know only that we know nothing. And
that is the highest degree of human wisdom."

Everything within him and around him seemed confused, senseless, and
loathsome. But in this very loathing for everything around him, Pierre took a
sort of irritating pleasure.

"May I be so bold as to ask Your Excellency to move over a little for this
gentleman?" asked the postmaster, coming into the room and bringing in
another traveller who was detained for lack of horses. This was a squat, large-
boned, sallow, wrinkled old man with grey, beetling brows over glittering eyes
of an indefinite greyish colour.

Pierre took his feet off the table, got up, and lay down on the bed prepared
for him, glancing from time to time at the man who had come in and, not looking at Pierre, with a sullenly weary air, was undressing with difficulty, helped
by a servant. Left in a fleece-lined nankeen coat, with felt boots on his skinny,
bony legs, the traveller sat down on the sofa, leaned his close-cropped head,
very big and broad at the temples, against the back, and looked at Bezukhov.

The stern, intelligent, and penetrating expression of this look struck Pierre. He wanted to start a conversation with this traveller, but, as he was preparing to address him with a question about the road, the traveller closed his eyes and, folding his wrinkled old man's hands, on the finger of one of which was a big cast-iron signet ring with a death's head, sat motionless, either resting or, as it seemed to Pierre, reflecting deeply and calmly on something. The traveller's servant was also a sallow old man, all covered with wrinkles, with no beard or moustache, which evidently had not been shaved, but had never grown. The agile old servant opened the cellaret, prepared the tea table, and brought a boiling samovar. When everything was ready, the traveller opened his eyes, moved to the table, and, having poured himself a glass, poured another for the beardless old man and handed it to him. Pierre was beginning to feel uneasiness and the necessity, even the unavoidability, of getting into conversation with this traveller.

The servant brought back his empty, overturned glass and a bitten lump of sugar,[2] and asked whether anything was needed.

"Nothing. Give me the book," said the traveller. The servant gave him a book, which looked like a spiritual one to Pierre, and the traveller immersed himself in reading. Pierre was looking at him. Suddenly the traveller set the book aside, having put in a bookmark and closed it, and, closing his eyes and leaning back, sat again in his former position. Pierre was looking at him and had no time to turn away before the old man opened his eyes and fixed his firm and stern gaze directly on Pierre's face.

Pierre felt embarrassed and wanted to avoid that gaze, but the old man's glittering eyes drew him irresistibly to them.

II

"I have the pleasure of speaking with Count Bezukhov, if I'm not mistaken," the traveller said unhurriedly and loudly. Pierre looked silently and questioningly at his interlocutor through his spectacles.

"I've heard about you," the traveller went on, "and about the misfortune that has befallen you, my dear sir." (He underlined, as it were, the word *misfortune,* as if to say: "Yes, misfortune, whatever you may call it, I know that what happened to you in Moscow was a misfortune.") "I am very sorry for it, my dear sir."

Pierre blushed and, hastily lowering his legs from the bed, leaned towards the old man, smiling unnaturally and timidly.

"I have mentioned it, my dear sir, not out of curiosity, but for more important reasons." He paused, not letting Pierre out of his gaze, and shifted on the sofa, inviting Pierre by this gesture to sit next to him. Pierre found it unpleasant to get into conversation with this old man, but, involuntarily submitting to him, he went over and sat down next to him.

"You are unhappy, my dear sir," he went on. "You are young, I am old. I should like to help you as much as I can."

"Ah, yes," said Pierre, with an unnatural smile. "I'm very grateful . . . Where are you coming from?" The traveller's face was not gentle, but even cold and stern, yet in spite of that, his new acquaintance's words and face had an irresistibly attractive effect on Pierre.

"But if for some reason you find conversation with me unpleasant," said the old man, "say so, my dear sir." And he suddenly smiled an unexpectedly gentle, fatherly smile.

"Ah, no, not at all, on the contrary, I'm very glad to make your acquaintance," said Pierre, and, glancing once again at his new acquaintance's hands, he took a closer look at his ring. He saw a death's head on it, a Masonic sign.

"Allow me to ask," he said, "are you a Mason?"

"Yes, I belong to the brotherhood of Freemasons,"[3] said the traveller, peering more and more deeply into Pierre's eyes. "And I give you a brotherly handshake on my own behalf and on theirs."

"I'm afraid," said Pierre, smiling and hesitating between the trust which the Mason personally inspired in him and his habit of mocking Masonic beliefs, "I'm afraid I'm very far from understanding—how shall I put it—I'm afraid my way of thinking about the universe is so much the opposite of yours that we won't understand each other."

"Your way of thinking is known to me," said the Mason, "and this way of thinking of yours, which you are talking about and which seems to you the result of your own mental work, is the way of thinking of the majority of people, the monotonous fruit of pride, laziness, and ignorance. Forgive me, my dear sir, but if I did not know it, I would not be talking with you. Your way of thinking is a lamentable error."

"Just as I may suppose you to have fallen into error," Pierre said with a weak smile.

"I shall never dare to say that I know the truth," said the Mason, amazing Pierre more and more with his definite and firm speech. "No one can attain to the truth by himself; only stone by stone, with the participation of all, over millions of generations, from our forefather Adam down to our time, is the temple being built which is to become a worthy dwelling place for the great God," said the Mason, and he closed his eyes.

"I must tell you that I don't believe, don't . . . believe in God," Pierre said with regret and effort, feeling the need to speak the whole truth.

The Mason looked at Pierre attentively and smiled, as a rich man, holding millions in his hands, would smile at a poor man who has said to him that he, the poor man, did not have the five roubles that would make his happiness.

"But you don't know Him, my dear sir," said the Mason. "You cannot know Him. You don't know Him, and that is why you are unhappy."

"Yes, yes, I am unhappy," Pierre agreed, "but what am I to do?"

"You don't know Him, my dear sir, and that is why you are very unhappy. You don't know Him, but He is here, He is in me, He is in my words, He is in you, and even in that blasphemous talk you have just produced," the Mason said in a stern, trembling voice.

He paused and sighed, obviously trying to calm himself.

"If He did not exist," he said softly, "we would not be talking about Him, my dear sir. What, whom are we talking about? Whom have you denied?" he said suddenly with rapturous sternness and power in his voice. "Who invented Him, if He does not exist? Why has the supposition appeared in you that there is such an incomprehensible being? Why do you and the whole world suppose the existence of such an unfathomable being, a being almighty, eternal, and infinite in all His qualities? . . ." He stopped and was silent for a long time.

Pierre could not and did not want to break that silence.

"He exists, but it is hard to understand Him," the Mason spoke again, not looking at Pierre's face, but straight ahead, leafing through his book with his old man's hands, which could not remain still because of his inner turmoil. "If you doubted the existence of some man, I would bring this man to you, I would take him by the hand and show him to you. But how can I, an insignificant mortal, show all His almightiness, all His eternity, all His goodness to one who is blind, or who closes his eyes so as not to see, not to understand his own loathsomeness and depravity?" He paused. "Who are you? What are you? You fancy that you're wise, because you were able to utter those blasphemous words," he said with a gloomy and scornful smile, "but you are more foolish and mad than a little child who, playing with part of a skilfully made clock, would dare say that, since he does not understand the purpose of this clock, he does not believe in the master who made it. It is hard to know Him. For centuries, starting with our forefather Adam and down to our days, we have been working towards that knowledge and are infinitely far from reaching our goal; but we see our incomprehension only as our weakness and His grandeur . . ."

With a swelling heart, with glittering eyes, Pierre gazed into the Mason's face, listened to him, did not interrupt him, did not ask anything, and believed with his whole soul what this stranger was telling him. Whether he believed those reasonable arguments in the Mason's speech, or believed, as children do, the intonations, convictions, and heartfelt emotion in the Mason's speech, the trembling of his voice, which sometimes almost interrupted him, or those glittering old man's eyes, grown old in that conviction, or the calmness, firmness, and knowledge of purpose which shone in the Mason's whole being and which struck him especially strongly, compared with his own slackness and hopelessness, in any case he wanted to believe with his whole soul, and did believe, and experienced a joyful feeling of peace, renewal, and return to life.

"He is not apprehended by reason, but by life," said the Mason.

"I don't understand," said Pierre, fearfully sensing doubt arising in him. He feared the vagueness and weakness of his interlocutor's arguments, he feared not believing him. "I don't understand," he said, "how is it that human reason cannot apprehend the knowledge you speak of?"

The Mason smiled his meek, fatherly smile.

"The highest wisdom and truth is like the most pure liquid, which we want to receive into ourselves," he said. "Can I receive this pure liquid in an impure vessel and then judge its purity? Only by purifying myself inwardly can I keep the liquid I receive pure to some degree."

"Yes, yes, that's so!" Pierre said joyfully.

"The supreme wisdom is based not on reason alone, not on the secular sciences of physics, history, chemistry, and so on, into which rational knowledge is divided. The higher knowledge has one science—the science of the all, the science that explains the whole universe and the place man occupies in it. To contain this science, it is necessary to purify and renew one's inner man, and thus before one can know, one must believe and perfect oneself. And to achieve that, a divine light, called conscience, has been put in our soul."

"Yes, yes," Pierre agreed.

"Look at your inner man with spiritual eyes and ask if you are pleased with yourself. What have you achieved, being guided by reason alone? What are you? You are young, you are rich, you are educated, my dear sir. What have you done with all these good things that have been given you? Are you content with yourself and your life?"

"No, I hate my life," Pierre said, wincing.

"If you hate it, change it, purify yourself, and insofar as you purify yourself, you will learn wisdom. Look at your life, my dear sir. How have you been spending it? In riotous orgies and depravity, taking everything from society and giving it nothing. You received wealth. How have you used it? What have you done for your neighbour? Have you thought about the tens of thousands of your slaves, have you helped them physically and morally? No. You have used their labour in order to lead a debauched life. That is what you have done. Have you chosen some position in which you could be useful to your neighbour? No. You have been spending your life in idleness. Then, my dear sir, you married, taking upon yourself the responsibility for guiding a young woman, and what did you do? You did not help her, my dear sir, to find the path of truth, you hurled her into an abyss of deceit and misfortune. A man insulted you, and you shot him, and you say that you do not know God and hate your life. That is no wonder, my dear sir!"

After these words, the Mason, as if tired after talking for so long, again leaned back on the sofa and closed his eyes. Pierre looked at this stern, motionless, almost dead old face and moved his lips soundlessly. He wanted to say: "Yes, a loathsome, idle, depraved life," but he dared not break the silence.

The Mason cleared his throat hoarsely, as old people do, and called for his servant.

"What about the horses?" he asked, not looking at Pierre.

"The relay has been brought," the servant answered. "Won't you get some rest?"

"No, tell them to harness up."

"Can it be he'll go away and leave me alone, without finishing what he was saying and without promising to help me?" thought Pierre, getting up and beginning to pace the room with his head lowered, glancing occasionally at the Mason. "Yes, I didn't think about it, but I've led a contemptible, depraved life, and I didn't like it or want it," thought Pierre, "but this man knows the truth, and if he wanted, he could reveal it to me." Pierre wanted to say that to the Mason, but did not dare. The traveller, having packed his things, was buttoning up his coat with his old, accustomed hands. When he finished, he turned to Bezukhov and said to him indifferently, in a polite tone:

"Where are you going now, my dear sir, if I may ask?"

"Me? . . . To Petersburg," Pierre replied in a childish, irresolute voice. "Thank you. I agree with you in everything. But don't think that I'm so bad. I wish with all my soul to be what you want me to be; but I've never found help from anybody . . . However, I am to blame for it all in the first place. Help me, teach me, and maybe I'll . . ." Pierre could not go on; he snuffed his nose and turned away.

The Mason was silent for a long time, evidently thinking something over.

"Help is given only by God," he said, "but that measure of help which our order has in its power to give you, it will give you, my dear sir. You are going to Petersburg. Give this to Count Willarski" (he took out his pocket-book and wrote a few words on a large sheet of paper folded in four). "Allow me to give you one piece of advice. When you arrive in the capital, devote the initial time to solitude, to examining yourself, and do not set out on the former ways of life. With that I wish you a good journey, my dear sir," he said, noticing that his servant had come into the room, "and success . . ."

The traveller was Osip Alexeevich Bazdeev, as Pierre learned from the postmaster's register. Bazdeev had been one of the best-known Masons and Martinists even back in Novikov's time.[4] Long after his departure, Pierre, neither going to bed nor asking for horses, paced the station-house room, thinking over his depraved past and, with a rapture of renewal, picturing to himself his blissful, irreproachable, and virtuous future, which seemed so easy to him. He had been depraved, it seemed to him, only because he had somehow accidentally forgotten how good it was to be virtuous. In his soul there remained no trace of his former doubts. He firmly believed in the possibility of the brother-hood of people, united with the purpose of supporting each other on the path of virtue, and that was what he imagined Masonry to be.

III

On arriving in Petersburg, Pierre did not inform anyone of his arrival, did not go out anywhere, and started spending whole days reading Thomas à Kempis,[5] a book which some unknown person had delivered to him. Pierre understood one thing and one thing only while reading this book; he understood the delight, previously unknown to him, of the possibility of achieving perfection and the possibility of brotherly and active love among people, which Osip Alexeevich had revealed to him. A week after his arrival, the young Polish count Willarski, whom Pierre knew superficially in Petersburg society, came into his room in the evening with that official and solemn look with which Dolokhov's second had come to him, and, closing the door behind him and making sure that there was no one in the room except Pierre, addressed him.

"I have come to you with a suggestion and a message, Count," he said, with-out sitting down. "A person very highly placed in our brotherhood has solicited for you to be received into the brotherhood before the fixed term, and has suggested that I be your sponsor. I consider it my sacred duty to fulfil the will of this person. Do you wish, under my sponsorship, to enter the brother-hood of Freemasons?"

The cold and severe tone of this man whom he had almost always seen at balls with an amiable smile, in the society of the most brilliant women, struck Pierre.

"Yes, I do," he said.

Willarski inclined his head.

"One more question, Count," he said, "which I ask you to answer not as a future Mason, but as an honest man *(galant homme)*, in all sincerity: have you renounced your former convictions, do you believe in God?"

Pierre reflected.

"Yes . . . yes, I believe in God," he said.

"In that case . . ." Willarski began, but Pierre interrupted him.

"Yes, I believe in God," he said once more.

"In that case we can go," said Willarski. "My carriage is at your service."

Willarski was silent the whole way. To Pierre's question of what he must do and how to answer, Willarski said only that brothers more worthy than he would test him and that Pierre need do nothing more than tell the truth.

Having driven through the gates of a big house where the lodge was quar-tered and gone up a dark stairway, they went into a small, well-lit anteroom, where they took off their fur coats without the help of servants. From the ante-room they went into another room. Some man in strange attire appeared at the door. Willarski, going to meet him, said something to him quietly in French and went over to a small wardrobe, in which Pierre noticed kinds of attire he had never seen before. Taking a cloth from the wardrobe, Willarski put it over Pierre's eyes and knotted it behind, catching Pierre's hair painfully. Then he drew him to himself, kissed him, and, taking his hand, led him somewhere. The hair caught in the knot caused him pain, he winced and smiled from pain and shame at something. His enormous figure, with lowered arms and winc-ing, smiling physiognomy, moved after Willarski with uncertain, timid steps.

Having led him by the hand for some ten paces, Willarski stopped.

"Whatever happens to you," he said, "you must courageously endure every-thing, if you are firmly resolved to enter our brotherhood." (Pierre responded affirmatively by inclining his head.) "When you hear knocking on the door, you will unbind your eyes," added Willarski. "I wish you courage and suc-cess." And, pressing Pierre's hand, Willarski went out.

Left alone, Pierre went on smiling in the same way. He shrugged his shoul-ders a couple of times, put his hand to the cloth as if wishing to take it off, and lowered it again. The five minutes he spent blindfolded seemed like an hour to him. His hands became swollen, his legs gave way under him; it seemed to him that he was tired. He experienced the most complex and varied feelings. He was afraid of what was going to happen to him, and still more afraid that he would show his fear. He was curious to know what he was about to go through, what would be revealed to him; but most of all he felt joy that the moment had come when he would finally enter the path of renewal and an actively virtuous life which he had been dreaming of since his meeting with Osip Alexeevich. There was loud knocking at the door. Pierre took off the blindfold and looked around. The room was pitch-dark: only in one place a lamp was burning inside something white. Pierre went closer and saw that the lamp was standing on a black table on which lay an open book. The book was the Gospel; the white thing in which the lamp was burning was a human skull with its holes and teeth. Having read the first words of the Gospel: "In the beginning was the Word, and the Word was with God,"[6] Pierre went round the table and saw a large open box filled with something. This was a coffin with bones. He was not surprised in the least by what he saw. Hoping to enter a totally new life, totally different from his former one, he expected everything to be extraordinary, still more extraordinry than what he saw. A skull, a coffin, the Gospel—it seemed he had expected it all, had expected still more. Trying to call up a tender feeling in himself, he looked around. "God, death, love, the brotherhood of men," he said to himself, connecting vague but joyful notions of something with these words. The door opened and someone came in.

By the faint light, to which Pierre's eyes, however, had become accustomed, a short man came in. Evidently having come from light into darkness, the man stopped; then he moved with cautious steps towards the table and placed on it his small hands covered with leather gloves.

This short man was wearing a white leather apron that covered his chest and part of his legs, on his neck there was some sort of necklace, and behind the necklace rose a high white jabot, framing his elongated face, which was lit from below.

"Why have you come here?" asked the man, turning in the direction of Pierre, who had made a slight rustle. "Why have you, who do not believe in the truths of the light and do not see the light, why have you come here, what do you want from us? Wisdom, virtue, enlightenment?"

At the moment when the door opened and the unknown man came in, Pierre experienced a feeling of fear and awe similar to what he had experienced in childhood at confession; he felt himself alone with a man who was a total stranger in the circumstances of life, yet close in the brotherhood of men. With a pounding heart that took his breath away, Pierre moved towards the rhetor (so the Masons call a brother who prepares a *seeker* to enter the brotherhood). Coming closer, Pierre recognized the rhetor as an acquaintance, Smolyaninov, but it offended him to think that he was an acquaintance: the man who had come in was only a brother and a virtuous preceptor. For a long time, Pierre could not utter a word, so that the rhetor had to repeat his question:

"Yes, I . . . I . . . want renewal," Pierre uttered with difficulty.

"Very well," said Smolyaninov, and he went on at once: "Do you have any idea of the means by which our holy order can help you to achieve your goal? . . ." the rhetor asked calmly and quickly.

"I . . . hope . . . for guidance . . . help . . . in my renewal," Pierre said in a trembling voice and speaking with difficulty, owing to his excitement and to being unused to speaking about abstract subjects in Russian.

"What is your notion of Freemasonry?"

"I presume that Freemasonry is the *fraternité* and equality of men with virtuous goals," said Pierre, embarrassed, even as he was speaking, by the unsuitability of his words to the solemnity of the moment. "I presume . . ."

"Very well," the rhetor said hastily, evidently fully satisfied with this reply. "Have you sought the means of achieving your goal in religion?"

"No, I considered it incorrect and did not follow it," Pierre said, so softly that the rhetor did not hear and asked him what he had said. "I was an atheist," Pierre replied.

"You seek the truth in order to follow its laws in life; consequently, you seek wisdom and virtue, is that it?" the rhetor said after a moment's silence.

"Yes, yes," Pierre agreed.

The rhetor cleared his throat, folded his gloved hands on his chest, and began to speak.

"Now I must reveal to you the main goal of our order," he said, "and if this goal coincides with yours, it will be useful for you to enter our brotherhood. The first main goal and withal the foundation of our order, on which it is established and which no human power can cast down, is the preservation and handing on to posterity of a certain important mystery . . . which has come down to us from ancient times and even from the first man, on which mystery, perhaps, the fate of the human race depends. But as it is the nature of this mystery that no one can know it and use it unless he has been prepared by long and diligent self-purification, not everyone can hope soon to attain it. Therefore we have a second goal, which consists in preparing our members as much as possible, setting their hearts to rights, purifying and enlightening their reason by means revealed to us by tradition from men who laboured in search of this mystery, and thereby making them capable of apprehending it.

"In purifying and setting to rights our members, we try, thirdly, to set to rights the whole human race, offering it, through our members, an example of piety and virtue, and thereby trying with all our might to oppose the evil that reigns in the world. Think it over, and I will come to you again," he said and left the room.

"To oppose the evil that reigns in the world . . ." Pierre repeated, and he pictured his future activity on this path. He pictured people such as he himself had been two weeks ago, and he mentally addressed to them a didactic and admonitory speech. He pictured depraved and unfortunate people whom he helped in word and deed; he pictured oppressors whose victims he saved. Of the three goals mentioned by the rhetor, this last one—setting mankind to rights—was especially close to Pierre. The certain important mystery which the rhetor had mentioned, though it aroused his curiosity, did not seem essential to him; and the second goal, purifying and setting himself to rights, interested him little, because at that moment he enjoyed feeling himself already fully set to rights from his former vices and ready only for the good.

Half an hour later the rhetor came back to transmit to the seeker the seven virtues, corresponding to the seven steps of Solomon's temple, which every Mason was supposed to cultivate in himself. These virtues were: (1) *discretion,* keeping the secrets of the order; (2) *obedience* to the higher ranks of the order; (3) *good morals;* (4) *love of mankind;* (5) *courage;* (6) *generosity;* and (7) *love of death.*

"*Seventh,*" said the rhetor, "try by frequent thoughts of death to bring yourself to the point where it no longer seems a fearsome enemy to you, but a friend . . . who delivers the soul grown weary in the labours of virtue from this calamitous life and leads it to the place of recompense and peace."

"Yes, that should be so," thought Pierre, when, after these words, the rhetor went away again, leaving him to his solitary reflections. "That should be so, but I'm still so weak that I love my life, the meaning of which is only now being gradually revealed to me." But he did feel in his soul the other five virtues that he remembered, counting them on his fingers: *courage,* and *generosity,* and *good morals,* and *love of mankind,* and especially *obedience,* which even seemed to him not a virtue, but happiness itself. (It was so joyful for him now to be delivered of his arbitrariness and submit his will to a person or persons who knew the unquestionable truth.) Pierre forgot the seventh virtue and simply could not recall what it was.

The third time the rhetor came back sooner and asked Pierre whether he was still firm in his intention and was determined to submit himself to everything that was demanded of him.

"I'm ready for everything," said Pierre.

"I must also inform you," said the rhetor, "that our order conveys its teaching not only by words, but by other means which affect the true seeker of wisdom and virtue perhaps even more strongly than verbal explanations. This temple, with its decorations, which you see, must already have explained to your heart, if it is sincere, more than words can do; you will see, perhaps, during your further initiation, a similar means of explanation. Our order imitates ancient societies, which revealed their teaching through hieroglyphics. A hieroglyph," said the rhetor, "is the designation of something not subject to the senses, which contains in itself qualities similar to what it is imaging."

Pierre knew very well what a hieroglyph was, but did not dare speak. He listened silently to the rhetor, feeling from it all that the testing was about to begin.

"If you are firm, then I must commence your induction," said the rhetor, coming closer to Pierre. "As a sign of generosity, I ask you to give me all your valuables."

"But I have nothing with me," said Pierre, thinking that he was being asked to hand over everything he owned.

"That is, what you have with you: a watch, money, rings . . ."

Pierre hurriedly took out his purse, his watch, but for a long time could not get the wedding ring off his fat finger. When that was done, the Mason said:

"As a sign of obedience, I ask you to undress." Pierre took off his tailcoat, his waistcoat, and his left boot, as the rhetor directed. The Mason opened his shirt on his left breast and, bending down, pulled up his left trouser leg above the knee. Pierre wanted hurriedly to take off his right boot and pull up his trouser, to spare the stranger the effort, but the Mason said there was no need for that and handed him a slipper for his left foot. With a childish smile of embarrassment, doubt, and self-mockery, which came to his face against his will, Pierre stood with lowered arms and straddled legs before his brother rhetor, waiting for new orders from him.

"And, finally, as a sign of open-heartedness, I ask you to reveal to me your main predilection," he said.

"My predilection! I *had* so many," said Pierre.

"The predilection which, more than all others, made you vacillate on the path of virtue," said the Mason.

Pierre paused, searching.

"Wine? Gluttony? Idleness? Laziness? Hot temper? Anger? Women?" he went through his vices, weighing them mentally, and did not know which to give preference to.

"Women," Pierre said in a low, barely audible voice. The Mason did not stir and did not speak for a long time after this reply. At last he moved towards Pierre, took the cloth that was lying on the table, and again blindfolded him.

"I tell you for the last time: turn all your attention to yourself, lay chains upon your feelings, and seek blessedness not in passions, but in your own heart . . . The source of blessedness is not outside, but inside us . . ."

Pierre already felt in himself that refreshing source of blessedness which now filled his soul with joy and tender feeling.

IV

Soon after that, it was not the rhetor who came into the dark temple for Pierre, but his sponsor Willarski, whom he recognized by his voice. To renewed questions about the firmness of his intentions, Pierre replied:

"Yes, yes, I agree," and with a radiant, childish smile, with his fat chest bared, walking unevenly and timidly with one shod foot and the other unshod, he went ahead, with Willarski holding a sword to his bared chest. From the room he was led down corridors, turning back and forth, and was finally led to the doors of the lodge. Willarski coughed, the response was a Masonic rapping of hammers, and the door opened before him. Someone's bass voice (Pierre was still blindfolded) asked him questions about who he was, where and when he was born, and so on. Then he was again led somewhere with his eyes still covered, and as he walked, they told him allegories about the labours of his journey, about sacred friendship, about the pre-eternal architect of the world, about the courage with which he must endure toils and dangers. During the journey, Pierre noticed that they referred to him now as *the seeker,* now as *the sufferer,* now as *the postulant,* and made various noises with hammers and swords. Just as he was brought to some sort of object, he noticed that there was perplexity and confusion among his guides. He heard the men around him arguing among themselves in whispers, and one of them insisting that he had to be led across some sort of rug. After that, they took his right hand, put it on something, and told him to hold a compass to his left breast with his left hand, and made him recite the oath of fidelity to the laws of the order, repeating words that someone else read. Then they put out the candles, lit a spirit lamp, as Pierre knew by the smell, and told him he would see the lesser light. The blindfold was removed from his eyes, and Pierre saw as in a dream, by the faint light of the spirit lamp, several men who stood facing him in the same aprons as the rhetor and holding swords pointed at his breast. Among them stood a man in a bloody white shirt. Seeing that, Pierre moved his chest towards the swords, wishing them to pierce him. But the swords withdrew, and his eyes were covered again.

"Now you have seen the lesser light," someone's voice said to him. Then candles were lit again, the voices said he must see the full light, and his eyes were uncovered again, and more than ten voices suddenly said: *"Sic transit gloria mundi."** *

Pierre gradually began to come to himself and look around at the room he was in and the men who were in it. Some twelve men were sitting around a long table covered in black, all in the same attire as he had already seen. Pierre knew some of them from Petersburg society. In the chairman's place sat an unknown young man with a special cross on his neck. To his right sat the Italian abbé Pierre had seen two years before at Anna Pavlovna's. There was a rather important dignitary, and a Swiss tutor who formerly lived with the Kuragins. They were all solemnly silent, listening to the words of the chairman, who was holding a hammer in his hand. The wall had a burning star embedded in it; on one side of the table was a small rug with various images, on the other something like an altar with a Gospel book and a skull. Around the table stood seven large candle stands, as in a church. Two of the brothers led Pierre to the altar, placed his feet at right angles, and ordered him to lie down, saying that he now prostrates himself at the gates of the temple.

"He should receive the trowel first," one of the brothers said in a whisper.

"Ah, enough, I beg you!" said another.

Pierre looked around perplexedly with his near-sighted eyes, not obeying, and doubt suddenly came over him: "Where am I? What am I doing? Aren't they laughing at me? Won't I be ashamed to remember it?" But this doubt lasted only a moment. Pierre looked at the serious faces of the people around him, remembered all he had already gone through, and realized that he could not stop halfway. He was horrified at his doubt, and, trying to recall his former tender feeling, he prostrated at the gates of the temple. And indeed a tender feeling still stronger than before came over him. After he had lain there for some time, they told him to get up and put on a white leather apron such as the others were wearing, handed him a trowel and three pairs of gloves, and then the grand master addressed him. He told him to try not to stain in any way the whiteness of this apron, which represented strength and blamelessness; then, of the unexplained trowel, he told him to work with it to purify his heart of vice

---

*Thus passes the world's glory.

and tolerantly smooth over the heart of his neighbour. Then, of the first pair of men's gloves, he said that Pierre could not know their meaning, but had to keep them; of the second pair of men's gloves, he said that he was to wear them at meetings; and, finally, of the third pair, which were women's gloves, he said:

"My gentle brother, these women's gloves are destined for you as well. Give them to the woman whom you honour most of all. By this gift you will give assurance of the blamelessness of your heart to the one whom you elect as your worthy lady Mason." After a pause, he added: "But preserve these gloves, gentle brother, that they not adorn unclean hands." Just as the grand master pronounced these last words, it seemed to Pierre that the chairman became embarrassed. Pierre became still more embarrassed, blushed to the point of tears, as children do, started looking around uneasily, and an awkward silence ensued.

This silence was broken by one of the brothers, who, leading Pierre to the rug, began reading to him from a notebook the explanation of all the images depicted on it: the sun, the moon, a hammer, a plumb line, a trowel, a rough stone and a squared stone, a pillar, three windows, and so on. Then Pierre was assigned his place, shown the signs of the lodge, told the password, and finally allowed to sit down. The grand master began to read the rules. The rules were very long, and Pierre, from joy, excitement, and abashedness, was unable to understand what was being read to him. He heard well only the last words of the rules, which stayed in his memory:

"In our temples we know no other distinctions," the grand master read, "than those between virtue and vice. Beware of making any distinction that may violate equality. Fly to aid your brother, whoever he may be, instruct him who errs, raise up the fallen, and never nurse any malice or enmity against your brother. Be gentle and affable. Arouse the fire of virtue in all hearts. Share your happiness with your neighbour, and let envy never cloud this pure delight.

"Forgive your enemy, take no revenge upon him, unless it be by doing him good. Having thus fulfilled the higher law, you will recover the traces of the ancient majesty you have lost," he concluded and, standing up, he embraced Pierre and kissed him.

Pierre looked around with tears of joy in his eyes, not knowing how to reply to the congratulations and renewals of acquaintance that surrounded him. He did not recognize any acquaintances; in all these people he saw only brothers, and he burned with impatience to start working with them.

The grand master rapped with his hammer, everyone sat down in their places, and one brother read a sermon about the necessity of humility.

The grand master suggested that they fulfil the last duty, and the important dignitary, who bore the title of alms collector, started making the round of the brothers. Pierre wanted to write down all the money he had on the list of alms, but was afraid of showing pride and wrote down the same amount as the others did.

The meeting was over, and on his return home it seemed to Pierre that he had come back from some distant journey, where he had spent dozens of years, had changed completely, and had detached himself from the former order and habits of his life.

V

The day after his reception into the lodge, Pierre was sitting at home, reading a book and trying to make out the meaning of a square, one side of which represented God, another the moral, the third the physical, and the fourth their mixture. From time to time he tore himself away from the book and the square, and in his imagination put together a new plan of life for himself. The day before, he had been told in the lodge that the rumour of his duel had reached the sovereign, and that it would be sensible for Pierre to leave Petersburg. Pierre planned to go to his southern estates and occupy himself with his peasants. He was joyfully contemplating this new life when Prince Vassily unexpectedly came into the room.

"My friend, what have you done in Moscow? Why did you quarrel with Lelya, *mon cher?* You are mistaken," said Prince Vassily as he came in. "I've found out everything and can tell you for certain that Hélène is as innocent before you as Christ before the Jews."

Pierre was about to reply, but he interrupted him.

"And why didn't you turn to me directly and simply as a friend? I know it all, I understand it all," he said. "You behaved as befits a man who cherishes his honour; perhaps too hastily, but we won't discuss that. Only understand in what position you have placed her and myself in the eyes of the whole of society and even of the court," he added, lowering his voice. "She's living in Moscow, you here. Come, my dear," he pulled his hand downwards, "this is nothing but a misunderstanding; I think you feel that yourself. Let's write her a letter right now, and she'll come here, everything will be explained, and all this talk will end, or else, I tell you, you may very well suffer for it, my dear."

Prince Vassily looked imposingly at Pierre.

"I have it from good sources that the dowager empress is taking a lively interest in this whole affair. You know, she's very favourable to Hélène."

Pierre was on the point of speaking several times, but, on the one hand, Prince Vassily would not let him, hastily cutting off all conversation, and on the other hand, Pierre himself was afraid he might not begin speaking in the tone of resolute refusal and disagreement in which he was firmly resolved to answer his father-in-law. Besides, the words of the Masonic rule—"Be gentle and affable"—came to his mind. He winced, blushed, rose up, sank back, working on himself in what was for him the most difficult thing in life—to say something unpleasant to a person's face, to say something that the person, whoever he might be, was not expecting. He was so used to obeying Prince Vassily's tone of casual self-assurance that this time, too, he felt he would be unable to oppose it; yet he felt that his whole future destiny would depend on what he said right now: whether he would follow the old former way, or the new one which had been shown to him so attractively by the Masons, and on which he firmly believed he would find rebirth into a new life.

"Well, my dear," Prince Vassily said jokingly, "say 'yes' to me, and I'll write to her myself, and we can kill the fatted calf."[7] But Prince Vassily had no time to finish his joke, because Pierre, with a fury in his face that was reminiscent of his father, without looking his interlocutor in the eye, said in a quiet whisper:

"Prince, I did not invite you here—go, please, go!" He jumped up and opened the door for him. "Go now," he repeated, not believing himself and glad of the expression of embarrassment and fear that appeared on Prince Vassily's face.

"What's the matter with you? Are you ill?"

"Go!" the menacing voice said once more. And Prince Vassily was forced to leave without receiving any explanation.

A week later, having said goodbye to his new Mason friends and having left them large sums for alms, Pierre went off to his estates. His new brothers gave him letters to the Masons of Kiev and Odessa and promised to write to him and guide him in his new activity.

VI

The affair between Pierre and Dolokhov was hushed up, and, despite the sovereign's severity concerning duels, neither the two adversaries nor their seconds suffered. But the story of the duel, confirmed by Pierre's separation from his wife, spread in society. Pierre, who had been viewed indulgently, patronizingly, when he was an illegitimate son, who had been coddled and made much of when he was the best suitor in the Russian empire, had lost much in the opinion of society after his marriage, when brides and mothers had nothing to expect from him, the more so as he neither could nor would seek its favour. Now he alone was blamed for what had happened; it was said that he was a jealous dunderhead, subject to the same fits of bloodthirsty rage as his father. And when Hélène returned to Petersburg after Pierre's departure, she was received by all her acquaintances not only cordially, but with a shade of deference, in view of her misfortunes. When talk turned to her husband, Hélène assumed a dignified expression, which she—though without understanding its significance—adopted with her own special tact. This expression meant that she was resolved to endure her misfortune without complaining, and that her husband was a cross sent her by God. Prince Vassily voiced his opinion with more candour. He would shrug his shoulders when the talk turned to Pierre and say, tapping his forehead:

"Un cerveau fêlé—je le disais toujours."[*]

"I said it first thing," Anna Pavlovna would say of Pierre, "I said at once then and before everyone else" (she insisted on her priority), "that he is a crazy young man, spoiled by the depraved ideas of our time. I said it back when everyone admired him, and he had just come from abroad and, remember, played some sort of Marat at one of my soirées. And how did it end? Even then I didn't want this marriage, and predicted everything that's happened."

As before, Anna Pavlovna, on free evenings, held soirées at her home such as she alone had the gift to organize—evenings at which, first of all, there gathered *la crème de la véritable bonne société, la fine fleur de l'essence intellectuelle de la société de Pétersbourg*,[†] as Anna Pavlovna herself put it. Besides this refined selection of society, Anna Pavlovna's soirées were also distinguished in that, at each soirée, Anna Pavlovna served up for her guests some new, interesting person, and that nowhere as at these soirées did the level of the political thermometer indicate the mood of legitimist Petersburg court society so clearly and firmly.

At the end of 1806, when all the sad details had been received of Napoleon's destruction of the Prussian army at Jena and Auerstädt and the surrender of most of the Prussian fortresses, when our army had already entered Prussia and our second war with Napoleon had begun,[8] Anna Pavlovna gathered a soirée in her home. *La crème de la véritable bonne société* consisted of the enchanting and unfortunate Hélène, abandoned by her husband, of Mortemart, of the enchanting Prince Ippolit, just come from Vienna, two diplomats, the aunt, a young man who in this drawing room simply bore the title of *un homme de beaucoup de mérite*,[‡] a newly appointed lady-in-waiting with her mother, and some other less conspicuous persons.

The person to whom Anna Pavlovna treated her guests as a novelty that evening was Boris Drubetskoy, who had just come as a courier from the Prussian army, where he was an adjutant attached to a very important person.

The level of the political thermometer shown to the company that evening was the following: however hard all European sovereigns and military leaders try to pander to Bonapartius, in order to cause *me*, and *us* in general, unpleasantness and grief, our opinion of Bonapartius cannot change. We will not cease to voice our unfeigned way of thinking on that account, and we can only say to the Prussian king and others: "So much the worse for you. *Tu l'as voulu, Georges Dandin*,[§9] that's all we can say." That was what the political thermometer indicated at Anna Pavlovna's soirée. When Boris, who was to be

---

[*]A crackbrain—I always said so.
[†]The cream of truly good society, the fine flower of the intellectual essence of Petersburg society.
[‡]A man of great merit.
[§]You asked for it, Georges Dandin.

served up to the guests, entered the drawing room, nearly the entire company had gathered, and the conversation, guided by Anna Pavlovna, had to do with our diplomatic relations with Austria and the hope of alliance with her.

Boris, in a dashing adjutant's uniform, matured, fresh, and red-cheeked, walked freely into the drawing room and was duly taken to greet the aunt, and then reattached to the general circle.

Anna Pavlovna gave him her dry hand to kiss, introduced him to some strangers, and whispered her definitions of them to him.

"*Le prince Hyppolite Kouragine—charmant jeune homme. Monsieur Kroug, chargé d'affaires de Kopenhague—un esprit profond,*" and simply: "*Monsieur Shittoff, un homme de beaucoup de mérite,*"* of the one who bore that title.

Boris, during the time of his service, thanks to the efforts of Anna Mikhailovna, his own tastes, and the qualities of his reserved character, had managed to put himself in a most advantageous position in the service. He was an adjutant to a very important person, had a very important mission in Prussia, and had just returned from there as a courier. He had fully adopted the unwritten subordination he had liked so much in Olmütz, according to which an ensign could have incomparably higher standing than a general, and according to which, for success in the service, one needed not efforts, not labours, not courage, not perseverance, but only skill in dealing with those who give rewards for service—and he was often surprised at his quick success and at how others could fail to understand it. Thanks to this discovery, his whole way of life, all his relations with former acquaintances, and all his plans for the future had changed completely. He was not rich, but he spent his last penny to dress better than others; he would sooner deprive himself of many pleasures than allow himself to drive in a shabby carriage or appear in an old uniform in the streets of Petersburg. He made friends and sought acquaintances only with people who were above him and therefore could be of use to him. He loved Petersburg and despised Moscow. The memory of the Rostovs' house and his childhood love for Natasha was disagreeable to him, and he had never once visited the Rostovs since joining the army. He considered his presence in Anna Pavlovna's drawing room as an important promotion in the service, and he now understood at once his role there and left it to Anna Pavlovna to exploit the interest contained in him, while studying every person attentively and evaluating the advantages and possibilities of making friends with each of them. He sat down in the place shown him by the beautiful Hélène and listened to the general conversation.

" '*Vienne trouve les bases du traité proposé tellement hors d'atteinte, qu'on*

---

*Prince Ippolit Kuragin—a charming young man. Monsieur Krug, envoy from Copenhagen—a deep mind . . . Monsieur Shitov, a man of great merit . . .

*ne saurait y parvenir même par une continuité de succès les plus brillants, et elle met en doute les moyens qui pourraient nous les procurer.' C'est la phrase authentique du cabinet de Vienne,"*¹⁰* the Danish chargé d'affaires was saying.

"*C'est le doute qui est flatteur,*"† said *l'homme à l'esprit profond*¹¹ with a subtle smile.

"*Il faut distinguer entre le cabinet de Vienne et l'Empereur d'Autriche,*" said Mortemart. "*L'Empereur d'Autriche n'a jamais pu penser à une chose pareille, ce n'est que le cabinet qui le dit.*"‡

"*Eh, mon cher vicomte,*" Anna Pavlovna mixed in, "*l'Urope*" (for some reason she pronounced it *l'Urope,* as if it was some special subtlety of the French language, which she could allow herself when speaking with a Frenchman), "*l'Urope ne sera jamais notre alliée sincère.*"§

After which Anna Pavlovna led the conversation towards the courage and firmness of the Prussian king, in order to bring Boris into things.

Boris listened attentively to what was being said, waiting for his turn, but at the same time he managed to glance several times at his neighbour, the beautiful Hélène, who several times met the eyes of the handsome young adjutant with a smile.

Quite naturally, in speaking of the position of Prussia, Anna Pavlovna asked Boris to tell them about his trip to Glogau and the situation in which he found the Prussian army. Boris, unhurriedly, in pure and correct French, told quite a few interesting details about the army and the court, taking care all through his account to avoid stating his own opinion concerning the facts he conveyed. For some time Boris commanded general attention, and Anna Pavlovna felt that the novelty she had treated them to was received with pleasure by all the guests. Hélène paid the most attention of all to Boris's story. She asked him several times about certain details of his trip and seemed to be very interested in the position of the Prussian army. As soon as he finished, she turned to him with her usual smile.

"*Il faut absolument que vous veniez me voir,*" she said to him in a tone implying that, for certain considerations, which he could not know, this was an absolute necessity. "*Mardi entre les huit et neuf heures. Vous me ferez grand plaisir.*"#

Boris promised to fulfil her wish and was about to get into conversation with her, when Anna Pavlovna called him away, on the pretext that her aunt wanted to hear him.

"You do know her husband?" said Anna Pavlovna, closing her eyes and pointing to Hélène with a sad gesture. "Ah, she's such an unhappy and lovely woman! Don't speak of him in her presence, please don't speak of him. It's too painful for her!"

VII

When Boris and Anna Pavlovna returned to the general circle, the conversation there had been taken over by Prince Ippolit. Leaning forward in his armchair, he said:

"*Le Roi de Prusse!*" and, having said it, he began to laugh. Everyone turned to him. "*Le Roi de Prusse?*" Ippolit asked, laughed again, and again calmly and seriously sat back in the depths of his armchair. Anna Pavlovna waited a little, but as it seemed that Ippolit decidedly had no intention of saying more, she began to tell about how the godless Bonaparte purloined the sword of Frederick the Great in Potsdam.

"*C'est l'épée de Frédéric le Grand que je . . .*"* she began, but Ippolit interrupted her with the words:

"*Le Roi de Prusse . . .*" and again, as soon as they turned to him, he apologized and fell silent. Anna Pavlovna winced. Mortemart, Ippolit's friend, addressed him resolutely:

"*Voyons à qui en avez vous avec votre Roi de Prusse?*"†

Ippolit laughed, as if he was ashamed of his own laughter.

"*Non, ce n'est rien, je voulais dire seulement . . .*" (He intended to repeat a joke that he had heard in Vienna and that he had been trying to put in all evening.) "*Je voulais dire seulement que nous avons tort de faire la guerre 'pour le Roi de Prusse.'*"‡12

Boris smiled cautiously, so that his smile could be understood either as mockery or as approval of the joke, depending on how it was received. Everyone laughed.

"*Il est très mauvais, votre jeu de mots, très spirituel, mais injuste,*" said Anna Pavlovna, shaking her shrivelled finger. "*Nous ne faisons pas la guerre pour le Roi de Prusse, mais pour les bons principes. Ah, le méchant, ce prince Hyppolite!*"§ she said.

---

*It's the sword of Frederick the Great that I . . .
†Come, who are you getting at with your King of Prussia?
‡No, it's nothing, I only wanted to say . . . I only wanted to say that we are wrong to make war "for the King of Prussia."
§Your play on words is very bad, very witty, but unfair . . . We are not making war for the king of Prussia, but for good principles. Ah, that wicked Prince Ippolit!

The conversation did not flag all evening, turning mostly around political news. At the end of the evening it became especially lively when things got around to the rewards bestowed by the sovereign.

"Last year N. N. received a snuffbox with a portrait," said *l'homme à l'ésprit profond,* "why shouldn't S. S. receive the same reward?"

"Je vous demande pardon, une tabatière avec le portrait de l'Empereur est une récompense, mais point une distinction," said the diplomat, *"un cadeau plutôt."**

"Il y eu plutôt de antécédents, je vous citerai Schwarzenberg."†

"C'est impossible,"‡ another objected to him.

"Let's bet on it. *Le grand cordon, c'est différent . . ."*§

When they all got up to leave, Hélène, who had spoken little all evening, again turned to Boris with the request and the gentle, meaningful order that he visit her on Tuesday.

"It's very necessary for me," she said with a smile, glancing at Anna Pavlovna, and Anna Pavlovna, with the same sad smile that accompanied her words when her exalted patroness was mentioned, seconded Hélène's wish. It seemed as though, from certain words that Boris had spoken that evening about the Prussian troops, Hélène had suddenly discovered the necessity of seeing him. It was as if she were promising him that, when he came on Tuesday, she would explain that necessity to him.

Having come on Tuesday evening to Hélène's magnificent salon, Boris was not given a clear explanation of why it had been necessary for him to come. There were other guests, the countess spoke little to him, and only as he kissed her hand on taking his leave did she, with a strange absence of a smile, unexpectedly, in a whisper, say to him:

"Venez demain dîner . . . le soir. Il faut que vous veniez . . . Venez."#

During this stay in Petersburg, Boris became an intimate of Countess Bezukhov's house.

---

*I beg your pardon, a snuffbox with the emperor's portrait is a reward, but hardly a distinction . . . a gift, rather.
†There have been antecedents, rather. I will remind you of Schwarzenberg.
‡It's impossible.
§The grand cordon is a different matter . . .
#Come to dine tomorrow . . . in the evening. You must come . . . Do come.

VIII

The war was heating up, and its theatre was approaching the borders of Russia. Everywhere curses were heard on the enemy of the human race Bonapartius; militia and recruits were being gathered from the villages, and divergent news kept coming from the theatre of the war, false as usual and therefore reinterpreted in various ways.

The life of old Prince Bolkonsky, Prince Andrei, and Princess Marya had changed much since 1805.

In 1806 the old prince was made one of the eight commanders in chief of the militia then appointed all over Russia. The old prince, despite the weakness of age, which had become especially noticeable during the time when he counted his son as killed, did not believe he had the right to refuse the function assigned to him by the sovereign himself, and this activity newly opened up for him roused and strengthened him. He travelled continually around the three provinces entrusted to him; he was thorough to the point of pedantry in his duties, strict to the point of cruelty with his subordinates, and personally entered into the minutest details of things. Princess Marya now stopped taking lessons in mathematics from her father, and merely went to her father's study in the mornings, whenever he was at home, accompanied by the wet-nurse and little Prince Nikolai (as his grandfather called him). The nursing Prince Nikolai lived with his wet-nurse and the nanny Savishna in the rooms of the late princess, and Princess Marya spent the greater part of the day in the nursery, replacing her little nephew's mother as well as she could. Mlle Bourienne also seemed to love the boy passionately, and Princess Marya, often depriving herself, yielded to her friend the pleasure of dandling the "little angel" (as she called her nephew) and playing with him.

Near the altar of the church at Bald Hills there was a chapel over the grave of the little princess, and in the chapel had been placed a marble memorial, brought from Italy, in the form of an angel with spread wings ready to soar into the sky. The angel had a slightly raised upper lip, as if he was about to smile, and once, as they were leaving the chapel, Prince Andrei and Princess Marya confessed to each other that the angel's face strangely reminded them of the face of the deceased woman. But stranger still was something that Prince Andrei did not tell his sister, which was that in the expression which the artist had chanced to give the angel's face, Prince Andrei read the same words of meek reproach he had once read on his dead wife's face: "Ah, why have you done this to me? . . ."

Soon after Prince Andrei's return, the old prince separated his son's share of the inheritance and gave him Bogucharovo, a large estate thirty miles from

Bald Hills. Partly on account of the painful memories connected with Bald Hills, partly because Prince Andrei did not always feel able to bear calmly with his father's character, and partly because he needed solitude, Prince Andrei took advantage of Bogucharovo, began building, and spent most of his time there.

After the Austerlitz campaign, Prince Andrei had firmly decided never to serve in the army again; and when war began and everyone had to serve, he took a post raising militia under his father's leadership, in order to get out of active service. It was as if, after the campaign of 1805, the old prince and his son had exchanged roles. The old prince, roused by his activity, expected nothing but good from the present campaign; Prince Andrei, on the contrary, not taking part in the war, and regretting it deep in his heart, saw nothing but bad.

On the twenty-sixth of February 1807, the old prince left on his rounds. Prince Andrei stayed at Bald Hills, as he did most often during his father's absence. Little Nikolushka had been ill for three days now. The coachman who drove the old prince came back from town bringing papers and letters for Prince Andrei.

The valet with the letters did not find the young prince in his study and went to Princess Marya's side; but he was not there either. The valet was told that the prince had gone to the nursery.

"If you please, Your Excellency, Petrusha has come with papers," said one of the maids who assisted the nanny, addressing Prince Andrei, who was sitting on a child's little chair, frowning, his hands trembling, pouring drops of medicine from a vial into a glass half filled with water.

"What's that?" he said crossly, and his hand carelessly twitched, pouring an extra number of drops from the vial into the glass. He dumped the medicine on the floor and asked for more water. The maid gave it to him.

In the room stood a baby's crib, two trunks, two armchairs, a table, and a child's table with the little chair on which Prince Andrei was sitting. The curtains were drawn, and a candle burned on the table, screened by a bound music book to shield the bed from the light.

"My friend," said Princess Marya, addressing her brother from beside the crib where she was standing, "it's better to wait . . . later . . ."

"Ah, for pity's sake, you keep saying stupid things, and you keep wanting to wait—see, we've waited," said Prince Andrei in a spiteful whisper, clearly with the wish to sting his sister.

"My friend, really, it's better not to wake him, he's asleep," the princess said in a pleading voice.

Prince Andrei got up and, holding the glass, tiptoed towards the crib.

"So you really think we shouldn't wake him?" he said hesitantly.

"As you wish—really . . . I think . . . but as you wish," said Princess Marya, clearly abashed and ashamed that her opinion had triumphed. She pointed to the maid, who was calling to her brother in a whisper.

It was the second night that the two of them had not slept, looking after the boy, who was burning with fever. For two whole days, not trusting their house doctor and expecting the one they had sent for from town, they had been trying now one, now another remedy. Worn out by sleeplessness and anxiety, they shifted their grief onto each other, reproached each other, and quarrelled.

"Petrusha's here with papers from your father," the girl whispered. Prince Andrei stepped out.

"Well, what now!" he said crossly and, having listened to the verbal orders from his father and taking the envelopes and his father's letter, he went back to the nursery.

"Well, how is he?" asked Prince Andrei.

"Still the same, just wait, for God's sake. Karl Ivanych always says that sleep is best of all," Princess Marya whispered with a sigh. Prince Andrei went over to the baby and felt him. He was burning.

"Devil take you and your Karl Ivanych!" He picked up the glass with the drops of medicine in it and went back again.

"André, don't!" said Princess Marya.

But he glowered at her angrily and at the same time sufferingly, and bent over the baby with the glass.

"But I want it," he said. "Well, give it to him, I beg you."

Princess Marya shrugged her shoulders, but took the glass obediently and, calling to the nanny, began to administer the medicine. The baby cried and wheezed. Prince Andrei, wincing, clutched his head, went out, and sat on a sofa in the next room.

He still had the letters in his hand. He opened them mechanically and began to read. On blue paper, in his large, elongated hand, occasionally using abbreviations, the old prince wrote the following:

I have this moment received most joyful news through a courier. If it is not a lie, Bennigsen is supposed to have won a full victory over Bonapartius at Preussisch-Eylau.[13] In Petersburg there is general rejoicing, and no end of rewards have been sent to the army. Though he is a German, I congratulate him. The commander in Korchevo, a certain Khandrikov, is doing something I cannot fathom: up to now additional men and provisions have not been delivered. Gallop there at once and tell him that his head will roll unless everything is done within a week. I have also received a letter about the battle of Preussisch-Eylau from Petenka, who took part in it—everything is true. When those who should not interfere do not interfere, even a German can beat Bonapartius. They say he is fleeing in great disarray. See that you gallop to Korchevo without delay and carry out my orders!

Prince Andrei sighed and opened another envelope. This was a two-page, closely written letter from Bilibin. He folded it without reading it and read his father's letter again, ending with the words: "Gallop to Korchevo and carry out my orders!"

"No, excuse me, I won't go now, not until the baby gets well," he thought and, going to the door, he peeked into the nursery. Princess Marya was still standing by the crib, gently rocking the baby.

"Yes, what's that other unpleasantness he writes?" Prince Andrei recalled the contents of his father's letter. "Yes. Our side has won a victory over Bonaparte precisely when I'm not serving. Yes, yes, he keeps making fun of me . . . well, he's welcome to . . ." And he began to read Bilibin's letter, written in French. He read, not understanding half of it, read only so as to stop thinking for at least a minute about what he had been thinking of exclusively and painfully for all too long.

IX

Bilibin was now attached to army headquarters in the capacity of a diplomatic functionary, and though he wrote in French, with French jokes and turns of phrase, he described the whole campaign with an exclusively Russian fearlessness of self-condemnation and self-derision. Bilibin wrote that his diplomatic *discrétion* tormented him, and that he was happy to have a faithful correspondent in Prince Andrei, before whom he could pour out all the bile that had accumulated in him while watching what was happening in the army. The letter was an old one, from before the battle of Preussisch-Eylau. Bilibin wrote:

*Depuis nos grands succès d'Austerlitz vous savez, mon cher Prince, que je ne quitte plus les quartiers généraux. Décidément j'ai pris le goût de la guerre, et bien m'en a pris. Ce que j'ai vu ces trois mois, est incroyable.**

Je commence ab ovo. *"L'ennemi du genre humain," comme vous savez, s'attaque aux Prussiens. Les Prussiens sont nos fidèles alliés, qui ne nous ont trompés que trois fois depuis trois ans. Nous prenons fait et cause pour eux. Mais il se trouve que l'ennemi du genre humain ne fait nulle attention à nos beaux discours, et avec sa manière impolie et sauvage se jette sur les Prussiens sans leur donner le temps de finir la parade commencée, en deux tours de main les rosse à plate couture et va s'installer au palais de Potsdam.*

---

*Since our great successes at Austerlitz, you know, my dear prince, that I no longer leave general headquarters. I have decidedly got the taste for war and have really taken to it. What I've seen in these three months is incredible.

I'll begin *ab ovo*. "The enemy of the human race," as you know, is attacking the Prussians. The Prussians are our faithful allies, who have betrayed us only three times in three years. We take up their cause. But it turns out that the enemy of the human race pays no attention to our fine speeches, and in his savage and impolite manner falls upon the Prussians without giving them time

"J'ai le plus vif désir," écrit le Roi de Prusse à Bonaparte, "que V. M. soit accueillie et traitée dans mon palais d'une manière, qui lui soit agréable et c'est avec empressement, que j'ai pris à cet effet toutes les mesures que les circonstances me permettaient. Puisse-je avoir réussi!" Les généraux Prussiens se piquent de politesse envers les Français et mettent bas les armes aux premières sommations.

Le chef de la garnison de Glogau avec dix mille hommes demande au Roi de Prusse, ce qu'il doit faire s'il est sommé de se rendre? . . . Tout cela est positif.

Bref, espérant en imposer seulement par notre attitude militaire, il se trouve que nous voilà en guerre pour tout de bon, et ce qui plus est, en guerre sur nos frontières avec et pour le Roi de Prusse. Tout est au grand complet, il ne nous manque qu'une petite chose, c'est le général en chef. Comme il s'est trouvé que les succès d'Austerlitz auraient pu être plus décisifs si le général en chef eut été moins jeune, on fait la revue des octogénaires et entre Prosorofsky et Kamensky, on donne la préférence au dernier. Le général nous arrive en kibik à la manière de Souvoroff, et est accueilli avec des acclamations de joie et de triomphe.

Le 4 arrive le premier courrier de Pétersbourg. On apporte les malles dans le cabinet du maréchal, qui aime à faire tout par lui-même. On m'appelle pour aider à faire le triage des lettres et prendre celles qui nous sont destinées. Le maréchal nous regarde faire et attend les paquets qui lui sont adressés. Nous cherchons—il n'y en a point. Le maréchal devient impatient, se met lui-même à la besogne et trouve des lettres de l'Empereur pour le comte T., pour le prince V. et autres. Alors le voilà qui se met dans une de ses

---

to finish the parade they've begun, beats the stuffing out of them in two seconds, and installs himself in the palace at Potsdam.

"I have the strongest desire," the King of Prussia writes to Bonaparte, "that Your Majesty be welcomed and treated in my palace in a manner agreeable to him, and to that end I have hastened to take all the measures which circumstances allowed. I hope to have succeeded!" The Prussian generals pride themselves on their politeness towards the French and lay down their arms at the first invitation.

The head of the garrison at Glogau, with ten thousand men, asks the King of Prussia what to do if he is invited to surrender . . . All this is undeniable.

In short, hoping to impress only by our military bearing, it turns out that we find ourselves at war in earnest, and what's more, at war on our own frontiers *with and for the King of Prussia.* We have everything, we only lack one little thing, a commander in chief. Since it has been found that the successes at Austerlitz would have been more decisive if the commander in chief had been less young, they make a review of all the octogenarians and, between Prozorovsky and Kamensky, give the preference to the latter. The general comes to us in a kibitka, like Suvorov, and is welcomed with acclamations of joy and triumph.

On the 4th the first mail arrives from Petersburg. The pouches are taken to the office of the marshal, who likes doing everything himself. I am sent for to help sort the letters and take those intended for us. The marshal watches us work and waits for the packets addressed to him. We search—there aren't any. The marshal grows impatient, sets to work himself, and finds letters from the Emperor to Count T., to Prince V. and others. Then he gets into one of his blue fits. He

*colères bleues. Il jette feu et flamme contre tout le monde, s'empare des let-
tres, les decachète, et lit celles de l'Empereur adressées à d'autres.* "Ah, so
that's how they deal with me. They don't trust me! Ah, there's an order to keep
an eye on me—very well, away with you!" *Et il écrit le fameux ordre du jour
au général Bennigsen.*

"I am wounded, I cannot mount a horse, and therefore cannot command an
army. You have brought your crushed *corps d'armée* to Pultusk: here it is
exposed, without firewood, and without forage, and thus in need of help, and
since you yourself were in touch with Count Buxhöwden yesterday, thought
should be given to retreating to our border, which should be done today."

"From all this riding around," *écrit-il à l'Empereur,** "I have got a saddle
sore, which, on top of my previous bandages, totally prevents me from riding
and commanding such a vast army, and therefore I have turned over the command to the general next in seniority to myself, Count Buxhöwden, sending
him all my staff and everything pertaining to it, advising them, if there is no
bread, to retreat further into the interior of Prussia, because there was only
enough bread left for one day, and some regiments had none, as division commanders Ostermann and Sedmoretsky announced, and everything the peasants had has been eaten; and I myself am staying in a hospital in Ostrolenka
until I am cured. Your most devoted servant submits this report, dating it, and
observing that if the army remains in its present bivouac for another two
weeks, by spring we will not have one healthy man left.

"Dismiss an old man to his country estates, who is left disgraced as it is that
he cannot fulfil the great and glorious destiny for which he was chosen. I shall
await your most merciful permission here in the hospital, to avoid playing the
role of a *scrivener* rather than a *commander* of troops. My removal from the
army will cause no greater stir than if a blind man was leaving it. There are
thousands like me in Russia."

*Le maréchal se fâche contre l'Empereur et nous punit tous; n'est-ce pas
que c'est logique!†*

*Voilà le premier acte. Aux suivants l'interêt et le ridicule montent comme
de raison. Après le départ du maréchal il se trouve que nous sommes en vue
de l'ennemi, et qu'il faut livrer bataille. Boukshevden est général en chef par
droit d'ancienneté, mais général Bennigsen n'est pas de cet avis; d'autant*

---

breathes fire and flame on everybody, seizes the letters, unseals them, and reads those the Emperor
has addressed to others . . . And he writes the famous order of the day to General Bennigsen.
*He wrote to the Emperor.
†The marshal is angry with the Emperor and is punishing us all; isn't that logical!

There you have the first act. In those that follow the interest and the ridiculousness increase, as
you might expect. After the marshal's departure, it turns out that we are in sight of the enemy and
must offer battle. Buxhöwden is commander in chief by right of seniority, but General Bennigsen is
not of that opinion; the more so as it is he with his corps that is in sight of the enemy, and he wants

plus qu'il est lui, avec son corps en vue de l'ennemi, et qu'il veut profiter de l'occasion d'une bataille "aus eigener Hand," comme disent les Allemands. Il la donne. C'est la bataille de Poultousk qui est sensée être une grande victoire, mais qui à mon avis ne l'est pas du tout. Nous autres pékins avons comme vous savez, une très vilaine habitude de décider du gain ou de la perte d'une bataille. Celui qui s'est retiré après la bataille, l'a perdu, voilà ce que nous disons, et à titre nous avons perdu la bataille de Poultousk. Bref, nous nous retirons après la bataille, mais nous envoyons un courrier à Pétersbourg, qui porte les nouvelles d'une victoire, et le général ne cède pas le commandement en chef à Boukshevden, espérant recevoir de Pétersbourg en reconnaissance de sa victoire le titre de général en chef. Pendant cet interrègne, nous commençons un plan de manoeuvres excessivement intéressant et original. Notre but ne consiste pas, comme il devrait l'être, à éviter ou à attaquer l'ennemi; mais uniquement à éviter le général Boukshevden, qui par droit d'ancienneté serait notre chef. Nous poursuivons ce but avec tant d'énergie, que même en passant une rivière qui n'est pas guéable, nous brûlons les ponts pour nous séparer de notre ennemi, qui pour le moment, n'est pas Bonaparte, mais Boukshevden. Le général Boukshevden a manqué d'être attaqué et pris par des forces ennemies supérieures à cause d'une de nos belles manoeuvres qui nous sauvait de lui. Boukshevden nous poursuit—nous filons. À peine passe-t-il de notre côté de la rivière, que nous repassons de l'autre. À la fin notre ennemi Boukshevden nous attrappe et s'attaque à nous. Les deux généraux se fâchent. Il y a même une provocation en duel de la part de Boukshevden et une attaque d'épilepsie de la part de Bennigsen. Mais au moment critique le courrier, qui porte la nouvelle de notre victoire de Poultousk, nous apporte de Pétersbourg notre nomination

---

to profit from the occasion of a battle *"on his own hand,"* as the Germans say. He offers it. This is the battle of Pultusk, which is considered to be a great victory, but which in my opinion is not one at all. We muftis have, as you know, a very nasty habit of deciding the winning or losing of a battle. He who retreats after the battle has lost it, that's what we say, and on that head we have lost the battle of Pultusk. In short, we retreat after the battle, but we sent a courier to Petersburg with news of a victory, and the general does not yield up the chief command to Buxhöwden, hoping to receive from Petersburg the title of commander in chief in recognition of his victory. During this interregnum, we begin an excessively interesting and original plan of manoeuvres. Our aim does not consist, as it should, of evading or attacking the enemy; but solely of evading General Buxhöwden, who by right of seniority should be our chief. We pursue this goal with so much energy that in crossing a river that is not fordable, we burn our bridges to separate ourselves from the enemy, who for the moment is not Bonaparte but Buxhöwden. General Buxhöwden was nearly attacked and taken by superior enemy forces because of one of our pretty manoeuvres that saved us from him. Buxhöwden pursues us—we slip away. He has barely crossed to our side of the river, when we cross back again. In the end our enemy Buxhöwden catches us and attacks us. The two generals become angry. There is even a challenge to a duel on Buxhöwden's part and an attack of epilepsy on Bennigsen's part. But at the critical moment, the courier who brought the news of our victory at Pultusk brings us from Petersburg our nomination as commander in chief, and the first

de général en chef, et le premier ennemi Boukshevden est enfoncé: nous pou-
vons penser au second, à Bonaparte. Mais ne voilà-t-il pas qu'a ce moment
se lève devant nous un troisième ennemi, c'est les Orthodox Armed Forces
qui demande à grands cris du pain, de la viande, des souchary, du foin—que
sais-je! Les magasins sont vides, les chemins impraticables. Les Orthodox
Armed Forces *se met à la maraude, et d'une manière dont la dernière cam-*
pagne ne peut vous donner la moindre idée. La moitié des régiments forme
des troupes libres, qui parcourent la contrée en mettant tout à feu et à sang.
Les habitants sont ruinés de fond en comble, les hôpitaux regorgent de
malades, et la disette est partout. Deux fois le quartier général a été attaqué
par des troupes de maraudeurs et le général en chef a été obligé lui-même de
demander un bataillon, pour les chasser. Dans une de ces attaques on m'a
emporté ma malle vide et ma robe de chambre. L'Empereur veut donner
droit à tous les chefs de division de fusiller les maraudeurs, mais je crains
fort que cela n'oblige une moitié de l'armée de fusiller l'autre.

Prince Andrei began by reading with his eyes alone, but then involuntarily (though he knew how far Bilibin was to be trusted) became more and interested in what he was reading. Having read to this point, he crumpled the letter and threw it down. It was not what he read in the letter that made him angry; what made him angry was that the life there, now foreign to him, could excite him. He closed his eyes, rubbed his forehead with his hand, as if driving away all concern for what he had read, and began listening to what was happening in the nursery. Suddenly he seemed to hear some strange noise behind the door. Fear came over him; he was afraid something had happened to the baby while he was reading the letter. He tiptoed to the door of the nursery and opened it.

The moment he went in, he saw that the nanny was hiding something from him with a frightened look, and that Princess Marya was no longer by the crib.

"My friend," he heard behind him what sounded like the desperate whisper of Princess Marya. As often happens after long sleeplessness and long anxiety, a groundless fear came over him: it occurred to him that the baby had died. Everything he saw and heard seemed to him to confirm his fear.

---

enemy, Buxhöwden, is sunk: we can think about the second, Bonaparte. But lo and behold if a third enemy doesn't rise up before us, the *Orthodox Armed Forces,* with loud cries for bread, meat, biscuits, fodder—and whatnot else! The stocks are empty, the roads are impracticable. The *Orthodox Armed Forces* start looting, and in a way of which the last campaign cannot give you the least idea. Half the regiments form free bands, which roam the countryside putting everything to fire and sword. The inhabitants are utterly ruined, the hospitals overflow with sick, and there is famine everywhere. Twice general headquarters has been attacked by bands of looters, and the commander in chief has asked for a battalion to drive them away. In one of those attacks they carried off my empty trunk and my dressing gown. The Emperor wants to give the heads of divisions the right to shoot the looters, but I'm very much afraid that this will oblige one half of the army to shoot the other.

"It's all over," he thought, and cold sweat broke out on his forehead. Bewildered, he went over to the crib, certain that he would find it empty, that the nanny was hiding the dead baby. He opened the curtain, and for a time his frightened, unfocused eyes could not find the baby. At last he saw him: the red-cheeked boy lay sprawled across the crib, his head lower than the pillow, smacking and moving his lips in his sleep, and breathing regularly.

Prince Andrei, on seeing the boy, was as glad as if he had already lost him. He bent down and, as his sister had taught him, tested with his lips whether the baby had a fever. The tender forehead was moist; he touched his head with his hand—even the hair was wet: the baby had sweated so much. Not only had he not died, but it was obvious now that the crisis was past and that he was getting well. Prince Andrei wanted to snatch up, to squeeze, to clutch to his heart this helpless little being; he did not dare to do it. He stood over him, gazed at his head, his arms, his legs outlined under the blanket. He heard a rustling beside him, and some shadow appeared under the canopy of the crib. He did not turn and, gazing at the baby's face, kept listening to his regular breathing. The dark shadow was Princess Marya, who had come over to the crib with inaudible steps, raised the canopy, and lowered it behind her. Prince Andrei recognized her without turning to look, and reached his hand towards her. She pressed his hand.

"He's been sweating," said Prince Andrei.

"I was coming to tell you that."

The baby stirred slightly in his sleep, smiled, and rubbed his forehead against the pillow.

Prince Andrei looked at his sister. Princess Marya's luminous eyes, in the dim half-light of the canopy, glistened more than usual from the happy tears that welled up in them. Princess Marya leaned towards her brother and kissed him, catching slightly in the canopy of the crib. They shook their fingers at each other and stood a little longer in the dim light of the canopy, as if reluctant to part with that world in which the three of them were separated from everything on earth. Prince Andrei was the first to leave the crib, his hair tangling in the muslin of the canopy. "Yes, this is the one thing left to me now," he said with a sigh.

X

Soon after he was received into the brotherhood of the Masons, Pierre left for the province of Kiev, where the greater part of his peasants were, with a full set of instructions he had written out for himself about what he was to do on his estates.

On reaching Kiev, Pierre summoned all his stewards to the main office and explained his intentions and wishes to them. He told them that measures would immediately be taken for the complete liberation of the peasants from bondage, that meanwhile the peasants should not be overburdened with work, that women with children should not be sent to work, that the peasants should be given assistance, that punishments should be administered hortatorily, not corporeally, that there should be hospitals, almshouses, and schools in each village. Some of the stewards (there were half-literate managers among them) listened fearfully, taking what he said to imply that the young count was displeased with their stewardship and their concealing of money; others, after the first fright, were amused by Pierre's lisp and the new words they had never heard before; a third group simply took pleasure in hearing how the master spoke; a fourth group, the most intelligent, the head steward among them, understood from his speech how they ought to treat the master in order to achieve their own aims.

The head steward expressed great sympathy with Pierre's intentions; but he observed that, besides these transformations, it was generally necessary to take care of things, which were in a bad state.

Despite Count Bezukhov's enormous wealth, ever since Pierre had received it—and he received, so it was said, a yearly income of five hundred thousand— he had felt himself much less rich than when he had received his ten thousand from the late count. In general terms he was vaguely aware of the following budget. Around eighty thousand was paid to the Council for all the estates; around thirty thousand went to the upkeep of the suburban Moscow estate, the Moscow house, and the princesses; around fifteen thousand was distributed in pensions and the same amount to charitable institutions; a hundred and fifty thousand was sent to the countess for her expenses; around seventy thousand was paid as interest on debts; the building of a new church, already begun, had been costing around ten thousand over the past two years; the rest, around a hundred thousand, got spent, he did not know how himself, and he was obliged to borrow almost every year. Besides that, every year the head steward wrote now about fires, now about poor harvests, now about the necessity of rebuilding mills and factories. And so, the first thing facing Pierre was that for which he had least ability or inclination—business matters.

Every day Pierre *busied* himself with his head steward. But he felt that his busying did not move things one step foward. He felt that his busying went on independently of things, that it did not mesh with things and did not make them move. On the one hand, the head steward, presenting things in the worst light, showed Pierre the necessity of paying off debts and undertaking new works using serf labour, to which Pierre would not agree; on the other hand, Pierre demanded a start to the business of liberation, against which the steward advanced the necessity of first paying the debt to the Trust Council, and hence the impossibility of a speedy liberation.

The steward did not say it was completely impossible; to achieve that goal, he suggested selling the woodlands in Kostroma province, selling the bottom-lands and the Crimean estate. But all these operations, as the steward spoke of them, became bound up with such a complexity of processes of lifting prohibitions, requesting permissions, and so on, that Pierre was at a loss and only said to him: "Yes, yes, do that."

Pierre did not have the practical tenacity that would have given him the possibility of undertaking the business directly, and therefore he did not like it, and only tried to pretend to the steward that he was occupied with it. And the steward tried to pretend to the count that he considered this occupation quite useful for the master and inconvenient for himself.

In the big town acquaintances turned up; strangers hastened to make the acquaintance and greet cordially the newly arrived rich man, the biggest proprietor in the province. Temptations in connection with Pierre's main weakness, the one he had confessed when he was being received into the lodge, were also so strong that Pierre could not resist them. Again whole days, weeks, months of Pierre's life passed busily taken up with soirées, dinners, lunches, balls, giving him no time to recover his senses, just as in Petersburg. Instead of the new life Pierre had hoped to lead, he still lived the same life as before, only in different surroundings.

Of the three precepts of Masonry, Pierre realized that he was not fulfilling the one which required every Mason to be an example of the moral life, and of the seven virtues he was totally lacking in two: good character and the love of death. He comforted himself by thinking that he was fulfilling another duty instead—the setting to rights of the human race—and had other virtues—love of his neighbour and, especially, generosity.

In the spring of 1807, Pierre decided to go back to Petersburg. On the way back he intended to visit all his estates and personally ascertain what of all he had prescribed had been done, and what the situation now was of the people whom God had entrusted to him and whose benefactor he was trying to be.

The steward—who considered all the young count's ventures near madness, unprofitable for himself, for Pierre, and for the peasants—made concessions. Continuing to present the business of emancipation as impossible, he ordered the construction of large buildings for schools, hospitals, and almshouses on all the estates; had receptions prepared everywhere for the master's arrival, not sumptuously festive, which he knew Pierre would not like, but of religious thanksgiving, with icons and bread and salt,[14] precisely such as would impress and deceive the master, as he understood him.

The southern spring, the comfortable, quick travel in a Viennese carriage, and the solitude on the way worked joyfully on Pierre. The estates he had not yet been to were one more picturesque than the other; the people everywhere seemed prosperous and touchingly grateful for the benefactions he had done them. Everywhere there were welcomes, which, though they sometimes embarrassed Pierre, at the bottom of his heart called up a joyful feeling in him. In one place the peasants offered him bread and salt and the icon of Peter and Paul,[15] and asked his permission, in honour of his patron saints Peter and Paul, as a sign of love and gratitude for his benefactions, to build a new chapel in the church at their own expense. In another place he was met by women with nursing babies, who thanked him for their deliverance from hard work. On a third estate he was met by the priest with a cross, surrounded by children whom, thanks to the count, he was instructing in reading, writing, and religion. On all the estates Pierre saw with his own eyes stone buildings under construction or already constructed according to the same plan, to serve as hospitals, schools, and almshouses, which were to be opened in a short time. Everywhere Pierre saw the stewards' reports on the reduction of the corvée compared to previous norms and heard touching thanks for it from deputations of peasants in blue kaftans.

Pierre did not know that the village where he was offered bread and salt and where a chapel to Peter and Paul was being built was a market village with a fair on St. Peter's Day, that the chapel had been begun long ago by the wealthy peasants, who were the ones that welcomed him, and that nine-tenths of the peasants in that village were completely destitute. He did not know that since, on his orders, women with nursing babies were no longer sent to do corvée, these same women had to do still harder work on their own land. He did not know that the priest who met him with the cross burdened the peasants with his exactions and that the pupils gathered around him had been sent off with tears by their parents and were bought back for large sums of money. He did not know that the stone buildings were constructed to plan by his own workers and increased their corvée, which was only reduced on paper. He did not know that where a steward showed him in the books that the quitrent had been reduced by a third, as he had ordered, the corvée had been augmented by half. And therefore Pierre was delighted by his visits to the estates and returned fully to that philanthropic state of mind in which he had left Petersburg, and wrote rapturous letters to his mentor-brother, as he called the grand master.

"How easy it is, how little effort it takes, to do so much good," thought Pierre, "and how little we care about it!"

He was happy with the gratitude shown him, but ashamed as he received it. This gratitude reminded him *how much more* he could do for these simple, good people.

The steward, a very stupid but cunning man, understood the intelligent but naïve count perfectly and played with him as with a toy. When he saw the effect these prearranged receptions had on Pierre, he addressed him more resolutely with arguments about the impossibility and, above all, the needlessness of emancipating the peasants, who were perfectly happy even without that.

In his heart of hearts Pierre agreed with the steward that it was hard to imagine happier people and that God knows what awaited them in freedom; yet Pierre insisted, albeit reluctantly, on what he considered right. The steward promised to put all his powers to use in fulfilling the count's will, clearly understanding that the count not only would never be able to check on whether all the measures had been taken for selling the woodlands and estates, so as to pay off the Council, but would probably never ask and never find out that the buildings constructed were standing empty and that the peasants went on giving in work and money all that peasants gave other masters—that is, all they could.

XI

Returning from his southern journey in the happiest state of mind, Pierre carried out a long-standing intention of his—to go and visit his friend Bolkonsky, whom he had not seen for two years.

Having learned at the last posting station that Prince Andrei was not at Bald Hills, but at his newly allotted estate, Pierre went to him there.

Bogucharovo lay in flat, unattractive country covered with fields and first- and second-growth stands of fir and birch. The manor stood at the end of a village that stretched along the high road, behind a newly dug, well-filled pond, its banks not yet overgrown with grass, in the middle of a young woods, amidst which stood a few big pines.

The manor consisted of a threshing floor, outbuildings, stables, a bathhouse, a cottage, and a big stone house with a semicircular façade, which was still under construction. Around the house a young garden was planted. The fences were sturdy and new; under a shed stood two fire hoses and a barrel painted green; the paths were straight, the bridges strong, with handrails. Everything bore the stamp of neatness and efficiency. To the question of where the prince lived, some domestics he met pointed him to the small, new cottage that stood just by the pond. Anton, Prince Andrei's old tutor, helped Pierre out of the carriage, said that the prince was at home, and led him to a clean little front hall.

Pierre was struck by the modesty of this small though clean house, after those magnificent conditions in which he had last seen his friend in Petersburg. He went quickly into the little reception room, unplastered and still smelling of pine, and wanted to go further, but Anton ran ahead on tiptoe and knocked on the door.

"Well, what is it?" came a sharp, unpleasant voice.

"A visitor," replied Anton.

"Ask him to wait," and there was the sound of a chair being moved. Pierre went up to the door with quick steps and ran face-to-face into the frowning and aged Prince Andrei, who was coming out to him. Pierre embraced him and, raising his spectacles, kissed him on the cheeks and looked at him close up.

"How unexpected, I'm very glad," said Prince Andrei. Pierre said nothing; he looked at his friend in astonishment and could not take his eyes off him. He was struck by the change that had taken place in Prince Andrei. His words were affectionate, there was a smile on Prince Andrei's lips and face, but his gaze was extinguished, dead, and despite his obvious desire, Prince Andrei could not give it a joyful and merry lustre. It was not that his friend had grown thinner, paler, more mature; it was this gaze and the wrinkle on his forehead, expressive of a long concentration on some one thing, which struck and alienated Pierre, until he got used to them.

In this meeting after a long separation, as always happens, the conversation could not settle on anything for a long time; they asked and gave brief replies about things they knew should have been discussed at length. At last the conversation gradually began to dwell on what had previously been said in fragments, on questions of past life, on plans for the future, on Pierre's journey, on his occupations, on the war, and so on. The concentration and dejection Pierre had noticed in Prince Andrei's eyes were now expressed still more strongly in the smile with which he listened to Pierre, especially when Pierre spoke with animated joy about his past or future. It was as if Prince Andrei would have liked to enter into what he was saying, but could not. Pierre was beginning to feel that raptures, dreams, hopes for happiness and the good were improper in front of Prince Andrei. He was ashamed to voice all his new Masonic thoughts, especially renewed and stirred up in him by his last journey. He restrained himself, he was afraid of being naïve; along with that he had an irrepressible desire to show his friend the more quickly that he was now quite a different, better Pierre than the one he had been in Petersburg.

"I can't tell you how much I've lived through in this time. I wouldn't recognize myself."

"Yes, we've changed very much, very much, since then," said Prince Andrei.

"Well, and you?" asked Pierre. "What are your plans?"

"Plans?" Prince Andrei repeated ironically. "My plans?" he repeated, as if astonished at the meaning of such a word. "As you see, I'm building, by next year I want to have moved completely . . ."

Pierre peered silently and intently into Andrei's aged face.

"No, I'm asking . . ." said Pierre, but Prince Andrei interrupted him:

"Why talk about myself . . . you tell me, tell me about your journey and all you did there on your estates."

Pierre began telling about what he had done on his estates, trying as far as possible to hide his own share in the improvements he had made. Prince Andrei prompted Pierre beforehand several times in what he was telling, as if everything Pierre had done was a long-known story, and he listened not only without interest, but even as if ashamed at what Pierre was telling him.

Pierre felt awkward and even oppressed in his friend's company. He fell silent.

"Well, the thing is, dear heart," said Prince Andrei, who obviously also felt oppressed and embarrassed with his visitor, "I'm on bivouac here, I've just come to have a look. And tonight I'm going to my sister's. I'll introduce you to them. But it seems you know her," he said, obviously entertaining a visitor with whom he no longer felt anything in common. "We'll go after dinner. And now would you like to look over my estate?" They went out and spent the time before dinner discussing political news and mutual acquaintances, like people who have little closeness to each other. Prince Andrei showed some animation and interest only when he talked about the new estate he was setting up and his construction projects, but here, too, in the midst of the conversation, on the scaffolding, as Prince Andrei was describing to Pierre the future layout of the house, he suddenly stopped. "However, there's nothing interesting in it, let's have dinner and go." Over dinner the conversation turned to Pierre's marriage.

"I was very surprised when I heard of it," said Prince Andrei.

Pierre blushed, as he always blushed about that, and said hastily:

"Some day I'll tell you how it all happened. But, you know, it's all over, and for ever."

"For ever?" said Prince Andrei. "Nothing is for ever."

"But you do know how it all ended? You heard about the duel?"

"Yes, you went through that, too."

"The one thing I thank God for is that I didn't kill the man," said Pierre.

"Why so?" asked Prince Andrei. "It's even very good to kill a vicious dog."

"No, to kill a man is bad, it's wrong . . ."

"Why is it wrong?" Prince Andrei repeated. "It's not given to people to judge what's right or wrong. People have eternally been mistaken and will be mistaken, and in nothing more so than in what they consider right and wrong."

"What's evil for another person is wrong," said Pierre, pleased to feel that for the first time since his arrival Prince Andrei was becoming animated and was beginning to talk and wanted to speak out everything that had made him the way he was now.

"But who has told you what's evil for another person?" he asked.

"Evil? Evil?" said Pierre. "We all know what's evil for us."

"Yes, we know, but what I know as evil for myself, I cannot do to another person," Prince Andrei was speaking more and more animatedly, clearly wishing to voice his new view of things to Pierre. He spoke in French. "*Je ne connais dans la vie que deux maux bien réels: c'est le remords et la maladie. Il n'est de bien que l'absence de ces maux.** To live for myself, only avoiding these two evils—that is all my wisdom now."

---

*I know only two very real evils in life: remorse and illness. The only good is the absence of these evils.

"And love of one's neighbour, and self-sacrifice?" Pierre began. "No, I can't agree with you! To live only so as not to do evil, so as not to repent, is too little. I used to live that way, I lived for myself, and I ruined my life. And only now, when I live, or at least try to live" (Pierre corrected himself out of modesty) "for others, only now have I understood all the happiness of life. No, I won't agree with you, and you don't really think what you're saying." Prince Andrei silently gazed at Pierre with a mocking smile.

"You'll be seeing my sister, Princess Marya. You'll get along well with her," he said. "Maybe you're right for yourself," he went on after a brief pause, "but each man lives in his own way: you lived for yourself and you say with that you almost ruined your life, and knew happiness only when you began to live for others. But I experienced the opposite. I used to live for glory. (What is glory? The same as love for others, the desire to do something for them, the desire for their praise.) So I lived for others and ruined my life—and not almost, but completely. And I've been at peace since I began living for myself alone."

"But how can you live for yourself alone?" asked Pierre, becoming heated. "What about your son, your sister, your father?"

"But they're the same as myself, they're not others," said Prince Andrei, "and others, one's 'neighbours,' *le prochain,* as you and Princess Marya call them, are the chief source of error and evil. *Le prochain*—that's those Kievan peasants of yours, to whom you want to do good."

And he gave Pierre a mockingly defiant look. He was clearly defying Pierre.

"You're joking," said Pierre, growing more and more animated. "What error and evil can there be in my wish (though fulfilled very little and poorly), my wish to do good, and in my doing at least something? What evil can there be if those wretched people, our peasants, people like us, who grow up and die with no other notion of God and truth than an icon and a meaningless prayer, are taught comforting beliefs about the future life, retribution, reward, comfort? What evil and error are there if people are dying of disease without any help, when it's so easy to help them materially, and I give them a doctor, and a hospital, and a shelter for the aged? And isn't it a palpable, unquestionable good if a peasant or a woman with a baby has no peace day or night, and I give them rest and leisure? . . ." said Pierre, hurrying and lisping. "And I've done that, though poorly, though very little, but I've done something to that end, and you not only won't convince me that what I've done was not good, but you also won't convince me that you don't think so yourself. And above all," Pierre went on, "this I know and know for certain, that the pleasure of doing good is the only certain happiness in life."

"Yes, if you put the question that way, it's another matter," said Prince Andrei. "I build a house and cultivate a garden, and you build hospitals. Both can serve to pass the time. But what's right, what's good—that is for the one who knows all to judge, not for us. Well, you want to argue," he added, "so let's argue." They left the table and sat on the porch, which took the place of a balcony.

"Well, let's argue, then," said Prince Andrei. "Schools, you say," he went on, raising a finger, "instruction, and so on—that is, you want to lead him out of his animal condition," he said, pointing to a muzhik who took off his hat as he passed by, "and give him moral needs. But it seems to me that the only possible happiness is animal happiness, and you want to deprive him of it. I envy him and you want to make him into me, but without giving him my intelligence, or my feelings, or my means. Second, you say lighten his work. But in my opinion physical labour is as much a necessity for him, as much a condition of his existence, as mental labour is for you and me. You cannot not think. I go to bed past two o'clock, I have thoughts and can't sleep, I toss about, I don't fall asleep until morning, because I'm thinking and cannot not think, as he cannot not plough or mow—otherwise he'll go to the pot-house or fall ill. Just as I could not stand his terrible physical labour and would die in a week, so he could not stand my physical idleness, he'd grow fat and die. Third—what was it you said?"

Prince Andrei raised a third finger.

"Ah, yes. Hospitals, medicines. He has a stroke, he's dying, but you let his blood, you cure him, and he'll go around crippled for another ten years, a burden on everyone. It's far more simple and easy for him to die. Others will be born, there are lots of them as it is. You might be sorry to lose an extra worker—that's how I look at him—but no, you want to cure him out of love for him. And he doesn't need that. Besides, what is this fantasy that medicine has ever cured anybody . . . Killed, yes!" he said, frowning spitefully and turning away from Pierre.

Prince Andrei spoke his mind so clearly and distinctly that it was evident he had thought about it more than once, and he spoke eagerly and quickly, like a man who has not spoken for a long time. His gaze became the more animated, the more hopeless his opinions were.

"Ah, that's terrible, terrible!" said Pierre. "Only I don't understand how one can live with such thoughts. Such moments have come over me, it was not long ago, in Moscow and on the road, but then I go so much to seed that I don't live, I find everything vile, above all myself. I don't eat then, don't wash . . . well, how is it with you . . ."

"Why don't you wash, it's not clean," said Prince Andrei. "On the contrary, one must try to make one's life as pleasant as possible. I'm alive and it's not my fault, which means I must somehow go on living the best I can, without bothering anybody, until I die."

"But what makes you live? With such thoughts, you'll sit without moving, without undertaking anything . . ."

"Life won't leave one alone as it is. I'd be glad to do nothing, but then, on the one hand, the local nobility deemed me worthy of being elected their marshal;[16] I barely got out of it. They couldn't understand that I don't have what it takes, don't have the sort of good-natured and bustling banality needed for it. Then there's this house, which had to be built so as to have a corner where I could be at peace. Now it's the militia."

"Why aren't you serving in the army?"

"After Austerlitz!" Prince Andrei said gloomily. "No, I humbly thank you, I promised myself that I would not serve in the active Russian army. And I won't. If Bonaparte was camped here in Smolensk, threatening Bald Hills, even then I wouldn't serve in the Russian army. Well, as I was saying," Prince Andrei went on, calming down. "Now it's the militia, my father is commander in chief of the third district, and my only means of avoiding service is to be with him."

"Which means you do serve?"

"I do." He paused briefly.

"So why do you serve?"

"Here's why. My father is one of the most remarkable men of his time. But he's getting old, and it's not that he's cruel, but he has all too active a character. He's frightening in his habit of unlimited power and now with this power bestowed on him by the sovereign as a commander in chief of the militia. If I had been two hours late a couple of weeks ago, he would have hanged a protocolist in Yukhnovo," Prince Andrei said with a smile. "So I serve because no one except for me has any influence on my father, and at some point I may have to save him from an act from which he might suffer later."

"Ah, well, so you see!"

"Yes, *mais ce n'est pas comme vous l'entendez*,"* Prince Andrei went on. "I never wished, nor do I wish now, any good to that scoundrel of a protocolist, who stole some boots from the militiamen; I'd even be very pleased to see him hanged, but I pity my father—that is, again, myself."

Prince Andrei was becoming more and more animated. His eyes shone feverishly all the while he was trying to prove to Pierre that there never was any wish for his neighbour's good in his action.

"Well, here you want to emancipate the peasants," he went on. "That's very good; but not for you (I suppose you've never whipped anyone to death or sent them to Siberia), and still less for the peasants. If they're beaten, whipped, and sent to Siberia, I don't think that makes it any worse for them. In Siberia he'll go on with his brutish life, and the welts on his body will heal, and he'll be as happy as he was before. But it's needed for those people who are morally ruined, live to repent it, suppress this repentance, and turn coarse, because they have the possibility of punishing justly and unjustly. Those are the ones I pity and for whose sake I would wish for the emancipation of the peasants. Maybe you haven't seen it, but I've seen good people brought up in this tradition of

*But it's not as you understand it.

unlimited power, as they become more irritated over the years, become cruel, coarse, know it, can't help themselves, and become more and more unhappy."

Prince Andrei said this with such enthusiasm that it involuntarily occurred to Pierre that these thoughts had been suggested to Prince Andrei by his father. He made no reply.

"So there is what and whom to be sorry for—human dignity, peace of conscience, purity, and not their backs and heads, which, however much you whip them and shave them, will still remain the same backs and heads."

"No, no, a thousand times no! I'll never agree with you," said Pierre.

XII

In the evening Prince Andrei and Pierre got into a carriage and drove to Bald Hills. Prince Andrei, glancing at Pierre, broke the silence from time to time with speeches which proved that he was in a good state of mind.

Pointing to the fields, he told him about his improvements in management.

Pierre was gloomily silent, answered monosyllabically, and seemed to be immersed in his own thoughts.

Pierre was thinking about Prince Andrei, that he was unhappy, that he was mistaken, that he did not know the true light, that Pierre had come to his aid, to enlighten him and raise him up. But as soon as Pierre thought of how and what he was going to say, he had the feeling that Prince Andrei would discredit his entire teaching with a single word, a single argument, and he was afraid to begin, afraid to expose his favourite, sacred thing to the possibility of ridicule.

"No, why do you think," Pierre suddenly began, lowering his head and looking like a butting bull, "why do you think that way? You shouldn't think that way."

"About what?" Prince Andrei asked in surprise.

"About life, about man's purpose. It can't be. I thought the same, and do you know what saved me? Masonry. No, don't smile. Masonry is not a religious, not a ritual sect, as I also thought, Masonry is the best, the only expression of the best, the eternal sides of mankind." And he began to explain Masonry to Prince Andrei as he understood it.

He said that Masonry is the teaching of Christianity, freed of state[17] and religious fetters; the teaching of equality, brotherhood, and love.

"Only our holy brotherhood has real meaning in life; all the rest is a dream," said Pierre. "Understand, my friend, that outside this union everything is filled with lies and falsehood, and I agree with you that an intelligent and good man has nothing left but to live out his life, like you, trying only not to bother others. But adopt our basic convictions, join our brotherhood, give yourself to us, let yourself be guided, and you will at once feel yourself, as I did, a part of this huge, invisible chain, the beginning of which is hidden in heaven," said Pierre.

Prince Andrei, looking straight ahead, listened silently to Pierre's speech. A few times he asked Pierre to repeat words he had not heard because of the noise of the carriage. By a particular gleam that lit up in Prince Andrei's eyes, and by his silence, Pierre saw that his words were not in vain, that Prince Andrei would not interrupt him or laugh at what he was saying.

They approached a flooded river, which they had to cross by ferry. While the carriage and horses were being loaded, they boarded the ferry.

Prince Andrei, leaning his elbow on the rail, looked silently down the flood-waters sparkling in the setting sun.

"Well, what do you think about that?" asked Pierre. "Why are you silent?"

"What do I think? I've been listening to you. That is all so," said Prince Andrei. "But you say, 'Join our brotherhood, and we'll show you the goal of life and the purpose of man and the laws that govern the world.' But who are *we*?—just people. How do you know everything? How is it that I alone do not see what you see? You see the kingdom of the good and the true on earth, and I don't see it."

Pierre interrupted him.

"Do you believe in a future life?" he asked.

"A future life?" Prince Andrei repeated, but Pierre gave him no time to reply, and took this repetition for a denial, the more so as he knew Prince Andrei's former atheistic convictions.

"You say you can't see the kingdom of the good and the true on earth. I didn't see it either; and it can't be seen if you look at our life as the end of everything. On *earth,* I mean this earth" (Pierre pointed to the fields), "there is no truth—everything is falsehood and evil; but in the universe, in the whole universe, there is the kingdom of the true, and we are now children of the earth, but eternally—children of the whole universe. Don't I feel in my soul that I make up a part of that huge, harmonious whole? Don't I feel that, among the countless number of beings in which the divinity—the higher power—whatever you like—is manifest, I make up one link, one step from lower beings to higher? If I see, see clearly, this ladder that leads from plant to man, then why should I suppose that this ladder, the lower end of which I do not see, is lost in the plants? Why should I suppose that this ladder stops with me and does not lead further and further to higher beings? I feel not only that I cannot disappear, as nothing disappears in the world, but that I will always be and have always been. I feel that, besides me, above me; spirits live, and that in this world there is truth."

"Yes, that's Herder's teaching,"[18] said Prince Andrei, "but that, dear heart, does not convince me; life and death are what convince me. What convinces me is to see a being dear to you, who is bound up with you, before whom you were guilty and hoped to vindicate yourself" (Prince Andrei's voice quavered and he turned away), "and suddenly this being suffers, agonizes, and ceases to be . . . Why? It cannot be that there's no answer! And I believe there is one . . . That is what convinces, that is what has convinced me," said Prince Andrei.

"Yes, ah, yes," said Pierre, "and isn't that the same as what I'm saying?"

"No. All I say is that what convinces one of the necessity of a future life is not arguments, but when one goes through life hand in hand with a person, and suddenly that person disappears *there* into *nowhere,* and you yourself stop before that abyss and look into it. And I did look . . ."

"Well, that's just it! You know there's a *there* and there's a *someone? There* is the future life. The *someone* is—God."

Prince Andrei did not reply. The carriage and horses had long been led out on the other side and hitched up, and the sun had already half disappeared, and the evening frost had covered the pools by the crossing with stars, but Pierre and Andrei, to the astonishment of the lackeys, coachmen, and ferry-men, were still standing on the ferry and talking.

"If there is God and if there is a future life, then there is truth, there is virtue; and man's highest happiness consists in striving to attain them. We must live, we must love, we must believe," said Pierre, "that we do not live only today on this scrap of earth, but have lived and will live eternally there, in the all" (he pointed to the sky). Prince Andrei stood with his elbow resting on the rail of the ferry, and, listening to Pierre, did not take his eyes off the red gleam of the sun on the blue floodwaters. Pierre fell silent. It was completely still. The ferry had long been moored, and only the waves of the current lapped with a faint sound against the ferry's bottom. It seemed to Prince Andrei that this splash of waves made a refrain to Pierre's words, saying: "It's true, believe it."

Prince Andrei sighed, and with a luminous, childlike, tender gaze looked into the flushed, rapturous face of Pierre, who still felt timid before his superior friend.

"Yes, if only it were so!" he said. "Anyhow, let's go and get in," Prince Andrei added and, stepping off the ferry, he looked at the sky Pierre had pointed to, and for the first time since Austerlitz saw that high, eternal sky he had seen as he lay on the battlefield, and something long asleep, something that was best in him, suddenly awakened joyful and young in his soul. This feeling disappeared as soon as Prince Andrei re-entered the habitual conditions of life, but he knew that this feeling, which he did not know how to develop, lived in him. The meeting with Pierre marked an epoch for Prince Andrei, from which began what, while outwardly the same, was in his inner world a new life.

XIII

It was already dusk when Prince Andrei and Pierre drove up to the main entrance of the house at Bald Hills. As they were driving up, Prince Andrei, smiling, drew Pierre's attention to the bustling that was going on by the back porch. A bent old woman with a bundle on her back and a short man dressed in black and with long hair, seeing the carriage drive up, went running back to the gate. Two women ran out after them, and all four, glancing at the carriage, ran fearfully up the back porch.

"Those are Masha's people of God," said Prince Andrei. "They took us for father. And this is the only thing in which she doesn't obey him: he orders these wanderers[19] driven away, but she receives them."

"But what are these people of God?" asked Pierre.

Prince Andrei had no time to answer him. The servants came out to meet them, and he asked them where the old prince was and how soon they expected him.

The old prince was still in town, and he was expected at any moment.

Prince Andrei took Pierre to his rooms, which always awaited him in perfect order in his father's house, and went himself to the nursery.

"Let's go to my sister," said Prince Andrei, returning to Pierre. "I haven't seen her yet, she's hiding now and sitting with her people of God. It will serve her right, she'll get embarrassed, but you'll see the people of God. *C'est curieux, ma parole.*"*

"*Qu'est-ce que c'est que* people of God?"† asked Pierre.

"You'll see."

Princess Marya indeed became embarrassed and covered with red spots when they came to her. In her cosy room, with icon lamps before the icons, a young boy with a long nose and long hair and in a monk's cassock was sitting on the sofa beside her at the samovar.

In an armchair next to them sat a thin, wrinkled old woman with a meek expression on her childlike face.

"*André, pourquoi ne pas m'avoir prévenu?*"‡ she said in mild reproach, standing in front of her wanderers like a hen in front of her chicks.

"*Charmée de vous voir. Je suis très contente de vous voir,*"§ she said to Pierre as he was kissing her hand. She had known him as a child, and now his friendship with Andrei, the misfortune with his wife, and, above all, his kind,

*It's curious, I swear.
†What are *people of God*?
‡André, why didn't you warn me?
§Delighted to see you. I'm very pleased to see you.

simple face disposed her towards him. She looked at him with her beautiful, luminous eyes and seemed to be saying: "I like you very much, but please don't laugh at *my people*." Having exchanged the first phrases of greeting, they sat down.

"Ah, Ivanushka's here, too," said Prince Andrei, indicating the young wanderer with his smile.

"*André!*" Princess Marya said pleadingly.

"*Il faut que vous sachiez que c'est une femme,*"* Andrei said to Pierre.

"*André, au nom de Dieu!*"† Princess Marya repeated.

It was clear that Prince Andrei's mocking attitude towards the wanderers and Princess Marya's useless intercession for them were habitual, well-established relations between them.

"*Mais, ma bonne amie,*" said Prince Andrei, "*vous devriez au contraire m'être reconnaissante de ce que j'explique à Pierre votre intimité avec ce jeune homme.*"‡

"*Vraiment?*"§ said Pierre, studying the face of Ivanushka curiously and gravely through his spectacles (for which Princess Marya was especially grateful to him). Realizing that they were talking about him, Ivanushka looked around at them all with cunning eyes.

Princess Marya's embarrassment for *her people* was totally unnecessary. They were not in the least intimidated. The little old woman, her eyes lowered and casting sidelong glances at the newcomers, turned her teacup bottom up on the saucer and, placing the nibbled piece of sugar beside it, sat calm and motionless in her armchair, waiting to be offered more tea. Ivanushka, sipping from the saucer, looked at the young men from under his brows with his sly feminine eyes.

"Where have you been, to Kiev?" Prince Andrei asked the old woman.

"So I have, good sir," the old woman replied garrulously. "Just before Christmas I was deemed worthy to partake of the holy, heavenly mysteries[20] with the monks there. And now I'm coming from Kolyazin, where a great blessing has been revealed . . ."

"And Ivanushka has come with you?"

"I've come on my own, my provider," Ivanushka said, trying to speak in a bass voice. "I met Pelageyushka only in Yukhnovo."

Pelageyushka interrupted her companion; she obviously wanted to tell what she had seen.

"In Kolyazin, good sir, a great blessing has been revealed."

---

*You should know that this is a woman.
†André, in God's name!
‡But, my good friend . . . you should on the contrary be grateful to me for explaining to Pierre your intimacy with this young man.
§Really?

"What, new relics?" asked Prince Andrei.

"Enough, Andrei," said Princess Marya. "Don't tell him, Pelageyushka."

"And what's wrong, good lady, why shouldn't I tell him? I like him. He's kind. God's chosen, he gave me ten roubles, my benefactor, I remember. When I was in Kiev, Kiriusha, a holy fool[21]—truly a man of God, he goes barefoot winter and summer—'Why do you go about where you don't belong,' he says, 'go to Kolyazin, there's a miracle-working icon revealed, the holy Mother of God.' At that word I took leave of the monks and went . . ."

Everyone was silent, only the wanderer woman spoke in a measured voice, drawing in her breath.

"I came, my good sir, and people tell me: a great blessing has been revealed, the holy Mother of God has blessed oil dripping from her cheek . . ."

"Well, all right, all right, you can tell it later," Princess Marya said, blushing.

"Allow me to ask her," said Pierre. "Did you see it yourself?" he asked.

"Of course, good sir, I was deemed worthy. There was radiance on her face, like a heavenly light, and it dripped from the holy Mother's cheek, just dripped and dripped . . ."

"But it's a trick," Pierre said naïvely, having listened attentively to the wanderer woman.

"Ah, good sir, what are you saying!" Pelageyushka said in horror, turning to Princess Marya for defence.

"They trick the people," he repeated.

"Lord Jesus Christ," the wanderer woman said, crossing herself. "Don't say it, good sir. There was this one gener'l who didn't believe it and said, 'The monks are tricking you.' As soon as he said it, he went blind. And he had a dream that the Mother of God of the Caves[22] comes to him and says: 'Believe in me and I will heal you.' So he started begging: 'Take me to her, take me.' It's the real truth I'm telling you, I saw it myself. They brought him, blind as he was, straight to her; he goes to her, falls down, says: 'Heal me! I'll give you everything the tsar has bestowed on me.' I saw the medal myself, a star, set into the icon. So he got his sight back! It's a sin to speak as you do. God will punish you," she addressed Pierre didactically.

"How did the star get into the icon?" asked Pierre.

"So the Mother of God has been promoted to general?" said Prince Andrei, smiling.

Pelageyushka suddenly turned pale and clasped her hands.

"Good sir, good sir, it's a sin, a sin. You have a son!" she began, her pallor suddenly turning to bright red.

"Good sir, what have you said, God forgive you!" She crossed herself. "Lord, forgive him. Good lady, what is this? . . ." she turned to Princess Marya. She got up and, all but in tears, began packing her bag. She was clearly frightened, and sorry for the one who had said it, and ashamed that she had received benefactions in a house where such things could be said, and sorry that she now had to be deprived of those benefactions.

"Well, what on earth did you do that for?" said Princess Marya. "Why did you come to me? . . ."

"No, I was joking, Pelageyushka," said Pierre. "*Princesse, ma parole, je n'ai pas voulu l'offenser,** I just said it. Never mind, I meant it as a joke," he said, smiling timidly and wishing to smooth over his guilt.

Pelageyushka paused mistrustfully, but Pierre's face showed such sincere regret and Prince Andrei looked so meekly and gravely now at Pelageyushka, now at Pierre, that she gradually calmed down.

XIV

The wanderer woman calmed down and, urged to go on, spent a long time telling about Father Amphilokhy, whose life was so holy that his dear hand smelled of incense, and about how, during her last pilgrimage to Kiev, some monks she knew gave her the keys to the caves, and how she took some rusks and spent two days in the caves with the saints. "I'd pray to one, recite a little, and go to another. I'd doze, go again and kiss the relics; and it was so quiet, dearie, so blissful, that I didn't even feel like going out into God's world."

Pierre listened to her attentively and gravely. Prince Andrei left the room. And after him, Princess Marya left the people of God to finish their tea and took Pierre to the drawing room.

"You're very kind," she said to him.

"Ah, really, I didn't mean to offend her, I understand those feelings and value them highly."

Princess Marya silently looked at him and smiled tenderly.

"I've known you a long time and love you like a brother," she said. "How do you find Andrei?" she asked hastily, not giving him time to say anything to her affectionate words. "He worries me very much. This winter his health has improved, but last spring his wound reopened, and the doctor said he should go abroad for treatment. And morally I fear very much for him. He's not of the same character as us women, who suffer and weep out our grief. He carries it inside him. Today he's merry and lively; but it's your arrival that has had that effect on him: he's rarely that way. If only you could persuade him to go abroad! He needs activity, and this regular, quiet life is ruining him. Others don't notice, but I see it."

Towards ten o'clock the manservants rushed out to the porch, hearing the

---

*Princess, I swear, I didn't want to offend her.

bells of the old prince's carriage as it drove up. Prince Andrei and Pierre also went out to the porch.

"Who's that?" the old prince asked, getting out of the carriage and seeing Pierre.

"Ah! Very glad! Kiss me!" he said on learning who the unknown young man was.

The old prince was in good spirits and treated Pierre affectionately.

Before supper Prince Andrei, returning to his father's study, found the old prince in hot dispute with Pierre. Pierre insisted that a time would come when there would be no more war. The old prince, mockingly, but without getting angry, argued against him.

"Drain the blood from their veins, put in water, then there'll be no more war. Nonsense, old women's nonsense," he said, but even so he patted Pierre affectionately on the shoulder and went over to the desk, where Prince Andrei, evidently unwilling to enter the conversation, was looking through the papers that the old prince had brought from town. The old prince went over to him and began talking about business.

"The marshal, Count Rostov, failed to produce half the men. He came to town and decided to invite me to dinner. I gave him a real dinner . . . And look at this one . . . Well, my boy," Prince Nikolai Andreich said to his son, slapping Pierre on the shoulder, "your friend's a fine fellow, I've come to love him! He fires me up. Another man talks cleverly, and you don't want to listen to him, but he talks nonsense, yet he fires me up, old as I am. Well, go, go," he said, "maybe I'll come and sit with you at supper. And argue again. Love my foolish Princess Marya," he called to Pierre from the door.

Only now, during his visit to Bald Hills, did Pierre appreciate all the strength and charm of his friendship with Prince Andrei. This charm expressed itself not so much in his relations with him, as in his relations with the whole family and household. With the severe old prince and the meek and timid Princes Marya, Pierre felt at once like an old friend, though he barely knew them. They all loved him already. Not only did Princess Marya, won over by his meek attitude towards the wanderers, give him her most luminous looks, but the little one-year-old Prince Nikolai, as his grandfather called him, smiled at Pierre and went to his arms. And Mikhail Ivanych and Mlle Bourienne looked at him with joyful smiles when he talked with the old prince.

The old prince came out for supper: this was obviously for Pierre's sake. He was extremely affectionate with him on both days of his stay at Bald Hills and told him to come to visit.

When Pierre left and all the members of the family came together, they began to discuss him, as always happens after the departure of a new person, and, as rarely happens, they all said only good things about him.

XV

Returning from leave this time, Rostov felt and realized for the first time how strong his bond was with Denisov and the whole regiment.

As Rostov approached the regiment, he experienced a feeling similar to what he had experienced on approaching his house on Povarskaya. When he saw the first hussar in the unbuttoned uniform of his regiment, when he recognized the red-haired Dementyev, saw the red-coated horses at the tethering rail, when Lavrushka shouted joyfully to his master: "The count's here!"—and the dishevelled Denisov, who had been asleep in bed, came running out of the dugout, embraced him, and the officers gathered around him, Rostov experienced the same feeling as when his mother, father, and sisters had embraced him, and the tears of joy that welled up in his throat prevented him from speaking. The regiment was also a home, and a home as unchangingly dear and precious as his parental home.

When he had reported to the regimental commander, had obtained an assignment to his former squadron, had been on duty and gone foraging, had entered into all the little concerns of the regiment, and had felt himself deprived of freedom and bound within one narrow, unchanging frame, Rostov experienced the same peace, the same support, and the same awareness that here he was at home, where he belonged, as he felt under the parental roof. There was not all that disorder of the free world, in which he found no place for himself and made wrong choices; there was no Sonya, with whom he had or did not have to talk things over. There was no possibility of going or not going here or there; there were not those twenty-four hours in a day which could be spent in so many different ways; there was no numberless multitude of people, of whom no one was close, no one was distant; there were none of those unclear and undefined money relations with his father; there was no recollection of that terrible loss to Dolokhov! Here in the regiment everything was clear and simple. The whole world was divided into two unequal parts: one was our Pavlogradsky regiment, the other—all the rest. And with this rest he had nothing to do. In the regiment, everything was known: who was a lieutenant, who a captain, who was a good and who a bad man, and—above all—who was a comrade. The sutler gives you credit, your salary comes three times a year; there is nothing to think up or choose between, only do not do anything that is considered bad in the Pavlogradsky regiment; when you are sent out, do what is clearly and distinctly defined and ordered—and all will be well.

Having entered once more into these definite conditions of regimental life, Rostov experienced a joy and peace similar to what a weary man feels when he lies down to rest. This regimental life was the more pleasurable for Rostov during this campaign in that, after losing to Dolokhov (an act for which, despite all his family's reassurances, he could not forgive himself), he had resolved to serve not as before, but, in order to smooth over his guilt, to serve well and be a perfectly excellent comrade and officer, that is, a fine human being—which seemed so difficult in the *world,* but so possible in the regiment.

Since the time of his gambling loss, Rostov had resolved to pay back the debt to his parents within five years. They used to send him ten thousand a year, but now he resolved to take only two and leave the rest to his parents in repayment of his debt.

Our army, after repeated retreats, advances, and battles around Pultusk and Preussisch-Eylau, was concentrated near Bartenstein. It was awaiting the arrival of the sovereign and the start of a new campaign.

The Pavlogradsky regiment, belonging to that part of the army that had been in the 1805 campaign, had been replenishing its ranks in Russia and was late for the first actions of the campaign. It had not been at Pultusk nor at Preussisch-Eylau, and, joining the active army in the second half of the campaign, was included in Platov's detachment.

Platov's detachment acted independently of the army. Several times parts of the Pavlogradsky regiment participated in exchanges of fire with the enemy, took prisoners, and once even captured the carriages of Marshal Oudinot. In the month of April, the regiment camped for several weeks near a totally devastated, empty German village, not budging from the spot.

There was a thaw, mud, cold, the ice on the river broke up, the roads became impassable; for several days provisions had not been issued either to the horses or to the men. Since transport became impossible, men scattered over the abandoned, desolate villages looking for potatoes, but found little even of them.

Everything had been eaten, and the local people had all fled; those who had stayed were worse than destitute, there was nothing to take from them, and the soldiers, little given to pity, often even gave them the last food they had, instead of taking from them.

The Pavlogradsky regiment lost only two men wounded in action; but it lost nearly half of its men to famine and disease. In the hospitals death was such a certainty that soldiers sick with fever and bloated from bad food preferred to go on serving, forcing themselves to drag their feet to the front rather than go to the hospital. With the coming of spring, the soldiers began to find sprouting from the ground a plant resembling asparagus, which for some reason they called "Mashka's sweet root," and they scattered over the meadows and fields hunting for this Mashka's sweet root (which was very bitter), digging it up with their sabres and eating it, in spite of orders not to eat this noxious plant. In spring a new disease broke out among the soldiers—a swelling of the hands, feet, and face, the cause of which the medics took to be the consuming of this root. But in spite of the prohibition, the Pavlogradsky soldiers of Denisov's squadron mostly ate Mashka's sweet root, because for two weeks already the last supply of biscuits had been stretched, each man receiving only half a pound per day, and the potatoes of the last shipment had frozen or sprouted.

It was also the second week that the horses had been eating straw from the roofs of houses; they were hideously skinny and still covered with their winter coat, which was matted in clumps.

Despite such destitution, the soldiers and officers lived just as always; now, too, though with pale and swollen faces and in tattered uniforms, the hussars lined up for roll call, did the cleaning, groomed the horses, polished their arms, pulled straw from the roofs to feed the horses, and sat down to eat around the cauldrons, going away hungry, joking about their vile food and their hunger. Just as always, in their time off from service, the soldiers made bonfires, steamed themselves naked by the flames, smoked, sorted and baked the sprouted, fusty potatoes, and told or listened to stories about Potemkin's or Suvorov's campaigns, or tales about Alyosha the Rogue and the priest's farmhand Mikolka.

The officers, just as usual, lived two or three together in gaping, half-ravaged houses. The senior officers busied themselves with obtaining straw and potatoes, and the means of nourishing the men in general; the lower ranks were taken up, as always, some with cards (there was plenty of money, though no provisions), some with harmless games like horseshoes and ninepins. There was little talk about the general course of the war, partly because nothing positive was known, partly because it was vaguely felt that the general business of the war was going badly.

Rostov lived with Denisov, as before, and their bond of friendship had become still stronger since their time on leave. Denisov never spoke about Rostov's family, but from the tender friendship which the commander showed his officer, Rostov felt that the elder hussar's unlucky love for Natasha played a part in the strengthening of this friendship. Denisov clearly tried to expose Rostov to danger as rarely as possible, protected him, and met him with particular joy when he returned from action safe and sound. During one of his missions, in an abandoned, ravaged village, where he had gone for provisions, Rostov found a family made up of an old Pole, his daughter, and a nursing baby. They were poorly clothed, hungry, and could not leave, having no means of moving anywhere. Rostov brought them to the camp, placed them in his quarters, and kept them for several weeks, while the old man was recovering. One of Rostov's comrades got to talking about women, and began to tease Rostov, saying he was the cleverest of them all, and that it would not be a bad thing if he introduced his comrades to the pretty Polish woman he had saved. Rostov took the joke as an insult, flared up, and said such unpleasant things to the officer that Denisov barely managed to keep them from a duel. When the officer left and Denisov, who did not know himself what Rostov's relations with the Polish woman were, began to rebuke him for being hot-tempered, Rostov said to him:

"Think what you will . . . She's like a sister to me, and I can't describe to you how hurt I felt . . . because . . . well, since I . . ."

Denisov slapped him on the shoulder and quickly began pacing the room without looking at Rostov, something he did in moments of inner turmoil.

"It's your cghrazy Ghrostov bghreed," he said, and Rostov noticed tears in Denisov's eyes.

XVI

In the month of April, the troops were enlivened by news that the sovereign was coming to the army. Rostov did not manage to get to the review that the sovereign held in Bartenstein: the Pavlogradsky regiment was stationed at outposts far forward of Bartenstein.

They were on bivouac. Denisov and Rostov lived in a dugout covered with branches and turf that the soldiers had made for them. The dugout was made in the following way, which had then come into fashion: a trench was dug four feet wide, five feet deep, and nine feet long. At one end of the dugout, steps were made, and this was the way down, the entrance; the trench itself was the room, in which the lucky ones, such as the squadron commander, had a board lying on four posts at the far end—this was a table. Along both sides of the trench, earth was removed to a width of two and a half feet, and this made two beds or couches. The roof was constructed in such a way that one could stand up in the middle, and one could even sit up on the beds if one moved closer to the table. Denisov, who lived in luxury, because the soldiers of his squadron loved him, also had a board in the pediment of the roof with a piece of broken but mended glass set into it. When it was very cold, hot coals from the soldiers' bonfires were brought to the steps (the anteroom, as Denisov called this part of the shed) on a bent piece of sheet iron, and it became so warm that the officers, of whom there were always many with Rostov and Denisov, sat in nothing but their shirts.

In the month of April, Rostov was on duty. Past seven in the morning, coming home after a sleepless night, he ordered hot coals brought, changed his rain-soaked underclothes, said his prayers, drank some tea, got warm, tidied things up in his corner and on the table, and with a wind-burned face, in nothing but his shirt, lay on his back with his hands behind his head. He thought pleasantly about the promotion he was supposed to receive one of those days for his last reconnoitring, and waited for Denisov, who had stepped out somewhere. Rostov wanted to talk with him.

From behind the hut came the rolling shout of Denisov, obviously in a fit of temper. Rostov moved to the window to see whom he was dealing with, and saw Sergeant Major Topcheenko.

"I oghrdered you not to let them eat that ghroot, Mashka's or whatever!" shouted Denisov. "I saw it myself, Lazarchuk was bghringing some fghrom the fields."

"I ordered them, Your Honour, they don't obey," said the sergeant major.

Rostov lay down again on his bed and thought with pleasure: "Let him fuss and bustle now, I've done my job and I'm lying down—that's splendid!" Through the wall he heard that, besides the sergeant major, Lavrushka, Denisov's pert and roguish lackey, was also talking. Lavrushka was telling something about some sort of wagons, biscuits, and oxen he had seen when he went for provisions.

From behind the shed came the shouting of Denisov again, moving away, and the words: "Saddle up—second section!"

"Where are they going?" Rostov wondered.

Five minutes later Denisov came into the shed, climbed onto the bed in his muddy boots, angrily smoked his pipe, scattered all his belongings around, strapped on his riding whip and sabre, and started out of the dugout. To Rostov's question, where to?—he answered angrily and vaguely that there was business to be done.

"Let God and the ghreat soveghreign judge me for it!" Denisov said as he went out; and Rostov heard the hoofs of several horses splash through the mud behind the shed. Rostov did not even bother to find out where Denisov had gone. Having warmed up in his corner, he fell asleep and emerged from the hut only towards evening. Denisov had not come back yet. The evening turned clear; by the next dugout two officers and a junker were pitching horseshoes, laughing as the horseshoes stuck in the loose, muddy soil. Rostov joined them. In the middle of the game, the officers saw some wagons driving up to them. They were followed by about fifteen hussars on skinny horses. The wagons with their hussar convoy drove up to the tethering posts, and a crowd of hussars surrounded them.

"Well, so Denisov got all upset," said Rostov, "and here come the provisions."

"Right you are!" said the officers. "The soldiers must be overjoyed!" Denisov rode a little behind the hussars, accompanied by two infantry officers with whom he was talking about something. Rostov walked towards them.

"I warn you, Captain," said one of the officers, thin, small, and clearly very angry.

"I said I won't give them up," replied Denisov.

"You'll answer for this, Captain, it's violence—to seize your own army's transport! Our men haven't eaten for two days!"

"And mine haven't eaten for two weeks," replied Denisov.

"It's highway robbery, my dear sir, you'll answer for it!" the infantry officer repeated, raising his voice.

"What are you botheghring me for? Eh?" shouted Denisov, suddenly flaring up. "I'm the one who'll answer for it, not you, so stop buzzing aghround here while you're still in one piece. Maghrch!" he shouted at the officers.

"All right, then!" shouted the little officer, not intimidated and not going away. "This is highway robbery, so I'll . . ."

"Maghrch off to the devil, quick step, while you're still in one piece." And Denisov turned his horse towards the officer.

"All right, all right," the officer said menacingly, and, turning his horse, he rode off at a trot, bouncing in the saddle.

"A dog on a fence, a ghreal live dog on a fence," Denisov said behind him, a cavalryman's highest mockery of an infantryman on horseback, and riding up to Rostov, he burst out laughing.

"I took it fghrom the infantghry, took the whole tghransport by foghrce!" he said. "What, should people dghrop dead of hunger?"

The wagons that were driven up to the hussars had been intended for an infantry regiment, but learning from Lavrushka that the transport was unescorted, Denisov and his hussars took it by force. The soldiers were given biscuits in plenty, and they even shared them with other squadrons.

The next day the regimental commander summoned Denisov and told him, covering his eyes with his spread fingers: "I look at it this way, I know nothing, and will not start proceedings; but I advise you to go to the staff and settle matters there in the provisions department, and, if possible, to sign a receipt that you received such-and-such provisions; in the contrary case—since the request was put in by the infantry regiment—proceedings could be started and might end badly."

Denisov rode to the staff straight from the regimental commander, with a sincere wish to follow his advice. In the evening he returned to his dugout in such a state as Rostov had never yet seen him in. Denisov could not speak and was gasping for breath. When Rostov asked what was the matter with him, he only uttered incomprehensible oaths and threats in a hoarse and weak voice.

Alarmed by Denisov's state, Rostov suggested he should undress, drink some water, and send for the doctor.

"Me tghried for ghrobbery—ach! Give me more water—let them tghry me, but I'll beat the scoundghrels, I'll always beat them, and I'll tell the soveghreign. Give me ice," he kept murmuring.

The regimental doctor came and said it was necessary to bleed him. A deep dish of dark blood came from Denisov's shaggy arm, and only then was he able to tell what had happened to him.

"I arrive," Denisov told them. " 'Well, where's your superior here?' They point. 'Kindly wait.' 'I have duties, I've ghridden twenty miles, I have no time to wait, announce me.' Very good, this super-thief comes out and starts teaching me. 'This is ghrobbery!' 'Ghrobbery,' I say, 'is not when somebody takes pgrrovisions to feed his soldiers, but when he takes them so as to line his pockets!' Very good. 'Give your signature to the commissioner,' he says, 'and your case will be passed on through the chain of command.' I go to the commissioner. I enter—at the table sits . . . who do you think?! No, just think! . . . Who is it that's starving us?" Denisov shouted, pounding the table with the fist of his just-bled arm so hard that the table almost fell and the glasses on it jumped. "Telyanin!! 'So it's you who are starving us to death?!' One-two in the mug, they landed nicely. . . 'Ah! . . . you this, this, this, and that . . .' and I started pummelling him! Anyhow it was good fun, I can tell you," Denisov cried, baring his white teeth gleefully and spitefully under his black moustache. "I'd have killed him if they hadn't pulled us apart."

"But what are you shouting for? Calm down," said Rostov. "Here you're bleeding again. Wait, your bandage should be changed."

Denisov's bandage was changed, and he was put to bed. The next day he woke up cheerful and calm.

But at noon the regimental adjutant came with a grave and mournful face to Denisov and Rostov's dugout and regretfully showed them an official paper to Major Denisov from the regimental commander, in which questions were raised about yesterday's occurrence. The adjutant informed them that the affair was bound to take a rather bad turn, that a court martial had been appointed, and that, considering the present strictness about marauding and insubordination among the troops, in the best case the affair might end in demotion.

The affair was presented by the offended side in such guise that, after seizing the transport, Major Denisov, uninvited, in a drunken state, appeared at the quartermaster general's, called him a thief, threatened him with a beating, and, when removed, rushed into the office, attacked two clerks, and dislocated the arm of one.

To Rostov's renewed questions, Denisov, laughing, said that it seemed somebody else had turned up there, but it was all nonsense, trifles, that he did not even dream of being afraid of any courts, and that if those scoundrels dared to provoke him, he would give them an answer they would remember.

Denisov spoke disdainfully of the whole affair; but Rostov knew him too well not to notice that, in his soul (concealing it from others), he was afraid of the trial and suffered over the affair, which was obviously going to have bad consequences. Every day papers of enquiry came, summonses from the court, and on the first of May, Denisov was ordered to turn over command of the squadron to the next in seniority and report to the division staff for explanations of the case of violence in the provisions commission. On the eve of that day, Platov made a reconnaissance of the enemy with two Cossack regiments and two hussar squadrons. Denisov, as always, rode out in front of the line, showing off his courage. A bullet fired by a French rifleman hit him in the fleshy upper part of the leg. Perhaps at another time Denisov would not have left the regiment with such a slight wound, but now he took advantage of this chance, excused himself from appearing at the division, and went to the hospital.

XVII

In the month of June, the battle of Friedland took place,[23] in which the Pavlogradsky regiment did not participate, and after it a truce was declared. Rostov, who painfully felt his friend's absence, having no news of him since the time of his departure and worried about the course of his case and his wound, took advantage of the truce and obtained permission to visit Denisov in the hospital.

The hospital was in a little Prussian village twice ravaged by Russian and French troops. Precisely because it was summer, when it was so pleasant in the fields, this little village, with its broken roofs and fences and its littered streets, with ragged inhabitants and drunken or sick soldiers wandering about in it, presented an especially dismal sight.

The hospital was housed in a stone buidling with a portion of its windows and window frames broken, which stood in a yard with the remains of a dismantled fence. Several soldiers, bandaged, pale, and swollen, were walking about or sitting in the yard in the sun.

As soon as Rostov went through the door of the house, he was enveloped by the stench of rotting flesh and hospital. On the stairs he met a Russian military doctor with a cigar in his mouth. The doctor was followed by a Russian assistant.

"I can't tear myself in two," said the doctor. "Come to Makar Alexeevich's in the evening, I'll be there." The assistant asked him about something else.

"Eh! do it your own way! Isn't it all the same?" The doctor saw Rostov coming up the stairs.

"What do you want here, Your Honour?" asked the doctor. "What do you want here? The bullet missed you, so you want to catch typhus? This is a pesthouse, old boy."

"How so?" asked Rostov.

"Typhus, my lad. Anyone who comes here is a dead man. There's only the two of us, me and Makeev" (he pointed to the assistant) "still hanging on here. Five of our fellow doctors have already died. A new one comes, after one little week he's finished," the doctor said with visible pleasure. "Prussian doctors were invited, but our allies don't find it to their liking."

Rostov explained to him that he would like to see the hussar major Denisov, who was a patient there.

"I don't know, I can't say, my lad. Just think, I've got three hospitals to myself, four hundred and some patients! It's a good thing some Prussian charitable ladies send us two pounds of coffee and lint²⁴ a month, otherwise we'd have perished." He laughed. "Four hundred, my lad, and they keep sending new ones. It is four hundred? Eh?" he turned to the assistant.

The assistant looked exhausted. He was clearly waiting with vexation for the garrulous doctor to leave.

"Major Denisov," Rostov repeated, "he was wounded at Moliten."

"Seems he died. Eh, Makeev?" the doctor asked the assistant indifferently.

The assistant, however, did not confirm the doctor's words.

"What, a tall man, with reddish hair?" asked the doctor.

Rostov described Denisov's appearance.

"There was one, there was one like that," the doctor said as if joyfully. "Must have died, but anyhow I'll check, I had lists. Do you have them, Makeev?"

"Makar Alexeich has the lists," said the assistant. "But if you'd be pleased to go to the officers' ward, you can see for yourself there," he added, turning to Rostov.

"Eh, you'd better not, my lad," said the doctor, "or you may wind up staying yourself!" But Rostov took leave of the doctor and asked the assistant to accompany him.

"Just don't go blaming me!" the doctor shouted from the bottom of the stairs.

Rostov and the assistant went into the corridor. The hospital stench in this dark corridor was so strong that Rostov held his hand to his nose and had to stop and gather his strength to go further. A door to the right opened, and a thin, yellow man on crutches stuck himself out, barefoot and in nothing but his underwear. Leaning against the door frame, he looked at the passing men with glittering, envious eyes. Glancing through the door, Rostov saw sick and wounded men lying there on the floor, on straw and overcoats.

"What's this?" he asked.

"The soldiers' wards," the assistant replied. "Nothing to be done," he added, as if apologizing.

"May I go in and look?" asked Rostov.

"What's there to look at?" said the assistant. But precisely because the assistant obviously did not want to let him go in, Rostov entered the soldiers' wards. Here the stench, which he had managed to get used to in the corridor, was still stronger. The stench here was slightly different: it was sharper, and one could sense that it was coming precisely from here.

In the long room, brightly lit by the sun through the large windows, sick and wounded men lay in two rows, their heads towards the walls, leaving a passage in the middle. Most of them were oblivious and paid no attention to the visitors. Those who were conscious all sat up or raised their thin, yellow faces, and fastened their eyes on Rostov with the same expression of hope for help, of reproach and envy of another man's health. Rostov went to the middle of the room, glanced into the next two rooms through the open doors, and on both sides saw the same thing. He stopped, silently looking around him. He had never expected to see what he saw. Right in front of him, almost across the middle passage, on the bare floor lay a sick man, probably a Cossack, because his hair was cut square. This Cossack lay on his back, his huge arms and legs spread. His face was purple-red, his eyes were completely rolled up so that only the whites showed, and the veins on his bare feet and arms, also red, were taut as ropes. He struck his head on the floor and said something hoarsely, and started repeating a word. Rostov listened to what he said and figured out the word he was repeating. This word was "drink, drink, drink!" Rostov looked around, hoping to find someone who could put this patient in his place and give him some water.

"Who looks after the patients here?" he asked the assistant. Just then a commissariat soldier, a hospital attendant, came out of the next room and, stamping his feet, snapped to attention in front of Rostov.

"Good day to you, Your Honour, sir!" the soldier shouted out, rolling his eyes at Rostov and obviously taking him for a hospital superior.

"Take him away, give him water," Rostov said, pointing to the Cossack.

"Yes, sir, Your Honour," the soldier said with pleasure, rolling his eyes and drawing himself up still more zealously, but not budging from his place.

"No, there's nothing to be done here," thought Rostov, lowering his eyes, and he was already about to leave, but he felt a meaningful gaze directed at him from the right and turned to look. Almost in the corner, on an overcoat, sat an old soldier with a yellow, stern face, gaunt as a skeleton's, and an unshaven grey beard, looking fixedly at Rostov. The old soldier's neighbour on one side was whispering something to him, pointing at Rostov. Rostov understood that the old man meant to ask him something. He went closer and saw that only one of the old man's legs was bent under him; the other was missing above the knee. The old man's other neighbour, who lay without moving, his head thrown back, some distance from him, was a young soldier with a waxen pallor on his snub-nosed, still freckled face, and only the whites of his eyes showing. Rostov looked at this snub-nosed soldier and a chill ran down his spine.

"But this one seems to be . . ." he turned to the assistant.

"We've been asking and asking, Your Honour," said the old soldier, his lower jaw trembling. "He passed away this morning. We're people, too, not dogs . . ."

"I'll send someone at once, he'll be taken away, he'll be taken away," the assistant said hastily. "If you please, Your Honour."

"Let's go, let's go!" Rostov said hastily, and, lowering his eyes and shrinking, he tried to pass unnoticed through the line of those reproachful and envious eyes directed at him as he left the room.

XVIII

Going down the corridor, the assistant led Rostov to the officers' wards, which consisted of three rooms with open doors. In these rooms there were beds; wounded and sick officers were sitting and lying on them. Some walked about the room in hospital gowns. The first person Rostov met in the officers' ward was a small, thin man without an arm, in a nightcap and hospital gown, with a little pipe in his teeth, who was walking about the first room. Rostov peered at him intently, trying to remember where he had seen him.

"See where God granted us to meet again," said the small man. "Tushin, Tushin—remember, I gave you a ride at Schöngraben? I've had a bit cut off, see . . ." he said, smiling and showing the empty sleeve of the robe. "It's Vassily Dmitrich Denisov you're looking for? He's my roommate," he said, on learning who Rostov wanted. "This way, this way." And Tushin led him to the other room, from which came the loud laughter of several voices.

"How can they not only live here, but even laugh?" thought Rostov, still sensing that smell of dead flesh he had picked up in the soldiers' section, and still seeing around him those envious looks that had followed after him on both sides and the face of the young soldier with rolled-up eyes.

Denisov, the blanket pulled over his head, was asleep in bed, though it was nearly noon.

"Ah! Ghrostov! Ghreetings, ghreetings!" he shouted, in the same voice he used in the regiment; but Rostov noticed sadly that, behind this habitual casualness and liveliness, some new, bad, hidden feeling showed in the expression of Denisov's face, in his intonations and words.

His wound, despite its insignificance, still had not healed, though it was now six weeks since he was wounded. His face had the same pale swollenness of all the hospital faces. But it was not this that struck Rostov: what struck him was that Denisov did not seem glad to see him and smiled at him unnaturally. Denisov did not ask about the regiment, nor about the general course of affairs. When Rostov mentioned it, Denisov did not listen.

Rostov even noticed that Denisov found it unpleasant to be reminded of the regiment and generally of that other, free life that went on outside the hospital. It seemed he was trying to forget that former life and was interested only in his case with the provision officials. To Rostov's question about how the case stood, he immediately pulled from under the pillow a paper he had received from the commission and the draft of his reply to it. When he started reading his paper, he became animated and particularly drew Rostov's attention to the biting remarks in it directed at his enemies. Denisov's hospital friends, who surrounded Rostov as a newly arrived person from the free world, gradually began to disperse as soon as Denisov started reading his paper. From their faces, Rostov understood that these gentlemen had all heard the story more than once already and were tired of it. Only the man in the next bed, a fat uhlan, stayed sitting on his cot, frowning gloomily and smoking his pipe, and little one-armed Tushin went on listening, shaking his head disapprovingly. In the middle of the reading, the uhlan interrupted Denisov.

"In my view," he said, turning to Rostov, "he ought simply to beg the sovereign for mercy. They say there will be lots of rewards now, and surely he'd be forgiven . . ."

"Me beg the soveghreign!" Denisov said in a voice which he wanted to endow with its former energy and ardour, but which rang with futile irritability. "For what? If I were a ghrobber, I'd ask for meghrcy, but I'm on tghrial because I bghrought the ghrobbers to light. Let them take me to court, I'm not afghraid of anybody; I've seghrved the tsar and the fatherland honoughrably, and didn't steal! To demote me and . . . Listen, I just wghrite to them stghraight out, here's what I wghrite: 'If I were an embezzler . . .' "

"It's cleverly written, there's no saying it's not," said Tushin. "But that's not the point, Vassily Dmitrich," he also turned to Rostov, "a man ought to submit, but Vassily Dmitrich here doesn't want to. The auditor told you your case was going badly."

"Well, let it go badly," said Denisov.

"The auditor wrote a petition for you," Tushin went on, "and you ought to sign it, and, see, you can send it with him" (he pointed to Rostov). "He's surely got a hand in at the staff. There couldn't be a better chance."

"Yes, but I told you I won't go ghrovelling," Denisov interrupted and continued reading the letter.

Rostov did not dare to persuade Denisov, though he felt instinctively that the way suggested by Tushin and the other officers was the surest, and though he would have considered himself very happy if he could have been of help to Denisov: he knew Denisov's inflexible will and righteous ardour.

When the reading of Denisov's venomous papers, which lasted more than an hour, was over, Rostov said nothing and spent the rest of the day in a very sad state of mind, in the company of Denisov's hospital friends, who again gathered around him. He told them things he knew and listened to what others had to say. Denisov was gloomily silent throughout the evening.

Late in the evening, Rostov got ready to go and asked Denisov whether there would be any errands.

"Yes, wait," said Denisov, glancing at the officers, and, taking his papers from under the pillow, he went to the window, where there was an inkstand, and sat down to write.

"It seems you can't bghreak an axehead with a stghraw," he said, coming from the window and handing Rostov a large envelope. This was a petition addressed to the sovereign, drawn up by the auditor, in which Denisov, without mentioning anything about the failures of the provisions department, merely begged for mercy.

"Hand it in, since it seems . . ." He did not finish and smiled a painfully false smile.

XIX

Having returned to the regiment and told the commander about the state of Denisov's case, Rostov rode on to Tilsit with the letter to the sovereign.

On the thirteenth of June, the French and Russian emperors met at Tilsit.[25] Boris Drubetskoy asked the important person to whom he was attached that he be included in the suite appointed to be stationed in Tilsit.

*"Je voudrais voir le grand homme,"** he said, referring to Napoleon, whom, until then, like everyone else, he had always called Buonaparte.

"Vous parlez de Buonaparte?"† his general said to him, smiling.

Boris looked questioningly at his general and understood at once that this was a joking test.

"Mon prince, je parle de l'empereur Napoléon,"‡ he replied. The general smiled and patted him on the shoulder.

"You'll go far," he said to him, and took him along.

Boris was among the few who were at the Niemen on the day of the emperors' meeting; he saw the rafts with monograms and Napoleon riding along the other bank past the French guards; saw the emperor Alexander's pensive face as he sat silently in a tavern on the bank of the Niemen awaiting Napoleon's arrival; saw how both emperors got into boats and how Napoleon, who was the first to reach the raft, stepped forward quickly to meet Alexander and gave him his hand, and how the two disappeared into the pavilion. Since the time of his entrance into the higher world, Boris had made it his habit to observe attentively what was happening around him and to write it down. During the meeting in Tilsit, he asked the names of the persons who arrived with Napoleon, about the uniforms they were wearing, and listened attentively to the words spoken by important persons. At the moment when the emperors went into the pavilion, he looked at his watch, and he did not forget to look again when Alexander came out of the pavilion. The meeting had lasted an hour and fifty-three minutes; and he wrote it down that evening, among other facts which he supposed were of historic significance. Since the emperor's suite was very small, for a man who valued his success in the service to be in Tilsit at the time

---

*I would like to see the great man.
†Do you mean Buonaparte?
‡My prince, I mean the emperor Napoleon.

of the emperors' meeting was a very important matter, and Boris, having gone to Tilsit, felt that from then on his position was completely assured. He was not only known, he was an accustomed and familiar figure. Twice he had been entrusted with messages to the sovereign himself, so that the sovereign knew his face, and all his attendants were now not only not aloof, as before, considering him a new person, but would have been surprised if he were not there.

Boris roomed with another adjutant, the Polish count Zhilinsky. Zhilinsky, a Pole brought up in Paris, was rich, passionately loved the French, and almost every day during their stay in Tilsit, Zhilinsky and Boris gathered French officers from the guards and French headquarters for dinners and lunches.

In the evening of the twenty-fourth of June, Count Zhilinsky, Boris's roommate, gave a supper for his French acquaintances. At this supper there was a guest of honour—one of Napoleon's adjutants—as well as several officers of the French guards, and a young boy from an old French aristocratic family, Napoleon's page. On that same day, Rostov, taking advantage of the darkness so as not to be recognized, in civilian dress, arrived in Tilsit and went to the apartment of Zhilinsky and Boris.

In Rostov, as in the whole army from which he came, that change in relations with Napoleon and the French, turning them from enemies into friends, was still far from being accomplished as it had been at headquarters and in Boris. In the army they still went on experiencing a mixed feeling of anger, contempt, and fear for Bonaparte and the French. Still recently Rostov, talking with one of Platov's Cossack officers, had argued that if Napoleon were ever taken prisoner, he would be treated not as a sovereign, but as a criminal. Still recently, meeting a wounded French colonel on the road, Rostov had become heated, proving to him that there could be no peace between a legitimate sovereign and the criminal Bonaparte. Therefore Rostov was oddly struck in Boris's apartment by the sight of French officers in those same uniforms which he was used to looking at quite differently from the flank line. As soon as he saw a French officer thrust himself out of the door, that warlike, hostile feeling which he always experienced at the sight of the enemy suddenly took hold of him. He stopped on the threshold and asked in Russian whether Drubetskoy lived there. Boris, hearing a stranger's voice in the front hall, came out to meet him. His face, when he recognized Rostov, at first expressed annoyance.

"Ah, it's you, very glad, very glad to see you," he said anyhow, smiling and going up to him. But Rostov had noticed his first reaction.

"It seems I chose the wrong time," he said. "I wouldn't have come, but I'm on business," he said coldly . . .

"No, I was only surprised that you've left the regiment. *Dans un moment je suis à vous,*"* he replied to a voice that was calling him.

*I'll be with you in a moment.

"I can see it's the wrong time," Rostov repeated.

The expression of annoyance had already disappeared from Boris's face; evidently having reflected and decided what to do, he took him by both hands with a particular calm and led him to the neighbouring room. Boris's eyes, looking calmly and firmly at Rostov, were as if veiled by something, as if some sort of screen—the blue spectacles of convention—had been put on them. So it seemed to Rostov.

"Ah, enough, please, as if you could come at the wrong time," said Boris. He led him into the room, where the supper table had been laid, introduced him to his guests, giving his name and explaining that he was not a civilian, but a hussar officer and his old friend. "Count Zhilinsky, *le comte N. N., le capitaine S. S.,*" he named his guests. Rostov looked frowningly at the Frenchmen, made his bows reluctantly, and said nothing.

Zhilinsky clearly took this new Russian person into his circle without any joy and said nothing to Rostov. Boris seemed not to notice the constraint caused by the appearance of a new person and, with the same agreeable calm and veiling of the eyes with which he had met Rostov, tried to enliven the conversation. One of the Frenchmen turned with habitual French politeness to the stubbornly silent Rostov and said to him that he had probably come to Tilsit to see the emperor.

"No, I'm on business," Rostov answered curtly.

Rostov felt ill-humoured immediately after he noticed the displeasure on Boris's face, and, as always happens with people who are ill-humoured, it seemed to him that everyone was looking at him hostilely and that he was hampering them all. And indeed he was hampering them all and alone remained outside the newly initiated general conversation. "Why is he sitting here?" said the glances cast at him by the guests. He got up and went over to Boris.

"Anyhow I'm in your way," he said softly to him. "Let's go and talk business, and I'll leave."

"Why no, not in the least," said Boris. "But if you're tired, let's go to my room, and you can lie down to rest."

"Yes, in fact . . ."

They went into the small room where Boris slept. Rostov, not sitting down, at once, with irritation—as if Boris was guilty before him for something—began telling him about Denisov's case, asking whether he could and would intercede for Denisov with the sovereign through his general and deliver his letter through him. When they were alone, Rostov realized for the first time that it was awkward for him to look Boris in the eye. Boris, crossing his legs, and stroking the slender fingers of his right hand with his left, listened to Rostov the way a general listens to the report of a subordinate, now looking away, now looking directly into Rostov's eyes with the same veiled gaze. Each time that happened, Rostov felt awkward and lowered his eyes.

"I've heard about cases of that sort, and I know that the sovereign is very severe on such occasions. I think it should not get as far as his majesty. In my opinion, it would be better to ask the corps commander directly . . . But generally I think . . ."

"If you don't want to do anything, just say so!" Rostov nearly shouted, not looking into Boris's eyes.

Boris smiled.

"On the contrary, I'll do what I can, only I thought . . ."

Just then Zhilinsky's voice was heard at the door, calling Boris.

"Well, go, go," said Rostov, and, declining supper and remaining alone in the little room, he paced up and down for a long time and listened to the merry French talk in the next room.

XX

Rostov had come to Tilsit on the day least suitable of all for interceding on Denisov's behalf. He could not go to the general on duty himself, because he was wearing a tailcoat and had come to Tilsit without permission of the authorities, while Boris, even if he wanted to, could not do it on the day after Rostov's arrival. On that day, the twenty-seventh of June, the preliminary conditions for peace were signed. The emperors exchanged decorations: Alexander received the Legion of Honour, and Napoleon the St. Andrew of the first degree, and on that day a dinner was arranged for the Preobrazhensky battalion, given by the battalion of the French guards.[26] Both sovereigns were to be present at this banquet.

For Rostov it was so awkward and unpleasant to be with Boris that, when Boris looked in on him after supper, he pretended to be asleep, and the next day he left the house early in the morning, trying not to see him. Nikolai wandered around town in a tailcoat and a round hat, gazing at the French and their uniforms, and at the streets and houses where the Russian and French emperors lived. In the square he saw tables being set up and preparations being made for the dinner; in the streets he saw draperies hung across with flags in the Russian and French colours and huge monograms of A and N. In the windows of the houses there were also flags and monograms.

"Boris doesn't want to help me, and I don't want to turn to him. That's settled," thought Nikolai, "it's all over between us, but I won't leave here without doing all I can for Denisov and, above all, without delivering the letter to the sovereign. To the sovereign?! He's here!" thought Rostov, involuntarily coming up again to the house occupied by Alexander.

Saddle horses stood by this house, and the suite was gathering, evidently preparing for the sovereign's levee.

"I may see him any moment," thought Rostov. "If only I could deliver the letter to him directly and tell him everything . . . Would they really arrest me for my tailcoat? It can't be! He would understand whose side justice is on. He understands everything, knows everything. Who can be more just and magnanimous than he? Well, and if they arrest me for being here, what's so bad about that?" he thought, looking at an officer going into the house occupied by the sovereign. "People do go in. Eh! it's all nonsense! I'll go and deliver the letter to the sovereign myself: so much the worse for Drubetskoy, who drove me to it." And suddenly, with a resoluteness which he did not expect of himself, Rostov felt for the letter in his pocket and went straight to the house occupied by the sovereign.

"No, I'm not going to let the chance slip now as I did after Austerlitz," he thought, expecting to meet the sovereign any moment and feeling the blood rush to his heart at the thought of it. "I'll fall at his feet and plead with him. He'll raise me up, listen to me, and even thank me. 'I'm happy when I can do good, but to set right an injustice is the greatest happiness,' " Rostov imagined the words that the sovereign would say to him. And he walked past curious onlookers up the porch of the house which the sovereign occupied.

From the porch a broad stairway led straight up; to the right he saw a closed door. Under the stairway was the door leading to the ground floor.

"Whom do you want?" someone asked.

"To deliver a letter, a petition to His Majesty," Nikolai said in a trembling voice.

"A petition—go to the officer on duty, this way, please" (he pointed him to the downstairs door). "Only you won't be received."

Hearing this indifferent voice, Rostov became frightened of what he was doing; the thought of meeting the sovereign at any moment was so seductive and therefore so frightening for him that he was ready to flee, but an attendant, meeting him, opened the door of the officer on duty, and Rostov went in.

A short, stout man of about thirty, in white trousers, top boots, and nothing but an evidently just-put-on cambric shirt, was standing in this room; a valet behind him was buttoning on a pair of splendid new silk-embroidered braces, which Rostov noticed for some reason. This man was talking to someone in the next room.

"*Bien faite et la beauté du diable,*"* this man was saying, and, seeing Rostov, he stopped speaking and frowned.

"What can I do for you? A petition? . . ."

"*Qu'est-ce que c'est?*"† asked someone from the other room.

"*Encore un petitionnaire,*"‡ replied the man in braces.

"Later, tell him. He'll be coming out in a minute, we have to go."

---

*Well-built and fresh as a daisy.
†What is it?
†Another petitioner.

"Later, later, tomorrow. There's no time . . ."

Rostov turned and was about to leave, but the man in braces stopped him.

"Who sent you? Who are you?"

"From Major Denisov," Rostov replied.

"Who are you? An officer?"

"Lieutenant Count Rostov.

"What boldness! Appeal through the chain of command. And take yourself away, away! . . ." And he began getting into the tunic that the valet was holding for him.

Rostov went to the front hall again and noticed that there were already many officers and generals in full-dress uniform past whom he would have to walk.

Cursing his boldness, his heart sinking at the thought that he could meet the sovereign at any moment, be disgraced before him and put under arrest, fully understanding all the inappropriateness of his behaviour and regretting it, Rostov, with lowered eyes, was making his way out of the house, surrounded by the crowd of the brilliant suite, when someone's familiar voice called him and someone's hand stopped him.

"What are you doing here in a tailcoat, my lad?" the bass voice asked him.

It was a cavalry general who had earned special favour from the sovereign during this campaign, the former commander of the division in which Rostov served.

Rostov fearfully began to justify himself, but seeing the general's good-naturedly joking face, led him aside and in an agitated voice told him the whole affair, begging the general to intercede for Denisov, whom he knew. The general listened to Rostov, shaking his head gravely.

"A pity, a pity for the fine fellow; give me the letter."

Rostov barely had time to hand him the letter and tell him all about Denisov's case before the sound of quick footsteps with spurs was heard from the stairway, and the general, leaving him, moved towards the porch. The gentlemen of the sovereign's suite ran down the steps and went to their horses. The groom Hayne, the same one who had been at Austerlitz, led up the sovereign's horse, and from the stairs came a light creak of footsteps which Rostov knew at once. Forgetting the danger of being recognized, Rostov, with some curious townsfolk, moved close to the porch and again, after two years, saw the same adored features, the same face, the same gaze, the same gait, the same combination of majesty and mildness . . . And the feeling of rapture and love for the sovereign rose again with its old force in Rostov's soul. The sovereign, in the Preobrazhensky tunic, white buckskin breeches, and high top boots, with a star Rostov did not know (it was the *Légion d'honneur*), came out to the porch, holding his hat under his arm and putting on a glove. He stopped, looked about, and illuminated everything around him with his gaze. He spoke a few words to one of the generals. He also recognized the former commander of Rostov's division, smiled to him, and called him over.

The entire suite now drew back, and Rostov saw the general speak about something with the sovereign for a rather long time.

The sovereign said a few words to him and took a step towards his horse. Again the crowd of the suite and the crowd of the street, in which Rostov stood, moved towards the sovereign. Stopping by his horse and placing his hand on the saddle, the sovereign turned to the cavalry general and spoke in a loud voice, obviously wishing everyone to hear him.

"I cannot, General, and the reason why I cannot is that the law is stronger than I," said the sovereign, and he raised his foot to the stirrup. The general inclined his head deferentially, the sovereign mounted and rode down the street at a gallop. Rostov, beside himself with rapture, ran after him with the crowd.

XXI

On the square to which the sovereign was riding there stood facing each other on the right the Preobrazhensky battalion and on the left the battalion of the French guards in their bearskin hats.

As the sovereign was approaching one flank of the battalions, which presented arms, another group of horsemen was riding up to the opposite flank, and at the head of them Rostov recognized Napoleon. It could not have been anyone else. He rode at a gallop, in a small hat, with the sash of St. Andrew across his shoulder, in a blue tunic unbuttoned over a white camisole, on an extraordinary purebred grey Arabian stallion, on a gold-embroidered crimson shabrack. Riding up to Alexander, he raised his hat, and as he did so Rostov's cavalry eye could not help noticing that Napoleon sat his horse poorly and unsteadily. The battalions shouted "Hurrah!" and *"Vive l'Empereur!"* Napoleon said something to Alexander. The two emperors got off their horses and took each other's hands. Napoleon's face wore an unpleasantly false smile. Alexander was saying something to him with a benign expression.

Rostov, not taking his eyes away, despite the trampling of the French gendarmes' horses, attempting to move the crowd back, followed every movement of the emperor Alexander and Bonaparte. He was struck, as if it was unexpected, by the fact that Alexander behaved as an equal with Bonaparte, and that Bonaparte, quite freely, as if such closeness to the sovereign was natural and habitual to him, treated the Russian tsar as an equal.

Alexander and Napoleon, with the long tail of their suite, approached the right flank of the Preobrazhensky battalion, riding straight at the crowd that was standing there. The crowd unexpectedly found itself so close to the emperors that Rostov, who was standing in the first rows, was afraid he would be recognized.

*"Sire, je vous demande la permission de donner la Légion d'honneur au plus brave de vos soldats,"** said a sharp, precise voice, articulating every letter.

This was spoken by the short Bonaparte, looking from below straight into Alexander's eyes. Alexander listened attentively to what was said to him and, inclining his head, smiled pleasantly.

"À celui qui s'est le plus vaillamment conduit dans cette dernière guerre,"† Napoleon added, rapping out every syllable with a calm and assurance that Rostov found outrageous, and looking over the ranks of Russian soldiers standing at attention before him, still presenting arms and looking fixedly at the face of their emperor.

"Votre Majesté me permettra-t-elle de demander l'avis du colonel,"‡ said Alexander, and took a few hasty steps towards Prince Kozlovsky, the commander of the battalion. Bonaparte meanwhile began to remove the glove from his small white hand, tore it, and threw it down. An adjutant, hastily rushing forward from behind, picked it up.

"To whom should it be given?" the emperor Alexander said softly to Kozlovsky in Russian.

"To whomever you order, Your Majesty."

The sovereign winced with displeasure and, looking around, said:

"But I must give him an answer."

Kozlovsky, with a resolute air, looked over the ranks and in that look took in Rostov.

"What if it's me?" thought Rostov.

"Lazarev!" the colonel commanded, frowning, and Lazarev, the first soldier in the rank, briskly stepped forward.

"Where are you going? Stop right there!" voices whispered to Lazarev, who did not know where to go. Lazarev stopped, casting a fearful sidelong glance at the colonel, and his face twitched, as happens with soldiers called out of line.

Napoleon turned his head slightly and held out his small, plump hand behind him, as if wishing to take something. The persons of his suite, guessing that very second what was wanted, began fussing, whispering, handing something on, and the page, the same one Rostov had seen the day before at Boris's, ran forward and, bending deferentially over the proffered hand, and without making it wait a single second, placed in it the decoration on its red ribbon. Napoleon, not looking, closed two fingers. The decoration was between them. Napoleon went up to Lazarev, who, staring wide-eyed, stubbornly went

*Sire, I ask your permission to give the Legion of Honour to the bravest of your soldiers.
†To him who bore himself most valiantly in this last war.
‡Your majesty will allow me ask the opinion of the colonel.

on looking only at his sovereign, and gave the emperor Alexander a glance, showing thereby that what he was now doing, he was doing for his ally. The small white hand with the decoration touched the soldier Lazarev's button. It was as if Napoleon knew that, for this soldier to be happy, rewarded, and distinguished from everyone else in the world, it was only necessary that his, Napoleon's, hand deign to touch the soldier's breast. Napoleon merely laid the cross on Lazarev's breast and, lowering his hand, turned to Alexander, as if he knew that the cross must stick to Lazarev's breast. The cross did stick, because obliging Russian and French hands instantly picked it up and fastened it to the tunic. Lazarev glanced darkly at the little man with white hands who had done something to him, and, motionless, continuing to present arms, again began gazing straight into Alexander's eyes, as if asking Alexander if he should go on standing there or would now be ordered to take a few steps or perhaps to do something else. But he was not ordered to do anything, and he remained in that motionless state for a rather long time.

The sovereigns got on their horses and left. The Preobrazhensky battalion, breaking ranks, mingled with the French guards and sat down at the tables prepared for them.

Lazarev sat in the place of honour; he was embraced, congratulated, his hands were shaken by Russian and French officers. Crowds of officers and people came merely to look at Lazarev. A droning of Russian and French talk and laughter hung over the tables on the square. Two officers with flushed faces, merry and happy, walked past him.

"What a treat, brother—all on silver," said one. "Have you seen Lazarev?"

"Yes."

"Tomorrow, they say, the Preobrazhensky battalion will be the hosts."

"No, but what luck for Lazarev! A twelve-hundred-franc pension for life."

"How's that for a hat, boys!" cried a Preobrazhensky soldier, putting on a Frenchman's shaggy hat.

"Charming, suits you perfectly!"

"Did you hear the passwords?" one officer of the guards said to another. "Two days ago they were '*Napoléon, France, bravoure,*' yesterday '*Alexandre, Russie, grandeur*'; one day our sovereign gives the passwords, the next day Napoleon. Tomorrow our sovereign will send a St. George to the bravest of the French guards. No way out of it! He has to respond in kind."

Boris, with his comrade Zhilinsky, also came to look at the Preobrazhensky banquet. On his way home, Boris noticed Rostov standing by the corner of a house.

"Rostov! Greetings! We haven't seen each other," he said and could not help asking what had happened to him: so strangely dark and upset was Rostov's face.

"Never mind, never mind," replied Rostov.

"Will you stop by?"

"Yes."

Rostov stood at the corner for a long time, looking at the feasting men from a distance. Painful work was going on in his mind, which he could not bring to an end. Terrible doubts arose in his soul. Now he remembered Denisov with his changed expression, his submission, and the whole hospital with those torn-off arms and legs, that filth and disease. He imagined so vividly now that hospital stench of dead flesh that he looked around to see where the stench could be coming from. Then he remembered that self-satisfied Bonaparte with his white little hand, who was now an emperor, whom the emperor Alexander liked and respected. Why, then, those torn-off arms and legs, those dead people? Then he remembered the rewarded Lazarev and Denisov punished and unforgiven. He caught himself in such strange thoughts that it made him frightened.

The smell of the Preobrazhenskys' food and his own hunger brought him out of that state: he had to eat something before he left. He went to the inn he had noticed in the morning. In the inn he found so many people and officers who had come, as he had, in civilian dress, that he had a hard time getting dinner. Two officers of his division joined him. The conversation naturally turned to the peace. The officers, Rostov's comrades, like the greater part of the army, were displeased with the peace concluded after Friedland. They said that if we had held out a little longer, Napoleon would have been done for, that there were no biscuits or shot left in his army. Nikolai ate silently and mostly drank. He drank two bottles of wine by himself. The inner work that had arisen in him, not being resolved, still pained him. He was afraid to give himself to his thoughts and yet could not get rid of them. Suddenly, to the words of one of the officers, that it was offensive to look at the French, Rostov began shouting with a vehemence that was in no way justified and therefore surprised the officers very much.

"And how can you judge what would have been better!" he shouted, his face suddenly suffused with blood. "How can you judge the sovereign's actions, what right have we to discuss it?! We can understand neither the goals nor the actions of the sovereign!"

"But I didn't say a word about the sovereign," the officer defended himself, unable to explain Rostov's outburst otherwise than by his being drunk.

But Rostov was not listening.

"We're not diplomatic officials, we're soldiers and nothing more," he went on. "We're told to die—and we die. If we're punished, it means we're guilty; it's not for us to judge. If it pleases the sovereign emperor to recognize Bonaparte as emperor and conclude an alliance with him—it means it has to be so. And if we start judging and reasoning about everything, then there'll be nothing sacred left. Next we'll be saying there's no God, no anything," shouted

Nikolai, banging the table, quite inappropriately in his interlocutors' opinion, but quite in keeping with his own train of thought.

"Our business is to do our duty, to cut and slash, not to think, that's all," he concluded.

"And to drink," said one of the officers, unwilling to quarrel.

"Yes, and to drink," Nikolai picked up. "Hey, you! Another bottle!" he shouted.

Part Three

I

In 1808 the emperor Alexander went to Erfurt for a new meeting with the emperor Napoleon, and there was much talk in Petersburg high society about the grandeur of this solemn meeting.[1]

In 1809 the closeness of the two rulers of the world, as Napoleon and Alexander were called, had reached the point that, when Napoleon declared war on Austria that year, a Russian corps went abroad to assist their former enemy, Bonaparte, against their former ally, the Austrian emperor, and there was talk in high circles about the possibility of marriage between Napoleon and one of the emperor Alexander's sisters. But, besides considerations of foreign policy, the attention of Russian society at that time was turned with particular keenness to the internal reforms that were then being carried out in all parts of the government.

Life meanwhile, people's real life with its essential concerns of health, illness, work, rest, with its concerns of thought, learning, poetry, music, love, friendship, hatred, passions, went on as always, independently and outside of any political closeness or enmity with Napoleon Bonaparte and outside all possible reforms.

Prince Andrei had been living in the country for two years without a break. All those undertakings which Pierre had initiated on his estates and had not brought to any result, constantly changing from one thing to another—all these undertakings, without talking about them to anyone and without any noticeable effort, had been carried out by Prince Andrei.

He possessed in the highest degree that practical tenacity, lacking in Pierre, which kept things in motion without any big gestures and efforts on his part.

On one of his estates of three hundred souls, the peasants were registered as free ploughmen (this was one of the first examples in Russia), on some others the corvée was replaced by quitrent.[2] A trained midwife was invited to Bogucharovo at his expense to help women in childbirth, and a priest was paid to teach the children of the peasants and servants to read and write.

Prince Andrei spent half his time at Bald Hills with his father and his son, who was still in the care of nannies; the other half in his Bogucharovo cloister, as his father called his estate. Despite the indifference he had displayed to

Pierre towards all external events in the world, he followed them assiduously, received many books, and, to his own astonishment, noticed, when people from Petersburg came to visit him or his father, fresh from the very whirlwind of life, that these people, in their knowledge of all that was happening in external and internal politics, were far behind him, who sat all the time in the country.

Besides being taken up with his estates, besides being generally taken up with reading the most varied books, Prince Andrei was taken up at that time with a critical analysis of our last two unfortunate campaigns and with drawing up a project for change in our military regulations and statutes.

In the spring of 1809, Prince Andrei went to his son's Ryazan estates, of which he was the trustee.

Warmed by the spring sun, he sat in his open carriage, looking at the first grass, the first birch leaves, and the first billows of white spring clouds racing across the bright blue sky. He was not thinking about anything, but looked around cheerfully and meaninglessly.

They crossed the ferry on which he had talked with Pierre a year before. They drove past a dirty village, threshing floors, sprouting fields, down a slope with residual snow by a bridge, up a slope of muddy clay, past strips of stubble and bushes greening here and there, and entered a birch woods on both sides of the road. It was almost hot in the woods, the wind was not felt. The birches, all strewn with sticky green leaves, did not stir, and the first green grass and purple flowers were poking through and lifting up last year's leaves. Small fir trees, scattered here and there among the birches, were an unpleasant reminder of winter with their crude evergreen needles. The horses began to snort as they drove into the woods and sweated more visibly.

The footman Pyotr said something to the coachman; the coachman answered affirmatively. But evidently the coachman's sympathy was not enough for Pyotr: he turned on the box towards his master.

"Your Excellency, how light it feels!" he said, smiling respectfully.

"What?"

"It feels light, Your Excellency."

"What's he talking about?" thought Prince Andrei. "Ah, the spring, probably," he thought, looking about. "So it is, everything's green already . . . so quickly! Birches, and bird cherry, and alders already beginning . . . But no sign of oaks. Ah, there's one."

At the side of the road stood an oak. Probably ten times older than the birches of the woods, it was ten times as thick and twice as tall as any birch. It was an enormous oak, twice the span of a man's arms in girth, with some limbs broken off long ago, and broken bark covered with old scars. With its huge, gnarled, ungainly, unsymmetrically spread arms and fingers, it stood, old, angry, scornful, and ugly, amidst the smiling birches. It alone did not want to submit to the charm of spring and did not want to see either the springtime or the sun.

"Spring, and love, and happiness!" the oak seemed to say. "And how is it you're not bored with the same stupid, senseless deception! Always the same, and always a deception! There is no spring, no sun, no happiness. Look, there sit those smothered, dead fir trees, always the same; look at me spreading my broken, flayed fingers wherever they grow—from my back, from my sides. As they've grown, so I stand, and I don't believe in your hopes and deceptions."

Prince Andrei turned several times to look at this oak as he drove through the woods, as if he expected something from it. There were flowers and grass beneath the oak as well, but it stood among them in the same way, scowling, motionless, ugly, and stubborn.

"Yes, it's right, a thousand times right, this oak," thought Prince Andrei. "Let others, the young ones, succumb afresh to this deception, but we know life—our life is over!" A whole new series of thoughts in connection with the oak, hopeless but sadly pleasant, emerged in Prince Andrei's soul. During this journey it was as if he again thought over his whole life and reached the same old comforting and hopeless conclusion, that there was no need for him to start anything, that he had to live out his life without doing evil, without anxiety, and without wishing for anything.

II

On business to do with the trusteeship of the Ryazan estates, Prince Andrei had to see the provincial marshal of nobility. The marshal was Count Ilya Andreevich Rostov, and in the middle of May Prince Andrei went to see him.

It was now the hot period of spring. The woods were now fully clothed, it was dusty and so hot that, passing by water, one wanted to go for a swim.

Prince Andrei, cheerless and preoccupied by considerations of one thing and another that he had to ask the marshal to do with business, was driving up the garden avenue to the Rostovs' house in Otradnoe. From behind the trees on the right, he heard merry feminine cries and saw a crowd of girls running across the path of his carriage. Ahead of the others, closer, a dark-haired girl came running towards the carriage, very slender, strangely slender, dark-eyed, in a yellow cotton dress, her head tied with a white kerchief, from under which strands of loose hair escaped. The girl was shouting something, but, seeing the stranger, ran back laughing without looking at him.

For some reason, Prince Andrei suddenly felt pained. The day was so beautiful, the sun was so bright, everything around was so cheerful; and this slender and pretty girl did not know and did not want to know of his existence and was content and happy with some separate—probably stupid—but cheerful and happy life of her own. "What is she so glad of? What is she thinking about? Not about military regulations, not about setting up quitrenters in Ryazan. What is she thinking about? And what makes her happy?" Prince Andrei asked himself with involuntary curiosity.

In 1809 Count Ilya Andreich was living in Otradnoe in the same way as before, that is, receiving almost the entire province, with hunts, theatricals, dinners, and musicians. He was glad to see Prince Andrei, as he was to see any new guest, and almost forced him to spend the night.

In the course of a boring day, during which Prince Andrei was entertained by the older hosts and the most respected guests, who filled the old count's house on the occasion of an approaching name-day party, Bolkonsky glanced several times at Natasha, who was laughing at something and having fun among the other, young half of the company, still asking himself: "What is she thinking about? What is she so glad of?"

In the evening, left alone in a new place, he could not fall asleep for a long time. He read, then put out the candle, but lit it again. The room, with the shutters closed from inside, was hot. He was vexed with this stupid old man (as he called Rostov), who had detained him, assuring him that the necessary papers had not yet been brought from town, and vexed with himself for having stayed.

Prince Andrei got up and went to open the window. As soon as he opened the shutters, moonlight, as if it had been watching at the window a long time waiting for that, burst into the room. He opened the window. The night was fresh and stilly bright. Just under his window was a row of trimmed trees, black on one side and silvery bright on the other. Under the trees was some juicy, wet, curly growth, with touches of silver on its leaves and stems. Further beyond the black trees was some roof glistening with dew, to the right a big, curly tree with a bright white trunk and branches, and above it a nearly full moon against the light, nearly starless spring sky. Prince Andrei leaned his elbows on the windowsill and fixed his eyes on this sky.

Prince Andrei's room was on the middle floor; there were also people in the rooms above him, and they were not asleep. He heard feminine talk overhead.

"Just one more time," said a feminine voice overhead, which Prince Andrei recognized at once.

"But when are you going to sleep?" another voice replied.

"I don't want to, I can't sleep, what am I to do? Well, one last time . . ."

Two feminine voices sang some musical phrase which made up the end of something.

"Ah, how lovely! Well, now let's sleep, that's the end."

"You sleep, I can't," the first voice answered, coming close to the window. She evidently leaned all the way out of the window, because he could hear the rustle of her dress and even her breathing. Everything became hushed and stone-still, like the moon and its light and shadows. Prince Andrei was also afraid to stir, lest he betray his involuntary presence.

"Sonya! Sonya!" the first voice was heard again. "How can you sleep! Just look how lovely it is! Ah, how lovely! Wake up, Sonya," she said almost with tears in her voice. "There's never, never been such a lovely night."

Sonya made some grudging reply.

"No, just look, what a moon! . . . Ah, how lovely! Come here. Darling, dear heart, come here. Well, you see? I'd like to sit on my heels, like this, take myself by the knees—tight, as tight as possible, you've got to strain—and fly away! Like this!"

"Enough, you'll fall."

Sounds of a struggle were heard, and Sonya's displeased voice:

"It's past one o'clock."

"Oh, you just spoil everything for me. Well, go, go."

Everything fell silent again, but Prince Andrei knew that she was still sitting up there, he heard an occasional quiet stirring, an occasional sigh.

"Ah, my God! my God! what on earth is it!" she suddenly cried. "If it's sleep, it's sleep!" and she slammed the window.

"She doesn't care at all about my existence!" Prince Andrei thought all the while he was listening to her talk, for some reason expecting and fearing that she would say something about him. "And she again! As if on purpose!" he thought. In his soul there suddenly arose such an unexpected tangle of youthful thoughts and hopes, contradictory to his whole life, that, feeling himself unable to comprehend his own state, he fell asleep at once.

III

The next day, having taken leave of the count alone, without waiting for the ladies to come out, Prince Andrei drove home.

It was already the beginning of June when Prince Andrei, on his way home, drove again into that birch woods, where that gnarled old oak had struck him so strangely and memorably. The ringing of the harness bells was still more muffled in the woods than a month ago; everything was filled out, shady, and dense; and the young firs scattered through the woods did not disrupt the overall beauty and, imitating the general character, showed the tender green of their fluffy young shoots.

The whole day had been hot, there was a thunderstorm gathering somewhere, but only a small cloud had sent a sprinkle over the dust of the road and the juicy leaves. The left side of the woods was dark, in the shade; the right side, wet, glossy, sparkled in the sun, barely swayed by the wind. Everything was in flower; nightingales throbbed and trilled, now near, now far.

"Yes, here, in this woods, was that oak that I agreed with," thought Prince Andrei. "But where is it?" he thought again, looking at the left side of the road, and, not knowing it himself, not recognizing it, he admired the very oak he was looking for. The old oak, quite transformed, spreading out a canopy of juicy, dark greenery, basked, barely swaying, in the rays of the evening sun. Of the gnarled fingers, the scars, the old grief and mistrust—nothing could be seen. Juicy green leaves without branches broke through the stiff, hundred-year-old bark, and it was impossible to believe that this old fellow had produced them. "Yes, it's the same oak," thought Prince Andrei, and suddenly a causeless springtime feeling of joy and renewal came over him. All the best moments of his life suddenly recalled themselves to him at the same time. Austerlitz with the lofty sky, and the dead, reproachful face of his wife, and Pierre on the ferry, and a girl excited by the beauty of the night, and that night itself, and the moon—all of it suddenly recalled itself to him.

"No, life isn't over at the age of thirty-one," Prince Andrei suddenly decided definitively, immutably. "It's not enough that I know all that's in me, everyone else must know it, too: Pierre, and that girl who wanted to fly into the sky, everyone must know me, so that my life is not only for myself; so that they don't live like that girl, independently of my life, but so that it is reflected in everyone, and they all live together with me!"

Having returned from this trip, Prince Andrei decided to go to Petersburg in the autumn, and thought up various reasons for this decision. A whole series of reasonable, logical arguments for why it was necessary that he go to Petersburg and even serve, was at his disposal every moment. He did not even understand now how he could ever have doubted the necessity of taking an active part in life, just as a month earlier he had not understood how it could ever occur to him to leave the country. It seemed clear to him that all his experience of life must go for naught and be meaningless, if he did not put it to work and again take an active part in life. He did not even understand how, on the basis of such poor rational arguments, it could have been obvious before that he would humiliate himself if now, after his lessons in life, he should again believe in the possibility of being useful and in the possibility of happiness and love. Now reason suggested something quite different. After his journey, Prince Andrei began to be bored in the country, his former occupations did not interest him, and often, sitting alone in his study, he would get up, go to the mirror, and look at his face for a long time. Then he would turn away and look at the portrait of the late Liza, who, with her hair curled *à la grecque,* looked at him tenderly and cheerfully from the gilt frame. She no longer said terrible words to her husband as before, she looked at him simply and cheerfully with curiosity. And Prince Andrei, putting his hands behind his back, would pace the room for a long time, now frowning, now smiling, thinking over those irrational thoughts, inexpressible in words, secret as a crime, that were connected with Pierre, with glory, with the girl on the windowsill, with the oak, with feminine beauty and love, which had changed his whole life. In those moments, if anyone came into his room, he was particularly dry, stern, resolute, and, in particular, unpleasantly logical.

"*Mon cher*," Princess Marya would say, coming in at such a moment, "Nikolushka mustn't go for a walk today: it's too cold."

"If it were warm," Prince Andrei would answer his sister with particular dryness at such a moment, "he would go only in his shirt, but since it's cold, you must put warm clothes on him, which is why they were invented—that's what follows from the fact that it is cold, and not that the child should stay at home when he needs air," he would say with particular logicality, as if punishing someone for all that secret illogical work that was going on inside him. On these occasions Princess Marya reflected on how such mental work dries men up.

IV

Prince Andrei arrived in Petersburg in August 1809. This was the time when the glory of the young Speransky and the energy of the reforms he carried through were at their apogee.[3] That same August, the sovereign was overturned while driving in his carriage, injured his leg, and stayed in Peterhof[4] for three weeks, seeing Speransky daily and exclusively. This was the time of the preparation not only of the two famous decrees which so alarmed society, on the abolition of court ranks and on examinations for the ranks of collegiate assessor and state councillor,[5] but also of an entire state constitution, which was supposed to change the existing judicial, administrative, and financial order of management in Russia, from the council of state to the local board. Now came the realization and embodiment of those vague liberal dreams with which Alexander had taken the throne and which he had been striving to realize with the aid of his helpers Czartoryski, Novosiltsev, Kochubey, and Stroganov, whom he himself jokingly referred to as his *comité de salut publique.**[6]

Now they had all been replaced by Speransky on the civil side and Arakcheev on the military. Soon after his arrival, Prince Andrei, being a gentleman of the chamber, appeared at court and at a levee. The sovereign met him twice and did not deign to say even one word to him. It had always seemed to Prince Andrei, even before, that he was antipathetic for the sovereign, that the sovereign disliked his face and his whole being. In the dry, distant gaze with

---

*Committee of Public Safety.

which the sovereign looked at him, Prince Andrei found still more confirmation of this supposition than before. The courtiers explained the sovereign's inattention to him by the fact that his majesty was displeased that Bolkonsky had not served since 1805.

"I know myself how little control we have over our sympathies and antipathies," thought Prince Andrei, "and therefore there's no use thinking of presenting my memorandum on military regulations to the sovereign personally, but the matter will speak for itself." He told an old field marshal, his father's friend, about his project. The field marshal appointed a time, received him benignly, and promised to report to the sovereign. A few days later, Prince Andrei was told that he had to appear before the minister of war, Count Arakcheev.

At nine o'clock in the morning of the appointed day, Prince Andrei appeared in Count Arakcheev's anteroom.

Prince Andrei did not know Arakcheev personally and had never seen him, but everything he knew about him inspired little respect in him for this man.

"He is minister of war, the sovereign emperor's trusted man; his personal qualities are nobody's business; he was entrusted with considering my memorandum—consequently, he alone can set it in motion," thought Prince Andrei, waiting among many significant and insignificant persons in Count Arakcheev's anteroom.

During his service, mostly as an adjutant, Prince Andrei had seen many anterooms of significant persons, and the differing characters of these anterooms were very clear to him. Count Arakcheev's anteroom had a completely special character. The insignificant persons waiting in line for an audience in Count Arakcheev's anteroom had feelings of abashedness and submission written on their faces; the persons of higher rank had faces expressing a general feeling of awkwardness, concealed behind an appearance of casualness and mockery of oneself, of one's position, and of the person they were waiting to meet. Some paced up and down pensively, others whispered and laughed, and Prince Andrei heard the sobriquet "Sila Andreich"[7] and the phrase "Uncle will give you what for," referring to Arakcheev. One general (a significant person), apparently insulted at having to wait so long, sat crossing and recrossing his legs and smiling contemptuously to himself.

But as soon as the door opened, all the faces instantly expressed only one thing—fear. Prince Andrei asked the officer on duty to announce him once more, but he was looked at with mockery and told that his turn would come in due time. After several persons were led into and out of the minister's office by the adjutant, the fearsome door received an officer who had struck Prince Andrei with his humiliated and frightened look. The officer's audience lasted a long time. Suddenly the thunder of an unpleasant voice was heard from behind the door, and the officer emerged, pale, his lips trembling, and, clutching his head, passed through the anteroom. After that, Prince Andrei was led to the door, and the officer on duty said in a whisper: "To the right, by the window."

Prince Andrei entered a tidy, unostentatious office and saw by the desk a forty-year-old man with a long waist, a long, close-cropped head, and thick wrinkles, with scowling brows over dull, hazel-green eyes and a drooping red nose. Arakcheev turned his head towards him without looking at him.

"What's your petition?" asked Arakcheev.

"I am not . . . petitioning for anything, Your Excellency," Prince Andrei said softly. Arakcheev's eyes turned towards him.

"Sit down," said Arakcheev, "Prince Bolkonsky."

"I am not petitioning for anything, but the sovereign emperor has deigned to pass on to Your Excellency the memorandum I submitted . . ."

"You see, my most gentle sir, I have read your memorandum," Arakcheev interrupted, speaking only the first words benignly, again without looking him in the face and lapsing more and more into a grumblingly contemptuous tone. "Proposing new military regulations? There are many regulations, and no one to carry out the old ones. Everybody writes regulations these days; it's easier to write them than to follow them."

"I have come by the will of the sovereign emperor to learn from Your Excellency what chances you intend to give to the memorandum submitted," Prince Andrei said courteously.

"I wrote a decision on your memorandum and it was passed on to the committee. I *do not* approve," said Arakcheev, getting up and taking a paper from his desk. "Here," he handed it to Prince Andrei.

Across the paper was scrawled, in pencil, without capitals, without orthography, without punctuation: "unsoundly compiled since copied from french military regulations and unnecessarily deviating from military articles."

"To what committee has the memorandum been passed on?" asked Prince Andrei.

"To the commission on military regulations, and I have proposed that Your Honour be enrolled as a member. Only without salary."

Prince Andrei smiled.

"I do not wish any."

"Member, without salary," repeated Arakcheev. "My respects. Hey! Call 'em in! Who's next?" he shouted, bowing to Prince Andrei.

V

While waiting to hear about his enrolment as a member of the committee, Prince Andrei renewed old acquaintances, especially with those persons who he knew were in power and could be useful to him. He now experienced in

Petersburg a feeling similar to what he had experienced on the eve of battle, when he had fretted with anxious curiosity and was irresistibly drawn to the higher spheres, where the future was being prepared on which the fates of millions depended. He sensed by the spitefulness of the old men, by the curiosity of the uninitiate, by the reserve of the initiate, by the haste and preoccupation of all, by the countless number of committees and commissions—and he learned of the existence of new ones every day—that now, in the year 1809, here in Petersburg, some enormous civil battle was being prepared, of which the commander in chief was a mysterious person, still unknown to him, whom he imagined to be a genius—Speransky. And both the matter of the reform, which he vaguely knew, and Speransky, who was its chief promoter, began to interest him so passionately that the matter of military regulations was very soon shifted to a secondary place in his consciousness.

Prince Andrei occupied one of the most advantageous positions for being well received in all the highest and most diverse circles of Petersburg society at that time. The party of the reformers cordially welcomed and courted him, first, because he had the reputation of being intelligent and well-read, and second, because by granting freedom to his peasants, he had already earned himself a reputation as a liberal. The party of the disgruntled old men turned to him directly for sympathy, as his father's son, condemning the reforms. Feminine society, the *world*, welcomed him cordially because he was an eligible young man, rich and well-born, and almost a new personage, with the aura of the romantic story of his alleged death and his wife's tragic end. Besides that, the general opinion of him among all who had known him before was that he had changed greatly for the better in those five years, had softened and matured, and there was none of the former affectation, pride, and mockery in him, but there was that serenity which comes with age. People talked about him, were interested in him, and everyone wished to see him.

The day after his visit to Count Arakcheev, Prince Andrei went to a soirée at Count Kochubey's. He told the count about his meeting with "Sila Andreich" (as Kochubey called Arakcheev, with that vague mockery of something which Prince Andrei had noticed in the minister of war's anteroom).

"*Mon cher,*" said Kochubey, "even in this matter you cannot avoid Mikhail Mikhailovich. *C'est le grand faiseur.** I'll tell him. He promised to come this evening . . ."

"What concern does Speransky have with military regulations?" asked Prince Andrei.

Kochubey smiled and shook his head, as if surprised at Bolkonsky's naïveté.

"He and I were talking about you the other day," Kochubey went on, "about your free ploughmen . . ."

*He is the great doer.

"Ah, so it's you, Prince, who freed your muzhiks?" asked an old man of Catherine's time, glancing scornfully at Bolkonsky.

"It's a small estate that brought no income," replied Bolkonsky, so as not to vex the old man for nothing, and trying to soften his act before him.

"*Vous craignez d'être en retard,*"* said the old man, looking at Kochubey.

"One thing I don't understand," the old man went on. "Who's going to work the land if they're freed? Writing laws is easy, but governing is difficult. It's the same thing I ask you now, Count: who will be the heads of departments if everybody has to take examinations?"

"Those who pass them, I suppose," Kochubey replied, crossing his legs and looking around.

"Here I've got Pryanichnikov serving under me, a nice man, good as gold, but he's sixty—is he going to take examinations? . . ."

"Yes, that makes it difficult, since education is not very widespread, but . . ." Count Kochubey did not finish, stood up, and, taking Prince Andrei by the arm, went to meet a tall, balding, fair-haired man of about forty, with a large, open forehead and an elongated face of an unusual, strange whiteness. The entering man was wearing a dark blue tailcoat, a cross on his neck, and a star on the left side of his chest. It was Speransky. Prince Andrei recognized him at once, and something in his soul shook, as happens at important moments of life. Whether it was respect, envy, or expectation—he did not know. Speransky's entire figure was of a special type, by which he could be recognized at once. In no one of the society in which Prince Andrei lived had he seen this calm and self-assurance of clumsy and obtuse movements, in no one had he seen such a firm and at the same time soft gaze of half-closed and slightly moist eyes, such firmness of a totally meaningless smile, such a thin, smooth, soft voice, and, above all, such a tender whiteness of the face and especially of the hands, somewhat broad, but extraordinarily plump, tender, and white. Such whiteness and tenderness of face Prince Andrei had seen only in soldiers who had spent a long time in the hospital. This was Speransky, secretary of state, counsellor to the sovereign, and his companion at Erfurt, where he had seen and spoken with Napoleon more than once.

Speransky did not shift his eyes from one face to another, as one does involuntarily when entering a large company, and he was in no hurry to speak. He spoke softly, with assurance that he would be heard, and looked only at the person with whom he was speaking.

Prince Andrei followed every word and movement of Speransky with special attention. As happens with people, especially those who judge their neighbours severely, Prince Andrei, on meeting a new person, especially one whom, like Speransky, he knew by reputation, always expected to find in him the full perfection of human virtues.

---

*You are afraid of falling behind.

Speransky told Kochubey that he was sorry he could not come earlier, but he had been detained in the palace. He did not say he had been detained by the sovereign. And this affectation of modesty Prince Andrei noticed. When Kochubey named Prince Andrei for him, Speransky slowly transferred his eyes to him with the same smile and silently began to look at him.

"I am very glad to make your acquaintance, I have heard about you, as everyone has," he said.

Kochubey said a few words about the reception Arakcheev had given Bolkonsky. Speransky's smile widened.

"The director of the commission on military regulations is a good friend of mine—Mr. Magnitsky," he said, articulating each syllable and each word, "and if you wish, I could bring you together with him." (He paused at the period.) "I hope you will find sympathy in him and a desire to further everything sensible."

A circle formed itself at once around Speransky, and the old man who had spoken of his subordinate Pryanichnikov also turned to Speransky with a question.

Prince Andrei, without entering into the conversation, observed all the movements of Speransky, this man, recently an insignificant seminarian,[8] who now held the destiny of Russia in his hands—those white, plump hands—as Bolkonsky thought. Prince Andrei was struck by the extraordinary, scornful calm with which Speransky answered the old man. He seemed to address his condescending words to him from an immeasurable height. When the old man began talking too loud, Speransky smiled and said he could not judge the advantage or disadvantage of what pleased the sovereign.

Having talked for some time in the general circle, Speransky got up and, going over to Prince Andrei, called him away to the other end of the room. It was clear that he considered it necessary to concern himself with Bolkonsky.

"I had no time to talk with you, Prince, amidst the animated conversation I was drawn into by that venerable elder," he said with a mildly scornful smile, as if acknowledging by that smile that he and Prince Andrei understood the insignificance of the people with whom he had just been talking. This manner flattered Prince Andrei. "I've known you for a long time: first, from your dealing with your peasants, our first example, of which it would be desirable to have more followers; and second, because you are one of those gentlemen of the chamber who did not consider themselves offended by the new edict on court ranks, which has caused so much talk and discussion."

"Yes," said Prince Andrei, "my father didn't want me to take advantage of that right; I started service in the lower ranks."

"Your father, a man of the old days, obviously stands higher than our contemporaries who condemn this measure so much, though it merely restores natural justice."

"I think, however, that there are also grounds for these condemnations," said

Prince Andrei, trying to fight against Speransky's influence, which he was beginning to feel. He disliked agreeing with him in everything: he wanted to contradict. Prince Andrei, who usually spoke easily and well, had difficulty expressing himself now in talking with Speransky. He was too taken up with observing the person of the famous man.

"Grounds of personal ambition, perhaps," Speransky quietly put in his word.

"Also partly of the state," said Prince Andrei.

"How do you mean? . . ." said Speransky, quietly lowering his eyes.

"I am an admirer of Montesquieu," said Prince Andrei. "And his thought that *'le principe des monarchies est l'honneur'* me paraît incontestable. *Certains droits et privilèges de la noblesse me paraissent être des moyens de soutenir ce sentiment.*"*

The smile vanished from Speransky's white face, and his physiognomy gained much from it. He probably found Prince Andrei's thought interesting.

"*Si vous envisager la question sous ce point de vue,*"† he began, articulating in French with obvious difficulty and speaking still more slowly than in Russian, but perfectly calmly. He said that honour, *l'honneur,* could not be supported by privileges detrimental to the course of government service, that honour, *l'honneur,* was either a negative notion of not committing reprehensible acts, or a well-known source of competition for gaining approval and the rewards expressive of it.

His arguments were concise, simple, and clear.

"An institution supportive of this honour, the source of competition, is an institution like the *Légion d'honneur* of the great emperor Napoleon, which is not detrimental, but contributes to the success of the service, and not the privilege of rank or position at court."

"I don't argue, but it is impossible to deny that court privileges achieve the same goal," said Prince Andrei. "Every courtier considers it his duty to uphold his position with dignity."

"But you did not want to take advantage of it, Prince," said Speransky, showing by his smile that he wished to stop an argument awkward for his interlocutor by this compliment. "If you will do me the honour of joining me on Wednesday," he added, "then, once I've talked with Magnitsky, I will inform you of something that may interest you, and, besides that, I will have the pleasure of a more detailed conversation with you." He closed his eyes, bowed, and, *à la française,* without saying goodbye, trying not to be noticed, left the room.

---

* "The principle of monarchies is honour" seems incontestable to me. Certain rights and privileges of the nobility seem to me to be means of supporting that feeling.
† If you consider the question from that point of view.

VI

During the initial time of his stay in Petersburg, Prince Andrei felt that his whole way of thinking, developed in his solitary life, was completely over-shadowed by the petty cares that consumed him in Petersburg.

On coming home in the evening, he would jot down in his notebook four or five necessary visits or *rendez-vous* at appointed hours. The mechanism of life, the ordering of the day so as to get everywhere on time, took the greater part of the very energy of life. He did not do anything, he did not even think about anything and had no time to think, but only talked, and talked successfully, about what he had had time to think over previously in the country.

He sometimes noticed with displeasure that he had happened to repeat the same thing on the same day in different companies. But he was so busy for whole days that he had no time to think about the fact that he was doing nothing.

As in his first meeting with him at Kochubey's, Speransky also made a strong impression on Bolkonsky that Wednesday at home, where he received him alone and talked with him at length and trustfully.

Prince Andrei considered such a vast number of people as contemptible and insignificant beings, he wanted so much to find in someone else the living ideal of that perfection for which he strove, that he easily believed that in Speransky he had found that ideal of the fully reasonable and virtuous man. If Speransky had been from the same society as Prince Andrei, of the same upbringing and moral habits, Bolkonsky would soon have found his weak, human, unheroic sides, but as it was, this logical way of thinking, which was strange for him, inspired him with all the more respect because he did not quite understand him. Besides that, Speransky, either because he appreciated Prince Andrei's ability, or because he found it necessary to acquire him for himself, flaunted his impartial, calm reason before Prince Andrei and flattered Prince Andrei with that subtle flattery, combined with self-assurance, which consists in silently acknowledging one's interlocutor and oneself as the only people capable of understanding all the stupidity of *all* the rest, and the intelligence and profun-dity of one's own thoughts.

In the course of their long conversation on Wednesday evening, Speransky said more than once: "Among *us* everything that lies outside the general level of inveterate habit is considered . . ." or, with a smile: "But *we* want the wolves well-fed and the sheep safe . . ." or: "*They* cannot understand it . . ." And all that with an expression which said: "We, you and I, understand what *they* are and who *we* are."

This first long conversation with Speransky only strengthened in Prince

Andrei the feeling he had had on first seeing him. He saw in him a reasonable, rigorous-minded man of immense intelligence, who through his energy and perseverance had come to power and used it solely for the good of Russia. Speransky, in Prince Andrei's eyes, was precisely that man—explaining all phenomena of life reasonably, accepting as real only that which is reasonable, and capable of applying the standard of reasonableness to everything—whom he himself wanted so much to be. Everything seemed so simple, so clear in Speransky's explanations that Prince Andrei involuntarily agreed with him in everything. If he protested and argued, it was only because he purposely wanted to be independent and not to yield entirely to Speransky's opinions. Everything was right, everything was very well, but one thing disconcerted Prince Andrei: it was Speransky's cold, mirror-like gaze, which let no one penetrate to his soul, and his tender white hand, at which Prince Andrei stared involuntarily, as one stares at the hands of people who have power. The mirror-like gaze and that tender white hand for some reason irritated Prince Andrei. He was also unpleasantly struck by a too-great contempt for people that he noticed in Speransky, and the diversity of methods of proof he resorted to in confirming his opinions. He employed every possible intellectual tool, except for analogy, and seemed to pass too boldly from one to another. Now he would stand on the practical activist's ground and denounce dreamers, now on the satirist's ground and chuckle ironically at his adversaries; now he would become strictly logical, now he would suddenly rise into the spheres of metaphysics. (This last instrument of proof he made use of especially often.) He would transfer the question to metaphysical heights, go on to definitions of space, time, thought, and, deriving his refutations from there, descend again to the ground of the argument.

In general, the main feature that struck Prince Andrei in Speransky's mind was his unquestionable, unshakeable faith in the power and legitimacy of reason. It was clear that the notion, so usual for Prince Andrei, that it was after all impossible to express everything one thinks, would never have entered Speransky's head, and it never occurred to him to wonder: "Isn't everything I think and believe sheer nonsense?" And that special cast of Speransky's mind attracted Prince Andrei most of all.

During the first period of his acquaintance with Speransky, Prince Andrei had a passionate feeling of admiration for him, resembling what he used to feel for Bonaparte. The circumstance that Speransky was a priest's son whom stupid people could vulgarly despise, as many did, for being a little cleric and a "preacher's brat," made Prince Andrei treat his feeling for Speransky with special care and unconsciously strengthen it within himself.

On that first evening which Bolkonsky spent with him, talking about the legislative commission, Speransky told Prince Andrei ironically that this commission had existed for a hundred and fifty years, had cost millions, and had done nothing, except that Rosenkampf had glued little labels to all the articles of comparative legislation.

"And for that alone the state has paid millions!" he said. "We want to give new judicial powers to the senate, but we have no laws. Which is why it's a sin, Prince, for people such as you not to serve now."

Prince Andrei said that for that he needed a legal education, which he did not have.

"But no one has, so what do you want? It's a *circulus viciosus* which we must make an effort to break out of."

A week later Prince Andrei was a member of the commission on military regulations and, something he had never expected, head of a section of the legislative commission. At Speransky's request, he took the first part of the civil code, then in the process of being developed, and with the help of the *Code Napoléon* and the *Justiniani,*⁹ worked on putting together the section headed "Personal Rights."

VII

Some two years before then, in 1808, having returned to Petersburg from his trip to his estates, Pierre involuntarily became the head of the Petersburg Masons. He organized dinners and funerals for the lodges, recruited new members, saw to the uniting of various lodges and the acquiring of authentic charters. He donated his own money for the setting up of temples and made up, as far as he could, for the shortfall in the collection of alms, in which the majority of members were stingy and irregular. Almost alone, on his own means, he supported a poorhouse set up by the order in Petersburg.

His life meanwhile went on in the same way, with the same diversions and licentiousness. He liked to dine and drink well, and though he considered it immoral and humiliating, he could not refrain from the amusements of the bachelor companies he participated in.

In the daze of his activities and diversions, however, Pierre began to feel after a year that the ground of Masonry, on which he stood, was giving way all the more under his feet the more firmly he tried to stand on it. Along with that, he felt that the further the ground he stood on gave way under his feet, the more involuntarily he was bound to it. When he was starting out in Masonry, he experienced the feeling of a man who trustingly sets foot on the smooth surface of a swamp. Placing one foot on it, he sank. To verify fully the firmness of the ground on which he stood, he placed the other foot on it and sank still more, became stuck, and now involuntarily walked knee-deep through the swamp.

Iosif Alexeevich was not in Petersburg. (He had recently withdrawn from the activity of the Petersburg lodges and was living permanently in Moscow.) All the brothers, the members of the lodges, were people whom Pierre knew in life, and it was difficult for him to see in them only brothers in Freemasonry, and not Prince B., not Ivan Vassilievich D., whom he knew in life mainly as weak and insignificant people. Under the Masonic aprons and signs, he saw on them the uniforms and decorations they strove for in life. Often, collecting alms and counting up twenty or thirty roubles, written down as receipts and for the most part left owing, from ten members, half of whom were as rich as he was, Pierre remembered the Masonic vow in which each brother promised to give all his possessions to his neighbour, and doubts arose in his soul which he tried not to dwell on.

He divided all the brothers he knew into four categories. In the first category he included brothers who took no active part either in the affairs of the lodges or in the affairs of the people, but were taken up exclusively with the mysteries of the order's science, with questions of the triple name of God or of the three basic elements of things—sulphur, mercury, and salt, or with the meaning of the square and all the figures on Solomon's temple.[10] Pierre respected this category of brother Masons, to which mainly the old brothers and Iosif Alexeevich himself belonged, in Pierre's opinion, but he did not share their interests. His heart was not inclined to the mystical side of Masonry.

In the second category Pierre included himself and similar brothers, seeking, vacillating, who had not yet found in Masonry a straight and clear path, but hoped to find one.

In the third category he included the brothers (they were the majority) who saw nothing in Masonry except external form and ritual, and who valued the strict observance of this external form, with no concern for its content and meaning. Such were Willarski and even the grand master of the main lodge.

In the fourth category, finally, there were also a great many brothers, especially those who had entered the brotherhood recently. These were people who, from Pierre's observation, did not believe in anything, did not desire anything, and joined the Masons only to be close to the rich young brothers, powerful through their connections and nobility, of whom there were many in the lodge.

Pierre was beginning to feel dissatisfied with his activity. Masonry, at least the Masonry he knew here, sometimes seemed to him to be based on appearance alone. He never thought of doubting Masonry itself, but he suspected that Russian Masonry had taken the wrong path and deviated from its source. And therefore, at the end of the year, Pierre went abroad to be initiated into the highest mysteries of the order.

. . .

In the summer of 1809 Pierre returned to Petersburg. From the correspondence of our Masons with those abroad, it was known that Bezukhov had managed while abroad to gain the confidence of many highly placed persons, had penetrated many mysteries, had been raised to a higher degree, and was bringing much back with him for the common good of the Freemasons' cause in Russia. All the Petersburg Masons came to him, fawned on him, and it seemed to them all that he was concealing and preparing something.

A solemn session of the lodge of the second degree was convened, at which Pierre promised to tell what he had to convey to the Petersburg brothers from the highest leaders of the order. The session was full. After the usual rituals, Pierre got up and began his speech.

"Beloved brothers," he began, blushing and faltering and holding the written text in his hand, "it is not enough to observe our mysteries in the quiet of the lodge—we must act . . . act. We are somnolent, but we must act." Pierre took out his notebook and began to read. "In order to spread the pure truth and bring about the triumph of virtue," he read, "we must purify people of prejudice, spread rules that correspond to the spirit of the time, take upon ourselves the upbringing of the young, unite the most intelligent people with indissoluble bonds, boldly and yet reasonably overcome superstition, unbelief, and stupidity, and form those devoted to us into people bound together by a single goal and having power and strength.

"For the achievement of this goal, we must assure a preponderance of virtue over vice, we must try to make it so that the honest man already attains in this world the eternal reward for his virtues. But we are very much hindered in these great intentions by present-day political institutions. What are we to do in such a state of affairs? Are we to favour revolutions, overthrow everything, drive out force by force? . . . No, we are very far from that. Every violent reform is blameworthy, because it will not set evil to rights in the least, as long as people remain as they are, and because wisdom has no need of violence.

"The entire project of the order should be based on forming people who are firm, virtuous, and bound together by unity of conviction, a conviction that consists of persecuting vice and stupidity everywhere and with all their might, and of patronizing talent and virtue: drawing worthy people up from the dust and uniting them to our brotherhood. Only then will our order have power— to bind imperceptibly the hands of those who condone disorder and rule them in such a way that they do not notice it. In short, a universal, sovereign form of government should be established, which will be spread over the whole world, without destroying civil bonds, and under which all other governments may continue in their usual way and do all except that which hinders the great goal of our order, that is, the achievement of the triumph of virtue over vice. This was the goal of Christianity itself. It taught people to be wise and kind and to follow, for their own benefit, the example and precepts of the best and wisest men.

"Back then, when all was plunged in darkness, preaching alone was, of course, sufficient: the newness of the truth endowed it with special strength, but now we require much stronger means. It is now necessary that men, governed by their own feelings, find sensual delight in virtue. It is impossible to eradicate the passions; we must only try to point them towards a noble goal, and therefore it is necessary that every man be able to satisfy his passions within the limits of virtue, and that our order provide the means for it.

"As soon as we have a certain number of worthy people in every state, each of them will in turn form two more, and they will all be closely united with each other—then everything will be possible for the order, which has already secretly succeeded in doing much for the good of mankind."

This speech produced not only a strong impression, but also agitation in the lodge. The majority of the brothers, who saw the dangerous designs of Illuminism[11] in the speech, received it with a coldness that surprised Pierre. The grand master began to object to Pierre. Pierre started developing his thoughts more and more ardently. It was long since they had had such a stormy session. Parties formed: some accused Pierre, condemning him for Illuminism; others supported him. Pierre was struck for the first time at this meeting by the infinite diversity of human minds, which makes it so that no truth presents itself to two people in the same way. Even those members who seemed to be on his side understood him in their own fashion, with limitations and alterations which Pierre could not agree to, since his main need consisted precisely in conveying his thought to others exactly as he understood it himself.

At the end of the session the grand master reprimanded Bezukhov with ill will and irony for his hot-headedness, saying that it was not love of virtue alone, but also a passion for struggle that had guided him in his argument. Pierre did not reply to him and asked curtly whether his suggestion would be accepted or not. He was told that it would not be, and Pierre, without waiting for the usual formalities, left the lodge and went home.

VIII

Pierre was again overcome by that anguish he feared so much. For three days after delivering his speech at the lodge, he lay at home on the sofa, receiving no one and going nowhere.

During that time a letter came from his wife, who begged him to agree to see her, wrote of her sadness without him and of her wish to devote her whole life to him.

At the end of her letter she informed him that in a few days she would be arriving in Petersburg from abroad.

Following the letter, one of the brother Masons he respected less than the others broke in upon Pierre's solitude and, turning the conversation to Pierre's marital relations, in the guise of brotherly advice came out with the thought that his severity towards his wife was unjust, and that Pierre was departing from the primary rules of Masonry in not forgiving the penitent.

At the same time his mother-in-law, Prince Vassily's wife, sent for him, begging him to visit her at least for a few minutes to discuss a very important matter. Pierre saw that there was a conspiracy against him, that they wanted to reunite him with his wife, and the idea was even not unpleasant for him in the state he was in. It was all the same to him: Pierre considered nothing in his life to be of great importance, and under the influence of the anguish that now possessed him, he valued neither his freedom nor his persistence in punishing his wife.

"No one is right, no one is wrong, so she's not wrong either," he thought. If Pierre did not consent at once to a reunion with his wife, it was only because, being in a state of anguish, he was not able to undertake anything. If his wife had come to him, he would not have sent her away. Was it not all the same, compared to what preoccupied Pierre, whether he lived or did not live with his wife?

Without replying either to his wife or to his mother-in-law, Pierre got ready for the road late one night and left for Moscow to see Iosif Alexeevich. Here is what Pierre wrote in his diary:

Moscow, 17 November.

Just back from my benefactor and hasten to write down everything I experienced. Iosif Alexeevich lives in poverty and has been suffering for three years from a painful bladder ailment. No one has ever heard a groan or a word of protest from him. From morning till late at night, except for the times when he eats the plainest food, he works at science. He received me graciously and seated me by him on the bed where he lay: I made the sign of the knights of the East and of Jerusalem, he responded with the same and asked me with a meek smile what I had learned and acquired in the Prussian and Scottish lodges. I told him everything, as well as I could, conveyed the principles I had suggested to our Petersburg lodge, and informed him of the bad reception I had received, and of the rift that had occurred between me and the brothers. Iosif Alexeevich, after quite a long and thoughtful silence, explained to me his view of it all, which instantly lit up for me the whole past and the whole future path that lay before me. He surprised me, asking whether I remembered the triple goal of the order: (1) keeping and knowing the mystery; (2) purifying and correcting oneself for the receiving of it; and (3) correcting the human race through striving for this purification. Which is the chiefest and first goal of the three? Of course, the purifying and correcting of oneself. It is the only goal we can strive for regardless of all circumstances. But at the same time, this goal precisely calls for our greatest effort, and therefore, deluded by pride, we neglect this goal and pursue either the mystery, which we are unworthy to partake of because of our impurity, or the correction of the human race, while we ourselves are an example of vileness and depravity. Illuminism is not a pure teaching precisely because it became concerned with social activity and is all filled with pride. On that basis, Iosif Alexeevich condemned my speech and my whole activity. I agreed with him in the depths of my soul. As our conversation turned to my family affairs, he told me: "The main duty of a true Mason, as I've told you, consists in perfecting one's own self. But we often think that, by removing all difficulties from our life, we will the sooner reach this goal. On the contrary, my dear sir," he said to me, "only amidst the world's troubles can we achieve the three main goals: (1) self-knowledge—for man can only know himself through comparison; (2) perfection—for it is achieved only through struggle; and (3) achieving the main virtue—the love of death. Only life's adversities can show us its vanity and contribute to our innate love of death, or rebirth into a new life." These words are the more remarkable in that Iosif Alexeevich, despite his great physical suffering, is never burdened by life, but loves death, for which, despite all the purity and loftiness of his inner man, he still does not feel himself sufficiently prepared. Then my benefactor fully explained to me the meaning of the great square of creation, and pointed out that the numbers three and seven are the foundation of everything. He advised me not to shun the company of the Petersburg brothers and, occupying only positions of the second degree in the lodge, to try, while keeping the brothers from the passions of pride, to turn them to the true path of self-knowledge and perfection. Besides that, for me personally, he advised first of all that I keep watch over myself, and with that purpose he gave me a notebook, the one in which I am writing and will henceforth write down all my acts.

Petersburg, 23 November.

I am living with my wife again. My mother-in-law came to me in tears and said that Hélène was here and that she begged me to hear her out, that she was innocent, that she was unhappy at being abandoned by me, and many other things. I knew that if I merely allowed myself to see her, I would no longer be able to refuse her wish. In my doubt, I did not know whose help and advice to resort to. If my benefactor had been here, he would have told me. I retreated to my room, reread my letters from Iosif Alexeevich, recalled my conversations with him, and concluded from it all that I should not refuse one who asks and should offer a helping hand to anyone, all the more to someone so bound to me, and that I should bear my cross. But if I forgave her for the sake of virtue, then let my union with her have only a spiritual goal. So I decided and so I wrote to Iosif Alexeevich. I told my wife that I asked her to forget all the past, asked her to forgive me for whatever I might be guilty of before her, but that I had nothing to forgive her. It gave me joy to tell her that. Let her not know how hard it was for me to see her again. I have settled upstairs in the big house and am experiencing a happy feeling of renewal.

IX

Then, as always, high society, assembling at court and at large balls, was subdivided into several circles, each having its own nuance. Among them, the most extensive one was the French circle of the Napoleonic alliance—the circle of Count Rumyantsev and Caulaincourt. In this circle, one of the most conspicuous places was occupied by Hélène, as soon as she settled with her husband in Petersburg. She was frequented by gentlemen from the French embassy and a great number of people, known for their intelligence and courtesy, who belonged to that trend.

Hélène had been in Erfurt during the famous meeting of the emperors, and from there had brought these connections with all the noteworthy Napoleonists of Europe. In Erfurt she had brilliant success. Napoleon himself, noticing her in the theatre, asked who she was and praised her beauty. Her success as a beautiful and elegant woman did not surprise Pierre, because with the years she had become still more beautiful than before. But what did surprise him was that in these two years his wife had succeeded in acquiring a reputation *"d'une femme charmante, aussi spirituelle que belle."** The famous prince de Ligne wrote eight-page letters to her. Bilibin saved up his *mots* so as to speak them for the first time in front of the countess Bezukhov. To be received in the countess Bezukhov's salon was considered a diploma in intelligence; young men read books before Hélène's soirées so as to have something to talk about in her salon, and embassy secretaries, and even ambassadors, confided diplomatic secrets to her, so that Hélène was a power in a certain sense. Pierre, who knew that she was very stupid, sometimes, with a strange feeling of perplexity and fear, attended her soirées and dinners, where politics, poetry, and philosophy were discussed. At these soirées, he experienced a feeling similar to what a conjurer experiences, expecting each time that his trick will be exposed. But either because stupidity was precisely necessary for keeping such a salon, or because those who were tricked found pleasure in the trick itself, the trick was not exposed, and the reputation of Elena Vassilievna Bezukhov as *une femme charmante et spirituelle* was so firmly established that she could utter the greatest banalities and stupidities, and still they all admired her every word and sought for a deep meaning in them, which she herself never suspected.

---

* A charming woman, as witty as she is beautiful.

Pierre was precisely the husband necessary for this brilliant society woman. He was that absent-minded eccentric, a *grand seigneur* of a husband, who got in nobody's way and not only did not spoil the general impression of high tone in the drawing room, but, by way of contrast to his wife's gracefulness and tact, served as an advantageous backdrop for her. As a result of his constant, concentrated occupation with non-material interests over those two years, and his sincere scorn of everything else, Pierre adopted in his wife's society, which did not interest him, that tone of indifference, negligence, and benevolence towards everyone, which cannot be acquired artificially and which, for that reason, inspires an involuntary respect. He came into his wife's drawing room as into a theatre, was acquainted with them all, was equally glad to see them all, and was equally indifferent to them all. Occasionally he got into a conversation that interested him, and then, without considering whether *les messieurs de l'ambassade* were there or not, mumbled his opinions, which were sometimes completely out of tone with the present moment. But the opinion about the eccentric husband *de la femme la plus distinguée de Pétersbourg** was so well established that no one took his quirks *au sérieux*.

Among the many young men who daily visited Hélène, Boris Drubetskoy, already quite successful in the service, was, after Hélène's return from Erfurt, the most intimate person in the Bezukhovs' house. Hélène called him *mon page* and treated him like a child. She addressed him with the same smile as she did everyone else, but sometimes Pierre found it unpleasant to see that smile. Boris treated Pierre with a special, dignified, and sad deference. This nuance of deference also troubled Pierre. Pierre had suffered so painfully three years ago from the offence inflicted on him by his wife that he now protected himself from the possibility of a similar offence, first, by not being his wife's husband, and second, by not allowing himself to suspect.

"No, now that she's become a *bas-bleu*,† she has for ever renounced her former passions," he said to himself. "There is no example of a *bas-bleu* having passions of the heart," he repeated to himself a rule drawn from who knows where and which he undoubtedly believed. But, strangely, Boris's presence in his wife's drawing room (and he was there almost all the time) affected Pierre physically: it bound all his limbs, and destroyed the spontaneity and freedom of his movements.

"Such a strange antipathy," thought Pierre, "and before I even liked him very much."

In the eyes of the world, Pierre was a great lord, the somewhat blind and ridiculous husband of a famous wife, an intelligent eccentric, a do-nothing, but

*Of the most distinguished lady of Petersburg.
†Bluestocking.

one who harmed nobody, a nice and kind fellow. Yet in Pierre's soul all that time a complex and difficult work of inner development was taking place, which revealed much to him and led him to many spiritual doubts and joys.

X

He continued his diary, and here is what he wrote in it during this time:

24 November.

Got up at eight o'clock, read the Holy Scriptures, then went to work [on the advice of his benefactor, Pierre had taken a post on one of the committees], came home for dinner, ate alone (the countess has many guests I find disagreeable), ate and drank with moderation, and after dinner copied out passages for the brothers. In the evening went down to the countess and told a funny story about B., and only remembered that I shouldn't have done it when everybody was laughing loudly.

I go to bed in a happy and calm mood. Great Lord, help me to walk in Thy ways: (1) to overcome the part of wrath by gentleness and slowness; (2) of lust by restraint and repulsion; (3) to withdraw from vanity, yet not lose the habit of (a) work in government service, (b) family cares, (c) friendly relations, and (d) economic concerns.

27 November.

Woke up late, and before getting up lay in bed for a long time, indulging in laziness. My God, help me and strengthen me so that I may walk in Thy paths. Read the Holy Scriptures, but without the proper feeling. Brother Urusov came, we talked about the vanity of the world. He told me about the sovereign's new projects. I began to object, but remembered my rules and the words of our benefactor, that a true Mason ought to be a zealous worker for the state when his participation is needed, and a calm contemplator of that to which he is not called. My tongue is my enemy. Brothers G. V. and O. visited me, there was a preparatory talk before the reception of a new brother. They laid upon me the duty of rhetor. I feel myself weak and unworthy. Then we talked about the explanation of the seven pillars and the seven steps of the temple: the seven sciences, the seven virtues, the seven vices, the seven gifts of the Holy Spirit. Brother O. was very eloquent. In the evening the reception took place. The new arrangement of the space contributed greatly to the magnificence of the spectacle. The one received was Boris Drubetskoy. I had nominated him, and I was the rhetor. A strange feeling kept troubling me all the while I was with him in the dark temple. I found that I had in me a feeling of hatred for him which I tried in vain to overcome. And therefore I would truly have wished to save him from evil and lead him to the path of truth, but bad thoughts about him did not leave me. It occurred to me that the goal of his entering the brotherhood consisted only in his desire to get close to and find favour with the people who belong to our lodge. Besides the fact that he asked several times whether N. and S. belonged to our lodge (to which I could not reply), besides the fact that, from my observation, he is not able to feel respect for our holy order and is too concerned and contented with his external man to wish for spiritual improvement, I had no grounds for doubting him; but he seemed insincere to me, and all the while I stood face to face with him in the dark temple, it seemed to me that he was smiling contemptuously at my words, and I really wanted to prick his bare chest with the sword I held pointed at it. I could not be eloquent and could not sincerely inform the brothers and the grand master of my doubts. Great Architect of nature, help me to find the true paths that lead out of the labyrinth of the lie!

After that three pages were skipped in the diary and then the following was written:

Had a prolonged, instructive conversation alone with brother V., who advised me to hold on to brother A. Much has been revealed to me, unworthy though I am. Adonai is the name of the creator of the world. Elohim is the name of the ruler over all. The third name, the unutterable name, has the meaning of *All*. Conversations with brother V. strengthen, refresh, and confirm me on the path of virtue. In his presence there is no room for doubt. The difference between the poor teaching of social science and our holy, all-embracing teaching is clear to me. Human science fragments everything in order to understand it, kills everything in order to examine it. In the order's holy science, everything is one, everything is known in its entirety and life. The Trinity—the three basic elements of things—sulphur, mercury, and salt. Sulphur has the properties of oil and fire; united with salt, by its fiery quality, it arouses a craving in it through which it attracts mercury, seizes it, retains it, and together they produce separate bodies. Mercury is a liquid and volatile spiritual essence— Christ, the Holy Spirit, He.

3 December.
Woke up late, read the Holy Scriptures, but was unfeeling. Afterwards went out and paced the reception room. Wanted to reflect, but instead my imagination presented me with an event that happened four years ago. Mr. Dolokhov, meeting me in Moscow after my duel, told me that he hoped I was enjoying total inner peace, despite the absence of my spouse. I made no reply then. But now I recalled all the details of this meeting and in my mind said the most spiteful words and caustic replies to him. I came to my senses and abandoned this thought only when I saw myself inflamed with wrath; but I am insufficiently repentant of it. Then Boris Drubetskoy came and began recounting various

adventures; but I was displeased with his visit from the moment he came in and said something contrary to him. He objected. I flared up and told him a host of unpleasant and even rude things. He fell silent, and I thought better of it only when it was too late. My God, I'm totally unable to deal with him! This is caused by my self-love. I set myself above him and therefore make myself much worse than he, for he is indulgent towards my rudeness, but I, on the contrary, am contemptuous of him. My God, grant me to see better my own vileness in his presence and to act in such a way that it will be useful to him as well. After dinner I fell asleep, and as I was falling asleep, I clearly heard a voice say in my left ear: "Your day."

I dreamed that I was walking in the darkness and was suddenly surrounded by dogs, but I walked on without fear; suddenly one small dog seized my left thigh with its teeth and would not let go. I began to strangle it with my hands. And I had only just torn it off when another bigger one seized me by the chest. I tore that one off, but a third, still bigger, began to bite me. I started to lift it up, but the more I lifted it, the bigger and heavier it became. And suddenly brother A. came and, taking me by the arm, led me with him and brought me to a building, to enter which one had to pass over a narrow plank. I stepped on it, and the plank bent and fell, and I started climbing up a fence which I could barely reach with my hands. With great effort I dragged myself over it in such a way that my legs hung on one side and my body on the other. I turned and saw that brother A. was standing on the fence and pointing out to me a big avenue and garden, and in the garden a big and beautiful building. I woke up. Lord, Great Architect of nature! help me to tear off the dogs—my passions—and the last of them, which combines in itself the strength of all the previous ones, and help me to enter that temple of virtue the contemplation of which I attained to in my dream.

7 December.

Dreamed that Iosif Alexeich was sitting in my house, and I was very glad and wanted to make him welcome. That I was babbling incessantly with other people and suddenly remembered that he would not like it, and I wanted to get close to him and embrace him. But as soon as I got close to him, I saw that his face was transfigured, had become young, and he was telling me something very, very softly about the teaching of the order, so softly that I couldn't hear it. That we all left the room, and then something complicated happened. We were sitting or lying on the floor. He was saying something to me. And I wanted to show him my sensitivity, and, without listening to what he said, I began to imagine to myself the state of my inner man and the grace of God coming upon me. And tears came to my eyes, and I was pleased that he noticed it. But he looked at me with vexation and jumped up, breaking off his conversation. I grew timid and asked whether what he was saying referred to me; but he did not reply, looked at me gently, and after that we were suddenly in my bedroom, where there was a double bed. He lay on the edge of it, and I, as if burning with the desire to caress him, lay beside him. And he asked me: "Tell me truly, what is your main predilection? Do you know it? I think you've already found it out." Embarrassed by this question, I replied that laziness was my main predilection. He shook his head mistrustfully. And, still more embarrassed, I replied that, though I was living with my wife on his advice, I was not a husband to my wife. To this he objected that my wife should not be deprived of my caresses, and gave me to understand that this was my duty. But I replied that I was ashamed of it; and suddenly everything disappeared. And I woke up and found in my thoughts the text of Holy Scripture: "And the life was the light of men. And the light shineth in the darkness and the darkness comprehended it not."¹² Iosif Alexeevich's face had been youthful and bright. That day I received a letter from my benefactor about the duty of married life.

9 December.

Had a dream from which I awakened with a pounding heart. I dreamed that I was in Moscow, in my own house, in the big sitting room, and Iosif Alexeevich came out of the drawing room. That I recognized at once that the process of rebirth had already been accomplished with him, and I rushed to meet him. That I kissed him and his hands, and he said: "Have you noticed that I now have a different face?" I looked at him, still holding him in my embrace, and saw that his face was young, but there was no hair on his head and his features were quite different. And that I said to him: "I would recognize you if I met you by chance"—and at the same time I thought: "Was I telling the truth?" And suddenly I saw that he was lying there like a dead body; then he gradually recovered and went with me into a big study, holding a big book written on royal paper. And I said: "I wrote this." And he answered me by inclining his head. I opened the book, and there were beautiful pictures on all the pages. And I knew that these pictures represented the amorous adventures of a soul with its beloved. And I saw on the pages a beautiful image of a girl in transparent clothing and with a transparent body, flying up to the clouds. And I knew that this girl was none other than the image of the Song of Songs.¹³ And looking at these pictures, I felt that I was doing a bad thing, and I could not tear myself away from them. Lord, help me! My God, if Thy forsaking of me is Thy doing, then Thy will be done; but if I myself am the cause of it, then teach me what to do. I will perish of my own depravity if Thou forsakest me altogether.

XI

The financial affairs of the Rostovs did not improve during the two years they spent in the country.

Though Nikolai Rostov, keeping firmly to his intention, went on serving in an obscure regiment, spending comparatively little money, the way of life at Otradnoe was such, and Mitenka in particular so conducted business, that the debts mounted irresistibly every year. The only help the old count could evidently envisage was government service, and he went to Petersburg to seek a post; to seek a post and at the same time, as he said, to amuse the girls for the last time.

Soon after the Rostovs came to Petersburg, Berg proposed to Vera, and his proposal was accepted.

Despite the fact that in Moscow the Rostovs belonged to high society without knowing or thinking what society they belonged to, in Petersburg their society was mixed and indefinite. In Petersburg they were provincials to whom the very people that the Rostovs fed in Moscow without asking what society they belonged to would not lower themselves.

In Petersburg the Rostovs lived as hospitably as in Moscow, and the most diverse people came together at their suppers: their neighbour in Otradnoe, a poor, elderly landowner with daughters, and the maid of honour Peronsky; Pierre Bezukhov, and the son of a provincial postmaster who served in Petersburg. Among the men who very soon became familiars of the Rostovs' house in Petersburg were Boris, Pierre, whom the old count met in the street and dragged home, and Berg, who spent whole days at the Rostovs' and showed the eldest daughter, Countess Vera, such attention as can only be shown by a young man who intends to propose.

Not in vain had Berg displayed to everyone his right arm wounded at Austerlitz and held his utterly useless sword in his left hand. He recounted the incident to everyone so persistently and with such importance that they all believed in the expediency and merit of this action—and Berg received two decorations for Austerlitz.

He had also managed to distinguish himself in the Finnish war.[14] He had picked up a shell splinter that had killed an adjutant standing next to the commander in chief and offered this splinter to his superior. Just as after Austerlitz, he recounted this incident to everyone at such length and with such persistence that they all also believed it had to have been done—and Berg received two decorations for the Finnish war. In 1809 he was a beribboned captain of the guards and occupied some sort of especially profitable posts in Petersburg.

Though some freethinkers smiled when told of Berg's virtues, it was impossible not to admit that Berg was a good, brave officer, highly regarded by his superiors, and a modest, moral young man with a brilliant career ahead of him and even a solid position in society.

Four years earlier, having met a German friend in the stalls of a Moscow theatre, Berg had pointed Vera Rostov out to him and said in German: *"Das soll mein Weib werden"**—and from that moment on had determined to marry her. Now, in Petersburg, having figured out the Rostovs' situation, he decided that the time had come and proposed.

Berg's proposal was received at first with a perplexity unflattering to him. At first it seemed strange that the son of an obscure Livonian nobleman should propose to Countess Rostov; but Berg's chief quality was such naïve and good-natured egoism that the Rostovs involuntarily thought it would be a good thing, since he himself was so firmly convinced that it would be good and even very good. What was more, the Rostovs' affairs were in great disorder, which the suitor could not help knowing, and, above all, Vera was twenty-four, she had come out everywhere, and, despite her being unquestionably beautiful and sensible, up to then no one had ever proposed to her. The proposal was accepted.

"So you see," Berg said to his comrade, whom he called his friend only because he knew that all people had friends. "You see, I figured it all out, and I wouldn't be getting married if I hadn't thought it all over and if it were awkward for some reason. But now, on the contrary, my papa and mama are provided for, I've arranged that lease for them in the Ostzee region, and I can live with my wife in Petersburg on my salary, her fortune, and my carefulness. We can get along quite well. I'm not marrying for money, I consider that ignoble, but a wife ought to bring in hers and a husband his. I have my service, she has her connections and some small means. In our time that means something, doesn't it? And, above all, she's an excellent, respectable girl, and she loves me . . ."

Berg blushed and smiled.

"And I love her, because she has a sensible character—a very good one. Take the other sister—same family, but something quite different, an unpleasant character, and none of that intelligence, and all that, you know? . . . It's unpleasant . . . But my fiancée . . . You must come to . . ." Berg went on; he was about to say "to dinner," but changed his mind and said "to tea," and with a quick movement of his tongue let out a small, round smoke ring that fully embodied his dreams of happiness.

After the first feeling of perplexity that Berg's proposal aroused in the parents, the festivity and joy usual on such occasions installed themselves in the family, yet the joy was not sincere, but external. In the feelings of the family

*She will be my wife.

regarding this marriage confusion and abashedness could be noticed. It was as if they were ashamed that they loved Vera so little and were now so eager to get her off their hands. The old count was the most embarrassed of all. He probably would have been unable to give a name to the cause of his embarrassment, but that cause was his financial affairs. He decidedly did not know what he had, how far in debt he was, and what he would be able to give Vera as a dowry. When the daughters were born, each was assigned three hundred souls as a dowry; but one of the estates had already been sold, another had been mortgaged and was so long overdue that it had to be sold; therefore it was impossible to give her an estate. There was no money either.

Berg had been a fiancé for over a month, and only a week remained before the wedding, but the count still had not resolved the question of the dowry for himself and had not discussed it with his wife. First the count wanted to allot Vera the Ryazan estate, then to sell some woodlands, then to borrow money on a promissory note. Several days before the wedding, Berg came into the count's study early in the morning and, with a pleasant smile, respectfully asked his future father-in-law to tell him what Countess Vera's dowry would be. This long-anticipated question embarrassed the count so much that he unthinkingly said the first thing that came to his head.

"I like that you're concerned about it, I like it, you'll be satisfied . . ."

And, patting Berg on the shoulder, he got up, wishing to end the conversation. But Berg, smiling pleasantly, explained that unless he knew for certain what Vera's dowry would be, and received at least part of what was allotted her in advance, he would be forced to renounce.

"Because consider, Count, if I were to allow myself to marry now, not having definite means of supporting my wife, I would be acting basely . . ."

The conversation ended with the count, who wished to be magnanimous and not be subjected to new requests, saying he would give him a promissory note for eighty thousand. Berg smiled meekly, kissed the count on the shoulder, and said that he was very grateful, but that he was quite unable to settle into the new life now without receiving thirty thousand in cash.

"Or at least twenty thousand, Count," he added, "and then a promissory note for only sixty thousand."

"Yes, yes, all right," the count said quickly, "only, excuse me, my friend, I'll give you twenty thousand, and a promissory note for eighty thousand besides. So there, kiss me."

XII

Natasha was sixteen, and it was the year 1809, the same she had counted up to on her fingers with Boris four years ago, after they had kissed. Since then she had not seen Boris once. To Sonya and her mother, when the conversation turned to Boris, she said quite freely, as a decided thing, that all that had gone before was childishness, not worth talking about and long forgotten. But in the most secret depths of her soul the question whether her engagement to Boris was a joke or an important, binding promise tormented her.

Since Boris left Moscow for the army in 1805, he had not seen the Rostovs. He had visited Moscow several times, had passed by not far from Otradnoe, but had never once been to the Rostovs'.

It sometimes occurred to Natasha that he did not want to see her, and these surmises were confirmed by the sad tone in which the older people spoke of him.

"Nowadays people don't remember old friends," the countess used to say when Boris was mentioned.

Anna Mikhailovna, who had visited the Rostovs less often of late, also behaved with some special dignity and each time spoke rapturously and gratefully of her son's merits and of the brilliant career he had entered upon. When the Rostovs came to Petersburg, Boris came to visit them.

He went to them not without emotion. The remembrance of Natasha was Boris's most poetic remembrance. But at the same time he went with the firm intention of letting her and her family feel clearly that the childhood relations between himself and Natasha could not be binding either on her or on him. He had a brilliant position in society owing to his intimacy with the countess Bezukhov, a brilliant position in the service owing to the patronage of an important person, whose confidence he fully enjoyed, and he had a nascent project of marrying one of the richest eligible girls in Petersburg, which could very easily be realized. When Boris entered the Rostovs' drawing room, Natasha was in her room. Learning of his arrival, she blushed and almost ran into the drawing room, beaming with a more than affectionate smile.

Boris remembered the Natasha of four years ago, in a short dress, with dark eyes shining from under her curls and a desperate, childish laugh, and therefore when quite a different Natasha came in, he became embarrassed and his face showed a delighted surprise. Natasha was glad of that expression on his face.

"Well, do you recognize your old mischievous friend?" asked the countess. Boris kissed Natasha's hand and said he was surprised at the change in her.

"How pretty you've grown!"

"What else!" Natasha's shining eyes replied.

"And has papa aged?" she asked. Natasha sat down and, without entering into the conversation between Boris and the countess, silently studied her childhood wooer in the minutest detail. He felt the weight of that persistent and affectionate gaze upon him and glanced at her from time to time.

Boris's uniform, spurs, tie, haircut—all this was of the most fashionable and *comme il faut*. Natasha noticed it at once. He sat slightly sideways on the armchair next to the countess, smoothing with his right hand the cleanest of moulded gloves on the left, spoke with an especially refined pursing of the lips about the amusements of Petersburg high society, and with mild mockery recalled the old times in Moscow and Moscow acquaintances. It was not by chance, as Natasha could feel, that in naming the high aristocracy, he mentioned a ball he had attended at the ambassador's and invitations from N. N. and S. S.

Natasha sat silently all the while, gazing at him from under her brows. This gaze disturbed and embarrassed Boris more and more. He interrupted his conversation and turned to look at Natasha more frequently. He stayed for no more than ten minutes and got up, bowing his way out. The same curious, defiant, and somewhat mocking eyes were looking at him. After his first visit, Boris said to himself that he found Natasha as attractive as ever, but that he was not going to give in to that feeling, because to marry her—a girl with almost no fortune—would be to ruin his career, and to renew their former relations without aiming at marriage would be an ignoble thing to do. Boris decided in himself to avoid meeting Natasha, but, despite that decision, came a few days later and began to visit often and spend whole days at the Rostovs'. He fancied he had to have a talk with Natasha, to tell her that all the old things must be forgotten, that despite all . . . she could not be his wife, that he had no fortune, and she would never be allowed to marry him. But he kept failing and felt awkward about starting this talk. He became more and more entangled every day. Natasha, in her mother's and Sonya's observation, seemed to be as in love with Boris as before. She sang his favourite songs for him, showed him her album, made him write in it, and did not allow him to talk about old things, giving him to understand how beautiful the new things were; and every day he left in a fog, without having said what he meant to say, not knowing himself what he was doing, or why he came, or how it would end. Boris stopped frequenting Hélène, received reproachful notes from her, and even so spent whole days at the Rostovs'.

XIII

One evening, when the old countess, sighing and groaning, in nightcap and bed jacket, without false curls and with one poor little knot of hair sticking out from under the white cotton cap, was bowing to the ground on the rug as she said her evening prayers, her door creaked and Natasha came running in, her bare feet in slippers, also in her bed jacket and her hair in curling papers. The countess looked at her and frowned. She was just finishing the last prayer: "Will this couch be my grave?" Her prayerful mood was destroyed. Natasha, red, animated, seeing her mother praying, suddenly stopped running, crouched down, and involuntarily stuck out her tongue, chiding herself. Seeing that her mother went on praying, she ran on tiptoe to the bed, quickly rubbed one small foot against the other, shaking off her slippers, and jumped onto the "couch" which the old countess feared might become her grave. This "couch" was high, with a featherbed and five pillows, each smaller than the last. Natasha jumped up, sank into the featherbed, rolled over to the wall, and began fidgeting under the blanket, settling herself, bending her knees towards her chin, kicking her feet, and laughing barely audibly, now covering her head, now peeking out to look at her mother. The countess finished her prayer and went to the bed with a stern look; but, seeing that Natasha had pulled the covers over her head, she smiled her kind, weak smile.

"Well, well, well," said the mother.

"Mama, can we talk? Say yes," said Natasha. "Well, so one kiss here, another, and that's it." And she embraced her mother's neck and kissed her under the chin. There was an outward crudeness in Natasha's treatment of her mother, but she was so sensitive and adroit that, no matter how she embraced her mother, she was always able to do it so that it was neither painful, nor unpleasant, nor awkward for her.

"Well, what is it tonight?" asked her mother, settling on the pillows and waiting until Natasha, having kicked her feet and turned over twice, lay next to her under the same blanket, her arms on top it, her expression serious.

These nightly visits of Natasha, which took place before the count's return from the club, were one of the favourite pleasures of both mother and daughter.

"What is it tonight? But I've got to tell you . . ."

Natasha covered her mother's mouth with her hand.

"About Boris . . . I know," she said seriously, "that's what I came for. Don't tell me, I know. No, tell me!" She took her hand away. "Tell me, mama. Isn't he sweet?"

"Natasha, you are sixteen years old. At your age I was married. You say Borya is sweet. He's very sweet, and I love him like a son, but what do you want? . . . What do you think? You've turned his head completely, I can see that . . ."

Saying this, the countess glanced at her daughter. Natasha lay looking straight ahead fixedly at one of the carved mahogany sphinxes at the corners of the bed, so that the countess could see her daughter's face only in profile. This face struck the countess by its especially serious and concentrated expression.

Natasha listened and reflected.

"Well, so what?" she said.

"You've turned his head completely—but why? What do you want from him? You know you can't marry him."

"Why not?" said Natasha, without changing her position.

"Because he's young, because he's poor, because he's a relation . . . because you don't love him yourself."

"How do you know?"

"I know. It's not nice, my dear."

"But if I want to . . ." said Natasha.

"Stop this silly talk," said the countess.

"But if I want to . . ."

"Natasha, I'm serious . . ."

Natasha did not allow her to finish, pulled the countess's big hand towards her and kissed it on the back, then on the palm, then turned it again and began to kiss it on one knuckle, then in between, then on the next knuckle, murmuring in a whisper: "January, February, March, April, May."

"Speak, mama, why are you silent? Speak," she said, glancing at her mother, who was looking at her daughter with a tender gaze and, while contemplating her like that, seemed to forget everything she wanted to say.

"It won't do, dearest. Not everyone will understand your childhood ties, and to see him so close to you may harm you in the eyes of other young men who visit us, and, above all, it torments him for nothing. He might have found a rich match for himself; but now he's going out of his mind."

"Out of his mind?" Natasha repeated.

"I'll tell you about myself. I had a cousin . . ."

"I know—Kirila Matveich; but isn't he an old man?"

"He wasn't always an old man. But I tell you what, Natasha, I'll have a talk with Borya. He oughtn't to come so often . . ."

"Why oughtn't he, if he wants to?"

"Because I know it will end in nothing."

"How do you know? No, mama, don't talk with him. Don't you dare talk with him. How stupid!" Natasha said in the tone of a person whose property is being taken away. "Well, I'm not going to marry him, so let him come if it's fun for him and fun for me." Natasha looked at her mother, smiling.

"Not to get married, but *just so*," she repeated.

"How's that, my dear?"

"*Just so.* Well, it's very necessary that I not marry him, but . . . *just so.*"

"Just so, just so," the countess repeated and, shaking all over, she laughed a kindly, unexpected, old woman's laugh.

"Enough laughing, stop it!" cried Natasha. "You're shaking the whole bed. You're a terrible laugher, just like me . . . Wait . . ." She seized the countess by both hands, kissed the knuckle of her little finger—June—and went on kissing July and August on the other hand. "Mama, is he very much in love? How does it look to you? Was anyone ever so in love with you? And he's very sweet, very, very sweet! Only not quite to my taste—he's so narrow, like a dining-room clock . . . You don't understand? . . . Narrow, you know, grey, light grey . . ."

"What nonsense!" said the countess.

Natasha went on:

"You mean you don't understand? Nikolenka would understand . . . Bezukhov—he's blue, dark blue with red, and he's rectangular."

"You flirt with him, too," the countess said, laughing.

"No, he's a Freemason, I found out. He's nice, dark blue with red, how can I explain to you . . ."

"Little countess," the count's voice came from outside the door. "Are you asleep?" Natasha jumped up barefoot and, snatching her slippers, ran to her room.

She could not fall asleep for a long time. She kept thinking that no one could understand all that she understood and all that was in her.

"Sonya?" she thought, looking at the curled-up, sleeping little cat with her enormous braid. "No, it's beyond her! She's virtuous. She fell in love with Nikolenka and doesn't want to know anything else. Even mama doesn't understand. It's astonishing how intelligent I am and how . . . sweet she is," she went on, speaking of herself in the third person and imagining that it was some very intelligent man saying it about her, the most intelligent and best of men . . . "There's everything in her, everything," this man went on, "she's extraordinarily intelligent, sweet, and then, too, pretty, extraordinarily pretty, nimble—she swims, she's an excellent horsewoman, and the voice! One may say, an astonishing voice!" She sang her favourite musical phrase from Cherubini's opera, threw herself on the bed, laughed at the joyful thought that she was about to fall asleep, called Dunyasha to put out the candle, and before Dunyasha had left the room, had already passed into a different, happier world of dreams, where everything was as light and beautiful as in reality, only still better, because it was different.

The next day the countess, having asked to see Boris, had a talk with him, and from that day on he stopped visiting the Rostovs.

XIV

On December 31, the eve of the new year 1810, for *le réveillon*,* a ball was given by a grand dignitary of Catherine's time. The ball was to be attended by the diplomatic corps and the sovereign.

The dignitary's well-known house on the English Embankment[15] shone with countless lights. Police stood by the brightly lit porch laid with red baize, and not merely gendarmes, but a mounted police chief and dozens of police officers. Carriages drove away and new ones drove up with red-liveried footmen and footmen with feathers in their hats. Men in uniforms, stars, and sashes emerged from the carriages; ladies in satin and ermine carefully descended the noisily flipped down footrests, and stepped hastily and soundlessly over the baize of the porch.

Almost every time a new carriage drove up, a whisper ran through the crowd and hats were doffed.

"The sovereign? . . . No, a minister . . . prince . . . ambassador . . . Don't you see the feathers? . . ." came from the crowd. One person in the crowd, better dressed than the others, seemed to know everyone and called by name the most distinguished dignitaries of that time.

A third of the guests had already arrived at the ball, but the Rostovs, who were to be there, were still hurriedly preparing to dress.

There had been many discussions and preparations for this ball in the Rostov family, many fears that they would not receive an invitation, the dresses would not be ready, and everything would not be arranged as it ought to be.

The Rostovs were going to the ball together with Marya Ignatievna Peronsky, the countess's friend and relation, a skinny and yellow lady-in-waiting of the old court, who guided the provincial Rostovs through Petersburg high society.

At ten o'clock in the evening they were to pick up the lady-in-waiting near the Tavrichesky Garden;[16] yet it was five minutes to ten, and the young ladies were still not dressed.

Natasha was going to the first grand ball of her life. She had got up that day at eight o'clock in the morning and had spent the whole day in feverish anxiety and activity. Since morning all her powers had been directed towards getting all of them—herself, mama, Sonya—dressed in the best possible way. Sonya and the countess put themselves entirely in her hands. The countess was to wear a damson velvet dress, and the two girls white gauze dresses over pink silk slips, with roses at the bodice. Their hair was to be done *à la grecque*.

*The New Year's Eve party.

All the essentials had already been done: feet, hands, neck, ears had been washed, perfumed, and powdered with special thoroughness for the ball; they already had on their silk lace stockings and white satin booties with bows; their hairdressing was nearly done. Sonya was finishing dressing, as was the countess; but Natasha, who had fussed over everybody, lagged behind. She was still sitting in front of the mirror, a peignoir thrown over her thin shoulders. Sonya, already dressed, stood in the middle of the room and, pressing painfully with her small finger, was pinning on a last ribbon, which squeaked as the pin went through it.

"Not that way, not that way, Sonya!" said Natasha, turning her head and putting both hands to her hair, which the maid who was holding it did not have time to let go of. "The bow's wrong, come here." Sonya crouched down. Natasha pinned the ribbon on another way.

"Please, miss, it's impossible this way," said the maid who was holding Natasha's hair.

"Ah, my God, wait, then! Like that, Sonya."

"Won't you hurry?" the countess's voice was heard. "It's already ten."

"Right away, right away. Are you ready, mama?"

"I only have to pin on my toque."

"Don't do it without me," cried Natasha, "you won't manage!"

"But it's already ten."

It had been decided to appear at the ball at half past ten, but Natasha still had to dress, and they still had to drive to the Tavrichesky Garden.

Having finished doing her hair, Natasha, in a short petticoat, her ball slippers showing from under it, and wearing her mother's bed jacket, ran up to Sonya, looked her over, and then ran to her mother. She turned her mother's head, pinned on the toque, and, quickly kissing her grey hair, again ran to the maids who were taking up her skirt.

The only thing now was Natasha's skirt, which was too long. Two maids were taking it up, hurriedly biting off the thread. A third, holding pins in her lips and between her teeth, kept running from the countess to Sonya; a fourth held the whole gauze dress on her high-raised arm.

"Mavrusha, darling, be quick!"

"Hand me the thimble there, miss."

"Will you hurry up, finally?" the count said, coming through the door. "Here's your scent. Mme Peronsky must be waiting."

"It's ready, miss," said the maid, lifting the taken-up gauze dress with two fingers, and shaking it and blowing at something, showing by this gesture an awareness of the airiness and purity of what she was holding.

Natasha began to put the dress on.

"One moment, one moment, don't come in, papa!" she cried to her father, who had opened the door, still under the gauze of her skirt, which covered her whole face. Sonya slammed the door. A moment later the count was admitted. He was wearing a dark blue tailcoat, stockings and shoes, was perfumed and pomaded.

"Papa, you look so handsome, it's lovely!" said Natasha, standing in the middle of the room and spreading the folds of the gauze.

"Let me, miss, let me," said the maid, getting on her knees, pulling at the dress, and moving the pins with her tongue from one side of her mouth to the other.

"Say what you like," Sonya cried with despair in her voice, looking at Natasha's dress, "say what you like, it's still too long!"

Natasha stepped back to look at herself in the pier glass. The dress was too long.

"By God, miss, it's not too long at all," said Mavrusha, who was crawling on the floor following her young lady.

"Well, if it's long, we can take it up, we can take it up in a minute," said the resolute Dunyasha, taking a needle out of the fichu on her breast and setting to work again on the floor.

Just then the countess came in bashfully, with quiet steps, in her toque and velvet dress.

"Ohh! my beauty!" cried the count. "Better than any of you! . . ." He was about to embrace her, but she retreated, blushing, so as not to have her dress rumpled.

"Mama, the toque more to one side," said Natasha. "I'll re-pin it," and she rushed forward, and the sewing girls, who had no time to follow her, tore off a piece of gauze.

"My God! What is this? It's not my fault, I swear . . ."

"Never mind, I'll stitch it up, it won't show," said Dunyasha.

"My beauty, my queen!" the nanny said, coming through the door. "And Sonyushka, too, what beauties! . . ."

At a quarter past ten they finally got into carriages and drove off. But they still had to stop by the Tavrichesky Garden.

Mme Peronsky was ready. Despite her old age and unattractiveness, the same things had gone on with her as at the Rostovs', though not as hurriedly (it was a habitual thing for her). Her old, unattractive body had been perfumed, washed, powdered in just the same way, she had been scrubbed behind the ears just as carefully, and, just as at the Rostovs', her old maid had delightedly admired her mistress's outfit, when she came out to the drawing room in a yellow dress with a monogram. Mme Peronsky praised the attire of the Rostovs.

The Rostovs praised her taste and attire and, mindful of their dresses and hair, put themselves into the carriages at eleven o'clock and drove off.

XV

Natasha had not had a free moment since the morning of that day and had never once had time to think about what lay ahead of her.

In the damp, cold air, in the incomplete darkness of the crowded, rocking carriage, she imagined vividly for the first time what awaited her there at the ball, in the brightly lit rooms—music, flowers, dancing, the sovereign, all the brilliant youth of Petersburg. What awaited her was so beautiful that she did not even believe it could happen: so out of keeping it was with the impression of the cold, the crowdedness, the darkness of the carriage. She understood what awaited her only when, having stepped over the red baize of the porch, she entered the front hall, took off her fur coat, and walked beside Sonya in front of her mother between the flowers on the lighted stairway. Only then did she remember how one had to behave at a ball and try to assume the majestic manner she considered necessary for a girl at a ball. But, luckily for her, she felt her eyes looking everywhere at once: she saw nothing clearly, her pulse beat a hundred times a minute, and the blood began to throb in her heart. She was unable to assume that manner which would have made her ridiculous, and walked on, faint with excitement and only trying as hard as she could to conceal it. And this was the manner that was most becoming to her. Before them, behind them, also talking quietly and also in ball gowns, other guests were entering. The mirrors on the stairway reflected ladies in white, blue, pink dresses, with diamonds and pearls on their bare arms and necks.

Natasha looked in the mirrors and in the reflections could not distinguish herself from the others. Everything mixed into one brilliant procession. At the entrance to the first room, the monotonous noise of voices, footsteps, greetings deafened Natasha, the light and brilliance dazzled her still more. The host and hostess, who had already been standing by the door for half an hour saying the same words to the entering people—*"Charmé de vous voir"** *—greeted the Rostovs and Mme Peronsky in the same way.

The two girls in white dresses, with identical roses in their dark hair, curtsied identically, but the hostess involuntarily rested her gaze longer on the slender Natasha. She looked at her and smiled at her alone with a special smile, in addition to her hostess smile. Gazing at her, the hostess may have remembered the golden, irretrievable time of her girlhood, and her own first ball. The host also followed Natasha with his eyes and asked the count which one was his daughter.

"Charmante!" he said, kissing the tips of his fingers.

*Delighted to see you.

The guests stood in the ballroom, crowding by the door, waiting for the sovereign. The countess placed herself in the first rows of this crowd. Natasha heard and felt that several voices were asking about her and looking at her. She realized that she was liked by those who paid attention to her, and this observation reassured her somewhat.

"There are some like us, and some worse than us," she thought.

Mme Peronsky named for the countess the most important persons at the ball.

"That one is the Dutch ambassador, see, the grey-haired one," she said, pointing to a little old man with abundant, curly silver-grey hair, surrounded by ladies whom he made laugh at something.

"And here she is, the queen of Petersburg, Countess Bezukhov," she said, pointing to the entering Hélène.

"How beautiful! She yields nothing to Marya Antonovna.[17] See how the men dangle after her, young and old. Both beautiful and intelligent. They say Prince——has lost his mind over her. But these two here, though they're not beautiful, are still more surrounded."

She pointed to a lady who was crossing the room with a very unattractive daughter.

"She's a millionaire bride," said Mme Peronsky. "And here come the wooers."

"That's Madame Bezukhov's brother, Anatole Kuragin," she said, pointing to a handsome horse guard who walked past them, looking somewhere above the ladies from the height of his raised head. "Handsome, isn't he? They say he's to marry this rich one. And your cousin, Drubetskoy, is also dangling after her very much. Millions, they say. Why, but that's the French ambassador himself," she replied to the countess's question about who Caulaincourt was. "Look at him, like some sort of tsar. But all the same the French are nice, very nice. There's nothing nicer for society. Ah, here she is! No, she's the best, our Marya Antonovna! And so simply dressed. Lovely!"

"And that fat one in spectacles is the universal Freemason," said Mme Peronsky, pointing to Bezukhov. "Set him next to his wife: a real tomfool!"

Pierre walked along, rolling his fat body, parting the crowd, nodding to right and left as casually and good-naturedly as if he was walking through a marketplace crowd. He moved through the crowd, evidently searching for someone.

Natasha looked joyfully at the familiar face of Pierre, that tomfool, as Mme Peronsky had called him, and knew that Pierre was looking for them in the crowd, and for her in particular. Pierre had promised to be at the ball and to introduce partners to her.

But before he reached them, Bezukhov stopped beside a very handsome dark-haired man of medium height, in a white uniform, who was standing by a window talking to a tall man with stars and a sash. Natasha immediately rec-

ognized the young man of medium height in the white uniform: it was Bolkonsky, who seemed to her to have grown younger, more cheerful, and better
looking.

"Here's another acquaintance, Bolkonsky, see, mama?" said Natasha, pointing to Prince Andrei. "Remember, he spent the night with us at Otradnoe."

"Ah, you know him?" said Mme Peronsky. "I can't bear him. *Il fait à
présent la pluie et le beau temps.* * And such boundless pride! Takes after his
papa. Got in with Speransky, drafting some sort of projects. Look how he
treats the ladies! She's talking to him, and he turns away," she said, pointing to
him. "I'd give it to him, if he behaved with me the way he does with these
ladies."

XVI

Suddenly everything stirred, the crowd began to talk, moved together, parted
again, and between the two rows of people, to the sounds of the struck-up
music, the sovereign came in. Behind him walked the host and hostess. The
sovereign walked quickly, nodding to right and left, as if trying to get quickly
past this first moment of meeting. The musicians played a polonaise well-
known then from the words written to it. These words began: "Alexander,
Elizaveta, how we all admire you." The sovereign walked into the drawing
room; the crowd surged towards the door; several persons with changed
expressions hurriedly went there and back. The crowd surged away from the
drawing-room door again, and the sovereign appeared in it, talking with the
hostess. A young man with a perplexed look pressed up to the ladies, asking
them to step aside. Some ladies with faces that expressed a total obliviousness
to all social conventions pushed forward, ruining their fancy dresses. Men
began to approach the ladies and form couples for the polonaise.

Everyone made way, and the sovereign, smiling and out of step with the
music, led the hostess through the drawing-room door. After him came the
host with Mme M. A. Naryshkin, then ambassadors, ministers, various generals, whom Mme Peronsky kept naming without pause. More than half of the
ladies had partners and were joining or preparing to join the polonaise.
Natasha sensed that she would be left with her mother and Sonya among the
smaller part of the ladies pushed back against the wall and not asked to the
polonaise. She stood, her thin arms lowered, her barely defined bosom rising
rhythmically, holding her breath, her shining, frightened eyes looking straight
ahead with an expression of readiness either for the greatest happiness or for
the greatest grief. She was interested neither in the sovereign nor in any of the

*He runs the whole show now.

important persons Mme Peronsky pointed out—she had one thought: "Can it be that no one will come up to me, can it be that I won't dance among the first, can it be that all these men won't notice me, who now don't even seem to see me, and if they look at me, it's with such an expression as if they were saying: 'Ah! it's not her, there's no point in looking!' No, it can't be!" she thought. "They must know how I want to dance, and how well I dance, and what fun it will be for them to dance with me."

The sounds of the polonaise, which had continued for quite a long time, were already beginning to seem sad—a reminiscence in Natasha's ears. She wanted to cry. Mme Peronsky left them. The count was at the other end of the room; the countess, Sonya, and she stood alone, as if in a forest, in this crowd of strangers, of no interest or need to anyone. Prince Andrei walked past them with some lady, obviously not recognizing them. The handsome Anatole, smiling, was saying something to the lady he was leading, and glanced at Natasha's face as one would glance at a wall. Boris walked past them twice and turned away each time. Berg and his wife, who were not dancing, came up to them.

For Natasha, this family intimacy here, at a ball, seemed offensive, as if there were no other place for family conversations except at a ball. She did not look at and did not listen to Vera, who was saying something to her about her green dress.

Finally, the sovereign stopped beside his last partner (he had danced with three), and the music ceased. A preoccupied adjutant ran up to the Rostovs, asking them to step aside somewhere, though they were standing at the wall, and from the gallery came the distinct, careful, and engagingly rhythmic sounds of a waltz. The sovereign looked over the room with a smile. A minute passed—no one began yet. The adjutant master of ceremonies went up to Countess Bezukhov and asked her to dance. Smiling, she raised her arm and placed it, without looking at him, on the adjutant's shoulder. The adjutant master of ceremonies, an expert in these matters, confidently, unhurriedly, and rhythmically, keeping firm hold of his partner, set off with her at first in a glissade round the edge of the circle, then, at the corner of the room, took her left arm, turned her, and now, above the ever-quickening sounds of the music, one could hear only the rhythmic jingle of the spurs on the adjutant's quick and nimble feet, and at every third beat, the velvet dress of his partner seemed to flash, flying, as she turned. Natasha looked at them and was ready to weep that it was not she dancing this first turn of the waltz.

Prince Andrei, in his white cavalry colonel's uniform, stockings, and low boots, animated and merry, stood in the first rows of the circle, not far from the Rostovs. Baron Vierhoff was talking to him about the first session of the State Council,[18] planned for the next day. Prince Andrei, being close to Speransky and taking part in the work of the legislative commission, could give accurate information about the next day's meeting, of which various rumours were circulating. But he was not listening to what Vierhoff was telling him, and looked now at the sovereign, now at the gentlemen preparing to dance, who had not yet ventured into the circle.

Prince Andrei was observing these gentlemen grown timid in the sovereign's presence and ladies faint with the desire to be invited.

Pierre came over to Prince Andrei and took him by the arm.

"You always dance. My protégée, the young Miss Rostov, is here. Ask her," he said.

"Where?" asked Bolkonsky. "I beg your pardon," he said, turning to the baron, "we can finish this conversation elsewhere—at a ball one must dance." He stepped forward, in the direction Pierre had indicated to him. Natasha's desperate, rapt face caught Prince Andrei's eye. He recognized her, guessed her feeling, realized that she was a débutante, remembered her conversation on the window ledge, and with a merry expression on his face went up to Countess Rostov.

"Allow me to introduce you to my daughter," the countess said, blushing.

"I have the pleasure of being acquainted, if the countess remembers me," said Prince Andrei, with a courteous and low bow, totally contradicting Mme Peronsky's remark about his rudeness, going up to Natasha and raising his arm to put it round her waist even before he finished asking her to dance. He suggested a turn of the waltz. That rapt expression of Natasha's face, ready for despair and for ecstasy, suddenly lit up with a happy, grateful, childlike smile.

"I've been waiting a long time for you," this frightened and happy girl seemed to say by her smile, shining through ready tears, as she raised her arm to Prince Andrei's shoulder. They were the second couple to enter the circle. Prince Andrei was one of the best dancers of his time. Natasha's dancing was excellent. Her little feet in satin ball slippers did their work quickly, lightly, and independently of herself, and her face shone with the rapture of happiness. Her bared neck and arms were thin and unattractive compared to Hélène's shoulders. Her shoulders were thin, her bosom undefined, her arms slender; but on Hélène there was already a sort of varnish from all the thousands of gazes that had passed over her body, while Natasha looked like a young girl who was bared for the first time and would have been very ashamed of it, if she had not been assured that it had necessarily to be so.

Prince Andrei liked to dance and, wishing to rid himself quickly of the political and intellectual conversations with which everyone addressed him, and wishing to break quickly this vexatious circle of embarrassment caused by the presence of the sovereign, had gone to dance and had asked Natasha because Pierre had pointed her out to him and because she was the first pretty woman his eyes fell on; but as soon as he put his arm round her slender, mobile, quivering waist, and she began to move so close to him and smile so close to him, the wine of her loveliness went to his head: he felt himself revived and rejuvenated when, catching his breath and leaving her, he stopped and began to look at the dancers.

XVII

After Prince Andrei, Boris came up to Natasha and asked her to dance, then also that dancer adjutant who had opened the ball, and other young men, and Natasha, sending her surplus partners to Sonya, happy and flushed, did not stop dancing all evening. She noticed nothing and did not see any of what interested everyone at this ball. Not only did she not notice how the sovereign had a long talk with the French ambassador, how he talked with particular graciousness with a certain lady, how prince so-and-so did and said such-and-such, how Hélène had great success and was granted the special attentions of so-and-so; she did not even see the sovereign, and noticed that he had gone only because the ball became more animated after his departure. In one of the merry cotillions before supper, Prince Andrei danced again with Natasha. He reminded her of their first meeting in the Otradnoe avenue, and how she could not fall asleep on that moonlit night, and how he involuntarily overheard her. Natasha blushed at this reminder and tried to justify herself, as if there was something shameful in that feeling which Prince Andrei had involuntarily over-heard from her.

Prince Andrei, like all people who have grown up in society, liked to encounter things in society that did not have the general society stamp on them. And Natasha was just that, with her astonishment, joy, and timidity, and even her mistakes in French. He treated her and talked to her with particular tenderness and care. Sitting next to her, talking with her about the simplest and most insignificant subjects, Prince Andrei admired the joyful shining of her eyes and smile, which referred not to what they were saying, but to her inner happiness. At those times when Natasha was chosen, and she got up with a smile and danced through the room, Prince Andrei especially admired her timid grace. In the middle of the cotillion, Natasha, having finished a figure, still breathing hard, was going to her seat. A new partner again asked her to dance. She was tired and out of breath, and obviously wanted to refuse, but then again cheerfully raised her arm to her partner's shoulder and smiled to Prince Andrei.

That smile said: "I'd be glad to rest and sit with you; I'm tired; but you see, I've been asked to dance, and I'm glad of it, and I'm happy, and I love everybody, and you and I understand all that," and much, much more. When her partner left her, Natasha ran across the room to invite two ladies for the figures.

"If she goes to her cousin first and then to another lady, she'll be my wife,"

Prince Andrei quite unexpectedly said to himself, looking at her. She went to her cousin first.

"What nonsense sometimes comes into one's head!" thought Prince Andrei. "But the one sure thing is that this girl is so sweet, so special, that she won't spend a month dancing here before she gets married . . . It's a rarity here," he thought, as Natasha, straightening a rose that had gone awry on her corsage, was sitting down beside him.

At the end of the cotillion, the old count in his dark blue tailcoat came over to the dancers. He invited Prince Andrei to come and see him, and asked his daughter whether she was having a good time. Natasha did not reply and only smiled a smile which said with reproach: "How can you ask that?"

"I've never enjoyed myself so much in my life!" she said, and Prince Andrei noticed how her thin arms rose quickly to embrace her father and at once dropped again. Natasha was happier than she had ever been before in her life. She was in that highest degree of happiness when a person becomes perfectly kind and good, and does not believe in the possibility of evil, unhappiness, and grief.

At this ball Pierre felt insulted for the first time by the position his wife occupied in high spheres. He was sullen and distracted. There was a deep furrow across his brow, and, standing by the window, he looked through his spectacles, seeing no one.

Natasha walked past him on her way to supper.

Pierre's gloomy, unhappy face struck her. She stopped in front of him. She wanted to help him, to transfer to him the overflow of her own happiness.

"Such a merry time," she said, "isn't it, Count?"

Pierre smiled distractedly, obviously not understanding what was being said to him.

"Yes, I'm very glad," he said.

"How can they be displeased with anything," thought Natasha. "Especially such a nice man as this Bezukhov?" In Natasha's eyes, all who were at the ball were equally kind, nice, wonderful people, and loved each other: no one could offend anyone, and therefore they should all be happy.

XVIII

The next day Prince Andrei remembered yesterday's ball, but his thought did not dwell on it for long. "Yes, it was a very brilliant ball. And then, too . . . yes, Miss Rostov is very sweet. There's something fresh in her, something special, non-Petersburg, that makes her different." That was all he thought about the ball, and, having had tea, he sat down to work.

But from fatigue or lack of sleep, the day was not good for work, and Prince Andrei could do nothing, kept criticizing his own efforts, as often happened with him, and was glad when he heard someone arrive.

The visitor was Bitsky, who worked on various commissions, frequented all the societies of Petersburg, was a passionate admirer of the new ideas and of Speransky, an anxious Petersburg newsmonger, one of those people who choose a trend as they do their clothes—according to the fashion, but who, because of it, look like the most ardent partisans of the trend. He rushed into Prince Andrei's room and, barely managing to take his hat off, anxiously began talking. He had just learned the details of the session of the State Council that morning, opened by the sovereign, and was recounting it with rapture. The sovereign's speech had been extraordinary. It had been one of those speeches that only constitutional monarchs make. "The sovereign said straight out that the Council and the Senate were *estates* of the realm; he said that the government should be based not on arbitrariness, but on *firm principles*. The sovereign said that the finances should be reformed and the accounting made public," Bitsky recounted, emphasizing certain words and widening his eyes significantly.

"Yes, today's event marks an epoch, the greatest epoch in our history," he concluded.

Prince Andrei listened to his account of the opening of the State Council, which he had awaited with such impatience and to which he had ascribed such importance, and marvelled that this event, now that it had taken place, not only did not move him, but seemed less than insignificant. With quiet mockery he listened to Bitsky's rapturous account. The simplest thought occurred to him: "What do Bitsky and I have to do with what the sovereign was pleased to say in the Council? Can any of it make me happier and better?"

And this simple reflection suddenly destroyed for Prince Andrei all his former interest in the reforms being carried out. That same day Prince Andrei was supposed to dine at Speransky's *"en petit comité,"** as the host had said when inviting him. This dinner in the circle of family and friends of the man whom Prince Andrei so admired had formerly interested him very much, the more so as he had not yet seen Speransky in his domestic surroundings; but now he did not want to go.

At the appointed dinner hour, however, Prince Andrei was already entering Speransky's modest private house[19] near the Tavrichesky Garden. In the parqueted dining room of the modest house, distinguished by its extraordinary cleanliness (reminiscent of monastic cleanliness), Prince Andrei, who was slightly late, found that at five o'clock the whole company of that *petit comité* of Speransky's intimate acquaintances had already gathered. There were no ladies, except for Speransky's little daughter (with a long face resembling her

*In an informal meeting.

father's) and her governess. The guests were Gervais, Magnitsky, and Stolypin. In the front hall Prince Andrei already heard loud voices and ringing, clipped laughter—laughter similar to what one hears on the stage. Some voice similar to Speransky's rapped out a distinct "ha, ha, ha." Prince Andrei had never heard Speransky laugh, and this ringing, high-pitched laughter from a statesman struck him as strange.

Prince Andrei entered the dining room. The whole company was standing between two windows, by a small table with hors d'oeuvres. Speransky, in a grey tailcoat with a star, and evidently in the same white waistcoat and high white necktie he had worn at the famous session of the State Council, stood by the table with a merry face. The guests stood around him. Magnitsky, addressing Mikhail Mikhailovich, was telling an anecdote. Speransky listened, laughing beforehand at what Magnitsky was about to say. Just as Prince Andrei entered the dining room, Magnitsky's words were again drowned by laughter. Stolypin produced a loud bass, chewing a piece of bread and cheese; Gervais hissed out a quiet chuckle; and Speransky laughed his high and clipped laugh.

Speransky, still laughing, gave Prince Andrei his white, tender hand.

"Very glad to see you, Prince," he said. "Just a moment . . ." he turned to Magnitsky, interrupting his story. "We've agreed that tonight will be a dinner for pleasure and not a word about business." He turned back to the speaker and laughed again.

Prince Andrei listened to his laughter and looked at the laughing Speransky with surprise and sad disappointment. This was not Speransky but another man, as it seemed to Prince Andrei. Everything in Speransky that had formerly seemed mysterious and attractive to Prince Andrei suddenly became clear and unattractive to him.

At the table the conversation did not let up for a moment and seemed to consist of a collection of funny anecdotes. Before Magnitsky finished his story, someone else announced his readiness to tell something still funnier. The anecdotes were for the most part concerned, if not with the world of government service, then with persons in the service. It seemed that the insignificance of those persons had been so definitely decided upon in this company that the only possible attitude towards them was a good-naturedly comic one. Speransky told how at the Council that morning a deaf dignitary, when asked his opinion, had replied that he was of the same opinion. Gervais recounted a whole case about an audit, remarkable for the senselessness of all the persons involved. Stolypin, stuttering, mixed into the conversation and began talking vehemently about abuses under the former order of things, threatening to give the conversation a serious character. Magnitsky began to make fun of Stolypin's vehemence. Gervais put in a joke, and the conversation resumed its former merry course.

Obviously, Speransky liked to relax after work and make merry in a friendly circle, and all his guests, understanding his wish, tried to make him merry and be merry themselves. But this merriment seemed heavy and cheerless to Prince Andrei. Speransky's high-pitched voice struck him as unpleasant, and his constant laughter for some reason offended Prince Andrei's feelings by its false note. Prince Andrei did not laugh and feared he would be a deadweight on the company. But no one noticed his lack of harmony with the general mood. They all seemed to be very merry.

He wanted several times to enter the conversation, but each time his word was thrown out, like a cork out of water; and he was unable to joke along with them.

There was nothing bad or inappropriate in what they said, everything was witty and might have been funny; but that something which constitutes the salt of merriment was not only missing, but they did not even know it existed.

After dinner Speransky's daughter and her governess got up. Speransky stroked his daughter with his white hand and kissed her. And this gesture seemed unnatural to Prince Andrei.

The men remained at the table over the port, English style. In the middle of the conversation that started up about Napoleon's Spanish campaign,[20] of which they all held the same approving opinion, Prince Andrei began to contradict them. Speransky smiled and, obviously trying to divert the conversation from the direction it had taken, told an anecdote that had no relation to it. They all fell silent for several moments.

Having sat at the table for a while, Speransky corked the wine bottle and saying: "Good wine costs a pretty penny these days," handed it to the servant and got up. They all got up and with the same noisy talk went to the drawing room. Speransky was handed two envelopes brought by a courier. He took them and went to his study. As soon as he left, the general merriment died down, and the guests began talking sensibly and quietly with each other.

"Well, now for a declamation!" said Speransky, coming out of his study. "An astonishing talent!" he said to Prince Andrei. Magnitsky at once assumed a pose and began to recite humourous verses he had composed in French about certain persons well-known in Petersburg, and was interrupted several times by applause. When the verses were over, Prince Andrei went up to Speransky to take his leave.

"Leaving so early?" said Speransky.

"I promised to be at a soirée . . ."

They fell silent. Prince Andrei looked closely into those mirror-like eyes which did not let anything in, and felt how ridiculous it was that he could have expected anything from Speransky and from all his activity connected with him, and that he could have ascribed importance to what Speransky was doing. That precise, mirthless laughter went on ringing in Prince Andrei's ears long after he had left Speransky.

On returning home, Prince Andrei began to recall his Petersburg life of those last four months as if it was something new. He recalled his solicitations, his petitioning, the story of his project for military regulations, which had been taken into consideration, but which they had tried to silence, solely because another project, a very bad one, had already been developed and presented to the sovereign; he recalled the sessions of the committee of which Berg was a member; he recalled how, at these sessions, everything to do with the form and procedure of the committee's sessions was discussed carefully and at length, and everything to do with the essence of the matter was carefully and briefly dispensed with. He recalled his work on legislation, the concern with which he had translated the articles of the Roman and French codes into Russian, and he felt ashamed of himself. Then he vividly pictured Bogucharovo, his occupations in the country, his trip to Ryazan, recalled the muzhiks, the headman Dron, and applying to them the personal rights he had classified by paragraphs, he felt astonished that he could have been occupied with such idle work for so long.

XIX

The next day Prince Andrei went to visit certain houses he had not been to yet, among them the house of the Rostovs, with whom he had renewed his acquaintance at the last ball. Besides the rules of courtesy, according to which he ought to call on the Rostovs, Prince Andrei wanted to see at home that special, animated girl who had left him with such a pleasant memory.

Natasha was one of the first to meet him. She was wearing a dark blue everyday dress, in which she seemed still better to Prince Andrei than in a ball gown. She and the whole Rostov family received Prince Andrei like an old friend, simply and cordially. The whole family, which Prince Andrei used to judge so severely, now seemed to him to consist of wonderful, simple, and kind people. The old count's hospitality and good-nature, which struck one especially nicely in Petersburg, was such that Prince Andrei could not refuse to stay for dinner. "Yes, they're kind, nice people," thought Bolkonsky, "who of course don't understand a whit of the treasure they have in Natasha; but kind people, who constitute the best backdrop for setting off this special girl, so poetic, lovely, and overflowing with life."

Prince Andrei sensed in Natasha the presence of a special world, completely foreign to him, filled with joys of a sort as yet unknown to him, that foreign world which even then, in the Otradnoe avenue and at the window on that moonlit night, had enticed him so. Now that world no longer enticed him, it was no longer foreign; but he himself, having entered it, found in it a new delight.

After dinner Natasha, at Prince Andrei's request, went to the clavichord and began to sing. Prince Andrei stood by the window, talking with the ladies, and listened to her. In the middle of a phrase, Prince Andrei fell silent and suddenly felt choked with tears, which he did not know was possible for him. He looked at the singing Natasha and something new and happy occurred in his soul. He was happy, but at the same time he felt sad. He had decidedly nothing to weep about, but he was ready to weep. About what? His former love? The little princess? His disappointments? . . . His hopes for the future? . . . Yes and no. The main thing he wanted to weep about was a sudden, vivid awareness of the terrible opposition between something infinitely great and indefinable that was in him, and something narrow and fleshly that he himself, and even she, was. This opposition tormented him and gladdened him while she sang.

As soon as Natasha finished singing, she went over to him and asked him how he liked her voice. She asked it and became embarrassed just after she said it, realizing that it was not a question to be asked. He smiled, looking at her, and said that he liked her singing just as he liked everything she did.

Prince Andrei left the Rostovs' late in the evening. He went to bed as was his habit, but soon realized that he could not sleep. Lighting a candle, he would sit on the bed, then get up, then lie down again, not troubled in the least by his insomnia: he felt as joyful and new in his soul as if he had gone from a stuffy room into God's open world. It did not occur to him that he was in love with Miss Rostov; he was not thinking of her; he only pictured her to himself, and owing to that his whole life appeared to him in a new light. "Why do I thrash about, why do I fuss inside this narrow, limited frame, when life, the whole of life, with all its joys, is open to me?" he said to himself. And for the first time in a long while he began making happy plans for the future. He decided that he must occupy himself with the education of his son, by finding a tutor for him and entrusting the boy to the tutor; then he must retire from the service and go abroad, to see England, Switzerland, Italy. "I must use my freedom while I feel so much youth and strength in me," he said to himself. "Pierre was right when he said that one must believe in the possibility of happiness in order to be happy, and I now believe in it. Let the dead bury their dead,[21] but while I'm alive, I must live and be happy," he thought.

XX

One morning Colonel Adolf Berg, whom Pierre knew, as he knew everyone in Moscow and Petersburg, came to see him in a spanking-new uniform and with his side-whiskers brushed and pomaded forward, as the sovereign Alexander Pavlovich wore them.

"I just called on the countess, your spouse, and was so unlucky as to have my request go unfulfilled; I hope that with you, Count, I shall have more luck," he said, smiling.

"What can I do for you, Colonel? I'm at your service."

"I am now fully settled in the new apartment, Count," Berg informed him, obviously knowing that it could not be unpleasant to hear it, "and therefore would like to arrange a small soirée for my and my wife's acquaintances." (He smiled still more pleasantly.) "I wanted to ask the countess and you to do me the honour of joining us for a cup of tea and . . . supper."

Only Countess Elena Vassilievna, considering the company of some sort of Bergs humiliating to her, could be so cruel as to refuse such an invitation. Berg explained so clearly why he wished to gather a small and good company at his place, and why this would be a pleasure for him, and why he would be sorry to spend money on cards or on something bad, but on good company he was ready to suffer the expense, that Pierre could not refuse and promised to come.

"Only not late, Count, if I may ask; around ten minutes to eight, if I may ask. We'll have a game of cards. Our general will join us. He's very kind to me. We'll have supper, Count. So do me the favour."

Contrary to his habit of being late, Pierre came to the Bergs' that day at a quarter to eight, instead of ten minutes to eight.

The Bergs, having prepared everything necessary for the soirée, were ready to receive their guests.

In the new, clean, bright study, decorated with little busts, and little pictures, and new furniture, sat Berg and his wife. Berg, in a brand-new, buttoned-up uniform, sat beside his wife, explaining to her that one can and must have acquaintances among people above oneself, because only then can one find pleasure in one's acquaintances.

"You can imitate something, you can ask for something. Just look how I've fared since the lower ranks." (Berg reckoned up his life not in years but in imperial rewards.) "My comrades are still nobodies now, but I already occupy the post of a regimental commander, and I have the happiness of being your husband" (he got up and kissed Vera's hand, but on his way straightened the turned-back corner of the carpet). "And how have I acquired it all? Mainly by knowing how to choose my acquaintances. It goes without saying that one must be virtuous and precise."

Berg smiled with a consciousness of his superiority over a weak woman and fell silent, thinking that all the same this sweet wife of his was a weak woman, who could not comprehend all that made up the dignity of a man—*ein Mann zu sein.** At the same time, Vera also smiled with a consciousness of her superiority over her virtuous, good husband, who all the same understood life wrongly, as, in Vera's view, all men did. Berg, judging by his wife, considered

*Of being a man.

all women weak and stupid. Vera, judging by her husband alone and extending the observation to everyone, supposed that all men ascribed reason only to themselves, and at the same time understood nothing, were proud and egoistic.

Berg got up and, embracing his wife carefully, so as not to rumple her lace pelerine, for which he had paid dearly, kissed her in the middle of the lips.

"Only we shouldn't have children too soon," he said, following an unconscious association of ideas.

"Yes," replied Vera, "I don't want that at all. One must live for society."

"That's exactly the same as Princess Yusupov wore," said Berg with a happy and kindly smile, pointing to the pelerine.

Just then the arrival of Count Bezukhov was announced. The two spouses exchanged self-satisfied smiles, each silently claiming the honour of this visit.

"That's what it means to know how to make acquaintances," thought Berg, "that's what it means to know how to behave!"

"Only, please, when I'm entertaining the guests," said Vera, "don't interrupt me, because I know how to entertain each of them and what to say in all kinds of company."

Berg also smiled.

"Impossible: sometimes men must have a male conversation," he said.

Pierre was received in the nice new drawing room, in which it was impossible to sit down anywhere without violating the symmetry, cleanliness, and order, and therefore it was quite comprehensible and not strange that Berg magnanimously suggested disturbing the symmetry of an armchair or a sofa for his dear guest, and, obviously in a painful dilemma himself in this respect, left the resolving of this question to his guest's choice. Pierre upset the symmetry by moving a chair towards him, and Berg and Vera at once began the evening, interrupting each other and entertaining the guest.

Vera, having decided in her own mind that Pierre must be entertained by a conversation about the French embassy, began this conversation at once. Berg, having decided that there was also need for a male conversation, interrupted his wife and touched upon the question of war with Austria, and involuntarily shifted the general conversation to his personal considerations about the offers made him in regard to taking part in the Austrian campaign, and to the reasons why he had not accepted them. Though the conversation was very incoherent, and Vera was angry at the interference of the male element, the two spouses felt with satisfaction that, even though there was only one guest, the soirée had begun very well, and that it was as like any other soirée, with conversation, tea, and lighted candles, as two drops of water.

Soon Boris arrived, Berg's old comrade. He treated Berg and Vera with a certain tinge of superiority and patronage. After Boris came a lady with a colonel, then the general himself, then the Rostovs, and the soirée now became quite indisputably like all other soirées. Berg and Vera could not contain their joyful smiles at the sight of this movement about the drawing room, at the sound of this disjointed talk, the rustling of dresses and bowing. Everything was like at everyone else's house, and especially like was the general, who praised the little apartment, patted Berg on the shoulder, and with paternal authority ordered the tables set for boston. The general sat down to play with Count Ilya Andreevich, as the most distinguished guest after himself. The old with the old, the young with the young, the hostess by the tea table, on which there were exactly the same cakes in a silver basket as the Panins had at their soirée—everything was exactly the same as with everyone else.

XXI

Pierre, as one of the most honoured guests, had to sit down to boston with Ilya Andreevich, the general, and the colonel. At the boston table, Pierre happened to sit facing Natasha, and he was struck by the odd change that had taken place in her since the day of the ball. Natasha was silent and not only was not as beautiful as she had been at the ball, but would even have been plain if she had not had such a look of meekness and indifference to everything.

"What's the matter with her?" Pierre wondered, glancing at her. She was sitting beside her sister at the tea table and replied reluctantly, without looking at him, to something Boris said as he sat down by her. Having gone through a whole suit and taken five tricks, much to his partner's delight, Pierre, who heard an exchange of greetings and the sound of someone's footsteps coming into the room as he was gathering in his tricks, looked at her again.

"What's going on with her?" he said to himself with still greater surprise.

Prince Andrei was standing before her with a solicitously tender expression and saying something to her. She, having raised her head, was looking at him, blushing deeply and clearly trying to restrain her fitful breathing. And the bright light of some inner fire, previously extinguished, again burned in her. She was quite transformed. From plain she again became as she had been at the ball.

Prince Andrei went over to Pierre, and Pierre noticed a new, young expression in his friend's face.

Pierre changed his place several times during the game, sitting now with his back to Natasha, now facing her, and in the course of all six rubbers observed her and his friend.

"Something very important is going on between them," thought Pierre, and a joyful and at the same time bitter feeling stirred him and made him forget the game.

After six rubbers, the general got up, saying it was impossible to play that way, and Pierre was set free. Natasha stood to one side, talking with Sonya and Boris. Vera, with a subtle smile, was talking with Prince Andrei. Pierre went over to his friend and, having asked whether what they were talking about was a secret, sat down beside them. Vera, having noticed Prince Andrei's attention to Natasha, had decided that at a soirée, at a real soirée, it was necessary to have subtle allusions to feelings, and, seizing a moment when Prince Andrei was alone, began a conversation with him about feelings in general and about her sister. With such an intelligent guest (as she considered Prince Andrei to be), she had to employ her diplomatic art.

When Pierre came up to them, he noticed that Vera was conversing with self-satisfied enthusiasm, while Prince Andrei seemed embarrassed (which seldom happened to him).

"What do you think?" Vera said with a subtle smile. "You're so perceptive, Prince, and understand people's characters so well at once. What do you think about Natalie? Can she be constant in her attachments? Can she, like other women" (Vera meant herself), "fall in love with a man once and remain faithful to him for ever? That is what I consider real love. What do you think, Prince?"

"I don't know your sister well enough," Prince Andrei replied with a mocking smile, behind which he hoped to hide his embarrassment, "to answer such a subtle question. And besides, I've observed that the less attractive the woman, the more constant she is," he added and looked at Pierre, who approached them just then.

"Yes, that's true, Prince; in our time," Vera went on (mentioning our time as limited people generally like to do, supposing that they have discovered and appreciated the particularities of our time and that people's qualities change with time), "in our time a girl has so much freedom that *le plaisir d'être courtisée* often stifles true feeling in her. *Et Natalie, il faut l'avouer, y est très sensible.*"* The return to Natalie again made Prince Andrei wince unpleasantly; he wanted to get up, but Vera continued with a still more subtle smile.

"I think no one has been so *courtisée* as she," Vera said, "but till recently she never liked anyone seriously. You know, Count," she turned to Pierre, "even our dear cousin Boris, who, *entre nous*, was quite, quite *dans le pays du tendre* . . ."† she said, alluding to the then popular map of love.[22]

Prince Andrei frowned and said nothing.

"But you're friends with Boris, aren't you?" Vera asked him.

"Yes, I know him . . ."

"Surely he has told you about his childhood love for Natasha?"

"Was there a childhood love?" Prince Andrei asked, suddenly blushing.

---

*The pleasure of being courted . . . And Natalie, it must be admitted, is very susceptible to that.
†Between us . . . in the land of tenderness.

"Yes. *Vous savez entre cousin et cousine cette intimité mène quelquefois à l'amour: le cousinage est un dangereux voisinage. N'est-ce pas?"*

"Oh, undoubtedly," said Prince Andrei, and suddenly, with unnatural animation, he began joking with Pierre about how he ought to be careful in dealing with his fifty-year-old Moscow cousins, and in the middle of the banter got up and, taking Pierre by the arm, drew him aside.

"What now?" said Pierre, looking with surprise at his friend's strange animation and noticing the glance he cast at Natasha as he got up.

"I must, I must have a talk with you," said Prince Andrei. "You know those women's gloves" (he meant the Masonic gloves which were given to a newly initiated brother to be presented to a beloved woman). "I . . . But no, I'll talk with you later . . ." And Prince Andrei, with a strange gleam in his eyes and with uneasy movements, went over to Natasha and sat down beside her. Pierre saw how Prince Andrei asked her something, and she, blushing, answered him.

But just then Berg came up to Pierre, insistently begging him to take part in an argument between the general and the colonel about Spanish affairs.

Berg was pleased and happy. The smile of joy never left his face. The soirée went very well and exactly like other soirées he had seen. Everything was similar. The ladies' subtle conversation, and the cards, and the general raising his voice over cards, and the samovar, and the cakes; but there was one thing missing that he had always seen at the soirées he wished to imitate. The missing thing was loud conversation among the men and an argument about something important and intellectual. The general began that conversation, and Berg drew Pierre into it.

XXII

The next day Prince Andrei went to the Rostovs' for dinner, as Count Ilya Andreich had invited him, and spent the whole day with them.

Everyone in the house sensed for whose sake Prince Andrei had come, and he, without concealing it, tried to be with Natasha the whole day. Not only in Natasha's soul, frightened, but happy and enraptured, but in all the house there was a sense of fear in the face of something important that was about to be accomplished. The countess looked at Prince Andrei with her sad and sternly serious eyes as he talked with Natasha, and timidly pretended to begin some insignificant conversation as soon as he turned to look at her. Sonya was afraid to leave Natasha and afraid of being a nuisance when she was with

---

*You know that between cousins this intimacy sometimes leads to love: cousinhood is a dangerous neighbourhood. Isn't it so?

them. Natasha turned pale from fearful expectation when she was left alone with him for a moment. Prince Andrei amazed her by his timidity. She felt that he had to tell her something, but could not resolve to do it.

When Prince Andrei left in the evening, the countess went over to Natasha and said in a whisper:

"Well?"

"Mama, for God's sake, don't ask me anything now. It's impossible to talk about it," said Natasha.

But in spite of that, Natasha, now excited, now frightened, her eyes staring, lay for a long time in her mother's bed that evening. She told her how he had praised her, then how he had said he would be going abroad, then had asked where they would spend the summer, then how he had asked her about Boris.

"But nothing, nothing like this . . . has ever happened to me before!" she said. "Only I'm frightened, I'm always frightened with him—what does it mean? It means it's something real, doesn't it? Mama, are you asleep?"

"No, dearest, I'm frightened myself," her mother replied. "Go."

"I won't sleep anyway. How stupid it is to sleep! Mama, mama, nothing like this has ever happened to me!" she repeated with astonishment and fear before the feeling she was aware of within her. "Who could have thought! . . ."

It seemed to Natasha that when she had first seen Prince Andrei in Otradnoe, she had fallen in love with him. She was as if frightened by this strange, unexpected happiness, that the one she had already chosen then (she was firmly convinced of it), that that same one had now met her again and seemed not to be indifferent to her. "Why did he have to come to Petersburg precisely now, when we're here? Why did we have to meet at that ball? It's all fate. It's clearly fate, everything has been leading up to it. Back then, when I'd only just seen him, I felt something special."

"What else did he say to you? There were some verses? Read them . . ." her mother said pensively, asking about the verses that Prince Andrei had written in Natasha's album.

"Mama, it's not shameful that he's a widower?"

"Enough, Natasha. Pray to God. *Les mariages se font dans les cieux.*"*

"Mama, darling, how I love you, how good I feel!" Natasha cried, shedding tears of happiness and excitement and embracing her mother.

At that same time, Andrei was sitting with Pierre and telling him of his love for Natasha and of his firm intention to marry her.

That evening there was a reception at Countess Elena Vassilievna's, there was the French ambassador, there was a prince who had lately become a frequent

---

*Marriages are made in heaven.

visitor to the countess's house, and there were many brilliant ladies and gentlemen. Pierre came downstairs, strolled through the rooms, and struck all the
guests by his concentratedly distracted and gloomy look.

Since the time of the ball, Pierre had been feeling in himself the approach of
an attack of hypochondria and had been making desperate efforts to fight it
off. Since the time of his wife's closeness to the prince, Pierre had been unexpectedly granted the rank of gentleman of the chamber, and since that time he
had begun to feel the burden and shame of grand society, and his former
gloomy thoughts about the vanity of all human things had begun to visit him
more often. At the same time, the feeling he had noticed between his protégée
Natasha and Prince Andrei, his contrasting of his own position with that of his
friend, intensified this gloomy mood still more. He tried equally to avoid
thoughts of his wife and of Natasha and Prince Andrei. Again everything
seemed insignificant to him compared with eternity, again the question "What
for?" presented itself. And he made himself work day and night over Masonic
writings, hoping to ward off the approaching evil spirit. Towards midnight,
having left the countess's rooms, Pierre was sitting at his desk upstairs in the
low-ceilinged, smoke-filled study, wearing a shabby dressing gown, copying
the original Scottish charters, when someone came into his room. It was Prince
Andrei.

"Ah, it's you," said Pierre, with a distracted and displeased air. "And here I
am working," he said, pointing to his notebook with that look of escaping
from life's adversities with which unhappy people look at their work.

Prince Andrei, with a radiant, rapturous face, renewed towards life, stopped
before Pierre and, not noticing his sad face, smiled at him with the egoism of
happiness.

"Well, dear heart," he said, "I wanted to tell you yesterday, and I've come to
tell you today. I've never experienced anything like it. I'm in love, my friend."

Pierre suddenly sighed deeply, and dropped his heavy body onto the sofa
beside Prince Andrei.

"With Natasha Rostov, is it?" he said.

"Yes, yes, who else? I'd never have believed it, but this feeling is stronger
than I am. Yesterday I was tormented, I suffered, but I wouldn't trade that torment for anything in the world. I've never lived before. Only now am I alive,
but I can't live without her. But can she love me? . . . I'm too old for her . . .
Why don't you speak? . . ."

"I? I? What was I telling you?" Pierre said suddenly, getting up and beginning to pace the room. "I've always thought so . . . This girl is such a treasure,
such a . . . She's a rare girl . . . My dear friend, I beg you, don't be clever, don't
doubt, marry, marry, marry . . . And I'm sure there'll be no man happier than
you."

"But she?"

"She loves you."

"Don't talk nonsense . . ." said Prince Andrei, smiling and looking into Pierre's eyes.

"She loves you, I know it," Pierre shouted angrily.

"No, listen," said Prince Andrei, stopping him by the arm. "Can you know what state I'm in? I must tell it all to somebody."

"Well, well, talk, I'm very glad," said Pierre, and indeed his face changed, the furrow smoothed out, and he listened joyfully to Prince Andrei. Prince Andrei seemed and was quite a different, new man. Where was his anguish, his contempt for life, his disillusionment? Pierre was the only man before whom he would venture to speak himself out; but then he spoke everything that was in his heart. First he lightly and boldly made plans far into the future, saying how he could not sacrifice his happiness to his father's whim, how he would make his father agree to this marriage and love her, or else he would do without his consent; then he was astonished, as at something strange, alien, independent of him, at the feeling that possessed him.

"I wouldn't have believed it if someone had told me I could love so much," said Prince Andrei. "It's quite a different feeling from what I knew before. The whole world is divided for me into two parts: one is she, and there is all happiness, hope, light; the other is where she is not, and there everything is dejection and darkness . . ."

"Darkness and gloom," Pierre repeated, "yes, yes, I understand that."

"I can't help loving the light, it's not my fault. And I'm very happy. Do you understand me? I know you're glad for me."

"Yes, yes," Pierre agreed, looking at his friend with tender and sad eyes. The brighter Prince Andrei's fate seemed to him, the gloomier seemed his own.

XXIII

For marriage he needed his father's consent, and for that Prince Andrei set off the next day to see his father.

The father received the son's communication with outward calm, but with inner spite. He could not understand why anyone would want to change his life, to introduce anything new into it, when for him life was already over. "Only let me live out my life as I want, and then they can do what they want," the old man said to himself. With his son, however, he used the diplomacy he made use of on important occasions. Assuming a calm tone, he discussed the whole matter:

First, the marriage was not a brilliant one in terms of family, wealth, and distinction. Second, Prince Andrei was not in his early youth and his health was weak (the old man especially emphasized that), while she was very young.

Third, there was his son, and it would be a pity to hand him over to a young girl. Fourth, and finally, the old man said, with a mocking glance at his son, "I beg you to put the matter off for a year, go abroad, take a cure, look, as you want to, for a German tutor for Prince Nikolai, and then, if this love, passion, obstinacy, call it whatever you like, is so great, you can marry. And that is my last word, be it known to you, my last . . ." the prince concluded, in a tone which showed that nothing would make him change his decision.

Prince Andrei saw clearly that the old man hoped that either his feeling or his future bride's would not endure the test of a year, or that he, the old prince, would die himself before then, and decided to do his father's will: to propose and to put off the wedding for a year.

Exactly three weeks after his last evening at the Rostovs', Prince Andrei returned to Petersburg.

The day after her talk with her mother, Natasha waited the whole day for Bolkonsky, but he did not come. On the next day and the third it was the same. Pierre also did not come, and Natasha, not knowing that Prince Andrei had gone to see his father, could not explain his absence.

Three weeks went by that way. Natasha did not want to go anywhere and, like a shadow, idle and dejected, wandered through the rooms, in the evenings wept in secret from everybody, and did not go to her mother. She blushed constantly and was irritable. It seemed to her that everyone knew about her disappointment, was laughing at her, and pitied her. With all the strength of her inner grief, this grief of vanity intensified her unhappiness.

One day she came to the countess, was about to say something to her, and suddenly began to cry. Her tears were the tears of an offended child who does not know why it is being punished.

The countess began to calm Natasha. Natasha first listened to her mother's words, then suddenly interrupted her:

"Stop it, mama, I'm not thinking and I don't want to think! So he came, and then stopped, and then stopped . . ."

Her voice trembled, she almost began to cry, but controlled herself and calmly went on:

"I don't want to get married at all. And I'm afraid of him; I'm calm now, completely calm . . ."

The day after this conversation, Natasha put on that old dress which was especially known for making her cheerful in the mornings, and with that morning began her former way of life, which she had abandoned since the ball. After having tea, she went to the reception room, which she especially liked for its strong resonance, and began to sing her solfeggio (singing exercises). Having finished the first exercise, she stopped in the middle of the room and repeated a musical phrase which she especially liked. She listened joyfully (as if it was unexpected for her) to the loveliness with which these sounds, rippling, filled the whole emptiness of the room and slowly died away, and she suddenly felt cheerful. "Why think much about it, things are good as it is," she said to herself and began walking up and down the room, not simply stepping on the resounding parquet but beginning each step on the heel (she was wearing new shoes that she liked), then going onto the toe, and listening joyfully, as she had to the sound of her voice, to the rhythmic stamping of the heel and the creaking of the toe. Going past a mirror, she looked into it. "Here I am!" the expression of her face seemed to say at the sight of her. "And that's good. I don't need anybody."

A servant wanted to come in to straighten something in the room, but she did not let him in, and, closing the door behind him, went back to her walk. That morning she returned again to her favourite state of love and admiration for herself. "How lovely that Natasha is!" she said of herself again, in the words of some collective male third person. "Pretty, a good voice, young, and doesn't bother anybody, only leave her in peace." But however much she was left in peace, she could no longer be at peace, and she felt it at once.

In the front hall the outside door opened, someone asked, "Are they at home?" and someone's footsteps were heard. Natasha was looking in the mirror, but did not see herself. She was listening to the sounds in the front hall. When she did see herself, her face was pale. It was *he*. She knew it for certain, though she had barely heard the sound of his voice through the closed door.

Pale and frightened, Natasha ran into the drawing room.

"Mama, Bolkonsky's here!" she said. "Mama, it's terrible, it's unbearable! I don't want . . . to suffer! What am I to do? . . ."

Before the countess had time to reply, Prince Andrei, with an anxious and serious face, came into the drawing room. As soon as he saw Natasha, his face lit up. He kissed the countess's and Natasha's hand and sat down near the sofa . . .

"It is long since we've had the pleasure . . ." the countess began, but Prince Andrei interrupted her, answering her question and obviously hurrying to say what he had to.

"I haven't called on you all this time, because I was at my father's: I had to discuss a very important matter. I came back only last night," he said, glancing at Natasha. "I must talk with you, Countess," he added after a moment's silence.

The countess, with a deep sigh, lowered her eyes.

"I am at your service," she said.

Natasha knew she must leave, but she could not do it: something clenched her throat, and she looked at Prince Andrei impolitely, directly, with wide-open eyes.

"Now? This minute! . . . No, it can't be!" she thought.

He glanced at her again, and this glance convinced her that she was not mistaken. Yes, her fate was decided, now, this minute.

"Go, Natasha, I'll call you," the countess said in a whisper.

Natasha glanced at Prince Andrei and her mother with frightened, pleading eyes, and went out.

"I have come, Countess, to ask for your daughter's hand," said Prince Andrei.

The countess's face blushed, but she said nothing.

"Your proposal . . ." the countess began gravely. He was silent, looking into her eyes. "Your proposal . . ." (she became embarrassed) "is pleasing to us and . . . I accept your proposal, I am glad. My husband, too . . . I hope . . . but it depends on her . . ."

"I'll tell her, once I have your consent . . . will you give it to me?" asked Prince Andrei.

"Yes," said the countess, and she gave him her hand and pressed her lips to his forehead with a mixed feeling of alienation and tenderness when he bent over her hand. She wished to love him as a son; but she felt that for her he was an alien and frightening man.

"I'm sure my husband will consent," said the countess, "but your father . . ."

"My father, whom I told of my plans, made it an absolute condition for his consent that the marriage not take place for a year. And I wanted to tell you that," said Prince Andrei.

"It's true that Natasha is still young, but—so long!"

"It cannot be otherwise," Prince Andrei said with a sigh.

"I'll send her to you," said the countess, and she left the room.

"Lord, have mercy on us," she repeated as she was looking for her daughter. Sonya said that Natasha was in her bedroom. Natasha was sitting on her bed, pale, dry-eyed, looking at the icon and whispering something, crossing herself quickly. Seeing her mother, she jumped up and rushed to her.

"What, mama? . . . What?"

"Go, go to him. He's asking for your hand," the countess said coldly, as it seemed to Natasha . . . "Go . . . go," the mother said sadly and reproachfully after her running daughter, and she sighed deeply.

Natasha did not remember how she entered the drawing room. Going through the door and seeing him, she stopped. "Can it be that this stranger has now become *everything* for me?" she asked herself, and instantly answered: "Yes, everything. He alone is now dearer to me than anything in the world." Prince Andrei went up to her with lowered eyes.

"I loved you the moment I saw you. May I hope?"

He glanced at her, and the serious passion in the expression of her face struck him. Her face said: "Why ask? Why doubt what you cannot help knowing? Why speak when it's impossible to put everything you feel into words?"

She came closer to him and stopped. He took her hand and kissed it.

"Do you love me?"

"Yes, yes," Natasha said as if with vexation, sighed loudly, then again and again, and burst into sobs.

"Why? What's the matter?"

"Ah, I'm so happy," she replied, smiling through her tears, leaned closer to him, thought for a second, as if asking herself whether she could, and kissed him.

Prince Andrei held her hand, looked into her eyes, and did not find the former love for her in his soul. Something suddenly turned over in his soul: the former poetic and mysterious delight of desire was not there, but there was pity for her woman's and child's weakness, there was fear before her devotion and trust, a heavy but at the same time joyful consciousness of duty that bound him to her for ever. The actual feeling, though not as bright and poetic as the former one, was more serious and strong.

"Did *maman* tell you that it can't be sooner than in a year?" Prince Andrei asked, still looking into her eyes.

"Can it be me, that 'baby girl' (as everybody said of me)," thought Natasha, "can it be that from this moment on I'm a *wife*, equal to this strange, dear, intelligent man, whom even my father respects? Can it be true? Can it be true that now there is to be no more toying with life, that I'm grown up now, that responsibility is laid upon me now for my every deed and word? Ah, what was it he asked me?"

"No," she replied, but she did not understand what he was asking.

"Forgive me," said Prince Andrei, "but you're so young, and I've already experienced so much of this life. I fear for you. You don't know yourself."

Natasha listened with concentrated attention, trying to understand the meaning of his words, and not understanding.

"Hard as this year that postpones my happiness will be for me," Prince Andrei went on, "during this time you will test yourself. I ask you to make me happy in a year; but you're free: our engagement will remain a secret, and if you become convinced that you don't love me, or that you love . . ." Prince Andrei said with an unnatural smile.

"Why are you saying this?" Natasha interrupted him. "You know I've loved you from the very day you first came to Otradnoe," she said, firmly convinced that she was speaking the truth.

"In a year you will know yourself . . ."

"A whole ye-e-ear!" Natasha said suddenly, only now understanding that the wedding was to be postponed for a year. "But why a year? Why a year? . . ." Prince Andrei began to explain to her the reasons for this postponement. Natasha did not listen to him.

"And it can't be otherwise?" she asked. Prince Andrei said nothing, but his face expressed the impossibility of changing this decision.

"That's terrible! No, it's terrible, terrible!" Natasha said suddenly and sobbed again. "I'll die, waiting a year: it's impossible, it's terrible!" She looked into her fiancé's face and saw there an expression of compassion and bewilderment.

"No, no, I'll do it all," she said suddenly, stopping her tears. "I'm so happy!" Her father and mother came into the room and blessed the betrothed couple. From that day on Prince Andrei began going to the Rostovs' as a fiancé.

XXIV

There was no formal betrothal, nor was anyone told of the engagement of Bolkonsky and Natasha; Prince Andrei insisted on that. He said that, as he was the cause of the delay, he must bear all the burden of it. He said that he had for ever bound himself by his word, but that he did not want to bind Natasha and gave her full freedom. If in six months she felt that she did not love him, she would be within her rights to refuse him. Of course it went without saying that neither the parents nor Natasha wanted to hear about it; but Prince Andrei insisted on having his way. Prince Andrei came to the Rostovs' every day, but he did not behave like a fiancé with Natasha: he addressed her formally and kissed only her hand. Between Prince Andrei and Natasha, after the day of the proposal, close and simple relations were established, quite different from before. It was as if they had not known each other till then. He and she both liked to remember how they had looked at each other when they were still *nothing*: now they both felt themselves completely different beings; then they had been false, now they were simple and sincere. At first there was a feeling of awkwardness in the family in dealing with Prince Andrei; he seemed a man from an alien world, and Natasha spent a long time getting the household accustomed to Prince Andrei and proudly assured them all that he only seemed so peculiar, but that he was the same as everybody else, and that she was not afraid of him, and that no one should be afraid of him. After a few days, the family got used to him, and, without restraint, carried on their usual way of life, in which he participated. He was able to talk about estate management with the count, about dresses with the countess and Natasha, about albums and embroidery with Sonya. Occasionally the Rostov household expressed surprise among themselves and in Prince Andrei's presence at how it had all happened and how obvious the portents of it had been: Prince Andrei's coming to Otradnoe, and their coming to Petersburg, and the resemblance between Natasha and Prince Andrei, which the nanny had noticed during Prince Andrei's first visit, and the clash between Andrei and Nikolai in 1805, and many other portents of what had happened were noted by the household.

In the house that poetic boredom and silence reigned which always accompanies the presence of an engaged couple. Often, while sitting together, they all fell silent. Sometimes they all got up and left, and the couple, alone together, were still just as silent. They rarely spoke of their future life. Prince Andrei was afraid and embarrassed to speak of it. Natasha shared that feeling, as she did all his feelings, which she invariably guessed. Once Natasha began to ask about his son. Prince Andrei blushed, which often happened to him now and which Natasha especially liked, and said that his son would not live with them.

"Why not?" Natasha asked in alarm.

"I cannot take him from his grandfather, and then, too . . ."

"How I'd love him!" said Natasha, guessing his thought at once, "but I know you want there to be no pretexts for blaming yourself or me."

The old count sometimes went up to Prince Andrei, kissed him, and asked his advice about Petya's education or Nikolai's service. The old countess sighed, looking at them. Sonya feared every moment to be in the way and tried to find pretexts for leaving them alone, when they did not even want it. When Prince Andrei spoke (he was a very good storyteller), Natasha listened to him with pride; when she spoke, she noticed with fear and joy that he looked at her attentively and searchingly. She asked herself in perplexity: "What is he looking for in me? What is he seeking with his eyes? What if what he's looking for isn't in me?" Sometimes she got into her wildly merry state, and then she especially liked to hear and see how Prince Andrei laughed. He laughed rarely, but when he did, he gave himself wholly to his laughter, and each time after this laughter she felt closer to him. Natasha would have been perfectly happy, if the thought of the imminent and approaching separation had not frightened her.

On the eve of his departure from Petersburg, Prince Andrei brought along Pierre, who had not once been to the Rostovs' since the time of the ball. Pierre looked perplexed and embarrassed. He was talking with the mother. Natasha sat down with Sonya by the chess table, thereby inviting Prince Andrei to join her. He went over to them.

"You've known Bezukhov for a long time, haven't you?" he asked. "Do you like him?"

"Yes, he's nice, but very funny."

And, as always when she spoke of Pierre, she began telling anecdotes about his absent-mindedness, anecdotes which had even been made up about him.

"You know, I've entrusted him with our secret," said Prince Andrei. "I've known him since childhood. He has a heart of gold. I beg you, Natalie," he suddenly said earnestly, "I'm going away. God knows what may happen. You may stop lov . . . Well, I know I mustn't talk about that. One thing—whatever happens with you while I'm not here . . ."

"What's going to happen?"

"Whatever misfortune there may be," Prince Andrei went on, "I beg you, Mademoiselle Sophie, whatever may happen, turn to him alone for advice and help. He's the most absent-minded and ridiculous man, but he has a heart of gold."

Neither her father and mother, nor Sonya, nor Prince Andrei himself could have foreseen how parting with her fiancé would affect Natasha. Flushed and agitated, her eyes dry, she wandered about the house that day, occupying herself with the most insignificant things, as if not understanding what awaited her. She did not cry when, at the moment of taking leave of her, he kissed her hand for the last time.

"Don't leave!" was all she said to him, in a voice which made him wonder whether he ought indeed to stay, and which he remembered long afterwards. When he was gone, she also did not cry; but for several days she sat, not crying, in her room, not interested in anything and only saying from time to time: "Ah, why did he go?"

But two weeks after his departure, just as unexpectedly for those around her, she recovered from her moral illness and became the same as before, only with a changed moral physiognomy, as children get up with a different face after a prolonged illness.

XXV

The health and character of Prince Nikolai Andreevich Bolkonsky, during that last year after his son's departure, declined considerably. He became still more irritable than before, and all the outbursts of his groundless wrath fell mainly upon Princess Marya. He seemed to carefully seek out all her sorest spots so as to torment her morally as cruelly as possible. Princess Marya had two passions and therefore two joys: her nephew Nikolushka and religion—and the two were the favourite topics of the prince's attacks and mockery. Whatever the talk was about, he always brought the conversation down to the superstitions of old maids or to the pampering and spoiling of children. "You want to make Nikolushka into an old maid like yourself. You shouldn't: Prince Andrei needs a son, not an old maid," he would say. Or, turning to Mlle Bourienne, he would ask her, in front of Princess Marya, how she liked our priests and icons, and would joke . . .

He insulted Princess Marya constantly and painfully, but his daughter did not even have to force herself to forgive him. How could he be guilty before her, and how could her father who (she knew all the same) loved her, be unjust to her? And what is justice? The princess never thought about this proud word *justice*. All the complicated laws of mankind were concentrated for her in one simple and clear law—the law of love and self-denial taught us by Him who suffered for mankind with love, though He Himself was God. What did the justice or injustice of other people matter to her? She herself had to suffer and to love, and that she did.

In the winter Prince Andrei came to Bald Hills, and was cheerful, meek, and affectionate, as Princess Marya had not seen him for a long time. She sensed that something had happened to him, but he said nothing to Princess Marya about his love. Before his departure, Prince Andrei had a long talk about something with his father, and Princess Marya noticed that before his departure they were both displeased with each other.

Soon after Prince Andrei's departure, Princess Marya wrote to Petersburg from Bald Hills, to her friend Julie Karagin, whom Princess Marya had dreamed, as girls always do, of marrying to her brother, and who at that time was in mourning on the occasion of the death of her brother, killed in Turkey.[23]

Sorrows are clearly our common lot, my dear and tender friend Julie.

Your loss is so terrible that I cannot explain it to myself otherwise than as a special mercy of God, who—loving you—wants to test you and your excellent mother. Ah, my friend, religion and religion alone can—I do not say comfort—but deliver us from despair; religion alone can explain to us that which man cannot understand without its help: wherefore, why kind and lofty beings, who know how to find happiness in life, who not only harm no one but are necessary for the happiness of others, are called to God, while the evil, the useless, the harmful, or such as are a burden to themselves and to others, are left to live. The first death I saw, which I will never forget—the death of my dear sister-in-law—made that impression on me. Just as you ask fate why your wonderful brother had to die, so I used to ask why this angel—Liza—had to die, who not only did no wrong to anyone, but never had anything but kind thoughts in her soul. And what then, my friend? Five years have gone by, and I, with my small mind, am now beginning to understand clearly why she had to die and in what way this death was the expression of the infinite goodness of the Creator, all of whose actions, though for the most part we do not understand them, are nothing but manifestations of His infinite love for His creation. It may be, I often think, that she was too angelically innocent to have the strength to bear all the duties of a mother. She was irreproachable as a young wife; perhaps she could not have been so as a mother. Now, she has not only left us, and Prince Andrei especially, with the purest regret and memory, but she will probably obtain there the place which I dare not hope for myself. But, not to speak only of her, this early and terrible death, despite all our grieving, had the most beneficent influence on me and on my brother. Then, at the moment of loss, these thoughts could not have come to me; then I would have driven them away with horror; but now it is so clear and unquestionable. I am writing all this to you, my friend, only so as to convince you of the Gospel truth that has become life's truth for me: not a single hair will fall from our heads without His will. And His will is guided only by His boundless love for us, and therefore everything that happens to us, everything, is for our own good.

You ask whether we shall spend next winter in Moscow. Despite all my wish to see you, I do not think so and do not wish to. And you will be surprised to learn that the reason for it is Buonaparte. And here is why. My father's health has noticeably declined: he cannot bear to be contradicted, he becomes irritated. This irritation, as you know, is turned mostly towards political affairs. He cannot bear the thought that Buonaparte deals as an equal with all the sovereigns of Europe, and especially with ours, the grandson of the great Catherine! As you know, I am totally indifferent to political affairs, but from my father's words and from his conversations with Mikhail Ivanovich, I know all that is happening in the world, and especially about all the honours rendered Buonaparte, who, it seems, only in Bald Hills, of all places in the world, is not recognized as a great man, still less as the French emperor. And my father cannot bear that. It seems to me that my father, mostly owing to his view of political affairs, and foreseeing the clashes he will have, owing to his manner of voicing his opinions without any restraint, is reluctant to speak of going to Moscow. All that he gains from treatment, he will lose owing to his arguments about Buonaparte, which are inevitable. In any case, this will be decided very soon.

Our family life goes on as before, except for the absence of my brother Andrei. As I've already written to you, he has changed very much recently. After his grief, it is only now, during this present year, that he has completely revived morally. He has become the way I knew him as a child: kind, affectionate, with that heart of gold of which I do not know the equal. He has understood, it seems to me, that his life is not over. But, along with this moral change, he has grown very weak physically. He has become thinner than before, more nervous. I fear for him, and I am glad he has undertaken this trip abroad which the doctors prescribed for him long ago. I hope this will cure him. You write me that he is spoken of in Petersburg as one of the most active, educated, and intelligent young men. Forgive my family vanity, but I never doubted that. It's impossible to calculate the good he has done here for everyone, from his peasants to the gentry. On coming to Petersburg, he only received his due. I wonder how rumours generally get from Petersburg to Moscow, and especially such false ones as the one you write to me about—the rumour of the supposed marriage of my brother to the little Rostov girl. I do not think Andrei will ever marry anyone, and especially not her. And here is why: first, I know that, though he rarely speaks of his late wife, the grief of that loss is too deeply rooted in his heart for him ever to decide to give her a successor and a stepmother to our little angel. Second, because, as far as I know, this girl does not belong at all to the category that could please Prince Andrei. I do not think that Prince Andrei would choose her for his wife, and I will tell you frankly: I do not wish it. But I am babbling away, coming to the end of my second sheet. Goodbye, my dear friend; may God keep you under His holy and mighty protection. My dear friend, Mlle Bourienne, kisses you.

Marie.

XXVI

In the middle of summer, Princess Marya received an unexpected letter from Prince Andrei in Switzerland, with a strange and unexpected piece of news. Prince Andrei announced his engagement to Miss Rostov. His whole letter breathed a loving rapture for his fiancée and a tender friendship and trust for his sister. He wrote that he had never loved as he loved now, and that only now did he know and understand life. He asked his sister to forgive him for not telling her of this decision during his visit to Bald Hills, though he had spoken of it with his father. He had not told her of it, because Princess Marya would have asked their father to give his consent, and without achieving that goal, would have irritated their father and brought upon herself the whole burden of his displeasure. However, he wrote, the matter had not been as finally decided then as it was now.

Then, father appointed me a year's term, and now *six* months, half the appointed term, have gone by, and I remain as firm in my decision as ever. If the doctors did not keep me here at the spa, I would be in Russia myself, but as it is I must put off my return for another three months. You know me and my relations with father. I need nothing from him, I am and always will be independent, but to go against his will, to incur his wrath, when he will perhaps not be with us much longer, would spoil half my happiness. I am now writing a letter to him about the same thing, and I ask you to choose a good moment to give him the letter, and to let me know how he looks at it all and whether there is any hope that he will agree to shorten the term by three months.

After many hesitations, doubts, and prayers, Princess Marya gave her father the letter. The next day the old prince calmly said to her:

"Write your brother that he should wait till I die . . . It won't be long—I'll soon unbind him . . ."

The princess was about to make some objection, but her father did not let her, and began raising his voice more and more.

"Marry, marry, dear boy . . . They're of good stock! . . . Clever people, eh? Rich, eh? Yes. A fine stepmother for Nikolushka. Write him that he can marry tomorrow even. She'll be Nikolushka's stepmother, and I'll marry little Bourienne! . . . Ha, ha, ha, so he won't be without a stepmother himself! Only one thing, there's no need for more women in my house; let him marry and live separately. Maybe you'll move in with him?" he turned to Princess Marya. "God help you, and good riddance . . . good riddance! . . ."

After this outburst, the prince never once spoke of the matter again. But his suppressed vexation with his son's faint-heartedness showed itself in the relations between father and daughter. To the previous subjects of mockery a new one was added—talk about stepmothers and his amiability towards Mlle Bourienne.

"Why shouldn't I marry her?" he said to his daughter. "She'd make a nice princess!" And lately, to her perplexity and astonishment, Princess Marya began to notice that her father had indeed become more and more intimate with the Frenchwoman. Princess Marya wrote to Prince Andrei about how their father had taken his letter; but she comforted her brother, giving him hope of reconciling their father to the thought.

Nikolushka and his upbringing, André, and religion were Princess Marya's comforts and joys; but, besides that, since every human being needs his personal hope, Princess Marya had in the deepest recesses of her soul a hidden dream and hope, which provided the main comfort of her life. This comforting dream and hope were given her by the people of God—the fools for Christ and wanderers who visited her in secret from the old prince. The longer Princess Marya lived, the more of life she experienced and observed, the more astonished she was at the short-sightedness of people who sought pleasure and happiness here on earth; who worked, suffered, struggled, and did evil to each other to achieve this impossible, illusory, and fallacious happiness. "Prince Andrei loved his wife, she dies, it's not enough for him, he wants to bind up his happiness with another woman. Father doesn't want it, because he wants a more aristocratic and wealthy marriage for Andrei. And they all struggle and suffer, and torment and ruin their souls, their eternal souls, to achieve blessings that last a moment. Not only do we know it ourselves—Christ, the Son of God, came down to earth and told us that this life is a momentary life, a trial, yet we keep holding on to it and hope to find happiness in it. How is it no one understands that?" thought Princess Marya. "No one except these contemptible people of God, who come to me at the back door with bags over their shoulders, afraid of being noticed by the prince, not because they would suffer from him, but so as not to lead him into sin. To leave family, birthplace, all cares for worldly goods, so as to walk, without clinging to anything, in coarse rags, under an assumed name, from place to place, without harming people, and praying for them, praying for those who persecute and for those who protect: there is no truth and life higher than this truth and life!"

There was one woman wanderer, Fedosyushka, a fifty-year-old, small, quiet, pockmarked woman, who had been walking barefoot and in chains[24] for thirty years already. Princess Marya had a special love for her. Once, when in the dark room, by the light of the icon lamp, Fedosyushka was telling about her life, the thought that Fedosyushka alone had found the right way of life suddenly came to Princess Marya with such force that she herself decided to go wandering. When Fedosyushka went to bed, Princess Marya thought about it for a long time, and finally decided that, however strange it was, she had to become a wanderer. She confided her intention only to her father confessor, the monk Akinfy, and the monk approved of it. Under the pretext of a gift for the wanderers, Princess Marya provided herself with a full wanderer's outfit: a shirt, bast shoes, a kaftan, and a black kerchief. Often, going to the secret chest, Princess Marya would pause, unable to decide whether the time had come to fulfil her intention.

Often, listening to the stories of the women wanderers, she would become excited by their simple talk, mechanical for them, but full of deep meaning for her, so that several times she had been ready to drop everything and flee the house. In her imagination, she already saw herself and Fedosyushka in coarse rags, walking with a stick and a bag down a dusty road, guiding her wandering without envy, without love of human things, without desires, from one holy place to another, and in the end to the place where there is no sorrow or sighing, but eternal joy and bliss.[25]

"I'll come to one place and pray; before I have time to get used to it and love it, I'll go on. And I'll keep going until my legs give out, and I lie down and die somewhere, and come finally to that eternal, quiet haven, where there is no sorrow or sighing! . . ." thought Princess Marya.

But then, seeing her father and especially little Coco, her intention would weaken, she would weep in quiet and feel she was a sinful woman: she loved her father and her nephew more than God.

Part Four

I

Biblical tradition says that absence of work—idleness—was the condition of the first man's blessedness before his fall. The love of idleness remained the same in fallen man, but the curse still weighs on man, and not only because we must win our bread in the sweat of our face,[1] but because our moral qualities are such that we are unable to be idle and at peace. A secret voice tells us that we should feel guilty for being idle. If man could find a condition in which, while idle, he felt that he was being useful and was fulfilling his duty, he would have found one side of primordial blessedness. And this state of obligatory and irreproachable idleness is enjoyed by an entire class—the military. In this obligatory and irreproachable idleness consists and will consist the chief attraction of military service.

Nikolai Rostov experienced this blessedness to the full as he continued serving after 1807 in the Pavlogradsky regiment, where he was already a squadron commander, having taken over from Denisov.

Rostov had become a bluff, good-natured fellow, whom his Moscow acquaintances would have found slightly *mauvais genre,** but who was loved and respected by his comrades, subordinates, and superiors, and who was content with his life. Lately—that is, in 1809—in letters from home, he often found complaints from his mother that their affairs were falling into worse and worse disorder, and that it was time for him to come home, to bring joy and peace to his old parents.

Reading these letters, Nikolai experienced a fear that they wanted to make him leave the milieu in which he lived calmly and peacefully, protected from life's confusion. He felt that sooner or later he would have to enter the deep water of life again, with its affairs disordered and straightened out, with its stewards' accounts, with its quarrels, intrigues, connections, with its society, with Sonya's love and his promise to her. All this was terribly difficult, confused, and he answered his mother's letters with cold, classical ones that began "*Ma chère maman*" and ended "*votre obéissant fils,*"† and omitted saying when he intended to return. In 1810 he received letters from his parents in

*The wrong sort.
†My dear mama ... your obedient son.

which they informed him of Natasha's engagement to Bolkonsky and that the wedding would take place in a year, because the old prince was against it. This letter upset and insulted Nikolai. First of all, he felt sorry that Natasha, whom he loved most of all in the family, would be leaving home; second, from his hussar point of view, he was sorry he was not there to show this Bolkonsky that connection with him was by no means so great an honour, and that if he loved Natasha, he could do without the permission of his crack-brained father. For a moment he hesitated whether he should not ask for a leave in order to see Natasha as a fiancée, but then came manoeuvres, considerations about Sonya, about the confusion, and Nikolai put it off again. But in the spring of that year he received a letter from his mother, written in secret from the count, and this letter persuaded him to go. She wrote that if Nikolai did not come and take things in hand, their property would be sold at auction, and they would all go begging. The count was so weak, so trusting in Mitenka, and so kind, and everyone deceived him so, that it was all getting worse and worse. "For God's sake, I beg you, come at once, if you don't want to make me and your whole family miserable," wrote the countess.

This letter made an impression on Nikolai. He had that common sense of mediocrity which told him what he *ought* to do.

Now he ought to go, if not into retirement, then at least on leave. Why he had to go, he did not know; but, having slept after dinner, he gave orders to saddle his grey Mars, a long unridden and terribly ill-tempered stallion, and returning home with the stallion all in a lather, he announced to Lavrushka (Denisov's footman, who had remained with Rostov) and the comrades who came in the evening that he was taking a leave and going home. Difficult and strange as it was for him to think that he would go without having learned from staff what especially interested him—whether he was to be promoted to captain or get an Anna[2] for the last manoeuvres; strange as it was to think that he would go without selling to Count Goluchowski a troika of greys that the Polish count wanted to buy, and that Rostov had bet he could sell for two thousand; incomprehensible as it seemed that he would not be at the ball the hussars were to give for *Panna* Przazdiecka, to spite the uhlans, who were giving a ball for their *Panna* Borzozowska—he knew that he had to go from this clear, good world to somewhere where everything was nonsense and confusion. A week later the leave came through. The hussars, his comrades not only of the regiment but of the brigade, gave Rostov a subscription dinner that cost them fifteen roubles each—two bands played, two choruses sang songs; Rostov danced the *trepak* with Major Basov; drunken officers tossed, embraced, and dropped Rostov; the soldiers of the third squadron also tossed him and shouted "Hurrah!" Then Rostov was laid in a sleigh and accompanied to the first posting station.

For half the journey, as always happens, from Kremenchug to Kiev, all Rostov's thoughts still lay behind him, in his squadron; but having passed the mid-point, he began to forget the troika of greys, his sergeant major, and *Panna* Borzozowska, and began asking himself uneasily what he would find at Otrad-noe and how it would be. The closer he came, the more strongly, far more strongly (as if moral feeling was also subject to the law of attraction, which increases in inverse proportion to the square of the distance), he thought of his home; at the last station before Otradnoe, he gave the driver three roubles for vodka and soon, breathless as a boy, was running up the front porch of the house.

After the raptures of the meeting and after that strange feeling of dissatisfac-tion compared with what one expected ("it's all just the same, why was I hur-rying so!"), Nikolai began to live his way into his old world of home. His father and mother were the same, only a little older. What was new in them was a sort of anxiety and sometimes disagreement, which had never happened before, and which, as Nikolai soon learned, came from the bad state of their affairs. Sonya was already going on twenty. She had already stopped growing prettier, nothing more was promised than what was there; but even that was enough. She breathed out happiness and love from the moment Nikolai arrived, and the faithful, unshakeable love of this girl had a gladdening effect on him. Petya and Natasha surprised Nikolai most. Petya was now a big, handsome thirteen-year-old boy, merry and wittily mischievous, whose voice was already breaking. As for Natasha, Nikolai looked at her for a long time, wondering and laughing.

"Not her at all," he said.

"What, worse?"

"On the contrary, but there's a sort of dignity. A princess?" he said to her in a whisper.

"Yes, yes, yes," Natasha said joyfully.

Natasha told him about her romance with Prince Andrei, his visit to Otrad-noe, and showed him his last letter.

"Well, are you glad?" asked Natasha. "I'm so calm and happy now."

"Very glad," Nikolai replied. "He's an excellent man. Well, are you very much in love?"

"How shall I tell you," Natasha replied. "I was in love with Boris, with my teacher, with Denisov, but this is not the same at all. I feel peaceful, firm. I know that there's no one better than he, and I feel so calm, so good now. Not at all like before . . ."

Nikolai expressed his displeasure at the wedding being put off for a year; but Natasha fiercely attacked her brother, proving to him that it could not be otherwise, that it would be bad to enter the family against the father's will, that she herself wanted it that way.

"You don't understand at all, not at all," she said. Nikolai fell silent and agreed with her.

Her brother often wondered, looking at her. It did not seem at all as if she was a loving fiancée separated from her future husband. She was level-headed, calm, altogether as cheerful as before. This surprised Nikolai, and it even made him look mistrustfully at this alliance with Bolkonsky. He did not believe that her fate was already decided, the less so as he had not seen her together with Prince Andrei. He kept thinking there was something wrong with this projected marriage.

"Why the postponement? Why no betrothal?" he thought. Talking with his mother once about his sister, he found, to his surprise and partly to his satisfaction, that deep in her heart his mother also sometimes looked mistrustfully at this marriage.

"Here he writes," she said, showing her son Prince Andrei's letter with that hidden feeling of ill-will a mother always has against her daughter's future marital happiness, "he writes that he won't come before December. What can be keeping him? It must be illness! His health is very weak. Don't tell Natasha. Never mind her cheerfulness. She's living out the last of her girlhood, but I know what happens to her each time a letter comes from him. But anyhow, God willing, all will be well," she concluded each time. "He's an excellent man."

II

In the initial time of his visit Nikolai was serious and even dull. He suffered from the impending necessity of intervening in these stupid matters of estate management for which his mother had summoned him. To get the burden off his shoulders, on the third day of his visit, angry, scowling, not answering Natasha's question of where he was going, he went to the wing to see Mitenka and demanded a *full accounting* from him. What this *full accounting* was, Nikolai knew still less than the frightened and bewildered Mitenka. The conversation and the accounting with Mitenka did not last long. The headman, the delegate, and the village clerk, who were waiting in the front hall of the wing, listened at first with fear and satisfaction to the sound of the young count's rapping voice rising higher and higher, pouring out terrible and abusive words one after another.

"Robber! Ungrateful creature! . . . cut you to pieces like a dog . . . not dealing with papa . . . thievery . . . *racaille!*"*

Then the same people, with undiminished satisfaction and fear, saw how the young count, all red, with bloodshot eyes, dragged Mitenka out by the scruff of the neck, chose a convenient moment between his words, applied foot and knee with great deftness to his rear end, and shouted: "Out, scoundrel, and don't leave a trace behind!"

*Scum!

Mitenka flew headlong down the six steps and ran off into the flower garden. (This flower garden was a well-known place of refuge for wrongdoers in Otradnoe. Mitenka himself, when coming back drunk from town, hid in this flower garden, and many inhabitants of Otradnoe, hiding from Mitenka, knew the saving power of this flower garden.)

Mitenka's wife and sisters-in-law stuck their frightened faces into the front hall from the door to their room, where a clean samovar was boiling and the steward's bed rose up high under its patchwork quilt.

The young count, breathless, paying no attention to them, walked by with resolute strides and went into the house.

The countess, learning at once through the maids of what had happened in the wing, was, on the one hand, calmed by the reflection that their situation should now be set to rights, but, on the other hand, was troubled by the thought of how her son would put up with it. She tiptoed to his door several times, listening as he smoked one pipe after another.

The next day the old count called his son aside and told him with a timid smile:

"You know, dear heart, you needn't have flown into a temper! Mitenka has told me everything."

"I knew," thought Nikolai, "that I'd never understand anything here in this foolish world."

"You got angry that he hadn't written down those seven hundred roubles. But he had carried them over, and you didn't look at the next page."

"Papa, he's a blackguard and a thief, I know it. What's done is done. But if you don't want it, I won't say anything to him."

"No, dear heart." (The count was also embarrassed. He felt he had managed his wife's estate poorly and was guilty before his children, but he did not know how to set things to rights.) "No, I ask you to take care of things, I'm old, I . . ."

"No, papa, forgive me if I've caused you unpleasantness; I'm less capable than you are."

"Devil take them, these muzhiks, and money, and carrying over to the next page," he thought. "I used to understand something about doubling on a six-card run, but about carrying over on pages I know nothing," he said to himself, and from then on he did not enter into the business any more. Only once the countess summoned her son, informed him that she had a promissory note for two thousand from Anna Mikhailovna, and asked Nikolai how he thought of acting upon it.

"Here's how," Nikolai replied. "You told me it depends on me. I don't like Anna Mikhailovna, and I don't like Boris, but they've been our friends and they're poor. So here's how!" and he tore up the note, and this action caused the old countess to burst into tears of joy. After that the young Rostov, not entering into such business any more, with passionate enthusiasm took up the occupation, new for him, of hunting with dogs, which the old count managed on a grand scale.

III

It was already turning winter, morning frosts gripped the earth moistened by autumn rains, the winter wheat was already tufting up and stood out bright green against the strips of brownish, cattle-trampled winter stubble and pale yellow summer stubble with red strips of buckwheat. The hilltops and woods, which at the end of August were still green islands among the black winter croplands and stubble, had become golden and bright red islands amidst the bright green winter crops. The hares had already half shed their summer coats, the fox cubs were beginning to disperse, and the young wolves were bigger than dogs. It was the best time for hunting. The dogs of the ardent young hunter Rostov had not only reached good hunting form, but were so footsore that at a general council of hunters it was decided to give the dogs a three-day rest and move off on the sixteenth of September, beginning in Oak Grove, where there was an intact family of wolves.

This was where things stood on the fourteenth of September.

All that day the hunt stayed at home; it was frosty and biting, but in the evening it became overcast and turned warmer. On the fifteenth of September, when young Rostov, in his dressing gown, glanced out of the window in the morning, he saw a morning than which nothing could be better for hunting: it was as if the sky was melting and, without wind, descending to earth. The only movement in the air was the slow movement from above to below of descending microscopic drops of mist or fog. Transparent drops hung on the bare branches of the garden and dripped onto the just-fallen leaves. The soil in the kitchen garden, glistening wet and black as poppy seed, merged in the near distance with the dull and damp curtain of the mist. Nikolai went out to the wet, mud-tracked porch; there was a smell of fading leaves and dogs. The black-spotted, broad-haunched bitch Milka, with big, black, bulging eyes, seeing her master, got up, stretched her hind legs, and lay down harelike, then suddenly jumped up and licked him right on the nose and moustache. Another borzoi, seeing his master from the garden path, rushed headlong, arching his back, towards the porch and, raising his stern (tail), began to rub himself against Nikolai's legs.

"Hal-loo!" Just then came that inimitable hunting call, which unites in itself the deepest bass and the highest tenor; and round the corner came the head kennelman and huntsman Danilo, a wrinkled old hunter, his grey hair cut round in Ukrainian fashion, a hooked hunting whip in his hand, and with that expression of independence and scorn for everything in the world that only hunters have. He took off his Circassian hat before his master and looked at him scornfully. This scorn was not offensive for the master: Nikolai knew that this Danilo, who scorned everything and was above everything, was still his serf and his hunter.

"Danilo!" said Nikolai, timidly sensing that, at the sight of this hunting weather, these dogs, and his hunter, he was already being seized by that irresistible hunting feeling in which a man forgets all his former intentions, like a lovesick man in the presence of his beloved.

"What orders, Your Excellency?" asked a protodeacon's bass, hoarse from hallooing, and two black, brilliant eyes looked from under their brows at the silent master. "So you can't stand it?" these two eyes seemed to say.

"A pretty nice day, eh? For a chase and a gallop, eh?" said Nikolai, scratching Milka behind the ears.

Danilo did not reply and blinked his eyes.

"I sent Uvarka to listen at dawn," his bass said after a moment's silence. "He says she *transferred* them to the Otradnoe reserve, they were howling there." ("Transferred" meant that the she-wolf they both knew about had gone with her cubs to the Otradnoe woods, which was a mile and a half from the house and was a small preserve.)

"We've got to go, then?" said Nikolai. "Meet me here with Uvarka."

"As you say, sir!"

"And hold off the feeding."

"Yes, sir."

Five minutes later Danilo and Uvarka were standing in Nikolai's big study. Though Danilo was of small stature, seeing him in the room produced an impression similar to seeing a horse or a bear standing there amidst the furniture and accessories of human life. Danilo felt it himself and, as usual, stayed near the door, trying to speak softly, not moving, so as not to break anything somehow in his master's room, and trying to say everything as quickly as possible and get out into the open, from under the ceiling to under the sky.

Having finished his questioning and extorted from Danilo the admission that the dogs were all right (Danilo himself wanted to go), Nikolai ordered the horses saddled. But Danilo was just about to leave when Natasha, not yet dressed, her hair still undone, in her nanny's big shawl, came into the room with quick steps. Petya ran in with her.

"You're going?" said Natasha. "I just knew it. Sonya said you wouldn't. I knew that on a day like this you couldn't help going."

"We're going," Nikolai answered reluctantly, being intent on some serious wolf hunting that day and not wanting to bring Natasha and Petya along. "We're going, but only for wolves: you'd be bored."

"You know it's my greatest pleasure," said Natasha. "That's not nice—

you're going yourself, you've ordered the horses saddled, and you haven't told us anything."

" 'Vain are all barriers to Russians'[3]—we're going!" cried Petya.

"But you're not allowed: mama said you're not allowed," said Nikolai, turning to Natasha.

"No, I'm going, I'm certainly going," Natasha said resolutely. "Danilo, order horses saddled for us, and have Mikhailo ride out with my pack," she turned to the huntsman.

And if being in the room like that seemed improper and burdensome to Danilo, having any sort of dealings with a young lady seemed simply impossible to him. He lowered his eyes and hurried out, as if it had nothing to do with him, trying not to injure the young lady somehow accidentally.

IV

The old count, who had always maintained an enormous hunt, having now handed the whole hunt over to his son's keeping, on that day of the fifteenth of September, feeling quite cheered up, made ready to go with them.

An hour later the entire hunt was at the porch. Nikolai, with a stern and serious air, showing that it was no time for bothering with trifles, walked past Natasha and Petya as they were telling him something. He examined all parts of the hunt, sent a pack and some hunters ahead to circle around, mounted his chestnut Don stallion, and whistling up the dogs of his pack, set out across the threshing floor to the field leading to the Otradnoe reserve. The old count's horse, a sorrel gelding named Viflyanka, was led by the count's groom; the count himself was to drive directly to the covert assigned to him in a little droshky.

In all, fifty-four hounds were led out under six kennelmen and whippers-in. Besides the gentlemen, there were eight borzoi handlers, around whom roamed more than forty borzois, so that, with the gentlemen's packs, there were about a hundred and thirty dogs in the field and twenty mounted hunters.

Each dog knew its master and its name. Each hunter knew his task, place, and purpose. As soon as they went beyond the fence, everybody, with no noise or talk, spread out evenly and calmly along the road and field leading to the Otradnoe woods.

As over a plush carpet, the horses walked over the field, splashing in puddles now and then as they crossed the roads. The misty sky went on imperceptibly and evenly descending to earth; the air was still, warm, soundless. Now and then came the whistle of a hunter, the snort of a horse, the crack of a whip, or the squeal of a hound strayed from its place.

They had not yet ridden a mile when the Rostov hunt was met by another five riders with dogs emerging from the mist. At their head rode a fresh, hand-some old man with big grey moustaches.

"Greetings, uncle!" said Nikolai, when the old man rode up to him.

"Right you are! . . . I just knew," the uncle began (he was a distant relation, a none-too-wealthy neighbour of the Rostovs), "I just knew you wouldn't stay home, and it's a good thing you didn't. Right you are!" (This was the uncle's favourite saying.) "Take the reserve at once, because my Girchik told me the Ilagins are at Korniki with their hunt. They'll snatch the litter—right you are!—straight out from under your nose."

"That's where I'm going. Shall we combine the packs?" asked Nikolai. "Combine . . ."

The hounds were united into a single pack, and the uncle and Nikolai rode side by side. Natasha, wrapped in shawls, from which her lively face peeked out with its bright eyes, galloped up to them, accompanied by Petya, who never left her side, and Mikhailo, a hunter and riding master, who was assigned to look after her. Petya laughed at something, and whipped and pulled his horse. Natasha adroitly and confidently sat her black Arabchik and with a sure hand effortlessly reined him in.

The uncle glanced disapprovingly at Petya and Natasha. He did not like combining play with the serious business of hunting.

"Greetings, uncle, we're coming, too," cried Petya.

"If it's greetings, it's greetings, but don't go trampling the dogs," the uncle said sternly.

"Nikolenka, what a lovely dog Trunila is! He recognized me," Natasha said of her favourite hound.

"First of all, Trunila's not a dog, he's a bloodhound," thought Nikolai, and he glanced sternly at his sister, trying to make her feel the distance that should separate them at that moment. Natasha understood it.

"Don't think we'll get in anybody's way, uncle," said Natasha. "We'll stay in our places and not move."

"And a good thing, too, little Countess," said the uncle. "As long as you don't fall off your horse," he added, "because—right you are!—there's not much there to hold on with."

The island of the Otradnoe reserve could be seen about two hundred yards away, and the kennelmen were approaching it. Rostov, having come to a final decision with the uncle about where to set on the hounds, and pointing Natasha to a place where she could stand and where nothing could ever run out, he went to circle round above the ravine.

"Well, dear nephew, you're up against a seasoned one," said the uncle, "mind you don't go petting him."

"We'll see," replied Rostov. "Karai, phweet!" he cried, answering his uncle's words with this call. Karai was an ugly and whiskery old he-dog, famous for having gone alone against a seasoned wolf. Everybody took their places.

The old count, knowing his son's hunting ardour, hurried so as not to be late, and before the kennelmen managed to reach their places, Ilya Andreich, merry, red-cheeked, with quivering jowls, drove up with his black horses across the green winter wheat to the covert left for him, and having straightened his fur jacket and put on his hunting gear, mounted his sleek, well-fed, placid, and kind Viflyanka, gone as grey as himself. The horses and droshky were sent away. Count Ilya Andreich, who, though not a hunter at heart, had a firm knowledge of the rules of hunting, rode to the edge of the bushes where he was to stand, straightened out the reins, settled in the saddle, and, feeling himself ready, looked around, smiling.

Next to him stood his valet, Semyon Chekmar, an old horseman now grown heavy in the saddle. Chekmar held in leash three wolfhounds, spirited but grown fat, like their master and his horse. Two clever old dogs lay down without a leash. A hundred paces away, inside the edge of the woods, stood the count's other groom, Mitka, a desperate horseman and passionate hunter. The count, by ancient habit, drank a silver tumbler of hunter's spiced brandy, had a bite to eat, and washed it down with half a bottle of his favourite Bordeaux.

Ilya Andreevich was slightly flushed from the wine and the driving; his eyes, veiled with moisture, had a special glitter, and, wrapped in his fur coat, sitting in his saddle, he had the look of a child made ready to go for a walk.

The thin, hollow-cheeked Chekmar, having set everything up for himself, kept glancing at his master, with whom he had lived in perfect harmony for thirty years, and understanding his pleasant state of mind, expected some pleasant conversation. A third person also rode up cautiously (clearly he had already learned his lesson) from beyond the woods, and stopped behind the count. This person was an old, grey-bearded man in a woman's coat and tall hat. He was the buffoon Nastasya Ivanovna.

"Well, Nastasya Ivanovna," the count said in a whisper, winking at him, "if you frighten the beast away, Danilo will give it to you."

"I'm a big boy myself," said Nastasya Ivanovna.

"Shh!" the count shushed and turned to Semyon.

"Have you seen Natalya Ilyinichna?" he asked Semyon. "Where is she?"

"She and Pyotr Ilyich are standing across from the Zharovo thicket," Semyon replied, smiling. "She may be a lady, but she knows a lot about hunting."

"And aren't you amazed at how she rides . . . eh, Semyon?" said the count. "The equal of any man!"

"How could I not be amazed? She's bold, skilful!"

"And where's Nikolashka? Over at the Lyadovsky knoll, is he?" the count went on asking in a whisper.

"Just so, sir. He knows where to stand. He's got such fine knowledge of horsemanship, me and Danilo just marvel sometimes," said Semyon, knowing how to please his master.

"Rides well, eh? And how he sits a horse, eh?"

"A real picture! Like the other day when we chased a fox from the Zavarzinsky thicket. The master went hurtling to cut it off from the forest, something fearsome—a thousand-rouble horse, but the rider's priceless! Yes, a fine fellow like that is hard to find!"

"Hard to find . . ." repeated the count, obviously sorry that Semyon had stopped talking so soon. "Hard to find," he said, pulling back the skirt of his jacket and taking out his snuffbox.

"The other day, when he came out of church in full regalia, Mikhail Sidorych . . ." Semyon did not finish, hearing in the still air the clear music of no more than two or three hounds baying in pursuit. Inclining his head, he listened and frowned silently to his master. "They've struck on the litter . . ." he whispered, "they're heading straight for the Lyadovsky knoll."

The count, forgetting to wipe the smile from his face, looked straight into the distance along the line of trees, and held the snuffbox in his hand without taking a pinch. Following the dogs' barking came the bass sound of Danilo's horn, calling after the wolf; the pack joined the first three dogs, and one could hear the baying of the hounds in full cry, with that special yelping that signals the pursuit of a wolf. The kennelmen no longer shouted, but hallooed, and Danilo's voice rose above all the others, now bass, now piercingly shrill. Danilo's voice seemed to fill the whole woods, emerge, and spread far across the field.

Listening silently for a few seconds, the count and his groom realized that the hounds had broken up into two packs: one, a big one, baying with particular fervour, began to move away; the other part of the pack raced through the woods, past the count, and in this pack Danilo's hallooing could be heard. These two chases merged, alternated, but both were moving away. Semyon sighed and bent down to straighten the leash in which a young dog had become entangled. The count also sighed and, noticing the snuffbox in his hand, opened it and took a pinch.

"Back!" Semyon shouted at a dog that had stepped out of the bushes. The count gave a start and dropped the snuffbox. Nastasya Ivanovna dismounted and went to pick it up.

The count and Semyon looked at him. Suddenly, as often happens, the sound of the chase instantly drew close, as if the dogs' baying muzzles and Danilo's hallooing were just in front of them.

The count turned and to his right saw Mitka, who was looking at the count with popping eyes and, raising his cap,[4] was pointing ahead of him to the other side.

"Look out!" he cried in a voice which made it clear that this word had been asking long and painfully to be let out. And, releasing his dogs, he galloped towards the count.

The count and Semyon leaped out of the bushes and to their left saw a wolf, which, swaying softly, was moving at a gentle lope to the left of them, towards the same bushes by which they were standing. The angry dogs squealed and, loosed from their leashes, raced towards the wolf past the horses' legs.

The wolf slowed his flight, turned his big-browed head towards the dogs awkwardly, as if suffering from angina, and, swaying just as softly, leaped once, twice, and, with a wag of his tail, disappeared into the bushes. At that same moment, from the bushes opposite, with a baying that sounded like a lament, perplexedly leaped one hound, a second, a third, and the whole pack raced across the field to the same place where the wolf had gone through. After the hounds, the hazel bushes parted, and Danilo's brown horse appeared, dark with sweat. On its long back, in a little lump, thrown forward, sat Danilo, hatless, his grey hair tousled above his red, sweaty face.

"Hallooloo, halloo! . . ." he cried. When he saw the count, his eyes flashed lightning.

"A——!" he cried, raising his whip threateningly at the count. "You b——ed the wolf! . . . Some hunters!"

And as if not deeming the abashed, frightened count worthy of further conversation, he whipped the hollow, wet flanks of his brown gelding with all the anger he had prepared for the count, and raced after the hounds. The count stood as if punished, looking around and trying with a smile to evoke some sympathy for his position in Semyon. But Semyon was no longer there: he was circling around the bushes to cut the wolf off from the timber. On both sides the borzoi men also came leaping after the beast. But the wolf got through the bushes, and not one hunter intercepted him.

V

Nikolai Rostov meanwhile stood in his place waiting for the beast. From the way the chase approached or withdrew, from the giving tongue of the dogs he knew, from the approaching, withdrawing, and rising voices of the kennelmen, he could sense what was happening in the island. He knew that there were growing (young) and seasoned (old) wolves; he knew that the hounds had broken up into two packs, that they were chasing somewhere, and that something had gone wrong. He expected the beast on his side every second. He made thousands of different conjectures about how and on which side the beast would come running, and how he would chase him down. Hope alternated with despair. Several times he addressed God with a plea that the wolf come out at him; he prayed with that passionate and guilty feeling with which people pray at moments of strong agitation arising from insignificant causes. "What would it cost You?" he said to God. "Do it for me! I know You are great, and it's a sin to ask it of You, but, for God's sake, make it so that the old wolf comes my way and Karai, before my uncle's eyes, gets a death grip on his throat." A thousand times during that half hour, Rostov cast intent, strained, and anxious glances around the edge of the woods, with two meagre oaks above the aspen undergrowth, and the ravine with its eroded edge, and his uncle's hat barely showing from behind a bush to the right.

"No, such luck is not to be," thought Rostov, "and yet what would it cost? It's not to be! I'm always unlucky, in cards, in war, in everything." Austerlitz and Dolokhov vividly but fleetingly flashed in his imagination. "If only once in my life I could chase down a seasoned wolf, I'd ask for nothing more!" he thought, straining his hearing and sight, looking to the left and then to the right, and listening to the smallest nuances in the sounds of the chase. He again looked to the right and saw that something was running towards him across the empty field. "No, it can't be!" thought Rostov, sighing deeply, as a man sighs at the accomplishment of something he has long awaited. What was accomplished was his greatest happiness—and so simply, without noise, without splendour, without portent. Rostov could not believe his eyes, and this doubt continued for more than a second. The wolf ran on and jumped heavily over a hole that lay in his path. He was an old beast, with a grey back and a well-stuffed, reddish belly. He ran unhurriedly, obviously convinced that no one could see him. Rostov, holding his breath, glanced at the dogs. They were lying down or standing, not seeing the wolf and understanding nothing. Old Karai turned his head and, baring his yellow teeth, clacked them along his haunch, angrily searching for a flea.

"Hallooloo," Rostov said in a whisper, protruding his lips. The dogs, jingling the metal rings of their collars, jumped up, cocking their ears. Karai finished scratching his haunch and stood up, cocking his ears and slightly wagging his tail, from which tufts of fur hung.

"Loose them, or not?" Nikolai was saying to himself all the while the wolf moved towards him, drawing away from the woods. Suddenly the wolf's entire physiognomy changed; he shuddered at the sight of human eyes, which he had probably never seen before, directed at him, and turning his head slightly towards the hunter, stopped—go back or go on? "Eh! it makes no difference, I'll go on!" he seemed to say to himself and started forward, not looking around now, at a soft, long, free, but resolute lope.

"Halloo!" Nikolai shouted in a voice not his own, and of itself his good horse raced headlong down the hill, leaping over gullies, to head off the wolf; and still more quickly, outstripping the horse, raced the dogs. Nikolai did not hear his own shouts, did not feel that he was galloping, did not see the dogs or the space over which he was galloping; he saw only the wolf, who, quickening his pace, loped down the hollow without changing direction. The first to turn up near the beast was the black-spotted, broad-haunched Milka, who began to close in on him. Closer, closer . . . there she was right next to him. But the wolf barely gave her a sidelong glance, and, instead of pushing on, as she always did, Milka, raising her tail, suddenly began braking with her forelegs.

"Halloolooloo!" shouted Nikolai.

The red Lyubim overtook Milka, precipitously threw himself at the wolf, and seized him by the hindquarters, but in the same second became frightened and jumped over to the other side. The wolf crouched, clacked his teeth, got up again, and loped on, accompanied at two yards' distance by all the dogs, who would not go nearer to him.

"He'll get away! No, it's impossible," thought Nikolai, continuing to shout in a hoarse voice.

"Karai! Halloo! . . ." he shouted, his eyes seeking the old dog, his only hope. Karai, with all his aged strength, stretching out as much as he could, looking at the wolf, galloped heavily alongside the beast, trying to head him off. But it was clear from the speed of the wolf and the slowness of the dog that Karai's calculation was wrong. Not far ahead of him now, Nikolai saw the woods, on reaching which the wolf would certainly get away. Ahead of them dogs appeared, and a hunter galloping almost straight towards them. There was still hope. A young, lanky, brindled dog, unknown to Nikolai, from another pack, flew swiftly at the wolf from the front and nearly bowled him over. The wolf got up more quickly than might have been expected of him, rushed at the brindled dog, snapped his teeth—and the bloodied dog, its side ripped open, let out a piercing squeal, burying its head in the ground.

"Karayushka! Old boy! . . ." wept Nikolai.

Thanks to the delay, the old dog, his matted fur hanging from his haunches, headed off the wolf, and was now within five paces of him. The wolf, as if sensing the danger, gave Karai a sidelong glance, tucked his tail still further between his legs, and increased his pace. But here—Nikolai only saw that something happened with Karai—he was instantly on top of the wolf and rolled head over heels with him into a ditch in front of them.

That moment, when Nikolai saw the dogs swarming over the wolf in the ditch, saw under them the wolf's grey fur, his outstretched hind leg, and his frightened and gasping head with its ears laid back (Karai had him by the throat)—the moment when Nikolai saw that was the happiest moment of his life. He had already taken hold of the pommel so as to dismount and stab the wolf, when the beast's head suddenly thrust itself out from the mass of dogs, then his front legs stood up on the edge of the ditch. The wolf clacked his teeth (Karai no longer had him by the throat), leaped out of the ditch with his hind legs, and, tucking in his tail, moved off, drawing away from the dogs again. Karai, his fur bristling, probably bruised or wounded, had difficulty climbing out of the ditch.

"My God! Why? . . ." Nikolai cried in despair.

The uncle's hunter rode across the wolf's path from the other side, and his dogs again stopped the beast. He was again surrounded.

Nikolai, his groom, the uncle, and his hunter all rode round and round the beast, hallooing, shouting, preparing to dismount at any moment, when the wolf sat on his haunches, and leaping forward each time the wolf shook himself and made a move towards the timber, which would save him.

From the beginning of this chase, Danilo, hearing the hallooing, had ridden out to the edge of the woods. He saw Karai take the wolf and stopped his horse, supposing the business was over. But when the hunters did not dismount, when the wolf shook himself and again began to make off, Danilo sent his brown horse not towards the wolf, but in a straight line towards the timber, just as Karai had done, to head off the wolf. Thanks to this direction, he rode up to the wolf just as the uncle's dogs stopped him a second time.

Danilo rode silently, holding an unsheathed dagger in his left hand, and threshing the taut flanks of his brown horse with his whip as if it was a flail.

Nikolai did not see or hear Danilo until the brown horse, breathing heavily, snorted past him, and he heard the sound of a body falling and saw that Danilo was already lying on the wolf's rump in the midst of the dogs, trying to catch him by the ears. It was obvious to the hunters, and to the dogs, and to the wolf himself that it was all over now. The beast, his ears laid back fearfully, tried to get up, but the dogs clung to him. Danilo, standing up, made a falling step and, with his whole weight, as if lying down to rest, collapsed on the wolf, seizing him by the ears. Nikolai wanted to stab him, but Danilo whispered, "Don't, we'll truss him up," and, changing position, he placed his foot on the wolf's neck. They put a stick in the wolf's mouth, tied it with a leash like a bridle, bound his legs, and Danilo rolled the wolf from side to side a couple of times.

With happy, exhausted faces, they hoisted the live, seasoned old wolf onto a shying, snorting horse and, accompanied by the squealing dogs, took him to the place where they were all supposed to assemble. The hounds had taken two young wolves and the borzois three. The hunters came together with their quarry and their stories, and everybody went to look at the seasoned old wolf, who, lolling his big-browed head with the stick gripped in his mouth, looked with wide, glassy eyes at this whole crowd of dogs and people surrounding him. When touched, he jerked his bound legs and looked at them all wildly and at the same time simply.

Count Ilya Andreich also rode up and touched the wolf.

"Oh, what a big old seasoned one!" he said. "A seasoned one, eh?" he asked Danilo, who was standing next to him.

"Yes, a seasoned one, Your Excellency," replied Danilo, hastily doffing his hat.

The count remembered how he had let the wolf slip and his confrontation with Danilo.

"You do get angry, though, brother," said the count. Danilo said nothing and just shyly smiled his childishly meek and pleasant smile.

VI

The old count rode home. Natasha and Petya stayed with the hunt, promising to come at once. The hunt went further on, because it was still early. At midday the hounds were loosed into a ravine overgrown with dense, young forest. Nikolai, standing in the stubble, could see all his hunters.

Across from Nikolai was a field of winter wheat, and there stood one of his hunters, alone, in a hollow behind an upthrust hazel bush. As soon as the hounds were loosed into the ravine, Nikolai heard the intermittent baying of a dog he knew—Voltorn; other dogs joined him, now falling silent, now giving tongue again. A moment later from the woods came a foxhunting cry, and the whole pack, joining together, went racing along the edge of the ravine in the direction of the field, away from Nikolai.

He saw the whippers-in in their red hats riding along the edge of the overgrown ravine; he even saw the dogs, and expected every second that a fox would appear on the other side, on the green field.

The hunter who was standing in the hollow stirred and loosed his dogs, and Nikolai saw a strange, low-slung red fox which, puffing up its tail, raced swiftly across the field. The dogs bore down on it. Now they drew close, now it started dodging among them, circling more and more quickly, and twining its puffed-up brush (tail) round itself; and now someone's white dog flew at it, and after it a black one, and everything became confused, and then the dogs stood forming a star, their rumps pointing outwards, swaying slightly. Two hunters rode up to the dogs, one in a red hat, the other, a stranger, in a green kaftan.

"What's this?" thought Nikolai. "Where did that hunter appear from? He's not uncle's."

The hunters took the fox from the dogs, and stood dismounted for a long time without strapping it on. The horses, their bridles free and their saddles jutting up, stood nearby, and the dogs lay down. The hunters waved their arms and did something with the fox. The sound of a horn rang out from there—the conventional signal of a fight.

"It's Ilagin's hunter and our Ivan acting up over something," said Nikolai's groom.

Nikolai sent his groom to call his sister and Petya to him and rode at a walk to the place where the kennelmen were gathering the hounds. Several hunters galloped to the scene of the fight.

Nikolai dismounted and stood by the hounds with Natasha and Petya, who joined him, waiting for news of how the matter would end. The hunter who had been fighting left the edge of the woods with the fox strapped to his saddle and rode over to his young master. He took off his hat while still some distance away and tried to speak respectfully; but he was pale, breathless, and his face was angry. He had a black eye, but he probably did not know it.

"What was that about?" asked Nikolai.

"Why, as if he's going to hunt out from under our hounds! It was my mouse-grey bitch that caught it. Go on, take it to court! He grabs hold of the fox! I whacked him with it. You want it, it's strapped on here. And how would you like a bit of this?" said the hunter, pointing to his dagger and probably imagining that he was still talking to his enemy.

Nikolai, not responding to the hunter, asked his sister and Petya to wait for him and rode to the place where Ilagin's hostile hunt stood.

The victorious hunter rode into the crowd of hunters and there, surrounded by curious sympathizers, told of his exploit.

The thing was that Ilagin, with whom the Rostovs had had a quarrel and a lawsuit, used to hunt in places that customarily belonged to the Rostovs, and now as if on purpose had sent his men to the reserve where the Rostovs were hunting and had allowed his hunter to take the quarry hunted down by the Rostovs' hounds.

Nikolai had never seen Ilagin, but, as usual, knowing no middle way in his opinions and feelings, judging by the rumours of this landowner's violence and wilfulness, hated him with all his heart and considered him his bitterest enemy. He was now riding to him in angry agitation, firmly gripping his whip and fully prepared for the most resolute and dangerous actions against his enemy.

He had barely ridden out beyond the projecting arm of the forest when he saw a fat gentleman in a visored beaver cap coming towards him on a beautiful black horse, accompanied by two grooms.

Instead of an enemy, Nikolai found in Ilagin a respectable, courteous gentleman, especially desirous of making the young count's acquaintance. Riding up to Rostov, Ilagin raised his beaver cap and said that he very much regretted what had happened, said that he would order the hunter punished for allowing himself to hunt from under another man's dogs, asked to make the count's acquaintance, and offered him his own hunting spots.

Natasha, fearing that her brother would do something terrible in his agitation, followed not far behind him. Seeing the enemies greet each other amicably, she rode up to them. Ilagin raised his beaver cap still higher before Natasha and, smiling pleasantly, said that the countess represented Diana[5] both in her passion for hunting and in her beauty, of which he had heard so much.

To smooth over his hunter's offence, Ilagin insistently invited Rostov to come to his upland, which was less than a mile away, which he kept for himself, and which, according to him, was all strewn with hares. Nikolai accepted, and the hunt, having doubled in size, moved on.

To reach Ilagin's upland, they had to go across the fields. The hunters spread out. The gentry rode together. The uncle, Rostov, and Ilagin kept glancing at each other's dogs on the sly, trying to keep the others from noticing, and sought worriedly among those dogs for rivals to their own.

Rostov was especially struck by the beauty of a small, purebred, red-spotted bitch in Ilagin's pack, slender, but with muscles of steel, narrow pincers (muzzle), and prominent black eyes. He had heard about the swiftness of Ilagin's dogs and in this beautiful bitch saw a rival to his Milka.

In the middle of a sedate conversation about that year's harvest, begun by Ilagin, Nikolai pointed to his red-spotted bitch.

"That's a good bitch you've got!" he said in a casual tone. "Swift-footed?"

"This one? Yes, she's a good dog, a catcher," Ilagin said in an indifferent voice of his red-spotted Yerza, for whom he had given his neighbour three families of house serfs a year before. "So with you, too, Count, there's no boasting about flour production this year?" he continued the conversation. And, considering it polite to pay the young count back in kind, Ilagin looked over his dogs and picked out Milka, whose broadness struck his eye.

"She's a good one, that black-spotted one of yours—well-built!" he said.

"Yes, she's all right. Good speed," Nikolai replied. "If only there was a seasoned hare running through the field, I'd show you what kind of dog she is!" he thought. And turning to his groom, he said he would give a rouble to the hunter who could spot a hare in its form.

"I don't understand," Ilagin went on, "how it is that other hunters can be jealous over game and dogs. I'll tell you about myself, Count. I enjoy having a ride, you know; you get together with company like this . . . what could be better?" (He again took his beaver cap off to Natasha.) "But this counting skins, who brought in how many—it's all the same to me!"

"Well, yes."

"Or that I should get upset that another man's dog catches it and not mine—all I want is to admire the chase, isn't that so, Count? Then, in my opinion . . ."

"Halloo!" came the long-drawn cry of one of the borzoi men, who had stopped. He was standing on a low knoll amidst the stubble with his whip raised, and once more called out: "Hallo-o-o!" (This sound and the raised whip signified that he had spotted a hare in its form in front of him.)

"Ah, seems he's spotted one," Ilagin said casually. "Well, let's course it, Count."

"Yes, we should ride over . . . together, shall we?" Nikolai replied, looking at Yerza and at his uncle's red Rugai, two rivals with whom he had never yet had his dogs compete. "And what if they pull my Milka off its ears?" he thought, heading for the hare alongside his uncle and Ilagin.

"A seasoned one?" asked Ilagin, approaching the hunter who had spotted the hare and turning, not without excitement, to whistle up Yerza . . .

"And you, Mikhail Nikanorych?" he turned to the uncle. The uncle rode along, scowling.

"Why should I get into it! Your dogs—right you are!—you paid a village for each of them, they cost thousands. You match yours, and I'll watch!

"Rugai! Here, here!" he cried. "Rugayushka!" he added, involuntarily expressing by this diminutive his tenderness and the hope he placed in this red dog. Natasha saw and felt the hidden excitement of these two old men and her brother, and was excited herself.

The hunter on the knoll stood with his whip raised; the gentlemen rode up to him at a walk; the hounds, running just on the horizon, were turning away from the hare; the rest of the hunters were also riding away. Everything moved slowly and sedately.

"Where's his head pointing?" asked Nikolai, riding up within a hundred paces of the hunter who had spotted the hare. But before the hunter had time to reply, the hare, sensing which way the wind was turning, leaped up from his form. The pack of hounds, linked in pairs, raced baying down the hill after the hare; from all sides the borzois, which were not on leashes, rushed after the hounds and the hare. All those slowly moving hunters and whippers-in crying "Hold up!"—throwing off their dogs—and the borzoi men crying "Sic him!" and driving their dogs on—galloped across the field. The calm Ilagin, Nikolai, Natasha, and the uncle flew along, not knowing how or where, seeing only the dogs and the hare, and only fearing to lose sight, even for a moment, of the course of the chase. The hare happened to be seasoned and swift-footed. Jumping up, he did not run at once, but moved his ears, listening to the shouting and stamping that suddenly arose on all sides. He made some ten leaps, not quickly, letting the dogs get closer to him, and finally, choosing his direction and realizing the danger, laid his ears back and dashed off as fast as his legs would carry him. He had been lying in the stubble, but ahead of him were the green fields, where the ground was soggy. The two dogs of the hunter who had spotted the hare, being closest to him, were the first to view and start after the hare; but they were still far from him when Ilagin's red-spotted Yerza flew up from behind, got within a dog's length of him, raced on at a terrible speed, aiming at the hare's tail, and, thinking she had seized him, went rolling head over heels. The hare arched his back and raced on still more swiftly. Yerza was overtaken from behind by the broad-haunched, black-spotted Milka, who sped quickly towards the hare.

"Good girl, Milushka!" Nikolai cried triumphantly. It seemed that Milka was about to hit the hare and snatch him up, but she drew level and missed him. The hare leaped aside. Again the beautiful Yerza was on the hare and hovering right over his tail, as if measuring so as not to miss this time and take him by the haunch.

"Yerzinka! Dearie!" wailed Ilagin in a voice not his own. Yerza did not heed his prayer. At the very moment she was expected to seize the hare, he swerved and flew out to the boundary between the green fields and the stubble. Again Yerza and Milka, like a team of horses, straightened up and sped after the hare; it was easier for him to run along the boundary, and dogs could not close in on him so quickly.

"Rugai! Rugayushka! Right you are!" a new voice cried just then, and Rugai, the uncle's red, hunchbacked dog, stretching out, then arching his back, caught up with the first pair of dogs, went ahead of them, raced with a terrible selflessness right onto the hare, knocked him from the boundary into the green field, raced on still more fiercely over the muddy green growth, sinking up to his knees, and one could only see him go rolling head over heels, dirtying his back in the mud, together with the hare. The dogs surrounded him in a star. A moment later everyone was standing by the crowding dogs. The happy uncle dismounted alone and cut off the hare's foot. Shaking the hare to make the blood run down, he looked around uneasily, his eyes darting, not knowing where to put his arms and legs, and spoke, himself not knowing what or to whom. "There's a right good piece of work . . . There's a dog . . . outran them all, a thousand roubles or one—right you are!" he said, gasping and looking around angrily, as if scolding someone, as if they were all his enemies, as if they had all offended him, and he had only now finally managed to vindicate himself. "There's your thousand-rouble dogs for you—right you are!"

"Catch, Rugai!" he said, tossing him the cut-off paw with dirt stuck to it. "You earned it—right you are!"

"She's worn out, she ran him down three times by herself," Nikolai said, also not listening to anyone and not caring whether anyone was listening to him.

"He cut in!" Ilagin's groom was saying.

"She almost had him, and after that any mongrel could have caught him!" Ilagin was saying at the same time, red-faced, trying to catch his breath after the galloping and excitement. At the same time, Natasha, without pausing for breath, let out a joyful and rapturous shriek, so shrill that it made their ears ring. With this shriek she expressed everything the other hunters had expressed with their simultaneous talk. And this shriek was so odd that she herself would have been embarrassed at such wild shrieking, and they all would have been surprised at it, if it had happened at any other time. The uncle strapped up the hare, flipped it nimbly and deftly across his horse's croup, as if reproaching them all by this flipping, and, mounting his chestnut with such a look as though he did not even want to speak with anyone, rode off. Everyone else but he, sad and offended, rode along and only after a long time could they recover their former sham indifference. For a long time they kept glancing at the red Rugai, who, his hunched back dirty with mud, jingling his collar, trotted behind the uncle's horse's legs with the calm look of a conqueror.

"So I'm just like all the rest, when it's not a matter of the chase. Well, but when it is, watch out!" was, as it seemed to Nikolai, what the dog's look said.

When, a long time later, the uncle rode up to Nikolai and began speaking to him, Nikolai felt flattered that, after all that had happened, his uncle still condescended to speak to him.

VII

When Ilagin took leave of Nikolai in the evening, Nikolai was so far from home that he accepted his uncle's offer to quit the hunt and spend the night with him (the uncle) in his village of Mikhailovka.

"And if you come to my place—right you are!—that will be even better," said the uncle. "You see, it's wet weather," the uncle said, "you'd get some rest, the little countess would be taken in the droshky." The uncle's offer was accepted, a hunter was sent to Otradnoe for the droshky, and Nikolai went to the uncle's with Natasha and Petya.

Some five men servants, big and small, ran out to the front porch to meet the master. Dozens of women, old, big and little, stuck themselves out from the back porch to look at the arriving hunters. The presence of Natasha, a woman, a lady, on horseback, raised the curiosity of the uncle's people to such a degree of astonishment that many, unabashed by her presence, went up to her, looked into her eyes, and made remarks about her, as about some wonder on display, which was not a human being and could not hear or understand that they were talking about her.

"Arinka, look, she sits sideways! She sits and her skirt hangs down . . . See, there's a little horn!"

"Saints alive, a little knife! . . ."

"See, like a Tartar woman!"

"How is it you don't go head over heels?" the boldest of them said, addressing Natasha directly.

The uncle dismounted by the porch of his small wooden house sunk in a garden, and, looking over his domestics, shouted peremptorily that the superfluous people should take themselves off and everything necessary should be done to receive the guests and the hunt.

They all dispersed. The uncle helped Natasha down from the horse and led her by the arm up the shaky plank steps of the porch. The house, unplastered, with timber walls, was not very clean inside—one could see that the aim of those living in it did not consist in keeping it spotless—but there were also no signs of neglect. The entryway smelled of fresh apples and was hung with wolf and fox pelts.

The uncle led his guests through the front hall into a small reception room with a folding table and red chairs, then to a drawing room with a round birch table and a sofa, then to the study, with a torn sofa, a worn rug, and portraits of Suvorov, the host's father and mother, and himself in military uniform. The study smelled strongly of tobacco and dogs.

In the study the uncle asked his guests to sit down and make themselves at home, and he himself left. Rugai with his still dirty back came into the study and lay on the sofa, cleaning himself with his tongue and teeth. From the study led a corridor in which one could see screens with torn curtains. From behind the screens came women's laughter and whispering. Natasha, Nikolai, and Petya took their coats off and sat down on the sofa. Petya leaned on his arm and immediately fell asleep; Natasha and Nikolai sat silently. Their faces were burning, they were very hungry and very merry. They looked at each other (after the hunt, inside the house, Nikolai no longer considered it necessary to display his male superiority before his sister); Natasha winked at her brother, the two restrained themselves for a time, then burst into ringing laughter, before they managed to think up a pretext for their laughter.

A little later the uncle came in wearing a jerkin, dark blue trousers, and low boots. And Natasha felt that this same costume, in which she had looked upon her uncle with astonishment and mockery at Otradnoe, was a genuine costume, in no way worse than frock coats and tailcoats. The uncle was also merry; not only was he not offended by the laughter of the brother and sister (it would not have entered his head that they might laugh at his way of life), but he joined in their causeless laughter himself.

"That's the young countess—right you are!—I've never seen another like her!" he said, handing a pipe with a long chibouk to Rostov, and, with a habitual gesture, tucking another, its chibouk cut short, between three fingers.

"She's ridden all day, enough for a man, and it seems like nothing to her!"

Soon after the uncle, the door was opened by a girl—evidently barefoot, by the sound of her feet—and through it came a fat, red-cheeked, beautiful woman of about forty, with a double chin and full, red lips, carrying a big, heavily laden tray. She looked around at the guests with hospitable dignity and affability in her eyes and in her every movement, and with an amiable smile bowed respectfully to them. Despite her more than usual stoutness, which made her thrust her chest and stomach forward and hold her head back, this woman (the uncle's housekeeper) had an extremely light step. She went to the table, set down the tray, and with her plump, white hands deftly took the bottles, snacks, and treats, and arranged them on the table. Having finished that, she stepped away and, with a smile on her face, stood by the door. "Here I am! Now do you understand your uncle?" her appearance said to Rostov. How could he not understand? Not only Rostov, but Natasha as well understood the uncle and the meaning of the frowning brows and happy, self-contented smile that puckered his lips slightly the moment Anisya Fyodorovna came in. On the tray were an herb cordial, liqueurs, mushrooms, flat cakes made from dark flour and buttermilk, honey in the comb, still and foaming mead, apples, fresh and roasted nuts, and nuts in honey. Then Anisya Fyodorovna brought preserves made with honey and with sugar, and a ham, and a just-roasted chicken.

All this was tended, gathered, and cooked by Anisya Fyodorovna. All this smelled, and spoke, and had the taste of Anisya Fyodorovna. It all spoke of juiciness, cleanness, whiteness, and a pleasant smile.

"Have some, little Miss Countess," she repeated, serving Natasha one thing, then another. Natasha ate everything, and it seemed to her that she had never seen or tasted anywhere such buttermilk flat cakes, preserves so fragrant, such nuts in honey, or such a chicken. Anisya Fyodorovna left. Rostov and the uncle, washing their dinner down with cherry liqueur, spoke of past and future hunts, of Rugai, and of Ilagin's dogs. Natasha, her eyes shining, sat straight-backed on the sofa, listening to them. She tried several times to wake up Petya and give him something to eat, but he mumbled incomprehensibly, evidently without waking up. Natasha was in such merry spirits, she felt so good in these new surroundings, that she only feared the droshky would come for her too soon. After a chance moment of silence, as almost always happens with people who receive acquaintances in their house for the first time, the uncle said, answering a thought that was in his guests' minds:

"So this is how I'll live out my life . . . I'll die—right you are!—there'll be nothing left. No use sinning!"

The uncle's face was very significant and even handsome as he said it. Rostov involuntarily remembered all the good things he had heard from his father and the neighbours about his uncle. In this whole part of the province, his uncle had the reputation of a most noble and disinterested eccentric. He was called in to judge family matters, he was asked to be an executor, secrets were entrusted to him, he was elected to a judgeship and to other posts, but he always stubbornly refused social service, spending the autumn and spring in the fields riding his chestnut gelding, sitting at home in the winter, and lying in his overgrown garden in the summer.

"How is it you don't serve, uncle?"

"I did, but I quit. Unfit for it—right you are!—I don't understand a thing. It's your sort of business, I don't have brains enough. As for hunting, that's another matter—it's right you are! Open the door there," he shouted. "Why did you close it?" The door at the end of the corridor (which the uncle called a collidor) led to the bachelor hunters' room, as the hunters' common room was known. Bare feet quickly pattered off, and an invisible hand opened the door to the hunters' room. From the corridor the sounds of a balalaika became clearly audible, played by someone who was obviously a master at it. Natasha had long been listening to those sounds, and now went to the corridor to hear them better.

"That's my Mitka the coachman . . . I bought him a good balalaika, I like it," said the uncle. It was the uncle's custom that, when he came back from the hunt, Mitka would play the balalaika in the bachelor hunters' room. The uncle liked listening to this music.

"How good! Excellent, really," said Nikolai with a sort of involuntary disdain, as if he was ashamed to confess that he found the sounds very pleasing.

"What do you mean, excellent?" Natasha said with reproach, feeling the tone with which her brother had said it. "It's not excellent, it's simply lovely!" Just as the uncle's mushrooms, honey, and liqueurs seemed the best in the world to her, so this song, too, seemed to her at that moment the height of musical loveliness.

"More, please, more," Natasha said through the door, as soon as the balalaika fell silent. Mitka tuned up and again began picking out "Barinya,"⁶ with runs and leaps. The uncle sat and listened, his head inclined to one side, with a barely perceptible smile. The melody of "Barinya" was repeated some hundred times. The balalaika was tuned several times, and again the same sounds rippled out, and the listeners were not bored, but only wanted to hear this playing again and again. Anisya Fyodorovna came in and leaned her corpulent body against the doorpost.

"Listen, if you please, little Countess," she said to Natasha with a smile very much like the uncle's smile. "He plays nicely," she said.

"This part here he doesn't do right," the uncle said suddenly with an energetic gesture. "He should pour it on—right you are!—pour it on."

"And can you do it?" Natasha asked. The uncle smiled without answering. "Go, Anisyushka, see whether my guitar has all its strings or not. Haven't set hand to it for a long time, right you are! Gave it up."

Anisya Fyodorovna went eagerly with her light step to fulfil her master's request and fetched the guitar.

The uncle, not looking at anyone, blew the dust off, rapped on the face of the guitar with his bony fingers, tuned it up, and settled comfortably in his armchair. He took hold of the guitar (with a slightly theatrical gesture, cocking his left elbow) a little higher on the neck and, with a wink to Anisya Fyodorovna, did not begin "Barinya," but struck one sonorous, pure chord, and measuredly, calmly, but firmly began at a very slow tempo to pick out the well-known song "Down the ro-o-oadway . . ." At once, in time with that sober merriment (the same that was breathed out by Anisya Fyodorovna's whole being), the tune of the song began to sing in the souls of Nikolai and Natasha. Anisya Fyodorovna blushed and, covering her face with her kerchief, left the room laughing. The uncle continued to pick out the song clearly, assiduously, and with energetic firmness, gazing with an altered, inspired gaze at the place Anisya Fyodorovna had left. Something laughed slightly in his face, on one side, under his grey moustache, and it laughed especially when, as the song got going, the tempo quickened and in running passages there would be a sudden break.

"Lovely, lovely, uncle! More, more!" cried Natasha as soon as he finished. She jumped up from her place, embraced her uncle, and kissed him. "Nikolenka, Nikolenka!" she said, glancing at her brother, as if asking him: what on earth is it?

Nikolai also liked the uncle's playing very much. The uncle played the song a second time. Anisya Fyodorovna's smiling face again appeared in the doorway, and behind her some other faces.

> Fetching water clear and cold,
> He cries out, oh maiden, hold!

the uncle played, again made a skilful run, broke off, and twitched his shoulders.

"Come, come, dearest uncle," Natasha moaned in such an imploring voice as though her life depended on it. The uncle got up, and it was as if there were two men in him—one smiled gravely at the jolly fellow, while the jolly fellow performed a naïve and precise little caper before dancing.

"Come, niece!" cried the uncle, waving to Natasha with the hand that had broken off the chord.

Natasha threw off the kerchief she had wrapped round her, ran and placed herself in front of her uncle and, arms akimbo, made a movement with her shoulders and stopped.

Where, how, and when had this little countess, brought up by an émigré Frenchwoman, sucked this spirit in from the Russian air she breathed, where had she got these ways, which should have been long supplanted by the *pas de châle*?* Yet that spirit and these ways were those very inimitable, unstudied Russian ones which the uncle expected of her. As soon as she stood there, smiling triumphantly, proudly, and with sly merriment, the fear which had first seized Nikolai and all those present—that she would not do it right—went away, and they began to admire her.

She did it exactly right, and so precisely, so perfectly precisely, that Anisya Fyodorovna, who at once handed Natasha the kerchief she needed for it, wept through her laughter, looking at this slender, graceful countess, brought up in silk and velvet, so foreign to her, who was able to understand everything that was in Anisya and in Anisya's father, and in her aunt, and in her mother, and in every Russian.

"Well, little Countess, right you are!" the uncle said, laughing joyfully, finishing the dance. "What a niece! Now all we need is to choose you a fine young fellow for a husband, right you are!"

"He's already been chosen," said Nikolai, smiling.

"Oh?" the uncle said with surprise, looking questioningly at Natasha. Natasha, with a happy smile, nodded affirmatively.

*Shawl dance.

"And such a one!" she said. But as soon as she said it, another, new train of thoughts and feelings arose in her. "What did Nikolai's smile mean, when he said, 'He's already been chosen'? Is he glad of it or not? He seems to be thinking that my Bolkonsky wouldn't approve of, wouldn't understand this joy of ours. No, he'd understand everything. Where is he now?" thought Natasha, and her face suddenly became serious. But that lasted only a second. "Don't think, don't dare think of it," she said to herself and, smiling, sat down again beside her uncle, asking him to play something else.

The uncle played another song, then a waltz; then, after a pause, he cleared his throat and struck up his favourite hunting song:

> Late that evening in the wood
> It was snowing well and good . . .

The uncle sang as the folk sing, with the full and naïve conviction that the whole meaning of a song is contained in the words alone, that the tune comes of itself, and that the tune does not exist on its own, but only just so, for the sake of the rhythm. Which was why this unconscious tune of the uncle's, as in the songs of birds, was so extraordinarily good. Natasha was delighted with the uncle's singing. She decided that she would no longer study the harp, but would only play the guitar. She took the uncle's guitar and at once found the chords for the song.

Some time past nine a break, a droshky, and three mounted men came looking for Natasha and Petya. The count and countess did not know where they were and were very worried, as the messenger said.

Petya was carried out and laid like a dead body in the break; Natasha and Nikolai got into the droshky. The uncle wrapped Natasha up and said goodbye to her with a completely new tenderness. He went with them on foot to the bridge, which they had to wade round, and ordered the hunters to ride in front with lanterns.

"Goodbye, dear niece!" his voice cried out in the darkness, not the voice Natasha used to know, but the one that had sung "Late that evening in the wood."

In the village they drove through, there were little red lights and a cheerful smell of smoke.

"How lovely this uncle is!" said Natasha, when they came out on the high road.

"Yes," said Nikolai. "Are you cold?"

"No, I'm perfect, perfect. I feel so good," Natasha said, even with perplexity. They were silent for a long time.

The night was dark and damp. The horses could not be seen; they only heard them splashing through the unseen mud.

What was going on in that childishly receptive soul, so greedily grasping and absorbing all the diverse impressions of life? How did it all get laid away in her? But she was very happy. As they drove up to the house, she began to sing the tune of the song "Late that evening in the wood," the melody she had been trying to get all the while they rode and finally did get.

"Got it?" asked Nikolai.

"What are you thinking about now, Nikolenka?" asked Natasha. They liked asking each other that.

"Me?" said Nikolai, trying to recall. "You see, first I was thinking that Rugai, the red dog, resembles uncle, and that if he were a man, he would always keep uncle with him, if not for the chase, then for his tunefulness. How tuneful uncle is! Isn't it so? Well, and you?"

"Me? Wait, wait. Yes, at first I was thinking, here we are driving along and we think we're driving home, but God knows where we're going in this darkness, and suddenly we'll arrive and see that we're not in Otradnoe, but in a magic kingdom. And then I was also thinking . . . No, nothing else."

"I know, you must have been thinking about *him,*" said Nikolai, smiling, as Natasha could tell from the sound of his voice.

"No," said Natasha, though in fact she had also been thinking at the same time about Prince Andrei and how he would have liked their uncle. "And I've also been repeating, all the way I've been repeating: how well Anisyushka stepped out, how well . . ." said Natasha. And Nikolai heard her ringing, causeless, happy laughter.

"You know," she suddenly said, "I know I'll never again be as happy and peaceful as I am now."

"That's nonsense, silliness, rubbish," said Nikolai, and thought: "How lovely my Natasha is! I have no other friend like her and never will. Why is she getting married? We could keep driving around together!"

"How lovely my Nikolai is!" thought Natasha.

"Ah! there's still light in the drawing room," she said, pointing to the windows of the house, shining beautifully in the wet, velvet darkness of the night.

VIII

Count Ilya Andreich resigned as marshal of the nobility because the post entailed very great expenses. But his affairs did not improve. Often Natasha and Nikolai saw secret, worried conversations between their parents and heard talk of selling the Rostovs' magnificent ancestral house and the estate near Moscow. Without the marshalship, he did not have to have such large receptions, and life in Otradnoe took a quieter course than in former years; but still, the huge house and wing were full of people, and, as before, more than twenty sat down at table. These were all people who had been accustomed to the house, almost members of the family, or such as, it seemed, had necessarily to live in the count's house. These were the musician Dimmler[7] and his wife, the dancing master Iogel and his family, the old maiden lady Belov, who lived in the house, and many others as well: Petya's teachers, the girls' former governess, and simply people who for some reason found it better or more advantageous to live in the count's house than in their own. There were not such big receptions as before, but they maintained the same way of life, for without it the count and countess could not imagine life at all. There was the same hunt, increased still more by Nikolai, the same fifty horses and fifteen coachmen in the stable; the same expensive presents to each other on name days and festive dinners for the whole district; the same whists and bostons, during which the count, holding his cards fanlike for everyone to see, allowed himself to lose hundreds daily to his neighbours, who looked upon their right to play cards with Count Ilya Andreich as upon a most profitable source of income.

The count walked about in his affairs as in an enormous net, trying not to believe that he was entangled and with each step getting more and more entangled, and feeling himself unable either to break the meshes that ensnared him or to begin carefully and patiently to disentangle them. The countess felt with her loving heart that her children were being ruined, that it was not the count's fault, that he could not help being what he was, that he was suffering himself (though he concealed it) from the consciousness of his own and his children's ruin, and she sought for a means to remedy the situation. From her feminine point of view, there was only one way—for Nikolai to marry a rich bride. She felt that it was their last hope and that if Nikolai refused the match she had found for him, they would have to say goodbye for ever to the possibility of mending their affairs. This match was Julie Karagin, the daughter of an excellent, virtuous mother and father, whom the Rostovs had known from childhood and who was now a rich bride owing to the death of the last of her brothers.

The countess had written directly to Mrs. Karagin in Moscow, suggesting the marriage of her daughter to her son, and had received a favourable answer from her. Mrs. Karagin had replied that she, for her part, gave her consent, and that everything would depend on her daughter's inclination. Mrs. Karagin invited Nikolai to come to Moscow.

Several times the countess said to her son, with tears in her eyes, that, now that both her daughters were settled, her sole desire was to see him married. She said she would go peacefully to her grave if that happened. Then she said that she had her eye on a wonderful girl and tried to draw out his opinion concerning marriage.

In other conversations she praised Julie and advised Nikolai to go to Moscow for the holidays to amuse himself. Nikolai guessed what his mother's conversations were driving at, and during one of these conversations he got her to speak quite openly. She told him that all her hope for straightening out their affairs now lay in his marrying Miss Karagin.

"And what, if I loved a girl with no fortune, would you really demand, *maman*, that I sacrifice my feeling and honour for the sake of money?" he asked his mother, not understanding the cruelty of his question and wishing only to make a show of his nobility.

"No, you haven't understood me," said his mother, not knowing how to justify herself. "You haven't understood me, Nikolenka. I wish for your happiness," she added, and felt that she was not speaking the truth, that she was confused. She began to cry.

"Don't cry, mama, only tell me that you want it, and you know I'll give my whole life, everything, for you to be at peace," said Nikolai. "I'll sacrifice everything for you, even my feeling."

But the countess did not want to put the question that way: she did not want a sacrifice from her son, she would have liked to sacrifice herself for him.

"No, you haven't understood me, let's not talk about it," she said, wiping her tears.

"Yes, maybe I do love a poor girl," Nikolai said to himself, "and what, should I sacrifice my feeling and honour for money? I'm surprised that mama could say it to me. Because Sonya's poor," he thought, "does it mean I can't love her, can't respond to her faithful, devoted love? And I'd surely be happier with her than with some doll of a Julie. I can't command my feelings," he said to himself. "If I love Sonya, my feeling is stronger and higher than everything for me."

Nikolai did not go to Moscow, the countess did not renew the conversation about marriage with him, and saw with sadness, and sometimes with anger, the signs of a greater and greater intimacy between her son and the dowerless Sonya. She reproached herself for that, but could not keep from grumbling and picking on Sonya, often interrupting her without reason, grumbling at her, and calling her "my dear miss." Most of all, the kindly countess was angry with Sonya precisely because this poor, dark-eyed niece was so meek, so kind, so devotedly grateful to her benefactors, and so faithfully, so unfailingly, so selflessly in love with Nikolai, that there was nothing to reproach her for.

Nikolai spent the rest of his leave with his family. A fourth letter came from the fiancé Prince Andrei, from Rome, in which he wrote that he would long ago have been on his way to Russia if it had not been for his wound, which had unexpectedly reopened in the warm climate, making him postpone his departure until the beginning of the new year. Natasha was just as much in love with her fiancé, just as much at peace because of that love, and just as receptive to all the joys of life; but at the end of the fourth month of separation from him, moments of sadness began to come over her, against which she could not struggle. She was sorry for herself, sorry that she had been going to waste for nothing, for nobody, all that while, throughout which she had felt herself capable of loving and of being loved.

Things were not cheerful in the Rostovs' house.

IX

Christmastime came and, besides the festal liturgy, besides the solemn and boring felicitations of the neighbours and the servants, besides the new dresses everybody put on, there was nothing special to mark it as Christmastime, yet in the windless twenty degrees of frost, in the bright, blinding sunlight of day and the starry winter light at night, one felt called upon to mark this time somehow.

On the third day of the feast, after dinner, the entire household dispersed to various rooms. It was the most boring time of the day. Nikolai, who had gone to the neighbours in the morning, fell asleep in the sitting room. The old count rested in his study. Sonya sat at the round table in the drawing room copying a pattern. The countess laid out cards. Nastasya Ivanovna, the buffoon, sat by the window with two old ladies, his face sad. Natasha came into the room, went over to Sonya, looked at what she was doing, then went to her mother and stopped silently.

"Why are you wandering about so forlorn?" her mother asked her. "What do you want?"

"I want *him* . . . now, this minute, I want *him*," Natasha said, her eyes glistening and not smiling. The countess raised her head and looked intently at her daughter.

"Don't look at me, mama, don't look at me, I'm going to cry now."

"Sit down, sit with me," said the countess.

"Mama, I want *him*. Why am I going to waste like this, mama? . . ." Her voice broke off, tears flowed from her eyes, and to conceal them she quickly turned and left the room. She went to the sitting room, stood, thought, and went to the maids' quarters. There an old maidservant was grumbling at a young girl who came in breathless from the cold outside.

"Enough playing," the old woman said, "there's a time for everything."

"Let her be, Kondratyevna," said Natasha. "Go, Mavrusha, go."

And, having dismissed Mavrusha, Natasha went through the reception room to the front hall. An old servant and two young ones were playing cards. They broke off their game and stood up when the young lady came in. "What shall I do with them?" thought Natasha.

"Yes, Nikita, please go . . ." ("but where shall I send him?"). "Yes, go to the yard and bring a rooster, please; yes, and you, Misha, bring some oats."

"Just a bit of oats is it?" Misha said merrily and eagerly.

"Go, go quickly," the old man confirmed.

"And you, Fyodor, go and get me some chalk."

Passing by the butler's pantry, she ordered a samovar served, though it was not the right time.

The butler Foka was the most ill-tempered man in the whole house. Natasha liked to test her power over him. He did not believe her and went to ask if it was true.

"This young lady, really!" said Foka, pretending to frown at Natasha.

No one in the house ordered so many people around or gave them so much work as Natasha. She could not look at people indifferently, without sending them somewhere. It seemed as if she were testing whether any of them would get angry or upset with her, but people liked carrying out Natasha's orders as they did no one else's. "What shall I do? Where shall I go?" thought Natasha, walking slowly down the corridor.

"Nastasya Ivanovna, what will I give birth to?" she asked the buffoon, who came from the opposite direction in his short quilted jacket.

"Fleas, dragonflies, grasshoppers," the buffoon replied.

"My God, my God, it's all the same thing! Ah, where shall I go? What shall I do with myself?" And, stamping her feet, she quickly ran upstairs to Iogel, who lived on the upper floor with his wife. Iogel had two governesses sitting with him; there were plates of raisins, walnuts, and almonds on the table. The governesses were discussing whether it was cheaper to live in Moscow or in Odessa. Natasha sat down, listened to their conversation with a serious, thoughtful face, and got up.

"The island of Madagascar," she said. "Ma-da-gas-car," she repeated each syllable distinctly and, not answering Mme Schoss's question about what she was saying, left the room.

Petya, her brother, was also upstairs: he and his tutor were preparing fireworks to be set off at night.

"Petya! Petka!" she cried to him. "Give me a ride dowstairs." Petya ran over and offered his back. She jumped on it, put her arms round his neck, and he went skipping about with her. "No, never mind . . . the island of Madagascar," she said and, jumping off his back, she went downstairs.

Having gone around her kingdom, as it were, tested her power, and convinced herself that everyone was submissive, but that it was still boring, Natasha went to the reception room, took her guitar, sat in a dark corner behind a little cupboard, and began to pluck at the bass strings, picking out a phrase she remembered from an opera she had heard in Petersburg with Prince Andrei. For an uninitiated listener, what came of her playing would have been something that had no meaning, but in her imagination a whole series of memories arose from these sounds. She sat behind the little cupboard, her eyes fixed on a strip of light coming from the pantry door, listened to herself, and remembered. She was in a state of remembrance.

Sonya walked across the reception room to the pantry with a glass in her hand. Natasha looked at her, at the crack of the pantry door, and it seemed to her that she remembered light coming through the crack in the pantry door and Sonya passing by with a glass. "Yes, that happened, too, in the same way," Natasha thought.

"Sonya, what's this?" Natasha cried, plucking a thick string with her fingers.

"Ah, you're here!" said Sonya, giving a start, and she came over and listened. "I don't know. A storm?" she said timidly, afraid of being wrong.

"She gave a start in just the same way, came over in just the same way, and smiled timidly when it happened before," thought Natasha, "and in just the same way . . . I thought there was something lacking in her."

"No, it's a chorus from *The Water-Carrier*,[8] don't you hear?" And Natasha finished singing the chorus to give Sonya the idea.

"Where did you go?" asked Natasha.

"To change the water in the glass. I'm just finishing a pattern."

"You always keep busy, but I don't know how," said Natasha. "And where's Nikolenka?"

"Asleep, I think."

"Go and wake him up, Sonya," said Natasha. "Tell him I'm calling him to sing." She went on sitting, thinking about what it meant that it had all happened before, and, not resolving the question and not regretting it in the least, was again carried back in her imagination to the time when she was with him and he was looking at her with amorous eyes.

"Ah, if only he'd come soon. I'm so afraid it won't happen! And above all, I'm getting old, that's the thing! What's in me now won't be there any more. But maybe he'll come today, right now. Maybe he has come and is sitting there in the drawing room. Maybe he already came yesterday and I forgot." She stood up, set aside the guitar, and went to the drawing room. All the household people, tutors, governesses, and guests were already sitting at the tea table. The servants stood around the table—Prince Andrei was not there, and it was still the old habitual life.

"Ah, here she is," said Ilya Andreich, seeing Natasha come in. "Well, sit here with me." But Natasha stopped by her mother, looking around, as if searching for something.

"Mama!" she said. "Give *him* to me, mama, quickly, quickly," and she again had difficulty holding back her sobs.

She sat down at the table and listened to the conversation of the older people and of Nikolai, who had also come to the table. "My God, my God, the same faces, the same conversations, papa holding his cup in the same way and blowing in exactly the same way!" thought Natasha, horrified at the feeling of revulsion rising in her against the whole household for being always the same.

After tea, Nikolai, Sonya, and Natasha went to the sitting room, to their favourite corner, where their most heartfelt conversations always began.

X

"Does it ever happen to you," Natasha said to her brother, when they had settled in the sitting room, "does it ever happen to you that you feel there's nothing more—nothing; that everything good has already happened? And it's not
really boring, but sad?"

"As if it doesn't!" he said. "It's happened to me that everything's fine, everybody's merry, and it suddenly comes into my head that it's all tiresome and we
all ought to die. Once in the regiment I didn't go to an outdoor fête, and there
was music there . . . and I suddenly felt so bored . . ."

"Ah, I know that. I know, I know," Natasha picked up. "I was still little
when it happened to me. Remember, I was punished once for the plums, and
you were all dancing, but I sat in the schoolroom and cried. I cried so much, I'll
never forget it. I felt sad, and sorry for everybody, myself and everybody else.
And the main thing was that I wasn't guilty," said Natasha, "remember?"

"Yes," said Nikolai. I remember that I came to you later and wanted to comfort you, and, you know, I was ashamed. We were terribly funny. I had a little
toy figure then, and I wanted to give it to you. Remember?"

"And do you remember," Natasha said with a pensive smile, "how long,
long ago, when we were still very little, our uncle called us to his study, in his
old house, and it was dark—we came, and suddenly there stood . . ."

"A blackamoor," Nikolai finished with a joyful smile, "as if I don't remember! And I don't even know now if it was a blackamoor, or we dreamed it up,
or somebody told it to us."

"He was grey, remember, and his teeth were white—he stood and looked
at us . . ."

"Do you remember, Miss Sonya?" asked Nikolai.

"Yes, yes, I also remember something," Sonya replied timidly.

"I asked papa and mama about that blackamoor," said Natasha. "They say
there wasn't any blackamoor. But you do remember!"

"Of course, I remember his teeth as if it was now."

"How strange it was, as if in a dream. I like that."

"And do you remember how we were rolling eggs in the reception room and
suddenly there were two old women, and they started twirling on the carpet.
Did that happen or not? Remember how good it was . . ."

"Yes. And do you remember how papa in his dark blue overcoat fired a gun
on the porch?" Smiling with pleasure, they went through their memories, not
sad, old people's memories, but poetic, youthful ones, those impressions from
the very distant past where dream merges with reality, and they laughed softly,
rejoicing at something.

Sonya, as always, lagged behind them, though they had memories in common.

Sonya did not remember much of what they remembered, and what she did remember did not evoke in her the poetic feeling they experienced. She only delighted in their joy, trying to imitate it.

The only moment she took a real part in was when they remembered Sonya's first arrival. Sonya told how she was afraid of Nikolai, because he had a jacket with cords on it, and her nanny told her that she, too, would be stitched with cords.

"And I remember being told that you were born under a cabbage," Natasha said, "and I remember not daring to disbelieve it then, but I knew it wasn't true, and I felt so awkward."

During this conversation, a maid stuck her head in at the back door of the sitting room.

"They've brought the rooster, miss," the girl said in a whisper.

"Never mind, Polya, tell them to take it away," said Natasha.

In the midst of the conversation going on in the sitting room, Dimmler came in and went to the harp that stood in the corner. He took the cloth off it, and the harp gave out a false sound.

"Edward Karlych, please play my favourite *Nocturne* by Monsieur Field,"[9] the voice of the old countess said from the drawing room.

Dimmler struck a chord and, turning to Natasha, Nikolai, and Sonya, said: "You young people sit so quietly!"

"We're philosophizing," said Natasha, glancing at him for a moment, and continuing the conversation. The conversation had gone on to dreams.

Dimmler began to play. Inaudibly, on tiptoe, Natasha went to the table, picked up the candle, took it out, came back, and quietly sat down in her place. The room was dark, especially on the sofa where they were sitting, but the silver light of the full moon fell on the floor through the big windows.

"You know," said Natasha in a whisper, moving closer to Nikolai and Sonya, when Dimmler had finished and still sat there, lightly thrumming the strings, clearly undecided whether to stop or begin something new, "I think that when you remember, remember, remember everything like that, you could go on until you remember what was there before you were in the world."

"That's metempsychosis," said Sonya, who had always been a good student and remembered everything. "The Egyptians believed that our souls were in animals and will go back into animals."

"No, you know, I don't believe we were in animals," Natasha said in the same whisper, though the music had stopped. "I know for certain that we were angels somewhere, and visited here, and so we remember everything . . ."

"May I join you?" asked Dimmler, quietly approaching and sitting down with them.

"If we were angels once, why did we end up lower?" asked Nikolai. "No, that can't be!"

"Not lower, who told you it's lower? . . . How do I know what I used to be?" Natasha objected with conviction. "The soul is immortal . . . which means, if I will live for ever, then I also lived before, lived for the whole eternity."

"Yes, but it's hard for us to imagine eternity," said Dimmler, who had approached the young people with a mildly scornful smile, but was now speaking as softly and seriously as they were.

"Why is it hard to imagine eternity?" asked Natasha. "There will be today, there will be tomorrow, there will be always, and there was yesterday, and there was the day before . . ."

"Natasha, it's your turn now! Sing something for me," said the countess's voice. "Why are you sitting there like conspirators?"

"Mama, I really don't want to!" said Natasha, but at the same time she got up.

None of them, not even the not-so-young Dimmler, wanted to break off the conversation and leave the sitting room, but Natasha got up and Nikolai sat at the clavichord. As always, Natasha stood in the middle of the room, choosing the most advantageous place for resonance, and began to sing her mother's favourite piece.

She had said she did not want to sing, but for a long time before and a long time after she did not sing as she sang that evening. Count Ilya Andreich heard her singing from the study, where he was talking with Mitenka, and, like a schoolboy who finishes his lesson while hurrying to go and play, he became confused as he gave orders to his steward, and finally fell silent, and Mitenka, also listening, stood before the count smiling silently. Nikolai could not take his eyes off his sister and paused for breath together with her. Sonya, listening, thought of what an enormous difference there was between her and her friend, and how impossible it would be for her to be ever so slightly as bewitching as her cousin. The old countess sat with a happily sad smile and tears in her eyes, shaking her head from time to time. She was thinking of Natasha, and of her own youth, and of how there was something unnatural and frightening in this forthcoming marriage of Natasha and Prince Andrei.

Dimmler, having sat down by the countess, closed his eyes and listened.

"No, Countess," he said finally, "that is a European talent, there's nothing for her to learn, that softness, tenderness, power . . ."

"Ah, I'm so afraid for her, so afraid!" said the countess, forgetting whom she was talking with. Her maternal intuition told her that there was too much of something in Natasha, and that because of it she would not be happy. Natasha had not yet finished singing when the enraptured fourteen-year-old Petya came running into the room with news that the mummers had come.

Natasha suddenly stopped.

"Fool!" she shouted at her brother, ran to a chair, fell on it, and burst into such sobbing that she could not stop for a long time. "It's nothing, mama, really, it's nothing—Petya just startled me," she said, trying to smile, but her tears still flowed and sobs choked her.

Servants dressed up as bears, Turks, innkeepers, ladies, frightening and funny, brought cold air and merriment in with them, first huddling timidly in the front hall; then, hiding behind each other, they crowded into the reception room; and, shyly at first, then more merrily and concertedly, songs, jigs, round dances, and Christmas games began. The countess recognized the faces, laughed at the costumes, and went to the drawing room. Count Ilya Andreich sat in the reception room with a beaming smile, approving of the games. The young people disappeared somewhere.

Half an hour later an old lady in a farthingale appeared in the room among the other mummers—this was Nikolai. The Turkish woman was Petya. A clown—this was Dimmler; the hussar was Natasha, and the Circassian was Sonya, with moustache and eyebrows drawn with burnt cork.

After indulgent surprise, non-recognition, and praise from the non-costumed side, the young people decided their disguises were so good that they had to be shown to somebody else.

Nikolai, who wanted to give everyone a ride over the excellent road in his troika, suggested that they take a dozen or so of the dressed-up servants and go to their uncle's.

"Ah, you'll just disturb the old man!" said the countess. "And there's no room to turn round in his place. If you go anywhere, it should be to the Melyukovs'."

Mrs. Melyukov was a widow with children of various ages, along with their governesses and governors, who lived three miles from the Rostovs.

"That, *ma chère,* is a bright idea," the old count picked up, all aroused. "Let me dress up now, and I'll go with you. I'll rouse Pashette, too."

But the countess did not consent to let the count go: he had had a pain in his leg all those days. It was decided that Ilya Andreich should not go, but that if Louisa Ivanovna (Mme Schoss) went, then the young ladies could go to Mrs. Melyukov's. Sonya, always timid and shy, was the most insistent in begging Louisa Ivanovna not to refuse them.

Sonya's outfit was the best of all. Her moustache and eyebrows were remarkably becoming. Everyone told her that she was very beautiful, and she was in an animatedly energetic mood unusual for her. Some inner voice told her that her fate was to be decided that night or never, and in a man's clothes she seemed a completely different person. Louisa Ivanovna consented and in half an hour four troikas with harness bells and sleigh bells, their runners screeching and squeaking over the frosty snow, drove up to the porch.

Natasha first set the tone for the holiday merriment, and that merriment, reflected from one to another, intensified more and more, and reached its highest point at the moment when they all went out into the cold and, talking, calling out to each other, laughing, and shouting, got into the sleighs.

Two of the troikas were for everyday driving; the third was the old count's, with an Orel trotter in the shafts; the fourth was Nikolai's own, with a small, shaggy black shaft horse. Nikolai, in his old lady's outfit, over which he put a belted hussar's cape, stood in the middle of his sleigh with a short grip on the reins.

It was so bright that he could see the harness plates gleaming in the moonlight and the eyes of the horses glancing fearfully at their passengers, who were making a great noise under the dark roof of the porch.

Natasha, Sonya, Mme Schoss, and two maids got into Nikolai's sleigh. Dimmler, his wife, and Petya got into the old count's sleigh; the dressed-up servants got into the other two.

"You go ahead, Zakhar!" Nikolai cried to his father's coachman, so as to have the chance to outrun him on the road.

The old count's troika, with Dimmler and the other mummers, set off ahead, its runners screeching as if freezing to the snow, its deep-toned bell clanging. The outrunners pressed themselves to the shafts and sank deeply, churning up the snow, compact and sparkling like sugar.

Nikolai set out after the first troika; behind him the rest came rattling and screeching. At first they went at a slow trot along the narrow road. As they drove past the garden, shadows from the bare trees often lay across the road and obscured the bright light of the moon, but as soon as they drove beyond the fence, a plain of snow, sparkling like diamonds, with a dove-blue sheen, bathed in moonlight and motionless, opened out on all sides. Once, twice the front sleigh jolted over a bump; the next sleigh jolted in the same way, then the next, and, boldly breaking the frost-bound stillness, the sleighs strung out one after the other.

"Hare's tracks, lots of them!" Natasha's voice rang out in the frost-bound air.

"How clear it is, Nicolas!" Sonya's voice said. Nikolai turned to look at Sonya and bent down to see her face more closely. A totally new, dear face with black eyebrows and moustache, both near and distant in the moonlight, peeked from the sable fur.

"That used to be Sonya," thought Nikolai. He looked at her more closely and smiled.

"What is it, Nicolas?"

"Nothing," he said and turned to the horses again.

Having driven out to the smooth high road, slicked down by runners and all cut up by the tracks of calked horseshoes, visible in the moonlight, the horses began to pull at the reins and speed up by themselves. The left outrunner, thrusting its head back, leaped and tugged at its traces. The shaft horse swayed, twitching its ears, as if asking: "Shall we start? Or is it still too early?" Ahead, already far away and clanging its deep-toned bell, Zakhar's black troika was clearly visible against the white snow. From his sleigh came shouts and laughter and the voices of the mummers.

"Well, now, my gentles!" cried Nikolai, tugging the reins to one side and raising the whip in his hand. And only by the keener wind that seemed to rush at them, and by the straining tug and ever-increasing gallop of the outrunners, could they tell how quickly the troika was flying. Nikolai turned and looked back. The other troikas hastened after them, with shouting and shrieking, the waving of whips and urging on of the shaft horses. His shaft horse rolled steadily under the bow, not even thinking of slowing down, but promising to push on more and more when necessary.

Nikolai caught up with the first troika. They drove down some sort of hill and came out on a wide trampled road across a meadow by the river.

"Where are we going?" thought Nikolai. "Across Sloping Meadow, it must be. But no, this is something new, I've never seen it before. This isn't Sloping Meadow, or Diomkin Hill, it's God knows what! It's something new and magical. Well, whatever!" And, urging his horses on, he began to pass the first troika.

Zakhar reined in his horses and turned his face, already covered with hoarfrost up to the eyebrows.

Nikolai gave his horses free rein; Zakhar, stretching his arms forward, clucked his tongue and let his own go.

"Hold on now, master," he said. The troikas flew on still faster side by side, and faster moved the legs of the galloping horses. Nikolai began to pull ahead. Zakhar, without changing the position of his outstretched arms, raised the hand that held the reins.

"No you don't, master," he cried to Nikolai. Nikolai sent his horses into a gallop and outstripped Zakhar. The horses sent a spray of fine, dry snow into the faces of the passengers; beside them was a rapid tinkling of bells and the tangle of quickly moving legs and shadows of the troika they were outstripping. From all sides came women's shrieks and the whistle of runners over snow.

Stopping his horses again, Nikolai looked around. Around him was the same magical plain drenched in moonlight, with stars strewn over it.

"Zakhar is shouting that I should turn to the left, but why to the left?" Nikolai wondered. "Are we driving to the Melyukovs'? Can this be Melyukovka? We're driving God knows where, and God knows what's going on with us—and it's very strange and good, what's going on with us." He glanced back into the sleigh.

"Look, his moustache and eyelashes are all white," said one of those strange, pretty, and unfamiliar-looking people with fine eyebrows and moustache.

"That one, I think, was Natasha," thought Nikolai, "and that one Mme Schoss, or maybe not; and this Circassian with the moustache—I don't know who she is, but I love her."

"Aren't you cold?" he asked. They did not reply and burst out laughing. Dimmler shouted something from the sleigh behind, probably something funny, but it was impossible to hear what it was.

"Yes, yes," voices answered, laughing.

Here, however, is some sort of magical forest with flowing dark shadows and the sparkle of diamonds, and with flights of some sort of marble steps, and magical buildings with some sort of silver roofs, and the piercing shrieks of some sort of animals. "And if this is indeed Melyukovka, then it's all the more strange that we drove God knows where and arrived at Melyukovka," thought Nikolai.

It actually was Melyukovka, and maids and footmen with candles and joyful faces ran out to the porch.

"Who are you?" they asked from the porch.

"Mummers from the count's, I can see by the horses," voices replied.

XI

Pelageya Danilovna Melyukov, a broad, energetic woman in spectacles and an open housecoat, was sitting in the drawing room, surrounded by her daughters, whom she was trying to keep from being bored. They were quietly pouring wax and looking at the shadows of the figures that emerged,[10] when the footsteps and voices of the visitors were heard in the front hall.

Hussars, ladies, witches, clowns, bears, clearing their throats and wiping their frost-covered faces in the front hall, came into the reception room, where candles were hastily lighted. The clown Dimmler and the lady Nikolai opened the dance. Surrounded by shouting children, the mummers, covering their faces and altering their voices, bowed before the hostess and took their places in the room.

"Ah, it's impossible to recognize them! And Natasha! See what she looks like! She really looks like somebody. And Edward Karlych is something! I didn't recognize him. How well he dances! Ah, dear me, there's a Circassian here, too; it really suits you, Sonyushka. And who's this one? Well, how amusing! Nikita, Vanya, take the tables away. And we were sitting here so quietly!"

"Ha, ha, ha! . . . That hussar, that hussar! Just like a boy, and the legs! . . . I can't stand it! . . ." voices said.

Natasha, the young Melyukovs' favourite, disappeared with them into the back room, asking to be brought cork and various house robes and men's clothing, which the girls' bare arms received from a footman through a slightly open door. In ten minutes all the young people of the Melyukov family had joined the mummers.

Pelageya Danilovna, having ordered a space cleared for the guests and snacks served to the masters and servants, not removing her spectacles, with a suppressed smile, walked among the mummers, looking closely at their faces and not recognizing anybody. She not only did not recognize the Rostovs or Dimmler, but she could not recognize her own daughters, or her husband's robes and uniforms, which they were wearing.

"And who's this one?" she said, addressing her governess and looking into the face of her daughter, who was dressed as a Kazan Tartar. "Seems to be one of the Rostovs. Well, and you, Mister Hussar, which regiment do you serve in?" she asked Natasha. "That Turk, give that Turk some fruit jelly," she said to the butler with a tray, "their law doesn't prohibit it."

Sometimes, looking at the strange but funny steps the dancers made, having decided once and for all that, as they were dressed up, no one could recognize them, and therefore not feeling embarrassed—Pelageya Danilovna covered her face with her handkerchief, and her whole corpulent body shook with unrestrainable, kindly, old-woman's laughter.

"Sashinette, look at my Sashinette!" she said.

After Russian dances and singing, Pelageya Danilovna joined all the servants and masters together in one big circle; they brought a ring, a piece of string, and a one-rouble coin, and played games together.

An hour later all the costumes were crumpled and disordered. The burnt cork moustaches and eyebrows were smeared over sweaty, flushed, and merry faces. Pelageya Danilovna began to recognize the mummers, admired how well the costumes had been made, how they especially suited the young ladies, and thanked them all for entertaining her so well. The guests were invited for supper in the drawing room, and food was arranged for the servants in the reception room.

"No, fortune-telling in the bathhouse, that's the scary thing!" an old maid who lived with the Melyukovs said over supper.

"Why so?" asked the eldest Melyukov daughter.

"You wouldn't go, it takes courage . . ."

"I'd go," said Sonya.

"Tell us what happened with that young lady?" the second Melyukov girl said.

"Here's what," said the old maid. "A girl once went, took a cock, set the table for two—all very proper—and sat down. She sat for a while, only suddenly she hears . . . harness bells, sleigh bells, a sleigh drives up; she hears him coming. He walks in, looking just like a man, like an officer, goes over, and sits down with her at the table."

"Ah! Ah! ..." Natasha cried, rolling her eyes in terror.

"But how was he, could he speak?"

"Yes, like a man, everything as it should be, and so he started, he started persuading her, and she should have kept him busy talking till cockcrow, but she got timid; she just got timid and covered her face with her hands. So he up and grabbed her. It's a good thing the maids came running in right then ..."

"Now, why go scaring them!" said Pelageya Danilovna.

"Mother, you did fortune-telling yourself ..." said the daughter.

"And how do you tell fortunes in a barn?" asked Sonya.

"You could do it even now. You go to the barn and listen. If you hear banging or knocking, it's bad; if you hear grain pouring, it's good. But it also happens ..."

"Mama, tell us what happened to you in the barn."

Pelageya Danilovna smiled.

"Why, I've forgotten by now ..." she said. "None of you would go, would you?"

"No, I'll go. Let me, Pelageya Danilovna, I'll go," said Sonya.

"All right, go, if you're not afraid."

"May I, Louisa Ivanovna?" asked Sonya.

Whether playing with the ring, the string, or the rouble coin, or talking as they were now, Nikolai never left Sonya's side and looked at her with totally new eyes. It seemed to him that it was only today, for the first time, owing to that cork moustache, that he had known her fully. Indeed, that evening Sonya was merrier, livelier, and prettier than Nikolai had ever seen her before.

"So this is how she is, and I'm a fool!" he thought, looking at her shining eyes and happy, rapturous smile, such as he had never seen before, which made dimples on her cheeks under the moustache.

"I'm not afraid of anything," said Sonya. "May I go now?" She got up. They told Sonya where the barn was, how she should stand silently and listen, and gave her her coat. She threw it over her head and glanced at Nikolai.

"What a lovely girl she is!" he thought. "And what have I been thinking about all this time!"

Sonya went out to the corridor, so as to go to the barn. Nikolai hastily went to the front porch, saying that he was hot. Indeed, it was stuffy in the house because of the crowd of people.

Outside there was the same immobile cold, the same moon, only it was still brighter. The light was so strong and there were so many stars on the snow, that one did not want to look at the sky, and the real stars went unnoticed. The sky was black and dull, the earth was merry.

"Fool, fool that I am! What have I been waiting for all this time?" thought

Nikolai, and, running down from the porch, he went round the corner of the house and along the path that led to the back porch. He knew Sonya would pass that way. Halfway down the path there lay some stacked firewood; it was covered with snow and cast a shadow; the shadows of bare old lindens, intertwining, fell across and beside it on the snow and on the path. The path led to the barn. The log wall of the barn and the snow-covered roof gleamed in the moonlight as if cut from some precious stone. A tree cracked in the garden, and again everything was perfectly silent. His breast seemed to breathe in, not air, but some eternally young strength and joy.

There was a patter of feet on the steps of the servants' porch, a loud creak on the last step, where the snow lay drifted, and the old maid's voice said:

"Straight, straight down that path, miss. Only don't look back!"

"I'm not afraid," Sonya's voice replied, and her little feet, screeching and squeaking in their thin shoes, went down the path towards Nikolai.

Sonya walked wrapped in her fur coat. She was two steps away before she saw him; she also saw him not as she had known him and had always been a little afraid of him. He was in a woman's dress, with tousled hair and a happy smile that was new for Sonya. Sonya quickly ran to him.

"Quite different and yet the same," thought Nikolai, looking at her face all lit up by the moonlight. He slipped his hands under the coat that covered her head, embraced her, pressed her to him, and kissed her on the lips, which had a moustache on them and smelled of burnt cork. Sonya kissed him right in the middle of the lips and, freeing her small hands, put them to his cheeks.

"Sonya! . . . Nicolas! . . ." was all they said. They ran to the barn and came back, each by a separate porch.

XII

When they all set out for home from Pelageya Danilovna's, Natasha, who always saw and noticed everything, arranged it so that she and Louisa Ivanovna got into the sleigh with Dimmler, and Sonya got in with Nikolai and the maids.

Nikolai, no longer racing, drove smoothly on the way back and, in that strange moonlight, kept peering at Sonya, seeking, in that ever-changing light, behind the eyebrows and moustache, the former and the present Sonya, from whom he had now resolved never to be parted. He peered, and, when he recognized the same one and the other and remembered the smell of cork mixed with the feeling of the kiss, he drew in the frosty air and, gazing at the earth speeding past and the brilliant sky, he again felt himself in a magical kingdom.

"Do you feel good, Sonya?" he asked now and then.

"Yes," replied Sonya, "and you?"

In the middle of the way, Nikolai handed the horses over to the coachman, ran to Natasha's sleigh for a moment, and stood on the fender.

"Natasha," he whispered to her in French, "you know, I've made up my mind about Sonya."

"Have you told her?" asked Natasha, suddenly all beaming with joy.

"Ah, Natasha, you're so strange with that moustache and those eyebrows! Are you glad?"

"I'm so glad, so glad! I was getting angry with you. I didn't tell you, but you behaved badly towards her. She's such a heart, Nicolas, I'm so glad! I can be nasty, but I was ashamed to be happy alone, without Sonya," Natasha went on. "Now I'm so glad! Well, run to her."

"No, wait, ah, how funny you are!" said Nikolai, peering at her and finding in his sister as well something new, unusual, and enchantingly tender, which he had not seen in her before. "Natasha, it's something magical, isn't it?"

"Yes," she said, "you've done a wonderful thing."

"If I'd seen her before as she is now," thought Nikolai, "I'd have asked her long ago what I should do, and I'd have done whatever she told me, and everything would be right."

"So you're glad, and I've done right?"

"Oh, so right! I recently quarrelled with mama about it. Mama said she was trying to snare you. How could she say that! I nearly had a fight with mama. And I'll never let anybody say or think anything bad about her, because there's nothing but good in her."

"So it's right?" said Nikolai, once more searching into the expression of his sister's face to find out if it was true, and, his boots creaking, he jumped off the fender and ran to his sleigh. The same happy, smiling Circassian with a little moustache and shining eyes, looking from under a sable hood, sat there, and this Circassian was Sonya, and this Sonya was certainly his future happy and loving wife.

Having come home and told their mother how they spent the time at the Melyukovs', the girls went to their room. They undressed, but without wiping off their cork moustaches, and sat for a long time talking about their happiness. They talked about how they would live when they were married, how their husbands would be friends, and how they would be happy. Mirrors prepared by Dunyasha since evening stood on Natasha's table.

"Only when will it all be? Never, I'm afraid . . . It would be too good!" said Natasha, getting up and going over to the mirrors.

"Sit down, Natasha, maybe you'll see him," said Sonya. Natasha lit the candles and sat down.

"I see someone with a moustache," said Natasha, seeing her own face.

"Don't laugh, miss," said Dunyasha.

With the help of Sonya and the maid, Natasha found the right position for the mirror; her face acquired a grave expression, and she fell silent. For a long time she sat looking at the row of candles going into the depths of the mirrors, supposing (according to stories she had heard) that she would see a coffin, or that she would see *him*, Prince Andrei, in that last dim, blurry square. But however ready she was to take the smallest spot for the image of a man or a coffin, she saw nothing. She started blinking rapidly and left the mirror.

"Why is it others see things, and I don't?" she said. "Well, you sit down, Sonya; you must do it tonight," she said. "In my place . . . I feel so frightened tonight!"

Sonya sat down before the mirror, got into the right position, and began to look.

"Now, Sofya Alexandrovna's sure to see something," Dunyasha said in a whisper, "because you just laugh all the time."

Sonya heard those words and heard Natasha say in a whisper:

"And I know she'll see something; she did last year."

For about three minutes they were all silent. "She's sure to!" Natasha whispered and did not finish . . . Suddenly Sonya moved away the mirror she was holding and covered her eyes with her hand.

"Ah, Natasha!" she said.

"Did you see something? Did you? What did you see?" Natasha cried.

"I told you so," said Dunyasha, holding up the mirror.

Sonya had not seen anything, she had been just about to blink her eyes and get up when she heard Natasha's voice say "She's sure to . . ." She did not want to disappoint either Dunyasha or Natasha, and it was hard to go on sitting there. She did not know how and why that cry had escaped her when she covered her eyes with her hand.

"Did you see him?" asked Natasha, seizing her hand.

"Yes. Wait . . . I . . . saw him," Sonya said involuntarily, still not knowing who Natasha meant by *him*: *him* Nikolai, or *him* Andrei.

"But why shouldn't I say what I saw? Other people see things! And who can catch me out about whether I did or didn't see anything?" flashed in Sonya's head.

"Yes, I saw him," she said.

"How? How? Standing up or lying down?"

"No, I saw . . . First there was nothing, then I suddenly saw him lying down."

"Andrei lying down? Is he sick?" Natasha asked, looking at her friend with fearfully fixed eyes.

"No, quite the opposite—he had a cheerful face, and he turned to me," and the moment she said it, she herself thought she had seen what she said.

"And then, Sonya?"

"Then I didn't quite see, there was something blue and red . . ."

"Sonya! When will he come back? When will I see him? My God, how I fear for him and for myself, and I'm frightened about everything . . ." Natasha said, and, without a word of reply to Sonya's consolations, she went to bed and, long after the candle was put out, lay motionless, open-eyed, on her bed, looking at the frosty moonlight through the windows.

XIII

Soon after Christmastime, Nikolai told his mother about his love for Sonya and his firm decision to marry her. The countess, who had long noticed what was happening between Sonya and Nikolai, and had been expecting this talk, listened silently to his words and said to her son that he could marry whomever he wanted, but that neither she nor his father would give their blessing to such a marriage. For the first time, Nikolai felt that his mother was displeased with him, and that, despite all her love for him, she would not yield. Coldly and without looking at her son, she sent for her husband; and when he came, the countess was going to tell him, briefly and coldly, in Nikolai's presence, what the matter was, but she could not stand it: she wept tears of vexation and left the room. The old count began hesitantly to admonish Nikolai and beg him to renounce his intention. Nikolai replied that he could not go back on his word, and his father sighed and, obviously embarrassed, very quickly broke off their talk and went to the countess. In all his confrontations with his son, the count had always been aware of his guilt before him for the disorder of his affairs, and therefore he could not be angry with his son for his refusal to marry a rich bride and his choice of the dowerless Sonya—he only remembered more vividly that, if their affairs had not been in disorder, they could not have hoped for a better wife for Nikolai than Sonya; and that he alone, with his Mitenka and his insuperable habits, was to blame for the disorder of their affairs.

The father and mother spoke no further with their son about this matter; but several days later the countess summoned Sonya to her and, with a cruelty neither of them expected, reproached her niece for luring her son away and for ingratitude. Sonya listened to the countess's cruel words silently, with lowered eyes, and did not understand what was being demanded of her. She was ready to sacrifice everything for her benefactors. The thought of self-sacrifice was her favourite thought; but in this case she could not understand to whom and what she must sacrifice. She could not help loving the countess and the whole Rostov family, but neither could she help loving Nikolai and knowing that his happiness depended on that love. She was silent and sad and made no reply. Nikolai, as it seemed to him, could not bear this situation any longer and went to talk with his mother. Nikolai first begged his mother to forgive him and Sonya and agree to their marriage, then threatened his mother that, if Sonya was persecuted, he would secretly marry her at once.

The countess, with a coldness such as her son had never seen, replied to him that he was of age, that Prince Andrei was going to marry without his father's consent, and that he could do the same, but that she would never recognize this *intriguer* as her daughter.

At the word *intriguer,* Nikolai exploded, raised his voice, and said to his mother that he had never thought she would make him sell his feelings, and that if it was so, he was saying for the last time . . . But he had no time to say the decisive word, which, judging by the expression on her face, his mother anticipated with horror, and which might have remained a bitter memory between them for ever. He had no time to finish, because Natasha, with a pale and serious face, came into the room from the door behind which she had been eavesdropping.

"Nikolenka, you're talking nonsense—keep quiet, keep quiet! Keep quiet, I tell you!" she almost shouted, in order to drown out his voice.

"Mama, darling, it's not at all because of . . . my poor, dear heart," she was saying to her mother, who, feeling herself on the verge of a break-up, looked at her son with horror, but, being stubborn and carried away by the struggle, would not and could not give in.

"Nikolenka, I'll explain, you just go . . . Listen, mama darling," she said to her mother.

Her words were meaningless, but they achieved the result she was striving for.

The countess, sobbing heavily, hid her face on her daughter's breast, and Nikolai got up, clutched his head, and left the room.

Natasha took up the cause of reconciliation and brought it to a point where Nikolai obtained his mother's promise that Sonya would not be oppressed, and promised himself that he would not undertake anything in secret from his parents.

With the firm intention of settling his affairs in the regiment, resigning from the service, coming home and marrying Sonya, Nikolai, sad and serious, in discord with his family, but, as it seemed to him, passionately in love, left for his regiment at the beginning of January.

After Nikolai's departure, the Rostovs' house became sadder than ever. The countess was so emotionally upset that she fell ill.

Sonya grieved both at being parted from Nikolai and still more at the hostile tone with which the countess could not help treating her. The count was more preoccupied than ever with the bad state of his affairs, which called for some decisive measures. It was necessary to sell the Moscow house and nearby estate, and to sell the house it was necessary to go to Moscow. But because of the countess's health, they had to put off the departure from day to day.

Natasha, who had borne the initial time of her separation from her fiancé lightly and even cheerfully, now grew more and more troubled and impatient with every day. The thought that her best time, which she could have used in loving him, was being wasted like that, for nothing, tormented her unremit-tingly. His letters mostly made her angry. It offended her to think that, while she lived only by thoughts of him, he was living a real life, seeing new places and new people who interested him. The more diverting his letters were, the more vexed she felt. Her own letters to him not only did not furnish her with any comfort, but were a boring and false duty. She was unable to write, because she could not conceive the possibility of truthfully expressing in a let-ter even a thousandth part of what she was used to expressing with her voice, smile, and gaze. She wrote him classically monotonous, dry letters, to which she herself did not ascribe any significance, and in the drafts of which the countess corrected the spelling errors.

The countess's health still did not improve; but it was no longer possible to put off the trip to Moscow. A dowry had to be prepared, the house had to be sold, and, besides, Prince Andrei was first expected in Moscow, where Prince Nikolai Andreich was spending that winter, and Natasha was sure that he had already arrived.

The countess stayed in the country, and the count, taking Sonya and Natasha with him, went to Moscow at the end of January.

Part Five

I

After the engagement of Prince Andrei and Natasha, Pierre, without any obvious reason, suddenly felt the impossibility of going on with his former life. However firmly convinced he was of the truths revealed to him by his benefactor, however joyful for him had been that first time of enthusiastic inner work of self-improvement, to which he had given himself with such ardour—after Prince Andrei's betrothal to Natasha, and after the death of Iosif Alexeevich, of which he received news at almost the same time, the whole charm of that former life suddenly vanished for him. Only the skeleton of life remained: his house with his brilliant wife, who now enjoyed the favours of an important person; acquaintance with all Petersburg; and service with its dull formalities. And that former life suddenly presented itself to Pierre with unexpected vileness. He ceased writing in his diary, avoided the company of the brothers, began going to the club again, began drinking heavily again, became close again with bachelor companies, and began leading such a life that Elena Vassilievna felt it necessary to reprimand him sternly. Pierre felt that she was right and, to avoid compromising his wife, left for Moscow.

In Moscow, as soon as he moved into his huge house with the dried- and drying-up princesses, with its enormous staff, as soon as he saw—on driving through the city—the Iverskaya Chapel[1] with countless candles burning before the gold casing, saw the Kremlin Square with its untrampled snow, the cabbies, the hovels of the Sivtsev Vrazhek, saw old Moscow men, who desired nothing and were not hurrying anywhere as they lived out their lives, saw little old women, Moscow ladies, Moscow balls, and the Moscow English Club—he felt himself at home, in a quiet haven. For him Moscow was comfortable, warm, habitual, and dirty, like an old dressing gown.

All Moscow society, from old women to children, received Pierre like a long-awaited guest, whose place was always kept ready and vacant. For Moscow society, Pierre was the most dear, kind, intelligent, merry, and magnanimous of eccentrics, absent-minded and warm-hearted, a Russian squire of the old stamp. His purse was always empty, because it was open to everyone.

Benefit performances, bad paintings and statues, philanthropic societies, Gypsies, schools, subscription dinners, carousing, the Masons, churches, books—no one and nothing met with refusal, and had it not been for two friends of his, who had borrowed a good deal of money from him and taken him under their tutelage, he would have given everything away. No evening or dinner at the club could do without him. As soon as he dropped into his place on the sofa after two bottles of Margaux, he was surrounded, and the talk, arguments, and jokes began. Where people quarrelled, he—merely by his kindly smile and an appropriately uttered joke—made peace. Dinners at the Masonic lodges were dull and sluggish if he was not there.

When, after a bachelor supper, with a sweet and kindly smile, yielding to the entreaties of the merry company, he got up to go with them, joyful, triumphant cries came from the young men. At balls he danced, if there was a need for partners. The young ladies and girls liked him, because, without paying court to anyone, he was equally amiable with them all, especially after supper. *"Il est charmant, il n'a pas de sexe,"** they said of him.

Pierre was one of those retired gentlemen-in-waiting of whom there were hundreds good-naturedly living out their lives in Moscow.

How horrified he would have been if, seven years ago, when he had just come from abroad, someone had told him that there was no need to seek or invent anything, that his rut had long been carved out for him and determined from all eternity, and that, however he twisted and turned, he would be that which everybody was in his position. He could not have believed it. Had he not wished with all his soul to establish a republic in Russia, then to become a Napoleon himself, a philosopher, a tactician, the defeater of Napoleon? Had he not seen the possibility and passionately wished to transform depraved mankind and bring his own self to the highest degree of perfection? Had he not established schools and hospitals and liberated his peasants?

But instead of all that, here he was—the rich husband of an unfaithful wife, a retired gentleman-in-waiting, who liked to eat, drink, and, unbuttoning himself, to denounce the government a little, a member of the Moscow English Club, and a universally beloved member of Moscow society. For a long time he could not reconcile himself to the thought that he was that very same retired Moscow gentleman-in-waiting the type of which he had so deeply despised seven years ago.

He sometimes comforted himself with the thought that he happened to be leading this life just so, in the meantime; but then he would be horrified by another thought, that it was just so, in the meantime, that so many people had entered this life, this club, as he had, with all their teeth and hair, and come out of it with not a single tooth or hair left.

In moments of pride, when he thought of his position, it seemed to him that he was quite different, distinct from those retired gentlemen-in-waiting whom he had formerly despised, that they were banal and stupid, content and at

*He's charming, he has no sex.

peace in their position, "while I am not at all content even now, and keep wanting to do something for mankind," he said to himself in moments of pride. "And maybe all these comrades of mine struggled just like me, sought some new path of their own in life, and, just like me, by force of circumstances, society, breeding, by that elemental force against which man is powerless, were brought to where I am now," he said to himself in moments of modesty, and, having lived in Moscow for a time, he no longer despised, but was beginning to love, respect, and pity his comrades in fate as he did himself.

Pierre was not, as formerly, overcome by moments of despair, spleen, and loathing for life; but the same illness that formerly expressed itself in abrupt fits was now driven inside and never left him for a moment. "What for? Why? What's going on in the world?" he asked himself with perplexity several times a day, involuntarily beginning to ponder the meaning of life's phenomena; but knowing from experience that there were no answers to these questions, he hastily attempted to turn away from them, picked up a book, or hurried off to the club or to Apollon Nikolaevich's to chat about the gossip of the town.

"Elena Vassilievna, who has never loved anything except her own body, and is one of the stupidest women in the world," thought Pierre, "appears to people as the height of intelligence and finesse, and they bow down to her. Napoleon Bonaparte was scorned by everyone as long as he was great, but now that he's become a pathetic comedian, the emperor Franz seeks to offer him his daughter as an illegitimate wife.[2] The Spanish offer up prayers to God through the Catholic clergy in thanksgiving for having defeated the French on the fourteenth of June, and the French offer up prayers through the same Catholic clergy for having defeated the Spanish on the fourteenth of June.[3] My brother Masons swear in blood that they are ready to sacrifice everything for their neighbour, but they won't pay a single rouble into the collection for the poor and have Astrea intrigue against the Manna Seekers, and fuss over an authentic Scottish rug and about charters the meaning of which is unknown even to those who wrote them and which nobody needs.[4] We all confess the Christian law of forgiveness of offences and love of one's neighbour, a law in consequence of which we have erected forty times forty churches in Moscow—but yesterday a deserter was flogged to death, and a priest, a servant of that same law of love and forgiveness, gave him the cross to kiss before the execution." So Pierre reflected, and accustomed as he was to it, this whole general, universally acknowledged lie amazed him each time like something new. "I understand this lie and confusion," he thought, "but how can I tell them all that I understand it? I've tried, and I've always found that in the depths of their souls, they understand the same thing I do, but they simply try not to see *it*. Therefore it must be so! But I, what am I to do with myself?" Pierre thought. He experienced the unfortunate ability of many people, especially Russians—the ability to see and believe in the possibility of goodness and truth, and to see the evil and falsehood of life too clearly to be able to participate in it seriously. Every sphere of work was, in his eyes, bound up with evil and deceit. Whatever he tried to be, whatever he undertook—evil and falsehood repulsed him and barred him from all paths of activity. And yet he had to live, he had to keep busy. It was too frightening to be under the burden of all the insoluble questions of life, and he gave himself to the first amusements that came along, only so as to forget them. He frequented every possible society, drank heavily, bought paintings, built, but, above all, he read.

He read, he read everything that came to hand, so that, on coming home, while the footmen were still undressing him, he would take up a book and read—and from reading he would pass into sleep, and from sleep to chatter in drawing rooms and the club, from chatter to carousing and women, from carousing back to chatter, reading, and wine. Drinking wine became more and more of a physical and at the same time moral need for him. Though the doctors told him that, with his corpulence, wine was dangerous for him, he drank a great deal. He felt perfectly well only when, without noticing how, having poured several glasses of wine into his large mouth, he experienced a pleasant warmth in his body, an affection towards all his neighbours, and a mental readiness to respond superficially to every thought, without going deeply into its essence. Only when he had drunk a bottle or two of wine did he become dimly aware that the tangled, terrible knot of life, which had formerly terrified him, was not as frightening as it seemed to him. With a buzzing in his head, chattering, listening to conversation, or reading after dinner and supper, he constantly saw that knot from some one of its sides. But only under the influence of wine did he say to himself: "Never mind. I'll disentangle it—I've got a ready explanation right here. But I have no time now—I'll think it all over later!" But this *later* never came.

On an empty stomach, in the morning, all the old questions seemed as insoluble and frightening as ever, and Pierre would hastily seize a book and was glad when somebody came to see him.

Sometimes Pierre remembered stories he had heard about how soldiers at war, taking cover under enemy fire, when there is nothing to do, try to find some occupation for themselves so as to endure the danger more easily. And to Pierre all people seemed to be such soldiers, saving themselves from life: some with ambition, some with cards, some with drafting laws, some with women, some with playthings, some with horses, some with politics, some with hunting, some with wine, some with affairs of state. "Nothing is either trivial or important, it's all the same; only save yourself from it as best you can!" thought Pierre. "Only not to see *it,* that dreadful *it!*"

II

At the beginning of winter, Prince Nikolai Andreich Bolkonsky came to Moscow with his daughter. Because of his past, because of his intelligence and originality, and especially because of the weakening just then of the raptures over the reign of Alexander I, and because of the anti-French and patriotic tendencies which reigned at that time in Moscow, Prince Nikolai Andreich at once became an object of special deference among the Muscovites and the centre of Moscow opposition to the government.

The prince had aged very much that year. Distinct signs of senility appeared in him: falling asleep unexpectedly, a forgetfulness of recent events and a good memory of those long past, and the childish vanity with which he accepted the role of head of the Moscow opposition. Despite which, when the old man, especially in the evenings, came out to tea in his fur-trimmed jacket and powdered wig and, prompted by someone, began his curt stories of the past or his still more curt and cutting opinions of the present, he aroused in all his guests the same feeling of deferential respect. For his visitors, the whole of that old house, with its enormous pier glasses, its pre-revolutionary furniture, those powdered footmen, and the tough and intelligent old man, himself of the previous century, with his meek daughter and the pretty little Frenchwoman, who both stood in awe of him, presented a majestically agreeable spectacle. But the visitors did not consider that, besides those two or three hours during which they saw their hosts, there were another twenty-two hours in the day during which the secret inner life of the house went on.

Lately in Moscow that inner life had become very painful for Princess Marya. She was deprived in Moscow of her best joys—conversations with the people of God and solitude, which refreshed her in Bald Hills—nor did she have any of the advantages or joys of life in the capital. She did not go into society; everybody knew that her father would not let her go without him, and he could not go on account of ill health, and so she was never invited to dinners or soirées. Princess Marya had completely abandoned all hope of getting married. She saw the coldness and animosity with which Prince Nikolai Andreich received and sent away the young men, possible suitors, who occasionally appeared in their house. Princess Marya had no friends. During this time in Moscow, she had become disappointed in the two persons closest to her: Mlle Bourienne, with whom she could not be fully candid even before, now became disagreeable to her, and she, for certain reasons, began to withdraw from her; Julie, who lived in Moscow and with whom Princess Marya had corresponded for the last five years, turned out to be totally foreign to her when Princess Marya met her again in person. At that time Julie, who, owing to the deaths of her brothers, had become one of the richest prospective brides in Moscow, was in the full whirl of society pleasures. She was surrounded by young men who, she thought, had suddenly come to appreciate her merits. Julie had reached that stage when a young lady of society feels that her last chance to marry has come and her fate must be decided now or never. On Thursday, Princess Marya remembered with a sad smile that she now had no one to write to, since Julie, Julie whose presence brought her no joy, was there, and she saw her every week. Like the old émigré who refused to marry a lady with whom he had been spending his evenings for several years, because, once married, he would not know where to spend his evenings, she was sorry that Julie was there and that she had no one to write to. Princess Marya had no one in Moscow with whom she could talk, no one to whom she could confide her grief, and many new griefs had been added on during that time. The date of Prince Andrei's return and marriage was approaching, and his request that she prepare their father for it had not only not been fulfilled, but the matter, on the contrary, seemed to have deteriorated completely, and any reminder of Countess Rostov put the old prince beside himself, and he was almost always in a bad mood as it was. A new grief recently added to Princess Marya's burden was the lessons she gave to her six-year-old nephew. In her relations with Nikolushka, she recognized in herself with horror the quality of her father's irritability. No matter how many times she told herself that she must not allow herself to get angry while teaching her nephew, almost every time she sat down with a pointer over the French reader, she wanted so much to pour her knowledge quickly and easily from herself into the child, who was already afraid that his aunt was about to get angry, that at the least inattention on the boy's part, she jumped, hurried, became angry, raised her voice, sometimes pulled his arm, and made him stand in the corner. Having stood him in the corner, she herself would begin to weep over her wicked, bad character, and Nikolushka, imitating her weeping, would leave the corner without permission, come over to her, pull her wet hands away from her face, and comfort her. But the greatest, the greatest of all the princess's griefs, came from her father's irritability, which was always directed against her and lately had reached the point of cruelty. If he had made her bow to the ground all night, if he had beaten her, made her carry firewood and water, it would not even have occurred to her that her position was difficult; but this loving tormentor—the more cruel because he loved her and because of that tormented himself and her—knew not only how to insult and humiliate her deliberately, but also how to prove to her that she was always to blame for everything. Lately a new feature had appeared in him which tormented Princess Marya most of all—this was his increasing intimacy with Mlle Bourienne. The thought, which had occurred to him as a joke when he received news of his son's intention, that if Andrei got married, he himself would marry Bourienne, was evidently to his liking, and lately, only in order to insult her (as it seemed to Princess Marya), he had stubbornly shown a special affection for Mlle Bourienne, and had shown his displeasure with his daughter by showing his liking for Bourienne.

One day in Moscow, in Princess Marya's presence (it seemed to her that he did it in front of her on purpose), the old prince kissed Mlle Bourienne's hand, pulled her to him, and embraced her affectionately. Princess Marya flared up and ran out of the room. A few moments later, Mlle Bourienne came into Princess Marya's room smiling and talking about something cheerfully in her pleasant voice. Princess Marya hastily wiped her tears, went up to Bourienne with resolute steps, and, apparently not realizing it herself, began shouting at the Frenchwoman with wrathful haste and a breaking voice:

"It's vile, low, inhuman to take advantage of the weakness . . ." She did not finish. "Get out of my room," she cried and burst into sobs.

The next day the prince did not say a word to his daughter; but she noticed that over dinner he ordered the food served starting with Mlle Bourienne. At the end of dinner, when the butler, out of old habit, again served the coffee starting with the princess, the prince suddenly flew into a rage, flung his cane at Filipp, and at once gave orders for him to be sent as a soldier.

"They don't hear . . . I told them twice! . . . they don't hear! She's the first person in this house; she's my best friend," cried the prince. "And," he shouted wrathfully, addressing Princess Marya for the first time, "if you allow yourself once more, as you did yesterday . . . to forget yourself before her, I'll show you who is master in this house. Out! I don't want to see you! Apologize to her!"

Princess Marya apologized to Amalia Evgenievna and to her father for herself and for the butler Filipp, who asked her to intercede for him.

At such moments a feeling resembling the pride of sacrifice gathered in Princess Marya's soul. And suddenly at those same moments, in her presence, this father whom she had judged would either search for his spectacles, fumbling just next to them and not seeing them, or forget what had just happened, or make a false step with his weakening legs and look around to see if anyone had noticed his weakness, or, which was worst of all, over dinner, if there were no guests to excite him, would suddenly doze off, dropping his napkin, and hanging his shaking head over his plate. "He's old and weak, and I dare to judge him!" she would think with self-loathing at such moments.

III

In 1811 there was living in Moscow a French doctor who quickly became the fashion, a man of immense height, handsome, amiable as Frenchmen are, and, as all Moscow said, extraordinarily skilful in his profession—Métivier. He was received in houses of high society not as a doctor, but as an equal.

Prince Nikolai Andreich, who had always laughed at medical science, had recently, on the advice of Mlle Bourienne, admitted this doctor to his presence and grown used to him. Métivier called on the prince twice a week.

On St. Nicholas's day, the prince's name day, all Moscow came to his door, but he gave orders to receive no one and to invite only a few to dinner, the list of whom he gave to Princess Marya.

Métivier, arriving on that morning with his felicitations, found it appropriate in his quality as a doctor *de forcer la consigne*,* as he said to Princess Marya, and went to see the prince. It so happened that on that morning of his name day the old prince was in one of his worst moods. He had been going wearily about the house all morning, picking on everyone and pretending that he did not understand what was said to him and that he himself was not understood. Princess Marya knew only too well this mood of quiet and preoccupied grumbling, which usually resolved itself in an outburst of rage, and she went about all morning as if under a loaded and cocked gun, awaiting the inevitable shot. Until the doctor's arrival, the morning had gone fairly well. Having let the doctor in, Princess Marya sat down with a book in the drawing room, from where she could hear everything that was happening in the study.

First she heard only Métivier's voice, then her father's voice; then both voices began speaking at once, the door was thrown open, and on the threshold appeared the frightened, handsome figure of Métivier with his black forelock and the figure of the prince in his nightcap and robe, his face distorted by rage and the pupils of his eyes rolled downwards.

"You don't understand?" the prince was shouting. "But I do! French spy! Bonaparte's slave and spy, out of my house—out, I say!" and he slammed the door.

Métivier, shrugging his shoulders, went over to Mlle Bourienne, who, hearing the shouting, had come running from the neighbouring room.

"The prince is not entirely well—*la bile et le transport au cerveau. Tranquillisez-vous, je repasserai demain,*"† said Métivier, and, putting his finger to his lips, he hurriedly left.

---

*Disobey orders.
†Bile and a seizure of the brain. Calm yourself, I'll come back tomorrow.

Behind the door, slippered footsteps were heard and shouts: "Spies, traitors, traitors everywhere! Not a moment's peace in my own house!"

After Métivier's departure, the old prince called his daughter to him, and all the force of his wrath fell upon her. It was her fault that a spy had been let in to his rooms. Yet he had told her, he had told her to make a list and not let in anyone not on the list. Why had this scoundrel been let in? She was the cause of it all. "With her he could not have a moment's peace, he could not die in peace," he said.

"No, my dear, we must part, we must part, let it be known to you! I cannot have it any more," he said and left the room. And, as if fearing she might somehow comfort herself, he came back and, trying to assume a calm look, added: "Don't think I said it to you in a moment of anger, I am calm, and I have thought it over; and it will be—we must part, find yourself a place! . . ." But he could not control himself and with that spitefulness which belongs only to someone who loves, he shook his fists at her, obviously suffering, and screamed:

"If only some fool would marry her!" He slammed the door, summoned Mlle Bourienne, and quieted down in his study.

At two o'clock the six chosen persons gathered for dinner. The guests—the well-known Count Rastopchin, Prince Lopukhin with his nephew, General Chatrov, the prince's old wartime friend, and of the young men Pierre and Boris Drubetskoy—awaited him in the drawing room.

Having come to Moscow on leave a few days earlier, Boris had wished to be introduced to Prince Nikolai Andreich, and had managed to win his favour to such a degree that the prince had made him an exception among all the young bachelors, whom he did not receive.

The prince's house was not what was known as "society," but it was a small circle which, though not much talked about in town, it was very flattering to be received in. Boris had understood that a week ago, when, in his presence, Rastopchin had said to the commander in chief, in response to his invitation to dinner on St. Nicholas's day, that he could not come:

"On that day I always go to venerate the relics of Prince Nikolai Andreich."

"Ah, yes, yes," the commander in chief had said. "How is he? . . ."

The small company that gathered before dinner in the old-fashioned drawing room, with its high ceiling and old furniture, resembled a solemn court in session. Everyone was silent, and if they spoke, they spoke softly. Prince Nikolai Andreevich came out, serious and silent. Princess Marya seemed still more quiet and timid than usual. The guests were reluctant to address her, because they saw that she was not following their conversation. Count Rastopchin alone maintained the thread of the conversation, telling about the latest town or political news.

Lopukhin and the old general took little part in the conversation. Prince Nikolai Andreevich listened as a supreme court justice listens to a report being made to him, only occasionally indicating by a grunt or a brief phrase that he has taken into consideration what is being reported to him. The tone of the conversation made it clear that no one approved of what was happening in the political world. Events were recounted which obviously confirmed that everything was getting worse and worse; but it was striking that in each account and opinion, the narrator stopped or was stopped each time at that limit where disapproval might refer to the person of the sovereign emperor.

Over dinner the conversation turned to the latest political news, about Napoleon's seizure of the lands of the duke of Oldenburg[5] and about a Russian note denouncing Napoleon, which had been sent to all the European courts.

"Bonaparte behaves with Europe like a pirate on a captured ship," said Count Rastopchin, repeating a phrase he had already uttered several times. "One is only astonished at the patience or blindness of the sovereigns. It has now gone as far as the pope, and Bonaparte, feeling no scruples, wants to overthrow the head of the Catholic religion,[6] and everyone is silent. Only our sovereign protested against the seizure of the duke of Oldenburg's lands. And even then . . ." Count Rastopchin fell silent, sensing that he was standing at the limit where it was no longer possible to disapprove.

"They offered him other lands in place of the dukedom of Oldenburg," said Prince Nikolai Andreich. "He moves dukes around the way I move peasants from Bald Hills to Bogucharovo and my Ryazan estates."

"*Le duc d'Oldenbourg supporte son malheur avec une force de caractère et une résignation admirable,*"* said Boris, respectfully entering into the conversation. He said it because, on his way from Petersburg, he had had the honour of being introduced to the duke. Prince Nikolai Andreich looked at the young man as if he wanted to tell him something about that, but changed his mind, considering him too young for it.

"I read our protest about the Oldenburg affair and was astonished at the poor wording of this note," Count Rastopchin said in the careless tone of a man judging a matter that was very familiar to him.

Pierre looked at Rastopchin with naïve astonishment, not understanding why he was disturbed by the poor wording of the note.

"Does it make any difference how the note is worded, Count," he said, "if the content is strong?"

"*Mon cher, avec nos cinq cent mille hommes de troupes, il serait facile d'avoir un beau style,*"† said Count Rastopchin. Pierre understood why Count Rastopchin was disturbed by the wording of the note.

"It seems there are lots of scribblers around," said the old prince. "There

*The duke of Oldenburg bears his misfortune with admirable strength of character and resignation.
†My dear, with our five hundred thousand troops, it would be easy to have a good style.

in Petersburg they're writing all the time, not only notes but new laws. My Andryusha wrote a whole volume of laws for Russia there. Nowadays everybody writes!" And he laughed unnaturally.

The conversation ceased for a moment; the old general cleared his throat to draw attention to himself.

"Did you hear about the latest event at the review in Petersburg? What a show the new French ambassador made of himself!"

"What's that? Yes, I heard something; he said something awkward in his majesty's presence."

"His majesty drew his attention to the grenadier division and the ceremonial march past," the general went on, "and the ambassador supposedly paid no attention to it and supposedly allowed himself to say that 'we in France pay no attention to such trifles.' The sovereign did not deign to reply. At the next review, they say, the sovereign did not deign to address him even once."

Everyone fell silent: about this fact, which referred personally to the sovereign, it was impossible to express any opinion.

"Insolent fellows!" said the prince. "Do you know Métivier? I threw him out today. He was here, he was let in to see me, though I had asked them not to let anybody in," said the prince, looking angrily at his daughter. And he recounted the whole conversation with the French doctor and the reasons why he became convinced that Métivier was a spy. Though those reasons were quite insufficient and unclear, no one objected.

After the roast, champagne was served. The guests got up from their places to congratulate the old prince. Princess Marya also went up to him.

He gave her a cold, angry look and offered her his wrinkled, clean-shaven cheek. The whole expression of his face told her that he had not forgotten their morning conversation, that his decision remained in force, and that it was only owing to the presence of the guests that he did not tell her so now.

When they went out to the drawing room for coffee, the old men sat together.

Prince Nikolai Andreich became more animated and voiced his way of thinking about the impending war.

He said that our wars with Bonaparte would be unsuccessful so long as we sought alliance with the Germans and meddled in the affairs of Europe, which we had been drawn into by the peace of Tilsit. We had no need to fight either for or against Austria. Our politics all lie in the East, and in relation to Bonaparte there is one thing—armed borders and firm politics—and he will never dare cross Russian borders as in the year seven.

"And far be it from us to fight the French, Prince!" said Count Rastopchin. "How can we oppose our teachers and gods? Look at our youth, look at our ladies. The French are our gods, and our kingdom of heaven is Paris."

He began to speak more loudly, obviously so that everyone could hear him.

"French clothes, French thoughts, French feelings! Here you threw Métivier out because he's French and a scoundrel, but our ladies go crawling after him. Yesterday I was at a soirée, and out of five ladies there, three were Catholic and, with the pope's permission, were doing embroidery on Sunday. And they sat there all but naked, like a signboard for a public bathhouse, if I may say so. Eh, Prince, when you look at our young people, you want to take Peter the Great's old cudgel from the Kunstkamera[7] and give them a good drubbing, to beat all the foolishness out of them!"

They all fell silent. The old prince looked at Rastopchin with a smile on his face, shaking his head approvingly.

"Well, goodbye, Your Excellency, be well," said Rastopchin, getting up with his peculiarly quick movements and holding out his hand to the prince.

"Goodbye, dear heart—it's always like a harp, listening to him!" said the old prince, holding him by the hand and offering him his cheek for a kiss. The others got up along with Rastopchin.

IV

Sitting in the drawing room and listening to this talk and gossip among the old men, Princess Marya understood nothing of what she heard; she was thinking only of whether the guests had noticed her father's hostile attitude towards her. She did not even notice the special attention and courtesy shown her during that dinner by Drubetskoy, who was already visiting their house for the third time.

Princess Marya turned, with an absent-minded, questioning look, to Pierre, who, the last of the guests, hat in hand and a smile on his face, went up to her after the prince had gone and they were left alone in the drawing room.

"May I stay a while longer?" he asked, letting his fat body sink into an armchair beside Princess Marya.

"Oh, yes," she said, and her glance added, "Did you notice anything?"

Pierre was in a pleasant after-dinner mood. He looked straight ahead and smiled quietly.

"Have you known that young man for a long time, Princess?" he asked.

"Which one?"

"Drubetskoy."

"No, not long . . ."

"And do you like him?"

"Yes, he's a pleasant young man . . . Why do you ask me that?" said Princess Marya, still thinking about her morning conversation with her father.

"Because I've made an observation: a young man usually comes to Moscow from Petersburg only with the aim of marrying a rich bride."

"You have made that observation?" asked Princess Marya.

"Yes," Pierre went on with a smile, "and this young man now behaves himself in such a way that, wherever there's a rich bride, he's there, too. I can read him like a book. He's undecided now whom to attack: you or Mlle Julie Karagin. *Il est très assidu auprès d'elle.*"*

"Does he visit them?"

"Yes, very often. And do you know the new way of courting?" Pierre said with a merry smile, clearly being in that merry mood of good-natured mockery for which he reproached himself so often in his diary.

"No," said Princess Marya.

"Nowadays, in order to please Moscow girls, *il faut être mélancolique. Et il est très mélancolique auprès de mademoiselle Karagine,*"† said Pierre.

"*Vraiment?*"‡ said Princess Marya, looking into Pierre's kind face and never ceasing to think about her grief. "It would be easier for me," she thought, "if I decided to confide everything I feel to someone. And I'd like to tell it all precisely to Pierre. He's so kind and noble. It would make it easier for me. He could give me advice!"

"Would you consider marrying him?" asked Pierre.

"Ah, my God, Count, there are moments when I'd marry anybody!" Princess Marya said suddenly, to her own surprise, with tears in her voice. "Ah, how painful it is to love a person who is close to you and feel . . . that you can do nothing for him," she went on in a trembling voice, "except grieve him, and when you know that you cannot change that. There's only one thing left—to go away, but where will I go?"

"What is it, what's wrong, Princess?"

But the princess, without finishing, began to cry.

"I don't know what's the matter with me today. Don't listen to me, forget what I've told you."

All of Pierre's cheerfulness vanished. He asked the princess worried questions, begged her to tell him everything, to confide her grief to him; but she only repeated that she begged him to forget what she had said, that she did not remember what she had said, that she had no grief except the one he knew—that Prince Andrei's marriage threatened to make father and son quarrel.

"Have you heard anything about the Rostovs?" she asked in order to change the conversation. "I was told they would be here soon. I also expect André any day. I wish they could see each other here."

"And how does he look at the matter now?" asked Pierre, meaning the old prince. Princess Marya shook her head.

"But what's to be done? There are only a few months before the year is out.

---

*He is very attentive to her.
†One must be melancholy. And he is very melancholy with Mlle Karagin.
‡Really?

And it's bound to happen. I only wish I could spare my brother the first moments. I wish they'd come soon. I hope to become close with her . . . You've known them a long time," said Princess Marya, "tell me, hand on heart, the whole real truth: what kind of girl is she and how you find her? But the whole truth; because, you understand, Andrei is risking so much in doing this against his father's will that I'd like to know . . ."

A vague instinct told Pierre that all these reservations and repeated requests to tell *the whole truth* expressed Princess Marya's ill-will towards her future sister-in-law, that she wished Pierre to disapprove of Prince Andrei's choice; but Pierre said what he felt rather than what he thought.

"I don't know how to answer your question," he said, blushing without knowing why himself. "I decidedly don't know what kind of girl she is; I simply cannot analyse her. She's enchanting. But why, I don't know: that's all one can say about her."

Princess Marya sighed, and the expression of her face said: "Yes, that's what I expected and was afraid of."

"Is she intelligent?" asked Princess Marya. Pierre pondered.

"I don't think so," he said, "although—yes. She doesn't deign to be intelligent . . . Ah, no, she's enchanting, that's all."

Princess Marya again shook her head disapprovingly . . .

"Ah, I wish so much to love her! Tell her that if you see her before I do."

"I've heard they'll be here one of these days," said Pierre.

Princess Marya told Pierre that she planned, as soon as the Rostovs arrived, to become close with her future sister-in-law and to try to get the old prince used to her.

V

Boris had failed to marry a rich bride in Petersburg and had come with the same purpose to Moscow. In Moscow, Boris hesitated between the two richest brides—Julie and Princess Marya. Though Princess Marya, despite her plainness, seemed more attractive to him than Julie, he found it awkward, for some reason, to court Princess Bolkonsky. During his last meeting with her, on the old prince's name day, to all his attempts to talk about feelings with her, she had responded beside the point and had obviously not been listening to him.

Julie, on the contrary, though in her own peculiar way, willingly accepted his courtship.

Julie was twenty-seven years old. After the death of her brothers, she had become very rich. She was by now utterly plain, but she thought she was not only as good-looking, but was even far more attractive now than she had been before. She was maintained in this delusion by the fact that, first of all, she had become a very rich bride, and second, that the older she became, the less dangerous she was for men, the more freely men treated her and, without taking any obligations upon themselves, profited from her suppers, soirées, and the lively company that gathered in her house. A man who, ten years before, would have been afraid of going every day to a house where there was a seventeen-year-old girl, so as not to compromise her and bind himself, now boldly came to her every day and treated her not as a prospective bride, but as an acquaintance who had no sex.

That winter the Karagins' house was the most agreeable and hospitable house in Moscow. Besides formal soirées and dinners, each day at the Karagins' a large company gathered, especially of men, who had supper around midnight and stayed till three in the morning. There was no ball, theatrical, or prome-nade that Julie missed. Her dresses were always the most fashionable. But, in spite of that, Julie seemed disappointed in everything, said to everyone that she believed neither in friendship, nor in love, nor in any of the joys of life, and expected peace only *there*. She adopted the tone of a girl who has lived through a great disappointment, a girl who, as it were, has lost a beloved man or been cruelly deceived by him. Though none of it had happened to her, people looked at her as if it had, and she herself even believed that she had suffered much in her life. This melancholy, which did not keep her from making merry, also did not keep the young people who visited her from passing the time pleas-antly. Each guest who came to them gave its due to the hostess's melancholy mood and then occupied himself with society talk, and dancing, and parlour games, and tournaments of *bouts rimés,** which were fashionable at the Kara-gins'. Only some of the young men, Boris among them, entered more deeply into Julie's melancholy mood, and with these young men she had more pro-longed and solitary conversations on the vanity of worldly things, and opened for them her albums filled with sad images, sayings, and verses.

Julie was especially affectionate with Boris: she was sorry for his early disap-pointment in life, offering him what consolations of friendship she could offer, having suffered so much in life herself, and she opened her album for him.[8] Boris drew two trees in her album and wrote: "*Arbres rustiques, vos sombres rameaux secouent sur moi les ténèbres et la mélancolie.*"†

In another place he drew a tomb and wrote:

> *La mort est secourable et la mort est tranquille.*
> *Ah! contre les douleurs il n'y a pas d'autre asile.*‡

Julie said that this was charming.

"*Il y a quelque chose de si ravissant dans le sourire de la mélancolie,*" she

*Set rhymes.
†Rustic trees, your gloomy branches shake darkness and melancholy down on me.
‡Death is helpful and death is peaceful. / Ah! against sorrows there is no other refuge.

recited to Boris, word for word, a phrase she had copied from a book. "*C'est un rayon de lumière dans l'ombre, une nuance entre la douleur et le désespoir, qui montre la consolation possible.*"*

To this Boris wrote down verses for her:

> *Aliment de poison d'une âme trop sensible,*
> *Toi, sans qui le bonheur me serait impossible,*
> *Tendre mélancolie, ah, viens me consoler,*
> *Viens calmer les tourments de ma sombre retraite*
> *Et mêle une douceur secrète*
> *A ces pleurs, qui je sens couler.*†

Julie played the most mournful nocturnes on the harp for Boris. Boris read *Poor Liza*[9] aloud to her and interrupted his reading more than once from emotions that robbed him of breath. Meeting at a large gathering, Julie and Boris looked at each other as the only people in a sea of the indifferent who understood each other.

Anna Mikhailovna, who often visited the Karagins and played cards with the mother, meanwhile obtained trustworthy information about what would come with Julie (what would come were the two Penza estates and the woodlands in Nizhni Novgorod province). Anna Mikhailovna, given over to the will of providence, looked with tenderness upon the refined sorrow that bound her son to the rich Julie.

"*Toujours charmante et mélancolique, cette chère Julie,*"‡ she said to the daughter. "Boris says his soul is eased in your house. He has suffered so many disappointments, and he is so sensitive," she said to the mother.

"Ah, my friend, how attached I've become to Julie lately," she said to her son. "I can't describe it to you! And who could possibly not love her? She's such an unearthly being! Ah, Boris, Boris!" She would fall silent for a moment. "And how sorry I am for her *maman*," she would go on. "Today she showed me reports and letters from Penza (they have an enormous estate), and she does everything alone, poor thing: they deceive her so much!"

Boris smiled almost imperceptibly, listening to his mother. He laughed meekly at her simple-hearted slyness, but he listened to her and occasionally questioned her attentively about the Penza and Nizhni Novgorod estates.

Julie had long been expecting a proposal from her melancholy admirer and was prepared to accept it; but some secret feeling of aversion for her, for her

---

*There is something so enchanting in the smile of melancholy . . . It is a ray of light in the darkness, a nuance between sorrow and despair, which shows consolation possible.

†Poisonous food for too sensitive a soul, / Thou, without whom happiness would be impossible for me, / Tender melancholy, ah, come to console me, / Come to calm the torments of my gloomy retreat, / And mingle a secret sweetness / With these tears, which I feel flowing.

‡Ever charming and melancholy, this dear Julie.

passionate desire to get married, for her unnaturalness, and a feeling of horror at renouncing the possibility of true love, still stopped Boris. The time of his leave was coming to an end. All day and every blessed day he spent at the Karagins', and every day, reasoning with himself, Boris said to himself that he would propose the next day. But in Julie's presence, looking at her red face and chin, almost always daubed with powder, at her moist eyes, and the expression of her face, which showed a permanent readiness to change at once from melancholy to the unnatural rapture of marital happiness, Boris was unable to utter the decisive words—despite the fact that, in his imagination he had long considered himself the owner of the Penza and Nizhni Novgorod estates and had allocated the use of the income from them. Julie saw Boris's irresolution, and the thought sometimes occurred to her that she repulsed him; but at once her feminine self-deception furnished her with a consolation, and she said to herself that it was merely the shyness that comes from love. However, her melancholy began to turn into irritation, and shortly before Boris's departure, she undertook a decisive plan. At the same time that Boris's leave was coming to an end, Anatole Kuragin appeared in Moscow and, naturally enough, in the Karagins' drawing room, and Julie, unexpectedly abandoning her melancholy, became very cheerful and attentive to Kuragin.

"*Mon cher*," Anna Mikhailovna said to her son, "*je sais de bonne source que le prince Basile envoie son fils à Moscou pour lui fair épouser Julie.** I love Julie so much that I would find that a pity. What do you think, my friend?" said Anna Mikhailovna.

The thought of making a fool of himself and wasting this whole month of heavy melancholic duty around Julie for nothing, and seeing the income from the Penza estates, already allocated and properly put to use in his imagination, in the hands of another—especially in the hands of stupid Anatole—offended Boris. He went to the Karagins' with the firm intention of making a proposal. Julie met him with a cheerful and careless air, told him casually how merry she had been at last night's ball, and asked him when he was leaving. Though Boris had come with the intention of speaking of his love, and therefore intended to be tender, he began speaking irritably of women's inconstancy: of how easily women could go from sadness to joy, and that their mood depended only on who was courting them. Julie became offended and said that it was all true, that a woman needed diversity, that one and the same thing all the time would bore anyone.

"In that case I'd advise you . . ." Boris began, wishing to sting her. But at that moment the offensive thought occurred to him that he might leave Moscow without achieving his goal and having wasted his efforts (which never hap-

---

*My dear, I have it from a good source that Prince Vassily is sending his son to Moscow to have him marry Julie.

pened to him in anything). He stopped in mid-speech, lowered his eyes, so as
not to see her unpleasantly irritated and irresolute face, and said: "It's not at all
to quarrel with you that I've come today. On the contrary . . ." He glanced at
her to make sure he could go on. All her irritation suddenly vanished, and her
anxious, pleading eyes were directed at him in eager expectation. "I can always
arrange it so that I see her rarely," thought Boris. "The thing's started and must
be done!" He turned bright red, raised his eyes to her, and said: "You know my
feelings for you!" There was no need to say more: Julie's face beamed with triumph and self-satisfaction; yet she made Boris say everything that is said on
such occasions, that he loved her and had never loved any woman more than
her. She knew she could demand that in exchange for the Penza estates and the
Nizhni Novgorod woodlands, and she got what she demanded.

The bride- and groom-to-be, no longer mentioning trees showering darkness and melancholy on them, made plans for the future setting-up of a brilliant house in Petersburg, paid visits, and prepared everything for a brilliant
wedding.

VI

At the end of January, Count Ilya Andreich came to Moscow with Natasha
and Sonya. The countess was still unwell and could not come, but it was
impossible to wait for her recovery: Prince Andrei was expected in Moscow
any day; besides that, it was necessary to buy the trousseau, it was necessary to
sell the estate near Moscow, and it was necessary to take advantage of the old
prince's presence in Moscow to introduce his future daughter-in-law to him.
The Rostovs' house in Moscow had not been heated; besides that, they were
coming for a short time, the countess was not with them, and therefore Ilya
Andreich decided to stay in Moscow with Marya Dmitrievna Akhrosimov,
who had long been offering the count her hospitality.

Late at night, the Rostovs' four vehicles drove into Marya Dmitrievna's
courtyard on Old Konyushennaya Street. Marya Dmitrievna lived alone. Her
daughter was already married. Her sons were all in the army.

She held herself as straight as ever, and voiced all her opinions just as
directly, loudly, and resolutely, and her whole being seemed to reproach other
people for all sorts of weaknesses, passions, and enthusiasms, the possibility of
which she did not acknowledge. From early morning, in her dressing jacket,
she would busy herself with household chores; then, on feast days, she would
go to church, and from church to the jails and prisons, where she had some
business of which she spoke to no one, and on weekdays she would dress and
receive the petitioners of various social conditions who came to her every day,
and would then have dinner; at dinner, substantial and tasty, she always had
three or four guests; after dinner she would play a game of boston; in the

evening she would have newspapers and new books read to her, while she herself knitted. She rarely made an exception for visits, and if she went visiting, it was only to the most important persons in town.

She was still up when the Rostovs arrived, and the door to the front hall squeaked on its pulley, letting the Rostovs and their servants in from the cold. Marya Dmitrievna, her spectacles low on her nose, her head thrown back, stood in the doorway of the reception room and glared at the entering people with a stern, irate look. One might have thought she was angry with them and was about to drive them out, if she had not been giving solicitous orders to her people at the same time about where to put up the guests and their things.

"The count's? Over here," she said, pointing to the suitcases and not greeting anybody. "The young ladies' here to the left. Well, what are you dawdling for!" she yelled at the maids. "Heat up the samovar! You've grown plumper, prettier," she said, pulling Natasha, pink from the cold, to her by the hood. "Pah, you're cold! Go and take your things off quickly," she cried to the count, who was about to kiss her hand. "You must be freezing. Serve rum with the tea! Sonyushka, *bonjour*," she said to Sonya, giving a special shade by this French greeting to her slightly scornful and affectionate attitude towards Sonya.

When, having taken their things off and straightened themselves up after the journey, they all came to tea, Marya Dmitrievna kissed them all in proper order.

"I'm heartily glad you've come and are staying with me," she declared. "It's none too soon," she said, glancing significantly at Natasha . . . "The old man's here, and they're expecting the son any day. You must, must make his acquaintance. Well, we'll talk about it later," she added, her glance at Sonya indicating that she did not want to talk about it in her presence. "Now listen," she turned to the count, "what do you need for tomorrow? Whom will you send for? Shinshin?" she bent down one finger, "the crybaby Anna Mikhailovna— two. She's here with her son. Getting married, the son is! Then Bezukhov, I suppose? He's here, too, with his wife. He ran away from her, but she went galloping after him. He dined with me on Wednesday. Well, and they," she pointed to the girls, "will come with me tomorrow to the Iverskaya Chapel, and then we'll stop and see Over-Shameless.[10] I suppose you'll have to make everything new? Don't go by me, nowadays they wear sleeves like this! The other day the young princess Irina Vassilievna came to see me: a dreadful sight, as if she'd put two barrels on her arms. Why, nowadays there's a new fashion every day. And how are things with you?" she asked the count sternly.

"Everything suddenly comes at once," the count replied. "Rags to be bought, and now there's also a buyer for the estate and the house. If you could do me the kindness, I'll choose a little moment, drive over to Maryinskoe for a day, and leave my girls in your hands."

"All right, all right, with me they'll be safe. With me it's like state custody. I'll take them out wherever necessary, and scold them, and pet them," said Marya Dmitrievna, touching the cheek of Natasha, her goddaughter and favourite, with her big hand.

The next morning Marya Dmitrievna took the girls to the Iverskaya Chapel and to Mme Aubert-Chalmet, who was so afraid of Marya Dmitrievna that she always let her have dresses for less, so as to get rid of her quickly. Marya Dmitrievna ordered almost the whole trousseau. On coming home, she drove everyone but Natasha out of the room and called her favourite to her armchair.

"Well, now let's have a talk. I congratulate you on your fiancé. You've hooked a fine one! I'm glad for you. I've known him since he was this high," she indicated some two feet from the ground. Natasha was blushing joyfully. "I love him and his whole family. Now listen. You know, old Prince Nikolai was very much against his son's getting married. A crotchety old man! Of course, Prince Andrei is not a child and can do without him, but it's not nice to enter the family against his will. It should be done peacefully, lovingly. You're a clever girl, you'll find a way. Go about it nicely and cleverly. And then everything will be all right."

Natasha said nothing, out of shyness, as Marya Dmitrievna thought, but, in reality, Natasha disliked any interference in the matter of her love for Prince Andrei, which appeared to her so set apart from all human affairs that no one, to her mind, could understand it. She loved and knew only Prince Andrei; he loved her and was to come one day soon and take her. She needed nothing else.

"You see, I've known him for a long time, and I love Mashenka, your sister-in-law. A sister-in-law is a sharp claw, but this one wouldn't hurt a fly. She's asked me to get you together with her. You'll go to her tomorrow with your father. Be nice and affectionate with her: you're younger than she is. So your young man comes, and you're already acquainted with his sister and father, and they love you. Am I right or not? Won't it be better?"

"Yes," Natasha replied reluctantly.

VII

The next day, on Marya Dmitrievna's advice, Count Ilya Andreich went with Natasha to see Prince Nikolai Andreich. The count set out on this visit in a cheerless mood: deep in his heart he was frightened. Their last meeting, during the recruitment, when the count, in response to his invitation to dinner, had listened to a scathing reprimand for failing to provide men, had remained in Count Ilya Andreich's memory. Natasha, wearing her best dress, was, on the contrary, in a most cheerful mood. "It can't be that they won't come to love me," she thought, "everyone has always loved me. And I'm so ready to do everything they want for them, so ready to love him, because he's his father, and her, because she's his sister, there's no reason why they shouldn't love me!"

They drove up to the old, gloomy house on Vzdvizhenka Street and went into the vestibule.

"Well, God bless us," the count said, half jokingly, half seriously; but Natasha noticed that her father was flustered as he stepped into the front hall and asked timidly and softly whether the prince and princess were at home. The announcement of their visit caused a commotion among the prince's servants. The footman who went to announce them was stopped by another footman in the reception room, and they whispered about something. A maid ran out to the reception room and hastily said something as well, mentioning the princess. At last an old footman with an angry look came out and told the Rostovs that the prince could not receive them, but the princess asked them to come in. The first to meet the guests was Mlle Bourienne. She met the father and daughter especially courteously and took them to the princess. The princess, her agitated, frightened face covered with red blotches, ran out, treading heavily, to meet the guests, trying in vain to appear casual and affable. Princess Marya disliked Natasha at first sight. She seemed to her too well dressed, flightily merry, and vain. Princess Marya did not know that, before seeing her future sister-in-law, she had already been ill-disposed towards her, being involuntarily envious of her beauty, youth, and happiness, and jealous of her brother's love. Besides this insuperable feeling of antipathy for her, Princess Marya was also troubled just then because, when the arrival of the Rostovs was announced, the prince had cried out that he did not want them, that Princess Marya could receive them if she liked, but that they were not to be admitted to him. Princess Marya had decided to receive the Rostovs, but was afraid every moment that the prince might perform some escapade, being very agitated by the Rostovs' arrival.

"Well, dear princess, here I've brought you my singer," said the count, scraping and looking around uneasily, as if fearing the old prince might walk in. "I'm so glad you'll be getting acquainted. A pity, a pity the prince is unwell," and, having said a few more general phrases, he got up. "If you will permit me, Princess, to deposit my Natasha here for a quarter of an hour, I'll drive over to the Dogs' Square, just two steps away, to see Anna Semyonovna, and come back for her."

Ilya Andreich had invented this diplomatic ruse in order to give Natasha's future sister-in-law the freedom to talk with her (as he later explained to her) and also to avoid the possibility of meeting the prince, whom he feared. He had not said that to his daughter, but Natasha understood her father's fear and anxiety and felt offended. She blushed for her father, became still angrier for having blushed, and gave the princess a bold, defiant look, which said that she was not afraid of anyone. The princess told the count that she was very glad and only asked him to stay longer at Anna Semyonovna's, and Ilya Andreich left.

Mlle Bourienne, despite the anxious glances cast at her by Princess Marya, who wished to talk privately with Natasha, would not leave the room and carried on a steady conversation about Moscow pleasures and theatres. Natasha was offended by the confusion that had taken place in the front hall, by her father's uneasiness, and by the unnatural tone of the princess, who, as it seemed to Natasha, was doing her a favour by receiving her. And therefore she found everything disagreeable. She did not like Princess Marya. She found her very plain, affected, and dry. Natasha suddenly shrank morally and involuntarily adopted such a casual tone that it made her still more repellent to Princess Marya. After five minutes of painful, false conversation, they heard slippered footsteps rapidly approaching. Princess Marya's face showed fear, the door to the room opened, and the prince came in, wearing a white nightcap and a dressing gown.

"Ah, Miss," he said, "Miss, Countess . . . Countess Rostov, if I'm not mistaken . . . I beg your pardon, I beg your pardon . . . I didn't know, miss. As God is my witness, I had no idea you'd honoured us with a visit, I was coming to my daughter in this attire. I beg your pardon . . . As God is my witness, I didn't know," he repeated, stressing the word *God* so unnaturally and so unpleasantly that Princess Marya stood with her eyes cast down, not daring to look either at her father or at Natasha. Natasha, having risen and curtsied, also did not know what to do with herself. Mlle Bourienne alone smiled pleasantly.

"I beg your pardon! I beg your pardon! As God is my witness, I didn't know," the old man muttered, and, having looked Natasha up and down, he left. Mlle Bourienne was the first to recover after this apparition and began talking about the prince's ill health. Natasha and Princess Marya silently looked at each other, and the longer they looked at each other silently, without saying what they needed to say, the more ill-willed were their thoughts about each other.

When the count came back, Natasha was discourteously glad of it and hastened to leave: at that moment she almost hated this old, dry princess, who could put her in such an awkward position and spend half an hour with her while saying nothing about Prince Andrei. "I couldn't be the first to start talking about him in front of this Frenchwoman," thought Natasha. Princess Marya meanwhile was suffering over the same thing. She knew what she needed to say to Natasha, but she also could not do it because Mlle Bourienne hindered her, and because she herself did not know why it was so hard for her to start talking about this marriage. When the count was already leaving the room, Princess Marya went up to Natasha with quick steps, took her by the hands, and, sighing deeply, said: "Wait, I must . . ." Natasha looked at Princess Marya mockingly, not knowing why herself.

"Dear Natalie," said Princess Marya, "please know that I am glad my brother has found happiness . . ." She stopped, feeling that she was saying an untruth. Natasha noticed this pause and guessed the reason for it.

"I think, Princess, that now is not the right time to speak of it," Natasha said with outward dignity and coldness, and with tears that she could feel in her throat.

"What have I said, what have I done!" she thought as soon as she left the room.

They waited dinner a long time that day for Natasha. She sat in her room and wept like a child, blowing her nose and sobbing. Sonya stood over her and kissed her hair.

"Natasha, what is it?" she was saying. "What do you care about them? It will all pass, Natasha."

"No, if you only knew how offensive it was . . . as if I . . ."

"Don't say it, Natasha, it's not your fault, so what do you care? Kiss me," said Sonya.

Natasha raised her head, kissed her friend on the lips, and pressed her wet face to her.

"I can't tell, I don't know. It's nobody's fault," said Natasha, "it's my fault. But it's all terribly painful. Oh, why doesn't he come! . . ."

She came out for dinner with red eyes. Marya Dmitrievna, who knew how the prince had received the Rostovs, pretended not to notice Natasha's upset face and bantered, firmly and loudly, with the count and the other guests at the table.

VIII

That evening the Rostovs went to the opera, for which Marya Dmitrievna had obtained tickets.

Natasha did not want to go, but she could not reject Marya Dmitrievna's kindness, which was meant exclusively for her. When she came out, dressed, to the reception room, and, looking in the big mirror while waiting for her father, saw that she was pretty, very pretty, she felt still more sad; but this was a sweet and amorous sadness.

"My God! if he were here, I wouldn't do it like before, with such stupid shyness at something, I'd embrace him in a new way, simply, I'd press myself to him, make him look at me with those searching, curious eyes with which he looked at me so often, and then I'd make him laugh as he laughed then, and his eyes—how I see those eyes!" thought Natasha. "And what do his father and sister matter to me: I love him alone, him, with his face and eyes, with his manly and at the same time childlike smile . . . No, better not to think about him, not to think, to forget, forget completely for the time being. I won't survive this waiting, I'll start sobbing right now," and she left the mirror, making an effort not to burst into tears. "And how can Sonya love Nikolenka so steadily, so peacefully, and wait so long and patiently?" she wondered, looking at Sonya, who was coming in, also dressed, holding a fan. "No, she's quite different. I can't!"

Natasha felt so softened and tender-hearted at that moment that it was not enough for her to love and know that she was loved: she had to embrace the beloved man now, at once, and speak and hear from him the words of love which so filled her heart. While she was riding in the carriage, sitting beside her father, and looking pensively at the lights of the street lamps flashing in the frozen window, she felt herself still more in love and more sad, and forgot where she was going and with whom. Falling in with the line of carriages, its wheels squeaking slowly over the snow, the Rostovs' carriage drove up to the theatre. Natasha and Sonya quickly jumped out, holding up their skirts; the count got out, supported by the footmen, and the three walked among the entering ladies and gentlemen and the programme sellers to the aisle leading to the box seats. Sounds of music were already coming from behind the closed doors.

"*Natalie, vos cheveux,*"* Sonya whispered. An usher deferentially and hastily slipped sideways before the ladies and opened the door to the box. The sounds of music became more vivid; through the door shone the brightly lit rows of boxes, with the bare shoulders and arms of ladies, and the noisy parterre brilliant with uniforms. The lady who was entering the next box looked Natasha over with envious feminine eyes. The curtain had not yet gone up, and the overture was being played. Natasha, smoothing her dress, walked in together with Sonya and sat down, looking over the lit-up rows of boxes opposite. For a long time she had not experienced that feeling, both pleasant and unpleasant, of hundreds of eyes looking at her bare arms and neck, which suddenly seized her now, calling up a whole swarm of memories, desires, and emotions corresponding to that feeling.

The two remarkably pretty girls, Natasha and Sonya, along with Count Ilya Andreich, who had not appeared in Moscow for a long time, attracted general attention. Besides, everyone knew vaguely of Natasha's betrothal to Prince Andrei, knew that since then the Rostovs had been living in the country, and looked with curiosity at the fiancée of one of the best matches in Russia.

Natasha had grown prettier in the country, as everybody told her, and that evening, owing to her agitated state, she was especially pretty. She struck people by her fullness of life and beauty, combined with her indifference to everything around her. Her black eyes gazed at the crowd without seeking anyone, her slender arm, bared above the elbow, rested on the velvet rail, her hand opening and closing, obviously unconsciously, in time with the overture, crumpling the programme.

*Natalie, your hair.

"Look, there's Miss Alenin," said Sonya, "with her mother, I think."

"Good heavens! Mikhail Kirilych has grown still fatter!" said the old count.

"Look! What a toque Anna Mikhailovna's wearing!"

"The Karagins, Julie and Boris with them. You can see at once they're engaged."

"Drubetskoy's made a proposal! Yes, indeed, I found out today," said Shinshin, coming into the Rostovs' box.

Natasha followed the direction of her father's gaze and saw Julie, who, with pearls on her fat, red neck (which Natasha knew was daubed with powder), was sitting with a happy look next to her mother. Behind them Boris's head could be seen, handsome, smoothly combed, smiling, its ear inclined to Julie's mouth. He looked at the Rostovs from under his eyebrows and, smiling, said something to his fiancée.

"They're talking about us, about me and him!" Natasha thought. "And he must be calming his fiancée's jealousy of me. They needn't worry! If only they knew how little I care about them all!"

Behind them, in a green toque, with a happy, festive face, given over to the will of God, sat Anna Mikhailovna. In their box hung that atmosphere of an engaged couple which Natasha knew and loved so well. She turned away, and suddenly all that had been humiliating in her morning visit recalled itself to her.

"What right has he not to want to receive me into his family? Ah, better not to think about it, not to think till he comes!" she said to herself and began looking at the familiar and unfamiliar faces in the parterre. At the front of the parterre, right in the middle, his back leaning on the rail, stood Dolokhov, with a huge mop of curly hair combed upwards, in Persian dress. He stood in full view of the theatre, aware that he was attracting the attention of the entire audience, as freely as if he was standing in his own room. Around him in a cluster stood the most brilliant young men of Moscow, and he was clearly the first among them.

Count Ilya Andreich, laughing, nudged the blushing Sonya, pointing to her former admirer.

"Do you recognize him?" he asked. "But where has he appeared from?" the count asked Shinshin. "Didn't he vanish somewhere?"

"Yes," replied Shinshin. "He was in the Caucasus, ran away from there, and, they say, became minister to some reigning prince in Persia, and killed the shah's brother there. Well, so all the Moscow ladies are losing their minds! *Dolochoff le Persan,* and all's said. Now no word is spoken among us without Dolokhov; they swear by him, they invite people for him as if he was a sterlet," said Shinshin. "Dolokhov and Anatole Kuragin have driven all our ladies out of their minds."

A tall, beautiful lady entered the neighbouring box, with an enormous braid and very bared, white, full shoulders and neck, on which hung a double string of big pearls. She took a long time to settle herself, rustling her heavy silk gown.

Natasha involuntarily gazed at that neck, the shoulders, the pearls, the coiffure, and admired the beauty of the shoulders and pearls. As Natasha looked at her a second time, the lady turned and, meeting Count Ilya Andreich's eyes, nodded to him and smiled. This was Countess Bezukhov, Pierre's wife. Ilya Andreich, who knew everybody in the world, leaned over and addressed her.

"Have you been here long, Countess?" he said. "I'll come, I'll come and kiss your hand. I'm here on business, and I've brought my girls along. They say Semyonova is an incomparable performer," said Ilya Andreich. "Count Pyotr Kirillovich never used to forget us. Is he here?"

"Yes, he wanted to stop by," said Hélène, and she looked attentively at Natasha.

Count Ilya Andreich sat back in his place.

"Fine woman, isn't she?" he whispered to Natasha.

"Wonderful!" said Natasha. "One could just fall in love with her!" At that moment the last chords of the overture sounded and the conductor tapped with his baton. The late-coming men went to their seats in the parterre and the curtain rose.

As soon as the curtain rose, the boxes and parterre all fell silent, and all the men, old and young, in uniforms and tailcoats, all the women, in precious stones on bare bodies, with greedy curiosity turned their attention to the stage. Natasha also began to look.

IX

The stage consisted of flat boards in the middle, with painted pieces of cardboard on the sides representing trees, and canvas stretched over boards at the back. In the middle of the stage sat girls in red bodices and white skirts. One, very fat, in a white silk dress, sat apart on a low stool with a piece of green cardboard glued to the back of it. They were all singing something. When they finished their song, the girl in white went up to the prompter's box, and a man with tight silk breeches on his fat legs, and with a feather and a dagger, came up to her and began singing and spreading his arms.

The man in tight breeches sang alone, then she sang. Then they both fell silent, music began to play, and the man began to touch the hand of the girl in the white dress with his fingers, evidently waiting for the beat again so as to begin his part with her. They sang together, and everybody in the theatre clapped and shouted, and the man and woman on stage, who represented lovers, began to bow, smiling and spreading their arms.

After the country, and with the serious mood she was in, Natasha found all this wild and astonishing. She was unable to follow the course of the opera; she could not even hear the music: she saw only painted cardboard and strangely dressed-up men and women, who moved, talked, and sang strangely in the bright light; she knew what it was all supposed to represent, but it was all so pretentiously false and unnatural that she first felt embarrassed for the performers, and then found them ridiculous. She looked around at the faces of the spectators, seeking in them the same feeling of mockery and perplexity that was in her; but all the faces were attentive to what was taking place on stage and expressed admiration—feigned, as it seemed to Natasha. "That must be how it's supposed to be!" she thought. She kept looking alternately now at the rows of pomaded heads in the parterre, now at the bare women in the boxes, particularly at her neighbour Hélène, who, totally undressed, with a quiet and calm smile, never took her eyes off the stage. Sensing the bright light spread all through the theatre and the warm air heated by the crowd, Natasha was gradually beginning to get into a state of inebriation such as she had not experienced for a long time. She did not remember who she was and where she was and what was happening before her. She looked and thought, and the strangest thoughts flashed through her head unexpectedly, without connection. Now the thought came to her of jumping up to the footlights and singing the aria the actress was singing, then she wanted to touch a little old man who was sitting not far away with her fan, then to lean over to Hélène and tickle her.

At one of the moments when everything was hushed on stage, waiting for an aria to begin, the front door creaked, and over the carpet of the parterre on the side where the Rostovs' box was, the footsteps of a late arrival were heard. "Here's Kuragin!" Shinshin whispered. Countess Bezukhov turned, smiling, to the entering man. Natasha followed Hélène's gaze and saw an extraordinarily handsome adjutant approaching their box with a self-assured and at the same time courteous air. This was Anatole Kuragin, whom she had seen and noticed at a Petersburg ball long ago. He was now in an adjutant's uniform with one epaulette and an aiguillette. He walked with a restrained swagger that would have been ridiculous if he had not been so good-looking and if his handsome face had not borne an expression of such benevolent satisfaction and good cheer. Though the performance was going on, he walked down the slanting carpet of the aisle unhurriedly, lightly jingling his spurs and sabre, bearing his handsome, perfumed head smoothly aloft. Having glanced at Natasha, he went up to his sister, placed his tightly gloved hand on the edge of her box, nodded to her, and, leaning over, asked her something, pointing to Natasha.

"*Mais charmante!*"* he said, evidently about Natasha, as she did not so much hear as understand from the movement of his lips. Then he walked to the front row and sat down next to Dolokhov, nudging with his elbow in a friendly

*How charming!

and casual way that same Dolokhov whom others treated so fawningly. He smiled at him with a merry wink and rested his foot against the rail.

"How alike the brother and sister are!" said the count. "And both so handsome!"

Shinshin began telling the count in a low voice the story of some intrigue of Kuragin's in Moscow, which Natasha listened in on precisely because he had said *"charmante"* of her.

The first act was over. Everyone in the parterre stood up, mingled, began coming and going.

Boris came to the Rostovs' box, received their felicitations with great simplicity and, raising his eyebrows, with a distracted smile, conveyed to Natasha and Sonya his fiancée's request that they be present at her wedding, and left. Natasha spoke to him with a merry and flirtatious smile, and offered to that same Boris with whom she had once been in love her felicitations on his marriage. In the state of inebriation she was in, everything seemed simple and natural.

The bare Hélène sat next to her and smiled identically at everyone; and Natasha smiled at Boris in the same way.

Hélène's box was filled and surrounded on the parterre side by the most well-born and intelligent men, who seemed to vie with one another in their wish to show everyone that they were acquainted with her.

Throughout this entr'acte Kuragin stood with Dolokhov in front by the footlights, gazing at the Rostovs' box. Natasha knew he was talking about her, and that afforded her pleasure. She even turned so that he could see her in profile, which, to her mind, was the most advantageous position. Before the start of the second act, the figure of Pierre, whom the Rostovs had not seen since their arrival, appeared in the parterre. His face was sad, and he had grown still fatter since the last time Natasha saw him. Not noticing anyone, he walked to the front rows. Anatole went up to him and began saying something to him, looking and pointing at the Rostovs' box. Pierre, seeing Natasha, became animated and, hastening along the rows, went to their box. On reaching them, he leaned on his elbows and, smiling, talked with Natasha for a long time. During her conversation with Pierre, Natasha heard a man's voice in Countess Bezukhov's box and somehow knew it was Kuragin. She turned and their eyes met. He, almost smiling, looked her straight in the eye with such an admiring, tender gaze that it seemed strange to be so near him, to look at him that way, to be so certain that he liked her, and not be acquainted with him.

In the second act, there were pieces of cardboard representing monuments, and there was a hole in the canvas representing the moon, and the shades were raised over the footlights, and the horns and double basses began to play in the bass clef, and from right and left came many people in black mantles. The people began to wave their arms, and in their hands there were something like daggers; then some other people came running and began to drag away the girl who used to be wearing a white dress and was now wearing a light blue one. They did not drag her away at once, but sang with her for a long time, and only then dragged her away, and in the wings something iron was struck three times, and everyone knelt and began to sing a prayer. All this performing was interrupted several times by the rapturous shouts of the spectators.

During this act, Natasha, each time she glanced at the parterre, saw Anatole Kuragin, his arm flung over the back of his seat, looking at her. She was pleased to see that he was so captivated by her, and it never entered her head that there was anything bad in it.

When the second act was over, Countess Bezukhov got up, turned to the Rostovs' box (her bosom was now completely bared), beckoned to the old count with her gloved finger, and, ignoring the people who came into her box, began talking to him with an amiable smile.

"Do introduce me to your lovely daughters," she said. "The whole town is shouting about them, and I don't know them."

Natasha stood up and curtsied to the magnificent countess. Natasha was so pleased to be praised by this brilliant beauty that she blushed with pleasure.

"I, too, want to become a Muscovite now," said Hélène. "And you should be ashamed to bury such pearls in the country!"

Countess Bezukhov was entitled to her reputation as an enchanting woman. She was able to say what she did not think, and especially to flatter, with perfect simplicity and naturalness.

"No, dear count, you must allow me to occupy myself with your daughters. I'm not here for long, but then neither are you. I'll try to entertain them. I had already heard much about you in Petersburg and wanted to get to know you," she said to Natasha with her uniformly beautiful smile. "I had heard about you from my page, Drubetskoy—have you heard he's getting married?—and from my husband's friend, Bolkonsky, Prince Andrei Bolkonsky," she said with special emphasis, hinting by it that she knew of his relation to Natasha. She asked that, in order to become better acquainted, one of the girls be allowed to sit in her box for the rest of the performance, and Natasha went over to her.

In the third act, there was a representation of a palace on stage, in which many candles were burning and paintings were hung, portraying knights with little beards. In front stood, probably, a tsar and tsaritsa. The tsar waved his right arm and, evidently timid, sang something poorly, then sat down on a raspberry-coloured throne. The girl, who had first been in white, then in light blue, was now dressed in nothing but a shift, with her hair down, and stood by the throne. She sang ruefully about something, addressing the tsaritsa; but the tsar sternly waved his arm, and from the sides came men with bare legs and women with bare legs, and they began dancing all together. Then the violins began to play very shrilly and merrily. One of the girls, with fat bare legs and skinny arms, separated from the others, went into the wings, straightened her bodice, came out to the centre and started leaping and rapidly slapping one foot against the other. Everyone in the parterre clapped their hands and shouted bravo. Then one of the men went to the corner. In the orchestra the cymbals and trumpets struck up more loudly, and this one man with bare legs started leaping high in the air and shifting his feet. (This man was Duport, who earned sixty thousand silver roubles for this art.) Everyone in the parterre, in the boxes, and in the gallery started clapping and shouting with all their might, and the man stopped and started smiling and bowing on all sides. Then the other men and women with bare legs danced, then one of the tsars again shouted something to the music, and they all began to sing. But suddenly a storm broke, the orchestra played chromatic scales and diminished seventh chords, and everyone ran and again dragged one of those present into the wings, and the curtain fell. Again a terrible noise and clamour arose among the spectators, and everyone started shouting with rapturous faces:

"Duport! Duport! Duport!"

Natasha no longer found it strange. She looked around with pleasure, smiling joyfully.

"*N'est-ce pas qu'il est admirable—Duport?*"* said Hélène, turning to her.

"*Oh, oui,*" answered Natasha.

X

During the entr'acte there was a gust of cold in Hélène's box, the door opened, and Anatole came in, ducking his head and trying not to snag on anyone.

"Allow me to introduce my brother to you," said Hélène, her eyes darting uneasily from Natasha to Anatole. Natasha turned her pretty head and smiled at the handsome fellow over her bare shoulder. Anatole, who was as good-looking close up as from afar, sat down next to her and said that he had long wished to have this pleasure, ever since the Naryshkins' ball, where he had had the pleasure, which he had not forgotten, of seeing her. With women Kuragin was much more intelligent and simple than in the company of men. He spoke boldly and simply, and Natasha was strangely and pleasantly struck that there was not only nothing frightening in this man, of whom there was so much talk, but that, on the contrary, he had a most naïvely cheerful and good-natured smile.

Anatole Kuragin asked what her impression of the performance was, and told her that during the previous performance, Semyonova had fallen on stage.

"But you know, Countess," he said suddenly, addressing her like an old,

---

*Isn't he wonderful—Duport?

long-standing acquaintance, "we're organizing a costume carousel; you must take part in it: we'll have great fun. Everybody's getting together at the Arkharovs'. Please come, won't you?" he said.

While saying this, he never took his smiling eyes from Natasha's face, neck, and bared arms. Natasha knew beyond doubt that he admired her. She enjoyed that, but for some reason his presence made her feel constrained, hot, and oppressed. When she was not looking at him, she felt that he was looking at her shoulders, and she involuntarily intercepted his glance, preferring that he look into her eyes. But, looking into his eyes, she felt with fear that between him and her that barrier of modesty which she had always felt between herself and other men was not there at all. Without knowing how herself, after five minutes she felt terribly close to this man. Whenever she turned away, she was afraid he might take her bare arm from behind or kiss her on the neck. They talked about the simplest things, and she felt that they were closer than she had ever been with any man. Natasha glanced at Hélène and at her father, as if asking them what on earth it meant, but Hélène was taken up by a conversation with some general and did not respond to her glance, and her father's glance said nothing to her except what it always said: "You're enjoying yourself, and I'm glad."

In one of the moments of awkward silence during which Anatole calmly and persistently stared at her with his prominent eyes, Natasha, to break the silence, asked him how he liked Moscow. Natasha asked it and blushed. She kept feeling that she was doing something indecent in speaking with him. Anatole smiled, as if encouraging her.

"In the beginning I didn't like it much, because what is it that makes a city pleasant? *Ce sont les jolies femmes,** isn't that so? Well, but now I like it very much," he said, looking at her meaningfully. "Will you come to this carousel, Countess? Please do come," he said and, reaching his hand out to her bouquet and lowering his voice, he said: "*Vous serez la plus jolie. Venez, chère comtesse, et comme gage donnez-moi cette fleur.*"†

Natasha did not understand what he said, nor did he himself, but she felt that there was some indecent purpose in his incomprehensible words. She did not know what to say, and she turned away as if she had not heard what he said. But as soon as she turned away, she thought that he was there behind her, so near to her.

"How is he now? Is he embarrassed? Angry? Should I set things right?" she asked herself. She could not help turning to look. She looked straight into his eyes, and his nearness, and his confidence, and the good-natured tenderness of his smile won her over. She also smiled at him, just as he did, looking straight

---

*It's pretty women.

†You will be the prettiest one. Come, dear Countess, and as a pledge give me this flower.

into his eyes. And again she felt with horror that between him and her there was no barrier of any sort.

The curtain rose again. Anatole left the box calm and cheerful. Natasha returned to her father's box, now totally subjected to the world she was in. Everything that was happening before her now seemed perfectly natural to her; but instead all her former thoughts about her fiancé, about Princess Marya, about country life, never once entered her head, as if it was all long ago, long past.

In the fourth act there was a devil, who sang, waving his arm, until the boards were pulled out from under him, and he sank down below. That was all Natasha saw of the fourth act: something excited and tormented her, and the cause of it was Kuragin, whom she involuntarily followed with her eyes. As they were leaving the theatre, Anatole came up to them, hailed their carriage, and helped them in. Helping Natasha in, he pressed her arm above the wrist. Natasha, excited, red, and happy, glanced at him. He, flashing his eyes and smiling tenderly, was looking at her.

Only when she came home could Natasha clearly think through all that had happened to her, and suddenly, remembering Prince Andrei, she became horrified, and, in front of everyone, over the tea to which they all sat down after the theatre, gasped loudly, turned red, and ran out of the room. "My God! I'm lost!" she said to herself. "How could I have allowed it?" she thought. For a long time she sat, covering her flushed face with her hands, trying to give herself a clear accounting of what had happened to her, and she could understand neither what had happened nor what she felt. Everything seemed dark, unclear, and frightening to her. There, in that huge, brightly lit hall, where Duport, with bare legs and a sparkling jacket, had leaped over the wet boards to the music, and girls, and old men, and the bare Hélène, with her calm and proud smile, had rapturously shouted bravo—there, in the shadow of this Hélène, everything had been clear and simple; but now, alone with herself, it was incomprehensible. "What on earth is it? What is this fear that I feel before him? What is this remorse that I feel now?" she wondered.

Only to the old countess, in bed at night, would Natasha have been able to tell everything she thought. She knew that Sonya, with her strict and wholesome view, would either understand nothing or be horrified by her confession. Natasha, alone with herself, tried to resolve what was tormenting her.

"Am I lost for Prince Andrei's love, or not?" she asked herself, and with a placating smile, she answered herself: "What a fool I am to be asking that! What happened to me? Nothing. I did nothing, I didn't provoke it in any way. No one will know of it, and I will never see him again," she said to herself. "So it's clear that nothing happened, that there's nothing to repent of, that Prince Andrei can love me *like this*. But what's this *like this*? Ah, my God, my God! why isn't he here?" Natasha would calm down for a moment, but then again some instinct would tell her that, although it was all true and nothing had happened—the instinct would tell her that all the former purity of her love for Prince Andrei was lost. And again in her imagination she would repeat her whole conversation with Kuragin, and picture the face, the gesture, the tender smile of that handsome and bold man when he pressed her arm.

XI

Anatole Kuragin was living in Moscow because his father had sent him away from Petersburg, where he spent over twenty thousand a year in cash and the same amount in debts, which his creditors demanded from his father.

The father announced to the son that he would pay half his debts for the last time, but only on condition that he go to Moscow in his capacity as the commander in chief's adjutant, which he had solicited for him, and try finally to find a good match for himself there. He pointed out Princess Marya and Julie Karagin for him.

Anatole agreed and went to Moscow, where he stayed with Pierre. At first, Pierre received Anatole reluctantly, but then he got used to him, occasionally went carousing with him, and gave him money in the guise of loans.

Anatole, as Shinshin rightly said of him, had driven all the Moscow ladies out of their minds ever since his arrival, especially by neglecting them and apparently preferring Gypsy women and French actresses, with the foremost of whom, Mlle George, he was said to be in intimate relations. He never missed a single carouse at Dolokhov's and at other Moscow merrymakers', drank all night long, outdrank everybody, and attended all the high society soirées and balls. There was talk of several intrigues of his with Moscow ladies, and at balls he paid court to some. But he never approached young girls, especially rich, marriageable ones, who were for the most part plain, the less so in that Anatole—something no one but his closest friends knew—had got married two years before. Two years before, while his regiment was stationed in Poland, a modest Polish landowner had forced Anatole to marry his daughter.

Anatole quite soon abandoned his wife and, for the money he promised to send to his father-in-law, reserved for himself the right to pass himself off as a bachelor.

Anatole was always content with his position, with himself, and with others. He was instinctively convinced with his whole being that it was impossible for him to live otherwise than the way he lived, and that he had never in his life done anything bad. He was not capable of reflecting either on how his actions might affect others, or on what might come of one or another of his actions. He was convinced that, just as the duck was created so that it must always live in water, so he was created by God so that he must live on an income of thirty thousand and occupy a high position in society. He believed it so firmly that others, looking at him, were also convinced of it and refused him neither a high position in society, nor the money which he, obviously without paying it back, borrowed from anyone and everyone.

He was not a gambler, at least he never cared about winning, and never even regretted losing. He was not vain. To him it made absolutely no difference what people thought of him. Still less could he be accused of being ambitious. Several times he taunted his father by ruining his career, and he made fun of all honours. He was not stingy and never refused anyone who asked of him. There was one thing he loved—merrymaking and women—and since, to his mind, there was nothing ignoble in these tastes, and since he was unable to reflect on the consequences that the satisfaction of his tastes had for other people, at heart he considered himself an irreproachable man, sincerely despised scoundrels and bad people, and with an easy conscience carried his head high.

Carousers, those male Magdalenes, have a hidden sense of awareness of their innocence, just as female Magdalenes have, based on the same hope of forgiveness. "Everything will be forgiven her, for she loved much; and every-thing will be forgiven him, for he had much fun."[11]

Dolokhov, who had appeared again in Moscow that year after his banish-ment and his Persian adventures, and who was leading a magnificent gambling and carousing life, became close with his old Petersburg friend Kuragin and used him for his own purposes.

Anatole sincerely liked Dolokhov for his intelligence and daring; Dolokhov, who needed the name, noble birth, and connections of Anatole Kuragin to lure rich young men into his gambling company, used and toyed with Kuragin without letting him feel it. Apart from the calculation which made Anatole necessary for him, the very process of manipulating another person's will was a pleasure, a habit, and a necessity for Dolokhov.

Natasha had made a strong impression on Kuragin. Over supper after the theatre, in the manner of a connoisseur, he analysed for Dolokhov the merits of her arms, shoulders, feet, and hair, and announced his decision to dangle after her a bit. What the result of this courtship might be, Anatole could not reflect upon or know, as he never knew what the result of any of his actions would be.

"She's a nice one, brother, but not for us," Dolokhov said to him.

"I'll tell my sister to invite her to dinner," said Anatole. "Eh?"

"You'd better wait till she's married . . ."

"You know," said Anatole, "*j'adore les petites filles:** she'll get all flustered."

"You already got caught once over a *petite fille*," said Dolokhov, who knew about Anatole's marriage. "Watch out."

*I adore little girls.

"Well, as if it can't happen twice! Eh?" said Anatole, laughing good-naturedly.

XII

The day after the theatre, the Rostovs did not go anywhere, and no one came to them. Marya Dmitrievna discussed something with Natasha's father, concealing it from her. Natasha could guess that they were talking about the old prince, working something out, and that disturbed and offended her. She was expecting Prince Andrei any moment and had sent the yard porter to Vzdvizhenka twice that day to find out if he had come. He had not. It was now harder for her than in the first days after her arrival. To her impatience and sadness were added the unpleasant memory of meeting Princess Marya and the old prince, and a fear and uneasiness of which she did not know the cause. She kept fancying either that he would never come or that something would happen to her before he came. She could not, as before, think about him calmly and for a long time, alone with herself. As soon as she began thinking about him, to her memory of him were added the memories of the old prince, of Princess Marya, of last night's performance, and of Kuragin. She again faced the question of whether she was to blame, whether she had already broken faith with Prince Andrei, and she again found herself recalling in the minutest detail every word, every gesture, every shade of expression that had played on the face of this man, who was able to arouse in her an incomprehensible and frightening feeling. In the eyes of those around her, Natasha seemed more animated than usual, but she was far from being as calm and happy as she had been before.

On Sunday morning, Marya Dmitrievna invited her guests to the liturgy at her parish of the Dormition on Mogiltsy.[12]

"I don't like these fashionable churches," she said, obviously proud of her freedom of thought. "God is the same everywhere. We have a wonderful priest, he celebrates properly, with some nobility, and so does the deacon. Is it some sort of holiness if the choir sings a concert? I don't like it, it's nothing but indulgence!"

Marya Dmitrievna liked Sundays and knew how to make them festive. Her house was always all scrubbed and cleaned on Saturday; she and her servants did no work, everybody got dressed up festively, and everybody went to the liturgy. Courses were added to the mistress's dinner, and the servants were given vodka and a roast goose or sucking-pig. But in nothing in the whole house was the festivity so noticeable as in Marya Dmitrievna's broad, stern face, which on that day acquired a permanent expression of solemnity.

When they had finished coffee after the liturgy, in the drawing room, where the dustcovers had been removed, it was announced to Marya Dmitrievna that the carriage was ready, and she, with a stern look, dressed in the fancy shawl in which she went visiting, stood up and declared that she was going to see Prince Nikolai Andreevich Bolkonsky, to have a talk with him concerning Natasha.

After Marya Dmitrievna's departure, a dressmaker came to the Rostovs' from Madame Chalmet, and Natasha, shutting the door to the room next to the drawing room, very pleased to be diverted, began trying on the new dresses. As she was putting on a tacked together and still sleeveless bodice, turning her head to see in the mirror how the back fitted, she heard animated voices from the drawing room, one her father's and the other a woman's voice which made her blush. It was the voice of Hélène. Before Natasha had time to take off the bodice she was trying on, the door opened and Countess Bezukhov walked in, beaming with a good-natured and affectionate smile, in a dark purple velvet dress with a high collar.

"*Ah, ma délicieuse!*"* she said to the blushing Natasha. "*Charmante!* No, this will never do, my dear count," she said to Ilya Andreich, who came in after her. "To live in Moscow and not go anywhere! No, I won't let you be! Tonight at my house Mlle George will recite and there'll be some guests; and if you don't bring your beauties, who are better than Mlle George, then I don't want to know you. My husband isn't here, he's gone to Tver, otherwise I'd send him to fetch you. Do come without fail, after eight." She nodded to the dressmaker, whom she knew, and who curtsied to her deferentially, and sat down in an armchair near the mirror, picturesquely spreading the folds of her velvet dress. She kept babbling away gaily and good-naturedly, ceaselessly admiring Natasha's beauty. She examined her dresses and praised them, boasted of her own new dress *en gaze metallique,*† which she had received from Paris, and advised Natasha to order one like it.

"Though everything becomes you, my lovely one," she said.

The smile of pleasure never left Natasha's face. She felt herself happy and blossoming under the praises of this nice Countess Bezukhov, who had formerly seemed to her such an unapproachable and important lady, and who was now so kind to her. Natasha became cheerful, and she felt almost in love with this woman who was so beautiful and so good-natured. Hélène, for her part, sincerely admired Natasha and wished to entertain her. Anatole had asked her to bring him and Natasha together, and she had come to the Rostovs' for that. The thought of bringing her brother together with Natasha amused her.

Despite the fact that she had formerly been vexed with Natasha, in Petersburg, for having won Boris away from her, she did not think of that now, and

*Ah, my delightful one!
†Metallic gauze.

in her own way wholeheartedly wished Natasha well. As she was leaving the Rostovs', she called her *protégée* aside.

"Yesterday my brother dined with me—we died of laughter—he eats nothing and sighs after you, my lovely. *Il est fou, mais fou amoureux de vous, ma chère.*"*

Natasha flushed crimson, hearing these words.

"How she blushes, how she blushes, *ma délicieuse!*" said Hélène. "Be sure to come. *Si vous aimez quelqu'un, ma délicieuse, ce n'est pas une raison pour se cloîtrer. Si même vous êtes promise, je suis sûr que votre promis aurais désiré que vous alliez dans le monde en son absence plutôt que de dépérir d'ennui.*"†

"So she knows I'm betrothed, so she and her husband, Pierre, the upright Pierre," thought Natasha, "have talked and laughed about it. So it's nothing at all." And again, under Hélène's influence, that which formerly had appeared to be frightening, now seemed simple and natural. "And she's such a *grande dame,* such a sweet lady, and she clearly loves me with all her heart," thought Natasha. "And why shouldn't I have fun?" she thought, looking at Hélène with astonished, wide-open eyes.

Marya Dmitrievna came home for dinner, silent, grave, obviously having suffered a defeat at the old prince's. She was still too agitated after the confrontation that had occurred to be able to tell about it calmly. To the count's question, she replied that all was well and that she would tell him about it tomorrow. Learning of Countess Bezukhov's visit and the invitation for the evening, Marya Dmitrievna said:

"I don't like to keep company with the Bezukhov woman and I don't advise it; but if you've already promised, go, divert yourself," she added, addressing Natasha.

XIII

Count Ilya Andreich took his girls to Countess Bezukhov's. There were quite a few people at the soirée. But the company was almost entirely unfamiliar to Natasha. Count Ilya Andreich noticed with displeasure that this company consisted mostly of men and of ladies known for the frivolity of their behaviour. Mlle George, surrounded by young men, stood in the corner of the drawing room. There were several Frenchmen, among them Métivier, who, since Hélène's arrival, had become a familiar of her house. Count Ilya Andreich decided not

---

*He's madly, quite madly in love with you, my dear.
†If you love someone, my delightful one, that's no reason to cloister yourself. Even if you're betrothed, I'm sure your betrothed would want you to go into society in his absence sooner than perish from boredom.

to sit down to cards, not to go far from his daughters, and to leave as soon as the actress's performance was over.

Anatole was obviously waiting by the door for the Rostovs to come in. Having greeted the count, he at once went up to Natasha and followed her. As soon as Natasha saw him, she was seized by the same feeling as in the theatre, of vain pleasure at being liked by him, and of fear because of the absence of moral barriers between them.

Hélène joyfully welcomed Natasha and loudly admired her beauty and her attire. Soon after their arrival, Mlle George left the room to get dressed. In the drawing room they began arranging chairs and sitting down. Anatole moved a chair for Natasha and was about to sit next to her, but the count, who never took his eyes off Natasha, sat next to her. Anatole sat behind them.

Mlle George, with bared, fat, dimpled arms, wearing a red shawl over one shoulder, came out into the empty space left for her among the chairs and stopped in an unnatural pose. Rapturous whispering was heard.

Mlle George gave the public a stern and gloomy look and began to recite some verses in French in which the talk was of her criminal love for her son.[13] In places she raised her voice, in places she whispered, solemnly lifting up her head, in places she paused and gasped, rolling her eyes.

"*Adorable, divin, délicieux!*"* came from all sides. Natasha looked at the fat George, but heard nothing, saw and understood nothing of what went on before her; she only felt herself again quite irretrievably in that strange, insane world, so far from her former one, that world in which it was impossible to know what was good, what was bad, what was sane and what insane. Behind her sat Anatole, and she, sensing his nearness, waited fearfully for something.

After the first monologue, the whole company stood up and surrounded Mlle George, expressing their rapture.

"How beautiful she is!" Natasha said to her father, who stood up along with the others and moved through the crowd towards the actress.

"I don't find her so, looking at you," said Anatole, following Natasha. He said it at a moment when she alone could hear him. "You're lovely . . . from the moment I first saw you, I've never ceased . . ."

"Come along, come along, Natasha," said the count, turning back for his daughter. "How beautiful she is!"

Natasha, saying nothing, went up to her father and looked at him with questioningly astonished eyes.

After several recitations, Mlle George left, and Countess Bezukhov invited the company to the reception room.

The count wanted to leave, but Hélène begged him not to ruin her improvised ball. The Rostovs stayed. Anatole invited Natasha for a waltz, and dur-

*Adorable, divine, delightful!

ing the waltz he pressed her waist and her hand, told her that she was *ravissante* and that he loved her. During the *écossaise*, which she again danced with Kuragin, when they were left alone, Anatole said nothing and only looked at her. Natasha had doubts whether what he had said to her during the waltz was not a dream. At the end of the first figure, he again pressed her hand. Natasha raised her frightened eyes to him, but there was such a self-assured, tender expression in his affectionate gaze and smile that, looking at him, she could not tell him what she had to tell him. She lowered her eyes.

"Don't say such things to me, I am betrothed and love another man," she said quickly . . . She glanced at him. Anatole was not embarrassed or upset by what she told him.

"Don't talk to me about that. What do I care?" he said. "I say that I'm madly, madly in love with you. Is it my fault that you're exquisite? . . . It's our turn."

Natasha, animated and alarmed, looked around with wide-open, frightened eyes and seemed merrier than usual. She remembered almost nothing of what happened that evening. They danced the *écossaise* and the Grossvater, her father invited her to leave, she begged to stay. Wherever she was, whomever she talked with, she felt his eyes upon her. Then she remembered that she asked her father's permission to go to the dressing room and straighten her dress, that Hélène came after her, spoke to her, laughingly, of her brother's love, and that in a small sitting room she again met Anatole, that Hélène disappeared somewhere, the two of them were left alone, and Anatole, taking her hand, said in a tender voice:

"I cannot call on you, but can it be that I will never see you? I love you madly. Can it be never? . . ." And, blocking her way, he brought his face close to hers.

His shining, big, masculine eyes were so close to her eyes that she saw nothing except those eyes.

"Natalie?!" his voice whispered questioningly, and someone squeezed her hands painfully. "Natalie?!"

"I understand nothing, I have nothing to say," her gaze said.

Hot lips pressed themselves to her lips, and at the same moment she felt herself released again, and heard the rustle of Hélène's dress in the room and the sound of her footsteps. Natasha glanced at Hélène, then, red and trembling, gave him a fearfully questioning glance and went to the door.

"*Un mot, un seul, au nom de dieu,*"* Anatole was saying.

She stopped. She needed so much that he say that word which would explain to her what had happened and that she could answer him.

"*Natalie, un mot, un seul,*" he kept repeating, apparently not knowing what to say, and he repeated it until Hélène came up to them.

*One word, just one, in God's name.

Hélène came out to the drawing room again together with Natasha. Without staying for supper, the Rostovs left.

Having returned home, Natasha did not sleep all night; an insoluble question tormented her: whom did she love, Anatole or Prince Andrei? She did love Prince Andrei—she clearly remembered how strongly she loved him. But she also loved Anatole, that was beyond doubt. "Otherwise how could all this have happened?" she wondered. "If, after that, in saying goodbye to him, I could respond to his smile with a smile, if I could let it go that far, it means that I loved him from the first moment. It means that he is kind, noble, and beautiful, and it was impossible not to love him. What am I to do, if I love him and love the other?" she said to herself, finding no answers to these terrible questions.

XIV

Morning came with its cares and bustle. Everybody got up, began to move, to talk, again the dressmakers came, again Marya Dmitrievna came out, and tea was served. Natasha looked at them all uneasily, with wide-open eyes, as if she wanted to catch every glance directed at her, and tried to seem the same as she always was.

After breakfast Marya Dmitrievna (this was her best time) sat down in her armchair and called Natasha and the old count to her.

"Well, my friends, I've thought the whole matter over, and here's my advice to you," she began. "Yesterday, as you know, I called on Prince Nikolai; well, sir, and I talked with him . . . He took a notion to shout. But there's no out-shouting me! I sang it all out for him!"

"And what about him?" asked the count.

"What about him? A madcap . . . doesn't want to listen. Well, there's no point talking, we've worn the poor girl out as it is," said Marya Dmitrievna. "And my advice to you is to finish your business and go home to Otradnoe . . . and wait there . . ."

"Ah, no!" cried Natasha.

"No, go home," said Marya Dmitrievna. "And wait there. If her fiancé comes here now, there'll be no avoiding a quarrel, and here he can talk it over alone with the old man and then come to you."

Ilya Andreich approved of this suggestion, grasping its good sense at once. If the old man softens, it will be all the better if they come to him in Moscow or Bald Hills afterwards; if not, then they could marry against his will only in Otradnoe.

"That's the veritable truth," he said. "And I regret that I went to see him and took her," said the old count.

"No, what is there to regret? Being here, you couldn't help paying your respects. And if he doesn't want it, that's his business," said Marya Dmitrievna, looking for something in her reticule. "And the trousseau is ready, you have nothing else to wait for, and what isn't ready, I'll send to you. Though I'll miss you, it's better that you go with God." Having found what she was looking for in the reticule, she gave it to Natasha. It was a letter from Princess Marya. "She writes to you. She's suffering so, the poor thing! She's afraid you'll think she doesn't love you."

"But she doesn't love me," said Natasha.

"Don't talk nonsense," cried Marya Dmitrievna.

"I won't believe anyone: I know she doesn't love me," Natasha said boldly, taking the letter, and her face showed a dry and spiteful resolution that made Marya Dmitrievna look at her more intently and frown.

"Don't you answer me back like that, dearie," she said. "What I'm saying is true. Write a reply."

Natasha did not answer and went to her room to read Princess Marya's letter.

Princess Marya wrote that she was in despair because of the misunderstanding that had occurred between them. Whatever her father's feelings were, wrote Princess Marya, she asked Natasha to believe that she could not but love her as the one chosen by her brother, for whose happiness she was ready to sacrifice everything.

"However," she wrote, "do not think that my father is ill-disposed towards you. He is an old and ailing man who ought to be excused; but he is kind, magnanimous, and will love the one who will make for his son's happiness." Princess Marya also asked Natasha to set a time when she could see her again.

Having read the letter, Natasha sat down at the desk to write a reply. *"Chère Princesse!"* she wrote quickly and mechanically, and stopped. What could she write after all that had happened yesterday? "Yes, yes, all that was, and now it's all different," she thought, sitting over the started letter. "Must I refuse him? Must I really? It's terrible! . . ." And, so as not to think those dreadful thoughts, she went to Sonya and began sorting out patterns with her.

After dinner, Natasha went to her room and again took up Princess Marya's letter. "Can it all be over already?" she wondered. "Can it all have happened so quickly and have destroyed all the former things?" She recalled her love for Prince Andrei with all its former force, and at the same time she felt that she loved Kuragin. She vividly imagined herself as Prince Andrei's wife, imagined the picture of her happiness with him, repeated in her mind so many times, and together with that, burning with excitement, she pictured to herself all the details of yesterday's meeting with Anatole.

"Why can't it be both together?" she thought in moments of total darkening. "Only then would I be perfectly happy, but now I must make a choice, and

I can't be happy without either of them. The thing is," she thought, "that it's equally impossible to tell Prince Andrei what has happened or to conceal it. While with *this one* nothing's spoiled. But can I really part for ever with the happiness of loving Prince Andrei, which I've lived with for so long?"

"Miss," a maid said in a whisper, with a mysterious look, coming into the room. "A man told me to give you this." The maid handed her a letter. "Only, for Christ's sake, miss . . ." the maid was still talking, while Natasha, unthinkingly, with a mechanical movement, broke the seal and began reading Anatole's love letter, from which, not understanding a word of it, she understood only one thing, that this letter was from him, from the man she loved. "Yes, she loves him, otherwise how could what happened have happened? How could a love letter from him be in her hand?"

With trembling hands Natasha held this passionate love letter, composed for Anatole by Dolokhov, and, reading it, she found in it echoes of everything she thought she felt herself.

"Since last evening my fate is sealed: to be loved by you or to die. I have no other way out," the letter began. Then he wrote that he knew the family would not give her to him, that there were secret reasons for that which he could reveal only to her, but that if she loved him, she had only to say the word "yes" and no human powers would prevent their bliss. Love would overcome all. He would abduct her and carry her off to the ends of the earth.

"Yes, yes, I love him!" thought Natasha, rereading the letter for the twentieth time and seeking some special, deep meaning in each word.

That evening Marya Dmitrievna went to the Arkharovs and suggested that the girls come with her. Natasha stayed home under the pretext of a headache.

XV

Returning late in the evening, Sonya came into Natasha's room and, to her surprise, found her still dressed, asleep on the sofa. On the table next to her lay the opened letter from Anatole. Sonya picked up the letter and started reading it.

She was reading and glancing at the sleeping Natasha, searching her face for an explanation of what she was reading and unable to find it. The face was gentle, meek, and happy. Clutching her chest to keep from choking, Sonya, pale and termbling with fear and agitation, sat in an armchair and dissolved in tears.

"How is it I didn't see anything? How could it have gone so far? Can it be she no longer loves Prince Andrei? And how could she have allowed this Kuragin? He's a deceiver and a villain, that's clear. What will Nicolas, dear, noble Nicolas, do when he finds out about it? So this is what her excited, determined, and unnatural face meant two days ago, and yesterday, and today," thought

Sonya. "But it can't be that she loves him! She probably opened the letter not knowing whom it was from. She's probably offended. She can't do that!"

Sonya wiped her tears and went over to Natasha, again peering into her face.

"Natasha!" she said, barely audibly.

Natasha woke up and saw Sonya.

"Ah, you're back?"

And with the resolution and tenderness that occur in moments of awakening, she embraced her friend. But, noticing the embarrassment on Sonya's face, Natasha's face expressed embarrassment and suspicion.

"Sonya, you read the letter?" she asked.

"Yes," Sonya said softly.

Natasha smiled rapturously.

"No, Sonya, I can't any more!" said Natasha. "I can't conceal it from you any more. You know, we love each other! . . . Sonya, darling, he writes . . . Sonya . . ."

Sonya, as if not believing what she heard, stared all eyes at Natasha.

"And Bolkonsky?" she asked.

"Ah, Sonya, if only you could know how happy I am!" said Natasha. "You don't know what love is . . ."

"But, Natasha, can *that* be all over?"

Natasha looked at Sonya with big, open eyes, as if she did not understand her question.

"What, are you refusing Prince Andrei?" asked Sonya.

"Ah, you don't understand anything, don't say stupid things, just listen," Natasha said with instant vexation.

"No, I can't believe it," Sonya repeated. "I don't understand. How is it that you've loved a man for a whole year and suddenly . . . You've only seen him three times, Natasha, I don't believe you, you're joking. To forget everything in three days and so . . ."

"Three days," said Natasha. "It seems to me I've loved him for a hundred years. It seems to me I've never loved anyone before him. And never loved anyone the way I love him. You can't understand it, Sonya. Wait, sit here." Natasha embraced and kissed her. "I've been told it happens, and you've probably heard it, but only now have I experienced this love. This isn't like before. As soon as I saw him, I felt that he was my master and I was his slave, and that I couldn't help loving him. Yes, slave! What he tells me to do, I'll do. You don't understand it. What am I to do? What am I to do, Sonya?" Natasha said with a happy and frightened face.

"But think what you're doing," said Sonya. "I can't leave it like this. These secret letters . . . How could you let him go so far?" she said with a horror and revulsion she had difficulty hiding.

"I told you," replied Natasha, "that I have no will, how can you not understand that: I love him!"

"Then I won't let it go so far, I'll tell," cried Sonya, bursting into tears.

"For God's sake, what are you . . . If you tell, you're my enemy," Natasha began. "You want me to be unhappy, you want them to separate us . . ."

Seeing this fear of Natasha's, Sonya wept tears of shame and pity for her friend.

"But what has happened between you?" she asked. "What has he told you? Why can't he visit our house?"

Natasha did not answer her question.

"For God's sake, Sonya, don't tell anyone, don't torment me," Natasha pleaded. "Remember, it's wrong to interfere in such things. I revealed it to you . . ."

"But why these secrets? Why doesn't he come to the house?" Sonya kept asking. "Why doesn't he seek your hand directly? Prince Andrei gave you full freedom, if that's how it is; but I don't believe it. Natasha, have you thought what *secret reasons* there might be?"

Natasha looked at Sonya with astonished eyes. Clearly, this question had presented itself to her for the first time, and she did not know how to answer it.

"What reasons, I don't know. But it means there are reasons!"

Sonya sighed and shook her head mistrustfully.

"If there are reasons . . ." she began. But Natasha, guessing her doubts, interrupted her fearfully.

"Sonya, it's impossible to doubt him, impossible, impossible, do you understand?" she cried.

"Does he love you?"

"Love?" Natasha repeated with a smile of regret at her friend's incomprehension. "Haven't you read the letter, haven't you seen him?"

"But if he's an ignoble man?"

"*He*—an ignoble man? If you only knew!" said Natasha.

"If he's a noble man, then he should either declare his intentions or stop seeing you; and if you don't want to do it, I'll do it; I'll write to him and tell *papa*," Sonya said resolutely.

"But I can't live without him!" cried Natasha.

"Natasha, I don't understand you. What are you saying! Think of your father, of Nicolas."

"I don't need anybody, I don't love anybody but him. How dare you say he's ignoble? Don't you know that I love him?" cried Natasha. "Go away, Sonya, I don't want to quarrel with you, go away, for God's sake, go away: you see how tormented I am," Natasha cried angrily in a restrainedly irritated and desperate voice. Sonya burst into sobs and ran out of the room.

Natasha went to the table and, without a moment's thought, wrote that reply to Princess Marya which she had been unable to write all morning. In this letter she curtly wrote to Princess Marya that all their misunderstandings were over, that, taking advantage of the magnanimity of Prince Andrei, who, on leaving, had given her freedom, she asked her to forget everything and to forgive her if she was to blame before her, but that she could not be his wife. All this seemed so easy, simple, and clear to her at that moment.

On Friday the Rostovs were to go to the country, and on Wednesday the count went with a buyer to his estate near Moscow.

On the day of the count's departure, Sonya and Natasha were invited to a big dinner at the Kuragins', and Marya Dmitrievna brought them. At this dinner Natasha again met with Anatole, and Sonya noticed that Natasha discussed something with him, trying not to be heard, and all through dinner was still more agitated than before. When they returned home, Natasha was the first to begin that talk with Sonya which her friend was expecting.

"So, Sonya, here you were saying all kinds of stupid things about him," Natasha began in a meek voice, the sort of voice in which children speak when they want to be praised. "He and I had a talk tonight."

"Well, and what, what then? What did he say? Natasha, I'm so glad you're not angry with me. Tell me everything, the whole truth. What did he say?"

Natasha became thoughtful.

"Ah, Sonya, if you knew him as I do! He said . . . He asked me what sort of promise I had made to Bolkonsky. He was glad that it rested with me to refuse him."

Sonya sighed sadly.

"But surely you haven't refused Bolkonsky?" she asked.

"Maybe I even have refused him! Maybe it's all over with Bolkonsky. Why do you think so ill of me?"

"I don't think anything, I just don't understand it . . ."

"Wait, Sonya, you'll understand everything. You'll see what a man he is. Only don't think ill either of me or of him."

"I don't think ill of anybody: I love everybody and pity everybody. But what am I to do?"

Sonya would not yield to the tender tone in which Natasha addressed her. The more soft and ingratiating the expression of Natasha's face was, the more serious and stern was the face of Sonya.

"Natasha," she said, "you asked me not to speak to you, and I didn't, you yourself began it now. Natasha, I don't trust him. Why this secrecy?"

"Again, again!" interrupted Natasha.

"Natasha, I'm afraid for you."

"Why be afraid?"

"I'm afraid you'll ruin yourself," Sonya said resolutely, frightened herself at what she said.

Natasha's face again showed anger.

"And I will, I will, I'll ruin myself as soon as possible. It's none of your business. It will be bad for me, not for you. Leave me, leave me alone! I hate you!"

"Natasha!" Sonya implored her fearfully.

"I hate you, I hate you! You're my enemy for ever!"

Natasha ran out of the room.

Natasha did not speak with Sonya any more and avoided her. With the same expression of agitated surprise and criminality, she paced the rooms, taking up one thing, then another, and abandoning them at once.

Hard as it was for Sonya, she watched her friend without taking her eyes off her.

The day before the count was to come back, Sonya noticed that Natasha sat all morning by the window in the drawing room, as if waiting for something, and that she made a sign to a passing officer, whom Sonya took to be Anatole.

Sonya began to watch her friend still more attentively, and noticed that all through dinner and in the evening, Natasha was in a strange and unnatural state (responded beside the point to questions put to her, began phrases and did not finish them, laughed at everything).

After tea, Sonya saw a timorous maid waiting for her by Natasha's door. She let her in and, eavesdropping at the door, learned that a letter had been brought again.

And it suddenly became clear to Sonya that Natasha had some terrible plan for that night. Sonya knocked on her door. Natasha did not let her in.

"She's going to elope with him!" thought Sonya. "She's capable of anything. Tonight there was something especially pathetic and resolute in her face. She cried as she said goodbye to uncle," Sonya recalled. "Yes, it's certain, she's going to elope with him—but what am I to do?" Sonya wondered, recalling the signs which clearly proved to her that Natasha had some terrible intention. "The count isn't here. What am I to do? Write to Kuragin, demanding an explanation from him? But who will tell him to reply to me? Write to Pierre, as Prince Andrei asked me to do in case of misfortune? . . . But maybe she has indeed already refused Bolkonsky (she sent a letter to Princess Marya yesterday). Uncle's not here!"

To tell Marya Dmitrievna, who had such faith in Natasha, seemed terrible to Sonya.

"But one way or another," thought Sonya, standing in the dark corridor, "now or never, the time has come to prove that I remember the family's kindness to me and that I love Nicolas. No, even if I don't sleep for three nights, I won't leave this corridor, and I'll keep her back by force and not let shame fall upon their family," she thought.

XVI

Anatole had recently moved in with Dolokhov. The plan for abducting Miss Rostov had been thought out and prepared by Dolokhov several days ago, and on the day when Sonya, listening at Natasha's door, decided to keep watch on her, that plan was to be put into execution. Natasha had promised to come out to Kuragin on the back porch at ten o'clock in the evening. Kuragin was to put her into a waiting troika and take her to the village of Kamenka, forty miles from Moscow, where they had a defrocked priest waiting, who was to marry them. In Kamenka, a relay was ready to take them to the Warsaw road, and from there they were to go abroad by post.

Anatole had a passport, travel documents, ten thousand roubles taken from his sister, and ten thousand borrowed through the intermediary of Dolokhov.

Two witnesses—Khvostikov, a former clerk, whom Dolokhov made use of for gambling, and Makarin, a retired hussar, a kind-hearted and weak man, who had a boundless love for Kuragin—sat in the front room over tea.

In Dolokhov's big study, its walls decorated up to the ceiling with Persian rugs, bearskins, and weapons, sat Dolokhov, in a travelling jacket and boots, before an open bureau on which lay an abacus and wads of money. Anatole, in an unbuttoned uniform, paced from the room where the witnesses sat, through the study, into the back room, where his French valet and others were packing the last of his belongings. Dolokhov was counting money and writing it down.

"Well," he said, "you've got to give Khvostikov two thousand."

"Well, give it to him," said Anatole.

"Makarka" (as they called Makarin) "is disinterested, he'll go through fire and water for you. Well, there, that's the end of the accounting," said Dolokhov, showing him the note. "Is it right?"

"Yes, of course it's right," said Anatole, who obviously was not listening to Dolokhov, and, with a smile that never left his face, he looked straight ahead.

Dolokhov slammed the bureau shut and turned to Anatole with a mocking smile.

"You know what—drop it all. There's still time!" he said.

"Fool!" said Anatole. "Stop saying stupid things. If you knew . . . Devil knows what this is!"

"Drop it, really," said Dolokhov. "I mean it. Do you think it's a joke, what you're up to?"

"What, teasing again? Go to hell! Eh? . . ." Anatole said, wincing. "I can't keep on with your stupid jokes." And he left the room.

Dolokhov smiled scornfully and condescendingly as Anatole went out.

"You wait," he said behind him, "I'm not joking, I mean it, come here, come here."

Anatole came into the room again and, trying to focus his attention, looked at Dolokhov, obviously obeying him involuntarily.

"Listen to me, I'm saying it to you for the last time. Why would I joke with you? Did I thwart you? Who arranged everything, who found the priest, who ordered the passport, who got the money? All me."

"Well, and I thank you. Do you think I'm not grateful to you?" Anatole sighed and embraced Dolokhov.

"I helped you, but even so I have to tell you the truth: it's a dangerous business, and, once you look at it, stupid. So you take her away—good. But are they going to let it stop there? They'll find out you're married. You'll wind up in the criminal court . . ."

"Ah, nonsense, nonsense!" Anatole began, wincing again. "I explained it to you, didn't I?" And with that special partiality which dull-witted people have when they work out some conclusion for themselves, Anatole repeated the argument that he had repeated to Dolokhov a hundred times. "I explained to you that I've decided: if this marriage is invalid," he said, counting off one finger, "it means I'm not answerable; and if it's valid, it makes no difference: nobody abroad will know it—well, isn't it so? And not a word, not a word, not a word!"

"Drop it, really! You'll only bind yourself . . ."

"Go to hell," said Anatole, and seizing himself by the hair, he went to the next room, came back at once, and sat with his legs tucked under in an armchair in front of Dolokhov. "Devil knows what it is! Eh? Feel how it's pounding!" He took Dolokhov's hand and put it to his heart. "*Ah! quel pied, mon cher, quel regard! Une déesse!!** Eh?"

Dolokhov, with a cold smile and flashing his beautiful, insolent eyes, looked at him, clearly wanting to taunt him a little longer.

"Well, when the money's gone, what then?"

"What then? Eh?" Anatole repeated, genuinely puzzled by the thought of the future. "What then? I don't know what then . . . But why talk nonsense!" He looked at his watch. "It's time!"

Anatole went to the back room.

"Well, will you make it soon? No dawdling here!" he shouted at the servants.

Dolokhov put the money away and, shouting for his man, so as to order food and drinks served before the road, went to the room where Makarin and Khvostikov were sitting.

Anatole lay on the sofa in the study, propped on his elbows, smiling pensively and whispering tenderly to himself.

"Go and eat something. Or drink!" Dolokhov called to him from the other room.

_____

*Ah! what a foot, my dear, what a look! A goddess!!

"I don't want to!" Anatole replied, still smiling.

"Come, Balaga's here."

Anatole got up and went to the dining room. Balaga was a famous troika driver, who had known Dolokhov and Anatole for six years already and furnished them with his troikas. More than once, when Anatole's regiment was stationed in Tver, he had taken him from Tver in the evening, brought him to Moscow by dawn, and taken him back the next night. More than once he had driven Dolokhov, when he had had to elude pursuit; more than once he had taken them for a ride around town with Gypsies and "damsels," as Balaga called them. More than once, while in their employ, he had run down folk and cabbies in Moscow, and his "gentlemen," as he called them, had always helped him out. More than one horse had been overdriven under them. More than once he had been beaten by them; more than once they had got him drunk on champagne and Madeira, which he liked, and he knew a thing or two about each of them which would have sent an ordinary man to Siberia long ago. They often invited Balaga to go carousing with them, made him drink and dance with the Gypsies, and more than one thousand of their roubles had gone through his hands. While in their service, he risked his life and his hide twenty times a year, and he had driven more horses to death than they had paid him roubles. But he liked them, liked their mad rides at twelve miles an hour, liked overturning other cabbies, and running down Moscow pedestrians, and going at full gallop down the Moscow streets. He liked hearing the wild shouts of drunken voices behind him: "Faster! Faster!" when it was impossible to go any faster. He liked giving a painful lash on the neck to a peasant, who even without that was trying, more dead than alive, to get out of his way. "Real gentlemen!" he thought.

Anatole and Dolokhov also liked Balaga for his masterful driving, and for liking the same things they did. With others Balaga haggled, charged twenty-five roubles for a two-hour ride, and very rarely went himself, but sent the boys who worked for him. But with his gentlemen, as he called them, he always went himself and never asked anything for his work. Only when he learned through valets that there was money there would he come, once every few months, in the morning, sober, and with low bows ask them to help him out. The gentlemen always invited him to sit down.

"Do help me out, dear Fyodor Ivanych, or you, Your Excellency," he would say. "I've got no horses left, and it's time to go to the fair. Advance me what you can."

And Anatole and Dolokhov, if they had money, would give him a thousand roubles or two.

Balaga was a blond, squat, snub-nosed man, with a red face and an especially red, thick neck, about twenty-seven years old, with small, glittering eyes and a little beard. He was wearing a thin, blue, silk-lined kaftan over a winter jacket.

He crossed himself towards the front corner[14] and went up to Dolokhov, holding out his small, dark hand.

"My respects to Fyodor Ivanovich," he said, bowing.

"Greetings, brother. Well, there he is."

"How do you do, Your Excellency," he said to the entering Anatole, and held out his hand again.

"I say, Balaga," said Anatole, placing his hands on the man's shoulders, "do you love me, or not? Eh? Now do me a service . . . What horses have you brought? Eh?"

"As your messenger told me, it's your own beasts," said Balaga.

"Listen, then, Balaga! Do in the whole troika, but we've got to make it in three hours. Eh?"

"If I do them in, what'll I drive with?" Balaga said, winking.

"I'll smash you in the mug, this is no laughing matter!" Anatole shouted, suddenly goggling his eyes.

"Who's laughing?" the coachman said with a chuckle. "There's no sparing horses for my gentlemen. We'll go as fast as they can gallop."

"Eh!" said Anatole. "Well, sit down."

"Yes, sit down!" said Dolokhov.

"I'll stand, Fyodor Ivanovich."

"Nonsense, sit down, drink," said Anatole, and he poured him a big glass of Madeira. The coachman's eyes lit up at the sight of the wine. He declined out of propriety, then drank and wiped his mouth with a red silk handkerchief tucked inside his hat.

"When do we go, Your Excellency?"

"Let's see . . ." Anatole looked at his watch. "We'll go at once. Look sharp, Balaga. Eh? Will you make it?"

"If we start out with good luck, why shouldn't we make it?" said Balaga. "We used to get you to Tver in seven hours. You surely remember, Your Excellency."

"You know, I once drove from Tver on Christmas Eve," said Anatole with a smile of recollection, addressing Makarin, who tenderly gazed all eyes at Kuragin. "Would you believe, Makarka, it took our breath away, we flew so fast. We drove into a wagon train, leaped right over two wagons. Eh?"

"Some horses those were!" Balaga went on with the same story. "I hitched up young outrunners to the chestnut," he turned to Dolokhov, "and would you believe, Fyodor Ivanych, the beasts flew for forty miles; my hands froze, I couldn't hold on to the reins, it was so cold. I dropped the reins—'Take 'em, Your Excellency'—and just flopped down in the sleigh. And it's not that we urged 'em on—there was no holding 'em back till we got there. The devils made it in three hours. Only the left outrunner dropped dead."

XVII

Anatole left the room and came back in a few moments wearing a fur coat with a silver belt and a sable hat, dashingly cocked to one side, which was very becoming to his handsome face. After looking in the mirror, he stood in front of Dolokhov in the same posture he had assumed in front of the mirror and took a glass of wine.

"Well, Fedya, farewell, thanks for everything, farewell," said Anatole. "Well, comrades, friends . . ." he pondered ". . . of my . . . youth, farewell," he turned to Makarin and the others.

Though they were all going with him, Anatole evidently wanted to make something touching and solemn out of this address to his friends. He spoke in a slow, loud voice and, thrusting out his chest, moved one leg forward.

"Everybody take a glass; you, too, Balaga. Well, comrades, friends of my youth, we've caroused, lived, caroused. Eh? When will we see each other again? I'm going abroad. We've lived—farewell, lads. To your health! Hurrah! . . ." he said, drank his glass, and smashed it on the floor.

"Your health!" said Balaga, also drinking his glass and wiping his mouth with his handkerchief. Makarin, tears in his eyes, embraced Anatole.

"Ah, Prince, I feel so sad parting with you," he said.

"Let's go, let's go!" cried Anatole.

Balaga started for the door.

"No, wait," said Anatole. "Close the door, we have to sit down.[15] There." They closed the door and sat down.

"Well, off we go now, lads!" said Anatole, getting up.

The valet Joseph handed Anatole a bag and a sword, and they all went out to the front hall.

"And where's the fur coat?" said Dolokhov. "Hey, Ignashka! Go to Matryona Matveevna, ask for her sable coat. I've heard how people elope," Dolokhov said, winking. "She'll come running out more dead than alive, in whatever she had on at home; if there's any dawdling—there'll be tears, and papa and mama, and she'll get cold and go back. You must wrap her in a fur coat at once and carry her to the sleigh."

The valet brought a woman's fox coat.

"Fool, the sable one I told you. Hey, Matryoshka, the sable one!" he shouted so loudly that his voice echoed far off through the rooms.

A beautiful, thin, and pale Gypsy girl, with shining black eyes and black curly hair of a bluish sheen, in a red shawl, ran out with a sable coat over her arm.

"Here, I'm not sorry, take it," she said, obviously fearful before her master and sorry about the coat.

Dolokhov, without answering her, took the coat, threw it on Matryosha, and wrapped her up.

"Like this," said Dolokhov. "And then like this," he said and raised the collar round her head, leaving it slightly open only in front of her face. "And then like this, see?" and he moved Anatole's face to the opening in the collar, from which Matryosha's brilliant smile could be seen.

"Well, goodbye, Matryosha," said Anatole, kissing her. "Eh, my carousing's finished here! Greetings to Styoshka.[16] Well, goodbye! Goodbye, Matryosha; wish me happiness."

"Well, Prince, God grant you great happiness," Matryosha said to Anatole with her Gypsy accent.

At the porch stood two troikas, held by two fine-looking coachmen. Balaga got up on the first troika and, raising his elbows high, unhurriedly sorted out the reins. Anatole and Dolokhov got in with him. Makarin, Khvostikov, and the valet got into the other troika.

"Ready?" asked Balaga.

"We're off!" he cried, winding the reins round his hand, and the troika raced thudding down Nikitsky Boulevard.

"Whoa! Giddap, now! . . . Whoa!" the cries of Balaga and the young fellow sitting on the box were all that was heard. On Arbat Square the troika snagged a carriage, something cracked, there was a shout, and the troika flew along the Arbat.

Having driven up and down the length of Podnovinsky, Balaga began reining in and, turning back, stopped the horses at the intersection of Old Konyushennaya.

The coachman jumped down to hold the horses by the bridle, Anatole and Dolokhov went off down the pavement. Coming to the back gate, Dolokhov whistled. A whistle answered him, and following that a maid ran out.

"Come into the yard or you'll be seen; she'll come out at once," she said.

Dolokhov remained by the gate. Anatole followed the maid into the yard, turned the corner, and ran up to the porch.

Gavrilo, Marya Dmitrievna's enormous footman, met Anatole.

"To the mistress, if you please," the footman said in a bass voice, barring the way back.

"What mistress? Who are you?" Anatole asked in a breathless whisper.

"If you please, I was ordered to bring you in."

"Kuragin! Come back!" shouted Dolokhov. "We're betrayed! Come back!"

By the back gate where he had stopped, Dolokhov was struggling with the yard porter, who had tried to lock the gate after Anatole went in. With a final effort, Dolokhov shoved the porter away and, as Anatole ran out, seized him by the arm, pulled him through the gate, and ran back with him to the troika.

XVIII

Marya Dmitrievna, finding the weeping Sonya in the corridor, had made her confess everything. Having intercepted Natasha's note and read it, Marya Dmitrievna went to Natasha with the note in her hand.

"Mean, shameless girl," she said to her. "I don't want to hear anything!" She pushed back Natasha, who looked at her with astonished but dry eyes, locked her in with a key, and, having ordered the yard porter to let in the people who would be coming that evening, but not to let them out, and the valet to bring those people to her, she sat in the drawing room waiting for the abductors.

When Gavrilo came to report to Marya Dmitrievna that the people who had come had run away, she frowned, stood up, and, putting her hands behind her back, paced the rooms for a long time, reflecting on what to do. Towards midnight, feeling the key in her pocket, she went to Natasha's room. Sonya sat weeping in the corridor.

"Marya Dmitrievna, let me see her, for God's sake!" she said. Marya Dmitrievna, not answering her, unlocked the door and went in. "Vile, nasty . . . in my own home, mean girl, hussy . . . I'm only sorry for her father!" thought Marya Dmitrievna, trying to quench her wrath. "Hard as it is, I'll tell everybody to keep quiet and conceal it from the count." Marya Dmitrievna went into the room with resolute steps. Natasha lay on the sofa, covering her head with her hands, and did not stir. She lay in the same position in which Marya Dmitrievna had left her.

"A fine one! very fine!" said Marya Dmitrievna. "Setting up trysts with your lovers in my house! There's no use pretending. You listen when I speak to you." Marya Dmitrievna touched her arm. "You listen when I speak to you. You've disgraced yourself like the lowest wench. I know what I'd do with you, but I'm sorry for your father. I'll conceal it." Natasha did not change her position, but her whole body began to heave with noiseless, convulsive sobs that choked her. Marya Dmitrievna glanced at Sonya and sat on the sofa beside Natasha.

"He's lucky he got away from me; but I'll find him," she said in her rough voice. "Do you hear what I say?" She put her big hand under Natasha's face and turned it towards her. Both Marya Dmitrievna and Sonya were surprised, seeing Natasha's face. Her eyes were glittering and dry, her lips compressed, her cheeks sunken.

"Let me . . . be . . . what do I . . . I'll . . . die . . ." she said, freed herself from Marya Dmitrievna with an angry thrust, and lay in her former position.

"Natalya! . . ." said Marya Dmitrievna. "I wish you well. You're lying there, well, so lie there, I won't touch you, but you listen . . . I won't even speak of how guilty you are. You know it yourself. Well, now your father will come tomorrow, and what am I to tell him? Eh?"

Again Natasha's body shook with sobs.

"Well, so he finds out, and your brother, and your fiancé!"

"I have no fiancé, I refused him," cried Natasha.

"It makes no difference," Marya Dmitrievna went on. "So they'll find out, and what then, will they leave it at that? I know your father, he'll challenge him to a duel. Won't that be a fine thing? Eh?"

"Ah, let me be, why did you interfere with everything! Why? why? who asked you to?" cried Natasha, raising herself on the sofa and looking angrily at Marya Dmitrievna.

"And what would you have liked?" Marya Dmitrievna shouted, getting angry again. "You weren't locked up, were you? Who prevented him from coming to the house? Why carry you off like some Gypsy woman? . . . So he'd carry you off, and then what, do you think they wouldn't find him? Your father, or your brother, or your fiancé? He's a scoundrel, a villain, that's what!"

"He's better than all of you," Natasha cried, getting up. "If you hadn't interfered . . . Oh, my God, what is it, what is it! Why, Sonya! Go away! . . ." And she sobbed with that despair with which people weep only over a grief of which they feel themselves the cause. Marya Dmitrievna tried to speak again, but Natasha shouted: "Go away, go away, you all hate me and despise me!" and she threw herself onto the sofa again.

Marya Dmitrievna went on for some time admonishing Natasha and impressing upon her that all this must be kept from the count, that no one would learn anything, if only Natasha would take it upon herself to forget it all and not let anyone see that something had happened. Natasha did not answer. She was no longer weeping, but she became feverish and began to shiver. Marya Dmitrievna put a pillow under her head, covered her with two blankets, and herself brought her lime-flower tea, but Natasha did not respond to her.

"Well, let her sleep," said Marya Dmitrievna, going out of the room, thinking she was asleep. But Natasha was not asleep, and her fixed, wide-open eyes looked straight ahead from her pale face. Natasha did not sleep all that night, did not weep, and did not speak with Sonya, who got up several times and went over to her.

By lunchtime the next day, as promised, Count Ilya Andreich arrived from his estate near Moscow. He was very cheerful: the business with the buyer was working out, and nothing now kept him in Moscow and separated from the countess, whom he missed. Marya Dmitrievna met him and told him that Natasha had fallen quite ill the day before, that they had sent for the doctor, but that she was better now. Natasha did not leave her room that morning. With compressed, cracked lips and a dry, fixed gaze, she sat by the window and anxiously peered at people driving down the street, and hurriedly turned round when anyone came into the room. She was obviously waiting for news of him, waiting for him to come himself or write to her.

When the count came into her room, she anxiously turned at the sound of a man's footsteps, and her face assumed its former cold and even angry expression. She did not even get up to meet him.

"What is it, my angel, are you ill?" asked the count.

Natasha paused.

"Yes, ill," she replied.

To the count's anxious enquiries as to why she was so crushed and whether anything was wrong with her fiancé, she assured him that nothing was wrong and asked him not to worry. Marya Dmitrievna confirmed for the count Natasha's assurances that nothing had happened. The count, judging by the supposed illness, by his daughter's being upset, by the embarrassed faces of Sonya and Marya Dmitrievna, saw clearly that something must have happened in his absence; but it was so frightening for him to think that anything shameful had happened with his beloved daughter, and he so loved his cheerful tranquillity, that he avoided questions and kept trying to persuade himself that there was nothing in particular, and only grieved that, owing to her illness, they had to put off leaving for the country.

XIX

Since the day his wife arrived in Moscow, Pierre had been intending to go somewhere, only so as not to be there with her. Soon after the Rostovs' arrival in Moscow, the impression Natasha made on him forced him to hasten to carry out his intention. He went to Tver, to see the widow of Iosif Alexeevich, who had long ago promised to give him the deceased's papers.

When Pierre returned to Moscow, he was handed a letter from Marya Dmitrievna, who asked him to come to her on a very important matter concerning Andrei Bolkonsky and his fiancée. Pierre had been avoiding Natasha. It seemed to him that he had a stronger feeling for her than a married man ought to have for his friend's fiancée. Yet some sort of fate constantly brought them together.

"What's happened? What has it got to do with me?" he wondered as he was getting dressed to go to Marya Dmitrievna's. "If only Prince Andrei would come quickly and marry her!" thought Pierre on his way to see Mrs. Akhrosimov.

On Tverskoy Boulevard someone called to him.

"Pierre! Been back long?" a familiar voice cried to him. Pierre raised his head. In a double sleigh harnessed to two grey trotters that kicked snow back into the dashboard, Anatole flashed by with his usual friend Makarin. Anatole was sitting upright in the classical pose of a military fop, the lower part of his face wrapped in a beaver collar, his head bent slightly. His face was ruddy and fresh, his white-plumed hat was cocked, revealing his curled and pomaded hair sprinkled with fine snow.

"Yes, indeed, there's a true wise man!" thought Pierre. "He doesn't see anything beyond the present moment of pleasure, nothing troubles him—and therefore he's always cheerful, content, and calm. I'd give anything to be like him!" Pierre thought with envy.

In Mrs. Akhrosimov's front hall, the valet, helping Pierre out of his fur coat, said that Marya Dmitrievna asked him to come to her bedroom.

Opening the door to the reception room, Pierre saw Natasha sitting by the window with a thin, pale, and spiteful face. She glanced at him, frowned, and, with an expression of cold dignity, left the room.

"What's happened?" asked Pierre, coming into Marya Dmitrievna's bedroom.

"A fine business," answered Marya Dmitrievna. "Fifty-eight years I've lived in this world, and I've never seen such a disgrace." And, after asking Pierre to give his word of honour that he would keep silent about everything he was about to learn, Marya Dmitrievna told him that Natasha had refused her fiancé without her parents' knowledge, and that the cause of this refusal was Anatole Kuragin, with whom Pierre's wife had brought her together, and with whom Natasha was going to elope in her father's absence, so as to get married secretly.

Pierre, his shoulders hunched and his mouth gaping, listened to what Marya Dmitrievna was telling him and could not believe his ears. Prince Andrei's fiancée, so deeply loved, this once sweet Natasha Rostov, to exchange Bolkonsky for that fool Anatole, who was already married (Pierre knew the secret of his marriage), and fall in love with him so much as to agree to elope with him!—that Pierre could not understand and could not imagine.

The sweet impression of Natasha, whom he had known since she was a child, could not be combined in his soul with the new notion of her baseness, stupidity, and cruelty. He remembered his wife. "They're all the same," he said to himself, thinking that he was not the only one to have the sad lot of being connected with a vile woman. But still he pitied Prince Andrei to the point of tears, pitied his pride. And the more he pitied his friend, the greater was the contempt and even loathing with which he thought of this Natasha, who had just walked past him in the reception room with an expression of such cold dignity. He did not know that Natasha's soul was filled with despair, shame, humiliation, and that it was not her fault that her face happened to express calm dignity and severity.

"What do you mean, get married!" said Pierre to Marya Dmitrievna's words. "He can't get married: he is married."

"Worse and worse by the hour," said Marya Dmitrievna. "A fine lad! What a scoundrel! And she's waiting, she's been waiting for two days. We must tell her; at least she'll stop waiting."

Having learned from Pierre the details of Anatole's marriage, having vented her anger in abusive words, Marya Dmitrievna told him why she had summoned him. Marya Dmitrievna was afraid that the count or Bolkonsky, who might come any minute, would find out about the affair, which she intended to conceal from them, and challenge Kuragin to a duel, and therefore she asked him to order his brother-in-law, on her behalf, to leave Moscow and not dare let her set eyes on him again. Pierre promised to fulfil her wish, only now realizing the danger which threatened the old count, and Nikolai, and Prince Andrei. Briefly and precisely laying out her demands for him, she let him out to the drawing room.

"Mind you, the count doesn't know anything. You make as if you don't know anything either," she said to him. "And I'll go and tell her there's nothing to wait for! Stay for dinner if you like," Marya Dmitrievna called out to Pierre.

Pierre met the old count. He was embarrassed and upset. That morning Natasha had told him that she had refused Bolkonsky.

"Trouble, trouble, *mon cher,*" he said to Pierre, "these girls are trouble when their mother's not around. I'm so sorry I came. I'll be frank with you. Have you heard, she refused her fiancé without asking anyone. I must say, I was never very glad of this marriage. Suppose he's a good man, but there'd be no happiness against his father's will, and Natasha won't remain without suitors. But it's been going on for so long, and how is it she's taken such a step without telling her father or mother? And now she's sick, and God knows what will happen! It's bad, Count, it's bad with daughters and no mother . . ." Pierre saw that the count was very upset, he tried to change the subject of conversation, but the count kept coming back to his grief.

Sonya came into the drawing room with an alarmed face.

"Natasha's not very well. She's in her room and would like to see you. Marya Dmitrievna is with her and also asks you to come."

"Yes, you're close friends with Bolkonsky, she probably wants you to tell him something. Ah, my God, my God! Everything was so nice!" And, clutching at his sparse grey whiskers, the count left the room.

Marya Dmitrievna had told Natasha that Anatole was married. Natasha refused to believe her and demanded that Pierre himself confirm it. Sonya told that to Pierre as she was bringing him down the corridor to Natasha's room.

Natasha, pale, stern, was sitting next to Marya Dmitrievna, and her feverishly glittering, questioning gaze met Pierre just at the door. She did not smile, did not nod to him, she only looked at him fixedly, and her gaze asked him only this: was he a friend, or, like everybody else, an enemy in relation to Anatole? Pierre himself evidently did not exist for her.

"He knows everything," said Marya Dmitrievna, pointing to Pierre and addressing Natasha. "Let him tell you whether I've spoken the truth."

As a wounded animal at bay looks at the approaching dogs and hunters, Natasha looked from one to the other.

"Natalya Ilyinichna," Pierre began, lowering his eyes and feeling pity for her and loathing for the operation he had to perform, "it should make no difference to you whether it's true or not, because . . ."

"So it's not true that he's married?"

"No, it's true."

"He was married, and long ago?" she asked. "Word of honour."

Pierre gave her his word of honour.

"Is he still here?" she asked quickly.

"Yes, I just saw him."

She was obviously unable to speak and made signs with her hands that they should leave her.

XX

Pierre did not stay for dinner, but left the room at once and drove off. He drove around town looking for Anatole Kuragin, at the thought of whom now all the blood rushed to his heart and he found it difficult to catch his breath. He was not at the ice hills, not at the Gypsies', not at Comoneno's. Pierre drove to the club. In the club everything was going on in its usual order: the guests who had come for dinner were sitting in groups and greeted Pierre and talked about town news. The footman, having greeted him, told him, knowing his circle and his habits, that a place had been reserved for him in the small dining room, that Prince Mikhail Zakharych was in the library, and that Pavel Timofeich had not arrived yet. One of Pierre's acquaintances, in the middle of talking about the weather, asked him whether he had heard about Kuragin's abduction of Miss Rostov, of which there was talk in town, and whether it was true. Pierre laughed and said it was nonsense, because he had just been at the Rostovs'. He asked everyone about Anatole; one man told him that he had not come yet, another that he would be dining there that evening. Pierre found it strange to look at this calm, indifferent crowd of people who did not know what was happening in his soul. He paced about, waiting until everyone had come, and, having waited in vain for Anatole, did not stay for dinner but drove home.

Anatole, whom he had been seeking, dined that day at Dolokhov's and discussed with him how to mend the spoiled affair. It seemed necessary to him that he see Miss Rostov. In the evening, he went to his sister's, to discuss with her the means of arranging this meeting. When Pierre, having driven in vain all over Moscow, returned home, the valet told him that Prince Anatole Vassilievich was with the countess. The countess's drawing room was filled with guests.

Pierre, without greeting his wife, whom he had not seen since his arrival (she was more hateful to him than ever at that moment), entered the drawing room and, seeing Anatole, went up to him.

"Ah, Pierre," said the countess, going to her husband. "You don't know what position our Anatole . . ." She stopped, seeing in her husband's lowered head, his face, his flashing eyes, his resolute stride, that terrible expression of rage and strength which she knew and had experienced personally after his duel with Dolokhov.

"Wherever you are, there is depravity and evil," Pierre said to his wife. "Anatole, come, I must have a talk with you," he said in French.

Anatole glanced at his sister and got up obediently, ready to follow Pierre.

Pierre, having taken him by the arm, pulled him to himself and started out of the room.

"*Si vous vous permettez dans mon salon . . .*"* Hélène said in a whisper; but Pierre left the room without answering her.

Anatole walked behind him with his usual swaggering stride. But uneasiness could be noticed on his face.

Having gone into his study, Pierre closed the door and addressed Anatole without looking at him.

"So you promised Countess Rostov to marry her? You were going to elope with her?"

"My dear," Anatole answered in French (as the whole conversation went on), "I don't consider myself obliged to answer questions put in such a tone."

Pierre's face, pale before then, became distorted with rage. He seized Anatole by the collar of his uniform with his big hand and began shaking him from side to side, until Anatole's face acquired a sufficiently frightened expression.

"When I say *I must* talk with you . . ." Pierre repeated.

"Well, that's stupid. Eh?" said Anatole, feeling a button of his collar, which had been ripped out with a bit of cloth.

"You're a scoundrel and a villain, and I don't know what restrains me from the pleasure of smashing your head with this," said Pierre, expressing himself so artificially because he was speaking in French. He picked up a heavy paperweight and raised it threateningly, but at once hastened to set it down again.

"Did you promise to marry her?"

"I . . . I . . . I didn't think; anyhow, I never promised, because . . ."

Pierre interrupted him.

"Do you have letters from her? Do you?" Pierre repeated, stepping towards Anatole.

---

*If you allow yourself, in my drawing room . . .

Anatole looked at him and, thrusting his hand into his pocket, at once took out his wallet.

Pierre took the letter he handed him and, pushing aside the table that stood in his way, dropped onto the sofa.

"*Je ne serai pas violent, ne craignez rien,*"* said Pierre, responding to Anatole's gesture of fear. "Letters—one," said Pierre, as if repeating a lesson to himself. "Second," he went on after a moment's silence, getting up again and beginning to pace the room, "tomorrow you are to leave Moscow."

"But how can I . . ."

"Third," Pierre went on, not listening to him, "you are never to say a word about what happened between you and the countess. I know I can't forbid you that, but if there's a spark of conscience in you . . ." Pierre silently paced the room several times. Anatole sat by the table, frowning and biting his lips.

"Can't you understand finally that, besides your own pleasure, there is the happiness, the peace of other people, that you are ruining a whole life just because you want to have fun? Amuse yourself with women like my spouse— with them you're within your rights, they know what you want from them. They're armed against you with the same experience of depravity. But to promise a girl you'll marry her . . . to deceive her, make off . . . How can you not understand that it's as mean as to beat an old man or a child! . . ."

Pierre paused and looked at Anatole now not with a wrathful, but with a questioning gaze.

"That I don't know. Eh?" said Anatole, taking heart as Pierre overcame his wrath. "That I don't know and don't want to know," he said, not looking at Pierre and with a slight trembling of his lower jaw, "but you have spoken to me in such words—'mean' and the like—as I, *comme un homme d'honneur,*† will not allow to anyone."

Pierre looked at him in surprise, unable to grasp what he wanted.

"Though it was just between us," Anatole went on, "I cannot . . ."

"What, do you want satisfaction?" Pierre said mockingly.

"You might at least take your words back. Eh? If you want me to fulfil your wishes. Eh?"

"I take them back, I take them back," said Pierre, "and I beg you to forgive me." Pierre glanced involuntarily at the torn-off button. "And money, if you need it for the road."

Anatole smiled.

The expression of that timorous and mean smile, known to him from his wife, made Pierre explode.

"Oh, mean, heartless breed!" he said, and walked out of the room.

The next day Anatole left for Petersburg.

---

*I won't be violent, don't be afraid of anything.
†Being a man of honour.

XXI

Pierre went to Marya Dmitrievna's to inform her of the fulfilment of her wish, of the banishment of Kuragin from Moscow. The whole house was in fear and agitation. Natasha was very ill and, as Marya Dmitrievna told him in secret, on the same night when it was announced to her that Anatole was married, she had poisoned herself with arsenic, which she had obtained on the quiet. Having swallowed a little, she had become so frightened that she had awakened Sonya and told her what she had done. The necessary measures against the poison had been taken in time, and she was now out of danger, but still so weak that it was impossible to think of taking her to the country, and the countess had been sent for. Pierre saw the bewildered count and the tearful Sonya, but could not see Natasha.

Pierre dined at the club that day and heard talk on all sides about the attempted abduction of Miss Rostov, and he stubbornly refuted that talk, assuring everyone that there was nothing more to it than that his brother-in-law had made a proposal to the Rostovs and received a refusal. Pierre felt it was his duty to conceal the whole affair and restore Natasha's reputation.

He fearfully awaited Prince Andrei's return, and went to the old prince every day to ask about it.

Through Mlle Bourienne, Prince Nikolai Andreich knew all the rumours going around town and had read the note to Princess Marya in which Natasha refused her fiancé. He seemed more cheerful than usual and awaited his son with great impatience.

Several days after Anatole's departure, Pierre received a note from Prince Andrei, informing him of his arrival and asking Pierre to come to see him.

Prince Andrei, on the first moment of his arrival in Moscow, had received from his father Natasha's note to Princess Marya, in which she refused her fiancé (Mlle Bourienne had stolen this note from Princess Marya and given it to the prince), and had heard stories from his father about Natasha's abduction, with additions.

Prince Andrei had arrived the evening before. Pierre came to see him the next morning. Pierre expected to find Prince Andrei in almost the same state Natasha was in, and was therefore surprised when, going into the drawing room, he heard Prince Andrei's loud voice from the study, animatedly saying something about some Petersburg intrigue. Now and then the voice of the old prince and of someone else interrupted him. Princess Marya came out to meet Pierre. She sighed, indicating with her eyes the door of the room where Prince Andrei was, obviously wishing to express her sympathy for his grief; but Pierre saw from Princess Marya's face that she was glad both of what had happened and of how her brother had taken the news of his fiancée's betrayal.

"He said he had expected it," she said. "I know his pride won't allow him to express his feelings, but still he bore it better, much better, than I expected. Evidently this is how it had to be . . ."

"But can it all be over completely?" said Pierre.

Princess Marya looked at him with astonishment. She did not understand how it was even possible to ask about it. Pierre went into the study. Prince Andrei, quite changed, grown visibly healthier, but with a new crosswise wrinkle between his brows, in civilian dress, stood facing his father and Prince Meshchersky, arguing heatedly and making energetic gestures.

The talk was about Speransky, the news of whose sudden exile and alleged treason had just reached Moscow.[17]

"Now everybody who admired him a month ago denounces and accuses him," Prince Andrei was saying, "including those who were unable to understand his goals. It's very easy to judge a man in disgrace and shift the mistakes of others onto him; but I say that if there was anything good done during this reign, it was done by him—by him alone . . ." He stopped, seeing Pierre. His face twitched and at once assumed a spiteful expression. "And posterity will give him credit," he finished and at once turned to Pierre.

"Well, how are you? Still getting fatter," he said animatedly, but the newly appeared wrinkle cut still more deeply into his brow. "Yes, I'm in good health," he replied to Pierre's question and grinned. It was clear to Pierre that his grin said: "I'm in good health, but nobody needs my good health." Having said a few words to Pierre about the terrible road from the Polish border, and about having met people in Switzerland who knew Pierre, and about M. Dessales, whom he had brought from abroad as a tutor for his son, Prince Andrei again mixed heatedly into the conversation about Speransky, which was still going on between the two old men.

"If there was treason and there were proofs of his secret communications with Napoleon, they would be made public," he said heatedly and hastily. "Personally I don't like and have never liked Speransky, but I do like justice." Pierre now recognized in his friend the all too familiar need to worry and argue about things extraneous to him, only in order to stifle his all too painful innermost thoughts.

When Prince Meshchersky left, Prince Andrei took Pierre by the arm and invited him to the room he had been given. There was a rumpled bed in the room and open suitcases and trunks. Prince Andrei went over to one of them and took out a box. From the box he took a bundle of papers. He did it all silently and very quickly. He straightened up and cleared his throat. His face was frowning, his lips were compressed.

"Forgive me for troubling you . . ." Pierre realized that Prince Andrei wanted to talk about Natasha, and his broad face expressed regret and compassion. This expression of Pierre's face angered Prince Andrei; he went on resolutely, in

a ringing and unpleasant voice: "I have received a refusal from Countess Rostov, and rumours have reached me about her hand being sought by your
brother-in-law, or something like that. Is it true?"

"Both true and not true," Pierre began, but Prince Andrei interrupted him.

"Here are her letters," he said, "and her portrait." He took the bundle from
the table and handed it to Pierre.

"Give this to the countess . . . if you see her."

"She's very ill," said Pierre.

"So she's still here?" asked Prince Andrei. "And Prince Kuragin?" he asked
quickly.

"He left long ago. She was near death . . ."

"I deeply regret her illness," said Prince Andrei. He grinned coldly, spitefully,
unpleasantly, like his father.

"But Mr. Kuragin did not, then, bestow his hand upon Countess Rostov?"
Andrei asked. He snorted through his nose several times.

"He couldn't marry, because he's already married," said Pierre.

Prince Andrei laughed unpleasantly, again resembling his father.

"And where is he now, your brother-in-law, may I ask?" he said.

"He left for Peter . . . however, I don't know," said Pierre.

"It makes no difference," said Prince Andrei. "Tell Countess Rostov that she
was and is completely free and that I wish her all the best."

Pierre took the bundle of papers. Prince Andrei, as if trying to remember if
he had something else to say, or waiting for Pierre to say something, stood
looking at him with fixed eyes.

"Listen, do you remember our argument in Petersburg," asked Pierre,
"remember, about . . ."

"I do," Prince Andrei said hastily. "I said that a fallen woman should be forgiven, but I did not say that I could forgive. I cannot."

"But can this be compared . . . ?" said Pierre. Prince Andrei interrupted him.
He cried sharply:

"Yes, to ask for her hand again, to be magnanimous and all that? . . . Yes, it's
very noble, but I can't walk *sur les brisées de monsieur.** If you wish to be my
friend, never speak to me of that . . . of all that. Well, goodbye. You will deliver
it? . . ."

Pierre left and went to see the old prince and Princess Marya.

The old man seemed more animated than usual. Princess Marya was the
same as ever, but Pierre saw in her, beyond her compassion for her brother, her
joy that her brother's marriage had been thwarted. Looking at them, Pierre
realized what contempt and spite they all felt for the Rostovs, and realized that

*In that gentleman's tracks.

it was impossible in their presence even to mention the name of her who could exchange Prince Andrei for whomever it might be.

Over dinner the talk turned to the war, the approach of which was becoming obvious. Prince Andrei talked incessantly and argued now with his father, now with the Swiss tutor Dessalles, and seemed more animated than usual—an animation the moral cause of which Pierre knew so well.

XXII

That same evening Pierre went to the Rostovs to carry out his errand. Natasha was in bed, the count was at the club, and Pierre, having delivered the letters to Sonya, went to see Marya Dmitrievna, who was interested to know how Prince Andrei had taken the news. Ten minutes later, Sonya came into Marya Dmitrievna's room.

"Natasha absolutely wants to see Count Pyotr Kirillovich," she said.

"But how? Are we to take him to her, or what? It's not tidied up there," said Marya Dmitrievna.

"No, she's dressed and has come out to the drawing room," said Sonya.

Marya Dmitrievna only shrugged her shoulders.

"When will the countess come, she's got me completely worn out. You watch yourself, don't tell her everything," she turned to Pierre. "One doesn't have the heart to scold her, she's so pathetic, so pathetic!"

Natasha, wasted, with a pale and stern face (not at all shamefaced as Pierre expected her to be), was standing in the middle of the drawing room. When Pierre appeared in the doorway, she became flustered, obviously undecided whether to go to him or wait for him.

Pierre hastily went up to her. He thought that she would give him her hand, as always; but, coming close to him, she stopped, breathing heavily and lowering her arms lifelessly, in exactly the same pose in which she came out to the middle of the room to sing, but with quite a different expression.

"Pyotr Kirilyich," she began, speaking quickly, "Prince Bolkonsky was your friend—is your friend," she corrected herself (it seemed to her that everything only was and that now it was all different). "He told me then to turn to you . . ."

Pierre sniffed silently, looking at her. Up to then he had reproached her in his soul and had tried to despise her; but now he felt such pity for her that there was no room in his soul for reproach.

"He's here now, tell him . . . to for . . . forgive me." She stopped and began to breathe still more rapidly, but she did not cry.

"Yes . . . I'll tell him," said Pierre, "but . . ." He did not know what to say.

Natasha was evidently afraid of the thought that might have occurred to Pierre.

"No, I know it's all over," she said hastily. "No, it can never be. I'm only tormented by the wrong I've done him. Tell him only that I beg him to forgive me, to forgive me for everything . . ." Her whole body shook, and she sat down on a chair.

A feeling of pity such as he had never experienced before overflowed Pierre's soul.

"I'll tell him, I'll tell him everything once more," said Pierre, "but . . . I'd like to know one thing . . ."

"What?" asked Natasha's gaze.

"I'd like to know whether you loved . . ." Pierre did not know what to call Anatole, and he blushed at the thought of him, "whether you loved that bad man?"

"Don't call him bad," said Natasha. "But I don't know, I don't know anything . . ." She began to cry again.

A still greater feeling of pity, tenderness, and love took hold of Pierre. He felt tears flowing behind his spectacles and hoped they would not be noticed.

"Let's not talk any more, my friend," said Pierre.

It seemed so strange suddenly for Natasha to hear that meek, tender, heartfelt voice.

"Let's not talk, my friend, I'll tell him everything; but I ask one thing of you—consider me your friend, and if you need help, advice, or simply to pour out your soul to somebody—not now, but when your soul is clear—remember me." He took her hand and kissed it. "I'll be happy if I'm able to . . ." Pierre became confused.

"Don't talk to me like that: I'm not worthy of it!" cried Natasha, and she was about to leave the room, but Pierre held her back by the hand. He knew he had something more to tell her. But when he said it, he was surprised at his words himself.

"Stop it, stop it, your whole life is ahead of you," he said.

"Ahead of me? No! For me all is lost," she said with shame and self-abasement.

"All is lost?" he repeated. "If I were not I, but the handsomest, brightest, and best man in the world, and I was free, I would go on my knees this minute and ask for your hand and your love."

Natasha, for the first time in many days, wept tears of gratitude and tenderness and, after glancing at Pierre, left the room.

Pierre, too, following her, almost ran out to the front hall, holding back the tears of tenderness and happiness that choked him, put on his coat, missing the sleeves, and got into the sleigh.

"Where to now, sir?" asked the coachman.

"Where to?" Pierre asked himself. "Where can I go now? Not to the club or to pay visits." All people seemed so pitiful, so poor in comparison with the feeling of tenderness and love he experienced, in comparison with that softened, grateful glance she had given him at the last moment through her tears.

"Home," said Pierre, throwing open the bearskin coat on his broad, joyfully breathing chest, despite the ten degrees of frost.

It was cold and clear. Above the dirty, semi-dark streets, above the black roofs, stood the dark, starry sky. Only looking at the sky did Pierre not feel the insulting baseness of everything earthly compared with the height his soul had risen to. At the entrance to Arbat Square, the huge expanse of the dark, starry night opened out to Pierre's eyes. Almost in the middle of that sky, over Prechistensky Boulevard, stood the huge, bright comet of the year 1812—surrounded, strewn with stars on all sides, but different from them in its closeness to the earth, its white light and long, raised tail—that same comet which presaged, as they said, all sorts of horrors and the end of the world. But for Pierre this bright star with its long, luminous tail did not arouse any frightening feeling. On the contrary, Pierre, his eyes wet with tears, gazed joyfully at this bright star, which, having flown with inexpressible speed through immeasurable space on its parabolic course, suddenly, like an arrow piercing the earth, seemed to have struck here its one chosen spot in the black sky and stopped, its tail raised energetically, its white light shining and playing among the countless other shimmering stars. It seemed to Pierre that this star answered fully to what was in his softened and encouraged soul, now blossoming into new life.

VOLUME III

Part One

I

Since the end of the year 1811 an intense arming and concentration of western European forces had begun, and in the year 1812 those forces—millions of men (including those who transported and fed the army)—moved from west to east, to the borders of Russia, towards which, since the year 1811, the forces of Russia had been drawn in exactly the same way. On the twelfth of June, the forces of western Europe crossed the borders of Russia, and war began—that is, an event took place contrary to human reason and to the whole of human nature. Millions of people committed against each other such a countless number of villainies, deceptions, betrayals, thefts, forgeries and distributions of false banknotes, robberies, arsons, and murders as the annals of all the law courts in the world could not assemble in whole centuries, and which, at that period of time, the people who committed them did not look upon as crimes.

What produced this extraordinary event? What were its causes? Historians say with naïve assurance that the causes of this event were the offence inflicted upon the duke of Oldenburg, the non-observance of the Continental System,[1] Napoleon's love of power, Alexander's firmness, diplomatic mistakes, and so on.

Consequently, it needed only that Metternich, Rumyantsev, or Talleyrand, between levee and rout, make a little better effort and write a more skilful dispatch, or that Napoleon write to Alexander: *Monsieur, mon frère, je consens à rendre le duché au duc d'Oldenbourg**—and there would have been no war.

Understandably, that was how the matter presented itself to contemporaries. Understandably, it seemed to Napoleon that the war was caused by the intrigues of England (as he said, in fact, on the island of St. Helena[2]); understandably, to the members of the English Parliament it seemed that the war was caused by Napoleon's love of power; to Prince Oldenburg it seemed that the war was caused by the violence done him; to the merchants it seemed that the war was caused by the Continental System, which was ruining Europe; to the old soldiers and generals it seemed that the chief cause was the need to make use of them; to the legitimists of that time,[3] that it was necessary to

---

*Dear sir, my brother, I agree to give the duchy back to the duke of Oldenburg.

restore *les bons principes;** and to the diplomats of that time, that it had all happened because the alliance between Russia and Austria in 1809 had not been concealed skilfully enough from Napoleon and because memorandum no. 178 had been clumsily worded. Understandably, these and a countless, endless number of other causes, the number of which depends on countless different points of view, presented themselves to contemporaries; but for us, the descendants, who contemplate the enormity of the event in all its scope and delve into its simple and terrible meaning, these causes seem insufficient. For us it is not understandable that millions of Christians killed and tortured each other because Napoleon was a lover of power, Alexander was firm, English policy cunning, and the duke of Oldenburg offended. It is impossible to understand what connection there is between these circumstances and the fact of killing and violence; why, because the duke of Oldenburg was offended, thousands of men from the other end of Europe should kill and ravage the people of Smolensk and Moscow provinces and be killed by them.

For us descendants—who are not historians, who are not carried away by the process of research and therefore can contemplate events with unobscured common sense—a countless number of causes present themselves. The deeper we go in search of causes, the more of them we find, and each cause taken singly or whole series of causes present themselves to us as equally correct in themselves, and equally false in their insignificance in comparison with the enormity of the event, and equally false in their incapacity (without the participation of all other coinciding causes) to produce the event that took place. The willingness or unwillingness of one French corporal to enlist for a second tour of duty appears to us as good a cause as Napoleon's refusal to withdraw his army beyond the Vistula and give back the duchy of Oldenburg; for if he had been unwilling to serve, and another had been unwilling, and a third, and a thousandth corporal and soldier, there would have been so many less men in Napoleon's army, and there could have been no war.

If Napoleon had not been insulted by the demand to withdraw beyond the Vistula, and had not ordered his troops to advance, there would have been no war; but if all the sergeants had been unwilling to enlist for a second tour of duty, there also could have been no war. There also could have been no war if there had been no intrigues of the English, and if there had been no prince of Oldenburg and insulted feelings in Alexander, and if there had been no autocratic power in Russia, and if there had been no French revolution and subsequent dictatorship and empire, and all that produced the French revolution, and so on. Without any one of these causes, nothing could have happened. Therefore, all these causes—billions of causes—coincided so as

*Good principles.

to bring about what happened. And consequently none of them was the exclusive cause of the event, but the event had to take place simply because it had to take place. Millions of men, renouncing their human feelings and their reason, had to go from west to east and kill their own kind, just as, several centuries earlier, hordes of men had gone from east to west, killing their own kind.

The actions of Napoleon and Alexander, on whose word it seems to have depended whether the event took place or not, were as little willed as the action of each soldier who went into the campaign by lot or by conscription. This could not be otherwise, because for the will of Napoleon and Alexander (the men on whom the event seemed to depend) to be fulfilled, the coincidence of countless circumstances was necessary, without any one of which the event could not have taken place. It was necessary that millions of men, in whose hands the actual power lay, the soldiers who shot, transported provisions and cannon—it was necessary that they agree to fulfil this will of isolated and weak men and be brought to that by a countless number of complex, diverse causes.

Fatalism in history is inevitable for the explanation of senseless phenomena (that is, those whose sense we do not understand). The more we try to explain sensibly these phenomena of history, the more senseless and incomprehensible they become for us.

Each man lives for himself, uses his freedom to achieve his personal goals, and feels with his whole being that right now he can or cannot do such-and-such an action; but as soon as he does it, this action, committed at a certain moment in time, becomes irreversible and makes itself the property of history, in which it has not a free but a predestined significance.

There are two sides to each man's life: his personal life, which is the more free the more abstract its interests, and his elemental, swarmlike life, where man inevitably fulfils the laws prescribed for him.

Man lives consciously for himself, but serves as an unconscious instrument for the achievement of historical, universally human goals. An action once committed is irrevocable, and its effect, coinciding in time with millions of actions of other people, acquires historical significance. The higher a man stands on the social ladder, the greater the number of people he is connected with, the more power he has over other people, the more obvious is the predestination and inevitability of his every action.

"The hearts of kings are in the hands of God."[4]

Kings are the slaves of history.

History, that is, the unconscious, swarmlike life of mankind, uses every moment of a king's life as an instrument for its purposes.

.   .   .

Napoleon, though now, in 1812, it seemed to him more than ever that it depended on him *verser* or not *verser le sang de ses peuples** (as Alexander wrote in his last letter to him), had never been more subject than now to those inevitable laws which forced him (acting by his own free will, as it seemed to him, with respect to himself) to do for the common cause, for history, that which had to be accomplished.

Men of the west moved towards the east in order to kill each other. And by the law of the coincidence of causes, the thousands of minute causes of this movement and of the war fitted into and coincided with the event: reproaches for the non-observance of the Continental System, and the duke of Oldenburg, and the movement of troops into Prussia, undertaken (as it seemed to Napoleon) only to achieve an armed peace,⁵ and the French emperor's love and habit of war, which coincided with his nation's disposition, the enthusiasm for grandiose preparations, and the expense of the preparations, and the need to obtain advantages that would recover the expenses, and the intoxicating honours in Dresden,⁶ and diplomatic negotiations which, according to the views of contemporaries, were conducted with a sincere desire to achieve peace and which only wounded the vanity of both sides, and millions and millions of other causes which fitted into the event that was to be accomplished, coinciding with it.

When an apple ripens and falls—what makes it fall? Is it that it is attracted to the ground, is it that the stem withers, is it that the sun has dried it up, that it has grown heavier, that the wind shakes it, that the boy standing underneath wants to eat it?

No one thing is the cause. All this is only the coincidence of conditions under which every organic, elemental event of life is accomplished. And the botanist who finds that the apple falls because the cellular tissue degenerates, and so on, will be as right and as wrong as the child who stands underneath and says that the apple fell because he wanted to eat it and prayed for it. As he who says that Napoleon went to Moscow because he wanted to, and perished because Alexander wanted him to perish, will be both right and wrong, so he will be right and wrong who says that an undermined hill weighing a million pounds collapsed because the last worker struck it a last time with his pick. In historical events the so-called great men are labels that give the event a name, which, just as with labels, has the least connection of all with the event itself.

Their every action, which to them seems willed by themselves, in the historical sense is not willed, but happens in connection with the whole course of history and has been destined from before all ages.

---

*To spill *or not* to spill the blood of his peoples.

II

On the twenty-ninth of May, Napoleon left Dresden, where he had spent three weeks surrounded by a court composed of princes, dukes, kings, and even one emperor. Before his departure, Napoleon showed kindness to the princes, kings, and emperor who deserved it, and scolded the princes and kings with whom he was not entirely pleased, made a gift of his own—that is, taken from other kings—pearls and diamonds to the Austrian empress, and, tenderly embracing the empress Marie-Louise, as his historian says, left her upset by this separation, which she—this Marie-Louise who was considered his wife, though another wife had been left in Paris⁷—seemed unable to endure. Though the diplomats still firmly believed in the possibility of peace and were working hard towards that end, though the emperor Napoleon himself wrote a letter to the emperor Alexander calling him *Monsieur mon frère* and sincerely assuring him that he did not want war and would always love and respect him—he drove off to the army and gave new orders at every station, having the aim of hastening the movement of the army from west to east. He drove in a travelling coach-and-six, surrounded by pages, adjutants, and an escort, down the high road to Posen, Thorn, Danzig, and Königsberg. In each of these towns, thousands of people met him with trembling and ecstasy.

The army moved from west to east, and six-horse relays carried him there as well. On the tenth of June, he caught up with the army and spent the night in the Wilkowiski forest, in quarters prepared for him on the estate of a Polish count.

The next day Napoleon, going ahead of his army, drove to the Niemen in his carriage and, to look for a crossing place, changed into a Polish uniform and drove out on the bank.

Seeing Cossacks *(les Cosaques)* on the other side and the spreading steppe *(les Steppes)*, in the middle of which lay *Moscou la ville sainte,** capital of that state, similar to the Scythian state to which Alexander the Great had marched—Napoleon, unexpectedly for everyone, and contrary to both strategic and diplomatic considerations, ordered an advance, and the next day his troops started crossing the Niemen.

Early in the morning of the twelfth, he came out of the tent, pitched that day on the steep left bank of the Niemen, and watched through a field glass the streams of his troops flowing out of the Wilkowiski forest and pouring over the three bridges thrown across the Niemen. The troops knew of the emperor's presence, sought him with their eyes, and when they found a figure in a frock

*Moscow the holy city.

coat and hat, standing apart from his suite on a hill in front of a tent, they threw their hats in the air, shouted *"Vive l'Empereur!"* and one after another, inexhaustibly, kept pouring, pouring from the huge forest that had concealed them till then and, dividing up, crossed over the three bridges to the other side.

*"On fera du chemin cette fois-ci. Oh! quand il s'en mêle lui-même ça chauffe . . . Nom de Dieu . . . Le voilà! . . . Vive l'Empereur! Les voilà donc les Steppes de l'Asie! Vilain pays tout de même. Au revoir, Beauché; je te réserve le plus beau palais de Moscou. Au revoir! Bonne chance . . . L'as-tu vu, l'Empereur? Vive l'Empereur! . . . preur! Si on me fait gouverneur aux Indes, Gérard, je te fais ministre du Cachemire, c'est arrêté. Vive l'Empereur! Vive! vive! vive! Les gredins de Cosaques, comme ils filent. Vive l'Empereur! Le voilà! Le vois-tu? Je l'ai vu deux fois comme je te vois. Le petit caporal . . . Je l'ai vue donner la croix à l'un des vieux . . . Vive l'Empereur! . . ."** said the voices of old and young men of the most diverse characters and social positions. The faces of all these men had one common expression of joy at the beginning of the long-awaited campaign and of rapture and devotion to the man in the grey frock coat who stood on the hill.

On the thirteenth of June Napoleon was brought a small, purebred Arabian horse, and he mounted up and rode at a gallop to one of the bridges across the Niemen, constantly deafened by rapturous cries, which he evidently put up with only because it was impossible to forbid them to express their love for him by these cries; but these cries that accompanied him everywhere oppressed him and distracted him from the military concerns that had consumed him since the time he joined the army. He rode across one of the bridges rocking on pontoons to the other side, turned sharply to the left, and galloped off in the direction of Kovno, preceded by the horse guard chasseurs, thrilled with happiness, enraptured, who galloped ahead of him, clearing the way through the troops. Having come to the wide river Vilia, he stopped beside a regiment of Polish uhlans that stood on the bank.

"Vivat!" the Poles cried just as rapturously, breaking their lines and crushing each other in order to see him. Napoleon surveyed the river, dismounted, and sat on a log that lay on the bank. At a wordless sign he was handed a field glass, placed it on the back of a happy page who ran over, and began to look at the other side. Then he immersed himself in examining a map laid out among

---

*We'll get somewhere this time. Oh! when he mixes into it himself, things get hot . . . By God . . . There he is! . . . Long live the Emperor! So there are the Steppes of Asia! Vile country all the same. Goodbye, Beauché; I'm reserving the best palace in Moscow for you. Goodbye! Good luck . . . Did you see the Emperor? Long live the Emperor! . . . peror! If they make me governor of the Indies, Gérard, I'll made you minister of Kashmir, that's settled. Long live the Emperor! Long live! long live! long live! Those rascally Cossacks, how they scuttle off. Long live the Emperor! There he is! Do you see him? I saw him twice as I see you. The little corporal . . . I saw him give the cross to one of the old men . . . Long live the Emperor!

the logs. Without raising his head, he said something, and two of his adjutants rode over to the Polish uhlans.

"What? What did he say?" came from the lines of the Polish uhlans as one adjutant rode up to them.

The order was to find a ford and cross to the other side. The colonel of the Polish uhlans, a handsome old man, turned red, and, stumbling over his words from excitement, asked the adjutant whether he would be allowed to swim across the river with his uhlans, without looking for a ford. Obviously fearing a refusal, like a boy who asks permission to get on a horse, he begged to be allowed to swim across the river before the emperor's eyes. The adjutant said that the emperor would probably not be displeased by this excessive zeal.

As soon as the adjutant said it, the moustached old officer, with a happy face and flashing eyes, raising his sabre, shouted "*Vivat!*" and, commanding the uhlans to follow him, spurred his horse and rode to the river. He angrily spurred his horse, which hesitated under him, and threw himself into the water, heading for the depths where the current was swift. Hundreds of uhlans followed him. It was cold and scary in the middle and in the swift current. The uhlans grasped at each other, fell off their horses, some horses drowned, men drowned as well, others tried to swim for it, some in the saddle, others holding on to their horses' manes. They tried to swim forward to the other side, and, though there was a ford a quarter of a mile away, they were proud to swim and drown in this river before the eyes of the man who sat on a log and was not even looking at what they were doing. When the adjutant returned and, choosing the right moment, allowed himself to draw the emperor's attention to the devotion of the Poles to his person, the little man in the grey frock coat stood up and, summoning Berthier to him, began pacing up and down the bank with him, giving him orders and occasionally glancing with displeasure at the drowning uhlans, who distracted his attention.

For him it was no new conviction that his presence at all ends of the world, from Africa to the steppes of Muscovy, struck people in the same way and threw them into the madness of self-oblivion. He ordered his horse brought and rode to his camp.

Some forty uhlans drowned in the river, despite the boats that were sent to help. Most of the men were washed back to this side. The colonel and several other men crossed the river and barely managed to climb out on the bank. But as soon as they climbed out, their streaming wet clothes sticking to them, they shouted "*Vivat!*"—gazing rapturously at the spot where Napoleon had stood, but where he no longer was, and at that moment they considered themselves happy.

In the evening, between two orders—one about the speedy delivery of forged Russian banknotes prepared for distribution in Russia, and the other about the shooting of the Saxon caught with a letter containing information about the orders of the French army—Napoleon gave a third order about enrolling the Polish colonel who had needlessly thrown himself into the river in the *Légion d'honneur,* of which Napoleon himself was the head.[8]

Quos vult perdere—dementat.[9]

III

Meanwhile the Russian emperor had already spent more than a month in Vilno, holding reviews and manoeuvres. Nothing was prepared for the war which everybody expected and for the preparation of which the emperor had come from Petersburg. There was no general plan of action. Hesitation over which plan of all those proposed was to be accepted increased still more after the emperor's one-month stay at headquarters. Each of the three armies had a separate commander in chief,[10] but there was no supreme commander over all the armies, and the emperor would not take the title upon himself.

The longer the emperor stayed in Vilno, the less and less did they prepare for war, grown weary of expecting it. All the strivings of the people who surrounded the sovereign were, it seemed, aimed only at making the sovereign, while passing the time pleasantly, forget about the impending war.

In the month of June, after many balls and fêtes given by the Polish dignitaries, by the courtiers, and by the sovereign himself, the thought occurred to one of the sovereign's Polish adjutant generals of giving a dinner and ball for the sovereign on the part of his adjutant generals. This thought was greeted joyfully by everyone. The sovereign gave his consent. The adjutant generals collected money by subscription. The person who might be most pleasing to the sovereign was invited to be hostess of the ball. Count Bennigsen, a landowner of Vilno province, offered his country house for the fête, and the thirteenth of June was the day fixed for the dinner, ball, boat rides, and fireworks at Zakret, Count Bennigsen's country house.

On the same day on which Napoleon gave orders to cross the Niemen, and his vanguard troops, driving back the Cossacks, crossed the Russian border, Alexander spent the evening at Bennigsen's house—at the ball given by his adjutant generals.

It was a gay, brilliant fête; connoisseurs said that rarely had so many beauties gathered in one place. Countess Bezukhov, among other Russian ladies who had followed the sovereign from Petersburg to Vilno, was at this ball, eclipsing the refined Polish ladies by her heavy, so-called Russian beauty. She was noticed, and the sovereign favoured her with a dance.

Boris Drubetskoy, *en garçon* (playing the bachelor), as he put it, having left his wife in Moscow, was also at this ball, and, though not an adjutant general, contributed a large sum to the subscription for the ball. Boris was now a rich man, far advanced in honours, no longer seeking patronage, but standing on an equal footing with the highest of his peers.

At midnight the dancing was still going on. Hélène, who did not have a worthy partner, invited Boris for the mazurka herself. They sat out as the third couple. Boris, glancing coolly at Hélène's gleaming bare shoulders emerging from her gown of dark gauze with gold, talked of old acquaintances and at the same time, unnoticeably to himself and others, never ceased for a second to observe the sovereign, who was in the same room. The sovereign was not dancing; he stood in the doorway and stopped now one couple, now another, with gracious words that he alone knew how to utter.

At the start of the mazurka, Boris saw the adjutant general Balashov, one of the closest persons to the sovereign, go up to him and in uncourtly fashion stop very close to the sovereign, who was talking with a Polish lady. When he finished talking with the lady, the sovereign glanced around questioningly and, evidently realizing that Balashov was acting that way only because there were very important reasons for it, nodded slightly to the lady and turned to Balashov. As soon as Balashov began to speak, the sovereign's face showed astonishment. He took Balashov by the arm and walked across the room with him, unconsciously clearing a seven-yard path for himself on both sides as people made way for him. Boris noticed Arakcheev's troubled face as the sovereign walked with Balashov. Arakcheev, glancing at the sovereign from under his eyebrows and puffing through his red nose, stepped out from the crowd, as if expecting the sovereign to address him. (Boris realized that Arakcheev envied Balashov and was displeased that some obviously important news had reached the sovereign not through him.)

But the sovereign and Balashov went out, without noticing Arakcheev, through the door leading to the lighted garden. Arakcheev, holding his sword and looking around spitefully, followed some twenty paces behind them.

While performing the figures of the mazurka, Boris was ceaselessly tormented by the thought of the news brought by Balashov and how to find it out before anyone else.

During a figure in which he had to choose a lady, whispering to Hélène that he wanted to choose Countess Potocki, who seemed to have gone out to the balcony, he rushed, gliding over the parquet, to the door to the garden and, seeing the sovereign stepping onto the terrace with Balashov, stopped. The sovereign and Balashov were heading for the door. Boris, flustered, as if he had no time to retreat, pressed himself deferentially to the door frame and lowered his head.

The sovereign, with the agitation of a man personally offended, was finishing the following words:

"To enter Russia without a declaration of war. I will make peace only when not a single armed enemy remains on my soil," he said. It seemed to Boris that the sovereign enjoyed uttering these words: he was pleased with the form in which he had expressed his thought, but displeased that Boris had overheard it.

"No one must know anything!" the sovereign added, frowning. Boris understood that this referred to him and, closing his eyes, bowed his head slightly. The sovereign went back into the room and remained at the ball for another half hour.

Boris was the first to learn the news of French troops crossing the Niemen and thanks to that had the chance to show certain important persons that much of what was concealed from others was known to him, and thereby had the chance to rise higher in the opinion of those persons.

The unexpected news of the French crossing the Niemen was particularly unexpected after a month of unfulfilled expectation, and that at a ball! The sovereign, in the first moment of receiving the news, under the influence of indignation and offence, had found a phrase which later became famous, which he liked himself, and which fully expressed his feelings. On returning home from the ball, at two o'clock in the morning, the sovereign sent for his secretary Shishkov and told him to write an order to the army and a rescript to Field Marshal Prince Saltykov, in which he insistently demanded the insertion of the words that he would not make peace so long as a single armed Frenchman remained on Russian soil.

The next day the following letter was sent to Napoleon.

*Monsieur mon frère,**

J'ai appris hier que malgré la loyauté avec laquelle j'ai maintenu mes engagements envers Votre Majesté, ses troupes ont franchis les frontières de la Russie, et je reçois à l'instant de Pétersbourg une note par laquelle le comte Lauriston, pour cause de cette agression, annonce que Votre Majesté s'est considerée comme en état de guerre avec moi dès le moment où le prince Kourakine[11] *a fait la demande de ses passeports. Les motifs sur lesquels le duc de Bassano fondait son refus de les lui délivrer, n'auraient jamais pu me faire supposer que cette démarche servirait jamais de prétexte à l'agression. En effet cet ambassadeur n'y a jamais été autorisé comme il l'a déclaré lui-*

---

*Monsieur my brother,

I learned yesterday that despite the loyalty with which I have kept my promises to Your Majesty, your troops have crossed the borders of Russia, and I have just received a note from Petersburg in which Count Lauriston announces, as the cause of this aggression, that Your Majesty has considered himself in a state of war with me from the moment when Prince Kurakin asked for his passports. The motives upon which the duke of Bassano based his refusal to deliver them to him would never have made me suppose that this step could ever serve as a pretext for aggression. Indeed, this ambassador was never authorized to take it, as he has declared himself, and as soon as I was informed of it, I made known to him how much I disapproved of him by ordering him to

même, et aussitôt que j'en fus informé, je lui ai fait connaître combien je le désapprouvais en lui donnant l'ordre de rester à son poste. Si Votre Majesté n'est pas intentionnée de verser le sang de nos peuples pour un malentendu de ce genre et qu'elle consente à retirer ses troupes du territoire russe, je regarderai ce qui s'est passé comme non avenu, et un accomodement entre nous sera possible. Dans le cas contraire, Votre Majesté, je me verrai forcé de repousser une attaque que rien n'a provoquée de ma part. Il dépend encore de Votre Majesté d'eviter à l'humanité les calamités d'une nouvelle guerre.
Je suis etc.

(signé) Alexandre.

IV

On the fourteenth of June, at two o'clock in the morning, the sovereign, having summoned Balashov and read him his letter to Napoleon, ordered him to carry this letter and hand it personally to the French emperor. Sending Balashov on his way, the sovereign again repeated to him the words that he would not make peace so long as even one armed enemy remained on Russian soil, and ordered him to convey these words to Napoleon *without fail*. The sovereign did not include them in the letter, because he felt, with his innate tact, that it would be inappropriate to convey these words at the moment when a last attempt at reconciliation was being made; but he told Balashov to convey them without fail to Napoleon in person.

Having set out that same night of the thirteenth of June, accompanied by a bugler and two Cossacks, Balashov reached the French outposts at the village of Rykonty, on the Russian side of the Niemen, at dawn. He was stopped by French cavalry sentinels.

A French hussar under-officer in a raspberry-coloured uniform and shaggy hat shouted to the approaching Balashov, ordering him to stop. Balashov did not stop at once, but went on moving slowly down the road.

The under-officer, frowning and muttering some abuse, thrust his horse's breast towards Balashov, took hold of his sabre, and shouted rudely at the Russian general, asking him if he was deaf and had not heard what he was told. Balashov gave his name. The under-officer sent a soldier for an officer.

---

remain at his post. If Your Majesty is not intent on shedding the blood of our peoples for a misunderstanding of this sort and consents to withdraw his troops from Russian territory, I will regard what has occurred as cancelled and an agreement between us will be possible. In the contrary case, Your Majesty, I will find myself forced to repel an attack which nothing on my part has provoked. It still depends on Your Majesty to spare humanity the calamities of a new war.
I remain, etc.

(signed) Alexander.

Paying no attention to Balashov, the under-officer started talking with his comrades about regimental matters and did not glance at the Russian general.

It was extremely strange for Balashov, after his closeness to the highest power and might, after his conversation three hours earlier with the sovereign, and generally in the habit of being honoured in his service, to see here, on Russian soil, this hostile, and above all disrespectful, treatment of him by brute force.

The sun was just beginning to rise behind the clouds; the air was fresh and dewy. A herd of cattle was being driven down the road from the village. From the fields, one by one, trilling larks sprayed up like bubbles in water.

Balashov looked around him, awaiting the arrival of the officer from the village. The Russian Cossacks, and the bugler, and the French hussars silently glanced at each other now and then.

A French hussar colonel, obviously just out of bed, came riding from the village on a handsome, well-fed grey horse, accompanied by two hussars. The officer, the soldiers, and their horses had a contented and foppish look.

This was that initial period of a campaign when the troops still find themselves in good order, almost on the level of a peacetime review of manoeuvres, only with a tinge of warlike showiness in their dress, and with a moral tinge of that gaiety and enthusiasm that always accompany the beginning of a campaign.

The French colonel had a hard time stifling his yawns, but was courteous, and evidently realized the full significance of Balashov. He led him past his soldiers behind the line and informed him that his wish to be presented to the emperor would probably be fulfilled at once, because, as far as he knew, the emperor's quarters were close by.

They rode through the village of Rykonty, past French hussar tethering posts, sentinels, and soldiers, who saluted their colonel and looked with curiosity at the Russian uniform, and came out on the other side of the village. According to the colonel, they were a mile and a half from the commander of the division, who would receive Balashov and take him to his destination.

The sun had already risen and shone gaily on the bright greenery.

They had just ridden up a hill past a tavern, when a bunch of horsemen appeared, riding towards them from the foot of the hill, at the head of whom, on a black horse, its trappings gleaming in the sun, rode a tall man in a plumed hat, with black, curled, shoulder-length hair, in a red mantle, his long legs thrust forward, as Frenchmen ride. This man galloped to meet Balashov, his plumes flying, his jewels and gold galloons shining in the bright June sun.

Balashov was just two lengths away from the horseman riding to meet him with a theatrically solemn face, in bracelets, plumes, necklaces, and gold, when Ulner, the French colonel, whispered respectfully: *"le roi de Naples."** Indeed,

---

*The king of Naples.

it was Murat, who was now called the Neapolitan king. Though it was completely incomprehensible why he was the Neapolitan king, he was called that, and he was fully convinced of it himself, and therefore had a still more solemn and important air than before. He was so sure that he was indeed the Neapolitan king, that when, on the eve of his departure from Naples, while strolling with his wife through the streets of the city, several Italians had cried "*Viva il re!*" he had turned to his wife with a sad smile and said: "*Les malheureux, ils ne savent pas que je les quitte demain!*"*

But though he firmly believed that he was the Neapolitan king and was sorry for the grief of the subjects he was abandoning, lately, after being called back into the service, and especially after meeting Napoleon in Danzig, when his august brother-in-law had said to him: "*Je vous ai fait Roi pour régner à ma manière, mais pas à la vôtre*"†—he had cheerfully taken up his familiar business and, as a well-fed but not yet fat horse, still fit for work, feeling itself in harness, begins to frolic in the shafts, he, having dressed up as gaudily and expensively as possible, cheerful and content, went riding down the roads of Poland, not knowing where or why himself.

Seeing the Russian general, he threw back his head with its curled, shoulder-length hair in a kingly manner and gave the French colonel a questioning glance. The colonel deferentially conveyed to his majesty the meaning of Balashov, whose family name he could not pronounce.

"*De Bal-machève!*" said the king (overcoming by his resoluteness the difficulty that the colonel was faced with), "*charmé de faire votre connaissance, général,*"‡ he added with a gesture of kingly graciousness. As soon as the king began to speak loudly and quickly, all his kingly dignity instantly left him, and, not noticing it himself, he went over to his proper tone of good-natured familiarity. He placed his hand on the withers of Balashov's horse.

"*Eh bien, général, tout est à la guerre, à ce qu'il parait,*"§ he said as if regretting the circumstance, of which he could not judge.

"*Sire,*" replied Balashov, "*l'Empereur mon maître ne désire point la guerre, et comme Votre Majesté le voit,*"# said Balashov, using *Votre Majesté* at every turn, with inevitably affected frequency, addressing the person for whom this title was still a novelty.

Murat's face beamed with stupid satisfaction as he listened to *Monsieur de Balachoff.* But *royauté oblige:*** he felt it necessary to discuss state affairs with Alexander's envoy as a king and ally. He dismounted and, taking Balashov by

---

*The poor fellows, they don't know that I'm leaving them tomorrow!
†I made you a king so that you would reign in my fashion, not in yours.
‡Delighted to make your acquaintance, General.
§Well, General, it's all for war, it seems.
#Sire . . . the emperor, my master, has no desire for war, and that Your Majesty can see.
**Royalty obliges.

the arm and moving a few steps away from the suite, who waited respectfully, began walking up and down with him, trying to speak significantly. He mentioned that the emperor Napoleon was offended by the demand to withdraw his troops from Prussia, especially now, when the demand had become known to everybody and the dignity of France was offended by it. Balashov said that there was nothing offensive in this demand, because . . . Murat interrupted him:

"So you don't consider the emperor Alexander the instigator?" he said unexpectedly with a good-naturedly stupid smile.

Balashov told him why he actually supposed that the initiator of the war was Napoleon.

"Eh, mon cher général," Murat interrupted him again, "je désire de tout mon coeur que les Empereurs s'arrangent entre eux, et que la guerre commencée malgré moi se termine le plutôt possible,"* he said in the tone of a conversation between servants who wish to remain good friends despite a quarrel between their masters. And he went on to ask about the grand duke, about his health, and to reminisce about the gay and amusing time he spent with him in Naples. Then, as if suddenly recollecting his royal dignity, Murat straightened up solemnly, assumed the same pose he had at his coronation, and with a wave of the right hand, said: "Je ne vous retiens plus, général; je souhaite le succès de votre mission"†—and, his embroidered red mantle and plumes flying and his precious stones glittering, he went towards the suite that was respectfully waiting for him.

Balashov rode on, supposing from Murat's words that he would quite soon be introduced to Napoleon himself. But instead of meeting Napoleon soon, he was detained by sentinels of Davout's infantry corps at the next village, as he had been at the front line, and the summoned adjutant of the corps commander took him to the village to Marshal Davout.

V

Davout was the emperor Napoleon's Arakcheev—a non-cowardly Arakcheev, but equally efficient, cruel, and incapable of expressing his devotion otherwise than by cruelty.

In the mechanism of the state organism these people are necessary, as wolves are necessary in nature's organism, and they always exist, always appear and hold out, however incongruous their presence and closeness to the head of

---

*Eh, my dear General . . . I wish with all my heart that the emperors may settle things between them and that the war begun in spite of me may end as soon as possible.
†I will not keep you any longer, General; I wish you success in your mission.

the government may seem. Only this necessity can explain how the cruel Arakcheev, who personally tore out grenadiers' moustaches, whose nerves were too weak for him to endure danger, an uneducated and uncourtly man, could hold on to such power next to the chivalrously noble and gentle character of Alexander.

Balashov found Marshal Davout in the shed of a peasant cottage, sitting on a barrel and busy with written work (he was checking the accounts). An adjutant stood next to him. It would have been possible to find a better location, but Marshal Davout was one of those people who deliberately set themselves up in the most gloomy conditions of life, so as to have the right to be gloomy. For the same reason they are always in a hurry and stubbornly busy. "How can I think about the happy side of human life, when, as you see, I'm sitting on a barrel in a dirty shed and working," said the expression of his face. The chief pleasure and need of these people, on meeting life's animation, consists in throwing their gloomy, stubborn activity into the eyes of that animation. Davout allowed himself this pleasure when Balashov was brought to him. He immersed himself still more in his work when the Russian general came in, and, looking through his spectacles at Balashov's face, animated by the impression of the beautiful morning and the conversation with Murat, he did not stand up, did not even stir, but frowned still more and grinned spitefully.

Noticing on Balashov's face the unpleasant impression produced by this reception, Davout raised his head and coldly asked what he wanted.

Supposing that such a reception could be given him only because Davout did not know that he was the emperor Alexander's adjutant general and even his representative before Napoleon, Balashov hastened to inform him of his rank and purpose. Contrary to his expectation, Davout, having heard Balashov out, became still more stern and rude.

"Where's your packet?" he said. *"Donnez-le moi, je l'enverrai à l'Empereur."* *

Balashov said he was under orders to personally deliver the packet to the emperor.

"Your emperor's orders are carried out in your army, but here," said Davout, "you should do as you're told."

And, as if to let the Russian general feel still more his dependence on brute force, Davout sent his adjutant for the officer on duty.

Balashov took out the packet that contained the sovereign's letter and placed it on the table (a table consisting of a door with ripped-off hinges sticking out from it, laid over two barrels). Davout took the envelope and read what was written on it.

---

*Give it to me, I'll send it to the emperor.

"You are perfectly within your rights to show or not show respect for me," said Balashov. "But allow me to observe that I have the honour to bear the rank of his majesty's adjutant general . . ."

Davout looked at him silently, and the slight trouble and confusion expressed on Balashov's face clearly afforded him pleasure.

"You'll be rendered what's due you," he said and, putting the envelope in his pocket, he left the shed.

A minute later the marshal's adjutant, M. de Castries, came in and led Balashov to the lodgings prepared for him.

Balashov had dinner with the marshal that day, in the same shed, on the same board on barrels.

The next day Davout left early in the morning and, summoning Balashov, told him imposingly that he asked him to remain there, to move along with the baggage, if such were the orders, and to speak with no one except M. de Castries.

After four days of solitude, boredom, consciousness of his dependence and insignificance, felt especially sharply after the milieu of power in which he had been so recently, after several marches with the marshal's baggage and the French troops, who occupied the entire area, Balashov was brought to Vilno, now occupied by the French, through the same gate from which he had ridden out four days earlier.

The next day the emperor's gentleman-in-waiting, M. de Turenne, came to Balashov and conveyed to him the emperor Napoleon's wish to honour him with an audience.

Four days earlier, the sentinels of the Preobrazhensky regiment were standing by the house to which Balashov was brought; now two French grenadiers stood there, in blue uniforms open on the chest and shaggy hats. A convoy of hussars and uhlans, and a dazzling suite of adjutants, pages, and generals, expecting Napoleon to come out, waited by the porch near his saddle horse and his Mameluke Rustan.[12] Napoleon was to receive Balashov in the same house in Vilno from which Alexander had sent him off.

VI

Accustomed though Balashov was to court solemnity, the luxury and magnificence of the emperor Napoleon's court struck him.

Count Turenne led him into a large reception room, in which sat many generals, gentlemen-in-waiting, and Polish dignitaries, many of whom Balashov had seen at the court of the Russian emperor. Duroc said that the emperor Napoleon would receive the Russian general before his promenade.

After several minutes of expectation, the gentleman-in-waiting on duty that day came out to the large reception room and, with a courteous bow to Bala-shov, invited him to follow him.

Balashov went into a small reception room, from which there was one door to the study, the same study from which the Russian emperor had sent him off. Balashov stood alone for a couple of minutes. There was a sound of hurried footsteps behind the door. Both halves of the door opened quickly, the gentleman-in-waiting who opened them stopped respectfully; everything fell silent, and from the study came the sound of other firm, resolute footsteps: this was Napoleon. He had just finished dressing for his ride. He was in a dark blue uniform, open over a white waistcoat which went down over his round stom-ach, white buckskins stretched tight over the fat haunches of his short legs, and jackboots. His short hair had obviously just been brushed, but one strand hung loose over the middle of his wide forehead. His plump white neck stood out sharply against the black collar of his uniform; he smelled of cologne. His full, youthful face with its protruding chin bore an expression of gracious and majestic imperial greeting.

He came out, springing briskly at every step, his head slightly thrown back. The whole of his stout, short figure, with its broad, fat shoulders and involun-tarily thrust-out stomach and chest, had that imposing, stately look which pampered forty-year-old men have. Besides, it was clear that he was in very good spirits that day.

He nodded in response to Balashov's low and respectful bow and, going up to him, began speaking at once, like a man who values every minute of his time and who does not condescend to prepare his speeches, but is certain that he will always speak well and say what needs to be said.

"Good day, General!" he said. "I have received the emperor Alexander's letter, which you delivered, and am very glad to see you." He glanced into Balashov's face with his large eyes and at once began to look straight ahead past him.

It was obvious that Balashov's person did not interest him in the least. It was clear that only what went on in *his* soul was of interest to him. Everything that was outside him had no meaning for him, because everything in the world, as it seemed to him, depended only upon his will.

"I do not want and have never wanted war," he said, "but I was forced into it. Even *now*" (he emphasized this word) "I am prepared to accept all the explanations you can give me." And he began to lay out, clearly and briefly, the reasons for his displeasure with the Russian government.

Judging by the calmly moderate and friendly tone with which the French emperor spoke, Balashov was firmly convinced that he wanted peace and intended to enter into negotiations.

"*Sire! L'Empereur, mon maître,*" Balashov began his long-prepared speech, when Napoleon, having finished his own speech, looked questioningly at the

Russian envoy; but the gaze that the emperor's eyes directed at him confused him. "You're confused—pull yourself together," Napoleon seemed to be saying to him, looking over Balashov's uniform and sabre with a barely perceptible smile. Balashov pulled himself together and began to speak. He said that the emperor Alexander did not consider Kurakin's demand for passports a sufficient reason for starting a war, that Kurakin had acted thus by his own free will and without the consent of the sovereign, that the emperor Alexander did not want war, and that there were no relations with England.

"Not *yet*," Napoleon put in, and, as if afraid of giving way to his emotion, he frowned and inclined his head slightly, thereby letting Balashov feel that he could go on.

Having spoken out everything he had been ordered to, Balashov said that the emperor Alexander wanted peace, but would not enter into negotiations otherwise than on condition that . . . Here Balashov hesitated: he remembered the words that the emperor Alexander had not written in the letter, but which he had ordered to be inserted without fail in the rescript to Saltykov and which he had ordered Balashov to convey to Napoleon. Balashov remembered the words—"that not a single armed enemy remains on Russian soil"—but some complex feeling held him back. He could not say those words, though he wanted to. He hesitated and said: on condition that the French troops withdraw beyond the Niemen.

Napoleon noticed Balashov's confusion as he uttered these last words; his face twitched, his left calf began to tremble rhythmically. Without leaving his place, he began to speak in a higher and more hurried voice than before. During the speech that followed, Balashov, lowering his eyes more than once, involuntarily observed the trembling of Napoleon's left calf, which increased as he raised his voice.

"I want peace no less than the emperor Alexander," he began. "Have I not been doing everything during these eighteen months to obtain it? I have waited eighteen months for explanations. And what is demanded of me, in order to start negotiations?" he said, frowning and making an energetically questioning gesture with his small, white, and plump hand.

"The withdrawal of your troops beyond the Niemen, Sire," said Balashov.

"Beyond the Niemen?" Napoleon repeated. "So now you want me to withdraw beyond the Niemen? Merely the Niemen?" Napoleon repeated, looking straight at Balashov.

Balashov lowered his head respectfully.

Instead of the demand four months earlier that he withdraw from Pomerania, now they demanded only that he withdraw beyond the Niemen. Napoleon turned quickly and started pacing the room.

"You say that withdrawal beyond the Niemen is demanded of me in order to begin negotiations; but in just the same way it was demanded of me two months ago that I withdraw beyond the Oder and the Vistula, and, despite that, you agree to conduct negotiations."

He paced silently from one corner of the room to the other, and again stopped in front of Balashov. His face was as if petrified in its stern expression, and his left leg trembled still more rapidly than before. Napoleon knew that he had this trembling of the left calf. *"La vibration de mon mollet gauche est un grand signe chez moi,"** he would say later.

"Suggestions such as clearing the Oder and Vistula can be made to the prince of Baden, not to me," Napoleon nearly cried out, quite unexpectedly for himself. "If you were to give me Petersburg and Moscow, I would not accept these conditions. You say I started the war? And who was the first to join his army? The emperor Alexander, not I. And you offer me negotiations, when I've spent millions, while you are in alliance with England, and when your position is bad—you offer me negotiations! What is the goal of your alliance with England? What has it gained you?" he said hurriedly, obviously no longer directing his speech at stating the advantages of concluding a peace and discussing its possibility, but only at proving his rightness and his strength, and the wrongs and errors of Alexander.

The introduction to his speech was made, obviously, with the aim of bringing out the advantages of his position and showing that, in spite of that, he had accepted the opening of negotiations. But he now began to speak, and the more he spoke, the less able he was to control his speech.

The whole aim of his speech now was obviously to exalt himself and insult Alexander, that is, to do the thing he had least wanted to do at the beginning of the meeting.

"They say you've concluded a peace with the Turks?"

Balashov inclined his head affirmatively.

"Peace has been concluded . . ." he began. But Napoleon did not let him speak. He clearly needed to speak himself, and he went on to speak with that eloquence and unrestrained irritation to which spoiled people are so greatly inclined.

"Yes, I know you've concluded a peace with the Turks, without getting Moldavia and Wallachia. And I would have given your sovereign those provinces, just as I gave him Finland.[13] Yes," he went on, "I promised, and I would have given the emperor Alexander Moldavia and Wallachia, but now he won't have those beautiful provinces. He might, however, have joined them to his empire, and within one reign he would have expanded Russia from the Gulf of Bothnia to the mouth of the Danube. Catherine the Great couldn't have done more," Napoleon was saying, growing more and more flushed, pacing the room, and repeating to Balashov almost the same words he had spoken to Alexander him-

*The trembling of my left calf is a great sign with me.

self at Tilsit. *"Tout cela il l'aurait dû à mon amitié . . . Ah! quel beau règne, quel beau règne!"** he repeated several times, stopped, took a gold snuffbox from his pocket, and inhaled greedily through his nose.

"Quel beau règne aurait pu être celui de l'empereur Alexandre!"†

He glanced at Balashov with pity, and just as Balashov was about to observe something, he again hastily interrupted him.

"What could he desire and seek that he could not have found in my friendship? . . ." said Napoleon, with a shrug of perplexity. "No, he found it better to surround himself with my enemies—and who are they?" he went on. "He summoned the Steins, the Armfelts, the Wintzingerodes, the Bennigsens. Stein—a traitor driven from his fatherland; Armfelt—a debauchee and intriguer; Wintzingerode—a fugitive French subject; Bennigsen—a bit more of a soldier than the others, but all the same an incompetent, who was unable to do anything in 1807, and who must call up terrible memories in the emperor Alexander . . .[14] Let's suppose, if they were competent, they could be made use of," Napoleon went on, barely able to keep up verbally with the constantly emerging considerations showing him his rightness or power (which to his mind were the same), "but that is not the case: they're no good either for peace or for war. They say Barclay is more capable than the rest; but I wouldn't say so, judging by his first moves. And what are they doing? What are all those courtiers doing? Pfuel proposes, Armfelt argues, Bennigsen considers, and Barclay, called upon to act, doesn't know what to decide on, and the time passes. Bagration alone is a military man. He's stupid, but he has experience, a good eye, and determination . . . And what role does your young sovereign play in that outrageous crowd? They compromise him and shift onto him the responsibility for all that's happening. *Un souverain ne doit être à l'armée que quand il est général,"*‡ he said, obviously throwing these words as a challenge into the face of the sovereign. Napoleon knew how much Alexander wished to be a military commander.

"It's a week since the campaign began, and you failed to defend Vilno. You're cut in two and thrown out of the Polish provinces. Your army murmurs . . ."

"On the contrary, Your Majesty," said Balashov, barely managing to remember what had been told him and following with difficulty these verbal fireworks, "the troops are burning with desire . . ."

"I know everything," Napoleon interrupted him, "I know everything, and I know the number of your battalions as accurately as my own. You have less than two hundred thousand men, and I have three times that number. I give

*All that he would have owed to my friendship . . . Ah, what a fine reign, what a fine reign!
†What a fine reign the reign of the emperor Alexander *might have* been!
‡A sovereign should not be with the army unless he's a general.

you my word of honour," said Napoleon, forgetting that his word of honour could have no meaning, "I give you *ma parole d'honneur que j'ai cinq cent trente mille hommes de ce coté de la Vistule.** The Turks are no help to you: they're good for nothing and have proved it by making peace with you. The Swedes—their destiny is to be ruled by mad kings. Their king was insane, they changed him and took another, Bernadotte, who promptly went out of his mind—because no Swede who wasn't a madman would conclude alliances with Russia."[15] Napoleon grinned spitefully and again put his snuffbox to his nose.

To each of Napoleon's phrases, Balashov could and would have objected; he continually made the movement of a man who wishes to say something, but Napoleon interrupted him. For instance, about the madness of the Swedes, Balashov was about to say that Sweden was an island when Russia backed her; but Napoleon cried out angrily to stifle his voice. Napoleon was in that state of irritation in which a man has to talk and talk and talk, only so as to prove his rightness to himself. It was becoming oppressive for Balashov: as an envoy, he was afraid of losing his dignity and felt it necessary to object; but as a human being he shrank morally before the oblivion of groundless wrath in which Napoleon obviously found himself. He knew that all the words Napoleon was now saying meant nothing, that he would be ashamed of them himself once he came to his senses. Balashov stood, his eyes lowered, looking at the movements of Napoleon's fat legs, and tried to avoid his gaze.

"What do I care about your allies?" said Napoleon. "I have the Poles for allies: there are eighty thousand of them, they fight like lions. And there will be two hundred thousand of them."

And, probably becoming still more aroused because, in saying that, he had said an obvious untruth, and because Balashov, in the same pose of submission to his fate, stood silently before him, he turned round sharply, went up very close to Balashov's face, and, making energetic and rapid gestures with his white hands, nearly shouted:

"Know that if you stir up Prussia against me, know that I will wipe her off the map of Europe," he said with a pale face distorted by anger, beating one small hand against the other with an energetic gesture. "Yes, I'll hurl you back beyond the Dvina, beyond the Dnieper, and rebuild that barrier against you which Europe was criminal and blind to have allowed to be destroyed.[16] Yes, that's what will happen to you, that's what you've gained by distancing yourselves from me," he said and silently paced the room several times, his fat shoulders twitching. He put the snuffbox into his waistcoat pocket, took it out again, brought it to his nose several times, and stopped facing Balashov. He

---

*My word of honour that I have five hundred and thirty thousand men on this side of the Vistula.

paused, looking mockingly straight into Balashov's eyes, and said in a quiet voice: *"Et cependent quel beau règne aurait pu avoir votre maître!"**

Balashov, feeling it necessary to object, said that on the Russian side things did not look so gloomy. Napoleon said nothing, went on looking at him mockingly, and obviously was not listening to him. Balashov said that in Russia all sorts of good things were expected from the war. Napoleon nodded condescendingly, as if to say: "I know it's your duty to say so, but you don't believe it yourself, I have persuaded you."

At the end of Balashov's speech, Napoleon again took out his snuffbox, snuffed from it, and gave a signal by stamping his foot twice on the floor. The door opened; a respectfully flexing gentleman-in-waiting handed the emperor his hat and gloves, another handed him a handkerchief. Napoleon, without looking at them, turned to Balashov.

"Assure the emperor Alexander on my behalf," he said, taking his hat, "that I am as devoted to him as before: I know him perfectly and value his lofty qualities very highly. *Je ne vous retiens plus, général, vous recevrez ma lettre à l'Empereur.*"† And Napoleon quickly went to the door. Everyone in the reception room rushed forward and down the stairs.

VII

After all that Napoleon had said to him, after those outbursts of wrath, and after those last drily spoken words—*"Je ne vous retiens plus, général, vous recevrez ma lettre"*—Balashov was convinced that Napoleon not only would not wish to see him, but would try not to see him—the envoy he had insulted and, moreover, the witness to his unseemly vehemence. But, to his surprise, Balashov received that day, through Duroc, an invitation to the emperor's table.

Bessières, Caulaincourt, and Berthier were at dinner.

Napoleon met Balashov with a cheerful and benign air. Not only was there no expression in him of embarrassment or self-reproach for his morning's outburst, but, on the contrary, he tried to encourage Balashov. Clearly it was Napoleon's long-standing conviction that the possibility of mistakes did not exist for him, and to his mind everything he did was good, not because it agreed with any notion of what was good and bad, but because *he* did it.

The emperor was very cheerful after his promenade on horseback in Vilno, where crowds of rapturous people met him and followed him. In all the win-

---

*And yet what a fine reign your master *might have had!*
†I will not keep you any longer, General, you will receive my letter to the emperor.

dows of the streets he rode down, carpets, banners, and his monogram were put out, and Polish ladies greeted him waving their handkerchiefs.

At dinner, seating Balashov beside him, he treated him not only benignly but as if he counted Balashov among his courtiers, among the people who sympathized with his plans and were supposed to be glad of his successes. Among other subjects, he talked about Moscow and began to ask Balashov about the Russian capital, not merely as a curious traveller asks about a new place he intends to visit, but as if convinced that Balashov, as a Russian, must be flattered by his curiosity.

"How many inhabitants does Moscow have? How many houses? Is it true that *Moscou* is called *Moscou la sainte*? How many churches are there in *Moscou*?" he asked.

And to the reply that there were more than two hundred churches, he said: "Why such a profusion of churches?"

"The Russians are very pious," answered Balashov.

"However, a great number of monasteries and churches is always a sign of a nation's backwardness," said Napoleon, turning to Caulaincourt for an appreciation of this judgement.

Balashov respectfully allowed himself to disagree with the French emperor's opinion.

"Each country has its customs," he said.

"But there's nothing like that anywhere in Europe now," said Napoleon.

"I beg Your Majesty's pardon," said Balashov, "besides Russia there is also Spain, where there are just as many churches and monasteries."

This reply of Balashov's, alluding to the recent defeat of the French in Spain,[17] was highly appreciated later on, according to Balashov's account, at the court of the emperor Alexander, but very little appreciated now, at Napoleon's dinner, and went unnoticed.

From the indifferent and puzzled faces of the gentlemen marshals, one could see that they were puzzled by exactly what constituted the wittiness here, which Balashov's intonation implied. "If there was any, we didn't understand it, or else it wasn't witty at all," said the expressions of the marshals' faces. So little was this reply appreciated that Napoleon even decidedly failed to notice it and naïvely asked Balashov through what towns the direct route from there to Moscow passed. Balashov, who was on the alert all through dinner, replied that *comme tout chemin mène à Rome, tout chemin mène à Moscou,** that there were many roads, and that among those various roads was the road through *Poltawa*, which had been chosen by Charles XII, said Balashov, involuntarily blushing with pleasure at the happy response.[18] Balashov had not managed to finish saying the final word, "*Poltawa*," before Caulaincourt

---

* As all roads lead to Rome, so all roads lead to Moscow.

began talking about the inconvenience of the road from Petersburg to Moscow and about his Petersburg memories.

After dinner they went to have coffee in Napoleon's study, which four days earlier had been the study of the emperor Alexander. Napoleon sat down, sipped his coffee from a Sèvres cup, and motioned Balashov to the chair beside him.

There exists in men a certain after-dinner state of mind which, more strongly than any reasonable causes, makes a man feel content with himself and consider everyone his friend. Napoleon was in that state of mind. It seemed to him that he was surrounded by people who adored him. He was convinced that after his dinner Balashov, too, was his friend and adorer. Napoleon addressed him with a pleasant and slightly mocking smile.

"This is the same room, I've been told, in which the emperor Alexander lived. Strange, isn't it, General?" he said, obviously not doubting that this remark could be anything but pleasing to his interlocutor, as it proved his, Napoleon's, superiority to Alexander.

Balashov could make no reply to that and silently bowed his head.

"Yes, in this room, four days ago, Wintzingerode and Stein conferred," Napoleon went on with the same mocking, confident smile. "What I can't understand," he said, "is that the emperor Alexander made all these personal enemies of mine his intimates. That I don't . . . understand. Didn't he reflect that I might do the same?" He turned to Balashov with this question, and the recollection evidently pushed him back onto the track of his morning's wrath, which was still fresh in him.

"And let him know that I will do it!" said Napoleon, getting up and shoving his cup away with his hand. "I'll throw all his relatives out of Germany, all these Württembergs, Badens, Weimars . . .[19] Yes, I'll throw them out. Let him prepare a refuge for them in Russia!"

Balashov inclined his head, showing by his look that he would have liked to bow out, and was listening only because he could not help listening to what was said to him. Napoleon did not notice that expression; he addressed Balashov not as his enemy's envoy, but as a man who was now entirely devoted to him and was supposed to be glad of his former master's humiliation.

"And why has the emperor Alexander taken charge of the army? What for? War is my trade, and his business is to rule, not to command troops. Why has he taken such responsibility upon himself?"

Napoleon took out his snuffbox again, silently paced the room several times, and suddenly went up to Balashov unexpectedly, and with a slight smile, as confidently, quickly, and simply as if he was doing something not only important but pleasant to Balashov, raised his hand to the face of the forty-year-old Russian general and, taking him by the ear, pulled it slightly, smiling with his lips only.

*Avoir l'oreille tirée par l'Empereur** was considered the greatest honour and favour at the French court.

"Eh bien, vous ne dites rien, admirateur et courtisan de l'Empereur Alexandre?"† he said, as if it was ridiculous in his presence to be anyone else's *courtisan* and *admirateur* than his, Napoleon's.

"Are the horses ready for the general?" he added, inclining his head slightly in response to Balashov's bow.

"Give him mine, he has *far to go* . . ."

The letter Balashov brought back was Napoleon's last letter to Alexander. All the details of the conversation were conveyed to the Russian emperor, and the war began.

VIII

After his meeting with Pierre in Moscow, Prince Andrei left for Petersburg on business, as he told his family, but in reality in order to meet Prince Anatole Kuragin, whom he considered it necessary to meet. Kuragin, about whom he made enquiries when he reached Petersburg, was no longer there. Pierre had let his brother-in-law know that Prince Andrei was coming after him. Anatole Kuragin at once obtained an appointment from the minster of war and left for the army in Moldavia. At that same time in Petersburg, Prince Andrei met Kutuzov, his former general, who was always well-disposed towards him, and Kutuzov suggested that he go with him to the army in Moldavia, where the old general had been appointed commander in chief.[20] Prince Andrei, receiving an appointment to be attached to general headquarters, left for Turkey.

Prince Andrei considered it improper to write to Kuragin and challenge him. Without giving him a new pretext for a duel, Prince Andrei considered that a challenge on his part would compromise Countess Rostov, and therefore he sought to meet Kuragin personally with the intention of finding a new pretext for a duel. But in the Turkish army he again failed to meet Kuragin, who returned to Russia soon after Prince Andrei's arrival in Turkey. In a new country and in new conditions, Prince Andrei's life became easier. After his fiancée's betrayal, which struck him the more strongly the more he tried to conceal its effect on him from everyone, the conditions of life in which he had been happy became a burden for him, and still more of a burden were the freedom and independence that had once been so dear to him. He not only did not think those former thoughts that had first come to him as he gazed at the sky on the field of Austerlitz, which he had liked to enlarge upon with Pierre, and which

*To have your ear pulled by the emperor.
†Well, so you say nothing, admirer and courtier of the emperor Alexander?

had filled his solitude in Bogucharovo and then in Switzerland and Rome; but he was even afraid to remember those thoughts that had opened boundless and bright horizons. He was now concerned only with the most immediate, practical interests, unconnected with his former ones, which he grasped at the more eagerly the more closed to him the former ones were. As if that boundless, ever-receding vault of the sky that used to stand over him had suddenly turned into a low, definite, oppressive vault, in which everything was clear and nothing was eternal or mysterious.

Of the activities that presented themselves to him, military service was the simplest and most familiar. Occupying the post of general on duty in Kutuzov's headquarters, he performed his duties persistently and diligently, astonishing Kutuzov by his zeal for work and his conscientiousness. Not having found Kuragin in Turkey, Prince Andrei did not consider it necessary to gallop back to Russia after him; but all the same he knew that, no matter how much time passed, he could not, on meeting Kuragin, despite all the contempt he had for him, despite all the proofs he gave himself that it was not worth humiliating himself by a confrontation with him, he knew that, on meeting him, he could not help challenging him, as a hungry man cannot help falling upon food. And this awareness that the insult had not yet been avenged, that the anger had not yet been vented, but remained in his heart, poisoned the artificial calm that Prince Andrei arranged for himself in Turkey, in the form of a bustlingly busy and somewhat ambitious and vainglorious activity.

In the year twelve, when news of the war with Napoleon reached Bucharest (where Kutuzov had been staying for two months, spending the days and nights with his Wallachian woman), Prince Andrei asked Kutuzov to transfer him to the Western Army. Kutuzov, who by then was sick of Bolkonsky's activity, which served as a reproach to his idleness, quite willingly let him go and gave him an errand to Barclay de Tolly.

Before going to the army, which in May was encamped on the Drissa, Prince Andrei stopped at Bald Hills, which was directly on his way, being two miles from the Smolensk high road. In the last three years of Prince Andrei's life there had been so many upheavals, he had thought, felt, and seen so much (having travelled both in the west and in the east), that on entering Bald Hills, he was strangely and unexpectedly struck that everything was exactly the same, to the smallest details—there was exactly the same course of life. He rode down the avenue and through the stone gates of the Bald Hills house as if into an enchanted, sleeping castle. The same staidness, the same cleanliness, the same silence were in this house, the same furniture, the same walls, the same sounds, the same smell, and the same timid faces, only grown slightly older. Princess Marya was the same timid, plain, ageing maiden, uselessly and joylessly living through the best years of her life in fear and eternal moral suffering. Mlle Bourienne was the same coquettish girl, pleased with herself, joyfully making use of every moment of her life, and filled with the most joyful hopes for herself. She had only become surer of herself, as it seemed to Prince Andrei. The tutor Dessales, whom he had brought from Switzerland, was dressed in a frock coat of Russian cut, spoke distorted Russian with the servants, but was the same narrowly intelligent, well-educated, virtuous, and pedantic tutor. The old prince had changed physically only in that a missing tooth could be noticed on one side of his mouth; morally he was the same as before, only with more animosity and mistrust towards the reality of what was happening in the world. Nikolushka alone had grown, changed, become red-cheeked, with a head of dark curly hair and, unknowingly, when he was laughing and gay, he raised the upper lip of his pretty little mouth exactly as the deceased little princess used to do. He alone did not obey the law of changelessness in this enchanted, sleeping castle. But, though externally everything remained as before, the inner relations of all these persons had changed since Prince Andrei last saw them. The members of the family were divided into two camps, alien and hostile to each other, which came together now only because of him, changing their usual way of life for his sake. To one belonged the old prince, Mlle Bourienne, and the architect, to the other Princess Marya, Dessales, Nikolushka, and all the nurses and nannies.

During his stay at Bald Hills, all the household dined together, but everyone felt awkward, and Prince Andrei sensed that he was a guest for whom an exception was being made, that he inconvenienced everyone by his presence. During dinner on the first day, Prince Andrei, involuntarily sensing that, was silent, and the old prince, noticing the unnaturalness of his state, also fell sullenly silent and went to his room directly after dinner. When Prince Andrei came to him in the evening and, trying to stir him up, began telling him about the campaign of the young Count Kamensky, the old prince unexpectedly began telling him about Princess Marya, condemning her for her superstitiousness and for her dislike of Mlle Bourienne, who, according to him, was the only one truly devoted to him.

The old prince said that if he was ill, it was only because of Princess Marya; that she deliberately tormented and irritated him; that she spoiled little Prince Nikolai with pampering and stupid talk. The old prince knew very well that he tormented his daughter, that her life was very wretched, but he also knew that he could not help tormenting her and that she deserved it. "Why does Prince Andrei, who sees it, say nothing to me about his sister?" the old man wondered. "What, does he think I'm a villain or an old fool, distancing myself from my daughter for no reason and becoming close with the Frenchwoman? He doesn't understand it, and therefore I must explain it to him, he must hear me out," thought the old prince. And he began to explain the reasons why he could not bear his daughter's muddle-headed character.

"If you're asking me," said Prince Andrei, without looking at his father (for the first time in his life he was censuring his father), "I didn't want to say it, but if you're asking me, I'll tell you my frank opinion about it all. If there is any misunderstanding and discord between you and Masha, I can't blame her for it—I know how she loves and respects you. If you're asking me," Prince Andrei went on, becoming irritated, because lately he was always ready to become irritated, "I can say one thing: if there are misunderstandings, the cause of them is a worthless woman, who should never have been my sister's friend."

At first the old man stared at his son with fixed eyes and an unnatural smile that revealed his newly missing tooth, which Prince Andrei could not get used to.

"What friend, my dear? Eh? So you had to say it! Eh?"

"Papa, I didn't want to judge," Prince Andrei said in a bilious and hard tone, "but you challenged me, and I've said and will always say that Princess Marya is not to blame, but the one to blame. . . the one to blame is this Frenchwoman . . ."

"Ah, judging! . . . judging!" the old man said in a low voice and, it seemed to Prince Andrei, with embarrassment, but then he suddenly jumped up and shouted: "Out, out! Don't leave a trace behind! . . ."

Prince Andrei wanted to leave at once, but Princess Marya persuaded him to stay for one more day. That day Prince Andrei did not see his father, who did not come out and did not let anyone in except for Mlle Bourienne and Tikhon, and asked several times if his son was gone. The next day, before his departure, Prince Andrei went to his son's rooms. The healthy boy, curly-headed like his mother, sat on his lap. Prince Andrei began telling him a fairy tale about Blue-beard, but did not finish and fell to thinking. He was not thinking about this pretty boy, his son, as he held him on his lap, but about himself. With horror he sought and did not find in himself either remorse for having irritated his father or regret at leaving him (having quarrelled with him for the first time in his life). Worst of all for him was that he sought and did not find in himself the former tenderness for his son, which he had hoped to awaken in himself by caressing the boy and sitting him on his lap.

"Well, tell me, tell me," said the boy. Prince Andrei did not answer him, took him off his knees, and left the room.

As soon as Prince Andrei abandoned his everyday occupations, and especially as soon as he entered the former conditions of life, in which he had lived when he was still happy, life's anguish took hold of him with its former force, and he hastened to get away quickly from those memories and quickly find something to do.

"So, André, you're definitely leaving?" his sister said to him.

"Thank God I can," said Prince Andrei, "it's too bad you can't."

"Why do you say that?" said Princess Marya. "Why do you say that now, when you're going to this terrible war, and he's so old! Mlle Bourienne said he asked about you . . ." As soon as she began to speak of it, her lips trembled and tears began to fall. Prince Andrei turned away from her and started pacing the room.

"Ah, my God! My God!" he said. "And to think of who—of what nonentities—can be the cause of people's unhappiness!" he said with a malice that frightened Princess Marya.

She understood that, in referring to the people he called nonentities, he had in mind not only Mlle Bourienne, who had ruined her happiness, but also the man who had ruined his own.

"André, I ask you one thing, I beg you," she said, touching his elbow and looking at him through the tears in her shining eyes. "I understand you" (Princess Marya lowered her eyes). "Don't think that grief is caused by people. People are His instruments." She looked slightly over Prince Andrei's head with that confident, habitual look with which one looks at the place of a familiar portrait. "Grief is sent by Him, not by people. People are His instruments, they're not to blame. If it seems to you that someone is to blame before you, forget it and forgive. We have no right to punish. And you will know the happiness of forgiveness."

"If I were a woman, Marie, I would be doing that. It's a woman's virtue. But a man must not and cannot forget and forgive," he said and, though he had not thought of Kuragin till that moment, all his unvented anger suddenly rose in his heart. "If Princess Marya is now persuading me to forgive him, it means I ought to have punished him long ago," he thought. And, no longer responding to Princess Marya, he began thinking of that joyful, spiteful moment when he would meet Kuragin, who (as he knew) was with the army.

Princess Marya begged her brother to wait one more day; she said she knew how unhappy their father would be if Andrei left without making peace with him; but Prince Andrei replied that he would probably come back soon from the army, that he would be sure to write to their father, and that the longer he stayed now, the more aggravated the discord would be.

*"Adieu, André! Rappelez-vous que les malheurs viennent de Dieu, et que les hommes ne sont jamais coupables"** were the last words he heard from his sister as he was taking leave of her.

"So it must be!" thought Prince Andrei as he was driving out of the avenue of the house at Bald Hills. "She, a pathetic, innocent being, stays to be devoured by a senile old man. The old man feels he's to blame, but cannot

---

*Goodbye, Andrei! Remember that misfortunes come from God, and that men are never to blame.

change himself. My boy is growing up and rejoices at life, in which he will be the same as everybody else, the deceived or the deceiver. I'm going to the army—why? I don't know myself, and I wish to meet a man whom I despise, in order to give him an occasion to kill me and laugh at me!" Before, too, there had been the same conditions of life, but before they had all cohered, while now everything had fallen apart. Nothing but meaningless phenomena, without any connection with each other, presented themselves to Prince Andrei one after the other.

IX

Prince Andrei arrived in the general headquarters of the army at the end of June. The troops of the first army, whom the emperor was with, were stationed in a fortified camp on the Drissa; the troops of the second army were in retreat, with the aim of joining the first army, from which, it was said, they were cut off by large forces of the French. Everyone was displeased with the general course of military affairs in the Russian army; but of the danger of an invasion of the Russian provinces no one even thought, no one even supposed that the war would be carried further than the western Polish provinces.

Prince Andrei found Barclay de Tolly, to whom he had been assigned, on the bank of the Drissa. As there was not a single large village or settlement in the vicinity of the camp, all the huge number of generals and courtiers who were with the army settled within a radius of seven miles in the best houses of the hamlets on this and the other side of the river. Barclay de Tolly was staying some three miles from the sovereign. He received Bolkonsky drily and coldly, and said with his German accent[21] that he would report his arrival to the sovereign so as to determine an assignment for him, and meanwhile he invited him to stay with his staff. Anatole Kuragin, whom Prince Andrei had hoped to find with the army, was not there: he was in Petersburg, and that news pleased Bolkonsky. Prince Andrei was taken up by the interest of being at the centre of a huge, ongoing war, and he was glad to be free for a time of the vexation produced in him by the thought of Kuragin. In the course of the first four days, during which he was not called for anywhere, Prince Andrei rode around the entire fortified camp and, with the help of his knowledge and of conversations with well-informed people, tried to form some idea of it for himself. But the question of whether this camp was advantageous or not remained unresolved for Prince Andrei. He had already managed to draw from his military experience the conviction that in military matters the most profoundly devised plans meant nothing (as he had seen in the Austerlitz campaign), that everything depended on how one responded to the unexpected and unpredictable actions of the enemy, that everything depended on how and by whom the action was conducted. To clarify this last question for himself, Prince Andrei, using his position and acquaintances, tried to penetrate the character of the army's administration, of the persons and parties participating in it, and arrived at the following idea about the state of affairs.

While the sovereign was still in Vilno, the army was divided in three: the first army was under the command of Barclay de Tolly, the second under the command of Bagration, the third under the command of Tormasov. The sovereign was with the first army, but not as commander in chief. It was not stated in the orders that the sovereign would command, but only that the sovereign would be present in the army. Besides that, the sovereign personally did not have a commander in chief's staff with him, but the staff of the imperial headquarters. With him were the chief of the imperial staff, the quartermaster general Prince Volkonsky, generals, imperial adjutants, diplomatic officials, and a large number of foreigners, but there was no army staff. Besides them, the following persons were with the sovereign without any specific function: Arakcheev, the former minister of war; Count Bennigsen, the highest ranking of the generals; the Grand Duke Tsarevich Konstantin Pavlovich; Count Rumyantsev, the chancellor; Stein, a former Prussian minister; Armfelt, a Swedish general; Pfuel, the chief author of the plan of campaign; the adjutant general Paulucci, a native of Sardinia; Wolzogen, and many others. Though these people were with the army without any military function, they had influence through their position, and often a corps commander and even the commander in chief did not know in what capacity Bennigsen, or the grand duke, or Arakcheev, or Prince Volkonsky asked or advised one thing or another, and did not know whether it was from his own person or from the sovereign that this or that order in the form of advice proceeded and whether or not it was necessary to carry it out. But these were externals, while the essential meaning of the presence of the sovereign and of all these persons—from the court point of view (and in the sovereign's presence everyone becomes a courtier)—was clear to everyone. It was the following: the sovereign did not take upon himself the title of commander in chief, but he gave orders to all the armies; the people of his entourage were his assistants. Arakcheev was the faithful executor-protector of order and the sovereign's bodyguard; Bennigsen was a landowner of Vilno province, who was as if doing *les honneurs* for the province, but in reality was a good general, useful for his advice and for always being at hand to replace Barclay. The grand duke was there because such was his pleasure. The ex-minister Stein was there because he was useful for his advice and because the emperor Alexander valued his personal qualities highly. Armfelt was a vicious hater of Napoleon and a self-assured general, which always had an effect on Alexander. Paulucci was there because he was bold and resolute in his speech. The adjutant generals were there because they were wherever the sovereign was, and finally—above all—Pfuel was there because, having drawn up the plan of war against Napoleon and having made Alexander believe in the advisability of this plan, he was directing the whole business of the war. Pfuel had come with Wolzogen, who conveyed Pfuel's thoughts in a form more accessible than did Pfuel himself, a closet theoretician, abrupt, and self-confident to the point of despising everything.

Besides the persons listed, Russians and foreigners (especially the foreigners, who, with the boldness characteristic of people acting in an alien milieu, suggested new, unexpected ideas every day), there were also many secondary persons, who were with the army because their superiors were there.

Among all the ideas and voices in this immense, restless, brilliant, and proud world, Prince Andrei saw the following more sharply distinguished tendencies and parties.

The first party was Pfuel and his followers, military theorists, who believed that there was a science of war and that in this science there were immutable laws—the laws of the oblique movement, of outflanking, and so on. Pfuel and his followers called for retreat into the depths of the country, a retreat according to precise laws set down by the imaginary theory of war, and saw in every departure from that theory only barbarism, ignorance, or ill will. To this party belonged the German princes, Wolzogen, Wintzingerode, and others, predominantly Germans.

The second party was the opposite of the first. As always happens, to one extreme corresponded representatives of the other extreme. The people of this party were those who, ever since Vilno, had been calling for an advance into Poland and freedom from all previously made plans. Along with being representatives of bold action, the people of this party were at the same time representatives of nationalism, which made them still more one-sided in dispute. These were Russians: Bagration, Ermolov, who was at the beginning of his rise, and others. At that time a well-known joke of Ermolov's was spread, that he had supposedly asked the sovereign for just one favour—to promote him to German. The people of this party said, recalling Suvorov, that there was a need not to think, not to stick pins in the map, but to fight, to beat the enemy, not to let them into Russia, and not to let the troops lose heart.

To the third party, which the sovereign trusted most of all, belonged the courtiers who made little deals between these two tendencies. The people of this party, for the most part nonmilitary, and to whom Arakcheev belonged, thought and said what people usually say who have no convictions but wish to seem as if they do. They said that war, especially with such a genius as Bonaparte (he was again known as Bonaparte), undoubtedly called for the most profoundly pondered considerations, for a profound knowledge of science, and in this matter Pfuel was a genius; but along with that, one could not help admitting that theorists are often one-sided, and therefore one must not fully trust them, one must lend an ear to what Pfuel's opponents and practical people, experienced in military affairs, have to say, and choose a middle course. The people of this party insisted on holding on to the Drissa camp, according to Pfuel's plan, while changing the movements of the other armies. Though this course of action attained neither one goal nor the other, to the people of this party it seemed better that way.

The fourth tendency was the tendency of which the most conspicuous representative was the grand duke, the heir to the throne, who was unable to forget his disappointment at Austerlitz, where, as at a review, he had ridden out at the head of his guards in a casque and collet, counting on boldly crushing the French, and, ending up in the front line, had barely managed to escape amidst the general confusion. The people of this party had in their opinions both the merit and the defect of sincerity. They were afraid of Napoleon, saw strength in him and weakness in themselves, and said so outright. They said: "Nothing will come of it but shame, grief, and ruin! We abandoned Vilno, we abandoned Vitebsk, and we will abandon the Drissa. The one intelligent thing left for us to do is conclude a peace, and as soon as possible, before we're driven out of Petersburg!"

This view of things, widely spread in the higher spheres of the army, found support both in Petersburg and in the chancellor Rumyantsev, who, for other reasons of state, was also for peace.

The fifth were adherents of Barclay de Tolly, not so much as a man but as a minister of war and commander in chief. They said: "Whatever else he may be" (they always began that way), "he's an honest, practical man, and there's nobody better. Give him real power, because war cannot proceed successfully without unity of command, and he will show what he can do, as he showed himself in Finland. If there is order and strength in our army, and it has withdrawn to Drissa without suffering any losses, we owe that only to Barclay. If Barclay is now replaced by Bennigsen, all will be lost, because Bennigsen already showed his incompetence in 1807," said the people of this party.

The sixth, the Bennigsenists, said, on the contrary, that all the same there was no one more practical and experienced than Bennigsen, and that, however you twisted and turned, all the same you would come to him. And the people of this party kept maintaining that our whole withdrawal to the Drissa was a most disgraceful defeat and an unbroken series of errors. "The more errors they make the better," they said, "at least they'll understand sooner that it can't go on like this. And what's needed is not some sort of Barclay, but a man like Bennigsen, who already showed himself in 1807, who was even given credit by Napoleon himself—a man whose authority would be willingly recognized, and the only such man is Bennigsen."

The seventh were persons who always exist, especially around young sovereigns, and who were especially numerous around the emperor Alexander: generals and imperial adjutants who were passionately devoted to the sovereign, not as an emperor but as a man, adoring him sincerely and disinterestedly, as Rostov had adored him in 1805, and who saw in him not only all virtues, but all human qualities. These persons, while admiring the modesty of the sovereign in refusing to take command of the army, also disapproved of this excessive modesty and wished for and insisted upon only one thing, that the adored sovereign, abandoning his excessive distrust of himself, would openly announce that he was placing himself at the head of the army, would assemble around him the headquarters of a commander in chief, and, asking advice whenever necessary from experienced theoreticians and practicians, would himself lead his troops, whom this alone would bring to the state of highest inspiration.

The eighth and largest group of people, which was so enormous that it outnumbered the others ninety-nine to one, consisted of people who desired neither peace nor war, neither an offensive movement nor a defensive camp in Drissa, or wherever it might be, neither Barclay nor the sovereign, neither Pfuel nor Bennigsen, but who desired only one thing, and that the most essential: the greatest benefit and pleasure for themselves. In those muddy waters of crisscrossing and entangled intrigues that swirled about the sovereign's headquarters, one could succeed in a great deal that would have been unthinkable at another time. One, wishing only to hold on to his advantageous position, agreed with Pfuel today, with his adversary tomorrow, and two days later maintained that he had no opinion on the subject, only so as to avoid responsibility and please the sovereign. Another, in his wish to gain some advantage, drew the sovereign's attention to himself, loudly repeating what the sovereign had alluded to the day before, arguing and shouting at the council, beating his breast and challenging those who disagreed to a duel, thus demonstrating that he was prepared to be a victim for the common good. A third, between two councils and in the absence of his enemies, simply solicited a reward for his faithful service, knowing that there would be no time to bother with a refusal. A fourth kept trying to catch the sovereign's eye as if by chance, as one burdened by his labours. A fifth, in order to achieve a long-desired goal—dinner with the sovereign—fiercely insisted on the rightness or wrongness of a newly emerged opinion and to that end put forth more or less forceful and correct arguments.

All the people in this party were pursuing roubles, crosses, ranks, and in this pursuit merely followed where the weathervane of the tsar's favour pointed, and as soon as they noticed the weathervane turning in a certain direction, all this drone population of the army began to blow in the same direction, so that it was harder for the sovereign to change it for another. Amidst the uncertainty of the situation, with the threat of serious danger, which gave everything an especially disquieting character, amidst this whirlwind of intrigues, vanities, clashes of various views and feelings, with all these people of different tribes, this eighth and largest party of people concerned only with personal interests brought great confusion and perplexity to the common cause. Whatever question arose, this swarm of drones, not yet done humming over the previous topic, flew on to the new one, and their buzzing drowned out and obscured the sincerely disputing voices.

From all these parties, one more, the ninth party, emerged and began to raise its voice just as Prince Andrei came to the army. This was a party of older people, intelligent, experienced in statesmanship, and who were able, without sharing any of these contradictory opinions, to look at everything that went on at headquarters abstractly, and to reflect on the means of getting out of this uncertainty, irresolution, confusion, and weakness.

The people of this party said and thought that all the harm came primarily from the presence of the sovereign and his military court in the army; that it brought into the army that indefinite, conditional, and fluctuating instability of relations which was suitable to the court, but bad for the army; that the sovereign ought to rule and not command troops; that the only way out of this situation was the departure of the sovereign and his court from the army; that the mere presence of the sovereign paralysed the fifty thousand troops needed to ensure his personal safety; that the very worst, but independent, commander in chief would be better than the very best, but bound by the presence and authority of the sovereign.

At the time when Prince Andrei was living unoccupied on the Drissa, Shishkov, the secretary of state, who was one of the chief representatives of this party, wrote a letter to the sovereign which Balashov and Arakcheev agreed to sign. In this letter, taking advantage of the permission granted him by the sovereign to discuss the general course of affairs, he respectfully suggested that the sovereign leave the army under the pretext that it was necessary for him to inspire the people of the capital for war.

The sovereign's inspiring of the people and calling them to the defence of the fatherland—that very inspiring of the people (insofar as it was produced by the sovereign's presence in Moscow) which was the chief cause of Russia's triumph—was presented to and accepted by the sovereign as a pretext for leaving the army.

X

This letter had not yet been given to the sovereign when Barclay told Bolkonsky at dinner that the sovereign would like to see Prince Andrei in person, in order to question him about Turkey, and that Prince Andrei was to go to Bennigsen's quarters at six o'clock in the evening.

On that same day information was received in the sovereign's quarters about new movements of Napoleon that might prove dangerous to the army—information which subsequently proved incorrect. And that same morning Colonel Michaud, making the round of the Drissa fortifications with the sovereign, tried to persuade the sovereign that this fortified camp, set up by Pfuel, which till then had been considered a tactical *chef-d'oeuvre* that would be the destruction of Napoleon—that this camp was absurd and would be the destruction of the Russian army.

Prince Andrei arrived at the quarters of General Bennigsen, who occupied a small manor house right on the bank of the river. Neither Bennigsen nor the sovereign was there; but Chernyshov, the imperial adjutant, received Bolkonsky and announced to him that the sovereign had ridden with General Bennigsen and Marquis Paulucci to make a second round of the fortifications of the Drissa camp, the suitability of which had become a subject of strong doubts.

Chernyshov was sitting with a French novel by a window in the first room. This room was probably once the reception room; an organ still stood there, with some sort of rugs piled on it, and in one corner stood the camp bed of Bennigsen's adjutant. This adjutant was there. He sat on the rolled-up bedding and dozed, evidently worn out by carousing or work. There were two doors in the reception room: one led straight to the former drawing room, the other to the study on the right. From the first door came the sound of voices talking in German and occasionally in French. There, in the former drawing room, were assembled, at the sovereign's wish, not a council of war (the sovereign liked indefiniteness), but some persons whose opinion about the forthcoming difficulties he wished to know. It was not a council of war, but, as it were, a council of some people chosen to clarify certain questions personally for the sovereign. To this semi-council there had been invited the Swedish general Armfelt, the adjutant general Wolzogen, Wintzingerode, whom Napoleon had called a fugitive French subject, Michaud, Toll, Count Stein, who was not a military man at all, and finally Pfuel himself, who, as Prince Andrei had heard, was the *cheville ouvrière** of the whole thing. Prince Andrei chanced to have a good look at him, because Pfuel arrived soon after he did and went to the drawing room after stopping for a moment to talk with Chernyshov.

At first glance, Pfuel, in his poorly cut Russian general's uniform, which sat awkwardly on him like a mummer's costume, seemed familiar to Prince Andrei, though he had never seen him. There was in him something of Weyrother, and of Mack, and of Schmidt, and of many other German theorist-generals whom Prince Andrei had managed to see in 1805; but he was the most typical of them all. Such a German theorist, who combined in himself all that there was in those other Germans, Prince Andrei had never seen before.

*Linchpin.

Pfuel was of small stature, very thin, but broad-boned, of coarse, robust build, with broad hips and sharp shoulder blades. His face was very wrinkled, his eyes deep-set. His hair in front, at the temples, had obviously been hastily slicked down with a brush, but at the back it stuck up naïvely in little tufts. He came into the room looking around uneasily and angrily, as if he was afraid of everything in that big room he had come into. Keeping a hand awkwardly on his sword, he addressed Chernyshov, asking in German where the sovereign was. He clearly wanted to go inside as quickly as possible, have done with the bowings and greetings, and get down to work on the map, where he felt he belonged. He hastily nodded his head to Chernyshov's words and smiled ironically, listening to him say that the sovereign was inspecting the fortifications which he, Pfuel himself, had laid out according to his theory. He grumbled something to himself in a tough bass voice, the way self-assured Germans speak: *"Dummkopf . . ."* or *"Zu Grunde die ganze Geschichte . . ."* or *"S'wird was gescheites d'raus werden . . ."** Prince Andrei did not quite hear and would have passed by, but Chernyshov introduced him to Pfuel, observing that Prince Andrei had come from Turkey, where the war had ended so fortunately. Pfuel barely glanced not so much at as through Prince Andrei and said, laughing: *"Da muss ein schöner taktischer Krieg gewesen sein."*† And, with a contemptuous laugh, he walked into the room in which the voices were heard.

Clearly, Pfuel, always ready for ironic irritation anyway, was especially upset that day that they had dared to inspect and criticize his camp without him. From this one brief encounter with Pfuel, Prince Andrei, owing to his memories of Austerlitz, formed a clear notion of the man's character for himself. Pfuel was one of those hopelessly, permanently, painfully self-assured men as only Germans can be, and precisely because only Germans can be self-assured on the basis of an abstract idea—science, that is, an imaginary knowledge of the perfect truth. A Frenchman is self-assured because he considers himself personally, in mind as well as body, irresistibly enchanting for men as well as women. An Englishman is self-assured on the grounds that he is a citizen of the best-organized state in the world, and therefore, as an Englishman, he always knows what he must do, and knows that everything he does as an Englishman is unquestionably good. An Italian is self-assured because he is excitable and easily forgets himself and others. A Russian is self-assured precisely because he does not know anything and does not want to know anything, because he does not believe it possible to know anything fully. A German is self-assured worst of all, and most firmly of all, and most disgustingly of all, because he imagines that he knows the truth, science, which he has invented himself, but which for him is the absolute truth. Such, obviously, was Pfuel. He had science—the

---

*Stupid man . . . Down with the whole thing . . . Something really pretty will come of it . . .
†A fine tactical war that must have been.

theory of the oblique movement, which he deduced from the history of the wars of Frederick the Great—and everything he came across in contemporary military history seemed to him senselessness, barbarism, grotesque clashes in which so many mistakes were made on both sides that these wars could not be called wars: they did not fit the theory and could not serve as material for science.

In 1806 Pfuel had been one of the architects of the plan of war that had ended with Jena and Auerstädt;[22] but he did not see in the outcome of that war the least proof of the incorrectness of his theory. On the contrary, to his mind, the departures from his theory were the only cause of the whole failure, and he, with a gleeful irony all his own, used to say: *"Ich sagte ja, dass die ganze Geschichte zum Teufel gehen wird."** Pfuel was one of those theorists who so love their theory that they forget the purpose of the theory—its application in practice; in his love for theory, he hated everything practical and did not want to know about it. He was even glad of failure, because failure, proceeding from departures from theory in practice, only proved to him the correctness of his theory.

He exchanged a few words with Prince Andrei and Chernyshov about the present war, with the expression of a man who knows beforehand that it will all go badly and who is not even displeased by that. The unbrushed tufts of hair on his nape and his hastily slicked down side-whiskers were the most eloquent confirmation of it.

He went into the other room, and at once from there came the grumbling sounds of his bass voice.

XI

Prince Andrei was still following Pfuel with his eyes when Count Bennigsen hurriedly came into the room and, nodding to Bolkonsky without pausing, went to the study, giving some orders to his adjutant. The sovereign was coming behind him, and Bennigsen had hurried ahead, so as to prepare things and have time to meet the sovereign. Chernyshov and Prince Andrei went out to the porch. The sovereign, with a weary look, was getting off his horse. Marquis Paulucci was telling him something. The sovereign, his head inclined to the left, listened with a displeased air to Paulucci, who was speaking with particular vehemence. The sovereign started on, apparently wishing to finish the conversation, but the flushed, excited Italian, forgetting propriety, walked after him, still speaking.

---

*I said then that the whole thing would go to the devil.

"*Quant à celui qui a conseillé ce camp, le camp de Drissa,*" Paulucci was saying at the moment when the sovereign, going up the steps and noticing Prince Andrei, began peering at the unfamiliar face.

"*Quant à celui, Sire,*" Paulucci went on desperately, as if unable to restrain himself, "*qui à conseillé le camp de Drissa, je ne vois pas d'autre alternative que la maison jaune ou le gibet.*"* Not hearing out and as if not listening to the Italian's words, the sovereign, having recognized Bolkonsky, graciously addressed him:

"Very glad to see you. Go in where they've assembled, and wait for me." The sovereign went to the study. He was followed by Prince Pyotr Mikhailovich Volkonsky and Baron Stein, and the doors closed behind them. Prince Andrei, taking advantage of the sovereign's permission, went, along with Paulucci, whom he had known in Turkey, into the drawing room where the council was assembled.

Prince Pyotr Mikhailovich Volkonsky occupied a post as something like the sovereign's chief of staff. Volkonsky came out of the study and, bringing maps to the drawing room and spreading them on the table, told the assembled gentlemen the questions on which he would like to hear their opinion. The thing was that during the night information had been received (subsequently proved false) that the French were moving to outflank the Drissa camp.

The first to begin speaking was General Armfelt, who, to get round the difficulty presented, unexpectedly suggested a new position, totally inexplicable (except by his wish to show that he, too, could have an opinion), away from the Petersburg and Moscow roads, at which, in his opinion, the united army should await the enemy. It was clear that this plan had been put together by Armfelt long ago, and he was now expounding it not so much with the purpose of answering the questions posed, which this plan did not answer, as with the purpose of using the opportunity to speak about it. It was one of the millions of suggestions that could be made, as well-founded as any other, if one had no notion of what character the war would take. Some argued against his opinion, some defended it. The young Colonel Toll argued against the Swedish general's opinion more vehemently than the others, and during the argument took from his side pocket a notebook full of writing, which he asked permission to read. In an extensively composed project, Toll suggested another plan of campaign—the complete opposite of Armfelt's plan and Pfuel's plan. Paulucci, objecting to Toll, suggested a plan of advance and attack, which alone, he said, could take us out of the uncertainty and the trap, as he called the Drissa camp, in which we found ourselves. During this argument, Pfuel and his translator Wolzogen (his bridge in court relations) were silent. Pfuel merely

* As for the one who advised this camp, the camp of Drissa . . . As for the one, Sire . . . who advised the camp of Drissa, I see no other alternative than the madhouse or the gibbet.

snorted scornfully and looked away, showing that he would never lower himself to objecting to the nonsense he was listening to. But when Prince Volkonsky, who was leading the debate, called on him to express his opinion, he merely said:

"Why ask me? General Armfelt has suggested a beautiful position, with an exposed rear. Or the attack *von diesem italienischen Herrn, sehr schön*!* Or a retreat. *Auch gut.*† Why ask me?" he said. "You yourselves know everything better than I." But when Volkonsky, frowning, said that he was asking his opinion on behalf of the sovereign, Pfuel stood up and, suddenly animated, began to speak:

"You have ruined everything, confused everything, wanted to know everything better than I, and now you come to me: how can we fix it? There's nothing to fix. Everything should be carried out precisely according to the foundations I have laid down," he said, rapping his bony knuckles on the table. "What is the difficulty? Nonsense, *Kinderspiel*!‡ He went up to the map and started speaking quickly, jabbing his dry finger at the map and insisting that no chance could alter the expediency of the Drissa camp, that everything had been foreseen, and that if the enemy should indeed outflank it, they would inevitably be destroyed.

Paulucci, who did not know German, started asking questions in French. Wolzogen came to the aid of his principal, who spoke French poorly, and started translating his words, barely keeping up with Pfuel, who rapidly proved that not only everything that had happened, but everything that could happen, had been foreseen in his plan, and that if there were difficulties now, the whole blame lay only in the fact that everything had not been carried out precisely. He kept laughing ironically, demonstrated, and at last contemptuously stopped demonstrating, as a mathematician stops checking in various ways the once-proven correctness of a problem. Wolzogen replaced him, continuing to set forth his thoughts in French and saying to Pfuel every now and then: "*Nicht wahr, Exellenz?*"§ Pfuel, like a man who in the heat of battle strikes his own side, shouted angrily at Wolzogen as well:

"*Nun ja, was soll denn da noch expliziert werden?*"#

Paulucci and Michaud with two voices fell upon Wolzogen in French. Armfelt addressed Pfuel in German. Toll explained something to Volkonsky in Russian. Prince Andrei silently listened and observed.

Of all these persons, the one who most awakened Prince Andrei's sympathy was the embittered, resolute, and senselessly self-assured Pfuel. He alone of all

---

*Of this Italian gentleman, very fine!
†Also good.
‡Child's play!
§Isn't it so, Your Excellency?
#Of course, what is there to explain?

the persons present there obviously desired nothing for himself, felt no enmity against anyone, and desired only one thing: the putting into action of a plan worked out according to a theory arrived at through years of labour. He was ridiculous, he was unpleasant in his irony, but at the same time he inspired an involuntary respect by his boundless devotion to his idea. Besides that, in all the speeches of all the speakers, with the exception of Pfuel, there was one common feature which had not been there at the council of war in 1805: there was now, however concealed, a panic fear before the genius of Napoleon, a fear that voiced itself in every objection. Every possible supposition was made with regard to Napoleon, he was expected on all sides, and with his terrible name they demolished each other's suggestions. Pfuel alone, it seemed, considered him, Napoleon, as much a barbarian as all the opponents of his theory. But, besides a feeling of respect, Pfuel inspired a feeling of pity in Prince Andrei. From the tone in which the courtiers addressed him, from what Paulucci had allowed himself to say to the emperor, but above all from a certain desperation in Pfuel's own expressions, it was clear that the others knew and he himself sensed that his fall was near. And despite his self-assurance and grumbling German irony, he was pitiful with his hair slicked down on his temples and tufts sticking out on his nape. Though he concealed it behind an appearance of irritation and contempt, he was clearly in despair, because the sole remaining opportunity of making an enormous experiment and proving the correctness of his theory to the whole world was slipping away from him.

The debate went on for a long time, and the longer it went on, the more heated the argument became, reaching the point of shouting and personal remarks, and the less possible it was to draw any general conclusion from all that had been said. Listening to this multilingual talk, and these suggestions, plans, and refutations, and shouts, Prince Andrei was simply amazed at what they all said. The thoughts he often used to have long ago, during the time of his military activity, that there was not and could not be any military science, and therefore there could not be any so-called military genius, now acquired for him the perfect evidence of truth. "What theory and what science could there be in a matter of which the conditions and circumstances are unknown and cannot be determined, in which the strength of those active in war can still less be determined? No one could or can know what position our own and the enemy army will be in a day later, and no one can know the strength of this or that detachment. Sometimes, when there's no coward at the head who shouts 'We're cut off!' and runs away, but a cheerful, bold man who shouts 'Hurrah!'—a detachment of five thousand is worth thirty thousand, as at Schöngraben, and sometimes fifty thousand flee in the face of eight, as at Austerlitz. What science can there be in a matter in which, as in any practical matter, nothing can be determined and everything depends on countless circumstances, the significance of which is determined at a certain moment, and no one knows when that moment will come? Armfelt says our army is cut off, and Paulucci says we've put the French army between two fires; Michaud says the Drissa camp is no good because the river is behind it, and Pfuel says its strength lies in that. Toll suggests one plan, Armfelt another; they're all good, and they're all bad, and the advantages of any position can become evident only at the moment when the event occurs. And why do they all talk about military genius? Is that man a genius who manages to order a timely delivery of biscuits and tells this one to go right and that one to go left? It is only because military men are clothed in splendour and power, and masses of scoundrels flatter power, endowing it with qualities of genius it does not have, that they are called geniuses. On the contrary, the best generals I knew were stupid or absent-minded people. Bagration was the best—Napoleon himself recognized that. And Bonaparte himself! I remember his self-satisfied and limited face on the battlefield at Austerlitz. A good commander not only does not need genius or any special qualities, but, on the contrary, he needs the absence of the best and highest human qualities—love, poetry, tenderness, a searching philosophical doubt. He should be limited, firmly convinced that what he is doing is very important (otherwise he would not have patience enough), and only then will he be a brave commander. God forbid he should be a human being and come to love or pity someone, or start thinking about what is just and what isn't. Understandably, the theory of genius was cut to fit them of old, because they are—power. The merit of success in military affairs does not depend on them, but on the man in the ranks who shouts 'We're lost!' or shouts 'Hurrah!' And it is only in the ranks that one can serve with the assurance of being useful!"

So thought Prince Andrei as he listened to the debate, and he came to his senses only when Paulucci called him and everybody was leaving.

At the review the next day the sovereign asked Prince Andrei where he would like to serve, and Prince Andrei was for ever lost to the world of the court when he did not ask to remain with the person of the sovereign, but asked permission to serve in the army.

XII

Before the opening of the campaign, Rostov received a letter from his parents in which, informing him briefly of Natasha's illness and her break with Prince Andrei (this break was explained to him by Natasha's refusal), they again asked him to resign from the service and come home. Nikolai, on receiving this letter, did not even attempt to ask for a leave or resignation, but wrote to his parents that he was sorry about Natasha's illness and her break with her fiancé, and that he would do everything possible to fulfil their wishes. To Sonya he wrote separately.

Adored friend of my soul,

Nothing save honour could keep me from returning to the country. But now, before the opening of the campaign, I would consider myself dishonourable not only before all my comrades, but also before my own self, if I were to prefer happiness to my duty and love for the fatherland. But this is our last separation. Believe me, right after the war, if I am alive and you still love me, I will abandon everything and come flying to you, to press you for ever to my ardent breast.

Indeed, only the opening of the campaign detained Rostov and prevented him from coming—as he had promised—and marrying Sonya. Autumn in Otradnoe with its hunting, and winter with Christmastime and Sonya's love, had opened before him the prospect of quiet gentlemanly joys and a tranquillity that he had not known before and which now beckoned to him. "A nice wife, children, a good pack of hounds, ten or twelve leashes of dashing borzois, husbandry, neighbours, local elections!" he thought. But now there was the campaign, and he had to stay in the regiment. And since it had to be so, Nikolai Rostov's character was such that he was content with the life he led in the regiment and managed to make that life pleasant for himself.

On returning from leave, joyfully welcomed by his comrades, Nikolai had been sent for a remount and had brought excellent horses from Little Russia, which pleased him and earned him the praises of his superiors. During his absence, he had been promoted to captain, and when the regiment was put on wartime status with an increased complement, he was again given his old squadron.

The campaign began, the regiment was moved to Poland, the pay was doubled, new officers arrived, new men and horses, and above all that excitedly cheerful mood spread around which accompanies the beginning of war; and Rostov, conscious of his advantageous position in the regiment, gave himself up wholly to the pleasures and interests of military service, though he knew that sooner or later he would have to leave them behind.

The troops retreated from Vilno for various complex governmental, political, and tactical reasons. Every step of the retreat was accompanied by a complex play of interests, conclusions, and passions in the general staff. Yet for the hussars of the Pavlogradsky regiment, this whole march in retreat, during the best period of summer, well provided with supplies, was the simplest and merriest affair. To be despondent, to worry, to intrigue was possible at general headquarters, but in the depths of the army no one even asked himself where he was going or why. If they were sorry to be retreating, it was only because they had to leave their homey quarters or a pretty Polish *panna*. If it did enter anyone's head that things were bad, then, as a good military man should, the one whose head it had entered would try to be cheerful and not think about the

general course of things, but about the matters closest to him. First they cheerfully camped near Vilno, making the acquaintance of the Polish landowners,
and waiting, and performing reviews for the sovereign and other high commanders. Then orders came to retreat to Swienciany and destroy the provisions that could not be taken along. Swienciany was memorable to the hussars
only because it was a *drunken camp,* as the whole army named their stopping
place there, and because there were many complaints against the troops, who,
taking advantage of the order to gather provisions, also gathered horses, carriages, and rugs from the Polish gentry. Rostov remembered Swienciany
because, on the first day they entered this little town, he had dismissed his
sergeant major and had been unable to handle all the drunken men of the
squadron, who, without his knowledge, had got hold of five barrels of old
beer. From Swienciany they retreated further and further towards the Drissa,
then again retreated from the Drissa, and were now approaching the Russian
border.

On the thirteenth of July, the Pavlogradskies were to take part in serious
action for the first time.

During the night of the twelfth of June, on the eve of action, there was violent rain and a thunderstorm. The summer of 1812 was generally remarkable
for its storms.

Two of the Pavlogradsky squadrons made their bivouac in the middle of a
rye field, already in ear but totally trampled down by cattle and horses. It was
pouring rain, and Rostov, with the young officer Ilyin, whom he patronized,
was sitting under a hastily slapped-together lean-to. An officer of their regiment, with long moustaches that continued across his cheeks, who was coming
back from the staff and got caught by the rain, stopped to see Rostov.

"I'm coming from the staff, Count. Have you heard about Raevsky's feat?"
And the officer recounted the details of the battle of Saltanovo, which he had
heard at the staff.

Rostov, hunching his shoulders as water ran down his neck, was smoking
his pipe and listening inattentively, glancing now and then at the young officer
Ilyin, who huddled up to him. This officer, a sixteen-year-old boy who had
recently joined the regiment, was now in relation to Nikolai what Nikolai had
been in relation to Denisov seven years ago. Ilyin tried to imitate Rostov in
everything, and was in love with him like a woman.

The officer with the double moustaches, Zdrzhinsky, was pompously telling
about how the Saltanovo dam was the Russian Thermopylae, and that on that
dam General Raevsky had performed a deed worthy of antiquity. Zdrzhinsky
recounted the deed of Raevsky, who had led his two sons onto the dam under
fierce gunfire and had gone into the attack alongside them.[23] Rostov was listening to the story, and not only said nothing to confirm Zdrzhinsky's raptures,
but, on the contrary, had the look of a man who is ashamed of what he is being

told, though he has no intention of objecting. After the campaigns of Austerlitz and of 1807, Rostov knew from his own experience that, when telling about military events, people always lied, as he himself had lied in telling about them; second, he had enough experience to know that in war everything goes on quite otherwise than we can imagine and recount. And therefore he did not like Zdrzhinsky's story, and did not like Zdrzhinsky himself, who, with his moustaches growing across his cheeks, had the habit of bending close to the face of the one he was telling his story to and crowding him in the crowded lean-to. Rostov silently looked at him. "First of all, it surely must have been so confused and crowded on the dam being attacked that, even if Raevsky did bring his sons there, it couldn't have affected anyone, except a dozen or so men who were right there with him," thought Rostov. "The rest couldn't have seen how Raevsky went across the dam and with whom. But even the ones who saw it couldn't have felt much enthusiasm, because what did they care about Raevsky's tender paternal feelings, when it was a matter of saving their own skins? Besides that, the fate of the fatherland didn't depend on taking or not taking the Saltanovo dam, the way they say it was with Thermopylae. And, therefore, why offer up such a sacrifice? And then, why get your children mixed up in it, in a war? I wouldn't lead my brother Petya into it, or even Ilyin, a nice boy but a stranger to me; I'd try to find some safe place to put him," Rostov went on thinking as he listened to Zdrzhinsky. But he did not voice his thoughts: he already had experience with that, too. He knew that this story contributed to the glory of our arms, and therefore one had to make it seem that one did not doubt it. And so he did.

"Anyhow, I can't stand it," said Ilyin, noticing that Rostov did not like Zdrzhinsky's conversation. "My socks, and my shirt, and under me it's all soaked. I'll go and find some shelter. The rain seems to be letting up." Ilyin left, and Zdrzhinsky rode away.

Five minutes later Ilyin, splashing through the mud, came running to the lean-to.

"Hurrah! Let's go quick, Rostov. I found it! A tavern, about two hundred paces from here, our boys are already there. We can dry out, and Marya Genrikhovna's there."

Marya Genrikhovna was the wife of the regimental doctor, a young, pretty German woman, whom the doctor had married in Poland. Either because he lacked means, or because he did not want to part with a young wife so early in their marriage, the doctor took her along everywhere with the hussar regiment, and his jealousy had become a habitual subject of jokes among the hussar officers.

Rostov threw on a cloak, told Lavrushka to bring the things, and went with Ilyin, here slipping in the mud, there splashing straight on under the subsiding rain, in the evening darkness, occasionally broken by distant lightning.

"Rostov, where are you?"

"Here. What lightning!" they said to each other.

XIII

In an abandoned tavern, before which stood the doctor's little kibitka, there were already some five officers. Marya Genrikhovna, a plump, flaxen-haired German, in a bed jacket and nightcap, sat in the front corner on a wide bench. Her husband, the doctor, was asleep behind her. Rostov and Ilyin, greeted with merry exclamations and guffaws, came into the room.

"Hey, aren't you having fun!" Rostov said, laughing.

"And why are you missing it?"

"Fine ones! They're drenched! Don't get our drawing room wet!"

"Don't get Marya Genrikhovna's dress muddy," voices answered.

Rostov and Ilyin hastened to find a corner where they could change their wet clothes without offending Marya Genrikhovna's modesty. They went behind a partition, but the little closet was entirely taken up by three officers playing cards on an empty box with a single candle on it, who absolutely refused to let them in to change. Marya Genrikhovna allowed them to take her skirt, using it as a curtain, and behind that curtain Rostov and Ilyin, with the help of Lavrushka, who brought their packs, took off their wet clothes and put on dry.

A fire was made in the broken stove. They found a board and, placing it on two saddles, covered it with a horse blanket, found a little samovar, a cellaret, and half a bottle of rum, and the officers, having invited Marya Genrikhovna to be the hostess, crowded around her. One offered her a clean handkerchief to wipe her lovely little hands, another put a jacket under her little feet so that they would not get damp, yet another screened the window with his cloak to keep out the draft, yet another fanned the flies away from her husband's face so that he would not wake up.

"Let him be," Marya Genrikhovna said with a timid and happy smile, "he's sleeping well as it is after a sleepless night."

"Never, Marya Genrikhovna," the officer replied, "we must wait upon our doctor. Maybe he'll pity me when he's cutting off my leg or arm."

There were only three glasses; the water was so dirty that it was impossible to tell whether the tea was strong or weak, and the samovar only held water enough for six glasses, but the more pleasant it was to receive one's glass in turn and by seniority from the plump little hands of Marya Genrikhovna with their short, none-too-clean nails. All the officers, it seemed, were actually in love with Marya Genrikhovna that evening. Even the officers who were playing cards behind the partition soon stopped playing and went over to the samovar, yielding to the general atmosphere of courting Marya Genrikhovna.

Marya Genrikhovna, seeing herself surrounded by such brilliant and polite young men, shone with happiness, however she tried to hide it, and however timid she became at every movement her sleeping husband made behind her back.

Of spoons there was only one, sugar was more plentiful than anything else, but they could not all stir at the same time, and so it was decided that she would stir the sugar for each of them in turn. Rostov, receiving his glass, poured some rum into it and asked Marya Genrikhovna to stir it.

"But do you take it without sugar?" she asked, with the same smile as if everything she said and everything the others said was very funny and had some other meaning.

"Never mind the sugar, I just want you to stir it with your little hand."

Marya Genrikhovna agreed and began looking for the spoon, which someone had already snatched up.

"Use your finger, Marya Genrikhovna," said Rostov, "that will be even nicer."

"It's too hot!" said Marya Genrikhovna, blushing with pleasure.

Ilyin took a bucket of water and, pouring a drop of rum into it, came to Marya Genrikhovna, asking her to stir it with her finger.

"This is my cup," he said. "Only dip your finger into it, and I'll drink it all."

When the whole samovar had been drunk, Rostov took the cards and suggested a game of "kings" with Marya Genrikhovna. They drew lots for who would be Marya Genrikhovna's partner. The rules of the game were, at Rostov's suggestion, that whoever was the king had the right to kiss Marya Genrikhovna's hand, and that whoever was left the knave would go and prepare a new samovar for the doctor when he woke up.

"And what if Marya Genrikhovna is the king?" asked Ilyin.

"She's the queen as it is! And her orders are law."

The game had only just begun when the doctor's tousled head suddenly rose up behind Marya Genrikhovna. He had been awake for a long time and listening to what was being said, and he clearly found nothing gay, funny, or amusing in all that was being said and done. His face was sad and glum. He did not greet the officers, scratched himself, and asked to be allowed to step out, because they tried to bar his way. As soon as he left, all the officers burst into loud guffaws, and Marya Genrikhovna blushed to the point of tears and became still more attractive in the eyes of all the officers. When he came back in, the doctor said to his wife (who had already stopped smiling so happily and looked at him, fearfully awaiting her sentence) that the rain had stopped and they had to go and spend the night in their kibitka, or else everything would be stolen.

"But I'll send an orderly . . . two orderlies!" said Rostov. "Come on, Doctor."

"I'll stand watch myself!" said Ilyin.

"No, gentlemen, you've had enough sleep, and I haven't slept for two nights," the doctor said and gloomily sat down beside his wife, waiting for the game to end.

Seeing the gloomy face of the doctor, looking askance at his wife, the officers grew still merrier, and many could not keep from laughing, for which they hastily tried to find plausible pretexts. When the doctor left, taking his wife along, and settled with her in the little kibitka, the officers lay down in the tavern, covering themselves with their wet greatcoats; but for a long time they did not sleep, now talking, remembering the doctor's fright and his wife's merriment, now running out to the porch and reporting on what was going on in the kibitka. Several times Rostov covered his head and tried to fall asleep; but again someone's remark would distract him, again a conversation would begin, and again there would be causeless, merry, childlike laughter.

XIV

It was past two o'clock and no one was asleep yet when the quartermaster appeared with orders to set out for the little village of Ostrovna.

Still with the same talk and laughter, the officers quickly began to get ready; again they set up the samovar with dirty water. But Rostov, not waiting for tea, went to his squadron. Dawn was breaking; the rain had stopped, the clouds had scattered. It was damp and cold, especially in still-wet clothes. Leaving the tavern, Rostov and Ilyin, in the half-light of dawn, peeked into the doctor's little kibitka, its leather glistening from the rain, from the apron of which the doctor's legs stuck out, and in the middle of which they could see his wife's nightcap on the pillow and hear her sleepy breathing.

"She's really very sweet!" Rostov said to Ilyin, who was leaving with him.

"A lovely woman!" Ilyin replied with a sixteen-year-old's earnestness.

Half an hour later the lined-up squadron was standing on the road. The command "Mount up!" rang out, the soldiers crossed themselves and began to mount up. Rostov, riding ahead, gave the command, "March!" and, stretching out four abreast, the hussars, with the sounds of hoofs splashing on the wet road, the clank of sabres, and quiet talk, started down the big, birch-lined road, in the wake of the preceding infantry and artillery.

The ragged, bluish-purple clouds, turning red in the east, were driven quickly by the wind. It was growing lighter and lighter. The short, curly grass that always grows at the sides of country roads was clearly visible, still wet from last night's rain; the hanging branches of the birches, also wet, swayed in the wind and shed bright drops sideways. The soldiers' faces could be seen more and more clearly. Rostov rode with Ilyin, who never lagged behind him, along the side of the road, between the double row of birches.

While on campaign, Rostov allowed himself the liberty of riding a Cossack horse instead of a regimental one. A fancier and a hunter, he had recently obtained for himself a fine, big, dashing Don horse, light chestnut with a white mane and tail, on which no one could outgallop him. It was a pleasure for Rostov to ride this horse. He thought about the horse, about the morning, about the doctor's wife, and never once thought about the impending danger.

Formerly, going into action, Rostov had been afraid; now he did not feel the least fear. He was not afraid, not because he was used to gunfire (one cannot get used to danger), but because he had learned to control his soul in the face of danger. He got used, going into action, to thinking about everything except what would seem more interesting than anything else—the impending danger. However hard he had tried, however much he had reproached himself for cowardice during his first period of service, he had been unable to achieve this; but now, with the years, it had come by itself. He was now riding beside Ilyin between the birches, occasionally pulling leaves off the branches that happened in his way, occasionally touching the horse's flank with his foot, occasionally handing his finished pipe, without turning round, to the hussar behind him— all with such a calm and carefree air as though he was just out for a ride. He felt pity, looking at the troubled face of Ilyin, who was talking much and anxiously; he knew from his own experiece that tormenting state of awaiting fear and death in which the ensign found himself, and knew that nothing but time would help him.

The sun had only just appeared in the clear space under a cloud when the wind died, as if not daring to ruin this lovely summer morning after the storm; the drops were still falling, vertically now, and all became still. The sun came out completely, appeared on the horizon, and vanished into the long, narrow cloud that stood above it. A few minutes later, the sun appeared still more brightly on the upper edge of the cloud, tearing its edge. Everything lit up and glistened. And along with this light, as if in response to it, cannon fire rang out ahead.

Before Rostov had time to think and determine how far away those shots were, Count Ostermann-Tolstoy's adjutant came galloping from Vitebsk with orders to proceed down the road at a trot.

The squadron overtook the infantry and artillery, which also speeded up, went down a hill and, passing through some empty, deserted village, rode uphill again. The horses began to lather, the men's faces became flushed.

"Halt! Dress ranks!" rang out the order of the division commander ahead.

"Column right, march!" came the command from ahead.

And the hussars, following the line of troops, went to the left flank position and stopped behind our uhlans, who stood in the front line. To their right our infantry stood in a dense column—this was the reserve; higher up the hill, in the perfectly clear air, in the slanting, bright morning light, just on the horizon—our cannon could be seen. Ahead, beyond a hollow, the enemy's columns and cannon could be seen. In the hollow, our front line, which had already gone into action, could be heard merrily exchanging clacks with the enemy.

As if by the sounds of the most cheerful music, Rostov felt cheered at heart by these sounds, which he had not heard for so long. Trap-ta-ta-tap!— several shots clapped out, now together, now in rapid succession. Then all fell silent, and then came the crackling again, as if someone was walking on firecrackers.

The hussars stood for about an hour in the same place. A cannonade began. Count Ostermann and his suite rode up behind the squadron, stopped, talked with the commander of the regiment, and rode off towards the cannon on the hill.

After Ostermann rode off, a command to the uhlans was heard:

"Column, form up for the attack!" The infantry ahead of them doubled up their platoons to let the cavalry pass by. The uhlans set off, pennants flying on their lances, and trotted downhill towards the French cavalry, which had appeared at the foot of the hill to the left.

As soon as the uhlans had gone down the hill, the hussars were ordered to move up the hill to cover the battery. While the hussars took the place of the uhlans, bullets came flying from the front line, whining and whistling, missing their aim by far.

This sound, which he had not heard for a long time, had a still more joyful and rousing effect on Rostov than the previous sounds of shooting. Drawing himself up, he surveyed the battlefield that opened out from the hill, and participated wholeheartedly in the movements of the uhlans. The uhlans flew down close to the French dragoons, something became confused there in the smoke, and five minutes later the uhlans came racing back, not to the place where they had been, but more to the left. Among the orange uhlans on chestnut horses, and behind them in a large mass, the blue French dragoons on grey horses could be seen.

XV

Rostov, with his keen hunter's eye, was one of the first to see these blue French dragoons pursuing our uhlans. Closer and closer came the disorderly crowds of uhlans and the French dragoons pursuing them. It was already possible to see how these men, who looked small at the foot of the hill, clashed together, chased each other, and waved their arms or sabres.

Rostov watched what was happening before him as if it was a hunting scene. He sensed intuitively that if he were now to strike the French dragoons with his hussars, they would not hold out; but if he were to strike, it would have to be now, at this moment, otherwise it would be too late. He looked around. A captain was standing next to him, his eyes also fixed on the cavalry below.

"Andrei Sevastyanych," said Rostov, "you know, we could crush them . . ."

"It would be a daring thing," said the captain, "and in fact . . ."

Rostov, not hearing him out, nudged his horse, leaped ahead of the squadron, and before he had time to command it to move, the whole squadron, feeling the same as he, set out after him. Rostov did not know himself how and why he was doing it. He did it all as he did at the hunt, not thinking, not reflecting. He saw that the dragoons were near, that they were galloping in disorder; he knew that they would not hold, and he knew that there was only one moment, which would not return if he missed it. Bullets whined and whistled so stirringly around him, his horse strained forward so ardently, that he could not control himself. He spurred his horse, gave the command, and at the same moment, hearing the hoofbeats of his deployed squadron behind him, started down at a full trot towards the dragoons at the foot of the hill. They had barely reached the foot of the hill when their trot involuntarily turned into a gallop, which became faster and faster as they drew nearer to our uhlans and the French dragoons pursuing them. The dragoons were near. The ones in front, seeing the hussars, began to turn back; the ones behind began to slow down. With the feeling with which he raced to intercept a wolf, Rostov, giving his Don horse free rein, galloped to intercept the disordered lines of the French dragoons. One uhlan stopped, one on foot fell to the ground to avoid being crushed, one riderless horse mingled with the hussars. Almost all the French dragoons were galloping away. Rostov, picking himself one on a grey horse, raced after him. On the way he galloped into a bush; the good horse carried him over it, and, barely straightening himself in the saddle, Nikolai saw that in a few seconds he would overtake the enemy he had picked out as his target. The Frenchman—probably an officer, by his uniform—hunched over, was galloping along on his grey horse, urging it on with his sabre. A moment later Rostov's horse struck the officer's horse in the rump with its breast, almost knocking it down, and at the same moment Rostov, not knowing why himself, raised his sabre and struck the Frenchman with it.

The moment he did this, all Rostov's animation suddenly vanished. The officer fell, not so much from the stroke of the sword, which only cut his arm slightly above the elbow, as from the jolt to his horse and from fear. Reining in his horse, Rostov sought his enemy with his eyes, to see whom he had vanquished. The French dragoon officer was hopping on the ground with one foot, the other being caught in the stirrup. Narrowing his eyes fearfully, as if expecting a new blow any second, he winced, glancing up at Rostov from below with an expression of terror. His face, pale and mud-spattered, fairhaired, young, with a dimple on the chin and light blue eyes, was not at all for the battlefield, not an enemy's face, but a most simple, homelike face. Before

Rostov decided what to do with him, the officer cried out: *"Je me rends!"** He hurriedly tried but was unable to disentangle his foot from the stirrup, and his frightened, light blue eyes were fixed on Rostov. Some hussars galloped up to him, freed his foot, and sat him in the saddle. Hussars on all sides were busy with the dragoons: one was wounded, but, with his face all covered with blood, refused to surrender his horse; another, his arms round a hussar, sat on his horse's croup; a third, supported by a hussar, was getting on his horse. In front of them, French infantry came running and shooting. The hussars hurriedly galloped away with their prisoners. Rostov galloped away with the others, experiencing some unpleasant feeling which wrung his heart. Something unclear, confused, something he was unable to explain to himself, had been revealed to him in the capture of this officer and the blow he had given him.

Count Ostermann-Tolstoy met the returning hussars, sent for Rostov, thanked him, and said that he would report his daring action to the sovereign and request the St. George Cross for him. When Rostov was summoned to Count Ostermann, he, remembering that his attack had been begun without orders, was fully convinced that his superior had called for him in order to punish him for unwarranted action. Ostermann's flattering words and the promise of a reward should therefore have been a joyful surprise for Rostov; yet the same unpleasant, unclear feeling nauseated him morally. "What on earth is tormenting me?" he asked himself, as he rode back from the general. "Ilyin? No, he's safe. Did I disgrace myself somehow? No, it's not that!" Something else tormented him, something like remorse. "Yes, yes, that French officer with the dimple. And I remember very well how my arm stopped as I raised it."

Rostov saw the prisoners being taken away and rode after them to look at his Frenchman with the dimple in his chin. He was sitting in his strange uniform on a spare hussar horse and looking around uneasily. The wound on his arm was almost not a wound. He feigned a smile at Rostov and waved to him by way of greeting. Rostov still felt awkward and as if ashamed of something.

That whole day and the next, Rostov's friends and comrades noticed that he was not dull, not angry, but silent, pensive, and concentrated. He drank reluctantly, tried to stay alone, and kept thinking about something.

Rostov kept thinking about that brilliant feat of his, which, to his surprise, had gained him the St. George Cross and even given him the reputation of a brave man—and there was something in it that he was unable to understand. "So they're even more afraid than we are!" he thought. "So that's all there is to so-called heroism? And did I really do it for the fatherland? And what harm had he done, with his dimple and his light blue eyes? But how frightened he

*I surrender!

was! He thought I'd kill him. Why should I kill him? My hand faltered. And they gave me the St. George Cross. I understand nothing, nothing!"

But while Nikolai was working out all these questions within himself, still without giving himself a clear accounting of what confused him so much, the wheel of fortune of military service, as often happens, turned in his favour. After the Ostrovna action he was promoted, was given a battalion of hussars, and whenever a brave officer was called for, the mission was given to him.

XVI

On receiving the news of Natasha's illness, the countess, though not quite recovered and still weak, went to Moscow with Petya and all the household, and the whole Rostov family moved from Marya Dmitrievna's to their own house and settled in Moscow.

Natasha's illness was so serious that, fortunately for her and for her family, the thought of all that had been the cause of her illness—her act and the break with her fiancé—moved into the background. She was so ill that it was impossible to think of how much she was to blame in all that had happened, while she did not eat, did not sleep, grew noticeably thinner, coughed, and was, as the doctors let it be felt, in danger. They had to think only of how to help her. Doctors visited Natasha both singly and in consultation, spoke a good deal of French, German, and Latin, denounced one another, prescribed the most varied medications for all the illnesses known to them; but the simple thought never occurred to any of them that they could not know the illness Natasha was suffering from, as no illness that afflicts a living human being can be known: for each human being has his peculiarities, and always has his own peculiar, complex illness, unknown to medical science, not an illness of the lungs, the liver, the skin, the heart, the nerves, and so on, recorded in medicine, but an illness consisting in one of the countless combinations of afflictions of these organs. This simple thought did not occur to the doctors (just as it cannot occur to a sorcerer that he cannot do sorcery), because their life's activity consisted in treating patients, because that was what they were paid for, and because they had spent the best days of their lives doing it. But above all this thought could not occur to the doctors because they saw that they were unquestionably useful, and indeed they were useful to all the Rostov household. They were useful not because they made the patient swallow what were for the most part harmful substances (the harm was little felt, because the harmful substances were given in small quantities), but they were useful, necessary, inevitable (for the same reason that there are and always will be imaginary healers, fortune-tellers, homeopaths, and allopaths), because they satisfied the moral need of the sick girl and the people who loved her. They satisfied that eternal human need for the hope of relief, the need for compassion and action, which a human being experiences in a time of suffering. They satisfied that eternal human need—noticeable in a child in its most primitive form—to rub the place that hurts. When a child hurts himself, he runs at once to his mother's or nanny's arms, to have the hurt place kissed and rubbed, and he feels better once the hurt place is kissed or rubbed. The child does not believe that those who are stronger and wiser than he have no means to help his pain. And the hope of relief and the show of compassion comfort him, while his mother rubs his bump. The doctors were of use to Natasha because they kissed and rubbed her "boo-boo," assuring her that it would go away at once if the coachman drove to the Arbat pharmacy and bought one rouble and seventy kopecks' worth of powders and pills in a pretty box, and if the sick girl made sure to take them with boiled water every two hours, not more or less.

What would Sonya, the count and countess have done, how could they have looked at the weak, wasting Natasha without undertaking anything, if it had not been for this taking of pills at specific times, warm drinks, chicken cutlets, and all the details of life prescribed by the doctors, the observance of which constituted the occupation and comfort of everyone around her? The more strict and complicated the rules, the more comforting it was for everyone. How could the count have borne the illness of his beloved daughter, if he had not known that Natasha's illness was costing him thousands of roubles and that he would not spare thousands more to be of use to her; if he had not known that, if she did not get better, he would spend thousands more and take her abroad and hold consultations there; if he had had no occasion to talk in detail about how Métivier and Feller had not understood the illness, but Frieze had, and Mudrov had diagnosed it still better? What would the countess have done, if she had not been able to quarrel occasionally with the sick Natasha for not fully observing the doctor's prescriptions?

"That way you'll never get well," she said, forgetting her grief in her vexation, "if you don't want to listen to the doctor and take your medicine on time! You shouldn't joke with it, you might get pneumonia," said the countess, and in the pronouncing of this word, incomprehensible not only for herself, she already found great comfort. What would Sonya have done, if she had not been joyfully aware that in the beginning she had not undressed for three nights, so as to be ready to fulfil all the doctor's prescriptions precisely, and that now she did not sleep at night, so as not to miss the time for administering the not-too-harmful pills from the little gold box? Even Natasha herself, who said that no medicine could cure her and that it was all stupid—even she was glad to see that so many sacrifices were being made for her, and that she had to take medicine at certain times, and she was even glad that, by neglecting what had been prescribed, she could show that she did not believe in the treatment and did not value her life.

The doctor came every day, felt her pulse, looked at her tongue, and joked with her, paying no attention to her grief-stricken face. On the other hand, when he went out to the other room, the countess hurriedly followed him, and he, assuming a serious air and shaking his head pensively, said that, although there was danger, he had hopes for the effectiveness of this latest medicine, and that they must wait and see; that the illness was more moral, but . . .

The countess, trying to conceal this action from herself and the doctor, would put a gold piece in his hand and go back to her daughter each time with her heart more at ease.

The signs of Natasha's illness were that she ate little, slept little, coughed, and never became animated. The doctors said that the sick girl must not be left without medical help, and therefore she was kept in the close air of the city. In the summer of 1812, the Rostovs did not leave for the country.

Despite the large quantity of pills, drops, and powders she had swallowed, from little jars and boxes of which Madame Schoss, a great lover of such objects, had assembled a large collection, despite the absence of her accustomed country life, youth had its way: Natasha's grief began to be covered over by the impressions of ongoing life, it ceased to weigh with such tormenting pain on her heart, it began to become the past, and Natasha started to recover physically.

XVII

Natasha was more calm, but not more cheerful. She not only avoided all external conditions of joyfulness—balls, promenades, concerts, the theatre—but she never once laughed so that tears were not heard behind her laughter. She could not sing. As soon as she began to laugh or tried to sing when she was by herself, tears choked her: tears of remorse, tears of remembrance of that irretrievable time of purity, tears of vexation that just so, for nothing, she had ruined her young life, which might have been so happy. Laughter and singing especially seemed to her a blasphemy against her grief. Of coquetry she never even thought; there was no need for her to restrain herself. She said and felt that at that time all men were for her exactly like the buffoon Nastasya Ivanovna. An inner guard firmly forbade her every joy. And there were in her none of those former interests of life from the girlish, carefree, hope-filled life she used to lead. Most often and most painfully of all she remembered those autumn months, the hunting, the uncle, and Christmastime spent with Nicolas at Otradnoe. What would she not have given to bring back just one day of that time! But now it was over for ever. Her presentiment had not deceived her then, that that state of freedom and openness to all joys would never return again. Yet one had to live.

It comforted her to think that she was not better, as she had thought before, but worse, much worse, than everyone, everyone in the world. But that was not all. She knew it, and asked herself: "And what then?" And then there was nothing. There was no joy in life, and life was going by. Natasha clearly tried only not to be a burden to anyone or to bother anyone, but for herself she wanted nothing. She avoided everyone in the house, and only felt at ease with her brother Petya. She liked being with him more than with the others; and sometimes, when they were alone together, she laughed. She hardly ever left the house, and of those who came to see them, she was glad only of Pierre. It was impossible to treat her more tenderly, more carefully, and at the same time more seriously, than Count Bezukhov treated her. Natasha unconsciously felt this tenderness of his treatment and therefore found great pleasure in his company. But she was not even grateful to him for his tenderness; nothing good on Pierre's part seemed an effort to her. It seemed so natural for Pierre to be kind to everyone, that there was no merit in his kindness. Occasionally Natasha noticed Pierre's embarrassment and awkwardness in her presence, especially when he wanted to do something to please her, or when he was afraid that something in their conversation might lead Natasha to painful memories. She noticed it and ascribed it to his general kindness and timidity, which, to her mind, must be the same with her as with everyone else. After those inadvertent words, that if he were free he would go on his knees and ask for her hand and her love, spoken at a moment of such intense emotion for her, Pierre had never said anything about his feelings for her; and it was obvious to her that the words which had comforted her so much then had been spoken the way all sorts of meaningless words are spoken to comfort a weeping child. Not because Pierre was a married man, but because Natasha felt in the highest degree the strength of the moral barriers between them—the absence of which she had felt with Kuragin—it never entered her head that her relations with Pierre might lead not only to love on her side, still less on his, but even to that sort of tender, self-aware, poetic friendship between a man and a woman, of which she knew several examples.

At the end of St. Peter's fast, Agrafena Ivanovna Belov, the Rostovs' neighbour in Otradnoe, came to Moscow to venerate the Moscow saints. She suggested that Natasha prepare for communion,[24] and Natasha joyfully seized upon the idea. Despite the doctor's prohibition on going out early in the morning, Natasha insisted on preparing, and preparing not as it was usually done in the Rostovs' home, that is, by hearing three services at home, but as Agrafena Ivanovna did it, that is, for the whole week, without missing a single vespers, liturgy, or matins.

The countess liked this zeal of Natasha's; after the unsuccessful medical treatment, she hoped in her heart that prayer would help her more than medications, and she consented to Natasha's wish, though with fear and concealing it from the doctor, and entrusted her to Mrs. Belov. Agrafena Ivanovna would come at three o'clock in the morning to wake Natasha, and most often found her already up. Natasha was afraid to sleep through the time for matins. Washing hastily and dressing humbly in the poorest of her dresses and an old mantilla, shivering in the fresh air, Natasha would go out into the deserted streets, transparently lit up by the glow of dawn. On Agrafena Ivanovna's advice, Natasha went to the services not in her own parish, but in a church in which, according to the pious Mrs. Belov, there was a priest of quite strict and lofty life. In the church there were always few people; Natasha and Mrs. Belov would stand in their usual place before the icon of the Mother of God, built into the back of the left-hand choir, and a new feeling of humility would come over Natasha before the great, the unknowable, when at this unaccustomed hour of morning, looking at the blackened face of the Mother of God lit by candles and the light of morning coming from the window, she listened to the words of the service, which she tried to follow and understand.[25] When she understood them, her personal feeling, with its nuances, joined with her prayer; when she did not, the sweeter it was for her to think that the wish to understand everything was pride, that it was impossible to understand everything, that she only had to believe and give herself to God, who in those moments—she felt—was guiding her soul. She crossed herself, bowed, and, when she did not understand, only asked God, in horror at her own vileness, to forgive her for everything, everything, and to have mercy on her. The prayers she gave herself to most of all were prayers of repentance. Returning home at an early hour of the morning, when she met only masons going to work and yard porters sweeping the streets, and everyone in the houses was still asleep, Natasha experienced a new feeling of the possibility of correcting her vices and the possibility of a new, pure life and happiness.

During the whole week in which she led this life, that feeling grew every day. And the happiness of taking communion, or of "communicating," as Agrafena Ivanovna used to say, playing joyfully with the word, seemed so great to her that she thought she would never survive till that blessed Sunday.

But the happy day came, and when Natasha, on that Sunday so memorable for her, in a white muslin dress, came home after communion, for the first time in many months she felt calm and not burdened by the life that lay ahead of her.

The doctor came that day, examined Natasha, and said she should continue to take those last powders he had prescribed two weeks ago.

"Be sure to continue, morning and evening," he said, clearly pleased in all good conscience with his success. "Only, I beg you, be precise. Don't worry, Countess," the doctor said jokingly, catching the gold piece deftly in his soft palm, "she'll soon be singing and frolicking again. This last medicine is very, very good for her. She's quite refreshed."

The countess looked at her nails, spat on them a little for luck, and went back to the drawing room with a cheerful face.

XVIII

At the beginning of July, more and more alarming rumours spread in Moscow about the course of the war: there was talk of the sovereign's appeal to the people, about the sovereign coming himself from the army to Moscow. And since up to the eleventh of July the manifesto and appeal had not been received, exaggerated rumours about them and about the situation of Russia went around. It was said that the sovereign had left the army because it was in danger, it was said that Smolensk had surrendered, that Napoleon had a million troops, and that only a miracle could save Russia.

On the eleventh of July, a Saturday, the manifesto was received, but not yet printed; and Pierre, who was at the Rostovs', promised to come the next day, Sunday, for dinner, and bring the manifesto and appeal, which he was to obtain from Count Rastopchin.

That Sunday the Rostovs, as usual, went to the liturgy at the Razumovskys' house chapel. It was a hot July day. By ten o'clock, when the Rostovs were getting out of the carriage before the church, in the hot air, in the cries of the hawkers, in the light and gay-coloured summer clothes of the crowd, in the dusty leaves of the trees along the boulevard, in the sounds of the music and the white breeches of a battalion marching to change the guard, in the rattling of carriages over the cobblestones, and in the bright brilliance of the hot sun, there was already that summer languor, that content and discontent with the present, which is felt especially strongly on a clear, hot day in town. All the Moscow nobility, all the Rostovs' acquaintances, were in the Razumovskys' chapel (that year, as if expecting something, many wealthy families, who usually went off to their country estates, stayed in town). Walking behind the liveried footman who made way through the crowd before her mother, Natasha heard a young man's voice saying of her in much too loud a whisper:

"That's Miss Rostov, the one who . . ."

"She's thinner, but still pretty!"

She heard, or seemed to hear, the names of Kuragin and Bolkonsky mentioned. However, it always seemed so to her. It always seemed to her that everyone who looked at her thought only of what had happened to her. Suffering, and with a sinking heart, as always in a crowd, Natasha walked in her violet dress with black lace as women know how to walk—the more calmly and majestically, the more pained and ashamed she felt at heart. She knew she was pretty, and she was not mistaken, but that did not cause her joy as it used to. On the contrary, it tormented her most of all lately, and especially on this bright, hot summer day in town. "One Sunday later, one week later," she said to herself, remembering how she had been here the last Sunday, "and it's the same life without living, and the same conditions in which it used to be so easy to live. I'm pretty, I'm young, and I know that I'm good now, I was bad before, but now I'm good, I know it," she thought, "and yet my best years are going by for nothing, for nobody." She stationed herself next to her mother and exchanged words with acquaintances who stood nearby. Out of habit, Natasha studied the ladies' dresses, disapproved of the *tenue** of a lady near her and the improper way she crossed herself with a quick little movement, again thought with vexation that she was being judged, that she herself was judging, and suddenly, hearing the sounds of the service, was horrified at her own vileness, horrified that the former purity was again lost to her.

A seemly, gentle little old man was serving with that meek solemnity which has such an exalting and soothing effect on the souls of the praying people. The royal doors closed, the curtain was slowly drawn; a mysterious, gentle voice pronounced something from inside. Tears, incomprehensible to herself, rose in Natasha's breast, and a joyful and agonizing feeling stirred her.

"Teach me what I'm to do, how I'm to set myself right for ever, for ever, how I'm to live my life! . . ." she thought.

The deacon came out to the ambo, released his long hair from under his dalmatic with a wide-spread thumb, and, making a cross on his breast, began loudly and solemnly to read the words of the prayer:

"In peace let us pray to the Lord."

"As one world[26]—all together, without distinction of rank, without enmity, but united in brotherly love—let us pray," thought Natasha.

"For the peace from above and for the salvation of our souls!"

"For the world of the angels and the souls of all the bodiless beings who dwell above us," Natasha prayed.

When they prayed for the military forces, she remembered her brother and Denisov. When they prayed for those who travel by land and sea, she remembered Prince Andrei and prayed for him, and also prayed that God forgive her the wrong she had done him. When they prayed for those who love us, she prayed for everyone at home, for her father, mother, Sonya, now understanding for the first time all her guilt before them and feeling all the strength of her love for them. When they prayed for those who hate us, she invented enemies and those who hated her in order to pray for them. She counted as enemies the creditors and all those who had dealings with her father, and each time, at the thought of enemies and those who hate us, she remembered Anatole, who had done her so much wrong, and though he did not hate her, she joyfully prayed for him as an enemy. Only while praying did she feel herself able to recall

*Attire.

clearly and calmly both Prince Andrei and Anatole as people for whom her feelings were as nothing compared to her feeling of fear and reverence for God. When they prayed for the tsar's family and the synod,[27] she made especially low bows and crossed herself, thinking that even if she did not understand, she could not doubt, and all the same loved the ruling synod and prayed for it.

Having finished the prayers of petition, the deacon crossed his stole over his breast and said:

"Let us commend ourselves and all our life unto Christ our God."

"Let us commend ourselves unto God," Natasha repeated in her soul. "My God, I commend myself to Your will," she thought. "I want, I wish for nothing; teach me what to do, where to make use of my will! Yes, take me, take me!" Natasha said with tender impatience in her soul, not crossing herself, but lowering her thin arms, and as if waiting for some unknown power to take her and deliver her from herself, from her regrets, desires, reproaches, hopes, and vices.

Several times during the service, the countess turned to look at her daughter's face, touched by emotion, with shining eyes, and prayed to God that He help her.

Unexpectedly, in the middle and outside the order of the service, which Natasha knew well, a beadle brought out a little footstool, the same as was used for the kneeling prayers on the feast of the Trinity,[28] and placed it in front of the royal doors. The priest came out in his purple velvet cap, smoothed his hair, and knelt with effort. Everybody did the same and looked at each other with perplexity. This was a prayer just received from the synod, a prayer for the salvation of Russia from foreign invasion.

"Lord God of hosts, God of our salvation," the priest began in that clear, unostentatious, and meek voice in which only clergy reading in Slavonic read and which affects the Russian heart so irresistibly.

"Lord God of hosts, God of our salvation! Look down now in mercy and compassion upon Thy humble people, and in Thy love for mankind hear us, spare us, and have mercy upon us. Behold, the enemy who confounds Thy land and would lay waste the whole universe has risen up against us; behold, lawless people have gathered together to destroy Thine inheritance, to devastate Thine honourable Jerusalem, Thy beloved Russia; to defile Thy churches, to overthrow Thine altars, to violate our holy places. How long, O Lord, how long shall sinners rejoice? How long shall the transgressor hold sway?

"O Lord God! Hear us who pray to Thee: give Thy strength to our most pious, autocratic, and great sovereign emperor Alexander Pavlovich; remember his righteousness and meekness, reward him according to his goodness, by which he preserves us, Thy beloved Israel. Bless his councils, undertakings, and actions; with Thine almighty right hand uphold his kingdom and grant him victory over his enemy, as Thou didst to Moses over Amalek, to Gideon over

Midian, and to David over Goliath.²⁹ Preserve his army: place a bow of brass into the hands of those fighting in Thy name, and gird them with the power to make war. Take up Thine arms and shield, and arise to help us, so that those who contrive evil against us may be put to shame and disgrace, let them be before the face of Thy faithful army like dust before the face of the wind, and let Thy mighty angel discomfit them and drive them hence; let the net they know not of come upon them, let the trap concealed from them ensnare them; so that they fall under the feet of Thy servants, and our warriors may trample upon them. Lord! let Thy power to save in things great and small not be exhausted: Thou art God, let no man prevail against Thee.

"God of our fathers! Remember Thy compassion and mercy from all eternity; drive us not away from Thy face, neither scorn our unworthiness, but have mercy upon us according to Thy great mercy and in the abundance of Thy compassion regard not our sins and transgressions. Create in us a pure heart and renew a right spirit within us; strengthen us all with faith in Thee, establish us in hope, inspire us with true love for each other, arm us with oneness of spirit in righteous defence of the inheritance which Thou hast granted to us and to our fathers, so that the rod of the unrighteous be not raised against the destiny of the sanctified.

"Lord our God, in whom we believe and place our trust, disgrace us not in our hope of Thy mercy and make a sign for the good, so that those who hate us and our Orthodox faith may be put to shame and perish; and let all nations know that Thy name is the Lord and we are Thy people. Show us this day Thy mercy, O Lord, and grant us Thy salvation; make the hearts of Thy servants rejoice in Thy mercy; strike down our enemies and swiftly crush them under the feet of Thy faithful. For Thou art the defence, the succour, and the victory of those who put their trust in Thee, and to Thee we ascribe glory, to the Father, and to the Son, and to the Holy Spirit, now, and ever, and unto ages of ages. Amen."

In that state of inner openness in which Natasha found herself, this prayer had a strong effect on her. She listened to every word about the victory of Moses over Amalek, and Gideon over Midian, and David over Goliath, and about the destruction of "Thy Jerusalem," and asked God with that tenderness and softness with which her heart was overflowing—but she did not understand very well what she was asking of God in this prayer. With her whole soul she participated in the petition about a right spirit, about the strengthening of hearts with faith, hope, and inspiring them with love. But she could not pray about trampling her enemies under her feet, when a few moments before she had wished to have more of them, so as to love them and pray for them. But she also could not doubt the rightness of the kneeling prayer that was being read. She felt in her soul the reverent and trembling fear before the punishment that comes upon people for their sins, especially upon her for her sins, and asked God to forgive them all, and herself, and to grant them all, and herself, peace and happiness in life. And it seemed to her that God heard her prayer.

XIX

Since the day when Pierre, leaving the Rostovs' and remembering Natasha's grateful eyes, had looked at the comet that hung in the sky, and had felt that something new had been revealed to him—the question that eternally tormented him about the vanity and folly of all earthly things had stopped presenting itself to him. That terrible question—"Why? What for?"—which used to present itself to him amidst every occupation, was now replaced for him not by another question and not by the answer to the old question, but by *her* image. Listening to a trivial conversation, or engaged in one himself, or reading, or learning about the baseness and senselessness of people, he was not horrified as he used to be; he did not ask himself why people made a fuss, if everything was so brief and unknown, but he remembered her the way he had seen her the last time, and all his doubts vanished, not because she answered the questions that presented themselves to him, but because her image immediately transferred him to a different, bright realm of inner activity, in which no one could be right or wrong, into a realm of beauty and love for which it was worth living. Whatever vileness of life presented itself to him, he said to himself:

"Well, let so-and-so steal from the state and the tsar, and the state and the tsar confer honours on him; but yesterday she smiled at me and asked me to come, and I love her, and nobody will ever know it," he thought.

Pierre still went into society, still drank as much and led the same idle and dissipated life, because besides the hours he spent at the Rostovs', he had the rest of the time to spend, and the habits and acquaintances he had acquired in Moscow drew him irresistibly to the life he was caught up in. But lately, whenever more alarming rumours kept coming from the theatre of war, and Natasha's health began to improve, and she ceased to arouse in him the former feeling of protective pity, an anxiety he found more and more incomprehensible began to come over him. He felt that the situation in which he found himself could not continue for long, that a catastrophe was coming which was bound to change his whole life, and he impatiently sought signs of this approaching catastrophe in everything. One of his brother Masons revealed to Pierre the following prophecy concerning Napoleon and derived from the Apocalypse of St. John.[30]

In the Apocalypse, chapter 13, verse 18, it was said: "Here is wisdom. Let him that hath understanding count the number of the beast: for it is the number of a man; and his number is six hundred threescore and six."

And in verse 5 of the same chapter: "And there was given unto him a mouth speaking great things and blasphemies; and power was given unto him to continue forty and two months."

French letters, given numerical values like the Hebrew, in which the first nine letters represent units, and the rest tens, will have the following significance:

a	b	c	d	e	f	g	h	i	k	l	m
1	2	3	4	5	6	7	8	9	10	20	30

n	o	p	q	r	s	t	u	v	w	x	y	z
40	50	60	70	80	90	100	110	120	130	140	150	160

Writing the words *l'empereur Napoléon* in this alphabet of numbers, it turns out that the sum of the figures equals 666 and that Napoleon is therefore that beast prophesied in the Apocalypse. Moreover, if the word *quarante-deux,* that is, the term fixed for the beast "to speak great things and blasphemies," is written in the same alphabet, the sum of these figures representing *quarante-deux* again equals 666, from which it follows that the term of Napoleon's power was reached in the year 1812, when the French emperor turned forty-two. Pierre was very struck by this prophecy, and he often posed the question for himself of precisely what would set a limit to the power of the beast, that is, of Napoleon, and on the basis of the same correspondence of word numbers and calculations, he tried to find an answer to his question. In answer to the question, Pierre wrote out: *L'empereur Alexandre? La nation russe?* He counted up the letters, but the sum of the numbers came out much larger or smaller than 666. Once, taken up with these calculations, he wrote his own name—*Comte Pierre Besouhoff;* the sum of the numbers was also far from the right one. He changed the orthography, putting *z* in place of *s,* added *de,* added the article *le,* and still did not get the desired result. Then it occurred to him that, if the answer to the question he was seeking was contained in his name, then the answer would certainly mention his nationality. He wrote *Le russe Besuhof* and, counting up the numbers, got 671. It was only five too much; five was *e,* the same *e* that was dropped from the article in the words *L'empereur.* Having dropped the *e* in the same way, albeit incorrectly, Pierre got the sought-for answer: *L'russe Besuhof,* which equalled 666. This discovery excited him. He did not know how, by what connection he was bound up with that great event which had been predicted in the Apocalypse; but he did not doubt that connection for a moment. His love for Miss Rostov, the Antichrist, Napoleon's invasion, the comet, 666, *l'empereur Napoléon* and *l'russe Besuhof*—all that together must ripen, burst, and lead him out of that spellbound, worthless world of Moscow habits in which he felt himself imprisoned, and bring him to a great deed and great happiness.

· · ·

On the eve of that Sunday when the prayer was read, Pierre had promised the Rostovs that he would bring them from Count Rastopchin, whom he knew well, both the appeal to Russia and the latest news from the army. In the morning, stopping at Count Rastopchin's, Pierre found with him a just-arrived courier from the army.

The courier was an acquaintance of Pierre's from the Moscow ballrooms.

"For God's sake, can't you lighten it for me?" said the courier. "I've got a bag full of letters to parents."

Among those letters was Nikolai Rostov's letter to his father. Pierre took it. Besides that, Count Rastopchin gave Pierre the sovereign's appeal to Moscow, only just printed, the latest orders to the army, and his own latest bulletin. Looking through the orders to the army, Pierre found in one of them, amidst information about the wounded, killed, and decorated, the name of Nikolai Rostov, awarded the St. George, fourth degree, for bravery shown during the Ostrovna action, and in the same order the appointment of Prince Andrei Bolkonsky as commander of a regiment of chasseurs. Though he was reluctant to remind the Rostovs of Bolkonsky, Pierre could not refrain from his wish to give them the glad news of their son's decoration, and, keeping the appeal, the bulletin, and the other orders, so as to bring them to dinner in person, he sent the printed order and the letter to the Rostovs.

The conversation with Count Rastopchin, his preoccupied and hasty tone, the meeting with the courier, who told casually of things going poorly in the army, of rumours of spies found in Moscow, of a paper circulating in Moscow which said that Napoleon promised to occupy both Russian capitals before autumn, of talk of the expected arrival of the sovereign the next day—all this aroused with renewed force in Pierre that feeling of excitement and expectation which had not left him since the time of the comet's appearance and especially since the start of the war.

Pierre had long been thinking of entering military service, and he would have done so had he not been hindered, first, by his belonging to the Masonic order, to which he was bound by oath and which preached eternal peace and the abolition of war, and second, by looking at the great number of Muscovites donning uniforms and preaching patriotism, which somehow made him ashamed to take such a step. But the main reason why he would not carry out his intention of entering military service consisted in his vague notion that he, *l'russe Besuhof*, had the number of the beast, 666, that his participation in the great deed of setting a limit to the power of the *beast* that spoke great things and blasphemies was predestined from all eternity, and that he was therefore not to undertake anything, but to wait for what was to happen.

XX

At the Rostovs', as always on Sundays, some of their closest acquaintances were dining.

Pierre came early, so as to catch them alone.

During that year, Pierre had grown so fat that he would have been monstrous if he had not been so tall, so large of limb, and so strong that he obviously bore his corpulence lightly.

He went up the stairs, puffing and muttering something to himself. His coachman no longer asked if he should wait. He knew that when the count went to the Rostovs', it was till midnight. The Rostovs' footmen joyfully rushed to help him off with his cloak and take his stick and hat. From club habit, Pierre left his stick and hat in the front hall.

The first person he saw at the Rostovs' was Natasha. Even before he saw her, while taking off his cloak in the front hall, he heard her. She was singing her solfeggios in the reception room. He knew that she had not sung since the time of her illness, and therefore he was surprised and glad to hear the sound of her voice. He quietly opened the door and saw Natasha in her violet dress, which she had worn to church, strolling about the room and singing. She had her back to him when he opened the door, but when she turned abruptly and saw his fat, astonished face, she blushed and quickly went over to him.

"I want to try singing again," she said. "It's something to do, after all," she added, as if apologizing.

"Wonderful."

"How glad I am you've come! I'm so happy today!" she said with the old animation, which Pierre had not seen in her for a long time. "You know, Nicolas was awarded the St. George Cross. I'm so proud of him."

"Of course, it was I who sent the order. Well, I don't want to hinder you," he added and was about to go to the drawing room.

Natasha stopped him.

"Count, is it wrong of me to sing?" she said, blushing, but gazing at Pierre questioningly, not turning her eyes away.

"No . . . Why? On the contrary . . . But why do you ask me?"

"I don't know myself," Natasha replied quickly, "but I wouldn't want to do anything that you wouldn't like. I trust you in everything. You don't know how important you are to me and how much you've done for me! . . ." She spoke quickly and did not notice how Pierre blushed at those words. "I saw in the same order that *he*, Bolkonsky" (she uttered that name in a quick whisper), "is in Russia and serving again. What do you think," she said quickly, clearly hurrying to speak because she feared for her strength, "will he forgive me some day? Won't he always have an angry feeling towards me? What do you think? What do you think?"

"I think . . ." said Pierre. "There's nothing for him to forgive . . . If I were in his place . . ." By a connection of memory, Pierre was instantly transported in imagination to the time when, in comforting her, he had told her that if he were not himself, but the best man in the world and free, he would go on his knees and ask for her hand, and the same feeling of pity, tenderness, and love came over him, and the same words were on his lips. But she gave him no time to say them.

"Yes, you—you," she said, pronouncing the word *you* with delight, "are a different matter. I don't know a man who is kinder, better, more magnanimous than you, and there can't be one. If you hadn't been there then, and now, too, I don't know what would have happened to me, because . . ." Tears suddenly welled up in her eyes; she turned away, raised the music to her eyes, and began to sing and pace the reception room again.

Just then Petya came running from the drawing room.

Petya was now a handsome, ruddy fifteen-year-old boy with plump red lips, and resembled Natasha. He was preparing for the university, but lately, with his friend Obolensky, had secretly decided to join the hussars.

Petya had run out to his namesake in order to talk the matter over.

He had asked him to find out whether they would take him into the hussars.

Pierre walked towards the drawing room, not listening to Petya.

Petya pulled him by the arm to attract his attention.

"Well, what about my business, Pyotr Kirilych? For God's sake! You're my only hope," said Petya.

"Ah, yes, your business. About the hussars? I'll tell you, I'll tell you. Today I'll tell you everything."

"Well, *mon cher*, did you get the manifesto?" asked the old count. "My little countess went to the liturgy at the Razumovskys' and heard a new prayer. A very good one, she says."

"I've got it," replied Pierre. "Tomorrow the sovereign will be here . . . There will be an extraordinary assembly of the nobility and, they say, a conscription of ten men per thousand. Ah, yes, and I congratulate you."

"Yes, yes, thank God. Well, and what news from the army?"

"Our side has retreated again. Near Smolensk already, they say," replied Pierre.

"My God, my God!" said the count. "So where is the manifesto?"

"The appeal! Ah, yes!" Pierre started hunting for the papers in his pockets and could not find them. Continuing to slap his pockets, he kissed the hand of the countess, who came in, and looked around uneasily, evidently waiting for Natasha, who was no longer singing, but had not yet come to the drawing room.

"By God, I don't know where I put it," he said.

"Well, really, he's for ever losing things," said the countess.

Natasha came in with a face softened by emotion and sat down, looking silently at Pierre. As soon as she entered the room, Pierre's face, downcast till then, brightened, and, while he went on searching for the paper, he looked at her several times.

"By God, I'll go and fetch it, I left it at home. Certainly . . ."

"Well, you'll be late for dinner."

"Ah, and my coachman has driven off."

But Sonya, who had gone to the front hall to look for the papers, had found them in Pierre's hat, tucked carefully under the lining. Pierre was about to start reading.

"No, after dinner," said the old count, clearly anticipating great pleasure from this reading.

Over dinner, at which they drank champagne to the health of the new chevalier of St. George, Shinshin told them the town news about the illness of an old Georgian princess, about Métivier's disappearance from Moscow, and about how they brought some German to Rastopchin and announced to him that he was a *spine* (so Count Rastopchin told it himself), and how Count Rastopchin ordered the *spine* set free, telling the folk that he was not a *spine*, but just a prickly old German.[31]

"They catch them, they catch them," said the count. "I even told the countess to speak less French. Now's not the time."

"Have you heard?" said Shinshin. "Prince Golitsyn has hired a Russian teacher, he's taking lessons in Russian—*il commence à devenir dangereux de parler français dans les rues.*"*

"Well, now, Count Pyotr Kirilych, once they start calling up the militia, you'll have to get on a horse, too?" said the old count, addressing Pierre.

Pierre had been silent and pensive all through this dinner. As if not understanding, he looked at the count when he addressed him.

"Yes, yes, to war," he said, "no! What kind of warrior am I? Anyhow, it's all so strange, so strange! I don't understand it myself. I don't know, I'm so far from having any taste for the military, but nowadays nobody can answer for himself."

After dinner, the count settled comfortably in an armchair and with a serious face asked Sonya, who was famous for her skill at reading, to read.

"To our first-throned capital, Moscow:[32]

"The enemy has entered within the borders of Russia with great forces. He comes to devastate our beloved fatherland," Sonya read diligently in her high little voice. The count listened, his eyes closed, sighing fitfully in certain places.

---

*It's becoming dangerous to speak French in the streets.

Natasha sat erect, looking searchingly and directly now at her father, now at Pierre.

Pierre felt her gaze on him and tried not to look at her. The countess shook her head disapprovingly and crossly at each solemn phrase of the manifesto. In all these words she saw only that the dangers which threatened her son would not end soon. Shinshin, composing his mouth into a mocking smile, was obviously preparing to mock at the first thing that presented itself for mockery: at Sonya's reading, at what the count would say, even at the appeal itself, if no better pretext appeared.

Having read about the dangers that threatened Russia, about the hopes the sovereign placed in Moscow, and especially in its illustrious nobility, Sonya, with a tremor in her voice, caused mainly by the attention with which she was being listened to, read the last words: "We ourselves will not be slow to stand amidst our people in that capital and other places of our realm, for consultation and for the guidance of all our armed forces, both those who already obstruct the enemy's path and those newly formed for his defeat, wherever he may appear. May the ruin to which he hopes to reduce us turn back upon his own head, and may a Europe freed from slavery glorify the name of Russia!"

"That's the way!" the count cried, opening his wet eyes and breaking off several times to sniff, as if a vial of strong smelling salts had been put to his nose. "The sovereign need only say it, and we'll sacrifice everything with no regrets."

Before Shinshin had time to tell the joke he had prepared about the count's patriotism, Natasha jumped up from her place and ran over to her father.

"What a darling he is, this papa!" she said, kissing him, and she again glanced at Pierre with that unconscious coquetry which had come back to her along with her animation.

"There's a little patriot for you!" said Shinshin.

"Not a little patriot at all, but just . . ." Natasha replied touchily. "Everything's funny to you, but this isn't a joke at all . . ."

"Some joke!" the count repeated. "He need only say the word, and we'll all go . . . We're not some sort of Germans . . ."

"And did you notice," asked Pierre, "that it said 'for consultation'?"

"Well, whatever it's for . . ."

Just then Petya, to whom no one paid attention, went up to his father and, all red, in a breaking voice, now gruff, now shrill, said:

"Well, so, papa dear, I'd say definitely—and mama, too, like it or not—I'd say definitely that you'll let me go into military service, because otherwise I can't . . . that's all . . ."

The countess raised her eyes to heaven with horror, clasped her hands, and turned angrily to her husband.

"There's your talking for you!" she said.

But the count recovered from his excitement that same moment.

"Well, well," he said. "Another warrior! Forget this foolishness: you must study."

"It's not foolishness, papa. Fedya Obolensky is younger than I am and he's going, and the main thing is that anyhow I can't study anything now, when . . ." Petya stopped, blushed hotly, and managed to bring out: ". . . when the fatherland is in danger."

"Enough, enough, it's foolishness . . ."

"But you said yourself that we'd sacrifice everything."

"Petya, be quiet, I'm telling you," the count cried, glancing at his wife, who, turning pale, was looking with fixed eyes at her younger son.

"And I'm telling you. And Pyotr Kirillovich here will say . . ."

"I'm telling you it's nonsense, the milk isn't dry on your lips, and you want to serve in the army! Well, well, I'm telling you," and the count, taking the papers with him, probably in order to read them once more in his study before napping, started out of the room.

"Pyotr Kirillovich, what do you say we go for a smoke . . ."

Pierre found himself in confusion and irresolution. Natasha's unusually brilliant and animated eyes, constantly turning to him with more than affection, had brought him to that state.

"No, I think I'll go home . . ."

"What do you mean, home? You wanted to spend the evening with us . . . You come rarely as it is. And this girl of mine . . ." the count said good-naturedly, pointing to Natasha, "is only cheerful when you're here . . ."

"Yes, but I forgot . . . I really must go home . . . Things to do . . ." Pierre said hurriedly.

"Well, goodbye, then," said the count, leaving the room altogether.

"Why are you going? Why are you upset? Why? . . ." Natasha asked Pierre, looking challengingly into his eyes.

"Because I love you!" he wanted to say, but he did not say it, blushed to the point of tears, and lowered his eyes.

"Because it's better that I visit you less often . . . Because . . no, I simply have things to do . . ."

"But why? No, tell me," Natasha began resolutely, and suddenly fell silent. They both looked at each other in fright and confusion. He tried to smile, but could not: his smile expressed suffering, and he silently kissed her hand and left.

Pierre decided to himself that he would not visit the Rostovs any more.

XXI

After the resolute refusal he had received, Petya went to his room and, locking himself in, wept bitterly. Everyone pretended to notice nothing when he came to tea, silent and gloomy, with tearful eyes.

The next day the sovereign arrived. Several of the Rostovs' domestics asked permission to go and look at the tsar. That morning, Petya spent a long time getting dressed, combing his hair, and arranging his collar the way grown-ups do. He frowned into the mirror, gesticulated, shrugged his shoulders, and finally, without telling anyone, put on his peaked cap and left the house by the back door, trying not to be noticed. Petya had decided to go directly to the place where the sovereign was and explain directly to some gentleman-in-waiting (Petya thought that a sovereign was always surrounded by gentlemen-in-waiting) that he, Count Rostov, despite his youth, wished to serve the fatherland, that youth could be no hindrance to devotion, and that he was prepared . . . While getting ready to go, Petya had prepared many fine words which he would say to the gentleman-in-waiting.

Petya was counting on the success of his undertaking precisely because he was a child (Petya even thought how everyone would be astonished at his youth), and yet in the arrangement of his collar, in his hairstyle, and in his slow, sedate walk, he wanted to make himself look like an old man. But the further he went, the more distracted he was by the ever-increasing numbers of people near the Kremlin, the more he forgot to maintain the slowness and sedateness proper to grown-up people. As he approached the Kremlin, he already began to worry about being jostled, and with a menacing look he resolutely stuck out his elbows. But at the Trinity Gate, in spite of all his resoluteness, people who probably did not know with what a patriotic purpose he was going to the Kremlin so pressed him to the wall that he had to submit and stop, while carriages passed under the archway with a hollow rumble. Next to Petya stood a peasant woman, a footman, two merchants, and a retired soldier. After standing for a while in the gateway, Petya, unwilling to wait until all the carriages went by, wanted to start moving ahead before the others and resolutely began to work with his elbows; but the peasant woman standing in his way, to whom he first applied his elbows, angrily shouted at him:

"What are you shoving for, little master, see, everybody's standing. What's all this pushing for?"

"Anybody can push in that case," said the footman, and, also beginning to work with his elbows, he squeezed Petya into the stinking corner of the gateway.

Petya wiped his sweat-covered face with his hands and straightened the sweat-soaked collar he had arranged so well, like a grown-up's, at home.

Petya felt that he looked unpresentable and was afraid that, if he appeared before the gentlemen-in-waiting like that, he would not be admitted to the sovereign. But, owing to the crowd, it was quite impossible to set himself right and move to another place. One of the generals driving by was an acquaintance of the Rostovs'. Petya wanted to ask for his help, but considered that it would be unmanly. When all the carriages had gone past, the crowd poured through and brought Petya out on the square, which was all filled with people. Not only on the square, but on the glacis, on the roofs, everywhere there were people. As soon as Petya found himself on the square, he clearly heard the sounds of the bells and the joyful talk of people that filled the whole Kremlin.

For a time the square was less crowded, but suddenly all heads were uncovered, everyone rushed forward somewhere. Petya was pressed so hard that he could not breathe, and everyone shouted: "Hurrah! Hur-r-rah! Hurrah!" Petya stood on tiptoe, shoved, pinched, but could see nothing except the people around him.

On all faces there was the same general expression of tenderness and rapture. A merchant woman standing beside Petya sobbed, and tears poured from her eyes.

"Father, angel, dearest!" she murmured, wiping her tears with her fingers.

"Hurrah!" came from all sides.

For a moment the crowd stood in one place; but then again it rushed forward.

Petya, forgetting himself, clenched his teeth, rolled his eyes out wildly, and rushed forward, working with his elbows and shouting "Hurrah!" as if he was ready to kill himself and everyone else at that moment, but exactly the same wild faces came at him from the sides, with the same shouts of "Hurrah!"

"So this is what the sovereign is!" Petya thought. "No, it's impossible for me to hand him a petition myself, it's too bold!" In spite of which, he made his way forward just as desperately, and saw, flashing between the backs of those ahead of him, an empty space and a passage laid with red cloth; but just then the crowd heaved backwards (the policemen ahead shoved back those who got too close to the procession; the sovereign passed from the palace to the cathedral of the Dormition), and Petya unexpectedly received such a blow in the ribs from the side, and was so squeezed, that everything suddenly went dim in his eyes, and he lost consciousness. When he came to, some clergyman with a clump of greying hair tied behind, in a shabby blue cassock, probably a beadle, was holding him under the arm with one hand and protecting him from the pressing crowd with the other.

"The young gentleman has been crushed!" the beadle was saying. "Such goings on! . . . ease up . . . he's crushed, crushed!"

The sovereign went into the cathedral of the Dormition. The crowd subsided again, and the beadle led Petya, pale and barely breathing, to the Tsar-Cannon.[33] Several persons felt sorry for Petya, and suddenly the whole crowd turned to him, and now there was a crush around him. Those who stood near attended to him, unbuttoned his frock coat, sat him up on the cannon, and reproached somebody—whoever had crushed him.

"You could crush somebody to death that way. What is it! Committing murder! See, the dear heart, he's gone white as a sheet," voices said.

Petya soon recovered, the colour returned to his face, the pain disappeared, and for this temporary unpleasantness he acquired a place on the cannon from which he hoped to see the sovereign, who should be coming back that way. Petya was no longer thinking of petitioning. If only he could see him, he would consider himself happy!

During the service in the cathedral of the Dormition—which was a combined prayer service on the occasion of the sovereign's arrival, and a prayer of thanksgiving for the concluding of peace with the Turks—the crowd spread out; hawkers appeared, offering kvass, gingerbread, poppy-seed cakes, which Petya especially fancied, and ordinary conversations were heard. One merchant's wife displayed her torn shawl, telling how much she had paid for it; another said that today all silk fabrics had become expensive. The beadle, Petya's saviour, talked with an official about just who and who were serving that day with the bishop. The beadle several times repeated the word "concelebration," which Petya did not understand. Two young tradesmen bantered with servant girls who were cracking nuts. All this talk, especially the bantering with the girls, which for a boy of Petya's age was especially alluring, all this talk did not concern Petya now; he sat on his lofty cannon, as excited as ever at the thought of the sovereign and of his love for him. The feeling of pain and fear, when he was being crushed, blended with the feeling of rapture, and increased in him still more the awareness of the importance of this moment.

Suddenly cannon shots were heard from the embankment (the shooting was in celebration of the peace with the Turks), and the crowd swiftly rushed to the embankment to watch how they were shooting. Petya also wanted to run there, but the beadle, having taken the young gentleman under his protection, would not let him. The shooting was still going on when officers, generals, gentlemen-in-waiting came running out of the cathedral, then others came out less hurriedly, then hats were taken off again, and those who had run to look at the cannon came running back. Finally, four more men in uniforms and sashes came through the doors of the cathedral. "Hurrah! Hurrah!" the crowd shouted again.

"Which is he? Which is he?" Petya asked all around in a tearful voice, but no one answered him; they were all too carried away, and Petya, having selected one of these four persons, whom he could not make out clearly because of the tears of joy that welled up in his eyes, concentrated all his rapture on him, though he was not the sovereign, shouted "Hurrah!" in a frantic voice, and decided that tomorrow, whatever it might cost him, he would be in the military.

The crowd ran after the sovereign, accompanied him to the palace, and began to disperse. It was already late, Petya had eaten nothing, he was streaming with sweat; but he would not go home, and together with the diminished but still quite large crowd, stood before the palace, looking through the palace windows while the sovereign dined, expecting something further, and equally envious both of the dignitaries who drove up to the entrance, to the sovereign's dinner, and of the palace footmen who served at the table and flitted past the windows.

At dinner with the sovereign, Valuev said, glancing out of the window:

"The people still hope to see Your Majesty."

The dinner was already over, the sovereign stood up and, finishing a biscuit, went out to the balcony. The people, with Petya among them, rushed to the balcony.

"Angel! Father! Hurrah! Dearest! . . ." cried the people and Petya, and again peasant women and a few men of the weaker sort, including Petya, wept with happiness. A rather large piece of the biscuit that the sovereign was holding broke off, fell onto the railing of the balcony, and from there to the ground. A cabby in a jerkin, who was standing closest of all, rushed to this piece of biscuit and snatched it up. Some people in the crowd rushed to the cabby. Noticing that, the sovereign asked for a plate of biscuits to be brought and began tossing biscuits from the balcony.[34] Petya's eyes became bloodshot, the danger of being crushed aroused him still more, he rushed for the biscuits. He did not know why, but it was necessary to take a biscuit from the tsar's hands, and necessary not to give it up. He rushed and tripped up a little old woman who was trying to catch a biscuit. But the little old woman did not consider herself defeated, though she was lying on the ground (she tried to catch a biscuit, but kept missing). Petya knocked her arm aside with his knee, snatched a biscuit, and, as if afraid to be late, again shouted "Hurrah!" in a voice now grown hoarse.

The sovereign went in, and after that the greater part of the people began to disperse.

"See, I said to keep waiting—and I was right," people said joyfully from various sides.

Happy as Petya was, he still felt sad to go home and know that all the pleasure of that day was over. From the Kremlin Petya did not go home, but to his friend Obolensky, who was also fifteen and who also wanted to join a regiment. Returning home, he announced resolutely and firmly that, if they would not let him, he would run away. And the next day Count Ilya Andreich, though not yet quite giving in, went to find out how he could arrange to set Petya up in some less dangerous place.

XXII

On the fifteenth, in the morning, the third day after that, a countless number of carriages stood by the Slobodsky palace.[35]

The great halls were filled. In the first were noblemen in uniforms, in the second merchants with medals, in beards and dark blue kaftans. In the hall of the Assembly of the Nobility there was noise and movement. The most important dignitaries sat on high-backed chairs around a large table under a portrait of the sovereign; but the majority walked about the room.

All the nobility, the same ones Pierre saw every day, now in the club, now in their homes, were in uniforms, some of Catherine's time, some of Paul's, some in new ones of Alexander's time, some in generic noblemen's uniforms, and this general character of the uniform lent something strange and fantastic to these old and young, most diverse and familiar faces. Especially striking were the old men, weak-sighted, toothless, bald, swollen with yellow fat or shrivelled, gaunt. For the most part they sat silently in their places, and if they walked and talked, they attached themselves to someone younger. Just as on the faces of the crowd Petya had seen in the square, so on all these faces there was a striking feature of contrast: a general expectation of something solemn, and the ordinary and everyday—a game of boston, Petrushka the cook, Zinaïda Dmitrievna's health, and so on.

Pierre, squeezed since morning into an uncomfortable nobleman's uniform which had become too tight for him, was there in the halls. He was excited: the extraordinary assembly not only of noblemen but of merchants as well—of estates, *états généraux*—called up in him a whole series of thoughts, long abandoned but deeply imprinted in his soul, about the *Contrat social*[36] and the French revolution. The words he had noticed in the appeal, that the sovereign would come to the capital *for consultations* with his people, confirmed him in this view. And, supposing that something important in that sense was approaching, something he had long awaited, he walked about, observed, listened to what was said, but did not find anywhere an expression of those thoughts that interested him.

The sovereign's manifesto was read, evoked raptures, and then everyone wandered about, talking. Besides ordinary interests, Pierre heard talk of where the marshals of the nobility were to stand when the sovereign entered, when to give the ball for the sovereign, whether it should be done by districts or by the whole province . . . and so on; but as soon as things touched on the war and what the nobility had assembled for, the talk became indecisive and indefinite. Everyone wished more to listen than to speak.

A middle-aged man, manly, handsome, in the uniform of a retired naval officer, spoke in one of the halls, and a crowd formed around him. Pierre went over to the circle around the speaker and began to listen. Count Ilya Andreich, in his kaftan of a governor from Catherine's time, who was strolling with a pleasant smile among the crowd, with all of whom he was acquainted, also went over to this group and began listening with his kindly smile, as he always did, nodding approvingly to indicate his agreement with the speaker. The retired naval officer was speaking very boldly; that was evident from the expression of the faces of his listeners, and from the fact that people known to Pierre as most submissive and quiet objected or walked away from him disapprovingly. Pierre pushed his way to the middle of the circle, listened, and became convinced that the man speaking was indeed a liberal, but in quite a different sense than Pierre had thought. The naval officer spoke in that especially resounding, melodious nobleman's baritone, pleasantly swallowing his *r*s and dropping consonants, that voice in which one calls out, "Youtheah, a pipe!" and the like. He spoke with a voice accustomed to both revelry and authority.

"So what if Smolensk has offered the sovn a militiah? Does Smolensk lay down the law for us? If the honable nobility of Moscow province find it necessary, they can show their devotion to the sovn emprah some othah way. We've not forgotten the militiah of the year seven! The only ones who profited from it were little church folk and thieving robbahs . . ."

Count Ilya Andreich, smiling sweetly, nodded his head approvingly.

"And was our militiah of any use to the country? None at all! It just ruined our husbandry. Conscription's better . . . because when they come back, they're not soldiers, not peasants, they're sheer depravity. The nobility won't spare their own lives, we'll go ourselves to the last man, we'll conscript more soldiers, and the sovn" (that was how he said "sovereign") "only needs to sound the call, and we'll all die for him," the orator added with inspiration.

Ilya Andreich gulped with pleasure and nudged Pierre, but Pierre also wanted to speak. He moved forward, feeling inspired, not knowing by what himself, and not knowing himself what he was going to say. He had only just opened his mouth to speak when one senator, completely toothless, with an intelligent and angry face, who was standing near the orator, interrupted Pierre. With an obvious habit of leading the debate and sustaining questions, he spoke softly but audibly:

"I suppose, my dear sir," said the senator, maundering with his toothless mouth, "that we have been summoned here not in order to discuss what is more appropriate for the country at the present moment—conscription or a militia. We have been summoned to respond to the appeal the sovereign has deigned to make to us. And we can let higher authorities judge which is more opportune—conscription or a militia . . ."

Pierre suddenly found an outlet for his inspiration. He rose up against the senator who had introduced this correctness and narrowness of view into the tasks facing the nobility. Pierre stepped forward and stopped him. He did not know himself what he was going to say, but he began with animation, from time to time breaking into French words and expressing himself bookishly in Russian.

"Excuse me, Your Excellency," he began. (Pierre knew this senator well, but considered it necessary here to address him officially.) "Though I do not agree with the gentleman . . ." (Pierre hesitated. He wanted to say *mon très honorable préopinant**)—"with the gentleman . . . *que je n'ai pas l'honneur de connaître;†* but I suppose that the estate of the nobility, besides expressing its sympathy and delight, has also been summoned to discuss the measures by which we may help the fatherland. I suppose," he said, becoming inspired, "that the sovereign himself would be displeased if he were to find in us only owners of peasants, whom we give to him, and . . . *chair à canon,‡* which we make of ourselves, and did not find in us any co . . . co . . . counsel."

Many walked away from the circle, seeing the senator's contemptuous smile and that Pierre was speaking liberally. Only Ilya Andreich was pleased with Pierre's speech, as he had been pleased with the speech of the naval officer, the senator, and generally always with the speech he had heard last.

"I suppose that, before discussing these questions," Pierre went on, "we should ask the sovereign, most respectfully ask his majesty, to communicate to us how many troops we have, in what position our troops and the army find themselves, and then . . ."

But Pierre had not managed to finish these words, when he was suddenly attacked from three sides. The strongest attack came from his old acquaintance, the boston player Stepan Stepanovich Apraksin, who had always been well-disposed towards him. Stepan Stepanovich was wearing a uniform, and either because of the uniform, or for some other reason, Pierre saw a completely different person before him. With an old man's anger suddenly showing on his face, Stepan Stepanovich shouted at Pierre:

"First, I put it to you that we have no right to ask that of the sovereign, and second, if the Russian nobility did have that right, the sovereign could not answer us. Troops move in accordance with the movements of the enemy— troops decrease and increase . . ."

Another voice, of a man of medium height, about forty years old, whom Pierre in the old days used to see at the Gypsies' and knew for a dishonest card-player, and who, also changed by his uniform, moving closer to Pierre, interrupted Apraksin.

---

*My most honourable opponent.
†Whom I do not have the honour of knowing.
‡Cannon fodder.

"And this is not the time for debate," said the voice of this nobleman, "we must act: there's war in Russia. The enemy is coming to destroy Russia, to defile the graves of our fathers, to carry off our wives and children." The nobleman beat his chest. "We'll all stand up, we'll all go to the last man for our dearest tsar!" he cried, rolling his bloodshot eyes. Several approving voices were heard in the crowd. "We're Russian, and we won't spare our blood to defend the faith, the throne, and the fatherland. And the raving has to stop, if we are sons of the fatherland. We'll show Europe how Russia rises to defend Russia," cried the nobleman.

Pierre wanted to object, but could not say a word. He felt that the sound of his words, regardless of the thought they contained, would be heard less than the sound of the animated nobleman's words.

Ilya Andreich approved from outside the circle; some briskly turned their shoulders to the orator at the end of each phrase and said:

"Right, right! That's right!"

Pierre wanted to say that he did not mind donating money, or peasants, or sacrificing himself, but that it was necessary to know the state of affairs in order to help in any way, but he could not speak. Many voices shouted and talked all at once, so that Ilya Andreich had no time to nod to them all; and the group grew in numbers, broke up, came together again, and moved, with a buzz of voices, to the large hall, to the large table. Pierre not only had not succeeded in speaking, he had been rudely interrupted, pushed aside, turned away from as a common enemy. This had happened not because they were displeased with the meaning of what he said—that had been forgotten, after the great number of speeches that followed it—but because, for inspiration, a crowd needs to have a tangible object of love and a tangible object of hatred. Pierre had become the latter. Many orators spoke after the animated nobleman, and they all spoke in the same vein. Many spoke beautifully and originally.

The editor of the *Russian Messenger*, Glinka, who was recognized ("The writer, the writer!" came from the crowd), said that hell should be repulsed by hell, and that he had seen a child smile at lightning flashes and thunderclaps, but that we were not going to be that child.

"Yes, yes, at thunderclaps!" was repeated approvingly from the back rows.

The crowd came to the large table at which sat the seventy-year-old dignitaries in their uniforms and sashes, grey-haired and bald, almost all of whom Pierre had seen in their homes with their buffoons and in the clubs over boston. The crowd came to the table, not ceasing to buzz. One after another, and sometimes two together, pressed up against the high backs of the chairs by the pushing crowd behind, the orators spoke. Those standing behind noticed the things that the orator did not say and hastened to say them. Others, in that heat and closeness, racked their brains in search of some sort of thought, and hastily spoke it. The old dignitaries whom Pierre knew sat and glanced now at one, now at another, and their expression for the most part said only that they found it very hot. Pierre, however, felt excited, and the general sense of a wish to show that it was all nothing to us, which was manifested more in sounds and facial expressions than in the meaning of their speeches, communicated itself to him as well. He did not renounce his thoughts, but he felt guilty of something and wanted to vindicate himself.

"I only said that it would be more appropriate if we made donations when we know what's needed," he said, trying to outshout the other voices.

The nearest little old man glanced round at him, but was at once distracted by shouting that started at the other end of the table.

"Yes, Moscow will be surrendered! She will be our redeemer!" shouted one.

"He's the enemy of mankind!" shouted another. "Allow me to speak . . . Gentlemen, you're crushing me! . . ."

XXIII

Just then, stepping briskly through the parting crowd of noblemen, in a general's uniform, with a sash over his shoulder, with his protruding chin and darting eyes, Count Rastopchin came in.

"The sovereign emperor will be here presently," said Rastopchin. "I've just come from there. I suppose that, in the position in which we find ourselves, there is not much to discuss. The sovereign has deigned to assemble us and the merchants," said Count Rastopchin. "Millions will pour from there," he pointed to the merchants' hall, "and our task is to raise a militia and not spare ourselves . . . That is the least we can do!"

Deliberations began among the dignitaries sitting at the table. The deliberations all went more than quietly. It even seemed sad when, after all the previous noise, the old voices were heard singly, one saying, "I agree," and another, for the sake of variety, "And I am of the same opinion," and so on.

The secretary was told to write down the resolution of the Moscow nobility that the Muscovites, like the people of Smolensk, would donate ten men per thousand with full equipment. The gentlemen of the session stood up as if relieved, scraping their chairs, and walked about the hall to stretch their legs, some arm in arm and talking.

"The sovereign! The sovereign!" suddenly spread through the hall, and the entire crowd rushed to the door.

Down a wide passage between walls of noblemen, the sovereign came into the hall. A respectful and frightened curiosity was expressed on all faces. Pierre was standing rather far away and could not hear all that the sovereign said. From what he did hear, he understood only that the sovereign was speaking of the danger the country was in, and of the hopes he placed in the Moscow nobility. Another voice responded to the sovereign, telling of the resolution just arrived at by the Moscow nobility.

"Gentlemen!" said the faltering voice of the sovereign; the crowd rustled and grew still again, and Pierre clearly heard the sovereign's voice, so pleasantly human and touched with emotion, saying: "I have never doubted the zeal of the Russian nobility. But today it has exceeded my expectations. I thank you on behalf of the fatherland. Gentlemen, let us act—time is most precious . . ."

The sovereign fell silent, the crowd began to press around him, and rapturous exclamations were heard on all sides.

"Yes, most precious . . . spoken like a tsar," the sobbing voice of Ilya Andreich said from behind. He had heard nothing, but had understood it all in his own way.

From the hall of the nobility, the sovereign passed into the hall of the merchants. He stayed there for about ten minutes. Pierre, among others, saw the sovereign come out of the merchants' hall with tears of tenderness in his eyes. As was learned later, the sovereign had just begun his speech to the merchants when tears gushed from his eyes, and he had finished it in a trembling voice. When Pierre saw the sovereign, he was coming out accompanied by two merchants. One was a fat tax farmer known to Pierre, the other a mayor with a thin, narrow-bearded, yellow face. Both were weeping. The thin one's eyes were filled with tears, but the fat tax farmer sobbed like a child and kept insisting:

"Take my life and my property, Your Majesty!"

Pierre had no other feelings at that moment except the desire to show that it was all nothing to him, and he was ready to sacrifice everything. He saw his speech with its constitutional tendency as a reproach to himself; he sought an occasion to smooth it over. Learning that Count Mamonov had donated a regiment, Bezukhov at once declared to Count Rastopchin that he was giving a thousand men and their maintenance.

Old Rostov could not tell his wife what had happened without tears, and at once agreed to Petya's demand, and went himself to sign him up.

The sovereign left the next day. All the assembled noblemen took off their uniforms, planted themselves at home or in the clubs again, and, groaning, gave their stewards orders about the militia, astonished at what they had done.

Part Two

I

Napoleon started the war with Russia because he could not help going to Dresden, could not help getting befuddled with honours, could not help putting on a Polish uniform, yielding to the heartening impression of a June morning, could not refrain from outbursts of anger in the presence of Kurakin and then of Balashov.

Alexander refused all negotiations because he felt himself personally offended. Barclay de Tolly tried to lead his army in the best fashion, so as to fulfil his duty and earn the glory of a great general. Rostov rode to the attack against the French because he could not resist the wish to go galloping across a level field. And all the countless persons who participated in this war acted in just the same way, as a result of their personal qualities, habits, conditions, and aims. They feared, boasted, rejoiced, resented, reasoned, supposing that they knew what they were doing and that they were doing it for themselves, and yet they were all involuntary instruments of history, and performed work hidden from them but comprehensible to us. Such is the inevitable fate of all men of action, and the higher they stand in the human hierarchy, the less free they are.

Now all the active figures of the year 1812 have long left their places, their personal interests have vanished without a trace, and only the historical results of that time stand before us.

But assume that the people of Europe, led by Napoleon, *had* to go into the depths of Russia and perish there, and all the self-contradictory, senseless, cruel activity of the people who participated in this war becomes comprehensible to us.

Providence made all these people, while striving to achieve their personal aims, contribute to the fulfilment of one enormous result, of which not one man (neither Napoleon, nor Alexander, still less any of the participants in the war) had the least expectation.

It is now clear to us what, in the year 1812, was the cause of the destruction of the French army. No one will dispute that the cause of the destruction of Napoleon's French forces was, on the one hand, their advance late in the year, without preparations for a winter march, into the depths of Russia, and, on the other hand, the character that the war took on with the burning of Russian towns and the hatred of the foe aroused in the Russian people. But then not only did no one foresee (what now seems obvious) that this was the only way that could lead to the destruction of an army of eight hundred thousand men, the best in the world and led by the best of generals, in conflict with a twice weaker Russian army, inexperienced and led by inexperienced generals; not only did *no one foresee this,* but all efforts *on the part of the Russians* were constantly aimed at hindering the one thing that could save Russia, and, *on the part of the French,* despite Napoleon's experience and so-called military genius, all efforts were aimed at extending as far as Moscow by the end of summer, that is, at doing the very thing that was to destroy them.

In historical writings about the year 1812, French authors like very much to speak of how Napoleon sensed the danger of extending his line, how he sought a battle, how his marshals advised him to stop at Smolensk, and to bring forth other similar arguments to prove that even then the danger of the campaign was supposedly understood; and Russian authors like still more to speak of how from the beginning of the campaign there existed a Scythian war plan of luring Napoleon into the depths of Russia, and one ascribes this plan to Pfuel, another to some Frenchman, another to Toll, another to the emperor Alexander himself, pointing to reports, projects, and letters that indeed contain hints at such a way of action. But all these hints at the foreseeing of what happened, both on the part of the French and on the part of the Russians, are now put forward only because events justified them. If the events had not occurred, those hints would have been forgotten, as thousands and millions of contrary hints and suppositions that were current then, but turned out to be incorrect, are now forgotten. There are always so many suppositions about the outcome of every event which takes place that, however it ends, people will always be found who say, "I said back then that it would be like this," quite forgetting that among the numberless suppositions, there were some that were completely contrary.

The suppositions about Napoleon's awareness of the danger of extending his line and, on the Russian side, about luring the enemy into the depths of Russia, obviously belong to this category, and it is only by greatly stretching a point that historians can ascribe such considerations to Napoleon and his marshals and such plans to the Russian commanders. All the facts completely contradict such suppositions. Not only was there no wish on the Russian side, during the whole time of the war, to lure the French into the depths of Russia, but everything was done to stop them from the moment of their entry into Russia; and not only was Napoleon not afraid of extending his line, but he rejoiced, as at a triumph, at his every step forward, and was very lazy, not as in his previous campaigns, in seeking a battle.

At the very beginning of the campaign, our armies are cut in two, and the one goal we aim at consists in reuniting them, though for retreating and luring the enemy into the depths of the country, uniting the armies is not advantageous. The emperor is with the army to inspire it to defend every step of Russian soil, and not to retreat. The enormous camp on the Drissa is set up according to Pfuel's plan with no intention of retreating further. The sovereign reproaches the commanders in chief for every step in retreat. Not only the burning of Moscow, but even the enemy's advance as far as Smolensk cannot present itself to the emperor's imagination, and when the armies unite, the sovereign is indignant that Smolensk is taken and burned and no general battle is given before its walls.

So thinks the sovereign, but the Russian commanders and all Russian people are still more indignant at the thought that our forces are retreating into the depths of the country.

Napoleon, having cut our armies in two, moves into the depths of the country and lets slip several chances for battle. In the month of August, he is in Smolensk, and his only thought is of going further, though, as we now see, this movement forward obviously spells destruction for him.

The facts say the obvious thing, that Napoleon did not foresee the danger of moving on Moscow, nor did Alexander and the Russian commanders think then about luring Napoleon, but both thought the opposite. The drawing of Napoleon into the depths of the country occurred not according to someone's plan (no one even believed in such a possibility), but occurred as the result of the most complex interplay of intrigues, aims, and desires of the people participating in the war, who did not perceive what was to happen and what would be the only salvation of Russia. It all occurs by chance. At the beginning of the campaign, the armies are cut in two. We attempt to unite them with the obvious goal of giving battle and holding up the enemy's advance, but in this attempt to unite, avoiding battles with the stronger enemy and involuntarily retreating at a sharp angle, we draw the enemy as far as Smolensk. But it is not enough to say that we retreat at a sharp angle, because the French are moving between the two armies—the angle becomes sharper still, and we pull further back, because Barclay de Tolly, an unpopular German,[1] is hateful to Bagration (who is to be under his leadership), and Bagration, commanding the second army, tries to take as long as possible to unite with Barclay and put himself under his command. Bagration does not unite with him for a long time (though the main goal of the entire leadership lies in this union), because it seems to him that in this march he is putting his army in danger and that the most advantageous thing for him will be to retreat more to the left and south, worrying the enemy from the flank and the rear, and filling out his army in the Ukraine. But it seems he has thought up this plan because he does not want to submit to the hateful and junior-ranking German Barclay.

The emperor stays with the army in order to inspire it, but his presence, and his not knowing what to decide on, and the enormous number of advisers and plans, destroys the first army's energy for action, and the army retreats.

At the Drissa camp the army is supposed to stop; but Paulucci, who aims at becoming commander in chief, unexpectedly affects Alexander with his energy, and Pfuel's whole plan is dropped, and the whole business is entrusted to Barclay. But since Barclay does not inspire confidence, his power is restricted.

The armies are divided, there is no unity of leadership, Barclay is unpopular; but this confusion, division, and the unpopularity of the German commander in chief results, on the one hand, in indecision and the avoidance of battle (from which it would have been impossible to refrain if the armies had been together and had not had Barclay for commander in chief), and, on the other hand, in a greater and greater indignation against the Germans and the arousing of a patriotic spirit.

The sovereign finally leaves the army, and the sole and most convenient pretext chosen for his departure is the notion that he must inspire the people in the capitals to arouse a national war. And this visit of the sovereign to Moscow triples the forces of the Russian army.

The sovereign leaves the army so as not to get in the way of the commander in chief's unity of power, and hopes that more resolute measures will be taken; but the situation of the army leadership becomes still weaker and more confused. Bennigsen, the grand duke, and a swarm of adjutant generals remain in the army to watch over the actions of the commander in chief and rouse his energy, and Barclay, feeling himself still less free under the eyes of all these *eyes of the sovereign,* becomes still more wary of decisive actions and avoids battle.

Barclay stands for wariness. The grand duke hints at treason and demands a general battle. Lubomirski, Branicki, Wlocki, and their like fan this noise so much that Barclay, under the pretext of delivering some papers to the sovereign, sends the Polish adjutants to Petersburg and enters into open struggle with Bennigsen and the grand duke.

Finally, in Smolensk, much as Bagration did not wish it, the two armies unite.

Bagration drives up in a carriage to the house occupied by Barclay. Barclay puts on his sash, comes out to meet him, and reports to his senior in rank Bagration. Bagration, in this contest of magnanimity, despite his seniority of rank, subordinates himself to Barclay; but, while subordinating himself, agrees with him still less. Bagration, at the sovereign's order, reports to him personally. He writes to Arakcheev:

Be it as my sovereign wills, but I can in no way work with this *minister* [Barclay].[2] For God's sake, send me somewhere, even if it is to command a regiment, but I cannot be here; and the whole headquarters is full of Germans, so that it is impossible for a Russian to live, and it is to no avail. I thought I was truly serving the sovereign and the fatherland, but on closer inspection it turns out that I am serving Barclay. I confess, I do not want to.

The swarm of Branickis, Wintzingerodes, and their like poisons relations between the commanders still more, and the result is still less unity. They prepare to attack the French before Smolensk. A general is sent to reconnoitre the positions. The general, who hates Barclay, goes to his friend, the commander of a corps, spends the whole day with him, returns to Barclay, and condemns point by point the future battlefield, which he has not seen.

While the arguments and intrigues about the future battlefield go on, while we search for the French, mistaking their whereabouts, the French stumble upon Neverovsky's division and come right up to the walls of Smolensk.

It is necessary to accept the unexpected battle at Smolensk in order to save our lines of communication. Battle is given. Thousands are killed on both sides.

Smolensk is abandoned against the will of the sovereign and all the people. But Smolensk is burned by its own inhabitants, deceived by their governor, and the ruined inhabitants set an example for other Russians, going to Moscow, thinking only of their losses, and kindling hatred for the enemy. Napoleon goes further, we retreat, and the very thing is achieved that was to defeat Napoleon.

II

On the day after his son's departure, Prince Nikolai Andreevich summoned Princess Marya to him.

"Well, what, are you pleased now?" he said to her. "You've made me quarrel with my son! Are you pleased? That's all you needed! Are you pleased? . . . It pains me, pains me. I'm old and weak, and you wanted it. Well, rejoice, rejoice . . ." And after that Princess Marya did not see her father for a week. He was sick and did not leave his study.

To her surprise, Princess Marya noticed that during the time of his illness, the old prince did not admit Mlle Bourienne to his rooms either. Tikhon alone took care of him.

After a week, the old prince came out and took up his former life again, busying himself especially actively with constructions and gardens and stopping all his former relations with Mlle Bourienne. His look and cold tone with Princess Marya seemed to say to her: "See, you thought up things against me, you lied to Prince Andrei about my relations with this Frenchwoman, and made me quarrel with him; but you see, I need neither you nor the Frenchwoman."

One half of the day Princess Marya spent with Nikolushka, supervising his lessons, giving him lessons in Russian and music herself, and talking with Dessales; the other part of the day she spent in her rooms with books, her old nanny, and God's people, who sometimes came to her by the back door.

About the war Princess Marya thought as women think about war. She feared for her brother, who was there; was horrified, not understanding it, at the cruelty of people, which made them kill each other; but she did not understand the significance of this war, which seemed to her the same as all other wars. She did not understand the significance of this war, even though Dessales, her constant interlocutor, passionately interested in the course of the war, tried to explain his reflections to her, and even though God's people, who came to see her, spoke with horror, each in his own way, of popular rumours about the coming of the Antichrist, and even though Julie, now Princess Drubetskoy, who had again entered into correspondence with her, wrote her patriotic letters from Moscow.³

I write to you in Russian, my good friend, because I have hatred for all Frenchmen as well as their language, which I cannot hear to speak . . . We in Moscow are all ravished through enthusiasm for our adored emperor.

My poor husband suffers travails and hunger in Jewish pot-houses; but the news which I have inspires me still more.

You must have heard about the heroic deed of Raevsky, in embracing his two sons and saying: "I shall perish with them, but we will not waver!" And indeed, though the enemy was twice stronger, we did not waver. We pass our time as we can; but in war as in war. Princess Alina and Sophie sit whole days with me, and we, unfortunate widows of living husbands, make beautiful conversations over the lint;⁴ only you, my friend, are lacking . . .

And so on.

Princess Marya did not understand the whole significance of the war mainly because the old prince never spoke of it, did not acknowledge it, and at dinner laughed at Dessales when he talked of this war. The prince's tone was so calm and assured that Princess Marya unreasoningly believed him.

For the whole month of July the old prince was extremely active and even animated. He started a new garden and a new building, constructed for the servants. One thing that troubled Princess Marya was that he slept little, and, having abandoned his habit of sleeping in the study, changed his sleeping place every day. One day he would order his camp bed made up in the gallery, then he would remain on the sofa or the Voltaire armchair in the drawing room and doze off without undressing, while, instead of Mlle Bourienne, the boy Petrusha read to him, then he would spend the night in the dining room.

On the first of August, a second letter came from Prince Andrei. In his first letter, which had come soon after his departure, Prince Andrei had humbly asked his father's forgiveness for what he had allowed himself to tell him and asked to be restored to his favour. To this the old man had replied with an affectionate letter, and after that letter had distanced the Frenchwoman from himself. The second letter from Prince Andrei, written from near Vitebsk after the French had occupied it, consisted of a brief description of the whole campaign, with a map drawn in the letter, and of reflections on the further course of the campaign. In this letter, Prince Andrei pointed out to his father the inconvenience of his position near the theatre of war, directly in the line of movement of the troops, and advised him to go to Moscow.

That day at dinner, when Dessales said he had heard that the French had already entered Vitebsk, the old prince remembered about Prince Andrei's letter.

"I received a letter from Prince Andrei today," he said to Princess Marya. "Have you read it?"

"No, *mon père*," the princess replied fearfully. She could not have read a letter the reception of which she had not even heard about.

"He writes about this war," the prince said, with that contemptuous smile that had become habitual to him whenever he spoke about the ongoing war.

"It must be very interesting," said Dessales. "The prince is in a position to know . . ."

"Ah, very interesting!" said Mlle Bourienne.

"Go and fetch it for me," the old prince turned to Mlle Bourienne. "You know, on the little table under the paperweight."

Mlle Bourienne jumped up joyfully.

"Ah, no," he cried, frowning. "You go, Mikhail Ivanych."

Mikhail Ivanych got up and went to the study. But as soon as he left, the old prince looked around uneasily, threw down his napkin, and went himself.

"They can't do anything, they get it all muddled."

While he was gone, Princess Marya, Dessales, Mlle Bourienne, and even Nikolushka silently exchanged glances. The old prince came back with hurried steps, accompanied by Mikhail Ivanych, with the letter and a plan, which he put down next to him, not letting anyone read them during dinner.

Having moved to the drawing room, he gave the letter to Princess Marya and, spreading out in front of him the plan of the new construction, at which he directed his eyes, told her to read it aloud. When she had read the letter, Princess Marya gave her father a questioning glance. He was looking at the plan, obviously immersed in his thoughts.

"What do you think of that, Prince?" Dessales allowed himself to address him with a question.

"I? I? . . ." said the prince, as if unpleasantly awakened, without taking his eyes from the construction plan.

"It's quite possible that the theatre of war will get so close to us . . ."

"Ha, ha, ha! The theatre of war!" said the prince. "I have said and I still say that the theatre of war is Poland, and the enemy will never penetrate beyond the Niemen."

Dessales looked with astonishment at the prince, who spoke of the Niemen when the enemy was already at the Dnieper; but Princess Marya, who had forgotten the geographical position of the Niemen, thought that what her father had said was true.

"The snow will melt, and they'll drown in the Polish swamps. Only they could fail to see that," said the prince, evidently thinking of the campaign of 1807, which took place, as it seemed to him, so recently. "Bennigsen should have entered Prussia sooner, then things would have taken a different turn . . ."

"But, Prince," Dessales said timidly, "the letter mentions Vitebsk . . ."

"Ah, yes, the letter . . ." the prince said with displeasure, "yes . . . yes . . ." His face suddenly took on a dark expression. He paused. "Yes, he writes that the French were crushed—by what river was it?"

Dessales lowered his eyes.

"The prince writes nothing about that," he said softly.

"He doesn't? Well, I didn't think it up myself." Everyone was silent for a long time.

"Yes . . . yes . . . So, Mikhail Ivanych," he said suddenly, raising his head and pointing to the construction plan, "tell me how you want to change it . . ."

Mikhail Ivanych went over to the plan, and the prince, having talked with him about the plan for the new construction, glanced angrily at Princess Marya and Dessales and went to his room.

Princess Marya saw the embarrassed and astonished glance Dessales directed at her father, noticed his silence, and was struck to see that her father had forgotten his son's letter on the table in the drawing room; but she was afraid not only to speak and ask Dessales about the cause of his embarrassment and silence, but afraid even to think about it.

In the evening, Mikhail Ivanych, sent by the prince, came to Princess Marya for Prince Andrei's letter, which had been forgotten in the drawing room. Princess Marya handed him the letter. Though it was unpleasant for her, she allowed herself to ask Mikhail Ivanych what her father was doing.

"He keeps bustling about," Mikhail Ivanych said with a respectfully mocking smile, which made Princess Marya turn pale. "He's very anxious about the new building. He read for a while, and now," said Mikhail Ivanych, lowering his voice, "he's at his desk, must be busy with his will." (Lately one of the prince's favourite occupations had been busying himself with the papers that were to be left after his death and which he called his will.)

"And Alpatych is being sent to Smolensk?" asked Princess Marya.

"That he is, ma'am, he's been waiting a long time."

III

When Mikhail Ivanych came back to the study with the letter, the prince, wearing spectacles, with a shade over his eyes and over the candle, was sitting at the open bureau, with papers in his outstretched hand, reading in a somewhat solemn pose his "remarks" (as he called them), to be delivered to the sovereign after his death.

When Mikhail Ivanych came in, his eyes were filled with tears of remembrance of the time when he had been writing what he was now reading. He took the letter from Mikhail Ivanych's hands, put it in his pocket, put his papers away, and called the already long-waiting Alpatych.

He had written what he needed from Smolensk on a sheet of paper, and, walking across the room past Alpatych, who was waiting at the door, he began giving orders.

"First, some stationery, do you hear? Eight quires. Here's a sample; gilt-edged . . . a sample, get exactly the same thing. Varnish, sealing wax—as on Mikhail Ivanych's list."

He took a few steps around the room and glanced at his memorandum.

"Then deliver the letter about the deed to the governor in person."

Then door bolts were needed for the new construction, of exactly the design the prince himself had devised. Then an ironbound box had to be ordered to keep the will in.

The giving of instructions to Alpatych went on for more than two hours. The prince would not let him go. He sat down, fell to thinking, and, closing his eyes, dozed off. Alpatych stirred.

"Well, off you go, off you go. If I need anything, I'll send for you."

Alpatych left. The prince went over to the bureau again, looked into it, touched his papers with his hand, locked it again, and sat down at the desk to write the letter to the governor.

It was already late when he stood up, having sealed the letter. He wanted to sleep, but he knew he would not be able to fall asleep and that the worst thoughts came to him in bed. He called Tikhon and walked about the rooms with him, so as to tell him where to make up his bed for that night. He walked about, sizing up every little corner.

Everywhere seemed bad to him, but worst of all was his customary couch in the study. This couch was frightful to him, probably because of the painful thoughts that came to him as he lay on it. Nowhere was good, but in any case the best of all was the little corner in the sitting room behind the piano: he had never yet slept there.

Tikhon and another servant brought the bed and began to make it up.

"Not like that, not like that!" cried the prince, and he himself moved it a few inches further from the corner, then a little closer again.

"Well, I've finally done everything, now I can rest," thought the prince, and he allowed Tikhon to undress him.

Wincing vexedly at the efforts that had to be made in order to take off his kaftan and trousers, the prince undressed, lowered himself heavily onto the bed, and seemed to lapse into thought, looking contemptuously at his yellow, shrivelled legs. He did not lapse into thought, but hesitated before the labour that faced him of raising those legs and shifting himself onto the bed. "Oh, how hard it is! Oh, if only these labours would be over quickly, quickly, and *you* would release me!" he thought. Compressing his lips, he made this effort for the twentieth time and lay down. But just as he lay down, the whole bed suddenly began moving rhythmically back and forth under him, as if breathing heavily and jostling. This happened to him almost every night. He opened his just-closing eyes.

"No peace, curse you!" he growled angrily at someone. "Yes, yes, there was something important, something very important, that I was saving for the night in bed. The door bolts? No, I said that. No, it was something that was in the drawing room. Princess Marya blathered something. Dessales—that fool— said something. Something in my pocket—I don't remember."

"Tishka! What were we talking about at dinner?"

"About the prince, Mikhail . . ."

"Silence, silence." The prince slapped his hand on the table. "Yes! I know, Prince Andrei's letter. Princess Marya read it. Dessales said something about Vitebsk. I'll read it now."

He had the letter taken from his pocket and a little table with lemonade and a spiral wax candle moved closer to the bed, and, putting on his spectacles, began to read. Only now, in the quiet of night, by the faint light from under the green shade, reading through the letter, did he momentarily grasp its meaning for the first time.

"The French are in Vitebsk, in four days' march they may be in Smolensk; they may be there already."

"Tishka!" Tikhon jumped up. "No, never mind, never mind!" he cried.

He hid the letter under the candlestick and closed his eyes. And before him stood the Danube, bright noonday, bullrushes, the Russian camp, and he, a young general, without a wrinkle on his face, brisk, cheerful, red-cheeked, goes into Potemkin's decorated tent, and a burning feeling of envy of the favourite, as strong now as it was then, stirs him. And he remembers all the words that were said then at his first meeting with Potemkin. And before him stands a short, fat woman with a yellow tint to her fleshy face—the mother-empress, her smiles, her words when she received him, with favours, for the first time, and he remembers the same face on a catafalque, and his clash with Zubov, who then stood by her coffin, over his right to go up and kiss her hand.

"Ah, quickly, quickly go back to that time, and let all this now be finished as quickly as possible, and let them leave me in peace!"

IV

Bald Hills, the estate of Prince Nikolai Andreich Bolkonsky, lay forty miles east of Smolensk and two miles from the Moscow road.

The same evening that the prince gave orders to Alpatych, Dessales, having demanded to see Princess Marya, told her that, as the prince was not quite well, and was taking no measures for his own safety, and it was clear from Prince Andrei's letter that to stay at Bald Hills was unsafe, he respectfully advised her to write and send with Alpatych her own letter to the head of the province in Smolensk, asking him to inform her about the situation and the degree of danger Bald Hills was exposed to. Dessales wrote a letter to the governor for Princess Marya, she signed it, and this letter was given to Alpatych with orders to deliver it to the governor and, in case of danger, to return as soon as possible.

Having received all his orders, Alpatych, accompanied by the domestics, in a white felt hat (the prince's gift), with a stick, just like the prince, came out to get into the little leather kibitka, harnessed to a troika of well-fed roans.

The bell was tied up, and the harness bells were stopped with bits of paper. The prince did not allow anyone in Bald Hills to drive with bells. But Alpatych liked bells on a long journey. Alpatych's courtiers—the land reeve, the clerk, the scullery maid, the cook, two old women, a boy servant, the coachmen, and other domestics—saw him off.

His daughter tucked some down-filled chintz pillows behind his back and under him. His old sister-in-law gave him a little bundle on the sly. One of the coachmen supported his arm as he got in.

"Well, well, women's preparations! Women, women!" Alpatych, huffing, said in a patter, just the way the prince said it, and got into the kibitka. Giving the land reeve some last orders about work, Alpatych, no longer imitating the prince, took the hat from his bald head and crossed himself three times.

"If there's anything . . . you come back, Yakov Alpatych; for Christ's sake, have pity on us," his wife cried to him, hinting at the rumours about the war and the enemy.

"Women, women, women's preparations," Alpatych said to himself and drove off, looking at the fields around him, some with already yellow rye, some with bushy, still-green oats, some still black where the cross-ploughing was just beginning. Alpatych drove along, admiring the rare yield of this year's spring

crops, looking attentively at the strips of rye, in which the reaping was beginning here and there, and having a steward's thoughts about sowing and harvesting, and about not forgetting any of the prince's orders.

Having fed his horses twice on the way, on the evening of the fourth of
August Alpatych arrived in town.

On his way, Alpatych met and passed baggage trains and troops. Driving up
to Smolensk, he heard distant shooting, but these sounds did not strike him.
What struck him most strongly was when, nearing Smolensk, he saw a beautiful field of oats, which some soldiers were mowing, evidently for fodder, and
on which they had pitched their camp; this circumstance struck Alpatych, but
he soon forgot it, thinking about his own business.

All the interests of Alpatych's life for the past thirty years had been confined
to the prince's will alone, and he never went outside that circle. Anything that
did not concern the fulfilling of the prince's orders not only did not interest
Alpatych, but did not exist for him.

Alpatych, arriving in Smolensk on the evening of the fourth of August,
stopped across the Dnieper, in the suburb of Gachena, at the inn kept by
the innkeeper Ferapontov, where he had been accustomed to stay for the
past thirty years. Twelve years before, Ferapontov, with a bit of a hand from
Alpatych, had bought a woods from the prince, went into commerce, and now
owned a house, an inn, and a flour shop in the provincial capital. Ferapontov
was a fat, black-haired, red-faced forty-year-old man, with thick lips, a fat
lump of a nose, similar lumps on his forehead over his black, beetling brows,
and a fat belly.

Ferapontov, in a waistcoat and a chintz shirt, was standing in the street by
the door to his shop. Seeing Alpatych, he went up to him.

"Welcome, Yakov Alpatych. Folk are leaving, and you come," said the
innkeeper.

"Leaving? Why so?" asked Alpatych.

"And I say they're stupid folk. Always afraid of the French."

"Women's talk, women's talk!" said Alpatych.

"I reason the same way, Yakov Alpatych. I say there's orders not to let them
in—it's a sure thing. And the peasants are asking three roubles for a cart—
that's heathenish!"

Yakov Alpatych listened inattentively. He asked for a samovar and some hay
for the horses and, having had his tea, went to bed.

All night troops moved down the street past the inn. The next day, Alpatych
put on the tunic that he wore only in town and went about his business. The
morning was sunny, and by eight o'clock it was already hot. A precious day for
harvesting, Alpatych thought. Outside town, shooting had been heard since
early morning.

By eight o'clock, cannon fire had joined the musket shots. There were many people in the streets, hurrying somewhere, and many soldiers, but the cabbies drove around as usual, shopkeepers stood by their shops, and services went on in the churches. Alpatych went to the shops, to the government offices, to the post office, and to the governor. In the government offices, in the shops, at the post office, everyone was talking about the troops, about the enemy, who was already attacking the town; they were all asking each other what to do, and they were all trying to reassure each other.

At the governor's house, Alpatych found a large number of people, Cossacks, and a travelling carriage belonging to the governor. On the porch, Yakov Alpatych met two gentlemen, one of whom he knew. The gentleman he knew, a former district police captain, was speaking vehemently.

"It's no joking matter," he said. "It's all right if you're alone. A man alone can be poor alone, but if you have a family of thirteen and all your possessions . . . They've brought us all to ruin, what sort of authorities are they? . . . I'd hang all the brigands . . ."

"Well, that'll do," said the other.

"What do I care, let him hear! Why, we're not dogs," said the former police captain and, looking around, he saw Alpatych.

"Ah, Yakov Alpatych, what brings you here?"

"Orders from his excellency, to see the governor," replied Alpatych, proudly holding up his head and laying his hand on his bosom, as he always did when he mentioned the prince . . . "He was pleased to order me to enquire into the state of affairs," he said.

"Go ahead, enquire," cried the gentleman. "They've brought it to the point where there's no carts, nothing! . . . There, do you hear?" he said, pointing in the direction from which the shooting was heard.

"They've brought us all to ruin . . . brigands!" he said again and stepped off the porch.

Alpatych shook his head and went up the steps. In the waiting room there were merchants, women, officials, silently exchanging glances with each other. The door to the office opened; they all stood up and moved forward. An official ran out, said something to a merchant, told a fat official with a cross on his neck to follow him, and again disappeared behind the door, obviously avoiding all the glances and questions addressed to him. Alpatych moved to the front, and at the official's next emergence, placing his hand inside his buttoned tunic, addressed the official, handing him two letters.

"To Baron Asch from General in Chief Prince Bolkonsky," he intoned so solemnly and significantly that the official turned to him and took his letters. A few minutes later, the governor received Alpatych and hurriedly said to him:

"Inform the prince and princess that nothing was known to me: I have been acting on orders from above—here . . ."

He handed Alpatych a paper.

"However, as the prince is unwell, I advise them to go to Moscow. I am going there myself presently. Tell . . ." But the governor did not finish. A dusty and sweaty officer came running in and began saying something in French. A look of terror appeared on the governor's face.

"Go," he said, nodding to Alpatych, and he started asking the officer something. Greedy, frightened, helpless eyes turned to Alpatych when he came out of the governor's office. Involuntarily listening now to the near and ever-increasing gunfire, Alpatych hurried to the inn. The paper that the governor gave to Alpatych was the following:

I assure you that the town of Smolensk is not yet threatened with the least danger, and it is unlikely that it will be. I on one side and Prince Bagration on the other are moving to unite before Smolensk, which will take place on the twenty-second instant, and the joint forces of the two armies will defend the compatriots of the province entrusted to you, until their efforts have beaten back the enemy of the fatherland or until the last warrior of their valiant ranks has perished. From this you will see that you have full right to set the inhabitants of Smolensk at ease, for those defended by two such valiant armies can be certain of victory. (Directive from Barclay de Tolly to the civil governor of Smolensk, Baron Asch, 1812.)[5]

People were worriedly milling about in the streets.

Carts heaped high with household wares, chairs, cupboards kept coming out of the gates of houses and driving down the streets. At the house next to Ferapontov's, wagons stood and women, bidding farewell, wailed and murmured. A yard dog, barking, fidgeted about in front of the harnessed horses.

Alpatych, at a more hurried pace than usual, came into the yard and went straight to the shed for his horses and cart. The coachman was asleep; he woke him, told him to hitch up, and went into the front hall. From the innkeeper's room came the sound of a child crying, a woman's rending sobs, and the angry, hoarse shouting of Ferapontov. The cook, like a frightened hen, fluttered up in the front hall as soon as Alpatych came in.

"He killed her—he beat the mistress! . . . How he beat her, how he dragged her! . . ."

"What for?" asked Alpatych.

"She was begging to leave. It's a woman's thing! 'Take me away,' she says, 'don't let me and the little children perish. People have all left,' she says, 'what about us?' And he started beating her. How he beat her, how he dragged her!"

Alpatych seemed to nod his head approvingly at these words, and, not wishing to know any more, went to the door of the room opposite the innkeeper's, where he had left his purchases.

"You villain! Murderer!" a thin, pale woman cried out at that moment, and, a baby in her arms, the kerchief torn from her head, she burst through the door and ran down the steps to the yard. Ferapontov came out after her and, seeing Alpatych, straightened his waistcoat, smoothed his hair, yawned, and followed Alpatych into the room.

"So you mean to leave already?" he asked.

Without answering the question or turning to look at the innkeeper, Alpatych, sorting his purchases, asked how much he owed for his stay.

"I'll reckon up! Well, have you been to the governor's?" asked Ferapontov. "What's the decision?"

Alpatych replied that the governor had told him decidedly nothing.

"The way we are here, how can we leave?" said Ferapontov. "Seven roubles a cart as far as Dorogobuzh. Like I said, it's heathenish!" he said.

"Selivanov, he was in luck on Thursday, sold flour to the army at nine roubles a sack. Well, do you want tea?" he added. While the horses were being hitched up, Alpatych and Ferapontov drank their tea and talked about the price of wheat, about the crops and the good weather for harvesting.

"It's quieting down, though," said Ferapontov, having drunk three cups of tea and getting up. "Must be our side won. They said they wouldn't let them. So they're strong . . . And today I heard tell that Matvei Ivanych Platov drove them into the river Marina, got some eighteen thousand drownded in one day."

Alpatych gathered up his purchases, gave them to the entering coachman, and paid the innkeeper. From the gates came the sound of wheels, hooves, and bells from the little kibitka rolling out.

It was already long past noon; half the street was in shadow, the other half brightly lit by the sun. Alpatych glanced out of the window and went to the door. Suddenly there came the strange sound of a distant whistling and a thud, and after that the merging roar of cannon fire, which made the windows shake.

Alpatych went outside; two men were running down the street towards the bridge. From different sides came the whistle and thud of cannonballs and the explosions of shells falling on the town. But the inhabitants scarcely heard or paid attention to these noises in comparison with the sound of gunfire outside town. This was the bombardment of the town which Napoleon had ordered opened from a hundred and thirty cannon starting at four o'clock. At first people did not understand the meaning of this bombardment.

The sounds of the falling shells and cannonballs aroused only curiosity at first. Ferapontov's wife, who till then had not stopped wailing in the shed, fell silent and came out to the gates with the baby in her arms, looking silently at people and listening to the sounds.

The cook and the shop clerk came out to the gates. Everyone tried with merry curiosity to catch sight of the projectiles racing over their heads. Several men came round the corner, talking animatedly.

"Some force!" said one. "It just smashed the roof and ceiling to splinters."

"Rooted up the earth like a pig," said another. "That's a grand thing, that cheers you up!" he said, laughing. "Lucky you jumped out of the way, or it would have flattened you."

People began to address these men. They stopped and told how a cannonball had struck a house right next to them. Meanwhile more projectiles, now cannonballs with their quick, grim whistle, now shells with their pleasant whine, went on flying over people's heads; but not a single one fell nearby, they all carried too far. Alpatych was getting into the little kibitka. The innkeeper was standing at the gate.

"As if there's anything to see!" he shouted to the cook, who, her sleeves rolled up, in her red skirt, swinging her bare elbows, went to the corner to hear what was being said.

"What a wonder!" she kept saying, but, hearing the innkeeper's voice, she came back, straightening her tucked-up skirt.

Again, very close this time, something whistled, like a bird flying down from above, fire flashed in the middle of the street, something went off, and the street was covered with smoke.

"Villain, what did you do that for?" cried the innkeeper, running to the cook.

At the same moment, women wailed pitifully on all sides, a frightened child wept, and people with pale faces silently crowded around the cook. In this crowd, the cook's moaning and pleading were heard most of all.

"Ahh, my dear hearts! My dear, kind hearts! Don't let me die! My dear, kind hearts! . . ."

Five minutes later there was no one left in the street. The cook, her hip smashed by a shell splinter, had been carried to the kitchen. Alpatych, his coachman, Ferapontov's wife and children, the yard porter were sitting in the cellar listening. The noise of the guns, the whistle of projectiles, and the pitiful moaning of the cook rising above all the other sounds, did not stop for a moment. The innkeeper's wife now rocked and comforted the baby, now asked each person who came to the cellar what had become of her husband, who had stayed outside. The shop clerk, who came to the cellar, told her that the innkeeper had gone with other people to the cathedral, where the miracle-working icon of Smolensk had been taken up.[6]

Towards dusk the cannonade began to subside. Alpatych came out of the cellar and stopped in the doorway. The previously clear evening sky was all covered with smoke. And through this smoke the light of the young crescent moon, high in the sky, shone strangely. After the terrible roar of the guns ceased, silence seemed to hang over the town, broken only by the rustle of footsteps, groans, distant shouts, and the crackle of fires spread all over town. The cook's moans now subsided. On two sides, the black smoke of fires rose and spread. Soldiers walked and ran down the streets, not in ranks, but like ants from a demolished anthill, in various uniforms and in various directions. Several of them ran into Ferapontov's yard before Alpatych's eyes. Alpatych went to the gate. Some regiment, crowding and hurrying, blocked the street on its way out of town.

"The town has surrendered—leave, leave," an officer said, noticing his figure, and at once turned to the soldiers, shouting:

"I'll teach you to go running into yards!"

Apatych went back to the cottage and, calling the coachman, told him to set off. After Alpatych and the coachman, Ferapontov's entire household came out. Seeing the smoke and even the flames of the fires that had now become visible in the falling twilight, the women, so far silent, suddenly began to howl, looking at the fires. As if seconding them, the same lamenting came from the ends of the street. In the shed, Alpatych and the coachman, with trembling hands, straightened the tangled reins and harness of the horses.

As Alpatych was driving through the gate, he saw some ten soldiers in Ferapontov's open shop, talking loudly and filling sacks and bags with wheat flour and sunflower seeds. Just then Ferapontov came into the shop from the street. Seeing the soldiers, he was about to shout something, but suddenly stopped and, clutching his hair, burst into sobbing laughter.

"Take it all, lads! Don't leave it for those devils!" he shouted, seizing the sacks himself and throwing them outside. Some of the soldiers got frightened and ran away, some went on pouring. Seeing Alpatych, Ferapontov turned to him.

"Done for! Russia!" he cried. "Alpatych! She's done for! I'll set the fire myself! She's done for!" Ferapontov ran out to the yard.

A constant stream of soldiers went down the street, blocking it entirely, so that Alpatych could not drive out and had to wait. Ferapontov's wife and children were also sitting on a cart waiting until they could leave.

It was already night. There were stars in the sky, and the young moon shone, covered from time to time by the smoke. On the descent to the Dnieper, the wagons of Alpatych and the innkeeper's wife, moving slowly amidst the lines of soldiers and other vehicles, had to stop. Not far from the intersection at which the wagons stopped, in a lane, a house and some shops were burning. The fire was already going out. The flames died down and were lost in black smoke, then suddenly flared up brightly, lighting up with a strange distinctness the faces of the crowding people standing at the intersection. Before the fire the black figures of people flitted; talking and shouting could be heard through the ceaseless crackling of the flames. Alpatych, getting out of the wagon, saw that the way would not soon be free, and turned into the lane to look at the fire. Soldiers constantly darted up and down past the fire, and Alpatych saw two soldiers, and with them some man in a frieze overcoat, drag burning beams out of the fire and across the street to a neighbouring yard, while others carried armfuls of straw.

Alpatych went up to a large crowd of people standing in front of a tall barn that was burning at full blaze. The walls were all on fire, the back wall fell, the plank roof was caving in, the beams were in flames. The crowd was apparently waiting for the roof to fall. Alpatych also waited for that.

"Alpatych!" someone's familiar voice called to the old man.

"Your Excellency, dearest," replied Alpatych, instantly recognizing the voice of his young prince.

Prince Andrei, in a cloak, astride a black horse, was standing behind the crowd and looking at Alpatych.

"What are you doing here?" he asked.

"Your . . . Your Excellency," Alpatych said and burst into sobs . . . "Your . . . Your . . . and are we lost, then? Your father . . ."

"What are you doing here?" Prince Andrei repeated.

The flames flared up brightly just then, and lit up for Alpatych his young master's pale and exhausted face. Alpatych told him how he had been sent and how he had barely been able to leave.

"So, Your Excellency, are we lost?" he asked again.

Prince Andrei, without answering, took out a notebook and, raising his knee, began to pencil something on a torn-out page. He was writing to his sister:

Smolensk is being surrendered. Bald Hills will be occupied by the enemy within a week. Leave for Moscow at once. Reply to me the moment you leave; send a messenger to Usvyazh.

Having written the note and handed it to Alpatych, he told him how to arrange the departure of the prince, the princess, and his son with his tutor, and how and where to reply to him at once. Before he had time to finish these orders, a mounted staff officer, accompanied by his suite, rode up to him.

"Are you a colonel?" the officer cried with a German accent in a voice familiar to Prince Andrei. "Houses are set on fire in your presence, and you stand there? What does this mean? You will answer for it," cried Berg, who was now assistant to the chief of staff of the left flank of the infantry of the first army — a quite agreeable and visible post, as Berg put it.

Prince Andrei looked at him and, without replying, went on addressing Alpatych:

"Tell them that I will wait for a reply until the tenth, and if I don't know by the tenth that everyone is gone, I'll have to drop everything and come to Bald Hills myself."

"I said it, Prince," said Berg, recognizing Prince Andrei, "only because I must carry out orders, because I always carry them out precisely . . . Excuse me, please," Berg apologized for something.

Something cracked in the fire. The fire subsided for a moment; black clouds of smoke poured from under the roof. Something cracked still more fearfully in the flames, and something enormous collapsed.

"Hoo-hoo-hoo!" roared the crowd, seconding the collapsed ceiling of the barn, from which came a smell of pancakes produced by the burning grain. The flames flared up and illuminated the animatedly joyful and worn-out faces of the people who stood around the fire.

The man in the frieze overcoat, raising his arm, cried:

"That's grand! Went right up! That's really grand, lads!"

"It's the owner himself," voices said.

"So, then," said Prince Andrei, turning to Alpatych, "convey everything as I've told you." And without saying a word to Berg, who stood silent beside him, he spurred his horse and rode down the lane.

V

From Smolensk the troops continued to retreat. The enemy followed after them. On the tenth of August, the regiment under Prince Andrei's command was going down the high road past the avenue that led to Bald Hills. The heat and drought had lasted for more than three weeks. Every day fleecy clouds crossed the sky, occasionally covering the sun; but towards evening it cleared up again, and the sun set in a reddish brown murk. Only the heavy dews at night refreshed the earth. The standing wheat was scorched and spilled its grains. The swamps dried up. The cattle lowed from hunger, finding no food in the sun-parched meadows. It was cool only at night and in the woods, while the dew lasted. But on the road, on the high road along which the troops were marching, there was not that coolness even at night and in the woods. There was no dew to be seen on the sandy dust of the road, churned up more than half a foot deep. As soon as dawn broke, movement began. Baggage trains and artillery went noiselessly, sunk to the hubs, and infantry sunk to the ankles in the soft, suffocating, hot dust that did not cool down overnight. Part of this dust was kneaded by feet and wheels, the rest rose and hung in a cloud over the troops, filling the eyes, hair, ears, nostrils, and, above all, the lungs of the men and animals moving along this road. The higher the sun rose, the higher rose the cloud of dust, and through this fine, hot dust one could look with the naked eye at the sun, not covered by clouds. The sun looked like a large crimson ball. There was no wind, and the men suffocated in this unstirring atmosphere. They walked on, tying handkerchiefs over their noses and mouths. When they came to a village, they all rushed to the wells. They fought over the water and drank it down to the mud.

Prince Andrei was in command of a regiment, and the organization of the regiment, the well-being of his men, the necessity of receiving and giving orders, diverted him. The burning and abandoning of Smolensk marked an epoch for Prince Andrei. The new feeling of anger against the foe made him forget his own grief. He was devoted entirely to the affairs of his regiment, he was solicitous of his men and officers and affectionate with them. In his regiment he was known as *our prince;* they were proud of him and loved him. But he was kind and mild only with the men of his regiment, with Timokhin and the rest, totally new people and in strange surroundings, who could not know and understand his past; but as soon as he ran into someone from his former life, some staff officer, he at once bristled up again; he became spiteful, mocking, and contemptuous. He was repulsed by everything that bound him to the memory of the past, and therefore he tried, in relation to his former world, only not to be unfair and to fulfil his *duty.*

True, everything presented itself in a dark, gloomy light to Prince Andrei— especially after the abandoning of Smolensk (which, to his mind, could and should have been defended) on the sixth of August, and after his ailing father had to flee to Moscow and leave to be pillaged his beloved Bald Hills, which he had built and peopled; but despite that, thanks to his regiment, Prince Andrei could think about a subject completely independent of general problems— about his regiment. On the tenth of August, the column of which his regiment formed part drew level with Bald Hills. Two days earlier, Prince Andrei had received news that his father, son, and sister had left for Moscow. Though Prince Andrei had nothing to do there, he, with his own peculiar wish to exacerbate his grief, decided that he had to stop and see Bald Hills.

He ordered a horse saddled for him and while on the march rode to his father's estate, where he was born and spent his childhood. Going past the pond where there were always dozens of village women talking together, wielding battledores, and rinsing their laundry, Prince Andrei noticed that there was no one at the pond, and a little raft, torn free, half sunk in the water, was floating in the middle of it. Prince Andrei rode up to the watch box. There was no one by the stone gates of the entrance, and the door was open. The footpaths of the garden were already overgrown, and calves and horses wandered over the English park. Prince Andrei rode up to the conservatory: there was broken glass, some of the trees in tubs were overturned, and some were dry. He called out for Taras, the gardener. No one replied. Having ridden round the conservatory to the outdoor beds, he saw that the carved wooden fence was all broken and plums had been pulled off with their branches. An old peasant (Prince Andrei used to see him by the gates in his childhood) was sitting on a little green bench plaiting a bast shoe.

He was deaf and did not hear Prince Andrei ride up. He was sitting on the bench on which the old prince had liked to sit, and beside him strips of bast were hanging on the branches of a broken and withered magnolia.

Prince Andrei rode up to the house. Several lindens in the old garden had been cut down, a piebald mare with a foal was walking right in front of the house between the rosebushes. The shutters were closed. One window on the ground floor was open. A serf boy, seeing Prince Andrei, ran into the house.

Alpatych, having sent the family away, had remained alone at Bald Hills; he was at home reading *The Lives of the Saints*. Learning of Prince Andrei's arrival, he came out of the house with his spectacles on his nose, buttoning himself up, hastily went to the prince and, without saying anything, wept, kissing Prince Andrei on the knee.

Then he turned away, vexed at his own weakness, and began to report on the state of things. Everything valuable and costly had been transported to Bogucharovo. The grain, up to eight hundred bushels, had also been taken there; the hay and this year's spring crops, remarkable according to Alpatych, had been mowed while still green and taken—by the troops. The peasants were devastated, some had also left for Bogucharovo, a small number had remained.

Prince Andrei, not hearing him out, asked when his father and sister had left, meaning when they had left for Moscow. Alpatych, assuming he had been asked about their departure for Bogucharovo, replied that they had left on the seventh, and again expanded on details of the estate management, asking for orders.

"Shall I let the troops have oats on receipt? We still have nearly five thousand bushels left," asked Alpatych.

"What answer can I give him?" thought Prince Andrei, looking at the old man's bald head shining in the sun and reading in the expression of his face that he understood how inappropriate his questions were, but that he had asked them just to stifle his own grief.

"Yes, let them," he said.

"If you've been pleased to notice disorders in the garden," said Alpatych, "it was impossible to prevent them: three regiments passed through and spent the night, dragoons in particular. I wrote down the rank and name of the commander so as to present a petition."

"Well, and what are you going to do? Will you stay if the enemy takes it?" Prince Andrei asked him.

Alpatych, turning his face towards Prince Andrei, looked at him; and suddenly, in a solemn gesture, he raised his arm aloft.

"He is my protector, let His will be done!" he said.

A crowd of peasants and servants walked through the meadow with uncovered heads, approaching Prince Andrei.

"Well, goodbye!" said Prince Andrei, leaning down to Alpatych. "Go away yourself, take whatever you can with you, and tell the people to leave for Ryazan or the estate outside Moscow." Alpatych pressed himself to his leg and burst into sobs. Prince Andrei carefully removed him and, spurring his horse, galloped down the avenue.

By the outside beds the old man still sat as indifferently as a fly on the face of a dead loved one, tapping the bast shoe on its last, and two girls, their skirts filled with plums picked from the conservatory trees, ran out from there and met Prince Andrei. Seeing the young master, the older girl, with a frightened look on her face, seized her younger friend by the hand and hid with her behind a birch tree, having no time to pick up the spilled green plums.

Prince Andrei turned away from them in frightened haste, afraid of letting them notice that he had seen them. He felt sorry for this pretty, frightened girl. He was afraid to look at her, but at the same time he had an irresistible desire to do so. A new, comforting, and reassuring feeling came over him when, looking at these girls, he realized the existence of other human interests, totally foreign to him and as legitimate as those that concerned him. These girls obviously had a passionate wish for one thing—to take and finish eating those green plums without being caught—and together with them Prince Andrei wished success to their undertaking. He could not help glancing at them one more time. Supposing themselves out of danger, they left their cover and, piping something in their high little voices, holding up their skirts, ran merrily and quickly with their bare, suntanned little feet over the grass of the meadow.

Prince Andrei had been somewhat refreshed, leaving the dusty area of the high road along which the troops were moving. But not far from Bald Hills, he came back to the road and caught up with his regiment at a stopping place by a dam on a small pond. It was past one in the afternoon. The sun, a red ball in the dust, scorched and burned his back unbearably through his black tunic. Dust, the same as ever, hung motionless over the halted troops buzzing with talk. There was no wind. As he rode across the dam, Prince Andrei smelled the slime and freshness of the pond. He wanted to go into the water—however dirty it was. He glanced round at the pond, from which came shouts and loud laughter. The small, muddy green pond had evidently risen some eight inches, overflowing the dam, because it was filled with the naked human bodies of soldiers flopping about in it, white with brick-red hands, faces, and necks. All that naked, white human flesh, with whoops and guffaws, was flopping about in the dirty puddle like carp in a bucket. This flopping about suggested merriment, and that made it particularly sad.

One fair-haired young soldier—Prince Andrei knew him—from the third company, with a leather band on his ankle, was crossing himself as he backed up to make his run and dive into the water; another, a black-haired, always dishevelled non-commissioned officer, up to his waist in the water, his muscular torso twitching, grunted joyfully, raising his black, hairy arms and pouring water over his head. There were sounds of slapping, shrieking, and hooting.

On the banks, on the dam, in the pond, everywhere there was white, healthy,

muscular flesh. The officer Timokhin, with a little red nose, was wiping himself on the dam and, seeing the prince, became embarrassed, yet ventured to
address him:

"It's nice, Your Excellency, if you'd be so pleased!" he said.

"It's dirty," said Prince Andrei, wincing.

"We'll clear it for you right away." And Timokhin, still undressed, ran to
clear it.

"The prince wants to."

"Which? *Our* prince?" voices said and everybody started hurrying, so that
Prince Andrei barely managed to calm them down. He decided it would be better to have a shower in the shed.

"Flesh, the body, *chair à canon*!" he thought, looking at his naked body,
and he shuddered, not so much from the cold as from revulsion and horror,
incomprehensible to himself, at the sight of this enormous number of bodies
splashing about in the dirty pond.

On the seventh of August, Prince Bagration, from his quarters in Mikhailovka
on the Smolensk road, wrote the following letter to Arakcheev7 (but he knew
that his letter would be read by the sovereign, and therefore considered every
word, as far as he was capable of doing so):

Dear Count Alexei Andreevich,

I believe the minister has already reported that Smolensk has been left to the
enemy. It is painful, sad, and the whole army is in despair that the most important place has been abandoned to no purpose. I, for my part, begged him most
insistently in person and finally in writing; but nothing moved him to agree. I
swear to you on my honour that Napoleon was in such a sack as never before,
and he could have lost half his army, but not taken Smolensk. Our troops
fought and are fighting as never before. I held out with fifteen thousand men
for more than thirty-five hours and beat them; but he did not want to stay even
fourteen hours. It is shameful, and a blot on our army; and he himself, it seems
to me, should not even be alive in the world. If he reports that the losses were
great—it is not true; maybe round four thousand, not more, and not even that.
Even if it was ten, what can be done, it is war! But the enemy lost endless numbers . . .

What would it have cost to stay two more days? At least they would have
withdrawn on their own; for they had no water for their men and horses. He
gave me his word that he would not retreat, but suddenly sent a disposition
that he would leave during the night. It is impossible to make war that way,
and we may soon bring the enemy to Moscow . . .

The rumour is going round that you are thinking about peace. God forbid that we make peace! After all the sacrifices, and after such muddle-headed retreats—to make peace: you will set the whole of Russia against you, and every one of us will think it a shame to wear a uniform. If things have gone this way, we must fight as long as Russia can and as long as there are men left standing . . .

One person must be in command, not two. Your minister may be good as ministers go; but as a general, he is not merely bad but trash, and to him the fate of our whole Fatherland was entrusted . . . I am truly going out of my mind with vexation; forgive me that I write so boldly. Clearly, one who advises the concluding of peace and puts a minister in command of an army does not love the sovereign and wishes the destruction of us all. And so I am writing you the truth: call out the militia. For the minister, in a most masterly way, is bringing a guest with him to the capital. The great suspicion of the whole army falls on Mister Imperial Adjutant Wolzogen. They say he is more Napoleon's than ours, and he is the minister's adviser in everything. I am not merely polite with him, but I obey him like a corporal, though I am his senior. This is painful; but, loving my benefactor and sovereign, I obey. Only it is too bad that the sovereign entrusts our fine army to the likes of him. Imagine that on our retirade we lost over fifteen thousand men from fatigue and in hospitals; if we had been on the offensive, that would not have happened. Tell me, for God's sake, what will our Russia—our mother—say, seeing that we are so frightened, and that we are giving up such a good and zealous Fatherland to such rabble and instilling hatred and disgrace in every subject? Why are we cowardly, and who are we afraid of? It is not my fault that the minister is irresolute, cowardly, muddle-headed, temporizing, and has every bad quality. The whole army is completely in tears and scolds him to death . . .

VI

Among the innumerable subdivisions that can be made in the phenomena of life, one can subdivide them all into those in which content predominates and those in which form predominates. Among the latter, as opposed to the life of a village, a zemstvo, a province, even of Moscow, can be counted the life of Petersburg, especially its salon life. That life is unchanging.

Since 1805 we had made peace and quarrelled with Bonaparte, we had made constitutions and unmade them, yet the salon of Anna Pavlovna and the salon of Hélène were exactly the same as they had been—the one seven years earlier, the other five years earlier. In just the same way, people at Anna Pavlovna's talked with perplexity about Bonaparte's successes, and saw both in his successes and in the indulgence shown him by European sovereigns a malicious conspiracy aimed solely at causing unpleasantness and anxiety in the court circle, of which Anna Pavlovna was the representative. In the same way, at Hélène's, whom Rumyantsev himself favoured with his visits and considered a remarkably intelligent woman, as in 1808, so in 1812, they talked with rapture about the great nation and the great man, and looked with regret upon the rupture with France, which, in the opinion of the people who gathered in Hélène's salon, should end in peace.

Recently, after the sovereign's arrival from the army, some sort of flurry had gone on in these opposing salon circles, and there had been some sort of demonstrations against each other, but the tendencies of the circles remained the same. In Anna Pavlovna's circle, Frenchmen were accepted only from among the inveterate legitimists, and here the patriotic thought was upheld that one should not go to the French theatre and that maintaining a company of actors cost as much as maintaining an entire army corps. Military events were eagerly followed, and the most advantageous rumours were spread about our army. The pro-French circle of Hélène and Rumyantsev refuted the rumours about the cruelty of the enemy and the war, and discussed all of Napoleon's attempts at reconciliation. This circle reproached those who advised overly hasty arrangements to do with preparing the court and the girls' institutes, under the dowager empress's patronage, for departure to Kazan. In general, the whole matter of the war was presented in Hélène's salon as empty demonstrations, which would quite soon end in peace, and there reigned the opinion of Bilibin, now in Petersburg and a familiar at Hélène's (every intelligent person had to be received in her salon), that the matter would be resolved not by gunpowder, but by those who invented it.[8] This circle ironically and quite intelligently, though also quite cautiously, laughed at the Moscow raptures, news of which had come to Petersburg with the sovereign.

In Anna Pavlovna's circle, those raptures, on the contrary, were admired and spoken of as Plutarch speaks of the ancients. Prince Vassily, who occupied all the same important posts, was the connecting link between the two circles. He visited *ma bonne amie* Anna Pavlovna, and he visited *dans le salon diplomatique de ma fille,** and often, in his ceaseless moves from one camp to the other, became confused and said at Anna Pavlovna's what ought to have been said at Hélène's, and vice versa.

Soon after the sovereign's arrival, Prince Vassily got to talking at Anna Pavlovna's about matters of the war, harshly denouncing Barclay de Tolly and finding himself undecided about who should be named commander in chief. One of the guests, known under the name of *un homme de beaucoup de mérite,*[†9] having told how he had seen Kutuzov, who had just been chosen as commander of the Petersburg militia, sitting in the treasury office over the

*My good friend . . . in the diplomatic salon of my daughter.
†A man of great merit.

enlistment of soldiers, allowed himself to cautiously voice the suggestion that Kutuzov might be the man who would satisfy all the requirements.

Anna Pavlovna smiled sadly and observed that Kutuzov had never caused the sovereign anything but trouble.

"I said over and over at the Assembly of the Nobility," Prince Vassily interrupted, "but they didn't listen to me. I said that his selection as commander of the militia wouldn't please the sovereign. They didn't listen to me.

"It's all some sort of mania for 'fronding,' "[10] he went on. "And before whom? And it's all because we want to ape those stupid Moscow raptures," said Prince Vassily, becoming confused for a moment and forgetting that at Hélène's one had to make fun of the Moscow raptures, but at Anna Pavlovna's to admire them. But he corrected himself at once. "Well, is it suitable for Count Kutuzov, the oldest general in Russia, to sit in an office, *et il en restera pour sa peine!** Is it possible to appoint as commander in chief a man who cannot mount a horse, who falls asleep at a council, a man of the lowest morals! A nice reputation he made for himself in Bucharest! I'm not even speaking of his qualities as a general, but is it possible at such a moment to appoint a man who is decrepit and blind, plain blind? A fine thing to have a blind general! He can't see a thing. Like playing blindman's buff . . . he sees precisely nothing!"

No one argued against that.

On the twenty-fourth of July, that was perfectly correct. But on the twenty-ninth of July, princely dignity was bestowed upon Kutuzov. Princely dignity might also mean that they wanted to get rid of him—and therefore Prince Vassily's opinion continued to be correct, though he was no longer in a hurry to voice it. But on the eighth of August, a committee was assembled made up of General Field Marshal Saltykov, Arakcheev, Vyazmitinov, Lopukhin, and Kochubey, to discuss matters of war. The committee decided that the failures came from multiplicity of command, and though the persons who made up the committee knew that the sovereign was ill-disposed towards Kutuzov, the committee, after a brief consultation, suggested the appointment of Kutuzov as commander in chief. And that same day Kutuzov was appointed commander in chief, with full power over the armies and the entire region occupied by the troops.

On the ninth of August, Prince Vassily again met *l'homme de beaucoup de mérite* at Anna Pavlovna's. *L'homme de beaucoup de mérite* was paying court to Anna Pavlovna on the occasion of his wish to be appointed a trustee of the empress Maria Feodorovna's institute for girls. Prince Vassily came into the room with the air of a happy victor, of a man who has achieved the aim of his desires.

"*Eh bien, vous savez la grande nouvelle? Le prince Koutouzoff est maréchal.* All the disagreements are over. I'm so happy, so glad!" Prince Vassily was

---

* And he'll stay there for all his trouble.

saying. *"Enfin voilà un homme,"** he said, casting a significant and stern glance at everyone in the drawing room. *L'homme de beaucoup de mérite,* despite his wish to obtain a post, could not help reminding Prince Vassily of his former opinion. (This was impolite both towards Prince Vassily in Anna Pavlovna's drawing room and towards Anna Pavlovna, who had received the news with as much joy; but he could not help himself.)

"Mais on dit qu'il est aveugle, mon prince?"† he said, reminding Prince Vassily of his own words.

"Allez donc, il y voit assez,"‡ Prince Vassily said in his brisk bass voice with a little cough, the voice and the little cough with which he resolved all difficulties. *"Allez, il y voit assez,"* he repeated. "And what makes me glad," he continued, "is that the sovereign has given him full power over all the armies, over the entire region—a power that no commander in chief has ever had. He's another autocrat," he concluded with a victorious smile.

"God grant it, God grant it," said Anna Pavlovna. *L'homme de beaucoup de mérite,* still a novice in court society, wishing to flatter Anna Pavlovna by defending her former opinion on this judgement, said:

"They say the sovereign gave Kutuzov this power reluctantly. *On dit qu'il rougit comme une demoiselle à laquelle on lirait 'Joconde,'*[11] *en lui disant: 'Le souverain et la patrie vous decernent cet honneur.'* "§

"Peut-être que le coeur n'était pas de la partie,"# said Anna Pavlovna.

"Oh, no, no," Prince Vassily stepped in vehemently. Now he could not yield Kutuzov to anybody. In Prince Vassily's opinion, Kutuzov was not only good in himself, but everyone adored him. "No, that can't be, because the sovereign was able to value him so much before," he said.

"God grant only," said Anna Pavlovna, "that Prince Kutuzov may exercise real power without letting *anyone* put spokes in his wheels—*des bâtons dans les roues.*"

Prince Vassily understood at once who this *anyone* was. He said in a whisper:

"I know for certain that Kutuzov stated as an absolute condition that the grand duke should not be with the army. *Vous savez ce qu'il a dit à l'Empereur?"*** And Prince Vassily repeated the words Kutuzov was supposed to have said to the sovereign: " 'I can neither punish him if he does wrong, nor reward him if he does well.' Oh, he's a most intelligent man, Prince Kutuzov, *et quel caractère. Oh, je le connais de longue date."*††

*Well, do you know the great news? Prince Kutuzov is marshal . . . Here at last is a man.
†But they say he's blind, Prince?
‡Come now, he can see well enough.
§They say he blushed like a young lady to whom someone was reading "Joconde," saying to him: "The sovereign and the country bestow this honour on you."
#Perhaps his heart was not in it.
**Do you know what he said to the emperor?
††And what character. Oh, I've known him for a long time.

"They even say," said *l'homme de beaucoup de mérite*, who did not yet have courtly tact, "that his excellency laid down as an absolute condition that the sovereign himself not come to the army."

As soon as he said it, Prince Vassily and Anna Pavlovna turned away from him in an instant and looked at each other sadly, with a sigh at his naïveté.

VII

While this was going on in Petersburg, the French had already passed Smolensk and were moving closer and closer to Moscow. Napoleon's historian Thiers, like his other historians, says, trying to justify his hero, that Napoleon was lured to the walls of Moscow involuntarily. He is right, as all historians are right who seek explanations of historical events in the will of one man; he is right, just as the Russian historians are right who maintain that Napoleon was lured to Moscow by the skill of the Russian commanders. Here, besides the law of retrospection, which presents all the past as a preparation for the accomplished fact, there is also a reciprocity that confuses the whole matter. A good player who loses at chess is genuinely convinced that he has lost because of a mistake, and he looks for this mistake in the beginning of his game, but forgets that there were also mistakes at every step in the course of the game, that none of his moves was perfect. The mistake he pays attention to is conspicuous only because his opponent took advantage of it. How much more complex is the game of war, which takes place in certain conditions of time and where no single will is guiding lifeless mechanisms, but everything is the result of numberless collisions of various wills?

After Smolensk, Napoleon sought a battle beyond Dorogobuzh at the Vyazma, then at Tsarevo-Zaimishche; but it turned out that, owing to numberless collisions of circumstances, the Russians could not accept battle before Borodino, seventy-five miles from Moscow. From the Vyazma Napoleon gave orders to move directly upon Moscow.

*Moscou, la capitale asiatique de ce grand empire, la ville sacrée des peuples d'Alexandre, Moscou avec ses innombrables églises en forme de pagodes chinoises!** This *Moscou* gave Napoleon's imagination no rest. On the march from Vyazma to Tsarevo-Zaimishche, Napoleon rode on his bob-tailed light bay ambler, accompanied by his guards, bodyguard, pages, and adjutants. The chief of staff, Berthier, had dropped behind in order to interrogate a Russian prisoner his cavalry had taken. Accompanied by his translator, Lelorgne d'Ideville, he galloped to catch up with Napoleon and with a merry face reined in his horse.

*Moscow, the Asiatic capital of this great empire, the sacred city of Alexander's peoples, Moscow with its innumerable churches in the form of Chinese pagodas!

"*Eh bien?*" said Napoleon.

"*Un cosaque de Platow* says that Platov's corps is marching to join the main army, that Kutuzov has been appointed commander in chief. *Trés intelligent et bavard!*"*

Napoleon smiled and told them to give this Cossack a horse and bring him to him. He wanted to talk with him personally. Several adjutants galloped off, and an hour later, Lavrushka, Denisov's serf, whom he had let go to Rostov, in an orderly's jacket, on a French cavalry saddle, with a sly and drunken, merry face, rode up to Napoleon. Napoleon told him to ride beside him and began to ask:

"You're a Cossack?"

"Yes, Your Honour."

"*Le cosaque ignorant la compagnie dans laquelle il se trouvait, car la simplicité de Napoléon n'avait rien qui put révéler, à une imagination orientale la présence d'un souverain, s'entretenait avec la plus extrême familiarité des affaires de la guerre actuelle,*"† says Thiers, recounting this episode.[12] In fact, Lavrushka had received a whipping the day before for getting drunk and leaving his master without dinner, and had been sent to a village to get some chickens, and there, carried away by pillaging, had been taken prisoner by the French. Lavrushka was one of those coarse, insolent lackeys who had been round, who considered it their duty to do everything with meanness and cunning, who were ready to perform any service for their master, and who cunningly guess their master's bad thoughts, especially the vain and paltry ones.

Finding himself in the company of Napoleon, whose person he recognized very well and easily, Lavrushka was by no means thrown off, and only tried wholeheartedly to be of service to his new masters.

He knew very well that this was Napoleon himself, and the presence of Napoleon could not throw him off any more than the presence of Rostov or of a sergeant major with a whip, because there was nothing he could be deprived of either by a sergeant major or by Napoleon.

He blurted out everything that was the talk among the orderlies. Much of it was true. But when Napoleon asked what the Russians thought about defeating or not defeating Napoleon, Lavrushka narrowed his eyes and fell to thinking.

He saw a subtle cunning here, as people like Lavrushka always see cunning in everything, so he frowned and paused.

"It's like this: if there's a battle," he said thoughtfully, "and at the soonest,

---

*One of Platov's Cossacks . . . Very intelligent and talkative!

†The Cossack, unaware of the company he found himself in, for Napoleon's simplicity had nothing that could reveal to an Oriental imagination the presence of a sovereign, conversed with extreme familiarity about the affairs of the present war.

then that's just that. Well, but if it happens three days after that same date, then it means that same battle's going to put a drag on things."

This is how it was translated for Napoleon: "*Si la bataille est donnée avant trois jours, les Français la gagneraient, mais que si elle serait donnée plus tard, Dieu seul sait ce qui en arriverait,*"* Lelorgne d'Ideville conveyed with a smile. Napoleon did not smile, though he was clearly in the most cheerful state of mind, and asked these words to be repeated for him.

Lavrushka noticed it and, to cheer him up more, said, pretending not to know who he was:

"We know you've got Bonaparte, he's beaten everybody in the world—well, but with us things are different . . ." he said, not knowing himself how and why this boastful patriotism had slipped into his words towards the end. The translator conveyed these words to Napoleon without the end, and Bonaparte smiled. "*Le jeune Cosaque fit sourire son puissant interlocuteur,*"† says Thiers. Having ridden several paces in silence, Napoleon turned to Berthier and said he would like to test what effect would be produced *sur cet enfant du Don*‡ by the news that this man with whom the *enfant du Don* was speaking was the emperor himself, the same emperor who had written his immortally victorious name on the pyramids.

The news was conveyed.

Lavrushka (realizing that this had been done in order to take him aback, and that Napoleon thought he would become frightened), so as to cater to his new masters, instantly pretended to be amazed, dumbfounded, goggled his eyes, and made the same face he was accustomed to make when taken off to be whipped. "*À peine l'interprète de Napoléon,*" says Thiers, "*avait-il parlé, que le Cosaque, saisi d'une sorte d'ébahissement ne proféra plus une parole et marcha les yeux constamment attachés sur ce conquérant, dont le nom avait pénétré jusqu'à lui, à travers les steppes de l'Orient. Toute sa loquacité s'était subitement arrêtée, pour faire place à un sentiment d'admiration naïve et silencieuse. Napoléon, après l'avoir récompensé, lui fit donner la liberté, comme à un oiseau qu'on rend aux champs qui l'ont vu naître.*"§

Napoleon rode on, dreaming of that *Moscou* which so filled his imagination, and *l'oiseau qu'on rendit aux champs qui l'ont vu naître* galloped to the outposts, inventing beforehand everything that had not happened and that he

*If battle is given within three days, the French will win, but if it should be given later, God only knows what will happen.
†The young Cossack made his powerful interlocutor smile.
‡On this child of the Don.
§Hardly had Napoleon's translator spoken when the Cossack, seized by a sort of amazement, offered not a word more and rode on with his eyes constantly fixed on this conqueror, whose name had penetrated as far as him, across the steppes of the East. All his loquacity had suddenly stopped, to give place to a feeling of naïve and silent admiration. Napoleon, after rewarding him, set him free, like a bird that one sends back to the fields where it was born.

would tell to his comrades. What had actually happened to him he did not want to tell, precisely because he thought it was not worth telling. He rode out to the Cossacks, asked them the whereabouts of the regiment that was part of Platov's detachment, and towards evening found his master, Nikolai Rostov, who was staying in Yankovo and had just mounted up to go for a ride with Ilyin round the neighbouring villages. He gave Lavrushka another horse and took him along.

VIII

Princess Marya was not in Moscow and out of danger, as Prince Andrei thought.

After Alpatych's return from Smolensk, the old prince seemed suddenly to have awakened from sleep. He ordered the militia assembled in the villages, armed them, and wrote a letter to the commander in chief in which he informed him of the intention he had taken to remain in Bald Hills to the last and to defend it, leaving it up to the commander whether he would or would not take measures to defend Bald Hills, where one of the oldest Russian generals might be killed or taken prisoner, and he announced to the household that he was staying in Bald Hills.

But, while staying in Bald Hills himself, the prince gave orders for the princess and Dessales to be sent with the little prince to Bogucharovo, and from there to Moscow. Princess Marya, frightened at her father's feverish, sleepless activity, which replaced his former inertia, would not risk leaving him alone, and for the first time in her life allowed herself to disobey him. She refused to leave, and the terrible thunder of the prince's wrath fell upon her. He reminded her of everything in which he had been unfair to her. Trying to accuse her, he told her that she had worn him out, that she had caused him to quarrel with his son, that she had had nasty suspicions of him, that she had made it the goal of her life to poison his life, and he drove her out of his study, telling her that it was all the same to him whether she left or not. He said that he did not want to know of her existence, but gave her fair warning beforehand that she dare not show her face to him. The fact that, contrary to her apprehensions, he did not have her taken away by force, but only ordered her not to show her face to him, gladdened Princess Marya. She knew it proved that, in his heart of hearts, he was glad that she was staying at home and not leaving.

The day after Nikolushka's departure, the old prince put on his full uniform in the morning and prepared to go to the commander in chief. The carriage was already at the porch. Princess Marya saw him leave the house, in his uniform and all his decorations, and go to the garden to hold a review of the armed peasants and domestics. Princess Marya was sitting by the window, listening to his voice coming from the garden. Suddenly several people with frightened faces came running up the avenue.

Princess Marya ran out to the porch, down the garden path, and into the avenue. A large crowd of militiamen and domestics was moving towards her, and in the middle of this crowd several men were dragging under the arms a little old man in a uniform and decorations. Princess Marya ran to him, and in the play of light falling in small circles through the shade of the linden avenue, she could not account to herself for the change that had come over his face. The one thing she saw was that the former stern and resolute expression of his face had been replaced by an expression of timidity and submission. Seeing his daughter, he moved his strengthless lips and made a wheezing sound. It was impossible to tell what he wanted. They picked him up, carried him to his study, and laid him on that very couch which he had feared so much lately.

The doctor brought that same evening let his blood and announced that the prince had had a stroke on the right side.

To remain in Bald Hills was becoming more and more dangerous, and the day after the stroke the prince was taken to Bogucharovo. The doctor went with them.

When they arrived in Bogucharovo, Dessales and the little prince had already left for Moscow.

In the same condition, neither better nor worse, stricken with paralysis, the old prince lay for three weeks in Bogucharovo, in the new house built by Prince Andrei. The old prince was unconscious; he lay like a disfigured corpse. He ceaselessly muttered something, his eyebrows and lips twitching, and it was impossible to know whether or not he understood what was going on round him. One thing could be known for certain—that he was suffering and still felt a need to express something. But what it was, no one could understand: was it some whim of a sick and half-demented man, did it have to do with the general course of things, or did it have to do with family circumstances?

The doctor said that the anxiousness he showed meant nothing, that it had physical causes; but Princess Marya thought (and the fact that her presence always increased his anxiousness confirmed her supposition) that he wanted to tell her something. He was obviously suffering both physically and morally.

There was no hope of recovery. To transport him was impossible. What would happen if he died on the road? "Wouldn't the end, the final end, be better?" Princess Marya sometimes thought. She watched over him day and night, almost without sleeping, and, dreadful to say, she often watched over him not hoping to find signs of improvement, but *wishing* to find signs of the approaching end.

Strange as it was for the princess to be aware of this feeling within her, it was there. And still more terrible for Princess Marya was the fact that, since the time of her father's illness (if not even earlier, when, expecting something, she had stayed with him), all her personal desires and hopes, forgotten and dormant in her, had reawakened. Things that had not entered her head for years—thoughts of a free life without the eternal fear of her father, even thoughts of the possibility of love and family happiness—ceaselessly flitted through her imagination, like temptations of the devil. Try as she might to push them away from her, questions constantly entered her head of how she would arrange her life now, after *that*. These were temptations of the devil, and Princess Marya knew it. She knew that the only weapon against them was prayer, and she attempted to pray. She stood in a prayerful position, looked at the icons, recited the words of a prayer, but was unable to pray. She felt that now another world had taken hold of her—of the difficult and free activity of everyday life, completely the opposite of the moral world in which she had previously been confined and in which the best consolation had been prayer. She could not pray and could not weep, and everyday cares took hold of her.

It was becoming dangerous to remain in Bogucharovo. There was talk on all sides about the approaching French, and in one village ten miles from Bogucharovo an estate had been looted by French marauders.

The doctor insisted that the prince be taken further away; the marshal of the nobility sent an official to Princess Marya to persuade her to leave as soon as possible. A police chief came to Bogucharovo and insisted on the same thing, saying that the French were twenty-five miles away, that French leaflets were going about the villages, and that if the princess and her father did not leave before the fifteenth, he could not answer for anything.

The princess decided to leave on the fifteenth. The cares of the preparations, of giving orders, for which everyone turned to her, occupied her the whole day before. The night of the fourteenth she spent, as usual, without undressing, in the room next to the one in which the prince lay. Several times, on waking up, she heard his groaning, muttering, the creaking of the bed, and the footsteps of Tikhon and the doctor as they turned him over. Several times she listened at the door, and it seemed to her that he muttered more loudly than usual that night and tossed more frequently. She could not sleep and went to the door several times, listening, wishing to go in and not daring to. Though he could not speak, Princess Marya saw and knew how unpleasant he found any sign of fear for him. She noticed with what displeasure he turned away from the intent gaze she sometimes involuntarily directed at him. She knew that her coming at night, at an unusual time, would irritate him.

But never had she felt so sorry for him, so frightened of losing him. She recalled all her life with him, and found in his every word, his every act, an expression of his love for her. From time to time, amidst these memories, the devil's temptations would break in upon her imagination, the thoughts of what would happen after his death and how her new, free life would be arranged. But she drove those thoughts away with loathing. By morning he quieted down, and she fell asleep.

She woke up late. That sincerity which comes with waking showed her clearly what it was in her father's illness that concerned her most. She woke up, listened to what was happening behind the door, and, hearing his groaning, said to herself with a sigh that everything was still the same.

"But what else could there be? What did I want? I want his death," she cried out with loathing for herself.

She dressed, washed, said her prayers, and went out to the porch. At the porch stood carriages without horses, and things were being packed into them.

The morning was warm and grey. Princess Marya stopped on the porch, never ceasing to be horrified at her inner loathsomeness and trying to put her thoughts in order before going in to see him.

The doctor came downstairs and went out to her.

"He's a little better today," he said. "I've been looking for you. Some of what he says can be understood, his head is clearer. Come along. He's calling for you . . ."

Princess Marya's heart beat so hard at this news that she turned pale and leaned against the doorway so as not to fall. To see him, to talk to him, to have him look at her now, when her whole soul was filled with those dreadful criminal temptations, was painfully joyful and terrible.

"Come along," said the doctor.

Princess Marya entered her father's room and went up to his bed. He lay propped up on his back, his small, bony hands covered with purple, knotty veins, lying on the covers, his left eye looking straight ahead, his right squinting to one side, his eyebrows and lips motionless. He was all so thin, small, and pitiful. His face seemed to have shrivelled or melted away, the features had grown smaller. Princess Marya went up and kissed his hand. His left hand pressed hers so hard that it was clear he had long been waiting for her. He pulled at her hand, and his eyebrows and lips twitched angrily.

She looked at him in fear, trying to guess what he wanted from her. When she changed her position so that his left eye could see her face, he calmed down and did not take his gaze from her for several seconds. Then his lips and tongue moved, sounds came out, and he began to speak, looking at her timidly and imploringly, clearly afraid that she would not understand him.

Princess Marya, straining all her powers of attention, looked at him. The comic effort with which he moved his tongue made Princess Marya lower her eyes and force herself to suppress the sobs that rose in her throat. He said something, repeating his words several times. Princess Marya could not understand them; but she tried to guess what he was saying and repeated questioningly the words he had said to her.

"Ma-sa . . . eh . . . eh . . ." he repeated several times.

She could not understand these words. The doctor thought he could and, repeating his words, asked: "Marya afraid?" The prince shook his head negatively and again repeated the same thing . . .

"My soul, my soul aches," Princess Marya guessed and said. He grunted affirmatively, took her hand, and began pressing it to various places on his chest, as if trying to find the right place for it.

"All thoughts! of you . . . thoughts," he then pronounced much more clearly and understandably than before, now that he was sure they understood him. Princess Marya pressed her head to his hand, trying to hide her sobs and tears.

He moved his hand over her hair.

"I was calling you all night . . ." he brought out.

"If only I'd known . . ." she said through her tears. "I was afraid to come in."

He pressed her hand.

"You weren't asleep?"

"No, I wasn't," said Princess Marya, shaking her head negatively. Involuntarily submitting to her father, she now spoke the way he did, trying to speak more in signs, and as if also moving her tongue with difficulty.

"Dear heart . . ."—or "Dear friend . . ." Princess Marya could not make it out, but certainly, by the expression of his gaze, it was a tender, caressing word such as he had never spoken before. "Why didn't you come?"

"And I was wishing, wishing for his death!" thought Princess Marya. He fell silent.

"Thank you . . . daughter, dear friend . . . for everything, everything . . . forgive me . . . thank you . . . forgive me . . . thank you! . . ." And tears flowed from his eyes. "Call Andryusha," he said suddenly, and something childishly timid and mistrustful showed in his face as he made this request. It was as if he knew himself that his request made no sense. At least it seemed so to Princess Marya.

"I received a letter from him," she replied.

He looked at her with astonishment and timidity.

"Where is he?"

"He's in the army, *mon père*, in Smolensk."

He fell silent for a long time, closing his eyes; then he nodded his head affirmatively, as if in response to his doubts and to confirm that he now understood and remembered everything, and opened his eyes.

"Yes," he said distinctly and softly. "Russia's lost! They've lost her!" And again he sobbed and the tears flowed from his eyes. Princess Marya could no longer help herself and also wept, looking at his face.

He closed his eyes again. His sobbing stopped. He gestured towards his eyes. Tikhon understood and wiped his tears.

Then he opened his eyes and said something that no one could understand for a long time and that Tikhon alone finally understood and explained. Princess Marya sought the meaning of his words in the mood in which he had spoken a moment before. First she thought he was speaking of Russia, then of

Prince Andrei, then of her, of his grandson, of his death. And that kept her from guessing his words.

"Put on your white dress, I like it," he had said.

Having understood these words, Princess Marya burst into still louder sobs, and the doctor, taking her by the arm, led her from the room to the terrace, persuading her to calm down and busy herself with the preparations for departure. After Princess Marya left the prince, he again began talking about his son, about the war, the sovereign, twitched his eyebrows angrily, began raising his hoarse voice, and had a second and final stroke.

Princess Marya stopped on the terrace. The day had cleared, it was sunny and hot. She could not understand anything, or think about anything, or feel anything, except her passionate love for her father, a love which, it seemed to her, she had not known till that moment. She ran out to the garden and, sobbing, ran down to the pond along a path lined with young lindens planted by Prince Andrei.

"Yes . . . I . . . I . . . I. I wished for his death. Yes, I wished it would end sooner . . . *I* wanted to be at peace . . . But what will become of me? What do I need peace for, if he won't be there?" Princess Marya murmured aloud, pacing the garden with quick steps, her arms pressed to her breast, from which sobs burst convulsively. Making a circle round the garden, which led her back to the house, she saw Mlle Bourienne coming towards her (she had stayed on at Bogucharovo and did not want to leave) and an unknown man with her. It was the marshal of the district nobility, who had come in person to the princess in order to present to her all the necessity of a speedy departure. Princess Marya listened and did not understand him; she led him to the house, offered him lunch, and sat down with him. Then, apologizing to the marshal, she went to the old prince's door. The doctor came out to her with an alarmed face and said she could not come in.

"Go away, Princess, go away, go away!"

Princess Marya went back to the garden and sat down in the grass at the foot of the hill by the pond, where no one could see her. She did not know how long she had stayed there. A woman's footsteps running down the path brought her to her senses. She stood up and saw that Dunyasha, her maid, who had evidently come running to fetch her, had suddenly stopped, as if frightened at seeing her mistress.

"Please, Princess . . . the prince . . ." Dunyasha said in a faltering voice.

"At once, I'm coming, I'm coming," the princess said hurriedly, not giving Dunyasha time to finish what she had to say, and trying not to see Dunyasha, she ran towards the house.

"Princess, God's will is being done, you must be prepared for anything," said the marshal, meeting her at the front door.

"Let me be. It's not true!" she shouted at him angrily. The doctor wanted to stop her. She pushed him away and ran up to the door. "Why do these people with frightened faces stop me? I don't need anybody! What are they doing here?" She opened the door and was terrified by the bright daylight in this previously semi-dark room. There were women in the room, and the nanny. They all stepped back from the bed, making way for her. He lay on the bed in the same way; but the stern look of his calm face stopped Princess Marya on the threshold.

"No, he hasn't died, it can't be!" Princess Marya said to herself, went up to him, and, overcoming the horror that seized her, pressed her lips to his cheek. But she drew back from him at once. Instantly the whole force of the tenderness for him which she felt in herself vanished and was replaced by a feeling of horror at what lay before her. "No, he's no more! He's no more, and in the place where he was there is something alien and hostile, some dreadful, terrifying, and repulsive mystery . . ." And, covering her face with her hands, Princess Marya fell into the arms of the doctor, who supported her.

In the presence of Tikhon and the doctor, the women washed what had been he, bound his head with a handkerchief so that the open mouth would not stiffen, and with another handkerchief bound together the legs, which were beginning to spread. Then they dressed the small, shrivelled body in the uniform with decorations and laid it out on the table. God knows who took care of it or when, but everything got done as if by itself. Towards nighttime candles were burning round the coffin, on the coffin lay a pall, the floor was strewn with juniper boughs, under the dead man's withered head a printed prayer had been placed, and in the corner sat a beadle reading the psalter.

As horses shy, crowd, and snort over a dead horse, so people crowded round the coffin in the drawing room—strangers and familiars, the marshal, and the headman, and peasant women—and all with a fixed and frightened gaze crossed themselves and bowed, and kissed the cold and stiffened hand of the old prince.[13]

IX

Bogucharovo, before Prince Andrei settled there, had always been an absentee estate, and the Bogucharovo peasants had quite a different character from those of Bald Hills. They differed from them in speech, dress, and disposition. They were called steppe folk. The old prince had praised them for their endurance at work when they came to help out with the harvest at Bald Hills or to dig ponds and ditches, but had disliked them for their wildness.

Prince Andrei's last stay in Bogucharovo, with his innovations—clinics, schools, and the reducing of the quitrent—had not softened their disposition, but, on the contrary, had increased in them the traits of character which the old prince called wildness. Among them there was always some vague talk going round, now about enlisting them all as Cossacks, now about a new faith to which they were to be converted, now about some charters from the tsars, now about an oath to Pavel Petrovich in 1797 (of which it was said that they had already been granted their freedom then, but that the landowners had taken it away), now about Pyotr Feodorovich, who was to begin to reign in seven years,[14] and under whom everything would be free and so simple that there would be nothing at all. The rumours of war and Bonaparte and his invasion combined for them with equally vague notions of the Antichrist, the end of the world, and pure freedom.

The neighbourhood of Bogucharovo was all large villages belonging to the crown or to absentee landowners. Very few landowners actually lived there; there were also very few domestic and literate serfs, and in the lives of the peasants in this area there appeared, more noticeably and strongly than in others, those mysterious currents of popular Russian life the causes and meaning of which are inexplicable for contemporaries. One of those phenomena, which had manifested itself among the peasants of that locality twenty years before, was a movement to migrate to some "warm rivers." Hundreds of peasants, Bogucharovo peasants among them, suddenly began selling their cattle and leaving with their families for somewhere in the south-east. As birds fly somewhere beyond the seas, these people, with their wives and children, made for somewhere there, in the south-east, where none of them had ever been. They made up caravans, bought themselves out one by one, ran away, and drove, and walked there, to the warm rivers. Many were punished, exiled to Siberia, many died on the road of cold and hunger, many came back of themselves, and the movement died down, just as it had begun, without any obvious reason. But the undercurrents never ceased to flow among these people and were gathering some sort of new forces in order to manifest themselves just as strangely and unexpectedly, and at the same time as simply, naturally, and strongly. Now, in the year 1812, it was noticeable for a man living close to the people that these undercurrents were intensely at work and were close to manifesting themselves.

Alpatych, having come to Bogucharovo a short time before the old prince's passing, noticed that there was agitation among the people and that, contrary to what was happening in the region of Bald Hills, where over a forty-mile radius all the peasants were going away (leaving their villages to be devastated by the Cossacks), in the steppe region of Bogucharovo the peasants, it was heard, had communications with the French, received some sort of leaflets that circulated among them, and were staying put. He knew through the domestic servants, who were devoted to him, that the muzhik Karp, who had great influence on the community, had made a trip in a government-owned cart the other day and come back with the news that the Cossacks devastated villages abandoned by their inhabitants, but that the French did not touch them. He knew that another muzhik, the evening before, had even brought from the village of Visloukhovo—where the French were camped—a leaflet from a French general, which announced to the inhabitants that no harm would be done them, and that whatever was taken from them would be paid for, if they stayed. As proof of it, the muzhik brought from Visloukhovo a hundred roubles in banknotes (not knowing they were counterfeit), which he had been paid in advance for hay.

Finally, most important of all, Alpatych learned that, on the same day that he ordered the headman to prepare carts for transporting the princess's baggage from Bogucharovo, there had been a meeting of the village in the morning, at which it had been decided to wait and not go anywhere. And meanwhile time was running out. The marshal insisted, on the fifteenth of August, the day of the prince's death, that Princess Marya should leave that same day, as it was becoming dangerous. He said that after the sixteenth he could not answer for anything. On the day of the prince's death, he left in the evening, but promised to come for the funeral the next day. But the next day he could not come, because, according to news he had received, the French had advanced unexpectedly, and he had barely managed to remove his family and all his valuables from his estate.

For thirty years Bogucharovo had been managed by the headman Dron, whom the old prince had called Dronushka.

Dron was one of those physically and morally sturdy muzhiks who, once they come of age and grow a beard, live on that way, unchanging, until they are sixty or seventy, without a single grey hair or missing tooth, as straight and strong at the age of sixty as at thirty.

Dron, soon after the migration to the warm rivers, in which he had taken part like the others, had been made headman and mayor of Bogucharovo, and since then had remained in those duties irreproachably for twenty-three years. The muzhiks feared him more than the master. The gentlemen, both the old prince and the young, and the steward respected him and jokingly called him minister. In all the time of his service, Dron had never once been drunk or sick; never, either after sleepless nights or after any sort of labour, had he shown the slightest fatigue, and, though illiterate, never had he forgotten a single accounting of money and sacks of flour for the enormous shipments he sold, nor a single stack of grain on any acre of the Bogucharovo fields.

It was this Dron whom Alpatych, having come from the devastated Bald Hills, summoned to him on the day of the prince's funeral and ordered to prepare twelve horses for the princess's carriages and eighteen carts for a train that was to be made up at Bogucharovo. Though the peasants there were on quitrent, the fulfilment of this order could not present any difficulties, in Alpatych's opinion, because there were two hundred and thirty households at Bogucharovo, and the peasants were well-to-do. But the headman Dron, having heard the order, silently lowered his eyes. Alpatych named for him some muzhiks whom he knew and from whom he ordered the carts to be taken.

Dron replied that those muzhiks had their horses hired out. Alpatych named some other muzhiks, and they, too, had no horses, according to Dron; some were pulling government carts, others were too weak, still others had dropped dead from lack of fodder. In Dron's opinion, it was impossible to collect any horses, not only for the carting, but even for the carriages.

Alpatych looked at Dron attentively and frowned. Just as Dron was an exemplary headman and muzhik, so it was not for nothing that Alpatych had managed the prince's estates for twenty years and was an exemplary steward. He was capable in the highest degree of understanding intuitively the needs and instincts of the people he was dealing with, and that was why he was an excellent steward. Having glanced at Dron, he understood at once that Dron's replies were not the expression of Dron's thoughts, but the expression of that general mood of the Bogucharovo community in which the headman was already caught up. But along with that he knew that Dron, grown rich and therefore hated by the community, was bound to waver between the two camps—the masters and the peasants. He noticed this wavering in his eyes, and therefore Alpatych frowned and moved closer to Dron.

"Listen, Dronushka!" he said. "No empty talk with me. His Excellency Prince Andrei Nikolaich himself has ordered me to have all these people sent away and not left to the enemy, and there's a tsar's order for it. And whoever stays is a traitor to the tsar. Do you hear?"

"I hear," Dron replied without raising his eyes.

Alpatych was not satisfied with this response.

"Eh, Dron, it'll go badly for you!" Alpatych said, shaking his head.

"The power's yours!" Dron said ruefully.

"Drop it, Dron!" said Alpatych, taking his hand from behind his lapel and pointing with a solemn gesture at the floor under Dron's feet. "I not only see through you, I see through everything seven feet under you," he said, staring at the floor under Dron's feet.

Dron became troubled, glanced fleetingly at Alpatych, and again lowered his eyes.

"Drop this nonsense and tell the people to get ready to leave home for Moscow and to prepare carts tomorrow morning for the princess's baggage, and don't go to any meeting. Do you hear?"

Dron suddenly fell at his feet.

"Yakov Alpatych, release me! Take the keys from me, release me, for Christ's sake!"

"Drop it!" Alpatych said sternly. "I see through seven feet under you," he repeated, knowing that his skill in beekeeping, his knowledge of when to sow oats, and the fact that for twenty years he had been able to please the old prince had long since earned him the reputation of a sorcerer, and that the ability to see seven feet under a man was ascribed to sorcerers.

Dron stood up and was about to say something, but Alpatych interrupted him.

"What's this you've got into your heads? Eh? . . . What are you thinking? Eh?"

"What can I do with the people?" said Dron. "They're all riled up. I did tell them . . ."

"So you told them," said Alpatych. "Drinking?" he asked curtly.

"All riled up, Yakov Alpatych: brought a second barrel."

"Listen, then. I'll go for the police chief, and you tell that to the people, and that they should drop all this and furnish the carts."

"Yes, sir," replied Dron.

Yakov Alpatych did not insist further. He had been managing peasants for a long time and knew that the main means of getting people to obey consisted in not showing them any suspicion that they might not obey. Having obtained the obedient "Yes, sir" from Dron, Yakov Alpatych was satisfied with that, though he not only suspected but was almost certain that the carts would not be furnished without the help of the militia.

And indeed, no carts had been rounded up by evening. In the village there was again a meeting by the pot-house, and at the meeting it was decided to drive the horses into the forest and not supply any carts. Saying nothing about it to the princess, Alpatych ordered his own baggage that he had brought from Bald Hills unloaded, and those horses prepared to be harnessed to the princess's carriages, and he himself drove to the authorities.

X

After her father's funeral, Princess Marya locked herself up in her room and refused to see anyone. A maid came to the door to tell her that Alpatych had come to ask for orders about the departure. (This was before Alpatych's conversation with Dron.) Princess Marya got up from the couch she was lying on and, through the closed door, said that she would never go anywhere and asked to be left in peace.

The windows of the room in which Princess Marya was lying gave on the west. She lay on the couch facing the wall and, fingering the buttons on the leather cushion, saw nothing but that cushion, and her vague thoughts were concentrated on one thing: she was thinking of the irrevocability of death and of her own inner loathsomeness, which she had not known about till then, and which had shown itself during her father's illness. She wanted but did not dare to pray, did not dare to address herself to God in the state of soul she was in. She lay in that position for a long time.

The sun went down on the other side of the house, and its slanting evening rays shone through the open window into the room and onto part of the morocco cushion Princess Marya was looking at. The flow of her thoughts suddenly stopped. She unconsciously sat up, smoothed her hair, rose, and went to the window, involuntarily breathing in the coolness of the clear but breezy evening.

"Yes, it's easy for you to admire the evening now! He's gone, and nobody will hinder you," she said to herself and, sinking onto a chair, let her head drop to the windowsill.

Someone called her name in a tender and soft voice from the garden side and kissed her on the head. She glanced up. It was Mlle Bourienne, in a black dress and weepers. She quietly approached Princess Marya, kissed her with a sigh, and at once began to cry. Princess Marya glanced round at her. She remembered all her former clashes with her, her jealousy of her; she remembered, too, how *he* had recently changed towards Mlle Bourienne, could not bear the sight of her, and, therefore, how unfair were the reproaches she had made to her in her heart. "And is it for me, who wished for his death, to judge anyone?" she thought.

Princess Marya vividly pictured the position of Mlle Bourienne, who had been distanced from her company recently, and who at the same time depended on her and lived in a house not her own. And she felt sorry for her. She gave her a meekly questioning look and held out her hand to her. Mlle Bourienne at once began to cry, kiss her hand, and speak of the grief that had befallen the princess, making herself a sharer in that grief. She said that her sole consolation in her grief was that the princess allowed her to share it with her. She said that all the old misunderstandings should be turned to naught before their great grief, that she felt herself pure before everyone, and that *he* could see her love and gratitude from there. The princess listened to her without understanding her words, but glancing at her from time to time and listening to the sounds of her voice.

"Your position is doubly terrible, dear princess," said Mlle Bourienne after a brief pause. "I realize that you could not and cannot think about yourself; but my love for you obliges me to do so . . . Did Alpatych come to see you? Did he talk with you about leaving?" she asked.

Princess Marya did not reply. She did not understand who had to leave and for where. "Is it possible to undertake anything, to think about anything now? Does it make any difference?" She did not reply.

"Do you know, *chère Marie*," said Mlle Bourienne, "do you know that we are in danger, that we are surrounded by the French? To leave now is dangerous. If we go, we're almost certain to be taken prisoner, and God knows . . ."

Princess Marya gazed at her friend without understanding what she was talking about.

"Ah, if anyone knew how little difference it makes to me now," she said. "Naturally, I would not wish to leave *him* for anything . . . Alpatych said something to me about leaving . . . Talk with him, there's nothing, nothing I can or want to do . . ."

"I did talk with him. He hopes we will manage to leave tomorrow; but I think it would be better now to stay here," said Mlle Bourienne. "Because, you'll agree, *chère Marie,* to fall into the hands of soldiers or rebellious muzhiks on the road would be terrible." Mlle Bourienne took from her reticule and handed to the princess an announcement by the French general Rameau, on unusual non-Russian paper, that the inhabitants should not abandon their homes, that they would be duly protected by the French.

"I think it's better to turn to this general," said Mlle Bourienne, "and I'm sure you'll be treated with due respect."

Princess Marya read the leaflet, and her face twitched with dry sobs.

"Whom did you get this from?" she asked.

"They probably found out that I have a French name," Mlle Bourienne said, blushing.

Princess Marya, the leaflet in her hand, got up from the window and with a pale face went to Prince Andrei's former study.

"Dunyasha, send me Alpatych, Dronushka, somebody," said Princess Marya, "and tell Amalia Karlovna not to come in here," she added, hearing the voice of Mlle Bourienne. "To leave quickly! Quickly leave!" Princess Marya repeated, horrified at the thought that she might remain in the power of the French.

"That Prince Andrei should learn that she was in the power of the French! That she, the daughter of Nikolai Andreich Bolkonsky, should beg Mister General Rameau to protect her and be her benefactor!" This thought horrified her, made her shudder, blush, and experience fits of anger and pride such as she had never felt before. All that was painful and, above all, insulting in her position vividly presented itself to her. "They, the French, will settle in this house; Mister General Rameau will occupy Prince Andrei's study; will amuse himself going through and reading his letters and papers. *Mlle Bourienne lui fera les honneurs de* Bogucharovo.* I'll be given a small room as a favour; the soldiers will devastate my father's fresh grave to take his crosses and decorations; they'll tell me about their victories over the Russians, they'll feign sympathy with my grief . . ." thought Princess Marya, not according to her own mind,

---

*Mlle Bourienne will do him the honours of *Bogucharovo.*

but feeling it her duty to think for herself the thoughts of her father and brother. For herself personally it made no difference where she stayed or what happened to her; but she felt herself at the same time the representative of her late father and of Prince Andrei. She involuntarily thought their thoughts and felt their feelings. Whatever they would have said, whatever they would have done now, she felt it necessary to do the same. She went into Prince Andrei's study and, trying to be penetrated by his thoughts, reflected on her position.

The demands of life, which she had considered annihilated by her father's death, suddenly emerged before Princess Marya with a new, as yet unknown force, and gripped her.

Agitated, flushed, she paced the room, demanding to see Alpatych, then Mikhail Ivanovich, then Tikhon, then Dron. Dunyasha, the nanny, and all the maids could tell her nothing about the extent to which what Mlle Bourienne had told her was correct. Alpatych was not at home: he had gone to the authorities. The architect Mikhail Ivanovich, when summoned, appeared before Princess Marya with sleepy eyes and could tell her nothing. With the same smile of agreement with which it had been his habit over fifteen years to respond, without expressing his own opinion, to the old prince's remarks, he now responded to Princess Marya, so that nothing definite could be drawn from his responses. The old valet Tikhon, when summoned, came with a sagging and sunken face, which bore the stamp of incurable grief, answered "Yes, ma'am" to all Princess Marya's questions, and could barely hold back his sobs looking at her.

Finally the headman Dron came to the room and, bowing low to the princess, stopped on the threshold.

Princess Marya walked across the room and stopped, facing him.

"Dronushka," said Princess Marya, seeing in him an unquestionable friend, the same Dronushka who, from his annual trip to the fair in Vyazma, brought back each time a gingerbread he bought specially and handed it to her with a smile. "Dronushka, now, after our misfortune . . ." she began and fell silent, unable to speak further.

"We all walk under God," he said with a sigh. They were both silent.

"Dronushka, Alpatych has gone off somewhere, I have no one to turn to. Is it true what they say to me, that it's impossible for me to leave?"

"Why shouldn't you leave, Your Excellency, it's possible to leave," said Dron.

"They tell me there's danger from the enemy. Dear heart, I can do nothing, I understand nothing, I have nobody with me. I want to leave for certain during the night or early tomorrow morning." Dron was silent. He glanced at Princess Marya from under his eyebrows.

"There's no horses," he said, "I told Yakov Alpatych so."

"Why aren't there?" asked the princess.

"It's all from God's punishment," said Dron. "Whatever horses there were got taken for the army, and some dropped dead, it's been such a year. Not just for feeding horses, but to keep from starving to death ourselves! As it is they sometimes go three days without food. There's nothing, they're completely devastated."

Princess Marya listened attentively to what he said to her.

"The muzhiks are devastated? They have no bread?" she asked.

"Starving to death," said Dron, "it's not just carts . . ."

"But why didn't you tell me, Dronushka? Can anything be done? I'll do all I can . . ." It was strange for Princess Marya to think that now, at a moment when such grief filled her soul, there could be rich and poor people, and that the rich would not help the poor. She had vaguely known and heard that there was the master's grain and that it could be given to the muzhiks. She also knew that neither her brother nor her father would have refused muzhiks in need; she was only afraid of somehow making a mistake in words concerning this distributing of grain to the muzhiks, which she wanted to order. She was glad that the pretext presented itself to her of a concern which made it not shameful for her to forget her own grief. She started asking Dronushka for details about the needs of the muzhiks and about what belonged to the masters of Bogucharovo.

"But we do have the master's grain, my brother's?" she asked.

"The master's grain is all there," Dron said proudly, "our prince told us not to sell it."

"Give it to the muzhiks, give them as much as they need: I allow it in my brother's name," said Princess Marya.

Dron said nothing and sighed deeply.

"Distribute that grain among them, if it will be enough for them. Distribute all of it. I order it in my brother's name, and tell them: what's ours is also theirs. We don't grudge them anything. Tell them that."

Dron looked intently at the princess as she spoke.

"Release me, mistress, for God's sake, have the keys taken from me," he said. "I've served for twenty-three years, never did any wrong; release me, for God's sake."

Princess Marya did not understand what he wanted from her and what he was asking to be released from. She replied that she had never doubted his devotion and that she was ready to do everything for him and for the muzhiks.

XI

An hour later Dunyasha came to the princess with the news that Dron had come and that all the muzhiks, on the princess's order, had assembled by the barn, wishing to talk with their mistress.

"But I never called them," said Princess Marya, "I only told Dron to distribute grain to them."

"Only for God's sake, dear princess, order them chased away and don't go out to them. It's all a trick," said Dunyasha, "but Yakov Alpatych will come back, and we'll leave . . . and please don't . . ."

"What sort of trick?" the princess said in surprise.

"Only listen to me, for God's sake, I do know. You can ask the nanny. They say they don't agree to leave on your orders."

"There's something wrong in what you're saying. I never ordered them to leave . . ." said Princess Marya. "Call Dronushka."

Dron came and confirmed Dunyasha's words: the muzhiks had come on the princess's orders.

"But I never called them," said the princess. "You must have made a mistake in what you told them. I only said that you should give them grain."

Dron sighed and did not reply.

"If you order it, they'll go away," he said.

"No, no, I'll go to them," said Princess Marya.

Despite the protests of Dunyasha and the nanny, Princess Marya went out to the porch. Dron, Dunyasha, the nanny, and Mikhail Ivanych followed her.

"They probably think I'm offering them grain so that they'll stay here, and that I'll leave myself, abandoning them to the mercy of the French," thought Princess Marya. "I'll promise them monthly rations and quarters on the estate near Moscow; I'm sure André would do still more in my place," she thought, approaching in the twilight the crowd standing on the green by the barn.

The crowd, clustering together, stirred, and hats were quickly taken off. Princess Marya, her eyes lowered, her legs getting tangled in her dress, went up close to them. So many different old and young eyes were directed at her, and there were so many different faces, that Princess Marya did not see any one face, and feeling it necessary to talk to all of them at once, she did not know what to do. But again the awareness of being the representative of her father and brother gave her strength, and she boldly began her speech:

"I am very glad that you have come," Princess Marya began, without raising her eyes and feeling how fast and hard her heart was pounding. "Dronushka told me that you have been devastated by the war. That is our common grief, and I will spare nothing to help you. I am leaving myself, because it's dangerous here now, and the enemy is close . . . because . . . I am giving you everything, my friends, and I beg you to take everything, all our grain, so that you won't be in need. And if you were told that I am giving you grain so that you will stay here, that is not true. On the contrary, I beg you to leave with all your possessions for our estate near Moscow, and there I take it upon myself and promise you that you will not be in need. You will be given houses and grain." The princess stopped. Nothing but sighs came from the crowd.

"I am not doing it of myself," the princess went on, "I am doing it in the name of my late father, who was a good master to you, and of my brother and his son."

She stopped again. No one broke her silence.

"Ours is a common grief, and we shall share everything. All that is mine is yours," she said, looking at the faces that stood before her.

All eyes were looking at her with the same expression, the meaning of which she could not understand. Whether it was curiosity, devotion, gratitude, or fear and mistrust, the expression on all the faces was the same.

"Much obliged for your goodness, only it's not for us to go taking the master's grain," said a voice at the back.

"But why not?" said the princess.

No one answered, and Princess Marya, looking over the crowd, noticed that now all the eyes she met were lowered at once.

"Why don't you want to?" she asked again. No one answered.

Princess Marya began to be oppressed by this silence; she tried to catch someone's eyes.

"Why don't you speak?" the princess addressed an old man who stood in front of her, leaning on a stick. "Tell me if you think something else is needed. I'll do everything," she said, catching his eyes. But he, as if angered by that, lowered his head altogether and said:

"What's there to agree to, we don't need your grain."

"What, us abandon everything? We don't agree. We don't agree . . . We're sorry for you, but we're not in agreement. You go by yourself . . ." came from different sides of the crowd. And again one and the same expression appeared on all the faces in this crowd, and now it was certainly not an expression of curiosity and gratitude, but of angry resolve.

"But surely you haven't understood," Princess Marya said with a sad smile. "Why don't you want to leave? I promise to house you, to feed you. And here the enemy will devastate you . . ."

But her voice was drowned out by the voices of the crowd.

"We're not in agreement, let them devastate us! We don't take your grain, we're not in agreement!"

Princess Marya again tried to catch someone's eyes in the crowd, but not a single gaze was directed at her; they obviously avoided her eyes. She felt strange and awkward.

"See what clever teaching, follow her into bondage! Wreck your houses and go into servitude! What else! I'll give you my grain, she says!" voices said in the crowd.

Princess Marya, lowering her head, left the circle and went to the house. After repeating the order to Dron to have the horses ready for departure, she went to her room and remained alone with her thoughts.

XII

That night Princess Marya sat for a long time by the open window in her room, listening to the sounds of the muzhiks' talk, which reached her from the village, but she was not thinking about them. She felt that, however much she thought about them, she could not understand them. She kept thinking about one thing—her grief, which, after the interruption caused by the cares of the present, had already become her past. Now she could remember, she could weep, and she could pray. As the sun set, the wind died down. The night was still and fresh. Towards midnight the voices began to subside, a cock crowed, the full moon began to appear from behind the lindens, a fresh, white, dewy mist rose, and silence now reigned over the village and the house.

One after another she imagined pictures of the recent past—her father's illness and his last moments. And with sad joy she now dwelt on those images, driving away from her with horror only the one last picture of his death, which she felt unable to contemplate even in her imagination at this still and mysterious hour of the night. And these pictures appeared before her with such clarity and detail that they seemed to her now a reality, now the past, now the future.

Then she vividly pictured the moment when he had had the stroke and had been dragged under the arms from the garden in Bald Hills, and had muttered something with his strengthless tongue, twitched his grey eyebrows, and looked at her anxiously and timidly.

"He wanted to tell me even then what he told me on the day of his death," she thought. "He had always thought what he told me." And here Princess Marya remembered in all its details that night at Bald Hills, on the eve of his stroke, when, having a foreboding of disaster, she had stayed with him against his will. She had not slept and at night had tiptoed downstairs and, going to the door of the flower room, where her father was spending that night, had listened to his voice. In a suffering, weary voice he was saying something to Tikhon. He evidently wanted to talk. "Why didn't he call me? Why didn't he allow me to be there instead of Tikhon?" Princess Marya wondered then and now. "Now he'll never tell anyone all that was in his soul. Neither for him nor for me will the moment ever come back when he could say everything he wanted to say, and I, not Tikhon, could listen and understand him. Why didn't I go into the room then?" she wondered. "Maybe he would have told me then what he said on the day of his death. He did ask twice about me then, during his talk with Tikhon. He wanted to see me, and I stood there outside the door. It was sad, it was hard for him to talk with Tikhon, who didn't understand him. I remember he mentioned Liza to him, as though she were alive—he had forgotten she had died, and Tikhon reminded him that she was no more, and he cried: 'Fool.' It was hard for him. I heard from outside the door how he lay down, groaning, on his bed and cried loudly, 'My God!' Why didn't I go in then? What would he have done to me? What would I have lost? And perhaps then he would have been comforted and would have told me his word." And Princess Marya said aloud the endearing words he had said to her on the day of his death: "De-ear he-eart!" Princess Marya repeated the words and sobbed with tears that eased her soul. She now saw his face before her. Not the face she had known ever since she could remember, and which she had always seen from a distance, but the face—timid and weak—which on the last day, as she bent close to his mouth to hear what he said, she had seen for the first time close up, with all its wrinkles and details.

"Dear heart," she repeated.

"What was he thinking when he said those words? What is he thinking now?" the question suddenly came to her, and in response to it she saw him before her with the expression he had had in the coffin, on his face bound with a white handkerchief. And the horror that had seized her then, when she had touched him and become convinced not only that this was not he, but that it was something mysterious and repugnant, seized her now. She wanted to think about other things, wanted to pray, and could do nothing. She stared wide-eyed at the moonlight and shadows, expected every second to see his dead face, and felt that the silence that hung over the house and within it held her fast.

"Dunyasha!" she whispered. "Dunyasha!" she cried in a wild voice, and tearing free of the silence, she ran to the maids' room, towards the nanny and maids who came running to her.

XIII

On the seventeenth of August, Rostov and Ilyin, accompanied by Lavrushka, who had just returned from captivity, and a hussar orderly, leaving their camp in Yankovo, ten miles from Bogucharovo, went for a ride—to try out a horse Ilyin had just bought, and to see if there was any hay in the villages.

For the past three days, Bogucharovo had been between two enemy armies, so that the Russian rear guard could get there as easily as the French vanguard, and therefore Rostov, as a thoughtful squadron commander, wanted to avail himself of whatever provisions had been left in Bogucharovo before the French got there.

Rostov and Ilyin were in the most cheerful mood. On the way to Bogucharovo, a princely estate with a manor house, where they hoped to find a large staff and some pretty girls, they either questioned Lavrushka about Napoleon and laughed at his stories, or raced each other, trying out Ilyin's horse.

Rostov had no idea that the village he was going to was the estate of that Bolkonsky who used to be his sister's fiancé.

Rostov and Ilyin sent their horses into a last race down the slope before Bogucharovo, and Rostov, getting ahead of Ilyin, was the first to gallop into the street of the village.

"You came out ahead," said the flushed Ilyin.

"Yes, always ahead, both in the meadow and here," Rostov replied, stroking his lathered Don horse with his hand.

"And I'd have outraced you on this Frenchman, Your Excellency," Lavrushka said from behind, calling his scrubby cart horse a Frenchman, "but I didn't want to shame you."

They rode at a walk towards a barn, by which a large crowd of muzhiks was standing.

Some of the muzhiks took off their hats, some, without taking off their hats, looked at the approaching officers. Two tall old muzhiks, with wrinkled faces and sparse beards, came out of the pot-house and, smiling, swaying, and singing some nonsensical song, went up to the officers.

"Fine lads!" said Rostov, laughing. "Got any hay?"

"And so alike . . ." said Ilyin.

"A ve-e-ery me-e-erry ta-a-alk . . ." the muzhiks sang away with blissful smiles.

One muzhik stepped out of the crowd and approached Rostov.

"Whose might you be?" he asked.

"Frenchmen," Ilyin replied, laughing. "Here's Napoleon himself," he said, pointing to Lavrushka.

"So you'd be Russians?" the muzhik asked again.

"Have you got many forces here?" asked another rather short muzhik, going up to them.

"Many, many," replied Rostov. "But why are you gathered here?" he added. "Is there a feast?"

"The old men got together on village business," the muzhik replied, stepping away from him.

Just then two women and a man in a white hat appeared on the road from the manor house, walking towards the officers.

"The one in pink's mine, no haggling!" said Ilyin, noticing Dunyasha resolutely heading towards him.

"Ours!" Lavrushka said to Ilyin with a wink.

"What do you want, my beauty?" said Ilyin, smiling.

"The princess asked me to find out your names and regiment."

"This is Count Rostov, the squadron commander, and I am your obedient servant."

"A ta-a-alky ta-a-alk!" the drunken muzhik sang away, smiling blissfully and looking at Ilyin talking with the maid. Following Dunyasha, Alpatych went up to Rostov, taking off his hat while still some distance away.

"I make so bold as to trouble you, Your Honour," he said respectfully, but with relative scorn for the youth of this officer, and putting his hand behind his lapel. "My mistress, the daughter of General in Chief Prince Nikolai Andree-vich Bolkonsky, who passed away on the fifteenth instant, being in difficulty on the occasion of the ignorance of these persons," he pointed to the muzhiks, "asks you kindly . . . would you be so good," Alpatych said with a sad smile, "as to ride off a little, for it is not so convenient in front of . . ." Alpatych pointed to the two muzhiks, who flitted about behind him like gadflies round a horse.

"Eh! . . . Alpatych . . . Eh? Yakov Alpatych! . . . A grand thing! Forgive us, for Christ's sake! A grand thing! Eh? . . ." the muzhiks said, smiling joyfully at him. Rostov looked at the drunken old men and smiled.

"Or perhaps Your Excellency finds this amusing?" Yakov Alpatych said sedately, pointing to the old men with the hand not put behind his lapel.

"No, it's not very amusing," said Rostov, and he rode aside. "What's the matter?" he asked.

"I make so bold as to report to Your Excellency that the coarse local people do not want to allow our mistress to quit the estate and threaten to unharness the horses, so that, though everything has been packed since morning, her excellency cannot leave."

"It can't be!" cried Rostov.

"I have the honour of reporting the real truth to you," Alpatych confirmed.

Rostov got off his horse and, turning it over to the orderly, went to the house with Alpatych, questioning him about the details of the matter. Indeed, the princess's offer of grain to the muzhiks the evening before, and her talk with Dron and to the gathering, had so spoiled things that Dron had definitively handed over the keys, joined the muzhiks, and refused to come when summoned by Alpatych, and in the morning, when the princess ordered them to harness up for leaving, the muzhiks came to the barn in a large crowd and sent to tell the princess that they would not let her out of the village, that there was an order not to leave, and that they would unhitch the horses. Alpatych went to them, trying to bring them to reason, but they answered him (Karp did most of the talking; Dron did not appear in the crowd) that it was impossible to let the princess go, that there was an order about it; but let the princess stay, and they would serve her as before and obey her in everything.

Just when Rostov and Ilyin came galloping down the road, Princess Marya, despite the attempts of Alpatych, the nanny, and the maids to dissuade her, had ordered the harnessing and wanted to leave; but, seeing the two cavalrymen gallop by, they took them for Frenchmen, the coachmen fled, and the women in the house began to weep.

"Dearest! My dearest! God has sent you!" deeply moved voices were saying as Rostov passed through the front hall.

Princess Marya, at a loss and strengthless, was sitting in the reception room when Rostov was brought to her. She did not understand who he was, or why he was there, or what would happen to her. Seeing his Russian face and recognizing him, by the way he walked in and by his first words, as a person of her own circle, she looked at him with her deep and luminous gaze and began to speak in a faltering voice trembling with agitation. Rostov immediately imagined something romantic in this encounter. "A defenceless, grief-stricken girl, alone, left to the mercy of coarse, mutinous muzhiks! And what a strange fate has pushed me to come here!" thought Rostov, listening to her and looking at her. "And what meekness, what nobility in her features and expression!" he thought, listening to her timid account.

When she mentioned that it had all happened the day after her father's funeral, her voice trembled. She turned away and then, as if fearing that Rostov might take her words for a wish to move him to pity her, gave him a questioningly frightened glance. Tears welled up in Rostov's eyes. Princess Marya noticed it and looked at Rostov gratefully, with that luminous gaze which made one forget the plainness of her face.

"I cannot express to you, Princess, how happy I am that I have come here accidentally and will be in a position to show you my readiness," Rostov said, getting up. "Go, please, and I will answer to you on my honour that not a single person will dare cause you any trouble, if only you will allow me to escort you," and, bowing respectfully, as one bows to a lady of royal blood, he went to the door.

With the respectfulness of his tone, Rostov seemed to be showing that, though he would consider himself fortunate to make her acquaintance, he did not want to use the occasion of her misfortune to become closer to her.

Princess Marya understood and appreciated that tone.

"I am very, very grateful to you," the princess said to him in French, "but I hope it was all a misunderstanding and that no one is to blame for it." The princess suddenly began to cry. "Excuse me," she said.

Rostov frowned, gave her one more low bow, and left the room.

XIV

"Well, what, is she pretty? No, brother, my pink one's lovely, and her name is Dunyasha . . ." But, glancing at Rostov's face, Ilyin fell silent. He saw that his hero and commander was in quite a different frame of mind.

Rostov gave Ilyin an angry look and, without replying, headed at a quick pace for the village.

"I'll show them, I'll give it to them, the brigands!" he was saying to himself.

Alpatych, gliding along, all but running, followed behind Rostov, barely keeping up with him.

"What decision have you been pleased to take?" he asked, catching up with him.

Rostov stopped and, clenching his fists, suddenly turned on Alpatych threateningly.

"Decision? What decision? You old cod!" he yelled at him. "Where were you looking? Eh? The muzhiks are rebellious, and you can't handle them? You're a traitor yourself. I know you all, I'll have your hides . . ." And, as if fearing to expend his store of anger uselessly, he left Alpatych and quickly went on. Alpatych, suppressing his offended feeling, glided hurriedly after Rostov, and went on telling him his reflections. He said that the peasants were obdurate, that at the present moment it was not sensible to *antagonorize* them, with no military detachment round, that it would be better to send for a detachment first.

"I'll give them an army detachment . . . I'll antagonize them," Nikolai muttered senselessly, choking with unreasonable animal anger and the need to vent that anger. Without considering what he was going to do, unconsciously, at a quick, resolute pace, he moved towards the crowd. And the closer he came to it, the more Alpatych felt that his unreasonable action might produce good results. The muzhiks in the crowd had the same feeling, looking at his quick and firm stride and resolute, frowning face.

After the hussars rode into the village and Rostov went to the princess, confusion and discord arose in the crowd. Some of the muzhiks began to say that the men who had come were Russian and might take offence that the young lady was not allowed to leave. Dron was of the same opinion; but as soon as he expressed it, Karp and some other muzhiks fell upon the former headman.

"How many years have you been feeding off the community?" Karp yelled at him. "It's all the same to you! You'll dig up your money box and take it with you, so what's it to you if our houses are devastated?"

"We're told there's to be order, nobody's to leave their houses, so as not a single crumb gets taken away—and that's that!" shouted another.

"It was your son's turn, but no fear, you felt sorry for your chubsy," a little old man suddenly spoke quickly, attacking Dron, "so my Vanka got his head shaved. Ah, we'll all die!"

"Right, we'll all die!"

"I'm no holdout on the community," said Dron.

"So he's no holdout, grown himself a nice paunch! . . ."

The two tall muzhiks were having their say. As soon as Rostov, accompanied by Ilyin, Lavrushka, and Alpatych, came up to the crowd, Karp, putting his fingers behind his belt, smiling slightly, stepped forward. Dron, on the contrary, went to the back rows, and the crowd closed in more tightly.

"Hey! Who's your headman here?" shouted Rostov, coming up to the crowd with quick strides.

"Our headman? What do you want him for? . . ." asked Karp.

But before he finished speaking, his hat went flying and his head rocked sideways from a strong blow.

"Hats off, traitors!" cried the full-blooded voice of Rostov. "Where's the headman?" he shouted furiously.

"The headman, he's calling for the headman . . . You, Dron Zakharych," obedient voices said hurriedly, and hats began coming off heads.

"There's no rebelling with us, we keep order," said Karp, and several voices from the back suddenly spoke at the same time:

"It's like the old men decided . . . there's lots of you superiors . . ."

"Speaking out? . . . Rebellion! . . . Brigands! Traitors!" Rostov yelled senselessly, in a voice not his own, seizing Karp by the collar. "Bind him, bind him!" he shouted, though there was no one to bind him except Lavrushka and Alpatych.

Lavrushka, however, ran up to Karp and seized his arms from behind.

"Shall I call our boys from over the hill?" he shouted.

Alpatych turned to the muzhiks, calling two by name to come and bind Karp. The muzhiks obediently stepped out of the crowd and began taking off their belts.

"Where's the headman?" cried Rostov.

Dron, with a frowning and pale face, stepped out of the crowd.

"You're the headman? Bind him, Lavrushka!" cried Rostov, as if this order, too, could meet with no hindrance. And in fact, two more muzhiks began to bind Dron, who, as if to help them, took off his belt and handed it to them.

"And you all listen to me." Rostov turned to the muzhiks. "March off to your homes right now, and don't let me hear a peep from you."

"Why, we didn't do any harm. It was just out of stupidity. Just a lot of nonsense . . . I kept saying it was wrong," voices were heard reproaching each other.

"It's just as I told to you," said Alpatych, entering into his rights. "It wasn't nice, boys."

"Our own stupidity, Yakov Alpatych," voices responded, and the crowd immediately began to break up and scatter through the village.

The two bound muzhiks were taken to the yard of the manor house. The two drunken muzhiks followed.

"Eh, just look at you!" one of them said, addressing Karp. "As if you can talk like that with the masters! What were you thinking of?"

"A fool," the other confirmed, "a real fool!"

Two hours later the carts stood in the yard of the Bogucharovo house. The muzhiks were animatedly carrying out the masters' belongings and loading them on the carts, and Dron, freed at the princess's request from the storeroom in which he had been locked, stood in the yard ordering the muzhiks about.

"Be careful how you set it down," said one of the muzhiks, a tall man with a round, smiling face, taking a chest from a maid's hands. "It also costs money. If you throw it down like that or put a rope on it, it'll get scuffed. I don't like that. Everything should be honest, by the rules. Like this, under a bast mat, and covered with some straw, there, that's grand. Beautiful!"

"Books, look at the books," said another muzhik, taking out Prince Andrei's bookcases. "Don't snag on anything! It's a real load, boys, hefty books!"

"Yes, they wrote and didn't dote," said the tall, round-faced muzhik, with a meaningful wink, pointing to the fat dictionaries that lay on top.

Rostov, unwilling to thrust his acquaintance upon the princess, did not approach her, but stayed in the village awaiting her departure. Having waited until Princess Marya's carriages left the house, Rostov mounted his horse and accompanied her, riding as far as the road occupied by our troops, eight miles from Bogucharovo. In Yankovo, at the inn, he respectfully took leave of her, for the first time allowing himself to kiss her hand.

"Shame on you," he said, blushing, in reply to Princess Marya's expression of gratitude for her salvation (as she called what he had done), "any policeman would have done the same. If we only had to make war on muzhiks, we wouldn't have let the enemy get so far," he said, embarrassed at something and trying to change the subject. "I am only happy to have had the chance to make your acquaintance. Goodbye, Princess, I wish you happiness and consolation and wish to meet you under happier circumstances. If you don't want to make me blush, please, don't thank me."

But the princess, if she no longer thanked him with words, thanked him with the whole expression of her face, radiant with gratitude and tenderness. She could not believe that she had nothing to thank him for. On the contrary, for her it was unquestionable that, if he had not been there, she would certainly have perished, both from the rebels and from the French; that *he,* in order to save her, had subjected himself to the most obvious and terrible dangers; and it was still more unquestionable that he was a man of lofty and noble soul, who had been able to understand her position and her grief. His kind and honest eyes, with tears welling up in them, at that time when she herself, weeping, had spoken to him of her loss, would not leave her imagination.

When she said goodbye to him and was left alone, Princess Marya suddenly felt tears in her eyes, and here, not for the first time, a strange question presented itself to her: did she love him?

Further on the way to Moscow, despite the fact that the princess's position was not joyful, Dunyasha, who was riding in the carriage with her, noticed more than once that the princess, leaning out the window of the carriage, was smiling joyfully and sadly at something.

"Well, what if I really have fallen in love with him?" thought Princess Marya.

Ashamed as she was to admit to herself that she had fallen in love first with a man who, perhaps, would never love her, she comforted herself with the thought that no one would ever know of it, and that she would not be to blame if, to the end of her life, without speaking of it to anyone, she should love the one she loved for the first and last time.

Sometimes she remembered his glances, his sympathy, his words, and happiness did not seem impossible to her. And it was then that Dunyasha noticed her, smiling, looking out of the window of the carriage.

"And it had to be that he came to Bogucharovo, and at that very moment!" thought Princess Marya. "And his sister had to refuse Prince Andrei!" And in all of that Princess Marya saw the will of Providence.

The impression Princess Marya made on Rostov was very pleasant. Whenever he remembered her, he became cheerful, and when his comrades, having learned of his adventure in Bogucharovo, teased him with having gone for hay and picked up one of the wealthiest brides in Russia, Rostov became angry. He became angry precisely because, against his will, the thought of marrying the meek Princess Marya, whom he found pleasant and who had an enormous fortune, had occurred to him more than once. For himself personally, Nikolai could not have wished for a better wife than Princess Marya: his marriage to her would make for the happiness of the countess, his mother, and would straighten out the affairs of his father; and it would even—Nikolai felt this—make for the happiness of Princess Marya.

But Sonya? And the word he had given? That was what made Rostov angry when they teased him about Princess Bolkonsky.

XV

Having taken command of the armies, Kutuzov remembered Prince Andrei and sent him an order to report to headquarters.

Prince Andrei arrived in Tsarevo-Zaimishche on the same day and at the same time of day that Kutuzov held the first review of the troops. Prince Andrei stopped in the village at the house of the priest, in front of which the commander in chief's carriage stood, and sat down on a bench by the gate to wait for his serenity, as everyone now called Kutuzov. From the field beyond the village one could hear the sounds of regimental music, then the roaring of an enormous number of voices shouting "Hurrah!" to the new commander in chief. There by the gate, ten paces from Prince Andrei, taking advantage of the prince's absence and the splendid weather, stood two orderlies, a courier, and a butler. A small, dark-haired lieutenant colonel of hussars, all overgrown with moustaches and side-whiskers, rode up to the gate and, glancing at Prince Andrei, asked if his serenity was staying there and when he would be back.

Prince Andrei said that he did not belong to his serenity's staff and was also a new arrival. The hussar lieutenant colonel turned to a smartly dressed orderly, and the commander in chief's orderly said to him, with that special contempt with which a commander in chief's orderlies speak to officers:

"What, his serenity? Should be here shortly. What do you want?"

The hussar lieutenant colonel smiled into his moustaches at the orderly's tone, got off his horse, handed it over to the courier, and went up to Bolkonsky with a slight bow. Bolkonsky moved over on the bench. The hussar lieutenant colonel sat down beside him.

"Also waiting for the commander in chief?" said the hussar lieutenant colonel. "They say he's accessible to eveghrybody, thank God. With those sausage makers it was big tghrouble! Not for nothing did Eghrmolov ask to be made a Geghrman. Now maybe Ghrussians will be able to speak, too. Otherwise devil knows what they've been up to. Ghretghreating, ghretghreating all the time. Did you do the campaign?" he asked.

"I had the pleasure," replied Prince Andrei, "not only of taking part in the retreat, but also of losing in that retreat everything that was dear to me, not to speak of my estates and the house I was born in . . . my father, who died of grief. I'm from the province of Smolensk."

"Ah? . . . You're Pghrince Bolkonsky? Veghry glad to make your acquaintance: Lieutenant Colonel Denisov, better known as Vaska," said Denisov, shaking Prince Andrei's hand and peering into his face with especially kind attention. "Yes, I heard," he said with sympathy and, after a brief pause, went on: "That's Scythian war. It's all veghry well, only not for those who catch it in the ghribs. So you're Pghrince Andghrei Bolkonsky?" He nodded his head. "Veghry glad, Pghrince, veghry glad to make your acquaintance," he added, again with a sad smile, shaking his hand.

Prince Andrei knew Denisov from Natasha's stories about her first suitor. That memory now carried him back sweetly and painfully to those aching feelings which he had not thought of for a long time now, but which were still there in his soul. Recently he had received so many other and such serious impressions—the abandoning of Smolensk, his visit to Bald Hills, the recent news of his father's death—and had experienced so many feelings, that these memories had not come to him for a long time, and when they came, were far from affecting him with their former strength. And for Denisov that series of memories evoked by the name Bolkonsky was a distant, poetic past, when, after supper and Natasha's singing, not knowing how himself, he had proposed to a fifteen-year-old girl. He smiled at the memory of that time and of his love for Natasha, and went on at once to what now concerned him passionately and exclusively. It was a campaign plan he had thought up while serving at outposts during the retreat. He had presented this plan to Barclay de Tolly and now intended to present it to Kutuzov. The plan was based on the fact that the French line of operations was very extended, and that, instead of or along with acting from the front, blocking the road for the French, they ought to act against their communications. He began to explain this plan to Prince Andrei.

"They can't maintain that whole line. It's impossible, I'll answer for bghreaking thghrough them; give me five hundghred men, and I'll bghreak thghrough them, that's ceghrtain! The only system is the paghrtisan one."[15]

Denisov stood up and, gesticulating, set forth his plan for Bolkonsky. In the middle of the account, the shouts of the army, more incoherent, more prolonged, and merging with the music and songs, came from the place of the review. In the village, hoofbeats and shouts could be heard.

"Himself is coming," cried a Cossack who was standing by the gate, "he's coming!"

Bolkonsky and Denisov moved towards the gate, by which a bunch of soldiers (an honour guard) was standing, and saw Kutuzov moving down the street mounted on a small bay horse. An enormous suite of generals rode after him. Barclay rode almost beside him; a crowd of officers ran after them and round them and shouted "Hurrah!"

The adjutants rode into the yard ahead of him. Kutuzov, impatiently urging on his horse, which glided at an amble under his weight, and constantly nodding his head, kept putting his hand to the white cap of the horse guards he was wearing (with a red band and no visor). Coming up to the honour guard of dashing grenadiers, most of them decorated, who were saluting him, he studied them silently and attentively for a minute with a commander's intent gaze and turned to the crowd of generals and officers that stood round him.

His face suddenly assumed a subtle expression; he shrugged his shoulders in a gesture of perplexity.

"And with such fine fellows, to keep retreating and retreating!" he said. "Well, goodbye, General," he added and sent his horse through the gate past Prince Andrei and Denisov.

"Hurrah! Hurrah! Hurrah!" cries came behind him.

Since Prince Andrei last saw him, Kutuzov had grown still heavier, become flabby and swollen with fat. But his familiar white eye, and the wound, and the weary expression of his face and figure were the same. He was dressed in a uniform jacket (the whip hung on a thin strap over his shoulder) and the white horse guard's cap. He sat on his brisk horse, sagging and swaying heavily.

"Phew . . . phew . . . phew," he whistled barely audibly, riding into the courtyard. His face expressed the joy of relief a man feels who intends to rest after an official appearance. He took his left foot from the stirrup and with difficulty, swinging his whole body and wincing from the effort, lifted it over the saddle, leaned on his knee, grunted, and lowered himself into the arms of the Cossacks and adjutants, who supported him.

He straightened up, looked round with his narrowed gaze and, glancing at Prince Andrei, obviously without recognizing him, strode towards the porch with his dipping gait.

"Phew . . . phew . . . phew," he whistled and again glanced round at Prince Andrei. Only after several seconds did the impression of Prince Andrei's face (as often happens with old men) connect with the remembrance of his person.

"Ah, greetings, Prince, greetings, dear boy, come along . . ." he said wearily, looking round, and went heavily up the steps, which creaked under his weight. He unbuttoned his jacket and sat down on a bench that stood on the porch.

"Well, how's your father?"

"Yesterday I received news of his passing away," Prince Andrei said shortly.

Kutuzov looked at Prince Andrei with wide-open, startled eyes, then took off his cap and crossed himself: "God rest his soul! His will be done with us all!" He sighed deeply, with his whole chest, and fell silent. "I loved and respected him, and I sympathize with you wholeheartedly." He embraced Prince Andrei, pressed him to his fat chest, and did not let go of him for a long time. When he did, Prince Andrei saw that Kutuzov's swollen lips were trembling and there were tears in his eyes. He sighed and took hold of the bench with both hands in order to stand up.

"Come along, come to my place, we'll have a talk," he said; but just then Denisov, who quailed as little before his superiors as he did before the enemy, though the adjutants by the porch tried to stop him with angry whispers, boldly went up the steps, his spurs knocking against them. Kutuzov, leaving his hands propped on the bench, looked at Denisov with displeasure. Denisov gave his name and announced that he had to inform his serenity of a matter of great importance for the good of the fatherland. Kutuzov began to look at Denisov with his weary gaze and, in a gesture of vexation, taking his hands from the bench and folding them over his stomach, repeated: "For the good of the fatherland? Well, what is it? Speak." Denisov blushed like a girl (how strange it was to see a blush on that moustached, old, and drunken face), and boldly began to set forth his plan for cutting the enemy's line of operations between Smolensk and the Vyazma. Denisov used to live in that area and knew the terrain well. His plan seemed unquestionably good, especially from the power of conviction in his words. Kutuzov was looking at his feet and occasionally glanced at the courtyard of the neighbouring cottage, as if expecting something unpleasant from there. And in fact, during the time that Denisov was speaking, a general with a portfolio under his arm appeared from the cottage he was looking at.

"What?" Kutuzov said in the middle of Denisov's explanation. "Ready so soon?"

"Ready, Your Serenity," said the general. Kutuzov shook his head, as if to say, "How can one man have time for it all," and went on listening to Denisov.

"I give you the noble woghrd of honour of a Ghrussian officer," Denisov was saying, "that I will bghreak Napoleon's communications."

"What relation are you to Kirill Andreevich Denisov, the commissary general?" Kutuzov interrupted him.

"He's my uncle, Your Seghrenity."

"Oh! we were friends," Kutuzov said cheerfully. "Very well, very well, my dear boy, stay here at headquarters, we'll talk tomorrow." Nodding to Denisov, he turned away and held out his hand for the papers Konovnitsyn had brought him.

"Would you be so good as to come in, Your Serenity?" the general on duty said in a displeased voice. "It is necessary to study the plans and sign some papers." An adjutant came out of the door and announced that everything was ready in the apartment. But Kutuzov evidently wanted to be free before going in. He winced . . .

"No, my dear boy, have them bring out a little table, I'll look at them here," he said. "Don't go away," he added, turning to Prince Andrei. Prince Andrei stayed on the porch, listening to the general on duty.

During the report, Prince Andrei heard a woman's whispers and the rustle of a woman's silk dress behind the front door. Several times, glancing in that direction, he noticed behind the door a plump, red-cheeked, and beautiful woman in a pink dress, with a purple silk kerchief on her head, holding a platter and obviously waiting for the commander in chief to come in. Kutuzov's adjutant explained in a whisper to Prince Andrei that she was the mistress of the house, the priest's wife, who intended to meet his serenity with bread and salt.[16] Her husband had met his serenity in church with a cross, and she at home . . . "Very pretty," the adjutant added with a smile. At those words Kutuzov glanced up. Kutuzov listened to the report of the general on duty (the main subject of which was a critique of the position at Tsarevo-Zaimishche) in the same way as he had listened to Denisov, in the same way as he had listened, seven years earlier, to the debate at the Austerlitz council of war. He obviously listened only because he had ears, which, despite the fact that one of them was stopped up with hemp, could not help listening; but it was obvious not only that he could not be surprised or interested in anything the general on duty could tell him, but that he knew beforehand everything he was being told and listened to it only because he had to listen, as one has to listen to the singing of a prayer service. Everything Denisov had said was practical and intelligent. What the general on duty was saying was still more practical and intelligent, but it was obvious that Kutuzov despised both knowledge and intelligence, and knew something else that was to decide matters—something that did not depend on intelligence and knowledge. Prince Andrei followed attentively the expression of the commander in chief's face, and the only expression he was able to notice on it was one of boredom, of curiosity about the meaning of the woman's whispering behind the door, and of the wish to observe propriety. It was obvious that Kutuzov despised the intelligence, the knowledge, and even the patriotic feeling shown by Denisov, but he despised them not with his intelligence, or feeling, or knowledge (for he did not even try to show any), he despised them with something else. He despised them with his old age, with his experience of life. The one order Kutuzov added personally to this report was concerned with looting by Russian troops. At the end of his report, the general on duty presented his serenity with a paper to be signed concerning remuneration by the army commanders, at a landowner's request, for green oats that had been mowed down.

Kutuzov smacked his lips and shook his head, having listened to the matter.

"Into the stove . . . into the fire! And I tell you once and for all, my dear boy," he said, "into the fire with all these things. Let them cut grain and burn wood as much as they like. I don't order it or allow it, but neither can I punish them for it. It's impossible otherwise. When you chop wood, the chips fly." He glanced at the paper once more. "Oh, German scrupulosity!" he said, shaking his head.

XVI

"Well, that's all now!" said Kutuzov, signing the last paper and, getting up heavily and smoothing the folds of his plump, white neck, he headed for the door with a more cheerful face.

The priest's wife, the blood rushing to her face, seized the platter, which, though she had had it so long prepared, she still did not manage to present in time. With a low bow, she offered it to Kutuzov.

Kutuzov's eyes narrowed; he smiled, took her by the chin, and said:

"And such a beauty! Thank you, my dear girl!"

He took a few gold coins from the pocket of his wide trousers and put them on the platter for her.

"Well, how's your life?" said Kutuzov, heading for the room that had been assigned to him. The priest's wife, with dimples on her red-cheeked, smiling face, followed him into the room. The adjutant came out to the porch and invited Prince Andrei to lunch; half an hour later, Prince Andrei was again summoned to Kutuzov. Kutuzov was lying in an armchair, in the same unbuttoned coat. He was holding a French book in his hand, and when Prince Andrei came in, he closed it, using the paper knife as a bookmark. It was *Les chevaliers du Cygne*, by Mme de Genlis,[17] as Prince Andrei saw by the cover.

"Well, sit down, sit down here, let's talk," said Kutuzov. "It's sad, very sad. But remember, my dear friend, that I'm like a father to you, a second father . . ." Prince Andrei told Kutuzov all he knew about his father's passing away, and about what he had seen at Bald Hills as he passed through.

"See . . . see what they've brought us to!" Kutuzov suddenly said with deep feeling, obviously picturing clearly to himself, from Prince Andrei's account, the situation Russia was in. "Just wait, just wait," he added with a spiteful expression on his face and, obviously not wishing to continue this disturbing conversation, he said: "I sent for you so as to keep you with me."

"I thank Your Serenity," replied Prince Andrei, "but I'm afraid I'm no longer fit for the staff," he said with a smile, which Kutuzov noticed. Kutuzov looked at him questioningly. "And above all," Prince Andrei added, "I'm used to the regiment, I've come to love the officers, and the men seem to love me. I'd be sorry to leave the regiment. If I refuse the honour of being attached to you, believe me . . ."

An intelligent, kind, and at the same time subtly mocking expression lit up on Kutuzov's plump face. He interrupted Bolkonsky:

"I'm sorry, I would have had need of you; but you're right, you're right. It's not here that we need men. Advisers are always plentiful, but men are not. The regiments wouldn't be what they are if all the advisers served in them as you do. I remember you from Austerlitz . . . I remember, I remember you with the standard," said Kutuzov, and a flush of joy rose to Prince Andrei's face at this recollection. Kutuzov pulled him to him by the arm, offering him his cheek, and again Prince Andrei saw tears in the old man's eyes. Though Prince Andrei knew that Kutuzov wept easily and that his special gentleness and pity for him now was caused by a desire to show sympathy for his loss, Prince Andrei was both gladdened and flattered by this recollection of Austerlitz.

"Go your way with God. I know, your way is the way of honour." He paused. "I was sorry you weren't in Bucharest: I needed someone to send." And, changing the subject, Kutuzov began speaking about the Turkish war and the peace that had been concluded. "Yes, I've been reproached a good deal," said Kutuzov, "both for the war and for the peace . . . but everything came at the right time. *Tout vient à point à celui qui sait attendre.** And there, too, there were no fewer advisers than here . . ." he went on, returning to the advisers, who were clearly on his mind. "Ah, advisers, advisers!" he said. "If we'd listened to everybody there in Turkey, we wouldn't have made peace and brought the war to an end. Everything quickly, but quick turns out to be slow. If Kamensky hadn't died, he'd have been lost. He stormed fortresses with thirty thousand men.[18] It's not hard to take a fortress, it's hard to win a campaign. And for that there's no need to storm and attack, there's need for *patience and time*. Kamensky sent soldiers to Rushchuk, but I, with just those two (patience and time), took more fortresses than Kamensky and made the Turks eat horseflesh." He shook his head. "And the French will, too! Take my word for it," Kutuzov said, becoming animated and beating his chest, "they'll eat horseflesh for me!" And again his eyes glistened with tears.

"But won't we have to accept battle?" said Prince Andrei.

"We'll have to if everybody wants it, there's no way round it . . . And yet, my dear boy, there's nothing stronger than those two warriors, *patience and time;* they'd do it all, but the advisers *n'entendent pas de cette oreille, voilà le mal.†* Some want it, others don't. What can we do?" he asked, evidently expecting an answer. "Yes, what would you have us do?" he repeated, and his eyes shone with a profound, intelligent expression. "I'll tell you what to do," he went on, since Prince Andrei still gave no answer. "I'll tell you what to do, and what I do. *Dans le doute, mon cher,*" he paused, "*abstiens-toi,"‡* he pronounced measuredly.

"Well, goodbye, my dear friend; remember that I bear your loss with all my heart, and that for you I'm not a serenity, or a prince, or a commander in chief, but a father. If you need anything, come straight to me. Goodbye, my dear boy." Again he embraced him and kissed him. And before Prince Andrei had time to get through the door, Kutuzov sighed and again picked up the unfinished novel by Mme de Genlis, *Les chevaliers du Cygne*.

How and why it happened, Prince Andrei could in no way have explained, but after this meeting with Kutuzov, he went back to his regiment relieved with regard to the general course of things and with regard to the man to whom it had been entrusted. The more he saw the absence of anything personal in this

*Everything comes at the right time to him who knows how to wait.
†Don't hear with that ear, that's the trouble.
‡When in doubt, my dear . . . abstain.

old man, in whom there seemed to remain only the habit of passions, and, instead of intelligence (which groups events and draws conclusions), only the ability to calmly contemplate the course of events, the more calmed he felt over everything being as it had to be. "He won't have anything of his own. He won't invent, won't undertake anything," thought Prince Andrei, "but he'll listen to everything, remember everything, put everything in its place, won't hinder anything useful or allow anything harmful. He understands that there is something stronger and more significant than his will—the inevitable course of events—and he's able to see them, able to understand their significance, and, in view of that significance, is able to renounce participating in those events, renounce his personal will and direct it elsewhere. And the main reason why one believes him," thought Prince Andrei, "is that he's Russian, despite the Genlis novel and the French proverbs; it's that his voice trembled when he said, 'See what they've brought us to!' and had a catch in it when he said he'd 'make them eat horseflesh.' " On this feeling, which was more or less vaguely experienced by everyone, the unanimity and general approval were based which, contrary to the considerations of the court, accompanied the people's election of Kutuzov as commander in chief.

XVII

After the sovereign's departure from Moscow, Moscow life flowed on in its former, habitual way, and the course of that life was so habitual that it was hard to remember the recent days of patriotic rapture and enthusiasm, and it was hard to believe that Russia was actually in danger and that the members of the English Club were at the same time sons of the fatherland, ready for any sacrifice for its sake. The one thing that recalled the general rapturously patriotic mood during the sovereign's stay in Moscow was the call for contributions in men and money, which, as soon as it was made, acquired a legal, official form and seemed inevitable.

With the enemy's approach to Moscow, the Muscovites' view of their situation not only did not become more serious, but, on the contrary, became still more light-minded, as always happens with people who see great danger approaching. At the approach of danger, two voices always speak with equal force in a man's soul: one quite reasonably tells the man to consider the properties of the danger and the means of saving himself from it; the other says still more reasonably that it is too painful and tormenting to think about the danger, when it is not in man's power to foresee everything and save himself from the general course of things, and therefore it is better to turn away from the painful things until they come and think about what is pleasant. In solitude, a man most often yields to the first voice; in company, on the contrary, to the second. That is what now happened with the citizens of Moscow. It was long since there had been so much merrymaking in Moscow as there was that year.

Rastopchin's little posters,[19] with a picture at the top of a drinking house, a tapster, and the Moscow tradesman Karpushka Chigirin *who, being a militiaman and having taken a drop too much from the tap, heard that Bonaparte wanted to march on Moscow, became angry, denounced all the French in nasty terms, came out of the drinking house, and under the eagle began speaking to the assembled people,* were read and discussed on a par with the latest *bouts-rimés* of Vassily Lvovich Pushkin.[20]

People gathered in the corner room of the club to read these posters, and some liked the way Karpushka taunted the French, saying that they will *get bloated with cabbage, burst with kasha, choke on shchi, that they're all dwarfs, and that one peasant woman will toss three of them with a pitchfork.* Some disapproved of this tone and said it was banal and stupid. It was said that Rastopchin had banished all Frenchmen and even all foreigners from Moscow, that there were spies and agents of Napoleon among them; but this was said primarily in order to have an occasion to repeat the witticism Rastopchin had produced as they were being sent away. The foreigners were sent by barge to Nizhny, and Rastopchin said to them: *"Rentrez en vous-même, entrez dans la barque et n'en faites pas une barque de Charon."*[*][21] It was said that all the government offices had already been sent away from Moscow, and at once Shinshin's joke was added, that for that alone people should be grateful to Napoleon. The story went that Mamonov's regiment would cost him eight hundred thousand, that Bezukhov had spent still more on his militia, but that the best thing about Bezukhov's actions was that he was going to put on a uniform himself and ride at the head of his regiment, and charge no admission for those who wanted to look at him.

"You make no grace to anyone," said Julie Drubetskoy, gathering and pressing together a little pile of shredded lint with her slender, beringed fingers.

Julie was preparing to leave Moscow the next day and was giving a farewell soirée.

"Bezukhov *est ridicule,* but he's so kind, so sweet. What's the pleasure to be so *caustique?*"

"A fine!" said a young man in a militia uniform, whom Julie called *"mon chevalier,"* and who was going to Nizhny with her.

In Julie's circle, as in many other circles in Moscow, it had been decided to speak only Russian, and those who mistakenly spoke a French word had to pay a fine for the benefit of the donation committee.

"Another fine for the Gallicism," said a Russian writer who was in the drawing room. "One doesn't say 'the pleasure to be.' "

---

[*]Reflect well, get into the boat, and don't make it a boat of Charon.

"You make no grace to anyone," Julie went on to the militiaman, ignoring the writer's comment. "I plead guilty to the *caustique*," she said, "and will pay, and I'm prepared to pay more for the pleasure to tell you the truth, but I can't answer for the Gallicisms," she turned to the writer. "I have neither the money nor the time, as Prince Golitsyn does, to take a tutor and study Russian. Ah, here he is," said Julie. "*Quand on . . .** No, no," she turned to the militiaman, "you won't catch me. When one speaks of the sun, one sees its rays," said the hostess, smiling amiably at Pierre. "We were just talking about you," said Julie, with a society woman's aptitude for lying freely. "We were saying that your regiment would probably be better than Mamonov's."

"Ah, don't speak to me about my regiment," replied Pierre, kissing the hostess's hand and sitting down beside her. "I'm so sick of it!"

"But surely you're going to command it yourself?" said Julie, exchanging a sly and mocking glance with the militiaman.

In Pierre's presence, the militiaman was no longer so *caustique,* and his face showed perplexity over the meaning of Julie's smile. Despite his absent-mindedness and good nature, the person of Pierre immediately put a stop to all attempts at mockery in his presence.

"No," replied Pierre, laughing and looking over his big, fat body. "I'd be much too easy a target for the French, and I'm afraid I wouldn't be able to get on a horse."

Among the persons touched upon in conversation in Julie's circle there happened to be the Rostovs.

"People say things are very bad with them," said Julie. "He's so muddleheaded—the count himself. The Razumovskys wanted to buy their house and the estate near Moscow, and it's still dragging on. He's asking too much."

"No, it seems the sale will go through one of these days," someone said. "Though it's mad to buy anything in Moscow now."

"Why?" asked Julie. "Do you really think Moscow's in danger?"

"Why are you leaving, then?"

"I? What a strange question. I'm leaving because . . . well, because everybody's leaving, and anyway I'm not Joan of Arc or some sort of Amazon."

"Well, yes, yes, give me some more rags."

"If he's able to manage the deal, he'll be able to pay off his debts," the militiaman went on about Rostov.

"A kind old man, but a very *pauvre sire.*† And why have they stayed so long? They've been wanting to go to the country for a long time. Natalie seems to be well now?" Julie asked Pierre with a sly smile.

*When one . . .
†Poor specimen.

"They're waiting for their younger son," said Pierre. "He joined Obolensky's Cossacks and went to Belaya Tserkov. The regiment's being formed there. But now they've transferred him to my regiment and are expecting him any day. The count has wanted to leave for a long time, but the countess won't agree to leave Moscow for anything until their son arrives."

"I saw them two days ago at the Arkharovs'. Natalie has grown pretty and cheerful again. She sang a romance. How easily some people get over things!"

"Get over what?" Pierre asked with displeasure. Julie smiled.

"You know, Count, knights like you are found only in the novels of Mme de Souza."

"What knights? Why?" Pierre asked, blushing.

"Well, enough, dear Count, *c'est la fable de tout Moscou. Je vous admire, ma parole d'honneur.*"*

"A fine! A fine!" said the militiaman.

"Well, all right. How boring—it's impossible to speak!"

"*Qu'est-ce qui est la fable de tout Moscou?*"† Pierre asked angrily, getting up.

"Enough, Count. You know!"

"I don't know anything," said Pierre.

"I know that you were friends with Natalie, and so . . . No, I've always been friendlier with Vera. *Cette chère Véra!*"

"*Non, madame,*" Pierre went on in a displeased tone. "I did not take upon myself the role of Miss Rostov's knight at all, and I haven't been there for almost a month. But I do not understand the cruelty . . ."

"*Qui s'excuse, s'accuse,*"‡ Julie said, smiling and waving the lint, and to have the last word remain hers, she changed the subject immediately. "Imagine, I've just learned that poor Marie Bolkonsky arrived in Moscow yesterday. Have you heard she lost her father?"

"Is it true? Where is she? I'd very much like to see her," said Pierre.

"I spent the evening with her yesterday. Today or tomorrow morning she's going to her estate near Moscow with her nephew."

"Well, how is she?" asked Pierre.

"All right, but sad. But do you know who saved her? It's a whole romance: Nicolas Rostov. They surrounded her, wanted to kill her, wounded her people. He rushed in and saved her . . ."

"Another romance," said the militiaman. "Decidedly, this general flight has been done so as to get all the old maids married. Catiche is one, Princess Bolkonsky another."

*It's the talk of all Moscow. I admire you, word of honour.
†What is the talk of all Moscow?
‡He who excuses himself, accuses himself.

"You know, I think in fact that she is *un petit peu amoureuse du jeune homme.*"*

"A fine! A fine! A fine!"

"But how do you say it in Russian? . . ."

XVIII

When Pierre returned home, he was given two of Rastopchin's posters that had been brought that day.

The first said that the rumour about Count Rastopchin forbidding people to leave Moscow was false and that, on the contrary, Count Rastopchin was glad that ladies and merchants' wives were leaving. "There will be less fear, less gossip," said the poster, "but I answer with my life that the villain will never be in Moscow." These words showed Pierre clearly for the first time that the French would be in Moscow. The second poster said that our headquarters were in Vyazma, that Count Wittgenstein had beaten the French,[22] but since many of the inhabitants wished to be armed, there were weapons prepared for them in the arsenal—sabres, pistols, muskets—which the inhabitants could obtain at a low price. The tone of the posters was no longer as jocular as in Chigirin's former bantering. Pierre fell to pondering over these posters. Obviously, that dreadful storm cloud he had been calling up with all the powers of his soul and which at the same time aroused an involuntary terror in him—obviously, that storm cloud was approaching.

"Go into military service and leave for the army, or sit and wait?" Pierre asked himself this question for the hundredth time. He took a deck of cards that lay on his table and began to play patience.

"If this patience comes out," he said to himself, shuffling the deck, holding it in his hand, and looking up, "if it comes out, that means . . . what does it mean?" Before he decided what it meant, he heard the voice of the eldest princess behind the door, asking if she could come in.

"Then it will mean I must go to the army," Pierre finished to himself. "Come in, come in," he added, addressing the princess.

(Only the eldest princess, with the long waist and stony face, was still living in Pierre's house; the two younger ones had married.)

"Excuse me, *mon cousin,* for coming to you," she said in a reproachfully agitated voice. "Something must finally be decided on! What is going to happen? Everyone has left Moscow, and the people are rebellious. Why are we staying?"

*A bit in love with the young man.

"On the contrary, everything seems quite well, *ma cousine*," said Pierre, with that habitual jocularity which he, always embarrassed by his role as the princess's benefactor, adopted in his relations with her.

"Yes, quite well . . . well indeed! Varvara Ivanovna told me today how our troops have distinguished themselves. It can be set down to their honour. And the people are quite rebellious, they've stopped listening; even my maid has become rude. Soon they'll start beating us. It's impossible to walk in the street. And above all, the French will be here any day—what are we waiting for? One thing I ask, *mon cousin*," said the princess. "Order them to take me to Petersburg: however I may be, I cannot live under Bonaparte's rule."

"Enough now, *ma cousine,* where do you get your information? On the contrary . . ."

"I will not submit to your Napoleon. Others can do as they like . . . If you don't want to do this . . ."

"I'll do it, I'll give the order at once."

The princess was clearly annoyed that there was no one to be angry with. She sat down on a chair, whispering something.

"But you've been incorrectly informed," said Pierre. "The city's all quiet, and there isn't any danger. See what I've just read . . ." Pierre showed the little posters to the princess. "The count writes that he answers with his life that the enemy will not be in Moscow."

"Ah, this count of yours," the princess began with anger, "is a hypocrite, a villain, who set the people to rebelling himself. Didn't he write in these foolish posters that whoever it might be, just take him by the topknot and drag him to the precinct? How stupid! Anybody who gets one, they say, honour and glory to him. So much for his pretty words. Varvara Ivanovna says the people nearly killed her for speaking French . . ."

"But that's just . . . You take it all too much to heart," said Pierre, and he began laying out patience.

Though the patience came out, Pierre did not go to the army, but remained in deserted Moscow, still in the same anxiety, irresolution, in the fear and at the same time the joy of awaiting something terrible.

The princess left towards evening the next day, and Pierre's head steward arrived with news that it was impossible to get hold of the money needed to equip a regiment unless one of the estates was sold. In general, the head steward made it seem to Pierre that this whole undertaking with the regiment would ruin him. Pierre had a hard time concealing a smile as he listened to the steward's words.

"Well, sell one," he said. "What's to be done, I can't back out of it now!"

The worse the state of any affairs, and especially his own, the more pleasant it was for Pierre, the more obvious it was that the catastrophe he expected was approaching. By then Pierre had almost no acquaintances left in the city. Julie was gone, Princess Marya was gone. Of close acquaintances, only the Rostovs remained; but Pierre did not call on them.

That day, to distract himself, Pierre went to the village of Vorontsovo to look at the big hot-air balloon that was being constructed by Leppich to destroy the enemy,²³ and the testing of the balloon, which was to go up the next day. The balloon was not ready yet, but, as Pierre learned, it was being constructed at the wish of the sovereign. About this balloon, the sovereign wrote the following to Rastopchin:

Aussitôt que Leppich sera prêt, composez-lui un équipage pour sa nacelle d'hommes sûrs et intelligents et dépêchez un courrier au général Koutousoff pour l'en prévenir. Je l'ai instruit de la chose.

*Recommandez, je vous prie, à Leppich d'être bien attentif sur l'endroit où il descendra la première fois, pour ne pas se tromper et ne pas tomber dans les mains de l'ennemi. Il est indispensable qu'il combine ses mouvements avec le général-en-chef.**

Returning home from Vorontsovo and driving through Bolotnaya Square, Pierre saw a crowd at the execution ground, stopped, and got out of the droshky. It was the flogging of a French cook accused of spying. The flogging had just ended, and the executioner was releasing from the flogging-horse a fat man with red side-whiskers, in blue stockings and a green jacket, who was moaning pitifully. Another criminal, thin and pale, was standing nearby. Both, judging by their faces, were Frenchmen. With a morbidly frightened air, similar to that on the thin Frenchman's face, Pierre pushed his way through the crowd.

"What is this? Who? For what?" he asked. But the attention of the crowd— office clerks, tradesmen, shopkeepers, muzhiks, women in coats and jackets— was so eagerly concentrated on what was happening on the execution ground that nobody answered him. The fat man got up, frowning, shrugged his shoulders, and, evidently wishing to show firmness, began putting on his camisole without looking round him; but his lips suddenly trembled, and he began to cry, angry with himself, as sanguine grown-up people cry. The crowd began talking loudly—to stifle their feeling of pity, as it seemed to Pierre.

"Some prince's cook . . ."

"Well, Mo'sieu, looks like Russian sauce is too sour for a Frenchman . . . sets his teeth on edge," said a wrinkled clerk who was standing next to Pierre, when the Frenchman began to cry. The clerk looked round, evidently expect-

---

*As soon as Leppich is ready, make him up a cockpit crew of trustworthy and intelligent men and send a courier to General Kutuzov to inform him of it. I have told him about it. Urge Leppich, I beg you, to be very careful about where he lands for the first time, so as not to make a mistake and fall into the hands of the enemy. It is indispensable that he coordinate his movements with the general in chief.

ing his joke to be appreciated. Some laughed, some went on looking fearfully at the executioner, who was stripping the other man.

Pierre snuffed his nose, winced, and, turning round quickly, went back to the droshky, muttering to himself all the while as he walked, and got in. During the ride, he gave a start several times and cried out so loudly that the coachman asked him:

"What orders?"

"Where are you going?" Pierre cried out to the coachman, who was driving out to the Lubyanka.

"To the commander in chief's, as you ordered," replied the coachman.

"Fool! Brute!" cried Pierre, yelling at his coachman, which rarely happened with him. "Home, I told you; and drive quickly, blockhead. I must leave today," Pierre said to himself.

At the sight of the punished Frenchman and the crowd surrounding the execution ground, Pierre had decided so definitively that he could no longer remain in Moscow and would go to the army the same day, that it seemed to him he had either told the coachman about it, or the coachman should have known it himself.

On returning home, Pierre told his all-knowing, all-capable coachman Evstafyich, familiar to the whole of Moscow, that he would go to the army in Mozhaisk that night and ordered his riding horses sent there. To do everything on the same day was impossible, and therefore, to Evstafyich's mind, Pierre should postpone his departure until the next day, to leave time for the relay horses to get ahead of him.

On the twenty-fourth it cleared up after some bad weather, and that day, after dinner, Pierre left Moscow. During the night, while changing horses at Perkhushkovo, Pierre learned that there had been a major battle that evening. It was said that there in Perkhushkovo the ground shook from the cannon fire. To Pierre's question of who had won, no one could give an answer. (This was the battle of the twenty-fourth at Shevardino.) At dawn Pierre was riding up to Mozhaisk.

All the houses in Mozhaisk were occupied by stationed troops, and at the inn, where Pierre was met by his groom and coachman, there were no places in the rooms: it was all filled with officers.

Everywhere in Mozhaisk and beyond Mozhaisk troops were camped or marching. Cossacks, foot soldiers, horse soldiers, wagons, caissons, cannon could be seen on all sides. Pierre was in a hurry to move on quickly, and the further he went from Moscow and the deeper he immersed himself in that sea of troops, the more he was overcome by anxious restlessness and a new joyful feeling he had never experienced before. This was a feeling similar to what he had experienced at the Slobodsky palace at the time of the sovereign's arrival—a feeling of the need to undertake something and sacrifice something.

He now experienced a pleasant sense of awareness that everything that constitutes people's happiness, the comforts of life, wealth, even life itself, is nonsense, which it is pleasant to throw away, in comparison with something . . . With what, Pierre could not account for to himself, nor did he try to clarify to himself for whom and for what he found it so particularly delightful to sacrifice everything. He was not concerned with what he wanted to sacrifice it for, but the sacrificing itself constituted a new, joyful feeling for him.

XIX

On the twenty-fourth there was the battle at the Shevardino redoubt, on the twenty-fifth not a single shot was fired on either side, on the twenty-sixth came the battle of Borodino.

Why and how was battle offered and accepted at Shevardino and Borodino? Why was the battle of Borodino fought? Neither for the French nor for the Russians did it make the slightest sense. The most immediate result of it was and had to be—for the Russians, that we came nearer to the destruction of Moscow (which we feared more than anything in the world); and for the French, that they came nearer to the destruction of their whole army (which they also feared more than anything in the world). This result was perfectly obvious then, and yet Napoleon offered and Kutuzov accepted this battle.

If the commanders had been guided by reasonable causes, it would seem it should have been quite clear to Napoleon that, having gone thirteen hundred miles and accepting battle with the likely chance of losing a quarter of his army, he was marching to certain destruction; and it should have been as clear to Kutuzov that, in accepting battle and also risking the loss of a quarter of his army, he would certainly lose Moscow. For Kutuzov this was mathematically clear, as it is clear that, in a game of checkers, if I have one man less and keep trading man for man, I will certainly lose, and therefore I should not keep trading.

When my opponent has sixteen pieces and I have fourteen, I am only one-eighth weaker than he; but when I have traded thirteen pieces, he will be three times stronger than I.

Before the battle of Borodino, our forces were approximately five to six with the French, but after the battle they were one to two; that is, before the battle it was a hundred thousand to a hundred and twenty thousand, but after the battle it was fifty thousand to a hundred thousand. And yet the intelligent and experienced Kutuzov accepted battle. And Napoleon, a commander of genius, as they call him, offered battle, losing a quarter of his army and extending his line still more. If it is said that, by occupying Moscow, he thought to end the campaign, as he had by occupying Vienna, there are many arguments against it. Napoleon's historians themselves say that he already wanted to stop after Smolensk, that he knew the danger of his extended position, and knew that the occupation of Moscow would not be the end of the campaign, because after Smolensk he had seen the condition of the Russian towns abandoned to him, and he had not received a single response to his repeated announcements of his wish to negotiate.

In offering and accepting battle at Borodino, Kutuzov and Napoleon acted involuntarily and senselessly. And only later did historians furnish the already accomplished facts with ingenious arguments for the foresight and genius of the commanders, who, of all the involuntary instruments of world events, were the most enslaved and involuntary agents.

The ancients left us examples of heroic poems in which heroes constitute the entire interest of history, and we still cannot get used to the fact that, for our human time, history of this sort has no meaning.

To the other question, how the battle of Borodino and the one that preceded it at Shevardino were offered, there exists in the same way a quite definite and universally known, but completely false, notion. All historians describe the matter in the following way:

The Russian army, in its retreat from Smolensk, was supposedly seeking the best position for a general battle, and such a position was supposedly found at Borodino.

The Russians supposedly fortified this position beforehand, to the left of the road (from Moscow to Smolensk), almost at a right angle to it, from Borodino to Utitsa, on the very place where the battle was fought.

In front of this position, a fortified outpost was set up on the Shevardino barrow,[24] *supposedly to observe the enemy. On the twenty-fourth, Napoleon supposedly attacked the outpost and took it; and on the twenty-sixth he attacked the whole Russian army, which stood in position on the field of Borodino.*

So the histories say, and it is all completely incorrect, as anyone who wishes to get to the essence of the matter can easily satisfy himself.

The Russians were not seeking the best position; on the contrary, during their retreat they passed many positions that were better than Borodino. They did not stop at any of those positions, because Kutuzov did not want to accept a position that he had not chosen, and because the people's call for battle had not yet expressed itself strongly enough, and because Miloradovich had not yet arrived with the militia, and for countless other reasons. The fact is that the former positions were stronger, and the position at Borodino (the one on which the battle was fought) not only was not strong, but could no more be considered a position than any other place in the Russian empire on which, by guesswork, one might randomly stick a pin in a map.

The Russians not only did not fortify the position on the field of Borodino to the left, at a right angle to the road (that is, the place where the battle was fought), but never thought, until the twenty-fifth of August 1812, that the battle could be fought in that place. This is proved, first, by the fact that there not only were no fortifications in that place on the twenty-fifth, but that, having been begun on the twenty-fifth, they were not finished on the twenty-sixth; second, it is proved by the position of the Shevardino redoubt: the Shevardino redoubt, in front of the position on which battle was accepted, made no sense at all. Why was this redoubt fortified more than any other point? And why, in defending it until late at night on the twenty-fourth, were all efforts exhausted and six thousand men lost? A mounted Cossack patrol would have sufficed to observe the enemy. The third proof that the position on which the battle took place had not been foreseen and that the Shevardino redoubt was not an outpost of that position, is that until the twenty-fifth, Barclay de Tolly and Bagration were convinced that the Shevardino redoubt was the *left* flank of the position, and that Kutuzov himself, in his report written hot on the heels of the battle, called Shevardino the *left* flank of the position. Much later, when there was more leisure for writing reports about the battle of Borodino, the incorrect and strange testimony was invented (probably to justify the mistakes of the commander in chief, who must be infallible) that the Shevardino redoubt was supposedly an *outpost* (whereas it was only a fortified point on the left flank), and that the battle of Borodino was accepted by us at a fortified and previously chosen position, whereas it occurred in a completely unexpected and almost unfortified place.

This is evidently how it was: a position was chosen along the river Kolocha, which crossed the high road not at a right angle but at an acute angle, so that the left flank was in Shevardino, the right near the village of Novoe, and the centre in Borodino, by the confluence of the rivers Kolocha and Voyna. For an army that aims at stopping the enemy from moving down the Smolensk road towards Moscow, this position, under cover of the river Kolocha, is obvious to anyone who looks over the field of Borodino forgetting how the battle took place.

Napoleon, having ridden to Valuevo on the twenty-fourth, did not see (as the history books say) the position of the Russians from Utitsa to Borodino (he could not have seen that position because it did not exist), and did not see the outpost of the Russian army, but ran into the Shevardino redoubt as he pursued the Russian rear guard, and, unexpectedly for the Russians, had his troops cross the Kolocha. And the Russians, even before the general battle, withdrew their left wing from the position they had intended to occupy and took up a new position that had not been foreseen or fortified. By crossing to the left side of the Kolocha, to the left of the road, Napoleon shifted the whole future battle from right to left (viewed from the Russian side), and transferred it to the field between Utitsa, Semyonovskoe, and Borodino (a field no more advantageous as a position than any other field in Russia), and the whole battle of the twenty-sixth took place on that field. In crude form, the plan of the supposed battle and actual battle is as in the map opposite.[25]

If Napoleon had not ridden out to the Kolocha on the evening of the twenty-fourth and had not ordered an attack on the redoubt that same evening, but had begun the attack the next morning, no one would have questioned that the Shevardino redoubt was the left flank of our position, and the battle would have taken place as we had expected. In that case, we would probably have defended the Shevardino redoubt on our left flank still more tenaciously; we would have attacked Napoleon in the centre or on the right, and the general battle would have taken place on the twenty-fourth at a position that had been fortified and foreseen. But since the attack on our left flank took place in the evening, following the retreat of our rear guard, that is, immediately after the battle at Gridnevo, and since the Russian commanders did not want or did not manage to begin the general battle that same evening of the twenty-fourth, the first and main action of the battle of Borodino was already lost on the twenty-fourth, and obviously led to the loss of the one fought on the twenty-sixth.

After the loss of the Shevardino redoubt, we found ourselves on the morning of the twenty-fifth with no position on the left flank, and were forced into the necessity of pulling our left wing back and hastily fortifying it wherever it ended up.

But it was not just that the Russian troops on the twenty-sixth of August were defended by weak, unfinished fortifications—the disadvantage of this position was increased still more by the fact that the Russian commanders, not having fully grasped the accomplished fact (the loss of the position on the left flank and the transfer of the whole future battlefield from right to left), remained in their extended position from the village of Novoe to Utitsa, and as a result had to move their troops from right to left during the battle. Thus, throughout the battle, the Russians confronted the whole French army, directed against our left wing, with forces that were twice weaker. (The actions of Poniatowski against Utitsa and of Uvarov against the French on the right flank were separate from the main course of the battle's action.)

And so, the battle of Borodino took place not at all as it is described (in an attempt to conceal the mistakes of our commanders and thereby diminishing the glory of the Russian army and people). The battle of Borodino did not take place on a chosen and fortified position, with only slightly weaker forces on the Russian side, but, owing to the loss of the Shevardino redoubt, was accepted by the Russians on open, almost unfortified terrain with forces twice weaker than the French—that is, in conditions in which it was not only unthinkable to fight for ten hours and leave the battle undecided, but unthinkable to keep the army for as long as three hours from total destruction and flight.

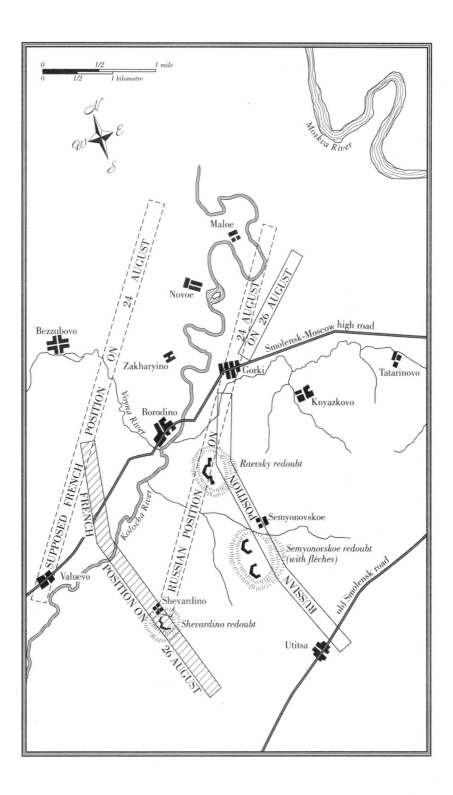

Moskva River

0 | 1/2 | 1 mile
0 | 1/2 | 1 kilometre

Maloe

Novoe

Bezzubovo

Zakharyino

Smolensk-Moscow high road

Gorki

Tatarinovo

Knyazkovo

Borodino

Raevsky redoubt

Semyonovskoe

Semyonovskoe redoubt
(with flèches)

Valuevo

Shevardino

Shevardino redoubt

Utitsa

old Smolensk road

Voyna River

Kolocha River

POSITION ON 24 AUGUST

ON 26 AUGUST

SUPPOSED FRENCH POSITION ON 24 AUGUST

FRENCH POSITION ON 26 AUGUST

RUSSIAN POSITION ON 24 AUGUST

RUSSIAN POSITION ON 26 AUGUST

XX

On the morning of the twenty-fifth, Pierre was driving out of Mozhaisk. Going down the huge, steep, and crooked hill that led out of the town, past the cathedral that stood on the hill to the right, in which a service was going on and the bells were ringing, Pierre got out of the carriage and went on foot. Behind him some mounted regiment was coming down the hill with singers at its head. In the opposite direction came a train of carts with men wounded in yesterday's action. The peasant drivers, shouting at the horses and whipping them with knouts, kept running from one side to the other. The carts with three or four wounded men lying or sitting in them bounced up and down on the stones scattered over the steep ascent in the guise of pavement. The wounded men, bandaged with rags, pale, with compressed lips and frowning brows, clinging to the sides, bounced and jostled in the carts. They all looked at Pierre's white hat and green tailcoat with an almost naïve, childlike curiosity.

Pierre's coachman shouted angrily at the train of wounded that they should keep to one side. The cavalry regiment, coming down the hill with songs, ran into Pierre's droshky and blocked the road. Pierre stopped, pressing himself to the edge of the road, which was dug out of the hillside. Because of the slope of the hill, the sun did not reach the dug-out road, and it was cold and damp; over Pierre's head was the bright August morning, and the bells rang out merrily. One cart with wounded stopped at the edge of the road just next to Pierre. The driver, in bast shoes, ran breathlessly to the cart, stuck a stone under the tyreless rear wheels, and began to straighten the breeching on his stopped little horse.

One wounded old soldier with his arm in a sling, who had been walking behind the cart, took hold of it with his good hand and glanced at Pierre.

"Well, countryman, are they setting us down here? Or taking us to Moscow?" he said.

Pierre was so deep in thought that he did not hear the question. He looked first at the cavalry regiment that had now run into the train of the wounded, then at the cart he was standing near and on which two wounded men were sitting and one was lying, and it seemed to him that there, in them, lay the solution to the problem that preoccupied him. One of the soldiers sitting on the cart had probably been wounded in the cheek. His whole head was bound in rags, and one cheek was swollen as big as a baby's head. His mouth and nose were askew. This soldier was looking at the cathedral and crossing himself. The second, a young boy, a recruit, fair-haired and as white as though there was no blood at all in his delicate face, looked at Pierre with a fixed, kindly smile. The third lay prone and his face could not be seen. The cavalry singers were just passing by the cart.

Ah, lost and gone . . . this bristly head . . .
Now living in some foreign land . . .

they poured out a soldiers' dance song. As if seconding them, but with another sort of merriment, the metallic ringing of the bells throbbed on high. And, with yet another sort of merriment, the sun's hot rays bathed the top of the slope opposite. But under the slope, by the cart with the wounded men, near the panting little horse, where Pierre was standing, it was damp, bleak, and sad.

The soldier with the swollen cheek looked angrily at the cavalry singers.

"Some songbirds!" he said reproachfully.

"Today it wasn't just soldiers, I saw peasants, too! They even drive peasants to it," a soldier standing behind the cart said with a sad smile, addressing Pierre. "No sorting them out nowadays . . . They want the whole people to throw their weight into it—Moscow, in short. They want to make an end of it." Despite the vagueness of the soldier's words, Pierre understood everything he meant to say and nodded approvingly.

The road cleared, and Pierre went down the hill and drove on.

Pierre drove along, looking on both sides of the road, searching for familiar faces, and everywhere meeting only the unfamiliar military faces of various kinds of troops, who stared with identical surprise at his white hat and green tailcoat.

Having gone about three miles, he met a first acquaintance and joyfully addressed him. This acquaintance was one of the chief doctors of the army. He was coming towards Pierre in a britzka, with a young doctor sitting beside him, and, recognizing Pierre, told his Cossack, who sat on the box in place of a coachman, to stop.

"Count! Your Excellency, what are you doing here?" asked the doctor.

"I just wanted to have a look . . ."

"Yes, yes, there'll be plenty to look at . . ."

Pierre got out and stopped to talk with the doctor, explaining to him his intention of taking part in the battle.

The doctor advised Bezukhov to address himself directly to his serenity.

"Why should you be God knows where, in obscurity, during the battle?" he said, exchanging glances with his young colleague. "And his serenity does know you, after all, and would receive you graciously. That's the thing to do, old boy," said the doctor.

The doctor seemed tired and hurried.

"You think so? . . . And I also wanted to ask you, where is the actual position?" asked Pierre.

"Position?" said the doctor. "That's not in my line. Go past Tatarinovo, where all the digging's going on. Climb up on the barrow there: you can see from there," said the doctor.

"You can see from there? . . . And if you'd . . ."

But the doctor interrupted him and moved towards his britzka.

"I'd take you there, but, by God—you see" (the doctor gestured at his throat) "I'm racing to the corps commander's. How are things with us? . . . You know, Count, tomorrow's the battle: for a hundred thousand troops we must figure on at least twenty thousand wounded; and we don't have enough stretchers, or beds, or medics, or doctors for even six thousand. There are ten thousand carts, but we need other things as well. So do as you like."

The strange notion that among those thousands of men, alive, healthy, young and old, who had stared with merry surprise at his hat, there were probably twenty thousand destined for wounds and death (maybe the same ones he had seen), struck Pierre.

"They may die tomorrow, how can they think of anything else but death?" And suddenly, by some mysterious linking of thoughts, he vividly pictured the descent of the hill in Mozhaisk, the carts with the wounded, the ringing bells, the slanting rays of the sun, and the songs of the cavalrymen.

"The cavalrymen go to battle and meet the wounded, and they don't stop to reflect for a moment on what awaits them, but go past and wink at the wounded. And twenty thousand of them are doomed to die, yet they get surprised at my hat! Strange!" thought Pierre, heading on towards Tatarinovo.

By a landowner's house on the left side of the road stood carriages, wagons, crowds of orderlies and sentries. His serenity was staying here. But at the time of Pierre's arrival, he was not there, and there was almost no one from his staff. They were all at a prayer service. Pierre drove on to Gorki.

Driving up a hill and coming to a small village street, Pierre saw muzhik militiamen for the first time, with crosses on their hats and white shirts, who with loud talk and laughter, lively and sweaty, were doing some sort of work to the right of the road, on an enormous barrow overgrown with grass.

Some of them were digging at the hill with shovels, others were transporting dirt over planks in handcarts, still others stood round doing nothing.

Two officers were standing on the barrow, giving them orders. Seeing these muzhiks, who obviously still enjoyed their new military situation, Pierre again recalled the wounded soldiers in Mozhaisk, and understood what the soldier had meant to express, saying "they want the whole people to throw their weight into it." The sight of these bearded muzhiks working on the battlefield, with their strange, clumsy boots, with their sweaty necks, and some with their side-buttoned shirts open, revealing their sunburned collarbones, impressed Pierre more strongly than anything he had seen or heard so far about the solemnity and significance of the present moment.

XXI

Pierre stepped out of the carriage and went past the labouring militiamen up the barrow from which, as the doctor had told him, the battlefield could be seen.

It was eleven o'clock in the morning. The sun was a little to the left and behind Pierre and, through the clear, rarefied air, shone brightly on the vast panorama that opened out before him like an amphitheatre over the rising terrain.

Cutting through the upper left of this amphitheatre, the Smolensk high road wound its way through a village with a white church that lay five hundred paces from the barrow and below it (this was Borodino). The road passed under the village, across a bridge and, ascending and descending, wound higher and higher up to the village of Valuevo (where Napoleon was now staying), visible some four miles away. Beyond Valuevo, the road disappeared into a forest that showed yellow on the horizon. In this birch and fir forest, to the right of the road, the distant cross and bell tower of the Kolotsky monastery shone in the sun. All over this blue distance, to right and left of the forest and the road, in various places, one could see smoking campfires and indefinite masses of troops, ours and the enemy's. To the right, along the courses of the Kolocha and Moskva Rivers, the terrain was all hills and gullies. Between their gullies, in the distance, the villages of Bezzubovo and Zakharyino could be seen. To the left the terrain was more level, there were grain fields, and one smoking, burned-down village could be seen — Semyonovskoe.

Everything Pierre saw to right and left was so indefinite that neither the left nor the right side of the field fully satisfied his notions. Everywhere there were fields, clearings, troops, woods, smoking campfires, villages, barrows, streams, but not the battlefield he had expected to see; and much as he tried to make it out, on this living terrain he could not find a position and could not even distinguish our troops from the enemy's.

"I must ask someone who knows," he thought and turned to an officer, who was looking with curiosity at his enormous, non-military figure.

"Allow me to ask," Pierre addressed the officer, "what village is that in front of us?"

"Burdino or something?" said the officer, turning to his comrade with the question.

"Borodino," the other replied, correcting him.

The officer, clearly pleased at the chance to talk, moved closer to Pierre.

"Those are ours there?" asked Pierre.

"Yes, and those further away are the French," said the officer. "Out there, out there you can see them."

"Those are ours?" asked Pierre.

"You can see them with your naked eye. There, there!" The officer pointed to some smoke visible to the left across the river, and that stern and serious expression appeared on his face which Pierre had seen on many of the faces he had met.

"Ah, they're the French! And there? . . ." Pierre pointed to a barrow on the left, near which troops could be seen.

"They're ours."

"Ah, ours! And there? . . ." Pierre pointed to another distant barrow with a big tree, near a village visible in a gully, where campfires were also smoking and something showed black.

"That's *him* again," said the officer. (This was the Shevardino redoubt.) "Yesterday it was ours, but now it's *his*."

"So what is our position?"

"Position?" said the officer with a smile of pleasure. "That I can tell you clearly, because I built nearly all our fortifications. There, you see, is our centre in Borodino, just there." He pointed to the village with the white church, straight ahead. "There's the crossing over the Kolocha. Over there, see, where rows of cut hay are still lying in a hollow, the bridge is right there. This is our centre. Our right flank is over there" (he pointed sharply to the right, far into the gully), "the Moskva River's there, and there we built three redoubts, very strong ones. The left flank . . ." Here the officer paused. "You see, it's hard to explain it to you . . . Yesterday our left flank was there, in Shevardino, see, where the oak tree is; but now we've moved the left wing back, now it's down there, there—see the village and the smoke?—that's Semyonovskoe, yes, it's there." He pointed to the Raevsky barrow. "Only it's unlikely the battle will be there. *He* shifted troops there, but it's a trick; *he* will probably go round to the right of the Moskva. Well, but wherever it is, we'll have a lot of men missing tomorrow!" said the officer.

An old sergeant, who came up to the officer while he was talking, was waiting silently for his superior to finish; but at this point, obviously displeased with the officer's words, he interrupted him.

"We have to go for gabions," he said sternly.

The officer seemed embarrassed, as if he realized that one might think of how many would be missing the next day, but one ought not to speak of it.

"Ah, yes, send the third platoon again," he said hastily. "And you are what—a doctor?"

"No, I'm just here," answered Pierre. And he went down the hill again past the militiamen.

"Ah, curse them!" the officer, who was following Pierre, said, holding his nose and running past the labourers.

"There they are! . . . They're carrying her, they're coming . . . There they

are . . . They'll be here in a moment . . ." Voices were suddenly heard, and officers, soldiers, and militiamen went running down the road.

A church procession from Borodino was coming up the hill. Ahead of them
all on the dusty road moved orderly ranks of infantry, their shakos off and
their muskets pointing down. From behind the infantry came the sound of
church singing.

Overtaking Pierre, soldiers and militiamen were running, hatless, to meet
the procession.

"It's our Mother they're carrying! Our intercessor! . . . The Iverskaya . . ."

"The Smolenskaya Mother of God,"[26] another corrected.

The militiamen—both those who were in the village and those who were
working on the battery—dropped their shovels and ran to meet the church
procession. Behind the battalion that marched down the dusty road came
priests in vestments, an old man in a cowl, other clergy, and a choir. Behind
them, soldiers and officers carried a large, dark-faced icon in a case. This
was the icon brought out of Smolensk, which had since been carried round
with the army. Behind the icon, round it, in front of it, on all sides, crowds of
bareheaded soldiers walked, ran, and bowed to the ground.

Having come up the hill, the icon stopped; the people who were holding the
icon on towels were replaced, the servers lit the censers, and the prayer service
began. The sun's hot rays beat down vertically from above; a faint, fresh breeze
played with the hair of the bared heads and the ribbons that decorated the
icon; the singing sounded subdued under the open sky. A huge crowd of bareheaded officers, soldiers, and militiamen surrounded the icon. Behind the priest
and the deacon, on a cleared space, stood men of higher rank. One bald general with a St. George on his neck stood directly behind the priest's back and,
not crossing himself (obviously a German), waited patiently for the end of the
service, which he considered it necessary to hear out, probably to arouse the
patriotism of the Russian people. Another general stood in a martial pose and
kept fluttering his hand in front of his chest, glancing round. Among this high-
ranking circle, Pierre, who was standing in the crowd of muzhiks, recognized
some acquaintances; but he was not looking at them: his whole attention was
absorbed by the serious expression of the faces in this crowd of soldiers and
militiamen who gazed with uniform eagerness at the icon. As soon as the
weary servers (who were singing their twentieth prayer service) began lazily
and habitually to sing: "Deliver thy servants from affliction, O Mother of
God," and the priest and deacon picked up: "For in God we flee unto thee as a
steadfast wall and intercessor"—all the faces lit up again with the same expression of awareness of the solemnity of the present moment that he had seen on
the faces at the foot of the hill in Mozhaisk and had glimpsed on many, many
faces he had met that morning: heads were bowed more frequently, hair was
tossed, and sighs and the thump of crossings on breasts were heard.

The crowd surrounding the icon suddenly parted and pressed against Pierre. Someone, probably a very important person, judging by the haste with which people made way for him, was approaching the icon.

It was Kutuzov going the rounds of the position. On his way back to Tatarinovo, he came up to the prayer service. Pierre recognized Kutuzov at once by his peculiar figure, which distinguished him from everyone else.

In a long coat on an immensely fat body, with a somewhat rounded back, an uncovered white head, a blinded white eye in a puffy face, Kutuzov entered the circle with his dipping, swaying gait, and stopped behind the priest. He crossed himself with a habitual gesture, touched the ground with his hand, and, sighing deeply, bowed his grey head. Behind Kutuzov came Bennigsen and the suite. Despite the presence of the commander in chief, who drew the attention of all the higher ranks, the militiamen and soldiers, without looking at him, went on praying.

When the service was over, Kutuzov went up to the icon, knelt down heavily, bowed to the ground, and for a long time tried and was unable to stand up because of his heaviness and weakness. His grey head twitched with the effort. Finally he stood up and, with a childishly naïve puckering of the lips, kissed the icon and bowed again, touching the ground with his hand. The generals followed his example; then the officers, and after them, crushing each other, stamping, puffing and jostling, with excited faces, came the soldiers and militiamen.

XXII

Reeling from the crush he was caught up in, Pierre glanced about.

"Count! Pyotr Kirilych! What are you doing here?" said someone's voice. Pierre turned to look.

Boris Drubetskoy, brushing his knees with his hand (he had probably dirtied them venerating the icon), smiling, was approaching Pierre. Boris was elegantly dressed, with a hint of the soldier on campaign. He was wearing a long tunic and a whip over his shoulder, just like Kutuzov.

Kutuzov meanwhile went to the village and sat down in the shade of the nearest house, on a bench which one Cossack ran to fetch and another quickly covered with a rug. An immense, brilliant suite surrounded the commander in chief.

The icon started off again, accompanied by the crowd. Pierre stopped some thirty paces from Kutuzov, talking to Boris.

Pierre explained his intention of taking part in the battle and looking over the position.

"Here's how to do it," said Boris. *"Je vous ferai les honneurs du camp.** You'll see everything best from where Count Bennigsen is. I'm attached to him. I'll tell him. And if you want to ride round the position, come with us: we're now going to the left flank. And then we'll come back, and you're welcome to spend the night with me, and we'll get up a game of cards. You know Dmitri Sergeich? He's staying here." He pointed to the third house in Gorki.

"But I'd like to see the right flank; they say it's very strong," said Pierre. "I'd like to start from the Moskva River and ride round the whole position."

"Well, you can do that later, but the main thing is the left flank . . ."

"Yes, yes. And where is Prince Bolkonsky's regiment? Can you point it out for me?" asked Pierre.

"Andrei Nikolaevich's? We'll go past it, I'll take you to him."

"So what about the left flank?" asked Pierre.

"To tell you the truth, *entre nous,*† our left flank is in God knows what state," said Boris, lowering his voice confidentially. "Count Bennigsen proposed something quite different. He proposed fortifying that barrow over there, not at all like . . . but." Boris shrugged his shoulders. "His serenity didn't want to, or somebody talked him out of it. You know . . ." And Boris did not finish, because just then Kaisarov, Kutuzov's adjutant, came up to Pierre. "Ah! Païssy Sergeich," said Boris, addressing Kaisarov with an easy smile. "I'm trying to explain the position to the count. It's astonishing how his serenity could guess the intentions of the French so correctly!"

"You mean the left flank?" said Kaisarov.

"Yes, yes, precisely. Our left flank is now very, very strong."

Though Kutuzov had chased out all the superfluous men of the staff, Boris, after the changes made by Kutuzov, had been able to maintain himself at headquarters. Boris had attached himself to Count Bennigsen. Count Bennigsen, like all the men on whom Boris had been in attendance, considered the young Prince Drubetskoy an invaluable man.

In the army's high command there were two clear-cut, well-defined parties: the party of Kutuzov and the party of Bennigsen, the chief of staff. Boris belonged to the latter party, and no one knew so well as he how, while rendering servile respect to Kutuzov, to make it felt that the old man was no good and that everything was being conducted by Bennigsen. Now the decisive moment of battle had come, which should either destroy Kutuzov and hand power over to Bennigsen, or, even if Kutuzov won the battle, make it felt that it had all been done by Bennigsen. In any case, for tomorrow big rewards should be given out and new men brought to the fore. And owing to that, Boris was in nervous animation all that day.

*I'll do you the honours of the camp.
†Between us.

After Kaisarov, other acquaintances came up to Pierre, and he had no time to answer all the questions about Moscow that they showered him with, or to listen to the stories they told him. Animation and anxiety showed on all their faces. But it seemed to Pierre that the cause of the agitation which showed on some of these faces lay mostly in questions of personal success, and he could not get out of his head those other expressions of agitation, which he had seen on other faces and which spoke of questions that were not personal but general, questions of life and death. Kutuzov noticed Pierre's figure and the group that had gathered round him.

"Call him over to me," said Kutuzov. The adjutant conveyed his serenity's wish, and Pierre went towards the bench. But before him a rank-and-file militiaman came up to Kutuzov. It was Dolokhov.

"What's that one doing here?" asked Pierre.

"He's such a sly fox, he slips in everywhere!" came the answer. "You see, he was reduced to the ranks. Now he has to get jumping. He's been submitting some projects, snuck behind the enemy's lines at night . . . but a fine fellow! . . ."

Pierre, taking off his hat, bowed respectfully to Kutuzov.

"I decided that if I report to Your Serenity, you can chase me away or tell me you already know what I'm reporting, and I'll be none the worse for it . . ." Dolokhov was saying.

"Yes, yes."

"But if I'm right, then I'll be of benefit to the fatherland, for which I'm prepared to die."

"Yes . . . yes . . ."

"And if Your Serenity needs a man who won't spare his hide, please remember me . . . Maybe I'll prove useful to Your Serenity."

"Yes . . . yes . . ." Kutuzov repeated, looking at Pierre with his laughing, narrowing eye.

Just then Boris, with his courtly adroitness, moved up next to Pierre, in proximity to his superior, and with the most natural air, and not loudly, as if continuing a conversation they had already begun, said to Pierre:

"The militiamen—they just went and put on clean white shirts, so as to be prepared for death. Such heroism, Count!"

Boris said it to Pierre in order to be heard by his serenity. He knew that Kutuzov would pay attention to these words, and in fact his serenity addressed him.

"What's that you're saying about the militia?" he said to Boris.

"They've put on white shirts, Your Serenity, getting ready for tomorrow, for death."

"Ah! . . . Wonderful, incomparable people!" said Kutuzov and, closing his eyes, he shook his head. "Incomparable people!" he said with a sigh.

"So you want a whiff of powder?" he said to Pierre. "Yes, a pleasant smell. I have the honour of being an admirer of your spouse. Is she well? My camp is at your service." And, as often happens with old people, Kutuzov started looking round absent-mindedly, as if forgetting all he had to say or do.

Evidently recalling what he was searching for, he beckoned to Andrei Sergeich Kaisarov, his adjutant's brother.

"How, how do they go, those verses of Marin's, how do they go? What he wrote on Gerakov: 'You'll be a teacher in the corps . . .'[27] Recite it, recite it," said Kutuzov, obviously getting ready to laugh. Kaisarov recited . . . Kutuzov, smiling, nodded his head in rhythm with the verses.

When Pierre left Kutuzov, Dolokhov, coming up to him, offered him his hand.

"Very glad to meet you here, Count," he said to him loudly and unembarrassed by the presence of strangers, with particular resoluteness and solemnity. "On the eve of a day when God knows who of us is destined to remain alive, I'm glad of the chance to tell you that I regret the misunderstandings that occurred between us and would wish that you not have anything against me. I ask you to forgive me."

Pierre, smiling, gazed at Dolokhov, not knowing what to say to him. Dolokhov, with tears in his eyes, embraced and kissed Pierre.

Boris said something to his general, and Count Bennigsen turned to Pierre and proposed that he come with him along the line.

"It will be interesting for you," he said.

"Yes, very interesting," said Pierre.

Half an hour later, Kutuzov left for Tatarinovo, and Bennigsen with the suite, Pierre among them, rode along the line.

XXIII

From Gorki Bennigsen went down by the high road to the bridge that the officer on the barrow had pointed out to Pierre as the centre of the position, and near which rows of mowed grass smelling of hay lay on the riverbank. Crossing the bridge, they rode to the village of Borodino, where they turned left and, passing huge numbers of troops and cannon, came to a high barrow, on which militiamen were digging up the ground. This was the redoubt, as yet unnamed, later known as the Raevsky redoubt or the battery of the barrow.

Pierre paid no particular attention to this redoubt. He did not know that for him it would be the most memorable place on the field of Borodino. Then they crossed the ravine to Semyonovskoe, where soldiers were pulling down the last logs of the cottages and barns. Then downhill and uphill they rode on through broken rye, beaten down as if by hail, along a road newly made by the artillery across the furrows of a ploughed field to the flèches,* which were still being dug.

Bennigsen stopped at the flèches and began looking ahead at the Shevardino redoubt (still ours yesterday), on which several horsemen could be seen. The officers said that Napoleon or Murat was there. And everybody looked eagerly at this bunch of horsemen. Pierre also looked, trying to guess which of those barely visible men was Napoleon. Finally the horsemen rode down off the barrow and disappeared from sight.

Bennigsen turned to a general who came up to him and started explaining the disposition of our troops. Pierre listened to Bennigsen's words, straining all his mental forces in order to understand the essence of the forthcoming battle, but felt with chagrin that his mental ability was insufficient for that. He understood nothing. Bennigsen stopped talking and, noticing the figure of the listening Pierre, suddenly said, turning to him:

"I suppose you find this uninteresting?"

"Oh, on the contrary, very interesting," Pierre said not quite truthfully.

From the flèches they rode still further to the left, on a road winding through a dense, not very tall birch woods. In the middle of this woods a brown hare with white legs jumped out onto the road in front of them and, frightened by the hoofbeats of the large number of horses, became so confused that it leaped along the road in front of them for a long time, arousing general attention and laughter, and only when several voices shouted at it did it dash to the side and disappear into the thicket. Having gone a mile and a half through the woods, they came out into a clearing where the troops of Tuchkov's corps were stationed, who were supposed to defend the left flank.

Here, at the extreme left flank, Bennigsen spoke a great deal and vehemently, and, as it seemed to Pierre, gave instructions that were important in a military respect. In front of the disposition of Tuchkov's troops, there was an elevation. This elevation was not occupied by troops. Bennigsen loudly criticized this error, saying that it was mad to leave a height that commanded the terrain unoccupied and place troops at the foot of it. Some generals expressed the same opinion. One in particular said with military vehemence that they had been put there to be slaughtered. Bennigsen ordered in his own name that the troops be moved to the height.

This instruction to the left flank made Pierre doubt still more his ability to understand military matters. Listening to Bennigsen and the generals discussing the position of the troops at the foot of the hill, Pierre fully understood them and shared their opinion; but, precisely for that reason, he could not understand how the one who had placed them there at the foot of the hill could have made such an obvious and crude mistake.

* A kind of fortification (Tolstoy's note).

Pierre did not know that these troops had been placed there not to defend the position, as Bennigsen thought, but had been put in a concealed spot for an ambush, that is, so as to remain unobserved and suddenly strike at the advancing enemy. Bennigsen did not know that and moved the troops forward for his own reasons, saying nothing about it to the commander in chief.

XXIV

On that clear August evening of the twenty-fifth, Prince Andrei lay propped on his elbow in a broken-up shed in the village of Knyazkovo, at the edge of his regiment's disposition. Through an opening in the broken wall, he looked at a row of thirty-year-old birches with chopped-off lower branches that ran along a fence, at a field with stacks of oats on it, and at some bushes in which the smoke of campfires—the soldiers' kitchens—could be seen.

Narrow, and unnecessary to anyone, and burdensome as Prince Andrei's life now seemed to him, he felt excited and nervous on the eve of battle, just as at Austerlitz seven years earlier.

The orders for tomorrow's battle had been given and received. He had nothing more to do. But the most simple, clear, and therefore dreadful thoughts would not leave him in peace. He knew that tomorrow's battle was to be the most dreadful of all he had taken part in, and the possibility of death presented itself to him, for the first time in his life, with no relation to the everyday, with no considerations of how it would affect others, but only in relation to himself, to his soul, vividly, almost with certainty, simply, and terribly. And from the height of that picture, all that used to torment and preoccupy him was suddenly lit up by a cold, white light, without shadows, without perspective, without clear-cut outlines. The whole of life presented itself to him as a magic lantern, into which he had long been looking through a glass and in artificial light. Now he suddenly saw these badly daubed pictures without a glass, in bright daylight. "Yes, yes, there they are, those false images that excited and delighted and tormented me," he said to himself, turning over in his imagination the main pictures of his magic lantern of life, looking at them now in that cold, white daylight—the clear notion of death. "There they are, those crudely daubed figures, which had presented themselves as something beautiful and mysterious. Glory, the general good, the love of a woman, the fatherland itself—how grand those pictures seemed to me, how filled with deep meaning! And it's all so simple, pale, and crude in the cold, white light of the morning that I feel is dawning for me." Three main griefs of his life especially held his attention. His love of a woman, the death of his father, and the French invasion that had seized half of Russia. "Love! That girl who seemed to me all filled with mysterious forces! How I loved her! I made poetic plans of love, of happiness with her. Oh, you dear boy!" he said angrily aloud. "What else! I believed in some sort of ideal love, which was to keep her faithful to me for the whole year of my absence! Like the tender dove in the fable, she was to pine away in my absence. But it's all so much simpler . . . It's all terribly simple, and vile!

"My father also built at Bald Hills and thought it was his place, his land, his air, his muzhiks; but Napoleon came and, not knowing of his existence, brushed him aside like a chip of wood, and Bald Hills and his whole life fell apart. And Princess Marya says it's a trial from on high. Why a trial, when he's no more and never will be? Never will be again! He's no more! So for whom is it a trial? The fatherland, the destruction of Moscow! And tomorrow I'll be killed—not even by a Frenchman, but by one of our soldiers, like the one yesterday who fired his gun just next to my ear—and the French will come, take me by the feet and head, and fling me into a pit, so as not to have me stink under their noses, and new conditions of life will take shape, which will become habitual for other people, and I won't know about them, and I won't be there."

He looked at the line of birches with their motionless yellow and green leaves and white bark gleaming in the sun. "To die, to be killed tomorrow, to be no more . . . so that all this is here and I am not." He pictured vividly to himself his absence from this life. And the birches with their light and shade, and the fleecy clouds, and the smoke of the campfires—everything round was transfigured for him and appeared as something dreadful and menacing. A chill ran down his spine. Getting up quickly, he left the shed, paced about, and went back in.

Voices came from outside the shed.

"Who's there?" Prince Andrei called out.

Red-nosed Captain Timokhin, formerly Dolokhov's company commander, and now, as the numbers of officers diminished, a battalion commander, timidly came into the shed. After him came an adjutant and the regimental paymaster.

Prince Andrei hastily got up, listened to what the officers had to tell him in the line of duty, gave them some further orders, and was about to dismiss them, when he heard a familiar, lisping voice from outside the shed.

"*Que diable!*"* said the voice of a man who had run into something.

Prince Andrei looked out of the shed and saw Pierre, who had stumbled over a pole that was lying there and nearly fallen. It was generally unpleasant for Prince Andrei to see people from his world, especially Pierre, who reminded him of all those painful moments he had lived through during his last visit to Moscow.

"Ah, look at that!" he said. "What fate brings you here? I'd never have expected it."

---

*What the devil!

As he said this, there was something more than dryness in his eyes and the expression of his whole face—there was a hostility that Pierre noticed at once. He was approaching the shed in the most animated state of mind, but, seeing the expression on Prince Andrei's face, he felt embarrassed and awkward.

"I've come . . . just . . . you know . . . I've come . . . it's interesting," said Pierre, who had repeated the senseless word "interesting" so many times that day. "I wanted to see the battle."

"Yes, yes, and what do your brother Masons say about war? Is there a way to prevent it?" Prince Andrei said mockingly. "Well, what about Moscow? What about my people? Have they finally come to Moscow?" he asked seriously.

"Yes. Julie Drubetskoy told me. I went to see them, but missed them. They'd gone to the estate outside Moscow."

XXV

The officers wanted to take their leave, but Prince Andrei, as if unwilling to be left alone with his friend, invited them to stay and have tea. Benches and tea were brought. The officers looked not without surprise at Pierre's fat, enormous figure, and listened to his stories about Moscow and about the disposition of our troops, which he had managed to ride round. Prince Andrei was silent, and his face was so unpleasant that Pierre addressed himself more to the good-natured battalion commander Timokhin than to Bolkonsky.

"So you've understood the whole disposition of the troops?" Prince Andrei interrupted him.

"How do you mean?" said Pierre. "As a non-military man I can't say I do fully, but anyhow I understand the general disposition."

"*Eh bien, vous êtes plus avancé que qui cela soit,*"* said Prince Andrei.

"Ah!" Pierre said with perplexity, looking through his spectacles at Prince Andrei. "Well, what do you say about the appointment of Kutuzov?" he asked.

"I was very glad of his appointment, that's all I know," said Prince Andrei.

"Well, and tell me, what's your opinion of Barclay de Tolly? In Moscow they're saying God knows what about him. How do you judge him?"

"Ask them," said Prince Andrei, pointing to the officers.

Pierre looked at Timokhin with the condescendingly questioning smile with which everyone involuntarily addressed him.

---

*Well, then you're ahead of everyone else.

"Light has shone on us, Your Excellency, since his serenity took over," Timokhin said timidly, glancing continually at his regimental commander.

"How so?" asked Pierre.

"Why, just as regards firewood and fodder, I must tell you. You see, we were retreating from Swienciany, not daring to touch a twig, or a wisp of hay there, or anything. You see, we were leaving, so *he* would get it, right, Your Excellency?" He turned to his prince. "But don't you dare! In our regiment, two officers were tried for that sort of thing. Well, as soon as his serenity took over, it got simple in that regard. Light has shone on us . . ."

"Then why was it forbidden before?"

Timokhin looked round in confusion, not understanding how and what to answer to such a question. Pierre turned with the same question to Prince Andrei.

"So as not to devastate the country we were abandoning to the enemy," Prince Andrei said with spiteful mockery. "It's very sound: troops shouldn't be allowed to pillage the countryside and get accustomed to looting. And in Smolensk he also reasoned correctly that the French might outflank us and that they had the greater force. But he could not understand," Prince Andrei cried in a high voice, as if suddenly bursting out, "he could not understand that there it was the first time we were fighting for Russian soil, that the spirit in the troops was such as I've never seen, that we beat back the French for two days in a row, and that that success increased our strength ten times. He ordered a retreat, and all our efforts and losses went for nothing. He wasn't thinking of treason, he was trying to do everything in the best possible way, he thought it all over: but that is why he's unfit. He's unfit now precisely because he thinks everything over very thoroughly and precisely, as every German ought to do. How shall I put it . . . Well, say your father has a German valet, and he's an excellent valet and will satisfy all his needs better than you, so let him serve; but if your father's mortally ill, you'll send the valet away and take care of your father with your unaccustomed, clumsy hands and comfort him better than any skilful stranger. That's what's been done with Barclay. As long as Russia was healthy, a stranger could serve her and be an excellent minister, but once she's in danger, she needs her own man, one of the family. But in your club you came up with the idea that he was a traitor! The only result of that slander will be that later, feeling ashamed of your own false reproach, you'll turn him from a traitor suddenly into a hero or a genius, which will be still more incorrect. He's an honest and very precise German . . ."

"However, they say he's a skilled commander," said Pierre.

"I don't understand what is meant by a skilled commander," Prince Andrei said mockingly.

"A skilled commander," said Pierre, "well, he's one who has foreseen all possibilities . . . well, who has guessed the thoughts of his adversary."

"That's impossible," said Prince Andrei, as if the matter had long been decided.

Pierre looked at him in astonishment.

"However," he said, "they do say that war is like a game of chess."

"Yes," said Prince Andrei, "only with this small difference, that in chess you can think over each move as long as you like, you're outside the conditions of time, and with this difference, too, that a knight is always stronger than a pawn, and two pawns are always stronger than one, while in war one battalion is sometimes stronger than a division and sometimes weaker than a company. Nobody can know the relative strength of the troops. Believe me," he said, "if anything depended on instructions from the staff, I'd be there giving instructions, but instead I have the honour of serving here in the regiment, with these gentlemen, and I think it's really on us that tomorrow depends, not on them . . . Success never did and never will depend on position, or on ammunition, or even on numbers; but least of all on position."

"But on what, then?"

"On the feeling that's in me, in him," he pointed to Timokhin, "in every soldier."

Prince Andrei glanced at Timokhin, who was looking fearfully and perplexedly at his commander. In contrast to his former restrained taciturnity, Prince Andrei now seemed excited. He clearly could not keep from expressing these thoughts, which came to him unexpectedly.

"A battle is won by him who is firmly resolved to win it. Why did we lose the battle of Austerlitz? The French losses were almost equal to ours, but we said to ourselves early on that we had lost the battle—and so we lost it. We said that because there was no need for us to fight: we wanted to leave the battlefield as soon as we could. 'We've lost—well, let's run for it!' And we ran. If we hadn't said it by evening, God knows what would have happened. But tomorrow we won't say it. You say: our position, the left flank is weak, the right is overextended," he went on. "That's all nonsense, it amounts to nothing. But what faces us tomorrow? A hundred million of the most varied possibilities, which will be decided instantly by who runs or will run away, theirs or ours, by whether this one or that is killed; but what's being done now is all just an amusement. The thing is that the men you rode round the position with not only don't contribute to the general course of things, but hinder it. They're concerned only with their own little interests."

"At such a moment?" Pierre said reproachfully.

"At *such a moment*," Prince Andrei repeated. "For them it's only the moment when they can undermine a rival and acquire one more little cross or ribbon. For me tomorrow is this: a hundred thousand Russian and a hundred thousand French troops have come together to fight, and the fact is that these two hundred thousand men will fight, and whoever fights hardest and spares himself least will win. And if you like, I'll tell you that, whatever goes on there, whatever muddle they make at the top, we'll win the battle tomorrow. Tomorrow, whatever goes on there, we'll win the battle."

"That's the truth, Your Excellency, that's the veritable truth," said Timokhin. "No sparing ourselves now! The soldiers in my battalion, if you can believe it, refused to drink their vodka: not on such a day, they said." Everybody fell silent.

The officers stood up. Prince Andrei went out of the shed with them, giving his last orders to the adjutant. When the officers had gone, Pierre went up to Prince Andrei and was just about to begin a conversation when, on the road not far from the shed, the hoofbeats of three horses were heard, and, glancing in that direction, Prince Andrei recognized Wolzogen and Clausewitz, accompanied by a Cossack. They passed close by, continuing to converse, and Pierre and Andrei involuntarily heard the following phrases:

"*Der Krieg muss im Raum verlegt werden. Der Ansicht kann ich nicht genug Preis geben,*"* said one.

"*O ja,*" said the other voice. "*Da der Zweck ist nur den Feind zu schwächen, so kann man gewiss nicht den Verlust der Privatpersonen in Achtung nehmen.*"†

"*O ja,*" the first voice confirmed.

"Yes, *im Raum verlegen,*" Prince Andrei repeated, snorting angrily, when they had ridden by. "*Im* this *Raum* I had a father, and a son, and a sister in Bald Hills. It's all the same to him. There's what I was saying to you— tomorrow these German gentlemen won't win the battle, they'll only muck things up as much as they can, because all there is in a German head is reasoning, which isn't worth a tinker's damn, but in their hearts they haven't got the one thing needed for tomorrow—which is what's in Timokhin. They gave *him* the whole of Europe and came to teach us! Fine teachers!" his voice shrieked again.

"So you think the battle will be won tomorrow?" said Pierre.

"Yes, yes," Prince Andrei said distractedly. "One thing I would do if I had power," he began again, "I would not take prisoners. What are prisoners? It's chivalry. The French devastated my home and are on their way to devastate Moscow, and they've offended me and offend me every second. They're my enemies, they're all criminals, to my mind. And Timokhin and the whole army think the same. They must be executed! If they're my enemies, they can't be friends, whatever they may have talked about in Tilsit."

*War must be extended in space. I cannot put too high a price on this view.
†Oh, yes . . . The aim is to weaken the enemy, so one cannot pay attention to the loss of private persons.

"Yes, yes," said Pierre, gazing at Prince Andrei with flashing eyes, "I agree with you completely, completely!"

The question that had been troubling Pierre ever since the hill in Mozhaisk and all that day, now presented itself to him as perfectly clear and fully resolved. He now understood the whole meaning and the whole significance of this war and the impending battle. Everything he had seen that day, all the significant, stern expressions on the faces he had seen flash by, appeared to him in a new light. He understood that hidden—*latente,* as they say in physics—warmth of patriotism which was in all the people he had seen, and which explained for him why all those people were calmly and as if light-mindedly preparing for death.

"Take no prisoners," Prince Andrei went on. "That alone would change the whole war and make it less cruel. As it is, we've been playing at war—that's the nasty thing, we act magnanimously and all that. It's like the magnanimity and sentimentality of the lady who swoons when she sees a calf slaughtered; she's so kind, she can't bear the sight of blood, but she eats the same calf in sauce with great appetite. We're told about the rules of war, about chivalry, about parleying, sparing the unfortunate, and so on. It's all nonsense. I saw chivalry and parleying in 1805: they cheated us, we cheated them. They loot other people's houses, spread false banknotes, and worst of all—kill my children and my father, and then talk about the rules of war and magnanimity towards the enemy. Take no prisoners, but kill and go to your death! Whoever has come to this, as I have, through the same sufferings . . ."

Prince Andrei, who had thought that it made no difference to him whether Moscow was or was not taken, as Smolensk had been, all at once stopped in his speech from an unexpected spasm that seized his throat. He silently paced up and down a few times, but his eyes glittered feverishly and his lips trembled when he began to speak again.

"If there was none of this magnanimity in war, we'd go to it only when it was worth going to certain death, as now. Then there would be no war because Pavel Ivanych offended Mikhail Ivanych. But if there's war like now, then it's war. And then the intensity of the troops would not be like now. Then all these Westphalians and Hessians led by Napoleon wouldn't follow him to Russia, and we wouldn't go to fight in Austria and Prussia, not knowing why ourselves. War isn't courtesy, it's the vilest thing in the world, and we must understand that and not play at war. We must take this terrible necessity sternly and seriously. That's the whole point: to cast off the lie, and if it's war it's war, and not a game. As it is, war is the favourite pastime of idle and light-minded people . . . The military estate is the most honoured. But what is war, what is needed for success in military affairs, what are the morals of military society? The aim of war is killing, the instruments of war are espionage, treason and the encouragement of it, the ruin of the inhabitants, robbing them or stealing to supply the army; deception and lying are called military stratagems; the morals of the military estate are absence of freedom, that is, discipline, idleness, ignorance, cruelty, depravity, and drunkenness. And in spite of that, it is the highest estate, respected by all. All kings except the Chinese wear military uniforms, and the one who has killed the most people gets the greatest reward . . . They come together, like tomorrow, to kill each other, they slaughter and maim tens of thousands of men, and then they say prayers of thanksgiving for having slaughtered so many people (inflating the numbers), and proclaim victory, supposing that the more people slaughtered, the greater the merit. How does God look down and listen to them!" Prince Andrei cried in a high, squeaky voice. "Ah, dear heart, lately it's become hard for me to live. I see that I've begun to understand too much. And it's not good for man to taste of the tree of the knowledge of good and evil . . . Well, it won't be for long!" he added. "However, you're falling asleep, and it's time I did, too. Go back to Gorki," Prince Andrei said suddenly.

"Oh, no!" Pierre replied, looking at Prince Andrei with frightened, commiserating eyes.

"Go, go: one needs a good night's sleep before a battle," Prince Andrei repeated. He went quickly up to Pierre, embraced and kissed him. "Goodbye, off with you," he cried. "Whether we see each other again or not . . ." And, turning hastily, he went into the shed.

It was already dark, and Pierre could not make out what the expression on Prince Andrei's face was, whether it was angry or tender.

Pierre stood for a while in silence, considering whether to follow him or go home. "No, he doesn't need it!" Pierre decided to himself, "and I know this is the last time we'll see each other." He sighed deeply and rode back to Gorki.

Prince Andrei, going back into the shed, lay down on the rug, but could not sleep.

He closed his eyes. One image succeeded another. He lingered long and joyfully over one of them. He vividly recalled one evening in Petersburg. Natasha was telling him with an animated, excited face how she had gone to pick mushrooms the previous summer and lost her way in a big forest. She incoherently described to him the dense forest and her feelings, and a talk with a beekeeper she met, and, interrupting herself every moment, said: "No, I can't, I'm not telling it right; no, you don't understand," even though Prince Andrei reassured her, saying that he did understand, and indeed he understood everything she wanted to say. Natasha was displeased with her own words; she sensed that she was not conveying the passionately poetic feeling which she had experienced that day and which she wanted to bring out. "He was so lovely, that old man, and it was so dark in the forest . . . and he had such a kind . . . No, I don't know how to tell it," she said, flushed and excited. Prince Andrei now smiled the same joyful smile that he had smiled then, looking in her eyes. "I understood her," thought Prince Andrei. "I not only understood her, but it was that inner force, that sincerity, that inner openness, that soul of hers, which was as if bound by her body, it was that soul that I loved . . . loved so strongly, so happily . . ." And suddenly he remembered what his love had ended with. "*He* didn't need any of that. *He* saw none of it and understood none of it. He saw in her a pretty and *fresh* girl, with whom he did not deign to join his fate. While I? . . . And to this day he's alive and cheerful."

Prince Andrei jumped up as if someone had burned him and again began pacing in front of the shed.

XXVI

On the twenty-fifth of August, the eve of the battle of Borodino, M. de Beausset, prefect of the French emperor's palace, and Colonel Fabvier came, the first from Paris, the second from Madrid, to see the emperor Napoleon in his camp at Valuevo.

Having changed into court uniform, M. de Beausset ordered the package he had brought with him carried to the emperor ahead of him, and entered the front section of Napoleon's tent, where, while talking to Napoleon's adjutants, who surrounded him, he occupied himself with opening the box.

Fabvier, not going into the tent, stood talking with some generals of his acquaintance by its entrance.

The emperor Napoleon had not yet left his bedroom and was finishing his toilette. Snorting and grunting, he turned now his fat back, now his hairy, fat chest under the brush with which a valet was rubbing his body. Another valet, stopping up the vial with his finger, sprayed eau de cologne over the emperor's pampered body, with a gesture which said that he alone could know how much eau de cologne must be sprayed and where. Napoleon's short hair was wet and tousled on his forehead. But his face, though swollen and yellow, expressed physical pleasure: "*Allez ferme, allez toujours . . .*"* he repeated, cringing and grunting, to the valet rubbing him. An adjutant who came into the bedroom to report to the emperor how many prisoners had been taken in yesterday's action, having said what he had to say, stood by the door waiting for permission to leave. Napoleon, wincing, gave the adjutant a frowning look from under his eyebrows.

"*Point de prisonniers,*" he repeated the adjutant's words. "*Ils se font*

*Do it hard, keep going. . .

*démolir. Tant pis pour l'armée russe,"** he said. *"Allez toujours, allez ferme,"* he said, hunching up and presenting his fat shoulders to the brush.

"C'est bien! Faites entrer monsieur de Beausset, ainsi que Fabvier,"† he said to the adjutant, nodding his head.

"Oui, Sire." And the adjutant disappeared through the door of the tent.

The two valets quickly dressed his majesty, and he, in the dark blue uniform of the guards, with firm, quick steps, went out to the reception room.

Just then Beausset, his hands hurrying, was setting up the present he had brought from the empress on two chairs facing the emperor's entrance. But the emperor dressed and came out so unexpectedly quickly that he did not quite have time to prepare the surprise.

Napoleon noticed at once what they were doing and realized that they were not ready yet. He did not wish to deprive them of the pleasure of giving him a surprise. He pretended he did not see Mr. Beausset, and called Fabvier over to him. Napoleon listened, frowning sternly and saying nothing, to what Fabvier was telling him about the bravery and loyalty of his troops who fought at Salamanca,[28] at the other end of Europe, and who had only one thought—to be worthy of their emperor, and only one fear—to displease him. The result of the battle was lamentable. During Fabvier's account, Napoleon kept making ironic comments, as if he had never supposed that things could go otherwise in his absence.

"I must make up for that in Moscow," said Napoleon. *"À tantôt,"*‡ he added and called for de Beausset, who meanwhile had had time to prepare the surprise, having set something on chairs and covered that something with a cloth.[29]

De Beausset bowed low with a French courtly bow, such as only old servitors of the Bourbons knew how to bow, and approached, holding out an envelope.

Napoleon turned to him cheerfully and pulled his ear.

"You were quick about it, I'm very glad. Well, what is Paris saying?" he said, suddenly changing his previously stern expression to a most benign one.

"Sire, tout Paris regrette votre absence,"§ replied de Beausset, as he ought. But though Napoleon knew that Beausset had to say that or something like it, though in his moments of clarity he knew that it was not true, he was pleased to hear it from de Beausset. He again honoured him by touching his ear.

"Je suis fâché de vous avoir fait faire tant de chemin,"# he said.

---

*No prisoners . . . They're getting themselves annihilated. So much the worse for the Russian army.
†That's enough! Have M. de Beausset come in, along with Fabvier.
‡See you later.
§Sire, all Paris is sorry for your absence.
#I regret having made you come such a long way.

*"Sire! Je ne m'attendais pas à moins qu'à vous trouver aux portes de Moscou,"** said Beausset.

Napoleon smiled and, raising his head distractedly, glanced to the right. The adjutant glided up to him with a gold snuffbox and held it out. Napoleon took it.

"Yes, it's a good chance for you," he said, putting the open snuffbox to his nose, "you like to travel. In three days you will see Moscow. You probably never expected to see an Asian capital. You'll have a pleasant journey."

Beausset bowed in gratitude for this attention to his (hitherto unknown to him) inclination for travel.

"Ah! What's this?" said Napoleon, noticing that the courtiers were all looking at something covered by a cloth. Beausset, with courtly adroitness, not showing his back, half turned and withdrew two steps, at the same time snatching off the cover, and said:

"A present for Your Majesty from the empress."

It was a portrait painted in bright colours by Gérard of the boy born to Napoleon and the daughter of the Austrian emperor, whom everyone for some reason called the king of Rome.

A quite handsome curly-headed boy with a gaze resembling the gaze of Christ in the Sistine Madonna was depicted playing bilboquet.[30] The ball represented the terrestrial globe and the stick in his other hand a sceptre.

It was not entirely clear precisely what the painter meant to express by presenting the so-called king of Rome skewering the terrestrial globe with a stick, but the allegory, to all those who had seen the picture in Paris, and to Napoleon himself, obviously seemed clear and quite pleasing.

"Le roi de Rome,"† he said, pointing to the portrait with a graceful gesture of the hand. *"Admirable!"* With a typically Italian capacity for changing facial expression at will, he went up to the portrait and assumed a look of thoughtful tenderness. He felt that what he said and did now—was history. And it seemed to him that the best thing he could do now—he with his grandeur, owing to which his son played bilboquet with the terrestrial globe—was to show, in contrast to that grandeur, the most simple fatherly tenderness. His eyes grew dim, he moved, glanced at a chair (the chair leaped under him), and sat down on it facing the portrait. One gesture from him—and everyone went out on tiptoe, leaving the great man alone with his feelings.

Having sat for a while and touched with his hand, not knowing why himself, the roughness of a highlight on the portrait, he stood up and called back Beausset and the officer on duty. He ordered the portrait taken out in front of

*Sire! I expected no less than to find you at the gates of Moscow.
†The king of Rome.

the tent, so as not to deprive the old guards standing near his tent of the happiness of seeing the king of Rome, the son and heir of their adored sovereign.

As he expected, while he was having breakfast with Mr. Beausset, who was deemed worthy of that honour, he heard in front of the tent the rapturous cries of the officers and soldiers of the old guard, who came running to the portrait.

"*Vive l'Empereur! Vive le Roi de Rome! Vive l'Empereur!*" came the rapturous voices.

After breakfast, Napoleon, in the presence of Beausset, dictated his order for the army.

"*Courte et énergique!*"* said Napoleon, when he had personally read over the proclamation, written straight off without corrections. The order ran:

Warriors! Here is the battle which you wanted so much. Victory depends on you. It is necessary for us; it will provide us with all that is needed: comfortable quarters and a speedy return to our fatherland. Act as you acted at Austerlitz, Friedland, Vitebsk, and Smolensk. Let posterity later remember with pride your exploits on this day. Let them say of each of you: he was in the great battle of Moscow.

"*De la Moskowa!*" Napoleon repeated and, having invited Mr. Beausset, the lover of travel, for a promenade, he came out of the tent to the saddled horses.

"*Votre Majesté a trop de bonté,*"† Beausset replied to the invitation to accompany the emperor: he wanted to sleep, and he did not know how and was afraid to ride on horseback.

But Napoleon nodded to the traveller, and Beausset had to go. When Napoleon came out of the tent, the cries of the guards before his son's portrait became louder still. Napoleon frowned.

"Take him away," he said, pointing to the portrait with a gracefully majestic gesture. "It is still too early for him to look upon a field of battle."

Beausset, closing his eyes and inclining his head, sighed deeply, showing thereby how he was able to appreciate and understand his emperor's words.

XXVII

The whole of that day of the twenty-fifth of August, as his historians say, Napoleon spent on horseback, studying the terrain, discussing plans presented to him by his marshals, and personally giving orders to his generals.

The original line of disposition of the Russian troops along the Kolocha had

*Brief and energetic!
†Your Majesty is too good.

been broken, and part of that line—namely, the Russian left flank—owing to the taking of the Shevardino redoubt on the twenty-fourth, had moved further back. That part of the line was no longer fortified, no longer protected by the river, and before it there was only a more open and level space. It was obvious to everyone, military and non-military, that this part of the line ought to be attacked by the French. It seemed that for that there was no need for much reflection, no need for such consideration and botheration on the part of the emperor and his marshals, and no need at all for that especially superior quality known as genius, which people like so much to ascribe to Napoleon; but the historians who later described the event, and the people who then surrounded Napoleon, and he himself thought otherwise.

Napoleon rode over the field, profoundly studying the terrain, nodding approvingly to himself or shaking his head mistrustfully, and, without informing the generals who surrounded him of that profound course of thought which guided his decisions, told them only his final conclusions in the form of orders. Having listened to a suggestion of Davout, known as the duke of Eckmühl, about turning the Russian left flank, Napoleon said that there was no need to do that, without explaining why there was no need. To the suggestion of General Compans (who was to attack the flèches) that he lead his division through the woods, Napoleon gave his consent, though the so-called duke of Elchingen—that is, Ney—allowed himself to observe that moving through the woods was dangerous and might break up the division.

Having examined the terrain in front of the Shevardino redoubt, Napoleon reflected for a time in silence and pointed to places on which two batteries were to be set up by tomorrow to go into action against the Russian fortifications, and to places next to them where the field artillery was to be lined up.

After giving this and other orders, he returned to his headquarters, and the disposition of the battle was drawn up at his dictation.

This disposition, which French historians speak of with rapture and other historians with deep respect, was the following:[31]

At dawn two new batteries, set up during the night on the plain occupied by the duke of Eckmühl, will open fire on the two opposing batteries of the enemy.

At the same time, the commander of artillery of the 1st corps, General Pernety, with thirty guns of Compans's division and all the howitzers of Dessaix and Friant's division, will move forward, open fire, and rain shells on the enemy battery, against which there will be in action:

> 24 guns of the guards' artillery
> 30 guns of Compans's division
> and 8 guns of Friant and Dessaix's division
> 62 guns in all.

The commander of artillery of the 3rd corps, General Fouché, will place the howitzers of the 3rd and 8th corps, sixteen in all, on the flanks of the battery designated to bombard the left fortification, which will bring against it a total of 40 guns.

General Sorbier should be ready at the first order to bring forward all the howitzers of the guards' artillery against one or the other fortification.

In the course of the cannonade, Prince Poniatowski will advance on the village through the woods and outflank the enemy's position.

General Compans will move through the woods in order to take the first fortification.

After entering into combat in this way, orders will be given in accordance with the enemy's actions.

The cannonade on the left flank will begin as soon as the cannonade on the right wing is heard. The riflemen of Morand's division and of the viceroy's[32] division will open heavy fire when they see the attack beginning on the right wing.

The viceroy will take the village* and cross its three bridges, proceeding at the same level as the divisions of Morand and Gérard which, under his leadership, will head for the redoubt and fall in with the other troops of the army.

All this is to be carried out in order *(le tout se fera avec ordre et méthode)*, sparing as far as possible the troops of the reserve.

In the imperial camp by Mozhaisk, 6th September 1812.[33]

This disposition, drawn up quite vaguely and confusedly—if one allows oneself to consider Napoleon's instructions without religious awe of his genius— contained four points, four instructions. Not one of these instructions was or could be carried out.

The disposition says, first, *that the batteries set up at the places chosen by Napoleon, along with the guns of Pernety and Fouché lined up with them, one hundred and two guns in all, should open fire and rain shells on the Russian flèches and redoubts.* That could not be done, since from the places designated by Napoleon the projectiles did not reach the Russian works, and those one hundred and two guns were shooting into the void, until the nearest commander, contrary to Napoleon's order, moved them forward.

The second instruction was that *Poniatowski, heading towards the village through the woods, would turn the left wing of the Russians.* That was not and could not be done, because Poniatowski, heading for the village through the woods, met Tuchkov there, who blocked his way, and so did not and could not outflank the Russian position.

The third instruction: *General Compans will move through the woods in*

*That is, Borodino (Tolstoy's note).

order to take the first fortification. Compans's division did not take the first fortification, but was repulsed, because, on emerging from the woods, it had to form up under canister shot, something Napoleon did not foresee.

The fourth: *The viceroy will take the village* (Borodino) *and cross its three bridges, proceeding at the same level as the divisions of Morand and Gérard* (of which it is not said where and when they would move), *which, under his command, will head for the redoubt and fall in with the other troops of the army.*

As far as one can tell—if not from this muddled sentence, then from the attempts that the viceroy made to carry out the orders given him—he was to move through Borodino from the left towards the redoubt, while the divisions of Morand and Gérard were to move simultaneously from the front.

All that, like the other points of the disposition, was not and could not be carried out. Having gone through Borodino, the viceroy was driven back on the Kolocha and could go no further; the divisions of Morand and Gérard did not take the redoubt, but were repulsed, and the redoubt was taken only at the end of the battle by the cavalry (probably something unforeseen by and unheard-of for Napoleon). Thus, none of the instructions of the disposition were or could be carried out. But it was said in the disposition that *after entering into combat in this way, orders will be given in accordance with the enemy's actions,* and therefore it would seem that, during the battle, Napoleon would be giving all the necessary instructions; but that was not and could not be done, because during the whole time of the battle, Napoleon was so far away from it that (as it turned out afterwards) the course of the battle could not be known to him and not one of his instructions during the battle could be carried out.

XXVIII

Many historians say that the battle of Borodino was not won by the French because Napoleon had a cold, that if he had not had a cold, his instructions before and during the battle would have been of still greater genius, and Russia would have perished, *et la face du monde eut été changée.** For historians who accept that Russia was shaped by the will of one man—Peter the Great—and that France was turned from a republic into an empire and French troops went to Russia by the will of one man—Napoleon—such an argument, that Russia remained a power because Napoleon had a bad cold on the twenty-sixth, such an argument for such historians is inevitably consistent.

If it had depended on Napoleon's will whether or not to fight the battle of

---

*And the face of the world would have been changed.

Borodino, and if it had depended on his will whether to give this or that instruction, then it is obvious that a cold, having an influence on the expression of his will, could have caused the salvation of Russia, and therefore the valet who forgot to give Napoleon his waterproof boots on the twenty-fourth was the saviour of Russia. By that way of thinking, this conclusion is indubitable—as indubitable as the conclusion which Voltaire drew jokingly (not knowing at what himself) when he said that the night of St. Bartholomew was the result of Charles IX having an upset stomach.[34] But for people who do not admit that Russia was shaped by the will of one man—Peter I—and that the French empire arose and the war with Russia began by the will of one man—Napoleon—this argument seems not only incorrect, unreasonable, but also contrary to all human essence. To the question of what constitutes the cause of historical events, a different answer presents itself, which is that the course of world events is predestined from on high, depends on the coincidence of all the wills of the people participating in those events, and that Napoleon's influence on the course of those events is only external and fictitious.

Strange as it may seem at first glance to suggest that the night of St. Bartholomew, the order for which was given by Charles IX, did not occur by his will, but that it only seemed to him that he had called for it, and that the slaughter of eighty thousand men at Borodino did not occur by the will of Napoleon (though he gave the orders for the beginning and the course of the battle), but that it only seemed to him that he called for it—strange as this suggestion may seem, human dignity, which tells me that each of us is, if not more, then certainly no less of a human being than the great Napoleon, calls for the allowance of this solution to the problem, and historical research abundantly confirms this suggestion.

In the battle of Borodino, Napoleon did not shoot at anyone and did not kill anyone. That was all done by the soldiers. Which means it was not he who killed people.

The soldiers of the French army went to kill Russian soldiers in the battle of Borodino not as the result of Napoleon's orders but by their own will. The whole army—the French, the Italians, the Germans, the Poles, hungry, ragged, and exhausted by the campaign—on seeing the army that blocked their way to Moscow, felt that *"le vin est tiré et qu'il faut le boire."** If Napoleon had now forbidden them to fight the Russians, they would have killed him and gone to fight the Russians, because it was necessary for them.

When they heard the order of Napoleon, who, in return for their mutilation and death, presented them in consolation with the words of posterity about their having been at the battle of Moscow, they cried *"Vive l'Empereur!"* just as they cried *"Vive l'Empereur!"* on seeing the depiction of the boy skewering

---

*The wine is drawn and it must be drunk.

the terrestrial globe with a bilboquet stick; just as they would cry *"Vive l'Em-pereur!"* to any nonsense that was told them. They had nothing left to do but cry *"Vive l'Empereur!"* and go to fight, in order to find food and rest as victors in Moscow. Which meant it was not as the result of Napoleon's order that they killed their own kind.

And it was not Napoleon who ordained the course of the battle, because nothing of his disposition was carried out and during the battle he did not know what was happening in front of him. Which meant also that the way these people were killing each other occurred not by the will of Napoleon, but went on independently of him, by the will of the hundreds of thousands of people who took part in the common action. To Napoleon *it only seemed* that the whole thing happened by his will. And therefore the question whether Napoleon had or did not have a cold is of no greater interest to history than the question of the last convoy soldier having a cold.

Napoleon's cold on the twenty-sixth of August has still less significance, since the evidence of writers that, owing to Napoleon's cold, his disposition and his instructions during the battle were not as good as previously, is totally incorrect.

The disposition quoted above was not at all worse, but even better than all the previous dispositions by which his battles had been won. His imaginary instructions during the battle were also no worse than previous ones, but exactly the same as ever. But the disposition and the instructions seem worse than previous ones because the battle of Borodino was the first that Napoleon did not win. All the most excellent and profoundly conceived dispositions and instructions seem very bad, and every military expert criticizes them with a significant air, when the battle is not won through them, and the worst dispositions and instructions seem very good, and serious men write whole volumes proving the merits of bad instructions, when the battle is won through them.

The disposition drawn up by Weyrother for the battle of Austerlitz was the picture of perfection in works of that sort, but all the same it was condemned, condemned for its perfection, for being excessively detailed.

In the battle of Borodino, Napoleon fulfilled his function as the representative of power just as well and even better than in other battles. He did nothing to harm the course of the battle; he bowed to the more well-reasoned opinions; he caused no confusion, did not contradict himself, did not get frightened, and did not run away from the battlefield, but with his great tact and experience of war calmly and worthily fulfilled his role of seeming to command.

XXIX

Having returned from a second preoccupied ride along the line, Napoleon said:

"The chessmen are set up, the game starts tomorrow."

Calling for punch to be served and sending for Beausset, he started a conversation with him about Paris, about some changes he intended to make in the *maison de l'impératrice,** astonishing the prefect by his memory of all the minute details of court relations.

He interested himself in trifles, joked about Beausset's love of travel, and chatted away casually, as a famous, self-assured surgeon, who knows his job, does as he rolls up his sleeves and puts on his apron, while the patient is being strapped to the cot: "The whole matter is in my hands and in my head, clearly and definitely. When I have to get down to it, I'll do it like nobody else, but now I can joke, and the more calm and jocular I am, the more assured, calm, and astonished at my genius you should be."

Having finished his second glass of punch, Napoleon went to rest before the serious business which, as it seemed to him, faced him the next day.

He was so concerned with the business facing him that he could not sleep and, despite his cold, aggravated by the evening dampness, at three o'clock that night, loudly blowing his nose, he went out to the large section of the tent. He asked if the Russians were still there. The reply was that the enemy's fires were still in the same places. He nodded his head approvingly.

The adjutant on duty came into the tent.

"*Eh bien, Rapp, croyez-vous que nous ferons de bonnes affaires aujourd'hui?*"† he addressed him.

"*Sans aucun doute, Sire,*"‡ answered Rapp.

Napoleon looked at him.

"*Vous rappelez-vous, Sire, ce que vous m'avez fait l'honneur de dire à Smolensk,*" said Rapp, "*le vin est tiré, il faut le boire.*"§

Napoleon frowned and sat silently for a long time, his head on his hand.

"*Cette pauvre armée,*" he said, "*elle a bien diminuée depuis Smolensk. La fortune est une franche courtisane, Rapp; je le disais toujours, et je commence à l'éprouver. Mais la garde, Rapp, la garde est intacte?*"# he said questioningly.

---

*Empress's household.
†Well, Rapp, do you think things will go well for us today?
‡Without any doubt, Sire.
§Remember, Sire, what you did me the honour of saying at Smolensk . . . the wine is drawn, it must be drunk.
#This poor army . . . has much diminished since Smolensk. Fortune is an arrant courtesan, Rapp; I always said so, and I'm beginning to experience it. But the guard, Rapp, the guard is intact?

"*Oui, Sire,*" answered Rapp.

Napoleon took a lozenge, put it in his mouth, and looked at his watch. He had no wish to sleep, morning was still far off; it was no longer possible to kill time by giving any sort of instructions, because they had all been given and were now being carried out.

"*A-t-on distribué les biscuits et le riz aux régiments de la garde?*"* Napoleon asked sternly.

"*Oui, Sire.*"

"*Mais le riz?*"†

Rapp answered that he had conveyed the sovereign's orders about the rice, but Napoleon shook his head in displeasure, as if he did not believe that his order had been carried out. A servant came in with punch. Napoleon called for another glass to be served to Rapp and silently sipped from his own.

"I have no taste or smell," he said, sniffing the glass. "I'm tired of this cold. They talk about medicine. What good is medicine, if they can't cure a cold? Corvisart gave me these lozenges, but they don't help at all. What can they cure? It's impossible to cure. *Notre corps est une machine à vivre. Il est organisé pour cela, c'est sa nature; laissez-y faire la vie à son aise, qu'elle s'y défende elle-même: elle fera plus que si vous la paralysiez en l'encombrant de remèdes. Notre corps est comme une montre parfaite qui doit aller un certain temps; l'horloger n'a pas la faculté de l'ouvrir, il ne peut la manier qu'à tâtons et les yeux bandés. Notre corps est une machine à vivre, voilà tout.*"‡ And as if entering on the path of definitions, *définitions*, which Napoleon liked, he suddenly made a new definition. "Do you know, Rapp, what the art of war is?" he asked. "It's the art of being stronger than the enemy at a certain moment. *Voilà tout.*"

Rapp said nothing.

"*Demain nous allons avoir affaire à Koutouzoff!*"§ said Napoleon. "We'll see! Remember, he was in command of the army in Braunau and in three weeks never once got on a horse to inspect the fortifications. We'll see!"

He glanced at his watch. It was only four o'clock. He did not want to sleep, the punch was finished, and there was still nothing to do. He stood up, paced back and forth, put on a warm tunic and a hat, and left the tent. The night was dark and damp; a barely perceptible dampness fell from above. Low fires burned nearby, among the French guards, and glimmered far off through the

---

*Have biscuits and rice been distributed to the regiments of the guard?
†Rice, too?
‡Our body is a machine for living. It is organized for that, such is its nature; leave life alone there and let it defend itself: it will do more than if you paralyse it by loading it down with remedies. Our body is like a perfect watch that must run for a certain time; the watchmaker is not able to open it, he can only handle it by feel and blindfolded. Our body is a machine for living, that's all.
§Tomorrow we'll be dealing with Kutuzov.

smoke along the Russian line. It was quiet everywhere, and one could clearly hear the rustling and tramping of the French troops, already beginning to move and take up their positions.

Napoleon walked about in front of his tent, looked at the fires, listened to the tramping, and, passing by a tall guard in a shaggy hat who was standing watch by his tent and, like a black post, drew himself to attention when the emperor appeared, stopped in front of him.

"What year did you join the service?" he asked with that habitual affectation of gruff and affectionate soldierliness with which he always addressed his men. The soldier told him.

"*Ah! un des vieux!** Did your regiment get rice?"

"Yes, Your Majesty."

Napoleon nodded his head and left him.

At half past five Napoleon was riding on horseback to the village of Shevardino.

It was beginning to grow light, the sky cleared, only one cloud lay in the east. The abandoned campfires were going out in the faint light of morning.

To the right a dense, solitary cannon shot rang out, raced by, and died away amidst the general silence. Several minutes passed. A second, a third shot rang out; the air shook; a fourth, a fifth rang out nearby and solemnly somewhere to the right.

The sound of the first shots still hung in the air when others rang out, more and more, merging and interrupting each other.

Napoleon and his suite rode up to the Shevardino redoubt and dismounted. The game had begun.

XXX

On returning to Gorki from seeing Prince Andrei, Pierre, having told his groom to prepare the horses and awaken him early in the morning, fell asleep at once behind the partition, in a corner that Boris had given up to him.

By the time Pierre fully awoke the next morning, there was no one in the cottage. The panes were rattling in the little windows. The groom was standing there trying to rouse him.

"Your Excellency, Your Excellency, Your Excellency . . ." the groom muttered insistently, without looking at Pierre, shaking him by the shoulder, and clearly having lost all hope of waking him up.

*Ah! an old-timer!

"What? It's begun? It's time?" said Pierre, now awake.

"Listen to the shooting, if you please," said the groom, a retired soldier. "All the gentlemen are gone, and his serenity rode by long ago."

Pierre hurriedly dressed and ran out to the porch. Outside it was clear, fresh, dewy, and cheerful. The sun, having just burst from behind the cloud that had covered it, sprayed its rays, half broken by the cloud, across the roofs of the street opposite, over the dew-covered dust of the road, over the walls of the houses, the windows, the fences, and Pierre's horses, which were standing by the cottage. The roar of cannon was clearly heard outside. An adjutant and a Cossack trotted down the road.

"It's time, Count, it's time," the adjutant called out.

Ordering the horse to be led after him, Pierre went down the road to the barrow, from which he had looked over the battlefield the day before. There was a crowd of military on this barrow, the French talk of the staff officers could be heard, and Kutuzov's grey head could be seen, in its white cap with the red band, and his grey nape sunk into his shoulders. Kutuzov was looking through a field glass down the high road in front of him.

Going up the steps to the barrow, Pierre looked ahead of him and froze in delight at the beauty of the spectacle. It was the same panorama he had admired from the barrow the day before; but now the whole terrain was covered with troops and the smoke of gunfire, and the slanting rays of the bright sun, rising behind and to the left of Pierre, cast over it, in the clear morning air, a piercing light of a pink and golden hue, and long, dark shadows. The distant woods, ending the panorama, as if carved from some precious yellow-green stone, displayed the curved line of its treetops on the horizon, and between them, beyond Valuevo, cut the Smolensk high road, all covered with troops. Golden fields and copses glistened closer by. Everywhere—ahead, to the right, to the left—troops could be seen. It was all lively, majestic, and unexpected; but what struck Pierre most of all was the sight of the battlefield itself, Borodino and the hollows above the Kolocha on both sides of it.

Above the Kolocha, in Borodino and on both sides of it, especially the left, where the Voyna, between its swampy banks, flows into the Kolocha, hung that mist which melts, dissolves, and turns translucent in the bright sun, and magically colours and outlines everything that shows through it. This mist merged with the smoke of gunfire, and everywhere over this mist and smoke gleams of morning light flashed—on the water, on the dew, on the bayonets of the soldiers who crowded along the banks and in Borodino. Through this mist the white church could be seen, and here and there the roofs of Borodino cottages, here and there solid masses of soldiers, here and there green caissons and cannon. And all this was moving, or seemed to be moving, because of the mist and smoke spreading over the entire expanse. As in this hollow terrain near Borodino, covered with mist, so outside it, higher and especially to the left, along the whole line, over the woods, over the fields, in the hollows, up on the heights, puffs of cannon smoke were ceaselessly born of themselves out of nothing, now singly, now in flocks, now sparse, now in rapid succession, and, swelling, spreading, billowing, merging, could be seen over the whole expanse.

This smoke of gunfire and, strange to say, the sound of it, made up the chief beauty of the spectacle.

Poof! Suddenly a round, compact puff of smoke was seen, a play of purple, grey, and milky white, and *boom!*—a second later came the sound of this smoke.

Poof-poof! Two puffs of smoke rose up, jostling and merging; and *boom-boom!*—came sounds confirming what the eyes had seen.

Pierre turned back to the first puff of smoke, which he had left as a round, compact ball, and in its place there were already balloons of smoke drawing to one side, and *poof* . . . (with a pause) *poof-poof*—another three, another four were born, and to each, with the same intervals, *boom* . . . *boom-boom-boom* came the beautiful, firm, sure sounds in response. It seemed that these puffs of smoke now raced along, now stood still, and past them raced woods, fields, and gleaming bayonets. On the left side, over the fields and bushes, these big puffs of smoke with their solemn echoes were ceaselessly being born, and still closer, over hollows and woods, burst out the small puffs of musket smoke, having no time to become round, and in the same way gave their own little echoes. *Trat-ta-ta-tat* rattled the muskets, rapidly but irregularly and meagrely in comparison with the firing of the ordnance.

Pierre wanted to be there where those puffs of smoke, those gleaming bayonets and cannons, those movements, those sounds were. He turned to look at Kutuzov and his suite, so as to compare his impressions with those of others. Everyone was looking ahead at the battlefield, as he was, and, it seemed to him, with the same feeling. On all faces there now shone that "hidden warmth" *(chaleur latente)* of feeling which Pierre had noticed the day before and which he had understood perfectly after his conversation with Prince Andrei.

"Go, dear boy, go, Christ be with you," Kutuzov was saying, without taking his eyes from the battlefield, to a general standing next to him.

Having heard the order, this general walked past Pierre to the path down from the barrow.

"To the crossing!" the general said coldly and sternly in reply, when one of the staff officers asked where he was going.

"So am I, so am I," thought Pierre, and he went in the same direction after the general.

The general was getting on his horse, brought him by a Cossack. Pierre went over to his groom, who was holding the horses. Asking which was the quieter, Pierre climbed onto the horse, clutched at its mane, pressed the heels of his splayed feet to the horse's belly, and, feeling that his spectacles were falling off and that he could not let go of the mane and the reins, galloped after the general, provoking smiles from the staff officers, who were watching him from the barrow.

XXXI

The general whom Pierre was galloping after, having gone down the hill, turned sharply to the left, and Pierre, losing sight of him, rode into the ranks of some infantry who were marching ahead of him. He tried to get out of them to the right, to the left; but everywhere there were soldiers with equally preoccupied faces, busy with some invisible but obviously important matters. They all looked with equally displeased and questioning eyes at this fat man in a white hat, who for some unknown reason was trampling them with his horse.

"Why go riding into the middle of a battalion?" one cried to him. Another shoved his horse with the butt of his musket, and Pierre, clinging to the pommel, barely controlling the shying horse, galloped out ahead of the soldiers, where there was more room.

Ahead of him was a bridge, and at the bridge more soldiers stood shooting. Pierre rode up to them. Without knowing it himself, Pierre had come as far as the bridge over the Kolocha, which was between Gorki and Borodino, and which the French (having taken Borodino) attacked in the first action of the battle. Pierre saw that there was a bridge ahead of him, and that on both sides of the bridge, and on the meadow, among those rows of mowed hay he had noticed the day before, soldiers were doing something in the smoke; but, despite the incessant shooting that was going on there, it never occurred to him that this was precisely the field of battle. He did not hear the sounds of the bullets whining on all sides, and of the shells that flew over his head, did not see the enemy on the other side of the river, and for a long time did not see the dead and wounded, though many fell not far from him. With a smile that never left his face, he looked about him.

"What's that one doing riding in front of the line?" someone again cried to him.

"Go left, go right," they shouted at him.

Pierre pulled to the right and unexpectedly ran into General Raevsky's adjutant, whom he knew. This adjutant also glanced angrily at Pierre, was obviously about to shout at him, but, recognizing him, nodded his head.

"What are you doing here?" he said and rode on.

Pierre, feeling out of place and having nothing to do, afraid of getting in someone's way again, rode after the adjutant.

"Is it here, or what? Can I come with you?" he asked.

"One moment, one moment," replied the adjutant and, riding up to a fat colonel who was standing in the meadow, he said something to him, and only then turned to Pierre.

"How did you end up here, Count?" he said to him with a smile. "Still curious?"

"Yes, yes," said Pierre. But the adjutant, turning his horse, was riding on.

"Here it's not bad, thank God," said the adjutant, "but on the left flank, with Bagration, it's getting terribly hot."

"Really?" asked Pierre. "Where's that?"

"Come to the barrow with me, you can see it from there. It's still bearable at our battery," said the adjutant. "Are you coming?"

"Yes, I'll come with you," said Pierre, looking round, his eyes seeking his groom. Only here for the first time did Pierre see the wounded, trudging on foot or carried on stretchers. On the same little meadow with the fragrant rows of hay over which he had ridden the day before, across the rows, his head twisted awkwardly, a soldier lay motionless, his shako fallen off. "Why didn't they pick up that one?" Pierre began; but seeing the stern face of the adjutant, who was looking in the same direction, he fell silent.

Pierre did not find his groom, and rode with the adjutant along the hollow towards the Raevsky barrow. Pierre's horse lagged behind the adjutant's and jolted him rhythmically.

"You're evidently not used to riding horseback, Count?" asked the adjutant.

"No, it's all right, but she's somehow bouncing a lot," Pierre said in perplexity.

"Ehh! . . . she's wounded," said the adjutant, "in the right foreleg, above the knee. Must have been a bullet. Congratulations, Count," he said, "*le baptême du feu.*"*

Having ridden in smoke through the sixth corps, behind the artillery, which, moved forward, was firing, deafening them with its gunfire, they came to a small woods. In the woods it was cool, quiet, and smelled of autumn. Pierre and the adjutant got off their horses and went up the hill on foot.

"Is the general here?" asked the adjutant, coming to the barrow.

"He was just here, he rode off that way," they answered him, pointing to the right.

The adjutant looked at Pierre as if not knowing what to do with him now.

"Don't worry," said Pierre, "I'll go up on the barrow if I may?"

"Yes, do. You can see everything from there, and it's not so dangerous. I'll come to fetch you."

Pierre went to the battery, and the adjutant rode on. They saw no more of each other, and much later Pierre learned that this adjutant had had his arm shot off that day.

*The baptism of fire.

The barrow that Pierre went up on was that famous place (later known to the Russians as the battery of the barrow, or the Raevsky battery, and to the French as *la grande redoute, la fatale redoute, la redoute du centre*) round which tens of thousands of men were brought down, and which the French considered the most important point of the position.

This redoubt consisted of a barrow in which trenches had been dug on three sides. In the area surrounded by the trenches stood ten cannon, firing through openings in the rampart.

In line with the barrow on both sides cannon also stood, firing steadily. Slightly behind the cannon stood infantry. Going up on this barrow, Pierre had no notion that this place surrounded by small trenches, where a few cannon stood firing, was the most important place in the battle.

On the contrary, it seemed to Pierre that this place (precisely because he was there) was one of the most insignificant places of the battle.

Having come up onto the barrow, Pierre sat down at the end of a trench that surrounded the battery and with an unconsciously joyful smile looked at what was happening round him. Now and then Pierre, with the same smile, got up and, trying not to bother the soldiers who were loading and rolling the guns, and who constantly ran past him with sacks and charges, strolled round the battery. The cannon of this battery fired steadily one after the other with a deafening roar and covered the whole area with powder smoke.

In contrast to the dread that was felt among the covering infantrymen, here at the battery, where a small number of people, busy with their work, were restricted, separated from the others by a trench—here one could feel a sort of family animation, the same and common to them all.

The appearance of Pierre's non-military figure in a white hat struck these men unpleasantly at first. The soldiers, passing by him, looked askance, with surprise and even fear, at his figure. The senior artillery officer, a tall, long-legged, pockmarked man, came up to Pierre, as if in order to check the action of the end cannon, and glanced at him curiously.

A young, round-faced little officer, still a perfect child, obviously just out of cadet school, commanding quite diligently the two cannon entrusted to him, addressed Pierre sternly.

"Allow me, sir, to ask that you clear the way," he said to him. "You cannot be here."

The soldiers shook their heads disapprovingly, looking at Pierre. But when they all became convinced that this man in the white hat not only was not doing any harm, but either sat peaceably on the slope of the rampart or, with a timid smile, politely making way for the soldiers, strolled round the battery under fire as calmly as if it were a boulevard, the feeling of hostile perplexity towards him gradually began to turn into a gentle and jocular sympathy, similar to what soldiers feel for their animals—the dogs, cocks, goats, and animals generally that live with military units. Then the soldiers mentally received Pierre into their family, adopted him, and gave him a nickname. "Our master" they nicknamed him, and gently made fun of him among themselves.

One cannonball ploughed up the dirt two steps from Pierre. He looked round with a smile, brushing off the earth it spattered on his clothes.

"How is it you're not afraid, master, really!" a stocky, red-mugged soldier addressed Pierre, baring his strong white teeth.

"Are you afraid?" asked Pierre.

"What else!" answered the soldier. "She's got no pity. She smacks down, and guts spill out. Impossible not to be afraid," he said, laughing.

Several soldiers with cheerful and gentle faces stopped near Pierre. It was as if they did not expect him to talk like everybody else and were glad of this discovery.

"Ours is soldierly business. But for a master it's amazing. Some master he is!"

"To your places!" cried the young officer to the soldiers gathered round Pierre. This young officer was clearly carrying out his duties for the first or second time, and therefore addressed both the soldiers and the superior with special precision and formality.

The rolling fire of cannon and muskets was growing more intense over the field, especially to the left, where Bagration's flèches were, but due to the smoke of gunfire in the place where Pierre was, almost nothing could be seen. Besides, observing the family-like circle of men (separated from all the others) who were there on the battery absorbed all Pierre's attention. His first unconsciously joyful excitement, produced by the sight and sounds of the battlefield, had now been replaced, especially after seeing the soldier lying solitarily on the field, by a different feeling. Sitting on the side of the trench now, he observed the faces round him.

By ten o'clock some twenty men had already been carried from the battery; two guns had been smashed, shells were hitting the battery more and more often, and bullets, buzzing and whistling, reached them from far away. But it was as if the men who were on the battery did not notice it; on all sides merry talk and joking were heard.

"A stuffed one!" a soldier cried at an approaching shell, whistling as it flew. "Not here! To the infantry!" another added with a laugh, noticing that the shell had flown over and hit the ranks of the covering troops.

"What, a friend of yours?" another soldier laughed at a muzhik who ducked under a flying cannonball.

Several soldiers gathered at the rampart, gazing at what was happening further ahead.

"They've drawn in the front line, you see, they've backed up," they said, pointing over the rampart.

"Mind your own business," an old sergeant shouted at them. "If they've backed up, it means they've got business back there." And he took one of the soldiers by the shoulder and kicked him with his knee. There was laughter.

"Roll up the fifth gun!" a cry came from one side.

"All at once now, together, like boatmen," merry cries were heard as they changed cannon.

"Aie, it almost knocked off our master's little hat," the red-mugged joker laughed at Pierre, showing his teeth. "Ah, clumsy girl," he added reproachfully to a cannonball that struck a wheel and a man's leg.

"Well, you foxes!" another laughed at the crouching militiamen who came to the battery to fetch the wounded.

"So you don't like the porridge? Ah, you crows, you're scared stiff!" they shouted at the militiamen, who faltered before a soldier with a shot-off leg.

"So it goes, lad," they mimicked the muzhiks. "They really don't like it!"

Pierre noticed how, after every cannonball that hit its mark, after every loss, the general animation flared up more.

As in an approaching storm cloud, there flashed more and more often, more and more brightly on the faces of all these men (as if in resistance to what was happening) the lightning of a hidden fire flaring up.

Pierre did not look ahead at the battlefield and was not interested in knowing what was going on there: he was entirely absorbed in contemplating this fire flaring up more and more, which (he felt it) was also flaring up in his soul.

At ten o'clock the infantrymen who had been in the bushes in front of the battery and along the Kamenka River retreated. From the battery they could be seen running back past it, carrying the wounded on muskets. Some general with his suite came up on the barrow and, having talked with the colonel, glared angrily at Pierre and went down again, ordering the covering infantry who stood behind the battery to lie down so as to be less exposed to fire. After that, from the ranks of infantry to the right of the battery came the sound of a drum, shouts of command, and it could be seen from the battery that those ranks of infantry were moving forward.

Pierre looked over the rampart. One face especially struck his eyes. It was the pale young face of an officer, who was marching backwards, carrying a lowered sword, and glancing uneasily over his shoulder.

The ranks of infantrymen disappeared into the smoke; their drawn-out cry was heard and then rapid musket fire. A few moments later, crowds of wounded and stretchers came back from there. Projectiles began falling still more frequently on the battery. Several men lay there and were not carried away. The soldiers bustled more animatedly round the cannon. No one paid any further attention to Pierre. He was shouted at a couple of times for being in the way. The senior officer, frowning, moved from one gun to another with big, quick strides. The young little officer, still more flushed, commanded the soldiers still more diligently. The soldiers handed on charges, turned, loaded, and did their work with tense jauntiness. They bobbed as if on springs as they walked.

The storm cloud came near, and the fire whose flaring up Pierre had been watching now burned brightly on all faces. He stood beside the senior officer. The young little officer, his hand to his shako, came running up to the older one.

"I have the honour to report, Colonel, that there are only eight charges left. Do you order us to continue firing?" he asked.

"Canister shot!" the senior officer cried without answering, looking over the rampart.

Suddenly something happened; the little officer said "Ah" and, curling up, sat on the ground like a bird shot down in flight. Everything became strange, vague, and bleak in Pierre's eyes.

One after another, cannonballs came whistling and struck the breastwork, the soldiers, the cannon. Pierre, who previously had not heard these sounds, now heard nothing else. To the right side of the battery, soldiers with cries of "Hurrah!" were running not forward, but back, as it seemed to Pierre.

A cannonball struck the very edge of the rampart before which Pierre was standing, scattering dirt, and in his eyes a black ball flashed and in that same instant smacked into something. The militiamen who were just coming into the battery ran back again.

"All canister shot!" cried the officer.

The sergeant ran up to the senior officer and in a frightened whisper (the way a butler reports to his master at dinner that they have run out of the wine he requested) said that they had run out of charges.

"The brigands, what are they doing!" shouted the officer, turning to Pierre. The senior officer's face was red and sweaty, his frowning eyes flashed. "Run to the reserves, bring the caissons!" he cried, angrily avoiding Pierre with his glance and turning to his soldier.

"I'll go," said Pierre. The officer, without answering him, walked off in the other direction with big strides.

"Hold your fire . . . Wait!" he cried.

The soldier who had been ordered to go for the charges collided with Pierre.

"Eh, master, this is no place for you," he said and ran down. Pierre ran after the soldier, avoiding the place where the young little officer sat.

One cannonball, a second, a third flew over him, landing in front, on the sides, behind. Pierre went running down. "Where am I going?" he suddenly tried to recall, already running up to the green caissons. He stopped, undecided whether to go back or go on. Suddenly a terrible shock threw him backwards onto the ground. At the same instant the flash of a big fire lit him up, and at the same instant a deafening roar, crash, and whistling rang in his ears.

When he came to, Pierre was sitting on his behind, his hands propped on the ground; the caisson he had been closest to was not there; only charred green boards and rags lay about on the scorched grass, and a horse dragging broken shafts trotted past him, while another, just like Pierre himself, lay on the ground and shrieked long and piercingly.

XXXII

Forgetting himself from fear, Pierre jumped up and ran back to the battery as the sole refuge from all the horrors that surrounded him.

Just as Pierre was entering the earthworks, he noticed that there was no shooting to be heard on the battery, but some people were doing something there. Pierre had no time to realize who these people were. He saw the senior colonel lying back to him on the rampart, as if studying something below, and saw one soldier he had noticed before, who, tearing away from the people who were holding him by the arm, was shouting "Brothers!"—and he saw something else strange.

But he had no time to realize that the colonel had been killed, that the one shouting "Brothers!" was a prisoner, that before his eyes another soldier was being bayoneted in the back. He had only just run into the earthworks, when a gaunt, yellow man with a sweaty face, in a blue uniform, with a sword in his hand, came charging at him, shouting something. Pierre, instinctively defending himself against the shock, because they were running into each other without seeing it, put his hands out and seized the man (it was a French officer) by the shoulder with one hand and by the throat with the other. The officer, letting go of his sword, seized Pierre by the collar.

For a few seconds the two men looked with frightened eyes into their mutually alien faces, and both were perplexed about what they had done and what they were to do. "Am I taken prisoner, or have I taken him prisoner?" each of them thought. But evidently the French officer was more inclined to the thought that he had been taken prisoner, because Pierre's strong hand, moved by involuntary fear, squeezed his throat more and more tightly. The Frenchman wanted to say something, but suddenly a cannonball came whistling, low and terrible, just over their heads, and Pierre fancied that the French officer's head had been torn off, he ducked so quickly.

Pierre also ducked his head and released his grip. No longer thinking of who had captured whom, the Frenchman ran back to the battery, and Pierre ran down the hill, stumbling over the dead and wounded, who, it seemed to him, tried to catch him by the legs. But before he got all the way down, dense crowds of Russian soldiers appeared before him, who, falling, stumbling, and shouting, ran merrily and stormily up to the battery. (This was the attack which Ermolov took credit for, saying that only his courage and good luck had made possible this exploit, during which he supposedly threw up onto the bar-row some St. George Crosses that he had in his pocket.)

The French who had taken the battery fled. Our troops, with shouts of "Hurrah!" chased the French so far beyond the battery that it was hard to stop them.

The prisoners were brought down from the battery, among them a wounded French general, who was surrounded by officers. Crowds of wounded, familiar and unfamiliar to Pierre, Russian and French, with faces disfigured by suffer-ing, walked, crawled, and were carried on stretchers from the battery. Pierre went up on the barrow, where he had spent more than an hour, and of that family circle which had taken him to itself, he found not a single one. There were many dead whom he did not know. But some he recognized. The young little officer sat in the same curled-up way, by the edge of the rampart, in a pool of blood. The red-mugged soldier was still twitching, but they did not take him away.

Pierre ran down.

"No, now they'll stop it, now they'll be horrified at what they've done!" he thought, aimlessly following behind the crowds of stretchers moving off the battlefield.

But the sun, veiled in smoke, was still high, and ahead, and especially to the left near Semyonovskoe, something seethed in the smoke, and the roar of gun-fire, musketry, and cannonades not only did not abate, but intensified to the point of despair, like a straining man crying out with his last strength.

XXXIII

The main action of the battle of Borodino took place over a stretch of seven thousand feet between Borodino and Bagration's flèches. (Outside that stretch, on one side, there was a show of Uvarov's cavalry in the middle of the day, and on the other side, beyond Utitsa, there was a clash between Poniatowski and Tuchkov; but these were separate and weak actions compared with what was happening in the middle of the battlefield.) On the field between Borodino and the flèches, by the woods, on a stretch open and visible from both sides, the main action of the battle took place in the most simple, artless way.

The battle began with a cannonade from both sides out of several hundred guns.

Then, when smoke lay over the whole field, through this smoke, from the right (on the French side), the two divisions of Dessaix and Compans moved against the flèches, and from the left the viceroy's regiments moved against Borodino.

From the Shevardino redoubt, where Napoleon stood, the flèches were two thirds of a mile away and Borodino more than a mile and a third away as the crow flies, and therefore Napoleon could not see what was going on there, the less so as smoke, merging with the mist, covered the whole terrain. The soldiers of Dessaix's division, sent against the flèches, could be seen only until they descended into the gully that separated them from the flèches. As soon as they descended into the gully, the smoke of the cannon and musket fire on the flèches became so thick that it obscured the whole ascent up the other side of the gully. There were glimpses of something black through the smoke— probably men—and an occasional gleam of bayonets. But whether they were moving or standing still, whether they were French or Russian, could not be seen from the Shevardino redoubt.

The sun rose brightly, and its slanting rays struck Napoleon straight in the face as he looked at the flèches from under his hand. Smoke spread in front of the flèches, and now it seemed that the smoke was moving, now that the troops were moving. The shouts of men were occasionally heard through the gunfire, but it was impossible to know what was being done there.

Napoleon, standing on the barrow, looked through a field glass, and through the small circle of the field glass he saw smoke and people, sometimes his own, sometimes Russians, but when he looked again with the naked eye, he could not tell where what he had seen was.

He went down from the barrow and began pacing in front of it.

Now and then he stopped, listened to the gunfire, and peered at the battlefield.

Not only from the place below, where he was standing, not only from the barrow where some of his generals now stood, but from the flèches themselves, on which, together or alternately, there were now Russian, now French soldiers, dead, wounded, and alive, frightened or panic-stricken, it was impossible to understand what was happening on that place. In the course of several hours on that place, amidst the incessant firing of muskets and cannon, there appeared now only Russian soldiers, now only French, now infantry, now cavalry; they appeared, fell, fired, collided, not knowing what to do with each other, shouted, and ran back again.

From the battlefield the adjutants he had sent and his marshals' orderlies constantly came galloping to Napoleon with reports on the course of events; but all these reports were false: both because in the heat of battle it is impossible to tell what is going on at a given moment, and because many of the adjutants did not reach the actual place of battle, but told what they had heard from others; and also because, while an adjutant was riding the mile or more that separated him from Napoleon, the circumstances changed, and the news he was bringing became incorrect. Thus an adjutant arrived from the viceroy with news that Borodino had been taken and the bridge over the Kolocha was in the hands of the French. The adjutant asked Napoleon if he ordered the troops to cross it. Napoleon ordered them to form ranks on the other side and wait; but not only as Napoleon was giving this order, but even as the adjutant was leaving Borodino, the bridge had already been retaken and burned by the Russians, in that same skirmish which Pierre took part in at the very beginning of the battle.

An adjutant came galloping from the flèches with a pale, frightened face to inform Napoleon that the attack had been repulsed and that Compans had been wounded and Davout killed, but meanwhile the flèches had been taken by another section of troops, just as the adjutant was being told that the French had been repulsed, and Davout was alive and only slightly bruised. On the weight of such unavoidably false reports, Napoleon gave his instructions, which either had been carried out before he even gave them or were not and could not be carried out.

The marshals and generals who were closer to the battlefield, but who, like Napoleon, did not take part in the battle itself, but only occasionally rode into the fire, gave their own instructions and orders about where to shoot and from where, and where the cavalry were to ride and the infantry to run, without asking Napoleon. But even their instructions were carried out as rarely and to as small a degree as Napoleon's instructions. For the most part, what came out was the opposite of what they had ordered. Soldiers who were told to advance would come under canister shot and run back; soldiers who were told to stay where they were, suddenly seeing the Russians appear unexpectedly before them, sometimes ran back and sometimes rushed forward, and the cavalry galloped without orders in pursuit of the fleeing Russians. Thus, two cavalry regiments galloped through the Semyonovskoe gully and, as soon as they rode up the hill, turned and galloped back at top speed. The infantrymen acted in the same way, sometimes getting nowhere near where they were told to go. All instructions about where and when to move cannon, when to send foot soldiers to shoot, when mounted soldiers to trample the Russian foot—all these instructions were given by the commanders closest to the units, in the ranks, without even asking Ney, Davout, and Murat, not to mention Napoleon. They were not afraid of being punished for non-fulfilment of orders or for unauthorized instructions, because in battle it is a matter of what is dearest to a man— his own life—and it sometimes seems that salvation lies in running back, sometimes in running forward, and these people, finding themselves in the very heat of battle, acted in conformity with the mood of the moment. In reality, all these movements forward and backward did nothing to alleviate or alter the situation of the troops. All their assaults and attacks on each other caused almost no harm; the harm, death, and mutilation were caused by the cannon- balls and bullets that flew everywhere through that space in which these men were rushing about. As soon as these men left that space through which the cannonballs and bullets flew, their commanders, who stood in the rear, formed them up, established discipline, and, under the effect of that discipline, again led them into the zone of fire, in which (under the effect of the fear of death) they again lost discipline and rushed about according to the chance mood of the crowd.

XXXIV

Napoleon's generals—Davout, Ney, and Murat, who were in proximity to the zone of fire and even occasionally rode into it—several times led huge and orderly masses of troops into that zone of fire. But contrary to what had invariably happened in all previous battles, instead of the expected news of the enemy's flight, the orderly masses of troops came back *from there* as disorderly, frightened crowds. They restored them to order, but the men were becoming fewer. Halfway through the day, Murat sent his adjutant to Napoleon to ask for reinforcements.

Napoleon was sitting at the foot of the barrow and drinking punch when Murat's adjutant galloped up to him with assurances that the Russians would be crushed if his majesty gave them one more division.

"Reinforcements?" said Napoleon, with stern astonishment, as if failing to understand his words and gazing at the handsome boy-adjutant with his long, curled black hair (the same way Murat did his hair). "Reinforcements!" thought Napoleon. "What sort of reinforcements can they ask for, when they've got half an army in their hands directed against a weak, unfortified Russian wing!"

"*Dites au roi de Naples,*" Napoleon said sternly, "*qu'il n'est pas midi et que je ne vois pas encore clair sur mon échiquier. Allez . . .*"*

The handsome boy-adjutant with long hair, not taking his hand from his hat, sighed deeply and galloped back to where people were being killed.

Napoleon stood up and, summoning Caulaincourt and Berthier, began talking with them about matters that did not concern the battle.

In the middle of the conversation, which had begun to interest Napoleon, Berthier's eyes turned towards a general with a suite, who was galloping towards the barrow on a lathered horse. It was Belliard. He dismounted, stepped quickly up to the emperor, and boldly, in a loud voice, began demonstrating the necessity for reinforcements. He swore on his honour that the Russians would be destroyed if the emperor gave one more division.

Napoleon heaved his shoulders and, saying nothing in reply, continued on

*Tell the king of Naples . . . that it's not yet midday, and that I still don't see my chessboard clearly. Go . . .

his walk. Belliard began talking loudly and animatedly with the generals of the suite who surrounded him.

"You're all fired up, Belliard," said Napoleon, coming to the newly arrived general again. "It's easy to make mistakes in the heat of the fire. Go and have a look, and then come back to me."

But Belliard had no time to disappear from view before a new messenger from the battlefield came galloping from the other side.

"*Eh bien, qu'est-ce qu'il y a?*"* Napoleon said in the tone of a man vexed at being constantly bothered.

"*Sire, le prince . . .*" began the adjutant.

"Asks for reinforcements?" Napoleon said with an angry gesture. The adjutant inclined his head affirmatively and began his report; but the emperor turned away from him, went two steps, stopped, came back, and summoned Berthier. "We must give them the reserves," he said, spreading his arms slightly. "Who should we send in, what do you think?" he addressed Berthier, that "*oison que j'ai fait aigle,*"† as he referred to him later.

"Shall we send in Claparède's division, Sire?" asked Berthier, who knew all the divisions, regiments, and battalions by heart.

Napoleon nodded his head affirmatively.

The adjutant galloped to Claparède's division. And a few minutes later the young guard unit that was stationed behind the barrow started from its place. Napoleon silently looked in that direction.

"No," he turned suddenly to Berthier, "I can't send Claparède. Send Friant's division," he said.

Though there was no advantage in sending Friant's division instead of Claparède's, and there was an obvious inconvenience and delay in stopping Claparède now and sending Friant, the order was carried out with precision. Napoleon did not see that, in relation to his troops, he was playing the role of the doctor whose medications are a hindrance—a role he so correctly understood and disapproved of.

Friant's division, like all the others, disappeared into the smoke of the battlefield. From all sides adjutants continued to come galloping, and all of them, as if by agreement, said one and the same thing. They all asked for reinforcements, they all said that the Russians were holding their positions and keeping up *un feu d'enfer*,‡ before which the French army was melting away.

Napoleon sat on his camp chair deep in thought.

Having grown hungry since morning, M. de Beausset, the lover of travel,

*Well, what is it?
†Gosling I made into an eagle.
‡A hellish fire.

came to the emperor and ventured to suggest respectfully that his majesty have lunch.

"I hope that I may already congratulate Your Majesty on a victory?" he said.

Napoleon said nothing and shook his head negatively. Supposing that the negation referred to the victory and not to lunch, M. de Beausset allowed himself to observe with playful respect that there was nothing in the world that could interfere with taking lunch, when it was possible to do so.

"*Allez-vous . . .*"* Napoleon suddenly said gloomily and turned away. A blissful smile of regret, repentance, and rapture lit up on Mr. Beausset's face and, with gliding steps, he went over to the other generals.

Napoleon was experiencing a painful feeling similar to that which is always experienced by a lucky gambler, who madly threw his money about, always won, and suddenly, precisely when he has calculated all the chances of the game, feels that the more he thinks over his move, the more certain he is to lose.

The troops were the same, the generals were the same, there were the same preparations, the same disposition, the same *proclamation courte et énergique,* he himself was the same, he knew it, he knew that he was even much more experienced and skilful now than he was before, even the enemy was the same as at Austerlitz and Friedland; but the terrible swing of the arm fell magically strengthless.

All the old methods, which had invariably been crowned with success—concentrating the batteries on a single point, attacking with the reserves to break the line, attacking with *les hommes de fer*† of the cavalry—all these methods had already been employed, and not only was there no victory, but from all sides the same news came of killed and wounded generals, of the need for reinforcements, of the impossibility of dislodging the Russians, and of disarray among the troops.

Formerly, after two or three instructions, two or three phrases, the marshals and adjutants had come galloping with congratulations and cheerful faces, had announced trophies of whole corps of prisoners, *des faisceaux de drapeaux et d'aigles ennemis,*‡ of cannon and baggage trains, and Murat had asked only for permission to let the cavalry take the baggage trains. It had been that way at Lodi, Marengo, Arcole, Jena, Austerlitz, Wagram,[35] and so on and so forth. But now something strange was happening with his troops.

Despite the news of the taking of the flèches, Napoleon saw that this was different, quite different, from all his previous battles. He saw that the same feeling he experienced was being experienced by all the people round him,

*Go . . .
†The men of iron.
‡Of bundles of standards and enemy eagles.

battle-seasoned as they were. All their faces were sad, they all avoided each other's eyes. Beausset alone could not understand the meaning of what was happening. But Napoleon, after his long experience of war, knew very well what it meant when, in the course of eight hours, after making every effort, the attacking army had not won the battle. He knew that this was almost a lost battle, and that the smallest chance—at that precarious point of indecision the battle had come to—could destroy him and his troops.

When he went through in imagination the whole of this strange Russian campaign, in which not a single battle had been won, in which no banners, no cannon, no corps of troops had been taken in two months, when he looked at the hidden sadness on the faces round him and listened to reports that the Russians still stood their ground—a terrible feeling, like one experienced in dreams, seized him, and all the unlucky chances that could destroy him came to his mind. The Russians could assault his left wing, could break through his centre, a stray cannonball could kill him. It was all possible. In his former battles, he had thought only of the chances of success, but now he imagined a countless number of unlucky chances, and he expected them all. Yes, it was as in a dream, when a man sees a villain coming at him, and in his dream the man swings and hits the villain with terrible force, which he knows should destroy him, and he feels his arm fall strengthless and limp as a rag, and the terror of irresistible destruction takes hold of the helpless man.

The news that the Russians were attacking the left flank of the French army awakened this terror in Napoleon. He sat silently on a camp chair at the foot of the barrow, his head lowered and his elbows on his knees. Berthier came up to him and suggested that they ride along the line to ascertain what position things were in.

"What? What's that you say?" said Napoleon. "Yes, tell them to bring my horse."

He mounted up and rode to Semyonovskoe.

In the slowly dispersing powder smoke over the whole space through which Napoleon was riding, horses and men lay in pools of blood, singly and in heaps. Never yet had Napoleon or any of his generals seen such horror, so many men killed on such a small space. The roar of guns, which for ten hours had never ceased to torment the ear, gave the spectacle a special significance (like the music in tableaux vivants). Napoleon rode out to the height of Semyonovskoe and saw ranks of men in uniforms of a colour his eyes were not accustomed to. These were Russians.

The Russians stood in close ranks behind Semyonovskoe and the barrow, and their guns roared and smoked without ceasing along their line. There was no longer any battle. There was a continuous slaughter, which could lead nowhere either for the Russians or for the French. Napoleon stopped his horse and again fell into that pensiveness which Berthier had brought him out of; he could not stop what was happening before him and round him, which was considered to be guided by him and dependent upon him, and which for the first time, owing to its unsuccess, appeared useless and terrible.

One of the generals who rode up to Napoleon allowed himself to suggest to him that he send the old guard into action. Ney and Berthier, who stood near Napoleon, exchanged glances and smiled contemptuously at the general's absurd suggestion.

Napoleon lowered his head and said nothing for a long time.

"*À huit cent lieux de France je ne ferai demolir ma garde,*"* he said and, turning his horse, rode back to Shevardino.

XXXV

Kutuzov sat, hanging his grey head and his heavy body sagging, on the rug-covered bench, in the same place where Pierre had seen him in the morning. He did not give any instructions, but only agreed or disagreed with what was suggested to him.

"Yes, yes, do that," he replied to various suggestions. "Yes, yes, go, dear boy, have a look," he said now to one of his attendants, now to another; or he said, "No, there's no need, we'd better wait." He listened to the reports brought to him, gave orders when his subordinates demanded it; but, as he listened to the reports, it seemed that he was not interested in the meaning of the words being said to him, but that something else in the expression of the face, in the tone of the reporter's speech interested him. By many years of military experience he knew, and by his old man's mind he understood, that one man cannot lead hundreds of thousands of men struggling with death, and he knew that the fate of a battle is decided not by the commander in chief's instructions, not by the position of the troops, not by the number of cannon or of people killed, but by that elusive force known as the spirit of the troops, and he watched this force and guided it, as far as that lay in his power.

The general expression of Kutuzov's face was one of concentrated, calm attention and a strain that barely overcame the weariness of a weak and old body.

At eleven o'clock in the morning, he was brought news that the flèches occupied by the French had been retaken, but that Prince Bagration had been wounded. Kutuzov said "Ah" and shook his head.

"Ride to Prince Pyotr Ivanovich and find out what and how in detail," he said to one of his adjutants and then turned to the duke of Württemberg, who was standing behind him.

*At eight hundred leagues from France I won't have my guard annihilated.

"May I ask Your Highness to accept command of the first army?"

Soon after the duke's departure, so soon that he could not yet have reached Semyonovskoe, the duke's adjutant came back from him and reported to his serenity that the duke requested more troops.

Kutuzov winced and sent an order to Dokhturov to assume command of the first army, and asked the duke to come back, saying he could not do without him in these important moments. When news was brought that Murat had been taken prisoner,[36] and the staff officers congratulated Kutuzov, he smiled.

"Wait, gentlemen," he said. "The battle is won, and the capture of Murat is nothing extraordinary. But we'd better wait before we rejoice." However, he sent an adjutant to spread this news among the troops.

When Shcherbinin came galloping from the left flank with a report that the French had taken the flèches and Semyonovskoe, Kutuzov, guessing by the sounds from the battlefield and Shcherbinin's face that the news was bad, got up as if to stretch his legs and, taking Shcherbinin's arm, led him aside.

"Go there, dear boy," he said to Ermolov, "see if anything can be done."

Kutuzov was in Gorki, at the centre of the Russian army's position. Napoleon's attack against our left flank had been repulsed several times. In the centre, the French had moved no further than Borodino. On their left flank, Uvarov's cavalry had put the French to flight.

After two o'clock the French attacks ceased. On all the faces of those who came from the battlefield and of those who stood round him, Kutuzov read an expression of tension that had reached the highest degree. Kutuzov was pleased with the success of the day, which was beyond expectation. But the old man's physical powers were failing him. Several times his head dropped as if falling, and he dozed off. They served him dinner.

The imperial adjutant Wolzogen, the same one who, riding past Prince Andrei, had said that war should be *im Raum verlegen,* and whom Bagration hated so much, rode up to Kutuzov during dinner. Wolzogen came from Barclay with a report on the course of things on the left flank. The sensible Barclay de Tolly, seeing crowds of retreating wounded and the disorderly rear guard of the army, having weighed all the circumstances, decided that the battle was lost, and sent his favourite to the commander in chief with that information.

Kutuzov was chewing roast chicken with difficulty and glanced at Wolzogen with narrowed, merry eyes.

Wolzogen, stretching his legs casually, with a half-contemptuous smile on his lips, went up to Kutuzov, touching the visor of his cap slightly.

Wolzogen treated his serenity with a certain affected casualness, intended to show that, as a highly educated military man, he left it to the Russians to make an idol of this old, useless man, while he knew whom he was dealing with. *"Der alte Herr"* (as the Germans called Kutuzov in their circle) *"macht sich*

*ganz bequem,"** thought Wolzogen, and glancing sternly at the plates in front
of Kutuzov, he began to report to the old gentleman the state of things on the
left flank, as Barclay had ordered him to do and as he himself had seen and
understood it.

"All the points of our position are in the hands of the enemy, and they cannot be repulsed, because there are no troops; they are running away, and it is
not possible to stop them," he reported.

Kutuzov stopped chewing and in astonishment, as if not understanding
what he was being told, fixed his eyes on Wolzogen. Wolzogen, noticing the
agitation *des alten Herrn,* said with a smile:

"I did not consider it right for me to conceal from Your Serenity what I
saw . . . The troops are in total disarray . . ."

"You saw? You saw? . . ." Kutuzov shouted, frowning, and rising quickly, he
went up close to Wolzogen. "How . . . how dare you! . . ." he shouted, making
threatening gestures with his trembling hands and spluttering. "How dare you,
my dear sir, say that to *me*! You know nothing. Tell General Barclay from me
that his information is incorrect and that the true course of the battle is known
better to me, the commander in chief, than to him."

Wolzogen was about to make some objection, but Kutuzov cut him off.

"The enemy has been repulsed on the left and beaten on the right flank. If you
see so poorly, my dear sir, don't allow yourself to speak of what you don't know.
Kindly go to General Barclay and tell him that I firmly intend to attack the enemy
tomorrow," Kutuzov said sternly. Everyone fell silent, and nothing was heard
but the heavy breathing of the puffing old general. "They've been repulsed everywhere, for which I thank God and our brave army. The enemy is defeated, and
tomorrow we will begin driving him out of the holy Russian land," said Kutuzov, crossing himself; and he suddenly choked from the tears welling up in him.
Wolzogen, shrugging his shoulders and twisting his lips, silently stepped away,
surprised *über diese Eingenommenheit des alten Herrn.*†

"Yes, here he is, my hero," said Kutuzov to the stout, handsome, black-
haired general who was coming up onto the barrow at that moment. This was
Raevsky, who had spent the whole day at the main point of the field of
Borodino.

Raevsky reported that the troops had stood their ground firmly, and that the
French no longer dared to attack.

Having heard him out, Kutuzov said in French:

*"Vous ne pensez donc pas comme les autres que nous sommes obligés de
nous retirer?"*‡

*The old gentleman . . . makes himself quite comfortable.
†At the old gentleman's self-conceit.
‡So you don't think *like others* that we are obliged to retreat?

"*Au contraire, votre altesse, dans les affaires indécises c'est toujours le plus opiniâtre qui reste victorieux,*" replied Raevsky, "*et mon opinion . . .*"*

"Kaisarov!" Kutuzov called his adjutant. "Sit down and write the order for tomorrow. And you," he turned to another, "ride to the line and announce that tomorrow we attack."

While the conversation with Raevsky was going on and the order was being dictated, Wolzogen came back from Barclay and reported that General Barclay de Tolly would like to have written confirmation of the order given by the field marshal.

Kutuzov, without glancing at Wolzogen, ordered the order to be written, which, on very good grounds, to avoid personal responsibility, the former commander in chief wished to have.

And by some indefinable, mysterious connection, which maintains the same mood through an entire army, which is known as the spirit of the army, and constitutes the central nerve of war, Kutuzov's words, his order to fight the next day, were conveyed simultaneously to all ends of the army.

It was far from the same words, the same order that passed through the last links of that chain. There was even no resemblance between the stories that were passed on from man to man at different ends of the army and what Kutuzov had said; but the sense of his words communicated itself everywhere, because what Kutuzov had said came not from clever considerations, but from the feeling that was in the soul of the commander in chief, just as it was in the soul of every Russian man.

And, learning that we would attack the enemy the next day, hearing from the high spheres of the army the confirmation of what they wanted to believe, the exhausted, vacillating men were comforted and reassured.

XXXVI

Prince Andrei's regiment was in the reserves, which till past one o'clock were stationed behind Semyonovskoe, inactive, under heavy artillery fire. Towards two o'clock the regiment, having lost over two hundred men already, was moved forward, onto a trampled oat field, to the space between Semyonovskoe and the battery of the barrow where thousands of men were killed that day, and at which, between one and two o'clock, the intensely concentrated fire of several hundred enemy guns was directed.

Without leaving the spot or firing a single shot, the regiment here lost another third of its men. In front and especially to the right, in the never-

---

*On the contrary, Your Highness, in undecided affairs it is always the most stubborn one who remains victorious . . . and my opinion . . .

dispersing smoke, cannon boomed, and out of the mysterious zone of smoke that lay over the whole terrain ahead, without ceasing, flew cannonballs with a hissing, rapid whistle, and slowly whistling shells. Sometimes, as if granting a respite, there would be a quarter of an hour when all the cannonballs and shells overshot, but sometimes several men were taken out of the regiment in the space of a single minute, and the dead and wounded were constantly being carried off.

With each new blow, the chances of survival for those who had not yet been killed grew less and less. The regiment stood by battalions in columns three hundred paces apart, but, despite that, the men of the regiment were all under the sway of the same mood. The men of the regiment were all equally silent and gloomy. Talk was heard rarely among the ranks, but that talk would fall silent each time they heard a shot strike home and the cry "Stretcher!" Most of the time the men of the regiment, on orders from their superiors, sat on the ground. One, taking off his shako, carefully undid and redid the gathers; another, crumbling some dry clay between his palms, polished his bayonet; a third worked the leather and readjusted the buckle of his bandolier; yet another carefully spread out his foot cloth, wound it up again, and put his boot back on. Some built little houses from the clods of the field or plaited little baskets out of straw. They all seemed fully immersed in these occupations. When men were wounded or killed, when stretchers were carried past, when our troops retreated, when large masses of the enemy were seen through the smoke, no one paid any attention to these circumstances. But when the artillery or cavalry advanced, or movements of our infantry could be seen, approving remarks could be heard on all sides. But the greatest attention was accorded to totally extraneous events, which had no relation to the battle. It was as if the attention of these morally exhausted men found rest in these ordinary everyday events. An artillery battery was passing by in front of the regiment. The outrunner of one of the artillery caissons stepped over a trace. "Hey, that outrunner! . . . Put it right! It'll fall . . . Eh, they don't see it! . . ." men shouted from the ranks all through the regiment. Another time, general attention was drawn to a little brown dog with a stiffly raised tail, who, coming from God knows where, trotted out in front of the ranks with a preoccupied air and, when a cannonball suddenly hit close by, squealed and dashed off, its tail between its legs. Guffaws and squeals came from all over the regiment. But distractions of this sort last only a few minutes, while the men had been standing for more than eight hours with no food and with nothing to do, under the relentless terror of death, and their pale and frowning faces grew more pale and frowning.

Prince Andrei, frowning and pale, like all the men of the regiment, paced up and down the meadow next to the oat field from one edge to the other, his hands behind his back, his head bowed. There was nothing for him to do or to order. Everything was being done by itself. The dead were dragged back behind the front line, the wounded were carried away, the ranks closed up. If soldiers ran off, they came hurrying back at once. At first Prince Andrei walked up and down the ranks, considering it his duty to rouse the courage of the soldiers and set them an example; but then he realized that he had nothing to teach them. All the forces of his soul, as of every soldier, were unconsciously bent solely on keeping himself from contemplating the horror of the situation they were in. He paced over the meadow, dragging his feet, scuffing up the grass, and observing the dust that covered his boots. Now he took big steps, trying to get into the footprints left on the meadow by the mowers; then he counted his steps, trying to reckon up how many times he had to go from edge to edge to make a mile; then he pulled off the flowers of the wormwood that grew along the edge, and rubbed those flowers between his palms, sniffing the fragrantly bitter, strong smell. Of all his mental work the day before, nothing remained. He was not thinking about anything. He listened with a weary ear to the same sounds, distinguishing the whistle of projectiles from the roar of cannon fire, looked at the familiar faces of the first battalion, and waited. "Here it comes . . . This one's for us again!" he thought, listening to the approaching whistle of something from the hidden zone of smoke. "One, another! More! A hit . . ." He stopped and looked at the ranks. "No, an overshot. But that one's a hit." And he began pacing again, trying to take big strides so as to reach the edge in sixteen steps.

A whistle and a thud! Five paces from him a cannonball dug up the dry earth and disappeared. An involuntary chill ran down his spine. He glanced at the ranks again. Many had probably been taken out; a large crowd gathered by the second battalion.

"Mr. Adjutant!" he shouted, "order them not to crowd round." The adjutant, having carried out the order, was coming towards Prince Andrei. From the other side the battalion commander rode up.

"Look out!" came a soldier's frightened cry, and, like a little bird whistling over in quick flight and alighting on the ground, a shell dully plopped down within two paces of Prince Andrei, near the battalion commander's horse. The horse first of all, not asking whether it was good or bad to show fear, snorted, reared up, nearly throwing the major, and leaped aside. The horse's terror communicated itself to the men.

"Get down!" cried the voice of the adjutant, throwing himself to the ground. Prince Andrei stood undecided. The shell was smoking, spinning like a top between him and the prone adjutant, on the border between the field and the meadow, near a bush of wormwood.

"Can this be death?" thought Prince Andrei, gazing with completely new, envious eyes at the grass, at the wormwood, and at the little stream of smoke curling up from the spinning black ball. "I can't, I don't want to die, I love life,

I love this grass, the earth, the air . . ." He was thinking all that and at the same time remembered that he was being looked at.

"Shame on you, officer!" he said to the adjutant. "What an . . ." He did not finish. At one and the same time there was the sound of an explosion, a whistling of splinters as if from a shattered window, a choking smell of powder—and Prince Andrei hurtled sideways and, raising his arm, fell on his chest.

Several officers ran to him. From the right side of his stomach a large stain of blood was spreading onto the grass.

The summoned militiamen stopped behind the officers. Prince Andrei lay on his chest, his face lowered to the grass, and was breathing in heavy gasps.

"Well, what are you standing there for, come here!"

The muzhiks went over and took hold of him by the shoulders and legs, but he moaned pitifully, and the muzhiks, exchanging glances, let go of him again.

"Pick him up, lay him out, it's all the same!" cried someone's voice. They took hold of him again by the shoulders and laid him on a stretcher.

"Ah, my God! My God! What is it? . . . The stomach! That's the end! Ah, my God!" voices were heard among the officers. "It whizzed just a hair away from my ear," said the adjutant. The muzhiks, hoisting the stretcher on their shoulders, started down the path they had trodden to the dressing station.

"Keep in step . . . Eh! . . . You clodhoppers!" cried an officer, stopping the muzhiks by the shoulders as they walked off unevenly, jolting the stretcher.

"Come on, fall in, Fyodor, fall in," said the muzhik in front.

"There we go, that's grand," the one behind said joyfully, falling into step.

"Your Excellency? Eh? Prince?" Timokhin said in a trembling voice, running up and looking into the stretcher.

Prince Andrei opened his eyes, looked out from the stretcher, into which his head had sunk deeply, at the one who was speaking, and lowered his eyelids again.

The militiamen brought Prince Andrei to the woods where the carts stood and where the dressing station was. The dressing station consisted of three tents with turned-back flaps pitched at the edge of a birch grove. In the birch grove stood carts and horses. The horses were eating oats from their nosebags, and sparrows flew down to them, pecking up the spilled grain. Crows, scenting blood, crowing impatiently, flew about in the birches. Around the tents, over more than five acres, bloodied men lay, sat, or stood in various clothes. Around the wounded, with dejected, attentive faces, stood crowds of stretcher bearers, whom the officers in charge of keeping order tried in vain to drive away from the place. Not heeding the officers, the bearers stood leaning on the stretchers and, as if trying to comprehend the difficult meaning of the spectacle, looked intently at what was going on before them. From the tents came now loud, angry screams, now a pitiful wailing. Occasionally surgeons' assistants ran out to fetch water and pointed to those who were to be carried in. The wounded, waiting their turn by the tents, wheezed, moaned, wept, shouted, cursed, begged for vodka. Some were delirious. As Prince Andrei was a regimental commander, the bearers, stepping among the not-yet-treated men, brought him close to one of the tents and stopped, waiting for orders. Prince Andrei opened his eyes and for a long time could not understand what was happening around him. He remembered the meadow, the wormwood, the field, the black, spinning ball, and his passionate fit of love for life. Two steps away from him, talking loudly and attracting general attention to himself, stood a tall, handsome, black-haired sergeant, leaning on a branch, his head bandaged. He had bullet wounds in his head and leg. Around him, listening eagerly to his talk, gathered a crowd of wounded and stretcher bearers.

"We just pounded him out of there, he dropped everything, we caught the king himself!" the soldier shouted, looking around him, his black, inflamed eyes glittering. "If only the reservers had come just then, brothers, he wouldn't even have left his name behind, it's the truth I'm telling you . . ."

Prince Andrei, like everyone else around the narrator, looked at him with shining eyes and experienced a comforting feeling. "But does it make any difference now?" he thought. "And what will be there, and what has there been here? Why was I so sorry to part with life? There was something in this life that I didn't and still don't understand . . ."

XXXVII

One of the doctors came out of the tent in a bloody apron and with small, bloody hands, in one of which, between the thumb and the little finger (so as not to stain it), he was holding a cigar. This doctor raised his head and began looking from side to side, but over the heads of the wounded. He obviously wanted to rest a little. Turning his head to right and left for some time, he sighed and lowered his eyes.

"Right now," he said to the words of the assistant, who was pointing to Prince Andrei, and ordered him brought into the tent.

A murmur arose in the crowd of waiting wounded.

"Looks like in the next world, too, only the masters'll have it good," one said.

Prince Andrei was brought in and laid on a just-vacated table, from which an assistant was rinsing something. Prince Andrei could not sort out separately what was in the tent. The pitiful moans on all sides, the tormenting pain in his hip, stomach, and back distracted him. Everything he saw around him merged for him into a general impression of bared, bloody human flesh, which seemed to fill this low tent, as several weeks ago, on that hot August day, that same flesh had filled the dirty pool on the Smolensk road. Yes, it was the same flesh, the same *chair à canon,* the sight of which already then, as if foretelling the present, had filled him with horror.

There were three tables in the tent. Two were occupied, Prince Andrei was laid on the third. He was left alone for a time, and he involuntarily saw what was taking place on the other two tables. On the near table sat a Tartar, probably a Cossack, judging by the uniform thrown down next to him. Four soldiers were holding him. A doctor in spectacles was cutting at something in his brown, muscular back.

"Unh, unh, unh! . . ." the Tartar was as if grunting, and suddenly, lifting up his high-cheeked, dark, snub-nosed face, and baring his white teeth, he began to strain, pull, and shriek in a piercingly ringing, drawn-out shriek. On the other table, around which many people crowded, a big, sturdy man lay on his back with his head thrown back (his curly hair, its colour, and the shape of his head seemed strangely familiar to Prince Andrei). Several assistants leaned their weight on the man's chest and held him down. One big, sturdy white leg kept jerking quickly and rhythmically with a feverish quivering. The man sobbed and spluttered convulsively. Two doctors—one was pale and trembling— were silently doing something to the man's other leg, which was red. Having finished with the Tartar, over whom an overcoat was thrown, the doctor in spectacles, wiping his hands, came up to Prince Andrei.

He looked at Prince Andrei's face and quickly turned away.

"Undress him! What are you standing there for?" he cried angrily to the assistants.

His very first, distant childhood came to Prince Andrei's mind as the assistant, his sleeves rolled up, unbuttoned and removed his clothes with hurrying hands. The doctor bent down over the wound, felt it, and sighed deeply. Then he made a sign to someone. And the tormenting pain inside his stomach made Prince Andrei lose consciousness. When he came to, the shattered hip bones had been removed, the shreds of flesh had been cut off, and the wound had been dressed. Someone sprayed water in his face. As soon as Prince Andrei opened his eyes, the doctor bent over him, silently kissed him on the lips, and hurried away.

After the suffering he had endured, Prince Andrei felt a bliss such as he had not experienced for a long time. All the best and happiest moments of his life, especially his most distant childhood, when he had been undressed and put in his little bed, when the nanny had sung to lull him to sleep, when, burying his head in the pillows, he had felt happy in the mere consciousness of life, presented itself to his imagination not as the past, but as a reality.

The doctors were bustling about a wounded man, the shape of whose head seemed familiar to Prince Andrei; they were lifting him and calming him.

"Show me . . . Oooh! oh! oooh!" his moaning, broken by sobs, was heard, frightened and resigned to his suffering. Hearing those moans, Prince Andrei wanted to weep. Whether it was because he was dying without glory, or because he was sorry to part with life, or from those memories of long-lost childhood, or because he was suffering, others were suffering, and this man was moaning so pitifully before him, he wanted to weep childlike, kind, almost joyful tears.

The wounded man was shown his cut-off leg in a boot caked with blood!

"Oh! Oooh!" he sobbed like a woman. The doctor, who was standing in front of the wounded man, screening his face, stepped away.

"My God! What is this? Why is he here?" Prince Andrei said to himself.

In the unfortunate, sobbing, exhausted man whose leg had just been removed, he recognized Anatole Kuragin. They were holding him up in their arms and offering him water in a glass, the rim of which he could not catch in his trembling, swollen lips. Anatole was sobbing deeply. "Yes, it's he; yes, this man is closely and painfully connected with me by something," thought Prince Andrei, not yet understanding clearly what he saw before him. "What is this man's connection with my childhood, with my life?" he asked himself, without finding an answer. And suddenly a new and unexpected memory from the world of childhood, purity, and love came to Prince Andrei. He remembered Natasha as he had seen her for the first time at the ball in 1810, with her slender neck and arms, with her frightened, happy face ready for rapture, and in his soul love and tenderness for her awakened, stronger and more alive than ever. He now remembered the connection between him and this man, who was looking at him dully through the tears that filled his swollen eyes. Prince Andrei remembered everything, and a rapturous pity and love for this man filled his happy heart.

Prince Andrei could no longer restrain himself, and he wept tender, loving tears over people, over himself, and over their and his own errors.

"Compassion, love for our brothers, for those who love us, love for those who hate us, love for our enemies—yes, that love which God preached on earth, which Princess Marya taught me, and which I didn't understand; that's why I was sorry about life, that's what was still left for me, if I was to live. But now it's too late. I know it!"

XXXVIII

The dreadful sight of the battlefield covered with corpses and wounded, combined with a heaviness of the head, and with the news that twenty generals he knew well had been killed or wounded, and with the awareness of the impotence of his once-strong arm, made an unexpected impression on Napoleon, who ordinarily liked to survey the dead and wounded, thereby testing his inner strength (as he thought). On that day the terrible sight of the battlefield overcame that inner strength, in which he placed his merit and greatness. He hastily left the battlefield and returned to the Shevardino barrow. Yellow, bloated, heavy, with dull eyes, a red nose, and a hoarse voice, he sat on a camp chair, involuntarily listening to the sounds of gunfire and not raising his eyes. With sickly anguish he awaited the end of this action, of which he considered himself the cause, but which he was unable to stop. Personal human feeling for a brief moment got the upper hand over that artificial phantom of life which he had served so long. He transferred to himself the sufferings and death he had seen on the battlefield. The heaviness in his head and chest reminded him of the possibility of his own suffering and death. At that moment he wanted for himself neither Moscow, nor victory, nor glory. (What more glory did he need?) The only thing he wished for now was rest, tranquillity, and freedom. But when he was on the Semyonovskoe heights, the artillery commander had suggested placing several batteries on those heights to increase the fire on the Russian troops crowding before Knyazkovo. Napoleon had agreed and ordered them to let him know what effect those batteries had.

An adjutant came riding to tell him that, on the emperor's orders, two hundred guns had been turned on the Russians, but the Russians still stood firm.

"Our fire takes them out by whole ranks, but they stand firm," said the adjutant.

"*Ils en veulent encore! . . .*"* Napoleon said in a hoarse voice.

"*Sire?*" said the adjutant, who had not caught what he said.

"*Ils en veulent encore,*" Napoleon, frowning, rasped in a husky voice, "*donnez-leur-en.*"†

And even without his order they were doing what he wanted, and he gave the instruction only because he thought an order was expected of him. And again he was transferred to his former artificial world of phantoms of some sort of greatness, and again (as a horse walking about a slanting treadmill imagines it is doing something for itself), he began to obediently fulfil that cruel, sad, oppressive, and inhuman role which had been assigned to him.

And not only for that hour and day were reason and conscience darkened in this man who, more than all the other participants in this affair, bore upon himself the whole weight of what was happening; but never to the end of his life was he able to understand goodness, or beauty, or truth, or the meaning of his own actions, which were too much the opposite of goodness and truth, and too far removed from everything human for him to be able to grasp their meaning. He could not renounce his actions, extolled by half the world, and therefore he had to renounce truth and goodness and everything human.

Not only on that day, riding around the battlefield strewn with dead and mutilated men (by his will, as he thought), did he, looking at these men, count

*They want more! . . .
†They want more . . . give it to them.

how many Russians there were to one Frenchman, and, deceiving himself, find cause to rejoice that for every Frenchman there were five Russians. Not only on that day did he write in a letter to Paris that *le champ de bataille a été superbe,** because there were fifty thousand corpses on it; but also on the island of St. Helena, in the quiet of solitude, where he said he intended to devote his leisure to setting forth the great deeds he had done, he wrote:

La guerre de Russie eut dû être la plus populaire des temps modernes: c'était celle du bon sens and des vrais intérêts, celle du repos et de la sécurité de tous; elle était purement pacifique et conservatrice.†

C'était pour la grande cause, la fin des hasards et le commencement de la sécurité. Un nouvel horizon, de nouveaux travaux allaient se dérouler, tout plein du bien-être et de la prospérité de tous. Le système européen se trouvait fondé; il n'était plus question que de l'organiser.

Satisfait sur ces grands points et tranquille partout, j'aurais eu aussi mon congrès et ma sainte-alliance. Ce sont des idées qu'on m'a volées. Dans cette réunion de grands souverains, nous eussions traités de nos intérêts en famille et compté de clerc à maître avec les peuples.

L'Europe n'eut bientôt fait de la sorte véritablement qu'un même peuple, et chacun, en voyageant partout, se fût trouvé toujours dans la patrie commune. Il eut demandé toutes les rivières navigables pour tous, la communauté des mers, et que les grandes armées permanentes fussent réduites désormais à la seule garde des souverains.

---

*The battlefield was superb.
†The war in Russia should have been the most popular of modern times: it was a war of good sense and true interests, of rest and security for all; it was purely pacific and conservative.

It was for the great cause, the end of uncertainties and the beginning of security. A new horizon, new works would unfold, all filled with well-being and the prosperity of all. The European system had been founded; it was only a question of organizing it.

Satisfied on these major points and at peace everywhere, I also would have had my *congress* and my *holy alliance.* Those are ideas that were stolen from me. In this meeting of the great sovereigns, we would have dealt with our interests as a family and accounted to the peoples as clerk to master.

In this way, Europe would soon have become truly one people, and each person, travelling everywhere, would always have found himself in a common fatherland. It would have called for all rivers to be navigable for everyone, the communality of the seas, and that the great standing armies be henceforth reduced to nothing but guards for the sovereigns.

On returning to France, to the bosom of the fatherland—great, strong, magnificent, peaceful, glorious—I would have proclaimed its limits immutable, all future wars purely *defensive;* and any new enlargement *antinational.* I would have associated my son with the Empire; my *dictatorship* would have ended, and his constitutional reign would have begun . . .

Paris would have been the capital of the world, and the French the envy of the nations! . . .

My ensuing leisure and my old age would have been devoted, in company of the empress and during the royal apprenticeship of my son, to visiting gradually and as a real country couple, with our own horses, every nook and cranny of the Empire, receiving complaints, redressing wrongs, and scattering monuments and benefactions all over and everywhere.

De retour en France, au sein de la patrie, grande, forte, magnifique, tranquille, glorieuse, j'eusse proclamé ses limites immuables, toute guerre future, purement défensive; tout agrandissement nouveau antinational. J'eusse associé mon fils à l'Empire; ma dictature eût fini, et son règne constitutionnel eut commencé . . .

Paris eût été la capitale du monde, et les Français l'envie des nations! . . .

Mes loisirs ensuite et mes vieux jours eussent été consacrés, en compagnie de l'impératrice et durant l'apprentissage royal de mon fils, à visiter lentement et en vrai couple campagnard, avec nos propres chevaux, tous les recoins de l'Empire, recevant les plaintes, redressant les torts, semant de toutes parts et partout les monuments et les bienfaits.[37]

He, predestined by Providence for the sad, unfree role of executioner of the peoples, assured himself that the goal of his actions was the good of the peoples, and that he could govern the destinies of millions and by means of power be their benefactor!

He wrote further of the Russian war:

Des 400,000 hommes qui passèrent la Vistule, la moitié était Autrichiens, Prussiens, Saxons, Polonais, Bavarois, Wurtembergeois, Mecklembourgeois, Espagnols, Italiens, Napolitains. L'armée impériale, proprement dit, était pour un tiers composée de Hollandais, Belges, habitants des bords du Rhin, Piémontais, Suisses, Génevois, Toscans, Romains, habitants de la 32ᵉ division militaire, Brême, Hambourg, etc.; elle comptait à peine 140,000 hommes parlant français. L'expédition de Russie coûta moins de 50,000 hommes à la France actuelle; l'armée russe dans la retraite de Wilna à Moscou, dans les différentes batailles, a perdu quatre fois plus que l'armée française; l'incendie de Moscou a coûté la vie à 100,000 Russes, morts de froid et de misère dans les bois; enfin dans sa marche de Moscou à l'Oder, l'armée russe fut aussi atteinte par l'intempérie de la saison; elle ne comptait à son arrivée à Wilna que 50,000 hommes, et à Kalisch moins de 18,000. *

He imagined that the war with Russia had came about by his will, and the horror of what happened did not strike his soul. He boldly took upon himself

---

*Of the 400,000 men who crossed the Vistula, half were Austrians, Prussians, Saxons, Poles, Bavarians, Württembergers, Mecklenburgers, Spanish, Italians, Neapolitans. The imperial army properly speaking was made up of one-third Dutch, Belgians, inhabitants of the banks of the Rhine, Piedmontese, Swiss, Genoans, Tuscans, Romans, inhabitants of the 32nd military division, Bremen, Hamburg, etc.; it counted barely 140,000 men who spoke French. The Russian expedition cost France herself less than 50,000 men; the Russian army in the retreat from Vilno to Moscow, in different battles, lost four times more than the French army; the burning of Moscow cost the lives of 100,000 Russians, dead of cold and starvation in the woods; finally, in its march from Moscow to the Oder, the Russian army also suffered from the bad weather of the season; it counted 50,000 men on its arrival in Vilno, and in Kalisch less than 18,000.

all responsibility for the event, and his darkened reason saw his justification in the fact that among the hundreds of thousands of men who perished, there were fewer Frenchmen than Hessians and Bavarians.

XXXIX

Several tens of thousands of men lay dead in various positions and uniforms in the fields and meadows that belonged to the Davydov family and to crown peasants, on fields and meadows where for hundreds of years peasants of the villages of Borodino, Gorki, Shevardino, and Semyonovskoe had at the same time gathered crops and pastured cattle. At the dressing stations, the grass and soil were soaked with blood over the space of three acres. Crowds of wounded and unwounded men of various units, with frightened faces, trudged on the one side back to Mozhaisk and on the other side back to Valuevo. Other crowds, exhausted and hungry, led by their commanders, moved forward. Still others stayed put and went on shooting.

Over the whole field, once so gaily beautiful, with its gleaming bayonets and puffs of smoke in the morning sun, there now hung the murk of dampness and smoke and the strangely acidic smell of saltpetre and blood. Small clouds gathered and rain began to sprinkle on the dead, the wounded, the frightened, and on the exhausted, and on the doubtful men. It was as if it were saying: "Enough, enough, men. Stop now . . . Come to your senses. What are you doing?"

Exhausted men on both sides, without food and rest, began alike to doubt whether they had to go on exterminating each other, hesitation was seen on all faces, and in every soul alike the question arose: "Why, for whom, should I kill and be killed? You kill whomever you like, do whatever you like, but I don't want any more of it!" Towards evening this thought ripened alike in each man's soul. At any moment all these men might become horrified at what they were doing, drop everything, and run away wherever their legs took them.

But though by the end of the battle the men felt all the horror of their actions, though they would have been glad to stop, some incomprehensible, mysterious power still went on governing them, and the artillery men, sweaty, covered with powder and blood, reduced to one in three, though stumbling and gasping from fatigue, kept bringing charges, loaded, aimed, applied the slow match; and the cannonballs, with the same speed and cruelty, flew from both sides and crushed human bodies flat, and the terrible thing continued to be accomplished, which was accomplished not by the will of men, but by the will of Him who governs people and worlds.

Anyone looking at the disordered rear of the Russian army would have said that the French needed to make one more little effort and the Russian army would have vanished; and anyone looking at the French rear would have said that the Russians needed to make one more little effort and the French would have perished. But neither the French nor the Russians made that effort, and the flame of battle slowly burned out.

The Russians did not make that effort, because it was not they who were attacking the French. At the beginning of the battle, they merely stood on the way to Moscow, shielding it, and they went on standing in the same way at the end of the battle as they had at the beginning. But even if the goal of the Russians had consisted in bringing down the French, they could not have made that last effort, because all the Russian troops were battered, there was not a single army unit that had not suffered in the battle, and the Russians, while staying in their places, had lost *half* their troops.

For the French, with the memory of all the previous fifteen years of victories, with their confidence in Napoleon's invincibility, with the awareness that they had taken part of the battlefield, that they had lost only a quarter of their men, and that they still had the intact twenty-thousand-man guard, it would have been easy to make that effort. The French, who had attacked the Russian army with the goal of dislodging it from its position, ought to have made that effort, because as long as the Russians barred the road to Moscow, as they had done before the battle, the goal of the French had not been attained, and all their efforts and losses were in vain. But the French did not make that effort. Some historians say that Napoleon needed only to send in his intact old guard for the battle to be won. To talk of what would have happened if Napoleon had sent in his guard is the same as talking about what would happen if autumn became spring. It could not be. It is not that Napoleon did not send in his guard because he did not want to, but that it could not be done. All the generals, officers, and soldiers of the French army knew that it could not be done, because the army's fallen spirits did not allow it.

It was not Napoleon alone who experienced that dreamlike feeling that the terrible swing of the arm fell strengthless, but all the generals, all the participating and non-participating soldiers of the French army, after all their experience of previous battles (where the enemy had fled after ten times less effort), experienced the same feeling of terror before an enemy who, having lost *half* his army, stood as formidably at the end as at the beginning of the battle. The moral strength of the attacking French army was exhausted. It was not the sort of victory that is determined by captured pieces of cloth on sticks, known as standards, and by the amount of ground the troops stood and stand on, but a moral victory, the sort that convinces the adversary of the moral superiority of his enemy and of his own impotence, that was gained by the Russians at Borodino. The French invasion, like an enraged beast mortally wounded as it charges, sensed its destruction; but it could not stop, just as the twice weaker Russian army could not help moving aside. After the shove it had been given, the French army could still roll on as far as Moscow; but there, with no new efforts on the part of the Russian army, it was to perish, bleeding from the mortal wound it had received at Borodino. The direct consequence of the battle of Borodino was Napoleon's causeless flight from Moscow, the return down the old Smolensk road, the destruction of an invading army of five hundred thousand men, and the destruction of Napoleonic France, upon which had been laid for the first time, at Borodino, the hand of an adversary stronger in spirit.

Part Three

I

For human reason, absolute continuity of movement is incomprehensible. Man begins to understand the laws of any kind of movement only when he examines the arbitrarily chosen units of that movement. But at the same time it is from this arbitrary division of continuous movement into discrete units that the greater part of human errors proceeds.

A well-known so-called sophism of the ancients posits that Achilles can never overtake a tortoise that is walking ahead of him, even though Achilles walks ten times faster than the tortoise: while Achilles covers the distance that separates him from the tortoise, the tortoise will get ahead of him by one tenth of that distance; Achilles covers that one tenth, the tortoise gets ahead by one hundredth, and so on to infinity. The ancients considered this problem insoluble. The nonsensical conclusion (that Achilles will never overtake the tortoise) resulted only from the fact that discrete units of movement were introduced arbitrarily, while the movement of both Achilles and the tortoise was continuous.

By taking smaller and smaller units of movement, we only approach the solution of the problem, but never reach it. Only by allowing for an infinitesimal quantity and the ascending progression from that up to one tenth, and by taking the sum of that geometrical progression, do we arrive at the solution of the problem. A new branch of mathematics, having attained to the art of dealing with infinitesimal quantities in other, more complex problems of movement as well, now gives answers to questions that used to seem insoluble.

This new branch of mathematics, unknown to the ancients, in examining questions of movement, allows for infinitesimal quantities, that is, such as restore the main condition of movement (absolute continuity), and thereby corrects the inevitable error that human reason cannot help committing when it examines discrete units of movement instead of continuous movement.

The same thing happens in the search for the laws of historical movement.

The movement of mankind, proceeding from a countless number of human wills, occurs continuously.

To comprehend the laws of this movement is the goal of history. But in order to comprehend the laws of the continuous movement of the sum of all individual wills, human reason allows for arbitrary, discrete units. The first method of history consists in taking an arbitrary series of continuous events and examining it separately from others, whereas there is not and cannot be a beginning to any event, but one event always continuously follows another. The second method consists in examining the actions of one person, a king, a commander, as the sum of individual wills, whereas the sum of individual wills is never expressed in the activity of one historical person.

Historical science in its movement always takes ever smaller units for examination, and in this way strives to approach the truth. But however small the units that history takes, we feel that allowing for a unit that is separate from another, allowing for the *beginning* of some phenomenon, and allowing for the notion that all individual wills are expressed in the actions of one historical person, is false in itself.

Any conclusion of historical science, without the least effort on the part of criticism, falls apart like dust, leaving nothing behind, only as a result of the fact that criticism selects as an object for observation a larger or smaller discrete unit, which it always has the right to do, because any chosen historical unit is always arbitrary.

Only by admitting an infinitesimal unit for observation—a differential of history, that is, the uniform strivings of people—and attaining to the art of integrating them (taking the sums of these infinitesimal quantities) can we hope to comprehend the laws of history.

The first fifteen years of the nineteenth century in Europe present an extraordinary movement of millions of people. People abandon their usual occupations, rush from one side of Europe to the other, plunder, kill each other, triumph and despair, and the whole course of life is altered for several years and presents an intense movement, which initially increases, then weakens. Human reason asks, what was the cause of this movement, or according to what laws did it occur?

Historians, in answer to this question, lay before us the deeds and speeches of several dozen men in one of the buildings in the city of Paris, calling these deeds and speeches by the name of *revolution;* then they give a detailed biography of Napoleon and of some persons sympathetic or hostile to him, tell of the influence of some of these persons on others, and say: here is the origin of this movement, and here are its laws.

But human reason not only refuses to believe in this explanation, but says straight out that this method of explaining is incorrect, because in this explanation a weaker phenomenon is taken as the cause of a stronger one. The sum of individual human wills produced the revolution and Napoleon, and only the sum of those wills endured them and then destroyed them.

"But every time there were conquests, there were conquerors; every time there were upheavals in the state, there were great men," says history. Indeed, each time conquerors appeared, there were wars, human reason replies, but that does not prove that the conquerors were the cause of the wars, and that it is possible to find the laws of war in the personal activity of one man. Every time I look at my watch and see the hand approaching ten, I hear the bells start to ring in the neighbouring church, yet from the fact that the bells start to ring every time the hand reaches ten, I have no right to conclude that the position of the hand is the cause of the movement of the bells.

Every time I see the movement of a locomotive, I hear a whistling sound, I see the opening of the valve and the movement of the wheels; but I have no right to conclude from this that the whistling and the movement of the wheels are the cause of the movement of the locomotive.

Peasants say that a cold wind blows in late spring because the leaf buds of the oak are sprouting, and indeed a cold wind blows every spring when the oak is sprouting. But though the cause of the cold wind that blows as the oak sprouts is unknown to me, I cannot agree with the peasants about the sprouting of the oak being the cause of the cold wind, if only because the force of the wind is beyond the influence of the leaf buds. I only see the coincidence of conditions that occurs in every phenomenon of life, and I see that however long and thoroughly I observe the hand of my watch, the valve and wheels of the locomotive, and the leaf buds, I will not learn the cause of the bells ringing, the movement of the train, and the spring wind. For that I must change my point of observation completely, and study the laws of the movement of steam, bells, and the wind. Historical science must do the same. And attempts at it have already been made.

To study the laws of history, we must change completely the object of observation, leave kings, ministers, and generals alone, and study the uniform, infinitesimal elements that govern the masses. No one can tell to what extent it is given to man to achieve in this way an understanding of the laws of history; but it is obvious that the possibility of grasping historical laws lies only on this path, and that on this path human reason has not yet made one millionth of those efforts the historians have made in describing the deeds of various kings, commanders, and ministers, and in setting forth their reflections on the occasion of those deeds.

II

The forces of two-and-ten European nations burst into Russia. The Russian army and populace retreat, avoiding a confrontation as far as Smolensk, and from Smolensk to Borodino. The French army, with an ever-increasing force of momentum, races on to Moscow, the goal of its movement. The force of its momentum increases as it nears its goal, just as the velocity of a falling body increases as it nears the earth. Behind are thousands of miles of famished, hostile country; ahead are a few dozen miles separating it from its goal. Every soldier of Napoleon's army feels that, and the invasion pushes on of itself, by the mere force of its momentum.

In the Russian army, as it retreats, the spirit of hostility towards the enemy flares up more and more; as it falls back, it concentrates and increases. At Borodino a confrontation takes place. Neither army falls apart, but immediately after the confrontation, the Russian army retreats of necessity, just as a ball rebounds of necessity after colliding with another ball coming towards it at a greater speed; and also of necessity (though losing all its force in the collision) the swiftly rolling ball of the invasion rolls on for a certain distance.

The Russians retreat another eighty miles beyond Moscow; the French reach Moscow and stop there. During the five weeks after that, there is not a single battle. The French do not move. Like a mortally wounded beast, which, losing blood, licks its wounds, they remain in Moscow for five weeks without undertaking anything, and suddenly, with no new cause, flee back: they rush down the Kaluga high road (and that after a victory, for the field remains theirs again after Maloyaroslavets), without entering a single serious battle, flee still more quickly back to Smolensk, beyond Smolensk, beyond Vilno, beyond the Berezina, and further.

On the evening of the twenty-sixth of August, both Kutuzov and the whole Russian army were convinced that the battle of Borodino had been won. Kutuzov wrote as much to the sovereign. Kutuzov ordered preparations for a new battle to finish off the enemy, not because he wanted to deceive anyone, but because he knew that the enemy was defeated, just as every participant in the battle knew it.

But that same evening and the next day, reports came in one after another about unheard-of losses, about the loss of half the army, and a new battle turned out to be physically impossible.

It was impossible to offer battle when not all the information had been gathered, when the wounded had not been taken away, the charges had not been replenished, the dead had not been counted, new commanders had not been appointed to replace those killed, and the men had not had enough food or sleep.

And at the same time, immediately after the battle, the next morning, the French army (by that impetuous force of movement, now increased in inverse proportion to the square of the distance) was of itself already making for the Russian army. Kutuzov had wanted to attack the next day, and the whole army had wanted it. But in order to attack, the wish to do so is not enough; what is needed is the possibility of doing so, and that possibility was not there. It was impossible not to retreat by one march, then it was just as impossible not to retreat by another, and by a third march, and finally, on the first of September, when the army got as far as Moscow, despite the strength of feeling that arose in the ranks of the army, the force of things demanded that those troops go beyond Moscow. And the troops retreated by one last march and surrendered Moscow to the enemy.

For those people who are accustomed to think that the plans of wars and battles are drawn up by the commanders, just as each of us sitting in his study over a map makes reflections on how he would have disposed such and such battles, questions present themselves as to why Kutuzov, as he retreated, did not act thus and so, why did he not take up a position before Fili, why did he not retreat directly to the Kaluga road, why did he abandon Moscow, and so on. People who are accustomed to think that way forget or do not know those inevitable conditions in which the activity of every commander in chief always takes place. The activity of a commander does not have the slightest resemblance to the activity we imagine to ourselves, sitting at ease in our study, analysing some campaign on a map with a known number of troops on one side and the other, and on known terrain, and beginning our reflections from some certain moment. A commander in chief is never in those conditions of the *beginning* of some event, in which we always consider events. A commander in chief always finds himself in the middle of a shifting series of events, and in such a way that he is never able at any moment to ponder all the meaning of the ongoing event. Imperceptibly, moment by moment, an event is carved into its meaning, and at every moment of this consistent, ceaseless carving of the event, a commander in chief finds himself in the centre of a most complex play of intrigues, cares, dependency, power, projects, advice, threats, deceptions, finds himself constantly in the necessity of responding to the countless number of questions put to him, which always contradict each other.

Learned military men tell us quite seriously that Kutuzov ought to have moved his troops to the Kaluga road long before Fili, that someone had even suggested such a plan. But a commander in chief, especially at a difficult moment, has before him not one plan, but always dozens simultaneously. And all these plans, based on strategy and tactics, contradict each other. The work of the commander in chief seems to be merely to choose one of these plans. But he cannot even do that. Events and time do not wait. Suppose a suggestion is made to move to the Kaluga road on the twenty-eighth, but just then an adjutant comes galloping from Miloradovich and asks whether they should go into action against the French now or retreat. An order must be given at once, that minute. And the order to retreat deflects us from the turn-off to the Kaluga road. After the adjutant, a commissary comes asking where to transport the food supplies, and the head of the hospitals asking where to transport the wounded; and a courier from Petersburg brings a letter from the sovereign that does not admit the possibility of abandoning Moscow, and the commander's rival, the one who tries to undermine him (there are always rivals—not one, but several), suggests a new plan, diametrically opposed to the plan of going to the Kaluga road; and the commander's own forces require sleep and fortification; and a venerable general, overlooked for a reward, comes to complain, and the inhabitants beg for protection; and an officer sent to survey the terrain comes and reports the complete opposite of what an officer sent out before him had said; and a spy, a prisoner, and a general who did some reconnoitring all describe the position of the enemy army differently. People accustomed to not understanding or to forgetting all these unavoidable conditions of the activity of any commander in chief present to us, for instance, the position of the army at Fili and in so doing suppose that on the first of September the commander in chief could quite freely decide the question of whether to abandon or defend Moscow, whereas, with the Russian army positioned within three miles of Moscow, this question could not exist. When, then, was the question decided? At Drissa, and at Smolensk, and most palpably at Shevardino on the twenty-fourth, on the twenty-sixth at Borodino, and every day, hour, and minute of our retreat from Borodino to Fili.

III

The Russian troops, having retreated from Borodino, were camped at Fili. Ermolov, who had gone to survey the position, rode up to the field marshal.

"It's not possible to fight in this position," he said. Kutuzov looked at him in surprise and made him repeat what he had said. When he did, Kutuzov held out his hand to him.

"Give me your hand," he said, and, turning it so as to feel the pulse, he said: "You're unwell, my dear boy. Think what you're saying."

On Poklonnaya Hill, four miles from the Dorogomilovo gate, Kutuzov got out of his carriage and sat down on a bench by the side of the road. A huge crowd of generals gathered around him. Count Rastopchin, having come from Moscow, joined them. All this brilliant society, breaking up into several circles, talked among themselves about the advantages and disadvantages of the position, about the situation of the troops, about the suggested plans, about the condition of Moscow, about military questions in general. Everyone felt that, though they had not been summoned for that, though it had not been called that, this was a council of war. All conversations kept to the area of general questions. If anyone reported or asked about personal news, he spoke of it in a whisper and at once went on to general questions again: no jokes, no laughter, no smiles even, could be noticed among all these people. Everyone, with obvious effort, tried to be equal to the occasion. And all the groups, talking among themselves, tried to keep in proximity to the commander in chief (whose bench constituted the centre of these circles), and spoke so that he was able to hear them. The commander in chief listened and occasionally asked them to repeat what had been said around him, but did not enter the conversation himself or express any opinion. Most often, having listened to the conversation in some circle, he turned away with a look of disappointment, as if what they were speaking about was not at all what he wished to know. One spoke of the position chosen, criticizing not so much the position as the mental abilities of those who had chosen it; another argued that the mistake had been made before, that battle should have been accepted two days earlier; a third discussed the battle of Salamanca, which the newly arrived Frenchman Crosart, in a Spanish uniform, told about. (This Frenchman, along with one of the German princes who served in the Russian army, was analysing the siege of Saragossa,[1] anticipating the possibility of defending Moscow in the same way.) In a fourth circle, Count Rastopchin said that he and the Moscow militia were ready to perish under the walls of the capital, but even so he could not help regretting the uncertainty in which he had been left, and had he known it earlier, things would have been different . . . A fifth, showing the profundity of its strategic reflections, spoke of the direction the troops would have to take. A sixth talked total nonsense. Kutuzov's face was growing more and more preoccupied and sad. From all these conversations, Kutuzov saw one thing: the defence of Moscow was *in no way physically possible,* in the full meaning of those words, that is, impossible to such a degree that if some insane commander in chief gave the order to offer battle, confusion would set in, and there would be no battle anyway; there would not be, because all the higher officers not only acknowledged that the position was impossible, but in their conversations discussed only what would take place after the undoubted abandoning of that position. How could the officers lead their troops to a battlefield they considered impossible? The lower officers, even the soldiers (who also reason), considered the position just as impossible, and therefore could not go to fight in the certainty of defeat. If Bennigsen insisted on the defence of that position and others still discussed it, the question no longer had any meaning in itself, but only as a pretext for argument and intrigue. Kutuzov understood that.

Bennigsen, having chosen the position, ardently displaying his patriotism (which Kutuzov could not listen to without wincing), insisted on defending Moscow. Kutuzov saw Bennigsen's aim as clear as day: if the defence failed, to throw the blame on Kutuzov, who had led the troops as far as Sparrow Hills without a battle; if it succeeded, to ascribe it to himself; in case of refusal—to clear himself of criminally abandoning Moscow. But this question of intrigue did not concern the old man now. One terrible question concerned him. And he heard no answer to this question from anyone. For him the question now consisted only in this: "Can it be that I allowed Napoleon to get as far as Moscow? And when, then, did I do it? When was it decided? Was it yesterday, when I sent Platov the order to retreat, or was it the evening before, when I dozed off and told Bennigsen to give the orders? Or still earlier? . . . But when, when was this terrible matter decided? Moscow must be abandoned. The troops must retreat, and the order has to be given." To give this terrible order seemed to him the same as giving up command of the army. And it was not just that he loved power and was used to it (the honours given to Prince Prozorovsky, to whom he had been attached in Turkey, piqued him), but he was convinced that he was destined to save Russia, and only because of that, against the will of the sovereign and by the will of the people, was he chosen commander in chief. He was convinced that he alone, in those difficult circumstances, could maintain himself at the head of the army, and that he alone in the whole world was capable of knowing without dread that his adversary was the invincible Napoleon; and he dreaded the thought of the order he had to give. But he had to decide something, had to stop these conversations around him, which were beginning to take on too free a character.

He called the senior generals to him.

*"Ma tête, fut-elle bonne ou mauvaise, n'a qu'à s'aider d'elle-même,"** he said, getting up from the bench and riding to Fili, where his carriages were waiting.

IV

In the spacious better side of the muzhik Andrei Savostyanov's cottage, a council gathered at two o'clock. The men, women, and children of the large peasant family crowded into the kitchen side, across the front hall. Only Andrei's granddaughter Malasha, a six-year-old girl whom his serenity caressed and gave a lump of sugar at tea, stayed on the stove in the big side. Malasha looked down timidly and joyfully from the stove on the faces, uniforms, and crosses of the generals, who came into the cottage one after another and sat down in the best corner, on wide benches under the icons. Grandpa himself, as Malasha mentally called Kutuzov, sat apart from them in a dark corner behind the stove. He sat deeply immersed in a folding armchair, constantly groaning and spreading the collar of his tunic, which, though unbuttoned, still seemed to chafe his neck. The entering men went up to the field marshal one after another; he shook hands with some, nodded to others. The adjutant Kaisarov was about to pull open the curtain on the window opposite Kutuzov, but Kutuzov waved his hand crossly, and Kaisarov understood that his serenity did not want people to see his face.

There were so many people gathered around the peasant pine table, on

---

*My head, be it good or bad, can only help itself.

which lay maps, plans, pencils, and papers, that the orderlies brought another bench and set it down at the table. On this bench sat the already arrived: Ermolov, Kaisarov, and Toll. Just under the icons, in the foremost place, a St. George on his neck, with a pale, sickly face, and with his high forehead merging into his bald head, sat Barclay de Tolly. It was the second day that he had been suffering from a fever, and just then he had chills and cramps. Next to him sat Uvarov, who, in a low voice (as they all spoke), was telling Barclay something, gesticulating rapidly. The small, round Dokhturov, with raised eyebrows, listened attentively, his hands folded on his stomach. On the other side, his broad head with its bold features and shining eyes propped on his hand, sat Count Ostermann-Tolstoy, who seemed to be immersed in his own thoughts. Raevsky, with an impatient expression, twirling the black hair on his temples with a habitual gesture, glanced now at Kutuzov, now at the door. The firm, handsome, and kindly face of Konovnitsyn shone with a tender and sly smile. He met Malasha's gaze and made signs to her with his eyes that made the girl smile.

They were all waiting for Bennigsen, who, on the pretext of making a new survey of the position, was finishing his delicious dinner. They waited for him from four to six o'clock, and all that while did not commence the deliberations, but conducted conversations in quiet voices.

Only when Bennigsen came into the cottage did Kutuzov stir from his corner and move towards the table, but only so far, so that his face would not be lit by the candles that had been placed on it.

Bennigsen opened the council with the question: "To abandon Russia's sacred and ancient capital without a fight, or to defend it?" A long and general silence ensued. All faces frowned, and in the silence Kutuzov's angry grunting and coughing could be heard. All eyes looked at him. Malasha also looked at Grandpa. She was closest to him of all and saw how his face winced; it was as if he was about to cry. But that did not last long.

"*Russia's sacred and ancient capital!*" he suddenly began in an angry voice, repeating Bennigsen's words and thereby indicating the false note in those words. "Allow me to tell you, Your Excellency, that this question has no meaning for a Russian." (He heaved his heavy body forward.) "Such a question cannot be posed, and such a question has no meaning. The question for which I have asked these gentlemen to meet is a military one. The question is this: Russia's salvation lies in the army. Is it more advantageous to risk losing the army and Moscow by accepting battle, or to surrender Moscow without a battle? That is the question on which I would like to know your opinion." (He heaved himself back in the armchair.)

A debate began. Bennigsen still did not consider the game lost. Allowing for the opinion of Barclay and others about the impossibility of accepting a defensive battle at Fili, he, imbued with Russian patriotism and love for Moscow, suggested shifting the troops during the night from the right flank to the left, and striking at the right wing of the French the next day. Opinions were divided, there were arguments for and against this opinion. Ermolov, Dokhturov, and Raevsky agreed with Bennigsen's opinion. Whether guided by a sense of the need for sacrifice before abandoning the capital, or by other more personal considerations, these generals seemed not to understand that the present council could not change the inevitable course of events, and that Moscow had already been abandoned. The rest of the generals understood that, and, leaving aside the question of Moscow, spoke of the direction the army should take in its retreat. Malasha, who looked at what was happening before her without taking her eyes away, understood the meaning of this council differently. It seemed to her that it was a matter only of a personal struggle between Grandpa and "Long-skirts," as she called Bennigsen. She saw that they were angry when they spoke to each other, and in her heart she took Grandpa's side. In the middle of the conversation, she noticed a sly glance that Grandpa cast at Bennigsen, and after that, to her joy, noticed that Grandpa had said something to Long-skirts that took him aback: Bennigsen suddenly turned red and angrily paced about the cottage. The words that had so affected Bennigsen were Kutuzov's opinion, expressed in a calm and soft voice, on the advantages and disadvantages of Bennigsen's suggestion about shifting the troops during the night from the right flank to the left for an attack on the French right wing.

"Gentlemen," said Kutuzov, "I cannot approve of the count's plan. Shifting troops in close proximity to the enemy is always dangerous, and military history confirms this consideration. Thus, for example . . ." (Kutuzov seemed to ponder, searching for an example, and looked at Bennigsen with a bright, naïve gaze.) "Yes, let's just take the battle of Friedland, which, as I believe the count remembers well,[2] was . . . not entirely successful, only because our troops were re-formed in much too close proximity to the enemy . . ." A moment's silence ensued, which seemed very long to all of them.

The debate began again, but there were frequent pauses, and the feeling was that there was nothing more to talk about.

During one such pause, Kutuzov sighed deeply, as if he was about to speak. They all turned to look at him.

"*Eh bien, messieurs! Je vois que c'est moi qui payerai les pots cassés,*"* he said. And, slowly getting up, he went to the table. "Gentlemen, I've heard your opinions. Some will disagree with me. But I," (he stopped), "by the power entrusted in me by my sovereign and the fatherland, I—order a retreat."

After that, the generals began to disperse with the same solemn and silent discretion as people dispersing after a funeral.

Some of the generals, in low voices, in quite a different register than when

---

*Well, gentlemen! I see it's I who will have to pay for the broken crockery.

they were speaking at the council, conveyed something to the commander in chief.

Malasha, who had long been expected at supper, carefully climbed down backwards from her stove shelf, resting her bare little feet on the ledges of the stove, and, getting tangled between the legs of the generals, darted through the door.

Having dismissed the generals, Kutuzov sat for a long time, his elbow leaning on the table, and thought about the same terrible question: "When, when was it decided, finally, to abandon Moscow? When was the thing done that decided this question, and who is to blame for it?"

"This, this I didn't expect," he said to the adjutant Schneider, who came into the room when it was already late at night, "this I didn't expect! This never occurred to me!"

"You must get some rest, Your Serenity," said Schneider.

"But no! They'll eat horseflesh, like the Turks," Kutuzov shouted, without replying, banging the table with his plump hand, "that they will, if only . . ."

V

In contrast to Kutuzov, at that same time, in an event still more important than the army's retreat without a battle, in the abandoning and burning of Moscow, Rastopchin, whom we picture as the guiding hand of this event, acted quite differently.

This event—the abandoning and burning of Moscow—was as inevitable as the army's retreat beyond Moscow without a battle, after the battle of Borodino.

Every Russian, not on the basis of reasoning, but on the basis of the feeling that is inside us and was inside our fathers, could have predicted what was to take place.

Beginning with Smolensk, the same thing that happened in Moscow had been happening in all the towns and villages on Russian soil, without the participation of Rastopchin and his posters. People nonchalantly awaited the enemy, did not riot, did not fret, did not tear anyone to pieces, but calmly awaited their fate, feeling themselves strong enough to find, at the most difficult moment, what needed to be done. And as soon as the enemy approached, the wealthiest elements of the population left, abandoning their property; the poorest stayed and set fire to and destroyed what remained.

The consciousness that it would be so and always would be so lay and lies in the soul of every Russian. And that consciousness and, what is more, the foreboding that Moscow would be taken, lay in Russian Moscow society in the year twelve. Those who started leaving Moscow already in July and the beginning of August showed that they expected it. Those who left, taking along whatever they could, abandoning houses and half their property, acted that way because of the hidden *(latent)* patriotism which is expressed not in phrases, not in the killing of children to save the fatherland, and similar unnatural acts, but inconspicuously, simply, organically, and therefore always produces the strongest results.

"It is shameful to flee from danger, only cowards are fleeing Moscow," they were told. Rastopchin in his little posters kept instilling in them that to leave Moscow was disgraceful. People were ashamed to be called cowards, were ashamed to go, but all the same they went, knowing that it had to be so. Why did they go? It is impossible to suppose that Rastopchin had frightened them with the horrors Napoleon had committed in conquered lands. The first to leave were the rich, educated people, who knew very well that Vienna and Berlin remained intact and that there, during Napoleon's occupation, the citizens passed the time gaily with the charming Frenchmen, whom the Russians, and especially the ladies, liked so much then.

They went because for Russians there could be no question of whether it would be good or bad under French rule in Moscow. To be under French rule was impossible: it was the worst thing of all. They were leaving before the battle of Borodino, and still more quickly after the battle of Borodino, despite the call to defence, despite the announcement by Moscow's commander in chief of his intention to take up the Iverskaya icon and go to fight, and the hot-air balloons that were to destroy the French, and despite all the nonsense Rastopchin wrote in his posters. They knew it was for the army to fight, and if it could not, it was impossible to go to the Three Hills with young ladies and servants to fight Napoleon, and they had to leave, however sorry they were to abandon their property to destruction. They were leaving without thinking of the majestic significance of that huge, wealthy capital being abandoned by its inhabitants and obviously burned (a large, wooden city was bound to be burned); each was leaving for his own sake, and at the same time it was only because they left that that majestic event took place which will for ever remain the finest glory of the Russian people. The lady who, in the month of June, was already moving out of Moscow to her estate near Saratov with her black-amoors and women jesters, with a vague awareness that she was not a servant to Bonaparte and fearing she might be stopped by an order from Count Rastopchin, was performing, simply and genuinely, that great deed which saved Russia. But Count Rastopchin, who now shamed those who were leaving, now evacuated government offices, now distributed good-for-nothing weapons among the drunken riffraff, now took up icons, now forbade Augustin to evacuate relics and icons, now confiscated all private carts, now transported the hot-air balloon constructed by Leppich on a hundred and thirty-six carts, now hinted that he would burn Moscow, now told how he had burned his own house and wrote a proclamation to the French in which he solemnly reproached them for destroying his orphanage; now he assumed the glory of having burned Moscow, now he renounced it, now he ordered the people to catch all the spies and bring them to him, now he reproached the people for it, now he banished all the French from Moscow, now he allowed Mme Aubert-Chalmet, the centre of all the French population of Moscow, to remain in the city[3] and ordered the old and venerable postmaster general Klyucharev, who had done nothing particularly wrong, to be arrested and exiled; now he gathered the people on the Three Hills to fight the French,[4] now, in order to be rid of those same people, he turned them loose to murder a man and escaped through the back gate himself; now he said he would not survive the misfortune of Moscow, now he wrote French verses in an album about his part in the affair*—this man did not understand the meaning of the event that was taking place, but only wanted to do something himself, to astonish someone or other, to accomplish something patriotically heroic, and, like a boy, frolicked over the majestic and inevitable event of the abandoning and burning of Moscow, and tried with his little hand now to encourage, now to stem the flow of the enormous current of people which carried him along with it.

VI

Hélène, having returned with the court from Vilno to Petersburg, found herself in a difficult situation.

In Petersburg Hélène enjoyed the special patronage of a dignitary who occupied one of the highest posts in the state. In Vilno she had become close with a young foreign prince. When she returned to Petersburg, both the prince and the dignitary were there, both claimed their rights, and Hélène was faced with a new task in her career: to maintain her close relations with them both without offending either.

What would have seemed difficult and even impossible for another woman, never once made Countess Bezukhov stop and think—clearly it was not in vain that she enjoyed the reputation of a most intelligent woman. If she had begun to conceal her actions, to extricate herself by cunning from an awkward situation, she would thereby have spoiled things for herself, acknowledging herself guilty; but Hélène, on the contrary, like a truly great person who can do whatever she likes, at once placed herself in the position of being right, in which she sincerely believed, and all the others in the position of being wrong.

*Je suis né Tartare. / Je voulus être Romain. / Les Français m'appelèrent barbare. / Les Russes— Georges Dandin. That is, "I was born a Tartar. / I wanted to be Roman. / The French will call me barbarian. / The Russians—Georges Dandin."[5] (Tolstoy's note.)

The first time the young foreign person allowed himself to reproach her, she proudly raised her beautiful head and, half turning to him, said firmly:

"*Voilà l'égoisme et la cruauté des hommes! Je ne m'attendais pas à autre chose. La femme se sacrifie pour vous, elle souffre, et voilà sa récompense. Quel droit avez vous, Monseigneur, de me demander compte de mes amitiés, de mes affections? C'est un homme qui a été plus qu'un père pour moi.*"*

The person wanted to say something. Hélène interrupted him.

"*Eh bien, oui,*" she said, "*peut-être qu'il a pour moi d'autres sentiments que ceux d'un père, mais ce n'est pas une raison pour que je lui ferme ma porte. Je ne suis pas un homme pour être ingrate. Sachez, Monseigneur, pour tout ce qui a rapport à mes sentiments intimes, je ne rends compte qu'à Dieu et à ma conscience,*"† she concluded, touching her high, beautiful breasts with her hand and glancing up at the sky.

"*Mais écoutez-moi, au nom de Dieu.*"

"*Epousez-moi, et je serai votre esclave.*"

"*Mais c'est impossible.*"

"*Vous ne daignez pas descendre jusqu'à moi, vous . . .*"‡ said Hélène, bursting into tears.

The person began to comfort her; Hélène said through her tears (as if forgetting herself) that nothing could prevent her from marrying, that there were examples (there were still few examples then, but she named Napoleon and other highly placed persons), that she had never been a wife to her husband, that she had been sacrificed.

"But laws, religion . . ." said the person, already yielding.

"Laws, religion . . . Why would they have been invented, if they couldn't do that!" said Hélène.

The important person was astonished that such a simple argument could have failed to occur to him, and turned for advice to the holy brothers of the Society of Jesus,[6] with whom he was in close relations.

Several days later, at one of the enchanting fêtes given by Hélène at her summer house on Kamenny Island, the enchanting M. de Jobert was introduced to her, a man no longer young, with snow-white hair and shining black eyes, *un Jésuite à robe courte,*§ who had a long conversation with Hélène, in the light

---

*There you have the egoism and cruelty of men! I expected nothing else. A woman sacrifices herself for you, she suffers, and there is her reward. What right do you have, My Lord, to ask me to account for my friendships, for my affections? He is a man who has been more than a father to me.
†Well, yes . . . perhaps he has other feelings for me than those of a father, but that is no reason for me to close my door to him. I'm not a man, that I should be ungrateful. Know, My Lord, that for all that concerns my intimate feelings, I give an accounting only to God and my conscience.
‡But listen to me, in God's name. / Marry me, and I will be your slave. / But that's impossible. / You don't want to lower yourself to me, you . . .
§A short-frocked Jesuit.

of the garden illuminations and to the sounds of music, about the love of God, of Christ, of the heart of the Mother of God, and about the comforts provided in this life and the next by the one true Catholic religion. Hélène was moved, and several times both she and M. de Jobert had tears in their eyes and a tremor in their voices. A dance to which a partner came to invite Hélène disrupted her conversation with her future *directeur de conscience;* but the next day M. Jobert came alone in the evening to see Hélène, and after that began to frequent her.

One day he took the countess to the Catholic church, where she knelt before the altar she had been brought to. The enchanting, not-too-young Frenchman placed his hands on her head and, as she herself recounted later, she felt something like a breath of fresh wind descend into her soul. It was explained to her that this was *la grâce.*

Then an *abbé à robe longue** was brought to her, and he confessed her and gave her absolution of her sins. The next day a box with communion in it was brought to her and left for home use. A few days later Hélène, to her satisfaction, learned that she had now joined the true Catholic church and that one of those days the pope himself would learn of her and send her some document.

All that was happening around her and to her at this time, all this attention paid to her by so many intelligent people and expressed in such pleasant, refined forms, and the dovelike purity in which she now found herself (she wore white dresses with white ribbons all that time)—all this afforded her pleasure; but never for a moment did she lose sight of her goal beyond that pleasure. And as it always happens in matters of cunning that a stupid person tricks the more intelligent, she, having realized that the goal of all this talk and fuss consisted primarily in converting her to Catholicism in order to take money from her for the benefit of Jesuit institutions (of which they had given her hints), Hélène, before giving money, insisted that various operations be performed over her that would free her from her husband. To her mind, the meaning of any religion consisted only in observing certain decencies while satisfying human desires. And with that purpose, in one of her talks with her spiritual director, she insistently demanded an answer to the question of the extent to which her marriage bound her.

They were sitting in the drawing room by the window. It was twilight. Through the window came the scent of flowers. Hélène was wearing a white dress, transparent on the shoulders and breast. The abbé, a well-fed man with a plump, clean-shaven chin, a pleasant, firm mouth, and white hands folded meekly on his knees, sat close to Hélène and, with a subtle smile on his lips, looked at her face now and then with a glance peacefully admiring of her

*A long-frocked abbot.

beauty, and expounded his view of the question that concerned them. Hélène, smiling uneasily, looked at his wavy hair, clean-shaven, plump, bluish cheeks, and expected the conversation to take a new turn any moment. But the abbé, though obviously enjoying the beauty and closeness of his interlocutrice, was carried away by his mastery of the case.

The course of the spiritual director's reasoning was as follows. In ignorance of the meaning of what you were undertaking, you gave a vow of marital fidelity to a man who, for his part, having entered into marriage without believing in its religious meaning, had committed blasphemy. This marriage did not have the double meaning it should have had. But despite that, you were bound by your vow. You departed from it. What did you commit in so doing? A *péché veniel* or a *péché mortel?** A *péché veniel,* because you committed your act without bad intent. If you now entered into a new marriage, with the purpose of having children, your sin could be forgiven. But again the question falls into two parts: first . . .

"But I think," said the suddenly bored Hélène with her enchanting smile, "that, having embraced the true religion, I cannot be bound by what a false religion imposed on me."

The *directeur de conscience* was astounded by this Columbus's egg that stood before him with such simplicity.[7] He was delighted with the unexpectedly quick success of his pupil, but could not renounce the edifice of arguments he had erected with such mental labour.

"*Entendons-nous, comtesse,*"[†] he said with a smile and began to refute the reasoning of his spiritual daughter.

VII

Hélène realized that the case was very simple and easy from the point of view of spiritual direction, but that her directors made difficulties only because they had apprehensions about how the secular authorities would look at it.

And as a result, Hélène decided that the case had to be prepared for in society. She provoked the jealousy of the old dignitary and told him the same thing as the first suitor, that is, put things so that the only way to obtain rights over her was to marry her. The old important person was as struck for the first moment by this proposal to marry her while her husband was living as the first, young person had been; but Hélène's unshakeable conviction that this was as simple and natural as a young girl getting married had its effect on him, too. If

*A venial sin or a mortal sin?
†Let us understand each other, Countess.

even the slightest signs of hesitation, shame, or secretiveness had been noticeable in Hélène herself, her case would undoubtedly have been lost; but not only
were there no signs of secretiveness or shame, but, on the contrary, with simplicity and good-natured naïveté, she told her close friends (and that meant all
Petersburg) that both the prince and the dignitary had proposed to her, and
that she loved them both and was afraid to upset either of them.

The rumour instantly spread through Petersburg, not that Hélène wanted
to divorce her husband (if such a rumour had spread, a great many people
would have risen up against such an unlawful intention), but simply that
the unfortunate, interesting Hélène was in perplexity about which of the
two men to marry. The question now consisted not in the degree to which
this was possible, but only in which match was the more advantageous
and how the court would look at it. There were indeed some obdurate
people who were unable to rise to the height of the question and saw in this
project a profanation of the sacrament of marriage; but they were few,
and they kept quiet, while the majority was interested in the questions of the
happiness that had befallen Hélène and which choice was better. As for
whether it was good or bad to marry while one's husband was living, no one
spoke of it, because this question had obviously already been decided by
people more intelligent than you and I (as they said), and to doubt the correctness of the decision would mean to risk showing one's stupidity and inability to
live in society.

Only Marya Dmitrievna Akhrosimov, who came to Petersburg that summer
to meet one of her sons, allowed herself to openly express her opinion, which
ran counter to that of society. Meeting Hélène at a ball, Marya Dmitrievna
stopped her in the middle of the ballroom and, amidst the general silence, said
to her in her gruff voice:

"So here you've started this marrying while the husband's still living. Maybe
you think you've invented some novelty? You've been forestalled, dearie. It
was invented long ago. They do it in all the ——." And with those words,
Marya Dmitrievna, with a habitual threatening gesture, pushing up her wide
sleeves and looking around sternly, strode through the room.

Marya Dmitrievna, though feared, was looked upon in Petersburg as a
jester, and therefore of the words she had spoken, only the crude word was
noticed and repeated among them in a whisper, supposing that that one word
contained all the salt of what she had said.

Prince Vassily, who forgot what he said especially often of late and repeated
the same thing a hundred times, said each time he happened to see his daughter:

"*Hélène, j'ai un mot à vous dire,*" he said, taking her aside, and pulling
her hand down. "*J'ai eu vent de certains projets relatifs à . . . Vous savez.
Eh bien, ma chère enfant, vous savez que mon coeur de père se réjouit
de vous savoir . . . Vous avez tant souffert . . . Mais, chère enfant . . . ne*

*consultez que votre coeur. C'est tout ce que je vous dis."** And, concealing ever the same emotion, he pressed his cheek to his daughter's cheek and walked away.

Bilibin, who had not lost his reputation as a most intelligent man and who was Hélène's disinterested friend, one of those friends that brilliant women always have, male friends who can never pass into the category of lovers, Bilibin once, in a *petit comité,*† voiced his view of this matter to his friend Hélène.

"*Écoutez, Bilibine*" (Hélène always called such friends as Bilibin by their last name). And she touched the sleeve of his tailcoat with her white, beringed hand. "*Dites-moi comme vous diriez à une soeur, que dois-je faire? Lequel des deux?*"‡

Bilibin gathered the skin over his eyebrows and, with a smile on his lips, fell to thinking.

"*Vous ne me prenez pas en* unawares, *vous savez,*" he said. "*Comme véritable ami j'ai pensé et repensé à votre affaire. Voyez vous. Si vous épousez le prince*" (this was the young man), he unbent one finger, "*vous perdez pour toujours la chance d'épouser l'autre et puis vous mécontentez la Cour. (Comme vous savez, il y a une espèce de parenté.) Mais si vous épousez le vieux comte, vous faites le bonheur de ses derniers jours, et puis comme veuve du grand . . . le prince ne fait plus de mésalliance en vous épousant,*"§ and he released the skin.

"*Voilà un veritable ami!*" said Hélène, brightening up and touching Bilibin's sleeve once again. "*Mais c'est que j'aime l'un et l'autre, je ne voudrais pas leur faire de chagrin. Je donnerais ma vie pour leur bonheur à tous deux,*"# she said.

Bilibin shrugged his shoulders, showing that even he could do nothing about such a plight.

"*Une maîtresse-femme! Voilà ce qui s'appelle poser carrément la question. Elle voudrait épouser tous les trois à la fois,*"** thought Bilibin.

---

*Hélène, I have a word for you . . . I've got wind of certain plans concerning . . . You know. Well, my dear child, you know that my father's heart rejoices to know that you . . . You've suffered so . . . But, dear child . . . consult only your own heart. That's all I have to say to you.
†Small group.
‡Listen, Bilibin . . . Tell me as you would a sister, what must I do? Which of the two?
§You're not catching me *unawares,* you know . . . As a true friend I have thought and rethought about your affair. Look. If you marry the prince . . . you lose for ever the chance to marry the other one and then, too, you displease the court. (As you know, there's some sort of relation.) But if you marry the old count, you make for the happiness of his last days, and then as the dignitary's widow . . . the prince will no longer be marrying beneath him by marrying you.
#There's a true friend! . . . But the thing is that I love them both, I wouldn't want to grieve them. I'd give my life for the happiness of them both.
**A masterful woman! That's what is known as putting the question squarely. She'd like to marry all three of them at once.

"But, tell me, how will your husband look at the matter?" he said, his reputation being so firmly founded that he was not afraid of harming himself by such a naïve question. "Will he consent?"

"*Ah! Il m'aime tant!*" said Hélène, who for some reason fancied that Pierre also loved her. "*Il fera tout pour moi.*"*

Bilibin gathered the skin to indicate that a *mot* was in preparation.

"*Même le divorce,*"† he said.

Hélène laughed.

Among the people who allowed themselves to doubt the lawfulness of the projected marriage was Hélène's mother, Princess Kuragin. She was constantly tormented by envy of her daughter, and now, when the subject of envy was closest to the princess's heart, she could not reconcile herself to this thought. She consulted with a Russian priest about the extent to which it was possible to divorce and enter into marriage while the husband was living, and the priest told her it was impossible, and, to her joy, pointed out to her a Gospel text which (as it seemed to the priest) rejected outright the possibility of entering into marriage while the husband is living.

Armed with these arguments, which to her seemed irrefutable, the princess went to her daughter early one morning, so as to find her alone.

Having heard her mother's objections, Hélène smiled meekly and mockingly.

"But it says straight out: whoever marries a divorced woman . . ."8 said the old princess.

"*Ah, maman, ne dites pas de bêtises. Vous ne comprenez rien. Dans ma position j'ai des devoirs,*"‡ Hélène began, switching to French from Russian, in which it always seemed to her there was some lack of clarity in her case.

"But, my friend . . ."

"*Ah, maman, comment est-ce que vous ne comprenez pas que le Saint Père, qui a le droit de donner des dispenses . . .*"§

Just then a lady companion who lived at Hélène's came to report that his highness was in the reception room and wished to see her.

"*Non, dites-lui que je ne veux pas le voir, que je suis furieuse contre lui, parce qu'il m'a manqué parole.*"#

"*Comtesse, à tout péché miséricorde,*"** said a fair-haired young man with a long face and nose, coming in.

* Ah! He loves me so! . . . He'll do anything for me.
† Even divorce.
‡ Ah, mama, don't say stupid things. You don't understand anything. In my position I have duties.
§ Ah, mama, how is it you don't understand that the Holy Father, who has the right to grant dispensations . . .
# No, tell him that I don't want to see him, that I'm furious with him, because he didn't keep his word to me.
** Countess, for every sin there is mercy.

The old princess respectfully rose and curtsied. The young man paid no attention to her. The princess nodded to her daughter and sailed towards the door.

"No, she's right," thought the old princess, all of whose convictions crumbled before the appearance of his highness. "She's right; but how is it we didn't know it in our long-lost youth? Yet it was so simple," thought the old princess, getting into her carriage.

At the beginning of August, Hélène's case became perfectly defined and she wrote a letter to her husband (who loved her very much, as she thought) in which she informed him of her intention to marry N. N., and of the fact that she had embraced the one true religion and that she asked him to go through all the necessary formalities for divorce, of which the bearer of the letter would inform him.

"*Sur ce je prie Dieu, mon ami, de vous avoir sous sa sainte et puissante garde. Votre amie Hélène.*"*

This letter was brought to Pierre's house at the time when he was on the field of Borodino.

VIII

Having run down from the Raevsky battery for the second time towards the end of the battle of Borodino, Pierre, with crowds of soldiers, made his way through the gully towards Knyazkovo, reached the dressing station, and, seeing blood and hearing cries and moans, hastened on, mixing with the crowds of soldiers.

The one thing Pierre now desired with all the forces of his soul was to get away as quickly as possible from those dreadful impressions in which he had lived that day, to return to the ordinary conditions of life, and fall peacefully asleep in a room on his own bed. He felt that only in the ordinary conditions of life would he be able to understand himself and all that he had seen and experienced. But there were no ordinary conditions of life anywhere.

Though there was no whistling of cannonballs and bullets here, on the road he was walking along, there was on all sides the same thing as there on the battlefield. There were the same suffering, tormented, and sometimes strangely indifferent faces, the same blood, the same soldiers' greatcoats, the same sounds of gunfire, distant now, but arousing terror all the same; besides, it was stifling and dusty.

---

*Upon which I pray God, my friend, to keep you under His holy and powerful protection. Your friend Hélène.

Having gone some two miles along the Mozhaisk high road, Pierre sat down by the roadside.

Dusk had fallen over the earth, and the roar of the artillery had died down. Pierre, propping himself on his elbow, lay down and stayed that way for a long time, gazing at the shadows that moved past him in the darkness. He kept fancying that a cannonball was flying at him with a frightful whistling; he would give a start and raise himself up. He did not remember how long he lay there. In the middle of the night three soldiers, bringing brushwood, settled next to him and began to make a fire.

The soldiers, glancing sidelong at Pierre, made the fire, put a kettle on it, crumbled some biscuits into it, and added some lard. The pleasant smell of edible and greasy viands mingled with the smell of smoke. Pierre sat up and sighed. The soldiers (there were three of them) were eating, without paying attention to Pierre, and talking among themselves.

"And what sort are you?" one of the soldiers suddenly addressed Pierre, obviously implying by this question what Pierre was thinking, namely: if you want to eat, we'll give you some, only tell us if you're an honest man.

"I? I? . . ." said Pierre, feeling it necessary to diminish his social position as much as possible, so as to be closer and more understandable to the soldiers. "I'm actually a militia officer, only my detachment isn't here; I was in the battle and lost my men."

"Just look at that!" said one of the soldiers.

Another soldier shook his head.

"Well, then, eat some of our mess if you want!" said the first, and he handed Pierre a wooden spoon, after licking it clean.

Pierre moved towards the fire and began to eat the mess that was in the kettle and that seemed to him the tastiest of all the dishes he had ever eaten. While he bent over the kettle, scooping up big spoonfuls and greedily chewing one after another, his face could be seen in the firelight, and the soldiers silently looked at him.

"Where are you headed? Tell us!" one of them again asked.

"To Mozhaisk."

"So you'd be a gentleman?"

"Yes."

"And what's your name?"

"Pyotr Kirillovich."

"Well, Pyotr Kirillovich, come on, we'll take you there."

In total darkness, the soldiers walked with Pierre towards Mozhaisk.

The cocks were already crowing when they reached Mozhaisk and began to climb the steep town hill. Pierre walked with the soldiers, having forgotten completely that his inn was below, at the foot of the hill, and that he had already gone past it. He would not have remembered it (he was in such a state of bewilderment) if halfway up the hill he had not run into his groom, who had gone looking for him all over the town and was now going back to the inn. The groom recognized Pierre by his hat, showing white in the darkness.

"Your Excellency," he said, "we've been in despair. Why are you on foot? Where are you going, if you please!"

"Ah, yes," said Pierre.

The soldiers stopped.

"Well, so you've found your people?" said one of them.

"Well, goodbye to you! Pyotr Kirillovich, is it? Goodbye to you, Pyotr Kirillovich!" said other voices.

"Goodbye," said Pierre, and he headed for the inn together with his groom.

"I should give them something!" Pierre thought, putting his hand to his pocket. "No, you shouldn't," some voice said to him.

There was no place left in the rooms of the inn: they were all taken. Pierre went out to the yard and, covering himself head and all, lay down in his carriage.

IX

Pierre had barely laid his head on the pillow when he felt himself falling asleep; but suddenly, with an almost lifelike clarity, he heard the boom-boom-boom of gunfire, heard groans, cries, the smack of projectiles, smelled blood and powder, and a feeling of terror and the fear of death seized him. Frightened, he opened his eyes and raised his head from under the greatcoat. All was quiet in the courtyard. Only some orderly came through the gate, talking with the yard porter and splashing through the mud. Some pigeons above Pierre's head, in the dark under the wooden eaves, were roused by the movement he made as he raised himself. The whole courtyard was filled with the peaceful, strong smell of an inn, which gladdened Pierre at that moment, the smell of hay, dung, and tar. Between the two black sheds the clear, starry night could be seen.

"Thank God there's no more of that," thought Pierre, covering his head again. "Oh, how terrible fear is and how disgracefully I yielded to it! And they . . . *they* were firm, calm all the time, till the end . . ." *They*, to Pierre's mind, were the soldiers—those who had been at the battery, and those who had fed him, and those who had prayed before the icon. *They*—these strange people, hitherto unknown to him—*they* were clearly and sharply separated in his mind from all other people.

"To be a soldier, simply a soldier!" thought Pierre, falling asleep. "To enter that common life with my whole being, to be pervaded by what makes them that way. But how to cast off all that's superfluous, devilish, all the burden of the outer man? At one time I could have been that. I could have run away from my father, as I wanted to. I could have been sent off as a soldier after the duel with Dolokhov." And there flashed in Pierre's imagination the dinner at the club, when he had challenged Dolokhov, and his benefactor in Torzhok. And now Pierre pictures to himself the solemn dining room of the lodge. This lodge is meeting in the English Club. And someone familiar, close, dear, is sitting at the head of the table. It is he! It is his benefactor. "But isn't he dead?" thought Pierre. "Yes, dead; but I didn't know he was alive. How sorry I am that he's dead; and how glad I am that he's alive again!" On one side of the table sat Anatole, Dolokhov, Nesvitsky, Denisov, and others like them (in his dream the category of these people was as clearly defined in Pierre's soul as the category of people he called *they*), and these people, Anatole, Dolokhov, were shouting and singing loudly; but from beyond their shouting the voice of his benefactor could be heard talking ceaselessly, and the sound of his words was as significant and constant as the noise of the battlefield, yet it was pleasant and comforting. Pierre did not understand what his benefactor was saying, but he knew (the categories of thought were just as clear in his dream) that the benefactor was speaking of the good, of the possibility of being what *they* were. And *they* surrounded his benefactor on all sides with their simple, kind, firm faces. But although they were kind, they were not looking at Pierre, they did not know him. Pierre wanted to attract their attention and speak. He rose a little, but just then his feet became cold and bare.

He was embarrassed and covered his feet with his hand, from which the overcoat had actually fallen. For a moment, as he straightened the overcoat, Pierre opened his eyes and saw the same sheds, posts, courtyard, but it was all bluish now, bright, and covered with sparkles of dew or frost.

"Day is breaking," thought Pierre. "But that's not it. I have to finish listening and understand the words of my benefactor." He covered himself again with the overcoat, but the dining room lodge and his benefactor were no longer there. There were only thoughts, clearly expressed in words, thoughts which someone spoke or Pierre himself pondered.

Recalling these thoughts afterwards, Pierre was convinced that, even though they had been called up by the impressions of the day, someone outside him had spoken them to him. Never, as it seemed to him, would he have been able to think and express his thoughts that way in a waking state.

"War is the most difficult subjection of man's freedom to the laws of God," the voice said. "Simplicity is obedience to God; you cannot get away from Him. And *they* are simple. *They* don't talk, they do. A word spoken is silver, unspoken is gold. Man cannot possess anything as long as he fears death. But to him who does not fear it, everything belongs. If there was no suffering, man would not know his limits, would not know himself. The most difficult thing" (Pierre went on thinking or hearing in his sleep) "consists in being able to unite the meaning of all things in his soul. To unite all things?" Pierre said to himself.

"No, not to unite. It's impossible to unite thoughts, but to *hitch together* all these thoughts—that's what's needed! Yes, *we must hitch together, hitch together!*" Pierre repeated to himself with inner rapture, feeling that precisely these and only these words expressed what he wanted to express and resolved the whole question that tormented him.

"Yes, we must hitch together, it's time to hitch together."

"We must hitch up, it's time to hitch up, Your Excellency! Your Excellency!" some voice repeated, "we must hitch up, it's time to hitch up . . ."

It was the voice of his groom, waking Pierre up. The sun was shining directly into Pierre's face. He glanced at the dirty inn yard, in the middle of which soldiers were watering some scrawny horses, and from which wagons were driving through the gate. Pierre turned away with revulsion, closed his eyes, and quickly fell back again on the seat of the carriage. "No, I don't want it, I don't want to see or understand it, I want to understand what was being revealed to me in my dream. One more second, and I'd have understood everything. What am I to do? Hitch together, but how hitch everything together?" And Pierre felt with horror that all the meaning of what he had seen and thought in his dream was destroyed.

The groom, the coachman, and the yard porter told Pierre that an officer had arrived with news that the French were advancing on Mozhaisk and that our troops were leaving.

Pierre got up and, ordering them to harness the carriage and catch up with him, set off on foot through the town.

The troops were leaving and abandoning about ten thousand wounded. These wounded could be seen in the courtyards and in the windows of houses and crowding in the streets. In the streets, around the wagons that were to take the wounded away, shouts, curses, and blows could be heard. Pierre's carriage caught up with him, and he offered it to a wounded general of his acquaintance, and drove with him to Moscow. On the way, Pierre learned of the death of his brother-in-law and the death of Prince Andrei.

X

On the thirtieth, Pierre returned to Moscow. Almost at the city gate, he ran into Count Rastopchin's adjutant.

"We've been looking everywhere for you," said the adjutant. "The count absolutely must see you. He asks you to come at once on very important business."

Pierre, without stopping at home, hired a cab and drove to the commander in chief.

Count Rastopchin had come to town from his suburban house in Sokolniki only that morning. The anteroom and waiting room in the count's house were full of officials who had come at his request or to receive orders. Vasilchikov and Platov had already seen the count and explained to him that to defend Moscow was impossible and that it would be surrendered. This news was concealed from the inhabitants, but the officials, the heads of various departments, knew that Moscow was to fall into the hands of the enemy, just as Count Rastopchin knew it; and to shift responsibility from themselves, they all came to the commander in chief, to ask what to do with the institutions they were in charge of.

Just as Pierre came into the anteroom, the courier who had come from the army was leaving the count's office.

The courier waved hopelessly to the questions people addressed to him and walked through the room.

While sitting in the anteroom, Pierre looked around with weary eyes at the various officials, old and young, military and civilian, significant and insignificant, who were in the room. They all seemed displeased and restless. Pierre went over to one group of officials, in which there was one of his acquaintances. Having greeted Pierre, they went on with their conversation.

"To send them away and bring them back again wouldn't do any harm; but in this situation one can't answer for anything."

"But look at what he writes," said another, pointing to a printed sheet he was holding in his hand.

"That's another matter. The people need it," said the first.

"What is it?" asked Pierre.

"A new poster."

Pierre took it and began to read:

The most serene prince, in order to join quickly with the troops coming to him, has passed through Mozhaisk and stopped at a fortified place where the enemy will not suddenly fall upon him. Forty-eight cannon with ammunition have been sent to him from here, and his serenity says he will defend Moscow to the last drop of his blood and is even ready to fight in the streets. Don't worry, brothers, about the closing of the government offices: we have to keep things in order, but we'll deal summarily with the villain! When it comes to that, I'll need stout fellows from the city and the country. I'll send out a call two days ahead, but there's no need yet, and so I'm silent. An axe would be a good thing, a spear wouldn't be bad, but a pitchfork would be best: a Frenchman is no heavier than a sheaf of rye. Tomorrow after dinner I'll have the Iverskaya icon taken up and brought to the wounded in the Ekaterininsky Hospital. We'll bless the water there: they'll recover the sooner. And I've now recovered: there was something wrong with my eye, but now I'm keeping them both open.

"But military men told me," said Pierre, "that it was impossible to fight in the city, and that the position . . ."

"Why, yes, that's what we're talking about," said the first official.

"But what does it mean: 'there was something wrong with my eye, but now I'm keeping them both open'?" asked Pierre.

"The count had a sty," the adjutant said, smiling, "and was very worried when I told him that people were coming to ask how he was. By the way, Count," the adjutant suddenly added, turning to Pierre with a smile, "we've heard you have family troubles? It seems that the countess, your wife . . ."

"I haven't heard anything," Pierre said indifferently. "And what have you heard?"

"No, you know, people often invent things. I'm talking about what I've heard."

"What have you heard?"

"They say," the adjutant said with the same smile, "that the countess, your wife, is preparing to go abroad. It's probably nonsense . . ."

"Maybe so," said Pierre, looking around distractedly. "And who is this?" he asked, pointing to a short old man in a clean blue merchant's kaftan, with a long, snow-white beard, similar eyebrows, and a ruddy face.

"This? This is the merchant, that is, the tavern keeper, Vereshchagin. Maybe you've heard that story about the proclamation?"

"Ah, so this is Vereshchagin!" said Pierre, peering into the old merchant's firm and calm face, and searching for an expression of treachery in it.

"This is not the man himself. This is the father of the one who wrote the proclamation," said the adjutant. "That one's young and sitting behind bars, and it looks like things will go badly for him."

An old man with a star and another, a German official with a cross on his neck, came up to the conversing men.

"You see," the adjutant was saying, "it's a tangled story. Back about two months ago this proclamation appeared. The count was informed. He ordered an investigation. Gavrilo Ivanych here found out that the proclamation had passed through exactly sixty-three hands. He comes to one: 'Who did you get it from?' 'From so-and-so.' He goes to that one: 'And you?' And so on. They got to Vereshchagin . . . a half-educated little merchant, you know, a piddler-diddler," the adjutant said, smiling. "They ask him: 'Who did you get it from?' And the thing is that we know who he got it from. He couldn't have got it from anyone else than the postmaster general. But there was clearly some collusion between them. He said: 'From nobody, I wrote it myself.' They threatened him and pleaded with him, but he stood by it: 'I wrote it myself.' They reported it to the count. The count told them to summon him. 'Who did you get the proclamation from?' 'I wrote it myself.' Well, you know the count!" the adjutant said with a proud and gay smile.

"He flew into a terrible temper, and just think: such brazenness, lying, and stubbornness! . . ."

"Ah, I see, the count wanted him to point to Klyucharev!" said Pierre.

"He didn't want that at all," the adjutant said in alarm. "Klyucharev had a few sins to his name without that, which is why he was banished. But the thing was that the count was highly indignant. 'How could you have written it?' says the count. He took the Hamburg *Gazette* from the table.⁹ 'It's here. You didn't write it, you translated it, and badly at that, because, fool that you are, you don't even know French.' And what do you think? 'No,' he says, 'I didn't read any newspapers, I wrote it myself.' 'If so, you're a traitor, I'll have you up in court, and you'll be hanged. Tell me, who did you get it from?' 'I haven't seen any newspapers, I wrote it.' And so it remained. The count summoned his father: he stood his ground. They took him to court and sentenced him, I believe, to hard labour. Now his father has come to petition for him. But what a nasty boy! You know that sort of little merchant's son, a dandy, a charmer, he listened to some lectures and thinks he can pluck the devil by the beard. Quite the fellow! His father keeps an inn here by the Kamenny Bridge, and in that inn there's a big icon of God Almighty, you know, holding a sceptre in one hand and an orb in the other; so he took the icon home for a few days, and what did he do! He found some scoundrel of a painter . . ."

XI

In the middle of this new story, Pierre was summoned to the commander in chief.

Pierre went into Count Rastopchin's study. Rastopchin, scowling, was rubbing his forehead and eyes with his hand as Pierre came in. A short man was saying something to him, but as soon as Pierre came in, he fell silent and left.

"Ah, greetings, great warrior!" said Rastopchin as soon as the man left. "We've heard about your *prouesses*!* But that's not the point. *Mon cher, entre nous,*† are you a Mason?" Count Rastopchin said in a stern tone, as if there was something wrong with it, but he intended to forgive it. Pierre said nothing. "*Mon cher, je suis bien informé,*‡ but I know that there are Masons and Masons, and I hope you don't belong to those who, on the pretence of saving mankind, want to ruin Russia."

"Yes, I am a Mason," Pierre replied.

"Well, there you see, my dear. I suppose you're not unaware of the fact that Messrs. Speransky and Magnitsky have been sent where they belong; the same

*Exploits.
†My dear, between us.
‡My dear, I am well informed.

has been done with Mr. Klyucharev,[10] and the same with some others, who, on the pretence of building the temple of Solomon, were trying to destroy the temple of their fatherland. You can understand that there are reasons for that, and that I could not have banished our postmaster general if he had not been a harmful man. Now I am informed that you sent him your carriage so that he could leave the city and that you even took some papers from him for safe-keeping. I like you and don't wish you any harm, and since you're half my age, I advise you like a father to stop all contacts with that sort of people and leave here as soon as possible."

"But what is Klyucharev guilty of, Count?" asked Pierre.

"That's for me to know and not for you to ask," exclaimed Rastopchin.

"If he's accused of distributing Napoleon's proclamations, that hasn't been proved," said Pierre (not looking at Rastopchin), "and Vereshchagin . . ."

"*Nous y voilà,*"* Rastopchin, suddenly frowning, exclaimed still more loudly than before, interrupting Pierre. "Vereshchagin is a traitor and a turncoat, who will get the punishment he deserves," said Rastopchin, with that hot anger with which people speak remembering an offence. "But I didn't send for you in order to discuss my affairs, but so as to give you a piece of advice, or an order, if you prefer that. I ask you to stop all contacts with gentlemen the likes of Klyucharev and to leave here. And I'll knock the foolishness out of anyone who has it in him." And, probably realizing that he seemed to be shouting at Bezukhov, who so far was not guilty of anything, he added, taking Pierre's hand amiably: "*Nous sommes à la veille d'un désastre publique, et je n'ai pas le temps de dire des gentillesses à tous ceux qui ont affaire à moi.* My head sometimes gets in a whirl! *Eh bien, mon cher, qu'est-ce que vous faites, vous personellement?*"†

"*Mais rien,*"‡ Pierre replied, still without raising his eyes or changing the expression of his pensive face.

The count frowned.

"*Un conseil d'ami, mon cher. Décampez et au plutôt, c'est tout ce que je vous dis. À bon entendeur salut!* Goodbye, my dear. Ah, yes," he called to him from the doorway, "is it true that the countess has fallen into the clutches *des saints pères de la Société de Jésus?*"§

Pierre made no reply and, frowning and angry as no one had ever seen him, left Rastopchin's office.

*There we are.
†We're on the eve of a public disaster, and I don't have time to say nice things to all those who have business with me . . . Well, my dear, what are you doing, you personally?
‡Why, nothing.
§A piece of friendly advice, my dear. Decamp, and as soon as possible, that's all I say to you. He's saved who listens well! . . . the holy fathers of the Society of Jesus?

. . .

When he reached home, it was already dusk. Some eight different people visited him that evening. The secretary of a committee, the colonel of his battalion, his steward, his butler, and various petitioners. They all had business with Pierre, which he was supposed to decide. Pierre understood nothing, was not interested in these matters, and to all questions gave such answers as would rid him of these people. Left alone at last, he opened and read his wife's letter.

"*They*—the soldiers at the battery, Prince Andrei killed . . . the old man . . . Simplicity is obedience to God. One must suffer . . . meaning of everything . . . must hitch together . . . my wife's getting married . . . Must forget and understand . . ." And going to his bed, he collapsed on it without undressing and fell asleep at once.

When he woke up the next morning, his butler came to tell him that a specially sent police official had come from Count Rastopchin to find out whether Count Bezukhov had left or was leaving.

Some ten people of various sorts, having business with Pierre, were waiting for him in the drawing room. Pierre hurriedly dressed and, instead of going to those who were waiting for him, went to the back door and from there left through the gate.

From then on until the end of the devastation of Moscow, no one of the Bezukhov household, in spite of all their searching, saw any more of Pierre or knew where he was.

XII

The Rostovs remained in the city until the first of September, that is, until the eve of the enemy's entrance into Moscow.

After Petya joined Obolensky's Cossack regiment and left for Belaya Tserkov, where the regiment was being formed, the countess was overcome with fear. The thought that both of her sons were at war, that they were both no longer under her wing, that today or tomorrow either one of them, and maybe both together, like the three sons of one of her acquaintances, might be killed, now for the first time, during that summer, came to her mind with a cruel clarity. She tried to call Nikolai back, tried to go to Petya herself, or to arrange a place for him somewhere in Petersburg, but both proved impossible. Petya could not be sent back except with his regiment or by means of a transfer to another active regiment. Nikolai was somewhere with the army and, after his last letter, in which he had described in detail his meeting with Princess Marya, had not been heard from again. The countess did not sleep at night or, when she did, saw her sons killed in her dreams. After many discussions and negoti-

ations, the count finally thought of a means to calm the countess. He transferred Petya from Obolensky's regiment to Bezukhov's regiment, which was
being formed outside Moscow. Though Petya remained in military service, the
countess, after this transfer, had the comfort of having at least one son under
her wing, and hoped to arrange things for her Petya so that he would not leave
her again and would always be assigned to places of service where there was no
chance of his getting into battle. While Nicolas alone was in danger, it seemed
to the countess (and she even felt sorry because of it) that she loved her eldest
more than the rest of her children; but when her youngest, the mischief, the
poor student, who broke everything in the house and pestered everybody, this
snub-nosed Petya, with his merry, dark eyes, fresh ruddy cheeks barely touched
with down, ended up there, with those big, frightening, cruel men, who were
fighting over *something,* and found something joyful in it—it seemed to the
mother that it was him that she loved more, much more than all her other children. The closer it came to the time when the awaited Petya was to return to
Moscow, the more the countess's anxiety grew. She thought she would never
live to see that happiness. The presence not only of Sonya, but of her favourite
Natasha, even of her husband, vexed the countess. "What do I care about
them, I don't need anyone but Petya!" she thought.

In the last days of August, the Rostovs received a second letter from Nikolai.
He wrote from Voronezh province, where he had been sent for horses. This letter did not calm the countess. Knowing that one son was out of danger, she
began to worry still more about Petya.

Though by the twentieth of August almost all the Rostovs' acquaintances
had left Moscow, though everyone tried to persuade the countess to leave as
soon as possible, she would hear nothing about departure until her treasure,
her adored Petya, returned. On the twenty-eighth of August, Petya arrived.
The sixteen-year-old officer did not like the morbidly passionate tenderness
with which his mother met him. Though his mother concealed from him her
intention of not letting him go again from under her wing, Petya understood
her designs and, instinctively afraid of going soft with his mother, of turning
womanish (as he thought to himself), he treated her coldly, avoided her, and,
during his stay in Moscow, kept exclusively to the company of Natasha, for
whom he had always had a special, almost amorous, brotherly tenderness.

Owing to the count's habitual insouciance, nothing was ready for departure
on the twenty-eighth of August, and the carts expected from the Ryazan and
Moscow estates to transport all the possessions from the house arrived only on
the thirtieth.

From the twenty-eighth to the thirty-first of August, Moscow was all bustle
and commotion. Every day thousands of men wounded at the battle of Borodino were brought through the Dorogomilovo gate and distributed all over
Moscow, and thousands of carts with citizens and their possessions left

through other gates. Despite Rastopchin's posters, or independently of them, or on account of them, the most strange and contradictory news spread about town. Some said that no one was allowed to leave; some, on the contrary, said that all the icons had been removed from the churches and everybody was being sent away by force; some said that there had been another battle after Borodino, in which the French had been crushed; some said that, on the contrary, the whole Russian army had been annihilated; some spoke of the Moscow militia going to the Three Hills with the clergy at their head; some said on the quiet that Augustin had been ordered not to leave, that some traitors had been caught, that the muzhiks were rioting and robbing those who were leaving, and so on, and so forth. But that was only talk, while in reality both those who were leaving and those who were staying (though the council in Fili at which it was decided to abandon Moscow had not taken place yet) felt, though without showing it, that Moscow would certainly be surrendered and that they had to take themselves away as soon as possible and save their possessions. They felt that everything was suddenly going to break up and change, but up to the first nothing had changed yet. As a criminal led out to execution knows that he is about to die, yet still looks around and straightens the hat he has put on askew, so Moscow involuntarily went on with her usual life, though she knew that the time of her destruction was near, when all the conventions of life, which people were accustomed to obey, would be broken.

In the course of those three days that preceded the capture of Moscow, the whole Rostov family found themselves bustling in various ways. The head of the family, Count Ilya Andreich, constantly drove around town gathering the rumours that came from all sides, and at home gave generally superficial and hasty instructions about preparing for departure.

The countess supervised the storing of things, was displeased with everything, and followed after Petya, who was constantly running away from her, jealous of Natasha over him, because he spent all his time with her. Sonya alone saw to the practical side of the matter: the packing of things. But Sonya had been especially sad and taciturn all the time recently. Nicolas's letter, in which he mentioned Princess Marya, had provoked the countess into talking joyfully in Sonya's presence about seeing God's providence in the meeting of Marya and Nicolas.

"I was never glad," said the countess, "when Bolkonsky was Natasha's fiancé, but I have always wished, and have a presentiment, that Nikolenka would marry the princess. And what a good thing it would be!"

Sonya felt that that was true, that the only possibility of mending the Rostovs' affairs was marriage to a rich girl, and the princess was a good match. But she felt very bitter. In spite of her grief, or maybe precisely because of it, she took upon herself all the difficulties of arranging for the storing and packing of things and was busy all day long. The count and countess turned to her when they needed to give some order. Petya and Natasha, on the contrary, not only did not help their parents, but mostly pestered and hindered everyone in the house. And for almost the whole day their running, shouting, and causeless laughter were heard in the house. They laughed and made merry not at all because there was any reason for laughter; but their souls were filled with joy and mirth because for them everything that happened was a cause of joy and laughter. Petya was merry because, having left home a boy, he had returned (so everyone told him) a fine man; he was merry because he was at home, because from Belaya Tserkov, where there was no hope of getting into battle, he had ended up in Moscow, where there would be fighting any day; and above all he was merry because Natasha, whose moods he was always subject to, was merry. Natasha was merry because she had been sad for too long, and now nothing reminded her of the cause of her sadness, and she was in good health. She was also merry because there was a person who admired her (the admiration of others was that grease for the wheels which was necessary if her machine was to run perfectly freely), and Petya admired her. And above all they were merry because there was war near Moscow, there would be fighting at the city gates, weapons were being distributed, everyone was fleeing, going somewhere, and in general something extraordinary was happening, which is always joyful for a person, especially a young one.

XIII

On Saturday, the thirty-first of August, everything in the Rostovs' house seemed turned upside down. All the doors were open, all the furniture had been taken out or moved around, the mirrors and paintings had been taken down. There were trunks in the rooms; straw, wrapping paper, and string lay about. Muzhiks and servants, carrying things out, tramped heavily over the parquet floors. The courtyard was crowded with peasant carts, some already filled to the top and tied up, some still empty.

The voices and footsteps of the huge number of servants and of the muzhiks coming with carts rang out, calling to each other in the courtyard and the house. The count had been away somewhere since morning. The countess, who had a headache from the fuss and noise, lay in the new sitting room, her head wrapped in a cloth with vinegar. Petya was not at home (he had gone to see a friend, with whom he intended to transfer from the militia to the active army). Sonya was in the reception room, seeing to the packing of the crystal and china. Natasha was sitting on the floor in her devastated room, amidst the scattered dresses, ribbons, scarves, staring fixedly at the floor, holding in her hands an old ball gown, the same one (already out of fashion) in which she had gone to a Petersburg ball for the first time.

Natasha was ashamed to be doing nothing in the house, when everybody was so busy, and since morning she had tried several times to do something, but her heart was not in it; and she could not and did not know how to do things if not with all her heart, with all her might. She stood over Sonya while she packed the china, wanted to help, but abandoned it at once and went to her room to pack her own things. At first she amused herself by giving her dresses and ribbons to the maids, but then, when she had to pack the rest of them, she found it boring.

"Dunyasha, darling, will you pack? Yes? Yes?"

And when Dunyasha willingly promised to do it all, Natasha sat on the floor, took her old ball gown in her hands, and fell to thinking of something that should not have concerned her at all now. She was brought out of her reverie by the talk of the girls in the maids' room next door and the sound of their footsteps hurrying from the room to the back porch. Natasha got up and looked out of the window. In the street an enormous train of wounded had stopped.

The girls, the footmen, the housekeeper, the nanny, the cooks, the coachmen, the postilions, the scullions, were standing at the gates, looking at the wounded.

Natasha covered her hair with a white kerchief and, holding it by the ends with both hands, went outside.

Their former housekeeper, old Mavra Kuzminishna, had separated from the crowd that stood by the gate and, going up to a cart with a bast hood over it, was talking with a pale young officer who lay in the cart. Natasha took several steps and stopped timidly, still holding her kerchief and listening to what the housekeeper was saying.

"What, have you got nobody in Moscow?" Mavra Kuzminishna was saying. "You'd be more comfortable staying somewhere . . . With us, even. The masters are leaving."

"I don't know if it's allowed," the officer said in a weak voice. "Here's my superior . . . ask him." And he pointed to a fat major who was coming back down the street along the row of carts.

Natasha peeked with frightened eyes into the wounded officer's face and immediately went to meet the major.

"May the wounded stay in our house?" she asked.

The major put his hand to his visor with a smile.

"Whom do you want, Mamzelle?" he said, narrowing his eyes and smiling.

Natasha calmly repeated her question, and her face and her whole manner, even though she went on holding her kerchief by the corners, were so serious that the major stopped smiling and, reflecting at first, as if asking himself to what extent it was possible, replied in the affirmative.

"Oh, yes, why not, they may," he said.

Natasha inclined her head slightly and with quick steps returned to Mavra

Kuzminishna, who was standing over the officer, talking to him with pitying sympathy.

"They may, he says they may!" Natasha said in a whisper.

The officer in the hooded cart turned into the Rostovs' courtyard, and dozens of carts with wounded, at the invitation of the town's inhabitants, began turning into the yards and driving up to the entrances of houses on Povarskaya Street. Natasha clearly liked these relations with new people, outside the ordinary conditions of life. Together with Mavra Kuzminishna, she tried to get as many of the wounded as possible to turn into their courtyard.

"All the same you must tell your father," said Mavra Kuzminishna.

"Never mind, never mind, it makes no difference! We'll move into the drawing room for a day. We can let them have our whole half."

"Well, miss, what an idea! Even if they just go to the wings, the spare room, and nanny's room, you still must ask."

"Well, I'll ask then."

Natasha ran into the house and went on tiptoe through the half-open door to the sitting room, from which came the smell of vinegar and Hoffmann's drops.

"Are you asleep, mama?"

"Ah, as if I could sleep!" the countess, who had just dozed off, said, waking up.

"Mama, darling," said Natasha, kneeling before her mother and putting her face close to hers. "It's my fault, forgive me, I'll never do it again, I woke you up. Mavra Kuzminishna sent me, they've brought some wounded officers, will you allow them to? . . . They've got nowhere to go; I know you'll allow them to . . ." she spoke quickly, without pausing for breath.

"What officers? Whom have they brought? I don't understand anything," said the countess.

Natasha laughed; the countess also smiled weakly.

"I knew you'd say yes . . . so I'll tell them." And Natasha kissed her mother, got up, and went to the door.

In the reception room she met her father, who had come home with bad news.

"We've sat ourselves out!" the count said with involuntary vexation. "The club's closed, the police are leaving."

"Papa, is it all right that I've invited the wounded into the house?" Natasha said to him.

"Of course it's all right," the count said absent-mindedly. "That's not the point. I'm now asking you not to be taken up with trifles, but to help pack and leave, leave tomorrow . . ." And the count gave the same orders to the butler and the servants. At dinner Petya, who had come home, told them his news.

He said that weapons had been distributed to the people that day in the

Kremlin, that, though Rastopchin's poster had said he would give the call two days beforehand, the orders had certainly already been given that all the people should go to the Three Hills tomorrow with their weapons, and a major battle would take place there.

The countess kept glancing with timid horror at her son's merry, flushed face as he was saying that. She knew that if she said a word about it, if she asked Petya not to go to this battle (she knew he was glad of this impending battle), he would say something about men, honour, the fatherland—something senseless, masculine, obstinate, against which it would be impossible to object—and the matter would be spoiled, and therefore, hoping to arrange everything so as to leave before then and take Petya along as a defender and protector, she said nothing to Petya, but summoned the count after dinner and tearfully implored him to take her away quickly, that same night if possible. With the involuntary feminine cunning of love, she, who so far had shown perfect fearlessness, said that she would die of fear unless they left that night. She was afraid of everything now, without feigning.

XIV

Mme Schoss, who had gone to see her daughter, increased the countess's fear still more by telling her what she had seen in Myasnitskaya Street at a drinking establishment on her way home. As she came down the street, she had been unable to reach home because of a drunken crowd of people rioting outside the establishment. She had hired a cab and come home by a back lane; and the cabby had told her that people were breaking open the barrels in the drinking establishment, that they had been ordered to.

After dinner the whole Rostov household, with enthusiastic haste, got to work packing things and preparing for departure. The old count, suddenly getting to work after dinner, kept going back and forth from the yard to the house, shouting senselessly at the hurrying people, telling them to hurry still more. Petya was in charge in the courtyard. Sonya did not know what to do under the influence of the count's contradictory orders, and was completely at a loss. People, shouting, arguing, and making noise, rushed about the rooms and the courtyard. Natasha, with her typical passion in everything, also suddenly got to work. At first her interference in the work of packing was met with mistrust. Everybody expected some joke from her and did not want to obey her; but she stubbornly and passionately demanded to be obeyed, became angry, all but wept that they did not listen to her, and finally got them to believe her. Her first exploit, which cost her enormous effort and gave her power, was packing the rugs. In the count's house there were costly Gobelin tapestries and Persian carpets. When Natasha got down to work, there were two open crates standing in the reception room: one was filled almost to the top with china, the other with carpets. There was also a good deal of china standing on the tables and more was being brought from the storeroom. A new, third crate had to be started, and people went for one.

"Wait, Sonya, we'll be able to fit everything in," said Natasha.

"It's impossible, miss, we've already tried," said the pantryman.

"No, please wait." And Natasha began taking the dishes and plates wrapped in paper out of the crate.

"The dishes ought to be put in here with the carpets," she said.

"We'll be lucky if we get the carpets into three crates as it is," said the pantryman.

"Wait, please." And Natasha quickly, deftly began sorting things. "Those we don't need," she said of the Kievan plates. "These, yes, these go in with the carpets," she said of the Saxony dishes.

"Let it be, Natasha. Enough, now, we'll pack," Sonya said with reproach.

"Eh, miss!" said the butler. But Natasha did not give in, threw all the things out, and quickly began repacking, deciding that the inferior domestic carpets and extra dishes should not be taken at all. When everything had been taken out, they began packing again. And indeed, having discarded almost all the cheap things that were not worth taking along, they fitted all the costly things into two crates. Only the lid of the carpet crate would not close. A few things could have been taken out, but Natasha insisted on having her way. She packed and repacked, pressed down, made the pantryman and Petya, whom she drew into the business of packing, press down on the lid, and made desperate efforts herself.

"Enough, Natasha," Sonya said to her. "I see you're right, just take out the one on top."

"I don't want to," cried Natasha, holding her loosened hair away from her sweaty face with one hand and pressing down on the carpets with the other. "Press on it, Petka, press on it! Vassilyich, press down on it!" she cried. The carpets got pressed down and the lid closed. Natasha clapped her hands and squealed with joy, and tears burst from her eyes. But that lasted only a second. She at once took up another task, and now they trusted her fully, and the count was not angry when he was told that Natalya Ilyinichna had cancelled his order, and the servants came to Natasha to ask if they should tie up a cart or not, and was it sufficiently loaded? The work went swimmingly owing to Natasha's directions: the unnecessary things were left and the most costly ones were packed in as tightly as possible.

But however everyone bustled, by late at night they could not get everything packed. The countess fell asleep, and the count, having postponed their departure till morning, went to bed.

Sonya and Natasha slept in the sitting room without undressing.

That night one more wounded man was transported down Povarskaya, and Mavra Kuzminishna, who was standing at the gate, had him turn in at the Rostovs'. This wounded man was, to Mavra Kuzminishna's mind, a very important one. He was being transported in a caleche with the apron completely closed and the hood down. On the box beside the driver sat an old man, a venerable valet. A doctor and two soldiers followed behind in a wagon.

"Do come to us, if you please. The masters are leaving, the whole house is empty," said the old woman, addressing the old servant.

"Why not," the valet answered, sighing, "we don't hope to make it! We have our own house in Moscow, but it's far, and there's nobody living there."

"Kindly come in, our masters have plenty of everything, if you please," said Mavra Kuzminishna. "What, is he very unwell?" she added.

The valet waved his hand.

"We don't hope to make it! You must ask the doctor." And the valet got down from the box and went to the wagon.

"All right," said the doctor.

The valet came back to the caleche, looked into it, shook his head, told the driver to turn into the courtyard, and stopped beside Mavra Kuzminishna.

"Lord Jesus Christ!" she said.

Mavra Kuzminishna suggested that the wounded man be taken into the house.

"My masters won't say anything . . ." she said. But they had to avoid carrying him upstairs, and therefore the wounded man was taken to the wing and put in Mme Schoss's former room. This wounded man was Prince Andrei Bolkonsky.

XV

Moscow's last day came. The weather was clear, cheerful, autumnal. It was Sunday. As on an ordinary Sunday, the bells were ringing for the liturgy in all the churches. No one, it seemed, could yet grasp what was in store for Moscow.

Only two indicators of the condition of society expressed the state Moscow was in: the mob, that is, the estate of the poor, and the prices of products. An enormous crowd of factory workers, servants, and muzhiks, mixed with clerks, seminarians, and noblemen, went out to the Three Hills early in the morning of that day. They stood there and waited in vain for Rastopchin, and, realizing that Moscow would be surrendered, this crowd dispersed to pothouses and taverns all over Moscow. The prices that day also indicated the state of things. The prices of weapons, gold, carts, and horses kept going up, while the prices of paper money and city things kept going down, so that by the middle of the day there were occasions when cabbies drove off with expensive goods, like broadcloth, for half the price, while a peasant horse was sold for five hundred roubles. Furniture, mirrors, bronze objects were given away for nothing.

In the sedate old household of the Rostovs, the breakdown of the former conditions of life expressed itself very faintly. In regard to the servants, the only thing was that three persons from the enormous staff disappeared during the night; but nothing was stolen; and in regard to the prices of things, it turned out that the thirty carts that had come from their country estates amounted to enormous wealth, which was envied by many and for which the Rostovs were offered enormous sums. Not only were enormous sums offered for these carts, but in the evening and early in the morning of the first of September, orderlies and servants sent by wounded officers kept coming to the Rostovs' courtyard, and wounded men placed with the Rostovs and neighbours came dragging themselves, imploring the Rostovs' servants to intercede for them to be given carts in order to leave Moscow. The butler, to whom these requests were addressed, though he pitied the wounded, resolutely refused, saying he would not dare even inform the count of it. However pitiful these abandoned wounded were, it was obvious that if they were to give them one cart, there would be no reason not to give them more, all—and their own carriages as well. Thirty carts would not save all the wounded, and amidst the general disaster, it was impossible not to think of oneself and one's own family. So the butler thought for his master.

Waking up on the morning of the first, Count Ilya Andreich quietly left the bedroom, trying not to wake the countess, who had fallen asleep only towards morning, and in his purple silk dressing gown went out to the porch. The tied-down carts stood in the courtyard. By the porch stood the carriages. The butler stood by the entrance, talking with an old orderly and a pale young officer with his arm in a sling. The butler, seeing the count, gave the officer and the orderly a meaningful and stern sign to withdraw.

"Well, is everything ready, Vassilyich?" said the count, rubbing his bald pate, glancing good-naturedly at the officer and the orderly and nodding to them. (The count liked new faces.)

"We can hitch up at once, Your Excellency."

"Well, that's nice, the countess will wake up, and God speed us! What about you, gentlemen?" he turned to the officer. "Are you staying in my house?" The officer moved closer. His pale face suddenly flushed with bright colour.

"Do me a favour, Count, allow me . . . for God's sake . . . to take refuge somewhere on one of your carts. I've got nothing with me. I'll get on top . . . it won't matter . . ." Before the officer finished, the orderly came up to the count with the same request for his master.

"Ah, yes, yes yes!" the count said quickly. "I'll be very glad to. Vassilyich, arrange it so that one or two carts are cleared there . . . whatever . . . whatever's necessary . . ." the count said, ordering something in some sort of indefinite terms. But at that same instant the ardent expression of gratitude from the officer confirmed what he had ordered. The count looked around: in the courtyard, in the gateway, in the windows of the wing, wounded men and orderlies could be seen. They were all looking at the count and moving towards the porch.

"If you please, Your Excellency, come to the gallery: what are your instructions concerning the paintings?" said the butler. And the count went into the house with him, repeating his order about not refusing the wounded who asked to ride along.

"Well, why not, you can take something out," he added in a soft, secretive voice, as if fearing that someone might overhear him.

At nine o'clock the countess woke up, and Matryona Timofeevna, her former maid, who carried out the functions of a police chief with the countess, came to report to her former young lady that Marya Karlovna was very offended and that the young ladies' summer dresses could not be left behind. On the countess's enquiries as to why Mme Schoss was offended, it was discovered that her trunk had been taken off the cart, and all the carts were being untied, the chattels taken out, and wounded men put in, whom the count, in his simplicity, had ordered to be taken along. The countess ordered her husband sent for.

"What is it, my friend, I hear things are being unloaded again?"

"You know, *ma chère,* here is what I wanted to tell you . . . *ma chère* little countess . . . an officer came to me, they ask to be given several carts for the wounded. These things all come and go; but think how it is for them to stay! . . . Really, there are officers here in our courtyard, we invited them in ourselves . . . You know, I think, really, *ma chère,* well, *ma chère,* let's take them . . . What's the hurry? . . ." The count said this timidly, as he always spoke when it had to do with money. The countess was accustomed to this tone, which always preceded something ruinous for their children, like some sort of building of a gallery or conservatory, the organizing of a home theatre or musical performances—and being accustomed to it, she considered it her duty always to fight against whatever was expressed in that timid tone.

She assumed her submissively tearful air and said to her husband:

"Listen, Count, you've brought it to the point that we're getting nothing for the house, and now you want to destroy all our—our *children's* property. You say yourself there's a hundred thousand roubles' worth of things in the house. I don't consent, my friend, I don't consent. As you wish! But it's for the government to take care of the wounded. They know it. Look: across the street, the Lopukhins cleared everything out two days ago. That's how people do it. We're the only fools. If you don't pity me, pity the children."

The count waved his hands and, saying nothing, left the room.

"Papa! What's this about?" said Natasha, who had followed him into her mother's room.

"Nothing! What business is it of yours!" the count said angrily.

"No, I heard," said Natasha. "Why doesn't mama want it?"

"What business is it of yours?" cried the count. Natasha went to the window and fell to thinking.

"Papa, Berg has come to see us," she said, looking out of the window.

XVI

Berg, the Rostovs' son-in-law, was already a colonel with a Vladimir and an Anna on the neck[11] and occupied the same quiet and agreeable post of assistant to the chief of staff, assistant to the first section chief of staff of the second corps.

On the first of September, he arrived in Moscow from the army.

He had nothing to do in Moscow; but he had noticed that everybody in the army asked to go to Moscow and had something to do there. He also considered it necessary to ask for leave on household and family business.

Berg, in his neat little droshky with a pair of well-fed grey horses, exactly like those of a certain prince, drove up to his father-in-law's house. He looked attentively at the carts in the courtyard and, going up on the porch, took out a clean handkerchief and tied a knot in it.[12]

From the front hall Berg ran with a gliding, impatient step into the drawing room and embraced the count, kissed Natasha's and Sonya's hands, and hastened to ask after mama's health.

"Who talks about health now? Well, go on, tell us," said the count, "what's with the troops? Are they retreating or will there be a battle?"

"Only the pre-eternal God can decide the fate of the fatherland, papa," said Berg. "The army is burning with the spirit of heroism, and now the leaders, so to speak, have gathered in council. No one knows what will happen. But I'll tell you in general, papa, that such a heroic spirit, the truly ancient courage of the Russian army, which they—it," he corrected himself, "showed or displayed in that battle of the twenty-sixth—no words can worthily describe . . . I'll tell you, papa" (he beat his breast the way a certain general, talking about it in his presence, had beaten his breast, though a little late, because he should have beaten his breast at the words "Russian army"), "I'll tell you openly that we superiors not only did not have to urge the soldiers on or anything like that, but we could hardly restrain those, those . . . yes, those courageous and ancient exploits," he said in a rapid patter. "General Barclay de Tolly risked his life everywhere at the head of his troops, I can tell you. Our corps was stationed on the side of a hill. Can you imagine it!" And here Berg told everything he could

remember from various stories he had heard since that time. Natasha, not taking her eyes away, which embarrassed Berg, looked at him as if seeking the
answer to some question in his face.

"In general, such heroism as the Russian troops displayed is impossible to
imagine and praise worthily!" said Berg, glancing at Natasha and smiling at
her, as if trying to placate her, in response to her stubborn gaze . . . " 'Russia is
not in Moscow, she is in the hearts of her sons!' Right, papa?" said Berg.

Just then the countess came in from the sitting room, with a weary and displeased air. Berg hastily jumped up, kissed the countess's hand, asked after her
health, and, expressing his sympathy with a wagging of the head, stood beside her.

"Yes, mama, I tell you truly, these are hard and sad times for any Russian.
But why worry so? You still have time to leave . . ."

"I don't understand what the servants are doing," said the countess, turning
to her husband. "I've just been told that nothing is ready. Somebody has to be
in charge. This is when I miss Mitenka. There'll be no end to it!"

The count was about to say something, but evidently restrained himself. He
got up from his chair and went to the door.

Berg took out his handkerchief just then, as if to blow his nose, and, looking
at the knot, fell to thinking, shaking his head sadly and significantly.

"I have a big favour to ask of you, papa," he said.

"Hm? . . ." said the count, stopping.

"I was just driving past Yusupov's house," Berg said, laughing. "The steward, an acquaintance of mine, ran out and asked if I'd like to buy anything. I
went in, out of curiosity, you know, and there was this little chiffonier and a
dressing table. You know how Verushka wanted one and how we argued over
it." (Berg involuntarily passed into a tone of joy at his comfortable life, when
he began talking about the little chiffonier and the dressing table.) "And it's so
lovely! It pulls out, and there's an English secret compartment, you know? And
Verushka has wanted one for a long time. I'd like so much to give her a surprise. I saw so many of those muzhiks in your courtyard. Please let me have
one, I'll pay him well, and . . ."

The count winced and began clearing his throat.

"Ask the countess, I'm not in charge."

"If it's any trouble, please don't bother," said Berg. "I just wanted it so much
for Verushka."

"Ah, go to the devil, all of you, to the devil, the devil, the devil! . . ." cried the
old count. "My head's spinning." And he left the room.

The countess began to cry.

"Yes, yes, mama, these are very hard times!" said Berg.

Natasha left with her father and, as if having difficulty figuring something
out, first followed after him, then ran downstairs.

Petya was standing on the porch, handing out weapons to the servants who were leaving Moscow. The hitched-up carts were still standing in the court-yard. Two of them had been unloaded, and an officer, supported by his orderly, was getting into one of them.

"Do you know why?" Petya asked Natasha (Natasha understood what Petya meant: why their father and mother had quarrelled). She did not reply.

"Because papa wanted to give all the carts to the wounded," said Petya. "Vassilyich told me. In my opinion . . ."

"In my opinion," Natasha suddenly almost shouted, turning her angry face to Petya, "in my opinion, this is so vile, so loathsome, so . . . I don't know what! Are we some sort of Germans? . . ." Her throat trembled with convulsive sobs, and, afraid of weakening and expending the charge of her anger for noth-ing, she turned and rushed precipitously up the stairs. Berg was sitting by the countess and, with respectful intimacy, was trying to comfort her. The count was pacing the room with his pipe in his hands, when Natasha, her face dis-torted by anger, stormed into the room and with quick steps went up to her mother.

"This is vile! This is loathsome!" she shouted. "It can't be that you ordered it."

Berg and the countess looked at her in perplexity and fear. The count stopped by the window, listening.

"Mama, this can't be; look at what's happening in the courtyard!" she shouted. "They're being left! . . ."

"What's the matter with you? Who are 'they'? What do you want?"

"The wounded, that's who! It can't be, mama; it's like nothing . . . No, mama, darling, it's not right, please, forgive me, darling . . . What do we care what we take, only look at what's happening in the courtyard . . . Mama! . . . It can't be! . . ."

The count stood by the window and, without turning his face, listened to Natasha's words. Suddenly he snuffed his nose and brought his face close to the window.

The countess glanced at her daughter, saw her face ashamed for her mother, saw her agitation, understood why her husband did not turn to look at her now, and glanced around her with a lost air.

"Ah, do as you like! As if I'm hindering anybody!" she said, still not surren-dering outright.

"Mama, darling, forgive me!"

But the countess pushed her daughter aside and went up to the count.

"*Mon cher*, you give the necessary orders . . . I don't know about such things," she said, lowering her eyes guiltily.

"The eggs . . . the eggs are teaching the hen . . ." the count said through happy tears, and he embraced his wife, who was glad to hide her ashamed face on his chest.

"Papa, mama! May I give the orders? May I? . . ." asked Natasha. "We'll take the most necessary things anyway . . ." she said.

The count nodded affirmatively to her, and Natasha, running quickly, as she used to run when playing blindman's buff, rushed through the reception room to the front hall, down the steps, and into the courtyard.

People gathered around Natasha and could not believe the strange instructions she gave them, until the count himself, in his wife's name, confirmed the instructions to hand over all the carts to the wounded and put the trunks in the storerooms. Once they understood the instructions, the people, joyful and bustling, got down to the new task. Now the servants not only did not find it strange, but, on the contrary, it seemed as though it could not be otherwise; just as, a quarter of an hour before, not only had no one found it strange that the wounded should be left behind and objects taken along, but it had seemed as though it could not be otherwise.

The whole household, as if making up for not having done it earlier, began bustling about the new task of accommodating the wounded. The wounded crawled out of their rooms and with pale, joyful faces surrounded the carts. Rumour also reached the neighbouring houses that there were carts available, and the wounded from other houses started coming to the Rostovs' courtyard. Many of the wounded asked them not to unload the things but just to sit them on top. But, once begun, the business of dumping things could not be stopped. It made no difference whether everything was left or only half. The courtyard was strewn with the trunks of dishes, bronzes, paintings, and mirrors that had been so carefully packed the night before, and people were still seeking and finding possibilities for unloading one thing or another and providing more and more carts.

"We can take four more," said the steward, "I'm handing over my carriage, otherwise where will they go?"

"Hand over my wardrobe cart, too," said the countess. "Dunyasha will ride in the carriage with me."

The wardrobe cart was handed over and sent to fetch some wounded men two houses away. All the household and the servants were cheerfully animated. Natasha was in a state of rapturously happy animation, such as she had not experienced for a long time.

"Where shall we tie it on?" asked the servants, trying to fix a trunk to the narrow tailboard of the carriage. "You must leave us at least one cart."

"What's in it?" asked Natasha.

"The count's books."

"Leave it. Vassilyich will put it away. It's not needed."

The britzka was full of people; the question was where Pyotr Ilyich would sit.

"On the box. Will you sit on the box, Petya?" cried Natasha.

Sonya also bustled about constantly; but the goal of her bustling was the opposite of Natasha's. She was putting away the things that had to be left behind; she made a list of them, as the countess wished, and tried to take along as much as possible.

XVII

Towards two o'clock the Rostovs' four carriages, harnessed and packed, stood by the entrance. The carts of wounded were driving out of the courtyard one after another.

The caleche in which Prince Andrei was being transported, driving past the porch, caught the attention of Sonya, who, along with a maid, was arranging a seat for the countess in her enormous, high carriage, which stood by the entrance.

"Whose caleche is that?" asked Sonya, leaning out of the window of the carriage.

"Don't you know, miss?" the maid replied. "The wounded prince: he spent the night here and is also going with us."

"But who is he? What's his name?"

"It's our former fiancé himself, Prince Bolkonsky!" the maid answered with a sigh. "They say he's dying."

Sonya jumped out of the carriage and ran to the countess. The countess, already dressed for travelling, in a shawl and a hat, tired out, was pacing the drawing room waiting for the household, so as to sit with the door closed and pray before their departure.[13] Natasha was not in the room.

"*Maman*," said Sonya, "Prince Andrei is here, wounded, dying. He's going with us."

The countess opened her eyes fearfully and, seizing Sonya's hand, looked around.

"Natasha?" she said.

For both Sonya and the countess, this news had in the first moment only one meaning. They knew their Natasha, and the dread of what would happen to her at this news stifled in them any sympathy for the man, whom they both liked.

"Natasha doesn't know yet; but he's going with us," said Sonya.

"You say he's dying?"

Sonya nodded her head.

The countess embraced Sonya and wept.

"The ways of God are inscrutable!" she thought, feeling that in all that was now happening an almighty hand, which had previously been hidden from people's eyes, was beginning to show.

"Well, mama, everything's ready. What's the matter? . . ." Natasha asked, running into the room with an animated look.

"Nothing," said the countess. "Everything's ready, so let's go." And the countess bent over her reticule to hide her upset face. Sonya embraced Natasha and kissed her.

Natasha looked at her questioningly.

"What's wrong? What's happened?"

"Nothing . . . No . . ."

"Something very bad for me? . . . What is it?" the sensitive Natasha asked.

Sonya sighed and said nothing. The count, Petya, Mme Schoss, Mavra Kuzminishna, and Vassilyich came into the drawing room, and having closed the door, they all sat down and silently, not looking at each other, remained seated for several seconds.

The count got up first and with a loud sigh began crossing himself before the icon. They all did the same. Then the count began to embrace Mavra Kuzminishna and Vassilyich, who were to remain in Moscow, and, while they tried to take hold of his hand and kissed his shoulder, he patted them lightly on the back, murmuring something vague and tenderly soothing. The countess went to the icon room, and Sonya found her there, kneeling before the few remaining icons that hung here and there on the wall. (The icons most precious for the family's past they brought with them.)

On the porch and in the courtyard, the servants who were leaving, armed by Petya with daggers and swords, their trousers tucked into their boots, and tightly girded with belts and sashes, were saying goodbye to those who were staying.

As is usual during a departure, many things were forgotten or wrongly packed, and for some time two liveried postilions stood on either side of the open door and steps of the carriage, ready to help the countess in, while maids ran about with pillows and bundles from the house to the carriages, the caleche, the britzka, and back.

"They eternally forget everything!" said the countess. "Why, you know I can't sit like that." And Dunyasha, clenching her teeth and not replying, with an expression of reproach on her face, rushed into the carriage to rearrange the seat.

"Ah, these folk!" said the count, shaking his head.

The old coachman Efim, who was the only one with whom the countess would venture to ride, sitting high up on the box, did not even turn to look at what was happening behind him. He knew with his thirty years of experience that it would be a while before they told him "Godspeed!" and that once they had told him, they would stop him twice more and send for things they had forgotten, and after that would stop him once again, and the countess herself would stick her head out and beg him in Christ's name to drive more carefully on the descents. He knew it and therefore waited for what was to come more patiently than his horses (especially the chestnut on the left, Sokol, who pawed the ground and champed at the bit). At last everybody was seated, the steps were folded and flipped back into the carriage, the door banged shut, the strongbox was sent for, the countess leaned out and said what she ought. Then Efim slowly took off his hat and began crossing himself. The postilion and all the servants did the same.

"Godspeed!" said Efim, putting on his hat. "Whip 'em up!" The postilion started the horses. The right trace horse lunged into the collar, the high springs creaked, and the body rocked. A footman jumped up on the box in motion. The carriage jolted as it drove out of the courtyard onto the bumpy pavement, the other equipages jolted in the same way, and the train started up the street. Everyone in the carriages, the caleche, and the britzka crossed themselves before the church across the street. Those staying in Moscow walked on both sides of the equipages, seeing them off.

Natasha had rarely experienced such a joyful feeling as she experienced now, sitting in the carriage next to the countess and gazing at the walls slowly moving past her of alarmed, abandoned Moscow. She occasionally leaned out of the carriage window and looked up and down the long train of wounded that preceded them. Almost at the head of it she could see the closed top of Prince Andrei's caleche. She did not know who was in it, and each time she looked over the extent of her train, she sought that caleche with her eyes. She knew it was at the head of them all.

From Nikitskaya, from Presnia, from Podnovinsky Boulevard, several trains like the Rostovs' came together in Kudrino, and now two lines of carriages drove down Sadovaya.

Driving around the Sukhareva tower, Natasha, who was curiously and quickly studying the people driving and walking by, suddenly cried out with joyful surprise:

"Good heavens! Mama, Sonya, look, it's him!"

"Who? Who?"

"Look, for God's sake, it's Bezukhov!" said Natasha, leaning out of the carriage window and gazing at a tall, fat man in a coachman's kaftan, obviously a disguised gentleman by his gait and bearing, who, side by side with a sallow, beardless little old man in a frieze overcoat, was walking out from under the archway of the Sukhareva tower.

"By God, it's Bezukhov, in a kaftan, with some sort of little old boy! By God," Natasha said, "look, look!"

"No, it's not him. How can you talk such nonsense."

"Mama," Natasha shouted, "it's him, I'll bet you anything! I assure you. Wait, wait!" she shouted to the driver; but the driver could not stop, because more carts and carriages were driving out of Meshchanskaya Street, and they were shouting at the Rostovs to move on and not hold up others.

Indeed, though now much further away than before, all the Rostovs saw Pierre, or a man extraordinarily like Pierre, in a coachman's kaftan, walking down the street with a bowed head and a serious face, beside a little beardless old man who looked like a footman. The little old man noticed a face thrust out at him from the carriage and, respectfully touching Pierre's elbow, said something to him, pointing at the carriage. For a long time Pierre could not understand what he was saying, so immersed he obviously was in his thoughts. When he finally understood him, he looked in the direction he was pointing in and, recognizing Natasha, yielded to his first impression that same second and quickly made for the carriage. But, having gone some ten steps, he evidently remembered something and stopped.

Natasha's face, thrust out of the carriage window, beamed with mocking tenderness.

"Pyotr Kirilych! Come here! We recognized you! It's astonishing!" she shouted, giving him her hand. "How can it be? Why are you like this?"

Pierre took the hand held out to him and clumsily, in motion (since the carriage went on moving), kissed it.

"What's the matter with you, Count?" the countess asked in an astonished and commiserating voice.

"What? What? Why? Don't ask me," said Pierre, and he glanced at Natasha, whose radiant, joyful gaze (he felt it without glancing at her) poured its loveliness upon him.

"But you're not staying in Moscow, are you?"

Pierre was silent for a moment.

"In Moscow?" he said questioningly. "Yes, in Moscow. Goodbye."

"Ah, I wish I were a man, I'd certainly stay with you. Ah, that's so good!" said Natasha. "Mama, please let me stay." Pierre looked distractedly at Natasha and was about to say something, but the countess interrupted him.

"You were in the battle, we've heard?"

"Yes, I was," answered Pierre. "Tomorrow there will also be a battle . . ." he began, but Natasha interrupted him.

"But what's the matter with you, Count? You don't look yourself . . ."

"Ah, don't ask me, don't ask me, I know nothing myself. Tomorrow . . . But no! Goodbye, goodbye," he said, "terrible times!" And, dropping behind the carriage, he went back to the pavement.

Natasha leaned out of the window for a long time, beaming at him with her tender and slightly mocking, joyful smile.

XVIII

Pierre, since disappearing from his house, had been living for two days in the empty apartment of the late Bazdeev. Here is how it happened.

On waking up the day after his return to Moscow and his meeting with Count Rastopchin, Pierre could not understand for a long time where he was and what was wanted of him. When, among the names of other persons waiting for him in the waiting room, he was told there was also a Frenchman who had brought a letter from Countess Elena Vassilievna, he was suddenly overcome by that feeling of confusion and hopelessness he was apt to succumb to. He suddenly imagined that everything was over now, everything was mixed up, everything was destroyed, that no one was right or wrong, that there would be nothing in the future, and there was no way out of this situation. Smiling unnaturally and muttering something, he sat on the sofa in a helpless pose, then got up, went to the door, peeked through the crack into the waiting room, then, waving his hands, went back and picked up a book. The butler came for a second time to inform Pierre that the Frenchman who had brought the letter from the countess wished very much to see him at least for a moment, and that someone had come from the widow of I. A. Bazdeev, asking him to take the books, since Mrs. Bazdeev herself had left for the country.

"Ah, yes, at once, wait a moment . . . Or no . . . no, go and tell them I'll come at once," Pierre said to the butler.

But as soon as the butler left, Pierre took his hat, which was lying on the table, and left by the back door of his study. There was no one in the corridor. Pierre walked the whole length of the corridor to the stairway and, wincing and rubbing his forehead with both hands, went down to the first-floor landing. The porter was standing by the front door. From the landing where Pierre stood, another stairway led to the back door. Pierre went down it and walked out to the courtyard. No one had seen him. But in the street, as soon as he went out of the gate, the coachmen who were standing by the carriages and the caretaker saw their master and took their hats off to him. Feeling their gazes directed at him, Pierre behaved like an ostrich, which hides its head in a bush so as not to be seen; he lowered his head and, quickening his pace, went down the street.

Of all the matters that faced Pierre that morning, to him the most important seemed to be sorting the books and papers of Iosif Alexeevich.

He took the first cab that came along and told the driver to take him to the Patriarch's Ponds, where the widow Bazdeev's house was.

Glancing constantly at the carts of those leaving Moscow, which were moving on all sides, and shifting his fat body so as not to slip off the old, rattling droshky, Pierre, experiencing a joyful feeling similar to that experienced by a boy who has run away from school, fell to talking with the cabby.

The cabby told him that weapons were being distributed that day in the Kremlin, and that the next day the people would all be driven out of the Three Hills gate and there would be a big battle.

Having reached the Patriarch's Ponds, Pierre found Bazdeev's house, where he had not been for a long time. He went to the gate. Gerasim, the same sallow, beardless little old man whom Pierre had seen five years before in Torzhok with Iosif Alexeevich, came out to his knocking.

"Is the lady at home?" asked Pierre.

"Owing to the present circumstances, Your Excellency, Sofya Danilovna has left with the children for the Torzhok estate."

"I'll come in anyway, I've got to sort the books," said Pierre.

"Please do, you're very welcome. Makar Alexeevich, the brother of the deceased—God rest his soul!—has stayed on here, but, as you are so good as to know, he's given to a certain weakness," said the old servant.

Makar Alexeevich was, as Pierre knew, the half-mad brother of Iosif Alexeevich, and given to heavy drinking.

"Yes, yes, I know. Let's go, let's go . . ." said Pierre, and he went into the house. A tall, bald old man in a dressing gown, with a red nose and galoshes on his bare feet, was standing in the front hall. Seeing Pierre, he angrily muttered something and went to the corridor.

"He was a great mind, but now, if you please, look how feeble he's become," said Gerasim. "Would you like to go to the study?" Pierre nodded. "The study has stayed the way it was when it was first sealed. Sofya Danilovna ordered that, if someone came from you, he was to be given the books."

Pierre entered the same gloomy study he used to enter with such awe while his benefactor was alive. This study, dusty and untouched since Iosif Alexeevich's demise, was gloomier still.

Gerasim opened one shutter and tiptoed out of the room. Pierre walked around the study, went to the bookcase in which the manuscripts lay, and took out what had once been one of the most important sacred objects of the order. These were the authentic Scottish charters, with his benefactor's notes and commentaries. He sat down at the dusty writing table and placed the manuscripts before him, opened them, closed them, and, finally, moving them aside, propped his head in his hands and lapsed into thought.

Gerasim cautiously peeked into the study several times and saw Pierre sitting in the same position. More than two hours went by. Gerasim allowed himself to make some noise by the door so as to attract Pierre's attention. Pierre did not hear him.

"Do you wish me to dismiss the cabby?"

"Ah, yes," said Pierre, coming to his senses and hastening to stand up. "Listen," he said, taking Gerasim by the button of his frock coat and looking down on the old man with shining, moist, rapturous eyes. "Listen, do you know that there will be a battle tomorrow? . . ."

"There's been talk of it," replied Gerasim.

"I ask you to tell no one who I am. And to do what I tell you . . ."

"Yes, sir," said Gerasim. "Do you wish to be served some food?"

"No, but I need something else. I need peasant clothes and a pistol," said Pierre, suddenly blushing.

"Yes, sir," said Gerasim, after a moment's thought.

All the rest of that day Pierre spent alone in his benefactor's study, pacing restlessly, as Gerasim could hear, from one corner to the other, talking to himself, and he spent the night on a bed made up for him there.

Gerasim, with the habit of a servant who had seen all sorts of strange things in his life, accepted Pierre's moving in without surprise and seemed pleased that he had someone to serve. That same evening, without even asking himself what they were needed for, he obtained a kaftan and hat for Pierre and promised to get the requested pistol the next day. That evening Makar Alexeevich, shuffling in his galoshes, twice came to the door and stopped, looking ingratiatingly at Pierre. But as soon as Pierre turned to him, he bashfully and angrily wrapped his dressing gown round him and hastily retreated. It was when Pierre, in a coachman's kaftan, acquired and steam-cleaned for him by Gerasim, was going with him to buy a pistol near the Sukhareva tower, that he met the Rostovs.

XIX

On the night of the first of September, Kutuzov's order was given for the retreat of the Russian troops through Moscow to the Ryazan road.

The first troops set out at night. The troops moving by night did not hurry and moved slowly and measuredly; but at dawn the moving troops, approaching the Dorogomilovo bridge, saw ahead of them, on this side, endless masses of troops crowding, hurrying over the bridge and, on the other side, climbing up and clogging the streets and lanes, while more troops were pressing behind them. And they were seized by a groundless haste and anxiety. They all rushed ahead towards the bridge, onto the bridge, to the fords and into the boats. Kutuzov had ordered himself taken round by the back streets to the other side of Moscow.

By ten o'clock in the morning of the second of September, only the troops of the rear guard remained at large in the Dorogomilovo suburb. The army was already on the other side of Moscow and beyond Moscow.

At that same time, at ten o'clock in the morning of the second of September,

Napoleon was standing among his troops on Poklonnaya Hill and looking at the spectacle spread out before him. Beginning with the twenty-sixth of August and until the second of September, from the battle of Borodino to the enemy's entry into Moscow, in all the days of that anxious, memorable week, there had been that extraordinary autumn weather, always astonishing for people, when the low sun gives more heat than in spring, when everything glistens in the rarefied, clear air so that the eyes hurt, when the chest feels stronger and fresher inhaling the fragrant autumn air, when even the nights are warm, and when in those dark, warm nights the sky, frightening and gladdening, ceaselessly pours down golden stars.

On the second of September, at ten o'clock in the morning, the weather was like that. The brilliance of the morning was magical. Moscow, from Poklonnaya Hill, spread out spaciously with its river, its gardens and churches, and seemed to be living its life, its cupolas glittering like stars in the sunlight.

At the sight of the strange city with the never-seen forms of its extraordinary architecture, Napoleon experienced that somewhat envious and restless curiosity which people experience at the sight of alien forms of life that know nothing of them. Obviously, this city lived with all the forces of its own life. By those indefinable signs which, even from a distance, unmistakably distinguish a living body from a dead one, Napoleon saw from Poklonnaya Hill the quivering of life in the city and felt, as it were, the breathing of that big and beautiful body.

Every Russian, looking at Moscow, feels that she is a mother; every foreigner, looking at her and not knowing her maternal significance, must feel the feminine character of this city, and Napoleon felt it.

"*Cette ville asiatique aux innombrables églises, Moscou la sainte. La voilà donc enfin, cette fameuse ville! Il était temps,*"* said Napoleon and, getting off his horse, he ordered a map of this *Moscou* spread out before him and summoned the interpreter Lelorgne d'Ideville. "*Une ville occupée par l'ennemi ressemble à une fille qui a perdu son honneur,*"† he thought (as he had also said to Tuchkov in Smolensk). And from that point of view he looked for the first time upon the Oriental beauty lying before him. It was strange for him that his long-standing wish, which had seemed impossible, had finally been fulfilled. In the clear morning light he looked now at the city, now at the map, checking the details of the city, and the certainty of possession excited and awed him.

"But how could it be otherwise?" he thought. "Here it is, this capital, at my feet, awaiting her destiny. Where is Alexander now, and what is he thinking? A

---

*This Asiatic city with her numberless churches, holy Moscow. So here she is at last, this famous city! It was time.
†A city occupied by the enemy is like a girl who has lost her honour.

strange, beautiful, majestic city! And a strange and majestic moment! In what light do they see me?" he thought of his troops. "Here it is, the reward for all those of little faith," he thought, looking at his retinue and at the troops approaching and forming up. "One word from me, one movement of my hand, and this ancient capital *des Czars* is destroyed. *Mais ma clémence est toujours prompte à descendre sur les vaincus.** I must be magnanimous and truly great . . . But no, it's not true that I'm in Moscow" suddenly came into his head. "Yet here she is lying at my feet, her golden cupolas and crosses playing and glittering in the sunlight. But I will spare her. On the ancient monuments of barbarism and despotism, I will write great words of justice and mercy . . . Alexander will take precisely that most painfully of all—I know him." (It seemed to Napoleon that the main significance of what was happening lay in his personal struggle with Alexander.) "From the heights of the Kremlin—yes, yes, that's the Kremlin—I will give them the laws of justice, I will show them the meaning of true civilization; I will make the generations of boyars[14] remember the name of their conqueror with love. I will tell their deputation that I did not and do not want war, that I have waged war only with the faulty policy of their court, that I love and respect Alexander, and that I will accept conditions of peace in Moscow which are worthy of me and of my people. I do not want to use the fortunes of war to humiliate a respected sovereign. 'Boyars,' I will say to them, 'I do not want war, I want peace and the well-being of all my subjects.' However, I know that their presence will inspire me, and I will speak to them as I always do: clearly, solemnly, and grandly. But can it be true that I'm in Moscow? Yes, there she is!"

"*Qu'on m'amène les boyards,*"† he turned to his suite. A general with a brilliant suite galloped off at once for the boyars.

Two hours went by. Napoleon had lunch and again stood in the same place on Poklonnaya Hill, waiting for the deputation. His speech to the boyars had already taken clear shape in his imagination. This speech was filled with dignity and with grandeur as Napoleon understood it.

He himself was carried away by the tone of magnanimity he intended to employ in Moscow. In his imagination, he appointed days for the *réunion dans le palais des Czars,*‡ where Russian dignitaries would get together with the dignitaries of the French emperor. He mentally appointed a governor who would be able to attract the populace to him. Having learned that there were many charitable institutions in Moscow, he decided in his imagination that all those institutions would be showered with his favours. He thought that, as in Africa he had had to sit in a burnous in a mosque, so in Moscow he had to be

---

*But my clemency is always swift to descend upon the vanquished.
†Have the boyars brought to me.
‡Meeting in the palace of the Tsars.

merciful like the tsars. And, so as to definitively touch the hearts of the Russians, he, like all Frenchmen, who could not imagine anything sentimental without mentioning *ma chère, ma tendre, ma pauvre mère,* he decided that he would write in large letters on all those institutions: *Établissement dédié à ma chère Mère.* "No, simply: *Maison de ma Mère,*"* he decided to himself. "But can it be that I'm in Moscow? Yes, there she is in front of me. But why is the deputation from the city so long in appearing?" he thought.

Meanwhile at the back of the emperor's suite a worried debate was going on in whispers among his generals and marshals. Those sent for the deputation had come back with the news that Moscow was empty, that everyone had left. The faces of the debating men were pale and worried. They were frightened not by the fact that Moscow had been abandoned by its inhabitants (important as that event might seem), but by how to announce it to the emperor, how, without putting his majesty into that dreadful position known to the French as *le ridicule,* to announce to him that he had been awaiting the boyars so long for nothing, that there were crowds of drunken men and nothing else. Some said that at least some sort of deputation had to be assembled; others argued against that opinion and insisted that they had to prepare the emperor cautiously and intelligently and tell him the truth.

"*Il faudra le lui dire tout de même . . .*" said the gentlemen of the suite. "*Mais, messieurs*† . . ." The situation was the more difficult in that the emperor, thinking over his plans for magnanimity, was patiently walking up and down in front of the map, occasionally glancing from under his hand at the road to Moscow, and smiling cheerfully and proudly.

"*Mais c'est impossible. . .*"‡ the gentlemen of the suite said, shrugging their shoulders, not daring to utter the terrible word in their minds: *le ridicule . . .*

Meanwhile the emperor, tired of vainly waiting and sensing with his actor's intuition that the majestic moment, having gone on too long, was beginning to lose its majesty, made a sign with his hand. The solitary shot of a signal gun rang out, and the troops that surrounded Moscow on all sides moved into the city through the Tver, Kaluga, and Dorogomilovo gates. Quicker and quicker, overtaking each other, the troops moved at a rapid walk or at a trot, disappearing in the clouds of dust they raised, and filling the air with the merging noise of their cries.

Drawn along by the movement of the troops, Napoleon went with them as far as the Dorogomilovo gate, but there stopped again and, getting off his horse, paced for a long time by the Kamerkollezhsky rampart, awaiting the deputation.

---

*My dear, my tender, my poor mother . . . Establishment dedicated to my dear Mother . . . House of my Mother.
†He must be told all the same . . . But, gentlemen . . .
‡But it's impossible . . .

XX

Meanwhile Moscow was empty. There were still people in it, there was still a fiftieth part of all the former inhabitants left in it, but it was empty. It was empty as a dying-out, queenless beehive is empty.

There is no life in a queenless beehive, but to a superficial glance it seems as alive as the others.

In the hot rays of the noonday sun, the bees hover just as merrily around a queenless hive as around the other living hives; from afar it has the same smell of honey; bees fly in and out of it in the same way. But we need only take a closer look at it to realize that there is no longer any life in this hive. The bees do not fly in the same way as in a living hive, the smell is not the same, it is not the same sound that strikes the beekeeper's ear. To the beekeeper's tapping on the wall of an ailing hive, instead of the former instantaneous, concerted response, the hissing of tens of thousands of bees, menacingly tucking their behinds under and producing this vital, airy sound by the rapid beating of their wings, there comes in response a scattered buzzing that resonates at various points of the empty hive. The entrance does not give out, as before, a spiritous, fragrant smell of honey and venom, no feeling of the warmth of fullness comes from it, but the smell of honey is mingled with a smell of emptiness and rot. At the entrance there are no more sentinels ready to defend it to the death, their behinds turned up, sounding the alarm. There is no longer that measured and quiet sound, the throb of work, like the sound of seething water, but one hears the discordant, scattered noise of disorder. Black, elongated, honey-smeared robber bees fly in and out of the hive, warily and shiftily; they do not sting, but slip away from danger. Formerly only laden bees flew in and empty bees flew out; but now laden bees fly out. The beekeeper opens the lower chamber and peers into the lower part of the hive. Instead of the black strands of juicy bees, pacified by labour, that formerly hung down to the very bottom, holding each other's legs and drawing out the wax with an incessant whisper of labour — sleepy, dried-up bees wander absent-mindedly in various directions over the bottom and sides of the hive. Instead of a floor neatly plastered with glue and swept by fanning wings, the bottom is covered with crumbs of wax, bee excrement, and bees, half-dead and barely moving their legs or completely dead and not cleared away.

The beekeeper opens the upper chamber and examines the superhive. Instead of solid rows of bees covering all the spaces between the combs and warming the brood, he sees the artful, complex workmanship of the combs, but no longer in the virginal form they used to have. Everything is neglected and dirty. Robbers—the black bees—dart swiftly and stealthily over the works; the native bees, dried-up, shrunken, sluggish, as if old, wander about slowly, hindering nothing, desiring nothing, having lost the awareness of life. Drones, hornets, bumblebees, butterflies beat senselessly against the walls of the hive in their flight. Here and there among the cells with their dead brood and honey, an angry grumbling is occasionally heard from different sides; in one place two bees, cleaning the nest by old habit and memory, assiduous, overstraining, drag away a dead bee or a bumblebee, not knowing themselves why they are doing it. In another corner, another two old bees fight lazily, or clean themselves, or feed each other, not knowing themselves whether they are doing it out of hostility or friendship. In a third place, a crowd of bees, crushing each other, attack some victim and beat and smother it. And the weakened or dead bee slowly, lightly, like a bit of fluff, falls from above into the heap of corpses. The beekeeper opens two central frames so as to see into the nest. Where formerly the entire space was covered by the black circles of thousands of bees sitting tightly back to back, guarding the lofty mysteries of generation, he now sees hundreds of dejected, half-alive and somnolent husks of bees. They are almost all dead, not knowing it themselves, sitting over the sacred thing they were guarding, which is no longer there. They smell of decay and death. Only some of them stir, rise, fly sluggishly, and land on the enemy's hand, not strong enough to die stinging him—the rest, dead, sift down lightly, like fish scales. The beekeeper closes the frames, marks the hive with chalk, and, when he finds time, breaks it open and burns it out.

So Moscow was empty when Napoleon, weary, restless, and scowling, paced back and forth by the Kamerkollezhsky rampart, awaiting what to his mind was a necessary, though external, observance of propriety—a deputation.

In various corners of Moscow only a few people still stirred meaninglessly, keeping to old habits and not understanding what they were doing.

When with due caution it was announced to Napoleon that Moscow was empty, he glared angrily at the one who announced it and, turning away, went on pacing in silence.

"Bring my carriage," he said. He got into the carriage beside the adjutant on duty and drove to the outskirts.

"*Moscou déserte. Quel événement invraisemblable!*"* he said to himself.

He did not drive into the city, but stayed at an inn in the suburb of Dorogomilovo.

Le coup de théâtre avait raté.†

---

*Moscow deserted. What an unlikely occurrence!
†The coup de théâtre had not come off.

XXI

Russian troops were passing through Moscow from two o'clock at night until two o'clock in the afternoon and carrying along with them the last departing inhabitants and the wounded.

The biggest crush during this movement of troops occurred on the Kamenny, Moskvoretsky, and Yauzsky bridges.

At the time when, after dividing in two around the Kremlin, the troops jammed together on the Moskvoretsky and Kamenny bridges, a great number of soldiers, taking advantage of the pause and the congestion, turned back from the bridges and darted furtively and silently past Basil the Blessed and under the Borovitsky gate, back up the hill to Red Square, where by some intuition they sensed that other people's things could be taken without trouble. The same crowd of people as at cut-rate sales filled all the passes and passageways of the Shopping Arcade. But there were no caressingly sweet, enticing voices of shopkeepers, there were no pedlars or motley crowds of women shoppers—there were only the uniforms and greatcoats of soldiers without guns, silently coming out of the rows laden and going in unladen. The shopkeepers and assistants (there were few of them) walked among the soldiers like lost men, unlocking and locking up their shops, and carrying their goods off somewhere themselves with the help of some stalwart young men. On the square by the Shopping Arcade drummers stood and beat to muster. But the sound of the drum did not make the looting soldiers come running to the call as formerly, but, on the contrary, made them run further away from the drum. Among the soldiers, in the shops and passageways, people in grey kaftans and with shaved heads could be seen. Two officers, one with a sash over his uniform, on a lean, dark grey horse, the other in a greatcoat, on foot, were standing at the corner of Ilyinka Street and talking about something. A third officer rode up to them.

"The general orders them all driven away at whatever cost. Who has ever seen the like! Half the men are scattered around."

"Where are you going? . . . And you two? . . ." he shouted at three infantrymen without guns, who, hoisting the skirts of their greatcoats, slipped past him into the rows. "Stop, you rascals!"

"Yes, go and round them up, if you please!" the other officer replied. "There's no rounding them up; we must get a move on, so that the last of them don't escape, that's all!"

"How, get a move on? They're standing there jammed on the bridge, not moving. Or shall we set up a cordon so that the last ones don't run for it?"

"Go in there! Drive them out!" cried the senior officer.

The officer in the sash got off his horse, called the drummer, and went into the arcade with him. A group of several soldiers broke into a run. A shop-keeper, with red pimples on his cheeks near the nose, with a calmly unshake-able expression of calculation on his well-fed face, went up to the officer hastily and jauntily, swinging his arms.

"Your Honour," he said, "be so good as to protect us! We won't count any trifles, it's our pleasure! If you please, I'll bring out a bolt of cloth right now, even two for an honourable person, it's our pleasure! Because we've got feel-ings; and this is—sheer robbery! Please! Set a watch or something, at least let us lock up . . ."

Several shopkeepers crowded around the officer.

"Eh! why blather for nothing!" said one of them, a lean man with a stern face. "Why weep for your hair when your head's cut off. Let them take what they like!" And with an energetic wave of the hand, he turned sideways to the officer.

"It's all right for you to talk, Ivan Sidorych," the first shopkeeper said angrily. "Please, Your Honour."

"It's all right for me to talk, is it!" the lean one cried. "I've got a hundred thousand worth of goods in three shops here. As if I can keep it when the army's gone! Eh, you folk, man proposes, God disposes!"

"Please, Your Honour," the first shopkeeper repeated, bowing. The officer stood perplexed, and hesitation could be seen in his face.

"Ah, what business is it of mine!" he cried suddenly and walked with quick steps down the row. From one open shop came the sound of blows and abuse, and just as the officer reached it, a man in a grey coat and with a shaved head was sent flying out of the door.

This man, bending double, flashed past the shopkeepers and the officer. The officer fell upon the soldiers who were in the shop. But just then the terrible cries of an enormous crowd came from the Moskvoretsky bridge, and the offi-cer ran out to the square.

"What is it? What is it?" he asked, but his comrade was already galloping in the direction of the cries, past Basil the Blessed. The officer got on his horse and followed him. When he rode up to the bridge, he saw two cannon dismounted from their carriages, infantry going across the bridge, several overturned wag-ons, several frightened faces, and the laughing faces of soldiers. Near the can-non stood a cart hitched to two horses. Behind the cart, four wolfhounds in collars pressed up close to the wheels. The cart was heaped with chattels, and on the very top, next to a child's chair turned legs up, sat a woman, shrieking piercingly and desperately. His comrades told the officer that the cries of the crowd and the shrieking of the woman came from the fact that General Ermolov had come upon this crowd and, learning that the soldiers had scat-tered to the shops and crowds of inhabitants were blocking the bridge, had ordered the cannon dismounted from their carriages, and had pretended that he was about to fire on the bridge. The crowd, overturning carts, crushing each other, crying desperately, shoving, had cleared the bridge, and the troops were now moving forward.

XXII

The city itself, meanwhile, was empty. There was almost no one in the streets. The gates and shops were all locked; here and there around the pot-houses, solitary shouts or drunken singing could be heard. No one drove through the streets, and the footsteps of pedestrians were rarely heard. Povarskaya Street was completely quiet and deserted. In the huge courtyard of the Rostovs' house, leftover hay and dung from the cart horses lay about, and not a single person was to be seen. In the big drawing room of the Rostovs' house, where all their belongings had been left behind, there were two people. They were the yard porter Ignat and the servant boy Mishka, Vassilyich's grandson, who had stayed in Moscow with his grandfather. Mishka opened the clavichord and played on it with one finger. The yard porter, arms akimbo, smiling joyfully, stood before the big mirror.

"That's neat, though! Eh, Uncle Ignat?" said the boy, suddenly beginning to bang on the keys with both hands.

"See there!" replied Ignat, marvelling at the smile spreading across his face in the mirror.

"Shameless! Really shameless!" the voice of Mavra Kuzminishna, who had come in quietly, spoke behind them. "Look at you, fat mug, baring your teeth. That's all you're good for! Nothing's been tidied up, Vassilyich is running his feet off. Just you wait!"

Ignat stopped smiling and, straightening his belt and lowering his eyes obediently, started out of the room.

"I did it gently, auntie," said the boy.

"I'll give it to you gently. Rapscallion!" shouted Mavra Kuzminishna, swinging her arm at him. "Go and start the samovar for your grandfather."

Mavra Kuzminishna, wiping the dust off, closed the clavichord and, with a heavy sigh, left the drawing room and locked the door.

Going out to the courtyard, Mavra Kuzminishna pondered where to go next: to have tea with Vassilyich in the wing, or to the pantry to put away what had not been put away yet?

In the quiet street there was the sound of quick footsteps. The footsteps stopped by the door in the gate; the latch rattled under a hand that tried to open it.

Mavra Kuzminishna went up to the gate.

"Who do you want?"

"The count, Count Ilya Andreich Rostov."

"But who are you?"

"I'm an officer. I must see him," said a pleasant and gentlemanly Russian voice.

Mavra Kuzminishna opened the door. An officer of about eighteen, with a round face of a type resembling the Rostovs, came into the courtyard.

"They're gone, dearie. Left yesterday afternoon, if you please," Mavra Kuzminishna said kindly.

The young officer, standing in the doorway as if undecided whether to go in or not, clucked his tongue.

"Ah, how vexing!" he said. "Yesterday I should have . . . Ah, what a pity! . . ."

Mavra Kuzminishna meanwhile was attentively and sympathetically studying the familiar features of the Rostov breed in the young man's face, and the worn greatcoat and down-at-heel boots he had on.

"What did you want the count for?" she asked.

"Ah, well . . . nothing to be done!" the officer said vexedly and grasped the door as if intending to leave. Again he stopped in indecision.

"You see?" he said suddenly. "I'm a relative of the count's, and he's always been very kind to me. Well, so you see" (he looked at his cloak and boots with a kind and cheerful smile), "I'm a bit shabby, and I've got no money; so I wanted to ask the count . . ."

Mavra Kuzminishna did not let him finish.

"You wait one little minute, dearie. Just one little minute," she said. And as soon as the officer let go of the gate, Mavra Kuzminishna turned and with a quick, old-womanish step went to her wing in the back yard.

While Mavra Kuzminishna was running to her room, the officer, lowering his head and gazing at his torn boots, strolled about the courtyard, smiling slightly. "What a pity I didn't find my uncle. But she's a nice old woman! Where did she run off to? And how am I to find out by what streets it will be closest for me to catch up with my regiment, which must now be approaching the Rogozhsky gate?" the young officer was thinking. Just then Mavra Kuzminishna, with a frightened and at the same time determined face, carrying a folded checkered handkerchief in her hands, came round the corner. While still a few steps away, she unfolded the handkerchief, took a white twenty-five rouble note from it, and hastily handed it to the officer.

"If his excellency had been at home, goodness knows, he'd just have given it to you, since you're a relation . . . so, maybe . . . now . . ." Mavra Kuzminishna became timid and confused. But the officer, not refusing and not hurrying, took the note and thanked Mavra Kuzminishna. "If the count had been at home," Mavra Kuzminishna kept saying apologetically. "Christ be with you, dearie!

God save you," she said, bowing and seeing him off. The officer, smiling and shaking his head, as if laughing at himself, ran almost at a trot down the empty street towards the Yauzsky bridge to catch up with his regiment.

And Mavra Kuzminishna went on standing for a long time with moist eyes before the closed gate, pensively shaking her head and feeling a sudden flood of maternal tenderness and pity for the unknown little officer.

XXIII

In an unfinished house on Varvarka Street, with a pot-house on the ground floor, drunken shouting and singing was heard. Some ten factory workers were sitting on benches by the tables in a small, dirty room. Drunk, sweaty, bleary-eyed, straining and opening their mouths wide, they were all singing some song. They sang discordantly, with difficulty, with effort, obviously not because they wanted to sing, but only in order to prove that they were drunk and carousing. One of them, a tall, blond fellow in a clean blue coat, was standing over them. His face with its thin, straight nose would have been handsome, if it were not for the thin, compressed, constantly moving lips and dull, fixed, frowning eyes. He stood over those who were singing, and, evidently imagining something to himself, swung his white arm, bared to the elbow, solemnly and awkwardly above their heads, trying to spread the dirty fingers of his hand unnaturally. The sleeve of his coat kept coming down, and the fellow would carefully push it up again with his left hand, as if there was something especially important in having this white, sinewy, waving arm be unfailingly bared. In the midst of the song, shouts of fighting and blows were heard in the front hall and on the porch. The tall fellow waved his arm.

"Enough!" he cried imperiously. "There's a fight, boys!" And, ceaselessly pushing up his sleeve, he went out to the porch.

The factory workers followed him. The factory workers drinking in the pot-house that morning, under the leadership of the tall fellow, had brought the landlord some leather from the factory, and for that he had given them vodka. The blacksmiths from the neighbouring smithies, hearing noises of carousing in the pot-house and supposing it had been broken into, wanted to force their way in. A fight started on the porch.

The landlord was fighting with a blacksmith in the doorway, and just as the factory workers came out, the blacksmith tore himself away from the landlord and fell face down on the pavement.

Another blacksmith was straining in the doorway, heaving the whole weight of his chest against the landlord.

The fellow with the pushed-up sleeve, still in motion, hit the blacksmith straining in the doorway in the face and shouted wildly:

"Hey! they're beating our boys!"

Just then the first blacksmith got up from the ground and, scraping at the blood on his smashed-in face, cried in a tearful voice:

"Help! Murder! . . . A man's been killed! Brothers! . . ."

"Good heavens, they've killed him, they've killed a man!" shrieked a woman who came out of the neighbouring gates. A crowd of people gathered around the blood-smeared blacksmith.

"It's not enough that you rob people, take the shirts off their backs," someone's voice said, addressing the landlord, "did you have to go and kill the man? Brigand!"

The tall fellow, standing on the porch, shifted his bleary eyes from the landlord to the blacksmiths and back, as if considering whom he should fight now.

"Fiend!" he suddenly cried to the landlord. "Tie him up, boys!"

"Sure, just you try it!" cried the landlord, waving away the men who came at him, and, tearing his hat off, he flung it on the ground. As if this act had some mysterious threatening significance, the workmen who surrounded the landlord stopped in indecision.

"I know the rules, brother, I know them perfectly! I'll take it to the police. You think I won't? Nobody's given any orders for robbery lately!" cried the landlord, picking up his hat.

"Let's go, then! Let's go! . . ." the landlord and the tall fellow repeated one after the other, and they both set off down the street. The blood-smeared blacksmith walked beside them. The workmen and some other people, talking and shouting, followed after them.

At the corner of Maroseika, across from a big house with closed shutters on which a cobbler's shingle hung, stood some twenty cobblers with glum faces— thin, worn-out men in smocks and tattered coats.

"He ought to square it properly with people!" a skinny artisan with a sparse beard and frowning eyebrows was saying. "Or else, what, he's sucked our blood—and he's quits. He led us on, led us on—for a whole week. And now he's brought it to the final end, and off he goes."

Seeing the people and the blood-smeared man, the talking workman fell silent, and the cobblers, with hasty curiosity, all joined the moving crowd.

"Where are these people going?"

"To the authorities, sure enough."

"So, is it true our forces weren't up to it?"

"And what do you think? Look at what people are saying."

There were more questions and answers. The landlord, taking advantage of the increased crowd, fell behind and went back to his pot-house.

The tall fellow, not noticing the disappearance of his enemy, the landlord, swinging his bared arm, never stopped talking, attracting general attention to himself. People pressed mainly around him, supposing they would receive answers from him to the questions that occupied them.

"He should show order, show the law, that's what the authorities are there for! Is it right what I'm saying, good Christian people?" the tall fellow said with a barely perceptible smile.

"Does he think there are no authorities? Can we do without the authorities? There's enough thievery as it is."

"Why this empty talk!" a response came from the crowd. "They can't abandon Moscow just like that! They told you for a joke, and you believed it. There's enough of our troops coming. As if they'd let him in here! That's what the authorities are for. Just listen to what people are telling," some said, pointing to the tall fellow.

By the wall of Kitaigorod, another small bunch of people surrounded a man in a frieze overcoat who was holding a paper in his hand.

"A ukase, they're reading a ukase! They're reading a ukase!" voices said in the crowd, and the people streamed towards the reader.

The man in the frieze overcoat was reading a poster from the thirty-first of August. When the crowd surrounded him, he seemed embarrassed, but at the demand of the tall fellow, who pushed his way through to him, he began, with a slight tremor in his voice, to read the poster from the beginning.

"Early tomorrow morning I'll be going to see his serenity the prince," he read ("His serenity," the tall fellow repeated solemnly, smiling with his mouth and frowning with his eyebrows), "to talk things over with him, to act, and to help the troops exterminate the villains; we'll eradicate . . ." the reader went on and then paused ("See?" the fellow cried victoriously. "He'll undo the whole distance for you . . .") . . . "the spirit in them, and send these guests to the devil. I'll come back by dinnertime, and we'll get down to business, do it, finish doing it, and have done with the villains."

The last words were read by the reader amidst total silence. The tall fellow hung his head sadly. It was obvious that no one understood those last words. In particular, the words "I shall come by dinnertime tomorrow" clearly even upset both the reader and the listeners. People's understanding was tuned to a higher pitch, and this was too simple, needlessly simple; it was something any of them could have said, and that a ukase issuing from the highest authority therefore could not say.

They all stood in dejected silence. The tall fellow moved his lips and swayed slightly.

"Let's ask him! . . . Is it him himself? Sure, try asking him! . . . Why not . . . He'll show . . ." suddenly came from the back rows of the crowd, and general attention turned to the police chief's droshky, which was driving out to the square accompanied by two mounted dragoons.

The police chief, who had gone that morning at the count's order to burn the barges, and who, on the occasion of this errand, had made a large sum of money, which at that moment was in his pocket, saw the crowd of people moving towards him and ordered his coachman to stop.

"Who are these people?" he cried to the men, who were approaching the droshky singly and timidly. "Who are these people, I ask you?" the police chief repeated, without getting an answer.

"Your Honour," said the clerk in the frieze overcoat, "Your Honour, in accordance with the proclamation of his excellency the count, they wished to serve, not sparing their lives, and it is not some sort of mutiny, but, as his excellency the count said . . ."

"The count hasn't left, he's here, and there will be an order concerning you," said the police chief. "Drive on!" he said to the coachman. The crowd stopped, clustering around those who had heard what the official said, and gazing at the departing droshky.

The police chief glanced back fearfully at that moment, said something to the coachman, and his horses picked up speed.

"It's a trick, boys! Take us to the man himself!" cried the voice of the tall fellow. "Don't let him go, boys! Let him give an accounting! Hold him!" voices shouted, and the people went running after the droshky.

The crowd, talking noisily, followed the police chief in the direction of the Lubyanka.

"What, the gentry and the merchants have all gone, and we're to perish for that? What, are we dogs or something?" was frequently heard in the crowd.

XXIV

On the evening of the first of September, after his meeting with Kutuzov, Count Rastopchin, upset and offended that he had not been invited to the council of war, that Kutuzov had paid no attention to his suggestion of taking part in the defence of the capital, and astonished at the new view revealed to him in the camp, in which the question of the tranquillity of the capital and its patriotic spirit appeared not only secondary, but completely unnecessary and insignificant—upset, offended, and astonished at all that, Count Rastopchin returned to Moscow. After supper, without undressing, the count lay down on the couch and was awakened past midnight by a courier who brought him a letter from Kutuzov. The letter said that, as the troops were retreating to the Ryazan road beyond Moscow, would the count be so good as to send police officers to lead the troops through the city. This came as no news to Rastopchin. Not only since the previous day's meeting with Kutuzov on Poklonnaya Hill, but ever since the battle of Borodino, when all the generals who came to Moscow said with one voice that it was still impossible to offer battle, and when, with the count's permission, government property was being evacuated every night and half the inhabitants had left, Count Rastopchin had known that Moscow would be abandoned. Nevertheless, this news, conveyed in the form of a simple note with an order from Kutuzov and received during the night, just as he was falling asleep, astonished and vexed the count.

Afterwards, explaining his activity during this time, Count Rastopchin wrote several times in his notes[15] that he then had two important goals: *De maintenir la tranquillité à Moscou et d'en faire partir les habitants.** If we allow for this double goal, every one of Rastopchin's acts turns out to be irreproachable. Why were the holy objects, the weapons, shot, powder, stores of grain, not evacuated, why were thousands of inhabitants deceived about Moscow not being surrendered, and thereby ruined? In order to maintain tranquillity in the capital, replies Count Rastopchin's explanation. Why were heaps of useless papers from government offices evacuated, along with Leppich's balloon and other objects? In order to leave the city empty, replies Count Rastopchin's explanation. One need only allow that something threatened the tranquillity of the people, and every action becomes justified.

All the horrors of the Reign of Terror[16] were based only on concern for public tranquillity.

On what, then, did Count Rastopchin base his fear for public tranquillity in Moscow in the year 1812? What reason was there to suppose there was a tendency to revolt in the city? The inhabitants were leaving, the retreating troops were filling Moscow. Why should the result of that be a popular revolt?

Neither in Moscow nor anywhere in Russia did anything resembling an insurrection occur at the entrance of the enemy. On the first of September, on the second of September, there were more than ten thousand people still in Moscow, and, apart from the crowd that gathered in the commander in chief's courtyard and was drawn there by the man himself—there was nothing. Obviously, there would have been still less reason to expect a disturbance among the people if, after the battle of Borodino, when the surrender of Moscow became obvious, or at least probable, instead of stirring people up by distributing weapons and posters, Rastopchin had taken measures to evacuate all the holy objects, powder, shot, and money, and had announced directly to the people that the city would be abandoned.

Rastopchin, an ardent, sanguine man who had always gone about in the highest administrative circles, though he did have patriotic feelings, did not have the least notion of the people he thought to govern. At the very beginning of the enemy's entry into Smolensk, Rastopchin had fashioned in his imagination a role for himself as a guide of popular feelings—the heart of Russia. It seemed to him (as it does to every administrator) that he was not only managing the external activities of the people of Moscow, but was also guiding their mood by means of his appeals and posters, written in that boorish language

---

*To maintain tranquillity in Moscow and to get the inhabitants to leave.

which the people despise in their own milieu, and which they do not understand when they hear it from above. The beautiful role of guide of popular feelings was so much to Rastopchin's liking, he grew so accustomed to it, that the
necessity of quitting that role, the necessity of abandoning Moscow without
any heroic effects, caught him unawares, and he suddenly lost the ground
under his feet, on which he had been standing, and decidedly did not know
what he was to do. He knew, but with all his soul did not believe until the last
moment, that Moscow would be abandoned, and did nothing in view of that.
The inhabitants were leaving against his will. If the government offices were
evacuated, it was done only on the demand of the officials, with whom the
count agreed reluctantly. He personally was concerned only with the role he
had created for himself. As often happens with people gifted with an ardent
imagination, he had known for a long time that Moscow would be abandoned, but had known it only with his reason, while with all his soul he
had not believed it, and he was not transported in imagination into that new
situation.

All his activity, painstaking and energetic (how far it was useful and had an
effect on the people is another question), was aimed only at arousing in the
inhabitants the feeling he himself experienced—patriotic hatred of the French
and confidence in himself.

But when the event assumed its real, historical dimensions, when a merely
verbal expression of hatred of the French proved insufficient, when it was
impossible to express that hatred even in battle, when self-confidence proved
useless with regard to the one question of Moscow, when the entire population, as one man, abandoned their property and poured out of Moscow, showing by this negative act all the force of their national feeling—then the role
chosen by Rastopchin suddenly proved meaningless. He suddenly felt himself
alone, weak, and ridiculous, with no ground under his feet.

When, having been awakened from sleep, he received the cold and peremp-
tory note from Kutuzov, Rastopchin felt the more vexed, the more he felt himself to blame. All that he had precisely been charged with, all the government
property he was supposed to have evacuated, was still in Moscow. To evacuate
everything was impossible.

"Who is to blame, who allowed this to happen?" he thought. "Certainly
not I. I had everything ready, I held Moscow like this! And see what they've
brought things to! Scoundrels! Traitors!" he thought, without defining very
well who these scoundrels and traitors were, but feeling it necessary to hate
whoever the traitors might be who were to blame for the false and ridiculous
position he was in.

All that night Count Rastopchin gave orders, for which people came to him
from all ends of Moscow. Those close to him had never seen him so gloomy
and irritated.

"Your Excellency, they've come from the Department of Records, from the director, for instructions . . . From the Consistory, from the Senate, from the University, from the Foundling Hospital, the auxiliary bishop has sent . . . he asks . . . What are your orders for the fire brigade? The warden of the prison . . . the warden of the madhouse . . ."—all night announcements kept coming to the count.

To all these questions the count gave brief and angry replies, showing that his instructions were no longer needed, that everything he had so carefully prepared had been spoiled by someone, and that this someone would bear all the responsibility for everything that was happening now.

"Well, tell that blockhead," he replied to the request from the Department of Records, "that he should stay and keep watch over his documents. What's that nonsense you asked about the fire brigade? They've got horses—let them go to Vladimir. No leaving them to the French."

"Your Excellency, the superintendent of the insane asylum is here, what are your instructions?"

"My instructions? Let them all leave, that's all . . . And let the madmen go free in the city. If we've got madmen commanding the armies, these will fill the bill, too."

To his question about the convicts in prison, the count shouted angrily at the warden:

"What, do you want me to give you a convoy of two battalions that don't exist? Let them go free, and enough!"

"There are political prisoners, Your Excellency: Meshkov, Vereshchagin."[17]

"Vereshchagin! He hasn't been hanged yet?" cried Rastopchin. "Bring him to me."

XXV

By nine o'clock in the morning, when troops were already moving through Moscow, no one came any more to ask the count for instructions. Everyone who could go was going on his own; those who stayed decided on their own what they should do.

The count ordered horses prepared in order to go to Sokolniki, and, frowning, yellow, and taciturn, sat in his office with folded arms.

To every administrator, in peaceful, unstormy times, it seems that the entire population entrusted to him moves only by his efforts, and in this consciousness of his necessity every administrator finds the chief reward for his labours and efforts. It is understandable that, as long as the historical sea is calm, it must seem to the ruler-administrator in his frail little bark, resting his pole against the ship of the people and moving along with it, that his efforts are moving the ship. But once a storm arises, the sea churns up, and the ship begins to move by itself, and then the delusion is no longer possible. The ship follows its own enormous, independent course, the pole does not reach the moving ship, and the ruler suddenly, from his position of power, from being a source of strength, becomes an insignificant, useless, and feeble human being.

Rastopchin felt that, and it irritated him.

The police chief, whom the crowd had stopped, entered the count's study along with the adjutant, who came to announce that the horses were ready. Both were pale, and the police chief, having reported that his mission had been accomplished, told the count that a huge crowd of people was standing in the courtyard and wished to see him.

Rastopchin, without a word of reply, stood up and with quick steps headed for his bright, luxurious drawing room, went to the door of the balcony, took hold of the handle, let go again, and went to the window, from which the whole crowd was better seen. The tall fellow was standing in front, waving his arm with a stern look, and saying something. The blood-smeared blacksmith was standing next to him with a gloomy air. Through the closed windows came the noise of voices.

"Is the carriage ready?" asked Rastopchin, stepping away from the window.

"Yes, Your Excellency," said the adjutant.

Rastopchin again went up to the door of the balcony.

"What do they want?" he asked the police chief.

"They say, Your Excellency, that they have gathered on your orders to go against the French. They shouted something about treason. It's a violent crowd, Your Excellency. I barely got away. Your Excellency, I venture to suggest . . ."

"Kindly leave, I know what to do without you," Rastopchin cried angrily. He stood at the door of the balcony, looking at the crowd. "See what they've done to Russia! See what they've done to me!" Rastopchin thought, feeling an irrepressible wrath rising in his soul against someone to whom he could ascribe the cause of all that was happening. As often happens with hot-tempered people, wrath had already taken hold of him, but he was still seeking an object for it. "*La voilà la populace, la lie du peuple,*" he thought, looking at the crowd, "*la plèbe qu'ils ont soulevée par leur sottise. Il leur faut une victime*"* occurred to him as he looked at the tall fellow swinging his arm. And it occurred to him precisely because he needed that victim himself, that object for his wrath.

"Is the carriage ready?" he asked once more.

"Yes, Your Excellency. What are your orders concerning Vereshchagin? He's waiting by the porch," said the adjutant.

*There is the rabble, the dregs of the people . . . the plebs they've stirred up by their stupidity. They need a victim.

"Ah!" cried Rastopchin, as if struck by some unexpected recollection.

And, quickly opening the door, he stepped resolutely onto the balcony. The talk suddenly ceased, hats and caps were taken off, and all eyes were raised to the emerging count.

"Greetings, lads!" the count said quickly and loudly. "Thank you for coming. I'll come out to you presently, but first of all we must deal with the villain. We must punish the villain who has brought ruin to Moscow. Wait for me!" And the count went inside just as quickly, slamming the door.

An approving murmur of satisfaction ran through the crowd. "It means he'll deal with all the villains! And you say Frenchmen . . . he'll undo the whole distance for you!" people said, as if reproaching each other for lack of faith.

A few minutes later an officer came hastily out of the front door, gave some order, and the dragoons stood to attention. The crowd eagerly moved from the balcony towards the porch. Coming out to the porch with wrathfully quick steps, Rastopchin hastily looked around, as if seeking someone.

"Where is he?" said the count, and the moment he said it, he saw coming round the corner of the house, between two dragoons, a young man with a long, thin neck, half of his head shaved and covered with new stubble. This young man was dressed in a once-foppish but now shabby coat of dark blue broadcloth lined with fox fur and dirty canvas convict's trousers tucked into unpolished, thin, down-at-heel boots. Irons hung heavily on his thin, weak legs, hampering the young man's irresolute steps.

"Ah!" said Rastopchin, hastily turning his gaze from the young man in the fox fur coat and pointing to the lowest step of the porch. "Put him there!" The young man, clanking his irons, climbed heavily onto the step indicated, pulled with his finger at the chafing collar of his coat, turned his long neck twice, and, with a sigh, folded his slender, non-working hands over his stomach in a submissive gesture.

For a few seconds, while the young man was settling himself on the step, the silence continued. Only in the back rows, from among the people pressing towards that one point, came grunts, groans, the sounds of shoving and the stamping of shifting feet.

Rastopchin, waiting for the man to stand still on the appointed place, frowningly rubbed his face with his hand.

"Lads!" Rastopchin said in a ringing, metallic voice, "this man, Vereshchagin—is the very scoundrel who has brought ruin to Moscow."

The young man in the fox fur coat stood in a submissive pose, stooping slightly, his hands clasped together over his stomach. His emaciated young face, with a hopeless expression, disfigured by the shaven head, was lowered. At the count's first words, he slowly raised his head and looked at him from below as if wishing to say something to him or at least to meet his eyes. But Rastopchin was not looking at him. On the young man's long, thin neck, behind his ear, a vein swelled like a cord and turned blue, and his face suddenly reddened.

All eyes were directed at him. He looked at the crowd, and, as if encouraged by the expression he read on people's faces, smiled sadly and timidly, and, lowering his head again, shifted his feet on the step.

"He has betrayed his tsar and his fatherland, he has gone over to Bonaparte, he alone of all Russians has disgraced the Russian name, and he has brought ruin on Moscow," Rastopchin was saying in a flat, shrill voice; but suddenly he gave a quick glance down at Vereshchagin, who went on standing in the same submissive pose. It was as if this glance blew him up. Raising his arm, he almost shouted, turning to the people: "Deal summarily with him! I hand him over to you!"

The people were silent and only pressed closer and closer from behind. To hold on to each other, to breathe in that infected atmosphere, having no strength to stir, and to wait for something unknown, incomprehensible, and dreadful, was becoming unbearable. The people standing in the front rows, seeing and hearing all that was going on before them, with frightened, wide-open eyes and gaping mouths, strained all their forces to hold back the pressure of those behind them.

"Beat him! . . . Let the traitor perish and not disgrace the Russian name!" Rastopchin began shouting. "Cut him down! I order it!"

Hearing not the words but the wrathful sound of Rastopchin's voice, the crowd groaned and moved closer, but stopped again.

"Count! . . ." Vereshchagin's voice, timid and at the same time theatrical, said in the momentary silence that again ensued. "Count, there is one God over us . . ." said Vereshchagin, raising his head, and again the fat vein on his thin neck swelled with blood and colour quickly rose to his face and left it again. He did not finish what he wanted to say.

"Cut him down! I order it! . . ." Rastopchin shouted out, suddenly turning as pale as Vereshchagin.

"Sabres out!" the officer cried to the dragoons, drawing his own sabre.

Another, still stronger wave swept over the people and, reaching the front rows, this wave pushed those in front and carried them, swaying, to the very steps of the porch. The tall fellow, with a stony expression on his face and his arm permanently raised, stood beside Vereshchagin.

"Cut him down!" the officer almost whispered to the dragoons, and one of the soldiers, his face disfigured by rage, suddenly struck Vereshchagin on the head with the flat of his broadsword.

"Ah!" Vereshchagin cried out briefly and surprisedly, looking around in fright, as though he could not understand why this thing had been done to him. The same groan of surprise and horror passed through the crowd.

"Oh, Lord!" someone exclaimed ruefully.

But after the exclamation of surprise that escaped Vereshchagin, he uttered a pitiful cry of pain, and that cry was the end of him. The barrier of human feeling, strained to the utmost in holding back the crowd, instantly broke. The crime had begun, it was necessary to go through with it. The pitiful moan of reproach was stifled by the menacing and wrathful roar of the crowd. Like the seventh and last wave that breaks up ships, this last irrepressible wave surged from the back rows, raced towards the front ones, knocked them down, and engulfed everything. The dragoon who had struck Vereshchagin was about to repeat his blow. Vereshchagin, with a cry of terror, shielding himself with his hands, rushed towards the people. The tall fellow, whom he ran into, seized Vereshchagin's thin neck with his hands and, uttering a wild cry, fell with him under the feet of the pushing, tearing people.

Some beat and tore at Vereshchagin, others at the tall fellow. And the shouts of the crushed men and of those who were trying to save the tall fellow only excited the fury of the crowd. For a long time the dragoons were unable to free the factory worker, bloody, beaten almost to death. And for a long time, despite all the feverish haste with which the crowd tried to finish the thing they had begun, the people who beat, strangled, and tore at Vereshchagin were unable to kill him; the crowd pressed at them from all sides, with them in the middle, heaving from side to side like a single mass, and not giving them the opportunity either to finish him off or to abandon him.

"Hit him with an axe or something? . . . Crush him . . . The traitor, he sold Christ! . . . alive . . . living . . . serves the thief right. Use a bar! . . . Is he alive?"

And only when the victim ceased to struggle and his cries were replaced by a drawn-out, rhythmic wheezing, did the crowd hurriedly begin moving round the prone, bloodstained body. Everyone went up, glanced at what had been done, and with horror, reproach, and astonishment, pressed back again.

"Oh, Lord, the people are like beasts, how could he be alive!" was heard in the crowd. "And he's a young fellow . . . must be a merchant . . . that's the people for you! . . . they say he's not the one . . . how, not the one . . . Oh, Lord! . . . The other one got beaten, they say he's barely alive . . . Eh, people . . . No fear of sin . . ." the same people now said, looking with painfully pitying expressions at the dead body with its blue face all smeared with blood and dust, and with its long, thin, slashed neck.

An assiduous police officer, finding the presence of a corpse in his excellency's courtyard inappropriate, ordered the dragoons to take the body outside. Two dragoons took hold of the mangled legs and dragged the body away. The bloody, dust-smeared, dead, shaven head, lolling on its long neck, trailed on the ground. The people shrank from the corpse.

As Vereshchagin fell and the crowd, with a wild roar, closed and swayed over him, Rastopchin suddenly turned pale and, instead of going to the back entrance where the horses were waiting for him, lowered his head and, not knowing where or why himself, went quickly down the corridor that led to the ground-floor rooms. The count's face was pale, and he could not stop the feverish trembling of his lower jaw.

"Your Excellency, this way . . . Where are you going? . . . This way, please," a trembling, frightened voice said behind him. Count Rastopchin was unable to make any reply and, turning obediently, went where he was told. A caleche was standing by the back entrance. The distant noise of the roaring crowd was heard there, too. Count Rastopchin hurriedly got into the caleche and ordered that he be taken to his country house in Sokolniki. Driving out to Myasnit-skaya and no longer hearing the cries of the crowd, the count began to have regrets. He now recalled with displeasure the agitation and fear he had shown before his subordinates. *"La populace est terrible, elle est hideuse,"* he thought in French. *"Ils sont comme les loups qu'on ne peut apaiser qu'avec de la chair."** "Count! there is one God over us!" he suddenly remembered Vereshchagin's words, and an unpleasant sensation of chill ran down Count Rastopchin's spine. But the sensation was momentary, and Count Rastopchin smiled scornfully at himself. *"J'avais d'autres devoirs,"* he thought. *"Il fallait apaiser le peuple. Bien d'autres victimes ont peri et perissent pour le bien publique,"†* and he began to think about those general responsibilities he had in relation to his family, to his (entrusted to him) capital, and about himself— not as Fyodor Vassilievich Rastopchin (he supposed that Fyodor Vassilievich Rastopchin had sacrificed himself for the *bien publique*), but as commander in chief, representative of the authorities, and the tsar's plenipotentiary. "If I were merely Fyodor Vassilievich, *ma ligne de conduite aurait été tout autre-ment tracée,‡* but I had to preserve the life and dignity of the commander in chief."

Rocking slightly on the soft springs of his caleche and no longer hearing the dreadful sounds of the crowd, Rastopchin calmed down physically and, as always happens, simultaneously with physical calm, his mind also devised causes for him to be morally calm. The thought that calmed Rastopchin was not new. As long as the world has existed and people have been killing each other, no one man has ever committed a crime upon his own kind without calming himself with this same thought. This thought was *le bien publique*, the supposed good of other people.

For a man not gripped by passion, that good is never known; but the man who commits the crime always knows for certain what that good consists in. And Rastopchin now knew it.

---

*The rabble is terrible, it's hideous . . . They're like wolves who can only be appeased by flesh.
†I had other duties . . . The people had to be appeased. Many other victims have perished and are perishing for the public good.
‡My line of conduct would have been drawn quite differently.

In his reasoning he not only did not reproach himself for his action, but even found cause for self-satisfaction in having been able to make use so successfully of this *à propos**—to punish the criminal and at the same time calm the crowd.

"Vereshchagin was tried and sentenced to death," thought Rastopchin (though the Senate had only sentenced Vereshchagin to hard labour). "He was a traitor and a turncoat; I couldn't let him go unpunished, and besides *je faisais d'une pierre deux coups;*† for the sake of calm I gave the people a victim and punished a villain."

On reaching his country house and busying himself with household instructions, the count became perfectly calm.

Half an hour later, the count was driving with fast horses across the Sokolniki field, no longer recalling what had happened, and thinking and considering only what was going to happen. He was now driving to the Yauzsky bridge, where he had been told Kutuzov was. Count Rastopchin was preparing in his imagination those wrathful and stinging reproaches he would make to Kutuzov for his deception. He would give that old fox of a courtier to feel that the responsibility for all the misfortunes that would proceed from the abandoning of the capital, from the ruin of Russia (as Rastopchin thought), would lie solely on his old, senile head. Thinking over beforehand what he was going to tell him, Rastopchin turned wrathfully in the caleche and glanced angrily to both sides.

The Sokolniki field was deserted. Only at the end of it, by the hospice and the madhouse, could bunches of men in white clothes be seen, and several solitary ones dressed the same way, walking across the field, shouting something and waving their arms.

One of them ran to intercept Count Rastopchin's caleche. And Count Rastopchin himself, and his driver, and the dragoons all looked with a vague feeling of horror and curiosity at these released madmen and especially at the one who was running towards them.

Swaying on his long, thin legs, his robe flying, the madman was running headlong, his eyes fixed on Rastopchin, shouting something to him in a hoarse voice and making signs for him to stop. The madman's sombre and solemn face, overgrown with uneven tufts of beard, was thin and yellow. His jet-black pupils shifted low and anxiously in their saffron-yellow whites.

"Wait! Stop, I tell you!" he called out piercingly and then cried something else, breathlessly, with imposing intonations and gestures.

He drew even with the carriage and ran alongside it.

"Thrice they killed me, thrice I rose from the dead. They have stoned me,

*Opportunity.
†I killed two birds with one stone.

they have crucified me . . . I shall rise . . . rise . . . rise. They have rent my body. The kingdom of God will be destroyed . . . Thrice will I destroy it, thrice will I raise it up," he cried, raising his voice more and more. Count Rastopchin suddenly grew pale, just as he had grown pale when the crowd fell upon Vereshchagin. He turned away.

"Dr . . . drive faster!" he cried to the coachman in a trembling voice.

The carriage raced as fast as the horses could pull it; but for a long time Count Rastopchin heard the ever more distant, mad, desperate shouting, and before his eyes saw only the surprised, frightened, bloody face of the traitor in the fur-lined coat.

Fresh as that memory was, Rastopchin felt that it was now deeply, bloodily engraved in his heart. He felt clearly now that the bloody trace of that memory would never heal, but that, on the contrary, the longer he lived, the more cruelly and tormentingly that terrible memory would live in his heart. He now fancied he could hear the sound of his own words: "Cut him down, or you'll answer to me with your heads!" "Why did I say those words! They came out somehow accidentally . . . I might not have said them," he thought, "then *nothing* would have happened." He saw the frightened and then suddenly cruel face of the dragoon who struck him, and the look of silent, timid reproach cast at him by that boy in the fox-lined coat . . . "But I didn't do it for myself, I had to act that way. *La plèbe, le traître . . . le bien publique,*" he thought.

Troops were still crowding around the Yauzsky bridge. It was hot. Kutuzov, frowning, glum, was sitting on a bench by the bridge and playing in the sand with his whip, when a caleche noisily galloped up to him. A man in a general's uniform, in a plumed hat, his shifting eyes either wrathful or frightened, came up to Kutuzov and began saying something to him in French. It was Count Rastopchin. He said to Kutuzov that he had come there because Moscow and the capital were no more and there was only the army.

"It would be different if Your Serenity had not told me you would not surrender Moscow without offering another battle: none of this would have happened!" he said.

Kutuzov was looking at Rastopchin and, as if not understanding the meaning of the words being addressed to him, was trying hard to read something special written at that moment on the face of the man who was speaking to him. Rastopchin, embarrassed, fell silent. Kutuzov shook his head slightly and, not taking his searching gaze from Rastopchin's face, said softly:

"No, I won't give up Moscow without offering battle."

Whether Kutuzov was thinking of something completely different as he said those words, or he spoke them deliberately, aware of their meaninglessness, Count Rastopchin said nothing and hastily walked away from Kutuzov. And strange thing! The commander in chief of Moscow, the proud Count Rastopchin, took a whip in his hand, went to the bridge, and began shouting and dispersing the clustering carts.

XXVI

Towards four o'clock in the afternoon, Murat's troops were entering Moscow. At their head rode a detachment of Württemberg hussars; on horseback behind them, with a large suite, rode the king of Naples himself.

Around the middle of the Arbat, by St. Nicholas the Revealed, Murat stopped to wait for news from the advanced detachment about the state of things in the city's fortress, *"le Kremlin."*

A small bunch of people from among the inhabitants who had remained in Moscow gathered around Murat. They all looked with timid perplexity at the strange, long-haired commander adorned with feathers and gold.

"What, is he their tsar himself or something? Not bad!" quiet voices were heard.

An interpreter rode up to the bunch of people.

"Take your hat off . . . your hat," they said in the crowd, addressing each other. The interpreter turned to an old yard porter and asked if it was far to the Kremlin. The yard porter, listening in perplexity to the Polish accent, which was foreign to him, and not recognizing the sounds of the interpreter's talk as Russian speech, did not understand what was being said to him and hid behind the others.

Murat approached the interpreter and told him to ask where the Russian troops were. One of the Russians understood what was asked and several voices suddenly began to answer the interpreter. A French officer from the advanced detachment rode up to Murat and reported that the gates of the fortress were closed and there was probably an ambush inside.

"Very well," said Murat, and, turning to one of the gentlemen of his suite, he ordered four light guns moved forward to fire on the gates.

The artillery trotted out from behind the column following Murat and went along the Arbat. Going down to the end of Vzdvizhenka Street, the artillery stopped and lined up on the square. Several French officers took charge of the guns, setting them up and looking at the Kremlin through field glasses.

Inside the Kremlin, the bells were ringing for vespers,[18] and this ringing confused the French. They supposed it was a call to arms. Several infantrymen ran to the Kutafyevsky gates. In the gateway lay beams and wooden screens. Two musket shots rang out from the gateway, as soon as an officer with a unit began running towards it. The general who stood by the guns shouted a command, and the officer and soldiers came running back.

Three more shots were heard from the gateway.

One shot grazed a French soldier's leg, and the strange shouting of a few voices came from behind the screens. On the faces of the French general, officers, and soldiers the former expression of cheerfulness and calm was replaced all at once, as if on command, by the stubborn, concentrated expression of a readiness to fight and suffer. For all of them, from marshal to the last soldier, this place was not Vzdvizhenka, Mokhovaya, Kutafaya, and the Troitsky gates, but the new terrain of a new and probably bloody battle. And they all prepared for that battle. The shouting from the gateway ceased. The guns were moved forward. The artillerymen blew the snuff from their wicks. The officer commanded, *"Feu!"** and the whistling sounds of two tin canisters rang out one after the other. Shot rattled against the stone of the gateway, the beams, the screens; and two clouds of smoke billowed over the square.

A few moments after the rolling of the shots over the stone Kremlin died away, a strange noise was heard over the heads of the French. A huge flock of jackdaws rose above the walls and, crowing and flapping thousands of wings, circled in the air. Along with that sound came a solitary human shout in the gateway, and from behind the smoke appeared the figure of a man without a hat, wearing a kaftan. He was holding a musket and aiming at the French. *"Feu!"* repeated the artillery officer, and one musket shot and two cannon shots rang out simultaneously. Smoke again covered the gateway.

Nothing stirred any more behind the screens, and the French soldiers and officers walked up to the gates. In the gateway lay three wounded and four dead men. Two men in kaftans were fleeing along the foot of the wall towards Znamenka Street.

"Enlevez-moi ça,"† said the officer, pointing to the beams and the corpses; and the French, having finished off the wounded, threw the corpses down behind the fence. Who these men were, no one knew. *"Enlevez-moi ça"* was all that was said of them, and they were thrown out and taken away later so that they would not stink. Thiers alone devoted a few eloquent lines to their memory: *"Ces misérables avaient envahi la citadelle sacrée, s'étaient emparés des fusils de l'arsenal, et tiraient (ces misérables) sur les Français. On en sabra quelques-uns et on purgea le Kremlin de leur présence."*‡

It was reported to Murat that the way had been cleared. The French entered the gates and began setting up camp on Senate Square. Soldiers threw chairs out of the windows of the Senate onto the square and built campfires.

*Fire!
†Rid me of that.
‡These wretches had invaded the sacred citadel, had taken guns from the arsenal, and had fired (the wretches) on the French. Some were put to the sword and the Kremlin was purged of their presence.

Other detachments passed through the Kremlin and settled along Maroseika, Lubyanka, and Pokrovka streets. Still others settled along Vzdvizhenka,
Znamenka, Nikolskaya, and Tverskaya. The French, finding no owners, settled everywhere not as in quarters in a town, but as in a camp located in a
town.

Though ragged, famished, exhausted, and reduced to a third of their former
number, the French soldiers still entered Moscow in an orderly manner. This
was an exhausted, emaciated, but still warlike and menacing army. But it was
an army only until the moment when the soldiers of that army dispersed to
quarters. As soon as the men of the regiments began to disperse among the
empty and wealthy houses, the army was annihilated for ever, and what
emerged were neither inhabitants nor soldiers, but something between the two,
known as looters. When the same men left Moscow five weeks later, they no
longer constituted an army. They were a mob of looters, each of whom drove
or carried with him a heap of things that seemed valuable or useful to him. The
goal of each of these men, as they were leaving Moscow, did not consist, as
before, in conquering, but only in keeping what they had acquired. Like the
monkey who, putting its hand into the narrow mouth of a jug and seizing a
handful of nuts, will not open its fist, so as not to lose what it has seized, and
thereby perishes, so the French, in leaving Moscow, were obviously bound to
perish as a result of dragging their loot with them, but to abandon that loot was
as impossible for them as it is for the monkey to let go of its handful of nuts. Ten
minutes after any French regiment entered some quarter of Moscow, there was
not a single soldier or officer left. In the windows of the houses, people in greatcoats and leggings could be seen laughing and strolling through the rooms; in
cellars and basements, the same sort of people were bustling about with provisions; in the courtyards, the same sort of people opened or broke down the
gates of sheds and stables; in the kitchens they made fires and, with their
sleeves rolled up, baked, kneaded, and cooked, frightened, amused, and fon-
dled the women and children. And there were many of these people everywhere in the shops and houses; but there was no more army.

On that same day, the French commanders issued order after order forbidding the troops to disperse through the city, strictly forbidding looting and
violence to the inhabitants, and announcing a general roll call for that very
evening; but despite all such measures, the men who formerly constituted an
army were spreading throughout the rich, empty city, abounding with comforts and supplies. As a hungry herd goes across a bare field in a group, but at
once irrepressibly scatters as soon as it comes upon rich pasture, so the troops
scattered as irrepressibly through the rich city.

There were no inhabitants in Moscow, and the soldiers were absorbed by it
like water by sand, and irrepressibly spread starwise in all directions from the
Kremlin, which they occupied first of all. Cavalrymen, entering a merchant's

house abandoned with all its goods, and finding stalls there not only for their own horses but extra ones as well, still went to occupy the house next door, which seemed better to them. Many occupied several houses, writing on them in chalk who the occupier was, and quarrelled and even fought with other units. Before they had time to settle, the soldiers ran outside to look over the city, and, hearing that everything had been abandoned, rushed wherever valuable things could be had for nothing. Officers went to stop the soldiers and were involuntarily drawn into the same acts. In Carriage Row there were abandoned shops with vehicles, and generals crowded there, picking out caleches and carriages for themselves. The remaining inhabitants invited the officers to stay with them, hoping to protect themselves from being looted. There was an abundance of riches and no end of them in sight; everywhere around the area occupied by the French, there were other areas, unknown and unoccupied, in which, as it seemed to the French, there were still greater riches. And Moscow absorbed them into itself more and more. Just as when water is poured onto dry ground, the result is that both water and dry ground disappear, so when the famished army entered the abundant, empty city, the result was that the army was annihilated and the abundant city was annihilated; there was mud, there were fires and looting.

The French ascribed the burning of Moscow *au patriotisme féroce de Rastopchine;** the Russians—to the savagery of the French. Yet in reality, with regard to the burning of Moscow, there were not and could not be any reasons for placing the responsibility for it on one or several persons. Moscow burned down because it was put into conditions in which any wooden town would have to burn down, regardless of whether the town had or did not have a hundred and thirty poor-quality fire pumps. Moscow had to burn down, because its inhabitants left it, and as inevitably as a pile of wood chips has to catch fire if sparks pour down on it for several days. A wooden town in which, in the presence of the inhabitants who own the houses and of the police, there are fires almost every day during the summer, cannot help burning down when there are no inhabitants there, but troops smoking pipes, making campfires on Senate Square out of the Senate's chairs, and cooking meals twice a day. Billet troops in the villages of some area during peacetime, and the number of fires in that area increases at once. How much greater, then, is the possibility of fires in an empty wooden town in which foreign troops are billeted? *Le patriotisme féroce de Rastopchine* and the savagery of the French are not to blame for anything here. Moscow caught fire from the pipes, the kitchens, the carelessness of enemy soldiers, who were living in houses they did not own. If there

*The fierce patriotism of Rastopchin.

was arson (which is very doubtful, because no one had any reason for it, and in any case it was troublesome and dangerous), that arson cannot be taken as the cause, since without any arson it would have been the same.

Flattering as it was for the French to blame the brutality of Rastopchin and for the Russians to blame the villain Bonaparte, or later to place the heroic torch in the hands of their own people, it is impossible not to see that there could be no such immediate causes for the burning, because Moscow had to burn down, just as any village, any factory, any house has to burn down which has been left by its owners, and in which strangers are allowed to take over and start cooking kasha for themselves. Moscow was burned by its inhabitants, true; but not by the inhabitants who stayed in it, but by those who left it. Occupied by the enemy, Moscow did not remain intact like Berlin, Vienna, and other cities, only because its inhabitants did not bring out bread and salt and the keys to the city for the French, but left it.

XXVII

The absorption of the French, which spread starwise over Moscow, reached the neighbourhood where Pierre was living only by the evening of the second of September.

After the past two days, spent solitarily and unusually, Pierre was in a state close to madness. His whole being was possessed by one importunate thought. He did not know how or when himself, but this thought had now taken such possession of him that he remembered nothing of the past, understood nothing of the present; and everything he saw and heard went on before him as in a dream.

Pierre had left his house only so as to be rid of the complicated tangle of life's demands which had taken hold of him, and which he, in the state he was in then, had been unable to disentangle. He had gone to Iosif Alexeevich's house under the pretext of sorting the books and papers of the deceased, only because he was seeking rest from life's anxieties, and the memory of Iosif Alexeevich was connected in his soul with the world of eternal, calm, and solemn thoughts, the complete opposite of the anxious tangle he felt himself being pulled into. He had sought a quiet refuge, and indeed had found one in Iosif Alexeevich's study. When, in the dead silence of the study, he sat down, resting his elbow on the deceased man's dusty writing table, memories of the last days began to appear calmly and meaningfully, one after another, in his imagination, especially of the battle of Borodino and of that indefinable feeling of his own insignificance and falseness in comparison with the truth, simplicity, and strength of that category of people imprinted in his soul under the name of *they*. When Gerasim roused him from his reflections, the thought came to Pierre that he would take part in the people's defence of Moscow, which he knew was pro-jected. And with that purpose he had at once asked Gerasim to obtain a kaftan and a pistol for him, and announced to him his intention of concealing his name and staying in Iosif Alexeevich's house. Later, in the course of his first day spent in solitude and idleness (Pierre tried several times, but was unable to fix his attention on Masonic manuscripts), a thought had vaguely presented itself to him several times, the same thought he had had before about the cabalistic connection between his name and the name of Bonaparte; but this thought that he, *l'Russe Besuhof,* was destined to set a limit to the power of the *beast,* still came to him only as one of those fantasies that, without cause or trace, flit through one's imagination.

When, having bought a kaftan (only with the aim of participating in the people's defence of Moscow), Pierre had met the Rostovs, and Natasha had said to him, "You're staying? Ah, that's so good!"—the thought had flashed through his head that it would indeed be good, even if Moscow were to be taken, for him to stay there and carry out what had been predestined.

The next day, with the one thought of not sparing himself and not lagging behind *them* in anything, he went out of the Three Hills gate with the people. But when he returned home, convinced that Moscow would not be defended, he suddenly felt that what formerly had been only a possibility had now turned into a necessity and an inevitability. He had to remain in Moscow, concealing his name, meet Napoleon, and kill him, so as either to perish, or to put an end to the misfortunes of all Europe, which proceeded, in Pierre's opinion, solely from Napoleon.

Pierre knew all the details of a German student's attempt on the life of Bona-parte in Vienna in 1809 and knew that this student had been shot.[19] And the danger to which he would subject his life while carrying out his intention excited him still more.

Two equally strong feelings drew Pierre irresistibly to his intention. The first was the feeling of the need for sacrifice and suffering in the awareness of the general calamity, that feeling on account of which he had gone to Mozhaisk on the twenty-fifth and ended up in the very heat of battle, and had now run away from his home and, instead of the habitual luxury and comforts of life, slept on a hard couch without undressing, and ate the same food as Gerasim; the other was that vague, exclusively Russian feeling of disdain for everything conven-tional, artificial, human, for everything that most people consider the highest good in the world. Pierre had experienced that strange and fascinating feeling for the first time in the Slobodsky palace, when he had suddenly felt that wealth, and power, and life—all that people arrange and preserve with such care—all this, if it is worth anything, is so only because of the pleasure with which one can abandon it all.

It was that feeling on account of which a volunteer recruit drinks up his last kopeck, a man on a drunken binge smashes mirrors and windows without any apparent reason and knowing that it will cost him his last penny; that feeling on account of which a man does (in the banal sense) insane things, as if testing his personal power and strength, claiming the presence of a higher judgement over life, which stands outside human conventions.

From that very day when Pierre had experienced this feeling for the first time in the Slobodsky palace, he had been constantly under its influence, but only now had found full satisfaction for it. Besides, at the present moment Pierre was supported in his intention and deprived of the possibility of renouncing it by what he had already done along that path. His flight from home, and his kaftan, and his pistol, and his declaration to the Rostovs that he would stay in Moscow—all this would not only lose its meaning, but would become contemptible and ridiculous (to which Pierre was sensitive), if, after all that, he left Moscow like everybody else.

Pierre's physical state, as always happens, coincided with his moral state. The unaccustomed, coarse food, the vodka he had been drinking during those days, the absence of wine and cigars, dirty, unchanged linen, two half-sleepless nights spent on a short sofa without bedding—all this kept Pierre in a state of irritation close to insanity.

It was already past one o'clock in the afternoon. The French were already entering Moscow. Pierre knew it, but instead of acting, he thought only about his undertaking, going through all its minutest future details. In his reveries, Pierre did not picture vividly to himself either the process of striking the blow itself or the death of Napoleon, but with extraordinary clarity and sad enjoyment pictured to himself his own destruction and his heroic courage.

"Yes, one for all, I must do it or perish!" he thought. "Yes, I'll go up . . . and then suddenly . . . Will it be a pistol or a dagger?" Pierre wondered. "However, it makes no difference. It is not I but the hand of Providence that punishes you, I'll say" (Pierre thought of the words he would utter as he killed Napoleon). "Well, so take me, punish me," Pierre went on saying to himself with a sad but firm expression on his face, bowing his head.

While Pierre stood in the middle of the room reasoning thus with himself, the door of the study opened and on the threshold appeared the totally transformed figure of the previously always timid Makar Alexeevich. His dressing gown hung open. His face was red and hideous. He was obviously drunk. Seeing Pierre, he was embarrassed at first, but, noticing embarrassment on Pierre's face, too, he at once took heart and, on staggering, thin legs, stepped into the middle of the room.

"They've turned coward," he said in a hoarse, trustful voice. "I say no surrender, I say . . . isn't it so, sir?" He reflected and suddenly, seeing the pistol on the table, seized it with unexpected swiftness and ran out to the corridor.

Gerasim and the yard porter, who followed Makar Alexeevich, stopped him in the front hall and tried to take the pistol from him. Pierre came out to the corridor and, with pity and revulsion, looked at this half-crazy old man. Makar Alexeich, wincing with the effort, clutched the pistol and cried out in a hoarse voice, clearly imagining something solemn to himself.

"To arms! Board 'em! No, you won't take it!" he cried.

"Enough, please, enough. Be so kind, please, leave off. Well, if you please, master . . ." Gerasim was saying, cautiously trying to steer Makar Alexeich towards the door by the elbows.

"Who are you? Bonaparte! . . ." cried Makar Alexeich.

"That's not nice, sir. Please go inside, have some rest. That little pistol, if you please."

"Away, contemptible slave! Don't touch me! See this?" cried Makar Alexeich, brandishing the pistol. "Board 'em!"

"Grab him," Gerasim whispered to the yard porter.

Makar Alexeich was seized by the arms and dragged towards the door.

The front hall was filled with the ugly noise of the scuffle and the drunken, wheezing sounds of a breathless voice.

Suddenly a new, piercing woman's cry came from the porch, and the cook rushed into the front hall.

"It's them! Saints alive! . . . It's them, by God! Four, on horseback! . . ." she cried.

Gerasim and the yard porter let go of Makar Alexeich, and in the hushed corridor they clearly heard the knocking of several hands on the front door.

XXVIII

Pierre, having decided to himself that, before carrying out his intention, he must reveal neither his rank nor his knowledge of French, stood in the half-opened doors to the corridor, intending to disappear as soon as the French came in. But the French came in, and Pierre still did not leave the doors: an invincible curiosity kept him there.

There were two of them. One was an officer, a tall, gallant, and handsome man; the other was obviously a soldier or an orderly, a low-slung, skinny, sun-burned man with sunken cheeks and a dull expression on his face. The officer, leaning on a stick and limping slightly, came in first. Having gone several steps, the officer, as if deciding to himself that the quarters were good, stopped, turned round to the soldiers who were standing in the doorway, and in a loud, commanding voice called to them to bring the horses. Having finished with that, the officer, raising his elbow high in a dashing gesture, smoothed his moustache and touched his hat with his hand.

"*Bonjour, la compagnie!*"* he said gaily, smiling and looking around him. No one made any reply.

"*Vous êtes le bourgeois?*"† the officer addressed Gerasim.

Gerasim gave the officer a fearfully questioning look.

"*Quartire, quartire, logement,*" said the officer, looking at the small man from above with an indulgent and good-natured smile. "*Les Français sont de bons enfants. Que diable! Voyons! Ne nous fâchons pas, mon vieux,*"‡ he added, patting the frightened and silent Gerasim on the shoulder.

"*Ah ça! Dites donc, on ne parle donc pas français dans cette boutique?*"§ he added, looking around and meeting Pierre's eyes. Pierre moved away from the door.

The officer turned to Gerasim again. He requested that Gerasim show him the rooms of the house.

"Master no here—not understand . . . my your . . ." said Gerasim, trying to make his words clearer by saying them incorrectly.

The French officer, smiling, spread his hands before Gerasim's nose, giving him to feel that he did not understand him either, and, limping, walked to the door where Pierre was standing. Pierre wanted to go away and hide from him, but just then he saw Makar Alexeich thrusting himself out of the open kitchen door with the pistol in his hand. With a madman's cunning, Makar Alexeich looked the Frenchman over, raised the pistol, and took aim.

"Board 'em!!!" shouted the drunk man, feeling for the trigger. The French officer turned at the shout, and at the same moment Pierre threw himself on the drunk man. Just as Pierre seized the pistol and raised it up, Makar Alexeich finally managed to put his finger on the trigger, and a shot rang out, deafening them all and drowning them in smoke. The Frenchman paled and rushed back to the door.

Forgetting his intention not to reveal his knowledge of French, Pierre, tearing the pistol away and dropping it, ran to the officer and began speaking to him in French.

"*Vous n'êtes pas blessé?*"# he said.

"*Je crois que non,*" replied the officer, feeling himself all over, "*mais je l'ai manqué belle cette fois-ci.*" he added, pointing to the broken plaster of the wall. "*Quel est cet homme?*"** the officer asked sternly, looking at Pierre.

"*Ah, je suis vraiment au désespoir de ce qui vient d'arriver,*" Pierre said

---

*Hello, everyone!
†Are you in charge?
‡*Kvartir, kvartir* [Russian], lodgings . . . The French are good fellows. Devil take it! Come now! Let's not be angry, old man.
§Well, now! Say, does nobody speak French in this shop?
#You're not wounded?
**I don't think so . . . but I had a lucky escape this time . . . Who is this man?

quickly, totally forgetting his role. *"C'est un fou, un malheureux qui ne savait pas ce qu'il faisait."**

The officer went up to Makar Alexeich and seized him by the collar.

Makar Alexeevich, slackening his lips as if falling asleep, swayed, leaning against the wall.

"Brigand, tu me la payeras," said the Frenchman, taking his hand away. *"Nous autres nous sommes cléments après la victoire: mais nous ne pardonnons pas aux traîtres,"*† he added with gloomy solemnity in his face and with a handsome, energetic gesture.

Pierre went on persuading the officer in French not to punish the drunken, insane man. The Frenchman listened silently, without changing his gloomy look, and suddenly turned to Pierre with a smile. For a few seconds he looked at him silently. His handsome face assumed a tragically tender expression, and he held out his hand.

"Vous m'avez sauvé la vie! Vous êtes français,"‡ he said. For a Frenchman that conclusion was unquestionable. Only a Frenchman could do a great deed, and the saving of his life, the life of M. Ramballe, *capitaine du 13ᵉ léger,*§ was without question a very great deed.

But however unquestionable this conclusion and the officer's conviction based on it were, Pierre found it necessary to disappoint him.

"Je suis russe,"# he said quickly.

"Tut, tut, tut, *à d'autres,"* said the Frenchman, wagging his finger before his nose and smiling. *"Tout à l'heure vous allez me conter tout ça,"* he said. *"Charmé de rencontrer un compatriote. Eh bien! qu'allons nous faire de cet homme?"*** he added, already addressing Pierre as his own brother. Even if Pierre was not a Frenchman, having received this highest title in the world, he could not renounce it, said the tone of the French officer and the expression of his face. To the last question, Pierre explained once again who Makar Alexeich was, explained that just before their arrival, this drunken, insane man had stolen a loaded pistol, which they had not managed to take away from him, and asked that his act go unpunished.

The Frenchman thrust out his chest and made a royal gesture with his hand.

"Vous m'avez sauvé la vie. Vous êtes français. Vous me demandez sa grâce? Je vous l'accorde. Qu'on emmène cet homme,"†† the French officer said

---

*Ah, I'm really in despair over what has just happened . . . He's a madman, an unfortunate, who didn't know what he was doing.

†Brigand, you'll pay me for that . . . We are merciful after victory: but we do not pardon traitors.

‡You've saved my life! You are French.

§Captain of the 13th light [horse].

#I am Russian.

***Tut, tut, tut,* tell that to others . . . You'll tell me all about it a little later . . . Delighted to meet a compatriot. Well, what are we going to do with this man?

††You have saved my life. You are French. You ask me for his pardon? I grant it to you. Take this man away.

quickly and energetically, taking the arm of Pierre, whom he had just promoted to Frenchman for saving his life, and going into the house with him.

The soldiers in the courtyard, hearing the shot, came into the front hall, asking what had happened, and showing a readiness to punish the guilty ones; but the officer sternly stopped them.

*"On vous demandera quand on aura besoin de vous,"** he said. The soldiers left. The orderly, who meanwhile had had time to visit the kitchen, came up to the officer.

"Capitaine, ils ont de la soupe et du gigot de mouton dans la cuisine," he said. *"Faut-il vous l'apporter?"†*

"Oui, et le vin,"‡ said the captain.

XXIX

When the French officer went into the house with Pierre, Pierre considered it his duty to assure the captain again that he was not French and wished to leave, but the French officer would not hear of it. He was so courteous, amiable, good-natured, and truly grateful for the saving of his life that Pierre did not have the heart to refuse him and sat down with him in the reception room, the first one they came to. To Pierre's assertion that he was not French, the captain, obviously not understanding how anybody could refuse such a flattering title, shrugged his shoulders and said that if he insisted so much on passing for a Russian, so be it, but in spite of that, he would be for ever bound to him all the same by a feeling of gratitude for saving his life.

If this man had been endowed with at least some ability to understand the feelings of other people and had guessed Pierre's feelings, Pierre would probably have left him; but this man's lively imperviousness to everything that was not himself won Pierre over.

"Français ou prince Russe incognito," said the Frenchman, examining Pierre's dirty but fine shirt and the signet ring on his finger, *"je vous dois la vie et je vous offre mon amitié. Un Français n'oublie jamais ni une insulte ni un service. Je vous offre mon amitié. Je ne vous dit que ça."§*

In the sounds of the voice, in the expression of the face, in the gestures of this officer there was so much good nature and nobility (in the French sense) that Pierre, responding with an unconscious smile to the smile of the Frenchman, pressed the hand held out to him.

---

* You'll be sent for when you're needed.
†Captain, they have soup and a leg of mutton in the kitchen . . . Shall I bring them to you?
‡Yes, and the wine.
§Frenchman or Russian prince incognito . . . I owe you my life and I offer you my friendship. A Frenchman never forgets an insult or a service. I offer you my friendship. That is all I say to you.

"Capitaine Ramballe du treizième léger, décoré pour l'affaire du Sept,"[20] he introduced himself with a self-satisfied, irrepressible smile that puckered his lips under his moustache. *"Voudrez-vous bien me dire à présent, à qui j'ai l'honneur de parler aussi agréablement au lieu de rester à l'ambulance avec la balle de ce fou dans le corps?"**

Pierre replied that he could not give his name and, blushing, tried to invent a name and talk about the reasons why he could not give it, but the Frenchman hastened to interrupt him.

"De grâce," he said. *"Je comprends vos raisons, vous êtes officier . . . officier supérieur, peut-être. Vous avez porté les armes contre nous. Ce n'est pas mon affaire. Je vous dois la vie. Cela me suffit. Je suis tout à vous. Vous êtes gentilhomme?"* he added with a slightly questioning tone. Pierre inclined his head. *"Votre nom de baptême, s'il vous plaît? Je ne demande pas davantage. Monsieur Pierre, dites-vous . . . Parfait. C'est tout ce que je désire savoir."*†

When the roast lamb, the omelette, the samovar, vodka, and wine from a Russian cellar, brought along by the French, were served, Ramballe invited Pierre to share this dinner and at once began eating himself, greedily and quickly, like a healthy and hungry man, quickly chewing with his strong teeth, constantly smacking his lips, and saying *excellent, exquis*!‡ His face was flushed and covered with sweat. Pierre was hungry and shared the dinner with pleasure. Morel, the orderly, brought a pan of warm water and put a bottle of red wine in it. He brought a bottle of kvass besides, which he had taken from the kitchen to try. This drink was already known to the French and had been given a name. They called it *limonade de cochon* ("pig's lemonade"), and Morel praised this *limonade de cochon*, which he had found in the kitchen. But since the captain had wine, procured as he was passing through Moscow, he left the kvass to Morel and took up the bottle of Bordeaux. He wrapped the bottle to the neck in a napkin, and poured wine for himself and for Pierre. Appeased hunger and the wine made the captain still more lively, and he talked ceaselessly during dinner.

"Oui, mon cher monsieur Pierre, je vous dois une fière chandelle de m'avoir sauvé . . . de cet enragé . . . J'en ai assez, voyez-vous, de balles dans le corps. En voilà une" (he pointed to his side) *"à Wagram et de deux à Smolensk"*— he pointed to the scar on his cheek. *"Et cette jambe, comme vous voyez, qui ne veut pas marcher. C'est à la grande bataille du 7 à la Moskowa que j'ai*

---

*Captain Ramballe of the thirteenth light, decorated for the business of the Seventh . . . Would you kindly tell me now with whom I have the honour of speaking so agreeably instead of lying in an ambulance with that madman's bullet in my body?

†Please . . . I understand your reasons, you are an officer . . . a superior officer, perhaps. You have borne arms against us. That is none of my business. I owe you my life. That is enough for me. I am entirely yours. You are a gentleman? . . . Your Christian name, if you please? I ask no more. Monsieur Pierre, you say . . . Perfect. That is all I want to know.

‡Excellent, exquisite!

*reçu ça. Sacré dieu, c'était beau. Il fallait voir ça, c'était un déluge de feu. Vous nous avez taillé une rude besogne; vous pouvez vous en vanter, nom d'un petit bonhomme. Et, ma parole, malgré l'atout que j'y ai gagné, je serais prêt à recommencer. Je plains ceux qui n'ont pas vu ça."**

"*J'y ai été,*"† said Pierre.

"*Bah, vraiment! Eh bien, tant mieux,*" said the Frenchman. "*Vous êtes de fiers ennemis, tout de même. La grande redoute a été tenace, nom d'une pipe. Et vous nous l'avez fait crânement payer. J'y suis allé trois fois, tel que vous me voyez. Trois fois nous étions sur les canons et trois fois on nous a culbuté et comme des capucins de cartes. Oh! c'était beau, monsieur Pierre. Vos grenadiers ont été superbes, tonnerre de Dieu. Je les ai vu six fois de suite serrer les rangs, et marcher comme à une revue. Les beaux hommes! Notre roi de Naples, qui s'y connait, a crié: bravo! Ah, ah! soldats comme nous autres!*" he said, smiling, after a moment's silence. "*Tant mieux, tant mieux, monsieur Pierre. Terribles en bataille . . . galants . . .*" he winked with a smile, "*avec les belles, voilà les Français, monsieur Pierre, n'est-ce pas?*"‡

The captain was so naïvely and good-naturedly merry, and wholesome, and pleased with himself, that Pierre glanced merrily at him and nearly winked himself. The word *galant* probably prompted the captain to thoughts about the state of Moscow.

"*À propos, dites donc, est-ce vrai que toutes les femmes ont quitté Moscou? Une drôle d'idée! Qu'avaient-elles à craindre?*"§

"*Est-ce que les dames françaises ne quitteraient pas Paris si les Russes y entraient?*"# asked Pierre.

*Yes, my dear Monsieur Pierre, I owe you a debt of gratitude for having saved me . . . from that madman . . . You see, I have enough bullets in me. Here's one . . . from Wagram and a second from Smolensk . . . And there's this leg, as you see, that doesn't want to walk. It was at the great battle of the 7th on the Moskova that I got that. Holy God, it was beautiful. You had to have seen it, it was a flood of fire. You carved out a rough task for us; you can be proud of it, by golly. And, on my word, despite the lick I came in for, I'd be ready to do it over again. I pity those who didn't see it.
†I was there.
‡Ah, really! Well, so much the better . . . You're tough enemies, anyhow. The great redoubt held out, bedad. And you made us pay pluckily for it. I went up it three times, as I'm here before you. Three times we were on the cannon and three times they knocked us over like cardboard hares. Oh! it was beautiful, Monsieur Pierre. Your grenadiers were superb, by God's thunder. I saw them close ranks six times in a row and march as if they were on review. Fine men! Our king of Naples, who knows something about it, shouted: Bravo! Ha, ha! Soldiers like the rest of us! . . . So much the better, so much the better, Monsieur Pierre. Terrible in battle . . . gallant . . . with the pretty women, that's the French for you, Monsieur Pierre, isn't it so?
§By the way, tell me, is it true that all the women have left Moscow? What a funny idea! What did they have to fear?
#Wouldn't the French ladies leave Paris if the Russians entered it?

"*Ah, ah, ah!* . . ." The Frenchman burst into merry, sanguine laughter, patting Pierre on the shoulder. "*Ah! elle est forte celle-là,*" he said. "*Paris?* . . . *Mais Paris . . . Paris . . .*"*

"*Paris la capitale du monde . . .*"† said Pierre, finishing his phrase.

The captain looked at Pierre. He had the habit of stopping in the middle of a conversation and gazing intently with laughing, tender eyes.

"*Eh bien, si vous ne m'aviez pas dit que vous êtes Russe, j'aurai parié que vous êtes Parisien. Vous avez ce . . . je ne sais quoi, ce . . .*"‡ and, having uttered this compliment, he again gave his silent look.

"*J'ai été à Paris, j'y ai passé des années,*"§ said Pierre.

"*Oh, ça se voit bien. Paris! . . . Un homme qui ne connaît pas Paris, est un sauvage. Un Parisien, ça se sent à deux lieues. Paris, c'est Talma, la Duchesnois, Potier, la Sorbonne, les boulevards,*"²¹ and, noticing that the conclusion was weaker than what had gone before, he hastily added: "*Il n'y a qu'un Paris au monde. Vous avez été à Paris et vous êtes resté Russe. Eh bien, je ne vous en estime pas moins.*"#

Under the influence of the wine he had drunk, and after the days he had spent alone with his dark thoughts, Pierre experienced an involuntary pleasure in conversing with this merry and good-natured man.

"*Pour en revenir à vos dames, on les dit bien belles. Quelle fichue idée d'aller s'enterrer dans les steppes, quand l'armée française est à Moscou. Quelle chance elles ont manqué celles-là. Vos moujiks c'est autre chose, mais vous autres gens civilisés vous devriez nous connaître mieux que ça. Nous avons pris Vienne, Berlin, Madrid, Naples, Rome, Varsovie, toutes les capitales du monde . . . On nous craint, mais on nous aime. Nous sommes bons à connaître. Et puis l'Empereur . . .*"** he began, but Pierre interrupted him.

"*L'Empereur,*" Pierre repeated, and his face suddenly acquired a sad and embarrassed expression. "*Est-ce que l'Empereur . . .*"††

---

*Ha, ha, ha! . . . Oh! that's a good one . . . Paris . . . But Paris . . . Paris . . .

†Paris, capital of the world . . .

‡Well, if you hadn't told me you were a Russian, I would have bet you were a Parisian. You have that . . . I don't know what, that . . .

§I was in Paris. I spent years there.

#Oh, that's quite obvious. Paris! . . . A man who doesn't know Paris is a savage. You can smell a Parisian two leagues away. Paris is Talma, la Duchesnois, Potier, the Sorbonne, the boulevards . . . There is only one Paris in the world. You've been in Paris and you've remained a Russian. Well, I don't respect you any the less for it.

**To come back to your ladies, they're said to be very beautiful. What an awful idea to go and bury themselves in the steppes when the French army is in Moscow. What a chance they've missed. Your muzhiks are another thing, but you more civilized people ought to know us better than that. We've taken Vienna, Berlin, Madrid, Naples, Rome, Warsaw, all the capitals of the world . . . We're feared, but we're loved. We're good to know. And then the emperor . . .

††The emperor . . . Is the emperor . . .

*"L'Empereur? C'est la générosité, la clémence, la justice, l'ordre, le génie, voilà l'Empereur! C'est moi, Ramballe, qui vous le dit. Tel que vous me voyez, j'étais son ennemi il y a encore huit ans. Mon père a été comte émigré ... Mais il m'a vaincu, cet homme. Il m'a empoigné. Je n'ai pas pu résister au spectacle de grandeur et de gloire dont il couvrait la France. Quand j'ai compris ce qu'il voulait, quand j'ai vu qu'il nous faisait une litière de lauriers, voyez-vous, je me suis dit: voilà un souverain, et je me suis donné à lui. Eh voilà! Oh, oui, mon cher, c'est le plus grand homme des siècles passés et à venir."**

"Est-il à Moscou?"† asked Pierre, faltering and with a criminal look. The Frenchman looked at Pierre's criminal face and smiled slightly.

"Non, il fera son entrée demain,"‡ he said and went on with his stories.

Their conversation was interrupted by the cries of several voices at the gate and the arrival of Morel, who came to tell the captain that the Württemberg hussars had arrived and wanted to put their horses in the same courtyard with the captain's horses. The difficulty came primarily from the fact that the hussars did not understand what was said to them.

The captain ordered the sergeant major brought to him and asked him in a stern voice what regiment he belonged to, who their commander was, and on what grounds he had allowed himself to occupy quarters which were already occupied. To the first two questions, the German, who had a poor understanding of French, named his regiment and his commander; but to the last question, which he did not understand, he answered, putting broken French words into German, that he was the regimental quartermaster, and that his commander had ordered him to occupy all the houses one after another. Pierre, who knew German, translated what the German said for the captain and gave the captain's reply in German to the Württemberg hussar. Having understood what was said to him, the German gave up and led his men away. The captain went out to the porch, giving instructions in a loud voice.

When he came back to the room, Pierre was sitting in the same place as before, his head lowered in his hands. His face expressed suffering. He was indeed suffering at that moment. When the captain went out and Pierre was left alone, he suddenly came to his senses and realized the position he was in. It was not that Moscow had been taken, and not that these happy victors were

---

*The emperor? He is generosity, clemency, justice, order, genius, that's the emperor! It is I, Ramballe, who tell you so. As I'm here before you, I was his enemy eight years ago. My father was an émigré count ... But the man won me over. He gripped me. I couldn't resist the spectacle of the greatness and glory with which he covered France. When I understood what he wanted, when I saw that he was making us a bed of laurels, you see, I said to myself: there's a real sovereign, and I gave myself to him. Well, there! Oh, yes, my dear, he's the greatest man of ages past and to come.
†Is he in Moscow?
‡No, he will make his entry tomorrow.

playing the masters in it and patronizing him—painful as it felt to Pierre, that was not what tormented him at the present moment. He was tormented by the consciousness of his own weakness. The several glasses of wine he had drunk, the conversation with this good-natured man, had destroyed the concentratedly grim state of mind in which Pierre had lived for those last days, and which was necessary for the carrying out of his intention. The pistol, and the dagger, and the peasant coat were ready; Napoleon would enter tomorrow. Pierre still considered it just as useful and worthy to kill the villain; but he felt that now he would not do it. Why? He did not know, but it was as if he had a presentiment that he would not carry out his intention. He struggled against the consciousness of his weakness, but he dimly sensed that he would not overcome it, that his former grim way of thinking about revenge, murder, and self-sacrifice had fallen into dust at the first contact with a human being.

The captain, limping slightly and whistling something, came into the room.

The Frenchman's chatter, which had previously amused Pierre, now seemed disgusting to him. The tune he whistled, and the way he walked, and the gesture of twirling his moustache, all now seemed offensive to Pierre.

"I'll leave now, I won't say another word to him," thought Pierre. He thought it, and meanwhile he went on sitting in the same place. Some strange feeling of weakness chained him to his place: he wanted to get up and leave, but could not.

The captain, on the contrary, seemed very merry. He paced the room a couple of times. His eyes gleamed, and his moustache twitched slightly as if he was smiling to himself at some amusing fancy.

"*Charmant,*" he said suddenly, "*le colonel de ces Wurtembourgeois! C'est un Allemand; mais brave garçon, s'il en fut. Mais Allemand.*"*

He sat down facing Pierre.

"*À propos, vous savez donc l'allemand, vous?*"†

Pierre looked at him silently.

"*Comment dites-vous 'asile' en allemand?*"‡

"*Asile?*" Pierre repeated. "*Asile en allemand—Unterkunft.*"

"*Comment dites-vous?*" the captain asked again, mistrustfully and quickly.

"*Unterkunft,*" Pierre repeated.

"*Onterkoff,*" said the captain, and he looked at Pierre for a few seconds with laughing eyes. "*Les Allemands sont de fières bêtes. N'est-ce pas, monsieur Pierre?*"§ he concluded.

---

*Charming . . . the colonel of these Württemburgers [sic]! He's a German, but a good fellow if there ever was one. But German.
†By the way, you know German, then?
‡How do you say "shelter" in German?
§The Germans are downright fools. Isn't it so, Monsieur Pierre?

*"Eh bien, encore une bouteille de ce Bordeaux Moscovite, n'est-ce pas? Morel, vas nous chauffer encore une petite bouteille. Morel!"** the captain cried merrily.

Morel brought candles and a bottle of wine. The captain looked at Pierre in the light and was evidently struck by his interlocutor's upset face. Ramballe went up to Pierre with a look of genuine distress and concern and bent over him.

"Eh bien, nous sommes tristes," he said, touching Pierre's arm. *"Vous aurai-je fait de la peine? Non, vrai, avez-vous quelque chose contre moi?"* he asked insistently. *"Peut-être rapport à la situation?"*†

Pierre made no reply, but looked affectionately into the Frenchman's eyes. This expression of concern was pleasing to him.

"Parole d'honneur, sans parler de ce que je vous dois, j'ai de l'amitié pour vous. Puis-je faire quelque chose pour vous? Disposez de moi. C'est à la vie et à la mort. C'est la main sur coeur que je vous le dis,"‡ he said, striking himself on the chest.

"Merci," said Pierre. The captain looked intently at Pierre, as he had looked at him when he learned what shelter was in German, and his face suddenly brightened.

"Ah! dans ce cas je bois à notre amitié!"§ he cried merrily, pouring two glasses of wine. Pierre took the filled glass and drank it. Ramballe drank his, shook Pierre's hand once more, and leaned his elbow on the table in a pensively melancholic pose.

"Oui, mon cher ami, voilà les caprices de la fortune," he began. *"Qui m'aurait dit que je serai soldat et capitaine de dragons au service de Bonaparte, comme nous l'appelions jadis. Et cependant me voilà à Moscou avec lui. Il faut vous dire, mon cher,"* he went on in the sad and measured voice of a man who is about to tell a long story, *"que notre nom est l'un de plus anciens de la France."*#

And with the easy and naïve candour of a Frenchman, the captain told Pierre the history of his ancestors, his childhood, adolescence, and maturity, all his genealogical, proprietary, and familial relations. *"Ma pauvre mère"* naturally played an important role in the story.

"Mais tout ça ce n'est que la mise en scène de la vie, le fond c'est l'amour.

*Well, one more bottle of this Muscovite Bordeaux, shall we? Morel, go and warm us up another little bottle. Morel!
†Well, so we're sad . . . Have I upset you? No, really, have you got something against me? . . . Maybe to do with the situation?
‡Word of honour, not to speak of what I owe you, I feel friendship for you. Can I do something for you? I'm at your disposal. That is for life and for death. With my hand on my heart I say it to you.
§Ah! In that case I drink to our friendship!
#Yes, my friend, such are the caprices of fortune . . . Who would have said that I would be a soldier and a captain of dragoons in the service of Bonaparte, as we used to call him. And yet here I am in Moscow with him. I must tell you, my dear . . . that our name is one of the oldest in France.

L'amour! N'est-ce pas, monsieur Pierre?" he said, growing animated. *"Encore un verre."**

Pierre drank again and poured a third glass.

"Oh, les femmes, les femmes!"† And the captain, looking at Pierre with unctuous eyes, began talking about love and about his amorous adventures. There were a great many of them, which was easy to believe, looking at the officer's self-satisfied, handsome face and the rapturous animation with which he talked about women. Despite the fact that all of Ramballe's love stories had that smutty character in which the French see the exceptional charm and poetry of love, the captain told his stories with such a genuine conviction that he alone had experienced and known all the charms of love, and described women so enticingly, that Pierre listened to him with curiosity.

It was obvious that the *amour* which the Frenchman liked so much was neither that low and simple kind of love that Pierre had once felt for his wife, nor the romantic love he felt for Natasha and fanned so much himself (Ramballe equally despised both these kinds of love—one was *l'amour de charretiers*, the other *l'amour des nigauds‡*); the *amour* which the Frenchman venerated consisted mainly in unnatural relations with women and in the combinations of abnormalities that endowed the feeling with its main charm.

Thus, the captain told a touching story of his love for an enchanting thirty-five-year-old marquise and at the same time for a charmingly innocent seventeen-year-old child, the enchanting marquise's daughter. The contest of magnanimity between the mother and daughter, which ended with the mother sacrificing herself and offering her daughter in marriage to her own lover, excited the captain even now, though it was a long-past memory. Then he recounted an episode in which the husband played the role of the lover and he (the lover) the role of the husband, and several other comic episodes from his *souvenirs d'Allemagne*, where *asile* means *Unterkunft*, where *les maris mangent de la choucroute* and *les jeunes filles sont trop blondes.§*

Finally, the latest episode in Poland, still fresh in the captain's memory, which he recounted with quick gestures and a flushed face, consisted in the fact that he had saved the life of a Pole (in general, episodes of saving lives occurred constantly in the captain's stories) and the Pole had entrusted his enchanting

---

*But all that is only the setting for life, the essence is love. Love! Isn't it so, Monsieur Pierre? . . . Another glass.

†Oh, women, women!

‡The love of wagoners . . . the love of simpletons.

§The husbands eat sauerkraut *and* the young girls are too blonde.

wife to him *(Parisienne de coeur*)*, while he himself entered into the service of the French. The captain was happy, the enchanting Polish lady wanted to run off with him; but, moved by magnanimity, the captain had returned the wife to her husband with the words: *"Je vous ai sauvé la vie, je sauve votre honneur!"*† Having repeated these words, the captain rubbed his eyes and shook himself, as if to drive away the weakness that came over him at this touching memory.

Listening to the captain's stories, as often happens late at night and under the influence of wine, Pierre followed everything he said, understood everything, and at the same time followed a line of personal memories that for some reason suddenly arose in his imagination. As he listened to these stories of love, suddenly, unexpectedly, he remembered his own love for Natasha, and going over the pictures of that love in his imagination, he mentally compared them with Ramballe's stories. Following the story of the struggle between duty and love, Pierre saw before him all the minutest details of his last meeting with the object of his love by the Sukhareva tower. Then this meeting had made no effect on him; he had not recalled it even once. But now it seemed to him that this meeting had had something very significant and poetic about it.

"Pyotr Kirilych, come here, I recognized you," he now heard the words she had said, saw before him her eyes, her smile, her travelling bonnet, a stray lock of hair . . . and something touching, something deeply moving, appeared to him in all this.

Having finished his story about the enchanting Polish woman, the captain turned to Pierre with the question whether he had ever experienced the same feeling of self-sacrifice for the sake of love and envy of the lawful husband.

Challenged by this question, Pierre raised his head and felt it necessary to voice the thoughts that occupied him; he began to explain that he understood love for a woman somewhat differently. He said that he loved and had loved only one woman in all his life and that that woman could never belong to him.

"Tiens!"‡ said the captain.

Then Pierre explained that he had loved this woman from a very early age, but had not dared to think of her, because she was too young and he was an illegitimate son without a name. Later, when he had acquired a name and wealth, he had not dared to think of her because he loved her too much, placed her too high above the whole world, and the more so, therefore, above himself. Reaching this point in his story, Pierre turned to the captain with the question whether he understood it.

The captain made a gesture which said that, even if he did not, he still asked him to go on.

---

*A Parisian woman at heart.
†I saved your life, I am saving your honour!
‡Well, now!

"*L'amour platonique, les nuages . . .*"* he murmured.

The wine he had drunk, or the need for openness, or the thought that this man did not and never would know any of the persons active in his story, or all of it together, loosened Pierre's tongue. And with a maundering mouth, his unctuous eyes looking somewhere into the distance, he told his whole story: his marriage, the story of Natasha's love for his best friend, and her betrayal, and all his own uncomplicated relations with her. Urged on by Ramballe's questions, he even told him what he had concealed at first—his social position—and even revealed his name to him.

Of all that Pierre told him, the captain was most struck by the fact that Pierre was very rich, that he had two mansions in Moscow, and that he had abandoned everything, and had not left Moscow, but had stayed in the city, concealing his name and rank.

Late at night they went outside together. The night was warm and bright. To the left of the house the first Moscow fire, started on the Petrovka, glowed brightly. To the right, high in the sky, was a young crescent moon, and opposite the crescent hung that bright comet which in Pierre's soul was connected with his love. By the gate stood Gerasim, the cook, and two Frenchmen. Their laughter and talk in mutually incomprehensible languages could be heard. They were looking at the glow that was visible in the city.

There was nothing terrible about a small, distant fire in a huge city.

Looking at the high, starry sky, at the crescent moon, at the comet, and at the glow, Pierre experienced a joyful tenderness. "See how good it is! What more does one need?!" he thought. And suddenly, remembering his intention, his head whirled, he felt sick, and had to lean on the fence so as not to fall.

Without saying goodbye to his new friend, Pierre left the gates with unsteady steps and, going back to his room, lay down on the sofa and fell asleep at once.

XXX

The glow of the first fire that started on the second of September was watched from different roads and with different feelings by the inhabitants fleeing Moscow in carriages and on foot and by the retreating soldiers.

The Rostovs' train stopped that night in Mytishchi, thirteen miles from Moscow. On the first of September they had set out so late, the road had been so encumbered with carts and troops, so many things had been forgotten, for which people had to be sent back, that it had been decided to spend that night three miles from Moscow. The next morning they started late and again

*Platonic love, clouds . . .

stopped so many times that they only reached Great Mytishchi. At ten o'clock the Rostov family and the wounded who were travelling with them, all settled in the yards and cottages of the big village. The servants, the Rostovs' drivers, and the orderlies of the wounded, after taking care of the masters, had supper, fed the horses, and went out to the porch.

In a cottage next door lay Raevsky's wounded adjutant with a shattered hand, and the terrible pain he felt made him moan pitifully, ceaselessly, and those moans had a terrible sound in the autumnal darkness of the night. This adjutant had spent the first night in the same courtyard as the Rostovs. The countess said she had not slept a wink on account of that moaning, and in Mytishchi they took an inferior cottage only so as to be further away from this wounded man.

One of the servants noticed, in the dark of the night, above the high body of a carriage that stood by the porch, another small glow of a fire. One glow had been visible for a long time already, and everyone knew it was Little Mytishchi, set on fire by Mamonov's Cossacks.

"But that, brothers, is a different fire," said an orderly.

They all turned their attention to the glow.

"Didn't they say Mamonov's Cossacks set fire to it?"

"Them! No, that's not Mytishchi, it's further away."

"Looks like it's in Moscow."

Two of the men stepped off the porch, went round the carriage, and sat on the footboard.

"It's more to the left! Come on, Mytishchi's over there, and that's on a completely different side."

Several people joined the first ones.

"Look at it blazing up," said one. "That, gentlemen, is a fire in Moscow: either in Sushchevskaya or in Rogozhskaya."

Nobody replied to this observation. And for some time all these people silently watched the flames of the new fire blazing up in the distance.

Old Danilo Terentyich, the count's valet (as he was called), went up to the crowd and called out to Mishka.

"What are you gaping at, you halfwit . . . The count will ask, and there'll be nobody. Go and get the clothes ready."

"I just ran to fetch some water," said Mishka.

"And what do you think, Danilo Terentyich, might that glow be in Moscow?" asked one of the servants.

Danilo Terentyich made no reply, and again everyone was silent for a long time. The glow spread and wavered further and further.

"Lord have mercy! . . . it's windy and dry . . ." a voice spoke again.

"Look how it's got going. Oh, Lord! you can even see the sparks flying! Lord, have mercy on us sinners!"

"They'll put it out, no fear."

"Who is there to put it out?" came the voice of Danilo Terentyich, who had been silent until then. His voice was calm and slow. "That's our Moscow, brothers," he said, "she, our dear mother of white st . . ."²² His voice broke, and he suddenly gave an old man's sob. And it was as if they had only been waiting for that to understand the meaning which this glow they were looking at had for them. Sighs were heard, words of prayer, and the sobbing of the count's old valet.

XXXI

The valet, coming back in, told the count that Moscow was burning. The count put on his dressing gown and went to look. Madame Schoss and Sonya, who had not undressed yet, went with him. Only Natasha and the countess stayed in the room (Petya was no longer with the family; he had gone ahead with his regiment, which was marching towards the Trinity monastery²³).

The countess began to cry on hearing the news about the Moscow fire. Natasha, pale, with a fixed gaze, sitting on a bench under the icons (in the same place where she had sat when they arrived), paid no attention to her father's words. She kept listening to the ceaseless moaning of the adjutant coming from three houses away.

"Ah, how terrible!" said the chilled and frightened Sonya, coming in from outside. "I think the whole of Moscow will burn down, it's such a terrible glow! Natasha, look now, you can see it from here through the window," she said to her cousin, evidently wishing to distract her with something. But Natasha looked at her as if she did not understand what was being asked of her, and again fixed her gaze on the corner of the stove. Natasha had been in this state of stupor since morning, when Sonya, to the countess's astonishment and vexation, had found it necessary, no one knew why, to tell Natasha about Prince Andrei's wound and his presence with them in the train. The countess had rarely been so angry with Sonya. Sonya had wept and asked forgiveness, and now, as if trying to smooth over her guilt, constantly attended to her cousin.

"Look, Natasha, how terribly it's burning," said Sonya.

"What's burning?" asked Natasha. "Ah, yes, Moscow."

And so as not to hurt Sonya by refusing and also to get rid of her, she moved her head towards the window, looked in such a way that she obviously could not see anything, and again sat in her former position.

"But you didn't see?"

"No, really, I did," she said in a voice pleading to be left in peace.

The countess and Sonya both understood that neither Moscow, nor the Moscow fire, nor anything else, of course, could have any meaning for Natasha.

The count went behind the partition again and lay down. The countess went up to Natasha, touched her head with the back of her hand, as she did when her daughter was sick, then touched her forehead with her lips, as if to see whether she had a fever, and kissed her.

"You're chilled. You're trembling all over. You should lie down," she said.

"Lie down? All right, I'll lie down. I'll lie down in a minute," said Natasha.

When Natasha had been told that morning that Prince Andrei had been badly wounded and was travelling with them, only at first had she asked many questions about where? how? was the wound dangerous? and could she see him? But after she was told that she could not see him, that he was badly wounded, but that his life was not in danger, she stopped asking and talking, obviously not believing what she was told, but convinced that no matter how much she talked, she would be told the same thing. All along the way, with her wide eyes, which the countess knew so well and the expression of which she feared so much, Natasha had sat motionless in the corner of the carriage, and was now sitting in the same way on the bench she had sat down on. She was planning something, deciding something, or had now already decided it in her mind—the countess knew that, but what it was she did not know, and that frightened and tormented her.

"Natasha, darling, undress and get into my bed." (The countess alone had a real bed made up for her: Mme Schoss and the two girls had to sleep on straw on the floor.)

"No, mama, I'll lie down here on the floor," Natasha said crossly, went to the window, and opened it. Through the open window, the moaning of the adjutant could be heard more clearly. She thrust her head out into the damp night air, and the countess saw her slender shoulders shake and beat against the windowsill. Natasha knew it was not Prince Andrei moaning. She knew that Prince Andrei was lying in the same cottage where they were, in the room on the other side of the front hall; but this terrible, ceaseless moaning made her burst into sobs. The countess exchanged glances with Sonya.

"Lie down, darling, lie down, my dear," said the countess, touching Natasha's shoulder lightly with her hand. "Do lie down."

"Ah, yes . . . I'll lie down right now," said Natasha, hastily undressing and tearing the lacings of her petticoat. Having thrown off her dress and put on her night jacket, she sat on the bed that had been prepared for her on the floor, tucking her legs under, and, throwing her thin and not very long braid over her shoulder, began rebraiding it. Her long, thin, accustomed fingers quickly, deftly undid, plaited, and tied up the braid. Natasha's head, with a habitual gesture, turned one way, then the other, but her eyes, feverishly wide, looked straight ahead fixedly. When the preparations for the night were over, Natasha slowly lowered herself onto the sheet that covered the straw, on the side nearest the door.

"Natasha, lie in the middle," said Sonya.

"No, I'll lie here," said Natasha. "Do go to bed, all of you," she added with vexation. And she buried her face in the pillow.

The countess, Mme Schoss, and Sonya hastily undressed and went to bed. Only the icon lamp remained lit in the room. But outdoors the fire in Little Mytishchi made it bright for two miles around, and there was the noise of drunk men shouting in the pot-house on the opposite corner of the street, which Mamonov's Cossacks had broken into, and the adjutant's constant moaning could still be heard.

Natasha listened for a long time to the sounds that reached her from outside and inside, and did not stir. First she heard her mother praying and sighing, the creaking of the bed under her, the familiar whistling snore of Mme Schoss, the quiet breathing of Sonya. Then the countess called Natasha's name. Natasha did not answer.

"She seems to be asleep, mama," Sonya replied softly. The countess, after a brief pause, called once more, but now no one answered her.

Soon after that, Natasha heard her mother's regular breathing. Natasha did not stir, though her bare little foot, sticking out from under the covers, felt cold on the bare floor.

As if celebrating a victory over everyone, a cricket chirped in a crack. A cock crowed far away, others responded nearby. The shouts died down in the pot-house, and only the adjutant's moaning could be heard. Natasha sat up.

"Sonya, are you asleep? Mama?" she whispered. No one answered. Natasha got up slowly and carefully, crossed herself, and stepped carefully with her slender and supple foot on the dirty, cold floor. A board creaked. Moving her feet quickly, she ran several steps like a kitten, and grasped the cold door handle.

It seemed to her that something heavy, throbbing rhythmically, was beating on all the walls of the cottage: it was the pounding of her own heart, sinking with fear, breaking with terror and love.

She opened the door, stepped across the threshold and onto the damp, cold, earthen floor of the front hall. The cold enveloped and refreshed her. With her bare foot, she felt a sleeping man, stepped over him, and opened the door to the room where Prince Andrei was. The room was dark. In the back corner by the bed, on which something lay, a tallow candle with a big mushroom of snuff stood on a bench.

Already that morning, when she had been told about the wound and Prince Andrei's presence, Natasha had decided that she must see him. She did not know why it had to be so, but she knew that the meeting would be painful, and was all the more convinced that it was necessary.

All day she had lived only in the hope of seeing him that night. But now that the moment had come, she was terrified of what she was going to see. How disfigured was he? What was left of him? Was he the same as that ceaseless moaning of the adjutant? Yes, that was how he was. In her imagination, he was the embodiment of that terrible moaning. When she saw an obscure mass in the corner, and took his knees raised under the blanket for his shoulders, she imagined some terrible body and stopped in horror. But an invincible power drew her on. She carefully took one step, another, and came into the middle of the small, cluttered room. Another man was lying in this room on the bench under the icons (this was Timokhin), and two more men were lying on the floor (these were the doctor and the valet).

The valet rose a little and whispered something. Timokhin, suffering from the pain in his wounded leg, was not asleep and stared all eyes at the strange apparition of a girl in a white nightgown, a jacket, and a nightcap. The valet's sleepy and frightened words—"What is it, why?"—only made Natasha approach more quickly what lay in the corner. However frightening and unlike anything human this body was, she had to see it. She went past the valet: the mushroom of snuff fell from the candle, and she clearly saw Prince Andrei lying with his arms on the covers, the same as she had always seen him.

He was the same as always; but the inflamed colour of his face, his glittering eyes, rapturously fixed on her, and especially his tender, childlike neck, rising from the turned-down collar of his shirt, gave him a special, innocent, boyish look, which she had never seen in Prince Andrei before. She went up to him, and with a quick, supple, youthful movement dropped to her knees.

He smiled and gave her his hand.

XXXII

For Prince Andrei seven days had gone by since the time he had come to himself in the dressing station on the field of Borodino. For all that time he had been almost continuously unconscious. In the opinion of the doctor, who accompanied the wounded man, his feverish state and the inflammation of his injured intestines were bound to carry him off. But on the seventh day he ate with pleasure a piece of bread with tea, and the doctor observed that his overall fever had gone down. Prince Andrei regained consciousness in the morning. The first night after they left Moscow had been quite warm, and Prince Andrei had been left to spend the night in the caleche; but in Mytishchi the wounded man himself had asked to be taken out and given tea. The pain caused by the transfer to the cottage had made Prince Andrei moan loudly and lose consciousness again. When he had been placed on the camp bed, he lay for a long time with his eyes closed, not moving. Then he opened them and whispered softly: "What about the tea?" This memory of the small details of life struck the doctor. He took his pulse and, to his astonishment and displeasure, noticed that the pulse had improved. The doctor was displeased to notice it, because he was convinced from experience that Prince Andrei could not live and that, if he did not die now, he would die with greater suffering some time later. Timokhin, the major of his regiment with the little red nose, who had been wounded in the leg at the same battle of Borodino and had joined them in Moscow, was being transported along with Prince Andrei. They were accompanied by the doctor, the prince's valet, his driver, and two orderlies.

Prince Andrei was given tea. He drank it greedily, looking with feverish eyes at the door straight ahead of him, as if trying to understand and recall something.

"I don't want any more. Is Timokhin here?" he asked. Timokhin crawled towards him along the bench.

"I'm here, Your Excellency."

"How's the wound?"

"Mine, sir? It's all right. What about you?" Prince Andrei lapsed into thought again, as if trying to recall something.

"Is it possible to get hold of a book?" he said.

"What book?"

"The Gospel! I don't have it."

The doctor promised to get hold of it and began to ask the prince about what he felt. Prince Andrei answered all the doctor's questions reluctantly but reasonably, and then said he would like to be propped on a bolster, because he was uncomfortable and in great pain. The doctor and the valet lifted the great-coat that covered him and, wincing from the strong smell of rotting flesh that spread from the wound, began to examine this dreadful place. The doctor remained very displeased with something, changed something, turning the wounded man over so that he moaned again and, while he was being turned, again fainted from the pain and began to rave. He kept saying that they should quickly get hold of that book for him and put it there under him.

"What will it cost you!" he said. "I don't have it—get it, please, put it under me for a moment," he said in a pitiful voice.

The doctor went to the front hall to wash his hands.

"Ah, shame on you, really," the doctor said to the valet, who was pouring water over his hands. "I just looked away for a moment. You laid him right on his wound. It's such pain, I'm amazed he can bear it."

"I thought we put something under him, Lord Jesus Christ," said the valet.

For the first time Prince Andrei understood where he was and what had happened to him, and remembered that he had been wounded and how, the moment the caleche stopped in Mytishchi, he had asked to be taken into the cottage. Confused again by the pain, he had come to his senses in the cottage while drinking tea, and here again, repeating in his memory everything that had happened to him, he pictured most vividly to himself that moment in the dressing station when, at the sight of the suffering of a man he had no love for, those new thoughts, promising happiness, had come to him. And those thoughts, though vaguely and indefinitely, now took possession of his soul again. He remembered that he now had a new happiness, and that that happiness had something to do with the Gospel. That was why he had asked for the Gospel. But the position they had put him in, which was bad for his wound, and the new turning over, had confused his thoughts again, and he came back to life for the third time in the total silence of the night. Everyone around him was asleep. A cricket chirped in the room across the hall, someone shouted and sang outside, the cockroaches rustled on the table and the icons, and a fat autumnal fly beat against his headboard and around the candle with its big, mushroom-like snuff that stood next to him.

His soul was not in a normal state. A healthy man usually thinks, feels, and remembers a countless number of subjects simultaneously, but has the power and strength to select one sequence of thoughts or phenomena and fix all his attention on it. A healthy man in a moment of the deepest reflection can tear himself away to say a few polite words to someone coming in and then return to his thoughts. But Prince Andrei's soul was not in a normal state in this respect. The forces of his soul were all clearer and more active than ever, but they acted outside his will. The most diverse thoughts and notions took hold of him simultaneously. Sometimes his thought suddenly began to work, and with such strength, clarity, and depth as it had never been able to do in healthy conditions; but suddenly, in the middle of its work, it broke off and was replaced by some unexpected notion, and he was unable to return to it.

"Yes, a new happiness was revealed to me, inalienable from man," he thought, lying in the quiet, semi-dark cottage and looking straight ahead with a feverishly wide, fixed gaze. "A happiness that is beyond material forces, beyond external material influences on man, a happiness of the soul alone, the happiness of love! Every person can understand it, but only God could conceive and prescribe it. But how did God prescribe this law? Why the Son? . . ." And suddenly this course of thoughts broke off, and Prince Andrei heard (not knowing whether it was in delirium or in reality) some soft, whispering voice ceaselessly repeating in rhythm: "Piti-piti-piti" and then "ti-ti," and again "piti-piti-piti" and again "ti-ti." And at the same time, to the sound of this whispering music, Prince Andrei felt that above his face, above the very middle of it, a strange airy edifice of fine needles or splinters was being raised. He felt (though it was hard for him) that he had to try to keep his balance, so that this rising edifice would not collapse; but even so it kept collapsing and was raised again to the sounds of the measured, whispering music. "It stretches! stretches! stretches out, and keeps stretching!" Prince Andrei said to himself. While listening to the whisper and feeling this stretching edifice of needles being raised, Prince Andrei had glimpses of the red circle of light around the candle and heard the rustling of cockroaches and of the fly striking against the pillow and his face. And each time the fly touched his face, it made a burning sensation, and at the same time he was surprised that, hitting against the very area of his face where the edifice was being raised, the fly did not destroy it. But besides that, there was something else important. It was the white thing in the doorway, it was the statue of a sphinx, which also weighed on him.

"But maybe it's my shirt on the table," thought Prince Andrei, "and these are my legs, and that's the door, but why is everything stretching and thrusting out and piti-piti-piti and ti-ti—and piti-piti-piti . . . Enough, stop, please, let me be," Prince Andrei begged someone painfully. And suddenly his thought and feeling emerged again with extraordinary clarity and force.

"Yes, love" (he thought again with perfect clarity), "but not the love that loves for something, for some purpose, or for some reason, but the love I experienced for the first time when, as I lay dying, I saw my enemy and loved him all the same. I experienced the feeling of love, which is the very essence of the soul and which needs no object. Now, too, I am experiencing that blissful feeling. To love my neighbours, to love my enemies. To love everything—to love God in all His manifestations. You can love a person dear to you with a human love, but an enemy can only be loved with divine love. That's why I experienced such joy when I felt that I loved that man. What's become of him? Is he alive . . . Loving with a human love, one can pass from love to hatred; but divine love cannot change. Nothing, not even death, nothing can destroy it. It is the essence of the soul. But I've hated so many people in my life. And of all people, I have loved and hated no one so much as her." And he vividly pictured Natasha to himself, not as he had pictured her before, with her loveliness alone, which brought him joy; but for the first time he pictured her soul. And he understood her feeling, her suffering, shame, repentance. For the first time now he understood all the cruelty of his refusal, saw the cruelty of his break with her. "If it were possible to see her just one more time. One time, looking into those eyes, to say . . ."

And piti-piti-piti and ti-ti, and piti-piti—boom, the fly struck. And his attention suddenly raced on to another world of reality and delirium, in which something special was happening. In that world, the edifice was still being raised without collapsing, something was still stretching, there was the same circle of red light around the candle, the same shirt-sphinx was lying by the door; but, besides all that, something creaked, there was a breath of fresh air, and a new white sphinx appeared, standing before the door. And the head of this sphinx had the pale face and shining eyes of that same Natasha, of whom he had just been thinking.

"Oh, how painful this constant delirium is!" thought Prince Andrei, trying to drive that face from his imagination. But that face stood before him with the force of reality, and that face was coming nearer. Prince Andrei wanted to return to the former world of pure thought, but he could not, and delirium was drawing him into its realm. The quiet, whispering voice continued its measured prattle, something weighed on him, stretched, and the strange face stood before him. Prince Andrei gathered all his forces so as to keep his senses; he stirred and suddenly there was a ringing in his ears, his eyes clouded, and, like a man plunging into water, he lost consciousness. When he came to himself, Natasha, that same living Natasha whom of all people in the world he most wanted to love with that new, pure, divine love which had now been revealed to him, was kneeling beside him. He understood that this was the living, real Natasha, and was not surprised, but quietly glad. Natasha, kneeling, gazed at him fearfully but fixedly (she was unable to move), trying to stifle her sobs. Her face was pale and motionless. Only in the lower part of it something trembled.

Prince Andrei sighed with relief, smiled, and held out his hand.

"You?" he said. "What happiness!"

With a quick but careful movement, Natasha moved closer to him on her knees and, carefully taking his hand, bent her head over it and began to kiss it, barely touching it with her lips.

"Forgive me!" she said in a whisper, raising her head and glancing at him. "Forgive me!"

"I love you," said Prince Andrei.

"Forgive . . ."

"Forgive what?" asked Prince Andrei.

"Forgive me for what I di . . . did," Natasha said in a barely audible, faltering whisper, and she began to kiss his hand more quickly, barely touching it with her lips.

"I love you more, better, than before," said Prince Andrei, raising her face with his hand so that he could see her eyes.

Those eyes filled with happy tears looked at him timidly, with compassion and joyful love. Natasha's thin and pale face with its swollen lips was more than unattractive, it was frightful. But Prince Andrei did not see that face, he saw radiant eyes, which were beautiful. Behind them talking could be heard.

The valet Pyotr, now fully awake, aroused the doctor. Timokhin, who had not slept all that time because of the pain in his leg, had long been watching everything that was happening, and fidgeted on the bench, trying to keep his undressed body covered by the sheet.

"What is this?" said the doctor, getting up from his bed. "Kindly leave, young lady."

Just then the maid, sent by the countess, who had found her daughter missing, knocked on the door.

Like a somnambulist awakened in the middle of her sleep, Natasha went out of the room and, returning to her side of the cottage, fell sobbing on her bed.

· · ·

From that day on, through all the rest of the Rostovs' journey, at every stopping or sleeping place, Natasha never left the wounded Bolkonsky, and the doctor had to admit that he had not expected from a young lady either such firmness or such skill in looking after a wounded man.

Terrible as the thought seemed to the countess that Prince Andrei might (and, according to the doctor, quite probably would) die in her daughter's arms during the journey, she was unable to oppose Natasha. Though it was conceivable that, owing to the closeness now established between the wounded Prince Andrei and Natasha, their former engagement might be renewed in case he recovered, no one spoke of it, least of all Natasha and Prince Andrei; the unresolved question of life and death hanging not only over Bolkonsky but over Russia shut out all other conjectures.

XXXIII

Pierre woke up late on the third of September. His head ached, the clothes he had slept in without undressing felt heavy on his body, and on his soul lay a vague consciousness of something shameful committed the day before. This shameful thing was yesterday's conversation with Captain Ramballe.

The clock showed eleven, but it seemed peculiarly overcast outside. Pierre got up, rubbed his eyes, and, seeing the pistol with its carved butt, which Gerasim had again placed on the writing table, he remembered where he was and precisely what lay before him that day.

"Am I already too late?" thought Pierre. "No, *he* would probably enter Moscow no earlier than noon." Pierre did not allow himself to reflect on what lay before him, but hastened to act quickly.

Having straightened his clothes, Pierre took the pistol in his hand and was about to leave. But here the thought occurred to him for the first time of how he was to carry this weapon outside, if not in his hand. Even under a loose kaftan it was hard to hide a big pistol. Neither in his belt nor under his arm was it possible to carry it unnoticed. Besides, the pistol had been fired, and Pierre had not had time to reload it. "Never mind, there's still the dagger," Pierre said to himself, though more than once, in thinking about carrying out his intention, he had decided to himself that the chief mistake of the student in 1809 had consisted in wanting to kill Napoleon with a dagger. But as if his main goal consisted not in carrying out the thing he had in mind, but in proving to himself that he had not renounced his intention and was doing everything to carry it out, Pierre quickly took the dull, nicked dagger in the green scabbard, which he had bought at the Sukhareva tower along with the pistol, and hid it under his waistcoat.

Having belted his kaftan and pulled down his hat, Pierre, trying not to make noise or meet the captain, walked down the corridor and went outside.

The fire, which he had looked at so indifferently the evening before, had grown significantly overnight. Now Moscow was burning on different sides. Carriage Row, Zamoskvorechye, the Shopping Arcade, Povarskaya Street, the barges on the Moskva River, and the firewood market by the Dorogomilovo bridge were burning at the same time.

Pierre's path lay through back lanes to Povarskaya and from there to the Arbat, to St. Nicholas the Revealed, which had long been designated in his imagination as the place where his deed was to be accomplished. Most of the houses had their gates and shutters closed. The streets and lanes were deserted. There was a smell of smoke and burning in the air. Now and then he met Russians with anxiously timid faces and Frenchmen with a non-city, camplike look walking down the middle of the streets. Both looked at Pierre with astonishment. Besides his great height and fatness, besides the strange, gloomily concentrated and suffering expression of his face and his whole figure, the Russians studied Pierre with interest, because they could not figure out what estate this man might belong to. The French followed him with astonished eyes particularly because, unlike all other Russians, who looked at the French with fear or curiosity, Pierre paid no attention to them. By the gates of one house, three Frenchmen, explaining something to some Russians who did not understand them, stopped Pierre to ask if he knew French.

Pierre shook his head negatively and went on. In another lane, a sentry standing by a green box called out to him, and only after the repetition of the threatening cry and the sound of the sentry cocking his musket did Pierre understand that he should go over to the other side of the street. He heard and saw nothing around him. With haste and horror, he carried his intention inside him like something dreadful and alien, afraid—having been taught by the previous night's experience—of somehow losing it. But Pierre was not destined to bring his state of mind intact to the place he was heading for. Besides, even if nothing held him up on his way, his intention could no longer be carried out, because more than four hours ago Napoleon had ridden from the suburb of Dorogomilovo down the Arbat to the Kremlin, and, in the darkest mood, was now sitting in the tsar's office in the Kremlin palace, issuing detailed, thorough instructions about the measures to be taken immediately to put out the fires, prevent looting, and reassure the inhabitants. But Pierre did not know that; entirely absorbed by what lay before him, he suffered, as people suffer who stubbornly undertake something impossible—not because of its difficulty, but because of its unsuitability to their nature; he suffered from fear that he would weaken at the decisive moment and, as a result, would lose repect for himself.

Though he saw and heard nothing around him, he found his way by instinct and without mistake took the lanes that led him to Povarskaya.

As Pierre approached Povarskaya, the smoke became thicker and thicker, and it even became warm from the flames of the fire. Fiery tongues occasionally soared up from behind the roofs of the houses. There were more people in the streets, and those people were more alarmed. But, though he felt that something extraordinary was happening around him, he was not aware that he was approaching the fire. Walking down a path that led across a big vacant lot adjoining Povarskaya on one side and the gardens of Prince Gruzinsky's house on the other, Pierre suddenly heard a woman's desperate cry just next to him. He stopped as if awakening from sleep and raised his head.

By the side of the path, on the dry, dusty grass, lay a heap of household belongings: featherbeds, a samovar, icons, and trunks. On the ground by the trunks sat a thin, middle-aged woman, with long, protruding front teeth, dressed in a black coat and bonnet. This woman, rocking and muttering something, was weeping heartrendingly. Two girls, between ten and twelve years old, dressed in dirty, short dresses and coats, looked at their mother with an expression of perplexity on their pale, frightened faces. A smaller boy, about seven years old, in a long coat and someone else's oversized cap, was weeping in the arms of an old nanny. A dirty, barefooted wench was sitting on a trunk and, having undone her pale braid, was pulling off the singed hairs and smelling them. The husband, a short, stoop-shouldered man in a civil uniform, with wheel-shaped side-whiskers and smooth temples, which could be seen from under the peaked cap that sat straight on his head, with an immobile face was pushing apart the trunks piled one on the other and pulling some sort of clothing out from under them.

The woman almost threw herself at Pierre's feet when she saw him.

"Dear hearts of mine, good Orthodox Christians, save us, save us, dear hearts! . . . Somebody help us," she managed to say through her sobs. "My little girl! . . . My daughter! . . . My youngest daughter got left behind! . . . She's burned up! O-o-oh! was it for this I nursed you . . . O-o-oh!"

"Enough, Marya Nikolaevna," the husband said to his wife in a soft voice, obviously only so as to justify himself before an outsider. "My sister must have taken her, where else could she be!" he added.

"Block of wood! Villain!" the woman shouted spitefully, suddenly ceasing to weep. "You have no heart, you don't pity your own child. Another man would have got her out of the flames. But this one's a block of wood, not a man, not a father. You're a gentleman," the woman pattered on, sobbing and turning to Pierre. "There was a fire next door, and it leaped over to us. The maid shouted 'Fire!' We rushed to gather things up. We ran out in whatever we had on . . . This is all we had time to take . . . God's blessing and our marriage bed, the rest is lost. I looked for the children, Katechka wasn't there. Oh, Lord! O-o-oh! . . ." and she burst into sobs again. "My dear, wee child, she's burned up! burned up!"

"But where, where did you leave her?" asked Pierre. From the expression of his suddenly animated face, the woman understood that this man might help her.

"Dear heart! Father!" she cried, seizing him by the legs. "Benefactor, ease my heart . . . Aniska, go, you vile thing, show him," she cried to the maid, opening her mouth angrily and with that displaying her long teeth still more.

"Show me, show me, I . . . I . . . I'll do it," Pierre said hurriedly in a breathless voice.

The dirty wench came from behind the trunk, fixed up her braid, sighed, and walked down the path on her blunt, bare feet. Pierre was as if he had come to life after a heavy swoon. He raised his head higher, his eyes lit up with a gleam of life, and he followed the maid with quick steps, overtook her, and came out on Povarskaya. The whole street was covered with a cloud of black smoke. Here and there tongues of flame burst from this cloud. A large crowd of people thronged in front of the fire. A French general stood in the middle of the street, saying something to those around him. Pierre, accompanied by the maid, wanted to reach the place where the general was standing, but French soldiers stopped him.

"*On ne passe pas,*"* a voice cried to him.

"This way, mister," said the maid. "We'll take the lane past the Nikulins'."

Pierre turned round and walked on, skipping now and then to keep up with her. The maid crossed the street, turned left into the lane, went past three houses, and turned right through the gates.

"It's just here," said the maid, and, running across the courtyard, she opened a little gate in a wooden fence and, stopping, pointed Pierre to a small wooden wing that was burning brightly and hotly. One side of it had collapsed, the other was burning, and bright flames burst from the window holes and from under the roof.

When Pierre went through the gate, a wave of heat hit him, and he involuntarily stopped.

"Which, which is your house?" he asked.

"O-o-oh!" the girl wailed, pointing to the wing. "That one, that was our place. You're burned up, my little treasure, Katechka, my precious little miss, o-o-oh!" wailed Aniska, looking at the fire and feeling a need to show her feelings as well.

Pierre tried to get to the wing, but the heat was so intense that he involuntarily swerved round the wing and ended up by the main house, which was burning only on one side of the roof and around which a crowd of Frenchmen swarmed. At first Pierre did not understand what these Frenchmen, who were dragging something out, were doing; but seeing a Frenchman in front of him who was beating a muzhik with the flat of his sword and trying to take a fox fur coat from him, Pierre vaguely realized that looting was going on there, but he had no time to stop at that thought.

*No further.

The sound of cracking and the crash of falling walls and ceilings, the whistling and hissing of the flames, and the lively cries of the people, the sight of billowing clouds of smoke, now frowningly thick and black, now soaring up brightly, with flashes of sparks, and, here and there, of solid, sheaflike red or scaly golden flames creeping over the walls, the sensation of heat and smoke and quick movement, produced on Pierre the usual exhilarating effect of fires. This effect was especially strong on him because, at the sight of this fire, he suddenly felt freed of his burdensome thoughts. He felt young, cheerful, adroit, and resolute. He ran round the little wing from the direction of the house and was about to run to the part of it that was still standing, when just by his head he heard the cries of several voices and after that the crash and clang of something heavy falling next to him.

Pierre turned to look and saw Frenchmen in the windows of the house, throwing out the drawer of a chest filled with some sort of metal objects. Other French soldiers, standing on the ground, went up to the drawer.

"*Eh bien, qu'est-ce qu'il veut celui-là?*"* one of the Frenchman called out to Pierre.

"*Un enfant dans cette maison. N'avez-vous pas vu un enfant?*"† said Pierre.

"*Tiens, qu'est-ce qu'il chante celui-là? Va te promener,*"‡ voices said, and one of the soldiers, probably fearing that Pierre would start taking from them the silver and bronze that were in the drawer, moved towards him menacingly.

"*Un enfant?*" a Frenchman shouted from above. "*J'ai entendu piailler quelque chose au jardin. Peut-être c'est son moutard au bonhomme. Faut être humain, voyez-vous . . .*"§

"*Où est-il? Où est-il?*"# asked Pierre.

"*Par ici! Par ici!*" the Frenchman called from the window, pointing to the garden behind the house. "*Attendez, je vais descendre.*"**

And, in fact, a moment later the Frenchman, a dark-eyed fellow with a spot on his cheek, in his shirtsleeves, jumped out of a ground-floor window and, slapping Pierre on the shoulder, ran to the garden with him.

"*Dépêchez-vous, vous autres,*" he cried to his comrades, "*il commence à faire chaud.*"††

Having run behind the house onto a sand-strewn path, the Frenchman pulled Pierre by the arm and pointed him to the circle. Under a garden bench lay a three-year-old girl in a pink dress.

---

*Well, what does this one want?
†A child in that house. Haven't you seen a child?
‡Say, what's this one singing about? Go take a walk.
§A child? . . . I heard something squealing in the garden. Maybe it's this fellow's kid. Got to be human, you see . . .
#Where is it? Where is it?
**This way! This way! . . . Wait, I'm coming down.
††Hurry up, the rest of you . . . it's beginning to get hot.

"*Voilà votre moutard. Ah, une petite, tant mieux,*" said the French-man. "*Au revoir, mon gros. Faut être humain. Nous sommes tous mortels, voyez-vous.*"* And the Frenchman with the spot on his cheek ran back to his comrades.

Pierre, breathless with joy, ran to the girl and wanted to pick her up. But see-ing a stranger, the sickly, scrofulous, unpleasant-looking little girl, who resem-bled her mother, screamed and tried to run away. Pierre picked her up anyhow and took her in his arms; she shrieked in a desperately angry voice and began tearing Pierre's hands away with her own little hands and biting them with her slobbery mouth. Pierre was seized by a feeling of horror and squeamishness, such as he had experienced on touching some little animal. But he forced him-self not to drop the child and ran with her back to the big house. But it was no longer possible to go back the same way; the wench Aniska was not there, and Pierre, with a feeling of pity and revulsion, pressing the suffering, sobbing, and wet little girl to him as tenderly as he could, ran through the garden to look for another way out.

XXXIV

When Pierre, having run round through courtyards and lanes, got back with his burden to the Gruzinskys' garden at the corner of Povarskaya, he did not at first recognize the place from which he had gone to look for the child, it was so cluttered with people and belongings taken from the house. Besides Russian families with their chattels, escaped from the fire, there were also several French soldiers in various dress. Pierre paid no attention to them. He was in a hurry to find the official's family, so as to give the daughter to the mother and go again to save someone. It seemed to Pierre that he had to do much more of some-thing and do it quickly. Flushed from the heat and the running, Pierre at that moment experienced even more strongly than before that feeling of youth, ani-mation, and determination which had taken hold of him as he was running to save the child. The girl had quieted down now and, holding on to Pierre's kaf-tan with her little hands, sat on his arm and looked around like a wild animal. Pierre occasionally glanced at her and smiled slightly. It seemed to him that he saw something touchingly innocent and angelic in that frightened and sickly little face.

Neither the official nor his wife was in the former place now. Pierre strode quickly among the people, looking at various faces he came upon. He involun-tarily noticed a Georgian or Armenian family, which consisted of a very old,

---

*There's your brat. Ah, a little girl, so much the better . . . Goodbye, my fat friend. Got to be human. We're all mortal, you see.

handsome man with a face of the Oriental type, dressed in a new fur-lined coat and new boots, an old woman of the same type, and a young woman. This very young woman seemed to Pierre the perfection of Oriental beauty, with her sharply outlined, arched eyebrows and long face, of an extraordinarily delicate pink, beautiful and expressionless. Among the scattered belongings, in the crowd on the square, she, in her costly satin-covered winter coat and bright purple shawl, which covered her head, resembled a tender hothouse flower thrown out on the snow. She sat on some bundles slightly behind the old woman, and her big, dark, elongated eyes, with their long lashes, looked motionlessly at the ground. She clearly knew her own beauty and feared for it. Her face struck Pierre, and, hastening along the fence, he turned several times to look at her. On reaching the fence and still not finding those he wanted, Pierre stood looking around.

The figure of Pierre with the child in his arms was now even more noticeable than before, and several Russian men and women gathered around him.

"Have you lost someone, dear man? You're a gentleman yourself, aren't you? Whose child is it?" he was asked.

Pierre replied that the child belonged to a woman in a black coat who had been sitting in that place with her children, and asked if anyone knew her and where she had gone.

"That must be the Anferovs," said an old deacon, addressing a pockmarked woman. "Lord have mercy, Lord have mercy," he added in an accustomed bass.

"What Anferovs!" said the old woman. "The Anferovs left in the morning. It must be either Marya Nikolavna or the Ivanovs."

"He says it was a woman, but Marya Nikolavna is a lady," said a servant.

"You must know her—long teeth, thin," said Pierre.

"That's Marya Nikolavna. They went to the garden when these wolves swooped down on us," said the woman, pointing to the French soldiers.

"Oh, Lord have mercy," the deacon added again.

"Go that way, they're over there. It's her. She kept grieving, weeping," the woman said again. "It's her. Over there."

But Pierre was not listening to the woman. For several seconds now, not taking his eyes away, he had been watching what was going on a few steps from him. He had been watching the Armenian family and two French soldiers who had gone up to them. One of the soldiers, a fidgety little man, was wearing a dark blue greatcoat tied with a rope. There was a cap on his head; his feet were bare. The other, who especially struck Pierre, was a tall, stooping, thin, flaxen-haired man with sluggish movements and an idiotic expression on his face. This one was dressed in a long frieze coat, dark blue trousers, and big, torn jackboots. The bootless little Frenchman in the dark blue greatcoat went up to the Armenians, said something, and at once took hold of the old man's legs, and the old man at once began to take off his boots. The other one, in the woman's coat, stood in front of the beautiful Armenian girl and looked at her silently, fixedly, with his hands in his pockets.

"Take the child, take her," said Pierre, addressing the woman peremptorily and hurriedly, and handing her the girl. "Give her to them!" he almost shouted at the woman, sitting the screaming little girl on the ground, and he again looked at the Frenchmen and the Armenian family. The old man was already sitting without his boots. The little Frenchman had taken the remaining boot off him and was slapping the two boots against each other. The old man, sobbing, was saying something, but Pierre saw it only fleetingly; his whole attention was turned to the Frenchman in the long coat, who meanwhile moved towards the young woman, swaying slowly, and, taking his hands out of his pockets, put them to her neck.

The Armenian beauty went on sitting in the same motionless position, with her long lashes lowered, as if she did not see or feel what the soldier was doing to her.

While Pierre was running the few steps that separated him from the Frenchman, the tall looter in the long coat was already tearing the necklace that the Armenian girl was wearing from her neck, and the young woman, seizing her neck with her hands, cried out in a piercing voice.

"*Laissez cette femme!*"* Pierre rasped in a furious voice, seizing the tall, stooping soldier by the shoulders and flinging him away. The soldier fell, got up, and ran off. But his comrade, throwing down the boots, drew his sword and moved threateningly towards Pierre.

"*Voyons, pas de bêtises!*"† he cried.

Pierre was in that ecstasy of fury in which he was oblivious to everything and his strength increased tenfold. He fell upon the barefoot Frenchman and, before he had time to draw his sword, had already knocked him off his feet and was pummelling him with his fists. An approving cry came from the surrounding crowd, and at the same time a mounted patrol of French uhlans appeared from round the corner. The uhlans trotted up to Pierre and the Frenchman and surrounded them. Pierre remembered nothing of what came after that. He remembered beating something, being beaten, and in the end felt that his hands were tied and that a crowd of French soldiers was standing round him, searching his clothes.

"*Il a un poignard, lieutenant,*"‡ were the first words Pierre understood.

*Leave that woman alone!
†Come on, no stupidities!
‡He has a dagger, Lieutenant.

"*Ah, une arme!*"* said the officer, and he turned to the barefoot soldier who had been taken together with Pierre.

"*C'est bon, vous direz tout cela au conseil de guerre,*" said the officer. And then he turned to Pierre. "*Parlez-vous français, vous?*"†

Pierre looked around with bloodshot eyes and did not reply. His face probably looked very frightful, because the officer said something in a whisper, and four more uhlans separated from the unit and stood on either side of Pierre.

"*Parlez-vous français?*" the officer repeated the question, keeping his distance from him. "*Faites venir l'interprète.*"‡

A little man in Russian civil dress rode out of the ranks. By his clothes and pronunciation, Pierre recognized him at once as a Frenchman from one of the Moscow shops.

"*Il n'a pas l'air d'un homme du peuple,*"§ said the interpreter, looking Pierre over.

"*Oh, oh! ça m'a bien l'air d'un des incendiaires,*" said the officer. "*Demandez-lui ce qu'il est?*"# he added.

"Who you?" asked the interpreter. "You must answer the superiority," he said.

"*Je ne vous dirai pas qui je suis. Je suis votre prisonnier. Emmène-moi,*"** Pierre suddenly said in French.

"*Ah! Ah!*" said the officer, frowning. "*Marchons!*"††

A crowd had gathered around the uhlans. Closest to Pierre stood the pockmarked woman with the girl; when the patrol started off, she moved forward.

"Where are they taking you, my dearest?" she asked. "The girl, what am I to do with the girl, if she's not theirs?" said the woman.

"*Qu'est-ce qu'elle veut cette femme?*"‡‡ asked the officer.

Pierre was like a drunk man. His ecstatic state increased still more at the sight of the girl he had saved.

"*Ce qu'elle dit?*" he said. "*Elle m'apporte ma fille que je viens de sauver des flammes,*"§§ he said. "*Adieu!*" and, not knowing himself how this pointless lie had escaped him, he walked with resolute, solemn steps between the Frenchmen.

The French patrol was one of those that had been sent out on Durosnel's

---

*Ah, a weapon!
†All right, you can say all that at the court martial . . . And you, do you speak French?
‡Bring the interpreter.
§He doesn't look like a man of the people.
#Oh, oh! it has all the look of one of these incendiaries . . . Ask him what he is.
**I will not tell you who I am. I am your prisoner. Take me away.
††Let's go!
‡‡What does this woman want?
§§What is she saying? . . . She's bringing me my daughter whom I just saved from the flames.

orders to various streets in Moscow, to stop looting and especially to catch the incendiaries, who, in the general opinion for that day among the French higher command, were the cause of the fires. Having gone around a few streets, the patrol had picked up some five more suspicious Russians—one shopkeeper, two seminarians, a muzhik, a servant—and a few looters. But of all the suspicious people, Pierre seemed the most suspicious. When they were all taken to spend the night in a big house on the Zubovsky rampart, where a guardhouse had been set up, Pierre was placed separately under strict guard.

VOLUME IV

Part One

I

In Petersburg, in the highest circles, a complex struggle was going on with greater heat than ever between the parties of Rumyantsev, the French, Maria Feodorovna, the grand duke, and others, drowned as always by the humming of the court drones. But the calm, luxurious life of Petersburg, concerned only with phantoms, with reflections of life, went on as of old; and beyond this course of life it took great effort to realize the danger and the difficult situation the Russian people were in. There were the same levees and balls, the same French theatre, the same interests of the courts, the same interests of the service and intrigues. Only in the very highest circles were efforts made to keep in mind the difficulty of the present situation. It was recounted in whispers how differently from each other the two empresses[1] behaved in these difficult circumstances. The empress Maria Feodorovna, concerned with the welfare of the almshouses and orphanages in her charge, made arrangements to move all the institutions to Kazan, and the belongings of these establishments had already been packed. The empress Elizaveta Alexeevna, however, to the question of what orders she would be pleased to give, kindly replied, with characteristic Russian patriotism, that she could give no orders about state institutions, since that was the sovereign's concern; as for what depended on her personally, she kindly replied that she would be the last to leave Petersburg.

On the twenty-sixth of August, the very day of the battle of Borodino, Anna Pavlovna had a soirée, the centrepiece of which was to be the reading of a letter from the metropolitan, written on the occasion of sending the sovereign an icon of St. Sergius.[2] This letter was considered a model of patriotic, spiritual eloquence. It was to be read by Prince Vassily, famous for his artistic recitations. (He also used to read at the empress's.) Artistic recitation consisted in pouring out words loudly, melodiously, alternating between a desperate howl and a tender murmur, quite regardless of their meaning, so that it was quite by chance that one word fell in with the howling and others with the murmuring. This reading, like all of Anna Pavlovna's soirées, had a political significance. Several important persons were to be there, who had to be shamed for going to the French theatre and inspired with patriotic sentiments. A good many people had already gathered, but Anna Pavlovna still did not see everyone she needed in her drawing room, and therefore would not let the reading begin, but initiated a general conversation.

The news of the day for that day in Petersburg was the illness of Countess Bezukhov. Several days earlier the countess had unexpectedly fallen ill, had missed several gatherings of which she was the adornment, and rumour had it that she was not receiving anyone, and that, instead of the famous Petersburg doctors who usually treated her, she had entrusted herself to some Italian doctor who was treating her in some new and unusual way.

Everyone knew very well that the lovely countess's illness came from the inconvenience of marrying two husbands at once, and that the Italian's treatment consisted in removing that inconvenience; but in Anna Pavlovna's presence not only did no one dare to think about it, but it was as if no one knew it.

"*On dit que la pauvre comtesse est très mal. Le médecin dit que c'est l'angine pectorale.*"*

"*L'angine? Oh, c'est une maladie terrible!*"†

"*On dit que les rivaux se sont réconciliés grâce à l'angine . . .*"‡

The word *angine* was repeated with great pleasure.

"*Le vieux comte est touchant à ce qu'on dit. Il a pleuré comme un enfant quand le médecin lui a dit que le cas était dangereux.*"§

"*Oh, ce serait une perte terrible. C'est une femme ravissante.*"#

"*Vous parlez de la pauvre comtesse,*" said Anna Pavlovna, approaching. "*J'ai envoyé savoir de ses nouvelles. On m'a dit qu'elle allait un peu mieux. Oh, sans doute, c'est la plus charmante femme du monde,*" said Anna Pavlovna with a smile at her own rapturousness. "*Nous appartenons à des camps différents, mais cela ne m'empêche pas de l'éstimer, comme elle le mérite. Elle est bien malheureuse,*"** Anna Pavlovna added.

Supposing that by these words Anna Pavlovna had slightly lifted the veil of secrecy over the countess's illness, one imprudent young man allowed himself to express surprise that, instead of calling in famous doctors, the countess was being treated by a charlatan who might give her dangerous remedies.

"*Vos informations peuvent être meilleures que les miennes,*" Anna Pavlovna suddenly fell venomously upon the inexperienced young man. "*Mais je sais de bonne source que ce médecin est un homme très savant et très habile.*

---

*They say the poor countess is very ill. The doctor says it's angina pectoris.

†Angina? Oh, that's a terrible illness!

‡They say the rivals have become reconciled thanks to the angina . . .

§The old count is touching, they say. He wept like a child when the doctor told him it was a dangerous case.

#Oh, it would be a terrible loss. She's a ravishing woman.

**You are speaking of the poor countess . . . I sent to learn her news. I'm told she's doing a little better. Oh, unquestionably, she's the most charming woman in the world . . . We belong to different camps, but that does not keep me from appreciating her as she deserves. She's very unfortunate.

*C'est le médecin intime de la reine d'Espagne."** And having thus annihilated the young man, Anna Pavlovna turned to Bilibin, who, in another circle, having gathered his skin and clearly preparing to release it again in order to utter *un mot*, was talking about the Austrians.

"Je trouve que c'est charmant,"† he said of a diplomatic paper sent to Vienna together with the Austrian standards taken by Wittgenstein, *le héros de Pétropol³* (as he was known in Petersburg).

"How, how is that?" Anna Pavlovna addressed him, inducing silence for the hearing of the *mot*, which she already knew.

And Bilibin repeated the following actual words from the diplomatic dispatch he had composed:

"L'Empereur renvoie les drapeaux Autrichiens," said Bilibin, *"drapeaux amis et égarés qu'il a trouvé hors de la route,"‡* Bilibin concluded, releasing his skin.

"Charmant, charmant," said Prince Vassily.

"C'est la route de Varsovie peut-être,"§ Prince Ippolit said loudly and unexpectedly. Everyone turned to him, not understanding what he meant to say by that. Prince Ippolit also looked around with merry surprise. Like everyone else, he did not understand the meaning of the words he had spoken. In the course of his diplomatic career, he had noticed more than once that words spoken suddenly like that turned out to be very witty, and, just in case, he had spoken these words, the first that came to his tongue. "Maybe it will turn out very well," he thought, "and if it doesn't, they'll be able to fix things up." Indeed, during the awkward silence that ensued, the insufficiently patriotic person whom Anna Pavlovna was waiting for in order to convert came in, and she, smiling and shaking her finger at Ippolit, invited Prince Vassily to the table and, giving him two candles and the manuscript, asked him to begin. Everything became silent.

"Most Gracious Sovereign Emperor!" Prince Vassily proclaimed sternly and looked the public over as if asking if anyone had anything to say against it. But no one said anything. "The first capital, Moscow, the New Jerusalem, receives *her* Christ," he suddenly emphasized the word *her*, "as a mother her zealous sons into her embrace, and through the gathering darkness, foreseeing the brilliant glory of thy dominion, sings in ecstasy: 'Hosanna, blessed is He that comes!' "⁴ These last words Prince Vassily uttered in a tearful voice.

Bilibin was attentively examining his fingernails, and many, clearly grown

*Your information may be better than mine . . . But I know from good sources that this doctor is a very learned and very able man. He is the personal physician of the queen of Spain.
†I find it charming.
‡The emperor returns these Austrian standards . . . friendly standards gone astray, which he found off the road.
§The road to Warsaw, perhaps.

timid, seemed to be asking what they were guilty of. Anna Pavlovna, like a little old woman repeating the prayer before communion, whispered in advance: "Let the brazen and insolent Goliath . . ."

Prince Vassily continued:

"Let the brazen and insolent Goliath from the borders of France encompass the ends of Russia in deathly horror; meek faith, that sling of the Russian David, will suddenly crush the head of his bloodthirsty pride. Behold the image of St. Sergius, zealous of old after the good of our fatherland, is being offered to Your Imperial Majesty. I lament that my failing strength prevents me from delighting in seeing Your most gentle face. I have sent up to heaven my warm prayers that the Almighty may exalt the generation of the righteous and fulfil among the blessed the wishes of Your Majesty."

*"Quelle force! Quel style!"** were heard in praise of the reader and of the writer. Inspired by this speech, Anna Pavlovna's guests talked for a long time about the situation of the fatherland and made various conjectures about the outcome of the battle which was to be offered one of those days.

"Vous verrez,"† said Anna Pavlovna, "tomorrow, on the sovereign's birthday, we'll receive news. I have a good presentiment."

II

Anna Pavlovna's presentiment indeed proved true. The next day, during the prayer service in the palace on the occasion of the sovereign's birthday, Prince Volkonsky was called out of the church and received an envelope from Prince Kutuzov. This was Kutuzov's report written from Tatarinovo on the day of the battle. Kutuzov wrote that the Russians had not retreated a step, that the French losses were much greater than ours, that he was reporting in haste from the battlefield, and had not yet had time to gather the latest information. Which meant it was a victory. And at once, before leaving church, thanks were offered up to the Creator for His help and for the victory.

Anna Pavlovna's presentiment proved true, and for the whole morning a joyfully festive mood reigned in the city. Everyone took the victory for an accomplished fact, and some already spoke of the capture of Napoleon himself, of his deposition and the choice of a new head for France.

Far from the action and amidst the conditions of court life, one could hardly expect events to be reflected in all their fullness and force. Involuntarily, general events group themselves around some specific occurrence. So now the main joy of the courtiers consisted as much in the fact that news of the victory

*What force! What style!
†You'll see.

arrived precisely on the sovereign's birthday, as in the fact that we had been victorious. This was like a successful surprise. In Kutuzov's report mention was also made of the Russian losses, and among them Tuchkov, Bagration, and Kutaisov were named. The sad side of the event, in the local Petersburg world, also involuntarily grouped itself around one event: the death of Kutaisov. Everyone knew him, the sovereign liked him, he was young and interesting. On that day people met each other with the words:

"How surprisingly it happened. During the prayer service. But what a loss Kutaisov is! Ah, what a pity!"

"What did I tell you about Kutuzov?" Prince Vassily now kept saying with the pride of a prophet. "I always said he alone was capable of defeating Napoleon."

But the next day no news came from the army, and the general voice became anxious. The courtiers suffered over the suffering of uncertainty in which the sovereign found himself.

"What a position the sovereign is in!" said the courtiers, and they no longer extolled Kutuzov as they had the day before, but denounced him for being the cause of the sovereign's worry. That day Prince Vassily no longer boasted of his protégé Kutuzov, but kept silent when the conversation turned to the commander in chief. Besides, towards the evening of that day it was as if everything combined to plunge the inhabitants of Petersburg into anxiety and worry; one more piece of terrible news was added: Countess Elena Bezukhov had died suddenly of that terrible illness, the name of which it had been so pleasant to articulate. Officially, in large gatherings, everyone said that Countess Bezukhov had died of a terrible attack of *angine pectorale,* but in intimate circles details were recounted of how *le médecin intime de la Reine d'Espagne* had prescribed Hélène small doses of some medicine to produce a certain effect; but Hélène, tormented by the old count's suspicions and by the fact that her husband, to whom she had written (that wretched, depraved Pierre), would not answer her, had suddenly taken a huge dose of the prescribed medicine and had died in agony before aid could be given. The story went that Prince Vassily and the old count were about to set upon the Italian; but the Italian showed them such notes from the unfortunate deceased woman that they let him go at once.

General conversation concentrated itself around three grievous events: the sovereign's uncertainty, the loss of Kutaisov, and the death of Hélène.

On the third day after Kutuzov's report, a landowner arrived in Petersburg from Moscow, and the news spread throughout the city about the surrender of Moscow to the French.[5] This was terrible! Imagine the sovereign's position! Kutuzov was a traitor, and Prince Vassily, during the *visites de condoléances**

---

*Visits of condolence.

paid to him on the occasion of his daughter's death, said of the formerly praised Kutuzov (it was forgivable for him, in his sorrow, to forget what he had said before) that nothing else could have been expected from a blind and depraved old man.

"I'm only surprised that the destiny of Russia could have been entrusted to such a man."

As long as this news remained unofficial, it could still be doubted, but the next day the following report came from Count Rastopchin:

Prince Kutuzov's adjutant has brought me a letter in which he requests police officers from me to lead the army to the Ryazan road. He says that he is abandoning Moscow with regret. Sovereign! Kutuzov's action decides the fate of the capital and of your empire. Russia will shudder on learning that the city in which Russia's greatness is centred, where the remains of your ancestors lie, is given up to the enemy. I will follow the army. I have evacuated everything, all that is left for me is to weep over the fate of my fatherland!

Having received this report, the sovereign sent Prince Volkonsky to Kutuzov with the following rescript:

Prince Mikhail Ilarionovich! I have had no reports from you since 29 August. Meanwhile I received on 1 September, through Yaroslavl, from the Moscow commander in chief, the grievous news that you and the army have decided to abandon Moscow. You can imagine the effect that this news has made on me, and your silence redoubles my astonishment. I am sending this by my adjutant general, Prince Volkonsky, in order to learn from you the situation of the army and the reasons that prompted you to such a grievous resolution.

III

Nine days after Moscow was abandoned, a messenger sent by Kutuzov reached Petersburg with an official announcement that Moscow had been abandoned. This messenger was the Frenchman Michaud, who did not know Russian, but *quoique étranger, Russe de coeur et d'âme,* * as he said of himself.

The sovereign received the messenger at once in his office in the palace on Kamenny Island. Michaud, who had never seen Moscow before the campaign and who did not know Russian, all the same felt deeply moved when he appeared before *notre très gracieux souverain* (as he wrote) with news of the Moscow fire, *dont les flammes éclairaient sa route.*†

---

*Though a foreigner, Russian in heart and soul.
†Our most gracious sovereign . . . the flames of which lighted his way.

Though the source of Mr. Michaud's *chagrin* was bound to be different from that which caused the grief of Russian people, Michaud, when he was led to the sovereign's office, had such a mournful face that the sovereign asked him at once:

"*M'apportez-vous de tristes nouvelles, colonel?*"*

"*Bien tristes, Sire,*" replied Michaud, lowering his eyes with a sigh, "*l'abandon de Moscou.*"†

"*Aurait-on livré mon ancienne capitale sans se battre?*"‡ the sovereign said quickly, suddenly flushing.

Michaud respectfully conveyed what he had been ordered to convey from Kutuzov—namely, that it had been impossible to fight near Moscow, and that, as one choice remained, to lose both the army and Moscow or Moscow alone, the field marshal had to choose the latter.

The sovereign listened silently, without looking at Michaud.

"*L'ennemi est-il en ville?*"§ he asked.

"*Oui, Sire, et elle est en cendres à l'heure qu'il est. Je l'ai laissée toute en flammes,*"# Michaud said resolutely, but, glancing at the sovereign, Michaud was horrified at what he had done. The sovereign began to breathe heavily and quickly, his lower lip trembled, and his beautiful blue eyes instantly became moist with tears.

But this lasted only a moment. The sovereign suddenly frowned, as if disapproving of himself for his weakness. And, raising his head, he addressed Michaud in a firm voice:

"*Je vois, colonel, par tout ce qui nous arrive,*" he said, "*que la providence exige de grands sacrifices de nous . . . Je suis prêt à me soumettre à toutes ses volontés; mais dites-moi, Michaud, comment avez-vous laissé l'armée, en voyant ainsi, sans coup férir, abandonner mon ancienne capitale? N'avez-vous pas aperçu du découragement? . . .*"**

Seeing that his *très gracieux souverain* had calmed down, Michaud also calmed down, but he had not yet had time to prepare an answer to the direct and essential question of the sovereign, which also required a direct answer.

"*Sire, me permettrez-vous de vous parler franchement en loyal militaire?*"†† he said, to gain time.

---

*Do you bring me sad news, Colonel?
†Very sad, Sire . . . the abandoning of Moscow.
‡Could they have given up my ancient capital without a fight?
§Is the enemy in the city?
#Yes, Sire, and it is in ashes by now. I left it all in flames.
**I see, Colonel, by all that is happening to us . . . that Providence demands great sacrifices from us . . . I am ready to submit to all of its whims; but tell me, Michaud, how was the army when you left it, seeing my ancient capital abandoned like this without striking a blow? Did you notice any discouragement?
††Sire, will you allow me to speak with you frankly as a loyal soldier?

"Colonel, je l'exige toujours," said the sovereign. *"Ne me cachez rien, je veux savoir absolument ce qu'il en est."**

"Sire!" said Michaud, with a fine, barely perceptible smile on his lips, having had time to prepare his answer in the form of a light and respectful *jeu de mots*. *"Sire! j'ai laissé toute l'armée depuis les chefs jusqu'au dernier soldat, sans exception, dans une crainte épouvantable, effrayante . . ."†*

"Comment ça?" the sovereign interrupted with a stern frown. *"Mes Russes se laisseront-ils abattre par le malheur . . . Jamais! . . ."‡*

Michaud was only waiting for that in order to put in his play on words.

"Sire," he said with a respectful playfulness of expression, *"ils craignent seulement que Votre Majesté par bonté de coeur ne se laisse persuader de faire la paix. Ils brûlent de combattre,"* said the plenipotentiary of the Russian people, *"et de prouver à Votre Majesté par le sacrifice de leur vie, combien ils lui sont dévoués . . ."§*

"Ah!" the sovereign said calmly now and with a benign twinkle in his eyes, slapping Michaud on the shoulder. *"Vous me tranquillisez, colonel."#*

The sovereign lowered his head and was silent for a time.

"Eh bien, retournez à l'armée," he said, drawing himself up to his full height and addressing Michaud with a benign and majestic gesture, *"et dites à nos braves, dites à tous mes bons sujets partout où vous passerez, que quand je n'aurais plus aucun soldat, je me mettrai moi-même à la tête de ma chère noblesse, de mes bons paysans, et j'userai ainsi jusqu'à la dernière ressource de mon empire. Il m'en offre encore plus que mes ennemis ne pensent,"* the sovereign spoke with ever increasing animation. *"Mais si jamais il fut écrit dans les decrets de la divine providence,"* he said, raising to heaven his beautiful, meek eyes, shining with emotion, *"que ma dynastie dût cesser de régner sur le trône de mes ancêtres, alors, après avoir épuisé tous les moyens qui sont en mon pouvoir, je me laisserai croître la barbe jusqu'ici"* (the sovereign put his hand to the middle of his chest), *"et j'irai manger des pommes de terre avec le dernier de mes paysans plutôt que de signer la honte de ma patrie et de ma chère nation, dont je sais apprécier les sacrifices! . . ."*** Having spoken

---

*Colonel, I always demand that . . . Conceal nothing from me, I absolutely want to know how it is.
†Sire! . . . play on words. Sire! I left the entire army, from the leaders down to the least soldier, without exception, in the most appalling, dreadful fear . . .
‡What's that? . . . My Russians let themselves be cast down by misfortune . . . Never! . . .
§Sire . . . they fear only that Your Majesty, in the goodness of his heart, will let himself be persuaded to make peace. They are burning to fight . . . and to prove how devoted they are to Your Majesty by the sacrifice of their lives . . .
#Ah! . . . You set me at ease, Colonel.
**Well, go back to the army . . . and tell our brave men, tell all my good subjects wherever you may go, that when I have no soldiers left, I will personally put myself at the head of my dear nobility, of my good peasants, and will thus use every last resource of my empire. It offers me much more than my enemies think . . . But if ever it were written in the decrees of divine Providence . . . that my

these words in an agitated voice, the sovereign suddenly turned away, as if wishing to conceal from Michaud the tears that had come to his eyes, and went further into his office. Having stood there for a few moments, he returned to Michaud with big strides and with a forceful gesture pressed his arm below the elbow. The sovereign's beautiful, meek face became flushed, and his eyes burned with the fire of resolution and wrath.

"*Colonel Michaud, n'oubliez pas ce que je vous dis ici; peut-être qu'un jour nous nous le rappellerons avec plaisir . . . Napoléon ou moi,*" said the sovereign, touching his breast. "*Nous ne pouvons plus régner ensemble. J'ai appris à le connaître, il ne me trompera plus . . .*"* And the sovereign frowned and fell silent.

Hearing these words, seeing the expression of firm resolution in the sovereign's eyes, Michaud, *quoique étranger, mais Russe de cœur et d'âme*, felt himself at this moment *enthousiasmé par tout ce qu'il venait d'entendre*† (as he said afterwards), and he expressed in the following terms his own feelings as well as the feelings of the Russian people, of whom he regarded himself as the plenipotentiary.

"*Sire!*" he said. "*Votre Majesté signe dans ce moment la gloire de la nation et le salut de l'Europe.*"‡

The sovereign inclined his head, dismissing Michaud.

IV

At that time when Russia was half conquered and the inhabitants of Moscow were fleeing to the distant provinces, and one popular militia after another was rising to the defence of the fatherland, we, who were not living at that time, involuntarily imagine that all Russian people, great and small, were taken up only with sacrificing themselves, saving the fatherland, or weeping over its loss. The stories and descriptions of that time all speak without exception of self-sacrifice, love of the fatherland, despair, grief, and the heroism of the Russians. In reality, it was not like that. It seems so to us only because all we see in the past is the general historical interest of the time, and we do not see all those

---

dynasty must cease to reign on the throne of my ancestors, then, after exhausting all the means in my power, I will let my beard grow to here . . . and I will go to eat potatoes with the least of my peasants, rather than put my signature to the shame of my country and of my dear people, whose sacrifices I know how to appreciate! . . .

*Colonel Michaud, do not forget what I say to you here; perhaps one day we will recall it with pleasure . . . Napoleon or me . . . We can no longer reign together. I have learned to know him, he will not deceive me again . . .

†Filled with enthusiasm by all he had just heard.

‡Sire! . . . Your Majesty is putting his signature at this moment to the glory of the people and the salvation of Europe.

personal, human interests that the people of that time had. And yet in reality the personal interests of the day are so much more significant than the general interests that as a result the general interests are never felt (or even noticed at all). The majority of the people of that time paid no attention to the general course of things, but were guided only by the personal interests of the day. And those people were the most useful figures of that time.

Those, however, who tried to understand the general course of things and wanted to take part in it with self-sacrifice and heroism, were the most useless members of society; they saw everything inside out, and everything they did to be useful turned out to be useless nonsense, like Pierre's and Mamonov's regiments, which looted Russian villages, like the lint that young ladies plucked and that never got to the wounded, and so on. Even those who were fond of being clever and expressing their feelings, when discussing the present situation of Russia, involuntarily gave their speeches the stamp either of pretence and falseness, or of useless condemnation and spite against the people, accusing them of something no one could be guilty of. In historical events what is most obvious is the prohibition against eating the fruit of the tree of knowledge. Only unconscious activity bears fruit, and a man who plays a role in a historical event never understands its significance. If he attempts to understand it, he is struck with fruitlessness.

The significance of the event that was then taking place in Russia was the less conspicuous the closer a man's participation in it was. In Petersburg and in provincial towns far from Moscow, ladies and men in militia uniform wept over Russia and the capital and spoke of self-sacrifice and so on; but in the army that was retreating beyond Moscow, there was almost no talk or thought of Moscow and, looking at it burning, no one swore revenge on the French, but they thought of the next pay day, of their next halt, of Matryoshka the sutler, and the like . . .

Nikolai Rostov, without any aim of self-sacrifice, but by chance, since the war found him in the service, took a direct and prolonged part in the defence of the fatherland, and therefore looked without despair and dark conclusions at what was then happening in Russia. If he had been asked what he thought of the present situation in Russia, he would have said that there was nothing for him to think, that Kutuzov and others were there for that, and that he had heard that regiments were being replenished, and that it must mean the fighting would go on for a long time yet, and that, in the present circumstances, it would be no wonder to him if he got a regiment within a couple of years.

Looking at things as he did, he took the news of his being sent to Voronezh to remount the division not only with no regret at not taking part in the coming fight, but with the greatest satisfaction, which he did not conceal, and which his comrades understood perfectly well.

Several days before the battle of Borodino, Nikolai received money, papers, and, sending his hussars on ahead, drove to Voronezh by post-chaise.

Only someone who has experienced it—that is, who has spent several months on end in an atmosphere of active duty—can understand the pleasure Nikolai experienced when he got out of the area over which the troops spread their foraging operations, supply trains, and hospitals; when, instead of soldiers, carts, the dirty traces of a camp's presence, he saw villages with peasant men and women, landowners' houses, fields with grazing cattle, posting stations with sleeping stationmasters. He felt such joy as if he were seeing it all for the first time. What especially surprised and gladdened him for a long time were the young, healthy women, who did not each have a dozen officers dangling after them, and who were glad and flattered that a travelling officer joked with them.

In the most cheerful state of mind, Nikolai arrived at night at a hotel in Voronezh, ordered everything that he had long been deprived of in the army, and the next day, clean-shaven and wearing his long-unworn full-dress uniform, went to report to the authorities.

The head of the militia was a civilian general, an old man who clearly enjoyed his military title and rank. He received Nikolai gruffly (thinking it was the military way), and questioned him imposingly, as if he had the right to do so, approving and disapproving, as if he were discussing the general course of things. Nikolai felt so cheerful that he found it merely amusing.

From the head of the militia, he went to the governor. The governor was a lively little fellow, very gentle and simple. He pointed Nikolai to the stud farms where he might get horses, recommended a dealer in town and a landowner fifteen miles out of town who had the best horses, and promised him every sort of assistance.

"Are you the son of Count Ilya Andreevich? My wife was great friends with your mother. We receive on Thursdays; today's a Thursday, kindly come to my place without any formalities," said the governor, dismissing him.

Straight from the governor's, Nikolai took relay horses and, putting the sergeant major in with him, galloped off to the landowner's stud farm fifteen miles away. Everything in this initial period of his stay in Voronezh was cheerful and easy, and as happens when a man is well-disposed himself, everything went smoothly and swimmingly.

The landowner Nikolai went to was an old bachelor, a cavalry officer, a horse fancier, a hunter, the owner of a carpet room,[6] of century-old honey vodka, old Hungarian wine, and superb horses.

After a couple of words, Nikolai bought seventeen stallions for six thousand, choice ones (as he said), to make a display of his remount. Having had dinner and drunk a bit too much Hungarian, Rostov exchanged kisses with the landowner, with whom he was already on familiar terms, and galloped back over the abominable road in the merriest spirits, constantly urging the driver on, so as to be back in time for the governor's soirée.

Changed, scented, his head doused with cold water, Nikolai, somewhat late, but armed with the phrase *vaut mieux tard que jamais,** arrived at the governor's.

It was not a ball, and no mention had been made of dancing, but everyone knew that Katerina Petrovna would play waltzes and *écossaises* on the clavichord and that there would be dancing, and, counting on that, everyone gathered as for a ball.

Provincial life in 1812 was exactly the same as ever, with the only difference that things were more lively in town because of the arrival of many rich families from Moscow, and that, as in everything that was going on at that time in Russia, some special boldness was noticeable in it—devil-may-care, harum-scarum—and also in that the banal conversation necessary among people, which formerly was about the weather and mutual acquaintances, was now about Moscow, the army, and Napoleon.

The society gathered at the governor's was the best society of Voronezh.

There were a great many ladies, there were several of Nikolai's Moscow acquaintances, but none of the men could in any way rival the bearer of the St. George, the remount officer of the hussars, who was at the same time the good-natured and well-bred Count Rostov. Among the men there was an Italian prisoner—an officer of the French army—and Nikolai felt that the presence of this prisoner further enhanced his significance as a Russian hero. He was like a trophy. Nikolai felt it, and it seemed to him that everyone looked at the Italian that way, and Nikolai treated this officer kindly, with dignity and restraint.

As soon as Nikolai entered in his hussar uniform, spreading about him the smell of scent and wine, and said himself and heard said to him several times the words *"vaut mieux tard que jamais,"* he was surrounded; all eyes turned to him, and he felt at once that he had stepped into the position of the universal favourite, which befitted him in the province, and was always agreeable, but now, after prolonged privation, made him drunk with pleasure. Not only in posting stations, inns, and the landowner's carpet room were the servant girls flattered by his attentions, but here, at the governor's soirée, there was (as it seemed to Nikolai) an inexhaustible number of young ladies and pretty girls who were waiting impatiently for him to pay attention to them. Ladies and girls flirted with him, and from the first day the old folk began bustling about to get this dashing scapegrace of a hussar married and settled down. Among the latter was the governor's wife herself, who received Rostov like a close relation, called him "Nicolas" and "my dear."

Katerina Petrovna indeed began to play waltzes and *écossaises,* and dancing began, in which Nikolai charmed the whole provincial society still more with his adroitness. He even surprised them with his special, casual way of dancing.

*Better late than never.

Nikolai was surprised himself at his way of dancing that evening. He had never danced that way in Moscow, and even would have considered such an all-too-casual way of dancing improper and *mauvais genre;* * but here he felt the need to astonish them all with something extraordinary, something which they would take as ordinary in the capital, but as yet unknown in the provinces.

All evening Nikolai paid most attention to a blue-eyed, plump, and sweet-looking blonde, the wife of one of the provincial officials. With the naïve conviction of young men making merry, that other men's wives were created for them, Rostov never left this lady's side and treated her husband in a friendly, somewhat conspiratorial way, as if, though there was no talk of it, they knew how nicely they would get along together—that is, Nikolai and this husband's wife. The husband, however, did not seem to share that conviction and tried to sulk with Rostov. But Nikolai's good-natured naïveté was so boundless that now and then the husband involuntarily yielded to his merry spirits. Towards the end of the evening, however, as the wife's face became ever more flushed and animated, her husband's face became sadder and paler, as if they had one portion of animation between them, and as it increased in the wife, it diminished in the husband.

V

Nikolai, with a smile that never left his face, slightly curved in an armchair, sat bending closely over the blonde, paying her mythological compliments.

Briskly shifting the position of his legs in their tight riding breeches, spreading the smell of scent around him, and admiring his lady, and himself, and the fine shape of his legs in their tight buckskins, Nikolai was saying to the blonde that there was a certain lady there in Voronezh that he wanted to abduct.

"What sort of lady?"

"Charming, divine. Her eyes" (Nikolai looked at his interlocutrice) "are blue, her mouth is coral, the whiteness" (he glanced at her shoulders) "of her figure is like Diana's . . ."

The husband came over to them and sulkily asked his wife what she was talking about.

"Ah! Nikita Ivanych," said Nikolai, politely getting up. And, as if wishing Nikita Ivanych to share in the joke, he began telling him, too, about his wish to abduct a certain blonde lady.

The husband smiled sullenly, the wife gaily. The governor's kindly wife came up to them with a disapproving air.

"Anna Ignatyevna wants to see you, Nicolas," she said, uttering the words

*Bad manners.

"Anna Ignatyevna" in such a tone that it became clear at once to Rostov that Anna Ignatyevna was a very important lady. "Come, Nicolas. You do allow me to call you that?"

"Oh, yes, *ma tante*.* Who is she?"

"Anna Ignatyevna Malvintsev. She has heard about you from her niece, how you rescued her . . . Can you guess?"

"As if I haven't rescued lots of them!" said Nikolai.

"Her niece, Princess Bolkonsky. She's here in Voronezh with her aunt! Oho, how he blushes! What, are you . . ."

"Never thought of it! Enough, *ma tante*."

"Well, all right, all right. Oh, what a one you are!"

The governor's wife led him to a tall and very fat old woman in a blue toque, who had just finished her game of cards with the most important persons in town. This was Mrs. Malvintsev, Princess Marya's aunt on her mother's side, a wealthy, childless widow who lived year-round in Voronezh. She was standing and settling up for the game when Rostov approached her. She narrowed her eyes sternly and imposingly, glanced at him, and went on scolding the general who had won from her.

"Delighted, my dear," she said, giving him her hand. "Kindly call on me."

After talking about Princess Marya and her late father, whom Mrs. Malvintsev evidently did not like, and asking Nikolai what he knew about Prince Andrei, who evidently was also not in her good graces, the imposing old lady let him go, repeating her invitation to visit her.

Nikolai promised and blushed again as he was taking leave of Mrs. Malvintsev. At the mention of Princess Marya, Rostov experienced a feeling of bashfulness, even fear, incomprehensible to himself.

On leaving Mrs. Malvintsev, Nikolai wanted to return to the dancing, but the governor's wife placed her plump little hand on his sleeve and, saying that she needed to talk to him, led him to the sitting room, which those who were there left at once, so as not to hinder her.

"You know, *mon cher*," said the governor's wife, with a serious expression on her small, kindly face, "it's just the match for you. Would you like me to arrange it?"

"With whom, *ma tante*?" asked Nikolai.

"With the princess. Katerina Petrovna says Lili, but I think, no—the princess. Would you like me to? I'm sure your *maman* will thank me. Really, such a girl, so lovely! And she's not at all so bad-looking."

"Not at all," Nikolai said, as if offended. "As befits a soldier, *ma tante*, I don't invite myself anywhere and don't refuse anything," said Rostov, before he had time to think what he was saying.

*My aunt.

"Remember, then: this is not a joke."

"Of course not!"

"Yes, yes," said the governor's wife, as if talking to herself. "And here's another thing, *mon cher, entre autres. Vous êtes trop assidu auprès de l'autre, la blonde.** The husband is pitiful, really . . ."

"Ah, no, we're friends," Nikolai said in the simplicity of his heart: it had never occurred to him that the pastime which he found so amusing might not be so for someone else.

"But what a stupid thing I said to the governor's wife!" Nikolai suddenly recalled at supper. "She's sure to start matchmaking. And Sonya? . . ." And on taking leave of the governor's wife, when she, smiling, told him once more: "Well, so remember," he took her aside.

"The thing is, to tell you the truth, *ma tante* . . ."

"What is it, what is it, my friend; let's go and sit down there."

Nikolai suddenly felt a desire and a need to tell all his innermost thoughts (such as he would not have told to his mother, sister, or friend) to this woman who was almost a stranger to him. Later, when he recalled this impulse of unprovoked, inexplicable candour, which, however, had very important consequences for him, it seemed to Nikolai (as it always seems to people) that it had been just a stupid whimsy; and yet this impulse of candour, along with other small events, had enormous consequences for him and for the whole family.

"Here's the thing, *ma tante. Maman* has long wanted me to marry a rich girl, but the very thought of marrying for money is repugnant to me."

"Oh, yes, I understand," said the governor's wife.

"But Princess Bolkonsky is another thing. First, to tell you the truth, I like her very much, she's a girl after my heart, and then, since I met her in such circumstances, so strangely, it has often occurred to me that it was fate. Especially if you consider that *maman* has long been thinking of it, but I never happened to meet her before, it just happened that we kept not meeting. And at the time when Natasha was engaged to her brother, it was impossible for me to think of marrying her. It had to be that I met her precisely when Natasha's engagement broke up, well, and then it all . . . But here's the thing. I've never told this to anyone and never will. Only to you."

The governor's wife gratefully pressed his elbow.

"You know Sophie, my cousin? I love her, I've promised to marry her, and will marry her . . . So you see, there can be no talk of it," Nikolai said incoherently and blushing.

"*Mon cher, mon cher,* how can you reason that way? Sophie has nothing, and you said yourself that your father's affairs are in disorder. And your

* Among others. You are being too attentive to the other one, the blonde.

maman? It will kill her, for one thing. Then Sophie, if she's a girl with a heart, what sort of life will it be for her? The mother in despair, affairs in disorder . . . No, *mon cher,* you and Sophie ought to understand that."

Nikolai was silent. It was pleasant for him to hear these conclusions.

"All the same, *ma tante,* it cannot be," he said with a sigh, after a brief pause. "And would the princess marry me? And then, too, she's in mourning now. Can there be any thought of it?"

"You're not thinking that I'll marry you off at once? *Il y a manière et manière,*"* said the governor's wife.

"What a matchmaker you are, *ma tante* . . ." said Nikolai, kissing her plump little hand.

<h1 style="text-align:center">VI</h1>

On arriving in Moscow after her meeting with Rostov, Princess Marya had found her nephew there with his tutor and a letter from Prince Andrei, who instructed them to proceed to Voronezh, to their aunt, Mrs. Malvintsev. The cares of moving, worry about her brother, organizing life in a new home, new faces, her nephew's upbringing—all this stifled in Princess Marya's soul that feeling of temptation, as it were, which had tormented her during the illness and after the death of her father, and especially after meeting Rostov. She was sad. Now, after a month spent in quiet conditions of life, the impression of the loss of her father, combined in her soul with the perishing of Russia, made itself felt in her more and more strongly. She was anxious: the thought of the dangers to which her brother—the only close person she had left—was exposed, tormented her ceaselessly. She was worried about the upbringing of her nephew, a task to which she constantly felt herself unequal. But in the depths of her soul there was a harmony with herself, coming from the consciousness that she had suppressed in herself the personal dreams and hopes that had begun to arise in her with the appearance of Rostov.

When the governor's wife went to Mrs. Malvintsev's the day after her soirée and, having talked over her plans with the aunt (mentioning that, though under the circumstances it was impossible even to think of a formal engagement, still the young people could be brought together and given a chance to know each other) and when, having obtained the aunt's approval, the governor's wife spoke of Rostov in Princess Marya's presence, praising him and telling how he had blushed at the mention of the princess—Princess Marya experienced not a joyful but a painful feeling: her inner harmony no longer existed, and again there arose desires, doubts, reproaches, and hopes.

*There are ways and ways.

In the two days that passed between the time of this announcement and Rostov's visit, Princess Marya never stopped thinking of how she ought to behave in relation to him. First she decided that she would not come out to the drawing room when he called on her aunt, that it was improper for her, in deep mourning, to receive guests; then she thought that that would be rude after what he had done for her; then it occurred to her that her aunt and the governor's wife had some sort of designs on her and Rostov (their glances and words occasionally seemed to confirm that conjecture); then she said to herself that only she, in her depravity, could think that of them: they could not help realizing that, in her position, when she was still in deep mourning, such matchmaking would be insulting both to her and to her father's memory. Supposing that she would come out to him, Princess Marya thought up the words he would say to her and she to him; and these words seemed to her now undeservedly cold, now too fraught with significance. Most of all she feared the embarrassment which, she felt, was bound to overcome her and betray her as soon as she saw him.

But on Sunday after the liturgy, when a footman came to the drawing room and announced that Count Rostov was there, the princess showed no embarrassment; only a slight flush came to her cheeks, and her eyes lit up with a new, luminous brightness.

"Have you seen him, aunt?" Princess Marya asked in a calm voice, not knowing herself how she could be so outwardly calm and natural.

When Rostov entered the room, the princess lowered her head for a moment, as if giving her guest time to greet her aunt, and then, just as Nikolai turned to her, she raised her head and her shining eyes met his gaze. In a movement full of dignity and grace, she rose with a joyful smile, gave him her slender, delicate hand, and began to speak in a voice in which, for the first time, new, throaty, feminine notes sounded. Mlle Bourienne, who was in the drawing room, looked at Princess Marya with bewildered astonishment. A skilful coquette herself, she could not have manoeuvred better on meeting a man she wanted to please.

"Either black is quite becoming to her, or she has really grown quite pretty, and I haven't noticed it. And, above all—that tact and grace!" thought Mlle Bourienne.

If Princess Marya had been able to reflect at that moment, she would have been more astonished than Mlle Bourienne at the change that had taken place in her. From the moment she saw that dear, beloved face, some new force of life had taken hold of her and made her speak and act apart from her own will. Her face, from the time Rostov entered, was suddenly transformed. As the complex, skilful artwork on the sides of a carved and painted lantern, which had seemed crude, dark, and meaningless before, suddenly emerges with unexpected, striking beauty when the light is lit inside: so was Princess Marya's face suddenly transformed. For the first time, all that pure, spiritual inner work, which she had so far lived by, emerged. All her inner work of discontent with herself, her suffering, her yearning for the good, obedience, love, self-sacrifice—all this now shone in those luminous eyes, in her fine smile, in every feature of her tender face.

Rostov saw it all as clearly as if he knew her whole life. He sensed that the being before him was quite different, and better, than all those he had met till then, and, above all, better than himself.

The conversation was most simple and insignificant. They talked of the war, involuntarily exaggerating, like everyone else, their grief at these events, talked of their last meeting, with Nikolai trying to turn the conversation to another subject, talked of the governor's kindly wife, of Nikolai's and Princess Marya's relatives.

Princess Marya did not speak of her brother, turning the conversation to another subject as soon as her aunt mentioned Prince Andrei. It was clear that she could speak artificially about the misfortunes of Russia, but her brother was a subject too close to her heart, and she would not and could not speak lightly of him. Nikolai noticed that, as he generally noticed, with a keenness of observation unusual for him, all the nuances of Princess Marya's character, which only confirmed his conviction that she was an utterly special and extraordinary being. Nikolai, just like Princess Marya, blushed and became embarrassed when someone talked to him about the princess, and even when he thought about her, but in her presence he felt perfectly free and said not at all what he had prepared, but what instantly and always appropriately came to his head.

During Nikolai's brief visit, as usual in a house where there are children, he resorted to Prince Andrei's little son when there was a moment of silence, stroking his head and asking if he wanted to be a hussar. He took the boy in his arms, began tossing him merrily, and turned to look at Princess Marya. Her tender, happy, and timid gaze followed the boy she loved in the arms of the man she loved. Nikolai noticed this gaze and, as if understanding its meaning, blushed with pleasure and began to kiss the boy merrily and good-naturedly.

Princess Marya did not go out because she was in mourning, and Nikolai did not consider it proper to visit them; but the governor's wife still went on with her matchmaking business and, having told Nikolai the flattering things Princess Marya had said about him and vice versa, insisted that Rostov should declare himself to Princess Marya. For that talk, she arranged a meeting between the young people at the bishop's before the liturgy.

Though Rostov told the governor's wife that he would not make any sort of declaration to Princess Marya, he did promise to come.

Just as in Tilsit Rostov had not allowed himself to doubt that what everyone recognized as good was indeed good, so also now, after a brief but sincere struggle between his effort to arrange his life according to his own reason and a humble submission to circumstances, he chose the latter and gave himself up to the power which (he felt) was irresistibly drawing him somewhere. He knew that, having given Sonya his promise, to speak out his feelings to Princess Marya would be what he called base. And he knew that he would never do anything base. But he also knew (or did not know, but felt in the depths of his soul) that, in yielding now to the power of the circumstances and the people who were guiding him, he was not only doing nothing bad, but was doing something very, very important, more important than anything he had ever done in his life.

After his meeting with Princess Marya, the form of his life outwardly remained the same, but all his former pleasures lost their charm for him, and he often thought of Princess Marya; but he never thought of her as he thought, without exception, of all the young ladies he met in society, nor as he had long thought, and at one time with rapture, about Sonya. Like almost every honourable young man, he had thought of all young ladies as future wives, applying to them in his imagination all the conditions of married life: a white dressing gown, a wife at the samovar, the wife's carriage, children, *maman* and *papa*, his relations with her, and so on, and so forth; and he had enjoyed these pictures of the future; but when he thought of Princess Marya, with whom they were matchmaking him, he never could imagine anything of their future married life. Even when he tried, everything came out incoherent and false. It only made him feel eerie.

VII

The dreadful news of the battle of Borodino, of our losses in dead and wounded, and the still more dreadful news about the loss of Moscow, were received in Voronezh in the middle of September. Princess Marya, learning of her brother's wound only from the newspapers and having no definite news of him, was getting ready to go in search of Prince Andrei, as Nikolai heard (he had not seen her himself).

On receiving the news of the battle of Borodino and the abandoning of Moscow, Rostov did not experience despair, anger, or vengefulness, and any similar feeling, but for him everything in Voronezh suddenly became dull and vexing, everything was somehow shameful and awkward. All the conversations he heard seemed artificial to him; he did not know how to judge it all, and he felt that only in the regiment would everything become clear to him again. He was in a hurry to finish buying the horses and often flew into a temper unfairly with his servant and the sergeant major.

A few days before Rostov's departure, a prayer service was offered on the occasion of the victory won by the Russian troops, and Nikolai went to the liturgy. He placed himself a little behind the governor, and with official staidness, thinking of the most various subjects, stood through the service. When the prayers were over, the governor's wife beckoned him to her.

"Did you see the princess?" she said, nodding towards a lady in black standing behind the choir.

Nikolai at once recognized Princess Marya, not so much by her profile, which could be seen under her hat, as by that feeling of carefulness, fear, and pity that at once came over him. Princess Marya, obviously immersed in her own thoughts, made a last sign of the cross before leaving the church.

Nikolai looked at her face with astonishment. It was the same face he had seen before, in it was the same general expression of fine, inner, spiritual work; but now it was lit completely differently. It bore a touching expression of sorrow, entreaty, and hope. As had happened with Nikolai before in her presence, he went up to her without waiting for the governor's wife to advise him to go to her, without asking himself whether or not it would be good or proper for him to address her there in church, and told her that he had heard about her grief and sympathized with her with all his soul. As soon as she heard his voice, a bright light suddenly shone in her face, lighting up both her sorrow and her joy.

"There is one thing I wanted to tell you, Princess," said Rostov. "It is that if Prince Andrei Nikolaevich was no longer alive, him being the commander of a regiment, it would have been announced at once in the newspapers."

The princess was looking at him, not understanding his words, but rejoicing at the expression of compassionate suffering in his face.

"And I know so many examples when a shrapnel wound" (the newspaper had said it was a shell) "is either fatal at once or, on the contrary, very light," said Nikolai. "You must hope for the best, and I'm sure . . ."

Princess Marya interrupted him.

"Oh, that would be so ter . . ." she began and, breaking off from emotion, she inclined her head gracefully (as she did everything in his presence) and, glancing at him with gratitude, followed after her aunt.

In the evening of that day, Nikolai did not go out visiting anywhere, but stayed home to finish some accounts with the horse dealers. When he finished his business, it was too late to go anywhere, but still too early to go to bed, and for a long time Nikolai paced up and down the room alone, thinking over his life, which rarely happened with him.

Princess Marya had produced a pleasant impression on him near Smolensk. That he had met her then in such particular conditions, and that it was precisely her that his mother had pointed to at one time as a wealthy match for him, had made him pay special attention to her. In Voronezh, during the time of his visit, the impression was not only pleasant, but strong. Nikolai was struck by that particular moral beauty which he noticed in her this time. However, he was getting ready to leave, and it never occurred to him to regret that, in leaving Voronezh, he was losing the chance of seeing the princess. But this last meeting with Princess Marya in church (Nikolai felt it) had lodged more deeply in his heart than he expected, and more deeply than he wished for his own peace of mind. That pale, fine, sorrowful face, that luminous gaze, those quiet, graceful movements, and above all that deep and tender sorrow which showed in all her features, stirred him and called for his sympathy. Rostov could not bear to see an expression of higher spiritual life in men (that was why he did not like Prince Andrei), he referred to it contemptuously as philosophy, dreaminess; but in Princess Marya it was precisely in that sorrow, which revealed the whole depth of a spiritual world foreign to him, that Nikolai felt an irresistible attraction.

"She must be a wonderful girl! Precisely an angel!" he said to himself. "Why am I not free, why did I rush things with Sonya?" And involuntarily he pictured to himself a comparison between the two: the poorness of the one and the richness of the other in those spiritual gifts, which Nikolai did not have and which he therefore valued so highly. He tried to picture how it would be if he were free. How would he propose to her, and how would she become his wife? No, he could not picture it to himself. It made him feel eerie, and no clear images came to him. With Sonya he had already made up a future picture, and it was all simple and clear, precisely because it was all invented, and he knew everything there was in Sonya; but with Princess Marya it was impossible for him to picture a future life, because he did not understand her, but only loved her.

Dreams about Sonya had something gay and toylike about them. But to think about Princess Marya was always difficult and a little frightening.

"How she prayed!" he remembered. "You could see that her whole soul was in the prayer. Yes, that's the kind of prayer that moves mountains, and I'm sure her prayer will be answered. Why don't I pray for what I want?" he wondered. "What do I want? Freedom, release from Sonya. What she said was true," he remembered the words of the governor's wife, "there will be nothing but unhappiness if I marry her. A tangle, *maman*'s grief . . . our affairs . . . a tangle, an awful tangle! And anyhow I don't love her. No, I don't love her as I should. My God! lead me out of this terrible, hopeless situation!" he suddenly began to pray. "Yes, prayer can move mountains, but one must believe and not pray, the way Natasha and I did as children, that snow turn into sugar, and then run outside to see if it did turn into sugar. No, I'm not praying about trifles now," he said, putting his pipe into a corner, crossing his arms, and standing before the icon. And, moved to tenderness by his memory of Princess Marya, he began to pray as he had not prayed for a long time. There were tears in his eyes and in his throat when Lavrushka came in with some papers.

"Fool! Why do you barge in unasked!" said Nikolai, quickly changing his position.

"From the governor," Lavrushka said in a sleepy voice, "a messenger came, there's mail for you."

"Well, all right, thanks, and off with you!"

Nikolai took the two letters. One was from his mother, the other from Sonya. He recognized them by the handwriting and opened Sonya's letter first. He had read only a few lines when his face turned pale and his eyes widened fearfully and joyfully.

"No, it can't be!" he said aloud.

Unable to sit still, he began pacing the room with the letter in his hand, reading it. He glanced through it, then read it once, twice, and, hunching his shoulders and spreading his arms, stopped in the middle of the room with gaping mouth and fixed eyes. The thing he had just prayed for with the certainty that God would grant his prayer, had been granted; but Nikolai was astonished by it, as if it was something extraordinary, and as if he had never expected it, and as if the fact that it had happened so quickly proved that it came not from God, whom he had asked, but from ordinary coincidence.

That seemingly indissoluble knot which had bound Rostov's freedom was dissolved by this unexpected (as it seemed to Nikolai) and quite unprovoked letter from Sonya. She wrote that the latest unfortunate circumstances, the loss of almost all of the Rostovs' Moscow property, the countess's oft-repeated wishes that Nikolai should marry Princess Bolkonsky, and his recent silence and coldness—all this together had made her resolve to renounce his promise and give him full freedom.

"It is too painful for me to think that I could be the cause of grief or discord in the family of my benefactors," she wrote, "and my love has no other aim than the happiness of those I love; and so I beg you, Nicolas, to consider yourself free and to know that, despite all, no one can love you more than—Your Sonya."

Both letters came from the Trinity monastery. The other letter was from the countess. This letter described the last days in Moscow, the departure, the fire, and the loss of all their property. Among other things, the countess wrote that Prince Andrei was travelling with them among the wounded. His condition was very grave, but the doctor now said there was greater hope. Sonya and Natasha were taking care of him as nurses.

The next day Nikolai took this letter and went to see Princess Marya. Neither Nikolai nor Princess Marya said a word about what the words "Natasha is taking care of him" might mean; but owing to this letter, Nikolai and the princess were suddenly brought together in almost familial relations.

The next day Nikolai saw Princess Marya off to Yaroslavl, and a few days later left himself for the regiment.

VIII

Sonya's letter to Nikolai, which was the realization of his prayer, had been written from the Trinity monastery. Here is how it came about. The old countess was more and more taken up with the idea of marrying Nikolai to a rich bride. She knew that Sonya was the chief obstacle to that. And Sonya's life recently, especially after Nikolai's letter describing his meeting with Princess Marya in Bogucharovo, was becoming more and more difficult in the countess's house. The countess never missed an opportunity to make an insulting or cruel hint to Sonya.

But a few days before leaving Moscow, moved and troubled by all that was going on, the countess, having sent for Sonya, addressed her in tears, instead of with reproaches and demands, begging her to pay back all that had been done for her by sacrificing herself and breaking her bond with Nikolai.

"I won't be at peace as long as you haven't given me that promise."

Sonya burst into hysterical sobs, answered through her sobs that she would do everything, that she was ready for everything, but promised nothing directly, and in her soul could not resolve to do what was demanded of her. She was to sacrifice herself for the happiness of the family that had nourished and raised her. To sacrifice herself for others was Sonya's habit. Her position in the house was such that it was only on the path of sacrifice that she could show her worth, and she was accustomed to sacrificing herself and loved it. But formerly, in all her acts of self-sacrifice, she had been joyfully aware that in sacrificing herself she thereby raised her value in her own and other people's eyes, and became more worthy of Nicolas, whom she loved more than anything in her life; but now her sacrifice was to consist in renouncing that which for her made up the whole reward for her sacrifice, the whole meaning of her life. And for the first time in her life she felt bitter towards the people who had been her benefactors only so as to torment her the more; she felt envy of Natasha, who had never experienced anything like that, who had never needed to sacrifice herself, but made others sacrifice themselves for her, and was loved even so. And for the first time Sonya felt her quiet, pure love for Nicolas suddenly begin to grow into a passionate feeling, which stood above the rules, and virtue, and religion; and, under the influence of that feeling, Sonya, having been taught by her life of dependence to be secretive, involuntarily answered the countess in general, indefinite terms, avoided talking further with her, and decided to wait for her meeting with Nikolai, not in order to free him at that meeting, but, on the contrary, to bind him to her for ever.

The bustle and horror of the Rostovs' last days in Moscow stifled in Sonya the gloomy thoughts that oppressed her. She was glad to find salvation from them in practical activity. But when she learned of Prince Andrei's presence in their house, despite all the sincere pity she felt for him and for Natasha, the joyful and superstitious feeling came over her that God did not want her to be separated from Nicolas. She knew that Natasha loved only Prince Andrei and had never ceased loving him. She knew that now, being brought together in such terrible conditions, they would love each other again, and that then, because of the family relations between them, Nikolai would be unable to marry Princess Marya. Despite all the horror of what had taken place in the last days and during the first days of the journey, this feeling, this consciousness of Providence interfering in her personal affairs, made Sonya happy.

In the Trinity monastery the Rostovs made their first day-long halt in their journey.

In the monastery hostel the Rostovs were given three big rooms, one of which was occupied by Prince Andrei. The wounded man was much better that day. Natasha sat with him. In the next room sat the count and countess, talking respectfully with the superior, who came to see his long-standing acquaintances and donors. Sonya sat with them, and she was tormented by curiosity as to what Prince Andrei and Natasha were talking about. She listened to the sound of their voices through the door. The door to Prince Andrei's room opened. Natasha came out with an agitated face and, not noticing the monk, who rose to meet her and took hold of the wide sleeve on his right arm, went to Sonya and took her by the hand.

"Natasha, what's the matter with you? Come here," said the countess.

Natasha went to receive the blessing, and the superior advised her to turn for help to God and to St. Sergius.

Immediately after the superior left, Natasha took her friend by the hand and went with her to the empty room.

"Sonya, he's going to live? Yes?" she said. "Sonya, how happy I am, and how unhappy! Sonya, darling—it's all like before. If only he lives! He can't . . . because, because . . ." And Natasha burst into tears.

"So! I knew it! Thank God," said Sonya. "He will live!"

Sonya was no less agitated than her friend—both by her fear and grief, and by her own personal thoughts, which she did not tell to anyone. Sobbing, she kissed and comforted Natasha. "If only he lives!" she thought. Having wept, talked, and wiped their tears, the two friends went up to Prince Andrei's door. Natasha, cautiously opening the door, peeked into the room. Sonya stood next to her by the half-open door.

Prince Andrei lay propped high on three pillows. His pale face was calm, his eyes closed, and they could see that he was breathing evenly.

"Ah, Natasha!" Sonya suddenly almost cried out, seizing her cousin's arm and stepping back from the door.

"What, what is it?" asked Natasha.

"It's that, it's that . . ." Sonya said with a pale face and trembling lips.

Natasha quietly closed the door and stepped to the window with Sonya, still not understanding what was being said to her.

"Do you remember," Sonya said with a frightened and solemn face, "do you remember when I looked into the mirror for you . . . In Otradnoe, at Christmas . . . Do you remember what I saw? . . ."

"Yes, yes!" said Natasha, opening her eyes wide, vaguely recalling that Sonya had said something then about seeing Prince Andrei lying down.

"Do you remember?" Sonya went on. "I saw it then and told everybody, you and Dunyasha. I saw him lying on a bed," she said, making a gesture with her raised finger at each detail, "and his eyes were closed, and he was covered precisely with a pink quilt, and his hands were folded," Sonya said, becoming convinced, as she described the details she had just seen, that she *had seen* those same details then. Then she had seen nothing, but had told that she saw whatever came into her head; but what she had invented then seemed to her as real as any other memory. What she had said then, that he had glanced at her and smiled, and was covered with something red, she remembered, but she was also firmly convinced that then, too, she had said and seen that he was covered with pink, precisely a pink quilt, and that his eyes were closed.

"Yes, yes, precisely pink," said Natasha, who also now seemed to remember the mention of "pink," and in this she saw the chief extraordinariness and mysteriousness of the prediction.

"But what does it mean?" Natasha asked thoughtfully.

"Ah, I don't know, it's all so extraordinary!" said Sonya, clutching her head.

A few minutes later Prince Andrei rang, and Natasha went to his room; and Sonya, feeling an agitation and a tenderness she had rarely felt, stayed by the window, thinking over all the extraordinariness of what had happened.

On that day there was a chance to send letters to the army, and the countess was writing a letter to her son.

"Sonya," said the countess, raising her head from the letter as her niece walked past her. "Sonya, why don't you write to Nikolenka?" the countess said in a soft, quavering voice, and in the gaze of her weary eyes looking through her spectacles, Sonya read all that the countess implied by these words. That gaze expressed entreaty, and fear of refusal, and shame at having to ask, and a readiness for implacable hatred in case of refusal.

Sonya went up to the countess and, kneeling, kissed her hand.

"I will, *maman*," she said.

Sonya was softened, agitated, and moved by all that had happened that day, especially by the mysterious fulfilment she had just seen of her divination. Now, when she knew that, because of the renewal of Natasha's relations with

Prince Andrei, Nikolai could not marry Princess Marya, she felt with joy the return of that mood of self-sacrifice in which she loved and was accustomed to live. And with tears in her eyes and a joyful awareness of performing a magnanimous act, she wrote, interrupted several times by the tears that clouded her velvety black eyes, that touching letter, the reception of which so struck Nikolai.

IX

In the guardhouse where Pierre was taken, the officers and soldiers who had arrested him treated him hostilely, but at the same time respectfully. In their attitude towards him, doubt could still be felt of who he was (perhaps a very important person), and hostility because of the still-fresh personal struggle with him.

But when another shift came the next morning, Pierre felt that for these new guards—both officers and soldiers—he did not have the same meaning he had had for those who arrested him. And indeed, in this large, fat man in a peasant kaftan the next day's guards no longer saw the living man who had fought so desperately with a looter and the convoy soldiers, and had spoken the solemn phrase about saving a child, but saw only the seventeenth arrested Russian, kept there for some reason on orders from the high command. If there was anything special in Pierre, it was only his untimid, concentratedly thoughtful air and the French which, surprisingly for the French, he spoke very well. Despite which, on that same day, Pierre was put together with the other arrested suspects, because the separate room he had occupied was needed for an officer.

All the Russians held together with Pierre were people of the lowest estate. And all of them, recognizing Pierre as a gentleman, shunned him, the more so as he spoke French. Pierre listened with sadness to their mockery of him.

That evening Pierre learned that all these prisoners (and probably he among them) were to be tried for arson. On the third day Pierre was taken with the others to some house where a French general with white moustaches sat with two colonels and other Frenchmen with armbands. With that precision and definiteness which is supposedly above human weakness, and with which the accused are usually treated, Pierre, like the others, was questioned about who he was, where he had been, with what purpose, and so on.

These questions, leaving aside the essence of life's business and excluding any possibility of discovering that essence, like all questions asked at trials, were aimed only at furnishing that channel down which the judges wished the answers of the accused to flow, leading him to the desired goal, that is, incrimination. As soon as he began to say something that did not conform to the purpose of incrimination, the channel was removed, and the water could flow wherever it liked. Besides that, Pierre experienced the same thing that an accused man experiences in any court: perplexity as to why all these questions were being asked him. He had the feeling that this trick of furnishing him with a channel was being used only out of indulgence or courtesy, as it were. He knew that he was in the power of these people, that it was only power that had brought him there, that only power gave them the right to demand answers to their questions, and that the only purpose of this gathering was to incriminate him. And therefore, since there was power and the wish to incriminate, there was no need for the trickery of questions and a trial. It was obvious that all answers should lead to finding him guilty. To the question of what he was doing when they arrested him, Pierre answered somewhat tragically that he was carrying a child *qu'il avait sauvé des flammes** to her parents. Why had he fought with the looter? Pierre answered that he was defending a woman, that to defend an offended woman was the duty of every man, that . . . He was stopped: that did not suit the case. Why was he in the yard of the burning house, where witnesses had seen him? He answered that he had gone out to see what was happening in Moscow. He was stopped again: he had not been asked where he was going, but why he was near the fire. Who was he? they repeated to him their first question, which he had told them he did not want to answer. Again he said that he could not tell them.

"Write that down, it's bad. Very bad," the general with the white moustaches and flushed, ruddy face said sternly to him.

On the fourth day fires broke out on the Zubovsky rampart.

Pierre and thirteen others were led to the Krymsky ford, to the carriage shed of a merchant's house. Going down the streets, Pierre choked from the smoke, which seemed to hang over the whole city. Fires could be seen on all sides. At that time Pierre still did not understand the significance of the burning of Moscow and looked at these fires with horror.

Pierre spent four more days in the carriage shed of the house near the Krymsky ford, and in the course of those days he learned from the conversation of the French soldiers that all those held there were awaiting the marshal's decision any day. What marshal, Pierre could not find out from the soldiers. Apparently for the soldiers a marshal was a supreme and somewhat mysterious link in the chain of power.

Those first days, until the eighth of September—the day when the prisoners were taken for a second interrogation—were the hardest for Pierre.

*That he had saved from the flames.

X

On the eighth of September an officer came into the prisoners' shed, a very important one, judging by the respect with which the guards addressed him. This officer, probably from the staff, with a list in his hands, made a roll call of all the Russians, referring to Pierre as *celui qui n'avoue pas son nom.** And, looking indifferently and lazily over all the prisoners, he ordered the officer of the guards to get them decently dressed and tidied up before bringing them to the marshal. An hour later a company of soldiers arrived, and Pierre and the other thirteen were led to the Devichye field. The day was clear and sunny after rain, and the air was extraordinarily pure. The smoke did not spread as low as on the day when Pierre was taken from the guardhouse of the Zubovsky rampart; the smoke rose in columns in the pure air. Flames were not to be seen anywhere, but columns of smoke rose on all sides, and the whole of Moscow, all that Pierre could see of it, was one charred ruin. On all sides one could see waste spaces with stoves and chimneys and occasionally the scorched walls of stone houses. Pierre looked at the charred ruins and did not recognize the familiar quarters of the city. Here and there he could see intact churches. The Kremlin, undestroyed, stood white in the distance, with its towers and Ivan the Great. Nearby, the dome of the Novodevichye Convent gleamed merrily, and the ringing of its bells could be heard especially clearly. This bell-ringing reminded Pierre that it was Sunday and the feast of the Nativity of the Mother of God. But it seemed there was no one to celebrate the feast: the fire's devastation was everywhere, and the only Russians to be met with now and then were ragged, frightened people who hid at the sight of the French.

Obviously, the Russian nest was devastated and destroyed; but beyond the destruction of the Russian order of life, Pierre felt unconsciously that the French had established their own quite different but firm order over this devastated nest. He felt it by the look of the soldiers who, marching briskly and cheerfully in regular ranks, escorted him along with the other criminals; he felt it by the look of some important French official in a carriage-and-pair, driven by a soldier, who came in the opposite direction. He felt it by the cheerful sounds of regimental music coming from the left side of the field, and he felt it and realized it especially by the list which, in the roll call of the prisoners, was read out by the French officer who had arrived that morning. Pierre had been arrested by one group of soldiers, had been taken to one place and then another with dozens of other people; it seemed they might have forgotten him

*He who does not divulge his name.

or confused him with others. But no: the answers he had given at the interrogation came back to him in the form of his designation: *celui qui n'avoue pas son nom.* And under this designation, which frightened Pierre, he was now led somewhere by people on whose faces was written the unquestioning certainty that all the other prisoners and he himself were precisely the necessary ones, and were being taken to the necessary place. Pierre felt like an insignificant chip of wood fallen into the wheels of a machine unknown to him but functioning well.

Pierre and the other criminals were taken to the right side of the Devichye field, not far from the convent, to a big white house with a huge garden. This was the house of Prince Shcherbatov, in which Pierre had often visited the owner, and in which, as he learned from the conversation of the soldiers, the marshal, the duke of Eckmühl, was now installed.

They were led up to the porch and brought into the house one by one. Pierre was brought in sixth. Through the glassed-in gallery, the front hall, the anteroom, familiar to Pierre, he was led into a long, low study, at the door to which stood an adjutant.

Davout was sitting at the end of the room, over a table, with spectacles on his nose. Pierre went up close to him. Davout, not raising his eyes, was evidently examining some document that lay before him. Without raising his eyes, he asked softly:

"*Qui êtes-vous?*"*

Pierre was silent, because he was unable to utter a word. For Pierre, Davout was not simply a French general; for Pierre, Davout was a man known for his cruelty. Looking at the cold face of Davout, who, like a stern teacher, agreed to be patient for a time and wait for an answer, Pierre felt that every second of delay might cost him his life; but he did not know what to say. He did not dare to say what he had said at the first interrogation; to reveal his title and position was both dangerous and shameful. Pierre was silent. But before he had time to decide on something, Davout raised his head, raised his spectacles to his forehead, narrowed his eyes, and looked fixedly at Pierre.

"I know this man," he said in a measured and cold voice, obviously calculated to frighten Pierre. The chill that had run down Pierre's spine earlier, now seized his head as in a vice.

"*Mon général, vous ne pouvez pas me connaître, je ne vous ai jamais vu . . .*"†

"*C'est un espion russe,*"‡ Davout interrupted him, addressing another general who was in the room and whom Pierre had not noticed. And Da-

*Who are you?
†General, you cannot know me, I have never seen you . . .
‡He's a Russian spy.

vout turned away. In an unexpectedly booming voice, Pierre began speaking quickly:

"*Non, monseigneur,*" he said, suddenly recalling that Davout was a duke. "*Non, monseigneur, vous n'avez pas pu me connaître. Je suis un officier militionnaire et je n'ai pas quitté Moscou.*"*

"*Votre nom?*"† asked Davout.

"*Besouhof.*"

"*Qu'est-ce qui me prouvera que vous ne mentez pas?*"‡

"*Monseigneur!*" exclaimed Pierre, not in an offended, but in a pleading voice.

Davout raised his eyes and looked fixedly at Pierre. For a few seconds they looked at each other, and that gaze saved Pierre. In that gaze, beyond all the conventions of war and courts, human relations were established between these two men. In that one moment, they both vaguely felt a countless number of things and realized that they were both children of the human race, that they were brothers.

At first glance, for Davout, who had only just raised his head from his list, where human deeds and life were known by numbers, Pierre was only a circumstance, and Davout could have shot him without taking a bad act on his conscience; but now he had seen him as a human being. He reflected for a moment.

"*Comment me prouverez-vous la vérité de ce que vous me dites?*"§ Davout said coldly.

Pierre remembered Ramballe and named him and his regiment and the street where the house was.

"*Vous n'êtes pas ce que vous dites,*"# Davout said again.

In a trembling, faltering voice, Pierre began to give proofs of the correctness of his evidence.

But just then an adjutant came in and reported something to Davout.

Davout suddenly beamed at the news told him by the adjutant and began to button up. He had clearly forgotten all about Pierre.

When the adjutant reminded him of the prisoner, he nodded, frowning, in Pierre's direction and said to take him away. But where he was to be taken, Pierre did not know: back to the shed or to the place prepared for executions, which his comrades had shown him as they walked through the Devichye field.

He turned his head and saw that the adjutant was again asking something.

---

*No, My Lord . . . No, My Lord, you could not have known me. I am a militia officer, and I have not left Moscow.
†Your name?
‡What will prove to me that you are not lying?
§How will you prove to me the truth of what you say?
#You are not what you say.

"*Oui, sans doute!*"* said Davout, but "yes" what, Pierre did not know.

Pierre did not remember how long he walked or where. In a state of total senselessness and torpor, seeing nothing around him, he moved his legs along with the others until they all stopped, and he stopped, too.

There was one thought in Pierre's head all that time. It was the thought of who, finally, had sentenced him to be executed. It was not the people of the commission that had interrogated him: not one of them would or obviously could have done it. It was not Davout, who had given him such a human look. Another moment and Davout would have understood that they were doing a bad thing, but the adjutant who came in had prevented that moment. And that adjutant obviously had not wanted anything bad, but he also might not have come in. Who was it, finally, who was executing, killing, depriving of life, him—Pierre—with all his memories, longings, hopes, thoughts? Who was doing it? And Pierre felt that it was no one.

It was the order of things, the turn of circumstances.

Some order of things was killing him—Pierre—depriving him of life, of everything, annihilating him.

XI

From Prince Shcherbatov's house, the prisoners were taken straight down the Devichye field, to the left of the Devichye Convent, and brought to the kitchen garden, where a post stood. Behind the post, a large pit had been dug, with freshly dug-up earth beside it, and a large crowd of people were standing in a semicircle around the pit and the post. The crowd consisted of a small number of Russians and a large number of Napoleonic troops out of rank: Germans, Italians, and French in various uniforms. To right and left of the post stood lines of French troops in blue uniforms with red epaulettes, in leggings and shakos.

The criminals were placed in a certain order, which was on the list (Pierre was sixth), and led to the post. Several drums suddenly began to beat on both sides, and Pierre felt that with this sound it was as if part of his soul was torn away. He lost the ability to think and reason. He could only see and hear. And he had only one desire—the desire that whatever terrible thing was to be done should be done more quickly. Pierre looked around at his comrades and studied them.

The first two men were convicts with shaven heads. One was tall and thin, the other dark, shaggy, and muscular, with a flattened nose. The third was a household serf of about forty-five, with greyish hair and a stout, well-stuffed

---

*Yes, undoubtedly.

body. The fourth was a muzhik, a very handsome one, with a bushy blond beard and dark eyes. The fifth was a factory worker, a thin, yellow-faced lad of about eighteen, in a smock.

Pierre heard the French debate about how to shoot them—by ones or by twos. "By twos," the senior officer said coldly and calmly. There was movement in the ranks of soldiers, and it was noticeable that they were all hurrying, and hurrying not as people hurry to do something everyone understands, but as they hurry in order to finish a necessary but unpleasant and incomprehensible business.

A French official in a sash went up to the right side of the file of criminals and read the sentence in Russian and in French.

Then two pairs of Frenchmen went up to the criminals and, on instructions from the officer, took the two convicts who stood first in line. The convicts, having gone to the post, stopped and, while the sacks were brought, looked silently around them, as a wounded animal looks at the approaching hunter. One kept crossing himself, the other kept scratching his back and made a movement with his lips similar to a smile. The soldiers, their hands hurrying, set about blindfolding them, putting sacks over their heads, and tying them to the post.

Twelve riflemen with muskets left the ranks with measured, firm strides and stopped eight paces from the post. Pierre turned away so as not to see what was going to happen. Suddenly there was a crackle and boom that to Pierre seemed louder than the most terrible peals of thunder, and he turned to look. There was smoke, and the French, with pale faces and trembling hands, were doing something by the pit. Another two were led up. In the same way, with the same eyes, these two also looked at everyone, in vain, with their eyes only, silently, begging for protection, and clearly not understanding and not believing what was going to happen. They could not believe it, because they alone knew what their life was for them, and therefore did not understand or believe that it could be taken from them.

Pierre did not want to look and again turned away; but again it was as if a terrible explosion struck his hearing, and along with these noises he saw smoke, someone's blood, and the pale, frightened faces of the Frenchmen, who again were doing something by the post, pushing each other with trembling hands. Pierre, breathing hard, looked around as if asking, "What does it mean?" The same question was in all the gazes that met Pierre's gaze.

On all the Russian faces, on the faces of the French soldiers and officers, on all without exception, he read the same fear, horror, and struggle that were in his heart. "But who, finally, is doing this? They're all suffering just as I am. Who is it? Who?" flashed for a second in Pierre's soul.

*"Tirailleurs du 86ᵉ, en avant!"** someone shouted. They led away the fifth

*Riflemen of the 86th, forward!

man, who was standing next to Pierre—alone. Pierre did not understand that he was saved, that he and all the rest had been brought there only to be present at the execution. With ever-increasing horror, feeling neither joy nor relief, he watched what was being done. The fifth man was the factory worker in the smock. As soon as they touched him, he jumped away in horror and clutched at Pierre (Pierre shuddered and tore free of him). The factory worker was unable to walk. He was dragged under the arms, and he was shouting something. When he was led to the post, he suddenly fell silent. It was as if he suddenly understood something. Either he understood that it was useless to shout, or that it was impossible that people should kill him, but he stood by the post, waiting to be bound as the others had been, and, like a wounded animal, looked around with glittering eyes.

Pierre could no longer make himself turn away and close his eyes. His own and the whole crowd's curiosity and agitation at this fifth murder had reached the highest pitch. Like the others, this fifth man seemed calm; he wrapped himself into his smock and scratched his leg with his bare foot.

When they set about blindfolding him, he himself straightened the knot at the back of his head, which hurt him; then, when he was put up against the bloody post, he leaned back, and, feeling uncomfortable in that position, straightened up, placed his feet level, and leaned back comfortably. Pierre did not take his eyes off him, not missing the slightest movement.

It must have been that the command was given, it must have been that after the command the shots of eight muskets rang out. But Pierre, much as he tried to recall later, did not hear the slightest sound of the shots. He only saw how the factory worker suddenly slumped down in the ropes for some reason, how blood appeared in two places, and how the ropes became loose under the weight of the sagging body, and the factory worker sat down, lowering his head and tucking his legs under unnaturally. Pierre ran to the post. No one held him back. Frightened, pale people were doing something around the factory worker. The lower jaw of one old, moustached Frenchman was trembling as he untied the ropes. The body sank down. The soldiers carried it clumsily and hastily behind the post and began to push it down into the pit.

They all obviously knew without question that they were criminals, who had to quickly conceal the traces of their crime.

Pierre glanced into the pit and saw the factory worker lying there, his knees up close to his head, one shoulder higher than the other. And that shoulder was rising and falling convulsively and regularly. But shovelfuls of earth were already being strewn over the whole body. One of the soldiers angrily, spitefully, and morbidly shouted at Pierre to get back. But Pierre did not understand him and stood by the post, and nobody drove him away.

When the pit was all filled, a command was heard. Pierre was taken to his place, and the French troops standing in line on both sides of the post made a half turn and started marching past it at a measured pace. The twenty-four riflemen with discharged muskets, who stood in the centre of the circle, ran to take their places as their companies marched past them.

Pierre now looked with senseless eyes at these riflemen who ran out from the circle in pairs. All except one joined their companies. A young soldier with a deathly pale face, his shako pushed back, his musket lowered, went on standing across from the pit in the place from which he had fired. He was reeling like a drunk man, taking a few steps forward, then back, to support his falling body. An old sergeant ran out from the ranks and, seizing the young soldier's arm, pulled him into the company. The crowd of Russians and Frenchmen began to disperse. They all walked silently, with lowered heads.

"*Ça leur apprendra à incendier,*"* someone among the Frenchmen said. Pierre glanced round at the speaker and saw that it was a soldier who wanted to comfort himself at least somehow for what had been done, but could not. Without finishing what he was saying, he waved his arm and walked away.

XII

After the execution, Pierre was separated from the other accused and left alone in a small, devastated and befouled church.

Before evening, a sergeant of the guards came into the church with two soldiers and announced to Pierre that he was pardoned and would now go to the barracks of the prisoners of war. Not understanding what was being said to him, Pierre got up and went with the soldiers. He was brought to some sheds built at the top of the field out of charred boards, beams, and rafters and led into one of them. In the darkness some twenty different people surrounded him. Pierre looked at them, not understanding who these people were, and why, and what they wanted of him. He heard the words said to him, but did not draw any conclusion from them or apply them to anything: he did not understand their meaning. He replied to what he was asked, but did not reflect on who was listening to him and how his replies would be taken. He looked at their faces and figures, but they all seemed equally meaningless to him.

From the moment when Pierre saw this horrible murder performed by people who did not want to do it, it was as if the spring that upheld everything and made it seem alive had been pulled from his soul, and it had all collapsed into a heap of meaningless trash. Though he did not account for it to himself, his faith in the world's good order, in humanity's and his own soul, and in God, was destroyed. Pierre had experienced this state before, but never with such force as now. Before, when doubts of this sort had come over Pierre, those doubts had had their source in his own guilt. And deep in his soul, Pierre had

*That'll teach them to set fires.

felt then that salvation from that despair and those doubts lay in himself. But now he felt that it was not his guilt that caused the world to collapse in front of his eyes and leave only meaningless ruins. He felt that to return to faith in life was not in his power.

People stood around him in the darkness: surely something in him interested them very much. They were telling him something, asking him about something, then they led him somewhere, and he finally found himself in a corner of the shed next to some people who were talking and laughing on all sides.

"And so, brothers . . . that same prince *who* . . ." the voice of someone in the opposite corner of the shed was saying, with special emphasis on the word "who."

Sitting silently and motionlessly by the wall on some straw, Pierre now opened, now closed his eyes. But as soon as he closed his eyes, he saw before him the same frightful face of the factory worker, especially frightening in its simplicity, and the faces of his involuntary murderers, still more frightful in their anxiety. And he would open his eyes again and look senselessly into the darkness around him.

Next to him, bending over, sat some little man whose presence Pierre first noticed by the strong smell of sweat that came from him with his every movement. This man was doing something with his feet in the darkness, and though Pierre could not see his face, he felt that this man was constantly glancing at him. When his eyes got used to the darkness, Pierre realized that this man was taking off his foot cloths. And the way he was doing it aroused Pierre's interest.

Having untied the strips with which one foot was bound, he folded them neatly and at once began on the other foot, glancing up at Pierre. While one hand was hanging up the first strips, the other was already beginning to unwrap the other foot. In this accurate fashion, with rounded, deft movements that followed one another without pause, the man unwrapped his feet, hung the wrappings on pegs above his head, took out a pocket knife, cut something off, folded the knife, put it under his pillow, and, settling himself more comfortably, put his arms round his raised knees, and fixed his eyes directly on Pierre. Pierre felt something pleasant, soothing, and rounded in these deft movements, in this well-arranged domain of his in the corner, even in the smell of this man, and he looked at him without taking his eyes away.

"So you've seen a lot of misery, master? Eh?" the little man suddenly said. And in the man's melodious voice there was such an expression of tenderness and simplicity that Pierre wanted to reply, but his jaw trembled, and he felt tears rising. The little man, in that same second, not giving Pierre time to show his confusion, spoke in the same pleasant voice.

"Ah, don't grieve, little falcon," he said with that tenderly melodious gentleness with which old Russian women speak. "Don't grieve, little friend: you suffer an hour, you live an age! So it is, my dear. And we live here, thank God, with no offence. There's bad people, and there's good," he said and, while speaking, shifted his weight to his knees in a supple movement, got up, and, clearing his throat, went somewhere.

"So she's come, the rascal!" Pierre heard the same gentle voice from the end of the shed. "She's come, the rascal, she remembers! Well, well, enough." And the soldier, pushing away a little dog that was jumping up to him, came back to his place and sat down. In his hands there was something wrapped in a rag.

"Here, have a bite to eat, master," he said, returning again to his respectful tone, and unwrapping and offering Pierre several baked potatoes. "There was soup for dinner. But the potatoes are grand!"

Pierre had not eaten all day, and the smell of the potatoes seemed extraordinarily pleasant to him. He thanked the soldier and began to eat.

"What, just like that?" the soldier said, smiling, and he took one of the potatoes. "Do it this way." He again took out his pocket knife, cut the potato into two equal halves on his palm, sprinkled them with salt from the rag, and offered them to Pierre.

"Grand potatoes," he repeated. "That's the way to eat them."

It seemed to Pierre that he had never eaten anything tastier.

"No, I'm all right," said Pierre, "but why did they shoot those unfortunate men! . . . The last one was about twenty."

"Tsk, tsk . . ." said the little man. "What a sin, what a sin . . ." he added quickly, and, as if his words had always been ready in his mouth and flew out of it inadvertently, he went on: "Why is it, master, that you stayed in Moscow like this?"

"I didn't think they'd come so quickly. I stayed by chance," said Pierre.

"How did they take you, little falcon? From your own house?"

"No, I went to the fire, and there they seized me and tried me for arson."

"Where there's law, there's lies," the little man put in.

"Have you been here long?" asked Pierre, chewing the last potato.

"Me? They took me on Sunday from a hospital in Moscow."

"And what are you, a soldier?"

"Soldiers of the Apsheronsky regiment. I was dying of fever. Nobody told us anything. There were about twenty of our men lying there. We never thought, never imagined."

"And what, is it sad for you here?" asked Pierre.

"How could it not be, little falcon? My name's Platon, last name Karataev," he added, evidently to make it easier for Pierre to address him. "They nicknamed me 'little falcon' in the service. How can you not be sad, little falcon! Moscow, she's the mother of cities. How can you not be sad looking at that. Well, the worm gnaws the cabbage, but dies before he's done: that's what the old folk used to say," he added quickly.

"What, what's that you said?" asked Pierre.

"Me?" asked Karataev. "I said: man proposes, God disposes," he said, thinking he was repeating what he had said. And he went on at once: "So then, master, have you got family estates? And a house? So the cup's overflowing! And a wife? Are your old parents still living?" he asked, and, though Pierre could not see it in the darkness, he sensed that the soldier's lips were puckered in a restrained smile of tenderness as he asked him these things. He was clearly upset that Pierre had no parents, especially no mother.

"A wife for advice, a mother-in-law for welcome, but no one's dearer than your own mother!" he said. "Well, but are there children?" he went on asking. Pierre's negative answer clearly upset him, and he hastened to add: "So what, you're young folk, God grant you'll still have some. Only live in good accord . . ."

"It doesn't matter now," Pierre said involuntarily.

"Ah, you dear man," Platon retorted. "There's no safety from the beggar's sack or the prison's bars." He settled himself more comfortably and cleared his throat, evidently preparing to tell a long story. "And so, my gentle friend, I used to live at home," he began. "Our estate was a prosperous one, there was lots of land, the muzhiks lived well, and so did our household, thank God. My good father went out to mow with the six of us. We lived well. We were real Christian peasants. Then once . . ." And Platon Karataev told a long story of how he went to another man's copse beyond the forest and got caught by the watchman, how they flogged him, tried him, and sent him for a soldier. "What then, little falcon," he said in a voice altered by a smile, "we thought it was grief, but it was joy! If it wasn't for my sin, my brother would have had to go. And my younger brother had four children, while I had only my wife left, you see. There was a daughter, but God took her before I was sent for a soldier. I came home on leave, I'll tell you. I look—they're living better than ever. A yard full of little stomachs, the women are at home, two brothers are off doing hired work. Only the youngest, Mikhailo, is there. My good father says: 'All my children are the same to me,' he says, 'whichever finger you bite, it hurts. But if Platon hadn't been sent, then Mikhailo would have had to go.' He called us all together—would you believe it?—stood us under the icons. 'Mikhailo,' he says, 'come here, bow down to his feet, and you, woman, bow down, and you grandchildren bow down, too. Understand?' he says. That's how things are, my gentle friend. Fate seeks a head. But we keep judging: this isn't good, this isn't right. Our luck is like water in a fishnet: drag it and it swells, pull it out and nothing's there. So it is." And Platon shifted on his straw.

After some silence, Platon got up.

"I suppose you must be sleepy?" he said, and he quickly began crossing himself, saying:

"Lord Jesus Christ, St. Nicholas, Frola and Lavra, Lord Jesus Christ, St. Nicholas, Frola and Lavra, Lord Jesus Christ, have mercy on us and save us!" he concluded, bowed to the ground, stood up, and, sighing, sat on his straw. "So there. Lord, lay me down like a stone, raise me up like a loaf," he said and lay down, pulling his greatcoat over him.

"What was that prayer you recited?" asked Pierre.

"Eh?" said Platon (he was already asleep). "What did I recite? I prayed to God. What, don't you pray?"

"No, I do pray," said Pierre. "But what was it you said: Frola and Lavra?"

"Of course," Platon replied quickly, "it's the horses' feast.[7] Beasts should also be pitied," said Karataev. "Look how she's curled up, the rascal. Got nice and warm, the daughter of a bitch," he said, touching the dog at his feet, and, turning over again, he fell asleep at once.

Outside, weeping and shouting could be heard somewhere in the distance, and fire could be seen through the cracks in the shed, but inside the shed it was quiet and dark. Pierre did not fall asleep for a long time and lay in his place in the dark with open eyes, listening to the regular snoring of Platon, who lay beside him, and he felt that the previously destroyed world was now arising in his soul with a new beauty, on some new and unshakeable foundations.

XIII

In the shed that Pierre entered and in which he stayed for four weeks, twenty-three soldiers, three officers, and two officials were held prisoner.

Later Pierre pictured them all as in a fog, but Platon Karataev remained for ever in Pierre's soul as the strongest and dearest memory and the embodiment of everything Russian, kindly and round. When at dawn the next day Pierre saw his neighbour, his first impression of something round was fully confirmed: the whole figure of Platon in his French greatcoat tied with a rope, in a peaked cap and bast shoes, was round, his head was perfectly round, his back, chest, shoulders, even his arms, which he held as if always about to embrace something, were round; his pleasant smile and his large, brown, tender eyes were round.

Platon Karataev must have been over fifty, judging by his stories of the campaigns he had taken part in long ago as a soldier. He himself did not know and had no way of determining how old he was; but his teeth, bright white and strong, which kept popping out in two semicircles when he laughed (which he often did), were all sound and intact; there was not a single grey hair in his beard or on his head, and his whole body had an air of suppleness and especially of firmness and hardiness.

His face, despite its small, round wrinkles, had an expression of innocence and youth; his voice was pleasant and melodious. But the main peculiarity of his speech consisted in its immediacy and promptness. He evidently never thought of what he had said or would say; and owing to that, there was in the quickness and certainty of his intonation a special, irresistible persuasiveness.

His physical strength and agility in the first period of captivity were such that it seemed he did not understand what fatigue and illness were. Every evening he said as he lay down: "Lord, lay me down like a stone, raise me up like a loaf"; in the morning, getting up, he always said, shaking his shoulders in the same way: "Lay down in a curl, got up in a whirl." And indeed he had only to lie down in order to fall asleep at once like a stone, and he had only to shake himself in order to set about doing something at once, without a second's delay, the way children, on getting up, take their toys. He knew how to do everything, not very well, but not badly either. He baked, cooked, sewed, planed, cobbled boots. He was always busy and only at night allowed himself to talk, which he liked to do, and to sing. He sang songs not as singers do who know they are being listened to, but as birds do, apparently because it was necessary for him to utter those sounds, as it is necessary to stretch one's arms or legs; and those sounds were always high, tender, almost feminine, mournful, and his face would be very serious as he sang them.

Having been taken prisoner and grown a beard, he had evidently thrown off everything assumed, alien, soldierly, and involuntarily returned to his former peasant, folkish ways.

"A soldier on leave is an untucked shirt," he used to say. He talked reluctantly about his time as a soldier, though he did not complain and often repeated that during all his time in the service he had never been beaten once. When he told stories, they were mostly stories from his old, and apparently dear, memories of "Christian," as he pronounced *krestyan,* life.[8] The proverbs that filled his speech were not those mostly indecent and bold proverbs that soldiers use, but those folk sayings which sound so insignificant taken separately, and which suddenly acquire a profoundly wise significance when spoken aptly.

He often said something completely opposite to what he had said before, but both the one and the other were right. He liked to speak, and spoke well, adorning his speech with endearments and sayings which, it seemed to Pierre, he made up himself; but the main charm of his stories was that, in what he said, the simplest events, sometimes the same that Pierre had seen without noticing them, acquired a character of solemn seemliness. He liked listening to folktales, which one soldier used to tell in the evenings (always the same ones), but most of all he liked listening to stories from real life. He smiled joyfully, listening to such stories, putting a word in and asking questions, tending towards clarifying for himself the seemliness of what he was being told. Karataev had no attachments, friendships, or love, as Pierre understood them; but he loved and lived lovingly with everything that life brought his way, especially other people—not any specific people, but those who were there before his eyes. He loved his mutt, his comrades, the French, he loved Pierre, who was his neighbour; but Pierre sensed that, despite all his gentle tenderness towards him (by which he involuntarily gave Pierre's spiritual life its due), Karataev would not have been upset for a moment to be parted from him. And Pierre was beginning to experience the same feeling towards Karataev.

Platon Karataev was for all the other prisoners the most ordinary of soldiers; they called him "little falcon" or Platosha, teased him good-naturedly, sent him on errands. But for Pierre he remained for ever as he had seen him the first night, the unfathomable, round, and eternal embodiment of the spirit of simplicity and truth.

Platon Karataev knew nothing by heart except his prayer. When he began to talk, it seemed he did not know how he was going to finish.

When Pierre, sometimes struck by the meaning of what he said, asked him to repeat it, Platon could not remember what he had said the moment before— just as he could not tell Pierre the words of his favourite song. There was in it "my dear one," "little birch tree," and "I'm sick at heart," but the words did not make any sense. He did not and could not understand the meaning of words taken separately from speech. Each of his words and each of his acts was the manifestation of an activity he knew nothing about, which was his life. But his life, as he looked at it, had no meaning as a separate life. It had meaning only as a part of the whole, which he constantly sensed. His words and acts poured out of him as evenly, necessarily, and immediately as fragrance comes from a flower. He was unable to understand either the value or the meaning of a word or act taken separately.

XIV

On receiving from Nikolai the news that her brother was with the Rostovs in Yaroslavl, Princess Marya, despite her aunt's dissuasions, at once made ready to go, and not just by herself, but with her nephew. Whether it was difficult or not difficult, possible or impossible, she did not ask and did not want to know: her duty was not only to be at the side of her, perhaps, dying brother, but to do everything possible so as to bring his son to him, and therefore she made ready to go. If Prince Andrei had not informed her himself, Princess Marya explained it by his being too weak to write or considering the long trip too difficult and dangerous for her and his son.

In a few days, Princess Marya was ready for the road. Her carriages consisted of the enormous princely coach, in which she had come to Voronezh, a britzka, and a cart. With her went Mlle Bourienne, Nikolushka and his tutor, the old nanny, three maids, Tikhon, a young servant, and a footman whom her aunt sent with her.

To go by the usual road to Moscow was unthinkable, and Princess Marya therefore had to take a roundabout way through Lipetsk, Ryazan, Vladimir, and Shuya, which was very long, and, post-horses being unavailable everywhere, very hard, and, near Ryazan, where (they said) the French had appeared, even dangerous.

During this difficult journey, Mlle Bourienne, Dessales, and Princess Marya's servants were astonished by her firmness of spirit and energy. She was the last to go to bed, the first to get up, and no difficulties could stop her. Thanks to her activity and energy, which aroused her companions, by the end of the second week they were approaching Yaroslavl.

In the latter part of her stay in Voronezh, Princess Marya had experienced the best happiness of her life. Her love for Rostov no longer worried or upset her. That love filled all her soul, became an inalienable part of her, and she no longer fought against it. Most recently, Princess Marya had become convinced—though she never said it definitely to herself in clear terms—that she loved and was loved. She had become convinced of it during her last meeting with Nikolai, when he came to her to announce that her brother was with the Rostovs. Nikolai had never hinted by so much as a word that now (in case of Prince Andrei's recovery) the former relations between him and Natasha might be renewed, but Princess Marya had seen by his face that he knew and thought it. And, in spite of that, his attitude towards her—careful, tender, and loving—not only had not changed, but he seemed to be glad that this family relation between him and Princess Marya now allowed him to express more freely his loving friendship for her, as Princess Marya sometimes thought of it. Princess Marya knew that she was in love for the first and last time of her life, and felt that she was loved, and was happy and calm in that respect.

But this happiness of one side of her soul not only did not prevent her from feeling the full force of her grief over her brother, but, on the contrary, this inner calm in one respect gave her a greater opportunity to give herself fully to her feeling for her brother. That feeling was so strong in the first moments of the departure from Voronezh that those who saw her off were convinced, looking at her careworn, desperate face, that she would certainly fall ill on the road; but it was precisely the difficulties and cares of the journey, which Princess Marya took in hand so energetically, that saved her for a time from grief and gave her strength.

As always happens during a journey, Princess Marya thought only about the journey itself, forgetting its goal. But as they approached Yaroslavl, when there again emerged what she might face, and not after many days, but that same evening, Princess Marya's agitation reached the utmost limits.

When the footman who had been sent ahead to find out where the Rostovs were staying in Yaroslavl, and what condition Prince Andrei was in, met the big coach entering town, he was horrified to see the princess's terribly pale face thrust out at him through the window.

"I've found out everything, Your Excellency. The Rostovs are staying on the square, in the house of the merchant Bronnikov. It's not far, just on the bank of the Volga," said the footman.

Princess Marya looked fearfully and questioningly into his face, not understanding why he did not answer the main question: how was her brother? Mlle Bourienne put this question instead of the princess.

"How is the prince?" she asked.

"His excellency is staying in the same house with them."

"That means he's alive," thought the princess, and she asked softly how he was.

"The people said he's still in the same condition."

What "still in the same condition" meant, the princess did not ask, but with only a fleeting, imperceptible glance at the seven-year-old Nikolushka, who sat facing her and was happy to see the city, she lowered her head and did not raise it until the heavy coach, rumbling, shaking, and heaving, stopped somewhere. The footboards banged as they were thrown down.

The doors were opened. To the left there was water—a big river; to the right was a porch; on the porch there were people, servants, and a red-cheeked girl with a big black braid, who smiled unpleasantly and falsely, as it seemed to Princess Marya (this was Sonya). The princess ran up the steps, the girl with the false smile said, "This way, this way!" and the princess found herself in a front room before an old woman with an Oriental type of face, who, with a moved expression, was quickly coming to meet her. It was the countess. She embraced Princess Marya and started kissing her.

"*Mon enfant!*" she said. "*Je vous aime et je vous connais depuis longtemps.*"*

Despite all her agitation, Princess Marya realized that this was the countess and that she had to say something to her. Not knowing why herself, she uttered some polite French words in the same tone in which she had been spoken to, and asked, "How is he?"

"The doctor says there's no danger," said the countess, but as she said it, she lifted up her eyes with a sigh, and the expression of this gesture contradicted her words.

"Where is he? May I see him? May I?" asked the princess.

"At once, Princess, at once, my dear friend. Is this his son?" she said, turning to Nikolushka, who was coming in with Dessales. "There's room for us all, the house is big. Oh, what a lovely boy!"

The countess led the princess into the drawing room. Sonya was talking with Mlle Bourienne. The countess caressed the boy. The old count came into the room and greeted the princess. The old count had changed greatly since

---

*My child! . . . I love you and have known you for a long time.

the princess had last seen him. Then he had been a sprightly, cheerful, self-confident old man; now he seemed a pitiful, lost person. Talking with the princess, he constantly looked around, as if asking everyone if he was doing the right thing. After the devastation of Moscow and his property, thrown out of his usual rut, he had clearly lost the awareness of his significance and felt that he no longer had any place in life.

Despite all her agitation, despite her one desire to see her brother as soon as possible and her vexation that, at that moment, when all she wanted was to see him, they distracted her and pretended to praise her nephew, the princess noticed everything that was going on around her and felt the need to submit for a time to this new order she was entering. She knew that all this was necessary, and though it was hard for her, she was not vexed with them.

"This is my niece," said the count, introducing Sonya, "have you met her, Princess?"

The princess turned to her and, trying to stifle the animosity for this girl that arose in her heart, kissed her. But she was beginning to be pained, because the mood of everyone around her was so far from all that was in her soul.

"Where is he?" she asked once more, addressing them all.

"He's downstairs, Natasha's with him," Sonya replied, blushing. "I've sent to enquire. You must be tired, Princess?"

Tears of vexation came to the princess's eyes. She turned away and was again about to ask the countess how to go to him, when light, impetuous, as if merry footsteps were heard at the door. The princess looked and saw Natasha almost running in, that Natasha whom she had so disliked when they had met in Moscow long ago.

But the princess had barely glanced at the face of this Natasha when she understood that this was a sincere companion in grief, and therefore her friend. She rushed to meet her and, embracing her, burst into tears on her shoulder.

As soon as Natasha, who had been sitting by Prince Andrei's head, learned of Princess Marya's arrival, she quietly left the room on those quick steps— merry, as it had seemed to Princess Marya—and ran to her.

On her anxious face, when she ran into the room, there was only one expression—an expression of love, of boundless love for him, for her, for everything that was close to the man she loved, an expression of pity, of suffering for others, and a passionate desire to give all of herself to help them. It was clear that at that moment there was not a single thought of herself or her relations to him in Natasha's soul.

The sensitive Princess Marya understood all that from her first glance at Natasha's face, and with grieving pleasure she wept on her shoulder.

"Come, come to him, Marie," said Natasha, leading her to the other room.

Princess Marya raised her face, wiped her tears, and turned to Natasha. She felt that from her she would understand and learn everything.

"How is . . ." she began the question, but suddenly stopped. She felt that it was impossible either to ask or to answer in words. Natasha's face and eyes would tell her more clearly and profoundly.

Natasha looked at her, but seemed to be afraid and doubtful whether to tell all she knew; it was as if she felt before those luminous eyes, which penetrated to the very bottom of her heart, that it was impossible not to tell the whole truth as she saw it. Natasha's lip suddenly trembled, ugly wrinkles formed round her mouth, and, bursting into sobs, she covered her face with her hands.

Princess Marya understood everything.

But even so she hoped and asked in words she did not believe in:

"But how is his wound? What condition is he in generally?"

"You . . . you'll see," was all Natasha could say.

They sat for a while downstairs, near his room, in order to stop crying and go in with calm faces.

"How has the whole illness gone? Has he been worse for long? When did *this* happen?" asked Princess Marya.

Natasha told her that at first there had been danger from his high fever and suffering, but in the Trinity monastery that had gone away, and the doctor had been afraid of only one thing—gangrene. But that danger, too, had passed. When they arrived in Yaroslavl, the wound had begun to fester (Natasha knew everything to do with festering and so on), and the doctor had said that the festering might take the right course. There was fever. The doctor had said that this fever was not dangerous.

"But two days ago," Natasha began, "*this* suddenly happened . . ." She suppressed her sobs. "I don't know, but you'll see how he's become."

"He's grown weaker? thinner? . . ." asked the princess.

"No, not that, but worse. You'll see. Ah, Marie, Marie, he's too good, he can't, he can't live, because . . ."

XV

When Natasha opened his door with a habitual movement, letting the princess go ahead of her, Princess Marya felt her sobs ready in her throat. Much as she had prepared herself, had tried to calm down, she knew she would not be able to see him without tears.

Princess Marya understood what Natasha had meant by the words "this happened to him two days ago." She understood that it meant he had suddenly softened, and that this softening and tender feeling were signs of death. As she was going to the door, she already saw in her imagination the face of the Andryusha she had known in childhood, gentle, mild, tender, which he showed so rarely and which therefore always affected her so strongly. She knew that he would speak quiet, gentle words to her, like those her father had spoken to her before his death, and she would be unable to bear it and would burst into sobs over him. But sooner or later it had to be, and so she went into the room. The sobs rose higher and higher in her throat as her near-sighted eyes made out his form more and more clearly and sought his features, and then she saw his face and met his gaze.

He was lying on a sofa, surrounded by pillows, in a squirrel-fur dressing gown. He was thin and pale. One thin, transparently white hand was holding a handkerchief, the other, with a quiet movement of the fingers, was touching his thin, newly grown moustache. His eyes were looking at the entering women.

Seeing his face and meeting his gaze, Princess Marya suddenly slowed her steps and felt that her tears had suddenly dried up and her sobs had ceased. Catching the expression of his face and gaze, she suddenly grew timid and felt guilty.

"But what am I guilty of?" she asked herself. "Of being alive and thinking about the living, while I . . ." his cold, stern gaze replied.

There was almost hostility in that deep gaze, looking not out of but into himself, as he slowly examined his sister and Natasha.

They took each other's hands and kissed each other, as was their habit.

"Hello, Marie, how is it that you got here?" he said in a voice as flat and alien as was his gaze. If he had shrieked in a desperate voice, that shriek would have terrified Princess Marya less than the sound of that voice.

"And you've brought Nikolushka?" he said just as flatly and slowly, and with an obvious effort of recollection.

"How is your health now?" asked Princess Marya, marvelling at herself as she said it.

"That, my friend, you must ask the doctor," he said, and, clearly making another effort to be gentle, he said with his lips only (it was clear that he did not at all think what he was saying): *"Merci, chère amie, d'être venue."**

Princess Marya pressed his hand. He winced barely noticeably from the pressure of her hand. He was silent, and she did not know what to say. She understood what had happened to him in those two days. In his words, in his tone, especially in that gaze—a cold, almost hostile gaze—there could be felt an alienation from everything of this world that was frightening in a living man. He clearly had difficulty now in understanding anything living; but at the same time it could be felt that he did not understand the living, not because he lacked the power of understanding, but because he understood something else, such as the living could not understand, and which absorbed him entirely.

---

*Thank you, dear friend, for coming.

"Yes, see how strangely fate has brought us together!" he said, breaking his silence and pointing to Natasha. "She's taking care of me."

Princess Marya listened and did not understand what he was saying. How could he, the sensitive, gentle Prince Andrei, say that in the presence of the one he loved and who loved him! If he had thought he would live, he would not have said it in such a coldly offensive tone. If he had not known he would die, how could he not have pitied her, how could he have said it in front of her! The only explanation could be that it made no difference to him, and it made no difference because something else, more important, had been revealed to him.

The conversation was cold, incoherent, and constantly interrupted.

"Marie came through Ryazan," said Natasha. Prince Andrei did not notice that she had called his sister "Marie." And Natasha, calling her that in his presence, noticed it herself for the first time.

"Well, and what about it?" he said.

"They told her that Moscow is all burned down, completely, that supposedly . . ."

Natasha stopped: it was impossible to speak. He was obviously making an effort to listen, and still could not.

"Yes, they say it's burned down," he said. "That's a great pity," and he began to look straight ahead, absent-mindedly stroking his moustache with his fingers.

"And you've met Count Nikolai, Marie?" Prince Andrei said suddenly, clearly wishing to please them. "He wrote here that he found you very much to his liking," he went on simply, calmly, clearly unable to understand all the complex significance his words had for living people. "If you should also like him, it would be very good . . . if you got married," he added somewhat more quickly, as if glad of the words he had long been searching for and had finally found. Princess Marya heard his words, but they had no other meaning for her than to prove how terribly far he now was from everything living.

"Why talk of me!" she said calmly, and glanced at Natasha. Natasha, feeling her gaze upon her, did not look at her. Again they all fell silent.

"André, would you li . . ." Princess Marya suddenly said in a shuddering voice, "would you like to see Nikolushka? He talks about you all the time."

Prince Andrei smiled barely perceptibly for the first time, but Princess Marya, who knew his face so well, understood with horror that this was a smile not of joy, not of tenderness for his son, but of quiet, mild mockery of Princess Marya, who, in his opinion, was using her last means of bringing him to his senses.

"Yes, I'm very glad Nikolushka is here. Is he well?"

. . .

When Nikolushka was brought to Prince Andrei, he looked at his father with fear, but did not cry, because no one was crying. Prince Andrei kissed him and obviously did not know what to say to him.

When Nikolushka was taken away, Princess Marya went up to her brother once more, kissed him, and, unable to control herself any longer, began to cry.

He looked at her intently.

"Is it about Nikolushka?" he asked.

Princess Marya, crying, nodded affirmatively.

"Marie, do you know the Gosp . . ." but he suddenly fell silent.

"What did you say?"

"Nothing. You mustn't cry here," he said, looking at her with the same cold gaze.

When Princess Marya began to cry, he understood that she was crying because Nikolushka would be left without a father. Making a great effort with himself, he attempted to come back into life and shift to their point of view.

"Yes, this must seem pitiful to them!" he thought. "Yet it's so simple!

" 'The birds of the air neither sow nor reap, but your Father feeds them,' "[9] he said to himself and wanted to say it to the princess. "But no, they'll understand it their own way, they won't understand! This they cannot understand, that all these feelings they value, all these thoughts of ours, which seem so important to us—that they're *unnecessary*. We cannot understand each other!" And he kept silent.

Prince Andrei's little son was seven years old. He could barely read, he knew nothing. He lived through many things after that day, acquiring knowledge, power of observation, experience; but if he had then possessed all these abilities he acquired later, he would not have been able to understand the full meaning of the scene he saw take place between his father, Princess Marya, and Natasha any better, any more profoundly, than he understood it now. He understood everything and, without crying, left the room, silently went up to Natasha, who came out after him, glanced at her bashfully with his thoughtful, beautiful eyes; his slightly raised, red upper lip quivered, he leaned his head against Natasha and began to cry.

From that day on he avoided Dessales, avoided the countess, who caressed him, and either sat by himself or timidly approached Princess Marya and Natasha, whom he seemed to have come to love more than his aunt, and quietly and bashfully caressed them.

Princess Marya, having left Prince Andrei, fully understood all that Natasha's face had said to her. She did not talk any more with Natasha about the hope of saving his life. She took turns with her by his sofa and did not cry any more, but prayed constantly, in her soul addressing the eternal, the unfathomable, whose presence over the dying man was now so palpable.

XVI

Prince Andrei not only knew that he would die, but felt that he was dying, that he was already half dead. He experienced an awareness of estrangement from everything earthly and a joyful and strange lightness of being. Without haste or worry, he waited for what lay ahead of him. The dread, the eternal, the unknown and far off, of which he had never ceased to feel the presence throughout his life, was now close to him and—by that strange lightness of being he experienced— almost comprehensible and palpable.

. . . .

Formerly he had been afraid of the end. Twice he had experienced that fright- ful, tormenting feeling of the fear of death, the end, and now he no longer understood it.

The first time he had experienced that feeling was when the shell was spin- ning before him like a top, and he looked at the harvested field, at the bushes, at the sky, and knew that death was before him. When he regained conscious- ness after being wounded, and in his soul, instantly, as if freed of the restrain- ing weight of life, that flower of love opened, eternal, free, not bound to this life, he was no longer afraid of death and did not think of it.

In those hours of suffering solitude and half delirium that he spent after being wounded, the more he pondered the new principle of eternal love revealed to him, the more, though without feeling it himself, he renounced earthly life. To love everything, everybody, always to sacrifice oneself for love, meant to love no one, meant not to live this earthly life. And the more imbued he was with this principle of love, the more he renounced life and the more completely he destroyed that dreadful barrier which, without love, stands between life and death. When, in that first time, he remembered that he had to die, he said to himself: "Well, so much the better."

But after that night in Mytishchi, when in his half delirium she whom he wished for appeared before him, and when, pressing her hand to his lips, he wept quiet, joyful tears, love for one woman crept imperceptibly into his heart and again bound him to life. Joyful and worried thoughts started com- ing to him. Remembering that moment at the dressing station when he had seen Kuragin, he now could not return to that feeling: he was tormented by the question of whether the man was still alive. And he did not dare ask it.

. . .

His illness was following its physical course, but what Natasha called "this happened to him" occurred two days before Princess Marya's arrival. It was the last moral struggle between life and death, in which death gained the victory. It was the unexpected awareness that he still valued life, as it presented itself to him in his love for Natasha, and a last, finally surmounted, attack of terror before the unknown.

It was in the evening. As usual after dinner, he was in a slightly feverish state, and his thoughts were extremely clear. Sonya was sitting at the table. He dozed off. Suddenly a sense of happiness came over him.

"Ah, it's that she's come!" he thought.

Indeed, Natasha, who had just come in with inaudible steps, was sitting in Sonya's place.

Since she had begun to take care of him, he had always experienced this physical sense of her nearness. She was sitting in an armchair, turned sideways to him, shielding the light of the candle from him, and knitting a stocking. (She had learned to knit stockings since Prince Andrei told her that no one could take such good care of the sick as old nannies who knit stockings, and that there was something soothing about the knitting of stockings.) Her slender fingers moved quickly, occasionally clicking the needles, and he could see clearly the thoughtful profile of her lowered face. She made a movement—the ball of yarn rolled off her lap. She gave a start, glanced round at him, and, shielding the candle with her hand, bent down in a cautious, supple, and precise movement, picked up the ball, and sat in her former position.

He looked at her without stirring, and saw that, after her movement, she needed to take a deep breath, but did not dare to do it, and caught her breath cautiously.

In the Trinity monastery they had talked about the past, and he had told her that, if he should live, he would eternally thank God for his wound, which had brought them together again; but since then they had never talked about the future.

"Could it be, or not?" he thought now, looking at her and listening to the slight noise of the steel needles. "Can it be that fate brought us together so strangely only so that I should die? . . . Can it be that the truth of life was revealed to me only so that I should live in a lie? I love her more than anything in the world. But what am I to do if I love her?" he said and suddenly moaned involuntarily, by a habit acquired during his sufferings.

Hearing this sound, Natasha put down the stocking, leaned in his direction, and suddenly, noticing his shining eyes, went over to him on light steps and bent down.

"You're not asleep?"

"No, I've been looking at you for a long time; I felt it when you came in. No one but you gives me that soft silence . . . that light. I want to weep for joy."

Natasha moved closer to him. Her face beamed with rapturous joy.

"Natasha, I love you too much. More than anything in the world."

"And I?" She turned away for a moment. "Why too much?" she asked.

"Why too much? . . . Well, what do you think, what do you feel in your soul, in your whole soul—will I live? How does it seem to you?"

"I'm sure of it, sure of it!" Natasha almost cried out, taking both his hands in a passionate movement.

He was silent for a moment.

"How good it would be!" And, taking her hand, he kissed it.

Natasha was happy and excited; and she remembered at once that this was forbidden, that he needed to be quiet.

"You didn't sleep, though," she said, suppressing her joy. "Try to fall asleep . . . please."

He let go of her hand after pressing it, and she went over to the candle and sat down again in the same position. Twice she turned to glance at him, and his eyes shone meeting hers. She set to work on the stocking and said to herself that she would not look at him until it was finished.

Indeed, soon after that he closed his eyes and fell asleep. He slept for a short time and suddenly woke up anxiously, in a cold sweat.

Falling asleep, he was thinking about the same thing he had been thinking about all that time—about life and death. And more about death. He felt himself closer to it.

"Love? What is love?" he thought. "Love hinders death. Love is life. Everything, everything I understand, I understand only because I love. Everything is, everything exists, only because I love. Everything is connected only by that. Love is God, and to die—means that I, a part of love, return to the common and eternal source." These thoughts seemed comforting to him. But they were only thoughts. Something was lacking in them, there was something one-sidedly personal, cerebral—there was no evidence. And there was the same uneasiness and vagueness. He fell asleep.

In a dream he saw himself lying in the same room in which he lay in reality, but he was not wounded, but healthy. Many sorts of persons, insignificant, indifferent, appear before Prince Andrei. He talks with them, argues about something unnecessary. They are preparing to go somewhere. Prince Andrei vaguely recalls that it is all insignificant and that he has other, more important concerns, but he goes on, to their surprise, speaking some sort of empty, witty words. Gradually, imperceptibly, all these people begin to disappear, and everything is replaced by the one question of the closed door. He gets up and goes to the door to slide the bolt and lock it. *Everything* depends on whether he does or does not manage to lock it. He walks, he hurries, his feet do not move, and he knows that he will not manage to lock the door, but still he painfully strains all his force. And a tormenting fear seizes him. And this fear is the fear of death: *it* is standing behind the door. But as he is crawling strength-lessly and awkwardly towards the door, this terrible something is already push-ing against it from the other side, forcing it. Something inhuman—death—is forcing the door, and he has to hold it shut. He lays hold of the door, strains in a last effort—to lock it is already impossible—just to hold it shut; but his attempts are weak, clumsy, and, pushed by the terrible thing, the door keeps opening and shutting again.

Once more it pushes from the other side. His last supernatural efforts are in vain, and the two halves open noiselessly. *It* comes in, and it is *death*. And Prince Andrei died.

But in the same instant that he died, Prince Andrei remembered that he was asleep, and in the same instant that he died, he made an effort with himself and woke up.

"Yes, that was death. I died—I woke up. Yes, death is an awakening." Clar-ity suddenly came to his soul, and the curtain that until then had concealed the unknown was raised before his inner gaze. He felt the release of a force that previously had been as if bound in him and that strange lightness which from then on did not leave him.

When, having come to in a cold sweat, he stirred on his sofa, Natasha went over to him and asked what was the matter. He did not answer, and, not under-standing her, gave her a strange look.

That was what had happened to him two days before Princess Marya's arrival. Since that day, the doctor said, the wasting fever had taken a turn for the worse, but Natasha was not interested in what the doctor said: she saw those dreadful moral signs, which were more unquestionable for her.

Since that day, there began for Prince Andrei, along with his awakening from sleep, an awakening from life. And it seemed no slower to him, in relation to the length of life, than an awakening from sleep in relation to the length of a dream.

There was nothing frightening and abrupt in this relatively slow awakening.

His last days and hours passed ordinarily and simply. Both Princess Marya and Natasha, who never left his side, felt it. They did not weep, did not shud-der, and during the last time they themselves felt that they were no longer tak-ing care of him (he was no longer there, he had left them), but of the nearest reminder of him—his body. The feelings of both were so strong that they were not affected by the external, dreadful side of death, and they found no need to exacerbate their grief. They did not weep either with him or without him, but also never spoke of him between themselves. They felt that they could not express what they understood in words.

They both saw how he sank deeper and deeper, slowly and peacefully, somewhere away from them, and they both knew that it had to be so and that it was good.

He confessed, took communion; everyone came to him for a last farewell. When his son was brought to him, he touched him with his lips and turned away, not because he felt grief or pity (Princess Marya and Natasha understood that), but only because he supposed that this was all that was expected of him; but when he was told to bless him, he did as they requested, and looked around as if asking if anything else needed to be done.

When the last shudderings of the body being left by the spirit occurred, Princess Marya and Natasha were there.

"Is it over?!" said Princess Marya, after his body had already lain motionless before them for several minutes, growing cold. Natasha went up, looked into the dead eyes, and hastened to close them. She closed them and did not kiss them, but pressed her lips to that which was her nearest reminder of him.

"Where has he gone? Where is he now? . . ."

When the clothed, washed body lay in the coffin on the table, they all went up to it for a last farewell and they all wept.

Nikolushka wept from a suffering bewilderment that rent his heart. The countess and Sonya wept from pity for poor Natasha and because he was no more. The old count wept because he felt that soon he, too, would have to take that dreadful step.

Natasha and Princess Marya also wept now, but they did not weep from their own personal grief; they wept from a reverent emotion that came over their souls before the awareness of the simple and solemn mystery of death that had been accomplished before them.

Part Two

I

The totality of causes of phenomena is inaccessible to the human mind. But the need to seek causes has been put into the soul of man. And the human mind, without grasping in their countlessness and complexity the conditions of phenomena, of which each separately may appear as a cause, takes hold of the first, most comprehensible approximation and says: here is the cause. In historical events (where the subject of observation is the actions of people), the most primordial approximation appears as the will of the gods, then as the will of those people who stand in the most conspicuous historical place—the historical heroes. But we need only enquire into the essence of any historical event, that is, into the activity of the entire mass of people who took part in the event, to become convinced that the will of the historical hero not only does not guide the actions of the masses, but is itself constantly guided. It would seem to make no difference whether we understand the meaning of historical events this way or that. But between a man who says that the people of the west went to the east because Napoleon wanted it, and the man who says that it happened because it had to happen, there is the same difference as between the people who maintained that the earth stood still and the planets moved around it and those who said that they did not know what upheld the earth, but knew that there were laws governing its movement and that of the other planets. There are not and cannot be any causes of a historical event, except for the one cause of all causes. But there are laws that govern events, which are partly unknown, partly groped for by us. The discovery of these laws is possible only when we wholly give up looking for causes in the will of one man, just as discovering the laws of planetary movement became possible only when people gave up the notion that the earth stands still.

After the battle of Borodino, the occupation of Moscow by the enemy and its burning, historians recognize as the most important episode of the war of 1812 the movement of the Russian army from the Ryazan to the Kaluga road and towards the Tarutino camp—the so-called flanking march beyond Krasnaya Pakhra.[1] Historians ascribe the glory of this feat of genius to various persons and argue over whom it essentially belongs to. Even foreign, even French historians acknowledge the genius of the Russian generals, when they speak of this flanking march. But why military writers, and everyone else after them, suppose this *flanking* march, which saved Russia and destroyed Napoleon, to be the most profound invention of some one person—is very hard to understand. First of all, it is hard to understand what the profundity and genius of this movement consisted in; for it takes no great mental effort to figure out that the best position for an army (when it is not under attack) is where there are most provisions. And anyone, even a stupid thirteen-year-old boy, would have no difficulty figuring out that the most advantageous position for the army in 1812, after the retreat from Moscow, was on the Kaluga road. And so it is impossible to understand, first, by what reasonings historians come to see anything profound in this manoeuvre. Second, it is still harder to understand precisely why historians see this manoeuvre as salutary for the Russians and destructive for the French; for this flanking march, under other preceding, accompanying, or following circumstances, could have been destructive for the Russian troops and salutary for the French. If, from the time this movement was accomplished, the position of the Russian army began to improve, it by no means follows that this movement was the cause of it.

This flanking march might not only have failed to produce any advantages, but might have destroyed the Russian army, had it not been accompanied by a coincidence of other conditions. What would have happened if Moscow had not burned down? If Murat had not lost sight of the Russians? If Napoleon had not remained inactive? If at Krasnaya Pakhra the Russian army, on the advice of Bennigsen and Barclay, had offered battle? What would have happened if the French had attacked the Russians as they moved beyond the Pakhra? What would have happened if Napoleon, later, coming to Tarutino, had attacked the Russians with at least one tenth of the energy with which he had attacked at Smolensk? What would have happened if the French had marched on Petersburg? . . . With all these suppositions, the salutariness of the flanking march might have turned to destruction.

The third and most incomprehensible thing consists in the fact that the people who study history deliberately refuse to see that the flanking march cannot possibly be ascribed to any one man, that no one ever foresaw it, that at that time this manoeuvre, just like the retreat from Fili, was never pictured by anyone in its entirety, but proceeded step by step, event by event, moment by moment, from a countless number of the most diverse conditions, and only presented itself in its entirety when it had been accomplished and become past.

At the council in Fili, the predominant thought of the Russian command was that a retreat straight back, that is, down the Nizhni Novgorod road, went without saying. The proofs of it are the fact that the majority of voices at the council voted in that sense, and, above all, the well-known conversation after the council between the commander in chief and Lanskoy, who was in charge of provisions. Lanskoy reported to the commander in chief that provender for the army was collected mainly along the Oka, in Tula and Kaluga provinces, and that in case of a retreat towards Nizhni, the supplies of provisions would be separated from the army by the large river Oka, transport across which was usually impossible at the beginning of winter. This was the first sign of the need to deviate from heading straight for Nizhni, the direction which had previously seemed most natural. The army kept more to the south, down the Ryazan road, and closer to the supplies. Later on, the inactivity of the French, who had even lost sight of the Russian army, the concern with defending the Tula factory,[2] and, above all, the advantages of being closer to the supplies, made the army deviate still further to the south, to the Tula road. In moving to the Tula road, in a desperate push beyond the Pakhra, the commanders of the Russian army had in mind staying near Podolsk, and there was no thought of the Tarutino position; but a countless number of circumstances, and the reappearance of French troops, who had previously lost sight of the Russians, and the plans for battle, and, above all, the abundance of provisions in Kaluga, made our army deviate still more to the south, and move to the middle of its supply lines, from the Tula to the Kaluga road, to Tarutino. Just as it is impossible to answer the question of when Moscow was abandoned, so it is impossible to answer precisely when and by whom it was decided to move to Tarutino. Only when the troops had already reached Tarutino, owing to countless differential forces, only then did people begin to assure themselves that they had wanted it and had long foreseen it.

II

The famous flanking march consisted only in that the Russian army, retreating straight back in the opposite direction of its advance, once the advance of the French stopped, deviated from the straight direction it had first followed and, not seeing anyone pursuing it, naturally tended towards the side it was drawn to by the abundance of provisions.

If we picture to ourselves, not commanders of genius at the head of the Russian army, but simply the army alone without any leaders, that army could not have done anything other than make a reverse movement towards Moscow, describing an arc on the side where there were more provisions and the land was more abundant.

This movement from the Nizhni Novgorod to the Ryazan, Tula, and Kaluga roads was so natural that the looters of the Russian army ran back in that same direction, and it was in that same direction that demands came from Petersburg for Kutuzov to move his army. In Tarutino, Kutuzov was almost reprimanded by the sovereign for leading the army to the Ryazan road, and that very position opposite Kaluga was pointed out to him which he was already in when he received the sovereign's letter.

Rolling back in the direction of the push given it during the whole campaign and at the battle of Borodino, the ball of the Russian army, with the exhaustion of the force of the push, and not receiving any new pushes, assumed the position that was natural for it.

Kutuzov's merit consisted not in some strategic manoeuvre of genius, as they call it, but in that he alone understood the significance of what was happening. He alone already understood then the significance of the French army's inactivity, he alone went on insisting that the battle of Borodino had been a victory; he alone—who, it would seem, in his position as commander in chief, should have been disposed to attack—he alone used all his powers to keep the Russian army from useless battles.

The beast wounded at Borodino lay there where the fleeing hunter had left it; but whether it was alive, whether it was strong or only lying low, the hunter did not know. Suddenly the groaning of that beast was heard.

The groaning of that wounded beast, the French army, which betrayed its destruction, was the sending of Lauriston to Kutuzov's camp with a request for peace.

Napoleon, with his assurance that the good was not what was good but whatever came into his head, wrote to Kutuzov the first words that came into his head, which had no meaning at all. He wrote:

Monsieur le prince Koutouzov,
J'envoie près de vous un de mes aides de camps généraux pour vous entretenir de plusieurs objets intéressants. Je désire que Votre Altesse ajoute foi à ce qu'il lui dira, surtout lorsqu'il exprimera les sentiments d'estime et de particulière considération que j'ai depuis longtemps pour sa personne . . . *Cette lettre n'étant à autre fin, je prie Dieu, Monsieur le prince Koutouzov, qu'il vous ait en sa sainte et digne garde.**

Moscou, le 3 Octobre 1812. Signé:
Napoléon.

Je serais maudit par la postérité si l'on me regardait comme le premier moteur d'un accommodement quelconque. Tel est l'esprit actuel de ma nation.†

---

*Monsieur le prince Koutouzov, I am sending you one of my adjutant generals to discuss several interesting subjects with you. I wish Your Highness to lend credence to what he will tell him, *above all when he expresses the feelings of esteem and of special consideration which I have long had for his person* . . . This letter having no other aim, I pray God, Monsieur le prince Koutouzov, that He keep you in His holy and worthy protection. Moscow, 3 October 1812. Signed: Napoleon.
†I would be cursed by posterity if I were looked upon as the prime mover of any accommodation whatsoever. *Such is the present spirit of my nation.*

So Kutuzov replied, and he went on using all his powers to keep the troops from attacking.

During the month that the French troops were looting Moscow and the Russian troops were quietly stationed at Tarutino, a change took place in the relative strength of the two armies (in spirit and numbers), as a result of which the advantage of strength turned out to be on the Russian side. Though the position of the French troops and their number were unknown to the Russians, as soon as the relations changed, the necessity of attacking expressed itself at once in a countless number of signs. These signs were: the sending of Lauriston, the abundance of provisions in Tarutino, the information coming from all sides about the inactivity and disorder of the French, the replenishing of our regiments with recruits, the good weather, the prolonged rest of the Russian soldiers, the impatience usually resulting from rest among troops to do what they had all been brought together for, curiosity about what was happening in the French army they had so long lost sight of, the boldness with which Russian outposts now poked around the French stationed at Tarutino, the news of easy victories of the peasants and partisans over the French, the envy it gave rise to, the desire for revenge that lay in each man's soul as long as the French were in Moscow, and (above all) the vague awareness which emerged in the soul of every soldier that the relations of strength had now changed and the advantage was now on our side. The essential relations of strength had changed, and it became necessary to attack. And at once, as surely as a clock begins to strike and chime as soon as the hand makes a full circle, so this essential change of strength was correspondingly reflected in higher spheres by an increased movement, hissing, and chiming.

III

The Russian army was governed by Kutuzov and his staff and by the sovereign from Petersburg. In Petersburg, before the news of the abandoning of Moscow had been received, a detailed plan for the whole war was drawn up and sent to Kutuzov for his guidance. Despite the fact that this plan was drawn up on the assumption that Moscow was still in our hands, it was approved by the staff and accepted for carrying out. Kutuzov wrote only that it is always difficult to carry out diversions from a distance. And in order to resolve the emerging difficulties, new directives and persons were sent, whose responsibility it was to follow his actions and report on them.

Besides that, the whole staff of the Russian army was now transformed. Bagration, who had been killed, and the offended Barclay, who had withdrawn, were replaced. Quite serious reflection was given to which would be better: to put A in B's place, and B in D's place, or, on the contrary, D in A's place, and so on, as if anything apart from the good pleasure of A and B could depend on it.

In the army staff, because of the enmity between Kutuzov and his chief of staff, Bennigsen, and the presence of the sovereign's confidential persons, and these replacements, a more than usually complex play of parties went on: A undermined B, D undermined C, and so on, in all possible transpositions and combinations. In all these underminings, the subject of the intrigues was for the most part the business of war, which all these people wanted to conduct; but this business of war went on independently of them, precisely as it had to go on, that is, never coinciding with what people devised, but proceeding from the essential correlation of the masses. Only in higher spheres were all these devisings, crisscrossing and entangling, taken as a faithful reflection of what ought to happen.

The sovereign wrote on the second of October, in a letter received only after the battle of Tarutino:

Prince Mikhail Ilarionovich!
Since September 2nd Moscow has been in the hands of the enemy. Your last reports are from the 20th; and in the course of all this time, not only has nothing been undertaken for action against the enemy and the deliverance of the first-throned capital, but, according to your latest reports, you have retreated even further back. Serpukhov is already occupied by an enemy detachment, and Tula, with its famous factory, so necessary for the army, is in danger. By the reports of General Wintzingerode, I see that an enemy corps of 10,000 men is moving down the Petersburg road. Another, of several thousand men, is also heading towards Dmitrov. A third has moved forward on the Vladimir road. A fourth, a rather considerable one, is stationed between Ruza and Mozhaisk. Napoleon himself was still in Moscow on the 25th. In the light of all these reports, when the enemy has broken up his forces into strong detachments, when Napoleon himself is still in Moscow with his guards, is it possible that the enemy forces you have before you are considerable and do not allow you to go on the offensive? In all probability, on the contrary, it is to be supposed that he is pursuing you with detachments or at most a corps, much weaker than the army entrusted to you. It would seem that, profiting from these circumstances, you could with advantage attack an enemy who is weaker than you and destroy him, or at least, by forcing him to retreat, keep in our hands the greater part of the provinces now occupied by the enemy and thus divert the danger from Tula and our other towns of the interior. It will remain your responsibility if the enemy is in a position to detach a considerable corps for Petersburg and threaten this capital, in which not many troops could remain, for with the army entrusted to you, acting resolutely and actively, you have all the means to prevent this new misfortune. Remember that you still owe the offended father-

land an answer for the loss of Moscow. You have had the experience of my readiness to reward you. That readiness will not weaken in me, but I and Russia have the right to expect on your part all the zeal, firmness, and success which your intelligence, your military talents, and the courage of the troops under your leadership presage for us.

But by the time this letter, which proved that the essential correlation of forces was already reflected in Petersburg, was on its way, Kutuzov could no longer keep the army he commanded from attacking, and battle had already been offered.

On the second of October, the Cossack Shapovalov, while on patrol, killed one hare with his musket and wounded another. Pursuing the wounded hare, Shapovalov wandered deep into the forest and ran into the left flank of Murat's army, which was camped there without any precautions. The Cossack, laughing, told his friends how he had almost been captured by the French. A cornet, hearing this story, told it to his commander.

The Cossack was summoned, questioned; the Cossack commanders wanted to use the occasion to capture some horses, but one of their superiors, who had acquaintances among the upper ranks of the army, reported this fact to a staff general. Lately the situation in the army staff had been strained to the utmost. Ermolov, a few days before, had come to Bennigsen and begged him to use his influence with the commander in chief to make him go on the offensive.

"If I didn't know you, I'd think you don't want what you're asking for. I need only advise something for his serenity to be sure to do the opposite," replied Bennigsen.

The news of the Cossacks, confirmed by patrols that were sent out, proved that the event had finally ripened. The taut string jumped, the clock hissed, the bells chimed. Despite all his imaginary power, his intelligence, experience, and knowledge of people, Kutuzov, taking into consideration the note from Bennigsen, who sent personal reports to the sovereign, the same wish expressed by all the generals, the supposed wish of the sovereign, and the information of the Cossacks, could no longer hold back the inevitable movement, and gave the order to do that which he considered useless and harmful—he blessed the accomplished fact.

IV

The note submitted by Bennigsen about the necessity to attack, and the information of the Cossacks about the exposed left flank of the French, were only the last signs of the necessity to order the attack, and the attack was fixed for the fifth of October.

On the morning of the fourth of October, Kutuzov signed the disposition. Toll read it to Ermolov, suggesting that he should occupy himself with the further arrangements.

"Very well, very well, I have no time now," said Ermolov, and he left the cottage. The disposition drawn up by Toll was very good. As in the Austerlitz disposition, it was written, though not in German:

"*Die erste Kolonne marschiert* to such and such place, *die zweite Kolonne marschiert** to such and such place," and so on. And on paper all these columns arrived where they were supposed to at the appointed time and destroyed the enemy. As in all dispositions, everything was beautifully thought out, and, as with all dispositions, not a single column arrived where it was supposed to at the appointed time.

When the disposition had been prepared in the proper number of copies, an officer was summoned and sent to Ermolov to hand him the papers for execution. The young officer of the horse guards, Kutuzov's orderly, pleased with the importance of the mission given to him, went to Ermolov's quarters.

"He left," said Ermolov's orderly. The officer of the horse guards went to a general whom Ermolov frequented.

"No, and the general's not here either."

The officer of the horse guards mounted up and rode to yet another.

"No, he left."

"I hope I won't have to answer for the delay! How vexing!" thought the officer. He rode around the whole camp. This one said Ermolov had been seen riding somewhere with some other generals, that one said he must have gone back home. The officer went without dinner and searched until six o'clock in the evening. Ermolov was nowhere to be found, and nobody knew where he was. The officer had a quick bite with a comrade and went back to Miloradovich in the vanguard. Miloradovich was also not at home, but here he was told that Miloradovich was at General Kikin's ball, and that Ermolov must be there, too.

"And where is that?"

"Over there in Yechkino," said the Cossack officer, pointing to a distant manor house.

"How can it be, beyond the line?"

"They sent two of our regiments to the line. There's such carousing going on there now, it's awful! Two bands, three choruses of singers."

The officer rode beyond the line to Yechkino. From a distance, as he approached the house, he could already hear the merry, concerted sounds of a soldiers' dancing song.

"Intheme-e-eadows . . . intheme-e-eadows! . . ." he heard, with whistling

*The first column will march . . . the second column will march . . .

and a torban,[3] occasionally overwhelmed by the shouting of voices. The officer felt cheered by these sounds, but at the same time afraid of being blamed for taking so long to convey the important order he had been entrusted with. It was already past eight o'clock. He dismounted and went up the porch and into the front hall of a big, intact landowner's mansion that stood between the Russians and the French. In the pantry and the front hall, servants bustled about with wines and food. The singers stood by the windows. The officer was led through the door, and he suddenly saw the most important generals of the army all together, among them the large, conspicuous figure of Ermolov. The generals were all standing in a semicircle, their tunics unbuttoned, their faces red and animated, laughing loudly. In the middle of the room a handsome, short, red-faced general was briskly and deftly dancing the *trepak*.

"Ha, ha, ha! Go to it, Nikolai Ivanovich! Ha, ha, ha!"

The officer felt that, coming in just then with an important order, he was doubly to blame, and he wanted to wait; but one of the generals saw him and, learning why he had come, told Ermolov. Ermolov, with a frowning face, came over to the officer and, having heard him out, took the paper from him without saying anything.

"You think he left by chance?" a comrade from the staff said that evening to the officer of the horse guards about Ermolov. "It's a trick, it was all on purpose. To undercut Konovnitsyn.[4] You'll see what a hash there'll be tomorrow!"

V

Early the next morning, the decrepit old Kutuzov got up, said his prayers, dressed, and, with the unpleasant awareness that he had to lead a battle of which he did not approve, got into a caleche and drove out of Letashevka, three miles behind Tarutino, to the place where the attacking columns were to assemble. Kutuzov rode along, falling asleep and waking up and trying to hear if there was gunfire to the right, if the action had begun. But everything was still quiet. A damp and overcast autumnal day was beginning to dawn. Approaching Tarutino, Kutuzov noticed some cavalrymen, who were taking their horses to water across the road on which his caleche was driving. Kutuzov looked at them closely, stopped the caleche, and asked what regiment they were from. The cavalrymen were from a column that should have been waiting in ambush far ahead. "An error, maybe," the old commander in chief thought. But, having driven further, Kutuzov saw infantry regiments, their muskets stacked, the soldiers in their underdrawers, eating kasha and toting firewood. An officer was sent for. The officer reported that there had been no order to advance.

"How's that, no or . . ." Kutuzov began, but fell silent at once and ordered the senior officer to be sent to him. Getting out of the caleche, his head lowered and breathing hard, he paced up and down, waiting silently. When Eichen, the summoned officer of the general staff, appeared, Kutuzov turned purple, not because this officer was guilty of an error, but because he was a worthy object for the expression of anger. And, shaking, choking, getting into that state of fury in which he was capable of rolling on the ground from wrath, the old man fell upon Eichen, making threatening gestures, shouting, and swearing in foul language. Another man who happened to turn up, Captain Brozin, suffered the same fate, though he was not guilty of anything.

"Who is this other swine? Shoot the scoundrels!" he cried hoarsely, waving his arms and reeling. He was suffering physically. He, the commander in chief, his serenity, who was assured by everyone that no one in Russia had ever had such power as he, had been put in such a position—held up to mockery before the entire army. "I bothered praying like that for the coming day, I spent a sleepless night thinking it all over—for nothing!" he thought to himself. "When I was a young brat of an officer, nobody dared to laugh at me like this . . . But now!" He was suffering physically, as if from corporal punishment, and could not help expressing it with wrathful and painful cries; but his strength soon began to fail, and, looking around, feeling that he had said a lot of bad things, he got into his caleche and silently drove back again.

The wrath he had poured out did not return, and Kutuzov, blinking weakly, heard out the justifications and words of defence (Ermolov himself did not come to him until the next day), and the insistences of Bennigsen, Konovnitsyn, and Toll, that the same miscarried movement could be done the next day. And Kutuzov again had to agree.

VI

The next day the troops assembled in the appointed places in the evening and advanced during the night. It was an autumnal night, with purplish black clouds, but without rain. The ground was damp, but there was no mud, and the troops walked noiselessly, only occasionally the clank of artillery could be faintly heard. Loud talk, pipe smoking, and striking a fire were forbidden; the horses were kept from neighing. The secrecy of the undertaking increased its attractiveness. The men marched cheerfully. Some columns halted, stacked their muskets, and lay down on the cold ground, assuming they had got where they were supposed to go; some columns (the majority) marched all night and obviously did not get where they were supposed to go.

Count Orlov-Denisov with his Cossacks (the most insignificant detachment of them all) was the only one who ended up in the right place and at the right time. This detachment halted at the edge of the forest, where a path led from the village of Stromilovo to Dmitrovskoe.

Before dawn the dozing Count Orlov was awakened. A deserter from the French camp was brought to him. He was a Polish sergeant from Poniatowski's corps. The sergeant explained in Polish that he had deserted because he had been passed over in the service, that he should have been a commissioned officer long ago, that he was braver than all of them, and therefore he had left them and wanted to punish them. He said that Murat was spending the night a mile away, and that if they gave him a hundred-man escort, he would take him alive. Count Orlov-Denisov consulted with his comrades. The offer was too tempting to refuse. Everyone volunteered to go, everyone advised making the attempt. After much arguing and considering, Major General Grekov with two Cossack regiments decided to go with the sergeant.

"But remember," said Count Orlov-Denisov as he dismissed the sergeant, "if you're lying, I'll have you hung like a dog, but if it's true, you'll get a hundred gold pieces."

Not replying to these words, the officer mounted his horse with a resolute air and rode off with the quickly prepared Grekov. They disappeared into the forest. Count Orlov, shivering from the chill of early dawn, excited by what he had undertaken on his own responsibility, having seen Grekov off, came out of the forest and began to study the enemy camp, which was now visible in the deceptive light of early morning and the dying campfires. Our columns were to appear to the right of Count Orlov-Denisov, on the open hillside. Count Orlov looked that way; but though these columns would have been visible from far off, they were nowhere in sight. It seemed to Count Orlov-Denisov, and especially to his very keen-sighted adjutant, that the French camp was beginning to stir.

"Ah, it really is late," said Count Orlov, glancing at the camp. As often happens once the person we have believed is no longer before our eyes, it suddenly became perfectly clear and obvious to him that this sergeant was a fraud, that he had lied to them, and would only spoil the whole business of the attack by the absence of those two regiments, which he would lead God knows where. How could anyone snatch a commander in chief out of such a mass of troops?

"He really lied, the rogue," said the count.

"They can be called back," said someone from his suite, who, like Count Orlov-Denisov, felt mistrustful of the undertaking, when he looked at the camp.

"Ah? Really? . . . What do you think, shall we leave it as is? Or not?"

"Do you order them called back?"

"Call them back, call them back!" Count Orlov suddenly said resolutely, looking at his watch. "It will be too late, it's quite light."

And an adjutant galloped into the forest after Grekov. When Grekov came back, Count Orlov-Denisov, upset by this cancelled attempt, and by the vain wait for the infantry columns, which were not yet in sight, and by the proximity of the enemy (all the men of his detachment experienced the same thing), decided to attack.

He whispered the command: "Mount!" They formed up; they crossed themselves . . .

"God be with you!"

"Hur-r-rah!" rang out through the forest, and, one by one, as if pouring from a sack, hundreds of Cossacks, their lances atilt, flew merrily across the brook towards the camp.

One desperate, frightened cry of the first Frenchman to see the Cossacks— and all who were in the camp, undressed, half-awake, abandoned cannon, muskets, horses, and ran off wherever they could.

If the Cossacks had pursued the French, paying no attention to what was behind and around them, they would have taken both Murat and everything that was there. The officers wanted that. But once the Cossacks got hold of the booty and the prisoners, they would not budge. No one obeyed orders. Fifteen hundred prisoners, thirty-eight cannon, standards, and, what was most important for the Cossacks, horses, saddles, blankets, and various objects were taken on the spot. All that had to be managed, the prisoners and cannon had to be taken in hand, the booty divided, with shouting and even fighting among themselves: the Cossacks were taken up with all that.

The French, no longer pursued, gradually began to recover, formed units, and started shooting. Orlov-Denisov waited for the rest of the columns and did not advance further.

Meanwhile, according to the disposition—"*die erste Kolonne marschiert*" and so on—the infantry of the belated columns, commanded by Bennigsen and directed by Toll, started out properly and, as always happens, got somewhere, but not where they were supposed to go. As always happens, the men, who had started out cheerfully, began to halt; displeasure was voiced, confusion was sensed, they began moving back somewhere. Adjutants and generals galloped about, shouted, became angry, quarrelled, said they had come to the wrong place and were late, denounced somebody, and so on; and finally they all waved their hands and went on, only so as to go somewhere. "We'll get somewhere!" And indeed they did, but not to the right place, though some also got to the right place, but so late that they were of no use and only got themselves shot at. Toll, who in this battle played the role of Weyrother at Austerlitz, galloped assiduously from place to place, and everywhere found things the wrong way round. Thus he ran into Bagovut's corps in the forest when it was already quite light and that corps was supposed to have long been with Orlov-Denisov. Agitated, upset by the failure, and supposing that someone was to blame for it, Toll rode up to the commander of the corps and began to upbraid him sternly, saying he ought to be shot for it. Bagovut, an old, calm, seasoned

general, also worn out by all those halts, confusions, contradictions, to everyone's surprise, completely contrary to his character, flew into a rage and said all
sorts of unpleasant things to Toll.

"I'm not going to take lessons from anybody, and I can die with my soldiers no worse than anybody else," he said and marched on with a single
division.

Coming out into the field under French fire, the agitated and brave Bagovut,
without considering whether his going into action now, and with only one
division, was useful or useless, marched straight ahead and led his troops
under fire. Danger, cannonballs, bullets were what he needed in his wrathful
state. One of the first bullets killed him, the bullets that followed killed many
of his soldiers. And for some time his division went on standing uselessly
under fire.

VII

Meanwhile, another column was supposed to attack the French on the front,
but Kutuzov was with that column. He knew very well that nothing but confusion would come of this battle begun against his will, and, as far as was in his
power, tried to hold back the troops. He did not move.

Kutuzov rode along silently on his little grey horse, lazily responding to the
suggestions to attack.

"You've got attack on your tongue all the time, and don't see that we can't
perform complicated manoeuvres," he said to Miloradovich, who was asking
to advance.

"We were unable to take Murat alive this morning and get in place on time:
now there's nothing to do!" he replied to another.

When word came to Kutuzov that in the French rear, where, according to a
Cossack report, there had previously been no one, there were now two battalions of Poles, he glanced sidelong at Ermolov behind him (he had not spoken
to him since the previous day).

"Here they're asking to go on the offensive, suggest several plans, but we
barely get down to business, and nothing's ready, and the alerted enemy takes
his measures."

Ermolov narrowed his eyes and smiled slightly, hearing these words. He
understood that the storm was over for him and that Kutuzov would limit
himself to this hint.

"He's having fun at my expense," Ermolov said softly, nudging Raevsky,
who was standing next to him, with his knee.

Soon after that, Ermolov stepped up to Kutuzov and reported respectfully:

"There's still time, Your Serenity, the enemy hasn't gone away yet. What if
you order an offensive? Otherwise the guards won't see any smoke."

Kutuzov said nothing, but when it was reported to him that Murat's troops were retreating, he ordered an offensive; but at every hundred paces, he halted for three quarters of an hour.

The whole battle consisted in what Orlov-Denisov's Cossacks had done; the rest of the troops merely lost several hundred men for nothing.

As a result of this battle, Kutuzov received a diamond decoration, Bennigsen also got diamonds and a hundred thousand roubles, others, according to their rank, also received many pleasant things, and after this battle there were more new transfers in the staff.

"That's how it's *always done with us,* all the wrong way round!" the Russian officers and generals said after the battle of Tarutino, just as people speak now, letting it be felt that some fool somewhere does things that way, the wrong way round, but we would not do things that way. But people who talk like that either do not know what they are talking about, or are deliberately deceiving themselves. No battle—Tarutino, Borodino, Austerlitz—comes off the way its organizers supposed. That is an essential condition.

A countless number of free forces (for nowhere is a man more free than in a battle, where it is a question of life and death) influence the direction of the battle, and that direction can never be known beforehand and never coincides with the direction of some one force.

If many simultaneous and variously directed forces act upon some body, the direction of that body's movement cannot coincide with any one of those forces; there will always be the shortest median direction, which in mechanics is expressed by the diagonal of the parallelogram of forces.

If in the descriptions of historians, French historians in particular, we find that their wars and battles were carried out according to a predetermined plan, the only conclusion we can draw from that is that these descriptions are not correct.

The battle of Tarutino obviously did not achieve the purpose Toll had in mind, of sending troops into action in good order according to the disposition; nor the one Orlov might have had, of capturing Murat; nor the goal of the instantaneous extermination of an entire corps, which Bennigsen and other persons may have had; nor the goal of the officer who wanted to go into action and distinguish himself; nor of the Cossack who would have liked to get more booty than he did; and so on. But if the goal was that which actually took place, and that which was then the general wish of all Russian people (to drive the French out of Russia and exterminate their army), then it will be perfectly clear that the battle of Tarutino, precisely owing to its incoherencies, was the very thing that was needed at that period of the campaign. It would be difficult and even impossible to think up any outcome of the battle more expedient than the one it had. With the least strain, with the greatest confusion, and with the most insignificant losses, the greatest results of the whole campaign were achieved, the transition was made from retreat to offence, the weakness of the French was exposed, and the push was given which Napoleon's army was only waiting for to begin its flight.

VIII

Napoleon enters Moscow after the brilliant victory *de la Moskowa;* there can be no doubt of the victory, since the battlefield remains with the French. The Russians retreat and surrender the capital. Moscow, filled with provisions, arms, ammunition, and incalculable riches, is in the hands of Napoleon. The Russian army, twice weaker than the French, does not make a single attempt to attack in the course of a month. Napoleon's position is most brilliant. To fall upon the remainder of the Russian army with double its forces and exterminate it, to negotiate an advantageous peace or, in case of refusal, to make a threatening move on Petersburg, even to return to Smolensk or Vilno in case of failure, or to remain in Moscow—in other words, to hold on to the brilliant position the French army was in at the time, would seem to require no special genius. For that one needed to do the simplest and easiest thing: to keep the army from looting, to provide a supply of winter clothing, of which there would be enough in Moscow for the whole army, and to organize the collection of provisions for the whole army, of which (on the evidence of French historians) there were enough in Moscow for more than six months. Napoleon, that genius of geniuses and having the power of control over the army, as the historians affirm, did none of that.

He not only did none of it, but, on the contrary, he used his power in order to choose, out of all the paths of action presented to him, the one which was the most stupid and destructive. Of all that Napoleon might have done: to winter in Moscow, to go against Petersburg, to go against Nizhni Novgorod, to go back more to the north, or to the south the way Kutuzov went later— whatever one thinks up, nothing stupider or more destructive than what Napoleon did, that is, to stay in Moscow until October, to allow his troops to loot the city, then, hesitating whether or not to leave a garrison, to quit Moscow, to approach Kutuzov without starting a battle, to turn to the right, reach Maly Yaroslavets, again without trying his chances of breaking through, to go, not by the road Kutuzov had taken, but back to Mozhaisk down the devastated Smolensk road—nothing stupider than that, or more destructive for his troops, could possibly have been thought up, as the consequences showed. Let the most skilful of strategists, imagining that Napoleon's goal was to destroy his army, think up another series of actions which would, as unquestionably and as independently of anything the Russian troops might have undertaken, destroy the whole French army so completely as what Napoleon did.

Napoleon the genius did that. But to say that Napoleon destroyed his army because he wanted to or because he was very stupid, would be just as unfair as to say that Napoleon brought his army as far as Moscow because he wanted to and because he was very intelligent and a genius.

In either case his personal activity, having no more power than the personal activity of each soldier, merely coincided with the laws according to which the phenomenon was accomplished.

Historians quite falsely (only because what followed did not justify his actions) describe for us the weakening of Napoleon's powers in Moscow. Just as earlier, and also later, in the year thirteen, he employed all his skill and powers to do the best for himself and his army. Napoleon's activity during this time was no less astounding than it was in Egypt, in Italy, in Austria, and in Prussia. We do not know for certain how great Napoleon's genius really was in Egypt, where forty centuries looked down upon his greatness, because all his great deeds are described for us only by the French. We cannot correctly judge his genius in Austria and Prussia, because information about his activity there must be drawn from French and German sources; and the incomprehensible surrender into captivity of whole corps without a battle and of fortresses without a siege was bound to incline the Germans towards recognizing his genius as the sole explanation of the war that was conducted in Germany. But we, thank God, have no reason to recognize his genius in order to cover up our shame. We paid for the right to look at the matter simply and directly, and we shall not give up that right.

His activity in Moscow is as astounding and marked by genius as everywhere else. Order after order and plan after plan proceed from him, from the time of his entry into Moscow until he leaves it. The absence of the inhabitants and the deputation and the burning of Moscow itself do not throw him off. He does not lose sight either of the welfare of his army, or of the doings of the enemy, or of the welfare of the peoples of Russia, or of the management of affairs in Paris, or of diplomatic considerations to do with terms for the coming peace.

IX

In the military respect, Napoleon, as soon as he enters Moscow, gives General Sébastiani strict orders to keep track of the movements of the Russian army, sends corps to various roads, and orders Murat to find Kutuzov. Then he makes careful arrangements for fortifying the Kremlin; then he draws up a brilliant plan for the future campaign over the whole map of Russia. In the diplomatic respect, Napoleon summons the robbed and bedraggled Captain Yakovlev, who does not know how to get out of Moscow, lays out for him in detail his policy and his magnanimity, and, having written a letter to the emperor Alexander in which he considers it his duty to inform his friend and brother that Rastopchin has arranged things badly in Moscow, he sends Yakovlev to Petersburg. Having laid out his plans and magnanimity in the same detail before Tutolmin,[5] he sends this old man, too, to Petersburg for negotiations.

In the legal respect, orders are given immediately after the fires to find the culprits and execute them. And the villain Rastopchin is punished by an order that his houses be burned down.

In the administrative respect, Moscow is granted a constitution, a city council is established, and the following is published:

Inhabitants of Moscow!

Your misfortunes are cruel, but His Majesty the Emperor and King wishes to put an end to the course thereof. Fearful examples have taught you how he punishes disobedience and crime. Strict measures have been taken to put an end to disorder and restore general safety. A paternal administration, chosen from among yourselves, will constitute your municipality or city council. The latter will attend to you, to your needs, to your well-being. The members thereof will be distinguished by a red ribbon worn over the shoulder, and the mayor will have besides a white sash. But, excluding their time of duty, they will wear only a red band round the left arm.

The city police force has been established on its former bases, and, through its activity, already better order exists. The government has appointed two commissaries general or police chiefs and twenty commissaries or district officers, placed in all districts of the city. You will recognize them by a white band worn round the left arm. Several churches of various confessions have been opened, and divine offices are celebrated in them without hindrance. Your fellow citizens daily return to their dwellings, and orders have been given so that they may find in them the help and protection owed to misfortune. These are the means that the government has employed to restore order and ease your situation; but to achieve that, it is necessary that you join your efforts to it, that you forget, if possible, the misfortunes you have suffered, give yourselves to the hope of a less cruel fate, be assured that an inevitable and shameful death awaits those who venture upon your persons or your remaining possessions, and finally that you not doubt that these latter will be safeguarded, for such is the will of the greatest and most just of monarchs. Soldiers and inhabitants, of whatever nation you may be! Restore public confidence, the source of the good fortune of the state, live as brothers, render mutual aid and protection to one another, unite to foil the intentions of the evil-minded, obey the military and civil authorities, and your tears will soon cease to flow!

In respect of supplies for the army, Napoleon prescribed to all his troops that they take turns going around Moscow *à la maraude** in order to stock up on provisions for themselves, so that in this way the army would be provided for in the future.

In the religious respect, Napoleon gave orders to *ramener les popes†* and resume church services.

In respect of trade and supplies for the army, the following was hung up everywhere.

PROCLAMATION

You, tranquil inhabitants of Moscow, artisans and working people whom misfortune has driven out of the city, and you, scattered tillers of the soil, whom a groundless fear still keeps in the fields, hear this! Stillness is returning to the capital, and order is being restored in it. Your compatriots are boldly leaving their refuges, seeing that they are respected. Every violence committed against them and their property is immediately punished. His Majesty the Emperor and King protects them and regards none among you as his enemies save those who disobey his orders. He wishes to put an end to your misfortunes and return you to your homes and families. Correspond to his beneficent intentions and come to us without any danger. Citizens! Return with confidence to your dwellings: you will soon find ways to satisfy your needs! Craftsmen and labour-loving artisans! Go back to your handiwork: houses, shops, protective guards are waiting for you, and you will be duly paid for your work! And, finally, you peasants, leave the forests where you have hidden yourselves from terror, return without fear to your cottages, in precise assurance that you will find protection. Depots are being set up in the city, where peasants can bring their surplus stocks and plants of the earth. The government has taken the following measures to provide them with a free market: (1) As of today, peasants, tillers of the soil, and those living in the environs of Moscow can without any danger bring to the city their supplies, of whatever sort they may be, to the two appointed depots, that is, to Mokhovaya Street and to Okhotny Row. (2) The said supplies will be purchased from them for the price agreed upon between the buyer and the seller; but if the seller does not obtain the fair price he demands, he is free to take them back to his village, and no one can prevent him by any means from doing so. (3) Each Sunday and Wednesday are appointed every week as major market days, for which reason a sufficient number of troops will be stationed on Tuesdays and Saturdays on all the main roads, at such distance from the city as will allow them to defend the supply trains. (4) Similar measures will be taken to prevent the hindering of those

---

*Marauding.
†Bring back the popes [Orthodox priests].

peasants with their carts and horses on their way back. (5) Immediately means will be employed for the restoration of normal trade. Inhabitants of the city and the villages, and you, workers and artisans, of whatever nation you may be! You are called to fulfil the paternal intentions of His Majesty the Emperor and King and contribute with him to the general well-being. Lay your respect and trust at his feet and do not be slow to unite with us![6]

In respect of raising the spirits of the troops and the people, reviews were constantly held and rewards distributed. The emperor rode about the streets and comforted the inhabitants; and, despite all his concern with state affairs, he personally visited the theatres established by his order.

In respect of philanthropy, the best virtue of monarchs, Napoleon also did all that depended on him. He ordered *Maison de ma mère** written on the almshouses, combining in this act a tender filial feeling with the grandeur of a sovereign's virtue.[7] He visited the orphanage, and, having allowed the orphans he had saved to kiss his helping hands, conversed graciously with Tutolmin. Then, according to Thiers's eloquent account, he ordered his troops to be paid in counterfeit Russian money he had made. *"Relevant l'emploi de ces moyens par un acte digne de lui et de l'armée française, il fit distribuer des secours aux incendiés. Mais les vivres étant trop précieux pour être donnés à des étrangers la plupart ennemis, Napoléon aima mieux leur fournir de l'argent afin qu'ils se fournissent au dehors, et il leur fit distribuer des roubles papiers."*[†]

In respect of army discipline, orders were constantly issued about severe punishments for the non-fulfilment of duty and about putting an end to looting.

X

But, strangely enough, all these instructions, concerns, and plans, while being by no means worse than others issued in similar cases, did not touch the essence of the matter, but, like the hands of a clock with the mechanism removed, turned arbitrarily and aimlessly, without catching the gears.

In the military respect, the brilliant plan of campaign, of which Thiers says, *"que son génie n'avait jamais rien imaginé de plus profond, de plus habile et de plus admirable,"*[‡] and concerning which Thiers, getting into polemics with

---

*My mother's house.

†Enhancing the use of these methods by an act worthy of himself and of the French army, he had aid distributed to the victims of the fire. But, food supplies being too precious to be given to strangers who were for the most part enemies, Napoleon preferred to provide them with money, so that they could provide for themselves elsewhere, and he had paper roubles distributed to them.

‡That his genius had never imagined anything more profound, more skilful, and more admirable.

Mr. Fain,[8] proves that the drawing up of this brilliant plan should be dated not to the fourth but to the fifteenth of October—this plan never was and never could have been carried out, because nothing in it was close to reality. The fortifying of the Kremlin, for which *la Mosquée* (as Napoleon called the church of Basil the Blessed) was to be razed, proved totally useless. The mining of the Kremlin only went towards fulfilling the emperor's wish that, as he left Moscow, the Kremlin should be blown up—that is, that the floor against which the little child hurt himself should be given a beating. The pursuit of the Russian army, which so preoccupied Napoleon, produced an unheard-of phenomenon. The French generals lost the sixty-thousand-man Russian army, and, in Thiers's words, it was only owing to the skill and, it seems, the genius of Murat that they managed to find, like a pin, this sixty-thousand-man Russian army.

In the diplomatic respect, all Napoleon's arguments about his magnanimity and fairness, both before Tutolmin and before Yakovlev, who was mostly concerned with acquiring an overcoat and a wagon, proved useless: Alexander did not receive these ambassadors or reply to their ambassage.

In the legal respect, after the execution of the supposed incendiaries, the other half of Moscow burned down.

In the administrative respect, the establishment of the municipality did not put an end to the looting and proved useful only to certain persons who took part in it and who, under the pretext of maintaining order, were themselves looting Moscow or saving their own property from being looted.

In the religious respect, the matter that had been settled so easily in Egypt by means of a visit to a mosque, here yielded no results. Two or three priests, found in Moscow, tried to carry out Napoleon's will, but one of them was slapped in the face by a French officer during a service, and of another a French official reported the following: *"Le prêtre, que j'avais découvert et invité à recommencer à dire la messe, a nettoyé et fermé l'église. Cette nuit on est venu de nouveau enfoncer les portes, casser les cadenas, déchirer les livres et commettre d'autres désordres."**

In respect of trade, the proclamation to the labour-loving artisans and all the peasants received no response. There were no labour-loving artisans, and the peasants caught the commissaries, who ventured too far afield with this proclamation, and killed them.

In respect of the entertainment of the people and the army with theatres, the business failed in exactly the same way. The theatres set up in the Kremlin and in Poznyakov's house closed at once, because the actresses and actors were robbed.

---

*The priest I had discovered and invited to begin saying mass again, cleaned and locked the church. That night people came again to break down the doors, smash the padlocks, tear up the books, and commit other disorders.

Even philanthropy did not yield the desired results. Counterfeit and non-counterfeit banknotes filled Moscow and had no value. For the French, who were collecting booty, there was need only for gold. Not only did the counterfeit notes that Napoleon so graciously distributed have no value, but silver was exchanged at below value for gold.

But the most striking manifestation of the ineffectiveness of orders from above at that time came from Napoleon's attempts to put an end to looting and restore discipline.

Here is what the army officers reported:

"Looting in the city continues, despite instructions to put an end to it. Order has not yet been restored, and there is not a single merchant who carries on trade in a legal way. Only the sutlers allow themselves to sell, and stolen goods at that."

"*La partie de mon arrondissement continue à être en proie au pillage des soldats du 3ᵉ corps, qui, non contents d'arracher aux malheureux réfugiés dans des souterrains le peu qui leur reste, ont même la férocité de les blesser à coups de sabre, comme j'en ai vu plusieurs exemples.*"*

"*Rien de nouveau outre que les soldats se permettent de voler et de piller. Le 9 octobre.*"†

"*Le vol et le pillage continuent. Il y a une bande de voleurs dans notre district qu'il faudra faire arrêter par de fortes gardes. Le 11 octobre.*"‡

"The emperor is extremely displeased that, despite strict orders to put an end to looting, all we see is detachments of marauding guards coming back to the Kremlin. Disorder and looting were renewed worse than ever among the old guard yesterday, last night, and today. The emperor regrets to see that the picked soldiers appointed to protect his person, and supposed to give an example of subordination, push their disobedience to such a degree that they break into the cellars and storerooms reserved for the army. Others have lowered themselves so far as to disobey sentries and guards officers, abusing and beating them."

"*Le grand maréchal du palais se plaint vivement,*" wrote the governor, "*que malgré les défenses réitérées, les soldats continuent à faire leurs besoins dans toutes les cours et même jusque sous les fenêtres de l'Empereur.*"§

---

*Part of my district continues to be prey to the looting of soldiers from the 3rd Corps, who, not content with wresting from the wretches hiding in basements the little they have left, even have the ferocity to wound them with jabs of their sabres, of which I have seen several examples.

†Nothing new, except that the soldiers allow themselves to steal and loot. 9 October.

‡The robbery and looting go on. There is a gang of thieves in our district that would need strong guards to arrest it. 11 October.

§The grand marshal of the palace complains loudly . . . that despite repeated prohibitions, the soldiers continue to satisfy their needs in all the courtyards and even right under the emperor's windows.

This army, like a herd let loose, trampling underfoot the fodder that might save it from starvation, was falling apart and perishing with every extra day it spent in Moscow.

Yet it did not budge.

It began to flee only when it was suddenly seized by panic fear, caused by the interception of its supply trains on the Smolensk road and by the battle of Tarutino. This same news of the battle of Tarutino, which Napoleon received unexpectedly during a review, aroused in him a desire to punish the Russians, as Thiers says, and he gave orders for departure, which was what the whole army was demanding.

Fleeing from Moscow, the men of this army took along everything they had looted. Napoleon also carted his own personal *trésor* with him. Seeing the baggage train that encumbered the army, Napoleon was horrified (as Thiers says). But, for all his experience of war, he did not order the burning of all superfluous wagons, as he had done with the wagons of a certain marshal when approaching Moscow, but looked at the caleches and carriages in which the soldiers were riding and said that it was very good, that these vehicles would be used for provisions, the sick, and the wounded.

The plight of the whole army was like the plight of a wounded animal that feels itself perishing and does not know what it is doing. To study the skilful manoeuvres and aims of Napoleon and his army from the moment of his entry into Moscow until the destruction of that army, is the same as studying the meaning of the dying leaps and convulsions of a mortally wounded animal. Very often a wounded animal, hearing a rustle, rushes towards the hunter's shot, runs forward, then back, and hastens its own end. That was what Napoleon was doing under the pressure of his whole army. The rustle of the battle of Tarutino frightened the beast, and it rushed ahead towards the shot, ran as far as the hunter, turned back, then ahead, then back again, and finally, like any beast, ran back over its old, familiar tracks—that is, over the most disadvantageous and dangerous path for it.

Napoleon, whom we imagine as guiding this whole movement (as a savage imagines that the figure carved on the prow of a ship is the force that guides it), Napoleon, during all this time of his activity, was like a child who, holding the straps tied inside a carriage, fancies that he is driving it.

XI

On the sixth of October, early in the morning, Pierre stepped out of the shed and, on his way back, stopped by the door, playing with a long, purplish dog on short, bowed legs that was fidgeting around him. This dog lived in their shed, spending the nights with Karataev, but occasionally went to town somewhere and came back again. It had probably never belonged to anyone, and now, too, it was no one's and had no name at all. The French called it Azor, the storytelling soldier called it Femgalka, Karataev and the others sometimes called it Grey, sometimes Floppy. Its not belonging to anyone, and the absence of a name and even of a breed, even of a definite colour, seemed not to bother the purplish dog in the least. Its fluffy tail stood up firm and rounded like a panache, its bowed legs served it so well that often, as if scorning to use all four legs, it raised one gracefully and ran very deftly and quickly on three. Everything was an object of pleasure for it. Now it lolled on its back, squealing with joy, now it warmed itself in the sun with a pensive and meaningful look, now it frolicked, playing with a wood chip or a straw.

Pierre's clothing now consisted of a dirty, tattered shirt, the only remains of his former attire, a soldier's trousers, tied with string at the ankles for the sake of warmth, on Karataev's advice, a kaftan, and a muzhik's hat. Physically Pierre had changed very much during that time. He no longer seemed fat, though he had the same look of massiveness and strength that was hereditary to his breed. The lower part of his face was overgrown with a beard and moustache; his hair, grown long and full of lice, now formed a tangled, curly cap. There was firmness, calm, and a lively readiness in the expression of his eyes, such as had never been there before. His former laxness, expressed even in his gaze, was now replaced by an energetic composure, ready for action and resistance. His feet were bare.

Pierre now looked down across the field, over which wagons and horsemen were moving about that morning, now into the distance beyond the river, now at the dog, who pretended that she was going to bite him in earnest, now at his bare feet, which he took pleasure in shifting into different positions, moving his dirty, fat, big toes. And each time he looked at his bare feet, a lively and self-satisfied smile passed over his face. The sight of those bare feet reminded him of all he had lived through and understood during that time, and he found that remembrance pleasant.

For several days already the weather had been calm, clear, with a light frost in the mornings—so-called "Indian Summer."

The air was warm in the sun, and that warmth, along with the invigorating freshness of the morning frost still felt in the air, was especially pleasant.

On all things far and near there was that magically crystalline sheen which occurs only at that time of autumn. In the distance he could see the Sparrow Hills, with the village, the church, and a large white house. The bared trees, and the sand, and the stones, and the roofs of the houses, and the green spire of the church, and the angles of the distant white house—all this was etched with unnatural distinctness, with the finest lines, in the transparent air. Nearby he could see the familiar ruins of a half-burnt manor house occupied by the French, with still dark green lilac bushes growing along the fence. And even that ruined and befouled house, repulsively ugly in overcast weather, now, in the bright, immobile brilliance, seemed something soothingly beautiful.

A French corporal, unbuttoned in a homey way, in a nightcap, with a short pipe in his teeth, came round the corner of the shed and, with a friendly wink, approached Pierre.

"Quel soleil, hein, monsieur Kiril?" (so all the Frenchmen called Pierre). *"On dirait le printemps."** And the corporal leaned against the door and offered Pierre a pipe, despite the fact that he always offered it and Pierre always refused it.

"Si l'on marchait par un temps comme celui-là . . ."† he began.

Pierre asked him what he had heard about the departure, and the corporal told him that almost all the troops were leaving, and that an order should come presently about the prisoners. In the shed where Pierre was, one of the soldiers, Sokolov, was sick and dying, and Pierre told the corporal that this soldier should be looked after. The corporal said that Pierre could rest assured, that there were ambulant and stationary hospitals for that, and there would be an order about the sick, and generally whatever might happen had all been foreseen by the superiors.

"Et puis, monsieur Kiril, vous n'avez qu'a dire un mot au capitaine, vous savez. Oh, c'est un . . . qui n'oublie jamais rien. Dites au capitaine quand il fera sa tournée, il fera tout pour vous . . ."‡

The captain the corporal was referring to conversed with Pierre frequently and at length, and was indulgent towards him in various ways.

" 'Vois-tu, St. Thomas,' qu'il me disait l'autre jour: 'Kiril c'est un homme qui a de l'instruction, qui parle français; c'est un seigneur russe, qui a eu des malheurs, mais c'est un homme. Et il s'y entend le . . . S'il demande quelque chose, qu'il me dise, il n'y a pas de refus. Quand on a fait ses études, voyez-vous, on aime l'instruction et les gens comme-il-faut.' C'est pour vous que je dis cela, monsieur Kiril. Dans l'affaire de l'autre jour, si ce n'était grâce à vous, ça aurait fini mal."§

And having chatted a while longer, the corporal left. (The business the corporal referred to, which had happened the other day, was a fight between the prisoners and the French, in which Pierre had managed to pacify his com-

---

*What sun, eh, Monsieur Kiril? . . . You'd think it was spring.

†If one was marching in weather like this . . .

‡And then, Monsieur Kiril, you have only to say a word to the captain, you know. Oh, he's a . . . who never forgets anything. Say it to the captain when he makes his rounds, he'll do everything for you . . .

§"You see, by St. Thomas," he said to me the other day: "Kiril is an educated man, who speaks French; he is a Russian nobleman, who has had misfortunes, but he's a man. And he understands the . . . If he asks for anything, let him tell me, there will be no refusal. When one has studied, you see, one likes education and proper people." I'm saying that for your sake, Monsieur Kiril. In that business the other day, if it hadn't been for you, things would have ended badly.

rades.) Several prisoners had listened to Pierre's talk with the corporal and at once began asking what he had said. While Pierre was telling his comrades what the corporal had said about the departure, a skinny, yellow, ragged French soldier came to the door of the shed. Raising his fingers to his forehead in a quick and timid movement as a sign of greeting, he addressed Pierre and asked whether the soldier *Platoche*, whom he had asked to sew a shirt for him, was in this shed.

About a week earlier, boot-making supplies and linen cloth had been distributed to the French, and the soldiers had asked the prisoners to make boots and shirts for them.

"It's ready, it's ready, little falcon!" said Karataev, coming out with a neatly folded shirt.

On account of the warmth and in order to work comfortably, Karataev was in nothing but drawers and a tattered shirt as black as earth. His hair, as is done among artisans, was tied with a strip of bast, and his round face looked still more round and comely.

"Promised and done are born brothers. I said by Friday, and so I did," said Platon, smiling and unfolding the shirt he had made.

The Frenchman glanced around uneasily and, as if overcoming his hesitations, quickly took off his jacket and put on the shirt. Under the jacket there was no shirt on the Frenchman, but on his bare, yellow, thin body he was wearing a long, greasy waistcoat of flowered silk. The Frenchman was clearly afraid that the prisoners would laugh, looking at him, and he hastily thrust his head into the shirt. None of the prisoners said a word.

"See, it's just right," Platon kept saying as he straightened the shirt on him. The Frenchman, having put his head and arms through without raising his eyes, studied the shirt on himself and examined the stitching.

"What, little falcon, this is no sewing shop, we've got no real tools; they say you can't even kill a louse without the right gear," Platon said, smiling roundly and clearly rejoicing over his own work himself.

"*C'est bien, c'est bien, merci, mais vous devez avoir de la toile de reste?*"* said the Frenchman.

"It'll fit better if you put it on your body," said Karataev, continuing to rejoice over his work. "See, it'll be fine and nice . . ."

"*Merci, merci, mon vieux, le reste? . . .*" the Frenchman repeated, smiling, and taking out a banknote, he handed it to Karataev, "*mais le reste. . .*"†

Pierre saw that Platon did not want to understand what the Frenchman was saying and watched them without interfering. Karataev thanked him for the

*It's good, it's good, thanks, but you must have some cloth left over?
†Thanks, thanks, old man, but the leftovers? . . . but the leftovers . . .

money and went on admiring his work. The Frenchman insisted on the left-overs and asked Pierre to translate what he said.

"What does he need the leftovers for?" said Karataev. "They'd make us some grand foot cloths. Well, God be with him." And Karataev, with a suddenly changed, sad face, took the bundle of scraps from his bosom and handed it to the Frenchman without looking at him. "Ah, well!" said Karataev, and he went back inside. The Frenchman looked at the cloth, fell to thinking, glanced questioningly at Pierre, and it was as if Pierre's gaze said something to him.

"*Platoche, dites-donc, Platoche,*" the Frenchman, suddenly blushing, called out in a squeaky voice. "*Gardez pour vous,*"* he said, handed him the scraps, turned and walked away.

"So there you have it," said Karataev, shaking his head. "People say they're heathenish, but they've got souls, too. It's like the old folks say: a sweaty hand's generous, a dry's ungiving. He's naked himself, and here he's given them to me." Karataev, looking at the leftovers with a pensive smile, was silent for a time. "And, dear friend, they'll make the grandest foot cloths," he said and went back into the shed.

XII

Four weeks had gone by since Pierre was taken prisoner. Though the French had offered to transfer him from the soldiers' shed to the officers', he had stayed in the shed he had entered on the first day.

In devastated and burnt Moscow, Pierre experienced almost the final limits of privation that a man can endure; but, owing to his strong constitution and health, which he had not been conscious of until then, and especially owing to the fact that these privations came so imperceptibly that it was impossible to tell when they began, he bore his situation not only lightly, but joyfully. And precisely in that time he received the peace and contentment with himself which he had previously striven for in vain. In his life he had long sought in various directions for that peace, that harmony with himself, which had struck him so much in the soldiers during the battle of Borodino—he had sought it in philanthropy, in Masonry, in the distractions of social life, in wine, in a heroic deed of self-sacrifice, in romantic love for Natasha; he had sought it by way of thought, and all this seeking and trying had disappointed him. And, without thinking, he had received that peace and harmony with himself only through the horror of death, through privation, and through what he had understood in Karataev. It was as if those terrible moments he had lived through during the execution had washed for ever from his imagination and memory the anxious

*Platosh, I say, Platosh . . . Keep them for yourself.

thoughts and feelings that had once seemed important to him. No thoughts of Russia, or of the war, or of politics, or of Napoleon came to him. It was obvious to him that all this did not concern him, that he was not called upon and therefore could not judge about all that. "Russia and hot weather don't go together," he repeated Karataev's words, and those words strangely calmed him. His intention of killing Napoleon and his calculation of the kabbalistic number and the beast of the Apocalypse now seemed incomprehensible and even ridiculous to him. His anger with his wife and his anxiety about his name being disgraced now seemed to him not only insignificant, but amusing. What did he care about this woman leading the life she liked somewhere? What did it matter to anyone, especially to him, whether or not they found out that their prisoner's name was Count Bezukhov?

He now often recalled his conversation with Prince Andrei and fully agreed with him, only he understood Prince Andrei's thought slightly differently. Prince Andrei had thought and said that happiness can only be negative, but had said it with a shade of bitterness and irony. It was as if, in saying it, he was voicing another thought—that all striving for positive happiness had been put into us solely in order to torment us without giving satisfaction. But Pierre acknowledged the correctness of it without any second thoughts. The absence of suffering, the satisfaction of one's needs, and the resulting freedom to choose one's occupation, that is, one's way of life, now seemed to Pierre the highest and most unquestionable human happiness. Here, only now, did Pierre fully appreciate for the first time the enjoyment of food when he wanted to eat, of drink when he wanted to drink, of sleep when he wanted to sleep, of warmth when he was cold, of talking to someone when he wanted to talk and to hear a human voice. The satisfaction of his needs—for good food, cleanliness, freedom—now that he was deprived of them all, seemed perfect happiness to Pierre, and the choice of an occupation, that is, of a life, now, when that choice was so limited, seemed to him such an easy matter that he forgot that a superfluity of life's comforts destroys all the happiness of the satisfaction of one's needs, and that a greater freedom to choose one's occupation, the freedom which in this life was granted him by education, wealth, social position—precisely that freedom made the choice of an occupation insolubly difficult and destroyed the very need and possibility of an occupation.

All Pierre's dreams were now turned to the time when he would be free. And yet afterwards and for the whole of his life Pierre thought and spoke with rapture of that month of captivity, of those irrevocable, strong, and joyful sensations, and above all of that full peace of mind, that perfect inner freedom, which he experienced only in that time.

When, on the first day, having got up early in the morning, he went out of the shed at dawn and saw the at first dark cupolas and crosses of the Novodevichye Convent, saw the frosty dew on the dusty grass, saw the heights of the

Sparrow Hills, and the wooded bank meandering along the river and disappearing into the purple distance, when he sensed the touch of the fresh air and heard the noise of jackdaws flying across the field from Moscow, and when the light then suddenly sprayed from the east and the rim of the sun floated majestically from behind a cloud, and the cupolas, and the crosses, and the dew, and the distance, and the river, everything began to play in the joyful light—Pierre felt a new, never yet experienced feeling of the joy and strength of life.

And that feeling not only did not abandon him through all the time of his captivity, but, on the contrary, kept growing in him as the hardships of his situation increased.

That feeling of readiness for anything, of moral fitness, was maintained still more in Pierre by the high opinion of him which, soon after he entered the shed, established itself among his comrades. With his knowledge of languages, the respect the French showed him, the simplicity with which he gave everything he was asked for (he received an officer's three roubles a week), his strength, which he showed to the soldiers by pushing nails into the wall of the shed, the meekness he manifested in his relations with his comrades, his ability, which they found incomprehensible, to sit motionless and think, doing nothing, Pierre seemed something of a mysterious and supreme being to the soldiers. The very qualities which, in the world he formerly lived in, were, if not harmful, at least a hindrance to him—his strength, his scorn of life's comforts, his absent-mindedness, his simplicity—here, among these people, gave him almost the status of a hero. And Pierre felt that this view obliged him.

XIII

In the night of the sixth to seventh of October, a movement of departure began among the French: kitchens and sheds were broken up, carts were loaded, and troops and baggage trains moved off.

At seven o'clock in the morning, a French convoy, in field uniform, in shakos, with muskets, knapsacks, and enormous sacks, stood in front of the sheds, and lively French talk, interspersed with oaths, rolled along the whole line.

In the shed, everyone was ready, dressed, belted, shod, and only waiting for the order to leave. The sick soldier Sokolov, pale, thin, with blue circles round his eyes, sat in his place, the only one unshod and undressed, staring questioningly, with eyes prominent in his emaciated face, at his comrades, who paid no attention to him, moaning softly and regularly. Clearly, what made him moan was not so much his suffering—he was sick with bleeding diarrhoea—as fear and grief at being left alone.

Pierre, belted with a rope and shod in shoes Karataev had made for him out of leather from a tea sack that a Frenchman had brought to mend his soles, went over to the sick man and squatted down in front of him.

"Come now, Sokolov, they're not leaving altogether! They've got a hospital here. Maybe you'll be better off than we are," said Pierre.

"Oh, Lord! It's the death of me! Oh, Lord!" the soldier moaned more loudly.

"I'll ask them again right now," said Pierre, and he got up and went to the door of the shed. As he was going to the door, the corporal who had offered Pierre his pipe the day before was coming to it from outside with two soldiers. The corporal and the soldiers were in field uniform, with knapsacks and shakos with buckled chin straps, which altered their familiar faces.

The corporal was coming to the door to close it by order of his superiors. The prisoners had to be counted before being let out.

"*Caporal, que fera-t-on du malade?* . . ."* Pierre began; but as he was saying it, he wondered whether this was the corporal he knew or some other unknown man: so unlike himself the corporal was at that moment. Besides that, just as Pierre was saying it, there came the noise of drums on both sides. The corporal frowned at Pierre's words and, uttering a senseless oath, slammed the door. The shed became semi-dark; on both sides there was a sharp noise of drums that drowned out the sick man's moans.

"Here it is! . . . Here it is again!" Pierre said to himself, and an involuntary chill ran down his spine. In the corporal's altered face, in the sound of his voice, in the arousing and engulfing noise of the drums, Pierre recognized that mysterious, indifferent force that made people kill their own kind against their will, that force the effect of which he had seen during the execution. To fear, to try to escape that force, to turn with requests or admonitions to the people who served as its tools, was useless. Pierre knew that now. One had to wait and endure. Pierre did not go back to the sick man or turn to look at him. He stood by the door of the shed frowning silently.

When the door of the shed was opened and the prisoners, like a herd of sheep, crushing one another, crowded in the doorway, Pierre pushed his way ahead of them and went up to that same captain who, on the corporal's assurance, was ready to do anything for him. The captain was also in field uniform, and out of his cold face looked the same "it" that Pierre had recognized in the words of the corporal and the noise of the drums.

"*Filez, filez,*"† the captain kept saying, frowning sternly and looking at the prisoners crowding past him. Pierre knew his attempt would be in vain, but he went up to him.

"*Eh bien, qu'est-ce qu'il y a?*"‡ said the officer, looking at him coldly, as if not recognizing him. Pierre told him about the sick man.

*Corporal, what will be done with the sick man?
†Step lively, step lively.
‡Well, what is it?

"*Il pourra marcher, que diable!*"* said the captain. "*Filez, filez,*" he went on repeating without looking at Pierre.

"*Mais non, il est à l'agonie . . .*"† Pierre began.

"*Voulez-vous bien?!*"‡ the captain cried, frowning angrily.

Tra-ta-ta-tam, tam, tam, beat the drums. And Pierre realized that the mysterious force now fully possessed these men and that to say anything more now was useless.

The captive officers were separated from the soldiers and told to march in front. There were about thirty officers, Pierre among them, and about three hundred soldiers.

The captive officers released from other sheds were all strangers, were much better dressed than Pierre, and looked at him, in his footgear, with mistrust and estrangement. Not far from Pierre walked a fat major with a puffy, yellow, angry face, in a Kazan dressing gown tied round with a towel, who was clearly held in general respect by his fellow prisoners. He kept one hand with a tobacco pouch in his bosom, the other he rested on his long-stemmed chibouk. The major, huffing and puffing, grumbled and was angry with everybody, because it seemed to him that everybody was pushing him and everybody was in a hurry, when there was nowhere to hurry to, that everybody was surprised at something, when there was nothing to be surprised at. Another, a small, thin officer, kept addressing everybody, making conjectures about where they were going now and how far they would manage to get that day. An official in felt boots and a commissariat uniform kept running off to different sides, looking at burnt-down Moscow, loudly reporting his observations on what had burned down and which was this or that part of Moscow that came into sight. A third officer, of Polish origin judging by his accent, argued with the commissariat official, proving to him that he was mistaken in identifying the neighbourhoods of Moscow.

"What's there to argue about?" the major said angrily. "St. Nicholas or St. Vlas, it's all the same. You can see it's all burned down, and that's the end of it . . . Why are you pushing, as if there's not road enough," he turned gruffly to a man walking behind him, who had not pushed him at all.

"Ai, ai, ai, what have they done!" the voices of the prisoners were heard, nevertheless, now on one side, now on another, as they looked at the charred ruins. "Zamoskvorechye, and Zubovo, and in the Kremlin, look, half of it's missing . . . I told you it was the whole of Zamoskvorechye, and so it is."

"Well, you know it's burned down, so what's there to talk about!" said the major.

---

*He can walk, devil take it!
†No, he is in the last agony.
‡If you please?!

Going past the church in Khamovniki (one of the few unburnt neighbour-hoods of Moscow), the whole crowd of prisoners suddenly pressed to one side, and exclamations of horror and revulsion were heard.

"See, the scoundrels! Real heathens! Yes, dead, he's dead . . . Smeared with something."

Pierre also moved towards the church, where that which had caused such exclamations was, and vaguely saw something propped against the church fence. From the words of his comrades, who could see better than he, he learned that this something was the corpse of a man stood upright against the fence and his face smeared with soot.

"*Marchez, sacré nom . . . Filez . . . trente mille diables! . . .*"* cursed the convoy guards, and with renewed animosity the French soldiers used their swords to disperse the crowd of prisoners looking at the dead man.

XIV

Through the lanes of Khamovniki, the prisoners walked alone with their convoy, and the carts and wagons belonging to the convoy followed behind; but, coming out to the supply storehouses, they found themselves in the middle of a huge, compactly moving artillery train, interspersed with private carts.

By the bridge they all stopped, waiting for those who were ahead to move on. From the bridge the prisoners could see endless lines of moving carts behind and ahead of them. To the right, where the Kaluga road curved round the Neskuchny Garden, endless lines of troops and carts stretched out, disappearing into the distance. These were the troops of Beauharnais's corps, which had started out before all the rest; behind, along the embankment and across the Kamenny Bridge, stretched the troops and trains of Ney.

The troops of Davout, to which the prisoners belonged, went across the Krymsky Ford and some had already entered Kaluga Street. But the trains were so strung out that the last trains of Beauharnais had not yet come out of Moscow onto Kaluga Street, and the head of Ney's troops was already leaving Bolshaya Ordynka.

Having crossed the Krymsky Ford, the prisoners moved on several steps, then stopped, then moved on again, and on all sides the people and vehicles grew more and more dense. It took them an hour to walk the several hundred steps that separated the bridge from Kaluga Street, and, having reached the square where Zamoskvoretskaya and Kaluga Streets met, the prisoners, pressed together in a mass, stopped and stood at that intersection for several hours. On all sides could be heard the rumble of wheels, incessant as the roar

*March, damn it . . . Step lively . . . thirty thousand devils! . . .

of the sea, and the tramp of feet, and incessant angry shouts and curses. Pierre stood pressed to the wall of a charred house, listening to that sound, which merged in his imagination with the sounds of a drum.

Several captive officers, in order to see better, climbed the wall of the charred house by which Pierre was standing.

"People! So many people! . . . Even the cannon are piled high! Look at those furs . . ." they said. "See what the vultures have looted . . . Behind there, on the cart . . . It's from an icon, by God. Must be Germans. And our peasants, too, by God! . . . Ah, the scoundrels! . . . See, he's loaded himself down, he can hardly walk! They even stole a droshky—really! . . . See, that one's sitting on some trunks. Good God! . . . They're fighting! . . ."

"That's it, in the mug, right in the mug! Like this we'll be waiting till evening. Look, look . . . that must be Napoleon's. See, what horses! with monograms and a crown. It's a folding house. He's dropped a sack and doesn't see it. Fighting again . . . A woman with a baby, and not bad-looking. Oh, yes, of course they'll let you pass . . . Look, there's no end to it. Russian wenches, by God, wenches! Sitting so comfortably in their caleches!"

Again a wave of general curiosity, as by the church in Khamovniki, pushed all the prisoners towards the road, and Pierre, thanks to his height, saw over the heads of the others what had attracted the prisoners' curiosity. In three carriages, mixed up among the ammunition caissons, sitting tightly packed together, rode women decked out in bright colours, heavily rouged, shouting something in squeaky voices.

From the moment Pierre recognized the appearance of the mysterious force, nothing seemed strange or frightful to him: not the corpse smeared with soot for the fun of it, not these women hurrying somewhere, not the charred ruins of Moscow. Everything that Pierre now saw made almost no impression on him—as if his soul, preparing for a difficult struggle, refused to receive impressions that might weaken it.

The train with the women passed by. Behind them again drew carts, soldiers, wagons, soldiers, flatbeds, carriages, soldiers, caissons, soldiers, and occasionally women.

Pierre did not see people separately, but saw their movement.

All these people and horses were as if driven by some invisible force. All of them, in the course of the hour during which Pierre observed them, came sailing out of various streets with one and the same desire to move on quickly; all of them, in the same way, running into the others, began to get angry and fight; white teeth were bared; brows frowned, the same oaths were exchanged, and all the faces had the same dashingly resolute and cruelly cold expression that had struck Pierre in the morning, at the sound of the drum, on the corporal's face.

Towards evening the leader of the convoy gathered his crew and with shouts and quarrels squeezed into the train, and the prisoners, surrounded on all sides, came out onto the Kaluga road.

They marched very quickly, without resting, and stopped only when the sun began to go down. The carts all drew up close to each other, and people began to prepare for the night. Everyone seemed angry and displeased. For a long time, curses, spiteful cries, and the sounds of fighting came from all sides. A carriage that was driving behind the convoy pulled up close to a convoy wagon and punched its shaft through it. Several soldiers came running to the wagon from different sides; some beat the horses hitched to the carriage on their heads, trying to get them to turn away, others fought among themselves, and Pierre saw that one German was badly wounded on the head by a sword.

It seemed that these men, once they stopped in the middle of a field in the chill twilight of the autumn evening, all experienced the same feeling of unpleasant awakening from the haste and headlong movement somewhere that had come over them at the start. Having stopped, it was as if they all realized that they did not yet know where they were going, and that in this movement there would be much that was painful and difficult.

At this halt the convoy treated the prisoners still worse than at the start. For the first time, the prisoners received their ration of meat in horseflesh.

From the officers to the last soldier, there could be noticed in each of them a personal animosity, as it were, against each of the prisoners, which quite unexpectedly replaced the former friendly relations.

This animosity increased still more when, on taking count of the prisoners, it turned out that, during the bustle as they were leaving Moscow, one Russian soldier, pretending to have a stomach ache, had escaped. Pierre heard how a Frenchman had beaten a Russian soldier for straying too far from the road, and heard his friend the captain reprimand the sergeant for the Russian prisoner's escape and threaten to court-martial him. To the sergeant's excuse that the soldier was ill and could not walk, the captain said that the order was to shoot those who lagged behind. Pierre felt that the fatal force which had crushed him during the execution, and which had been imperceptible during his imprisonment, now once again took possession of his existence. It frightened him; but he felt how, as the fatal force made efforts to crush him, a force of life independent of it arose and grew stronger in his soul.

Pierre ate his supper of rye-meal soup with horsemeat and talked with his comrades.

Neither Pierre nor any of his comrades spoke of what they had seen in Moscow, or of the rough treatment of the French, or of the instructions to shoot that had been announced to them: as if to ward off the worsening situation, they were all especially animated and cheerful. People talked of personal memories, of funny scenes witnessed during the march, and changed the subject when it came to the present situation.

The sun had set long ago. Bright stars lit up here and there; red as fire, the glow of the rising full moon spread on the edge of the horizon, and the enormous red ball wavered astonishingly in the greyish haze. It was growing light. The evening was already over, but night had not yet begun. Pierre got up and walked away from his new comrades, between the campfires, to the other side of the road, where he was told the captive soldiers were camped. He wanted to talk with them. On the road a French sentry stopped him and told him to go back.

Pierre went back, but not to the campfire, to his comrades, but to an unhitched cart, where there was no one. Crossing his legs and lowering his head, he sat on the cold ground by the wheel of the cart and stayed there motionless for a long time, thinking. More than an hour went by. No one disturbed Pierre. Suddenly he burst into his fat, good-natured laugh, so loudly that people from different sides turned in astonishment towards this strange, evidently solitary laughter.

"Ha, ha, ha," laughed Pierre. And he said aloud to himself: "The soldier wouldn't let me go. They caught me, they locked me up. They're holding me prisoner. Who, me? Me? Me—my immortal soul! Ha, ha, ha! . . . Ha, ha, ha! . . ." he laughed, with tears brimming his eyes.

Some man got up and came to see what the strange, big man was laughing about by himself. Pierre stopped laughing, got up, went further away from the curious fellow, and looked around.

The enormous, endless bivouac, noisy earlier with the crackling of campfires and the talking of men, was growing still; the red flames of the campfires were dying out and turning pale. The full moon stood high in the bright sky. Forests and fields, invisible earlier beyond the territory of the camp, now opened out in the distance. And further beyond these forests and fields could be seen the bright, wavering, endless distance calling one to itself. Pierre looked into the sky, into the depths of the retreating, twinkling stars. "And all this is mine, and all this is in me, and all this is me!" thought Pierre. "And all this they've caught and put in a shed and boarded it up!" He smiled and went to his comrades to lie down and sleep.

XV

In the first days of October, another envoy came to Kutuzov with a letter from Napoleon and an offer of peace, deceptively addressed from Moscow, while Napoleon was already not far ahead of Kutuzov on the old Kaluga road. Kutuzov's reply to this letter was the same as to the first, sent with Lauriston: he said there could be no question of peace.

Soon after that, information was received from Dorokhov's partisan detachment, moving about to the left of Tarutino, that troops had appeared in Fomin-skoe, that those troops consisted of Broussier's division, and that that division, separated from the other troops, could easily be exterminated. Again the sol-diers and officers called for action. The staff generals, stirred by the memory of the easy victory at Tarutino, insisted that Kutuzov act upon Dorokhov's sugges-tion. Kutuzov did not consider any offensive necessary. What happened was between the two, as it was bound to be: a small detachment was sent to Fomin-skoe to attack Broussier.

By a strange chance, this assignment—the most difficult and important, as it turned out later—fell to Dokhturov, that same modest little Dokhturov, whom no one has ever described to us as drawing up plans of battle, flying at the head of regiments, throwing crosses on batteries, and so on, who was considered and called irresolute and imperceptive, that same Dokhturov whom, during all the wars between the Russians and the French, from Austerlitz to the year thir-teen, we find in command wherever the situation is difficult. At Austerlitz, he is the last to remain at the dam of Augesd, gathering the regiments, saving what-ever is possible, when all are fleeing and perishing and there is not one general left in the rear guard. Sick, in a fever, he goes to Smolensk with twenty thou-sand men to defend the city against the entire Napoleonic army. In Smolensk, he has just dozed off by the Molokhovsky gate in a paroxysm of fever, when he is awakened by a cannonade aimed at Smolensk, and Smolensk holds out for the whole day. In the battle of Borodino, when Bagration has been killed and the troops of our left flank have been wiped out in a proportion of nine to one, and the full force of the French artillery is directed there—none other than the irresolute and imperceptive Dokhturov is sent there, and Kutuzov, having first sent someone else, hastily corrects his mistake. And quiet little Dokhturov goes there, and Borodino is the best glory of the Russian army. And many heroes have been described for us in verse and prose, but there is hardly a word about Dokhturov.

Again Dokhturov is sent to Fominskoe, and from there to Maly Yaroslavets, to the place where the last battle with the French was fought, to the place from which the destruction of the French army obviously begins, and again many geniuses and heroes are described for us from that period of the campaign, but of Dokhturov not a word, or very little, and that questionable. This silence about Dokhturov is the most obvious proof of his merit.

To a man who does not understand the workings of a machine, it naturally seems, when he sees it in operation, that the most important part of the machine is the chip of wood that accidentally got into it and is tossed about in it, interfering with its working. A man who does not know the construction of the machine cannot understand that it is not this harmful and interfering chip of wood, but that little transmission gear turning noiselessly that is one of the most essential parts of the machine.

On the tenth of October, the same day that Dokhturov got halfway to Fomin-skoe and halted in the village of Aristovo, preparing to carry out with precision the order he had been given, the entire French army, having reached in its con-vulsive movement the position of Murat, seemingly in order to give battle, sud-denly, without any reason, turned left onto the new Kaluga road and began to enter Fominskoe, which had previously been occupied only by Broussier. At that time Dokhturov had under his command, besides Dorokhov, the two small detachments of Figner and Seslavin.

In the evening of the eleventh of October, Seslavin came to the headquarters in Aristovo with a French guard who had been taken prisoner. The prisoner said that the troops that had just entered Fominskoe were the vanguard of the whole big army, that Napoleon was there, that the whole army had already left Moscow five days ago. That same evening a servant from Borovsk told how he had seen an enormous army enter the town. The Cossacks of Dorokhov's detachment reported that they had seen French guards going down the road to Borovsk. From all this information it became obvious that, where they had thought to find one division, there was now the whole French army, coming from Moscow in an unexpected direction—down the old Kaluga road. Dokh-turov did not want to undertake anything, since it was not clear to him now what his duty was. He had been ordered to attack Fominskoe. But earlier only Broussier had been in Fominskoe, now there was the whole French army. Ermolov wanted to act at his own discretion, but Dokhturov insisted that they had to have an order from his serenity. It was decided to send a report to the staff.

For that a sensible officer was chosen, Bolkhovitinov, who, besides the writ-ten report, was to recount the whole matter in his own words. It was past eleven when Bolkhovitinov, having received the envelope and verbal instruc-tions, galloped to staff headquarters, accompanied by a Cossack and spare horses.

XVI

The night was dark, warm, autumnal. Light rain was falling for the fourth day. Having changed horses twice and galloped twenty miles in an hour and a half over a muddy, sticky road, Bolkhovitinov reached Letashevka before two o'clock in the morning. Dismounting at a cottage where a sign reading "Staff Headquarters" was hung on a wattle fence, he left his horse and went into the dark front hall.

"The general on duty, quickly! A matter of great importance!" he said to someone who was getting up and puffing in the darkness of the front hall.

"He was very sick in the evening, it's the third night he hasn't slept," the solicitous voice of an orderly whispered. "Better wake the captain first."

"A very important message from General Dokhturov," said Bolkhovitinov, feeling his way to the door and opening it. The orderly went ahead of him and began waking someone up:

"Your Honour, Your Honour—a coullier."

"What, what? From whom?" said someone's sleepy voice.

"From Dokhturov and Alexei Petrovich. Napoleon is in Fominskoe," said Bolkhovitinov, not seeing in the darkness who was questioning him, but supposing by the voice that it was not Konovnitsyn.

The awakened man yawned and stretched.

"I really don't want to wake him up," he said, feeling for something. "He's quite ill! Maybe it's just rumours."

"Here is the report," said Bolkhovitinov. "The order was to hand it at once to the general on duty."

"Wait, I'll light a candle. You always stick it away somewhere, curse you," the stretching man said, addressing the orderly. It was Shcherbinin, Konovnitsyn's adjutant. "I've found it, I've found it," he added.

The orderly was striking a light, Shcherbinin was feeling for the candlestick.

"Ah, loathesome creatures," he said with revulsion.

By the light of the sparks, Bolkhovitinov saw the young face of Shcherbinin with the candle and in the front corner a still-sleeping man. This was Konovnitsyn.

When the sulphur crumbs caught fire from the tinder, giving first a blue, then a red flame, Shcherbinin lit a tallow candle, causing the cockroaches that were gnawing on it to flee from the candlestick, and looked at the messenger. Bolkhovitinov was all covered with mud, and, wiping it with his sleeve, he smeared it over his face.

"Whose report is it?" asked Shcherbinin, taking the envelope.

"The information is correct," said Bolkhovitinov. "The prisoners, the Cossacks, and the scouts all unanimously bear out the same thing."

"No help for it, we'll have to wake him up," said Shcherbinin, getting up and going over to the man in the nightcap, covered with a greatcoat. "Pyotr Petrovich!" he said. Konovnitsyn did not stir. "To staff headquarters!" he said, smiling, knowing that these words were sure to wake him up. And indeed, the head in the nightcap rose at once. The handsome, firm face of Konovnitsyn, with its feverishly inflamed cheeks, still kept for a moment an expression of dreamy sleep, far from the present situation, but then he suddenly gave a start: his face assumed his usual calm and firm expression.

"Well, what is it? From whom?" he asked unhurriedly but at once, blinking from the light. Listening to the officer's report, Konovnitsyn opened the letter and read it. Having barely read it, he lowered his feet in woollen stockings to the beaten-earth floor and began putting his boots on. Then he took off his nightcap, combed his side-whiskers, and put on his peaked cap.

"Were you quick in getting here? Let's go to his serenity."

Konovnitsyn realized at once that the news brought to him was of great importance and brooked no delay. Whether it was good or bad he did not consider or ask himself. That did not interest him. He looked at the whole business of war not with his mind, not with his reason, but with something else. There was a deep, unspoken conviction in his soul that all would be well, but that it was not to be believed, still less spoken about, and that he had only to do his duty. And this duty of his he did, giving all his forces to it.

Pyotr Petrovich Konovnitsyn, like Dokhturov, was put on the list of the so-called heroes of the year twelve—the Barclays, the Raevskys, the Ermolovs, the Platovs, the Miloradovichs—merely out of propriety, as it were; like Dokhturov, he had the reputation of a man of quite limited abilities and knowledge; and, like Dokhturov, Konovnitsyn never made plans of battles, but was always where things were most difficult; since his appointment as general on duty, he had always slept with the door open, giving instructions that every messenger should wake him up; in battle he was always under fire, so that Kutuzov reproached him for it and was afraid to send him in; and, like Dokhturov, he was one of those inconspicuous gears which, without clatter or noise, constitute the most essential part of the machine.

Coming out of the cottage into the damp, dark night, Konovnitsyn frowned, partly from an increased pain in his head, partly from the unpleasant thought that came to him about how that whole nest of influential staff people would now get stirred up at this news, especially Bennigsen, who, after Tarutino, was at daggers drawn with Kutuzov; how they would suggest, argue, order, cancel. And this presentiment was unpleasant to him, though he knew it was impossible to do without it.

In fact, Toll, to whom he came to report the fresh news, at once began laying out his considerations to the general who lived with him, and Konovnitsyn, who listened silently and wearily, reminded him that they must go to his serenity.

XVII

Kutuzov, like all old people, slept little at night. During the day he often dozed off unexpectedly, but at night, lying on his bed without undressing, he was for the most part sleepless and thinking.

So he was lying in bed now, propping his big, heavy, disfigured head on his plump hand and thinking, his one open eye peering into the darkness.

Since Bennigsen, who corresponded with the sovereign and had the most power on the staff, had been avoiding him, Kutuzov had been more at ease with regard to the fact that he and his troops would not be forced again to take part in useless offensive action. The lesson of the battle of Tarutino and its eve, painfully memorable to Kutuzov, should also have its effect, he thought.

"They should understand that we can only lose by going on the offensive. Patience and time, these are my mighty warriors!" thought Kutuzov. He knew that an apple should not be picked while it is green. It will fall by itself when it is ripe, but if you pick it green, you will spoil the apple and the tree, and you will set your teeth on edge. Like an experienced hunter, he knew that the beast was wounded, wounded as badly as the whole Russian force could wound it, but whether mortally or not was still an unclarified question. Now, by the dispatches of Lauriston and Barthélemy, and by the reports of the partisans, Kutuzov almost knew that it was mortally wounded. But more proofs were needed; he had to wait.

"They want to run and look at how they've killed him. Wait, you'll see. All this manoeuvreing, all this advancing!" he thought. "What for? All to distinguish themselves. As if there's something amusing in fighting. They're just like children whom you cannot get to tell you how the thing went, because all they want is to prove that they know how to fight. But that's not the point now.

"And what artful manoeuvres all of them suggest to me! It seems to them that if they think up two or three cases" (the general plan from Petersburg came to his mind), "they've thought of them all. But there's no counting them!"

The unresolved question of whether the wound inflicted at Borodino was mortal or not had been hanging over Kutuzov's head for a whole month. On the one hand, the French had occupied Moscow. On the other hand, Kutuzov felt unquestionably with his whole being that that terrible blow, in which he together with all the Russian people had strained all his forces, must be mortal. But in any case, proofs were needed, and he had been waiting for them for a month already, and the more time that passed, the more impatient he became. Lying on his bed during his sleepless nights, he did the same thing that all these young generals were doing, the same thing for which he reproached them. He thought up all the possible occasions in which this certain, already accomplished destruction of Napoleon could be manifested. He thought of them all, just as the young men did, but with the difference that he based no suppositions on them and saw not two or three of them but thousands. The longer he thought, the more of them he imagined. He thought up all sorts of movements of the Napoleonic army, as a whole or in parts—towards Petersburg, against him, skirting round him; thought up as well the case (which he was most afraid of) that Napoleon would start fighting him with his own weapon, that he would remain in Moscow waiting for him. Kutuzov even thought up the movement of the Napoleonic army back towards Medyn and Yukhnov; but the one thing he was unable to foresee was the thing that happened, that insane, convulsive rushing about of Napoleon's troops in the course of the first eleven days after leaving Moscow—a rushing about which made possible what Kutuzov did not yet dare to think of at that time: the total extermination of the French. Dorokhov's reports about Broussier's division, the news from the partisans about the distress of Napoleon's army, the rumours about preparations for abandoning Moscow—everything confirmed the supposition that the French army was beaten and preparing to flee; but these were only suppositions, which seemed important to the young men, but not to Kutuzov. With his sixty years of experience, he knew what weight should be ascribed to rumours, knew how capable people who desire something are of grouping all the information in such a way that it seems to confirm what they desire, and knew how willingly on such occasions they omit all that contradicts it. And the more Kutuzov desired it, the less he allowed himself to believe it. This question occupied all his inner forces. All the rest was for him only the habitual acting out of life. His conversations with the staff, his letters to Mme de Staël,[9] which he wrote from Tarutino, his reading of novels, distribution of rewards, correspondence with Petersburg, and so on, were the same habitual acting out of and submission to life. But the destruction of the French, foreseen by him alone, was his heartfelt, his sole desire.

On the night of the eleventh of October, he was lying propped on his hand and thinking about that.

There was a stir in the next room, and the footsteps of Toll, Konovnitsyn, and Bolkhovitinov were heard.

"Hey, who's there? Come in, come in! What's new?" the field marshal called to them.

While the footman was lighting a candle, Toll told him the content of the news.

"Who brought it?" asked Kutuzov, with a face that struck Toll, once the candle was lit, by its cold sternness.

"There can be no doubt, Your Serenity."

"Call him, call him here!"

Kutuzov sat up, one leg lowered from the bed and his big belly leaning on the other, bent leg. His good eye was narrowed the better to see the messenger, as if he wanted to read in his features what so preoccupied him.

"Tell me, tell me, friend," he said to Bolkhovitinov in his quiet, old man's voice, closing the shirt that had opened on his chest. "Come, come closer. What's the word you've brought me? Eh? Has Napoleon left Moscow? Truly? Eh?"

Bolkhovitinov first reported in detail what he had been ordered to.

"Speak, speak quicker, don't torment my soul," Kutuzov interrupted him.

Bolkhovitinov told him everything and fell silent, awaiting orders. Toll began to say something, but Kutuzov interrupted him. He wanted to say something, but suddenly his face shrivelled, wrinkled; waving his hand at Toll, he turned the other way, to the corner of the room with its blackened icons.

"Lord, my Creator! Thou hast heeded our prayer . . ." he said in a trembling voice, clasping his hands. "Russia is saved. I thank Thee, Lord!" And he wept.

XVIII

From the time of this news until the end of the campaign, Kutuzov's entire activity consists only of restraining his troops, by power, cunning, and entreaties, from useless attacks, manoeuvres, and clashes with the perishing enemy. Dokhturov goes to Maloyaroslavets, but Kutuzov hangs back with the whole army and gives orders to vacate Kaluga and retreat beyond it, which seems quite possible to him.

Kutuzov retreats everywhere, but the enemy, without waiting for him to retreat, flees back in the opposite direction.

Napoleon's historians describe to us his skilful manoeuvre towards Tarutino and Maloyaroslavets and make conjectures as to what would have happened if Napoleon had managed to penetrate to the rich southern provinces.

But, not to speak of the fact that nothing prevented Napoleon from going to those southern provinces (since the Russian army gave way to him), the historians forget that Napoleon's army could not have been saved by anything, because by then it already bore within itself the conditions of inevitable destruction. Why should this army, which found abundant provisions in Moscow and could not keep them, but trampled them underfoot, this army which, on coming to Smolensk, did not distribute provisions, but looted them—why should this army have been able to set itself to rights in Kaluga province, populated by the same Russians as in Moscow and where fire had the same property of burning up what was set aflame?

This army could not set itself to rights anywhere. Since the battle of Borodino and the looting of Moscow, it had borne within itself, as it were, the chemical conditions of its decomposition.

The men of this former army fled with their leaders, not knowing where themselves, wishing (Napoleon and every soldier) for only one thing: to extricate themselves personally as quickly as possible from the hopeless situation which they were all, albeit dimly, aware of.

It was only because of this, at the council in Maloyaroslavets, when the generals, pretending to confer, offered various opinions, that the last opinion, given by the simple soldier Mouton,[10] who said what they all thought, that they only had to get away as quickly as possible, sealed all their lips, and no one, not even Napoleon, could say anything against this truth which they were all aware of.

But though they all knew they had to get away, there still remained the shame of the awareness that they had to flee. And they needed an external push which would overcome that shame. And that push came at the right moment. It was what the French called *le Hourra de l'Empereur.*

The day after the council, early in the morning, pretending that he wanted to inspect the troops and the field of the past and future battles, Napoleon rode with his suite of marshals and an escort through the middle of the line of deployed troops. Some Cossacks poking around for booty ran into the emperor and nearly caught him. If the Cossacks did not catch Napoleon that time, what saved him was the very thing that destroyed the French: the plunder which, at Tarutino and here, the Cossacks fell upon, letting the men go. Paying no attention to Napoleon, they fell upon the booty, and Napoleon managed to get away.

If *les enfants du Don** could all but catch the emperor himself in the middle of his army, it was clear that there was nothing else to do but flee as quickly as possible down the nearest known road. Napoleon, with his forty-year-old's pot-belly, feeling himself no longer as nimble and brave as before, understood that hint. And under the influence of the scare the Cossacks had given him, he promptly agreed with Mouton and gave, as the historians say, the order to retreat back to the Smolensk road.

That Napoleon agreed with Mouton and that the troops marched back does not prove that he ordered it, but that the forces acting upon the whole army, in the sense of directing it down the Mozhaisk road, acted simultaneously upon Napoleon.

XIX

When a man finds himself in motion, he always thinks up a goal for that motion. In order to walk a thousand miles, a man needs to think that there is something good at the end of those thousand miles. One needs a vision of the promised land in order to have the strength to move.

The promised land for the advancing French was Moscow; for the retreat it was their native land. But their native land was too far away, and a man walking a thousand miles must say to himself, forgetting the final goal: "Today I will walk thirty miles to a resting place and spend the night," and during this first march, the resting place overshadows the final goal and concentrates all desires and hopes on itself. The yearnings manifested in a separate man are always magnified in a crowd.

For the French going back down the old Smolensk road, the final goal of their native land was too distant, and the nearest goal, the one towards which all their desires and hopes, increased in great proportion in the crowd, were directed—was Smolensk. Not because the men knew that there were abundant provisions and fresh troops in Smolensk, not because they were told so

*The children of the Don.

(on the contrary, the higher ranks of the army and Napoleon himself knew that there were few provisions there), but because that alone could give them the strength to move and to endure the present privations. They, both those who knew and those who did not know, equally deceiving themselves, yearned for Smolensk as for the promised land.

Coming out onto the high road, the French, with striking energy, with unheard-of speed, ran towards their imagined goal. Besides the cause of a general yearning that bound the crowds of the French into a single whole and endowed them with a certain energy, there was yet another cause that bound them together. This cause consisted in their numbers. Their enormous mass itself, as in the physical law of gravity, drew the separate atoms of men to it. Their mass of a hundred thousand men moved like a whole state.

Each man of them desired only one thing—to give himself up as a prisoner, to be delivered from all horrors and misfortunes. But, on the one hand, the force of their general yearning towards the goal of Smolensk drew each of them in one and the same direction; on the other hand, it was impossible for a corps to give itself up to a company, and though the French used every opportunity to get rid of each other and on every decent pretext gave themselves up as prisoners, those pretexts did not always occur. Their very numbers and compact, quick movement deprived them of that possibility and made it not only difficult but impossible for the Russians to stop that movement, to which all the energy of the mass of the French was directed. Beyond a certain limit, the mechanical rending of the body could not hasten the ongoing process of decomposition.

It is impossible to melt a ball of snow instantly. There exists a certain time limit before which no efforts at heating can melt the snow. On the contrary, the greater the heat, the more solid the remaining snow becomes.

Of the Russian military leaders, no one but Kutuzov understood that. When the direction of the flight of the French army down the Smolensk road became definite, what Konovnitsyn had foreseen on the night of the eleventh of October began to come true. All the higher ranks in the army wanted to distinguish themselves, to cut off, to intercept, to capture, to overrun the French, and they all called for an offensive.

Kutuzov alone used all his powers (those powers are not very great in any commander in chief) to oppose an offensive.

He could not tell them what we say now: why battles, why the blocking of roads, and the loss of our own men, and the inhuman finishing off of the unfortunate? Why all that, when from Moscow to Vyazma a third of that army melted away without any battle? But, guided by his old man's wisdom, he told them what they could understand—he spoke to them of the golden bridge, and they laughed at him, slandered him, stormed and raged, and swaggered over the slain beast.

At Vyazma, Ermolov, Miloradovich, Platov, and others, finding themselves in proximity to the French, could not restrain their desire to cut off and overrun two French corps. To inform Kutuzov of their intention, they sent him an envelope containing, instead of a message, a blank sheet of paper.

And however much Kutuzov tried to hold the troops back, our troops attacked, trying to block the way. Infantry regiments, as it was told, went into the attack with music and beating drums, and destroyed and lost thousands of men.

But as for cutting off—they cut off and overran nobody. And the French army, having drawn up more tightly in the face of danger, continued, melting away regularly, along their same fatal path to Smolensk.

Part Three

I

The battle of Borodino, with the subsequent occupation of Moscow by the French and their flight without any new battles, is one of the most instructive phenomena in history.

All historians agree that the external activity of states and nations, in their conflicts among themselves, is expressed in wars; that the political power of states and nations increases or decreases owing directly to their greater or lesser military successes.

However strange the historical descriptions of how some king or emperor, having quarrelled with another emperor or king, raised an army, fought with the army of the enemy, defeated it, killed three, five, ten thousand men, and as a result subjugated a state and a whole nation of several millions; however incomprehensible the reason why the defeat of one army, one hundredth of all the forces of the nation, made the nation submit—all the facts of history (insofar as it is known to us) confirm the correctness of the statement that the greater or lesser successes of the army of one nation against the army of another nation are the cause or at least the essential sign of an increase or decrease in the strength of the nation. An army wins a victory, and at once the rights of the victorious nation increase, to the detriment of the vanquished one. An army suffers a defeat, and at once, according to the degree of the defeat, the nation is deprived of rights, and in case of a total defeat of their army, is totally subjugated.

So it has been (according to history) from the most ancient times to the present. All the wars of Napoleon serve as a confirmation of this rule. To the degree that the Austrian army is defeated, Austria is deprived of her rights, and the rights and strength of France increase. The victories of the French at Jena and Auerstädt destroy the independent existence of Prussia.

But suddenly, in the year 1812, the French win a victory at Moscow, Moscow is taken, and following that, with no new battles, it is not Russia that ceases to exist, but the six-hundred-thousand-man French army ceases to exist, and after that Napoleonic France. To stretch the facts to fit the rules of history by saying that the battlefield of Borodino remained Russian, that there were battles after Moscow which destroyed Napoleon's army—is impossible.

After the victory of the French at Borodino, not only was there no general battle, but there was even none in any way significant, yet the French army ceased to exist. What does it mean? If it was an example from the history of China, we might say that it was not a historical event (the historians' loophole when something does not fit their yardstick); if it was a matter of a brief clash involving a small number of troops, we could take it for an exceptional phenomenon; but this event took place before the eyes of our fathers, for whom the question of the life or death of the fatherland was decided, and this war was the greatest of all known wars . . .

The period in the campaign of 1812 from the battle of Borodino to the expulsion of the French proved that a battle won is not only not the cause of a conquest, but is not even an invariable sign of conquest; it proved that the force that decides the destiny of nations lies not in conquerors, not even in armies and battles, but in something else.

French historians, describing the situation of the French army before leaving Moscow, affirm that everything in the Grand Army was in order, except the cavalry, the artillery, and the transport, and there was also no forage to feed the horses and cattle. There was no help for this calamity, because the muzhiks of the region burned their hay rather than give it to the French.

The battle won did not bring the usual results, because the muzhiks Karp and Vlas, who, after the French moved on, came to Moscow with their carts to loot the city and in general did not manifest any personal heroic sentiments, and all the countless number of muzhiks like them, did not bring hay to Moscow for the good money they were offered, but burned it.

Let us imagine two men who came with swords to fight a duel by all the rules of the art of fencing: the fighting went on for quite a long time; suddenly one of the adversaries, feeling himself wounded, realizing that it was not a joking matter, but something that concerned his life, threw down his sword and, picking up the first club he found, started brandishing it. But let us imagine that the man who so sensibly employed the best and simplest means to attain his goal, inspired at the same time by the traditions of chivalry, wished to conceal the essence of the matter, and insisted that he won the sword fight by all the rules of the art. One can imagine what confusion and obscurity would come from such a description of the duel that took place.

The French were the fencer who demanded a fight by the rules of the art; the Russians were the adversary who dropped his sword and picked up a club; those who attempt to explain everything by the rules of fencing are the historians who have written about this event.

From the time of the burning of Smolensk, a war began that did not fit any of the former traditions of war. The burning of towns and villages, the retreats after battles, the blow struck at Borodino and then another retreat, the abandoning and burning of Moscow, the hunt for marauders, the cutting off of transport, the partisan war—these were all deviations from the rules.

Napoleon sensed that, and from the moment when he stopped in Moscow, in the correct position of a fencer, and instead of his adversary's sword, saw a club raised over him, he never ceased complaining to Kutuzov and the emperor Alexander that the war was being conducted against all the rules (as if there existed some sort of rules for killing people). Despite the complaints of the French about the non-fulfilment of the rules, despite the fact that highly placed Russians thought it shameful for some reason to fight with a club and wanted to follow the rules and assume a position *en quatre* or *en tierce,* make a skilful thrust *en prime,* and so on—the club of a national war was raised with all its terrible and majestic power, and, not asking about anyone's tastes or rules, with stupid simplicity, but with expediency, not sorting anything out, rose and fell, and hammered on the French until the whole invasion was destroyed.

And blessed is that nation which, not like the French in the year 1813, who saluted by all the rules of the art and, turning the sword hilt first, graciously and courteously handed it to the magnanimous victor, but which, in the moment of trial, not asking how others have acted according to the rules on such occasions, simply and easily raises the first club that comes along and hammers with it until the feeling of outrage and revenge in its soul gives place to contempt and pity.

II

One of the most palpable and advantageous deviations from the so-called rules of war is the action of scattered people against people pressed together in a mass. This kind of action always emerges in a war that acquires a national character. These actions consist in the fact that, instead of a crowd opposing a crowd, people scatter, attack singly, and flee as soon as large forces attack them, then attack again as soon as the opportunity arises. This was done by the guerrillas in Spain;[1] it was done by the mountaineers in the Caucasus; it was done by the Russians in the year 1812.

Warfare of this kind has been named partisan warfare, and those who named it supposed that by doing so they were explaining its meaning. Yet this kind of warfare not only does not fit into any rules, but is directly opposed to a tactical rule that is well-known and acknowledged as infallible. This rule says that an attacker should concentrate his troops in order to be stronger at the moment of battle.

Partisan warfare (always successful, as history demonstrates) is directly opposed to this rule.

This contradiction proceeds from the fact that military science assumes the strength of an army to be identical with its numbers. Military science says that the bigger the army, the stronger it is. *Les gros bataillons ont toujours raison.**

In saying that, military science is like a mechanics which, considering forces only in relation to their masses, would say that forces are equal or not equal to each other because their masses are or are not equal.

Force (the quantity of motion) is the product of mass times velocity.

In military action, the force of an army is also a product of mass times something, some unknown x.

Military science, seeing from a countless number of examples in history that the mass of an army does not coincide with its force, that small detachments defeat large ones, vaguely recognizes the existence of this unknown multiplier and tries to find it either in geometric disposition, or in armaments, or—most commonly—in the genius of the commander. But the substitution of all these values for the multiplier does not produce results that agree with the historical facts.

And yet one need only renounce the false view, established to please the heroes, of the validity of orders from the higher powers in time of war, in order to find this unknown x.

This x is the spirit of the army, that is, the greater or lesser desire to fight and subject themselves to danger on the part of all the men who make up the army, regardless of whether they are fighting under the command of geniuses or not, in three lines or in two, with clubs or with guns that fire thirty rounds a minute. Men who have the greatest desire to fight will always put themselves in the most advantageous conditions for fighting.

The spirit of an army is the multiplier of the mass that yields the product of force. To determine and express the value of that unknown multiplier, the spirit of an army, is the task of science.

This task is possible only if we stop arbitrarily substituting for the value of the whole unknown x the conditions under which force is manifested—to wit: the orders of the commander, armaments, and so on—taking them for the value of the multiplier, and recognize this unknown in its entirety, that is, as the greater or lesser desire to fight and subject oneself to danger. Only then, expressing known historical facts in equations, may we hope, by comparing the relative values of this unknown, to define the unknown itself.

Ten men, battalions, or divisions, fighting against fifteen men, battalions, or divisions, defeated the fifteen, that is, killed or captured them all to a man, and lost four themselves; thus, on one side four and on the other side fifteen were cancelled. Therefore, four were equal to fifteen, and therefore: $4x = 15y$. Therefore, $x : y = 15 : 4$. This equation does not give us the value of the unknown, but

---

*Big battalions are always right.

it gives the ratio between two unknowns. And by bringing various historical units (battles, campaigns, periods of war) into such equations, we will obtain a series of numbers in which laws should exist and may be discovered.

The tactical rule that there should be massed action in attack and dispersed action in retreat only confirms unwittingly the truth that the strength of an army depends on its spirit. To lead men under cannonballs, there is a need for greater discipline, achieved only by mass action, than to repulse the attackers. But this rule, which loses sight of the spirit of the army, always proves wrong, and is in especially flagrant contradiction to reality wherever there exists a strong rise or fall in the spirit of the army—as in all national wars.

The French, retreating in 1812, though according to tactics they should defend themselves separately, press together in a mass, because the spirit of the army has fallen, and only its mass holds the army together. The Russians, on the contrary, should, according to tactics, be attacking in mass, but in fact they break up, because the spirit has risen so much that separate persons beat the French without any orders and need not be forced to subject themselves to difficulties and dangers.

III

The so-called partisan war began with the entrance of the enemy into Smolensk.

Before the partisan war was officially accepted by our government, thousands of men of the enemy army—lingering marauders, foragers—were exterminated by the Cossacks and muzhiks, who killed these men off as unconsciously as dogs bite to death a rabid stray dog. Denis Davydov, with his Russian intuition, was the first to understand the meaning of that terrible club which, without enquiring into the rules of military art, was destroying the French, and to him belongs the glory of the first step towards legitimizing this method of warfare.

On the twenty-fourth of August, Davydov's first partisan detachment was formed, and after that others began to be formed. The further the campaign moved, the greater the number of these detachments grew.

The partisans were destroying the Grand Army piecemeal. They gathered up the dry leaves that fell by themselves from the withered tree of the French army, and occasionally shook that tree. By October, when the French were fleeing towards Smolensk, there were hundreds of these parties, of various sizes and characters. There were parties that imitated all the methods of an army, with infantry, artillery, staffs, and the conveniences of life; there were some of Cossacks, of cavalry; there were small combined ones, foot and horse; there were peasants' and landowners' parties, unknown to anyone. There was a party commanded by a beadle, which took several hundred prisoners in a month.

There was Vassilisa, a village headman's wife, who destroyed hundreds of the French.

The last days of October were the hottest time of the partisan war. The initial period of this war—a time when the partisans, surprised at their own boldness, were afraid every moment of being caught and surrounded by the French, and hid in the forest without unsaddling their horses and hardly ever dismounting, expecting every moment to be pursued—had already passed. Now this war was already defined; it had become clear to everyone what could and could not be undertaken with the French. Now only those leaders of detachments who had staffs, followed rules, and moved about at a distance from the French considered many things impossible. The small partisan groups, who had long been in action and watched the French from close up, considered things possible that the leaders of large detachments did not dare to think of. The Cossacks and the peasants, who got in among the French, considered that anything was now possible.

On the twenty-second of October, Denisov, being one of the partisans, found himself with his party in the very heat of partisan passion. He and his party had been on the move since morning. All day, from the forest stretching along the high road, he had been watching a large French transport of cavalry supplies and Russian prisoners, which was separated from the rest of the army and, under heavy cover, as was known from scouts and prisoners, was heading for Smolensk. Not only Denisov and Dolokhov (also a partisan with a small party, who moved about close to Denisov), but the leaders of large detachments with staffs as well—all of them knew about this transport and, as Denisov said, were whetting their teeth for it. Two of these large detachment leaders—one a Pole, the other a German—almost simultaneously sent Denisov an invitation to join each of their detachments, in order to attack the transport.

"No, bghrother, I've been around long enough," said Denisov, having read these papers, and he wrote to the German that, despite his heartfelt wish to serve under the command of such a valiant and famous general, he had to deprive himself of that happiness, because he had already put himself under the command of the Pole. To the Polish general he wrote the same, informing him that he had already put himself under the German's command.[2]

Having arranged things in this way, Denisov, together with Dolokhov, intended, without reporting to the higher command, to attack and take this transport with their own small forces. The transport was going, on the twenty-second of October, from the village of Mikulino to the village of Shamshevo. To the left of the road from Mikulino to Shamshevo there were big forests, in some places coming right down to the road, in some moving back from the road to a distance of half a mile or more. Denisov and his party had been moving through these forests all day, now going deep into the middle of them, now riding out into the open, not losing sight of the moving French. In the morning, not far from Mikulino, where the forest came close to the road, Cossacks from Denisov's party had captured two wagons of cavalry saddles that were bogged down in the mud, and had driven them into the forest. From then on until evening, the party, without attacking, had followed the movement of the French. They had, without frightening them, to let them go peacefully as far as Shamshevo and then, joining up with Dolokhov, who was to arrive by evening for a meeting at a guardhouse (a mile from Shamshevo), to fall upon them at dawn, out of the blue, and kill or capture them all at once.

Six Cossacks were left behind, a mile and a half from Mikulino, where the forest came right down to the road, who were to inform them at once as soon as new French columns appeared.

On the other side of Shamshevo, Dolokhov was to keep an eye on the road in the same way, to find out how far away the other French troops were. There were supposed to be fifteen hundred men with the transport. Denisov had two hundred men, Dolokhov might rally the same number. But the superiority of numbers did not stop Denisov. There was only one thing he still needed to know, which was precisely what sort these troops were. For that purpose, Denisov needed to capture a "tongue" (that is, a soldier from the enemy column). In the morning attack on the wagons, the business had been done with such haste that all the French with the wagons had been killed, and the only one taken alive was a drummer boy, who was half-witted and could say nothing positive about what sort of troops were with the column.

Denisov considered it dangerous to attack another time, for fear of disturbing the whole column, and therefore he sent ahead to Shamshevo the muzhik Tikhon Shcherbaty, who was in his party, to capture at least one of the French vanguard, who were taking up quarters there.

IV

It was a warm, rainy autumn day. The sky and the horizon were both the colour of muddy water. Now the fog seemed to descend, now a slanting rain would suddenly come down in big drops.

Denisov, in a felt cloak and a papakha streaming with water, rode on a lean, purebred horse with drawn-in flanks. Like his horse, who kept moving its head sideways and laying its ears flat, he winced from the slanting rain and peered ahead worriedly. His emaciated face, overgrown with a thick, short, black beard, looked angry.

Beside Denisov, also in a felt cloak and papakha, on a big, well-nourished Don stallion, rode a Cossack esaul*—Denisov's associate.

*Captain.

The esaul Lovaisky was a tall, white-faced, fair-haired man, flat as a board, with narrow, pale eyes and a calmly smug expression in his face and bearing. Though it was impossible to say what made for the peculiarity of the horse and rider, from a first glance at the esaul and at Denisov, one could see that Denisov felt wet and awkward—that he was a man sitting on a horse; while, looking at the esaul, one could see that he felt as comfortable and at ease as ever, and that he was not a man sitting on a horse, but a man who was one with a horse, a being of twice-increased strength.

A little ahead of them walked a soaking wet little peasant—their guide—in a grey kaftan and a white cap.

A little behind them, on a skinny, slender Kirghiz nag, with an enormous mane and tail and lips so torn that they bled, rode a young officer in a dark blue French greatcoat.

Beside him rode a hussar, with a boy in a tattered French uniform and blue cap sitting behind him on his horse's croup. The boy held on to the hussar with hands red from the cold, moved his bare feet in an effort to warm them, and, raising his eyebrows, looked around in surprise. This was the French drummer boy captured in the morning.

Behind, by threes, by fours, along the narrow, sodden, and much-travelled forest road, stretched hussars, then Cossacks, some in felt cloaks, some in French greatcoats, some with horse blankets pulled over their heads. The horses, bay and sorrel, all looked black from the rain streaming off them. The horses' necks seemed strangely thin because of their drenched manes. Steam rose from the horses. Clothes, saddles, reins—everything was wet, slippery, and soggy, like the ground and the fallen leaves that covered the road. The men sat looking ruffled up, trying not to stir, so as to keep the water warm that had seeped through to the body and not let in the new, cold water that flowed under their seats, knees, and behind their necks. Between the strung-out Cossacks, the two wagons, hitched to French and saddled Cossack horses, rumbled over stumps and branches and gurgled through the water-filled ruts of the road.

Denisov's horse, swerving round a puddle that was in its way, pulled to the side and bumped its rider's knee against a tree.

"Ah, the devil!" Denisov cried angrily and, baring his teeth, he gave his horse three strokes of the whip, splashing himself and his comrades with mud. Denisov was in a foul mood because of the rain, and because he was hungry (no one had eaten anything since morning), and above all because there was no word from Dolokhov and the man sent to take a prisoner had not come back.

"There could hardly be another such occasion as today for attacking the transport. To attack alone is too risky, but put it off to another day and some bigger party will snatch the booty right from under our noses," thought Denisov, constantly glancing ahead, hoping to see the expected messenger from Dolokhov.

Emerging into a clearing, where one could see far to the right, Denisov stopped.

"Somebody's coming," he said.

The esaul looked in the direction in which Denisov was pointing.

"There are two coming—an officer and a Cossack. Only it's not *presupposable* that it's the lieutenant colonel himself," said the esaul, who liked to use words unknown to the Cossacks.

The riders descended the hill, disappeared from sight, and reappeared in a few minutes. In front, at a weary gallop, applying his whip, rode an officer—dishevelled, soaked through, his trousers bunched up above his knees. Behind him, standing in the stirrups, trotted a Cossack. This officer, a very young boy with a broad, red-cheeked face and quick, merry eyes, galloped up to Denisov and handed him a wet envelope.

"From the general," said the officer, "sorry it's not quite dry . . ."

Denisov, frowning, took the envelope and began to open it.

"They keep saying it's dangerous, dangerous," said the officer, turning to the esaul, while Denisov read the letter handed to him. "Anyhow, me and Komarov," he pointed to the Cossack, "are ready. Each of us has two pist . . . But what's that?" he asked, seeing the French drummer boy. "A prisoner? You've already been in battle? Can I talk to him?"

"Ghrostov! Petya!" Denisov cried out just then, having looked through the envelope handed to him. "Why didn't you tell me who you were?" And Denisov turned with a smile and gave the officer his hand.

This officer was Petya Rostov.

On the way there, Petya had been preparing the way he, as a grown man and an officer, without hinting at their former acquaintance, would behave with Denisov. But as soon as Denisov smiled at him, Petya at once beamed, blushed for joy, and, forgetting his prepared officialness, began to tell how he had ridden past the French, and how glad he was that he had been given such an errand, and that he had already been in battle at Vyazma, and that a certain hussar had distinguished himself there.

"Well, I'm veghry glad to see you," Denisov interrupted him, and his face again assumed a preoccupied expression.

"Mikhail Feoklitych," he turned to the esaul, "this one is from the German again. He's attached to him." And Denisov told the esaul that the content of the letter just brought consisted of a repeated request to join him in attacking the transport. "If we don't take it tomoghrrow, they'll snatch it fghrom under our noses," he concluded.

While Denisov was talking with the esaul, Petya, abashed by Denisov's cold tone and supposing that the cause of it was the state of his trousers, was straightening them under his greatcoat, so that no one would notice, trying to look as martial as possible.

"Will there be any orders from Your Honour?" he said to Denisov, putting his hand to his visor and returning again to the game of adjutant and general which he had prepared for, "or shall I stay with Your Honour?"

"Oghrders? . . ." Denisov said pensively. "But can you stay till tomoghrrow?"

"Ah, please . . . May I stay with you?" cried Petya.

"And exactly what did the geneghral tell you—to ghreturn at once?" asked Denisov. Petya blushed.

"He didn't tell me anything. I think I can?" he said questioningly.

"Well, all ghright," said Denisov. And turning to his subordinates, he gave instructions for the party to go to the appointed resting place by the guard-house in the forest and for the officer on the Kirghiz horse (this officer functioned as an adjutant) to go looking for Dolokhov, to find out where he was and whether he would come in the evening. Denisov himself, with the esaul and Petya, intended to ride up to the edge of the forest that came out at Shamshevo, in order to look over the place where the French were camped, at which the next day's attack should be directed.

"Well, ghreybeard," he turned to the muzhik guide, "lead us to Shamshevo."

Denisov, Petya, and the esaul, accompanied by several Cossacks and the hussar who was carrying the prisoner, rode left across a ravine to the edge of the forest.

V

The light rain stopped; only mist fell and drops of water from the branches of the trees. Denisov, the esaul, and Petya silently rode after the muzhik in the cap, who, stepping lightly and noiselessly over the roots and wet leaves with his splayed feet in bast shoes, led them to the edge of the forest.

Going up a slope, the muzhik paused, looked around, and made for the thinning wall of trees. By a big oak still covered with leaves, he stopped and beckoned mysteriously with his hand.

Denisov and Petya rode up to him. From the place where the muzhik had stopped, the French could be seen. Just beyond the forest, a field of spring wheat descended over a low knoll. To the right, across a steep ravine, a small village and a manor house with broken-down roofs could be seen. In this village, and in the manor house, and all over the knoll, in the garden, by the wells and the pond, and along the road uphill from the bridge to the village, no more than four hundred yards away, crowds of men could be seen through the undulating mist. One could clearly hear their non-Russian shouts at the horses pulling wagons up the hill and their calls to one another.

"Bghring the pghrisoner here," Denisov said in a low voice, without taking his eyes off the French.

The Cossack got off his horse, took the boy down, and went up to Denisov with him. Denisov, pointing to the French, asked what kind of troops these and those were. The boy, putting his chilled hands in his pockets and raising his eyebrows, looked at Denisov in fear and, despite his obvious wish to tell all he knew, became confused in his answers and only confirmed whatever Denisov asked. Denisov frowned, turned away from him, and addressed the esaul, telling him his considerations.

Petya, quickly turning his head, looked now at the drummer boy, now at Denisov, now at the esaul, now at the French in the village and on the road, trying not to miss anything important.

"Whether Dolokhov comes or not, we've got to take them! . . . Ghright?" said Denisov, with a merry sparkle in his eyes.

"It's a convenient place," said the esaul.

"We'll send the infantry from below, through the maghrshes," Denisov went on. "They'll sneak up on the garden. You and the Cossacks will ghride ghround from there," Denisov pointed to the forest behind the village, "and I'll come fghrom here with my hussars. And at the signal shot . . ."

"We can't go through the hollow—it's swampy," said the esaul. "The horses will get bogged down; we'll have to go round more to the left."

As they were talking like that in half whispers, a shot cracked below, in the hollow by the pond, they saw a puff of white smoke, then another, and heard the concerted, merry-sounding shout of hundreds of voices of the French who were on the hillside. At the first moment, Denisov and the esaul drew back. They were so close that they thought they were the cause of the shots and shouts. But the shots and shouts had nothing to do with them. Below, across the marsh, ran a man in something red. Obviously, the French were shooting and shouting at him.

"Why, that's our Tikhon," said the esaul.

"Him! It's him!"

"What a ghrascal!" said Denisov.

"He'll get away!" the esaul said, narrowing his eyes.

The man they called Tikhon ran to the river, plopped into it with a splash, disappeared for a moment, and clambered out on all fours, black from the water, and ran on. The French who were running after him stopped.

"That's nimble," said the esaul.

"What a ghrogue!" Denisov said with the same expression of vexation. "What's he been up to all this time?"

"Who is he?" asked Petya.

"Our *plastun*.* I sent him to take a 'tongue.' "

"Ah, yes," said Petya, nodding his head at Denisov's first words as if he understood everything, though he decidedly did not understand a single word.

---

*Scout.

Tikhon Shcherbaty was one of the most necessary men in the party. He was a muzhik from Pokrovskoe, near Gzhat. When, at the beginning of his operations, Denisov had come to Pokrovskoe and, as usual, summoned the headman and asked what they knew about the French, the headman had answered as all headmen would, as if defending himself, that he knew nothing, had seen nothing. But when Denisov explained that his aim was to kill the French and asked whether the French had happened to come there, the headman said that, in fact, some "marowders" had been there, but that in their village only Gaptoothed Tishka concerned himself with such doings. Denisov told him to summon Tikhon and, having praised him for his activity, said a few words in front of the headman about loyalty to the tsar and the fatherland, and the hatred for the French that the sons of the fatherland should observe.

"We do no harm to the French," said Tikhon, clearly cowed by these words of Denisov's. "We just went hunting and had some fun with the lads. We did kill some couple of dozen 'marowders,' but otherwise we did no harm . . ." The next day, when Denisov, forgetting entirely about this muzhik, left Pokrovskoe, it was reported to him that Tikhon had attached himself to the party and asked to be allowed to stay with it. Denisov said he could stay.

Tikhon, who at first did the dirty work of making campfires, carrying water, skinning horses, and so on, soon showed great zeal and ability for partisan warfare. At night he went after booty, and came back each time bringing some French clothing or weapons, and, when told to, also brought in prisoners. Denisov relieved Tikhon from work, began taking him with him on patrol, and enlisted him as a Cossack.

Tikhon did not like riding and always went on foot, never lagging behind the cavalry. His weapons were a musketoon, which he strapped on mainly for amusement, a pike, and an axe, which he used as a wolf does its teeth, with equal ease picking fleas out of its fur or biting through thick bones. Tikhon, with equal precision, would swing his ax to split logs or, taking it by the butt, whittle thin pegs or carved spoons. In Denisov's party, Tikhon occupied his own exceptional place. When there was a need to do something especially difficult and nasty—to haul a cart out of the mud with one's shoulder, to pull a horse out of a swamp by its tail or skin it, to slip right into the middle of the French, to walk thirty miles a day—everyone pointed, chuckling, at Tikhon.

"What harm will it do the devil—he's sturdy as an ox," they said of him.

Once a Frenchman Tikhon was about to capture shot at him with a pistol and hit him in the soft hindquarters. This wound, which Tikhon treated only with vodka, internally and externally, was the object of the merriest jokes in the whole party, jokes to which Tikhon willingly yielded.

"Never again, eh, brother? All doubled up?" the Cossacks laughed at him, and Tikhon, doubling up on purpose and making faces, pretending to be angry, denounced the French with the funniest oaths. The only influence this incident had on Tikhon was that, after his wound, he rarely brought in prisoners.

Tikhon was the bravest and most useful man in the party. Nobody found more chances for attacking than he, no one captured or killed more of the French; and as a result of that, he was a buffoon for all the Cossacks and hussars, and willingly accepted that rank. Now Tikhon had been sent by Denisov to Shamshevo during the night, in order to take a "tongue." But, either because he was not satisfied with one prisoner, or because he had slept through the night, he had slipped by day into some bushes, right in the middle of the French, and, as Denisov had seen from the hill, had been discovered by them.

VI

Having talked a while longer with the esaul about the next day's attack, which Denisov, seeing the closeness of the French, now seemed to have definitively resolved upon, he turned his horse and rode back.

"Well, bghrother, now let's go and get dghry," he said to Petya.

Riding up to the forest guardhouse, Denisov stopped, peering into the forest. In the forest, among the trees, a man was walking with big, light strides, on long legs, with long, swinging arms, wearing a jacket, bast shoes, and a Kazan hat, with a gun over his shoulder and an axe in his belt. Seeing Denisov, this man hastily flung something into the bushes and, taking off his soaked hat with its drooping brim, went up to his commander. It was Tikhon. His pockmarked and wrinkled face, with its small, narrow eyes, beamed with self-satisfied merriment. Raising his head high, and as if trying to keep from laughing, he fixed his eyes on Denisov.

"Well, where did you disappear to?" said Denisov.

"Disappear to? I went after the French," Tikhon replied boldly and quickly, in a hoarse but melodious bass.

"Why did you slip in there during the day? Bghrute! So you didn't take . . ."

"I took one, I did," said Tikhon.

"Where is he?"

"I took him first thing at dawn," Tikhon went on, moving his flat, splayed feet in their bast shoes further apart, "and I led him into the forest. I saw he wasn't the right sort. I thought, why don't I go and take another more proper one?"

"See, he's a ghrascal, that's what," Denisov said to the esaul. "Why didn't you bring that one?"

"Why bring him," Tikhon interrupted crossly and quickly, "if he's no good? Don't I know what kind you need?"

"Sly dog! . . . So? . . ."

"I went after another," Tikhon continued. "I crawled into the forest like this and lay there," Tikhon unexpectedly and nimbly lay on his belly, acting out how he had done it. "One of them came along," he continued. "I grabbed him like this." Tikhon jumped up quickly and lightly. " 'Let's go to the colonel,' I said. He started jabbering. Four of them came. Fell on me with their little swords. I swung my axe like this: 'Come on, Christ help you,' " Tikhon cried, swinging his arms, scowling terribly, and thrusting out his chest.

"We saw from the hill how you cut and ran through the puddles," said the esaul, narrowing his bright eyes.

Petya wanted very much to laugh, but he saw that they all kept from laughing. He quickly shifted his gaze from Tikhon's face to the esaul's and Denisov's, not understanding what it all meant.

"Don't play the fool," said Denisov, coughing crossly. "Why didn't you bghring the first one?"

Tikhon began to scratch his back with one hand, his head with the other, and suddenly his whole mug stretched into a beaming, foolish smile, revealing the missing tooth (for which he was nicknamed Shcherbaty—"Gap-toothed"). Denisov smiled, and Petya dissolved in merry laughter, in which Tikhon himself joined.

"No, but he was all wrong," said Tikhon. "Such poor clothes on him, there was no point bringing him here. And a crude one, Your Honour. 'It's like this,' he says, 'I'm a ginneral's son, I won't go,' he says."

"What a bghrute!" said Denisov. "I need to question . . ."

"But I did ask him," said Tikhon. " 'Things are bad,' he says—in *signs*. 'There's a lot of us,' he says, 'but in poor shape; just in name only,' he says. 'One good whack,' he says, 'and you'll take them all,' " Tikhon concluded, glancing merrily and resolutely into Denisov's eyes.

"When you get a hundghred hot ones fghrom me, that'll teach you to play the fool," Denisov said sternly.

"Why get angry," said Tikhon, "as if I haven't seen your Frenchmen? Wait till it gets dark, I'll bring you any sort you like, even three of them."

"Well, let's go," said Denisov, and rode on until they came to the guardhouse, silent and frowning angrily.

Tikhon walked behind, and Petya heard the Cossacks laughing with him and at him about some boots he had thrown into the bushes.

When the laughter that came over him at Tikhon's words and smile passed, and Petya realized for a moment that this Tikhon had killed a man, he felt uneasy. He glanced at the captive drummer boy and something stabbed his heart. But this uneasiness lasted only a moment. He felt a need to raise his head higher, to encourage himself, and to question the esaul about the next day's undertaking, assuming a significant air, so as not to be unworthy of the company he was in.

The officer who had been sent met Denisov on the way with the news that Dolokhov himself would come at once and that for his part all was well.

Denisov suddenly cheered up and called Petya to him.

"Well, tell me about yourself," he said.

VII

Petya, having left his family on their departure from Moscow, had joined his regiment, and soon after that was attached as an orderly to a general in command of a large detachment. Since the time of his promotion to officer, and especially since going on active duty, where he had taken part in the battle of Vyazma,[3] Petya had constantly been in a state of happily excited joy that he was grown up, and in constantly rapturous haste not to miss any occasion for real heroism. He was very happy with what he had seen and experienced in the army, but at the same time it seemed to him all the time that he was not where what was most real and heroic was now happening. And he hurried to get where he was not.

When, on the twenty-first of October, his general expressed the wish to send someone to Denisov's detachment, Petya begged so pitifully to be sent that the general could not refuse. But as he was sending him, the general, recalling Petya's mad behaviour at the battle of Vyazma, where, instead of taking to the road and going where he had been sent, he had galloped into the line under French fire and there twice shot off his pistol—as he was sending him, the general precisely forbade Petya to take part in any of Denisov's actions whatever. It was this that had made Petya blush and become confused when Denisov asked if he could stay. Until he rode out to the edge of the forest, Petya thought that, in strict fulfilment of his duty, he ought to return at once. But when he saw the French, saw Tikhon, learned that there would certainly be an attack in the night, he, with a young man's quickness in changing his views, decided to himself that his general, whom till then he had respected very much, was trash, a German, that Denisov was a hero, and the esaul was a hero, and Tikhon was a hero, and it was shameful to leave them at a difficult moment.

Night was already falling when Denisov, with Petya and the esaul, rode up to the guardhouse. In the semi-darkness they could see saddled horses, Cossacks, hussars, setting up little lean-tos in the clearing and making a glowing fire in the wooded ravine (so that the French would not see the smoke). In the front hall of the small cottage, a Cossack, his sleeves rolled up, was carving mutton. Inside the cottage itself, three officers from Denisov's party were setting up a table made from a door. Petya took off his wet things, handed them over to be dried, and at once began to assist the officers in setting up the dinner table.

Ten minutes later, the table was ready, covered with a cloth. On the table stood vodka, a flask of rum, white bread, and roast mutton with salt.

Sitting with the officers at the table and tearing at a greasy hunk of fragrant mutton with his hands, which dripped with fat, Petya was in a rapturous, childlike state of tender love for all people, and consequently of certainty that other people had the same love for him.

"So what do you think, Vassily Fyodorovich," he turned to Denisov, "is it all right if I stay with you for one little day?" And, not waiting for an answer, he answered himself: "I was told to find out, so I'll find out . . . Only let me go to the very . . . to the main . . . I don't need any rewards . . . But I'd like . . ." Petya clenched his teeth and looked around, tossing his raised head and swinging his arms.

"To the main . . ." Denisov repeated, smiling.

"Only, please, give me full command, so that I can be in command," Petya went on. "What is it to you? Ah, you need a knife?" he turned to an officer who wanted to cut some mutton. And he gave him his pocketknife.

The officer praised the knife.

"Keep it, please. I've got many like it . . ." Petya said, blushing. "Good heavens! I completely forgot," he suddenly cried. "I've got wonderful raisins, you know, the seedless kind. We have a new sutler—and such excellent things. I bought ten pounds. I'm used to something sweet. Would you like some? . . ." And Petya ran to the front hall, to his Cossack, and brought back bags with some five pounds of raisins. "Eat, gentlemen, eat."

"And don't you need a coffeepot?" he turned to the esaul. "I bought one from our sutler, it's wonderful! He has excellent things. And he's very honest. That's the main thing. I'll make sure to send you one. Or maybe you're out of flints—they get used up, you know. I brought some along, I've got them here," he pointed to the bags, "a hundred flints. I bought them very cheap. Please, take as many as you like, or even all of them . . ." And suddenly, afraid that he had let his tongue run away with him, Petya stopped and blushed.

He began to recall whether he had done any other stupid things. And, going through his memories of that day, he stopped at the memory of the French drummer boy. "It's fine for us, but how about him? Where have they put him? Have they fed him? Have they mistreated him?" he thought. But, realizing that he had got carried away with the flints, he was now wary.

"I could ask," he thought, "but they'll say: 'He's a boy himself and he feels sorry for a boy.' I'll show them tomorrow what sort of boy I am! Will it be shameful if I ask?" thought Petya. "Well, what difference does it make!"—and at once, blushing and looking fearfully at the officers to see if there was any mockery in their faces, he said:

"And can I call that boy you captured? to give him something to eat . . . maybe . . ."

"Yes, a pitiful lad," said Denisov, obviously finding nothing shameful in this reminder. "Call him here. His name's Vincent Bosse. Call him."

"I'll call him," said Petya.

"Call him, call him. A pitiful lad," Denisov repeated.

Petya was standing by the door when Denisov said that. He squeezed between the officers and went up close to Denisov.

"Allow me to kiss you, dear heart," he said. "Ah, how excellent! how good!" And, having kissed Denisov, he ran outside.

"Bosse! Vincent!" cried Petya, stopping by the door.

"Who do you want, sir?" a voice said from the darkness. Petya replied that it was the French boy who had been captured that day.

"Ah! Vesenny?" said a Cossack.

His name, Vincent, had already been changed into Vesenny by the Cossacks, into Visenya by the muzhiks and soldiers. Both changes brought together a reminder of springtime[4] with the idea of a young boy.

"He was warming up by the fire. Hey, Visenya! Visenya! Vesenny!" echoing voices and laughter were heard in the darkness.

"He's a sharp little lad," said a hussar who was standing by Petya. "We gave him something to eat earlier. He was dying of hunger!"

Footsteps were heard in the darkness, and the drummer boy, splashing barefoot through the mud, came up to the door.

"*Ah, c'est vous!*" said Petya. "*Voulez-vous manger? N'ayez pas peur, on ne vous fera pas de mal,*" he added, touching his hand timidly and tenderly. "*Entrez, entrez.*"*

"*Merci, monsieur,*" the drummer boy replied in a trembling voice, almost a child's, and began wiping his muddy feet on the threshold. Petya would have liked to say many things to the drummer boy, but he did not dare. He stood beside him in the front hall, shifting from foot to foot. Then he took his hand in the darkness and pressed it.

"*Entrez, entrez,*" he only repeated in a tender whisper.

"Ah, what can I do for him?" Petya said to himself and, opening the door, he let the boy go in past him.

When the drummer boy had entered the cottage, Petya sat down at some distance from him, considering that it was humiliating for him to pay attention to him. He only felt the money in his pocket, and wondered whether it would be shameful for him to give it to the drummer boy.

---

*Ah, it's you! . . . Would you like to eat? Don't be afraid, nobody will hurt you . . . Come in, come in.

VIII

From the drummer boy, who, on Denisov's instructions, was given vodka and mutton, and whom Denisov ordered dressed in a Russian kaftan, so that he could stay with the party and not be sent away with the prisoners, Petya's attention was distracted by the arrival of Dolokhov. In the army, Petya had heard many stories of Dolokhov's extraordinary courage and cruelty to the French, and therefore, once Dolokhov entered the cottage, Petya gazed at him without taking his eyes away, and kept encouraging himself by tossing his raised head, so as not to be unworthy even of such company as Dolokhov.

Dolokhov's appearance struck Petya strangely by its simplicity.

Denisov was dressed in a Cossack coat, wore a beard and an icon of St. Nicholas the Wonderworker on his chest, and in his manner of speaking, in all his ways, expressed the singularity of his position. Dolokhov, on the contrary, who formerly in Moscow had worn Persian dress, now had the look of a most prim officer of the guards. His face was clean-shaven, he was dressed in a padded guardsman's jacket with a St. George in the buttonhole and in a simple peaked cap set straight on his head. He took off his wet felt cape in the corner and, going up to Denisov, without greeting anyone, at once began asking him about business. Denisov told him about the designs that the large detachments had on their transport, about the sending of Petya, and about his response to the two generals. Then Denisov told him all he knew about the position of the French.

"That's all very well, but we must know what kind of troops they are and how many," said Dolokhov. "We'll have to go there. We can't go into action without knowing for certain how many they are. I like to do things neatly. So, gentlemen, does anyone want to go with me to their camp? I've got uniforms with me."

"Me, me . . . I'll go with you!" cried Petya.

"There's no need at all for you to go," said Denisov, addressing Dolokhov, "and him I won't let go for anything."

"That's just fine!" cried Petya. "Why can't I go? . . ."

"Because there's no need."

"Well, excuse me, because . . . because . . . I'm going, that's all. Will you take me?" he turned to Dolokhov.

"Why not . . ." Dolokhov answered distractedly, peering into the face of the French drummer boy.

"Have you had this little fellow long?" he asked Denisov.

"We took him today, but he doesn't know anything. I'm keeping him with me."

"And where do the rest disappear to?" asked Dolokhov.

"Meaning what? I send them off and take ghreceipts!" Denisov cried, suddenly turning red. "And I say boldly that I don't have a single man on my conscience. Is it hard for you to send thirty or even thghree hundghred men to town under escort, instead—I'll say it outghright—instead of besmighrching the honour of a soldier?"

"Such niceties would be fitting for the little sixteen-year-old count here," Dolokhov said with a cold smirk, "but it's time you gave them up."

"What, I'm not saying anything, I'm only saying that I'll definitely go with you," Petya said timidly.

"But for you and me, brother, it's time to drop these niceties," Dolokhov went on, as if he found a special pleasure in talking about this subject, which irritated Denisov. "Now, why have you taken this one with you?" he said, shaking his head. "Because you feel sorry for him? We know those receipts of yours. You send off a hundred men, thirty will arrive. The rest will starve to death or be killed. Does it make any difference if you don't take them?"

The esaul, narrowing his pale eyes, nodded approvingly.

"That makes no diffeghrence, there's nothing to discuss. I don't want to take it on my soul. You say they'll die. Veghry well. As long as it's not because of me."

Dolokhov laughed.

"Who told them not to capture me twenty times over? But if they do—for me and for you, with all your chivalry, it's the same aspen tree." He paused. "Anyhow, we've got to get down to business. Send for my Cossack with the bundle! I have two French uniforms. Well, are you coming with me?" he asked Petya.

"Me? Yes, yes, definitely," cried Petya, blushing almost to the point of tears and glancing at Denisov.

While Dolokhov was arguing with Denisov about what to do with the prisoners, Petya had again felt uneasy and hurried; but again he had not quite managed to understand what they were talking about. "If the big, famous ones think like that, it means it must be so, it means it's good," he thought. "And, above all, Denisov mustn't think that I'll obey him, that he can command me. I'll definitely go to the French camp with Dolokhov. If he can, I can!"

To all Denisov's persuasions not to go, Petya replied that he was also used to doing everything neatly and not any old way, and that he never thought about the danger to himself.

"Because—you yourself will agree—if we don't know for certain how many there are, the lives of hundreds may depend on it, and here it's just us, and I also want it very much, and I'll definitely go, I will, you won't hold me back," he said, "that will only be worse . . ."

IX

Having put on French uniforms and shakos, Petya and Dolokhov rode to the clearing from which Denisov had looked at the camp, and, riding out of the forest in total darkness, descended into the hollow. On reaching the bottom, Dolokhov told the Cossacks who accompanied them to wait there and rode at a sturdy trot down the road to the bridge. Petya, his heart thrilling with excitement, rode beside him.

"If we're caught, I won't surrender alive, I've got a pistol," Petya whispered.

"Don't speak Russian," Dolokhov said in a quick whisper, and at the same moment they heard a call from the darkness: *"Qui vive?"** and the cocking of a musket.

The blood rushed to Petya's face, and he gripped his pistol.

"Lanciers du 6ᵉ,"† said Dolokhov, without slowing or increasing the pace of his horse. The black figure of the sentry stood on the bridge.

"Mot d'ordre?"‡

Dolokhov reined in his horse and rode slowly.

"Dites donc, le colonel Gérard est ici?"§ he said.

"Mot d'ordre!" the sentry said without replying and barred his way.

"Quand un officier fait sa ronde, les sentinelles ne demandent pas le mot d'ordre . . ." cried Dolokhov, suddenly flaring up and riding his horse into the sentry. *"Je vous demande si le colonel est ici?"#*

And, not waiting for a reply from the sentry, who stepped aside, Dolokhov rode up the hill at a walk.

Noticing the black shadow of a man crossing the road, Dolokhov stopped him and asked where the commander and the officers were. This man, with a sack on his back, a soldier, stopped, came up close to Dolokhov's horse, touched it with his hand, and told him simply and amicably that the commander and the officers were further up the hill, to the right, in the courtyard of the farmhouse (as he called the manor house).

Riding up the road, from both sides of which came the sounds of French talk around the campfires, Dolokhov turned into the courtyard of the manor house. Riding through the gates, he got off his horse and went up to a big, blazing campfire, around which several men sat talking loudly. In a pot at the edge

*Who goes there?
†Lancers of the sixth.
‡Password?
§Tell me, is Colonel Gérard here?
#When an officer is making his rounds, the sentries do not ask for the password . . . I ask you, is the colonel here?

of the fire something was cooking, and a soldier in a cap and blue uniform, on his knees, brightly lit up by the fire, was stirring it with a ramrod.

"*Oh, c'est un dur à cuire,*"* said one of the officers, sitting in the shadow on the opposite side of the fire.

"*Il les fera marcher les lapins . . .*"† another said, laughing. They both fell silent, peering into the darkness at the sound of Dolokhov's and Petya's footsteps as they approached the fire with their horses.

"*Bonjour, messieurs!*" Dolokhov said loudly and distinctly.

The officers stirred in the shadow of the fire, and one, a tall officer with a long neck, went up to Dolokhov.

"*C'est vous, Clément?*" he said. "*D'où, diable . . .*"‡ but he did not finish, realizing his mistake, and, frowning slightly, greeted Dolokhov as a stranger, asking what he could do for him. Dolokhov told him that he and his comrade were trying to catch up with their regiment, and asked, addressing them all in general, whether the officers knew anything about the sixth regiment. No one knew anything, and Petya thought that the officers were beginning to look at him and Dolokhov with animosity and suspicion. For a few seconds they were all silent.

"*Si vous comptez sur la soupe du soir, vous venez trop tard,*"§ a voice said from behind the fire with restrained laughter.

Dolokhov replied that they were not hungry and had to be on their way that night.

He handed the horses to the soldier who was stirring the pot and squatted by the fire next to the officer with the long neck. This officer, not taking his eyes off Dolokhov, asked again what regiment he was from. Dolokhov did not reply, as if he had not heard the question, and, lighting up a short French pipe that he took from his pocket, asked the officers how far the road ahead was safe from Cossacks.

"*Les brigands sont partout,*"# replied the officer from behind the fire.

Dolokhov said that Cossacks were only a fear for stray ones like him and his comrade, but added questioningly that they probably did not dare to attack large detachments. No one made any reply.

"Well, now he'll leave," Petya kept thinking every moment, standing before the fire and listening to his conversation.

But Dolokhov began the stalled conversation again and started asking directly how many men were in their battalion, how many battalions, how many prisoners. Asking about the Russian prisoners who were with their detachment, Dolokhov said:

*Oh, he's a hard nut to crack.
†He'll make the rabbits scurry . . .
‡Is that you, Clément? . . . Where the devil . . .
§If you're counting on the evening soup, you're too late.
#The brigands are everywhere.

*"La vilaine affaire de trainer ces cadavres après soi. Vaudrait mieux fusiller cette canaille,"** and burst loudly into such strange laughter that Petya thought the French would see through the deceit at once, and he involuntarily stepped back from the fire. No one responded to Dolokhov's words and laughter, and the French officer who could not be seen (he was lying wrapped in his greatcoat) rose slightly and whispered something to his comrade. Dolokhov got up and called the soldier with the horses.

"Will they bring the horses or not?" wondered Petya, involuntarily moving close to Dolokhov.

The horses were brought.

"Bonjour, messieurs," said Dolokhov.

Petya wanted to say *bonsoir*[†] but could not bring the word out. The officers were whispering something among themselves. Dolokhov took a long time mounting his horse, which would not stand still; then he rode through the gates at a walk. Petya rode beside him, wishing and not daring to turn round to see if the French were running after them or not.

Coming out to the road, Dolokhov did not ride back to the field, but went through the village. In one place he stopped, listening.

"You hear?" he said.

Petya recognized the sounds of Russian voices and saw the dark figures of Russian prisoners by the fires. Descending to the bridge, Petya and Dolokhov rode past the sentry, who gloomily paced the bridge without saying a word, and went down into the hollow where the Cossacks were waiting.

"Well, and now goodbye. Tell Denisov it's set for dawn, at the first shot," said Dolokhov, and he was about to leave, but Petya seized him by the sleeve.

"No!" he cried, "you're such a hero! Ah, how good! How excellent! How I love you!"

"All right, all right," said Dolokhov, but Petya would not let go of him, and in the darkness Dolokhov made out that Petya was leaning towards him. He wanted to kiss. Dolokhov kissed him, laughed, and, turning his horse, disappeared into the darkness.

---

*Nasty business dragging these corpses behind you. Better to shoot the scum.
†Good night.

X

On returning to the guardhouse, Petya found Denisov in the front hall. Alarmed, anxious, and vexed with himself for having let Petya go, Denisov was waiting for him.

"Thank God!" he cried. "Well, thank God!" he repeated, listening to Petya's rapturous story. "Devil take you, I haven't slept because of you!" said Denisov. "Well, thank God, now go to bed. We can still get some sleep before morning."

"Yes . . . No," said Petya. "I don't want to sleep yet. And I know myself, if I fall asleep, that's the end. And then I usually don't sleep before a battle."

Petya sat for a while in the cottage, joyfully recalling the details of his ride and vividly imagining how tomorrow would be. Then, noticing that Denisov had fallen asleep, he got up and went outside.

Outside it was still quite dark. The rain had stopped long ago, but drops were still falling from the trees. Close to the guardhouse, he could see the black outlines of the Cossacks' lean-tos and the horses tethered together. Behind the cottage, the two wagons showed black, with horses standing by them, and the dying fire glowed in the ravine. Not all the Cossacks and hussars were asleep: here and there, along with the sound of falling drops and the closer sound of horses munching, he could hear soft, as if whispering, voices.

Petya stepped out of the front hall, looked around in the darkness, and went over to the wagons. Someone was snoring under the wagons, and around them stood saddled horses, munching oats. In the darkness, Petya made out his horse, whom he called Karabakh, though it was a Little Russian horse,[5] and went over to it.

"Well, Karabakh, tomorrow we'll do some service," he said, sniffing its nostrils and kissing it.

"What, master, you're not asleep?" said a Cossack who was sitting under a wagon.

"No, but . . . your name is Likhachev, I believe? I've just come back. We took a ride to the French."

And Petya told the Cossack in detail, not only about his ride, but also why he had gone and why he thought it was better to risk his life than to act any old way.

"Why don't you get some sleep?" said the Cossack.

"No, I'm used to it," Petya replied. "Maybe the flints in your pistols are worn out? I brought some with me. Don't you need some? Take them."

The Cossack stuck himself out from under the wagon to have a closer look at Petya.

"Because I like to do everything neatly," said Petya. "Some do things just like that, anyhow, without preparing, and then they're sorry. I don't like that."

"Right you are," said the Cossack.

"And another thing: please sharpen my sabre, dear heart; it's got bl . . ." (but Petya was afraid to lie)—"it's never been sharpened. Can it be done?"

"Why not?"

Likhachev stood up, rummaged in the packs, and Petya soon heard the martial sound of steel against a whetstone. He clambered onto the wagon and sat on its edge. The Cossack under the wagon was sharpening the sabre.

"And what, are the lads asleep?" asked Petya.

"Some are, and some are like us."

"Well, and what about the boy?"

"Vesenny? He's there in the front hall, just dropped off. Fright makes you sleep. He was so glad."

After that Petya was silent for a long time, listening to the sounds. Footsteps came from the darkness and a black figure appeared.

"What are you sharpening?" asked the man, coming up to the wagon.

"A sabre for the master here."

"That's a good thing," said the man, whom Petya took for a hussar. "Did I leave my bowl here?"

"There, by the wheel."

The hussar took the bowl.

"Likely it'll be light soon," he said, yawning, and went off somewhere.

Petya ought to have known that he was in the forest, in Denisov's party, a mile from the road, that he was sitting on a wagon captured from the French with horses tethered by it, and that under him sat the Cossack Likhachev, sharpening his sabre, that the big black spot to the right was the guardhouse, and the bright red spot down to the left was the dying campfire, that the man who had come for the bowl was a hussar who wanted a drink; but he knew nothing of that and did not want to know. He was in a magic kingdom, in which there was nothing resembling reality. Maybe the big black spot was indeed the guardhouse, but maybe it was a cave that led into the very depths of the earth. Maybe the red spot was a fire, but maybe it was the eye of a huge monster. Maybe he is indeed sitting on a wagon now, but it very well may be that he is sitting, not on a wagon, but on a terribly tall tower, from which, if you fell, it would take you a whole day, a whole month, to reach the earth— you would keep falling and never get there. Maybe it is simply the Cossack Likhachev sitting under the wagon, but it very well may be that he is the kindest, bravest, most wonderful, most excellent man in the world, whom nobody knows. Maybe it was indeed a hussar who came for water and went back into the hollow, but maybe he just vanished from sight, vanished completely, and never was.

Whatever Petya might have seen now, nothing would have astonished him. He was in a magic kingdom in which everything was possible.

He looked at the sky. The sky was as magical as the earth. The sky was clearing, and clouds raced over the treetops, as if uncovering the stars. Sometimes it seemed that the clouds dispersed and a black, clear sky appeared. Sometimes it seemed that these black patches were clouds. Sometimes it seemed that the sky rose high, high above his head; sometimes the sky came right down, so that he could touch it with his hand.

Petya began to close his eyes and rock.

Drops dripped. Quiet talk went on. Horses neighed and scuffled. Someone snored.

"Ozhik, zhik, ozhik, zhik . . ." whistled the sabre being sharpened. And suddenly Petya heard a harmonious chorus of music, playing some unknown, solemnly sweet hymn. Petya was musical, like Natasha, and more so than Nikolai, but he had never studied music or thought about music, and therefore the melodies that unexpectedly came to his head were especially new and attractive to him. The music played more and more audibly. The melody grew, passing from one instrument to another. What is known as a fugue was going on, though Petya had not the slightest idea of what a fugue was. Each instrument, now resembling a violin, now trumpets—but better and clearer than violins and trumpets—each instrument played its own part and, before finishing its motif, merged with another, starting out almost the same, and with a third, and with a fourth, and they all merged into one and scattered again, and merged again, now solemn and churchly, now brightly brilliant and victorious.

"Ah, yes, it's me dreaming," Petya said to himself, rocking forward. "It's in my ears. And maybe it's my music. Well, again. Go on, my music! Now! . . ."

He closed his eyes. And on all sides, as if from far away, sounds trembled, began to harmonize, scattered, merged, and again all joined in the same sweet and solemn hymn. "Ah, how lovely that is! As much as I like and however I like," Petya said to himself. He attempted to conduct this huge chorus of instruments.

"Softer, softer now, fade away." And the sounds obeyed him. "Fuller now, merrier. More, more joyful." And swelling, solemn sounds rose from an unknown depth. "Now, voices, join in!" Petya ordered. And voices, first men's, then women's, came from far away. The voices grew, grew in a measured, solemn effort. Petya felt frightened and joyful hearkening to their uncommon beauty.

The song merged with the solemn, victorious march, and drops dripped, and bzhik, zhik, zhik . . . whistled the sabre, and again the horses scuffled and neighed, not disrupting the chorus, but entering into it.

Petya did not know how long it went on; he enjoyed it, was surprised all the while at his enjoyment and sorry there was no one to share in it. He was awakened by Likhachev's gentle voice.

"It's ready, Your Honour, you'll split a Frenchman right in two."

Petya woke up.

"It's getting light already, really getting light!" he cried.

The formerly invisible horses could now be seen down to their tails, and a watery light was coming through the bared branches. Petya shook himself, jumped up, took a rouble from his pocket and gave it to Likhachev, swung the sabre to try it out, and put it in the scabbard. The Cossacks were untying the horses and tightening their saddle girths.

"And here's the commander," said Likhachev.

Denisov came out of the guardhouse and, calling Petya, told him to get ready.

<h1 style="text-align:center">XI</h1>

In the half darkness, horses were quickly taken, girths were tightened, and units were formed. Denisov stood by the guardhouse giving last-minute orders. The infantry of the party, splashing with a hundred feet, went ahead on the road and quickly disappeared among the trees in the pre-dawn mist. The esaul was giving some orders to the Cossacks. Petya was holding his horse by the bridle, waiting impatiently for the order to mount up. Washed with cold water, his face, especially his eyes, burned with fire, a chill ran down his spine, and something trembled rapidly and regularly all over his body.

"Well, is everything ghready?" asked Denisov. "Bghring the horses."

The horses were brought. Denisov got angry with the Cossack for the slack girth and, having rebuked him, mounted up. Petya took hold of the stirrup. The horse, out of habit, went to nip him in the leg, but Petya, not feeling his own weight, quickly leaped into the saddle and, looking back at the hussars who set out behind him in the darkness, rode up to Denisov.

"Vassily Fyodorovich, will you entrust me with something? Please . . . for God's sake . . ." he said. Denisov seemed to have forgotten about Petya's existence. He looked at him.

"One thing I ask of you," he said sternly, "listen to me and don't poke your nose anywhere."

During the whole traverse, Denisov did not say a word more to Petya and rode silently. When they rode up to the edge of the forest, it was beginning to grow noticeably light in the field. Denisov said something in a whisper to the esaul, and the Cossacks began to ride past Petya and Denisov. When they had all ridden past, Denisov touched up his horse and rode down the hill. Sitting back and sliding, the horses and riders descended into the hollow. Petya rode

beside Denisov. The trembling in his whole body kept increasing. It was growing brighter and brighter, only the mist hid distant objects. Having ridden
down and looked around, Denisov nodded to a Cossack who was standing
next to him.

"The signal!" he said.

The Cossack raised his hand, a shot rang out. And at the same moment
came the thud of horses galloping ahead, shouts from different sides, and more
shots.

At the same moment, as the sound of thudding hoofs and shouts rang out,
Petya, lashing his horse and loosing the reins, not listening to Denisov, who
was shouting to him, galloped forward. It seemed to Petya that it suddenly
became completely bright, like midday, just as the shot rang out. He rode up to
the bridge. Ahead of him Cossacks were galloping along the road. On the
bridge he ran into a Cossack who lagged behind and galloped on. Ahead of
him some people—it must have been the French—were running from the
right side of the road to the left. One fell into the mud under the feet of Petya's
horse.

By one cottage, Cossacks were crowded, doing something. A terrible cry
came from the midst of the crowd. Petya rode up to this crowd, and the first
thing he saw was the pale face of a Frenchman with a trembling lower jaw,
who was clutching the shaft of a pike pointed at him.

"Hurrah! . . . Lads . . . ours . . ." cried Petya, and, giving free rein to his
excited horse, he rode on up the street.

Shooting was heard ahead. Cossacks, hussars, and ragged Russian prisoners
were running along both sides of the street, shouting something loudly and
incoherently. A dashing Frenchman in a blue greatcoat, hatless, with a red,
frowning face, was fighting off some hussars with his bayonet. When Petya
galloped up, the Frenchman had already fallen. "Late again," flashed in Petya's
head, and he rode to where he heard the sounds of rapid gunfire. The shots
were coming from the courtyard of the manor house, where he had been the
night before with Dolokhov. The French had ensconced themselves there
behind the wattle fence, in a garden densely overgrown with bushes, and were
firing at the Cossacks crowding in the gateway. Riding up to the gate, Petya
saw Dolokhov amidst the powder smoke, with a pale, greenish face, shouting
something to the men. "Go round! Wait for the infantry!" he was shouting just
as Petya rode up to him.

"Wait? . . . Hurra-a-ah! . . ." shouted Petya, and, not losing a moment, he
galloped towards the place from which the shots were coming and where the
powder smoke was thickest. A volley of shots rang out, stray bullets whined
and splatted into something. The Cossacks and Dolokhov galloped after Petya
through the gates of the house. In the dense, undulating smoke some of the
French dropped their weapons and ran out of the bushes towards the Cos-

sacks, others ran down the hill to the pond. Petya galloped on his horse across the manor courtyard, and, instead of holding the reins, waved both arms somehow strangely and quickly, and kept slipping further and further to one side in his saddle. Running into the campfire smouldering in the morning light, the horse balked, and Petya fell heavily onto the wet ground. The Cossacks saw how his arms and legs jerked rapidly, though his head did not move. His head had been pierced by a bullet.

Having parleyed with the senior French officer, who came out to him from behind the house with a handkerchief on his sword and announced that they would surrender, Dolokhov got off his horse and went over to Petya, who lay motionless with outstretched arms.

"Finished," he said, frowning, and walked out of the gates to meet Denisov, who was riding towards him.

"Killed?!" cried Denisov, seeing from far off the familiar, undoubtedly lifeless, position in which Petya's body lay.

"Finished," Dolokhov repeated, as if uttering this word gave him pleasure, and walked quickly to the prisoners surrounded by dismounted Cossacks. "We won't take any!" he cried to Denisov.

Denisov did not reply. He rode up to Petya, got off his horse, and with trembling hands turned Petya's face towards him. It was stained with blood and mud and already turning pale.

"I'm used to something sweet. Excellent raisins, take them all," he recalled. And the Cossacks glanced round in surprise at the sounds, similar to a dog's barking, with which Denisov quickly turned away, went to the wattle fence, and caught hold of it.

Among the Russian prisoners retaken by Denisov and Dolokhov was Pierre Bezukhov.

XII

During the whole time of its movement from Moscow, there had been no new instructions from the French authorities about the party of prisoners that Pierre was in. On the twenty-second of October, that party was no longer with the same troops and trains with which it had left Moscow. Half of the train with biscuits, which had followed them during the first marches, had been taken by the Cossacks, the other half had gone further ahead. Not one of the dismounted cavalrymen who had marched before them was left; they had all disappeared. The artillery, which during the first marches could be seen ahead, had now been replaced by the huge train of Marshal Junot, escorted by Westphalians. Behind the prisoners came the train of cavalry supplies.

From Vyazma the French troops, formerly moving in three columns, now went in a single crowd. The signs of disorder, which Pierre had noticed at the first halt after Moscow, had now reached the final degree.

The road they followed was strewn on both sides with dead horses; the ragged men who fell behind various units changed constantly, now rejoining, then again falling behind the moving column.

Several times during the march there were false alarms, and the soldiers of the convoy raised their muskets, fired, and ran headlong, trampling each other, but then gathered again and denounced each other for needless fear.

These three assemblies moving together—the cavalry depot, the depot of prisoners, and Junot's train—still constituted separate entities, though the first, the second, and the third were quickly melting away.

In the first depot, in which there had been one hundred and twenty wagons to begin with, there now remained no more than sixty; the rest had been captured or abandoned. Of Junot's train, several wagons had also been abandoned or captured. Three wagons had been looted in a raid by straggling soldiers from Davout's corps. From the conversation of the Germans, Pierre heard that more guards had been placed on this train than on the prisoners, and that one of their comrades, a German soldier, had been shot on orders from the marshal himself, because a silver spoon belonging to the marshal had been found among the soldier's possessions.

Of these three assemblies, the depot of prisoners had melted away most of all. Of the three hundred and thirty men who had set out from Moscow, there now remained less than a hundred. The prisoners were a still greater burden to the soldiers of the convoy than the saddles of the cavalry depot or Junot's train. They understood that the saddles and Junot's spoons might be of some use, but why the hungry and cold soldiers had to stand guard and watch over equally cold and hungry Russians, who were dying and fell behind on the road, who were ordered to be shot—this was not only incomprehensible, but also repugnant. And the convoy, as if fearing, in the grievous position they found themselves, to give way to the pity they felt for the prisoners, and thereby worsen their own position, treated them especially grimly and sternly.

In Dorogobuzh, while the convoy soldiers, having locked the prisoners in a stable, had gone to loot their own storehouses, several of the imprisoned soldiers tunnelled under the wall and escaped, but they were caught by the French and shot.

The former order, introduced at the departure from Moscow, that the captive officers would go separately from the soldiers, had long since been abolished; all those who could walk went together, and since the third march Pierre had been reunited with Karataev and the bow-legged purplish dog, who had chosen Karataev for its master.

Karataev, on the third day after leaving Moscow, came down with that fever in which he had been lying in the Moscow hospital, and as he grew weaker,

Pierre withdrew from him. Pierre did not know why, but ever since Karataev had begun to weaken, he had had to make an effort to approach him. And approaching him and listening to the quiet moaning with which Karataev usually lay down during their halts, and sensing the increased smell that Karataev now gave off, Pierre moved further away from him and did not think about him.

In captivity, in the shed, Pierre had learned, not with his mind, but with his whole being, his life, that man is created for happiness, that happiness is within him, in the satisfying of natural human needs, and that all unhappiness comes not from lack, but from superfluity; but now, in these last three weeks of the march, he had learned a new and more comforting truth—he had learned that there is nothing frightening in the world. He had learned that, as there is no situation in the world in which a man can be happy and perfectly free, so there is no situation in which he can be perfectly unhappy and unfree. He had learned that there is a limit to suffering and a limit to freedom, and that those limits are very close; that the man who suffers because one leaf is askew in his bed of roses, suffers as much as he now suffered falling asleep on the bare, damp ground, one side getting cold as the other warmed up; that when he used to put on his tight ballroom shoes, he suffered just as much as now, when he walked quite barefoot (his shoes had long since worn out) and his feet were covered with sores. He learned that when, by his own will, as it had seemed to him, he had married his wife, he had been no more free than now, when he was locked in a stable for the night. Of all that he, too, later called suffering, but which at the time he hardly felt, the main thing was his bare feet, covered with sores and scabs. (Horsemeat was tasty and nutritious, the saltpetre bouquet of the gunpowder they used instead of salt was even agreeable, there were no great cold spells, and walking in the daytime always made him hot, while at night there were campfires; the lice that ate him warmed his body pleasantly.) One thing was painful at first—his feet.

On the second day of the march, when Pierre examined his sores by the campfire, he thought it would be impossible to step on them; but when everybody got up, he went along limping, and then, having warmed up, walked without pain, though by evening his feet were still more frightful to look at. But he did not look at them and thought of other things.

Only now did Pierre understand the full force of human vitality and the saving power of the shifting of attention that has been put in man, similar to the safety valve in steam engines, which releases the extra steam as soon as the pressure exceeds a certain norm.

He did not see or hear how the prisoners who fell behind were shot, though more than a hundred of them had already died in that way. He did not think about Karataev, who grew weaker every day and obviously would soon be subjected to the same lot. Still less did Pierre think about himself. The harder his situation became, the more terrible the future, the more independent of the situation he found himself in were the joyful and calming thoughts, memories, and images that came to him.

XIII

At noon on the twenty-second, Pierre was going up a hill on a muddy, slippery road, looking at his feet and the unevenness of the way. Now and then he glanced at the familiar crowd around him, then again at his feet. Both were equally his own and familiar to him. The bow-legged purplish Grey ran merrily along the side of the road, cocking its hind leg and hopping on three, to prove its agility and satisfaction, then dashing along again on all four, barking at the crows that sat on the carrion. Grey was sleeker and merrier than in Moscow. On all sides lay the flesh of various animals, from men to horses, in various stages of decay. The walking men kept the wolves from coming near, so that Grey could eat as much as he liked.

It had been raining all morning, and had seemed as if it were just about to stop and the sky to clear, when, after a short pause, the rain would come down harder still. The rain-soaked road no longer absorbed water, and streams flowed down the ruts.

Pierre walked along looking on all sides, counting his steps by threes, and bending his fingers. Addressing the rain, he was inwardly saying to it: "Well, well, go on, give us some more."

It seemed to him that he was not thinking of anything; but somewhere far and deep his soul was thinking something important and comforting. That something was the subtlest spiritual extract from his conversation the day before with Karataev.

The day before, at their nightly halt, having grown cold by a dead campfire, Pierre had got up and gone over to the nearest better-burning fire. By the fire he went to sat Platon, his greatcoat covering his head like a priest's vestment, telling the soldiers, in his quick, pleasant, but weak, sickly voice, a story Pierre knew.[6] It was already past midnight. This was the time when Karataev usually recovered from his bouts of fever and was especially animated. Coming up to the fire and hearing Platon's weak, sickly voice and seeing his pitiful face brightly lit by the fire, Pierre felt something stab his heart unpleasantly. He was afraid of his pity for this man and wanted to go away, but there was no other fire, and so, trying not to look at Platon, Pierre sat down by the fire.

"So, how's your health?" he asked.

"My health? Lament for your sickness, and God won't grant you death," said Karataev, and he went back at once to the story he had begun.

". . . And so, brother mine," Platon continued, with a smile on his thin, pale face, and with a special, joyful brightness in his eyes, "so, brother mine . . ."

Pierre had long known this story. Karataev had told it to him alone some six times, and always with a special, joyful feeling. But however well Pierre knew this story, he now listened to it as something new, and the quiet rapture that Karataev clearly felt as he told it communicated itself to Pierre. It was a story about an old merchant, who lived a seemly and God-fearing life with his family, and went once with a comrade, a rich merchant, to the Makary.[7]

Having stopped at an inn, the two merchants went to bed, and the next day the comrade was found murdered and robbed. The bloody knife was found under the old merchant's pillow. The merchant was tried, punished with the knout, and, having had his nostrils slit, was—in due order, as Karataev said—sent to hard labour.

"And so, brother mine" (Pierre arrived at this point in Karataev's story), "ten years or more go by after this affair. The old man lives at hard labour. Duly submits, does nothing bad. Only asks God for death. Good. And the convicts got together, a nightly thing, like you and me here, and the old man was with them. They started talking about who suffers for what, and what he's guilty of before God. They began telling: this one killed a man, that one killed two, another set a fire, another was a runaway, so he did nothing. They started asking the old man: 'What are you suffering for, grandpa?' 'I, my dear brothers,' he says, 'am suffering for my own and other people's sins. I didn't kill anybody, or take anything that wasn't mine, but even gave to beggars. I, my dear brothers, was a merchant; I had great wealth.' Thus and so, he says. That is, he told them how the whole thing went, in proper order. 'I don't grieve over myself,' he says. 'God, that is, has found me. I only pity my old woman and children.' And so the old man wept. In their company there happened to be the very man who had killed the merchant. 'Where did it happen, grandpa?' he says. 'When, in what month?'—he asked everything. His heart ached inside him. He goes up to the old man and—plop at his feet. 'You're perishing because of me, old man. It's the real truth. This man is suffering, lads,' he says, 'guiltlessly and needlessly. I did that deed,' he says, 'and put the knife under your head while you slept. Forgive me, grandpa,' he says, 'for Christ's sake.' "

Karataev fell silent, smiling joyfully, gazing at the fire, and he adjusted the logs.

"And the old man says: 'God will forgive you, and we're all sinful before God, I'm suffering for my own sins.' And he wept bitter tears. And what do you think, little falcon?" Karataev was speaking with a rapturous smile that beamed brighter and brighter, as if what he was about to tell contained the chief delight and the whole meaning of the story, "what do you think, little falcon, this same murderer denounced himself to the authorities. 'I killed six men,' he says (he was a great villain), 'but I'm sorriest for this old man. Let him not lament on account of me.' He declared it: they wrote it down, duly sent a letter. This was a far-off place, it was a while before everything got done, all the papers filled out as they ought, to the authorities, that is. It went all the way to the tsar. Time passed, the tsar's ukase came: release the merchant, give him a reward, as much as they decided. The paper came, they started searching for the old man. Where's that old man who has suffered guiltlessly and needlessly? A paper has come from the tsar. They started searching." Karataev's lower jaw quivered. "But God had already forgiven him—he was dead. There it is, little falcon," Karataev concluded and for a long time, smiling silently, he looked straight in front of him.

It was not the story itself, but its mysterious meaning, the rapturous joy that shone in Karataev's face as he told it, the mysterious significance of that joy, that now strangely and joyfully filled Pierre's soul.

XIV

"*À vos places!*"* a voice suddenly cried.

Among the prisoners and the convoy, a joyful commotion and expectation of something happy and solemn set in. Shouts of command were heard on all sides, and cavalrymen appeared to the left, well-dressed, on good horses, trotting around the prisoners. On all faces there was the expression of tension that people have at the proximity of high powers. The prisoners pressed together, they were pushed off the road; the convoy formed up.

"*L'Empereur! L'Empereur! Le maréchal! Le duc!*"—and the well-fed convoy had no sooner passed than a carriage rumbled by, drawn by grey horses in tandem. Pierre caught a glimpse of the calm, handsome, fat, and white face of a man in a three-cornered hat. It was one of the marshals. The marshal's gaze turned to the large, conspicuous figure of Pierre, and in the expression with which this marshal frowned and turned away, Pierre fancied he saw compassion and the desire to conceal it.

The general who led the depot, his face red and frightened, urging on his skinny horse, galloped after the carriage. Several officers came together, with soldiers surrounding them. They all had tensely excited faces.

"*Qu'est-ce qu'il a dit? Qu'est-ce qu'il a dit?. . .*"† Pierre heard.

As the marshal was driving by, the prisoners pressed together, and Pierre saw Karataev, whom he had not yet seen that morning. Karataev, in his meagre greatcoat, sat leaning against a birch tree. In his face, besides the expression of yesterday's joyful tenderness as he was telling the story of the merchant's guiltless suffering, there also shone an expression of quiet solemnity.

Karataev looked at Pierre with his kind, round eyes, now veiled with tears, and was evidently calling him over, wanting to say something. But Pierre was

*To your places!
†What did he say? What did he say? . . .

too afraid for himself. He pretended that he had not seen his look and hurriedly walked away.

When the prisoners started off again, Pierre looked back. Karataev was sitting at the edge of the road, by the birch, and two Frenchmen were saying something over him. Pierre did not look any longer. He went limping up the hill.

From behind, where Karataev had been sitting, came the sound of a shot. Pierre heard the shot clearly, but the moment he heard it, he recalled that he had not finished the calculation, begun before the marshal passed, of how many marches there remained to Smolensk. And he started to count. Two French soldiers, one of them holding a smoking gun in his hand, ran past Pierre. Both were pale, and the expression of their faces—one of them glanced timidly at Pierre— had something in it similar to what he had seen in the young soldier at the execution. Pierre looked at the soldier and remembered how, two days before, this soldier had burned his shirt while drying it over the campfire, and how everybody had laughed at him.

A dog began to howl behind, in the place where Karataev had been sitting. "What a fool, what's it howling about?" thought Pierre.

Like him, his soldier comrades, walking beside Pierre, did not turn to look at the place from which the shot had been heard and then the howling of the dog; but there was a stern look on all their faces.

XV

The depot, and the prisoners, and the marshal's train stopped in the village of Shamshevo. They all crowded in a mass by the campfires. Pierre went up to the fire, ate some roasted horsemeat, lay down with his back to the fire, and fell asleep at once. He slept again the same sleep as he had slept in Mozhaisk after the battle of Borodino.

Again the events of reality combined with dreams, and again someone, he himself or some other person, spoke thoughts to him, and even the same thoughts that had been spoken to him in Mozhaisk.

"Life is everything. Life is God. Everything shifts and moves, and this movement is God. And while there is life, there is delight in the self-awareness of the divinity. To love life is to love God. The hardest and most blissful thing is to love this life in one's suffering, in the guiltlessness of suffering."

"Karataev!" Pierre recalled.

And suddenly a long-forgotten, meek old teacher, who had taught him geography in Switzerland, emerged in Pierre's mind as if alive. "Wait!" said the old man. And he showed Pierre a globe. This globe was a living, wavering ball of no dimensions. The entire surface of the ball consisted of drops tightly packed together. And these drops all moved and shifted, and now merged from several into one, now divided from one into many. Each drop strove to spread and take up the most space, but the others, striving to do the same, pressed it, sometimes destroying, sometimes merging with it.

"This is life," said the old teacher.

"How simple and clear it is," thought Pierre. "How could I not have known before?"

"In the centre is God, and each drop strives to expand in order to reflect Him in the greatest measure. It grows, merges, and shrinks, and is obliterated on the surface, goes into the depths, and again floats up. Here he is, Karataev, see, he spread and vanished. *Vous avez compris, mon enfant?*"* said the teacher.

"*Vous avez compris, sacré nom?*"† shouted the voice, and Pierre woke up.

He raised himself and sat up. A Frenchman was squatting by the fire, having just shoved a Russian soldier aside, and was roasting some meat on a ramrod. His sleeves were rolled up, and his sinewy, hairy, stub-fingered red hands were deftly turning the ramrod. His brown, gloomy face with frowning eyebrows was clearly visible in the light from the coals.

"*Ça lui est bien égal,*" he growled, glancing quickly at the soldier, who was standing behind him, ". . . *brigand. Va!*"‡

And, turning the ramrod, he glanced gloomily at Pierre. Pierre turned away, peering into the shadows. One captive Russian soldier, the one whom the Frenchman had shoved aside, was sitting by the fire and patting something with his hand. Looking more closely, Pierre recognized the purplish dog, who was sitting by the soldier, wagging its tail.

"Ah, it's come?" said Pierre. "Ah, Pla . . ." he began, and did not finish. In his imagination suddenly, simultaneously, connecting among themselves, memories emerged of the gaze with which Platon had looked at him, sitting under the tree, of the shot he had heard from that spot, of the howling of a dog, of the criminal faces of the two Frenchmen who had run past him, of the smoking gun in the hand, of the absence of Karataev at this halt, and he was ready then to understand that Karataev had been killed, but at the same moment a memory emerged in his soul, coming from God knows where, of an evening he had spent with a beautiful Polish woman, in the summer, on the balcony of his house in Kiev. And still not connecting the memories of that day and not drawing any conclusions about them, Pierre closed his eyes, and the picture of summer nature mixed with the memory of bathing, of the liquid, wavering ball, and he sank somewhere into the water, so that the water closed over his head.

---

*Have you understood, my child?
†Have you understood, damn it?
‡It's all the same to him . . . brigand. Get out!

Before sunrise he was awakened by loud, rapid gunshots, and shouting French soldiers ran past him.

"*Les cosaques!*" one of them shouted, and a moment later Pierre was surrounded by a crowd of Russian faces.

For a long time Pierre could not understand what was happening to him. On all sides he heard his comrades' shouts of joy.

"Brothers! My dear ones, my darlings!" the old soldiers cried out, weeping, embracing the Cossacks and hussars. The hussars and Cossacks surrounded the prisoners and hastened to offer them—one clothes, another boots, another bread. Pierre sobbed, sitting among them, and could not utter a word; he embraced the first soldier who came up to him and kissed him, weeping.

Dolokhov stood by the gates of a ruined house, letting a crowd of disarmed French soldiers go past him. The French, shaken by all that had happened, talked loudly among themselves; but as they went past Dolokhov, who tapped himself lightly on the boots with a whip and looked at them with his cold, glassy gaze, which promised nothing good, the talk ceased. Opposite him stood Dolokhov's Cossack, counting the prisoners and marking the hundreds with a chalk line on the gate.

"How many?" Dolokhov asked the Cossack who was counting the captives.

"Going on the second hundred," replied the Cossack.

"*Filez, filez,*" Dolokhov kept repeating, having learned this expression from the French, and, meeting the eyes of the passing prisoners, his gaze flashed with a cruel gleam.

Denisov, with a gloomy face, taking off his papakha, followed behind some Cossacks who were carrying to a pit dug in the garden the body of Petya Rostov.

XVI

From the twenty-eighth of October, when the frosts set in, the flight of the French only acquired a more tragic character of men freezing or roasting to death by campfires, and of the emperor, kings, and dukes in fur coats continuing to drive on in carriages filled with stolen goods; but in essence the process of the flight and decomposition of the French army had not changed in the least since the departure from Moscow.

Between Moscow and Vyazma, of the French army of seventy-three thousand men, not counting the guards (who did nothing but loot during the entire war), there remained thirty-six thousand (though no more than five thousand had been lost in battle). This is the first member of a progression, which determines the subsequent members with mathematical certainty.

The French army melted away and was annihilated in the same proportion from Moscow to Vyazma, from Vyazma to Smolensk, from Smolensk to the Berezina, from the Berezina to Vilno, irrespective of the greater or lesser degree of the cold, the pursuit, the barring of roads, and all other conditions taken separately. After Vyazma the French army, instead of three columns, pressed together in a single mass, and so went on to the end. Berthier wrote to his sovereign (it is known how far superior officers allow themselves to depart from the truth in describing the situation of an army). He wrote:

Je crois devoir faire connaître à Votre Majesté l'état de ses troupes dans les différent corps d'armée que j'ai été à même d'observer depuis deux ou trois jours dans différents passages. Elles sont presque débandées. Le nombre des soldats qui suivent les drapeaux est en proportion du quart au plus dans presque tous les régiments, les autres marchent isolément dans différents directions et pour leur compte, dans l'espérance de trouver des subsistances et pour se débarrasser de la discipline. En général ils regardent Smolensk comme le point où ils doivent se refaire. Ces derniers jours on a remarqué que beaucoup de soldats jettent leurs cartouches et leurs armes. Dans cet état de choses, l'intérêt du service de Votre Majesté exige, quelles que soient ses vues ultérieurs, qu'on rallie l'armée à Smolensk en commençant à la débarrasser des non-combattants, tels que hommes démontés et des bagages inutiles et du matériel de l'artillerie qui n'est plus en proportion avec les forces actuelles. En outre les jours de repos, des subsistances sont nécessaires aux soldats qui sont exténués par la faim et la fatigue; beaucoup sont morts ces derniers jours sur la route et dans les bivouacs. Cet état de choses va toujours en augmentant et donne lieu de craindre que si l'on n'y prête un prompt remède, on ne soit plus maître des troupes dans un combat.

Le 9 novembre, à 30 verstes de Smolensk.*

---

*I believe it my duty to inform Your Majesty of the state of his troops in the different corps of the army that I have been able to observe over the past two or three days in different visits. They are on the point of disbanding. The number of soldiers following the colours is in the proportion of a quarter at most in almost all the regiments; the rest march separately in different directions and on their own, in the hope of finding subsistence and to be rid of discipline. In general they consider Smolensk as the point where they must recuperate. In the last few days many soldiers have been seen throwing down their cartridges and weapons. In this state of affairs, the interest of Your Majesty's service, whatever his further plans, demands that we rally the army at Smolensk, beginning by ridding it of noncombatants, such as men without horses, and of useless baggage and the artillery matériel, which is no longer in proportion to our present forces. Besides days of rest, subsistence is also necessary for the soldiers, who are exhausted by hunger and fatigue; many have died over these last days on the road and in the bivouacs. This state of affairs keeps worsening and makes one fear that, if a prompt remedy is not applied, one will no longer be in control of the troops in case of combat.

9 November, 30 versts from Smolensk.

Barging into Smolensk, which in their imagination was a promised land, the French killed each other over provisions, looted their own storehouses, and, when everything had been looted, ran further.

They all went, not knowing themselves where they were going or why. The genius Napoleon knew still less than others, since no one gave him orders. But even so he and his entourage observed their long-standing habits: wrote orders, letters, reports, the *ordre du jour;** addressed each other as *Sire, Mon Cousin, Prince d'Eckmühl, roi de Naples,* and so on. But the orders and reports existed only on paper, nothing was carried out according to them, because nothing could be carried out, and despite their calling themselves majesties, highnesses, and cousins, they all felt that they were pathetic and vile people who had done a great deal of evil, for which they now had to pay. And despite their pretence of looking after the army, each of them thought only of himself and of how to get away quickly and save himself.

XVII

The actions of the Russian and French armies during the reverse campaign from Moscow to the Niemen resemble a game of blindman's buff, when two players are blindfolded and one occasionally rings a little bell to let the catcher know where he is. At first the one to be caught rings without fearing the enemy, but, when things go badly for him, he runs away from his enemy, trying to move inaudibly, and often, thinking to escape, goes straight into his arms.

At first Napoleon's troops let their presence be known—this was in the initial period of their movement along the Kaluga road—but later, coming out to the Smolensk road, they began to run, holding the little bell's tongue, and often, thinking they were getting away, ran straight into the Russians.

Owing to the quickness of the French flight and the Russian pursuit, and the resulting exhaustion of the horses, the chief means of roughly ascertaining the position of the enemy—cavalry patrols—did not exist. Besides that, as a result of the frequent and rapid changes of position of the two armies, information, if there was any, could not arrive in time. If the news came on the second that the enemy army had been in such-and-such place on the first, then on the third, when something could have been done, the army had already gone two marches further and was in a completely different position.

One army ran, the other pursued. From Smolensk the French had many different roads before them; and it would seem that, staying for four days, the French could have found out where the enemy was, worked out something advantageous, and undertaken something new. But after the four-day halt, their

*Order of the day.

crowds again ran, not to the right, not to the left, but, without any manoeuvres or considerations, down the old, worst road to Krasnoe and Orsha—by the beaten track.

Expecting the enemy from behind, and not from in front, the French ran, stringing out and separating from each other, over a twenty-four-hour stretch. Ahead of them all ran the emperor, then the kings, then the dukes. The Russian army, thinking that Napoleon would bear to the right, beyond the Dnieper, which was the only reasonable thing, also bore to the right and came out on the main road to Krasnoe. And here, as in the game of blindman's buff, the French ran into our vanguard. Unexpectedly sighting the foe, the French became confused, stopped from the unexpectedness of the fright, but then ran on again, abandoning their comrades who followed behind. Here, for three days, separate units of the French, first the viceroy's, then Davout's, then Ney's, ran the gauntlet of the Russian troops. They all abandoned each other, abandoned their loads, artillery, half their men, and ran, getting around the Russians only by night, making semicircles to the right.

Ney, coming last, because he had busied himself with blowing up the walls of Smolensk, which were not hindering anyone (in spite of their unfortunate position, or precisely because of it, they wanted to give a beating to the floor on which they had hurt themselves)—coming last, Ney, who had a corps of ten thousand, came running to Napoleon in Orsha with only a thousand men, having abandoned all the other men and all his cannon and stolen away in the night, making his way through a forest and across the Dnieper.

From Orsha they ran further along the road to Vilno, playing blindman's buff with the enemy in the same way. At the Berezina they again fell into confusion, many were drowned, many surrendered, but those who got across the river ran further. Their supreme leader put on his fur coat and, getting into a sledge, galloped off alone, abandoning his comrades. Whoever could, also rode off, whoever could not surrendered or died.

XVIII

It would seem, in this campaign of the flight of the French, when they did everything they could to destroy themselves, when not a single movement of this crowd, from the turn onto the Kaluga road to the flight of the leader from his army, made the least sense—it would seem finally impossible, in this period of the campaign, for historians who ascribe the actions of the masses to the will of one man to describe this retreat in their sense. But no. Mountains of books have been written by historians about this campaign, and they all describe Napoleon's orders and his profound plans—the manoeuvres that guided the troops, and the brilliant orders of his marshals.

The retreat from Maloyaroslavets, when the road to abundant lands was given to him, and when the parallel road on which Kutuzov later pursued him was also open, the unnecessary retreat along a devastated road is explained to us by various profound considerations. His retreat from Smolensk to Orsha is described by means of the same profound considerations. Then his heroism at Krasnoe is described, where he is supposed to have been preparing to accept battle and command it himself, and walked about with a birch stick, saying:

"J'ai assez fait l'Empereur, il est temps de faire le général,"* and, despite that, immediately afterwards ran further, abandoning to their fate the scattered units of the army he left behind.

Then the greatness of soul of the marshals is described for us, especially of Ney, his greatness of soul consisting in his making a roundabout way by night through the forest and across the Dnieper, coming on the run to Orsha, minus banners and artillery and nine tenths of his troops.

And, lastly, the final departure of the great emperor from his heroic army is presented to us by historians as something great and marked by genius. Even this final act of flight, known in human language as the final degree of baseness, which every child is taught to be ashamed of, even this act receives justification in the language of the historians.

Then, when it is no longer possible to stretch the so-elastic threads of historical discourse any further, when an action clearly contradicts all that mankind calls good and even just, historians resort to the saving notion of greatness. It is as if greatness excludes the possibility of the measure of good and bad. For the great man there is no bad. There is no horror that can be laid to the blame of someone who is great.

"C'est grand!"† say the historians, and then there is no longer any good or bad, but there is "grand" and "not grand." Grand is good, not grand is bad. Grand, to their minds, is the property of some sort of special animals known as heroes. And Napoleon, in his warm fur coat, clearing off for home from his perishing men, who are not only comrades, but (in his opinion) people he has brought there, feels que c'est grand, and his soul is at peace.

"Du sublime" (he sees something sublime in himself) "au ridicule il n'y a qu'un pas,"‡ he says. And for fifty years the whole world repeats: "Sublime! Grand! Napoléon le grand! Du sublime au ridicule il n'y a qu'un pas."

And it never enters anyone's head that the recognition of a greatness not measurable by the measure of good and bad is only a recognition of one's own insignificance and immeasurable littleness.

---

*I have been emperor long enough, it is time to be a general.
†It is great.
‡There is only one step from the sublime to the ridiculous.

For us, with the measures of good and bad given us by Christ, nothing is immeasurable. And there is no greatness where there is no simplicity, goodness, and truth.

XIX

Who among Russian people, reading the descriptions of the last period of the campaign of 1812, has not experienced an oppressive feeling of vexation, dissatisfaction, and vagueness? Who has not asked himself the questions: why were all the French not captured, not destroyed, when three armies surrounded them in superior numbers, when the disordered French, starving and freezing, surrendered in masses, and when (as the historians tell us) the aim of the Russians consisted precisely in stopping, cutting off, and capturing all the French?

How did it happen that the Russian army, which, weaker in numbers than the French, gave battle at Borodino, how did it happen that this army, surrounding the French on three sides and having the aim of capturing them, failed to do so? Can it be that the French had such an enormous advantage over us that we, surrounding them with superior forces, could not beat them? How could that happen?

History (or what is called by that name), in answering these questions, says that this happened because Kutuzov, and Tormasov, and Chichagov, and so-and-so, and so-and-so did not execute such-and-such manoeuvres.

But why did they not execute all these manoeuvres? Why, if they were to blame for not achieving the intended aim—why were they not tried and executed? But, even if we allow that Kutuzov and Chichagov and so on were to blame for the *failure* of the Russians, it is impossible to understand why, in such conditions as the Russians were in at Krasnoe and the Berezina (in both cases the Russians had superior forces), why was the French army with its marshals, kings, and emperors not taken captive, if that was the aim of the Russians?

The explanation of this strange phenomenon as Russian military historians give it—that Kutuzov prevented the attack—is groundless, because we know that Kutuzov's will could not keep the troops from attacking at Vyazma and Tarutino.

Why was the same Russian army, which with weaker forces could gain the victory at Borodino over an enemy in full force, defeated at Krasnoe and the Berezina, where its forces were superior, by the disorderly crowds of the French?

If the aim of the Russians consisted in cutting off and capturing Napoleon and the marshals, and that aim was not only not achieved, but all the attempts to achieve it were thwarted each time in the most shameful way, then the last period of the campaign is quite correctly presented by the French as a series of victories, and is quite incorrectly presented by Russian military historians as victorious.

Russian military historians, insofar as they are bound by logic, involuntarily come to this conclusion, and, despite lyrical proclamations of courage and devotion, and so on, have had involuntarily to admit that the retreat of the French from Moscow was a series of victories for Napoleon and of defeats for Kutuzov.

But, leaving national vanity completely aside, one feels that this conclusion contains an inner contradiction, because the series of French victories brought them to total destruction, while the series of Russian defeats led them to the total destruction of the foe and the purging of the fatherland.

The source of this contradiction lies in the fact that historians who study the events from the letters of sovereigns and generals, from relations, reports, plans, and so on, posit a false, never-existing aim for the last period of the war of 1812—an aim which supposedly consisted in cutting off and capturing Napoleon with his marshals and his army.

This aim never existed and could not exist, because it made no sense and to achieve it was totally impossible.

This aim made no sense, first, because Napoleon's disordered army was fleeing Russia with all possible speed, that is, carrying out the very thing that any Russian could desire. What, then, was the need of performing various operations on the French, who were simply fleeing as fast as they could?

Second, it was senseless to stand in the way of people who had put all their energy into flight.

Third, it was senseless to waste our troops on the destruction of the French army, which was being annihilated without any external causes in such a progression that, without any blocking of the path, they were unable to bring across the border more than what they brought across in the month of December, that is, one hundredth of the entire army.

Fourth, it was senseless to wish to take prisoner the emperor, the kings, the dukes—people whose capture would have hampered the actions of the Russians in the highest degree, as was recognized by the most skilful diplomats of that time (Joseph de Maistre and others). Still more senseless would have been the wish to capture whole corps of the French, when our own troops had melted away by half before reaching Krasnoe, and for corps of prisoners it would have been necessary to detach divisions as a convoy, and when our own soldiers did not always receive full rations and the prisoners already taken were starving to death.

The whole profound plan of cutting off and capturing Napoleon and his army was like the plan of a farmer who, while driving out the cattle who were trampling his vegetable garden, would run to the gate and start beating those cattle on the head. The one thing that might be said to justify the farmer is that he was very angry. But it would be impossible to say even that about the devisers of this project, because it was not they who suffered from the trampled vegetable patch.

But, besides the fact that the cutting off of Napoleon and his army was senseless, it was also impossible.

It was impossible, first, because, as is clear from experience, in battle the movement of columns over a stretch of three miles never conforms to plans, so that the probability of Chichagov, Kutuzov, and Wittgenstein coming together on time in the appointed place would have been so slight that it was next to impossible, as Kutuzov thought, who, on receiving the plan, said that diversions over long distances do not bring the desired results.

Second, it was impossible because, in order to paralyse that force of inertia with which Napoleon's troops were moving back, an incomparably bigger army was needed than that which the Russians had.

Third, it was impossible because the military term "to cut off" has no meaning. One can cut off a piece of bread, but not an army. To cut off an army—to bar its way—is quite impossible, because there is always plenty of room for it to go round, and there is the night, during which nothing can be seen, of which military historians could satisfy themselves if only from the examples of Krasnoe and the Berezina. To take a prisoner is quite impossible, unless the one being taken prisoner agrees to it, just as it is impossible to catch a swallow, though you can catch one if it settles on your hand. It is possible to take prisoner someone who surrenders, like the Germans, according to the rules of strategy and tactics. But the French troops quite rightly did not find that suitable, since death from hunger and cold awaited them equally in flight and in captivity.

Fourth, and chiefly, it was impossible because never, as long as the world has existed, has there been a war under such terrible conditions as those in which the war of 1812 took place, and the Russian troops strained all their forces in their pursuit of the French and could not do more without destroying themselves.

In its movement from Tarutino to Krasnoe, the Russian army lost fifty thousand men, sick or fallen behind, which is a number equal to the population of a large provincial town. Half the men dropped out of the army without any battles.

And of this period of the campaign, when troops without boots and warm coats, without sufficient rations, without vodka, for months spending nights in the snow at fifteen degrees of frost; when the day is only seven or eight hours long, and the rest is night, during which discipline can have no influence; when, not as in a battle, in which men enter the realm of death, where there is no longer any discipline, for only a few hours, but when men live for months, fighting every moment with death from hunger and cold; when half the army perishes within a month—of this period of the campaign we are told by historians how Miloradovich was to have made a flanking movement here, and Tormasov there, and how Chichagov was to have moved over there (to move knee-deep in snow), and how so-and-so overran and cut off, and so on, and so forth.

The Russians, dying by half, did all they could do and should have done to achieve an aim worthy of the nation, and are not to blame if other Russian people, sitting in warm rooms, proposed doing what was impossible.

This whole strange, now incomprehensible contradiction between facts and historical descriptions comes only from the fact that the historians who wrote about this event wrote the history of the beautiful feelings and words of various generals, and not the history of the events themselves.

They find very interesting the words of Miloradovich, the decorations received by this or that general, and their own speculations; and the question of those fifty thousand men left in hospitals and graves does not even interest them, because it is not subject to their study.

And yet one need only turn from the study of reports and general plans and look into the movement of those hundreds of thousands of men who took a direct, immediate part in the event, and all the questions that previously seemed insoluble suddenly, with extraordinary ease and simplicity, receive an unquestionable solution.

The aim of cutting off Napoleon and his army never existed, except in the imaginations of several dozen people. It could not exist, because it was senseless, and to achieve it was impossible.

The aim of the people was one: to clear their land of the invasion. That aim was being achieved, first of all, by itself, since the French were running away, and therefore it only followed that this movement should not be stopped. Second, this aim was achieved by the actions of the national war in obliterating the French, and third, by the fact that a large Russian army was following the French, ready to use force in case the movement of the French stopped.

The Russian army had to act like a whip on a running animal. And the experienced driver knew that it was most advantageous to hold the whip raised, to threaten, but not to lash the running animal on the head.

Part Four

I

When a man sees a dying animal, horror comes over him: that which he himself is, his essence, is obviously being annihilated before his eyes—is ceasing to be. But when the dying one is a person, and a beloved person, then, besides a sense of horror at the annihilation of life, there is a feeling of severance and a spiritual wound which, like a physical wound, sometimes kills and sometimes heals, but always hurts and fears any external, irritating touch.

After the death of Prince Andrei, Natasha and Princess Marya equally felt that. Morally bowed down and shutting their eyes to the menacing cloud of death that hung over them, they did not dare to look life in the face. They carefully protected their open wounds from any offensive, painful touch. Everything—a carriage driving quickly down the street, a reminder of dinner, a maid's question about what dress to prepare; still worse, a word of insincere, weak sympathy—everything painfully irritated the wound, seemed offensive, and violated the necessary quiet in which they both tried to listen to the dread, stern choir not yet silenced in their imagination, and prevented them from peering into those mysterious, infinite distances which for a moment had opened before them.

Only together were they not offended or pained. They spoke little between themselves. When they spoke, it was of the most insignificant subjects. They both equally avoided mentioning anything that had a relation to the future.

To acknowledge the possibility of a future seemed to them an offence to his memory. Still more carefully did they avoid in their conversations all that might have a relation to the dead man. It seemed to them that what they had lived through and felt could not be expressed in words. It seemed to them that any mention in words of the details of his life violated the majesty and sacredness of the mystery that had been accomplished before their eyes.

A continual restraint of speech, a constant careful avoidance of all that might lead to words about him: these halts on all sides at the border of what could not be spoken of, brought out still more purely and clearly in their imagination what they both felt.

. . .

But pure, perfect sorrow is as impossible as pure and perfect joy. Princess Marya, in her position as the sole, independent mistress of her fate, the guardian and instructor of her nephew, was the first to be called away by life from the world of sorrow in which she had lived for the first two weeks. She received letters from relations, which had to be answered; the room in which Nikolenka had been placed was damp, and he began to cough. Alpatych came to Yaroslavl with business reports, and with suggestions and advice to move to Moscow, to the house on Vzdvizhenka, which had remained intact and only needed minor repairs. Life did not stop, and one had to live. Hard as it was for Princess Marya to leave the world of solitary contemplation in which she had lived till then, sorry and as if ashamed as she was to leave Natasha alone, the cares of life called for her participation, and she involuntarily surrendered to them. She went over the accounts with Alpatych, consulted with Dessales about her nephew, and gave instructions and made preparations for moving to Moscow.

Natasha remained alone and, once Princess Marya began preparing for departure, avoided her as well.

Princess Marya suggested that the countess allow Natasha to come with her to Moscow, and the mother and father gladly accepted this suggestion, noticing the daily decline in their daughter's physical strength, and supposing that the change of place and the help of Moscow doctors would be good for her.

"I won't go anywhere," replied Natasha, when the suggestion was made, "only please leave me alone," she said and ran out of the room, barely holding back her tears, not so much of grief as of vexation and anger.

After she felt herself deserted by Princess Marya and solitary in her grief, Natasha spent most of her time alone in her room, sitting with her legs tucked up at the corner of the sofa, and, while tearing or kneading something with her thin, tense fingers, stared with an intent, fixed gaze at whatever her eyes rested on. The solitude exhausted her, tormented her; but it was necessary for her. The moment someone came in, she quickly got up, changed her position and the expression of her gaze, and took up a book or some sewing, waiting with obvious impatience for whoever had troubled her to leave.

It kept seeming to her that she was just on the point of understanding, of penetrating, that terrible, overwhelming question at which her inner gaze was directed.

At the end of December, Natasha, in a black woollen dress, her braid carelessly done up in a knot, thin and pale, was sitting with her legs tucked up at the corner of the sofa, tensely crumpling and smoothing out the ends of her sash, and looking at a corner of the door.

She was looking there, where he had gone, to the other side of life. And that side of life, of which she had never thought before, which before had seemed so far off and unbelievable, was now closer and dearer, more comprehensible, to her than this side of life, where everything was either emptiness and ruin, or suffering and offence.

She was looking there, where she knew he was; but she could not see him otherwise than as he had been here. She saw him again as he had been in Mytishchi, at the Trinity, in Yaroslavl.

She saw his face, heard his voice, and repeated his words and the words she had said to him, and sometimes she invented new words for herself and for him, which might have been said then.

Here he is lying in an armchair in his velvet coat, his head propped on his thin, pale hand. His chest is terribly sunken, and his shoulders are hunched. His lips are firmly compressed, his eyes glitter, and a wrinkle springs up and then disappears on his pale forehead. One of his legs trembles rapidly, barely noticeably. Natasha knows that he is struggling with tormenting pain. "What is this pain? Why pain? What is he feeling? How it hurts him!" thinks Natasha. He noticed her attention, raised his eyes, and, without smiling, began to speak.

"One thing is terrible," he had said, "it is to bind yourself for ever to a suffering man. That is eternal torment." And he had looked at her—Natasha could see it now—with a searching gaze. Natasha, as always, had answered then before she had time to think of what answer she would give: "It cannot go on like this, it won't be, you'll get well—completely."

She now saw him anew and lived through all she had felt then. She remembered his prolonged, sad, stern gaze at those words, and understood the meaning of the reproach and despair in that prolonged gaze.

"I agreed," Natasha now said to herself, "that it would be terrible if he was left suffering always. I said it then only because it would be terrible for him, but he understood it differently. He thought it would be terrible *for me.* He still wanted to live then—he was afraid of death. And I said it to him so crudely, so stupidly then. I didn't think that. I thought quite differently. If I had said what I thought, I would have said: let him be dying, dying all the time before my eyes, I would still be happy compared to what I am now. Now . . . There's nothing, nobody. Did he know that? No. He didn't know, and he'll never know. And now it will never, never be possible to put it right." And again he was saying the same words to her, but now, in her imagination, Natasha answered him differently. She stopped him and said: "Terrible for you, but not for me. You know that for me there is nothing in life without you, and to suffer with you is the best happiness for me." And he took her hand and pressed it as he had pressed it on that terrible evening, four days before his death. And in her imagination she said other tender, loving things to him, which she might have said then, and which she was saying now: "I love you . . . you . . . I love, I love . . ." she said, convulsively pressing her hands together, clenching her teeth with a violent effort.

And a sweet sorrow came over her, and tears already welled up in her eyes, but suddenly she asked herself: to whom is she saying this? Where is he, and *who* is he now? And again everything was veiled in a dry, hard perplexity, and again, tensely knitting her brows, she peered there, where he was. And it seemed to her that she was just about to penetrate the mystery . . . But at the moment when the incomprehensible seemed about to be revealed, her hearing was painfully struck by a loud rattling of the door handle. Quickly and heedlessly, with a frightened look on her face, unconcerned with her, the maid Dunyasha came into the room.

"Please go to your father, quickly," said Dunyasha, with a peculiar and animated expression. "A misfortune, about Pyotr Ilyich . . . a letter," she said with a sob.

II

Besides a general feeling of alienation from all people, Natasha experienced at that time a particular feeling of alienation from the persons of her own family. All of them—her father, her mother, Sonya—were so close, so habitual, so humdrum, that all their words and feelings seemed to her an insult to that world in which she had been living recently, and she was not only indifferent, but looked at them with hostility. She heard Dunyasha's words about Pyotr Ilyich, about the misfortune, but she did not understand them.

"What sort of misfortune is there for them, what sort of misfortune could there be? With them it's all their old, habitual, and peaceful thing," Natasha said to herself.

When she entered the reception room, her father was quickly coming out of the countess's room. His face was pinched and wet with tears. He had clearly run out of that room in order to let loose the sobs that were choking him. Seeing Natasha, he waved his arms desperately and broke into painfully convulsive gasps, which disfigured his round, soft face.

"Pe . . . Petya . . . Go, go, she's . . . she's . . . calling . . ." And weeping like a child, quickly moving his weakened legs, he went over to a chair and almost fell into it, covering his face with his hands.

Suddenly it was as if an electric shock ran through Natasha's whole being. Something hit her terribly painfully in the heart. She felt a terrible pain; it seemed to her that something had torn inside her and she was dying. But after the pain, she suddenly felt free of the ban on life that had lain on her. Seeing her father and hearing her mother's terrible, coarse cry from behind the door, she instantly forgot herself and her grief. She ran to her father, but he, strengthlessly waving his hand, pointed at the door to her mother's room. Princess Marya, pale, with a trembling lower jaw, came out of the door and took Natasha by the hand, saying something to her. Natasha did not see, did not hear her. With quick steps she went through the door, stopped for a moment as if struggling with herself, and ran to her mother.

The countess was lying in an armchair, stretched out somehow strangely, awkwardly, and beating her head against the wall. Sonya and the maids were holding her by the arms.

"Natasha! I want Natasha! . . ." cried the countess. "It's not true, it's not true . . . He's lying . . . I want Natasha!" she cried, pushing away everyone around her. "Get out of here, all of you, it's not true! Killed! . . . ha, ha, ha! . . . it's not true!"

Natasha placed her knee on the chair, bent over her mother, embraced her, raised her with unexpected strength, turned her face towards her, and pressed herself to her.

"Mama! . . . darling! . . . I'm here, my dearest. Mama," she whispered to her, not pausing for a second.

She would not let go of her mother, struggled with her gently, called for pillows, water, unbuttoned and tore open her mother's dress.

"My dearest, my darling . . . mama . . . dear heart," she whispered ceaselessly, kissing her head, hands, face, and feeling the tears flowing irrepressibly, in streams, tickling her nose and cheeks.

The countess pressed her daughter's hand, closed her eyes, and became calm for a moment. Suddenly, with an unwonted quickness, she got up, looked around senselessly, and, seeing Natasha, began pressing her head with all her strength. Then she turned her daughter's face to her, which was wincing with pain, and peered into it for a long time.

"Natasha, you love me," she said in a soft, trustful whisper. "Natasha, you won't deceive me? You'll tell me the whole truth?"

Natasha looked at her with tear-filled eyes, and there was nothing in her face but a plea for forgiveness and love.

"My dearest mama," she repeated, straining all the force of her love towards her, so as to somehow shift onto herself the excess of grief that was crushing her.

And again, in her strengthless struggle with reality, her mother, by refusing to believe that she could live while her beloved boy had been killed in the flower of life, tried to save herself from reality in a world of insanity.

Natasha did not remember how that day passed, nor the night, the next day, the next night. She did not sleep and did not leave her mother's side. It was as if Natasha's love, persistent, patient, not as an explanation, not as a consolation, but as a summons to life, enveloped the countess on all sides every second. On the third night, the countess calmed down for a few minutes, and Natasha closed her eyes, resting her head on the arm of the chair. The bed creaked. Natasha opened her eyes. The countess was sitting on the bed and speaking softly.

"I'm so glad you've come. You're tired, would you like some tea?" Natasha went to her. "You've grown handsome and manly," the countess went on, taking her daughter by the hand.

"Mama, what are you saying? . . ."

"Natasha, he's no more, no more!" And, embracing her daughter, for the first time the countess began to weep.

III

Princess Marya postponed her departure. Sonya and the count tried to replace Natasha, but could not. They saw that she alone could keep her mother from insane despair. For three weeks Natasha was constantly with her mother, slept in the armchair in her room, made her drink and eat, and talked ceaselessly with her—talked, because only her gentle, caressing voice could soothe the countess.

The wound in the mother's soul could not heal. Petya's death tore away half of her life. A month after the news of Petya's death, which had found her a fresh and cheerful fifty-year-old woman, she came out of her room an old woman—half-dead and taking no part in life. But the same wound that half killed the countess, this new wound called Natasha to life.

A wound in the soul, coming from the rending of the spiritual body, strange as it may seem, gradually closes like a physical wound. And once a deep wound heals over and the edges seem to have knit, a wound in the soul, like a physical wound, can be healed only by the force of life pushing up from inside.

This was the way Natasha's wound healed. She thought her life was over. But suddenly her love for her mother showed her that the essence of life—love—was still alive in her. Love awoke, and life awoke.

Prince Andrei's last days had bound Natasha and Princess Marya together. The new misfortune brought them still closer. Princess Marya postponed her departure and for the last three weeks looked after Natasha like a sick child. Those last weeks, which Natasha spent in her mother's room, undermined her physical strength.

Once, in the middle of the afternoon, noticing that Natasha was shivering feverishly, Princess Marya brought her to her own room and made her lie down on her bed. Natasha lay down, but, when Princess Marya lowered the blinds and was about to leave, Natasha called her to her.

"I don't want to sleep. Sit with me, Marie."

"You're tired—try to sleep."

"No, no. Why did you take me away? She'll ask for me."

"She's much better. She talked so nicely today," said Princess Marya.

Natasha lay on the bed and studied Princess Marya's face in the semi-darkness of the room.

"Does she resemble him?" thought Natasha. "Yes, she does and doesn't. But she's special, a stranger, quite new, unknown. And she loves me. What's in her heart? All good things. But how? How does she think? How does she look at me? Yes, she's wonderful."

"Masha," she said, timidly drawing her hand towards her. "Masha, you don't think I'm bad, do you? No? Masha, darling. How I love you. Let's be best, best friends."

And embracing Princess Marya, Natasha started kissing her hands and face. Princess Marya was abashed and overjoyed at this expression of Natasha's feelings.

From that day on, a passionate and tender friendship was established between Princess Marya and Natasha such as occurs only between women. They constantly kissed each other, spoke tender words to each other, and spent most of their time together. If one went out, the other became uneasy and hastened to join her. The two felt a greater harmony between themselves than separately, each with herself. A feeling stronger than friendship was established between them: it was the exceptional feeling that life was possible only in each other's presence.

Sometimes they were silent for hours at a time; sometimes, already in bed, they would start talking and talk till morning. They talked mostly about the distant past. Princess Marya told about her childhood, about her mother, her father, her dreams; and Natasha, who formerly turned away with calm incomprehension from that life of devotion, submission, from the poetry of Christian self-denial, now, feeling herself bound by love to Princess Marya, also came to love Princess Marya's past and to understand a formerly incomprehensible side of life. She did not think of applying submission and self-denial to her own life, because she was used to seeking other joys, but she understood and came to love this formerly incomprehensible virtue in another. For Princess Marya, as she listened to the stories of Natasha's childhood and early youth, a formerly incomprehensible side of life was also revealed, faith in life, in the pleasures of life.

As before, they still never spoke of *him*, so as not to violate with words, as it seemed to them, that lofty feeling that was in them, and this silence about him had the effect that little by little, without believing it, they began to forget him.

Natasha had grown thin, pale, and become so weak physically that everyone constantly spoke of her health, and that pleased her. But sometimes she was unexpectedly overcome not only by the fear of death, but by the fear of illness, weakness, the loss of beauty, and involuntarily she sometimes studied her bare arm, amazed at its thinness, or in the morning contemplated in the mirror her drawn and, as it seemed to her, pathetic face. It seemed to her that it ought to be so, but at the same time she felt afraid and sad.

One time she went quickly up the stairs and got completely out of breath. At once she involuntarily thought up for herself some business downstairs, and from there ran up again, testing her strength and observing herself.

Another time she called Dunyasha, and her voice sounded cracked. She called her once more, though she heard her footsteps—called in that chesty voice in which she used to sing, and listened attentively to it.

She did not know it, she would not have believed it, but under the seemingly impenetrable layer of silt that covered her soul, thin, tender young needles of grass were already breaking through, which were to take root and so cover with their living shoots the grief that oppressed her, that it would soon not be seen or noticed. The wound was healing from inside.

At the end of January, Princess Marya left for Moscow, and the count insisted that Natasha go with her so as to consult the doctors.

IV

After the clash at Vyazma, where Kutuzov could not hold back his troops from their wish to overrun, cut off, and so on, the further movement of the fleeing French and pursuing Russians, until Krasnoe, went without battles. The flight was so swift that the pursuing Russian army could not keep up with the French, the horses of the cavalry and artillery balked, and the information about the movement of the French was always wrong.

The men of the Russian army were so exhausted by this constant movement at thirty miles a day that they could move no faster.

To understand the degree of exhaustion of the Russian army, one need only understand clearly the meaning of the fact that, having lost no more than five thousand wounded and killed since Tarutino, and no more than a hundred as prisoners, the Russian army, which had numbered a hundred thousand when it left Tarutino, numbered fifty thousand when it reached Krasnoe.

The swift movement of the Russians after the French had the same disastrous effect on the Russian army as the flight of the French on theirs. The only difference was that the Russian army moved voluntarily, without the threat of destruction which hung over the French army, and that the French sick, lagging behind, remained in the foe's hands, while the Russian sick remained at home. The chief cause of the diminution of Napoleon's army was the swiftness of its movement, and the corresponding diminution of the Russian army serves as an unquestionable proof of it.

Kutuzov's whole activity, as at Tarutino and Vyazma, was aimed only at not stopping, insofar as it was in his power, this movement so destructive for the French (as the Russian generals in Petersburg and in the army wanted to do), but at contributing to it, and at making the movement of his own troops easier.

But, besides that, once the troops had shown the fatigue and enormous losses caused by swiftness of movement, Kutuzov had one more reason for slowing down and waiting. The aim of the Russian army was to follow the

French. The path of the French was unknown, and therefore, the more closely our troops followed on the heels of the French, the greater the distance they covered. Only by following at a certain distance could they make shortcuts in the zigzag path the French took. All the skilful manoeuvring proposed by the generals was expressed in terms of moving troops and multiplying marches, while the only reasonable goal consisted in diminishing the marches. And it was towards this goal that Kutuzov's activity was directed throughout the campaign, from Moscow to Vilno—not accidentally, not temporarily, but so consistently that he never once betrayed it.

Kutuzov knew, not by reason or science, but with all his Russian being he knew and felt what every Russian soldier felt, that the French were defeated, that the foe was fleeing and had to be driven out; but along with that he felt, together with the soldiers, all the difficulty of this march, of unheard-of swiftness and at such a time of year.

But to the generals, especially the non-Russian ones, who wished to distinguish themselves, to astonish someone, to take prisoner, God knows why, some duke or king—to these generals it seemed that now, when any battle was both nasty and senseless, was just the right time to give battle and defeat someone or other. Kutuzov merely shrugged his shoulders when presented with projects, one after another, for manoeuvres involving those ill-shod, coatless, half-starved soldiers, who in a month, without any battles, had melted away by half, and who, under the best conditions for the continuing flight, would have to cover more space to reach the border than what they had already gone through.

This striving to be distinguished and to manoeuvre, to overrun and cut off, was especially manifest when the Russian troops ran across the French.

It happened that way at Krasnoe, where they thought they would find one of the three French columns and stumbled onto Napoleon himself with sixteen thousand men. Despite all the means employed by Kutuzov to avoid this disastrous clash and spare his troops, the worn-out men of the Russian army spent three days at Krasnoe finishing off the beaten mob of the French.

Toll wrote a disposition: *die erste Kolonne marschiert,* and so on. And, as always, everything was done not according to the disposition. Prince Eugene of Württemberg fired from a hill at crowds of Frenchmen running by and called for reinforcements, which did not come. The French, going round the Russians by night, scattered, hid in the forests, and made their way each man as he could.

Miloradovich, who used to say that he did not want to know anything about the material affairs of his detachment, who could never be found when he was needed, *"chevalier sans peur et sans reproche,"*[*][1] as he called himself, and a great lover of parleys with the French, kept sending envoys calling for surrender, and lost time, and did not do what he was ordered to do.

---

[*] A knight without fear and without reproach.

"I make you a gift of that column, lads," he would say, riding up to the troops and pointing out the French to his cavalrymen. And the cavalrymen, urging on their scrawny, battered, barely moving horses with spurs and sabres, after mighty exertions trotted up to the column given to them, that is, to a crowd of frostbitten, numb-with-cold, and hungry Frenchmen; and the column given to them dropped its weapons and surrendered, something it had long been wanting to do.

At Krasnoe they took twenty-six thousand prisoners, hundreds of cannon, some stick which was called a marshal's baton, and disputed over who had distinguished himself there, and were pleased with that, but very much regretted that they had not taken Napoleon or at least some hero or marshal, and for that reproached each other and especially Kutuzov.

These people, carried away by their passions, were merely the blind executors of the most grievous law of necessity; but they considered themselves heroes and imagined that what they had done was a most worthy and noble thing. They accused Kutuzov and said that, from the very start of the campaign, he had prevented them from defeating Napoleon, that he thought only about satisfying his passions and did not want to leave Polotnyany Zavody, because he felt comfortable there; that he had stopped moving at Krasnoe, because, having learned of Napoleon's presence, he was completely at a loss; that it was conceivable that he was in conspiracy with Napoleon, that he had been bribed by him,[2] and so on and so forth.

It is not enough that contemporaries, carried away by their passions, spoke this way—Napoleon has been recognized as *grand* by posterity and history, and Kutuzov, by the foreigners, as a cunning, depraved, feeble old courtier; by the Russians, as something indefinite, a sort of puppet, useful only because of his Russian name . . .

V

In the years twelve and thirteen, Kutuzov was directly accused of blunders. The sovereign was displeased with him. And in a history written not long ago at the highest injunction, it is said that Kutuzov was a cunning court liar, fearful of the name of Napoleon, who, through his blunders at Krasnoe and the Berezina, deprived the Russian army of the glory of a complete victory over the French.*

Such is the destiny, not of great men, not of the *grands hommes*, whom the Russian mind does not recognize, but of those rare, always solitary men who,

*Bogdanovich's *History of the Year 1812:* characteristics of Kutuzov and considerations of the insufficient results of the fighting at Krasnoe. (Tolstoy's note.)

discerning the will of Providence, submit their personal will to it. The hatred and contempt of the crowd punish these men for their insight into the higher law.

For Russian historians—strange and terrible to say—Napoleon, that most insignificant instrument of history, who never and nowhere, even in exile, displayed any human dignity—Napoleon is the object of admiration and enthusiasm; he is *grand*. While Kutuzov, a man who, from the beginning to the end of his activity in 1812, from Borodino to Vilno, while always being true to himself in all his acts and words, shows an example uncommon in history of self-denial and awareness in the present of the future significance of the event—Kutuzov seems to them something indefinite and pathetic, and when they speak of Kutuzov and the year twelve, it is as if they are always slightly embarrassed.

And yet it is hard to imagine a historical figure whose activity was so invariably and constantly directed towards one and the same goal. It is hard to imagine a goal more worthy and more concurrent with the will of the whole people. It is harder still to find another example in history in which the goal that the historical figure set for himself was so perfectly attained as the goal towards which the entire activity of Kutuzov was directed in the year twelve.

Kutuzov never spoke of forty centuries looking down from the pyramids, of the sacrifices he was making for the fatherland, of what he intended to accomplish or had accomplished: he generally said nothing about himself, did not play any role, always seemed a most simple and ordinary man, and said the most simple and ordinary things. He wrote letters to his daughters and to Mme de Staël, read novels, enjoyed the society of beautiful women, joked with generals, officers, and soldiers, and never contradicted people who wanted to prove something to him. When Count Rastopchin galloped up to Kutuzov on the Yauza bridge with personal reproaches, blaming him for the destruction of Moscow, and said, "Didn't you promise not to abandon Moscow without giving battle?"—Kutuzov replied: "And I won't abandon Moscow without a battle," though by then Moscow had already been abandoned. When Arakcheev, coming to him from the sovereign, said that Ermolov must be appointed commander of the artillery, Kutuzov said, "Yes, I just said the same thing"—though the moment before he had said something quite different. What did he care, who, amidst the muddle-headed crowd around him, alone then understood all the immense meaning of the event, what did he care if Count Rastopchin attributed the calamity of Moscow to him or to himself? Still less could he be concerned about who was appointed commander of the artillery.

Not only in these cases, but constantly, this old man, who, through the experience of life, had reached the conviction that thoughts and the words which serve to express them are not what move people, spoke completely meaningless words—the first that came to his head.

But this same man, so heedless of his words, never once in all his activity spoke a single word that was not consistent with the one goal towards the attainment of which he went during the whole time of the war. Obviously unwillingly, with the painful certainty that he would not be understood, he voiced his thought more than once in the most varied circumstances. Starting from the battle of Borodino, when his dissension with his entourage began, he alone said that *the battle of Borodino was a victory,* and he repeated it orally, and in reports, and in dispatches till the day he died. He alone said *that the loss of Moscow was not the loss of Russia.* In response to Lauriston's proposal of peace, he replied *that there could be no peace, because such was the will of the people;* he alone, during the French retreat, said that *all our manoeuvres are unnecessary, that everything was getting done by itself, better than we could wish, that the enemy should be given a golden bridge, that the battles of Tarutino, Vyazma, and Krasnoe were unnecessary, that they had to have some men left when they got to the border, that he would not give up one Russian even for ten Frenchmen.*

And he alone, this courtier, as they portray him for us, the man who lied to Arakcheev in order to curry favour with the sovereign—he alone, this courtier, says in Vilno, thereby earning disgrace from the sovereign, that *a further war beyond the border is harmful and useless.*

But words alone would not prove that he then understood the significance of the event. His actions—all without the least deviation—were directed towards one and the same goal, which was made up of three things: (1) to strain all his forces in the clash with the French, (2) to defeat them, and (3) to drive them out of Russia, alleviating, as far as possible, the distress of the people and the army.

He, this temporizer Kutuzov, whose motto is "patience and time," the enemy of decisive actions, gives battle at Borodino, clothing the preparations for it in unparalleled solemnity. He, this Kutuzov, who, before the battle of Austerlitz begins, says it will be lost, at Borodino, despite the assurances of the generals that the battle has been lost, despite the example unheard-of in history of an army having to retreat after winning a battle, he alone, contradicting everyone, maintains till his dying day that the battle of Borodino was a victory. He alone, during the whole time of the retreat, insists on not giving battle, which was now useless, on not beginning a new war, on not crossing the borders of Russia.

If we do not apply to the activity of the masses goals that existed only in the heads of a few dozen persons, it is easy now to understand the significance of the event, because the whole event and its consequences lie before us.

But how was it that this old man, alone, contrary to the opinion of all, could then guess so correctly the significance of the national meaning of the event that, during his whole activity, he never once betrayed it?

The source of this extraordinary power of penetration into the meaning of events taking place lay in that national feeling, which he bore within himself in all its purity and force.

Only the recognition of that feeling in him made the people choose him in such a strange way—him, an old man in disgrace—against the will of the tsar, as representative of the national war. And only that feeling placed him on that loftiest human height, from which he, the commander in chief, directed all his powers, not at killing and destroying people, but at sparing and pitying them.

This simple, modest, and therefore truly majestic figure could not fit into that false form of the European hero, the imaginary ruler of the people, which history has invented.

For a lackey there can be no great man, because a lackey has his own idea of greatness.

VI

The fifth of November was the first day of the so-called battle of Krasnoe. Before evening, already after many disputes and mistakes of the generals, who had not gone where they were supposed to, after the sending out of adjutants with counter-orders, when it had already become clear that the enemy was fleeing everywhere, and there could not and would not be any battle, Kutuzov left Krasnoe and rode to Dobroe, where the headquarters had been transferred that day.

The day was clear, frosty. Kutuzov, with an enormous suite of generals, who were displeased with him and whispered behind his back, rode towards Dobroe mounted on his fat white horse. Parties of French prisoners taken that day (seven thousand had been taken), crowded along the road, warming up by fires. Not far from Dobroe, an enormous crowd of ragged prisoners, wrapped and covered up in whatever they could find, buzzed with talk, standing on the road by a long line of unhitched French guns. As the commander in chief approached, the talk ceased, and all eyes were fixed on Kutuzov, who, in his white cap with the red band and a padded greatcoat that hunched up on his stooping shoulders, slowly moved along the road. One of the generals was reporting to Kutuzov about where the guns and prisoners had been taken.

Kutuzov seemed to be preoccupied with something and was not listening to the general's words. He narrowed his eyes with displeasure and peered attentively and fixedly at the figures of the prisoners, who were a particularly pathetic sight. The greater part of the French soldiers' faces were disfigured by frostbitten noses and cheeks, and almost all of them had red, swollen, and festering eyes.

One bunch of Frenchmen was standing close to the road, and two soldiers— the face of one was covered with sores—were tearing a piece of raw meat with their hands. There was something terrible and animal-like in the fleeting glance they cast at the passers-by and in the spiteful expression with which the soldier with the sores, having glanced at Kutuzov, immediately turned away and went on with what he was doing.

Kutuzov gazed long and attentively at these two soldiers; wrinkling his face still more, he narrowed his eyes and shook his head pensively. In another place he noticed a Russian soldier who was saying something affectionately to a Frenchman, laughing and patting him on the back. Kutuzov again shook his head with the same expression.

"What were you saying? What's that?" he asked the general, who went on reporting and was drawing the commander in chief's attention to the captured French standards that stood in front of the Preobrazhensky regiment.

"Ah, standards!" said Kutuzov, clearly having difficulty tearing himself away from the subject that occupied his thoughts. He looked around absent-mindedly. Thousands of eyes were looking at him from all sides, waiting for a word from him.

He stopped in front of the Preobrazhensky regiment, sighed deeply, and closed his eyes. Someone from the suite waved to the soldiers holding the standards to come and place them staff-down round the commander in chief. Kutuzov was silent for a few seconds, and, with evident reluctance, submitting to the necessity of his position, raised his head and began to speak. Crowds of officers surrounded him. He gazed attentively at the circle of officers, recognizing some of them.

"I thank you all!" he said, turning to the soldiers and again to the officers. In the silence that reigned around him, his slowly articulated words could be heard distinctly. "I thank you all for your difficult and faithful service. The victory is complete, and Russia will not forget you. Glory to you for ever!" He paused, looking around.

"Lower it, lower its head," he said to a soldier who was holding the French eagle and had inadvertently inclined it before the Preobrazhensky standards. "Further, further, like that. Hurrah, lads!" he said with a quick movement of his chin, addressing the soldiers.

"Hur-ra-ra-rah!" thousands of voices roared.

While the soldiers were shouting, Kutuzov, hunching up on his saddle, bent his head, and his eye lit up with a meek, as if mocking glint.

"Here's the thing, brothers," he said when the voices died down . . .

And suddenly his voice and the expression of his face changed: it was no longer a commander in chief speaking, but a simple old man, who obviously now wished to tell his comrades something they needed most of all.

There was a movement in the crowd of officers and in the ranks of soldiers, so that they could hear more clearly what he was going to say now.

"Here's the thing, brothers. I know it's hard for you, but what's to be done!

Be patient; it won't last long. We'll see our guests off, then we'll have a rest. The tsar will not forget your service. It's hard for you, but still you're at home; but they—see what they've come to," he said, pointing to the prisoners. "Worse than the lowest beggars. While they were strong, we took no pity on ourselves, but now we can pity them. They're also people. Right, lads?"

He looked around, and in the intent, respectfully puzzled eyes directed at him he read sympathy with his words: his face began to grow brighter and brighter, starting from the old man's meek smile that wrinkled, starlike, the corners of his mouth and eyes. He paused and hung his head as if in perplexity.

"But, that said, who invited them here? It's their own doing, f . . . th . . . in the f . . ." he suddenly said, raising his head. And, swinging his whip, he rode off at a gallop for the first time in the whole campaign, while the soldiers, breaking ranks, joyfully guffawed and roared "Hurrah!"

The words spoken by Kutuzov were hardly understood by the troops. No one would have been able to convey the contents of the field marshal's at first solemn and in the end simple-hearted old man's speech; but the heartfelt meaning of that speech was not only understood, but that same feeling of majestic triumph, combined with pity for the foe and the consciousness of his rightness, expressed precisely by that old man's good-natured oath— that same feeling lay in the soul of every soldier, and expressed itself in a joyful, long-drawn shout. When, after that, one of the generals addressed him with the question whether the commander in chief would be ordering a carriage brought, Kutuzov, in answering, sobbed unexpectedly, evidently deeply moved.

VII

The eighth of November, the last day of the battles at Krasnoe: it was already dark when the troops came to their night camp. The whole day had been quiet, frosty, with light, sparse snow falling; towards evening it began to clear. The deep purple, starry sky could be seen through the snowflakes, and the frost began to deepen.

The musketeer regiment, which on leaving Tarutino had numbered three thousand, now, numbering nine hundred men, was one of the first to come to the place appointed for the night camp, in a village by the high road. The quartermasters who met the regiment announced that all the cottages were taken up by sick and dead Frenchmen, cavalrymen, and staff. There was only one cottage for the regimental commander.

The regimental commander rode up to his cottage. The regiment went through the village and stacked muskets by the last cottage on the road.

Like a huge, many-limbed animal, the regiment began the work of arranging its den and food. One part of the soldiers wandered off, through knee-deep snow, into a birch woods to the right of the village, and at once the chopping of axes and swords, the crack of breaking branches, and merry voices were heard from the woods; another part pottered around the centre of the regimental carts and horses, bunched together, taking out pots, biscuits, and feeding the horses; a third part scattered through the village, arranging lodgings for the staff, carrying away the dead bodies of the French that lay in the cottages, and collecting boards, dry wood, and straw from the roofs for campfires, and wattle fences for shelter.

Behind the cottages, at the edge of the village, some fifteen soldiers, with merry shouts, were loosening the high wattle side of a shed from which the roof had already been removed.

"Ready now, all at once, heave!" cried the voices, and in the darkness of the night, a huge, snow-dusted section of the wall swayed with a frosty creaking. The lower stakes cracked more and more, and the wall finally fell over together with the soldiers pushing on it. There were loud, coarsely joyful shouts and guffaws.

"Take it by twos! Reach me that lever here! That's it. Where are you shoving?"

"Now, all at once . . . Wait up, lads! . . . At the shout!"

They all fell silent, and a soft, velvety, pleasant voice began singing a song. At the end of the third verse, just as the last sound ended, twenty voices shouted out together: "Hooo! Here goes! All at once! Up with it, boys! . . ." But despite their concerted efforts, the wall hardly budged, and in the ensuing silence heavy panting could be heard.

"Hey, you, sixth company! Damn you devils! Give us a hand . . . we'll also do for you."

Some twenty men of the sixth company, who were on their way to the village, joined the haulers, and the wattle wall, about thirty-five feet long and seven feet high, curving, crushing and cutting the shoulders of the panting men, moved on down the village street.

"Keep on, will you . . . Look out, it's falling . . . What did you stop for? That's it . . ."

The merry, outrageous cursing never ceased.

"What's with you?" suddenly came the commanding voice of a soldier who ran into the carriers. "There's gentry here; the gener'l himself's in the cottage, and you damned foul-mouthed devils . . . I'll give it to you!" cried the sergeant major, and he swung and struck the first soldier who came along on the back. "Can't you do it quietly?"

The soldiers fell silent. The soldier struck by the sergeant major, groaning, began to wipe the blood from his face, which he had scratched as he bumped against the wall.

"See how the devil fights! My mug's all bloody," he said in a timid whisper, when the sergeant major had walked on.

"Don't you love it?" said a laughing voice; and, holding down the sounds of their voices, the soldiers went on. Once outside the village, they again began to talk just as loudly, interspersing their talk with the same pointless curses.

In the cottage that the soldiers had passed, the high command had gathered and a lively conversation was going on over tea about the past day and the proposed manoeuvres to come. It was proposed to make a flanking march to the left, to cut off the viceroy and capture him.

When the soldiers came lugging the wattle wall, the cook fires were already kindled in various places. The firewood crackled, the snow melted, and the black shadows of soldiers darted here and there on the trampled snow all over the occupied space.

Axes and swords were at work on all sides. Everything got done without any orders. A supply of firewood was brought for the night, little lean-tos were set up for the officers, pots boiled, guns and ammunition were put in order.

The wattle wall brought by the eighth company was set up in a half circle on the north side, propped with stakes, and a campfire was built in front of it. They beat the tattoo, called the roll, ate supper, and settled for the night by the campfires—some mending their footgear, some smoking their pipes, some, stripped naked, steaming out lice.

VIII

It would seem that in those almost unimaginably hard conditions of existence in which the Russian soldiers found themselves at that time—without warm boots, without winter coats, without a roof over their heads, in the snow at eighteen degrees of frost, without even a full ration of provisions, which did not always keep up with the army—it would seem that the soldiers must present a very sad and dejected spectacle.

On the contrary, never, in the very best material conditions, did an army present a more cheerful, lively spectacle. That came from the fact that each day all those who began to lose heart or strength were thrown out of the army. All those who were physically and morally weak had long since stayed behind, leaving only the flower of the army—in strength of spirit and body.

The eighth company, sheltered by the wattle wall, gathered the most people of all. Two sergeants major joined them, and their campfire blazed brighter than the others. They demanded an offering of firewood for the right to sit by the wall.

"Hey, Makeev, you . . . did you get lost, or did the wolves eat you? Fetch that firewood," shouted a red-mugged, red-headed soldier, squinting and blinking from the smoke, but not moving away from the fire. "Crow, you go at least and fetch some firewood," this soldier addressed someone else. The redhead was not a sergeant or a corporal, but he was a lusty soldier and therefore ordered about those who were weaker than he. The skinny, small, sharp-nosed soldier who had been called "Crow" obediently got up and was about to go and carry out the order, but just then the slender, handsome figure of a young soldier carrying a load of firewood came into the light of the campfire.

"Give it here. That's great!"

The wood was broken up, laid on, blown at, fanned with the skirts of great-coats, and the flames hissed and crackled. The soldiers moved up and lit their pipes. The handsome young soldier who had brought the firewood set his arms akimbo and began stamping his chilled feet quickly and deftly in place.

"Cold is the dew, ah, mother dear, how good, I'll be a musketeer," he sang along, as if hiccuping at each syllable of the song.

"Hey, your soles'll fly off!" cried the redhead, noticing that one of the dancer's soles was loose. "Swallowed dancing poison!"

The dancer stopped, tore off the loose piece of leather, and threw it in the fire.

"Right you are, brother," he said, and, sitting down, he took a scrap of blue French broadcloth from his pack and began wrapping his foot in it. "It's the steam does it," he added, stretching out his feet to the fire.

"We'll get new ones soon. They say when we've killed them off, we'll all get double the goods."

"And see, that son of a bitch Petrov fell behind all right," said one sergeant major.

"I've had an eye on him for a long time," said the other.

"Some soldier boy . . ."

"And in the third company, I heard, there were nine men missing yesterday."

"Yes, but figure, once your feet are frozen, how are you going to walk?"

"Eh, empty chatter!" said the sergeant major.

"Or do you want the same thing?" said an old soldier, turning reproachfully to the one who had talked about frozen feet.

"And what do you think?" the sharp-nosed soldier known as "Crow" began in a squeaky and trembling voice, suddenly rising up from behind the campfire. "A sleek man gets thin, but for a thin man it's death. Me, for instance. I can't stand it any more," he suddenly said resolutely, turning to the sergeant major. "Order me sent to the hospital, I hurt all over; I'll fall behind anyway . . ."

"Well, that'll do, that'll do," the sergeant major said calmly.

The little soldier fell silent, and the conversation went on.

"Quite a few of these Frenchmen got taken today; but, to say it straight out, not a one had a real pair of boots on, just in name only," one of the soldiers began a new subject.

"The Cossacks always take them. When we cleaned the cottage for the colonel, we carried some of them out. It's a pity to see, lads," said the dancer. "We unwrapped them: one was still alive, believe me, he babbled something in his own talk."

"But they're clean folk, lads," said the first. "White, white as that birch, and gallant, you might say, noble fellows."

"But what did you think? He has them recruited from all the classes."

"But they don't know anything of our talk," the dancer said with a perplexed smile. "I say to him: 'Whose crown are you under?' and he babbles in his own way. Funny folk!"

"There's this puzzler, brothers," the one who had been surprised at their whiteness went on. "The muzhiks at Mozhaisk said, when they started clearing away the dead where the battle was, so you can reckon it's a whole month their dead were lying there—so, they say, some of them's lying there, they say, white as paper, clean, not a whiff off them."

"What, from the cold or something?" asked one.

"A smart one you are! From the cold! It was hot then. If it'd been from the cold, ours wouldn't have gone bad either. But, they say, you go up to one of ours, and he's all rotten and wormy. So, they say, we'd cover ourselves with handkerchiefs and turn our mugs away as we dragged them out. Couldn't stand it. But theirs, they say—white as paper, not a whiff off them."

They all fell silent.

"Must be the food," said the sergeant major. "They ate gentry's grub."

Nobody objected.

"That muzhik was telling, the one there at Mozhaisk where the battle was, it took ten villages to cart them off, and they were twenty days at it, and there were still some dead left. There were so many wolves, they say . . ."

"That was a real battle," said the old soldier. "So there's something to remember; but everything after . . . It's just only to make folk suffer."

"That's right, uncle. Two days ago we made a rush, but nothing doing, they wouldn't let us get at them. Dropped their muskets quick. Fell on their knees. '*Pardon*,' they say. That's just one example. They say Platov took Poleon himself twice. Doesn't know a word. So they take him: he turns into a bird in their hands and flies away, just flies away. And there's also no permit to kill him."

"You're lying your head off, Kiselev, as I'm looking at you."

"How, lying—it's the real truth."

"If I had it my way, I'd catch him and bury him right in the ground. And put an aspen stake through him. He's destroyed a lot of folk."

"We'll put an end to him one way or another, he won't be around long," the old soldier said, yawning.

The conversation ceased, the soldiers began settling down to sleep.

"Look at the stars, burning away something awful! You'd say it was women spreading sheets," a soldier said, admiring the Milky Way.

"That means a good harvest this year."

"We'll need more firewood."

"You warm your back and your belly gets cold. It's funny."

"Oh, Lord!"

"What are you shoving for—is the fire just for you alone or something? Look at him . . . sprawling."

Silence was now setting in, and several sleepers could be heard snoring; the others turned and warmed themselves, occasionally exchanging words. From a campfire some hundred paces away came a chorus of merry guffaws.

"Look how they're roaring in the fifth company," said one soldier. "And so many folk—it's awful!"

One soldier got up and went to the fifth company.

"They're having fun there," he said, coming back. "Two Frenchmen have joined them. One's completely frozen, but the other's pretty frisky! He's playing songs."

"Oh? Let's go and see . . ." Several soldiers went over to the fifth company.

IX

The fifth company was camped just by the forest. An enormous campfire burned brightly amidst the snow, lighting up the boughs of the trees heavy with hoarfrost.

In the middle of the night, the soldiers of the fifth company had heard footsteps in the snow of the forest and the cracking of twigs.

"That's a bear, lads," said one soldier. They all raised their heads and listened, and from the forest two human figures emerged into the bright light of the fire, holding on to each other and strangely dressed.

They were two Frenchmen who had been hiding in the forest. Saying something hoarsely in a language the soldiers did not understand, they came up to the fire. One was taller, wearing an officer's hat, and looked quite weak. Coming to the fire, he wanted to sit down, but fell to the ground. The other, a small, stocky soldier, his cheeks tied round with a kerchief, was stronger. He lifted up his comrade and, pointing to his mouth, said something. The soldiers surrounded the Frenchmen, laid the sick man on an overcoat, and brought some kasha and vodka for them both.

The weak French officer was Ramballe; the one tied round with a kerchief was his orderly, Morel.

When Morel had drunk some vodka and finished a mess tin of kasha, he suddenly became morbidly merry and began rattling something out to the soldiers, who did not understand him. Ramballe refused to eat and lay silently by the fire, propped on his elbow, looking at the Russian soldiers with vacant red eyes. From time to time he let out a long moan and fell silent again. Morel, pointing to his shoulders, tried to bring it home to the soldiers that this was an officer and that he needed to get warm. A Russian officer who came up to the fire sent to the colonel to ask if he would take in a French officer to get warm; the answer came back that the colonel ordered the officer brought. Ramballe was told to go. He stood up and tried to walk, but staggered and would have fallen if a soldier standing beside him had not supported him.

"What? You don't want to?" one soldier said, addressing Ramballe with a mocking wink.

"Eh, you fool! Don't talk nonsense! A lout, a real lout!" reproaches against the joking soldier came from all sides. Ramballe was surrounded, two men made a seat with their hands, picked him up, and carried him into the cottage. Ramballe put his arms round the soldiers' necks and, as they carried him, kept saying pitifully:

"*Oh, mes braves, oh, mes bons, mes bons amis! Voilà des hommes! oh, mes braves, mes bons amis!*"* and, like a child, he rested his head on one of the men's shoulders.

Meanwhile Morel was sitting in the best place, surrounded by soldiers.

Morel, a stocky little Frenchman with inflamed, watery eyes, with a kerchief tied woman-like over his cap, was dressed in a woman's coat. Evidently tipsy, he put his arm round the soldier sitting next to him and sang a French song in a hoarse, faltering voice. The soldiers held their sides, looking at him.

"Come on, come on, teach me, how does it go? I'll learn it right away. How does it go? . . ." said the joker-singer whom Morel was embracing.

> *Vive Henri quatre,*
> *Vive ce roi vaillant . . .*

sang Morel, winking.

> *Ce diable à quatre . . .*[†]

"Vivariká! Vif seruvaru! Sidyablyakà . . ." the soldier repeated, waving his arm, and indeed catching the motif.

"Well done! Ho, ho, ho, ho, ho! . . ." Coarse, joyful guffawing arose on all sides. Morel, puckering up, also laughed.

"Well, go on, more, more!"

*Oh, my fine fellows, oh, my good, my good friends! Here's men for you! Oh, my fine fellows, my good friends!
†Long live Henry the Fourth, / Long live that valiant king . . . / That quadruple devil . . .

Qui eut le triple talent
De boire, de battre,
Et d'être un vert galant . . .

"That also goes nicely. Well, well, Zaletaev! . . ."

"Kew . . ." Zaletaev brought out with effort. "Ke-e-ew . . ." he drew out, diligently protruding his lips, "letriptala, de bu de ba i detravagala," he sang.

"Ah, great! There's a Khrenchman for you! Ho, ho, ho, ho! What, you want more to eat?"

"Give him more kasha; you don't get full soon when you're starving."

They again offered him kasha; and Morel, chuckling, started on his third mess tin. Joyful smiles lingered on the faces of the young soldiers, looking at Morel. The old soldiers, who considered it improper to be taken up with such trifles, lay on the other side of the campfire, but, getting up on an elbow every once in a while, they glanced smiling at Morel.

"They're also people," one of them said, wrapping himself in his greatcoat. "Even wormwood grows on its root."

"Ohh! Lord, Lord! What an awful lot of stars! It'll be freezing cold . . ." And everything became still.

The stars, as if knowing that no one could see them now, frolicked in the black sky. Now flaring up, now going out, now quivering, they busily whispered among themselves about something joyful but mysterious.

X

The French troops uniformly melted away in a mathematically regular progression. And the crossing of the Berezina, of which so much has been written, was only one of the intermediate steps in the destruction of the French army, and not at all a decisive episode of the campaign. If so much has been written and is being written about the Berezina, that is so on the French side only because, on the broken bridge over the Berezina, the calamities that the French army had formerly been undergoing regularly, here suddenly grouped together in one moment and in one tragic spectacle that stayed in everyone's memory. On the Russian side, there has been so much talking and writing about the Berezina only because, away from the theatre of the war, in Petersburg, a plan was drawn up (by the same Pfuel) for catching Napoleon in a strategic trap on the river Berezina. Everyone was confident that in reality everything would be done exactly as in the plan, and therefore insisted that it was precisely the crossing of the Berezina that destroyed the French. As a matter of fact, the

*Who had the triple talent / To drink, to fight, / And to be a hearty gallant . . .

results of the crossing of the Berezina were far less destructive for the French in losses of ordnance and prisoners than Krasnoe, as the numbers show.

The sole significance of the crossing of the Berezina lies in the fact that this crossing proved obviously and unquestionably the fallacy of all the plans for cutting off and the correctness of the sole possible course of action, demanded by Kutuzov and the entire mass of troops—of merely following the enemy. The crowd of the French was running at a constantly increasing force of speed, with all its energy directed at achieving its goal. It ran like a wounded animal, and it was impossible to stand in its way. This was proved not so much by the arrangement of the crossing as by the movement on the bridges. When the bridges were broken down, the unarmed soldiers, the Moscow inhabitants, the women with children who were in the French transport—everyone, borne on by the force of inertia, did not surrender but ran ahead into the boats, into the freezing water.

That impulse was reasonable. The position of both fleers and pursuers was equally bad. Remaining with their own, each of them in his distress hoped for help from his comrades, hoped to occupy a definite place among his own. Surrendering to the Russians, he would be in the same situation of distress, but would stand on a lower step in sharing the satisfaction of the necessities of life. The French did not need to have correct information about the fact that half the prisoners, whom no one knew what to do with, perished of cold and hunger, despite all the desire of the Russians to save them; they sensed that it could not be otherwise. The most compassionate Russian commanders and lovers of the French, even the French in Russian service, could do nothing for the prisoners. The French perished from the distress in which the Russian army found itself. It was impossible to take bread and clothing from hungry and much-needed soldiers in order to give it to the not harmful, not hated, not guilty, but simply unneeded French. Some did so, but that was only an exception.

Behind lay certain destruction; ahead lay hope. The boats were burned; there was no other salvation except joint flight, and all the forces of the French were directed at that joint flight.

The further the French fled, the more pathetic their remnants, especially after the Berezina, in which, owing to the Petersburg plan, special hopes were placed, the more strongly burned the passions of the Russian commanders, as they accused each other and especially Kutuzov. Supposing that the failure of the Petersburg plan for the Berezina would be attributed to him, they expressed their dissatisfaction with him, their contempt for him and mockery of him more and more strongly. The mockery and contempt, it goes without saying, were expressed in respectful form, in such form that Kutuzov could not even ask what he was being accused of and why. They did not speak seriously with him; reporting to him or asking his permission, they had the air of fulfilling a mournful ritual, but behind his back they winked and tried to deceive him at every step.

All these people, precisely because they could not understand him, were convinced that there was no point in talking with the old man; that he would never understand all the profundity of their plans; that he would reply to them with his phrases (they thought they were only phrases) about a golden bridge, about the impossibility of crossing the border with a crowd of vagrants, and so on. They had already heard all that from him. And all that he said—for instance, that they should wait for provisions, that the men had no boots—all that was so simple, while all that they proposed was so complex and clever, that it was obvious to them that he was old and stupid, and they, though not in authority, were commanders of genius.

Especially after the union with the army of the brilliant admiral and Petersburg hero Wittgenstein, this mood and the staff gossip reached the highest limit. Kutuzov saw it and only shrugged his shoulders with a sigh. Only once, after the Berezina, did he get angry and write to Bennigsen, who reported separately to the sovereign, the following letter:

> By reason of your bouts of illness, be so good, Your Excellency, upon receipt of this present, to go to Kaluga and wait there for further commands and appointments from His Imperial Majesty.

But following the sending away of Bennigsen, the grand duke Konstantin Pavlovich came to the army; he had participated in the beginning of the campaign and had been removed by Kutuzov. Now the grand duke, having come to the army, informed Kutuzov of the displeasure of the sovereign emperor at the poor success of our troops and the slowness of their movement. The sovereign emperor intended to come to the army himself any day.

The old man, as experienced in court affairs as in military, the same Kutuzov who in August of that year had been chosen commander in chief against the will of the sovereign, the same one who had removed the heir and grand duke from the army, who, on his own authority, in opposition to the sovereign's will, had decreed the abandoning of Moscow, that Kutuzov now understood at once that his time was up, that his role had been played, and that he no longer had that imaginary authority of his. He understood it not only by the attitude of the court. On the one hand, he saw that the military business in which he had played his role was finished, and he felt that his mission was fulfilled. On the other hand, he began at the same time to feel physical weariness in his old body and the necessity of physical repose.

On the twenty-ninth of November, Kutuzov rode into Vilno—into his good old Vilno, as he used to say. Twice during his service, Kutuzov had been governor of Vilno.[3] In wealthy, unscathed Vilno, apart from the comforts of life he had been deprived of for so long, Kutuzov found old friends and memories.

And, suddenly turning away from all military and state cares, he immersed himself in the regular, habitual life, insofar as he was left in peace by the passions that boiled around him, as if all that was being accomplished now and had yet to be accomplished in the historical world did not concern him in the least.

Chichagov, one of the most passionate cutters-off and overrunners, Chichagov, who at first had wanted to make a diversion to Greece, and then to Warsaw, but had in no way wanted to go where he was ordered, Chichagov, known for his boldness of speech with the sovereign, Chichagov, who considered himself Kutuzov's benefactor, because, when he was sent in the year eleven to conclude a peace with the Turks, over Kutuzov's head, and found out that peace had already been concluded, he acknowledged before the sovereign that the merit of having concluded the peace belonged to Kutuzov—this same Chichagov was the first to meet Kutuzov in Vilno, at the castle where Kutuzov was to stay. Chichagov, in a naval undress uniform, with a dagger, holding his peaked cap under his arm, handed Kutuzov a formal report and the keys to the city. That contemptuously respectful attitude towards the senile old man expressed itself in the highest degree in the whole manner of Chichagov, who already knew the accusations made against Kutuzov.

While talking with Chichagov, Kutuzov told him, by the way, that the carriages with sets of dishes captured from him in Borisov were safe and would be returned to him.

"*C'est pour me dire que je n'ai pas sur quoi manger . . . Je puis au contraire vous fournir de tout dans le cas même où vous voudriez donner des dîners,*"* Chichagov said, flushing, with each of his words wishing to prove his rightness, and therefore supposing that Kutuzov was concerned with the same thing. Kutuzov smiled his subtle, perceptive smile and, shrugging his shoulders, replied:

"*Ce n'est que pour vous dire ce que je dis.*"†

Contrary to the will of the sovereign, Kutuzov stationed the greater part of the troops in Vilno. Kutuzov, as those around him said, went extraordinarily to seed and became weaker physically during this stay in Vilno. He was reluctant to occupy himself with army matters, leaving everything to his generals and, awaiting the sovereign, gave himself up to a dissipated life.

Leaving Petersburg on the seventh of December with his suite—Count Tolstoy, Prince Volkonsky, Arakcheev, and others—the sovereign arrived in Vilno on the eleventh of December and drove straight to the castle in his travelling sleigh. At the castle, despite the severe frost, stood several hundred generals

---

*You mean to say I have nothing to eat from . . . On the contrary, I can furnish you with everything in case you should want to give dinners.
†I only mean to say to you what I'm saying.

and staff officers in full-dress uniform and the honour guard of the Semyonovsky regiment.

A courier, galloping up to the castle with a sweating troika ahead of the sovereign, shouted: "He's coming!" Konovnitsyn rushed to the front hall to report to Kutuzov, who was waiting in the porter's little lodge.

A minute later the old man's large, fat figure, in full-dress uniform, with all his regalia covering his chest, and a sash tied tightly round his belly, came waddling out to the porch. Kutuzov put on his service cap, took his gloves in his hand, and, negotiating the steps with difficulty, went sideways down the stairs and took in his hand the report prepared for presentation to the sovereign.

Scurrying about, whispers, another troika desperately flying by, and all eyes turned to the jolting sleigh in which the figures of the sovereign and Volkonsky could already be seen.

From a habit of fifty years, all this had a physically agitating effect on the old general; he patted himself all over with anxious haste, straightened his cap, and, just as the sovereign, stepping out of the sleigh, raised his eyes to him, he at once braced himself, stood to attention, handed over the report, and began speaking in his measured, ingratiating voice.

The sovereign looked Kutuzov up and down with a quick glance, frowned momentarily, but then, getting the better of himself at once, went up and, spreading his arms, embraced the old general. Again, from an old, habitual impression and in relation to his innermost thoughts, this embrace, as usual, affected Kutuzov: he sobbed.

The sovereign greeted the officers, the Semyonovsky guard, and, shaking the old man's hand once more, went with him into the castle.

Left alone with the field marshal, the sovereign voiced to him his displeasure with the slowness of the pursuit, with the mistakes at Krasnoe and the Berezina, and informed him of his considerations about the future campaign abroad. Kutuzov made no objections or comments. The same submissive and vacant expression with which, seven years earlier, he had listened to the sovereign's orders on the field at Austerlitz now settled on his face.

When Kutuzov came out of the study and, with his heavy, dipping gait, lowering his head, went through the reception room, someone's voice stopped him.

"Your Serenity," someone said.

Kutuzov raised his head and looked for a long time into the eyes of Count Tolstoy, who stood before him with some small object on a silver salver. Kutuzov seemed not to understand what was wanted of him.

Suddenly it was as if he remembered: a barely noticeable smile flashed across his puffy face, and with a low, respectful bow, he took the object that lay on the salver. It was the Order of St. George, first degree.

XI

The next day the field marshal gave a dinner and a ball, which the sovereign honoured with his presence. The sovereign had conferred on Kutuzov the Order of St. George, first degree; he had shown him the highest honours; but the sovereign's displeasure with the field marshal was known to everyone. The proprieties were observed, and the sovereign showed the first example of it; but everyone knew that the old man was at fault and good for nothing. When, at the ball, by the old habit of a courtier of Catherine's time, Kutuzov, on the sovereign's entrance into the ballroom, ordered the captured standards thrown down at his feet, the sovereign winced unpleasantly and spoke some words, among which some heard: "old comedian."

The sovereign's displeasure with Kutuzov increased in Vilno, particularly because Kutuzov obviously would not or could not understand the significance of the coming campaign.

When the sovereign said the next morning to the officers gathered around him, "You have not only saved Russia, you have saved Europe"—they all understood that the war was not yet over.

Kutuzov alone would not understand that and openly voiced his opinion that a new war could not improve the situation and increase the glory of Russia, but could only worsen its position and diminish the highest degree of glory at which, in his opinion, Russia now stood. He tried to demonstrate to the sovereign the impossibility of recruiting new troops; spoke of the hard conditions of the population, the possibility of failure, and so on.

Given such a state of mind, the field marshal naturally seemed only a hindrance and an obstacle in the way of the coming war.

To avoid confrontations with the old man, a way out was found of itself, which consisted, as at Austerlitz and at the beginning of the campaign under Barclay, in removing the ground of authority he stood on from under the commander in chief, without disturbing him or informing him of it, and transferring it to the sovereign himself.

To this end, the staff was gradually reorganized, and all the essential authority of Kutuzov's staff was cancelled and transferred to the sovereign. Toll, Konovnitsyn, and Ermolov received other assignments. Everyone said aloud that the field marshal had grown very weak and his health was failing.

He had to be in weak health in order to give up his place and have someone else take over for him. And indeed his health was weak.

As naturally, and simply, and gradually as Kutuzov had come from Turkey to the treasury in Petersburg to raise a militia, and then to the army, precisely when he was needed, so now, just as naturally, gradually, and simply, when

Kutuzov's role had been played, there appeared in his place the new leader required.

The war of 1812, besides its national significance dear to the Russian heart, was to have another—this time European.

The movement of peoples from west to east was to be followed by a movement of peoples from east to west, and for this new war a new leader was needed, who had qualities and views different from Kutuzov's and was moved by different incentives.

Alexander I was as necessary for the movement of peoples from east to west and for the restoration of national frontiers, as Kutuzov had been necessary for the salvation and glory of Russia.

Kutuzov did not understand the significance of Europe, balance, Napoleon. He could not understand it. Once the foe was annihilated, once Russia was delivered and placed at the highest degree of her glory, for this Russian man, as a Russian, there was nothing more to do. For the representative of the national war there was nothing left but death. And so he died.[4]

XII

Pierre, as most often happens, felt the whole burden of the physical privations and strains he experienced during captivity only when those strains and privations were over. After being freed from captivity, he arrived in Orel, and on the third day after his arrival, as he was about to go to Kiev, he fell ill and spent three months lying ill in Orel; he had, as the doctors put it, "bilious fever." Though the doctors treated him, let his blood, and gave him medications to drink, he nevertheless recovered.

All that happened to Pierre from the time he was set free until his illness left almost no impression on him. He remembered only grey, gloomy, now rainy, now snowy weather, inner physical anguish, pain in his legs, in his side; remembered the general impression of people's misfortunes and sufferings; remembered the disturbing curiosity of officers and generals who asked him questions, his trouble finding a carriage and horses, and, above all, remembered his inability to think and feel at that time. On the day he was set free, he saw the corpse of Petya Rostov. On the same day, he learned that Prince Andrei had lived for over a month after the battle of Borodino and had died only recently in Yaroslavl, in the Rostovs' house. And on the same day, Denisov, who told this news to Pierre, mentioned Hélène's death, supposing that Pierre had already long known of it. All this only seemed strange then to Pierre. He felt that he could not understand the meaning of all this news. He only made haste then to get away quickly, quickly from those places where people were killing each other to some quiet haven, and there to recover, to rest, to rethink all these strange and new things that he learned during that time. But as soon as he arrived in Orel, he fell ill. On awakening from his illness, Pierre saw himself surrounded by his two servants from Moscow, Terenty and Vaska, and the eldest princess, who lived on Pierre's estate in Yelets and, having learned of his liberation and illness, came to look after him.

During his convalescence, Pierre only gradually fell out of the habit of the impressions he had grown used to over the past months, and became used to the fact that no one was going to herd him anywhere tomorrow, that no one was going to take away his warm bed, and that he was certain to have dinner, and tea, and supper. But for a long time in his dreams he still saw himself in the old conditions of captivity. In the same way, Pierre gradually came to understand the news he had learned after being freed from captivity: the death of Prince Andrei, the death of his wife, and the annihilation of the French.

The joyful feeling of freedom—that full, inalienable freedom proper to a human being, the awareness of which he had experienced for the first time at the first halt after leaving Moscow—filled Pierre's soul during his convalescence. He was astonished at how this inner freedom, independent of external circumstances, was now as if surrounded by the superfluity, the luxury of external freedom as well. He was alone in a strange town, without acquaintances. No one demanded anything of him; no one sent him anywhere. He had everything he wanted; the thought of his wife, which had eternally tormented him before, was no longer there, because she was no longer there.

"Ah, how good! How nice!" he said to himself, when they moved a laid table up to him with clean linen and fragrant broth, or when in the evening he lay down on the soft, clean bed, or when he remembered that his wife and the French were no more. "Ah, how good, how nice!" And by old habit he asked himself: "Well, and what then? What am I going to do?" And he answered himself at once: "Nothing. I'll live. Ah, how nice!"

That which he had been tormented by before, which he had constantly sought, the purpose of life—now did not exist for him. It was not that this sought-for purpose of life happened not to exist for him only at the present moment, but he felt that it did not and could not exist. And this very absence of purpose gave him that full, joyful awareness of freedom which at that time constituted his happiness.

He could have no purpose, because he now had faith—not faith in some rules, or words, or thoughts, but faith in a living, ever-sensed God. Before he had sought for Him in the purposes he set for himself. This seeking for a purpose had only been a seeking for God; and suddenly he had learned in his captivity, not through words, not through arguments, but through immediate sensation, what his nanny had told him long ago: that God is here, right here, everywhere. In captivity he had learned that God in Karataev was much

greater, more infinite and unfathomable, than in the Arkhitekton of the universe recognized by the Masons. He experienced the feeling of a man who has
found what he was seeking under his own feet, while he had been straining his
eyes looking far away from himself. All his life he had looked off somewhere,
over the heads of the people around him, yet there was no need to strain his
eyes, but only to look right in front of him.

Formerly he had been unable to see the great, the unfathomable and infinite,
in anything. He had only sensed that it must be somewhere and had sought for
it. In all that was close and comprehensible, he had seen only the limited, the
petty, the humdrum, the meaningless. He had armed himself with a mental
spyglass and gazed into the distance, where the petty and humdrum, disappearing in the distant mist, had seemed to him great and infinite, only because
it was not clearly visible. Thus he had looked at European life, politics,
Masonry, philosophy, philanthropy. But even then, in moments he regarded as
his own weakness, his mind had penetrated this distance, and there, too, he
had seen the petty, the humdrum, the meaningless. Now he had learned to see
the great, the eternal, and the infinite in everything, and therefore, in order to
see it, to enjoy contemplating it, he had naturally abandoned the spyglass he
had been looking through until then over people's heads, and joyfully contemplated the ever-changing, ever-great, unfathomable, and infinite life around
him. And the closer he looked, the calmer and happier he became. The terrible
question "Why?" which formerly had destroyed all his mental constructions,
did not exist for him now. Now, to this question "Why?" a simple answer was
always ready in his soul: because there is God, that God without whose will
not a single hair falls from a man's head.

XIII

Pierre was almost unchanged in his external ways. To look at, he was exactly
the same as he had been before. He was as absent-minded as before, and
seemed to be taken up not with what was in front of his eyes, but with something special of his own. The difference between his former and present states
consisted in the fact that, formerly, when he forgot what was in front of him or
what was being said to him, he would wrinkle his brow with suffering, as if
trying but unable to make out something far away. Now he forgot what was
being said to him and what was before him in the same way; but now, with
a barely perceptible, as if mocking smile, he peered at what was in front of
him and listened intently to what was being said to him, though he obviously
saw and heard something quite different. Formerly he had seemed a kind but
unhappy man, and therefore people had involuntarily shunned him. Now a
smile of the joy of life constantly played about his lips, and in his eyes shone a

sympathy for people—the question: are they as content as I am? And people enjoyed being in his presence.

Formerly he had talked a great deal, had become excited as he talked, and had listened little; now he was rarely carried away by a conversation, and was able to listen so well that people willingly told him their innermost secrets.

The princess, who had never had any love for Pierre, and had experienced an especially hostile feeling towards him because, ever since the old count's death, she had felt herself obliged to him, to her vexation and surprise, after her brief stay in Orel, where she had come with the intention of proving to Pierre that, despite his ingratitude, she considered it her duty to look after him, the princess soon felt that she loved him. Pierre in no way sought the princess's favour. He merely studied her with curiosity. Formerly the princess had felt indifference and mockery in his gaze, and she had shrunk from him as she did from others, and had exhibited only the combative side of her life; now, on the contrary, she felt as if he was trying to delve into the innermost sides of her life; and, first with mistrust, then with gratitude, she revealed to him the hidden good sides of her character.

The most cunning person could not have wormed himself into the princess's confidence more skilfully, calling up memories in her of the better time of her youth and showing sympathy for them. And yet Pierre's whole cunning consisted in his seeking his own pleasure in calling up human feelings in the embittered, dry, and, in her own way, proud princess.

"Yes, he's a very, very kind man, when he's under the influence, not of bad people, but of such people as me," the princess said to herself.

The change that had taken place in Pierre was also noticed, in their own way, by his servants, Terenty and Vaska. They found that he had become much simpler. Often Terenty, having undressed his master, with his boots and clothes in his hands, having wished him a good night, was slow to leave, waiting for his master to get into conversation. And most often Pierre would stop Terenty, noticing that he wanted to talk.

"Well, so tell me . . . how did you get food for yourself?" he would ask. And Terenty would begin a story about the devastation of Moscow, about the late count, and would stand for a long time holding the clothes, talking and sometimes listening to Pierre's stories, and, with a pleasant awareness of his closeness to the master and of friendliness for him, would go to the front hall.

The doctor who treated Pierre and visited him every day, though, as all doctors feel they must do, he considered it his duty to have the look of a man whose every moment is precious to suffering mankind, sat for hours with Pierre, telling his favourite stories and observations on the ways of the sick in general and of ladies in particular.

"Yes, it's pleasant to talk with such a man, not like what we have here in our province," he said.

Several captured officers of the French army were living in Orel, and the doctor brought one of them along, a young Italian officer.

This officer started visiting Pierre, and the princess laughed at the tender feelings the Italian expressed for him.

The Italian was evidently happy only when he could come to Pierre and talk and tell him of his past and his life at home, of his love, and pour out to him his indignation against the French and especially against Napoleon.

"If all Russians are at least a little like you," he said to Pierre, "*c'est un sacrilège que de faire la guerre à un peuple comme le vôtre.** You, who have suffered so much from the French, you don't even have any anger against them."

And Pierre had earned the Italian's passionate love only by calling up the best sides of his soul and admiring them.

At the end of Pierre's stay in Orel, his old acquaintance, the Mason Count Willarski, came to visit him, the one who had introduced him into the lodge in 1807. Willarski was married to a rich Russian woman who had large estates in Orel province, and he occupied a temporary position in that town in the provision sector.

Learning that Bezukhov was in Orel, Willarski, though he had never been closely acquainted with him, came to him with declarations of friendship and intimacy, such as people usually express to each other when they meet in the desert. Willarski was bored in Orel and was happy to meet a man of his circle and, as he supposed, with similar interests.

But, to his surprise, Willarski soon noticed that Pierre lagged very far behind real life and had fallen, as he defined Pierre to himself, into apathy and egoism.

"*Vous vous encroûtez, mon cher,*"† he said to him. Despite that, Willarski found it more pleasant to be with Pierre now than formerly, and he called on him every day. But for Pierre, looking at Willarski and listening to him now, it was strange and incredible to think that he himself had very recently been the same.

Willarski was married, a family man, occupied with the business of his wife's estate, with his service, and with his family. He considered all these occupations a hindrance to life and considered them all contemptible, because their purpose was the personal well-being of himself and his family. Military, administrative, political, and Masonic considerations constantly absorbed his attention. And Pierre, without trying to change his view, without judging him, with his now constant quiet, joyful mockery, admired this strange phenomenon he knew so well.

In his relations with Willarski, with the princess, with the doctor, with all the people he met now, there was a new feature in Pierre which won him the favour

*It is a sacrilege to make war on a people like yours.
†You're getting rusty, my dear.

of all people: this was the recognition of the possibility for each person of think-ing, feeling, and looking at things in his own way; the recognition of the impos-sibility of changing a person's opinion with words. This legitimate peculiarity of each person, which formerly had troubled and irritated Pierre, now constituted the basis of the sympathy and interest he took in people. The difference, some-times the complete contradiction of people's views with his own life and among themselves, delighted Pierre and evoked an amused and meek smile in him.

In practical matters, Pierre now felt unexpectedly that he had a centre of gravity which he had not had formerly. Formerly every monetary question, especially requests for money, which he, as a very rich man, was very often sub-ject to, had sent him into hopeless agitation and perplexity. "Should I give it or not?" he would ask himself. "I have it, and he needs it. But the other one needs it more. Who needs it more? And maybe they're both cheats?" And formerly he had not found any way out of these suppositions and had given to every-body, as long as he had something to give. He had formerly found himself in the same perplexity faced with any question concerning his fortune, when one said he ought to act this way and another that way.

Now, to his surprise, he discovered that there were no more doubts and per-plexities in all these questions. In him an arbiter now appeared, who by some laws unknown to him decided what must and must not be done.

He was as indifferent to monetary matters as formerly; but now he knew unquestionably what should be done and what should not. The first applica-tion of this new arbiter for him was the request of a captive French colonel, who came to him, told him a great deal about his exploits, and in the end almost demanded that Pierre give him four thousand francs to send to his wife and children. Without the slightest difficulty or strain, Pierre refused him, won-dering afterwards at how simple and easy what had formerly seemed insolubly difficult really was. Together with this refusal of the colonel, he decided that it was necessary to employ a ruse so that, on leaving Orel, he could make the Ital-ian officer accept some money, which he clearly needed. For Pierre, the new proof of his strengthened view of practical matters was his solution of the question of his wife's debts and of the restoration or non-restoration of his houses in Moscow and the country.

His chief steward came to him in Orel, and together with him Pierre made a general accounting of his changed income. The Moscow fire, by his chief stew-ard's calculation, had cost Pierre around two million.

By way of consolation for these losses, the chief steward presented Pierre with a calculation showing that, despite these losses, his income not only would not diminish, but would increase, if he refused to pay the debts left behind by the countess, which could not be imputed to him, and if he did not restore the houses in and near Moscow, which cost him eighty thousand a year and yielded nothing.

"Yes, yes, that's true," said Pierre, smiling cheerfully. "Yes, yes, I don't need any of it. My ruin has made me much richer."

But in January Savelyich came from Moscow, told him about the situation in Moscow, about the estimate an architect had given him for restoring the houses in and near Moscow, speaking of it as a decided thing. At the same time, Pierre received letters from Prince Vassily and other Petersburg acquaintances. The letters spoke of his wife's debts. And Pierre decided that his steward's plan, which he had liked so much, was wrong, and that he had to go to Petersburg to settle his wife's affairs and had to rebuild in Moscow. Why it had to be so, he did not know; but he knew unquestionably that it had to be. As a result of this decision, his income would be diminished by three quarters. But it had to be so; he felt it.

Willarski was going to Moscow, and they arranged to go together.

All through his convalescence in Orel, Pierre had experienced a feeling of joy, freedom, life; but when, during his journey, he found himself in the open world and saw hundreds of new faces, that feeling increased still more. All through the journey, he experienced the joy of a schoolboy on vacation. All persons—the coachman, the stationmaster, the muzhiks on the road or in the villages—everything had a new significance for him. The presence and observations of Willarski, who constantly complained about the poverty, the backwardness compared to Europe, the ignorance of Russia, only enhanced Pierre's joy. Where Willarski saw deadness, Pierre saw the extraordinary, mighty force of vitality, that force which, in the snow, over this vast expanse, maintained the life of this whole, special, and united people. He did not contradict Willarski and, as if agreeing with him (since pretending to agree was the shortest means of avoiding an argument that could not lead anywhere), listened to him with a joyful smile.

XIV

Just as it is hard to explain why and where ants hurry to from a demolished anthill, some away from the anthill carrying specks of dust, eggs, and dead bodies, and others back to the anthill—why they run into each other, chase each other, fight—so it would be hard to explain the reasons that made the Russian people, after the departure of the French, crowd into the place which was formerly called Moscow. But just as, when looking at the ants scattered around the destroyed anthill, despite its complete obliteration, one can see by the tenacity, the energy, the countless numbers of the swarming insects, that everything has been destroyed, except for something indestructible, immaterial, which made for the whole strength of the anthill—so Moscow, in the month of October, despite the fact that there were no authorities, no churches, no holy objects, no wealth, no houses, was the same Moscow it had been in

August. Everything was destroyed, except for something immaterial but mighty and indestructible.

The promptings of the people who rushed to Moscow from all sides after it was cleared of the foe were the most varied, personal, and, in the initial period, for the most part, wild, animal promptings. Only one prompting was common to them all—to rush to the place that was formerly called Moscow, so as to apply their activity there.

In a week there were already fifteen thousand inhabitants in Moscow, in two—twenty-five thousand, and so on. Rising ever higher and higher, this number, by the autumn of 1813, had reached a figure exceeding the population of the year 1812.

The first Russian people who entered Moscow were the Cossacks of Wintzingerode's detachment, the muzhiks of the neighbouring villages, and inhabitants who had fled and had been hiding in the vicinity. On entering devastated Moscow and finding it looted, the Russians also started looting. They went on with what the French had been doing. The muzhiks came to Moscow with trains of wagons to take back to their villages all that had been abandoned in the devastated Moscow houses and streets. The Cossacks carried off as much as they could to their headquarters; the house owners took everything they found in other houses and transported it to their own, under the pretext that it was their property.

But after the first looters came another wave, a third, and looting, in time with the increasing number of looters, became harder and harder every day and took on more definite forms.

The French had found Moscow empty but with all the forms of a city leading an organically regular life, with its various functions of trade, crafts, luxury, state government, religion. These forms were lifeless, but they still existed. There were rows of stalls, shops, storehouses, granaries, bazaars—most of them with stock; there were factories, workshops; there were palaces, wealthy houses filled with luxury objects; there were hospitals, jails, government offices, churches, cathedrals. The longer the French stayed, the more these forms of city life were obliterated, and in the end it all merged into one indistinct, lifeless field for looting.

The longer the looting of the French went on, the more it destroyed the wealth of Moscow and the strength of the looters. The longer the looting of the Russians, with which they began their takeover of the capital, went on, and the greater the number of people taking part in it, the more quickly it restored the wealth of Moscow and the regular life of the city.

Besides looters, the most varied people, some drawn by curiosity, some by official duties, some by calculation—house owners, clergy, high- and low-ranking officials, tradesmen, artisans, muzhiks—flowed into Moscow from all sides, like blood to the heart.

Within a week, muzhiks coming with empty carts to carry things off were stopped by the authorities and forced to cart the dead bodies out of the city. Other muzhiks, hearing of their comrades' failure, came to the city with wheat, oats, hay, and beat each other down to prices lower than before. Teams of carpenters, hoping for high pay, entered Moscow every day, and on all sides there were new houses under construction and burned-down houses being repaired. Merchants opened their stalls for trade. Cookshops and inns were set up in burnt houses. The clergy resumed services in many churches that had not burned down. Donors brought looted church objects. Officials set up their baize-covered tables and file cabinets in small rooms. The higher authorities and police took charge of distributing the goods left by the French. The owners of those houses in which many things had been brought together from other houses, complained of the unfairness of bringing them all to the Faceted Palace;[5] others insisted that the French had brought things together in one place from various houses, and therefore it was unfair to give the owner of the house the things found in it. The police were abused; they were bribed; the estimates of burned-down government property were inflated tenfold; there were demands for relief. Count Rastopchin wrote his proclamations.

XV

At the end of January, Pierre arrived in Moscow and settled in the surviving wing of his house. He called on Count Rastopchin and on some acquaintances who had returned to Moscow, and intended to go to Petersburg in two days. Everyone was celebrating the victory; everything was boiling with life in the destroyed and reviving capital. Everyone was glad to have Pierre back; everyone wanted to see him, and everyone asked him about what he had seen. Pierre felt especially amicably disposed towards all the people he met; but now he involuntarily kept himself on guard with all people, so as not to bind himself by anything. To all the questions put to him, important or quite trifling, he replied with equal vagueness. To whatever he was asked—where was he going to live? was he going to build? when would he be going to Petersburg and might he take a little box with him?—he replied: yes, maybe, I think so, and so on.

Of the Rostovs he heard that they were in Kostroma, and the thought of Natasha rarely crossed his mind. If it did, it was only as a pleasant memory of long ago. He felt not only free of the conventions of life, but also of that feeling which he, as it seemed to him, had deliberately affected.

On the third day after his arrival in Moscow, he learned from the Drubetskoys that Princess Marya was in Moscow. The death, the sufferings, the last days of Prince Andrei had often occupied Pierre, and now came to his mind again with new vividness. Having learned at dinner that Princess Marya was in

Moscow and living in her unburnt house on Vzdvizhenka, he went to see her that same evening.

On the way to Princess Marya, Pierre never stopped thinking of Prince Andrei, of his friendship with him, of his various meetings with him, and especially of the last one in Borodino.

"Can it be that he died in the spiteful mood he was in then? Can it be that the explanation of life was not revealed to him before death?" thought Pierre. He remembered about Karataev, about his death, and involuntarily started comparing these two men, so different and at the same time so similar, because of the love he had for both of them, and because both had lived and both had died.

Pierre drove up to the old prince's house in the most serious state of mind. The house was intact. There were traces of damage, but the character of the house was the same. An old servant, who met Pierre with a stern face, as if wishing to make it known to the visitor that the prince's absence had not disturbed the order of the house, said that the princess had been pleased to retire to her rooms and that she received on Sundays.

"Announce me; perhaps she'll receive me," said Pierre.

"Yes, sir," said the servant. "Please come to the portrait room."

A few minutes later the servant and Dessales came out to Pierre. Dessales told Pierre on the princess's behalf that she would be very glad to see him and asked, if he would forgive her lack of ceremony, that he come to her rooms upstairs.

In a room with a low ceiling, lit by one candle, sat the princess and with her someone else in a black dress. Pierre recalled that the princess always had lady companions, but who and what sort these companions were, Pierre did not know and did not recall. "It's one of her companions," he thought, glancing at the lady in the black dress.

The princess rose quickly to meet him and gave him her hand.

"Yes," she said, looking intently into his changed face after he had kissed her hand, "so this is how you and I meet. During the last days, he often spoke of you," she said, shifting her gaze from Pierre to the companion with a shyness that struck him for a moment.

"I was so glad to learn that you had been saved. It was the only joyful news we had received for a long time." Again, still more uneasily, the princess glanced at her companion and was about to say something, but Pierre interrupted her.

"Can you imagine, I knew nothing about him," he said. "I counted him as killed. All I knew, I knew from other people, at third hand. I know only that he ended up with the Rostovs . . . What a fate!"

Pierre was speaking quickly, animatedly. He glanced once at the face of the companion, saw an attentively tender, curious gaze directed at him, and, as often happens during a conversation, felt for some reason that this companion in the black dress was a sweet, kind, nice being, who would not hinder his heart-to-heart talk with Princess Marya.

But when he said the last words about the Rostovs, the perplexity on Princess Marya's face showed still more strongly. She again shifted her gaze from Pierre's face to the face of the lady in the black dress and said:

"Don't you recognize her?"

Pierre glanced once more at the pale, fine face of the companion, with its dark eyes and strange mouth. Something dear, long forgotten, and more than sweet looked at him from those attentive eyes.

"But no, it can't be," he thought. "This stern, thin, pale, aged face? It can't be her. It's only a reminiscence of that one." But just then Princess Marya said: "Natasha." And the face, with its attentive eyes, with difficulty, with effort, like a rusty door opening—smiled, and from that open door there suddenly breathed and poured out upon Pierre that long-forgotten happiness of which, especially now, he was not even thinking. It breathed out, enveloped, and swallowed him whole. When she smiled, there could no longer be any doubt: it was Natasha, and he loved her.

In that first moment, Pierre involuntarily told her, and Princess Marya, and above all himself, a secret he himself was unaware of. He blushed joyfully and painfully. He wanted to conceal his excitement. But the more he wanted to conceal it, the more clearly—more clearly than the most definite words—he said to himself, and to her, and to Princess Marya, that he loved her.

"No, it's just because of the unexpectedness," thought Pierre. But as he was about to continue the conversation he had started with Princess Marya, he again glanced at Natasha, and he blushed still more deeply, and a still greater excitement of joy and fear seized his soul. He became entangled in his words and stopped in the middle of his speech.

Pierre had not noticed Natasha because he had never expected to see her there, but he had not recognized her because the change that had taken place in her since he had last seen her was enormous. She had grown thinner and paler. But that was not what had made her unrecognizable: it had been impossible to recognize her in the first moment, as he came in, because on that face, in the eyes of which formerly there had always shone a secret smile of the joy of life, now, when he had come in and glanced at her for the first time, there had been not even the shadow of a smile; there had been only eyes—attentive, kind, and sadly questioning.

Pierre's confusion was not reflected as confusion in Natasha, but only as a pleasure that almost imperceptibly lit up her whole face.

XVI

"She's come to stay with me," said Princess Marya. "The count and countess will come any day now. The countess is in a terrible state. But Natasha herself needed to see a doctor. They forced her to come with me."

"Yes, is there a family without its grief?" said Pierre, turning to Natasha. "You know, it was on the same day that we were set free. I saw him. He was such a lovely boy!"

Natasha was looking at him, and in reply to his words her eyes only widened and lit up the more.

"What can one say or think in consolation?" said Pierre. "Nothing. Why did such a nice boy, so full of life, have to die?"

"Yes, in our time it would be hard to live without faith . . ." said Princess Marya.

"Yes, yes. That's really true," Pierre hastily interrupted.

"Why?" asked Natasha, looking attentively into Pierre's eyes.

"What do you mean, why?" said Princess Marya. "The mere thought of what awaits us there . . ."

Natasha, not hearing Princess Marya out, again glanced questioningly at Pierre.

"It's because," Pierre went on, "only a person who believes that there is a God who rules over us can endure such a loss as hers . . . and yours," said Pierre.

Natasha had already opened her mouth to say something, but suddenly stopped. Pierre hastened to turn away from her and again addressed Princess Marya with a question about the last days of his friend's life. Pierre's confusion had now almost vanished; but along with that he felt that all his former freedom had also vanished. He felt that now over his every word, his every deed, there was a judge, a judgement, which was dearer to him than the judgements of all the people in the world. He spoke now, and along with his words he considered the impression his words would make on Natasha. He did not deliberately say what would please her, but whatever he said, he judged himself from her point of view.

Princess Marya reluctantly, as always happens, began to tell him about the state in which she had found Prince Andrei. But Pierre's questions, his animatedly restless glance, his face trembling with emotion, gradually made her go into details which, on her own, she had been afraid to renew in her imagination.

"Yes, yes, so, so . . ." Pierre kept saying, bending over Princess Marya with his whole body and greedily listening to her story. "Yes, yes, so he calmed down? softened? He always sought one thing with all the forces of his soul: to be fully good, so that he could not be afraid of death. The shortcomings that were in him—if there were any—did not come from him. So he softened?" said Pierre. "What a happy thing that he met you," he said to Natasha, suddenly turning to her and looking at her with eyes full of tears.

Natasha's face twitched. She frowned and momentarily lowered her eyes. For about a minute she hesitated whether she should speak or not.

"Yes, it was happy," she said in a soft, chesty voice, "for me it certainly was happy." She paused. "And he . . . he . . . he said that he was wishing for it at the same moment that I came to him . . ." Natasha's voice broke. She blushed, pressed her hands to her knees, and all at once, obviously making an effort with herself, raised her head and began speaking quickly:

"We knew nothing as we were leaving Moscow. I didn't dare ask about him. And suddenly Sonya told me he was with us. I didn't think anything, I couldn't imagine what state he was in, I only needed to see him, to be with him," she said, trembling and breathless. And, not letting them interrupt her, she told what she had never yet told anyone: all that she had lived through during those three weeks of their journey and life in Yaroslavl.

Pierre listened to her open-mouthed, not taking his tear-filled eyes from her. Listening to her, he did not think of Prince Andrei, or of death, or of what she was telling. He listened to her and simply pitied her for the suffering she was experiencing now, as she spoke.

The princess, wincing from the desire to hold back her tears, sat beside Natasha and for the first time listened to the story of those last days of the love between her brother and Natasha.

This tormenting and joyful story was evidently necessary for Natasha.

She spoke, mixing the most trifling details with her innermost secrets, and it seemed she could never finish. She repeated the same things several times.

Dessales's voice was heard outside the door asking whether Nikolushka could come in to say good night.

"Well, that's all, that's all . . ." said Natasha. She quickly stood up, just as Nikolushka was coming in, and almost ran to the door, bumped her head against the door, which was covered by a curtain, and with a moan either of pain or of sorrow, burst out of the room.

Pierre looked at the door through which she had gone and could not understand why he was suddenly left all alone in the world.

Princess Marya called him out of his distraction, drawing his attention to her nephew, who had come into the room.

Nikolushka's face, which resembled his father's, so affected Pierre in that moment of inner softening in which he now found himself, that, having kissed him, he got up hastily, took out his handkerchief, and went over to the window. He wanted to take leave of Princess Marya, but she kept him.

"No, Natasha and I sometimes don't go to bed till after two; please stay. I'll order supper served. Go downstairs; we'll come presently."

Before Pierre went out, the princess said to him:

"It's the first time she's spoken of him like that."

XVII

Pierre was taken to the big, well-lit dining room; a few minutes later foot-steps were heard, and the princess and Natasha came into the room. Natasha was calm, though a stern, unsmiling expression had again settled on her face. Princess Marya, Natasha, and Pierre equally experienced that feeling of awk-wardness that usually follows the end of a serious and heartfelt talk. To go on with the previous conversation is impossible, to talk about trifles is shameful, and to be silent is unpleasant, because one wants to talk, and this silence is like a pretence. They silently went to the table. The servants moved chairs out and in. Pierre unfolded the cool napkin and, deciding to break the silence, glanced at Natasha and Princess Marya. They had both obviously just decided on the same thing: in the eyes of both shone a contentment with life and a recognition that, besides sorrow, there were also joys.

"Do you drink vodka, Count?" asked Princess Marya, and these words sud-denly dispersed the shadows of the past.

"Tell us about yourself," said Princess Marya. "They tell such incredible wonders about you."

"Yes," Pierre replied with his now habitual smile of mild mockery. "They even tell me such wonders as I've never seen even in dreams. Marya Abra-movna invited me to her house and told me everything that has happened to me or should have happened. Stepan Stepanych also taught me how to tell my story. Generally, I've noticed that being an interesting person is very convenient (I'm an interesting person now); people invite me and tell me about myself."

Natasha smiled and was about to say something.

"We've been told," Princess Marya interrupted her, "that you lost two mil-lion in Moscow. Is it true?"

"And I've become three times richer," said Pierre. Despite the fact that his wife's debts and the necessity of building had changed his affairs, he went on telling people that he had become three times richer.

"What I've unquestionably gained is freedom . . ." he began seriously; but he decided not to go on, noticing that it was too egotistical a subject for conversation.

"And are you building?"

"Yes, Savelyich orders me to."

"Tell us, did you not yet know of the countess's death when you stayed in Moscow?" Princess Marya asked and blushed at once, noticing that by asking this question right after his words about being free, she was ascribing a mean-ing to his words that they might not have had.

"No," answered Pierre, obviously not finding anything awkward in the interpretation Princess Marya had given to his mention of his freedom. "I learned of it in Orel, and you can't imagine how it struck me. We were not exemplary spouses," he said quickly, glancing at Natasha and noticing curiosity on her face about how he would speak of his wife. "But this death struck me terribly. When two persons quarrel, both are always guilty. And one's guilt suddenly becomes terribly heavy before a person who is no longer there. And then, such a death . . . without friends, without consolation. I'm very, very sorry for her," he finished, and was pleased to notice joyful approval on Natasha's face.

"Yes, and now you're a bachelor and eligible again," said Princess Marya.

Pierre suddenly blushed deeply and tried for a long time not to look at Natasha. When he ventured to glance at her, her face was cold, stern, and even contemptuous, as it seemed to him.

"But did you really see and speak with Napoleon, as we've been told?" asked Princess Marya.

Pierre laughed.

"Not once, never. It always seems to everybody that being in captivity means being Napoleon's guest. I not only didn't see him, but I didn't even hear about him. I was in much inferior company."

The supper was coming to an end, and Pierre, who at first refused to tell about his captivity, was gradually drawn into the story.

"But it's true that you stayed in order to kill Napoleon?" Natasha asked him, with a faint smile. "I guessed it then, when we met you by the Sukhareva tower—remember?"

Pierre acknowledged that it was true, and starting with that question, guided gradually by the questions of Princess Marya and especially Natasha, was drawn into a detailed account of his adventures.

At first he spoke with that mocking, meek attitude he now had towards people and especially towards himself, but then, when he came to the story of the horrors and suffering he had seen, he involuntarily got carried away without noticing it and started speaking with the restrained emotion of a man who is reliving strong impressions in recollection.

Princess Marya with a meek smile looked now at Pierre, now at Natasha. In this whole story she saw only Pierre and his kindness. Natasha, leaning on her arm, the expression of her face constantly changing with the story, followed Pierre without tearing herself away for a moment, clearly reliving what he was telling along with him. Not only her gaze, but her exclamations, and the brief questions she asked, showed Pierre that she understood precisely what he meant to convey in what he was telling. It was clear that she understood not only what he was telling, but also what he would have liked to but could not express in words. His episode with the child and the woman whom he was imprisoned for defending, Pierre told like this:

"It was a terrible spectacle, children were abandoned, some in the flames . . . In my presence, a child was pulled out . . . women had their things pulled off them, earrings torn out . . ."

Pierre blushed and faltered.

"Here the patrol arrived and took all the men, all those who weren't looting. And me, too."

"You're surely not telling us everything; you surely did something . . ." said Natasha, and she paused, "something good."

Pierre went on with what he was telling. When he told about the execution, he wanted to avoid the terrible details, but Natasha demanded that he not leave anything out.

Pierre began telling about Karataev (by then he had stood up from the table and was pacing; Natasha followed him with her eyes) and stopped.

"No, you can't understand what I learned from that illiterate man—a little simpleton."

"No, no, go on," said Natasha. "Where is he?"

"He was killed almost in my presence." And Pierre began telling about the last period of their retreat, Karataev's illness (his voice trembled constantly), and his death.

Pierre told of his adventures as he had never told them to anyone, as he had never yet recalled them to himself. It was as if he now saw a new significance in everything he had lived through. Now, as he told it all to Natasha, he experienced that rare pleasure which is granted by women when they listen to a man—not *intelligent* women, who, when they listen, try either to memorize what they are told in order to enrich their minds and on occasion retell the same thing, or else to adjust what is being told to themselves and quickly say something intelligent of their own, worked out in their small intellectual domain; but the pleasure granted by real women, endowed with the ability to select and absorb all the best of what a man has to show. Natasha, not knowing it herself, was all attention: she did not miss a word of Pierre's, not a waver in his voice, not a glance, not the twitch of a facial muscle, not a gesture. She caught the not-yet-spoken word in flight and brought it straight into her open heart, guessing the secret meaning of all Pierre's inner work.

Princess Marya understood the story, sympathized with it, but she now saw something else that absorbed all her attention; she saw the possibility of love and happiness between Natasha and Pierre. And that thought, which occurred to her for the first time, filled her soul with joy.

It was three o'clock in the morning. The servants came with sad and stern faces to change the candles, but no one noticed them.

Pierre finished his story. Natasha went on looking at him intently and attentively with her shining, animated eyes, as if wishing to understand the rest, which he had perhaps not expressed. Pierre, in shy and happy confusion, glanced at her from time to time, and tried to think of what to say now, in order to turn the conversation to another subject. Princess Marya was silent. It occurred to no one that it was three o'clock in the morning and time for bed.

"They say: misfortunes, sufferings," said Pierre. "Well, if someone said to me right now, this minute: do you want to remain the way you were before captivity, or live through it all over again? For God's sake, captivity again and horsemeat! Once we're thrown off our habitual paths, we think all is lost; but it's only here that the new and the good begins. As long as there's life, there's happiness. There's much, much still to come. I'm saying that to you," he said, turning to Natasha.

"Yes, yes," she said, responding to something quite different. "I, too, would wish for nothing except to live through it all over again."

Pierre looked at her attentively.

"Yes, and nothing more," Natasha confirmed.

"Not true, not true," cried Pierre. "I'm not to blame that I'm alive and want to live; and you do, too."

Suddenly Natasha lowered her head to her hands and began to cry.

"What is it, Natasha?" asked Princess Marya.

"Nothing, nothing." She smiled at Pierre through her tears. "Goodbye, it's time for bed."

Pierre got up and took his leave.

Princess Marya and Natasha, as always, came together in the bedroom. They talked about what Pierre had told them. Princess Marya did not voice her opinion of Pierre. Natasha also did not speak of him.

"Well, good night, Marie," said Natasha. "You know, I'm often afraid that we don't talk about *him*" (Prince Andrei), "as if we're afraid of lowering our feeling, and we're forgetting."

Princess Marya sighed deeply and by that sigh acknowledged the correctness of Natasha's words; but in words she did not agree with her.

"As if we could forget?" she said.

"It felt so good to me tonight to tell it all; hard, and painful, and good. Very good," said Natasha. "I'm sure he really loved him. That's why I told him . . . there was no harm in my telling him?" she asked, suddenly blushing.

"Pierre? Oh, no! He's so wonderful!" said Princess Marya.

"You know, Marie," Natasha said suddenly with a mischievous smile, which Princess Marya had not seen on her face for a long time. "He's become somehow clean, smooth, fresh—as if from the bathhouse, you understand?—morally from the bathhouse. Hasn't he?"

"Yes," said Princess Marya, "he's gained much."

"And his short little frock coat and cropped hair; just, well, just like from the bathhouse . . . papa used to . . ."

"I understand that *he*" (Prince Andrei) "loved no one as he did him," said Princess Marya.

"Yes, and he's different from him. They say men become friends when they're quite different. That must be true. Isn't it true that he's not like him at all?"

"Yes, and he's marvellous."

"Well, good night," answered Natasha. And that same mischievous smile, as if forgotten, remained on her face for a long time.

XVIII

Pierre could not fall asleep for a long time that night; he paced up and down the room, now frowning, thinking over something difficult, suddenly shrugging his shoulders and shivering, now smiling happily.

He was thinking about Prince Andrei, about Natasha, about their love, and now felt jealous of her past, now reproached himself, now forgave himself for it. It was already six o'clock in the morning, and he was still pacing the room.

"Well, nothing to be done. If it's impossible now without that! Nothing to be done! It means it has to be so," he said to himself, and, hastily undressing, he went to bed, happy and excited, but with no doubt or indecision.

"I must—however strange, however impossible this happiness—I must do everything to make it so that she and I are man and wife," he said to himself.

Several days before then, Pierre had fixed on Friday as the day of his departure for Petersburg. When he woke up on Thursday, Savelyich came to him for orders about packing things for the trip.

"Why to Petersburg? What's Petersburg? Who's in Peterburg?" he asked involuntarily, though only to himself. "Yes, there was something long, long ago, before this happened, that gave me a reason for going to Petersburg," he recalled. "And why not? Maybe I'll even go. How kind and attentive he is, how he remembers everything!" he thought, looking at Savelyich's old face. "And what a pleasant smile!" he thought.

"So you still don't want your freedom, Savelyich?" asked Pierre.

"What do I need freedom for, Your Excellency? We lived all right with the late count, God rest his soul, and with you we haven't seen any offences."

"Well, but your children?"

"The children will get along, Your Excellency: one can live with such masters."

"Well, but my heirs?" said Pierre. "If I suddenly get married . . . And it may happen," he added with an involuntary smile.

"And if I may be so bold: it would be a good thing, Your Excellency."

"He takes it so lightly," thought Pierre. "He doesn't know how frightening, how dangerous it is. Too early or too late . . . Frightening!"

"What are your orders, if you please? Will you be leaving tomorrow?" asked Savelyich.

"No, I'll postpone it a little. I'll tell you later. Forgive me for the trouble," said Pierre, and, looking at Savelyich's smile, he thought: "How strange, though, that he doesn't know there's no more Petersburg now and first of all this thing must be resolved. However, he surely does know and is only pretending. Shall I talk to him? What does he think?" Pierre wondered. "No, some other time."

At breakfast, Pierre told the princess that he had been at Princess Marya's yesterday and had found there—can you imagine whom?—Natalie Rostov.

The princess pretended that she saw nothing more extraordinary in this news than if he had seen some Anna Semyonovna.

"Do you know her?" asked Pierre.

"I've seen the princess," she replied. "I heard they were matching her with the young Rostov. That would be very good for the Rostovs; they say they're completely ruined."

"No, do you know Miss Rostov?"

"I only heard about that story then. A great pity."

"No, she doesn't understand, or she's pretending," thought Pierre. "I'd better not say anything to her either."

The princess was also preparing provisions for Pierre's trip.

"How kind they all are," thought Pierre, "to busy themselves with all this now, when it certainly can't interest them any more. And all for me; that's the astonishing thing."

That same day the police chief came to Pierre with an offer to send an agent to the Faceted Palace to retrieve things that were being distributed to their owners.

"And this one, too," thought Pierre, looking into the police chief's face, "such a nice, handsome officer, and so kind! To be concerned with such trifles *now*. And yet they say he's dishonest and profits from it. What nonsense! And anyhow, why shouldn't he profit? He was brought up that way. And they all do it. But such a pleasant, kind face, and he smiles, looking at me."

Pierre went to dine at Princess Marya's.

Driving along the streets amidst the charred ruins of houses, he was astonished at the beauty of these ruins. The chimney stacks of the houses, the broken-down walls, picturesquely reminiscent of the Rhine and the Colosseum, were strung out, hiding each other, through the burnt quarters. Cabbies and their passengers, carpenters notching frames, market women and shopkeepers all glanced at Pierre with merry, beaming faces and seemed to be saying: "Ah, here he is! We'll see what comes of it!"

As he was going into Princess Marya's house, doubt came over Pierre whether it was true that he had been there yesterday, had seen Natasha and spoken with her. "Maybe I invented it. Maybe I'll go in and not see anybody." But he had no sooner entered the room than he sensed her presence with his whole being, by the instant loss of his freedom. She was in the same black dress with soft folds, and her hair was done in the same way as yesterday, yet she was quite different. If she had been like that yesterday, when he came into the room, he would not have failed to recognize her for a moment.

She was the same as he had known her almost as a child and then as Prince Andrei's fiancée. Her eyes shone with a merry, questioning brightness; her face had a tender and strangely mischievous expression.

Pierre dined and would have sat there all evening, but Princess Marya went to vespers and Pierre left with them.

The next day Pierre came early, dined, and sat there all evening. Though Princess Marya and Natasha were obviously glad of their guest, though the whole interest of Pierre's life was now centred on this house, by evening they had talked everything over, and the conversation passed constantly from one insignificant subject to another, and frequently broke off. Pierre sat for so long that evening that Princess Marya and Natasha kept glancing at each other, obviously waiting for him to go. Pierre saw it, yet he could not go. It was becoming painful, awkward, but he went on sitting, because he *could not* get up and go.

Princess Marya, seeing no end to it, got up first and, complaining of a migraine, began saying goodbye.

"So you're going to Petersburg tomorrow?" she asked.

"No, I'm not," Pierre said hastily, with surprise and as if offended. "Ah, no, to Petersburg? Tomorrow—only I'm not saying goodbye. I'll come by for your errands," he said, standing in front of Princess Marya, blushing and not leaving.

Natasha gave him her hand and went out. Princess Marya, on the contrary, instead of leaving, lowered herself into an armchair and looked at Pierre sternly and attentively with her deep, luminous gaze. The fatigue she had clearly shown just before was now completely gone. She gave a deep and drawn-out sigh, as if preparing for a long conversation.

In Natasha's absence, all Pierre's confusion and awkwardness instantly vanished and were replaced by excited animation. He quickly moved an armchair quite close to Princess Marya.

"Yes, I wanted to tell you," he said, answering her gaze as if it were words. "Princess, help me. What am I to do? May I hope? Princess, my friend, listen to me. I know everything. I know I'm not worthy of her; I know it's impossible to talk about it now. But I want to be a brother to her. No, I don't . . . I can't . . ."

He stopped and rubbed his face and eyes with his hands.

"Well, there," he went on, clearly making an effort to speak coherently. "I don't know since when I've loved her. But I've loved only her, her alone, all my life, and I love her so much that I can't imagine my life without her. I don't dare ask for her hand now; but the thought that she might perhaps be mine and that I might miss this possibility . . . possibility . . . is terrible. Tell me, may I hope? Tell me, what am I to do? Dear princess," he said, after pausing briefly and touching her hand, since she did not reply.

"I'm thinking about what you've told me," Princess Marya replied. "Here is what I will tell you. You're right that to speak to her of love now . . ." The princess stopped. She was going to say that to speak to her of love now was impossible; but she stopped, because it was the third day since she had seen by the suddenly changed Natasha, not only that Natasha would not be offended if Pierre spoke to her of his love, but that she wished only for that.

"To speak to her now . . . is impossible," Princess Marya said all the same.

"But what am I to do?"

"Leave it to me," said Princess Marya. "I know . . ."

Pierre was looking into Princess Marya's eyes.

"Well? . . . Well? . . ." he said.

"I know that she loves . . . will love you," Princess Marya corrected herself.

She had barely managed to say these words when Pierre jumped up and with a frightened face seized Princess Marya by the hand.

"What makes you think so? You think that I may hope? You think so?!"

"Yes, I do," Princess Marya said, smiling. "Write to her parents. And leave it to me. I'll tell her, when it can be done. I wish it. And my heart tells me it will happen."

"No, it can't be! I'm so happy! But it can't be . . . I'm so happy! No, it can't be!" Pierre was saying, kissing Princess Marya's hands.

"You go to Petersburg; that will be best. And I'll write to you," she said.

"To Petersburg? Go? Very well, yes, I'll go. But may I come to you tomorrow?"

The next day Pierre came to say goodbye. Natasha was less animated than on the previous days; but that day, occasionally glancing in her eyes, Pierre felt that he was disappearing, that neither he nor she was there any more, but there was just one feeling of happiness. "Can it be? No, it can't," he said to himself at her every glance, gesture, word, which filled his soul with joy.

When, saying goodbye to her, he took her thin, slender hand, he involuntarily held it slightly longer in his.

"Can it be that this hand, this face, these eyes, all this treasure of feminine loveliness that is stranger to me now, can it be that it will all be eternally mine, habitual, the same as I am for myself? No, it's impossible! . . ."

"Goodbye, Count," she said to him aloud. "I'll be waiting very much for you," she added in a whisper.

And those simple words, the glance and expression of the face that went with them, in the course of two months constituted a subject of inexhaustible memories, explanations, and happy reveries for Pierre. " 'I'll be waiting very much for you . . .' Yes, yes, how did she put it? Yes, 'I'll be waiting very much for you.' Ah, I'm so happy! What is it—I'm so happy!" Pierre said to himself.

XIX

In Pierre's soul now nothing went on like what had gone on in it under similar circumstances during his engagement to Hélène.

He did not repeat, as then, with morbid shame, the words he had spoken, did not say to himself: "Ah, why didn't I say it, and why, why did I say *'je vous aime'* then?" Now, on the contrary, he repeated in his imagination every word of hers, of his, with all the details of her face and smile, and did not want either to add or subtract: he wanted only to repeat. There was now not the shadow of a doubt whether what he was undertaking was good or bad. Only one terrible doubt sometimes entered his head: "Isn't it all a dream? Isn't Princess Marya mistaken? Am I not too proud and presumptuous? I believe her; but what if suddenly, as is bound to happen, Princess Marya tells her, and she smiles and says: 'How strange! He's certainly mistaken. Doesn't he know that he is a man, simply a man, while I? . . . I am quite a different, higher being?' "

That was the only doubt that often came to Pierre. He also did not make any plans now. The happiness awaiting him seemed so incredible, that it needed only to come about, and there could be nothing after it. Everything ended there.

A joyful, unexpected madness, of which Pierre considered himself incapable, came over him. The whole meaning of life, not only for him, but for all the world, seemed to him to consist only in his love and the possibility of her love for him. Sometimes all people seemed to him to be occupied with only one thing—his future happiness. It sometimes seemed to him that they were all rejoicing as he was, and only tried to conceal their joy, pretending to be occupied with other interests. In every word and movement he saw hints at his happiness. He often surprised people who met him by his significant happy glances and smiles, expressive of a secret complicity. But when he realized that people could not know of his happiness, he pitied them with all his heart and felt a desire to explain to them somehow that everything they were occupied with was completely nonsensical and trifling, not worthy of attention.

When they offered him a post in the service or discussed some general matters of state and the war, supposing that the happiness of all people depended on this or that outcome of events, he listened with a meek, condoling smile and surprised the people who spoke to him with his odd remarks. But both those people who seemed to Pierre to understand the real meaning of life, that is, his feeling, and those unfortunates who obviously did not understand it—all people in that period of time appeared to him in such a bright light of the feeling shining within him, that without the least effort, meeting any person whatever, he at once saw in him all that was good and worthy of love.

In examining his late wife's business affairs and papers, he experienced no feeling for her memory, except pity that she had not known the happiness he knew now. Prince Vassily, especially proud now of his new post and star, appeared to him a touching, kind, and pathetic old man.

Later Pierre often remembered that time of happy insanity. All the judgements of people and circumstances he formed for himself in that period of time remained for ever true for him. He not only did not subsequently renounce those views of people and things, but, on the contrary, in inner doubt and contradiction he would resort to the views he had had in that time of insanity, and those views always turned out to be correct.

"Maybe I did seem strange and ridiculous then," he thought, "but I wasn't as insane as I seemed. On the contrary, I was more intelligent and perceptive then than ever, and I understood everything that's worth understanding in life, because . . . I was happy."

Pierre's insanity consisted in the fact that he did not wait, as before, for personal reasons, which he called people's merits, in order to love them, but love overflowed his heart, and, loving people without reason, he discovered the unquestionable reasons for which it was worth loving them.

XX

From that first evening, when Natasha, after Pierre's departure, told Princess Marya with a joyfully mocking smile that he was "just, well, just like from the bathhouse, with his short little frock coat and cropped hair," from that moment something hidden and unknown to her, but irresistible, had awakened in Natasha's soul.

Everything—her face, her step, her gaze, her voice—everything suddenly changed in her. Unexpectedly for herself, the force of life, her hopes for happiness, came to the surface and demanded to be satisfied. From the first evening, it was as if Natasha forgot all that had happened to her. After that she never once complained of her situation, said not a word about her past, and was no longer afraid to make cheerful plans for the future. She spoke little of Pierre, but when Princess Marya mentioned him, the long-extinguished brightness lit up in her eyes, and her lips puckered in a strange smile.

The change that took place in Natasha at first surprised Princess Marya but when she understood its meaning, this change upset her. "Can it be that she loved my brother so little, that she could forget him so soon?" Princess Marya thought, when she pondered by herself the change that had taken place. But when she was with Natasha, she was not angry with her and did not reproach her. The awakened force of life that took hold of Natasha was obviously so irrepressible, so unexpected for Natasha herself, that in her presence Princess Marya felt she had no right to reproach her even in her heart.

Natasha gave herself up so fully and sincerely to this new feeling that she did not even attempt to hide the fact that she was now not grieving but joyful and gay.

When Princess Marya returned to her room after her talk that night with Pierre, Natasha met her on the threshold.

"He said it? Yes? He said it?" she repeated. And a joyful and at the same time pathetic expression, as if asking forgiveness for her joy, lingered on Natasha's face.

"I wanted to listen at the door, but I knew you'd tell me."

Understandable and touching as she found the gaze with which Natasha looked at her, sorry as she was to see her agitation, for the first moment Natasha's words offended Princess Marya. She remembered her brother and his love.

"But what's to be done! She can't be otherwise," thought Princess Marya; and with a sad and somewhat stern face, she told Natasha everything Pierre had said to her. On hearing that he was going to Petersburg, Natasha was amazed.

"To Petersburg?" she repeated, as if she did not understand. But, looking intently into the sad expression of Princess Marya's face, she guessed the reason for that sadness and suddenly began to cry. "Marie," she said, "teach me what to do. I'm afraid to be bad. I'll do whatever you say; teach me . . ."

"You love him?"

"Yes," Natasha whispered.

"Then why are you crying? I'm happy for you," said Princess Marya, completely forgiving Natasha's joy on account of those tears.

"It won't be soon, but some day. Think what happiness when I'll be his wife and you'll have married Nicolas."

"Natasha, I asked you not to talk about that. Let's talk about you."

They were silent for a while.

"Only what's he going to Petersburg for!" Natasha said suddenly, and hastily answered herself: "No, no, it has to be so . . . Right, Marie? It has to be so . . ."

EPILOGUE

Part One

I

Seven years had passed since 1812. The churned-up historical sea of Europe settled back within its shores. It seemed to have grown still; but the mysterious forces that move mankind (mysterious because the laws that determine their movement are unknown to us) continued their action.

Though the surface of the historical sea seemed immobile, mankind moved as ceaselessly as the movement of time. Various groups of human connections were made and unmade; causes were prepared for the formation and decomposition of states, for the displacements of peoples.

The historical sea did not, as formerly, direct its surges from one shore to another: it seethed in its depths. Historical figures were not, as formerly, borne by the waves from one shore to another; they now seemed to turn in place. Historical figures, who formerly, at the head of armies, reflected the movement of the masses by ordering wars, marches, battles, now reflected the seething movement through political and diplomatic considerations, laws, treaties . . .

Historians call this activity of historical figures *the reaction*.

Describing the activity of these historical figures, who were, in their opinion, the cause of what they call *the reaction*, historians severely condemn them. All the well-known people of that time, from Alexander and Napoleon to Mme de Staël, Photius, Schelling, Fichte, Chateaubriand, and others, pass before their severe judgement and are either acquitted or condemned, depending on whether they contributed to *progress* or *the reaction*.

In Russia, according to their descriptions, a reaction was also going on in that period of time, and the chief perpetrator of this reaction was Alexander I—the same Alexander I who, according to their own descriptions, was the chief perpetrator of the liberal initiatives of his reign and of the salvation of Russia.

In present-day Russian literature, from the schoolboy to the learned historian, there is not a person who does not cast his little stone at Alexander I for his wrong actions during this period of his reign.

"He should have acted thus and so. In this case he acted well, in that badly. He behaved himself splendidly at the beginning of his reign and during the year twelve; but he acted badly in granting Poland a constitution, forming the Holy Alliance, giving power to Arakcheev, encouraging Golitsyn and mysticism, and then encouraging Shishkov and Photius. He did badly in occupying himself with the front-line units of the army; he acted badly in disbanding the Semyonovsky regiment, and so on."[1]

One would have to fill ten pages with writing in order to enumerate all that the historians reproach him with, on the basis of that knowledge of the good of mankind which they possess.

What do these reproaches mean?

The very actions for which the historians approve of Alexander I, such as the liberal initiatives of the reign, the struggle with Napoleon, the firmness he showed in the year twelve, and the campaign of the year thirteen—do they not all come from the same sources, from the conditions of blood, upbringing, life that made the person of Alexander what he was, and from which also come the actions for which the historians blame him, such as the Holy Alliance, the restoration of Poland, the reaction of the twenties?

In what consists the essence of these reproaches?

It is that a historical figure such as Alexander I, a figure who stood on the highest possible step of human power, as if at the focal point of the blinding light of all the historical rays concentrated upon him; a figure subject to the strongest influences in the world—of intrigues, deceptions, flattery, self-delusion—which are inseparable from power; a figure who felt upon himself at every moment of his life the responsibility for all that was happening in Europe; and not an invented figure, but a living one, and, like every man, with his personal habits, passions, strivings for goodness, beauty, truth—that this figure, fifty years ago, was not so much not virtuous (the historians do not reproach him for that), but did not have those views of the good of mankind now possessed by a professor who from his youth has been taken up with learning, that is, reading books, attending lectures, and copying things from these books and lectures into a notebook.

But even if we suppose that Alexander I was mistaken fifty years ago in his views of what the good of the peoples was, we must involuntarily suppose that the historian judging Alexander will in the same way, after the passing of some time, turn out to be incorrect in his view of what the good of mankind is. This supposition is the more natural and necessary in that, as we follow the development of historical science, we see that the view of what the good of mankind is changes with each new year, with each new writer; so that in ten years what seemed good looks like evil, and vice versa. What is more, in one and the same time we find completely opposite views among historians as to what was evil and what was good: some set the Holy Alliance and the granting of a constitution to Poland to the credit, others to the reproach of Alexander.

Of the activity of Alexander and Napoleon it is impossible to say that it was useful or harmful, for we cannot say what it was useful or harmful for. If that activity displeases someone, it displeases him only because it does not coincide with his limited notion of what the good is. The preservation of my father's house in Moscow in the year twelve, or the glory of the Russian army, or the flourishing of the universities of Petersburg and elsewhere, or the freedom of Poland, or the might of Russia, or the balance of Europe, or a certain sort of European enlightenment known as progress, may seem good to me, but I must acknowledge that, besides those purposes, the activity of every historical figure had other more general purposes, inaccessible to me.

But let us suppose that so-called science has the possibility of reconciling all contradictions and possesses an immutable yardstick of good and evil for historical figures and events.

Let us suppose that Alexander could have done everything otherwise. Let us suppose that, according to the prescriptions of those who accuse him, those who profess a knowledge of the ultimate purpose of mankind's movement, he could have arranged everything according to the programme of nationhood, freedom, equality, and progress (there seems to be no other), which his present-day accusers would have provided for him. Let us suppose that this programme was possible and was drawn up and that Alexander acted according to it. What would have become then of the activity of all those people who opposed the then tendency of the government—an activity which, in the opinion of the historians, was good and useful? There would have been no such activity; there would have been no life; there would have been nothing.

If we allow that human life can be governed by reason, the possibility of life is annihilated.

II

If we allow, as historians do, that great men lead mankind to the achievement of certain purposes, which consist either in the greatness of Russia or France, or in the balance of Europe, or in spreading the ideas of the revolution, or in general progress, or in whatever else, then it is impossible to explain the phenomena of history without the notions of *chance* and *genius*.

If the purpose of the European wars at the beginning of the present century was the greatness of Russia, that purpose could have been achieved without any of the preceding wars and without the invasion. If the purpose was the greatness of France, it could have been achieved without the revolution and without the empire. If the purpose was the spreading of ideas, printing would have carried it out far better than soldiers. If the purpose was the progress of civilization, it is quite easy to suppose that, besides the destruction of people and their wealth, there are other more expedient ways to spread civilization.

Why did it happen this way and not otherwise?

Because this is how it happened. "*Chance* made the situation; *genius* profited from it," says history.

But what is *chance*? What is *genius*?

The words *chance* and *genius* do not designate anything that actually exists and therefore cannot be defined. These words designate only a certain degree of understanding of phenomenon. I do not know why such-and-such a phenomenon occurs; I think that I cannot know it; therefore I do not want to know it, and I say: *chance*. I see a power that produces effects incommensurate with common human qualities; I do not know why that happens, and I say: *genius*.

For a flock of sheep, the sheep that the shepherd takes into a separate pen to be fed, and that grows twice as fat as the others, must seem a genius. And the circumstance that every evening precisely this same sheep ends up, not in the general fold, but in a separate pen to have oats, and that this, precisely this same sheep, spilling over with fat, is killed for meat, must appear as an astonishing conjunction of genius with a whole series of extraordinary chances.

But the sheep need only stop thinking that everything that happens to them occurs only to achieve their sheep purposes; they need only allow that what happens to them may have purposes incomprehensible to them—and they will immediately see the unity, the consistency in what happens to a fattened-up sheep. Even if they do not know the purpose for which he is being fattened up, they will at least know that all that happened to the sheep did not happen by chance, and they will no longer need the notions of *chance* or of *genius*.

Only by renouncing the knowledge of an immediate, comprehensible purpose and admitting that the final purpose is inaccessible to us, will we see the consistency and expediency in the life of historical figures; the cause will be revealed to us of that effect incommensurate with common human qualities which they produce, and we will not need the words *chance* and *genius*.

We need only admit that the purpose of the upheavals of the European peoples is unknown to us, while we know only facts, which consist in murders, first in France, then in Italy, in Africa, in Prussia, in Austria, in Spain, in Russia, and that the movements from west to east and from east to west constitute the essence and purpose of these events, and not only will we not need to see anything exceptional and marked by *genius* in the characters of Napoleon and Alexander, but it will be impossible for us to picture these figures otherwise than as the same people as all the rest; and not only will we no longer need to explain by *chance* those small events that made these men what they were, but it will be clear that all those small events were necessary.

In renouncing knowledge of the final purpose, we will clearly understand that, just as it is impossible to invent for any plant a flower and seed that correspond to it more than those it produces, so it is impossible to invent two other persons, with all their past, who would correspond to such a degree, in such minute detail, to the purpose they were meant to fulfil.

III

The fundamental, essential meaning of the European events of the beginning of the present century is the military movement of masses of European peoples from west to east and then from east to west. The initial movement was from west to east. For the peoples of the west to be able to perform that military movement to Moscow which they did perform, it was necessary (1) that they form a military group of such size as to be able to withstand a clash with the military group of the east; (2) that they renounce all established traditions and customs; and (3) that, in performing their military movement, they have at their head a man who could justify both to himself and to them the deceptions, robberies, and murders which were to be performed and which accompanied that movement.

And starting with the French revolution, the old, insufficiently large group is destroyed; old customs and traditions are obliterated; step by step a group of a new size is produced, along with new customs and traditions, and that man is prepared who is to stand at the head of the future movement and bear upon himself all the responsibility for what is to be performed.

A man without convictions, without customs, without traditions, without a name, not even a Frenchman, seemingly by the strangest chances, moves among all the parties stirring up France, and, without attaching himself to any of them, is borne up to a conspicuous place.

The ignorance of his associates, the weakness and insignificance of his opponents, the sincerity of his lies, and the brilliant and self-confident limitedness of this man move him to the head of the army. A brilliant complement of soldiers from the Italian army, the reluctance of his adversaries to fight, his childish boldness and self-confidence win him military glory. Countless numbers of so-called chances accompany him everywhere. The disgrace he falls into with the rulers of France turns to his advantage. His attempts to change the path he is destined for fail: he is not accepted into the Russian service, and fails to obtain an appointment in Turkey. During the wars in Italy, several times he is on the brink of destruction and is saved each time in an unexpected way. The Russian troops, the very ones who can destroy his glory, do not, for various diplomatic considerations, enter Europe while he is there.[2]

On his return from Italy, he finds the government in Paris in that process of decomposition in which the people who happen to be in this government are inevitably wiped out and obliterated. And a way out of this dangerous situation appears to him of itself, consisting in a senseless, groundless expedition to Africa. Again the same so-called chances accompany him. Impregnable Malta surrenders without a shot fired; the most imprudent orders are crowned with success. The enemy fleet, which afterwards will not let a single boat pass, lets pass a whole army.[3] In Africa a whole series of villainies is committed upon the all-but-unarmed inhabitants. And the people who commit these villainies, and in particular their leader, assure themselves that this is beautiful, that this is glory, that this is like Caesar and Alexander the Great, and that this is good.

That ideal of *glory* and *greatness* which consists not only in considering nothing that one does as bad, but in being proud of one's every crime, ascribing some incomprehensible supernatural meaning to it—that ideal, which was to guide this man and the people connected with him, is freely developed in Africa. Everything he does succeeds. The plague leaves him untouched. The cruel murder of prisoners is not imputed to him in fault. His childishly imprudent, groundless, and ignoble departure from Africa, leaving his comrades in trouble, is set to his credit, and again the enemy fleet misses him twice. At the time when, already completely intoxicated by the successful crimes he has committed, prepared for his role, he arrives in Paris without any aim, the decomposition of the republican government, which could have destroyed him a year earlier, has reached the ultimate degree, and his presence, clear of any parties, can now only elevate him.

He has no plan at all; he is afraid of everything; but the parties seize upon him and demand his participation.

He alone, with his ideal of glory and greatness worked out in Italy and Egypt, with his insane self-adoration, with his boldness in crime, with his sincerity in lying—he alone can justify what is to be performed.

He is needed for the place that awaits him, and therefore, almost independently of his will, and despite his irresolution, his lack of a plan, all the mistakes he makes, he is drawn into a conspiracy the purpose of which is the seizure of power, and the conspiracy is crowned with success.

He is pushed into a meeting of the rulers. Frightened, he wants to flee, considering himself lost; he pretends to faint; he says senseless things, which should have been his ruin. But the rulers of France, once sharp-witted and proud, now, sensing that their role has been played out, are still more confused than he is, and do not say the words that needed to be said in order to hold on to power and destroy him.

Chance, millions of *chances*, give him power, and all people, as if by arrangement, contribute to the strengthening of that power. *Chance* makes the characters of the then rulers of France submissive to him; *chance* makes the character of Paul I, who recognizes his power; *chance* makes a conspiracy against him which not only does not harm him, but strengthens his power. *Chance* sends d'Enghien into his hands and accidentally forces him to kill him,[4] thereby convincing the mob more forcefully than by any other means that he has the right, because he has the power. *Chance* makes it so that he strains all his forces towards an expedition to England, which obviously would have destroyed him, and never carries out his intention, but instead unexpectedly runs into Mack and his Austrians, who surrender without a battle. *Chance* and *genius* give him the victory at Austerlitz, and *by chance* all people, not only the French, but all of Europe as well, with the exception of England, which does not participate in the events about to take place, all people, despite their former horror and loathing for his crimes, now recognize his power, the title he has given himself, and his ideal of greatness and glory, which to all of them seems something beautiful and reasonable.

As if trying themselves out and preparing for the coming movement, the forces of the west, in 1805, '06, '07, '09, repeatedly push eastwards, gaining strength and growing in numbers. In 1811, the group of people formed in France merges into one huge group with the peoples of the centre. Along with the ever-increasing group of people, the power of justification of the man who stands at the head of the movement also develops further. During the ten-year preparatory period preceding the big movement, this man is brought together with all the crowned heads of Europe. The unmasked rulers of the world cannot oppose any intelligent ideal to Napoleon's ideal of *glory* and *greatness*, which has no meaning. One after another, they rush to demonstrate their nonentity to him. The king of Prussia sends his wife to seek favour with the great man; the emperor of Austria considers it a favour that this man receives a daughter of the Caesars in his bed; the pope, guardian of what the peoples hold sacred, lets his religion serve the great man's rise. It is not so much Napoleon himself who prepares for the fulfilling of his role, as everything around him prepares him to take upon himself all responsibility for what is being performed and is to be performed. There is no action, no villainy or petty deception committed by him that is not reflected at once, on the lips of those around him, in the form of a great deed. The best celebration the Germans can think up for him is to celebrate Jena and Auerstädt. Not only is he great, but his ancestors, his brothers, his stepsons, his brothers-in-law are great. Everything is done to deprive him of the last powers of reason and prepare him for his terrible role. And when he is ready, the forces are ready as well.

The invasion pushes eastwards; it reaches its final goal—Moscow. The capital is taken; the Russian army is annihilated more than any enemy armies were ever annihilated in previous wars from Austerlitz to Wagram. But suddenly, instead of the *chances* and *genius* that up to now have led him so consistently through an unbroken series of successes to the appointed goal, there appear a countless number of reverse *chances,* from a head cold at Borodino to the frosts and the spark that sets fire to Moscow; and instead of *genius* there appears an unexampled stupidity and baseness.

The invasion flees, returns, flees again, and now all the chances are constantly not for but against him.

A counter-movement is performed from east to west, which remarkably resembles the preceding movement from west to east. As in 1805, 1807, 1809, the same attempts at movement from east to west precede the big movement; there is the same merging into a group of huge dimensions; the same joining of peoples of the centre to the movement; the same hesitation midway, and the same swiftness as they near the goal.

Paris, the ultimate goal, is reached. The Napoleonic government and army are destroyed. Napoleon himself no longer has any meaning; all his actions are obviously pathetic and vile; but again an inexplicable chance occurs: the allies hate Napoleon, in whom they see the cause of their calamities; deprived of strength and power, exposed in his villainies and perfidies, he ought to appear to them as he appeared ten years earlier and one year later—as a bandit and outlaw. But by some strange chance no one sees it. His role is not finished yet. The man who ten years earlier and one year later was considered a bandit and outlaw is sent a two-day sail from France, to an island given into his possession, with his guards and several million, which are paid to him for some reason.

IV

The movement of peoples begins to settle within its shores. The waves of the big movement flood back, and on the calmed sea eddies form, over which diplomats skim, imagining that it is precisely they who have brought about the calming of the movement.

But the calmed sea suddenly rises. To the diplomats it seems that they, that their disagreements, are the cause of this new upsurge of forces; they expect war among their sovereigns; the situation seems insoluble to them. But the wave which they can feel rising does not break from where they expect. The same wave rises from the same point of departure—Paris. The last backwash of the movement from the west occurs, the backwash that is to resolve the seemingly unresolvable diplomatic difficulties and put an end to the military movement of that period.

The man who devastated France, alone, without conspiracy, without soldiers, comes back to France. Any guard can arrest him; but by a strange chance, not only does no one arrest him, but everyone greets with rapture the man whom they cursed the day before and will curse a month later.

This man is still needed to justify the last joint act.

The act is performed. The last role has been played. The actor is told to undress and wash off his greasepaint and rouge: there is no more need for him.

And several years go by during which this man, in solitude on his island, plays a pathetic comedy before himself, pettily intriguing and lying to justify his actions, when that justification is no longer needed, and showing to the whole world what it was that people took for strength while an unseen hand was guiding him.[5]

The stage manager, having finished the drama and undressed the actor, shows him to us.

"Look at what you believed in! Here he is! Do you see now that it was not he but *I* who moved you?"

But, blinded by the force of the movement, people long fail to understand that.

Still greater consistency and necessity are presented in the life of Alexander I, the figure who stood at the head of the counter-movement from east to west.

What does that man need who, overshadowing others, would stand at the head of this movement from east to west?

He needs a sense of justice, a concern for the affairs of Europe, but a distant concern, unobscured by petty interests; he needs a moral superiority over his associates—the sovereigns of the time; he needs a mild and attractive personality; he needs a personal grievance against Napoleon. And all this is there in Alexander I; all this has been prepared by countless so-called *chances* throughout his past life: his upbringing, his liberal initiatives, the advisers surrounding him, Austerlitz, Tilsit, Erfurt.

During the national war, this figure is inactive, since he is not needed. But once the necessity for a general European war appears, this figure at a given moment appears in his place and, uniting the peoples of Europe, leads them to their goal.

The goal is achieved. After the final war of 1815, Alexander finds himself at the height of all possible human power. How does he use it?

Alexander I, the pacifier of Europe, a man who from his youth strove only for the good of his people, the first initiator of liberal innovations in his fatherland, now, when he seems to possess the greatest power and therefore the possibility of doing good for his people, while Napoleon in exile makes childish and deceitful plans for how he would have made mankind happy if he had had power, Alexander I, having fulfilled his vocation and felt the hand of God upon him, suddenly recognizes the insignificance of this imaginary power, turns away from it, puts it into the hands of people he despises and who are despicable, and says only:

" 'Not unto us, not unto us, but unto Thy Name!' I am also a man, like you; let me live like a man, and think of my soul and of God."[6]

As the sun and every atom of the ether is a sphere complete in itself and at the same time only an atom of a whole that is inaccessible to man in its enormity— so, too, every person bears his own purposes within himself and yet bears them in order to serve general purposes that are inaccessible to man.

A bee sitting on a flower stung a child. And the child is afraid of bees and says that a bee's purpose consists in stinging people. A poet admires a bee sucking from the cup of a flower and says that a bee's purpose consists in sucking up the fragrance of flowers. A beekeeper, noting how a bee gathers flower pollen and brings it to the hive, says that a bee's purpose consists in gathering honey. Another beekeeper, who has studied the life of a hive more closely, says that a bee collects pollen in order to feed the young bees and rear a queen, and that its purpose consists in reproducing its kind. A botanist notes that, as a bee lands with pollen on the pistil of a dioecious flower, it fertilizes it, and in that the botanist sees the bee's purpose. Another, observing the migration of plants, sees that the bee contributes to that migration, and this new observer may say it is in this that the bee's purpose consists. But the final purpose of the bee is exhausted neither by the one, nor the other, nor the third purpose that human reason is able to discover. The higher human reason rises in the discovery of these purposes, the more obvious for it is the inaccessibility of the final purpose.

All that is accessible to man is the observation of the correspondence between the life of a bee and other phenomena of life. It is the same for the purposes of historical figures and peoples.

V

The wedding of Natasha, who married Bezukhov in the year thirteen, was the last joyful event in the family of the old Rostovs. Count Ilya Andreevich died that same year, and, as always happens, with his death the old family broke up.

The events of the past year—the Moscow fire and the flight from it, the death of Prince Andrei and Natasha's despair, the death of Petya, the countess's grief—all this, like one blow after another, fell on the old count's head. It seemed he did not understand and felt unable to understand the significance of all these events, and morally bowed his old head, as if expecting and asking for new blows that would finish him off. He seemed now frightened and perplexed, now unnaturally animated and enterprising.

Natasha's wedding occupied him for some time by its external side. He ordered dinners, suppers, and obviously wanted to appear cheerful; but his cheerfulness did not communicate itself as formerly, but, on the contrary, evoked compassion in people who knew and loved him.

After the departure of Pierre and his wife, he grew quiet and began to complain of anguish. A few days later he fell ill and took to his bed. Despite the doctors' reassurances, he understood from the first days of his illness that he would not get up again. The countess spent two weeks in an armchair by his bedside without undressing. Each time she gave him his medicine, he sobbed and silently kissed her hand. On the last day, weeping, he begged forgiveness of his wife and absent son for having ruined their property—the chief guilt he felt hanging over him. Having taken communion and been anointed, he died quietly, and the next day a crowd of acquaintances, who came to pay their last respects to the deceased, filled the Rostovs' rented apartment. All these acquaintances, who had dined and danced so many times in his house, who had laughed at him so many times, now said with the same feeling of inner reproach and affection, as if justifying themselves before someone: "Yes, be that as it may, he was an excellent man. You don't meet such men nowadays . . . And who doesn't have his weaknesses? . . ."

Precisely at a time when the count's affairs had become so entangled that it was impossible to imagine how it would all end if it went on a year longer, he unexpectedly died.

Nikolai was with the Russian troops in Paris when the news of his father's death reached him. He immediately sent in his resignation and, without waiting to be discharged, took a leave and went to Moscow. The state of their financial affairs became perfectly clear within a month after the count's death, astonishing everyone by the enormity of the sum of various little debts, the existence of which no one even suspected. The debts were twice greater than the property itself.

Relations and friends advised Nikolai to renounce the inheritance. But Nikolai saw renouncing the inheritance as an expression of reproach to his father's memory, which was sacred to him, and therefore would not hear of it and accepted the inheritance with the obligation to pay off the debts.

The creditors, who had been silent for so long, being bound, while the count was alive, by that undefined but powerful influence which his lax kindness had on them, suddenly all sued for recovery. There was, as always happens, a competition for who would get paid first, and those very people who, like Mitenka and others, held uncovered promissory notes as gifts, now turned out to be the most demanding creditors. Nikolai was given no time or respite, and those who, by the look of it, had felt sorry for the old man who was to blame for their losses (if there were losses), now fell mercilessly on the young heir, obviously guiltless before them, who voluntarily took the payment upon himself.

Not one of Nikolai's proposed schemes succeeded; the estate went under the hammer for half its value, and half of the debts still remained unpaid. Nikolai accepted the thirty thousand offered him by his brother-in-law Bezukhov to pay off the portion of debts he recognized as real debts of money. And to avoid being sent to jail for the remaining debts, as his creditors threatened, he went into the service again.

To go to the army, where he stood to get the first vacant post as regimental commander, was impossible, because his mother now clung to her son as her last enticement to life; and therefore, despite his reluctance to remain in

Moscow, in the circle of people who had known him formerly, despite his loathing of the civil service, he accepted a civil post in Moscow and, having taken off his beloved uniform, settled with his mother and Sonya in a small apartment on the Sivtsev Vrazhek.

Natasha and Pierre were living in Petersburg at the time and had no clear idea of Nikolai's situation. Having borrowed money from his brother-in-law, Nikolai tried to conceal his disastrous situation from him. His situation was especially bad because he not only had to support himself, Sonya, and his mother on his twelve-hundred-rouble salary, but had to support his mother in such a way that she did not notice they were poor. The countess could not understand the possibility of life without the conditions of luxury she had been accustomed to since childhood, and, not realizing how difficult it was for her son, she demanded now a carriage they did not have to send for a lady acquaintance, now some expensive food for herself and wine for her son, now money so as to make a surprise gift to Natasha, Sonya, or Nikolai himself.

Sonya ran the household, took care of her aunt, read aloud to her, put up with her caprices and secret dislike, and helped Nikolai to conceal from the old countess the situation of poverty in which they found themselves. Nikolai felt he owed an unrepayable debt of gratitude to Sonya for all she was doing for his mother, admired her patience and devotion, but tried to distance himself from her.

In his heart it was as if he reproached her for being too perfect and having nothing to be reproached for. In her there was everything for which people are appreciated; but there was little of what would make him love her. And he felt that, the more he appreciated her, the less he loved her. He took her at her word, in the letter in which she had given him his freedom, and behaved with her now as if all that had been between them was long forgotten and could by no means be repeated.

Nikolai's situation was becoming worse and worse. The thought of putting something aside from his salary proved a dream. He not only put nothing aside, but, in satisfying his mother's demands, accumulated small debts. No way out of his situation presented itself to him. The thought of marrying a rich heiress, which his female relations suggested to him, he found revolting. The other way out of his situation—his mother's death—never entered his head. He wished for nothing, hoped for nothing, and deep in his heart took a gloomy and stern pleasure in the unmurmuring endurance of his situation. He tried to avoid former acquaintances with their condolences and offers of insulting assistance, avoided all distractions and amusements, and even at home did nothing except lay out patience with his mother, silently pace the room, and smoke pipe after pipe. It was is if he was carefully maintaining in himself that gloomy state of mind which alone enabled him to endure his situation.

VI

At the beginning of winter, Princess Marya came to Moscow. From town rumours she learned about the situation of the Rostovs and how "the son was sacrificing himself for his mother"—as they said in town.

"I never expected anything else from him," Princess Marya said to herself, feeling a joyful confirmation of her love for him. Remembering her friendly and almost familial relations with their whole family, she considered it her duty to visit them. But remembering her relations with Nikolai in Voronezh, she was afraid of it. Nevertheless, making a great effort with herself, several weeks after her arrival in town, she went to see the Rostovs.

Nikolai was the first to meet her, because one could get to the countess's room only through his. At his first glance at her, Nikolai's face, instead of the expression of joy that Princess Marya expected to see on it, assumed an expression of coldness, dryness, and pride such as the princess had never seen before. Nikolai asked about her health, took her to his mother, and, having sat for about five minutes, left the room.

When she left the countess, Nikolai met her again and, with particular solemnity and dryness, saw her to the front hall. He did not say a word in reply to her remarks about the countess's health. "What is it to you? Leave me alone," his gaze said.

"What's she prowling around for? What does she want? I can't bear these ladies and all these gentilities!" he said aloud in Sonya's presence, evidently unable to hold back his vexation, once the princess's carriage had driven away from the house.

"Ah, Nicolas, how can you say such things!" said Sonya, barely concealing her joy. "She's so kind, and *maman* loves her so."

Nikolai said nothing and would have preferred not to talk about the princess any more. But since the time of her visit, the old countess began to talk about her several times a day.

The countess praised her, demanded that her son call on her, expressed a wish to see her more often, but along with that always became ill-humoured when she spoke of her.

Nikolai tried to say nothing when his mother spoke of the princess, but his silence vexed the countess.

"She's a very worthy and wonderful girl," she said, "and you must call on her. At least you'll see someone; because I think you're bored with us."

"But I don't have the slightest wish to, mama."

"First you wanted to see her, but now 'I don't wish to.' I really don't understand you, my dear. First you're bored, then you suddenly don't want to see anybody."

"I never said I was bored."

"Why, you yourself said you don't even wish to see her. She's a very worthy girl, and you always liked her; but now there are suddenly some sort of reasons. You hide everything from me."

"Not at all, mama."

"If I was asking you to do something unpleasant, but all I'm asking is that you go and return a visit. It would seem that courtesy demands it . . . I've asked you, and now I won't interfere any more, since you have secrets from your mother."

"I'll go, then, if you want."

"It makes no difference to me; I want it for your sake."

Nikolai sighed, bit his moustache, and laid out the cards, trying to divert his mother's attention to another subject.

The next day, and the third, and the fourth, the same conversation was repeated.

After her visit to the Rostovs and the unexpected, cold reception she was given by Nikolai, Princess Marya confessed to herself that she had been right in not wishing to go first to the Rostovs.

"I expected nothing else," she said to herself, calling on her pride for help. "I don't care about him at all, I merely wanted to see the old lady, who was always kind to me and to whom I owe a great deal."

But she could not pacify herself with these arguments: a feeling akin to repentance tormented her when she remembered her visit. Though she had firmly resolved not to call on the Rostovs any more and to forget it all, she constantly felt herself in an uncertain position. And when she asked herself what it was that tormented her, she had to confess that it was her relations with Rostov. His cold, courteous tone did not come from his feeling for her (she knew that), but was covering up something. That something she had to explain, and until then she felt she could not be at peace.

In the middle of winter, she was sitting in the schoolroom, following her nephew's lessons, when Rostov's arrival was announced. Firmly resolved not to give away her secret and not to show her confusion, she called Mlle Bourienne and together with her came out to the drawing room.

With the first glance at Nikolai's face, she saw that he had come only to fulfil his duty to courtesy, and she resolved to keep firmly to the same tone in which he addressed her.

They talked about the countess's health, about mutual acquaintances, about the latest news of the war, and when the ten minutes demanded by decency had passed, after which a guest may rise, Nikolai stood up to say goodbye.

The princess, with the help of Mlle Bourienne, had sustained the conversation very well; but at the very last moment, just as he stood up, she felt so tired of talking about things of no concern to her, and the thought that she alone was given so few joys in life occupied her so much, that in a fit of absent-mindednes, her luminous eyes staring straight ahead, she sat motionless, not noticing that he had stood up.

Nikolai looked at her and, wishing to make it seem that he did not notice her absent-mindedness, said a few words to Mlle Bourienne, and again glanced at the princess. She was sitting just as motionless, and her tender face expressed suffering. He suddenly felt sorry for her, and vaguely imagined that he might be the cause of the sorrow expressed on her face. He would have liked to help her, to say something nice to her, but he could not think of what to say.

"Goodbye, Princess," he said. She came to her senses, blushed, and sighed deeply.

"Ah, forgive me," she said, as if waking up. "You're leaving already, Count? Well, goodbye! What about the pillow for the countess?"

"Wait, I'll bring it at once," said Mlle Bourienne, and she left the room.

They were both silent, glancing at each other from time to time.

"Yes, Princess," Nikolai finally said, smiling sadly, "it doesn't seem long ago, but so much water has flowed by since you and I met for the first time in Bogucharovo. How unfortunate we all seemed—yet I'd pay dearly to bring that time back . . . but there's no bringing it back."

The princess was looking intently into his eyes with her luminous gaze while he said that. It was as if she were trying to grasp the hidden meaning of his words, which would explain to her his feeling for her.

"Yes, yes," she said, "but you shouldn't regret the past, Count. As I understand your life now, you'll always remember it with pleasure, because the self-sacrifice by which you live now . . ."

"I do not accept your praises," he hastily interrupted her. "On the contrary, I constantly reproach myself; but that is a quite uninteresting and cheerless subject."

And again his eyes acquired their former dry and cold expression. But the princess had already seen in him the same man she had known and loved, and she now spoke only with that man.

"I thought you would allow me to say that to you," she said. "I had become so close to you . . . and to your family, and I thought you would not consider my sympathy misplaced; but I was mistaken," she said. Her voice suddenly quavered. "I don't know why," she went on, having composed herself, "you were different before and . . ."

"There are thousands of reasons *why*" (he placed special emphasis on the word *why*). "Thank you, Princess," he said softly. "It's sometimes hard."

"So that's why! That's why!" an inner voice was saying in Princess Marya's soul. "No, it wasn't only that cheerful, kind, and open gaze, not only that handsome appearance that I loved in him; I guessed at his noble, firm, self-sacrificing soul," she said to herself. "Yes, he's poor now, and I'm rich . . . Yes, it's only because of that . . . Yes, if it weren't for that . . ." And, recalling his former tenderness and looking now at his kind and sad face, she suddenly understood the reason for his coldness.

"But why, Count, why?" she suddenly almost cried out involuntarily, moving towards him. "Why, tell me? You must tell me." He was silent. "I don't know your *why*, Count," she went on. "But it's hard for me, it's . . . I'll confess it to you. You want for some reason to deprive me of your former friendship. And that pains me." There were tears in her eyes and in her voice. "There has been so little happiness in my life that every loss is hard for me . . . Forgive me, goodbye." She suddenly began to weep and started out of the room.

"Princess, wait, for God's sake!" he cried, trying to stop her. "Princess!"

She glanced back. For a few seconds they looked silently into each other's eyes, and the distant and impossible suddenly became near, possible, and inevitable.   .   .   .   .
.   .   .   .

VII

In the autumn of 1814, Nikolai married Princess Marya and moved with his wife, mother, and Sonya to live at Bald Hills.

In three years, without selling his wife's estate, he paid off the remaining debts and, having received a small inheritance from a deceased cousin, also paid back his debt to Pierre.

In three more years, by 1820, Nikolai had so arranged his financial affairs that he bought another small estate near Bald Hills and was negotiating to buy back his father's Otradnoe, which was his fondest dream.

Having begun farming out of necessity, he quickly developed such a passion for it that it became his favourite and almost sole occupation. Nikolai was a simple farmer, did not like innovations, especially the English ones which were becoming fashionable then, laughed at theoretical writings on farming, did not like millworks, expensive products, expensive cereal crops, and generally was not taken up with any specific part of farming. Before his eyes there was always only the *estate* as a whole and not some separate part of it. And the chief thing on the estate was not nitrogen and not oxygen, which were in the soil or the air, not a special plough and manure, but the chief tool by means of which nitrogen, and oxygen, and manure, and the plough became operative—that is, the labouring muzhik. When Nikolai took up farming and began going into its various parts, his attention was especially drawn to the muzhik; the muzhik appeared to him not only as a tool, but as a goal and a judge. He began by studying the muzhik, trying to understand what he wanted, what he considered bad or good, and only pretended to give instructions and orders, but in essence was only learning the methods and speech of the muzhiks and their judgements of what was good and what was bad. And only when he understood the tastes and strivings of the muzhik, learned to speak his language and understand the hidden meaning of his speech, when he felt akin to him, only then did he begin boldly to manage him, that is, to fulfil in relation to the muzhiks that very duty the fulfilment of which was demanded of him. And Nikolai's farming produced the most brilliant results.

On taking up the management of the estate, Nikolai at once, unerringly, by some gift of insight, appointed as bailiff, headman, and delegate the very people who would have been chosen by the muzhiks themselves if it had been up to them, and his officers never changed. Before studying the chemical properties of manure, before getting involved with *debit* and *credit* (as he liked to say mockingly), he found out the number of cattle the peasants had and increased that number by every possible means. He maintained peasant families of the largest size, not allowing them to divide up. The lazy, the depraved, and the weak he persecuted equally and tried to drive them out of the community.

During the sowing and harvesting of hay and grain, he looked after his own and the muzhiks' fields in exactly the same way. And rare was the landowner who had his fields sown and harvested so early and so well and had such good returns as Nikolai.

He did not like having anything to do with house serfs, called them "freeloaders," and, as everyone said, spoiled and indulged them; when some sort of orders had to be given about a house serf, especially when one had to be punished, he would lapse into indecisiveness and consult everyone in the house; but when it was possible to send a house serf as a soldier in place of a muzhik, he did it without the slightest hesitation. In all his orders concerning muzhiks, he never experienced the slightest doubt. Any order from him—this he knew— would be approved by all against one or a few.

He never allowed himself either to burden or punish a man only because he wanted it that way, or to relieve and reward a man because it was his personal desire to do so. He would have been unable to say what constituted this yardstick of what should and should not be done, but this yardstick in his soul was firm and unwavering.

He often said with vexation of some failure or disorder: "That's our Russian folk"—and fancied that he could not bear muzhiks.

But with all the forces of his soul he loved these "Russian folk" and their life, and only because of that understood and adopted for himself the one way and method of farming that produced good results.

Countess Marya was jealous of this love of her husband's and was sorry that she could not share in it, but she could not understand the joys and griefs afforded him by that separate world so foreign to her. She could not understand why he was so especially animated and happy when, having got up at dawn and spent the whole morning in the fields or at the threshing floor, he came back to have tea with her from the sowing, mowing, or harvesting. She did not understand why he told her admiringly and with rapture about the rich, thrifty muzhik Matvei Ermishin, who spent whole nights with his family transporting sheaves, and before anyone else had anything harvested, already had his stacks built. She did not understand why, pacing from the window to the balcony, he smiled so joyfully under his moustache and winked to himself when a warm, fine rain fell on the withering oat sprouts, or why, when a menacing cloud was blown away during the mowing or harvesting, he would come from the threshing floor, red, sunburnt, and sweaty, with the smell of wormwood and bitterwort in his hair, joyfully rubbing his hands, and say, "Well, one more little day, and mine and the peasants' will all be threshed."

Still less could she understand why he, with his kind heart, with his usual readiness to anticipate her wishes, would almost be driven to despair when she conveyed to him the requests of some peasant women or muzhiks who had turned to her asking to be released from work, why he, her kind Nicolas, stubbornly refused her, angrily asking her not to interfere in what was not her business. She felt that he had his special world, which he passionately loved, with some sort of laws that she did not understand.

When, trying to understand him, she occasionally spoke to him of his merits, which consisted in being good to his subjects, he would get angry and say: "Not in the least; it never even enters my head; and I wouldn't do this much for their good. It's all poetry and old wives' tales—all this good of one's neighbour. I want our children not to go begging; I have to set up our fortune while I live; that's all. What's needed for that is order, strictness . . . That's what!" he said, clenching his sanguine fist. "And justice, of course," he added, "because if a peasant is naked and hungry, and has only one little nag, he won't work well either for himself or for me."

And—it must have been because Nikolai did not allow himself the thought that he was doing anything for others out of virtuousness—all that he did was fruitful: his fortune quickly increased; neighbouring muzhiks came asking him to buy them; and long after his death, the pious memory of his management was preserved among the people. "He was a master . . . The muzhiks' affairs first, and then his own. But he never went easy on us. In short—a master!"

VIII

The one thing that tormented Nikolai in his running of the estate was his hot temper, combined with the old hussar habit of making free with his fists. At first he saw nothing reprehensible in it, but in the second year of his marriage, his view of this sort of reprisal suddenly changed.

Once in the summer the headman from Bogucharovo was summoned, the one who had replaced the late Dron and who was accused of various frauds and irregularities. Nikolai came out to him on the porch, and with the headman's first answers, shouts and blows could be heard in the front hall. Returning home for lunch, Nikolai went up to his wife, who was sitting with her head bent low over her embroidery, and began telling her, as usual, everything he had been busy with that morning and, incidentally, about the Bogucharovo headman. Countess Marya, turning red, then pale, and pursing her lips, sat in the same way, her head bowed, and made no reply to her husband's words.

"Such an impudent scoundrel," he said, getting angry at the mere recollection. "He could have told me he was drunk, didn't see . . . What's wrong, Marie?" he suddenly asked.

Countess Marya raised her head, was about to say something, then quickly looked down again and pressed her lips.

"What is it? What's wrong, my dearest? . . ."

The homely Countess Marya always became pretty when she wept. She never wept from pain or vexation, but always from sadness and pity. And when she wept, her luminous eyes became irresistibly lovely.

As soon as Nikolai took her hand, she was unable to restrain herself and began to weep.

"Nicolas, I saw . . . he was wrong, but you, why did you! Nicolas! . . ." And she covered her face with her hands.

Nikolai fell silent, blushed deeply, and, moving away from her, silently began pacing the room. He understood what she was weeping about, but in his soul he could not suddenly agree with her that something he had lived with since childhood and considered most ordinary—was bad.

"Is this gentilities, old wives' tales, or is she right?" he asked himself. Without deciding the question for himself, he glanced once again at her suffering and loving face and suddenly understood that she was right, and he had long been in the wrong with himself.

"Marie," he said softly, going up to her, "it will never happen again; I give you my word. Never," he repeated in a quavering voice, like a boy asking forgiveness.

The tears flowed still more abundantly from the countess's eyes. She took her husband's hand and kissed it.

"Nicolas, when did you break the cameo?" she said, to change the subject, studying his hand, on which there was a signet ring with the head of Laocoön.

"Today, all that same thing. Ah, Marie, don't remind me of it." He blushed deeply again. "I give you my word of honour that it won't happen again. And let this always remind me of it," he said, pointing to the broken ring.

From then on, in talking with headmen and stewards, the moment the blood rushed to his face and his hands began clenching into fists, Nikolai turned the broken ring on his finger and lowered his eyes before the man who had angered him. However, about twice a year he would forget himself and would then come to his wife, confess, and again promise her that this was now the very last time.

"Marie, you surely despise me?" he would say to her. "I deserve it."

"You should walk away, walk away quickly, if you feel you can't control yourself," Countess Marya would say with sadness, trying to comfort her husband.

Among the gentry of the province, Nikolai was respected, but not liked. He was not concerned with the interests of the gentry. And for that some regarded him as a proud, others as a stupid man. All his time in the summer, from the spring sowing to the harvest, was spent on farm work. In the autumn, with the same business-like seriousness with which he occupied himself with farming, he gave himself to hunting, going off for a month or two with his hunt. In winter he rode around to his other estates and took up reading. His reading consisted mostly of history books, which he ordered each year for a certain sum. He was putting together, as he said, a serious library, and made it a rule to read all the books he bought. He would sit in his study with an important look over this reading, which was first self-imposed as a duty, but later became a habitual occupation that provided him with a special sort of pleasure and the awareness of being occupied with a serious matter. Except for business trips, he spent the greater part of the time in winter at home, sharing the life of his family and entering into the minute relations between mother and children. He became closer and closer with his wife, every day discovering new spiritual treasures in her.

From the time of Nikolai's marriage, Sonya had been living in his house. Before his marriage, blaming himself and praising her, Nikolai had told his fiancée everything that there had been between him and Sonya. He had asked Princess Marya to be gentle and kind with his cousin. Countess Marya felt the full guilt of her husband; she also felt her own guilt before Sonya; she thought that her fortune had influenced Nikolai's choice, could not reproach Sonya for anything, wished to love her, but not only did not love her, but often found wicked feelings against her in her heart and could not overcome them.

Once she got to talking with her friend Natasha about Sonya and about her unfairness towards her.

"You know what," said Natasha, "you've read the Gospels a great deal; there's a passage in them that's exactly about Sonya."

"What?" Countess Marya asked in astonishment.

" 'To him who has will be given, from him who has not will be taken,'[7] remember? She's the one who has not—why, I don't know; maybe she lacks egoism—I don't know, but from her will be taken, and everything has been taken. I feel terribly sorry for her sometimes; I used to want terribly for Nicolas to marry her; but I always had a sort of presentiment that it would never be. She's a *sterile blossom,* you know, like on strawberries? Sometimes I feel sorry for her, but sometimes I think she doesn't feel it the way we would."

And though Countess Marya explained to Natasha that those words of the Gospel should be understood differently—looking at Sonya, she agreed with the explanation given by Natasha. Indeed it did seem that Sonya was not burdened by her position and was completely reconciled with her destiny as a *sterile blossom.* It seemed she valued not so much the people as the whole family. Like a cat, she became accustomed not to the people, but to the house. She took care of the old countess, petted and pampered the children, was always ready to render the small services she was capable of; but all this was involuntarily taken with far too little gratitude . . .

The country seat at Bald Hills had been rebuilt, but no longer on the footing it had been on under the late prince.

The buildings, begun in the lean time, were more than simple. The enormous house, on the old stone foundations, was built of wood and plastered only inside. The big, roomy house with its bare plank floors was furnished with the simplest hard sofas and armchairs, tables and chairs, fashioned from their own birches by their own joiners. The house was spacious, with rooms for the servants and separate quarters for visitors. The relations of the Rostovs and Bolkonskys sometimes descended on Bald Hills by whole families, with their sixteen horses, with dozens of servants, and stayed for months. Besides that, four times a year, on the masters' birthdays and name days, up to a hundred guests would gather for a day or two. For the rest of the year, an inviolably regular life went on, with its usual occupations, teas, lunches, dinners, and suppers from the household's provisions.

IX

It was the eve of the winter feast of St. Nicholas, the fifth of December 1820. That year Natasha, her children and husband had been visiting with her brother since the early fall. Pierre was in Petersburg, where he had gone on his own special business, as he put it, for three weeks and had already stayed for seven. He was expected any moment.

On the fifth of December, besides the Bezukhov family, Nikolai's old friend, retired general Vassily Fyodorovich Denisov, also visited the Rostovs.

On the sixth, the feast day, when guests would gather, Nikolai knew he would have to take off his quilted jacket, put on a frock coat and narrow boots with narrow toes, and go to the new church he had built, and then receive congratulations, serve refreshments, and talk about the election of the marshal of nobility and about the harvest; but he still considered it his right to spend the eve of the day as usual. Before dinner Nikolai went through the bailiff's accounts from the Ryazan village, the estate of his wife's nephew, wrote two business letters, and strolled to the threshing floor, the cattle and horse yards. Having taken measures against the general drunkenness expected the next day on the occasion of the patron saint's feast, he came to dinner and, having no time for a private talk with his wife, sat down at the long table set for twenty, at which the whole household was gathered. At the table were his mother, the old Mrs. Belov, who lived with her, his wife, his three children, the governess, the tutor, his nephew with his tutor, Sonya, Denisov, Natasha, her three children, their governess, and old Mikhail Ivanych, the prince's architect, who was living in retirement at Bald Hills.

Countess Marya sat at the opposite end of the table. As soon as her husband sat in his place, by the gesture with which, having removed the napkin, he quickly shifted the goblet and wineglass that stood in front of him, Countess Marya decided that he was in a bad humour, as sometimes happened to him, especially before the soup, and when he had come to dinner straight from farmwork. Countess Marya knew that mood very well, and when she was in a good mood herself, she calmly waited until he had had his soup, and only then began to talk to him and make him admit that he was in a bad humour for no reason; but today she completely forgot this observation of hers; it pained her that he was angry with her for no reason, and she felt unhappy. She asked him where he had been. He told her. She also asked whether everything was all right on the farm. He winced unpleasantly from her unnatural tone and answered brusquely.

"So I wasn't mistaken," thought Countess Marya. "Why is he angry with me?" In the tone of his answer, Countess Marya heard ill will towards her and a wish to break off the conversation. She felt that her words were unnatural, but she could not keep from asking several more questions.

Thanks to Denisov, the conversation at dinner soon became general and lively, and Countess Marya did not talk to her husband. When they left the table and went to thank the old countess, Countess Marya kissed her husband, holding out her hand, and asked him why he was angry with her.

"You always have the strangest notions; I never thought of being angry," he said.

But the word *always* answered Countess Marya: "Yes, I'm angry, and I don't want to say so."

Nikolai and his wife got along so well that even Sonya and the old countess, who, out of jealousy, wished for some disagreement between them, could find no pretext for reproach; but there were also moments of hostility between them. Sometimes, precisely after the happiest periods, a feeling of estrangement and hostility suddenly came over them; this feeling appeared most often at the time of Countess Marya's pregnancies. She was in one of those periods now.

"Well, *messieurs et mesdames*," Nikolai said loudly and as if merrily (Countess Marya fancied it was deliberate, so as to offend her), "I've been on my feet since six o'clock. Tomorrow I'll have to suffer, but today I'll go and rest." And without saying anything more to Countess Marya, he went to the small sitting room and lay on the sofa.

"That's how it *always* is," thought Countess Marya. "He talks with everybody except me. I see, I see he finds me repulsive. Especially in this condition." She looked at her high stomach and in the mirror at her yellow, pale, emaciated face, its big eyes bigger than ever.

And everything became unpleasant for her: Denisov's shouting and laughing, and Natasha's talking, and especially the glance that Sonya hastily cast at her.

Sonya was always the first pretext that Countess Marya chose for her irritation.

Having sat with the guests and understood nothing of what they were saying, she quietly stepped out and went to the nursery.

The children were riding to Moscow on chairs and invited her to come with them. She sat down and played with them, but the thought of her husband and his groundless vexation never stopped tormenting her. She got up and, tiptoeing with difficulty, went to the small sitting room.

"Maybe he's not asleep; I'll have a talk with him," she said to herself. Andryusha, the elder boy, imitating her, came after her on tiptoe. Countess Marya did not notice him.

"*Chère Marie, il dort, je crois; il est si fatigué,*"* said Sonya (it seemed to Countess Marya that she met her everywhere) in the big sitting room. "Andryusha may wake him up."

Countess Marya turned, saw Andryusha behind her, felt that Sonya was right, and, precisely because of that, flared up and clearly had difficulty holding back a harsh word. She said nothing and, so as not to obey Sonya, made a sign with her hand for Andryusha not to make noise but still to follow her, and went to the door. Sonya left by the other door. From the room where Nikolai was sleeping, his wife could hear his regular breathing, familiar to her down to the smallest nuances. Hearing that breathing, she saw before her his smooth, handsome forehead, his moustache, his whole face, which she so often gazed at for a long time, while he slept, in the silence of the night. Nikolai suddenly stirred and grunted. And at the same time, Andryusha shouted through the door:

"Papa, mama's standing here."

Countess Marya turned pale from fright and began making signs to her son. He fell silent, and this silence, so terrible for Countess Marya, went on for

*Dear Marie, he's sleeping, I think; he's so tired.

about a minute. She knew how much Nikolai disliked being awakened. Suddenly from behind the door came a new grunt, movement, and the displeased voice of Nikolai said:

"They don't give me a moment's peace. Marie, is that you? Why have you brought him here?"

"I only came to look, I didn't see . . . excuse me . . ."

Nikolai cleared his throat and fell silent. Countess Marya stepped away from the door and took her son to the nursery. Five minutes later, unnoticed by her mother, the three-year-old, dark-eyed little Natasha, her father's favourite, having learned from her brother that papa was sleeping in mama's sitting room, ran to her father. The dark-eyed little girl boldly opened the creaking door, went up to the sofa, stepping energetically on her blunt little feet, and, making out the position of her father, who was sleeping with his back to her, got up on tiptoe and kissed his hand, which lay under his head. Nikolai turned with a tender smile on his face.

"Natasha, Natasha!" Countess Marya's frightened whisper was heard through the door, "papa wants to sleep."

"No, mama, he doesn't want to sleep," little Natasha answered with conviction, "he's laughing."

Nikolai lowered his feet, sat up, and took his daughter in his arms.

"Come in, Masha," he said to his wife. Countess Marya went in and sat down by her husband.

"I didn't see him run after me," she said timidly. "I'm so . . ."

Nikolai, holding his daughter with one arm, glanced at his wife and, noticing the guilty expression on her face, put his other arm round her and kissed her on the hair.

"May I kiss *mamà*?" he asked Natasha.

Natasha smiled shyly.

"Again," she said, pointing with an imperious gesture to the place where Nikolai had kissed his wife.

"I don't know why you think I'm in a bad humour," said Nikolai, answering the question that he knew was in his wife's mind.

"You can't imagine how unhappy and lonely I am when you're like that. It always seems to me . . ."

"Enough silliness, Marie. Shame on you," he said gaily.

"It seems to me that you can't love me, because I'm so plain . . . always . . . and now . . . in this cond . . ."

"Ah, how funny you are! Not dear for being pretty, but pretty for being dear. Men only love Malvina and the like because they're beautiful: but do I love my wife? It's not love, but just . . . I don't know how to tell you. Without you or, like today, when there's some falling-out between us, it's as if I'm lost and can't do anything. Well, do I love my finger? I don't love it, but try cutting it off . . ."

"No, I'm not like that, but I understand. So you're not angry with me?"

"Terribly angry," he said, smiling, and, standing up and smoothing his hair, he started pacing the room.

"Do you know what I was thinking about, Marie?" he began, now that they were reconciled, beginning at once to think aloud in his wife's presence. He did not ask whether she was prepared to listen to him; it made no difference to him. The thought had occurred to him, which meant to her, too. And he told her of his intention to persuade Pierre to stay with them until spring.

Countess Marya heard him out, made her comments, and in turn began to think her thoughts aloud. Her thoughts were about the children.

"How one sees the woman in her even now," she said in French, pointing to Natasha. "You reproach us women for being illogical. Here's our logic. I say to her, 'Papa wants to sleep,' and she says, 'No, he's laughing.' And she's right," said Countess Marya, smiling happily.

"Yes! yes!" And Nikolai, taking his daughter in his strong hands, lifted her up, seated her on his shoulder, and, holding her legs, began walking about the room with her. Both father and daughter had the same senselessly happy faces.

"But you know, maybe you're unfair. You love this one too much," Countess Marya whispered in French.

"Yes, but what can I do? . . . I try not to show it . . ."

Just then the sounds of the door pulley and footsteps came from the front hall and anteroom, like the sounds of an arrival.

"Someone's come."

"I'm certain it's Pierre. I'll go and find out," said Countess Marya, and she went out of the room.

In her absence, Nikolai allowed himself to give his daughter a gallop round the room. Out of breath, he quickly set down the laughing girl and hugged her to his breast. His leaps reminded him of dancing, and, looking at the child's round, happy face, he thought of how she would be when he, as an old man, started taking her out, and would do the mazurka with her, as his late father used to dance the Daniel Cooper with his daughter.

"It's him, it's him, Nicolas!" Countess Marya said a few minutes later, coming back into the room. "Now our Natasha's revived. You should have seen her delight, and how he got it from her for overstaying. Well, come along, come along, quickly! Do part, finally," she said, smiling, looking at the little girl, who pressed herself to her father. Nikolai went out, holding his daughter by the hand.

Countess Marya stayed in the sitting room.

"Never, never would I have believed," she whispered to herself, "that one could be so happy." Her face shone with a smile, but at the same time she sighed, and her profound gaze showed a quiet sadness. As if, besides the happiness she experienced, there was another happiness, unattainable in this life, which she involuntarily remembered at that moment.

X

Natasha was married in the early spring of 1813, and by 1820 she already had three daughters and one son, whom she had passionately wished for and was now nursing herself. She had filled out and broadened, so that it was difficult to recognize in this strong mother the former slender, nimble Natasha. The features of her face had defined themselves and bore an expression of softness and serenity. In her face there was not, as formerly, that ceaselessly burning fire of animation that had constituted her charm. Now one often saw only her face and body, while her soul was not seen at all. One saw only a strong, beautiful, and fruitful female. Very rarely was the former fire kindled in her now. It happened only when, as now, her husband returned home, or a sick child recovered, or she and Countess Marya remembered Prince Andrei (she never spoke of him with her husband, supposing that he was jealous of Prince Andrei's memory), and very rarely when something chanced to draw her into singing, which she had abandoned completely after marriage. And in those rare moments when the former fire was kindled in her developed, beautiful body, she was still more attractive than before.

Since the time of her marriage, Natasha and her husband had lived in Moscow, Petersburg, on the estate near Moscow, and with her mother, that is, with Nikolai. The young Countess Bezukhov was little seen in society, and those who saw her remained displeased. She was neither sweet nor amiable. It was not that Natasha liked solitude (she did not know whether she liked it or not; it even seemed to her that she did not), but, bearing, giving birth to, and nursing her children, and taking part in every minute of her husband's life, she was unable to satisfy those needs otherwise than by giving up society. Everyone who had known Natasha before her marriage was surprised at the change that had taken place in her as at something extraordinary. Only the old countess, with her mother's intuition, understood that all Natasha's impulses came only from the need to have a family, to have a husband, as she, not so much joking as in earnest, had cried out once in Otradnoe. Her mother was surprised at the surprise of the people who did not understand Natasha, and kept repeating that she had always known that Natasha would make an exemplary wife and mother.

"Only she carries her love for her husband and children to such an extreme," said the countess, "that it's even stupid."

Natasha did not follow that golden rule preached by intelligent people, especially the French, according to which a girl, once married, should not let herself go, should not abandon her talents, should be still more concerned with her appearance than when unmarried, should entice her husband just as she had enticed him before he was her husband. Natasha, on the contrary, at once abandoned all her charms, among which one was extraordinarily strong—her singing. She abandoned it precisely because it was a strong charm. She, as they put it, let herself go. Natasha took no trouble either about her manners, or about the delicacy of her speech, or about showing herself to her husband in the most advantageous poses, or about her toilette, or about not hampering her husband with her demands. She did everything contrary to these rules. She felt that the charms which her instinct had taught her to make use of before would now only be ridiculous in the eyes of her husband, to whom, from the first moment, she had given herself entirely—that is, with her whole soul, not leaving one little corner that was not open to him. She felt that her bond with her husband held, not by those poetic feelings that had attracted him to her, but by something else, indefinite but firm, like the bond between her own soul and body.

To fluff up her curls, wear hoop-skirts, and sing romances in order to attract her own husband would have seemed as strange to her as to adorn herself in order to be pleased with herself. And to adorn herself in order to be liked by others—maybe she would have enjoyed that now, she did not know, but she simply had no time for it. The main reason why she was not occupied with singing, with dressing, or with thinking over her words, was that she had absolutely no time to be occupied with them.

It is known that man has the ability to immerse himself entirely in one subject, however insignificant it might seem. And it is known that there is no subject so insignificant that it will not expand to infinity, if attention is concentrated on it.

The subject that absorbed Natasha fully was her family—that is, her husband, who had to be kept in such a way as to belong entirely to her, to the household; and her children, whom she had to carry, give birth to, nurse, and bring up.

And the more she entered into the subject that absorbed her, not with her mind, but with her whole soul, with her whole being, the more that subject expanded under her attention, and the weaker and more insignificant her own forces seemed to her, so that she concentrated them all on one thing, and still had no time to do everything that seemed necessary to her.

Discussions and arguments about women's rights, about the relations between spouses, about their freedom and rights, though they had not yet been called "questions," as they are now, were the same then as they are now; but these questions not only did not interest Natasha, but she decidedly did not understand them.

These questions, then as now, existed only for those people who see in marriage nothing but the pleasure the spouses get from each other, that is, nothing but the beginnings of marriage, and not its whole significance, which consists in the family.

These arguments and present-day questions, similar to the question of how to get as much pleasure as possible from a dinner, did not exist then, as they do not exist now, for people for whom the purpose of a dinner is nourishment and the purpose of marriage is the family.

If the purpose of a dinner is to nourish the body, then someone who suddenly eats two dinners will perhaps achieve greater pleasure, but will not achieve his purpose, because his stomach will not digest two dinners.

If the purpose of marriage is the family, then someone who wishes to have many wives or husbands will perhaps get much pleasure, but in any case will have no family.

If the purpose of a dinner is nourishment, and the purpose of marriage is the family, then the whole question is solved simply by not eating more than the stomach can digest and not having more wives and husbands than are needed for a family, that is, one of each. Natasha needed a husband. A husband was given her. And the husband gave her a family. And not only did she see no need for another, better husband, but, as all her inner forces were directed at serving this husband and family, she could not even imagine and saw no interest in imagining how it would be if it were different.

Natasha did not like society in general, but she valued all the more the society of her relations—Countess Marya, her brother, her mother, and Sonya. She valued the society of the people to whom, dishevelled, in a dressing gown, she could come striding out of the nursery with a joyful face and show a nappy with a yellow instead of a green stain, and hear comforting words that the baby was now much better.

Natasha let herself go to such a degree that her clothes, her hair, her words spoken out of place, her jealousy—she was jealous of Sonya, of the governess, of any woman, beautiful or not—were habitual subjects of jokes among all those close to her. The general opinion was that Pierre was under his wife's heel, and in fact it was so. From the very first day of their marriage, Natasha had announced her demands. Pierre was very surprised by his wife's view, which was completely new to him, that every minute of his life belonged to her and the family; Pierre was surprised by his wife's demands, but was flattered by them and submitted to them.

Pierre's subjection consisted in his not daring, not only to flirt, but even to talk smilingly with another woman, not daring to go to clubs or dinners just to pass the time, not daring to spend money on whims, not daring to leave for long periods of time except on business, in which his wife also included his intellectual pursuits, of which she understood nothing, but to which she ascribed great importance. In exchange for all that, Pierre had the full right at home to dispose as he liked, not only of himself, but of the whole family as well. At home Natasha put herself on the footing of her husband's slave; and the whole house went on tiptoe when Pierre was busy reading or writing in his study. Pierre needed only to show some predilection, for what he liked to be invariably fulfilled. He needed only to express a wish, for Natasha to jump up at once and run to fulfil it.

The entire household was governed only by the imaginary orders of the husband, that is, by Pierre's wishes, which Natasha tried to guess. The manner and place of their life, their acquaintances, their connections, Natasha's occupations, the raising of the children—not only was everything done according to the express will of Pierre, but Natasha tried to guess what might follow from Pierre's thoughts voiced in conversation. And she rightly guessed the essence of Pierre's wishes, and, having once guessed it, she firmly held to what she had chosen. When Pierre himself wanted to be unfaithful to his wish, she fought him with his own weapons.

Thus, during a difficult time, which Pierre remembered ever after, when Natasha had given birth to a first weak child, and they had had to change wet-nurses three times, and Natasha had become sick with despair, Pierre had told her once of Rousseau's thoughts, with which he was in complete agreement, about the unnaturalness and harmfulness of wet-nurses. With the next child, despite the opposition of her mother, the doctors, and the husband himself, who rose up against her nursing as a then unheard-of and harmful thing, she had stood her ground, and from then on had nursed all her children herself.

Quite often, in moments of irritation, it happened that the husband and wife would spend a long time arguing; then, after the argument, Pierre, to his joy and surprise, would find not only in his wife's words, but in her actions, the very thought she had been arguing against. And he not only found the same thought, but found it purified of whatever had been superfluous, provoked by passion and argument, in his expression of it.

After seven years of married life, Pierre felt a joyful, firm consciousness that he was not a bad man, and he felt it because he saw himself reflected in his wife. In himself he felt all the good and the bad mixed together and obscuring each other. But only what was truly good was reflected in his wife; all that was not entirely good was rejected. And this reflection came not by way of logical thinking, but otherwise—as a mysterious, unmediated reflection.

XI

Two months before then, Pierre, already visiting with the Rostovs, had received a letter from Prince Fyodor, summoning him to Petersburg to discuss important questions which interested the members of a society in Petersburg of which Pierre was one of the chief founders.

Having read this letter, as she read all her husband's letters, Natasha herself suggested that he go to Petersburg, hard as his absence was for her. To all that belonged to her husband's intellectual, abstract pursuits, without understanding them, she ascribed enormous importance, and she was in constant fear of being a hindrance to this activity of her husband's. To Pierre's timid, questioning glance after reading the letter, she responded by asking him to go, but only to determine for certain the time of his return. And he was granted a four-week leave.

Ever since the term of Pierre's leave had expired, two weeks before then, Natasha had been in a constant state of fear, sadness, and irritation.

Denisov, a retired general discontented with the current state of affairs, who came during those last two weeks, looked at Natasha with surprise and sadness, as at an unfaithful portrait of a once-loved person. A dull, despondent gaze, out-of-place replies, and conversation about the nursery was all he saw and heard from the former enchantress.

Natasha was sad and irritated all that time, especially when her mother, her brother, or Countess Marya, comforting her, tried to excuse Pierre and think up reasons for his delay.

"It's all foolishness, all trifles," said Natasha, "all his reflections, which don't lead to anything, and all these stupid societies," she said of the very things in the great importance of which she firmly believed. And she would go off to the nursery to nurse her only boy, Petya.

No one could tell her anything so soothing and sensible as this little three-month-old being, when he lay at her breast and she felt the movement of his mouth and the puffing of his little nose. This being said: "You're angry, you're jealous, you'd like to take revenge on him, you're afraid, but here I am. Here I am . . ." And there was nothing to reply. It was more than true.

In those two weeks of worry, Natasha so often resorted to the baby to be soothed, so fussed over him, that she overfed him and he fell sick. She was terrified by his illness, but at the same time it was what she needed. Taking care of him made it easier for her to endure the worry about her husband.

She was nursing when the noise of Pierre's sleigh was heard in the drive, and the nanny, who knew what would gladden her mistress, came through the door, inaudibly but quickly, with a beaming face.

"He's come?" Natasha asked in a quick whisper, afraid to move lest she awaken the baby, who was falling asleep.

"He's come, dearie," whispered the nanny.

The blood rushed to Natasha's face and her feet made an involuntary movement, but she could not jump up and run. The baby opened his eyes again and looked. "You're here," he seemed to say, and again lazily smacked his lips.

Having gently withdrawn her breast, Natasha rocked the baby, handed him over to the nanny, and went with quick steps to the door. But at the door she stopped, as if feeling a pang of remorse that, in her gladness, she had left the baby too quickly, and turned to look. The nanny, her elbows raised, was lifting the baby over the railing of his little bed.

"Just go, just go, dearie, don't worry, just go," the nanny whispered, smiling, with the familiarity that is usually established between a nanny and her mistress.

And Natasha ran with light steps to the front hall.

Denisov, with his pipe, coming out from the study to the reception room, here recognized Natasha for the first time. A bright, shining, joyful light was pouring in streams from her transformed face.

"He's come!" she said to him on the run, and Denisov felt that he was delighted by the fact that Pierre, for whom he had very little love, had come. Having run to the front hall, Natasha saw a tall figure in a fur coat unwinding his scarf.

"It's him! Really! Here he is!" she said to herself, and, flying to him, she embraced him, pressed his head to her breast, and then, pushing it away, looked at the frosty, red-cheeked, and happy face of Pierre. "Yes, it's him; happy, content . . ."

And suddenly she remembered all the torments of waiting that she had felt over the last two weeks: the joy shining on her face vanished; she frowned, and a stream of reproaches and angry words poured out on Pierre.

"Yes, it's fine for you! You're very glad, you had a good time . . . But what about me? You might at least feel sorry for the children. I'm nursing, my milk went bad. Petya almost died. And you're having a very good time. Yes, a good time."

Pierre knew he was not guilty, because he could not have come sooner; he knew that this outburst was improper on her part, and knew that in two minutes it would pass; he knew, above all, that he himself was cheerful and happy. He would have liked to smile, but did not even dare to think of it. He made a pitiful, frightened face and cowered.

"I couldn't, by God! But how's Petya?"

"He's all right now, let's go. You ought to be ashamed! If only you could see how I am without you, how I suffered . . ."

"Are you well?"

"Let's go, let's go," she said, still holding on to his hand. And they went to their rooms.

When Nikolai and his wife came looking for Pierre, he was in the nursery, holding his awakened nursling son on his enormous right palm, dandling him. A merry smile lingered on his broad face with its open, toothless mouth. The storm had long since spent itself, and a bright, joyful sun shone on the face of Natasha, who gazed tenderly at her husband and son.

"And you talked it all over well with Prince Fyodor?" Natasha was saying.

"Yes, perfectly."

"See, he holds it up" (his head, Natasha meant). "But how he frightened me! . . . And did you see the princess? Is it true that she's in love with that . . . ?"

"Yes, can you imagine . . ."

Just then Nikolai and Countess Marya came in. Pierre, without putting his son down, bent over, exchanged kisses with them, and answered their questions. But, obviously, despite the many interesting things that had to be discussed, the baby in his little hat, with his wobbly head, absorbed all Pierre's attention.

"How sweet he is!" said Countess Marya, looking at the baby and playing with him. "This is what I don't understand, Nicolas," she turned to her husband. "How is it you don't understand the charm of these charming little miracles?"

"I just don't, I can't," said Nikolai, looking at the baby with a cold gaze. "A piece of meat. Let's go, Pierre."

"Yet the main thing is, he's such an affectionate father," said Countess Marya, to justify her husband, "but only when they're a year old or so . . ."

"No, Pierre's an excellent nanny," said Natasha, "he says his hand was just made to fit a baby's bottom. Look."

"Well, not only for that," said Pierre, laughing suddenly, shifting the baby, and handing him to the nanny.

XII

As in every real family, several totally different worlds lived together in the house at Bald Hills, each maintaining its own particularity and yielding to the others, but merging into one harmonious whole. Every event that occurred in the house was equally—joyfully or sadly—important for all these worlds; but each world had its own reasons, independent of the others, for rejoicing or lamenting over whatever the event might be.

Thus, Pierre's coming was a joyful, important event, and as such it had an effect on everyone.

The servants—the most reliable judges of their masters, because they judge not by conversations and expressions of feelings, but by acts and manner of life—were glad of Pierre's coming, because with him there they knew the count would stop going to the farmwork every day, would be more cheerful and kind, and also because everybody would get costly presents for the feast day.

The children and governesses were glad of Bezukhov's coming, because no one else drew them into a common life so well as Pierre. He alone could play on the clavichord that écossaise (his only piece) to which one could dance, as he said, all possible dances, and he had surely brought everyone presents.

Nikolenka, who was now a thin fifteen-year-old boy with curly blond hair and beautiful eyes, sickly and intelligent, was glad because Uncle Pierre, as he called him, was the object of his admiration and passionate love. No one had instilled any special love for Pierre into Nikolenka, and he saw him only rarely. Countess Marya, who had brought him up, employed all her powers to make Nikolenka love her husband as she loved him, and Nikolenka did love his uncle; but he loved him with a barely noticeable shade of contempt. As for Pierre, he adored him. He did not want to be a hussar or a chevalier of St. George like Uncle Nikolai; he wanted to be learned and intelligent and kind, like Pierre. In Pierre's presence there was always a joyful radiance on his face, and he blushed and became breathless whenever Pierre addressed him. He never missed a single word of what Pierre said, and afterwards, with Dessales or alone with himself, would recall and ponder the meaning of Pierre's every word. Pierre's past, his misfortunes before the year twelve (of which he had put together a vague, poetic picture from what he had heard), his adventures in Moscow, his captivity, Platon Karataev (of whom he had heard from Pierre), his love for Natasha (whom the boy also loved with a special love), and, above all, his friendship with his father, whom Nikolenka did not remember—all this made Pierre a hero and a sacred figure for him.

From words he let fall about his father and Natasha, from the excitement with which Pierre spoke of the dead man, and from the cautious, reverential tenderness with which Natasha spoke of him, the boy, who was only beginning to suspect about love, put together the notion that his father had loved Natasha and had bequeathed her, upon dying, to his friend. This father, whom the boy did not remember, appeared to him as a deity, whom it was impossible to imagine and of whom he did not think otherwise than with a thrill in his heart and tears of sadness and rapture. And the boy was happy on account of Pierre's coming.

The guests were glad of Pierre as a man who always animated and united any company.

The adults of the household, not to mention his wife, were glad of him as a friend in whose presence life was easier and calmer.

The old ladies were glad of the presents he would be bringing, and above all that Natasha would come to life again.

Pierre felt the various views of these various worlds upon him, and hastened to give each person what was expected.

Pierre, the most absent-minded and forgetful of men, had this time bought everything, according to the list his wife had drawn up, not forgetting either the errands for her mother and brother, or the present of fabric for Mrs. Belov's dress, or the toys for his nephews. In the early days of his marriage, this demand of his wife's—that he do that and not forget anything he had undertaken to buy—had seemed strange to him, and he had been struck by her serious distress when, on his first trip, he had forgotten everything. But later on he got used to it. Knowing that Natasha never asked anything for herself, and asked for others only when he volunteered, he now, unexpectedly for himself, took a childlike pleasure in this buying of presents for the whole household and never forgot anything. If he did earn Natasha's reproach, it was only for buying things that were superfluous and too expensive. In the opinion of most people, to her other shortcomings (or qualities, in Pierre's opinion)—slovenliness, letting herself go—Natasha had also added stinginess.

From the time when Pierre began to live in a big household, a family, which required big expenses, he noticed, to his surprise, that he was spending twice less than before, and that his affairs, recently upset in particular by his first wife's debts, had begun to improve.

Life was cheaper because it was restricted: Pierre no longer had, nor wished to have, that most expensive luxury, which is the kind of life that can be changed at any moment. He felt that his way of life was now defined once and for all, till death, that to change it was not in his power, and therefore this way of life was cheap.

Pierre was sorting out his purchases with a merry, smiling face.

"Look at this!" he said, unfolding a length of cotton like a shopkeeper. Natasha sat facing him, holding her elder daughter on her lap and quickly shifting her shining eyes from her husband to what he was displaying.

"That's for Mrs. Belov? Excellent." She felt it for quality.

"A rouble, probably?"

Pierre told her the price.

"Expensive," said Natasha. "Well, how glad the children will be, and *maman*. Only you needn't have bought this for me," she added, unable to suppress a smile, and admiring a gold and pearl comb such as were only just coming into fashion.

"Adèle got me confused: buy it, buy it," said Pierre.

"When will I ever wear it?" Natasha put it into her braid. "It's for Mashenka's coming out; maybe they'll be wearing them again by then. Well, come on."

And, taking the presents, they went first to the nursery, then to the countess.

The countess, as usual, was sitting with Mrs. Belov over double patience when Pierre and Natasha, packages under their arms, came into the drawing room.

The countess was already past sixty. Her hair was completely white, and she wore a cap with a ruffle that went all the way round her face. Her face was wrinkled, her upper lip was sunken, and her eyes were dull.

After the deaths of her son and her husband, which had followed so quickly upon each other, she felt herself an accidentally forgotten being in this world, with no purpose or meaning. She ate, drank, slept, woke, but did not live. Life gave her no impressions at all. She needed nothing from life except peace, and that peace she could find only in death. But as long as death did not come, she had to live, that is, to make use of her time, her life forces. In her there was noticeable in the highest degree what one notices in very small children and very old people. In her life no external purpose could be seen, but what was evident was only the need to exercise her various inclinations and abilities. She needed to eat, to sleep, to think, to talk, to weep, to work, to get angry, and so on, only because she had a stomach, a brain, muscles, nerves, and a liver. She did all that without any external impulse, not as people do in the full force of life, when, behind the purpose they are striving towards, they do not notice another purpose—that of applying their forces. She talked only because she had a physical need to work her lungs and tongue. She wept like a baby, because she had to clear her nose, and so on. What for people in full force presented itself as a purpose, for her was obviously a pretext.

Thus, in the morning, especially if she had eaten something rich the day before, a need to be angry appeared in her, and then she chose the closest pretext—Mrs. Belov's deafness.

She would begin to say something softly to her from the other end of the room.

"It seems warmer today, my dear," she would say in a whisper. And when Mrs. Belov replied, "Why, of course they've come," the countess would grumble crossly: "My God, how deaf and stupid she is!"

Another pretext was her snuff, which seemed to her now dry, now damp, now poorly rubbed. After these irritations, bile would spread over her face, and her maids knew by sure signs when Mrs. Belov would again be deaf, and the snuff would again be damp, and when her face would turn yellow. As she needed her bile to work, so she also sometimes needed her remaining thinking capacity to work, and the pretext for that was a game of patience. When she needed to weep, the object was the late count. When she needed to worry, the pretext was Nikolai and his health; when she needed to speak caustically, the pretext was Countess Marya. When she needed to exercise her vocal organs—this happened mainly between six and seven, after a digestive rest in a dark room—then the pretext was the telling of ever the same stories to ever the same listeners.

Everyone in the house understood the old woman's condition, though no one ever spoke of it, and everyone made every possible effort to satisfy her needs. Only in an occasional glance and sad half smile exchanged among Nikolai, Pierre, Natasha, and Marya was this mutual understanding of her condition expressed.

But, besides that, these glances said something else; they said that she had already finished her business in life, that all of her was not in that which could be seen in her now, that we would all be the same, and that it was a joy to submit to her, to restrain oneself for the sake of this being, once so dear, once as full of life as we, and now so pathetic. *Memento mori*—said these glances.

Of all the household, only quite bad and stupid people, and the little children, did not understand that and avoided her.

XIII

When Pierre and his wife came to the drawing room, the countess was in the habitual state of needing to occupy herself with the mental work of double patience, and therefore, though she said out of habit the words she always spoke when Pierre or her son returned: "It's high time, high time, my dear; we've been waiting and waiting. Well, thank God," and as the presents were given to her, said other habitual words: "It's not the gift that's dear, my friend—thank you for thinking of an old woman like me . . ."—one could see that Pierre's coming was disagreeable to her at that moment, because it distracted her from her unfinished double patience. She finished the patience and only then received the presents. The presents consisted of a wonderfully worked case for cards, a bright blue Sèvres cup with a lid and pictures of shepherdesses, and a gold snuffbox with a portrait of the late count, which Pierre had ordered from a miniaturist in Petersburg. (The countess had long been wishing for that.) She did not feel like weeping now, and therefore glanced indifferently at the portrait and interested herself more in the case.

"Thank you, my friend, you've comforted me," she said, as she always did. "But the best thing is that you've brought yourself. I've never seen the like of it; you ought to give your wife a scolding. What is it? She's like a crazy person without you. Doesn't see anything, doesn't remember anything," she said her habitual words. "Look, Anna Timofeevna," she added, "what a case our boy's brought me."

Mrs. Belov praised the gifts and admired her cotton fabric.

Though Pierre, Natasha, Nikolai, Marya, and Denisov had much to talk about that they would not speak of in the countess's presence, not because anything was concealed from her, but because she was so behind in many things that, if one began to say something in her presence, it would be necessary to answer her questions, put in inappropriately, and repeat once more what had already been repeated to her several times—to tell her that this one had died, that that one had married, which she once more would not remember—but they sat over tea as usual by the samovar in the drawing room, and Pierre answered the countess's questions, needless for her and of interest to no one, saying that Prince Vassily had aged and that Countess Marya Vassilievna had sent her greetings and remembered her, and so on . . .

Such conversation, of interest to no one, but necessary, went on all through tea. For tea round the round table and the samovar, at which Sonya presided, all the grown-up members of the household gathered. The children, tutors, and governesses had already had tea, and their voices could be heard in the neighbouring sitting room. At tea everyone sat in their usual places. Nikolai sat at a little table by the stove, where tea was served to him. The old borzoi bitch Milka, daughter of the first Milka, with a totally grey-haired face, against which her big, black, protruding eyes showed more sharply, lay in an armchair beside him. Denisov with his half-grey curly hair, moustache, and side-whiskers, in an unbuttoned general's tunic, sat next to Countess Marya. Pierre sat between his wife and the old countess. He was talking about what he knew might interest the old lady and be understood by her. He spoke of external, social events and of the people who had once made up the circle of the old countess's contemporaries, who had once been an actual, living, definite circle, but who now, mostly scattered over the world, were living out their time, as she was, gleaning the remaining ears of what they had sown in their lives. But they, these contemporaries, seemed to the old countess the only serious and real world. From Pierre's animation, Natasha could see that his trip had been interesting, that he would have liked to tell about many things, but he did not dare speak in the countess's presence. Denisov, besides his not being a member of the family, and therefore not understanding Pierre's cautiousness, was quite interested, as a disgruntled man, in what was happening in Petersburg, and constantly provoked Pierre into telling now about some story that had just happened in the Semyonovsky regiment, now about Arakcheev, now about the Biblical Society. Pierre occasionally got carried away and began telling, but Nikolai and Natasha brought him back each time to the health of Prince Ivan and Countess Marya Antonovna.

"Well, what about all that madness, Gossner and the Tataghrinov woman— is it still going on?"[8]

"Still going on, hah!" cried Pierre. "Stronger than ever. The Biblical Society— that's now the whole government."

"What's that, *mon cher ami*?" asked the countess, who had finished her tea and clearly wished to find a pretext for getting angry after eating. "What's that you say: the government? I don't understand it."

"You know, *maman*," interrupted Nikolai, who knew how to translate everything into his mother's language, "it's that Prince Alexander Nikolaevich Golitsyn has organized a society, so they say it's become very influential."

"Arakcheev and Golitsyn," Pierre said imprudently, "that's now the whole government. And what a government! They see conspiracies everywhere, they're afraid of everything."

"Why, what fault is that of Prince Alexander Nikolaevich's? He's a very respectable man. I used to meet him at Marya Antonovna's," the countess said offendedly, and, still more offended that everyone fell silent, she went on: "Nowadays everybody finds fault. An evangelical society—well, what's wrong with that?" And she stood up (everyone also stood up) and with a stern look sailed back to her table in the sitting room.

Amidst the sad silence that ensued, children's laughter and voices were heard from the neighbouring room. Evidently some joyful excitement was going on among the children.

"Ready, ready!" little Natasha's joyful cry was heard over everyone else's. Pierre exchanged glances with Countess Marya and Nikolai (Natasha he always saw) and smiled happily.

"That's wonderful music!" he said.

"It's Anna Makarovna finishing her stocking," said Countess Marya.

"Oh, I'll go and see," said Pierre, jumping up. "Do you know why I especially love that music?" he said, stopping at the door. "They're the first to let me know that everything's all right. Coming today, the closer I got to the house, the more frightened I was. As I came into the front hall, I heard Andryusha laughing his head off about something—well, that meant everything was all right . . ."

"I know, I know that feeling," Nikolai agreed. "I mustn't go, the stockings are a surprise for me."

Pierre went to the children, and the laughter and shouting grew still louder. "Well, Anna Makarovna," Pierre's voice was heard, "come here to the middle, and at the command, one, two, and when I say three, you stand here. And you in my arms. Now, one, two . . ." said Pierre's voice; there was a hush. "Three!" and a rapturous groan of chidren's voices arose in the room.

"Two, two!" shouted the children.

That meant two stockings, which, by a secret known only to herself, Anna Makarovna knitted at once on her needles, and which she always drew triumphantly one out of the other before the children, when the stockings were finished.

XIV

Soon after that, the children came to say good night. The children kissed everyone, the tutors and governesses bowed and left. Only Dessales and his pupil remained. The tutor suggested in a whisper that his pupil go downstairs.

"*Non, monsieur Dessales, je demanderai à ma tante de rester,*"* Nikolenka Bolkonsky replied, also in a whisper.

"*Ma tante,* please let me stay," said Nikolenka, going up to his aunt. His face expressed entreaty, excitement, and rapture. Countess Marya glanced at him and turned to Pierre.

"When you're here, he can't tear himself away . . ." she said to him.

"*Je vous le ramènerai tout à l'heure, monsieur Dessales. Bonsoir,*"† said

---

*No, Monsieur Dessales, I'll ask my aunt to let me stay.
†I'll bring him back to you right away, Monsieur Dessales. Good evening.

Pierre, giving his hand to the Swiss, and, smiling, he addressed Nikolenka: "We haven't seen each other at all. Look at the resemblance, Marie," he added, turning to Countess Marya.

"To my father?" said the boy, blushing deeply and looking up at Pierre with admiring, shining eyes. Pierre nodded to him and went on with the story interrupted by the children. Countess Marya worked on her embroidery; Natasha looked at her husband without taking her eyes away. Nikolai and Denisov got up, asked for pipes, smoked, took tea from Sonya, who sat sullenly and stubbornly at the samovar, and questioned Pierre. The curly-headed, sickly boy, with his shining eyes, sat in the corner unnoticed by anyone and, only turning his curly head on its thin neck, emerging from a turned-down collar, to the side where Pierre was, occasionally trembled and whispered something to himself, clearly experiencing some new and strong feeling.

The conversation turned around that contemporary gossip from the highest government in which the majority of people ordinarily see the most important interest of internal politics. Denisov, discontented with the government for his own unsuccesses in the service, was glad to learn about all the stupid things which, in his opinion, were now being done in Petersburg, and made his observations on Pierre's words in strong and sharp terms.

"Before you had to be a Geghrman, now you have to dance with this Tataghrinov woman and Madame Kghrüdener, to ghread . . . Eckaghrtshausen[9] and the ghrest. Ah! I'd turn that fine fellow Bonapaghrte loose on them! He'd knock all this foolishness out of them. Well, have you ever seen anything like it—giving the Semyonovsky ghregiment to that foot soldier Schwaghrtz!" he shouted.

Nikolai, though without Denisov's wish to find everything bad, also considered it a very worthwhile and important thing to discuss the government, and considered that the fact that A was appointed minister here, and B governor general there, and that the sovereign said such-and-such, but the minister said such-and-such—that all this was a very significant matter. And he considered it necessary to be interested in it and questioned Pierre about it. Under the questioning of these two interlocutors, the conversation never departed from the usual character of gossip about high spheres of government.

But Natasha, knowing all the ways and thoughts of her husband, saw that Pierre had long wanted to but could not lead the conversation a different way and voice his innermost thought, the one for which he had gone to Petersburg to consult with his new friend, Prince Fyodor; and she helped him with a question: how was his business with Prince Fyodor?

"What is it about?" asked Nikolai.

"The same thing all over again," said Pierre, glancing around. "Everybody sees that things are taking such a nasty turn that they can't be left like this, and that it's the duty of all honest men to oppose it as far as they can."

"But what can honest men do?" Nikolai said, frowning slightly. "What can be done?"

"Here's what . . ."

"Let's go to my study," said Nikolai.

Natasha, who had long anticipated that they would come to fetch her to nurse the baby, heard the nanny call and went to the nursery. Countess Marya went with her. The men went to the study, and Nikolenka Bolkonsky, unnoticed by his uncle, went there, too, and sat in the shadow, by the window, at the writing table.

"Well, what are you going to do?" asked Denisov.

"Eternal fantasies," said Nikolai.

"Here's what," Pierre began, not sitting down, and now pacing the room, now stopping, lisping and making rapid gestures with his hands while he talked. "Here's what. The situation in Petersburg is like this: the sovereign doesn't enter into anything. He's totally given up to this mysticism" (Pierre could not forgive mysticism in anyone now.) "All he seeks is peace, and peace can be given him only by those people *sans foi ni loi** who hack up and stifle everything far and wide: Magnitsky, Arakcheev, and *tutti quanti*† . . . You'll agree that if you weren't personally taken up with farming, but only wanted peace, then the harsher your bailiff, the sooner you'd achieve your purpose?" he turned to Nikolai.

"Well, but what are you getting at?" said Nikolai.

"Well, and so everything's falling apart. There's thievery in the courts, in the army only the rod: drill, settlements¹⁰—they torment the people, stifle enlightenment. Whatever is young and honest, they destroy! Everybody sees that it can't go on like this. It's all too strained and bound to snap," Pierre said (as people have been saying as long as governments have existed, once they look attentively at any government whatever). "I said just one thing to them in Petersburg."

"To whom?" asked Denisov.

"Well, you know to whom," said Pierre, glancing significantly from under his eyebrows, "to Prince Fyodor and all of them. To contribute to enlightenment and philanthropy is all very well, of course. It's a splendid aim and all; but in the present circumstances, something else is needed."

Just then Nikolai noticed the presence of his nephew. His face darkened; he went over to him.

"What are you doing here?"

"Why? Let him be," said Pierre, taking Nikolai by the arm, and he went on: "That's not enough, I told them: something else is needed now. When you

---

*Without faith or law.
†All that sort.

stand and wait for that tightened string to snap any moment, when every-body's waiting for the inevitable upheaval—people must join hands, as many and as closely as possible, in order to oppose the general catastrophe. Every-thing young and strong is drawn there and gets corrupted. One is seduced by women, another by honours, a third by vainglory or money—and they go over to the other camp. There are no independent people like you and me left. I say: expand the circle of the society; let the *mot d'ordre** be not only virtue, but independence and activity."

Nikolai, having let his nephew be, angrily moved up his armchair, sat down in it, and, as he listened to Pierre, coughed discontentedly and frowned more and more.

"But what's the purpose of your activity?" he cried. "And in what relation will you stand to the government?"

"Here's in what! In the relation of helpers. The society may not be secret, if the government allows it. Not only is it not hostile to the government, but it is a society of true conservatives. A society of gentlemen in the full sense of the word. It's only so as not to have Pugachev come tomorrow and put a knife into my and your children, or to have Arakcheev send me to a military settlement—we're joining hands only for that, with the one purpose of the common good and common security."

"Yes, but a secret society—consequently a hostile and harmful one, which can breed only evil," said Nikolai, raising his voice.

"Why so? Did the Tugendbund,¹¹ which saved Europe" (they still did not dare to think then that Russia had saved Europe), "breed anything harmful? The Tugendbund is an alliance of virtue, it is love, mutual aid; it's what Christ preached on the Cross . . ."

Natasha, who had come into the room in the middle of the conversation, looked joyfully at her husband. She did not rejoice in what he was saying. She was not even interested in it, because it seemed to her that it was all extremely simple and that she had long known it (it seemed so, because she knew where it all came from—the whole soul of Pierre). But she rejoiced looking at his ani-mated, rapturous figure.

With still more joyful rapture, Pierre was looked at by the boy they had all forgotten, with his thin neck emerging from a turned-down collar. Every word of Pierre's burned his heart, and with a nervous movement of the fingers—not noticing it himself—he kept breaking the pens and sticks of sealing wax that lay on his uncle's table.

"What I'm proposing is not at all what you think, but something like what the German Tugendbund was."

---

*Watchword.

"Well, bghrother, the Tugendbund is fine for sausage makers. I don't understand it and can't even pghronounce it," the loud, resolute voice of Denisov rang out. "Eveghrything's nasty and vile, I aghree, only this Tugendbund I don't understand, but if you don't like things—*ghrebellion,* that's the way! *Je suis votghre homme!*"*

Pierre smiled, Natasha laughed, but Nikolai knitted his brows still more and began demonstrating to Pierre that no sort of upheaval was expected and that all the danger he was speaking of existed only in his imagination. Pierre demonstrated the contrary, and as his mental powers were stronger and more resourceful, Nikolai felt himself up against the wall. This made him still angrier, since in his heart, not by reasoning, but by something stronger than reasoning, he knew the unquestionable rightness of his opinion.

"Here's what I'll tell you," he said, getting up and trying to prop his pipe in the corner with a nervous gesture and finally abandoning it. "I can't prove anything to you. You say everything's bad with us and there'll be an upheaval; I don't see that; but you say an oath is a conventional thing, and to that I'll tell you: you're my best friend, you know that, but if you were to set up a secret society and start opposing the government, whatever it might be, I know that my duty is to obey it. And if Arakcheev ordered me right now to go against you with a squadron and cut you down—I'd go without thinking for a second. You can say whatever you like."

After these words, an awkward silence ensued. Natasha was the first to speak, defending her husband and attacking her brother. Her defence was weak and awkward, but her purpose was achieved. The conversation picked up again, and no longer in that unpleasantly hostile tone in which Nikolai's last words had been spoken.

When they all rose for supper, Nikolenka Bolkonsky went up to Pierre, pale, with shining, luminous eyes.

"Uncle Pierre . . . you . . . no . . . If papa were alive . . . He'd agree with you?" he asked.

Pierre suddenly realized what a special, independent, complex, and intense work of feeling and thought must have been going on in this boy while he was talking, and, recalling everything he had said, he was vexed that the boy had heard him. However, he had to give him an answer.

"I think so," he said reluctantly and left the study.

The boy bowed his head, and here it was as if he noticed for the first time what he had done on the table. He blushed and went over to Nikolai.

"Uncle, forgive me, I didn't mean to do it," he said, pointing to the broken pens and sticks of wax.

Nikolai gave an angry start.

---

*I'm your man!

"All right, all right," he said, throwing the pens and sticks of wax under the table. And, clearly having a hard time suppressing the wrath that had risen in him, he turned away.

"You shouldn't have been here at all," he said.

XV

Over supper the conversation was no longer about politics and societies but, on the contrary, started on what was most pleasant for Nikolai—memories of the year twelve—which Denisov evoked and in which Pierre was especially nice and amusing. And the family parted on the most friendly terms.

When Nikolai, having undressed in his study after supper and given instructions to the steward, who had long been waiting, went to the bedroom in his dressing gown, he found his wife still at the writing table: she was writing something.

"What are you writing, Marie?" asked Nikolai. Countess Marya blushed. She was afraid that her husband would not understand or approve of what she was writing.

She would have liked to hide what she had written from him, but at the same time she was glad that he had found her and that she could tell him.

"It's my diary, Nicolas," she said, handing him a blue notebook covered with her firm, large handwriting.

"Your diary? . . ." Nikolai said with a shade of mockery and took the notebook from her. It was written in French:

December 4. Today Andryusha [the elder son] woke up and did not want to get dressed, and Mlle Louise sent for me. He was capricious and headstrong. I tried to threaten him, but he became still more angry. Then I took it upon myself to let him be, and the nanny and I began getting the other children up, and I told him that I did not like him. He remained silent for a long time, as if he was surprised; then, in nothing but his nightshirt, he jumped up to me and burst into such sobs that it was long before I could calm him. It was clear that he suffered most of all from having upset me; then, in the evening, when I gave him his little ticket, he again wept pitifully as he kissed me. With him everything can be done by tenderness.

"What is a little ticket?" asked Nikolai.

"I've begun giving the older ones little reports in the evening on their behaviour."

Nikolai glanced into the luminous eyes that were looking at him and went on turning pages and reading. The diary contained everything from the children's life that the mother found noteworthy, expressing the children's character or inspiring general thoughts about methods of upbringing. These were for the most part the most insignificant trifles, but they did not seem so either to the mother or to the father as he now read this children's diary for the first time.

For December 5 there was written:

Mitya was mischievous at the table. Papa ordered that he not be given dessert. He was not; but he looked at the others so pitifully and greedily while they ate! I think that to punish by depriving of sweets develops greed. Tell Nicolas.

Nikolai set the book aside and looked at his wife. The luminous eyes gazed at him questioningly (did he approve of her diary or not?). There could be no doubt not only of Nikolai's approval, but also of his admiration of his wife.

"Maybe it needn't be done so pedantically; maybe it needn't be done at all," thought Nikolai; but this tireless, eternal inner effort, aimed only at the moral good of the children—this he admired. If Nikolai could have been conscious of his feeling, he would have found that his firm, tender, and proud love for his wife had always been based on this feeling of wonder before her inner life, before that lofty moral world, almost inaccessible to him, in which his wife lived always.

He was proud that she was so intelligent and good, being conscious of his own insignificance before her in the spiritual world, and rejoiced the more that she, with her soul, not only belonged to him, but made up a part of him.

"I approve, I approve very much, my dearest," he said with a significant air. And after some silence, he added: "And I behaved badly today. You weren't in the study. Pierre and I began to argue, and I got angry. It's impossible. He's such a child. I don't know what would happen to him if Natasha didn't keep him on a leash. Can you imagine why he went to Petersburg . . . They're setting up . . ."

"I know," said Countess Marya. "Natasha told me."

"Well, so you know," Nikolai went on, getting excited at the mere recollection of the argument. "He wants to convince me that it's the duty of every honest man to go against the government, whereas my oath and my duty . . . I'm sorry you weren't there. They all attacked me, Denisov and Natasha . . . Natasha's killingly funny. She really keeps him under her heel, but once it comes to arguments, she has no words of her own, she just speaks his words," Nikolai added, yielding to that irresistible impulse that makes us judge the nearest and dearest people. Nikolai forgot that what he was saying about Natasha could be said word for word about himself in relation to his wife.

"Yes, I've noticed that," said Countess Marya.

"When I told him that my duty and oath were highest of all, he began proving God knows what. It's a pity you weren't there; what would you have said?"

"In my opinion, you're completely right. And I told Natasha so. Pierre says that everybody's suffering, tormented, becoming depraved, and that our duty is to help our neighbours. Of course, he's right," said Countess Marya, "but he forgets that we have other, closer responsibilities, which God himself has indicated to us, and that we can risk ourselves, but not our children."

"Well, there, there, that's the same thing I told him," Nikolai picked up, fancying that he had indeed said that same thing. "But he keeps at it about love for one's neighbour and Christianity, and all that in front of Nikolenka, who also got into the study and broke everything."

"Ah, you know, Nicolas, I often suffer over Nikolenka," said Countess Marya. "He's such an extraordinary boy. And I'm afraid I forget about him because of my own. We all have children, we all have relations; but he has nobody. He's eternally alone with his thoughts."

"Well, I don't think you have anything to reproach yourself with on his account. You've done and are doing everything for him that a most tender mother could do for her son. And, naturally, I'm glad of that. He's a nice, nice boy. Today he was listening to Pierre in some sort of trance. And can you imagine: we go to supper; I look, and he's broken everything on my table to bits, and he told me at once. I've never seen him tell a lie. A nice, nice boy!" repeated Nikolai, who in his heart did not like Nikolenka, but whom he was always ready to acknowledge as nice.

"Still, it's not the same as a mother," said Countess Marya. "I feel it's not the same, and I suffer over it. A wonderful boy, but I'm terribly afraid for him. Company would do him good."

"Well, it won't be long; this summer I'll take him to Petersburg," said Nikolai. "Yes, Pierre has always been and will remain a dreamer," he went on, returning to the conversation in the study, which had clearly disturbed him. "Well, what do I care about all that—that Arakcheev is no good and the rest—what did I care, when I got married and had so many debts that they wanted to throw me into prison, and had a mother who was unable to see or understand it. And then you, the children, work. Is it for my own pleasure that I'm in the office and tending to business from morning till night? No, I know that I must work to comfort my mother, to pay you back, and not leave the children as poor as I was."

Countess Marya wanted to tell him that man does not live by bread alone, that he ascribed too much importance to this *business;* but she knew it was unnecessary and useless to say it. She only took his hand and kissed it. He accepted this gesture of his wife's as an approval and confirmation of his thoughts and, after some silent reflection, went on thinking aloud.

"You know, Marie," he said, "today Ilya Mitrofanych" (this was the business manager) "came from the Tambov estate and told me that they're now offering eighty thousand for the timber." And with an animated face, Nikolai began talking about the possibility of buying back Otradnoe in a very short time. "Ten more years of life, and I'll leave the children in an excellent situation."

Countess Marya listened to her husband and understood all that he said to her. She knew that, when he thought aloud like that, he sometimes asked her what he had said and was angry when he noticed that she had been thinking of something else. But it cost her great effort to do so, because what he said did not interest her at all. She looked at him and did not so much think about something else as feel about something else. She felt a submissive, tender love for this man, who would never understand all that she understood, and as if because of that she loved him still more strongly, with a shade of passionate tenderness. Besides this feeling, which wholly absorbed her and kept her from entering into the details of her husband's plans, thoughts flashed in her head that had nothing to do with what he was talking about. She was thinking about her nephew (her husband's account of his agitation over Pierre's talk had struck her deeply), imagined various traits of his gentle, sensitive character; and, thinking of her nephew, she also thought of her own children. She did not compare her nephew with her children, but compared her feeling for them, and found it sad that something was lacking in her feeling for Nikolenka.

Sometimes the thought occurred to her that this difference was caused by age; but she felt that she was guilty before him, and in her heart she promised herself to mend her ways and do the impossible—that is, in this life to love her husband, and her children, and Nikolenka, and all who were close to her as Christ loved mankind. Countess Marya's soul always strove towards the infinite, eternal, and perfect, and therefore could never be at peace. The stern expression of concealed, lofty suffering of a soul burdened by a body came to her face. Nikolai looked at her.

"My God! what will become of us if she dies, as it seems to me she will when she has such a face?" he thought and, standing in front of the icon, he began to recite the evening prayers.

XVI

Natasha, left alone with her husband, also talked as only a wife and husband can talk, that is, grasping thoughts and conveying them to each other with extraordinary clarity and quickness, in a way contrary to all the rules of logic, without recourse to opinions, conclusions, and deductions, but in a totally special way. Natasha was so used to talking with her husband in this way that for her a logical train of thought in Pierre served as a sure sign that something was wrong between them. When he began to prove, to speak reasonably and calmly, and when she, carried along by his example, began to do the same, she knew it would inevitably lead to a quarrel.

From the very moment they were left alone, and Natasha, with wide-open, happy eyes, went softly up to him and suddenly seized his head and pressed it to her breast, saying, "Now you're all mine, all mine! You won't get away!"—

from that moment such a conversation began, contrary to all the laws of logic, contrary if only because totally different subjects were discussed at one and the same time. This simultaneous discussion of many things not only did not hinder their clarity of understanding, but, on the contrary, was the surest sign that they fully understood each other.

As everything in a dream is false, senseless, and contradictory, except for the feeling that guides the dream, so in this sort of communication, contrary to all the laws of reason, it was not the words that were consistent and clear, but only the feeling that guided them.

Natasha told Pierre about her brother's daily life, about how she suffered and did not live without her husband, and about how she had come to love Marie still more, and how Marie was better than her in all respects. In saying that, Natasha was sincerely acknowledging that she saw Marie's superiority, but, while saying it, she demanded that Pierre still prefer her to Marie and to all other women, and now, especially after having seen so many women in Petersburg, that he repeat it to her again.

Pierre, in reply to Natasha's words, told her how unbearable it was for him to be at soirées and dinners with ladies in Petersburg.

"I've completely forgotten how to talk with ladies," he said, "it was simply boring. Especially since I was so busy."

Natasha looked at him intently and went on:

"Marie is so lovely!" she said. "How well she understands children. It's as if she sees only their souls. Yesterday, for instance, Mitenka began to fuss . . ."

"Ah, he's so much like his father," Pierre interrupted.

Natasha understood why he made this observation about Mitenka's resemblance to Nikolai: he had an unpleasant memory of the argument with his brother-in-law and wanted to know Natasha's opinion about it.

"Nikolenka has this weakness, that if something isn't generally accepted by everybody, he won't agree with it for anything. But I understand that you precisely value what can *ouvrir une carrière*,"* she said, repeating words that Pierre had said once.

"No, the main thing is," said Pierre, "that for Nikolai thoughts and arguments are an amusement, almost a pastime. Here he's collecting a library and has made it a rule not to buy a new book before he's read what he's bought—Sismondi, and Rousseau, and Montesquieu," Pierre added with a smile. "You know how he and I . . ." He was beginning to soften his words, but Natasha interrupted him, letting him feel that it was unnecessary.

"So you say thinking is an amusement for him . . ."

"Yes, and for me all the rest is an amusement. All the while I was in Peters-

*Open up a career.

burg, I saw everyone as if in a dream. When I'm taken up with a thought, all the rest is an amusement."

"Ah, what a pity I didn't see you greet the children," said Natasha. "Which of them was most glad? Liza, surely?"

"Yes," said Pierre, and he went on with what occupied him. "Nikolai says we shouldn't think. But I can't help it. Not to speak of the fact that in Petersburg I felt (I can tell you) that without me it would all fall apart, each one pulling in his own direction. But I succeeded in uniting them all, and besides, my thought is so simple and clear. I don't say we should oppose this or that. We may be mistaken. What I say is: let's join hands with those who love the good, and let there be one banner—active virtue. Prince Sergei is a nice man and intelligent."

Natasha would have had no doubt that Pierre's thought was a great thought, but one thing confused her. It was the fact that he was her husband. "Can it be that a man so important and necessary for society is at the same time my husband? How did it happen that way?" She wanted to express this doubt to him. "Who and what are the people who could decide whether he is really so much smarter than everyone else?" she asked herself, and went over in her imagination the people whom Pierre greatly respected. Judging by his accounts, there was no one he respected so much as Platon Karataev.

"You know what I'm thinking about?" she said. "About Platon Karataev. How about him? Would he approve of you now?"

Pierre was not surprised in the least by this question. He understood his wife's train of thought.

"Platon Karataev?" he said and fell to thinking, evidently trying in all sincerity to imagine Karataev's opinion on this subject. "He wouldn't understand, but anyhow, I think, yes."

"I love you terribly!" Natasha said suddenly. "Terribly. Terribly!"

"No, he wouldn't approve of me," said Pierre, having reflected. "What he would approve of is our family life. He wished so much to see seemliness, happiness, peace in everything, and I would have shown us to him with pride. Now, you say—parting. But you wouldn't believe what a special feeling I have for you after we've been parted . . ."

"Yes, there's also . . ." Natasha began.

"No, it's not that. I never stop loving you. And it's impossible to love more; and that's especially . . . Well, yes . . ." He did not finish, because their eyes met and said all the rest.

"What stupidity," Natasha said suddenly, "that the honeymoon and the first time is the happiest. On the contrary, now it's best. If only you didn't go away. Remember how we quarrelled? And it was always my fault. Always. And what we quarrelled about—I don't even remember."

"Always the same thing," said Pierre, smiling, "jealo . . ."

"Don't say it, I can't bear it," Natasha cried. And a cold, angry gleam lit up in her eyes. "Did you see her?" she added, after a pause.

"No, and if I had, I wouldn't have recognized her."

They fell silent.

"Ah, you know? As you were talking in the study, I was looking at you," Natasha began, clearly trying to ward off the intruding cloud. "You and he are as alike as two drops of water—the boy, I mean." (She referred to her son that way.) "Ah, it's time to go to him . . . Time . . . Too bad I have to leave."

They fell silent for a few seconds. Then they suddenly turned to each other and started saying something at the same time. Pierre began with self-satisfaction and enthusiasm, Natasha with a quiet, happy smile. Colliding, they both stopped, giving way to each other.

"No, what were you saying? Speak, speak."

"No, you tell me, mine was just something stupid," said Natasha.

Pierre said what he had started. It was a continuation of his self-satisfied discourse about his success in Petersburg. It seemed to him at that moment that he was called upon to give a new direction to the whole of Russian society and the whole world.

"I was going to say only that all thoughts that have great consequences are always simple. My whole thought is that, since vicious people band together and constitute a force, honest people need only do the same. It's that simple."

"Yes."

"And what were you going to say?"

"Just something stupid."

"No, but still."

"It's nothing, trifles," said Natasha, her smile shining still more brightly. "I only wanted to tell you about Petya: today the nanny came to take him from me, he laughed, closed his eyes, and pressed himself to me—he must have thought he was hiding. He's awfully sweet. That's him shouting. Well, goodbye!" And she left the room.

At that same time, downstairs, in Nikolenka Bolkonsky's part of the house, in his bedroom, an icon lamp was burning as always (the boy was afraid of the dark, and they could not get him to drop this bad habit). Dessales slept propped up high on his four pillows, and his Roman nose produced the steady sounds of snoring. Nikolenka, having just woken up in a cold sweat, his eyes wide open, sat up on his bed and looked around. A terrible dream had awakened him. In his dream he had seen himself and Pierre wearing helmets—the kind illustrated in his edition of Plutarch. He and Uncle Pierre were marching at the head of a huge army. This army consisted of slanting white lines that filled the air like the spiderwebs that fly about in the autumn and that

Dessales called *le fil de la Vierge.** Ahead was glory, just the same as these threads, only slightly denser. They—he and Pierre—were racing lightly and joyfully nearer and nearer to their goal. Suddenly the threads that moved them began to weaken, to tangle; the going became heavy. And Uncle Nikolai Ilyich stood before them in a stern and menacing pose.

"Did you do that?" he said, pointing to the broken-up wax and pens. "I loved you, but Arakcheev has given me orders, and I'll kill the first one who moves forward." Nikolenka turned to look at Pierre; but there was no longer any Pierre. Pierre was his father, Prince Andrei, and his father had no image or form, but he was there, and, seeing him, Nikolenka felt weak from love: he felt strengthless, boneless, and liquid. His father caressed and pitied him. But Uncle Nikolai Ilyich moved closer and closer to them. Nikolenka was overcome by terror and woke up.

"Father," he thought. "Father" (though there were two portraits of a good likeness in the house, Nikolenka never pictured Prince Andrei in his human image), "father was with me and caressed me. He approved of me, he approved of Uncle Pierre. Whatever he says—I'll do. Mucius Scaevola burned his hand.[12] Why shouldn't it be the same in my life? I know they want me to study. And I will study. But some day I'll stop. And then I'll do it. I ask God for only one thing: that it's the same with me as with the men in Plutarch, and I'll do the same. I'll do better. Everybody will know me, love me, admire me." And Nikolenka suddenly felt sobs seize his breast, and he burst into tears.

"*Êtes-vous indisposé?*"† Dessales's voice was heard.

"*Non,*" replied Nikolenka, and he lay back on the pillow. "He's kind and good, I love him," he thought of Dessales. "But Uncle Pierre! Oh, what a wonderful man! And father? Father! Father! Yes, I'll do something that even *he* would be pleased with . . ."

*The thread of the Virgin.
†Are you unwell?

I

The subject of history is the life of peoples and of mankind. To grasp directly and embrace in words—to describe—the life not only of mankind, but of one people, appears impossible.

All the ancient historians used one and the same method to describe and grasp the seemingly ungraspable—the life of a people. They described the activity of individual men who ruled the people; and this activity expressed for them the activity of the whole people.

To the questions of how individual men made peoples act according to their will, and what governed the will of these men themselves, the ancients answered the first question by recognizing the will of a divinity who subjected peoples to the will of one chosen man, and the second by recognizing that the same divinity guided the will of the chosen one towards a predestined goal.

For the ancients, these questions were decided by faith in the direct participation of a divinity in the affairs of mankind.

Modern history, in its theory, has rejected both of these propositions.

It would seem that, having rejected the beliefs of the ancients in the subjection of peoples to a divinity and in the definite goal towards which peoples are led, modern history should study not the manifestations of power, but the causes that form it. Modern history has not done that. Having rejected the views of the ancients in theory, it follows them in practice.

In place of men endowed with divine power and directly guided by the will of a divinity, modern history has put either heroes endowed with extraordinary, superhuman capacities, or simply men of the most diverse qualities, from monarchs to journalists, who guide the masses. In place of the former god-pleasing goals of the peoples—the Jews, the Greeks, the Romans—which the ancients took for goals of the movement of mankind, modern history has set up its own goals—the good of the French, the Germans, the English, and, in its highest abstraction, the goal of the good of all human civilization, usually understood as the people occupying the small north-west corner of a large continent.

Modern history has rejected the beliefs of the ancients without putting in their place a new view, and the logic of the situation has made historians, who fancied they had rejected the divine power of kings and the fatum of old, come by a different route to the same thing: to the recognition that (1) peoples are guided by individual men, and (2) there exists a certain goal towards which peoples and mankind move.

These two old, inevitable propositions lie at the basis of all the works of modern history, from Gibbon to Buckle, despite their apparent disagreement and the apparent novelty of their views.

First, the historian describes the activity of separate persons who, in his opinion, guide mankind (one considers monarchs, military commanders, ministers to be such; another, besides monarchs and orators, includes learned reformers, philosophers, and poets). Second, the historian knows the goal towards which mankind is being led (for one this goal is the greatness of the Roman, Spanish, or French state; for another it is freedom, equality, a certain kind of civilization in a small corner of the world known as Europe).

In 1789 a ferment arises in Paris; it grows, spreads, and expresses itself in a movement of peoples from west to east. Several times this movement directed to the east comes into collision with a counter-movement from east to west; in the year twelve it reaches its utmost limit—Moscow; and, with remarkable symmetry, the counter-movement from east to west is accomplished, drawing with itself, as the first movement had done, the peoples of the centre. The counter-movement reaches the point of departure in the west—Paris—and subsides.

During this twenty-year period of time an enormous number of fields go unploughed; houses are burned; trade changes direction; millions of people become poor, become rich, migrate; and millions of Christians, who profess the law of love of their neighbour, kill each other.

What does it all mean? Why did it happen? What made these people burn houses and kill their own kind? What were the causes of these events? What force made people act that way? These are the involuntary, simple-hearted, and most legitimate questions that mankind poses for itself, encountering the memorials and traditions of that past period of movement.

To settle these questions, mankind's common sense turns to the science of history, which has for its goal the self-knowledge of peoples and of mankind.

If history had maintained the view of the ancients, it would say that a divinity, to reward or punish its people, gave power to Napoleon and guided his will towards achieving its divine purposes. And that answer would be full and clear. One might believe or not believe in the divine significance of Napoleon; but for the believer in it, everything in the history of that time would be comprehensible, and there could not be a single contradiction.

But modern history cannot answer in that way. Science does not recognize the view of the ancients on the direct participation of a divinity in the affairs of mankind, and therefore it should give other answers.

Modern history, in answer to these questions, says: you want to know what this movement means, why it occurred, and what force produced these events? Listen:

"Louis XIV was a very proud and presumptuous man; he had such-and-such mistresses and such-and-such ministers, and he ruled France badly. Louis's heirs were also weak men and also ruled France badly. They, too, had such-and-such favourites and such-and-such mistresses. Besides, certain men were writing books at that time. At the end of the eighteenth century, some two dozen men got together in Paris and started talking about all men being equal and free. That led people all over France to start slaughtering and drowning each other. These people killed the king and many others. At the same time there was in France a man of genius—Napoleon. He defeated everybody everywhere—that is, he killed a lot of people—because he was a great genius. And he went off for some reason to kill Africans, and he killed them so well, and was so cunning and clever, that, on coming back to France, he ordered everybody to obey him. And everybody obeyed him. Having become emperor, he again went to kill people in Italy, Austria, and Prussia. And there he killed a lot. In Russia there was the emperor Alexander, who decided to restore order in Europe and therefore made war with Napoleon. But in the year seven, he suddenly made friends with him, then in the year eleven quarrelled again, and again they started killing a lot of people. And Napoleon brought six hundred thousand men to Russia and captured Moscow; then he suddenly ran away from Moscow, and then the emperor Alexander, helped by the advice of Stein and others, united Europe to take up arms against the disturber of its peace. All Napoleon's allies suddenly became his enemies; and this armed force marched against Napoleon, who had gathered new forces. The allies defeated Napoleon, entered Paris, made Napoleon abdicate, and exiled him to the island of Elba, not depriving him of the dignity of emperor and showing him every respect, though five years earlier and one year later everybody considered him a bandit and outlaw. And so began the reign of Louis XVIII, whom until then both the French and the allies had only laughed at. Napoleon, pouring out tears before his old guard, abdicated and went into exile. Then skilful statesmen and diplomats (in particular Talleyrand, who managed to sit in a certain chair before anyone else and thereby extended the borders of France)[1] talked in Vienna, and with these talks made people happy or unhappy. Suddenly the diplomats and monarchs nearly quarrelled; they were already prepared to order their troops to kill each other again; but at that moment Napoleon arrived in France with a battalion, and the French, who hated him, all submitted to him at once. But the allied monarchs were angered by that and again went to war with the French. And the genius Napoleon was defeated and taken to the island of St. Helena, having suddenly been recognized as a bandit. And there the exile, separated from those dear to his heart and from his beloved France, died a slow death on the rock and bequeathed his great deeds to posterity. But in Europe there was the reaction, and the sovereigns all started mistreating their own people again."

It would be wrong to think that this is a mockery, a caricature, of historical descriptions. On the contrary, it is the mildest expression of those answers, contradictory and answering no questions, which are given by *all* history, from the composers of memoirs and histories of separate states to general histories and the new genre of histories of the *culture* of that time.

The strangeness and comicality of these answers come from the fact that modern history is like a deaf man, answering questions that no one has asked him.

If the aim of history is to describe the movements of mankind and of peoples, then the first question, without answering which the rest will remain incomprehensible, is the following: what force moves peoples? To this question, modern history anxiously tells us either that Napoleon was a great genius, or that Louis XIV was very proud, or else that the writers so-and-so wrote such-and-such books.

All that may very well be, and mankind is ready to agree with it; but it is not asking about that. All that might be interesting, if we recognized the divine power, based on itself and always the same, that governs its peoples through Napoleons, Louis, and writers; but we do not recognize that power, and therefore, before talking about Napoleons, Louis, and writers, we must show the existing connection between these persons and the movement of peoples.

If in place of divine power there stands another force, then what this force consists in must be explained, for the whole interest of history is contained precisely in that force.

History seems to suppose that this force goes without saying and is known to everyone. But, despite all the desire to take this new force as a known thing, anyone who reads through very many historical works will involuntarily doubt that this new force, variously understood by the historians themselves, is well known to everyone.

II

What force moves peoples?

Specialized biographical historians and historians of separate peoples understand this force as the force inherent in heroes and rulers. In their descriptions, events are produced solely by the will of the Napoleons, the Alexanders, or generally of those persons the specialized historian is describing. The answers given by this sort of historian to the question of the force that moves events are satisfactory, but only so long as there is one historian for each event. But once historians of different nationalities and views begin to describe the same event, the answers they give immediately lose all meaning, because each of them understands this force not only differently but often in a totally opposite way. One historian insists that the event was produced by the power of Napoleon; another insists that it was produced by the power of Alexander; a third by the power of some third person. Besides that, historians of this sort contradict one another even in explaining that force on which the power of one and the same person is based. Thiers, a Bonapartist, says that Napoleon's power was based on his virtue and genius; Lanfrey, a republican, says it was based on his swindling and on duping the people. So that historians of this sort, by mutually demolishing each other's propositions, thereby demolish the concept of the force that produces events, and give no answer to the essential question of history.

General historians, who deal with all peoples, seem to recognize the incorrectness of the specialized historians' view of the force that produces events. They do not recognize this force as the power inherent in heroes and rulers, but as the result of many variously directed forces. In describing a war or the subjugation of a people, the general historian seeks the cause of an event not in the power of one person, but in the interaction of many persons connected with the event.

According to this view, it seems that the power of historical figures, conceived as the result of many forces, cannot be considered a force itself productive of events. Yet general historians in most cases happen to use the concept of power once again as a force in itself productive of events and related to them as a cause. By their account, a historical figure is now the product of his time and his power is only the product of various forces, now his power is a force productive of events. Gervinus, Schlosser, and others, for example, now prove that Napoleon was a product of the revolution, of the ideas of 1789, and so on, and now say outright that the campaign of the year twelve and other events they do not like are only products of Napoleon's misdirected will, and that those same ideas of 1789 were stopped in their development as a result of Napoleon's despotism. The ideas of the revolution, the general state of mind, produced the power of Napoleon. The power of Napoleon suppressed the ideas of the revolution and the general state of mind.

This strange contradiction is not accidental. Not only is it encountered at every step, but all the descriptions of the general historians are made up of a consecutive series of such contradictions. This contradiction comes from the fact that, having entered upon the path of analysis, the general historians stop halfway.

To find the component forces equal to a composite or resultant, it is necessary that the sum of the components equal the composite. This condition is never observed by general historians, and therefore, in order to explain the resultant force, they must necessarily allow for an unexplained force, besides the insufficient components, which acts upon the composite.

The specialized historian, describing the campaign of the year thirteen, or the restoration of the Bourbons, says directly that these events were produced by the will of Alexander. But the general historian Gervinus, disproving this view of the specialized historian, aims to show that the campaign of the year thirteen and the restoration of the Bourbons had as their causes, besides the will of Alexander, the activity of Stein, Metternich, Mme de Staël, Talleyrand, Fichte, Chateaubriand, and others. The historian has obviously broken down the power of Alexander into its components: Talleyrand, Chateaubriand, and so on; the sum of these components, that is, the mutual influence on each other of Chateaubriand, Talleyrand, Mme de Staël, and others, obviously does not equal the whole resultant, that is, the phenomenon that millions of Frenchmen submitted to the Bourbons. From the fact that Chateaubriand, Mme de Staël, and others said such-and-such words to each other, there follows only their relations among themselves, not the submission of millions. And therefore, in order to explain in what way the submission of millions followed from their relations, that is, how from components equal to one A there followed a resultant equal to a thousand times A, the historian must necessarily allow again for the same force of the power which he denies, recognizing it as the result of forces, that is, he must allow for the unexplained force acting upon the composite. This is what general historians do. And consequently they contradict not only the specialized historians, but also themselves.

Country dwellers, having no clear concept of what causes rain, say, depending on whether they would like to have rain or fair weather: the wind has scattered the clouds, the wind has gathered the clouds. It is the same with general historians: sometimes, when they want to, when it suits their theory, they say that power is the result of events; and sometimes, when they need to prove something else, they say that power produces events.

The third sort of historians, known as historians of *culture,* following the path laid down by the general historians, who sometimes recognize writers and ladies as forces productive of events, understand this force quite differently still. They see it in so-called culture, in intellectual activity.

Historians of culture are perfectly consistent in relation to their progenitors, the general historians, for if historical events can be explained by the fact that certain people had such-and-such relations with each other, then why not explain them by the fact that such-and-such people wrote such-and-such books? These historians select, from among the enormous number of symptoms that accompany any living phenomenon, the symptom of intellectual activity, and say that this symptom is the cause. But, despite all their attempts to show that the cause of an event lay in intellectual activity, only with great flexibility can one agree that there is something in common between intellectual activity and the movement of peoples, but in no case is it possible to allow that intellectual activity guides the activity of people, for such phenomena as the cruellest murders of the French revolution resulting from the preaching of the equality of man, and the wickedest wars and executions resulting from the preaching of love, do not confirm this supposition.

But, even allowing that all the cleverly woven arguments which fill these histories are correct, allowing that peoples are governed by some indefinable force known as an *idea*—the essential question of history either remains unanswered, or, to the former power of monarchs and to the influence of advisers and other persons introduced by the general historians, there is joined yet another new force, the *idea,* the connection of which with the masses calls for explanation. It is possible to understand that Napoleon had power, and therefore an event took place; with some flexibility it is possible to understand that Napoleon, along with other forces, was the cause of an event; but in what way the book *Le contrat social** brought it about that the French started drowning each other cannot be understood without explaining the causal connection of this new force with the event.

Undoubtedly there exists a connection among all that is alive at the same time, and therefore it is possible to find a certain connection between the intellectual activity of a people and their historical movement, just as this connection can be found between the movement of mankind and trade, crafts, gardening, or anything you like. But why the intellectual activity of people is presented by historians of culture as the cause or expression of the whole historical movement is hard to understand. Only the following considerations could lead historians to such a conclusion: (1) that history is written by scholars, and therefore it is natural and pleasant for them to think that the activity of their estate is the basis for the movement of all mankind, just as it is natural and pleasant for merchants, farmers, and soldiers to think so (this does not get expressed only because merchants and soldiers do not write history), and (2) that spiritual activity, education, civilization, culture, the idea are all vague, indefinite concepts, under the banner of which it is quite convenient to use words that have a still less clear meaning and therefore can easily be plugged into any theory.

But, not to speak of the inner merit of histories of this sort (perhaps they are even needed by someone or for something), the histories of culture, which all general histories are beginning to come down to more and more, are remarkable in that, while thoroughly and seriously analysing various religious, philosophical, and political teachings as causes of events, each time they have only to describe an actual historical event—for example, the campaign of the year twelve—they describe it involuntarily as a product of power, saying outright that this campaign is the product of Napoleon's will. In speaking this way, the historians of culture involuntarily contradict themselves, or prove that the new force they have invented does not express historical events, and that the sole means of understanding history is that power which they supposedly do not recognize.

The Social Contract.

III

A locomotive is moving. Someone asks: why does it move? A muzhik says: the devil moves it. Another man says the locomotive moves because its wheels turn. A third asserts that the cause of the movement is the smoke blown away by the wind.

The muzhik is irrefutable. In order to refute him, someone would have to prove to him that there is no devil, or another muzhik would have to explain to him that it is not the devil but a German who moves the locomotive. Only then, by way of contradiction, will they see that they are both wrong. But the one who says that the cause is the turning of the wheels refutes himself, because, if he enters upon the terrain of analysis, he must keep going: he must explain the cause of the turning of the wheels. And until he arrives at the ultimate cause of the locomotive's movement, the steam compressed in the boiler, he will have no right to stop in his search for the cause. The one who explained the movement of the locomotive by the smoke blown back, noticing that the explanation by the wheels did not furnish the cause, took the first symptom that came along and, in his turn, passed it on as the cause.

The only concept that can explain the movement of the locomotive is the concept of a force equal to its visible movement.

The only concept by means of which the movement of peoples can be explained is the concept of a force equal to the whole movement of the peoples.

Yet under this concept different historians understand completely different forces, none of them equal to the visible movement. Some see it as a force immediately inherent in heroes—like the muzhik who sees the devil in a locomotive; others as a force produced by certain other forces—like the turning of the wheels; still others as an intellectual influence—like the blown-away smoke.

As long as histories of separate persons are written—be they Caesars, Alexanders, or Luthers and Voltaires—and not the history of *all* the people, *all* without a single exception, who participate in an event, it is absolutely impossible to describe the movement of mankind without the concept of a force that makes people direct their activity towards a single goal. And the only such concept known to historians is power.

This concept is the one handle by means of which the material of history can be mastered in today's accounting of it, and he who breaks off that handle, as Buckle did, without having learned any other method of dealing with historical material, only deprives himself of the last possibility of dealing with it. The inevitability of the concept of power for the explanation of historical phenomena is proved best of all by the general historians and historians of culture themselves, who allegedly renounce the concept of power and inevitably make use of it at every step.

Up to now, in relation to the question of mankind, historical science has been like circulating money—paper and coin. Biographies and histories of separate peoples are like paper money. They pass and circulate, fulfilling their purpose, without harming anyone and even being useful, until the question arises of what backs them up. We need only forget the question of how the will of heroes produces events, and the histories of Thiers will be interesting, instructive, and besides that will acquire a tinge of poetry. But just as doubt of the actual value of paper money will arise, either because, as it is so easy to make, a great deal of it will be made, or because people will want to exchange it for gold—in just the same way doubt arises about the actual meaning of histories of this sort, either because too many of them appear, or because someone in the simplicity of his heart will ask: by what force did Napoleon do that?—that is, will want to exchange paper currency for the pure gold of actual understanding.

General historians and historians of culture are like people who, having recognized the inconvenience of paper money, decide instead to make coins out of a metal that lacks the density of gold. And the money will indeed come out having the *clink* of coin, but only the *clink*. Paper money might still deceive the unknowing, whereas a coin that clinks but has no value will deceive no one. As gold is only gold when it can be used not for exchange alone, but also for real things, so, too, general historians will only be gold when they are able to answer the essential question of history: what is power? The general historians answer this question contradictorily, and the historians of culture push it aside altogether, answering something else. And as tokens that resemble gold can only be used among a group of people who agree to take them for gold, and among those who do not know the properties of gold, so, too, general historians and historians of culture, without answering the essential questions of mankind, for some sort of purposes of their own, serve as current money for the universities and the mass of readers—lovers of serious books, as they put it.

IV

Having renounced the view of the ancients on the divine submission of the will of the people to a chosen one and on the submission of that will to a divinity, history cannot take a single step without contradiction unless it chooses one of two things: either to return to the former faith in the direct participation of the divinity in the affairs of mankind, or to explain definitely the meaning of that force productive of historical events which is known as power.

To return to the first is impossible: belief has been destroyed, and therefore it is necessary to explain the meaning of power.

Napoleon gave orders to gather troops and go to war. We are so accustomed to this notion, we have grown so used to this view, that the question of why six hundred thousand men go to war when Napoleon says such-and-such words seems senseless to us. He had power, and therefore what he ordered was done.

This answer is perfectly satisfactory, if we believe that power was given to him from God. But as soon as we do not acknowledge that, it becomes necessary to define what this power of one man over others is.

This power cannot be the direct power of physical domination of a strong being over a weak, a domination based on the application or threat of the application of physical force, like the power of Hercules; nor can it be based on the domination of moral force, as some historians think in the simplicity of their hearts, when they say that historical figures are heroes, that is, men endowed with a special force of soul and mind which is called genius. This power cannot be based on the domination of moral force, for, not to speak of heroic men like Napoleon, about whose moral virtues opinions differ greatly, history shows us that neither the Louis XIs nor the Metternichs, who ruled over millions of people, had any special qualities of spiritual force, but were, on the contrary, for the most part morally weaker than each of the millions of people they ruled over.

If the source of power lies neither in the physical nor in the moral qualities of the person who possesses it, then it is obvious that the source of this power must be found outside this person—in those relations to the masses in which the person who possesses power finds himself.

That is exactly how power is understood by jurisprudence, that money changer of history, which promises to exchange the historical understanding of power for pure gold.

Power is the sum total of the wills of the masses, transferred by express or tacit agreement to rulers chosen by the masses.

In the domain of jurisprudence, which consists of arguments about how the state and power must be organized, if all that can be organized, this is all very clear, but when applied to history, this definition of power calls for elucidation.

Jurisprudence considers the state and power as the ancients considered fire—as something absolutely existent. But for history, the state and power are only phenomena, just as for present-day physics fire is not an element but a phenomenon.

From this fundamental difference between the views of history and of jurisprudence comes the fact that jurisprudence can speak in detail of how, in its opinion, power must be organized and what power is, existing immutably outside time; but to historical questions about the meaning of power as it changes in time it can give no answer.

If power is the transfer of the sum total of wills to a ruler, then is Pugachev a representative of the wills of the masses? If he is not, then why is Napoleon I? Why was Napoleon III a criminal when he was caught in Boulogne,[2] while later the criminals were the ones he caught?

During palace revolutions, in which two or three men sometimes take part, is the will of the masses also transferred to a new person? In international relations, is the will of the popular masses transferred to their conqueror? Was the will of the Confederation of the Rhine transferred to Napoleon in 1808?[3] Was the will of the mass of the Russian people transferred to Napoleon in 1809, when our troops in alliance with the French went to make war on Austria?

These questions can be answered in three ways:

Either (1) by recognizing that the will of the masses is always unconditionally handed over to a ruler or rulers whom they have chosen, and that therefore any rise of a new power, any struggle against the power once handed over, should be considered only as a violation of the real power.

Or (2) by recognizing that the will of the masses is transferred to a ruler conditionally, under definite and known conditions, and by showing that all constraints, clashes, and even destructions of power come from the non-observation by the rulers of the conditions under which power was transferred to them.

Or (3) by recognizing that the will of the masses is transferred to a ruler conditionally, but under unknown, undefined conditions, and that the rise of many powers, their struggle, and their fall come only from the greater or lesser degree to which the rulers fulfil those unknown conditions under which the wills of the masses are transferred from some persons to others.

And these are the three ways in which historians explain the relations of the masses to the rulers.

Some historians, not understanding, in the simplicity of their hearts, the question of the meaning of power, those same specialized and biographical historians of whom we have spoken above, seem to recognize that the sum total of the wills of the masses is transferred to historical figures unconditionally, and therefore, while describing some one power, these historians suppose that that same power alone is absolute and real, and that any other force opposing that real power is not power but a breach of power—violence.

Their theory, fit for primitive and peaceful periods of history, when applied to complex and stormy periods in the life of peoples, during which various powers arise simultaneously and struggle with each other, has the inconvenience that a legitimist historian will prove that the Convention, the Directoire, and Bonaparte were only breaches of power, while a republican and Bonapartist will prove—the one, that the Convention, and the other, that the empire was the real power, and that all the rest were breaches of power. It is obvious that the explanations of power by these historians, mutually refuting each other in this fashion, can be fit only for children of the most tender age.

Recognizing the falseness of this view of history, another sort of historian says that power is based on the conditional handing over to rulers of the sum total of the wills of the masses, and that historical figures have power only on condition of carrying out the programme which the will of the people has tacitly agreed to prescribe to them. But what those conditions consist in the historians do not tell us, or if they do, they constantly contradict each other.

Each historian, according to his view of what constitutes the goal of the movement of a people, sees those conditions as the greatness, wealth, freedom, enlightenment of the citizens of France or some other state. But to say nothing of the contradictions of historians as to what those conditions are, even allowing for the existence of a single programme of those conditions common to all, we will find that the historical facts almost always contradict this theory. If the conditions under which power is handed over consist in wealth, freedom, enlightenment of the people, then why do a Louis XIV and an Ivan the Terrible quietly live out their reigns, while a Louis XVI and a Charles I are executed by their people? To this question the historians answer that the activity of Louis XIV, being contrary to the programme, affected Louis XVI. But why did it not affect Louis XIV and XV; why did it affect precisely Louis XVI? And what is the term of this effect? To these questions there neither are nor can be any answers. Equally little explanation is given by this view of the reason why the sum total of wills is not transferred from its rulers and their successors for several centuries, but then suddenly, in the course of fifty years, is transferred to the Convention, the Directoire, Napoleon, Alexander, Louis XVIII, again to Napoleon, to Charles X, to Louis Philippe, to the republican government, to Napoleon III. While explaining these quickly occurring transfers of wills from one figure to another, especially to do with international relations, conquests, and alliances, these historians must involuntarily recognize that part of these phenomena are not regular transfers of wills, but accidents, depending now on cunning, now on error, or perfidy, or the weakness of a diplomat, or a monarch, or a party leader. So that the majority of historical phenomena— civil wars, revolutions, conquests—are presented by these historians not as the results of transfers of free wills, but as results of the false application of the will of one or several men, that is, again, as breaches of power. And therefore historical events of this sort, too, are presented by historians as deviations from theory.

These historians are like the botanist who, having observed that some plants emerge from the seed with two cotyledons, would insist that everything that grows, grows only by doubling itself into two leaves, and that a palm, and a mushroom, and even an oak, branching out in its full growth and no longer having any resemblance to two leaves, deviate from the theory.

Historians of the third sort recognize that the will of the masses is transferred to historical figures conditionally, but that these conditions are unknown to us.

They say that historical figures have power only because they carry out the will of the masses transferred to them.

But in that case, if the force that moves peoples is not in historical figures, but in the peoples themselves, what then is the significance of historical figures?

Historical figures, say these historians, express in themselves the will of the masses; the activity of historical figures serves to represent the activity of the masses.

But in that case the question arises: does all the activity of historical figures serve to express the will of the masses, or only some side of it? If all the activity of historical figures serves to express the will of the masses, as some think, then the biographies of the Napoleons and Catherines, with all the details of court gossip, serve to express the life of the people, which is an obvious absurdity; if only one side of the activity of a historical figure serves to express the life of the people, as other alleged philosopher-historians think, then, in order to determine which side of the activity of a historical figure expresses the life of the people, we must first know what the life of the people is.

Running into this difficulty, historians of this sort think up the most vague, intangible, and general abstraction, to which the greatest number of events can be accommodated, and say that this abstraction is the goal of the movement of mankind. The most usual general abstractions, accepted by almost all historians, are freedom, equality, enlightenment, progress, civilization, culture. Having posited some such abstraction as the goal of the movement of mankind, historians study those who have left the greatest number of memorials behind—kings, ministers, generals, writers, reformers, popes, journalists—to the extent that all these figures, in their opinion, have furthered or hindered that abstraction. But since nothing proves that the goal of mankind consists in freedom, equality, enlightenment, or civilization, and since the connection of the masses with the rulers and enlighteners of mankind is based only on the arbitrary assumption that the sum total of the wills of the masses is always transferred to the figures who are conspicuous for us, the activity of the millions of people who migrate, burn houses, abandon farming, and destroy each other, is never expressed in the description of the activity of a dozen figures who do not burn houses, are not concerned with farming, and do not kill their own kind.

History proves that at every step. Is the ferment among the people of the west at the end of the last century and their striving towards the east explained by the activity of Louis XIV, XV, XVI, their mistresses and ministers, by the lives of Napoleon, Rousseau, Diderot, Beaumarchais, and others?

Is the movement of the Russian people to the east, to Kazan and Siberia, expressed in the details of the morbid character of Ioann IV and his correspondence with Kurbsky?[4]

Is the movement of people during the Crusades explained by studies of the Godefroys and Louis and their ladies? We still find incomprehensible the movement of people from west to east without any goal, without leadership, with a crowd of vagabonds, with Peter the Hermit.[5] And still less comprehensible remains the ceasing of this movement once a reasonable, holy purpose for the campaign—the deliverance of Jerusalem—had been set by the historical actors. Popes, kings, and knights urged the people to liberate the Holy Land, but the people did not go, because the unknown reason that had prompted them to move earlier no longer existed. The history of the Godefroys and minnesingers obviously cannot contain the life of the people. And the history of the Godefroys and minnesingers has remained the history of the Godefroys and minnesingers, while the history of the life of the people and their motives has remained unknown.

Still less will the history of writers and reformers explain the life of the people to us.

The history of culture will explain to us the motives, the conditions of life, and the thought of a writer or reformer. We will learn that Luther had a hot temper and said such-and-such things; we will learn that Rousseau was mistrustful and wrote such-and-such books; but we will not learn why, after the Reformation, the peoples slaughtered each other and why, during the French revolution, they executed each other.

If we combine these two sorts of history, as modern historians do, we will get the history of monarchs and writers, and not the history of the life of peoples.

V

The life of peoples cannot be contained in the lives of several men, for the connection between these several men and the peoples has not been found. The theory that this connection is based on the transfer of the sum total of wills to historical figures is a hypothesis not confirmed by the experience of history.

The theory of the transfer of the sum total of wills of the masses to historical figures may explain a great deal in the sphere of jurisprudence and may be necessary for its purposes; but in its application to history, once revolutions, conquests, civil wars appear, once history begins—this theory explains nothing.

This theory seems irrefutable precisely because the act of transferring the wills of the people cannot be verified, since it never took place.

Whatever event takes place, whoever stands at the head of the event, the theory can always say that this person stood at the head of the event because the sum total of wills was transferred to him.

The answers that this theory gives to historical questions are like the answers of a man who, looking at a moving herd, and taking no account either of the quality of pasture in different parts of the field or the urgings of the herdsman, would judge the reasons for this or that direction of the herd by which animal is at the head of the herd.

"The herd is going in this direction because the animal at the head of it is leading it, and the sum total of wills of all the rest of the animals is transferred to this ruler of the herd." So answers the first category of historians, who recognize the absolute transfer of power.

"If the animals at the head of the herd change, that happens because the sum total of wills of all the animals is transferred from one ruler to another, depending on whether he leads the herd in the direction the entire herd has chosen." So answer the historians who recognize that the sum total of wills of the masses is transferred to the rulers under conditions which they consider known. (Given this method of observation, it quite often happens that the observer, depending on the direction chosen by the herd, considers animals as leaders who, as a result of a change in the direction of the masses, are no longer in front, but on the side, and sometimes behind.)

"If the animals at the head change constantly and the direction of the entire herd changes constantly, that happens because, to attain the direction which is known to us, the animals hand over their wills to animals that are conspicuous to us, and thus, in order to study the movement of the herd, we must observe all the conspicuous animals going on all sides of the herd." So speak historians of the third category, who recognize all historical figures, from monarchs to journalists, as expressive of their time.

The theory of the transfer of the will of the masses to historical figures is only a paraphrase—only an expression of the words of the question in different words.

What is the cause of historical events? Power. What is power? Power is the sum total of wills transferred to one person. On what condition are the wills of the masses transferred to one person? On condition that the person express the will of the whole people. That is, power is power. That is, power is a word the meaning of which we do not understand.

If the domain of human knowledge were limited to abstract thinking alone, then, having subjected the explanation of power given by *science* to criticism, mankind would come to the conclusion that power is only a word and does not exist in reality. But for the apprehending of phenomena, besides abstract thinking, man has the tool of experience, with which he verifies the results of thinking. And experience says that power is not a word, but an actually existing phenomenon.

Not to mention the fact that, without the concept of power, no description of the sum total of human activity is possible, the existence of power is proved by history as well as by the observation of contemporary events.

Whenever an event takes place, a man or men always appear by whose will the event appears to take place. Napoleon III gives the command, and the French go to Mexico. The king of Prussia and Bismarck give the command, and troops go to Bohemia. Napoleon I gives the order, and troops go to Russia. Alexander I gives the order, and the French submit to the Bourbons.[6] Experience shows us that, whenever an event takes place, it is always connected with the will of one or several persons who have ordered it.

Historians, from the old habit of acknowledging divine participation in human affairs, want to see the cause of an event in the expression of the will of the person invested with power; but that conclusion is confirmed neither by reasoning nor by experience.

On the one hand, reasoning shows that the expression of the will of man in words is only part of the general activity expressed in an event such as a war or a revolution; and therefore, without recognizing an incomprehensible supernatural force—a miracle—it is impossible to allow that words could be the immediate cause of the movement of millions; on the other hand, even if we allow that words can be the cause of an event, history shows that the expression of the will of historical figures in the majority of cases produces no effect at all, that is, that their orders often are not only not carried out, but that sometimes what takes place is even the opposite of what they ordered.

Unless we allow for divine participation in human affairs, we cannot take power as the cause of events.

Power, from the point of view of experience, is only the dependence that exists between the expression of a person's will and the carrying out of that will by other people.

In order to explain the conditions of that dependence to ourselves, we must first of all restore the concept of the expression of will, referring it to man and not to a divinity.

If a divinity gives an order, expresses its will, as the history of the ancients shows us, the expression of that will does not depend on time and is not caused by anything, since the divinity is in no way connected with the event. But, speaking of orders as the expression of the will of people who act in time and are connected among themselves, we should restore, so as to explain to ourselves the connection of orders with events: (1) the condition of all that takes place—the continuity of the movement in time both of events and of the person who gives orders, and (2) the condition of the necessary connection of the person who gives orders to the people who carry out his orders.

VI

Only the expression of the will of a divinity not dependent on time can pertain to a whole series of events that are to take place over several years or centuries, and only a divinity, without cause, by its will alone, can determine the direction of mankind's movement. Man acts in time and himself participates in events.

In restoring the first omitted condition—the condition of time—we will see that not a single order can be carried out without the existence of a previous order that makes possible the carrying out of the later one.

Never does a single order appear spontaneously and not include in itself a whole series of events; but each order follows from another and never pertains to a whole series of events, but always only to one moment of the event.

When we say, for instance, that Napoleon ordered the army to go to war, we unite into one simultaneously expressed order a series of consecutive orders dependent on each other. Napoleon could not order a campaign against Russia and never did. Today he ordered such-and-such papers written to Vienna, Berlin, and Petersburg; tomorrow, such-and-such decrees and orders to the army, the fleet, the commissariat, and so on, and so forth—millions of orders, which formed a series of orders corresponding to a series of events which brought French troops to Russia.

If Napoleon, throughout his reign, keeps giving orders about the expedition to England, expends more effort and time on it than on any other of his undertakings, and, despite that, throughout his reign, never once attempts to carry out his intention, but makes an expedition to Russia, with which, by his more than once expressed conviction, he considers it more advantageous to be in alliance, this happens because the first series of orders did not correspond to a series of events and the second series of orders did.

To be certain that an order will be carried out, one must give such orders as can be carried out. But to know what can and cannot be carried out is impossible, not only for Napoleon's campaign in Russia, in which millions take part, but even for the most uncomplicated event, because the carrying out of the one and the other can always meet with millions of obstacles. Each order carried out is always one of a great many that are not carried out. All the impossible orders are not connected with the event and are not carried out. Only those that are possible are connected in a consecutive series of orders that correspond to a series of events and are carried out.

Our false notion that the order that precedes an event is the cause of the event comes from the fact that, once an event has taken place and out of thousands of orders only those connected with the event were carried out, we forget about those that were not, because they could not be carried out. Besides,

the chief source of our error in this sense comes from the fact that, in a historical account, a whole series of countless, diverse, minuscule events, such as all
that brought French troops to Russia, is generalized into one event, according
to the result this series of events produced, and in correspondence with this
generalization, the whole series of orders is also generalized into one expression of will.

We say: Napoleon wanted to and did campaign against Russia. In reality, we
will never find in all the activity of Napoleon anything resembling the expression of such a will, but we will see the series of orders or expressions of his will
directed in the most diverse and indefinite way. Out of a countless series of
Napoleon's orders that were not carried out, the series of orders carried out for
the campaign of the year twelve composed itself, not because those orders were
in any way different from the others that were not carried out, but because the
series of those orders corresponded to the series of events that brought French
troops to Russia; just as in stencilling, some figure or other gets painted, not
depending on the direction or manner in which the paint is applied, but because
the figure cut out of the stencil is smeared in all directions with paint.

So that, considering the relation of orders to events in time, we will find that
orders can in no way be the cause of events, but that there exists a certain
dependence between the one and the other.

To understand what this dependence is, it is necessary to restore another
omitted condition of any order proceeding not from a divinity, but from a man,
which consists in the fact that the man who orders participates in the event
himself.

This relation of the one who orders to those whom he orders is precisely
what is called power. This relation consists in the following:

For common activity people always form themselves into certain units
within which, despite the variety of purposes set for the joint action, the relation among the people participating in the activity is always the same.

In forming these units, people always arrive at such relations among themselves that the largest number of people take the largest direct part and the
smallest number of people the smallest direct part in the joint action for which
they have come together.

Of all the units that people form for carrying out joint actions, one of the
most distinct and definite is an army.

Every army is made up of members of the lowest military rank—privates—
of whom there is always the largest number; of members of the next higher
military rank—corporals, sergeants—who are fewer in number than the first;
of still higher rank, who are still fewer in number; and so on to the highest military power, which is concentrated in one person.

Military organization can be expressed with perfect precision in the figure of
the cone, in which the base with the largest diameter would be made up of the

privates; the higher, smaller sections of the higher ranks of the army, and so on to the apex of the cone, the point of which would be the commander in chief.

The soldiers, of whom there is the largest number, constitute the lowest points of the cone and its base. The soldier himself directly stabs, cuts, burns, loots, and always receives orders for these actions from higher-placed persons; he himself never gives orders. A sergeant (the number of sergeants is already smaller) performs the action itself more rarely than the soldier, but he does give orders. An officer still more rarely performs the action itself and still more often gives orders. A general only orders the troops to move, pointing to the goal, and almost never uses weapons. The commander can never take a direct part in the action itself and only gives general instructions about the movement of the masses. The same relations of persons among themselves is manifested in any group of people united for common activity—in farming, trade, and any management.

And so, without artificially separating all the converging points of the cone and ranks of the army, or the titles and positions of any management or common business, from lowest to highest, a law is manifested according to which, for the carrying out of a joint action, people always form themselves into such relations that the more immediately people participate in carrying out the action, the less they can give orders and the greater their number; and the smaller the direct part that people take in the action itself, the more they give orders and the smaller their number, rising in this way from the lowest layers to the one last man, who takes the least direct part in the event and more than all aims his activity at giving orders.

This relation of the persons who give orders to those whom they order constitutes the essence of the concept known as power.

Having restored the conditions of time under which all events occur, we found that an order is executed only when it refers to a corresponding series of events. Restoring the necessary condition of the connection between the one who orders and the one who carries out, we have found that it is an inherent property of those who order to take the least part in the event itself and that their activity is aimed exclusively at giving orders.

VII

When some event takes place, people express their opinions and wishes about the event, and since the event results from the joint action of many people, one of the opinions or wishes expressed is bound to be fulfilled, if only approximately. When one of the opinions expressed is fulfilled, that opinion is connected with the event as the order preceding it.

Men are dragging a log. Each of them expresses his opinion about how and where to drag it. The men drag the log out, and it is discovered that it was done the way one of them had said. He gave the order. Here are order and power in their primitive form.

The one who mainly worked with his hands was less able to think over what he was doing, to consider what might come of the common activity, and to give orders. The one who mainly gave orders, as a consequence of his verbal activity, was obviously less able to act with his hands. The greater the assembly of people aiming their activity at a single goal, the more sharply set off is the category of people who take a less direct part in the common activity, the more their activity is aimed at giving orders.

A man, when he acts alone, always bears within himself a certain series of considerations which guided, as it seems to him, his past activity, serve him as a justification for his present activity, and guide him in his suppositions about his future acts.

Assemblies of people do exactly the same thing, leaving it to those who do not participate in the action to think up considerations, justifications, and suppositions about their joint activity.

For reasons known or unknown to us, the French begin to drown and slaughter each other. And the event is correspondingly accompanied by its justification in the expressed wills of the people about the necessity of it for the welfare of France, for liberty, for equality. People stop slaughtering each other, and this event is accompanied by its justification in the necessity to unify power, to repulse Europe, and so on. People go from west to east, killing their own kind, and this event is accompanied by words about the glory of France, the baseness of England, and so on. History shows us that these justifications of the event have no general sense and contradict themselves, like killing a man in recognition of his rights, and killing millions in Russia to humiliate England. But in a contemporary sense, these justifications have a necessary significance.

These justifications take away the moral responsibility of the people who produce events. These temporary goals are similar to the brushes that go in front of a train to clear the way on the rails: they clear the way of people's moral responsibility. Without these justifications, there could be no explaining the simplest question, which presents itself with the examination of every event: how is it that millions of people commit joint crimes, wars, killings, and so on?

Given the complex present-day forms of state and social life in Europe, is it possible to think up any sort of event that would not have been prescribed, indicated, ordered by sovereigns, ministers, parliaments, the newspapers? Is there any joint action that would not find its justification in state unity, in nationality, in the balance of Europe, in civilization? Thus every event that takes place inevitably coincides with some expressed desire, and, receiving its justification, is seen as a product of the will of one or more persons.

Wherever a moving ship may be heading, at its bow will always be seen the swirl of the wave it cuts through. For people on the ship, the movement of that swirl will be the only noticeable movement.

Only by following closely, moment by moment, the movement of that swirl and comparing that movement with the movement of the ship, will we realize that at every moment the movement of the swirl is determined by the movement of the ship, and that we were misled by the fact that we ourselves were imperceptibly moving.

We will see the same thing if we follow moment by moment the movement of historical figures (that is, having restored the necessary condition of all that happens—the condition of the continuity of movement in time) and do not lose sight of the necessary connection of historical figures with the masses.

When a ship goes in one direction, there is one and the same swirl at its bow; when it frequently changes direction, the swirl running ahead of it also shifts frequently. But wherever it turns, there will always be a swirl preceding its movement.

Whatever happens, it will always turn out that that very thing had been foreseen and ordered. Wherever a ship heads, the swirl, without guiding it, without reinforcing its movement, foams at its bow, and from afar will appear to us not only to be moving by its own will, but to be guiding the movement of the ship.

Considering only those expressions of the will of historical figures which relate to events as orders, historians have supposed that events depend on orders. Considering the events by themselves and that connection with the masses in which historical figures find themselves, we have discovered that historical figures and their orders depend on the event. The unquestionable proof of this conclusion is the fact that, however great the number of orders, the event will not take place unless there are other reasons for it; but once the event— whatever it may be—takes place, there will be found, among the ceaselessly expressed wills of various persons, those which, by their sense and timing, will relate to the event as orders.

Having come to this conclusion, we can answer directly and positively those two essential questions of history:

(1) What is power?

(2) What force produces the movement of peoples?

(1) Power is that relation of a certain person to other persons in which the person takes the less part in the action the more he expresses opinions, suppositions, and justifications for the jointly accomplished action.

(2) The movement of peoples is produced, not by power, not by intellectual activity, not even by a combination of the two, as historians used to think, but by the activity of *all* the people taking part in the event and always joining together in such a way that those who take the greatest direct part in the event, take the least responsibility upon themselves, and vice versa.

In the moral respect, the cause of the event appears to be power; in the physical respect, those who submit to power. But since moral activity is unthinkable without physical activity, the cause of the event is neither the one nor the other, but a combination of the two.

Or, in other words, the concept of a cause is inapplicable to the phenomenon we are considering.

In the last analysis, we arrive at an eternal circle, at that utmost brink at which, in every domain of thought, the human mind always arrives, if it is not toying with its subject. Electricity produces heat, heat produces electricity. Atoms attract each other, atoms repel each other.

In speaking of the interaction of heat and electricity or of atoms, we cannot tell why it happens that way, and we say that it is that way because it is unthinkable otherwise, because it has to be that way, because it is a law. It is the same with respect to historical phenomena. Why does a war or a revolution take place? We do not know; we know only that for the accomplishment of the one action or the other, people form themselves into certain units and all participate; and we say that this is so because it is unthinkable otherwise, because it is a law.

VIII

If history had to do with no more than external phenomena, the positing of this simple and obvious law would be enough, and we would be done with our argument. But the law of history relates to man. A particle of matter cannot tell us that it feels no need at all to attract or repel and that it is not true; but man, who is the subject of history, says outright: I am free and therefore not subject to the law.

The presence of the question of man's free will, though unspoken, is felt at every step of history.

All serious-minded historians have involuntarily arrived at this question. All the contradictions and obscurities of history, the wrong path that this science has taken, are based only on the non-solution of this question.

If the will of each man were free, that is, if each could act as he pleased, the whole of history would be a series of incoherent accidents.

If even one man out of millions in a thousand-year period of time has had the possibility of acting freely, that is, as he pleased, then it is obvious that one free act of this man, contrary to the laws, destroys the possibility of the existence of any laws whatever for the whole of mankind.

If there is just one law that governs the actions of men, then there can be no free will, for the will of men would have to submit to that law.

In this contradiction lies the question of freedom of the will, which from ancient times has occupied the best minds of mankind and since ancient times has been posed in all its enormous significance.

The question consists in the fact that, in looking at man as an object of observation from any point of view—theological, historical, ethical, philosophical— we find a general law of necessity to which he is subject, like all that exists. While looking at him from within ourselves, as that which we are conscious of, we feel ourselves free.

This consciousness is a totally separate source of self-knowledge, independent of reason. Through reason man observes himself, but he knows himself only through consciousness.

Without consciousness of oneself, no observation and no application of reason are thinkable.

In order to understand, observe, deduce, man must first be conscious of himself as alive. A living man knows himself not otherwise than as wanting, that is, he is conscious of his will. And his will, which constitutes the essence of his life, man is conscious of and cannot be conscious of otherwise than as free.

If, subjecting himself to observation, man sees that his will is always directed according to one and the same law (whether he observes the necessity of taking food, or the activity of the brain, or whatever), he cannot understand this always identical direction of his will otherwise than as a limitation of it. That which is not free cannot be limited. Man's will appears limited to him precisely because he is conscious of it not otherwise than as free.

You say: I am not free. But I have raised and lowered my arm. Everyone understands that this illogical answer is an irrefutable proof of freedom.

This answer is the expression of a consciousness not subject to reason.

If the consciousness of freedom were not a separate source of self-knowledge, independent of reason, it would be subject to reasoning and experience; but in reality such subjection never occurs and is unthinkable.

A series of experiments and arguments shows each man that as an object of observation he is subject to certain laws, and man submits to them and never fights against the law of gravity or of impermeability, once he knows them. But that same series of experiments and arguments shows him that full freedom, which he is conscious of in himself, is impossible, that his every action depends on his constitution, his character, and the motives that influence him; yet man never submits to the conclusions of these experiments and arguments.

Having learned from experience and argument that a stone falls downwards, man believes it unquestioningly and in all cases expects the law he has learned to be fulfilled.

But, having learned as unquestionably that his will is subject to laws, he does not and cannot believe it.

However many times experience and argument have shown a man that in the same conditions, with the same character, he would do the same thing he did before, he, when he sets out for the thousandth time, in the same conditions, with the same character, on an action that has always ended the same way, undoubtedly feels no less certain that he can act as he pleases than he did before the experience. Every man, savage or sage, however irrefutably argument and experience prove to him that it is impossible to imagine two acts in the same conditions, feels that without this senseless notion (which constitutes the essence of freedom), he cannot imagine life. He feels that, impossible as it may be, it is so; for without this notion of freedom, he not only would not understand life, but could not live for a single moment.

He could not live, because all man's strivings, all his impulses to life, are but strivings towards greater freedom. Wealth and poverty, fame and obscurity, power and submission, strength and weakness, health and sickness, education and ignorance, work and idleness, satiety and hunger, virtue and vice are nothing but greater or lesser degrees of freedom.

It is impossible to imagine to oneself a man who has no freedom otherwise than as deprived of life.

If for reason the concept of freedom presents itself as senselessly contradictory, like the possibility of performing two acts in the same moment of time or an action without a cause, that only proves that consciousness is not subject to reason.

This consciousness of freedom, unshakable, irrefutable, not subject to experience or argument, recognized by all thinkers and sensed by all human beings without exception, a consciousness without which any notion of man is unthinkable, constitutes the other side of the question.

Man is the creation of an almighty, all-good, and all-knowing God. What then is sin, the concept of which follows from the consciousness of man's freedom? That is a question for theology.

Men's actions are subject to general, immutable laws expressed by statistics. In what, then, consists man's responsibility before society, the concept of which follows from the consciousness of man's freedom? That is a question for jurisprudence.

Man's acts follow from his innate character and the motives acting upon him. What is conscience and the consciousness of the good and evil of acts following from the consciousness of freedom? That is a question for ethics.

A man, in connection with the common life of mankind, appears subject to the laws defining that life. But the same man, independent of that connection, appears free. How should the past life of peoples and of mankind be regarded—as a product of the free or unfree activity of men? That is a question for history.

Only in our self-confident time of the popularization of knowledge, thanks to that most powerful tool of ignorance—the spread of printing—has the question of freedom of will been reduced to grounds on which the question itself cannot exist. In our time the majority of so-called advanced people, that is, a crowd of ignoramuses, have taken the works of the naturalists, who study one side of the question, for the solution of the whole question.

The soul and freedom do not exist, because the life of man is expressed in muscular movements, and muscular movements are conditioned by nervous activity; the soul and freedom do not exist, because at some unknown period of time we descended from the apes—they say, write, and print, not even suspecting that thousands of years ago all religions and all thinkers not only recognized but never tried to deny that very law of necessity which they now try so zealously to prove by means of physiology and comparative zoology. They do not see that the role of natural science in this question consists only in serving as an instrument to throw light on one side of it. For the fact that, from the point of view of observation, reason and will are only secretions of the brain, and man, following a general law, could develop from lower animals at an unknown period of time, only clarifies from a new side a truth recognized thousands of years ago by all religious and philosophical theories, that from the viewpoint of reason man is subject to the laws of necessity, but does not advance by a hair the solution of the question, which has another, opposite side, based on the consciousness of freedom.

If men descended from the apes at an unknown period of time, that is as comprehensible as that men descended from a handful of earth at a known period of time (in the first case the x is time, in the second the descent), and the question of how the consciousness of man's freedom can be combined with the law of necessity to which man is subject cannot be resolved by comparative physiology and zoology, for in the frog, the rabbit, and the ape we can observe only muscular and nervous activity, while in man both muscular and nervous activity and consciousness.

The naturalists and their admirers, who think to solve this question, are like plasterers assigned to plaster one side of a church wall, who, taking advantage of the foreman's absence, in a fit of zeal smear their plaster all over the windows, the icons, the scaffolding, and the as yet unreinforced walls, and rejoice at how, from their plastering point of view, everything comes out flat and smooth.

IX

For the solution of the question of freedom and necessity, history has the advantage over other branches of knowledge in which the same question is raised, that for history this question refers not to the essence of man's will, but to the notion of the manifestation of that will in the past and under certain conditions.

For the solution of this question, history stands to other sciences in the position of an experimental science to speculative sciences.

History has as its subject not the will of man itself, but our notion of it.

And therefore the insoluble mystery of the combining of the two opposites, freedom and necessity, does not exist for history, as it does for theology, ethics, and philosophy. History examines the notion of man's life in which the combining of these two opposites has already taken place.

In actual life, every historical event, every human action, is understood quite clearly and definitely, without the least sense of contradiction, even though each event appears partly free and partly necessary.

To solve the question of how freedom and necessity are combined and what constitutes the essence of these two concepts, the philosophy of history can and must follow a path opposite to the one other sciences have taken. Instead of defining the concepts of freedom and necessity in themselves, and then fitting the phenomena of life to the worked-out definitions, history must take the immense number of phenomena lying before it, which always appear dependent on freedom and necessity, and from them derive a definition of the concepts of freedom and necessity themselves.

Whatever notion of the activity of many people or one man we examine, we understand it not otherwise than as a product partly of freedom and partly of the law of necessity.

Whether we are speaking of the migration of peoples and the raids of barbarians, or of the decrees of Napoleon III, or of the act of a man, performed an hour ago, which consisted in choosing one direction out of many for a stroll— we see not the slightest contradiction. The measure of freedom and necessity that guided the acts of these men is clearly defined for us.

Quite often the notion of greater or lesser freedom varies according to the different points of view from which we examine a phenomenon; but—always in the same way—every human action appears to us not otherwise than as a certain conjunction of freedom and necessity. In every action examined, we see a certain portion of freedom and a certain portion of necessity. And always, the more freedom we see in whatever action, the less necessity; and the more necessity, the less freedom.

The ratio of freedom to necessity decreases or increases depending on the point of view from which the action is examined; but this ratio always remains inversely proportional.

A drowning man who clutches another and drowns him, or a hungry mother, exhausted from nursing her baby, who steals food, or a man accustomed to discipline who stands in a firing squad and kills a defenceless man on command, appears less guilty, that is, less free and more subject to the law of necessity, to someone who knows the conditions these people were in, and more free to someone who does not know that the man was himself drowning, that the mother was hungry, that the soldier was in a firing squad, and so on. In the same way, a man who twenty years ago committed a murder, and after that lived peacefully and harmlessly in society, appears less guilty—his act more subject to the law of necessity—for someone who examines it after a lapse of twenty years, and more free to someone who examined it the day after it was committed. And in the same way, every act of a crazy, drunk, or greatly agitated man appears less free and more necessary to someone who knows the inner state of the one who commits the act, and more free and less necessary to someone who does not know it. In all these cases, the concept of freedom increases or decreases and, correspondingly, the concept of necessity decreases or increases, depending on the point of view from which the act is examined. So that the greater the necessity appears, the lesser the freedom appears. And vice versa.

Religion, mankind's common sense, jurisprudence, and history itself understand this ratio between necessity and freedom in the same way.

All occasions without exception in which our notion of freedom and necessity increases and decreases have only three bases:

(1) The relation of the man committing the act to the external world,

(2) to time, and

(3) to the causes producing the act.

(1) The first basis is the relation more or less visible to us of the man to the external world, the more or less clear notion of that definite place which every man occupies in relation to everything that exists simultaneously with him. This is that basis owing to which it is obvious that the drowning man is less free and more subject to necessity than a man standing on dry land; that basis owing to which the actions of a man living in close connection with other people in a densely populated area, the actions of a man who is connected with family, work, enterprises, appear unquestionably less free and more subject to necessity than the actions of man who is single and solitary.

If we examine a man alone, without his relation to everything around him, his every action appears free to us. But if we see at least some relation to what is around him, if we see his connection with anything whatever—with the man who is talking to him, with the book he is reading, with the work he is doing, even with the air that surrounds him, even with the light that falls on things around him—we see that each of these conditions has an influence on him and guides at least one side of his activity. And insofar as we see these influences, so far our notion of his freedom decreases and our notion of the necessity he is subject to increases.

(2) The second basis is the more or less visible temporal relation of man to the world; the more or less clear notion of the place that the action of a man occupies in time. This is that basis owing to which the fall of the first man, which had as its consequence the origin of mankind, appears, obviously, less

free than a modern man's marriage. This is that basis owing to which the life and activity of people who lived centuries ago, and are connected with me in time, cannot appear as free to me as modern life, the consequences of which are still unknown to me.

The degree of our notion of greater or lesser freedom and necessity in this relation depends on the greater or lesser span of time between the committing of the act and our judgement of it.

If I examine an act I committed a moment ago, under approximately the same conditions as I am in now, my action seems unquestionably free to me. But if I review an act I committed a month ago, I involuntarily recognize, being in different conditions, that if that act had not been committed, many useful, agreeable, and even necessary things which resulted from that act would not have taken place. If I transport myself in memory to an act still more remote, ten years back or more, the consequences of my act will appear still more obvious to me; and it will be hard for me to imagine what would have happened if the act had not been done. The further back I transport myself in memory, or, what is the same, ahead in my judgement, the more questionable my argument about the freedom of the act will become.

In history we find exactly the same progression of convincingness about the portion of free will in the general affairs of mankind. A just-accomplished contemporary event appears to us as unquestionably proceeding from all known people; but in a more remote event we see its inevitable consequences, aside from which we cannot imagine anything else. And the further back we transport ourselves in examining events, the less arbitrary they appear to us.

The Austro-Prussian war appears to us as the unquestionable consequence of the actions of cunning Bismarck, and so on.

The Napoleonic wars, though questionably now, still appear to us as proceeding from the wills of heroes; in the Crusades we already see an event which occupies a definite place and without which the modern history of Europe is unthinkable, though in the same way, for the chroniclers of the Crusades, this event appeared only as proceeding from the wills of several persons. As for the migrations of peoples, it never occurs to anyone in our time that the renewal of the European world depended on the good pleasure of Attila. The further back in history we transport the object of our observation, the more questionable becomes the freedom of the men producing events, and the more obvious the law of necessity.

(3) The third basis is the greater or lesser accessibility for us of that endless linking of causes that constitutes the inevitable demand of reason and in which every phenomenon comprehended, and therefore every human action, should have its definite place, as a consequence of what precedes and a cause of what follows.

This is that basis owing to which our own and other people's actions appear to us, on the one hand, as more free and less subject to necessity, the more we know of those physiological, psychological, and historical laws man is subject to, deduced from observation, and the more correctly we perceive the physiological, psychological, or historical cause of the action; and on the other hand, the simpler the observed action itself and the less complex the character and mind of the man whose action we are examining.

When we totally fail to understand the cause of an act—whether an evil deed, a good deed, or even an act indifferent to good and evil—we recognize in such an act a greater share of freedom. If it is an evil deed, we most of all demand punishment for such an act; if it is a good deed, we most of all appreciate such an act. If it is indifferent, we recognize its greater individuality, originality, freedom. But if just one of the countless reasons is known to us, we already recognize a certain share of necessity and demand a lesser requital for the crime, recognize a lesser merit in the good deed, a lesser freedom in the seemingly original act. The fact that a criminal was brought up among evildoers already extenuates his guilt. The selflessness of a father, of a mother, selflessness with a possibility of reward, is more comprehensible than causeless selflessness, and therefore appears less deserving of sympathy, less free. The founder of a sect or party, the inventor, surprise us less when we know how and by what his activity was prepared for. If we have a large series of experiences, if our observation is constantly directed at finding the correlation of causes and effects in people's actions, their actions appear the more necessary and the less free to us, the more correctly we connect effects with causes. If the examined actions are simple, and we have for observation an enormous number of such actions, our notion of their necessity will be more complete. The dishonest act of the son of a dishonest father, the bad behaviour of a woman who ended up in a certain milieu, a drunkard's return to drinking, and so on, are actions which appear the less free to us, the more comprehensible we find their cause. And if the person himself whose actions we are examining stands on the lowest level of mental development, like a child, a madman, a simpleton, then, knowing the causes of the action and the incomplexity of his character and mind, we already see so large a share of necessity and so small of freedom, that once the cause that is to produce the action is known to us, we can predict the act.

Only on these three bases have irresponsibility for crimes and extenuating circumstances, which exist in all legal codes, been constructed. Responsibility appears greater or lesser, depending on a greater or lesser knowledge of the conditions in which the man whose action is being reviewed found himself, and on the greater or lesser span of time from the committing of the act to the judging of it, and on the greater or lesser understanding of the causes of the act.

X

Thus our notion of freedom and necessity gradually decreases or increases, depending on the greater or lesser connection with the external world, the greater or lesser distance in time, and the greater or lesser dependence on causes in which we examine the phenomenon of human life.

So that, if we examine a man in such a situation that his connection with the external world is most fully known, the period between the time of judgement and the time of committing the act is longest, and the causes of the act are most accessible, then we get the notion of the greatest necessity and the least freedom. But if we examine a man in least dependence on external conditions, if his action is committed in the moment closest to the present, and the causes of his action are inaccessible to us, then we will get the notion of the least necessity and the greatest freedom.

But neither in the one case nor in the other, however we may change our point of view, however we may try to grasp what connection the man finds himself in with the external world, or however inaccessible it seems to us, however much we lengthen or shorten the period of time, however intelligible or unfathomable the causes are for us—we can never imagine either total freedom or total necessity.

(1) However we may try to imagine a man excluded from the influences of the external world, we will never arrive at a concept of freedom in space. A man's every action is inevitably conditioned by what surrounds him and by his own body. I raise my arm and lower it. My action seems free to me; but asking myself if I could raise my arm in any direction, I see that I raised my arm in the direction in which there were fewest obstacles to that action either from bodies around me or from the structure of my own body. If, out of all possible directions, I chose one, I did so because there were fewer obstacles in that direction. For my action to be free, it is necessary that it not meet with any obstacles. To imagine man as free, we must imagine him outside space, which is obviously impossible.

(2) However close together we bring the time of judgement to the time of the act, we will never get a concept of freedom in time. For if I examine an act committed a second ago, I must still recognize the unfreedom of the act, since the act is bound to the moment of time in which it was committed. Can I raise my arm? I raise it, but I ask myself: could I have not raised my arm in that already past moment of time? To convince myself of it, I do not raise my arm in the next moment. But it is not in that first moment when I asked myself about freedom that I did not raise my arm. Time went by, it was not in my power to stop it, and the arm which I then raised and the air in which I then made that movement are no longer the air which now surrounds me and the arm with which I

now do not make that movement. The moment in which the first movement was performed is irretrievable, and at that moment I could make only one movement, and whatever movement I made, that movement could be the only one. The fact that I did not raise my arm the next moment does not prove that I could have not raised it. And since my movement could be the only one in one moment of time, it could not be any other. To imagine it as free, one must imagine it in the present, at the border of past and future, that is, outside time, which is impossible.

(3) However much the difficulty of comprehending causes may increase, we will never arrive at the notion of total freedom, that is, the absence of cause. However unfathomable for us is the cause of the expression of will in any act of mine or others, the first demand of intelligence is the assumption of and search for a cause, without which no phenomenon is conceivable. I raise my arm in order to perform an act independent of any cause, but the fact that I want to perform an act that has no cause, is the cause of my act.

But even if, imagining a man completely excluded from all influences, examining only his instantaneous act in the present, not provoked by any cause, we should allow the infinitesimally small remainder of necessity to equal zero, we would still not arrive at a notion of man's total freedom; for a being who is not affected by the influences of the external world, who is outside time and does not depend on causes, is no longer a man.

In the same way, we can never imagine the actions of a man without any participation of freedom and subject only to the law of necessity.

(1) However much our knowledge of the spatial conditions in which man finds himself may increase, that knowledge can never be complete, since the number of those conditions is as infinitely great as space is infinite. And therefore, so long as not *all* the conditions influencing man are defined, there is no complete necessity, and there is a certain share of freedom.

(2) However much we may lengthen the period of time between the phenomenon we are examining and the time of judgement, that period will be finite, while time is infinite, and therefore, in this respect, there can never be complete necessity.

(3) However accessible the chain of causes of any event, we will never know the entire chain, because it is endless, and again we will never get complete necessity.

But, besides that, even if, having allowed the smallest remainder of freedom to equal zero, we were to recognize in some case—for instance, a dying man, a foetus, an idiot—a total absence of freedom, we would thereby destroy the very concept of the man we are examining; because once there is no freedom, there is no man. And therefore to imagine the action of a man that is subject only to the law of necessity, without the slightest remainder of freedom, is as impossible as to imagine a totally free action.

Thus, to imagine the act of a man that is subject to the law of necessity alone, without freedom, we must allow for knowledge of an *infinite* number of spatial conditions, an *infinitely* great period of time, and an *infinite* series of causes.

To imagine a man who is completely free, not subject to the law of necessity, we must imagine him alone, *outside space, outside time,* and *outside any dependence on causes.*

In the first case, if necessity without freedom were possible, we would arrive at the definition of the law of necessity by that same necessity, that is, at form alone without content.

In the second case, if freedom without necessity were possible, we would arrive at unconditional freedom outside space, time, and causes, which, by the very fact of being unconditional and unlimited by anything, would be nothing, or content alone without form.

We would arrive generally at those two bases from which man's whole worldview is formed—at the unfathomable essence of life and at the laws which define that essence.

Reason says: (1) Space, with all the forms which its visibility—matter—gives it, is infinite and cannot be conceived otherwise. (2) Time is infinite movement without a moment's rest, and cannot be conceived otherwise. (3) The linking of causes and effects has no beginning and can have no end.

Consciousness says: (1) I am alone, and all that exists is only I; consequently, I include space; (2) I measure fleeting time by the unmoving moment of the present, in which alone I am conscious of myself as living; consequently, I am outside time; and (3) I am outside cause, for I feel myself to be the cause of every manifestation of my life.

Reason expresses the laws of necessity. Consciousness expresses the essence of freedom.

Freedom, not limited by anything, is the essence of life in the consciousness of man. Necessity without content is man's reason with its three forms.

Freedom is that which is examined. Necessity is that which examines. Freedom is content. Necessity is form.

Only by the separation of the two sources of cognition, which are related to each other as form to content, do we get the distinct, mutually exclusive, and unfathomable concepts of freedom and necessity.

Only by their union do we get a clear picture of the life of man.

Outside these two concepts, mutually defining in their union as form and content, no picture of life is possible.

All that we know about the life of men is only a certain relation of freedom to necessity, that is, of consciousness to the laws of reason.

All that we know about the external world of nature is only a certain relation of the forces of nature to necessity, or of the essence of life to the laws of reason.

The forces of the life of nature lie outside us and we are not conscious of them, and we call these forces gravity, inertia, electricity, animal force, and so on; but we are conscious of the force of man's life, and we call it freedom.

But just as the force of gravity, unfathomable in itself but sensed by every man, is only comprehensible to us insofar as we know the law of necessity it is subject to (from the primitive knowledge that all bodies are heavy, to Newton's law), so, too, the force of freedom, unfathomable in itself but of which each of us is conscious, is only comprehensible to us insofar as we know the laws of necessity which it is subject to (starting from the fact that every man dies and going as far as the knowledge of the most complex economic or historical laws).

Any knowledge is only the placing of the essence of life under the laws of reason.

Man's freedom differs from any other force in that man is conscious of this force; but for reason it is no different from any other force. The forces of gravity, electricity, or chemical agents differ from each other only in that they are differently defined by reason. In the same way, for reason the force of man's freedom differs from all other forces of nature only by the definition which that same reason gives it. Freedom without necessity, that is, without the laws of reason which define it, does not differ in any way from gravity, or heat, or vegetative force—for reason it is only a momentary, undefinable sensation of life.

And as the undefinable essence of the force that moves the heavenly bodies, the undefinable essence of the force of heat, electricity, or chemical agents, or the life force make up the content of astronomy, physics, chemistry, botany, zoology, and so on, so the essence of the force of freedom makes up the content of history. But just as the subject of any science is the manifestation of this unknown essence of life, while the essence itself can only be the subject of metaphysics, so the manifestation of the force of men's freedom in space, time, and dependence on causes, is the subject of history; freedom itself is the subject of metaphysics.

In experimental science, what is known to us we call the laws of necessity; what is unknown to us we call the life force. The life force is only the expression of the unknown remainder of what we know about the essence of life.

It is the same with history: what is known to us we call the laws of necessity; what is unknown—freedom. For history, freedom is only the expression of the unknown remainder of what we know about the laws of human life.

XI

History examines the manifestations of man's freedom in connection with the external world in time and in dependence on causes, that is, it defines that freedom by the laws of reason, and therefore history is only a science insofar as that freedom is defined by those laws.

For history to recognize men's freedom as a force capable of influencing historical events, that is, as not subject to laws, is the same as for astronomy to recognize a free force moving the heavenly bodies.

That recognition destroys the possibility of the existence of laws, that is, of any knowledge whatever. If at least one freely moving body exists, then the laws of Kepler and Newton no longer exist, nor does any notion of the movement of the heavenly bodies. If there exists one free act of man, then not a single historical law exists or any notion of historical events.

For history there exist the lines of movement of human wills, one end of which vanishes into the unknown, but at the other end of which the consciousness of men's freedom in the present moves in space, in time, and in dependence on causes.

The more this field of movement expands before our eyes, the more obvious are the laws of this movement. To grasp and determine those laws constitutes the task of history.

From the point of view from which historical science now looks at its subject, on the path it follows, seeking the causes of phenomena in the free will of men, it is impossible for it to express laws, for, however much we limit men's freedom, as soon as we recognize it as a force not subject to laws, the existence of law is impossible.

Only by limiting this freedom infinitely, that is, by looking upon it as an infinitely small quantity, will we be convinced of the total inaccessibility of causes, and then, instead of searching for causes, history will set itself the task of searching for laws.

The search for these laws has long since begun, and the new methods of thinking which history should adopt for itself are being worked out simultaneously with the self-destruction towards which, ever subdividing and subdividing the causes of phenomena, the old history is moving.

All of mankind's sciences have followed this path. Having arrived at the infinitely small, mathematics, the most exact of sciences, abandons the process of subdividing and starts on a new process of summing up the unknown infinitesimals. Renouncing the concept of cause, mathematics seeks laws, that is, properties common to all unknown infinitely small elements.

Other sciences, though in a different form, have followed this same path of thinking. When Newton formulated the law of gravity, he did not say that the sun or the earth has the property of attraction; he said that all bodies, from the largest to the smallest, have this property of attracting each other, as it were; that is, leaving aside the question of the cause of the movement of the bodies, he formulated the property common to all bodies, from the infinitely large to the infinitely small. The natural sciences do the same: leaving aside the question of cause, they seek for laws. History stands on the same path. And if history has for its subject of study the movements of peoples and of mankind, and not the description of episodes from people's lives, it should set aside the notion of causes and seek for the laws common to all the equal and inseparably bound together infinitely small elements of freedom.

XII

Ever since Copernicus's law was found and proved, the mere recognition of the fact that what moves is not the sun but the earth has destroyed the whole cosmology of the ancients. It might have been possible, by refuting the law, to retain the old view of the movement of bodies, but without refuting it, it would have been impossible, it seems, to go on studying the Ptolemaic worlds. Yet even after the discovery of Copernicus's law, the Ptolemaic worlds long went on being studied.

Ever since the first man said and proved that the number of births or crimes obeys mathematical laws, that certain geographic and politico-economic conditions determine one or another form of government, and that certain relations of the inhabitants to the land produce movements of peoples—ever since then the foundations on which history had been built were essentially destroyed.

It might have been possible, by refuting the new laws, to retain the former view of history, but without refuting them, it would have been impossible, it seems, to go on studying historical events as if they proceeded from men's free will. For, if a certain form of government has been established, or a certain movement of peoples has taken place owing to such-and-such geographic, ethnographic, or economic conditions, then the will of those men who appear to us as establishing a form of government or provoking a movement of peoples can no longer be considered the cause.

And yet the former history goes on being studied on a par with the laws of statistics, geography, political economy, comparative philology, and geology, which directly contradict its postulates.

A long and stubborn struggle went on in physical philosophy between the old and new views. Theology stood guard over the old view and accused the new of destroying revelation. But when the truth triumphed, theology established itself as firmly on the new soil.

Just as long and stubborn a struggle has gone on in our time between the old and new views of history, and in the same way theology stands guard over the old view and accuses the new of destroying revelation.

In the one case as in the other, the struggle on both sides arouses passions and stifles the truth. On one side of the struggle there is fear and pity for the whole edifice erected over the centuries; on the other the passion for destruction.

To the people who fought against the emerging truth of physical philosophy it seemed that, if they were to recognize that truth, faith in God, in the creation of the firmament, in the miracle of Joshua, son of Nun,[7] would be destroyed. To the defenders of the laws of Copernicus and Newton—Voltaire, for instance—it seemed that the laws of astronomy destroyed religion, and he used the law of gravity as a weapon against religion.

In the same way now it seems that we need only recognize the law of necessity and the notions of the soul, of good and evil, and all state and church institutions based on those notions will be destroyed.

In the same way now as with Voltaire in his time, the uninvited defenders of the law of necessity use that law as a weapon against religion; whereas—exactly like Copernicus's law in astronomy—the law of necessity in history not only does not destroy, but even consolidates the ground on which state and church institutions are built.

As in the question of astronomy then, so now in the question of history, all the difference in views is based on the recognition or non-recognition of an absolute unit serving as a measure of visible phenomena. In astronomy this was the immobility of the earth; in history it is the independence of the person—freedom.

As for astronomy the difficulty of recognizing the movement of the earth consisted in renouncing the immediate feeling of the immobility of the earth and the similar feeling of the movement of the planets, so for history the difficulty of recognizing the subjection of the person to the laws of space, time, and causes consists in renouncing the immediate feeling of the independence of one's person. But, as in astronomy the new view said: "True, we do not feel the movement of the earth, but by assuming its immobility, we arrive at an absurdity; whereas, by assuming the movement which we do not feel, we arrive at laws," so, too, in history the new view says: "True, we do not feel our dependence, but by assuming we are free, we arrive at an absurdity; whereas, by assuming our dependence on the external world, time, and causes, we arrive at laws."

In the first case, the need was to renounce the consciousness of a non-existent immobility in space and recognize a movement we do not feel; in the present case, it is just as necessary to renounce a non-existent freedom and recognize a dependence we do not feel.

THE END

APPENDIX

A Few Words Apropos of the Book *War and Peace*

Publishing a work on which I have spent five years of ceaseless and exclusive labour, under the best conditions of life, I would like in a preface to that work to state my view of it and thereby forestall those perplexities which may arise in readers. I would like readers not to see or seek in my book what I did not want or was not able to express, and to pay attention to precisely what I wanted to express, but on which (given the conditions of its production) I did not consider it appropriate to dwell. Neither time nor my skill allowed me to fully carry out my intention, and I avail myself of the hospitality of a specialized journal to state, however briefly and incompletely, for those readers whom it might interest, the author's view of his work.[1]

(1) What is *War and Peace*? It is not a novel, still less an epic poem, still less a historical chronicle. *War and Peace* is what the author wanted and was able to express, in the form in which it is expressed. Such a declaration of the author's disregard of the conventional forms of artistic prose works might seem presumptuous, if it were premeditated and if it had no previous examples. The history of Russian literature since Pushkin's time not only provides many examples of such departure from European forms, but does not offer even one example to the contrary. From Gogol's *Dead Souls* to Dostoevsky's *Dead House*,[2] there is not a single work of artistic prose in the modern period of Russian literature, rising slightly above mediocrity, that would fit perfectly into the form of the novel, the epic, or the story.

(2) The character of the time, as some readers expressed to me when the first part appeared in print, is insufficiently defined in my work. To this reproach I have the following rejoinder. I know what this character of the time is that people do not find in my novel—the horrors of serfdom, the immuring of wives, the whipping of adult sons, Saltychikha,[3] and so on; and this character of that time, which lives in our imagination, I do not consider correct and did not wish to express. Studying letters, diaries, legends, I did not find all the horrors of that brutality in a greater degree than I find them now or at any other time. In those times, too, people loved, envied, sought truth, virtue, were carried away by passions; there was the same complex mental and moral life, sometimes even more refined than now, among the upper classes. If in our minds we have formed an opinion of the arbitrariness and crude force characteristic of that

time, it is only because the legends, memoirs, stories, and novels that have come down to us record only the most outstanding cases of violence and brutality. To conclude that the prevailing character of that time was brutality is as incorrect as it would be for a man who sees only treetops beyond a hill to conclude that there is nothing but trees in that region. There is a character of that time (as there is of every epoch), which comes from the greater alienation of the upper circles from the other estates, from the reigning philosophy, from peculiarities of upbringing, from the habit of using the French language, and so on. And this character I have tried as far as I could to express.

(3) The use of French in a Russian work. Why is it that in my work not only the Russians but also the French speak partly in Russian, partly in French? The reproach that people speak and write in French in a Russian book is similar to the reproach made by a man who, looking at a painting, notices black spots in it (shadows) that are not found in reality. The painter is not to blame if the shadow he has made on the face in the painting looks to some like a black spot that does not exist in reality, but is to blame only if those shadows are laid on incorrectly and crudely. Studying the period of the beginning of the present century, portraying Russian figures of a certain society, and Napoleon, and the French, who took such a direct part in the life of that time, I was involuntarily carried away more than necessary by the form of expression of that French way of thinking. And therefore, without denying that the shadows I laid on are probably incorrect and crude, I wish only that those to whom it seems very funny that Napoleon speaks now in Russian, now in French, should know that it seems so to them because, like the man looking at the portrait, they see not a face with light and shadow, but only a black spot under its nose.

(4) The names of characters—Bolkonsky, Drubetskoy, Bilibin, Kuragin, and others—resemble well-known Russian names. In juxtaposing non-historical characters with other characters who are historical, it felt awkward to my ear to make Count Rastopchin talk with Prince Pronsky, Strelsky, or some other princes or counts with invented double or single last names. Bolkonsky and Drubetskoy, though they are neither Volkonsky nor Trubetskoy, have the ring of something familiar and natural in a Russian aristocratic circle. I was unable to invent names for all my characters, such as Bezukhov and Rostov, that did not seem false to my ear, and could not get around this difficulty otherwise than by taking the last names most familiar to a Russian ear and changing some letters in them. I would be very sorry if the similarity of the invented names to real ones should give anyone the idea that I meant to describe this or that real person; especially because the literary activity that consists in describing persons who really exist or existed has nothing in common with that which I was engaged in.

M. D. Akhrosimov and Denisov are exceptional characters to whom I involuntarily and thoughtlessly gave names that closely resemble those of two particularly distinctive and dear real persons of the society of that time. That was my mistake, which came from the particular distinctiveness of these two persons; but my mistake in this regard was limited to the introducing of these two characters alone; and readers will probably agree that nothing resembling reality happens to these characters. All the rest of the characters are completely invented and for me do not even have any specific prototypes in tradition or reality.

(5) The divergence between my descriptions of historical events and the accounts of historians. It is not accidental, but inevitable. A historian and an artist, describing a historical epoch, have two completely different objects. As a historian would be wrong if he should try to present a historical figure in all his entirety, in all the complexity of his relations to all sides of life, so an artist would not fulfil his task by always presenting a figure in his historical significance. Kutuzov did not always ride a white horse, holding a field glass and pointing at enemies. Rastopchin did not always take torch in hand and set fire to his Voronovo house[4] (in fact he never did it at all), and the empress Maria Feodorovna did not always stand in an ermine mantle, her hand resting on the code of law; but that is how they are pictured in the popular imagination.

For a historian, considering the contribution rendered by some person towards a certain goal, there are heroes; for the artist, considering the correspondence of this person to all sides of life, there cannot and should not be any heroes, but there should be people.

The historian is sometimes obliged, by bending the truth, to bring all the actions of a historical figure under the one idea he has put into that figure. The artist, on the contrary, sees the very singularity of that idea as incompatible with his task, and only tries to understand and show not the famous figure but the human being.

The distinction is still sharper and more substantial in the description of events themselves.

A historian has to do with the results of an event, the artist with the fact of the event. A historian, describing a battle, says: the left flank of such-and-such army was moved against such-and-such village, cut down the enemy, but was forced to retreat; then the cavalry, going into the attack, overthrew . . . and so on. The historian cannot speak otherwise. And yet these words have no meaning for an artist and do not even touch upon the event itself. The artist, using his own experience, or letters, memoirs, and accounts, derives for himself an image of the event that took place, and quite often (in a battle for example) the conclusion which the historian allows himself to draw about the activity of such-and-such army turns out to be the opposite of the artist's conclusion. The difference between the results obtained is explained by the sources from which the two draw their information. For the historian (we continue the example of a battle), the main source is the reports of individual commanders and the commander in chief. The artist can draw nothing from such sources, they tell him nothing, explain nothing. Moreover, the artist turns away from them, finding in them a necessary falsehood. To say nothing of the fact that with every battle the two enemies almost always describe it in a totally opposite way from each other, in every description of a battle there is a necessity for falsehood which comes from the need to describe in a few words the actions of thousands of men, scattered over several miles, who are in the most intense moral agitation under the influence of fear, shame, and death.

In descriptions of battles it is usually written that such-and-such army was sent to attack such-and-such point and was then ordered to retreat, and so on, as if supposing that the discipline that makes tens of thousands of men obey the will of one man on the drill ground will have the same effect where it is a matter of life and death. Anyone who has been to war knows how incorrect that is;* and yet official reports are based on this supposition, and military descriptions on them. Make the rounds of a whole army right after a battle, even on the second or third day, before the reports have been written, and ask all the soldiers, the senior and junior officers, how it went; they will tell you what all these men experienced and saw, and you will form a majestic, complex, infinitely diverse, oppressive, and vague impression; and from no one, least of all the commander in chief, will you learn how it all went. But after two or three days, the reports begin to be submitted, talkers begin telling how what they did not see happened; finally, a general account is put together, and the general opinion of the army is put together from this account. It is a relief to everyone to exchange his doubts and questions for this false but clear and always flattering picture. After a month or two, question a man who took part in the battle—you no longer feel in his story that raw material of life which had been there before; his account follows the report. So I was told about the battle of Borodino by many living, intelligent participants in that affair. They all told me the same thing, and all following the incorrect descriptions of Mikhailovsky-Danilevsky, Glinka, and others; even the details they recounted were the same, though the narrators had been several miles from each other.

After the loss of Sevastopol, the artillery commander Kryzhanovsky sent me the reports of the artillery officers from all the bastions and asked me to put those more than twenty accounts together into one. I am sorry I did not make copies of those reports. It was the best example of that naïve and necessary military falsehood from which descriptions are put together. I suppose that many

---

*After the publication of my first part and the description of the battle of Schöngraben, the words of Nikolai Nikolaevich Muravyov-Karsky were conveyed to me about this description of the battle, which confirmed my conviction. N. N. Muravyov, a commander in chief, said that he had never read a more faithful description of a battle, and that his own experience had convinced him that it was impossible to carry out the orders of a commander in chief during a battle. (Tolstoy's note.)

of my comrades who put together those accounts then will laugh, having read these lines, at the recollection of how, on orders from their superiors, they wrote something they could not have known. Everyone who has had the experience of war knows how capable Russians are of doing their duty in war and how little capable they are of describing it with the boastful falsity necessary to the task. Everyone knows that, in our armies, this duty of writing reports and accounts is for the most part carried out by our non-Russians.

I say all this in order to show the inevitability of falsehood in the military descriptions which serve as material for military historians, and therefore to show the inevitability of frequent disagreements between artists and historians in understanding historical events. But, besides the inevitability of untruths in their setting forth of historical events, I encountered in the historians of the epoch that interested me (probably as a result of the habit of grouping events, expressing them briefly, and conforming to the tragic tone of the events) a particular inclination to high-flown speech, in which falsehood and distortion often touch not only the events, but also the understanding of the meaning of an event. Often, in studying the two main historical productions of that epoch, Thiers and Mikhailovsky-Danilevsky, I would become perplexed at how these books could be printed and read. Not to speak of the setting forth of the same events in the most serious, significant tone, with references to the materials, and yet diametrically opposed to each other, I encountered in these historians such descriptions that I did not know whether to laugh or weep when I remembered that these two books are the sole memorials of that epoch and have millions of readers. I will give only one example from the book of the famous historian Thiers. Having told how Napoleon brought counterfeit money with him, he says: *"Relevant l'emploi de ces moyens par un acte de bienfaisance digne de lui et de l'armée française, il fit distribuer des secours aux incendiés. Mais les vivres étant trop précieux pour être donnés longtemps à des étrangers, la plupart ennemis, Napoléon aima mieux leur fournir de l'argent, et il leur fit distribuer des roubles papier."**

This passage, taken separately, strikes one by its deafening, one cannot say immorality, but sheer meaninglessness; but within the book as a whole it does not strike one, because it corresponds perfectly to the high-flown, solemn tone, lacking in any direct meaning, of its overall style.

And so the tasks of the artist and the historian are completely different, and the disagreements with historians in the description of events and figures in my book should not strike the reader.

---

*Augmenting the use of these means by an act of charity *worthy of himself and of the French army,* he had aid distributed to the victims of the fire. But food supplies being too precious to be given for long to foreigners, most of them enemies, Napoleon preferred to furnish them with money, and he had paper roubles distributed to them.

But the artist should not forget that the notion of historical figures and events formed among people is based not on fantasy, but on historical documents, insofar as historians have been able to amass them; and therefore, while understanding and presenting these figures and events differently, the artist ought to be guided, like the historian, by historical materials. *Wherever in my novel historical figures speak and act, I have not invented, but have made use of the materials, of which, during my work, I have formed a whole library, the titles of which I find it unnecessary to set down here, but for which I can always give the reference.*

(6) Finally, the sixth and for me the most important consideration concerns the small significance which, to my mind, so-called great men have in historical events.

In studying an epoch so tragic, so rich in the enormity of its events, and so near to us, of which such a variety of traditions still live, I arrived at the obviousness of the fact that the causes of the historical events that take place are inaccessible to our intelligence. To say (which seems quite simple to everyone) that the causes of the events of the year twelve are the conquering spirit of Napoleon and the patriotic firmness of the emperor Alexander Pavlovich, is as meaningless as to say that the causes of the fall of the Roman Empire are that such-and-such barbarian led his people to the west, and such-and-such Roman emperor ruled his people badly, or that an immense mountain that was being levelled came down because the last workman drove his spade into it.

Such an event, in which millions of men set about killing each other and killed half a million, cannot have the will of one man as its cause: just as one man alone could not undermine a mountain, so one man cannot make five hundred thousand die. But what then were the causes? Some historians say that the cause was the conquering spirit of the French, the patriotism of Russia. Others speak of the democratic element that Napoleon's host spread about, and of the necessity for Russia to enter into relations with Europe, and so on. But how is it that millions of men set about killing each other? Who ordered them to do it? It seems clear to everyone that no one would be the better for it, but all would be the worse; why then did they do it? A countless number of retrospective conjectures can be made and are being made about the causes of this senseless event; but the enormous number of these explanations and their convergence on one goal only proves that there is a countless multitude of these causes and that none of them can be called the cause.

Why did millions of men set about killing each other, if it has been known ever since the world began that it is both physically and morally bad?

Because it was so inevitably necessary that, in fulfilling it, men were fulfilling that elementary zoological law which the bees fulfil by exterminating each other in the autumn, and according to which male animals exterminate each other. No other answer can be given to this terrible question.

This truth is not only obvious, but is so innate in every man that it would not be worth proving, if there were not another feeling and consciousness in man, which convinces him that he is free at every moment as he performs some action.

Examining history from a general point of view, we are unquestionably convinced of the pre-eternal law according to which events take place. Looking from a personal point of view, we are convinced of the opposite.

A man killing another, Napoleon giving the order to cross the Niemen, you and I applying for a job, raising and lowering our arm, are all unquestionably convinced that each of our acts is based on reasonable causes and our own will, and that it depended on us to act that way and not otherwise, and that conviction is so inherent and dear to each of us that, despite the arguments of history and the statistics of crime, which convince us of the involuntariness of other people's actions, we extend the consciousness of our freedom to all our acts.

The contradiction seems insoluble: in committing an act, I am convinced that I am committing it according to my own good pleasure; examining this act in terms of its being part of the common life of mankind (in its historical significance), I am convinced that this act was predetermined and inevitable. Where does the mistake lie?

Psychological observations of man's ability to make an instantaneous retrospective adjustment of a whole series of allegedly free conjectures to an accomplished fact (I intend to set this forth in more detail elsewhere), confirm the assumption that man's consciousness of freedom in the committing of acts of a certain sort is mistaken. But those same psychological observations prove that there are acts of another sort in which the consciousness of freedom is not retrospective, but instantaneous and unquestionable. Whatever the materialists may say, I can unquestionably commit an action or refrain from it, insofar as that action concerns me alone. By my will alone I have unquestionably just raised and lowered my arm. I can presently stop writing. You can presently stop reading. Unquestionably, by my will alone and outside any obstacles, I can mentally transport myself right now to America or to any mathematical problem. Testing my freedom, I can raise and forcefully lower my arm in the air. I have just done so. But there is a child standing beside me: I raise my arm over him and want to lower it with the same force upon the child. I *cannot* do that. A dog attacks the child: I *cannot* help raising my arm against the dog. I stand in the ranks and cannot help following the movements of the regiment. In battle, I cannot help attacking with my regiment and fleeing when everyone around me flees. When I am standing in court as defender of an accused man, I cannot help speaking or knowing what I am going to say. I cannot help blinking when a blow is aimed at my eye.

And so there are two sorts of acts. One depends, the other does not depend on my will. And the mistake that produces a contradiction comes only from the fact that I wrongly transfer the consciousness of freedom, which legitimately accompanies any act connected with my *I*, with the highest abstraction of my existence, to my acts committed jointly with other people and depending on the coinciding of other wills with my own. To determine the boundaries of the domains of freedom and dependence is very difficult, and the determining of those boundaries is the essential and sole task of psychology; but, observing the conditions of the manifestation of our greatest freedom and greatest dependence, it is impossible not to see that the more abstract our activity is and therefore the less connected with the activity of others, the more free it is, and, on the contrary, the more our activity is connected with other people, the more unfree it is.

The most strong, indissoluble, burdensome, and constant connection with other people is the so-called power over other people, which in its true meaning is only the greatest dependence on them.

Mistakenly or not, having become fully convinced of that in the course of my work, it was natural that, in describing the historical events of 1805, 1807, and especially of 1812, in which this law of predetermination* stands out most prominently, I could not ascribe importance to the activity of those people who fancied they were governing events, but who introduced less free human activity into them than all the other participants in the events. The activity of those people was interesting to me only as an illustration of that law of predetermination which, in my conviction, governs history, and of that psychological law which makes a person who commits the most unfree act adjust in his imagination a whole series of retrospective conjectures aimed at proving his freedom to himself.

> COUNT LEO TOLSTOY
> *The Russian Archive*
> March 1868

---

*It is worth noting that almost all the writers who have written about the year twelve have seen something special and fateful in those events. (Tolstoy's note.)

NOTES

VOLUME I

Part One

1. *Gênes et Luques . . . la famille Buonaparte:* In 1797, after his first Italian campaign, Napoleon made Genoa into the Ligurian Republic, which was annexed to France in 1805. Lucca was taken by the French in 1799, and in 1805 became the centre of a princedom which Napoleon bestowed upon his sister Marie-Anne-Elisa (1777–1820), married to Felix Bacciochi, who thus became prince of Lucca and Piombino. Anna Pavlovna scornfully uses the Corsican form of Napoleon's family name, as others will later. He will also be referred to as "Boonapart" and "Bonapartius."

2. *la dépêche de Novosilzoff:* In 1804–5 England, Russia, Austria, Prussia, Sweden, and the kingdom of Naples planned to form a coalition against France. Napoleon, learning of the plan, made an offer of peace to England. England asked the Russian emperor, Alexander I, to mediate in the negotiations, and he sent his special emissary, Novosiltsev (here and further on called "Novosiltsov"), to Paris for that purpose. On reaching Berlin on 15 June 1805, Novosiltsev learned of Napoleon's taking of Genoa and Lucca, sent that information in a dispatch to the emperor, and remained in Berlin. No peace was concluded, and in the autumn of 1805 war began between France and the Austrian-Russian coalition.

3. *Austria . . . betraying us:* Austria had separated itself from Russia in several previous wars, with Turkey in 1787–91, with the French after the Italian campaign of 1799, and in 1801, when Austria signed the peace of Lunéville, which dissolved the second coalition against France.

4. *the righteous one:* The reference is to the murder of Louis-Antoine, duc d'Enghien (1772–1804), of the princely house of Condé, who lived in emigration in Germany after the revolution. Falsely accusing him of taking part in a plot to assassinate him, Bonaparte had him arrested, condemned by a summary court martial, and shot. Alexander I was the only European monarch to protest openly against this act.

5. *to evacuate Malta:* The Mediterranean island of Malta, which since the sixteenth century had belonged to the order of the knights of St. John, was taken by Napoleon in 1798 and by England in 1800. The English refusal to quit the island led to new hostilities in 1803, in which Russia participated against the French.

6. *Hardenberg . . . Haugwitz:* Prussia delayed in joining the coalition against Napoleon, who was in the process of conquering the southern and western German principalities. In 1805, Alexander I, sending Russian troops to Austria, ordered them to cross Prussian territory without permission and to act against the Prussian army in case of resistance. In 1805, Hardenberg was the Prussian minister of foreign affairs; Haugwitz was a Prussian diplomat.

7. *our dear Wintzingerode:* In May 1805 Alexander I sent General F. F. von Wintzingerode to Austria with an overall plan of action for the coalition against Napoleon; it was hoped that he would be able to convince Prussia to join them.

8. *the good émigrés:* Many members of the French nobility sought refuge abroad during the revolution. Tolstoy's Mortemart is a composite figure; the actual Mortemarts were a branch of

the house of Rochechouart. Montmorency and Rohan are indeed among the highest French nobility.

9. *the famous Prince Bolkonsky:* Tolstoy took many features of the old Prince Bolkonsky from his maternal grandfather, Prince Nikolai Sergeevich Volkonsky (1753–1821), a high military dignitary under the empress Catherine the Great, who was disgraced under her son, the emperor Paul I, and retired to his estate. Tolstoy similarly drew features from his paternal grandfather, Count Ilya Andreevich Tolstoy (1757–1820), in portraying Count Ilya Andreevich Rostov. The old prince Bolkonsky is called "the king of Prussia" because he continued, contrary to the new fashion, to wear a powdered "pigtail and bag" wig, knee breeches, and so on, like the Prussian king Frederick II, the Great (1712–86).

10. *with a monogram:* Gowns embroidered with the monograms of the tsaritsa were worn by the ladies-in-waiting of the imperial court.

11. *plan for eternal peace:* Tolstoy's abbé Morio is based on the Italian abbé Scipio Piatolli, sometime tutor to Prince A. A. Czartoryski. The prince became a councillor to the young Alexander I and in 1804–6 served as minister of foreign affairs, giving Piatolli access to the highest circles in Petersburg, where he presented his plan for eternal peace by means of a European union against Napoleon.

12. *the duc d'Enghien:* See note 4.

13. *Kutuzov . . . appointed commander in chief:* In 1802 Kutuzov was dismissed from his post as military governor of Petersburg, but in the summer of 1805 he was made commander in chief of the 50,000-man Russian army that was sent to Austria for the war with Napoleon.

14. *sacre de Milan:* In 1805 Napoleon proclaimed himself king of Italy and was crowned in Milan on 28 May.

15. *Louis XVI . . . la reine . . . madame Elisabeth:* Louis XVI and Marie-Antoinette were condemned to death by the Convention and beheaded in 1793, Elisabeth de France, the sister of Louis XVI, in 1794.

16. *the Condés:* The family of Condé was a collateral branch of the French royal house of Bourbon; many of its members played an important part in the history of France (see also note 4).

17. *Contrat social:* Rousseau's theoretical work, *Du Contrat social* ("Of the Social Contract"), published in 1762, caused a considerable stir and helped to inspire the French revolution. Its central idea is that social life is based on a contract in which each party resigns his freedom to the community and agrees to submit to the expression of the general will.

18. *the eighteenth Brumaire:* On 9 November 1799 (18 Brumaire of the year VIII according to the French republican calendar), Napoleon, having returned from Egypt, overthrew the Directoire in a bloodless coup d'état and instituted the Consulat, consolidating all power in his own hands as first consul.

19. *the prisoners . . . in Africa:* Four thousand Turkish soldiers, who had surrendered to Napoleon at the siege of the Palestinian port city of Jaffa in 1799 on condition that their lives would be spared, were shot on his orders, supposedly in punishment for the killing of a French peace envoy.

20. *the bridge of Arcole . . . plague victims:* On 17 November 1796, fighting the Austrians in northern Italy, Napoleon, at the head of his grenadiers and with a banner in his hand, charged onto the bridge at Arcole to keep the enemy from taking it. The plague that was raging in Jaffa (see previous note) when the French stormed the city afflicted both the local population and the French army. Napoleon visited the plague victims in the hospital with his marshals Berthier and Bessières, an incident commemorated by the French painter Jean-Antoine Gros (1771–1835) in *The Plague Victims of Jaffa* (1804).

21. *Commentaries:* That is, *De Bello Gallico* ("The Gallic Wars," ca. 50 B.C.), a year-by-year account of the Roman conquest of Gaul by the general and statesman Julius Caesar (100–44 B.C.), who carried out the conquest.

22. *a Mason:* A member of the fraternity of Free and Accepted Masons, derived ultimately from the medieval guild of stonemasons. In London in 1717 four of its "lodges" formed themselves into a "grand lodge" with a new constitution, a special ritual, and a system of secret signs, and from London it spread to many countries of the world. Masonry was (and is) a society of mutual aid and brotherhood, but in the eighteenth century it acquired political dimensions and

was of some significance in the beginnings of the French revolution. Masonry was alternately embraced and banned in a number of countries during the eighteenth and nineteenth centuries. Pierre's connections with Masonry will play a considerable part in what follows.

23. *Break the grip:* It was the Russian custom for those making a bet to join hands and have a third person separate them.

24. *the name day of the Natalyas:* On the day commemorating a certain saint, everyone bearing the name of that saint would celebrate.

25. *Forty thousand souls:* Before the emancipation of the serfs in 1861, Russian estates were evaluated in terms of the number of adult male serfs, or "souls," living on them. Forty thousand souls was a very large number; they would have been divided among a number of estates.

26. *a raspberry-coloured collar:* Russian university students wore uniforms with stiff round collars, the colour of which denoted their subject or school of study.

27. *in the archives and all:* Comfortable posts in the state archives were given to young noblemen at the end of their studies, while they waited to make a career.

28. *as a junker:* In the Russian army, the German term *Junker,* the equivalent of the English *cadet,* was used for young gentlemen who entered the service without a commission.

29. *the straw-laid street:* It was an old custom in Russia and Europe to lay straw over the cobblestones of a street where a person lay gravely ill in order to deaden the noise of carriage wheels.

30. *his last duty:* A dying man's "last duty" was to confess to a priest and receive holy communion and extreme unction.

31. *Boulogne expedition . . . Villeneuve:* In 1805–6 Napoleon set up a large military camp in Boulogne, on the English Channel, and prepared for a landing of troops in England. In the autumn of 1805 he ordered Admiral Villeneuve to move his ships from the Mediterranean to the Channel and join the squadron already there, but Villeneuve, blockaded in the Mediterranean by the English, was unable to carry out the order. On 21 October 1805, at the battle of Trafalgar, Admiral Nelson destroyed the allied French-Spanish fleet, and at the same time news came that Russia was sending troops to aid the Austrians, at which point Napoleon abandoned the Boulogne expedition and moved his army to Austria.

32. *manifesto . . . recruitment:* The manifesto of Alexander I about the war and recruitment was announced in Moscow on 1 September 1805, but on 10 August the Russian army, under Kutuzov's command, had already left Petersburg and gone to join the Austrians. Thus the manifesto could be talked about at the Rostovs' party on 26 August before its official announcement.

33. *when chance smiled on him:* Tolstoy uses a special eighteenth-century expression for men who made quick careers at court. During the reign of Catherine the Great, such men were usually her lovers.

34. *the achievement of that intention:* An actual quotation from the 1 September manifesto, taken from the entry for 7 September 1805 in *Diary of a Student,* by S. P. Zhikharev, which Tolstoy had in the library of his estate at Yasnaya Polyana.

35. *Take Suvorov:* Shinshin has in mind the Swiss campaign of 1799, in which the allied forces of Russia and Austria were defeated. In fact, however, though Suvorov and his 20,000 men were surrounded in the Alps by 80,000 French, they managed to break through and avoid capture.

36. *"The Spring":* A vocal quartet in the Italian style sometimes attributed to Mozart. Tolstoy himself used to sing it with the pupils of the school at Yasnaya Polyana.

37. *the metropolitan himself:* Marriage between cousins was permitted by the Russian Orthodox Church only with special permission. A metropolitan is a bishop having jurisdiction over all the bishops of a given area.

38. *a song he had just learned:* The words of the song are by Dmitri Alexandrovich Kavelin (1778–1851), director of the Chief Pedagogical Institute and its Pension for Nobility, and of St. Petersburg University. Pushkin refers to him in a letter as "doctor of theology Kavelin" (9 July 1819, to A. I. Turgenev). He was an amateur versifier and member of the literary group Arzamas, as was Pushkin himself. Tolstoy found the words in Zhikharev's *Diary of a Student.*

39. *trepak:* One of the fastest of Russian folk dances, with stamping of the heels and sudden bends.

40. *a blank confession:* A sacrament of confession administered to an unconscious, dying per-

son; the priest himself enumerates the standard human sins in the unconscious man's ear and proceeds to give him absolution.

41. *Breguet:* A well-known "repeater" pocket watch made by the French-Swiss clockmaker Abraham-Louis Breguet (1747–1823).

42. *the capitals:* It was customary to refer to Russia as having two capitals, the old capital of Moscow and the new imperial capital of Petersburg, founded in 1703 by a decree of Peter the Great, which became the administrative centre of the country.

43. *Héloïse:* The old prince is referring sarcastically to the epistolary novel *Julie ou la Nouvelle Héloïse* (1761), by Jean-Jacques Rousseau, which had considerable influence on the evolution of sensibilities in the later eighteenth century. Tolstoy based the letters of Princess Marya and Julie Karagin on a large collection of similar letters exchanged by two young ladies, M. A. Volkov and B. I. Lanskoy, which he read with great interest in 1863.

44. *Key to the Mystery:* The occult treatise *A Key to the Mysteries of Nature*, by Bavarian-born Karl von Eckartshausen (1752–1803), was widely read in Europe during the later eighteenth century and was translated into Russian several times. It was especially popular in Masonic circles. Eckartshausen was a prolific writer on such spiritual topics as magic, alchemy, and number mysticism.

45. *a Dusek sonata:* The Czech composers Frantisek Xaver Dusek (1731–99) and Jan Ladislav Dusek (1760–1812) both wrote piano sonatas.

46. *Mikhelson . . . Tolstoy . . . Sweden . . . Pomerania:* Wintzingerode's complex general plan (see note 7) involved attacking the French from several sides, with armies led by Mikhelson from the east, P. A. Tolstoy from the north, and Kutuzov from the south. The coalition of Swedish, English, and Russian troops led by Tolstoy was to cross from Sweden to Pomerania (a region on the Baltic, formerly part of Germany, now of Poland) and on through Hanover.

47. *Malbroug . . . reviendra:* Lines from a French popular song going back to the Wars of Spanish Succession in the Low Countries in the early eighteenth century, in which the English armies were led by John Churchill, duke of Marlborough (1650–1722).

48. *Suvorov . . . Moreau:* Prince Andrei misstates the facts about Suvorov, perhaps deliberately (see note 35). Not only was he not caught in Moreau's trap, but his troops defeated Moreau at the battle of Cassano in 1799.

49. *Hofs-kriegs-wurst-schnapps-rath:* The old prince makes fun of the Austrian Court Council of War (*Hofkriegsrath*), and of the German language, by calling it the "Court-war-sausage-schnapps-council."

50. *their own:* A play on the Slavonic translation of John 1:11: "He came unto his own, and his own received him not."

51. *the German Pahlen . . . Moreau:* Moreau was exiled for taking part in a conspiracy to overthrow Napoleon in 1804 and went to America. In 1805 Alexander I sent Count P. A. von Pahlen to invite him to serve in the Russian army, but von Pahlen turned back when he received news of the battle of Austerlitz and the end of the war.

52. *As Sterne says:* The English writer Laurence Sterne (1713–68) had a marked influence on the young Tolstoy, particularly with his *Sentimental Journey Through France and Italy* (1768), which stands behind Tolstoy's first piece of fiction, "A History of Yesterday" (1851), and part of which Tolstoy translated. Sterne's novel *The Life and Opinions of Tristram Shandy, Gentleman* (1760–7) has been seen as a formal precursor of *War and Peace*.

53. *a Lombard note:* "Lombard" was a general term for a private banker, money changer, or pawnbroker.

Part Two

1. *the Tsaritsyn Field:* A square in Petersburg used as a parade ground. In 1818 the name was changed to Marsovo Polie ("the Field of Mars").

2. *Izmail comrade:* Kutuzov served under Suvorov in the war with Turkey during the reign of Catherine the Great. In 1790 they took the Turkish fortress of Izmail on the Danube delta.

3. *the Germans sent us carriages:* That is, the Austrians (who, along with other central European Europeans, are often referred to by Russian soldiers under the general name of "Germans"). On 13 August 1805, the Russian army began to march slowly from Radzivilov in the Ukraine; the Austrians also moved slowly, thinking that Napoleon's army was still in Boulogne. When it was discovered in early September that the French were already on the Rhine, Kutuzov's troops were loaded onto wagons and the officers were given carriages to speed up their progress.

4. *so er verdient:* Tolstoy took this letter from *A Description of the First War of the Emperor Alexander with Napoleon in 1805,* by A. I. Mikhailovsky-Danilevsky (St. Petersburg, 1844).

5. *a Vladimir with a bow:* The civil and military order of St. Vladimir was founded in 1782 by Catherine the Great to commemorate the twentieth year of her reign; it was named for St. Vladimir, Grand Prince of Kiev (ca. 958–1015), who converted Kievan Rus to Orthodox Christianity. The military decoration was worn with a special bow in the ribbon.

6. *Lambach, Amstetten, and Mölk:* These three battles were given by a detachment of 6,000 men under Bagration, whom Kutuzov sent to delay the French while the Russian army retreated from Krems to Znaim. The same detachment also fought at Schöngraben.

7. *our ambassador in Vienna:* The Russian ambassador in Vienna at that time was Count Razumovsky, who is best known now for the "Razumovsky" string quartets he commissioned from Beethoven. He built a fine neoclassical embassy in Vienna at his own expense, and was the chief Russian negotiator at the Congress of Vienna in 1814–15, which reorganized Europe after the fall of Napoleon.

8. *Orthodox Russian armed forces:* An ironic reference to a phrase that occurs in the litanies of various church services.

9. *Bonaparte is in Schönbrunn . . . Count Vrbna . . . orders:* Having taken Vienna on 1 November 1805, Napoleon chose as his headquarters the superb imperial residence of the Hapsburgs in the Schönbrunn quarter of the city. Count Rudolf Vrbna acted as mediator in the negotiations between the Austrians and the French.

10. *those who invented gunpowder:* Russians say of a stupid person that he "won't invent gunpowder." Bilibin's *mot* reverses the saying.

11. *the meeting in Berlin . . . a new Campo Formio:* In October 1805, Alexander I went to Berlin to try to persuade the Prussian king Friedrich-Wilhelm III to join the war against Napoleon. They reached a secret agreement in Potsdam, but before the Prussian envoy Haugwitz could reach Napoleon with an ultimatum, the Russian-Austrian alliance had already been defeated, and it was Napoleon who dictated the terms of the peace. Eight years earlier, on 17 October 1797, in the Italian town of Campo Formio, a peace agreement had been signed between the French republic and the Austrian empire which ended Napoleon's campaign in Italy.

12. *pour les beaux yeux . . . separately:* In accordance with the treaty of Turin (1796), the king of Sardinia, Victor-Amadeus III, had to yield Nice, Savoy, and other fortresses and towns to the French. One of the conditions of the Potsdam ultimatum (see previous note) was recompense for the king of Sardinia. Before the French took Vienna, the Austrian emperor Franz I indeed sent an ambassador to Napoleon with an offer of a separate peace, and on the eve of abandoning the capital, he sent Napoleon another offer of a truce. Neither offer was accepted.

13. *Démosthène . . . bouche d'or:* The greatest of the Athenian orators, Demosthenes (384–22 B.C.) was said to have had a speech defect as a boy and to have corrected it by learning to speak clearly while holding a pebble in his mouth.

14. *here was that Toulon:* Napoleon's first victory was the taking of Toulon, which had become the centre of French royalist resistance, in 1793. Following it he was promoted from captain to general.

15. *I'm not joking . . . ni bêtise, ni lâcheté:* The historical facts of the French taking of the bridge of Tabor in Bohemia (now the Czech Republic) are very close to Bilibin's version.

16. *touched a Leiden jar:* The Leiden jar was the first electrical condenser, invented in 1745 by Pieter van Musschenbroek, professor of physics at Leiden University in the Netherlands. It is a jar partly filled with water with a copper wire projecting through its cork. Charged with static electricity by friction, it can give a painful shock when touched.

17. *Napoléon:* Tolstoy took this letter from *L'Histoire du Consulat et de l'Empire* ("The His-

tory of the Consulate and the Empire"), by the French statesman and historian Adolphe Thiers, which was one of his main sources in the writing of *War and Peace*.

18. *only atmosphere:* The officers' conversation about immortality has its source in an article entitled "Man Is Created to Expect Immortality," by the German philosopher Johann Gottfried von Herder (1744–1803). A Russian version, printed in the July 1804 issue of the *Vestnik Evropy* ("European Messenger"), has been preserved in Tolstoy's library at Yasnaya Polyana.

19. *Napoleon . . . St. Helena:* The source of Napoleon's words is *Le Mémorial de Sainte-Hélène* ("The Memorial of St. Helena"), a journal of conversations with Napoleon during his last years in exile on the island of St. Helena (1815–21), kept by Emmanuel, comte de Las Cases (1766–1842) and published in Paris in 1823–4.

20. *a unicorn:* A smooth-bored muzzle-loading cannon that tapered towards the mouth.

Part Three

1. *Potsdam . . . enemy of the human race:* See note 11 to Part Two.

2. *Vinesse:* A French miniaturist known to have been living in Petersburg in 1812.

3. *Arnauti:* A Turkish name for the Albanians, who served the Turks as cavalrymen.

4. *lost his Latin:* Since Dolgorukov is speaking in French, Tolstoy literally translates this French saying for him, which means "to be at a loss" or "to be all at sea."

5. *the old cunctators:* The nickname of *cunctator* (from the Latin *cunctatio* ["delay"] was given to the Roman general Fabius (ca. 275–03 B.C.), because of his tactic of avoiding direct confrontation with the Carthaginian general Hannibal (247–183 B.C.) as the latter marched towards Rome. Russian and Austrian generals gave the same nickname to Kutuzov.

6. *Prsch . . . Prsch:* Bilibin is trying to pronounce the name of the Polish general Przebyszewski, who will be named later.

7. *Hollabrunn:* This is the French name for the battle that Tolstoy refers to elsewhere as Schöngraben, from the nearby village of that name.

8. *Arcole:* See note 20 to Part One.

9. *the Tsaritsyn Field:* See note 1 to Part Two.

VOLUME II

Part One

1. *the English Club:* Founded in Moscow in 1770, the English Club was a meeting place for the high nobility, modelled on gentlemen's clubs in England.

2. *Ilyushka the Gypsy:* Nickname of Ilya Osipovich Sokolov (d. 1848), who for forty years conducted a famous Gypsy choir in Moscow and was admired by Pushkin, Liszt, and Denis Davydov.

3. *the treachery . . . Langeron:* All the reasons given here for the defeat at Austerlitz are wrong, apart from bad provisioning. Przebyszewski and his column of Russian soldiers surrendered to the French at the start of the battle; there was no treachery on the part of A. F. Langeron, a Frenchman serving in the Russian army, nor on the side of the Austrians, where there was only cowardice, poor strategy, and bad leadership.

4. *Bagration . . . Italian campaign . . . Suvorov:* Bagration had been one of Suvorov's closest associates during the campaign of 1799–1800 against the French revolutionary forces in northern Italy, which was a series of brilliant victories for the Russian generals.

5. *parodying . . . Voltaire:* Voltaire's famous phrase was *S'il n'était pas Dieu, il faudrait l'inventer* ("If there were no God, he would have to be invented").

6. *in powdered wigs and kaftans:* That is, dressed in the fashion of the previous century.

7. *had crowed like a cock:* Field Marshal Suvorov was indeed known for several oddities of behaviour, one of which was crowing like a cock.

8. *Glorify . . . :* The verses are by N. P. Nikolev (d. 1815), well-known in the eighteenth century as a poet and playwright. Tolstoy found them in Zhikharev's *Diary of a Student* (see note 34 to Volume I, Part I), the entry for 4 March 1806, from which he also drew many details of the banquet itself. Ripheus was the companion of Aeneas in Virgil's *Aeneid*; Alcides ("son of the mighty one") was one of the surnames of Hercules, whose father was the god Zeus. The line of the polonaise that follows ("Thunder of victory resound . . .") is from a victory ode by the great eighteenth-century poet G. R. Derzhavin (1743–1816) celebrating the taking of Izmail in 1790, which was set to music by Osip Kozlovsky (1751–1813).

9. *lenten and non-lenten:* The banquet falls within the Great Lent, the forty-day period of fast preceding Holy Week and Easter in the Orthodox Church. Count Ilya Andreich graciously allows for those who keep the fast and those who do not.

10. *Pavel Ivanovich Kutuzov:* Not the general, Mikhail Ilarionovich Kutuzov. He was a minor poet of the time, and his "cantata" was indeed performed during the banquet for Bagration, at which the author himself handed out copies to the guests.

11. *Louis XVI . . . Robespierre:* Louis XVI was arrested while trying to flee France in June 1791. Accused of treason, he was tried by the National Convention a year later and executed on 21 January 1793. Maximilien de Robespierre, a leading member of the Convention and of the Committee of Public Safety, which brought about the bloody "Reign of Terror" in France, was overthrown on 27 July 1794 and executed in his turn.

12. *que diable . . . dans cette galère:* A line spoken by Géronte in *Les Fourberies de Scapin* (1671), by Jean-Baptiste Poquelin, known as Molière (1622–73). It means literally "What the devil was he going to do in that galley?" but has become proverbial in a more general sense.

13. *Great Russia:* The old name for Russia proper, centred on Moscow, as distinct from the southern provinces of Little Russia (*Malorus*) and White Russia (*Belorus*).

14. *as for one of the living:* In the Orthodox tradition, there are special prayers for the living and for the dead, as there are special commemorations of the living and the dead in the sacrament of communion.

15. *wedding candles:* In the Russian Orthodox marriage service, the bride and groom hold candles, often specially decorated, which are carefully kept after the wedding.

16. *sat in another room:* It was traditional in Russia for the real parents not to participate in the baptismal ceremony, being replaced by the godparents. It was also customary to stick the baby's hair, cut during the ceremony, to melted wax and drop it into the baptismal font. If the hair floated, it meant the child would live.

17. *war with Napoleon:* In September 1806 Napoleon won significant victories over the Prussians at Jena and Auerstädt and occupied Berlin before the Russians could offer help. With the French army so close, Alexander I began preparations for defending his borders, including a new conscription of troops.

18. *Epiphany:* In the Orthodox festal calendar, the feast of the Epiphany, or Theophany, on 6 January, celebrates Christ's baptism by St. John in the Jordan River (Matthew 3:13–17, Mark 1:9–11, Luke 3:21–23).

19. *receiving tickets for lessons:* The Moscow dancing master Iogel arranged balls which he counted as lessons for his pupils, who were admitted with personal tickets which he then exchanged for money.

Part Two

1. *Mme Souza . . . Amélie de Mansfield:* Adelaide Filleul, marquise de Souza (1761–1836), gathered a brilliant salon in Paris before the revolution, which included Talleyrand among its habitués. She fled to England in 1792, but her husband was arrested in Boulogne and guillotined, after which she supported herself by writing novels. In his notes for *War and Peace* Tolstoy men-

tions the popularity of Mme de Souza's novels as a characteristic of Russian society of the early nineteenth century. *Amélie de Mansfield*, however, is a novel by her younger contemporary, Sophie Cottin (1773–1807).

2. *overturned glass . . . sugar:* Russians sometimes drink tea from a glass instead of a cup. It was a custom among lower-class people to turn the glass upside down to show that they had finished their tea, as it was a custom to nibble from a lump of sugar instead of stirring it into the tea.

3. *Freemasons:* See note 22 to Volume I, Part One. In the autumn of 1866, Tolstoy found a large collection of Masonic texts in the Rumyantsev Museum in Moscow, which he drew from for his descriptions of Masonic ceremonies in what follows.

4. *Bazdeev . . . Martinists . . . Novikov's time:* Tolstoy based his portrayal of Osip (later Iosif) Alexeevich Bazdeev on the actual figure of the well-known Moscow Mason Osip Alexeevich Pozdeev (d. 1811). The Martinists were followers of the theosophist and Rosicrucian teachings of the French writers Martines de Pasqually (1727–73) and his disciple, Louis Claude de Saint-Martin (1743–1803), who were both closely connected with Masonry. N. I. Novikov (1744–1818) was a Russian journalist, publisher, and devoted Mason, who spent time in prison for his beliefs. In 1785 he published Saint-Martin's first work, *Des Erreurs et de la vérité* ("On Errors and the Truth").

5. *Thomas à Kempis:* A German mystical writer and Benedictine monk (1379–1471), author of the *De Imitatione Christi* ("Of the Imitation of Christ"), one of the most widely read Christian devotional works.

6. *In the beginning . . . God:* The first words of the Gospel of John.

7. *kill the fatted calf:* In Christ's parable of the prodigal son (Luke 15: 11–32), the father kills the fatted calf in celebration of his son's return.

8. *our second war with Napoleon:* See note 17 to Volume I, Part Two. The Prussian army was virtually annihilated at the battles of Jena and Auerstädt, and well-supplied fortresses were surrendered one after another without resistance as the French army moved east into Poland. In November 1806, the vanguard of the Russian army, under the command of General Bennigsen, entered Warsaw.

9. *Tu l'as voulu . . . :* A line spoken by the protagonist in Molière's comedy *Georges Dandin, ou Le mari confondu* (see note 12 to Volume II, Part One), which has become proverbial.

10. *Vienne . . . Vienne:* A slight anachronism. The treaty of Bartenstein between Prussia, Austria, and Russia on the one side and France on the other was being negotiated in April 1807, after Napoleon's army fought several indecisive battles. Friedrich-Wilhelm III, who felt somewhat encouraged by Napoleon's unsuccess, found the French conditions too stiff.

11. *l'homme à l'esprit profond:* Tolstoy's mistake. Shitov is *l'homme de beaucoup de mérite*; the Danish envoy himself is the *esprit profond*.

12. *pour le Roi de Prusse:* In French, to do something *pour le Roi de Prusse* is to go to a lot of trouble for nothing.

13. *Preussisch-Eylau:* The battle of Preussisch-Eylau took place on 8 February 1807. On the Russian side, Bennigsen lost more than a third of his men, but there were also heavy losses on the French side. Both claimed the victory.

14. *bread and salt:* The meeting of guests (including sovereigns) with an offering of bread and salt was traditional in Russia, bread being the staff of life and salt, which had to be imported, being a luxury.

15. *Peter and Paul:* Pierre's patron saint is Peter, but the Orthodox Church gives the same feast day to Peter and Paul (29 June), who are often portrayed together on icons, and therefore they are both his patron saints.

16. *marshal:* Marshal of the nobility was the highest elective office in a Russian province before the reforms of the 1860s. Governors and administrators were appointed by the sovereign.

17. *freed of state . . . fetters:* The Russian Orthodox Church was traditionally headed by the patriarch of Moscow, who was elected by the bishops of the Church. In 1700, at the death of the patriarch Adrian, Peter the Great stopped the election of a new patriarch, and in 1721 he issued a decree effectively making himself the head of the Church, which was administered by a synod of bishops under a lay "procurator" appointed by the emperor. This "synodal" period lasted until the 1917 revolution.

18. *Herder's teaching:* See note 18 to Volume I, Part Two.

19. *wanderers:* In Russian popular religious life, "wanderers" were people who left home and and went on a sort of perpetual pilgrimage to various holy places, praying and living on charity.

20. *to partake of the holy, heavenly mysteries:* A naïvely ornate way of saying that she took communion, the central Christian sacrament of bread and wine.

21. *a holy fool:* A "holy fool" (or "fool in God," or "fool for Christ's sake"—*yurodivyi* in Russian) could be a harmless village idiot, but there are also saintly persons or ascetics whose saintliness is expressed as "folly." Holy fools of that sort were known from early in Orthodox tradition.

22. *the Mother of God of the Caves:* That is, the icon of the Mother of God from the Monastery of the Caves in Kiev, founded in the eleventh century by St. Anthony of the Caves, which became the most important cultural centre of the Kievan period of Russian history. The relics of many saints are venerated there, as Pelageyushka mentions in the next chapter.

23. *the battle of Friedland:* The Russian advance, begun with successful actions by Bagration and Platov, ended with defeat in June 1807 at the battle of Friedland in East Prussia.

24. *lint:* Noble ladies would get together and contribute to the war effort by shredding lint, which was used for dressing wounds.

25. *Tilsit:* Napoleon and Alexander I met at Tilsit on 25 June (13 June by the Julian calendar, used in Russia until 1917) to conclude a peace. The negotiations, to which the king of Prussia was not invited, took place during the night in a pavilion on a raft in the middle of the Niemen River. The peace lasted for five years.

26. *The emperors exchanged decorations . . . Preobrazhensky battalion:* The order of the *Légion d'honneur* was instituted by Napoleon in 1802 in recognition of military and civil services. The first class of the order of St. Andrew (the patron saint of Russia) was the highest award given in Russia. The Russian emperor traditionally held the rank of colonel in his Preobrazhensky regiment, which is why that specific battalion was honoured by the French emperor's guards.

Part Three

1. *Erfurt . . . meeting:* In September 1808, Alexander I, Napoleon, and some German monarchs met in Erfurt to confirm the validity of the Tilsit treaty and make a public show of the strength of the Franco-Russian alliance. Napoleon wanted assurance of Russia's support in case of a new war with Austria, but did not obtain it.

2. *free ploughmen . . . quitrent:* The status of "free ploughmen" was introduced by law in Russia in 1803, but only a few landowners released their peasants from serfdom. Serfs owed their masters a certain amount of labour on the land (the corvée), but some landowers allowed them to pay rent in place of the services required of them.

3. *the young Speransky:* Speransky was head of the Ministry of the Interior from 1803 to 1807. In 1808 he became the closest associate of Alexander I on questions of internal policy. In 1809 Speransky developed a plan for reform, *An Introduction to the Code of State Law*, only part of which was implemented.

4. *Peterhof:* A splendid complex of palaces, gardens, and fountains south-west of Petersburg, planned as a summer residence by Peter the Great and considerably enhanced in the mid-eighteenth century by the empress Elizaveta I, who employed the Italian architect Bartolomeo Rastrelli (1700–71) on her building projects.

5. *court ranks . . . state councillor:* In 1809 Speransky issued a decree abolishing the privilege of the nobility to have court rank from childhood and obliging courtiers to be in government service, and another decree on examinations for administrative ranks: for the eighth rank (collegiate assessor) a university diploma was required; for the fifth rank (state councillor), in addition to that, ten years of government service were required. As a result, many old officials had to retire, and others bought themselves diplomas.

6. *comité de salut publique:* See note 11 to Volume II, Part One.

7. *Sila Andreich:* A jocular name for Arakcheev. "Andreich" is the familiar form of his patronymic Andreevich; "Sila" is Russian for "strength" or "power."

8. *an insignificant seminarian:* Russian seminary education was open to poorer people who

1234 ～ ○ *Notes to pages 433–487*

could not afford private tutors or expensive schools, and did not necessarily mean that the student was preparing for a church career. Speransky was of humble origin, the son of a village priest.

9. *Code Napoléon . . . Justiniani:* The French code of civil law, or Code Napoléon, was established by the revolutionary assemblies, Napoleon, and his jurists in 1804 and is still the basis for most European civil law. The Codex Justiniani was the most important code of Roman law in the late empire, compiled and first issued in 529 at the order of the Byzantine emperor Justinian I (ca. 483–565). It has formed the basis for the study of law in Europe since the twelfth century.

10. *the figures on Solomon's temple:* King Solomon's temple in Jerusalem was ornamented with carved or moulded cherubs, palm trees, open flowers, pomegranates, lilies, gourds, lions, oxen, wreaths, and so on (see the description in I Kings 6–7).

11. *Illuminism:* The sect of the Illuminati (in German *Illuminaten*), founded in 1776, at Ingolstadt in Bavaria, by Prof. Ada Weishaupt, was close to the Masons in ideology and structure, but in addition had republican political goals. It was suppressed by the Bavarian government in 1785.

12. *And the life . . . comprehended it not:* Pierre quotes John 1:4–5.

13. *the Song of Songs:* Also known as "The Song of Solomon," a collection of mystical-erotic poems dating in its recorded form to the third century B.C. but containing much more ancient material.

14. *the Finnish war:* At the instigation of Napoleon, who wanted to punish Sweden for its alliance with England, Alexander I began a war with Sweden in February 1808, which ended with the Russian annexation of Finland.

15. *the English Embankment:* This section of the Neva embankment in Petersburg, just downstream from the imperial Winter Palace, was lined with wealthy palaces and mansions.

16. *the Tavrichesky Garden:* This mansion and garden, east of the city centre, in the large bend of the Neva, was at that time the residence of the dowager empress Maria Feodorovna.

17. *Marya Antonovna:* Princess Marya Antonovna Naryshkin (1779–1854) was for a long time the mistress of the emperor Alexander.

18. *the State Council:* At Speransky's suggestion, a State Council was instituted in Russia as an advisory body to the emperor, to examine legislative, administrative, and judicial matters. It met for the first time on 1 January 1810 and continued in existence until 1906.

19. *Speransky's modest private house:* This scene is based on the memoirs of Speransky's daughter, published in *The Life of Count Speransky*, by M. A. Korf (1861), which was in Tolstoy's library at Yasnaya Polyana. Tolstoy adds an ironic tone that is not found in Korf's book.

20. *Napoleon's Spanish campaign:* To establish a total blockade of England from European trade, Napoleon crossed the Pyrenees in 1807 and invaded Spain. In 1808 he placed his brother Joseph, then king of Naples, on the throne of Ferdinand VII and made his brother-in-law, Marshal Murat, king of Naples. But by 1813 the English under Wellington and the Spanish partisan forces (whose tactics were the origin of the word *guerrilla*, or "little war") had driven the French out of Spain.

21. *Let the dead bury their dead:* Prince Andrei quotes Christ's words in Luke 9:59.

22. *map of love:* Mlle Madeleine de Scudéry (1607–1701) set the style for the "precious" salons in seventeenth-century Paris. The "map of love," or "map of the land of tenderness" (*la carte du tendre*), first made its appearance in her novel *Clélie* (1654) and then in her salon, where it became a very popular game, as it did later in Russia.

23. *killed in Turkey:* At the negotiations in Tilsit and Erfurt, Napoleon had promised to give the east to Alexander I and take the west for himself. In the spring of 1809, the Russians resumed their military activity against the Turks on the lower Danube and in the Caucasus.

24. *in chains:* Ascetics would sometimes wear heavy lengths of chain wrapped about their bodies as a form of mortification of the flesh.

25. *no sorrow . . . bliss:* Words reminiscent of a prayer for the dead from the Orthodox burial and memorial services: "Give rest with the Saints, O Christ, to the soul of thy servant, where there is neither sickness, nor sorrow, nor sighing, but life everlasting."

Part Four

1. *in the sweat of our face:* In cursing Adam, God says, "In the sweat of thy face shalt thou eat bread, till thou return unto the ground: for out of it wast thou taken" (Genesis 3:19).

2. *get an Anna:* The Order of St. Anna, named for the mother of the Virgin Mary, was founded in 1735 by Karl-Friedrich, duke of Schleswig-Holstein, in honour of his wife, Anna Petrovna, daughter of the Russian emperor Peter the Great. It had four degrees, two civil and two military.

3. *Vain . . . Russians:* The first line of P. I. Kutuzov's "cantata" (see note 10 to Volume II, Part One).

4. *raising his cap:* A conventional sign among hunters indicating that the game has been sighted.

5. *represented Diana:* The Roman goddess Diana, daughter of Jupiter, was a huntress.

6. *"Barinya":* The title of this popular song means "lady" or "mistress."

7. *the musician Dimmler:* E. K. Dimmler is mentioned a number of times in Zhikharev's *Diary of a Student* (see note 34 to Volume I, Part One). He gave piano lessons in Moscow in the early nineteenth century.

8. *The Water-Carrier:* The opera *Les Deux journées* ("The Two Days"), better known as *The Water-Carrier*, by Luigi Cherubini (1760–1842), who directed the Paris Conservatory for twenty years and was known for his religious works, operas, and quartets. It was first produced in Vienna in 1805 and was much admired by Beethoven.

9. *Monsieur Field:* John Field (1782–1837) was an Irish-born composer who made his career in Petersburg, where he lived from 1804 to 1831. He was the first composer of "nocturnes" for the piano, which had a great influence on Chopin.

10. *quietly pouring wax:* A method of divination by pouring melted candle wax into water and interpreting the resulting shapes (which Tolstoy calls "shadows").

Part Five

1. *Iverskaya Chapel:* The Iverskaya Chapel, built on to the Voskresensky Gate of Red Square in Moscow, houses a copy—made in 1648 at the request of the tsar Alexei Mikhailovich (1629–76)—of a miracle-working icon known as the Iverskaya Mother of God, thought to have been painted in Byzantium in the eighth century and kept in the Iveron ("Iberian") Monastery on Mount Athos. One of the holiest sites in Moscow, the chapel was demolished in Soviet times and replaced by a statue of a worker, but it was rebuilt in 1999 and the icon has been put back.

2. *an illegitimate wife:* In 1809, Napoleon managed to annul his marriage to Josephine Beauharnais (1763–1814). After making unsuccessful overtures for the hand of the Russian grand duchess Ekaterina Pavlovna, in 1810 he married the archduchess Maria-Louisa of Austria (1791–1847), whose father, the emperor Franz I, had suffered a serious defeat in his last war with Napoleon and hoped that the marriage would improve the position of his empire.

3. *The Spanish . . . the fourteenth of June:* The reference is probably to the battle of Talavera de la Reina in July 1809, at which the French were defeated by a coalition of Spanish, Portuguese, and English troops under the command of Wellington.

4. *Astrea . . . Manna Seekers . . . an authentic Scottish rug . . . charters:* "Astrea" and "Manna Seekers" were the names of two Masonic lodges in Petersburg. One of the necessary accessories of a Masonic lodge was a rug with symbolic images, and each lodge sought to obtain such a rug from a venerable Masonic organization (the first lodges emerged in England and Scotland), along with "charters" listing the rites and regulations of the order.

5. *the duke of Oldenburg:* In 1810 Napoleon abolished the independence of the Hanseatic towns of Hamburg, Bremen, and Lübeck, in the north of Germany, because they did not or could not observe the strictures of his continental blockade, and for the same reason he drove out the duke of Oldenburg and seized his lands. The duke had been hastily married to the sister of Alexander I to make it impossible for her to marry Napoleon (see note 2 above), and this conflict, which broke the Tilsit accord, greatly displeased the Russian court. The emperor sent a note of protest to all the courts of Europe.

6. *to overthrow the head of the Catholic religion:* On 17 May 1809 Napoleon proclaimed the annexation of Rome and the Papal States to the French empire. On 10 June French troops entered Rome, and Pope Pius VII was arrested and taken to Savona on the Gulf of Genoa and later to Fontainebleau. He remained Napoleon's hostage until 1814.

7. *Peter the Great's old cudgel . . . Kunstkamera:* The Kunstkamera on the University Embankment in Petersburg was founded by Peter the Great in 1714 as a museum to house natural and human curiosities and rarities. Among the collections are various mementoes of its founder— some clothes, a copy of his death mask, a cast of his right hand, and his cudgel, suggestive of his forceful way of ruling Russia.

8. *her album:* Russian girls used to keep personal albums in which their friends and acquaintances would draw or write things for them.

9. *Poor Liza:* A novel by the Russian writer and historian Nikolai Mikhailovich Karamzin (1766–1826), published in 1792. It marked the shift in Russian literature from classicism to "sensibility."

10. *Over-Shameless:* Marya Dmitrievna plays on the name of the French dressmaker Mme Aubert-Chalmet. The Russian reads *Ober-Shelma*, which means something like "Super-Rogue." Napoleon put the dressmaker in charge of his table when he was in Moscow, and she set up a kitchen in the cathedral of the Archangel in the Kremlin. When the French left Moscow, she went with them.

11. *Everything will be forgiven her . . . much fun:* A common distortion of the sense of Christ's words in Luke 7:47: "Wherefore I say unto thee, Her sins, which are many, are forgiven; for she loved much." The woman in question is sometimes taken to be Mary Magdalene.

12. *the Dormition on Mogiltsy:* A modest neoclassical church which still stands on Chisty Lane in the Arbatskaya section of Moscow, dedicated to the Dormition (Assumption) of the Mother of God, built in 1799 on the site of an older church. While digging the foundation, the builders came upon deep pits filled with many human bones; hence the name of the church, which means "Dormition on the Graves."

13. *her criminal love for her son:* Mlle George is obviously reciting from the title role of the tragedy *Phèdre*, by Jean Racine (1639–99), for which she was famous. The actress, whose real name was Marguerite-Josephine Weymer (1787–1867), performed in Moscow and Petersburg in 1808–12.

14. *towards the front corner:* Icons are traditionally hung in the right corner opposite the entrance to a room. Balaga, being a good peasant, crosses himself towards the icon(s) on coming in.

15. *We have to sit down:* It is a Russian custom for people to sit down together for a few moments of silence and prayer before leaving on a journey or moving out.

16. *Styoshka:* The Gypsy singer Stepanida Soldatova (Styosha or Styoshka) was famous in Moscow in the early nineteenth century and greatly admired by the musical (and non-musical) elite.

17. *Speransky . . . Moscow:* After a period of almost unlimited authority following the treaty of Tilsit, Speransky was abruptly dismissed by Alexander I in 1812 and exiled to Perm. In foreign policy, he had been a strong advocate of alliance with France, and as a new war with France became inevitable, he was suspected of collusion with Napoleon and even of treason.

VOLUME III

Part One

1. *the Continental System:* The blockade imposed by Napoleon on trade between the European continent and England (see note 20 to Volume II, Part Three).

2. *as he said . . . St. Helena:* See note 19 to Volume I, Part Two.

3. *the legitimists of that time:* Those who upheld the rights of the legitimate ruling dynasty, in this case the Bourbons.

4. *The hearts of kings . . . :* See Proverbs 21:1: "The king's heart is in the hand of the Lord, as the rivers of water: he turneth it whithersoever he will."

5. *the movement of troops into Prussia . . . an armed peace:* In 1811, as Napoleon was preparing for war with Russia, he asked Prussia to support him with troops, but Prussia hesitated. Napoleon then told Marshal Davout to enter and occupy Prussia at the first sign from him. In 1812 a treaty was signed in Paris in which Prussia agreed to participate on Napoleon's side in his future wars.

6. *honours in Dresden:* Napoleon spent the month of May 1812 in Dresden in the company of his new allies the emperor of Austria, the king of Prussia, the king of Saxony, and the sixteen German princes of the Confederation of the Rhine, which was put together by Napoleon following his victory at Austerlitz, and which lasted from 1806 to 1813.

7. *another wife had been left in Paris:* See note 2 to Volume II, Part Five.

8. *Légion d'honneur:* On founding the order of the Legion of Honour, Napoleon made himself its first grand chancellor (see note 26 to Volume II, Part Two).

9. *Quos vult perdere—dementat:* An abbreviated form of the saying *Quos Deus vult perdere, prius dementat* ("Those whom God wants to destroy, he first drives mad").

10. *a separate commander in chief:* Barclay de Tolly was commander in chief of the first army in the west (later replaced by Kutuzov); Bagration of the second, further to the south; and Tormasov of the third, a reserve force being drawn up near the Austrian border.

11. *Kourakine. . . passeports:* On 25 April 1812, the Russian ambassador in Paris, Prince A. B. Kurakin, conveyed to Napoleon the request of Alexander I that he withdraw his troops from Prussia. The request was denied, and Kurakin then asked for papers allowing him to leave France.

12. *Mameluke Rustan:* The Mamelukes were a military force, originally formed of Circassian slaves, who seized control of Egypt in 1254 and remained a power until 1811, when they were crushed by the Egyptian viceroy Mohammed Ali (1769–1849). Napoleon had defeated them at the battle of the pyramids on 21 July 1798, and had brought one of the prisoners, Rustan, back to France as a bodyguard.

13. *peace with the Turks . . . Moldavia and Wallachia . . . Finland:* Following a series of victories and diplomatic efforts, Kutuzov signed a peace treaty with the Turks in Bucharest on 16 May 1812, to the great annoyance of Napoleon, who was hoping to make use of the Turkish army in his war on Russia. In the treaty, part of Moldavia (Bessarabia) went to the Russians, but the rest of Moldavia and Wallachia remained under Turkish rule. For Finland, see note 14 to Volume II, Part Three.

14. *the Steins, the Armfelts, the Wintzingerodes, the Bennigsens . . . Alexander:* The Prussian minister Baron von Stein, banished by Napoleon for sympathizing with Spain and seeking to free Prussia from French occupation, was living in Russia in 1812. The Swedish general and statesman G. M. Armfelt, who had been in the service of Russia since 1811 as president of the committee for Finnish affairs and was a member of the State Council, intrigued against Speransky and played a part in his exile. He accompanied Alexander I during the 1812 campaign. General Wintzingerode could be called a "French subject" only because Napoleon had included his native Hesse in the Confederation of the Rhine; he had been in service to Russia since 1797. General Bennigsen had been defeated by Napoleon at the battle of Friedland in 1807, but "terrible memories" is a reference to his participation in the plot to assassinate Alexander's father, the emperor Paul I.

15. *Bernadotte . . . Russia:* In 1810 the French marshal Jean-Baptiste Bernadotte was adopted as his heir by King Charles XIII of Sweden, who hoped to use French influence to get Finland back, but in 1812 Bernadotte went over to the anti-French alliance.

16. *that barrier . . . destroyed:* Napoleon is referring to the Polish territories bordering Russia, which Russia had acquired as a result of the partitioning of Poland in 1793.

17. *defeat of the French in Spain:* Under Wellington's command, the allied English, Spanish, and Portuguese forces won a series of victories over the French in 1812, culminating in the battle of Salamanca on 22 July. By August they were in Madrid.

18. *Poltawa . . . happy response:* King Charles XII of Sweden (1682–1718), up to then consid-

ered invincible, tried to get to Moscow through the Ukraine, but was crushed by Peter the Great at the battle of Poltava in 1709. Tolstoy deliberately uses the "foreign" spelling "Poltawa."

19. *Württembergs, Badens, Weimars . . . :* The mother of Alexander I, Maria Feodorovna, was princess of Württemberg before her marriage to Paul I; his sister Ekaterina Pavlovna was married to the duke of Oldenburg, and his sister Marya Pavlovna to the prince of Saxe-Weimar.

20. *in Moldavia . . . commander in chief:* Having fallen into disgrace after the battle of Austerlitz, Kutuzov was sent to administrative posts in Kiev and then Vilno, but in March 1811 he was brought back to lead the army in Moldavia.

21. *his German accent:* In fact, Barclay de Tolly was of Scottish ancestry and was born in Lithuania, but Tolstoy reflects the habit among Russian soldiers of considering all foreigners "Germans" (see note 3 to Volume I, Part Two).

22. *Jena and Auerstädt:* See note 17 to Volume II, Part One.

23. *the Russian Thermopylae . . . alongside them:* In 480 B.C. three hundred Spartans under the command of their king, Leonidas, defended the pass at Thermopylae in Thessaly against the entire army of the Persian king Xerxes and perished there. At Saltanovo, General Raevsky with a detachment of 15,000 men fought for ten hours against the five divisions of Marshals Davout and Mortier. Raevsky himself denied the truth of the story about his two sons, though his courage during the battle was well-known.

24. *St. Peter's fast . . . prepare for communion:* There is a two-week fast period preceding the feast of Sts. Peter and Paul on 29 June. Preparation for communion involves attendance at weekday and Sunday services, prayer, fasting, and confession.

25. *she tried to follow and understand:* The language of the Russian Orthodox Church is Church Slavonic, a liturgical language with its own alphabet, developed originally in the ninth century from Slavic dialects spoken in Thessaly and Bulgaria, which is only partly comprehensible for Russians.

26. *As one world:* A common example of the problems that can occur for Russians in understanding church prayers. In both Slavonic and Russian, the words for *peace* and *world* sound the same; hence when the deacon says "peace" here and further on, Natasha (or possibly Tolstoy himself) understands it as "the world." It is impossible to convey this confusion in English.

27. *the synod:* See note 17 to Volume II, Part Two.

28. *the feast of the Trinity:* Another name for the feast of Pentecost in the Orthodox Church, marking the end of the Pascal period. The priest and congregation kneel at vespers while the priest recites three long prayers.

29. *Moses . . . Gideon . . . David:* Three famous Old Testament confrontations. In Exodus 17:8–16, Moses sent Joshua to fight against Amalek and Joshua "mowed down Amalek and his people with the edge of the sword"; the battle of Gideon, the fifth of the Judges of Israel, with the Midianites is recounted in Judges 7–8; and the story of David's slaying of the Philistine champion Goliath is told in I Samuel 17.

30. *the Apocalypse of St. John:* The language of the final book of the New Testament, also called *The Revelation to St. John*, is so symbolic that it can easily be applied to all sorts of historical events. The "beast from the earth" whose number is 666 (Revelation 13:11–18) deceives the people and has been interpreted as symbolizing imperial power.

31. *spine . . . prickly old German:* In the original, there is a pun on the words for *spy* (*shpion*) and *mushroom* (*shampinion*). The incident is recounted in *Notes of the Year Twelve*, by Sergei Glinka, editor of the *Russian Messenger*, who served as a Moscow militiaman in 1805–7. The book, published in Petersburg in 1836, is in Tolstoy's library at Yasnaya Polyana. The pun is thought to be Rastopchin's own invention.

32. *our first-throned capital, Moscow:* A deferential title of the elder of the "two capitals" of Russia.

33. *the Tsar-Cannon:* An enormous bronze cannon, weighing forty tons, cast in 1586, which stands in the Kremlin not far from the cathedral of the Dormition.

34. *tossing biscuits from the balcony:* Despite his claim (see Appendix) that he could always give historical references for the passages in his novel in which historical figures speak and act, Tolstoy was unable, when challenged by the poet Prince P. A. Vyazemsky, to supply a reference for this unlikely behaviour of the emperor.

35. *the Slobodsky palace:* The seat of the Assembly of the Nobility in Moscow. The details come from *Notes of the Year Twelve,* by Sergei Glinka, who was present (see note 31 above).

36. *contrat social:* See note 17 to Volume I, Part One.

Part Two

1. *an unpopular German:* See note 21 to Volume III, Part One.

2. *minister:* Barclay de Tolly was the Russian minister of war from 1810 to 1812.

3. *patriotic letters from Moscow:* Like all upper-class young women of her time, Julie has difficulty writing in Russian and constantly lapses into French words and syntax.

4. *lint:* See note 24 to Volume II, Part Two.

5. *Directive . . . to . . . Baron Asch:* Tolstoy quotes from Barclay's actual directive of 20 August 1812, which is cited in *A History of the Fatherland War of 1812,* by M. I. Bogdanovich, published in Petersburg in 1859.

6. *the miracle-working icon of Smolensk:* It was customary in times of war, epidemic, or natural disaster to "take up" an icon of the Mother of God and carry it in procession, stopping on the way to serve offices of prayer for deliverance. The icon of the Smolensk Mother of God, the prototype of which was sent to Russia by the Byzantine emperor Constantine Monomakh in the eleventh century, has long been considered miracle-working.

7. *Bagration . . . wrote . . . to Arakcheev:* Bagration's letter was published in the appendix to Volume 2 of *A History of the Fatherland War of 1812* (see note 5 above).

8. *gunpowder . . . those who invented it:* See note 10 to Volume I, Part Two.

9. *un homme de beaucoup de mérite:* The "man of great merit" is generally thought to be the philosopher Joseph de Maistre (1753–1821), author of *Soirées de Saint-Pétersbourg* (1821), who served in Russia as ambassador of the king of Sardinia from 1803 to 1817. Tolstoy drew on his correspondence for details of this particular soirée.

10. *mania for 'fronding':* Prince Vassily makes a Russian verb out of the French verb *fronder* ("to criticize by mockery, to defy"). A *fronde* is a sling. Historically, the Fronde was a power struggle that took place in France during the minority of Louis XIV (1648–53).

11. *Joconde:* One of the early, licentious *Contes* ("Tales") by the French poet and fabulist Jean de La Fontaine (1621–95).

12. *Thiers, recounting this episode:* See note 17 to Volume I, Part Two. The details of the impression Napoleon makes on the Cossack were most probably invented by Thiers himself.

13. *kissed . . . the hand of the old prince:* It was customary in Russia to lay a body out on a table before the coffin arrived. The floor was strewn with juniper boughs for the sake of their strong fragrance. It is also customary to kiss the hand of the deceased in leave-taking before the burial.

14. *Pyotr Feodorovich . . . seven years:* Tolstoy uses the archaic spelling "Feodorovich" here, as with the dowager empress Maria Feodorovna. Peter III reigned for only six months before his assassination. The mysterious circumstances of his death gave rise to rumours among the people that he had escaped and would one day return to the throne, and Russian history knew a number of false Peters, the most famous being the Cossack rebel Emelyan Pugachev.

15. *the paghrtisan one:* Denisov is modelled—a little too closely, as Tolstoy himself admits (see Appendix)—on the famous Russian soldier-poet Denis Davydov, an older friend of Pushkin's, who initiated the partisan war against the retreating French army and afterwards published an *Essay Towards a Theory of Partisan Warfare* (1821).

16. *bread and salt:* See note 14 to Volume II, Part Two.

17. *Les chevaliers du Cygne:* The full title is *Les chevaliers du Cygne, ou la cour de Charlemagne* ("The Knights of the Swan, or the Court of Charlemagne"), a three-volume Gothic novel by Mme de Genlis, published in 1797 in Hamburg, while the author was living in exile in Berlin.

18. *Kamensky . . . thirty thousand men:* The gifted young general N. M. Kamensky (1778–1811) took part in several stormings of fortresses (Shumla, Batyn, Rushchuk) during the Turkish campaign of 1810–11, but fell ill and died before the end of the war, which was negotiated by Kutuzov.

19. *Rastopchin's little posters:* The aim of the posters devised by the military governor of Moscow was both to inform people of the state of affairs and to stir up patriotic feelings. They did neither: the information they contained was false, and their style was artificially jovial and folksy.

20. *Vassily Lvovich Pushkin:* Vassily Lvovich Pushkin (1767–1830), uncle of Russia's greatest poet, Alexander Pushkin (1799–1835), was a poet of light verse, famous for his epigrams, madrigals, and doggerel to set rhymes (*bouts-rimés*).

21. *une barque de Charon:* In Greek mythology, Charon is the ferryman who carries the shades of the dead across the river Styx to the house of Hades.

22. *Count Wittgenstein had beaten the French:* Count Wittgenstein with a corps of 25,000 men was protecting the road to Petersburg. On 30 July 1812 he repelled an attack of the French under Marshal Oudinot.

23. *hot-air balloon . . . Leppich:* Franz Leppich, a Dutch peasant, went to Moscow in 1812 to convince Rastopchin that he could build a hot-air balloon that would enable the Russians to attack the French from the air. (Leppich had made the same proposal a year earlier to Napoleon, who had ordered him removed from French territory.) When the balloon was finally tried out, it failed to rise, and nothing more was seen of its inventor.

24. *the Shevardino barrow:* The Kurgan or Barrow people (*kurgan* is Russian and Turkish for "barrow") were a Bronze Age culture that is thought to have originated in Russia and spread across northern Europe in the fifth to third millennia B.C., characterized by their practice of burying their dead in mounds or barrows, which survive to this day. The word *kurgan*, like *barrow*, may also mean a hill or hillock, and by extension a hill fort of the kind also built by the Kurgan people.

25. *the plan . . . is as in the map opposite:* Tolstoy spent two days in September 1867 studying the battlefield of Borodino and comparing the terrain with historical accounts of the battle, after which he sketched a map correcting the descriptions of the historians, which is the basis of the map included here.

26. *The Iverskaya . . . The Smolenskaya Mother of God:* See note 1 to Volume II, Part Five and note 6 above. The icons in question would have been copies.

27. *You'll be a teacher in the corps . . . :* S. N. Marin, imperial adjutant to Alexander I, was known for his parodies and comic verses. G. V. Gerakov was a teacher of history at the Petersburg Cadet Corps and a writer of ultrapatriotic works. Marin's verses read: "You'll be a writer, yes, you will, / And with words your readers drill, / You'll be a teacher in the corps, / You'll be a captain evermore."

28. *fought at Salamanca:* See note 17 to Volume III, Part One.

29. *Beausset . . . with a cloth:* The following passage is generally borne out by the memoirs of Beausset himself, but, as he does with other sources, Tolstoy adds an irony not found in the original.

30. *bilboquet:* A child's toy made up of a ball with a hole in it attached by a string to a stick with a peg at the tip. The point of the game is to catch the ball by landing the hole on the peg.

31. *This disposition . . . was the following:* The text of Napoleon's disposition is taken word for word from Bogdanovich's *History of the Fatherland War of 1812* (see note 5 above).

32. *the viceroy's:* The reference is to Napoleon's stepson, Eugène de Beauharnais, whom Napoleon made viceroy of Italy in 1805, when he created the "kingdom of Italy" with himself as king (see note 14 to Volume I, Part One). The viceroy took part in the battles of Borodino and Maloyaroslavets at the head of the army of Italy.

33. *6th September 1812:* French documents and reports cited by Tolstoy give dates according to the Gregorian calendar (the "New Style"), which in the nineteenth century was twelve days ahead of the Julian calendar (the "Old Style") still used in Russia. Elsewhere he gives the dates by the Julian calendar, according to which the date here is 25 August.

34. *Charles IX having an upset stomach:* On the night of the feast of St. Bartholomew, 24 August 1572, King Charles IX of France, at the instigation of his mother, Catherine de Medicis, and the family of the Guises, ordered a massacre of French Protestants.

35. *Lodi . . . Wagram:* A list of brilliant victories from Napoleon's campaigns against Austria and Prussia between 1796 and 1809, which had made him seem invincible.

36. *Murat had been taken prisoner:* The news was false. The captured general was Charles

Auguste Bonnamy de Bellefontaine (1764–1830), who had taken the Raevsky redoubt during the battle of Borodino, but then lost all his troops defending it and fell with twenty bayonet wounds. The Russians nursed him back to life, however, and returned him to France in 1814.

37. *La guerre de Russie . . . bienfaits:* This and the following quotation are from *The Memorial of St. Helena* (see note 19 to Volume I, Part Two).

Part Three

1. *the siege of Saragossa:* The siege of the Spanish city of Saragossa, capital of the province of Aragon, lasted for over two months, ending on 20 February 1809. The resistance of the citizens was so heroic that the French had to take the city piecemeal, storming each house.

2. *the battle of Friedland:* See note 23 to Volume II, Part Two.

3. *allowed Mme Aubert-Chalmet . . . to remain in the city:* However, see note 10 to Volume II, Part Five.

4. *he gathered the people . . . to fight the French:* Rastopchin's posters summoned the people to assemble at the Three Hills Gate in Moscow on 1 September "to exterminate the villain."

5. *Georges Dandin:* See note 9 to Volume II, Part Two.

6. *the holy brothers of the Society of Jesus:* Members of the Jesuit order, founded in 1543. The order was expelled from Portugal in 1759 and from France in 1762, and was briefly suppressed by Pope Clement XIV in 1773. Catherine the Great protected the Jesuits, as did the kings of Prussia, but Alexander I eventually expelled them from Russia. A *Jésuite à robe courte* was a sympathizer who was not a member of the order.

7. *Columbus's egg . . . simplicity:* The story goes that Columbus, angered when someone at a banquet said that anyone could have discovered America, asked if anyone there could balance an egg on its end. When they all failed, Columbus took a hard-boiled egg, flattened one end on the table, and stood it up.

8. *whoever marries a divorced woman:* It is said by Christ, in Matthew 5:32 and in Luke 16:18.

9. *Hamburg Gazette:* The story of Vereshchagin and his false "proclamations" is historically accurate, as is Tolstoy's account, in chapter XXV, of Vereshchagin's ultimate fate and Rastopchin's cynical role in it.

10. *Speransky and Magnitsky . . . Klyucharev:* For Speransky, see note 3 to Volume II, Part Three; note 17 to Volume II, Part Five; and note 14 to Volume III, Part One. M. L. Magnitsky was an associate of Speransky's in 1810–11 and shared his disgrace. F. P. Klyucharev, the director of the Moscow Post Office and a Mason from Novikov's circle (see note 4 to Volume II, Part Two), was totally innocent, but aroused Rastopchin's suspicions by interceding for young Vereshchagin, who was a friend of his son's.

11. *a Vladimir and an Anna on the neck:* See note 5 to Volume I, Part Two and note 2 to Volume II, Part Four respectively. The Order of St. Anna had two degrees, one worn on the breast, the other on a ribbon round the neck.

12. *tied a knot in it:* As a reminder to himself—a Russian custom that still persists.

13. *to sit . . . and pray before their departure:* See note 15 to Volume II, Part Five.

14. *boyars:* Tolstoy implies Napoleon's ignorance of Russian history: the boyars were a privileged order of the medieval Russian aristocracy, abolished a century earlier by Peter the Great.

15. *Rastopchin . . . notes:* Count Rastopchin's *La vérité sur l'incendie de Moscou* ("The Truth About the Burning of Moscow") was first published in Paris in 1823.

16. *the Reign of Terror:* See note 11 to Volume II, Part One. *La Terreur,* as it is known in French, directed by the Committee for Public Safety, lasted from 31 May 1793 to 27 July 1794; in the months of June–July 1794 alone, 1,400 people were sent to the guillotine.

17. *Meshkov, Vereshchagin:* P. A. Meshkov was a lawyer in Moscow. In 1812 he copied out Vereshchagin's "proclamations" (see note 9 above), for which he was sentenced to be stripped of rank and nobility and sent to the army as a simple soldier. He was pardoned by Alexander I in 1816.

18. *Inside the Kremlin, the bells were ringing for vespers:* There are five churches and the Ivan

the Great bell tower in the Kremlin. The French evidently did not know that and, confused by the ringing of so many bells, thought it was a call to arms.

19. *this student had been shot:* During a military review in front of the Schönbrunn palace in Vienna, on 12 October 1809, the seventeen-year-old German student Friedrich Staps attempted to assassinate Napoleon with a kitchen knife. He was sentenced by a military court and shot on 17 October 1809.

20. *l'affaire du Sept:* That is, the battle of Borodino. Ramballe, being French, gives the date in the New Style (see note 33 to Volume III, Part Two); in the Old Style, it is 26 August, as Tolstoy says elsewhere. Further on, Ramballe also refers to the battle of Borodino in the French manner as *la grande bataille de la Moskowa* ("the great battle of the Moskova [River]").

21. *Paris, c'est Talma . . . boulevards:* Ramballe, reflecting Tolstoy's view of French culture, produces an interesting list of the merits of Paris—the tragic actor Talma, the actress la Duchesnois, the comedian Potier, the boulevards associated with the theatres—and into it sticks the Sorbonne, the city's ancient university.

22. *our dear mother of white st . . . :* Belokamennaya ("white-stoned") was an endearing epithet for Moscow, because of the whitewashed stone churches of the Kremlin.

23. *the Trinity monastery:* The Trinity–St. Sergius Monastery, to the north of Moscow, is named for its founder, St. Sergius of Radonezh (ca. 1319–92), the greatest of the saints of ancient Russia.

VOLUME IV

Part One

1. *the two empresses:* The mother of Alexander I, the dowager empress Maria Feodorovna, and his wife, Elizaveta Alexeevna (1779–1826), daughter of the margrave of Baden-Durlach, who became empress on Alexander's accession to the throne after the assassination of Paul I.

2. *the metropolitan . . . St. Sergius:* Platon II (born Platon Levshin, 1737–1812) was metropolitan of Moscow from 1775 until his death a few months after the battle of Borodino. A former instructor of rhetoric in the theological academy of the Trinity–St. Sergius Monastery, he was famous for his sermons, which were published posthumously in twenty volumes. In 1380 St. Sergius (see note 23 to Volume III, Part Three) blessed the grand prince of Vladimir, Dmitri Donskoy, before the battle of Kulikovo, the first successful attempt of the Russians to resist the Tartars.

3. *a diplomatic paper . . . le héros de Pétropol:* The standards were sent back to Vienna to chide the Austrians for changing sides and fighting for Napoleon. The Germanic name St. Petersburg was changed to Petropol for the same reason.

4. *Hosanna, blessed is He that comes:* As Christ rides into Jerusalem, the people who go before him and follow him cry out: "Hosanna; Blessed is he that cometh in the name of the Lord" (Mark 11:9). The same words are sung in the eucharistic prayer of the Orthodox liturgy.

5. *the surrender of Moscow to the French:* Bogdanovich mentions "some sort of landowner" in his *History of the Fatherland War of 1812* (see note 5 to Volume III, Part Two). The landowner was in fact I. A. Yakovlev, whose illegitimate son was the well-known radical writer and publicist Alexander Herzen (1812–70).

6. *owner of a carpet room:* A room in a manor house decorated with carpets in the Oriental style.

7. *Frola and Lavra . . . the horses' feast:* Floros and Lavros, stonemasons in Illyria, were martyred in the early second century, and their bodies were thrown into a dry well. More than a century later, horses were seen drinking at this well, and the intact relics of the twin brothers were found in it. The well was said to have healing powers for horses. Their icon shows the two saints

with the archangel Michael and below them a number of horses and horsemen at the well. There is a fine example from Novgorod in the Tretyakov Gallery in Moscow.

8. *"Christian" . . . krestyan:* The Russian word *krestyanin* ("peasant") comes from the word *khristianin*, pronounced almost identically and meaning "Christian" or simply "human being."

9. *The birds of the air . . . your Father feeds them:* A shortened quotation of Christ's words in the Sermon on the Mount: "Behold the fowls of the air: for they sow not, neither do they reap, nor gather into barns; yet your heavenly Father feedeth them" (Matthew 6:26).

Part Two

1. *the so-called flanking march beyond Krasnaya Pakhra:* This movement was part of Kutuzov's plan. He withdrew the Russian army from Moscow on the Ryazan road, but then shifted to the Tula road, and at Krasnaya Pakhra turned the main body of the army sharply southwards to the Kaluga road and camped at Tarutino, thus barring the way for the French to the fertile Russian provinces to the south and to cities with military supplies (Tula, Briansk), while the two Cossack regiments of the Russian rear guard continued to retreat down the Ryazan road, misleading Murat, who was in command of the French vanguard and indeed lost sight of the enemy.

2. *defending the Tula factory:* The city of Tula, some 160 miles south of Moscow, was renowned for its metalworkers, particularly its gunsmiths.

3. *torban:* The torban is a multistringed east European musical instrument combining features of the lute and the psaltery, played mainly in the Ukraine. Its name may come from the west European theorbo.

4. *To undercut Konovnitsyn:* After Borodino, Konovnitsyn was appointed general on duty of the army and would have been responsible for the failure to carry out the commander in chief's order.

5. *Captain Yakovlev . . . Tutolmin . . . :* See note 5 to Volume IV, Part One. Alexander Herzen recounts this episode from his father's life in his autobiographical work, *My Past and Thoughts* (1867), the early chapters of which were first published in the magazine *Polar Star* in 1856, where Tolstoy read them. In 1812, Major General I. V. Tutolmin was director of the Moscow orphanage and remained in Moscow when the French occupied it.

6. *Inhabitants of Moscow! . . . do not be slow to unite with us!:* Tolstoy took these two proclamations word for word from Volume III of *A Description of the Fatherland War of 1812,* by A. I. Mikhailovsky-Danilevsky, published in Petersburg in 1839. They are written in very bad Russian.

7. *Maison de ma mère . . . a sovereign's virtue:* Tolstoy found this detail in excerpts from Moscow newspapers of 18 September 1812, published in the *Russian Archive.*

8. *Thiers . . . Mr. Fain:* Agathon Jean François, Baron Fain (1778–1837), Napoleon's secretary and archivist, published a number of works contributing to the history of the emperor's last years. Thiers polemicizes with Fain's *Manuscript About the Year 1812* (Paris, 1827) in his *History of the Consulate and the Empire* (see note 17 to Volume I, Part One).

9. *his letters to Mme de Staël:* The French novelist and essayist Anne-Louise-Germaine de Staël (1766–1817) was an outspoken critic of Napoleon, who banished her from Paris in 1802. In 1812 she was in Russia. She indeed exchanged letters with Kutuzov and was the first to congratulate him on his appointment as commander in chief.

10. *the simple soldier Mouton:* General Régis-Barthélemy Mouton-Duvernet (1769–1816) was a "simple soldier" only in the sense that he spoke directly and without useless gestures at the military council of 25 October.

Part Three

1. *the guerrillas in Spain:* See note 20 to Volume II, Part Three.

2. *under the German's command:* Tolstoy based Denisov's stratagem here on a passage from Denis Davydov's *Essay Towards a Theory of Partisan Warfare* (see note 15 to Volume III, Part Two).

3. *the battle of Vyazma:* The first major battle during Napoleon's retreat down the Smolensk road was at Vyazma on 2–3 November 1812, where the Russian vanguard under Miloradovich won an important victory which finally broke the spirit of the French forces.

4. *a reminder of springtime:* Both changes suggest *vesna*, the Russian word for spring.

5. *Karabakh . . . a Little Russian horse:* Karabakh is a mountainous region in the southern Caucasus, whereas Little Russia (*Malorus*) is in the Ukraine.

6. *a story Pierre knew:* Tolstoy reworked this story separately and published it in 1872 under the title "God Sees the Truth but Waits" in his didactic collection *A New Primer*.

7. *the Makary:* In the early nineteenth century, the trade fair in Nizhni Novgorod was called the Makaryevsky fair ("Makary" for short), after the nearby St. Makary monastery; later it became known as the Nizhni fair.

Part Four

1. *chevalier sans peur et sans reproche:* Pierre Terrail, seigneur de Bayard (1473–1524), one of the great military commanders of his time, was considered the epitome of chivalry. In Paris in 1527, his loyal follower Jacques de Mailles published *La Très joyeuse et très plaisante histoire du gentil Seigneur de Bayart, le bon chevalier sans peur et sans reproche* ("The Very Joyful and Very Pleasing Story of the Noble Lord of Bayart, the Good Knight Without Fear and Without Reproach"). The phrase became proverbial.

2. *They accused Kutuzov . . . that he had been bribed by him:* At this point Tolstoy supplies the terse footnote: "Wilson's Diaries." General Sir Robert Wilson was the English representative at the headquarters of the Russian army. Along with Bennigsen, who was chief of staff, he intrigued against Kutuzov, calling for decisive action and slandering him in his dispatches to the Russian emperor. Tolstoy undoubtedly read the passages of Wilson's journals published in the *Russian Messenger* in 1862.

3. *governor of Vilno:* Kutuzov had been military governor of Lithuania during the last years of the reign of Paul I (1799–1801) and again in 1809–11, before he was made commander in chief of the army in Moldavia.

4. *And he died:* Kutuzov died on 28 April 1813, during the Russian army's campaign abroad, in the small town of Bunzlau in what was then Prussian Silesia (now Poland).

5. *the Faceted Palace:* So called because of the distinctive stonework of its façade, the Faceted Palace is what remains of a fifteenth-century royal palace in the Kremlin. Its vast main hall (5,380 square feet) was once the throne room and banqueting hall of the tsars.

EPILOGUE

Part One

1. *he acted badly . . . and so on:* These "bad actions" all have to do with Alexander's increasing mysticism and conservatism. Alexander signed the constitution of the kingdom of Poland at the Congress of Vienna on 9 December 1815, but also declared there that Poland was indissolubly

bound to the Russian throne. The Holy Alliance of Austria, Prussia, and Russia was concluded in Paris in September 1815, after Napoleon's second abdication. Prince Golitsyn was a conservative statesman, head of the Biblical Society, minister of education, and procurator of the Holy Synod (see note 17 to Volume II, Part Two); retired admiral Alexander Semyonovich Shishkov, who headed the conservative Society of Lovers of the Russian Word (much mocked by Pushkin and his circle), had been a severe critic of Alexander's early liberal measures. The Semyonovsky regiment, founded in 1683, one of the two oldest and most prestigious of the emperor's lifeguard regiments, mutinied in October 1820 under the harsh treatment of its new German commander, Colonel Schwartz. The entire regiment was imprisoned in the Peter and Paul Fortress in Petersburg, the leaders of the mutiny were executed, and the rest were sent to hard labour in Siberia.

2. *The Russian troops . . . while he is there:* Suvorov's and Bagration's string of victories against the French in northern Italy (see note 4 to Volume II, Part One) took place while Napoleon was on his expedition to Egypt (1798–9).

3. *The enemy fleet . . . lets pass a whole army:* Napoleon tricked Admiral Nelson in 1798 by spreading a rumour that his fleet was going to pass through the Strait of Gibraltar and land in Ireland. In fact, the French fleet went to Malta, where the garrison surrendered without a fight.

4. *a conspiracy against him . . . forces him to kill him:* After General Moreau's conspiracy with the royalists (see note 51 to Volume I, Part One), on 18 May 1804 the French senate conferred imperial dignity on Napoleon. For the duc d'Enghien, see note 4 to Volume I, Part One.

5. *plays a pathetic comedy . . . while an unseen hand was guiding him:* The "pathetic comedy" refers to Napoleon's memoirs, dictated to his secretary Las Cases on St. Helena (see note 19 to Volume I, Part Two). Tolstoy considered that these memoirs exposed Napoleon more effectively than any other document.

6. *Not unto us . . . of my soul and of God:* The quotation, the opening line of Psalm 115, was inscribed on the medal Alexander I had struck to commemorate the victory of 1812. The second sentence expresses the emperor's new piety and withdrawal from worldly affairs.

7. *To him . . . will be taken:* An inexact quotation of Matthew 25:29: "For unto everyone that hath shall be given, and he shall have abundance: but from him that hath not shall be taken away even that which he hath."

8. *the Biblical Society . . . Gossner and the Tataghrinov woman:* The Biblical Society, dedicated to translating, printing, and distributing the Holy Scriptures in Russia, was founded in 1812 as a subsidiary of the English Biblical Society. Alexander I was a member, as were many church hierarchs. The Bavarian priest Johannes Gossner (1773–1858) left the Catholic Church because of his evangelical tendencies and became a Lutheran minister in Berlin. He was invited to Petersburg by the Biblical Society, was elected a director of the society (1820–4), and had great success as a preacher. In 1817 Elizaveta Filippovna Tatarinova (1783–1856), the daughter of General Buxhöwden, founded an ecstatic sect called the Spiritual Union. She claimed to have the gift of prophecy. Owing to her connections with Petersburg high society, the union continued in existence until 1837.

9. *Madame Kghrüdener . . . Eckaghrtshausen:* Varvara Juliana, Baroness von Krüdener (1764–1824), a Russian mystic and novelist, fell into the pietism of her time, travelled in Europe, met various famous preachers and visionaries, and eventually became one herself. In 1815 she met Alexander I in Heilbronn and preached her gospel to him. He was deeply taken with it and kept her with him when he went to Paris, where she achieved great social power and was the inspiration behind the Holy Alliance (see note 1 above). But the emperor soon separated himself from her influence. For Eckartshausen, see note 44 to Volume I, Part One.

10. *settlements:* Military colonies were established by Arakcheev in the provinces of White Russia and the Ukraine to assure a permanent military presence on the frontier. They combined the rigours of military and peasant life, were run with harsh discipline, imposed military service on the colonists' sons, and were very unpopular.

11. *the Tugendbund:* The "Union of Virtue," a political society founded in Königsberg in 1808 to free Prussia from the power of Napoleon. It was forbidden by Friedrich-Wilhelm III on Napoleon's order, but continued its activity illegally until it was dissolved in 1815.

12. *Mucius Scaevola burned his hand:* The story of Mucius Scaevola ("Left-handed Mucius") is told in Plutarch's *Life of Poplicola.* The Roman soldier Mucius impressed the hostile Etruscan

king Porsenna by holding his right hand in fire without flinching, which led Porsenna to make a truce with the Romans. Reading the *Parallel Lives of the Noble Greeks and Romans*, by the Greek historian Plutarch (ca. A.D. 46–ca. 126), was an indispensable part of a boy's education at that time.

Part Two

1. *Talleyrand . . . extended the borders of France:* At the Congress of Vienna (1814–15), which re-established order in Europe after Napoleon's first abdication, Talleyrand, who represented France, managed to have the former French borders restored with the addition of some 150 square miles of neighbouring territory.

2. *Napoleon III . . . caught in Boulogne:* Charles-Louis-Napoleon Bonaparte (1808–73), the emperor's nephew, made two attempts to overthrow the king, Louis Philippe, and have himself declared emperor. In 1840 he was arrested in Boulogne while attempting to flee France and condemned to life imprisonment in the fortress of Ham. He escaped in 1846 and by 1851, having arrested a certain number of republican leaders, managed to have himself declared emperor as Napoleon III, initiating the period of the Second Empire.

3. *the Confederation of the Rhine:* See note 6 to Volume III, Part One.

4. *Ioann IV . . . Kurbsky:* Tolstoy uses the Church Slavonic form of the name of the tsar Ivan IV, the Terrible (1530–84). Prince Andrei Mikhailovich Kurbsky (1528–83) was at first the tsar's close friend and adviser, then his bitter opponent. After Kurbsky fled to Lithuania, he and the tsar engaged in a remarkable correspondence (1564–79), alternating between invectives and profound reflections on the nature of power and the relations between the autocratic tsar and his boyars. Kurbsky also wrote a history of the reign of Ivan IV.

5. *Godefroys and Louis . . . Peter the Hermit:* Godefroy IV de Boulogne (1061–1100), known as Godefroy de Bouillon, one of the leaders of the second expedition of the First Crusade (1096–9), was proclaimed king of Jerusalem in 1099. Louis VII led the Second Crusade (1147–9), together with the Holy Roman Emperor Conrad III, and Louis IX led the Seventh Crusade (1248–54). Peter the Hermit (ca. 1050–1115) was a monk who led the first expedition of the First Crusade, which was decimated by the time it reached Asia Minor and was destroyed there by the Turks, though Peter himself survived. The minnesingers mentioned further on were medieval German courtly poets, who sang epic songs about Godefroy de Bouillon among others.

6. *Napoleon III gives the command . . . submit to the Bourbons:* In 1862 Napoleon III sent French troops to Mexico to intervene in the civil wars there. After some initial successes, he installed the archduke of Austria, Maximilian, as emperor of Mexico, but then abandoned him in 1867. Maximilian was overthrown and executed that same year. In the Austro-Prussian war of 1866, Otto von Bismarck (1815–98), chancellor of Wilhelm I of Prussia, seized lands in Bohemia that had formerly been part of the Austrian empire. The Bourbons were restored to the French throne in the person of Louis XVIII, younger brother of the executed Louis XVI, by the first treaty of Paris (1814), negotiated on strict terms by the allies under Alexander I.

7. Joshua, son of Nun: In the Old Testament book of Joshua, 10:12–13, Joshua, who succeeded Moses in leading the Israelites to the Promised land, commands the sun and moon to stand still and they obey him.

Appendix

1. *the author's view of his work:* This article appeared in the journal *Russian Archive*, March 1868, when the first four of the then-projected six volumes of the novel had been published and Tolstoy was working on the fifth.

2. *Dead Souls . . . Dead House:* Tolstoy makes a parallel between the titles of works by Nikolai Gogol and Fyodor Dostoevsky: the title of Dostoevsky's semi-fictional account of his term at hard labour in Omsk is generally mistranslated into English as *Notes from the House of the*

Dead. Notes from a Dead House (1860) was one of the very few works that Tolstoy later admitted to the category of "good art."

3. *Saltychikha:* A scornful variant of the last name of Darya Nikolaevna Saltykova (1730–1801), a notorious landowner who, widowed in 1756, abused her power by torturing to death a large number of serfs (the figures vary from 60 to 160), mainly women and young girls. She was denounced to the empress Elizaveta I in 1762, tried and condemned in 1768, pilloried for a day on Red Square, and imprisoned for life in a convent.

4. *Voronovo house:* Rastopchin's suburban estate near Moscow.

HISTORICAL INDEX

Alexander I (1777–1825): The emperor Alexander Pavlovich Romanov came to the Russian throne in 1801, following the assassination of his father, Paul I. He began his reign in a spirit of liberal reform, but later allowed conservative advisers to dictate policy, and in 1815 formed the Holy Alliance of Russia, Prussia, and Austria to oppose the revolutionary and liberal ideas that were spreading through Europe.

Apraksin, Count Stepan Stepanovich (1747–1827): Descended from a distinguished noble family, he entered military service early, took part in the Turkish wars under Catherine II, was promoted to lieutenant general, and in 1803 became military governor of Smolensk. He retired to his estate in 1809.

Arakcheev, Count Alexei Andreevich (1769–1834): General and statesman under the emperors Paul I and Alexander I. First served in the artillery, where he became known for his iron discipline and was generally detested. In 1808 he became minister of war and in 1810 was appointed to the first State Council. In the later years of Alexander's reign, he became the emperor's chief counsellor and closest friend.

Arcole: A village in the north of Italy on the Alpone River, a tributary of the Adige, where, on 17 November 1796, the bridge was hotly contested by the French, who were besieging Mantua, and the Austrian allies who were coming to relieve the city. The French under Napoleon eventually drove back the superior Austrian forces.

Armfelt, Count Gustaf Mauritz (1757–1814): A Swedish courtier and soldier of Finnish origin, who participated at the highest levels in the complex military and political events of the time. Eventually banished from Sweden, he went to Russia and swore allegiance to the young Alexander I, on whom he had great influence as an adviser and from whom he won independence for the grand duchy of Finland.

Auerstädt: Town in Saxony where Marshal Davout won a brilliant victory over the Prussians in 1806, on the same day that Napoleon defeated them at Jena. Napoleon rewarded Davout by making him "duke of Auerstädt."

Augustin (in the world, A. V. Vinogradsky, 1776–1819): Bishop Augustin was known as a spiritual writer and brilliant preacher; he also wrote verses in Latin. In 1812 he was virtually the head of the archdiocese of Moscow in place of Metropolitan Platon, who was seventy-five years old.

Austerlitz: Town in Moravia where Napoleon, in what was perhaps his greatest victory, defeated the combined forces of Austria and Russia on 2 December 1805. The battle is known as "the battle of the three emperors," because it pitted Napoleon against Alexander I and Franz I of Austria.

Bagovut, Karl (1761–1812): Russian general, fought in the Turkish wars and in the wars of 1806–8; in 1812 commanded the second corps of infantry in the army of Barclay de Tolly. Killed at the battle of Tarutino.

Bagration, Prince Pyotr Ivanovich (1765–1812): Russian general of Georgian descent. Served with Suvorov in northern Italy, took part in all the campaigns of 1805–7, was general in chief of the Russian army in the renewed hostilities with the Turks in 1809, and commanded one of the three Russian armies during the Napoleonic invasion. Mortally wounded at Borodino.

Balashov, Alexander Dmitrievich (1770–1837): Russian general and statesman. In 1804 he became chief of police of Moscow, and in 1808 of Petersburg. Alexander I raised him to the rank of adjutant general and made him military governor of Petersburg. In 1810 he became a member of the newly created State Council and minister of police. He accompanied the emperor to Vilno in 1812 and carried his letter to Napoleon.

Barclay de Tolly, Prince Mikhail Bogdanovich (1761–1818): Russian general of Scottish descent, born in Livonia. Commander in chief of the Russian army during the Swedish war, minister of war in 1810, commander in chief of the Russian army at the beginning of the 1812 campaign, before he was replaced by Kutuzov.

Beauharnais, Eugène de (1781–1824): Son of the viscount Alexandre de Beauharnais and Marie-Joseph (Josephine) Tascher de La Pagerie. His father was guillotined in 1794; in 1796 his mother married Napoleon, who adopted him officially in 1806 and later made him viceroy of Italy, prince of Venice, grand duke of Frankfurt, and prince of Eichstatt. Took part in a number of campaigns; in Russia commanded a corps of Italian, French, and Bavarian troops known as "the army of Italy."

Beauharnais, Josephine de (1763–1814): The first wife of Napoleon and mother of Eugène de Beauharnais by her previous marriage. She became empress in 1804, but Napoleon had their childless marriage annulled in 1809.

Bekleshov, Alexander Andreevich (1745–1808): Served in various posts of the Russian administration and at the end of his life worked closely with Speransky. He was governor general of Moscow in 1804–7.

Belliard, Auguste Daniel (1769–1832): Took part in Napoleon's Italian, Egyptian, and Spanish campaigns, was chief of staff of Murat's armies in 1805–8, and was named governor of Madrid in 1808. Promoted to major general, he took part in the Russian campaign in 1812.

Bennigsen, Count Leonty Leontievich (1745–1826): Russian general, born in Brunswick, joined the Russian army in 1773. Opposed to the policies of Paul I, he took an active part in the conspiracy to assassinate him. Appointed governor of Lithuania in 1801, commanded an army in the campaigns of 1805–7, was initially successful, but was badly defeated at Friedland, after which he retired. In 1812 he was called back to service, fought at Borodino, and defeated Murat at Tarutino. Following a dispute with Kutuzov, he retired a second time, but returned to service after Kutuzov's death.

Berezina: A river in Belorus, tributary of the Dnieper, which, on 26–29 November 1812, the remains of Napoleon's Grande Armée had to cross on hastily built bridges while fighting off the attacks of the pursuing Russian army.

Bernadotte, Jean-Baptiste (1763–1844): French general, made a marshal of the empire and, in 1805, prince of Pontocorvo. In 1810 King Charles XIII of Sweden adopted him as his son and heir, hoping that the French might help him to take Finland back from the Russians, but Bernadotte, having become the virtual ruler of Sweden, joined the anti-French coalition. In 1818 he became King Charles XIV. His dynasty still sits on the Swedish throne.

Berthier, Louis-Alexandre (1753–1815): Major general and marshal of the empire, prince of Wagram and of Neuchâtel, one of the most trusted generals of Napoleon, who made him minister of war under the Consulat. Took part in all of Napoleon's campaigns in Italy, Spain, Austria, and Russia.

Bessières, Jean-Baptiste (1768–1813): French marshal and cavalry commander, made prince of Istria in 1809, participated in all of Napoleon's major battles, and was commander in chief of cavalry during the Russian campaign. Killed in action at Weissenfels in eastern Germany.

Bonaparte, Joseph (1768–1844): Older brother of Napoleon, became king of Naples in 1806 and was king of Spain from 1808 to 1813. He retired to the United States after Waterloo but later returned to Europe.

Borodino: Village in the Mozhaisk district, between Moscow and Smolensk, on the Kolocha River, which, on 7 September (26 August by the Julian calendar), was the scene of the most important and bloody battle of the war of 1812, called *la bataille de la Moskowa* by the French, after the nearby Moskova River. There was great loss of life on both sides, but no decisive victory for either.

Broussier, Jean-Baptiste (1766–1814): French major general, campaigned in Lombardy, distinguished himself at the battle of Wagram (6 July 1809). Took part in the Russian campaign and the campaigns in Saxony. Sought refuge in Strasbourg after the fall of Napoleon and died suddenly of a stroke.

Buckle, Henry Thomas (1821–62): English historian and sociologist, author of *The History of*

Civilization in England (1857–62); formulated the idea that the development of civilization leads to the cessation of wars.

Buxhöwden, Count Fyodor Fyodorovich (1750–1811): Russian general, served under Suvorov in Poland and was made military governor of Warsaw; in 1805 joined Kutuzov's forces, commanded a corps at Austerlitz, was commander in chief during the Swedish war of 1808.

Catherine II, the Great (1729–98): Daughter of the duke of Anhalt-Zerbst, wife of the Russian emperor Peter III, became empress of Russia after the assassination of her husband in 1762. Her successful wars extended the southern and western boundaries of Russia into the Crimea, part of the Ukraine, Belorus, Lithuania, and Poland. The Russo-Turkish wars gave Russia access to the Black Sea. Catherine also brought the spirit of the French Enlightenment to Russia and personally corresponded with Voltaire and Diderot.

Caulaincourt, Armand Augustin Louis, Marquis of (1772–1827): French diplomat and general, made duke of Vicenza in 1808. In 1801 Napoleon sent him to Petersburg to congratulate Alexander I on his accession, and he served as ambassador to Russia in 1807–11. He advised Napoleon against invading Russia, but accompanied the emperor as his aide-de-camp throughout the campaign.

Chateaubriand, Viscount François-René de (1768–1848): French writer and diplomat, emigrated to England in 1792, returned to France in 1800, but was on bad terms with Napoleon. Under the restoration, he was ambassador to London and minister of foreign affairs. His fame rests on his books, above all his *Mémoirs d'outre-tombe* ("Memoirs from Beyond the Grave"), written from 1811 to 1841 and published after his death.

Chernyshov, Alexander Ivanovich (1785–1857): Russian adjutant general and cavalry commander, began his career at Austerlitz; after the peace of Tilsit, he was Russian military and diplomatic representative in Paris. Became an imperial adjutant in 1811, and commanded a partisan detachment during the French retreat in 1812. Minister of war from 1827 to 1852, and chairman of the State Council.

Chichagov, Pavel Vassilievich (1765–1849): Russian admiral and statesman, became assistant minister of the navy under Alexander I, was appointed to the new State Council, and became the emperor's adjutant general. In 1812 commanded the Danube flotilla, took part in the battle at the Berezina, and was blamed for allowing the French to cross the river. In 1813 he left Russia for medical treatment abroad and never returned.

Claparède, Michel-Marie (1770–1842): Was with Napoleon in the Italian campaign, fought at Austerlitz and Jena, and as a major general at Wagram in 1809. In the Russian campaign, he commanded a Polish corps which saw action at Borodino and the Berezina.

Clausewitz, Karl Philipp Gottfried von (1780–1831): Prussian general and military theoretician. After fighting against Napoleon, he worked at reforming the Berlin military academy. Opposed to Prussia's forced alliance with the French, he served in the Russian army from 1812–14, after which he wrote his book *The Year 1812*. His best-known work is the treatise *On War*.

Compans, Jean-Dominique (1769–1845): French general, chief of staff of the army of Italy in 1798. Badly wounded at Austerlitz, he won the rank of major general at Jena, and saw the entire campaign in Russia. Napoleon considered him one of his best generals.

Consulat: The government established after Napoleon's bloodless coup d'état of 18 Brumaire (9 November 1799), which provided for rule by three consuls, of whom Napoleon was named first consul. In 1802 Napoleon had himself named consul for life. The Consulat was abolished when he was made emperor in 1804.

Convention: The revolutionary national assembly that replaced the legislative assembly on 21 September 1792 and governed France until 1795. It condemned Louis XVI and Marie-Antoinette to death, and in 1793 entrusted dictatorial power to the Committee of Public Safety, which ruled by terror. It was replaced in 1795 by the Directoire.

Corvisart, Baron Jean-Nicolas (1755–1821): French physician, taught medicine at the Collège de France in 1797. In 1804 he became personal physician to Napoleon, who raised him to the nobility. Corvisart tended Napoleon from then until his exile to St. Helena in 1815.

Czartoryski, Prince Adam Adamovich (1770–1861): A Polish prince, descended from the distinguished old Lithuanian family of the Jagellons, who became a close confidant of the young

Alexander I, served as Russian minister of foreign affairs in 1804–6, and tried to persuade the emperor to restore the kingdom of Poland.

Davout, Louis-Nicolas (1770–1823): Served with Napoleon in the Egyptian campaign, fought as major general at Marengo, was made marshal of the empire in 1804, duke of Auerstädt after his victory in that battle, and prince of Eckmühl after the battles of Austerlitz, Eckmühl, and Wagram. He commanded the first corps of the Grande Armée in Russia and covered the French retreat with Marshal Ney.

Davydov, Denis Vassilievich (1784–1839): Russian major general, first organizer of partisan warfare against the retreating French army. A poet famous for the invention of "hussar poetry," he was admired by Pushkin and was a popular figure in society. He also wrote a treatise on partisan warfare and an autobiography, *Some Events from the Life of Denis Vassilievich Davydov,* which, in the words of D. S. Mirsky, contains "some of the best military reading in the language." He was the model for Tolstoy's Denisov.

Delzons, Alexis Joseph (1775–1812): Fought under Napoleon in the campaigns in Italy and Egypt, and as brigadier general in the Austrian campaigns of 1805–9. In Russia he served under Eugène de Beauharnais at Borodino and Maloyaroslavets, where he was killed leading the counter-attack against the Russians.

Dessaix, Count Joseph Marie (1764–1834): Served in the French republican army at the siege of Toulon, in the Pyrenees, and in the Italian campaign. Opposed the coup d'état of 18 Brumaire. As brigadier general and commander of the Legion of Honour, he fought at Wagram and in 1810 was made a count. Took part in the Russian campaign, in which he was wounded twice.

Diderot, Denis (1713–84): French writer and philosopher, one of the directors of the *Encyclopédie raisonné des sciences, des arts et des métiers* ("Descriptive Encyclopaedia of the Sciences, Arts, and Trades"). A materialist and atheist, he was one of the most effective advocates of eighteenth-century philosophical ideas. He corresponded with Catherine the Great and visited Russia in 1773.

Directoire: The government that replaced the Convention in France and functioned from October 1795 to November 1799, when it was overturned by Napoleon and replaced by the Consulat.

Dokhturov, Dmitri Sergeevich (1756–1816): Major general of Russian infantry. His action at Austerlitz and at the dam of Augesd earned him the nickname "the Iron General." At Borodino he replaced the mortally wounded Bagration on the left wing. At Maloyaroslavets his alert action forced Napoleon to retreat down the old Smolensk road instead of going to Kaluga, where there were abundant supplies and access to the rich and untouched southern provinces.

Dolgorukov, Prince Sergei Nikolaevich (1769–1829): Infantry officer, fought in the Swedish war, became major general in 1798. From 1805 to 1811 he served mainly on diplomatic missions, but returned to the army in 1812.

Dolgoruky, Prince Yuri Vladimirovich (1740–1830): Descendant of Grand Prince Yuri Vladimirovich Dolgoruky (ca. 1096–1157), the founder of Moscow. He was military commander of Moscow under Paul I.

Dorokhov, Ivan Semyonovich (1762–1815): Russian cavalry officer, took part in the Russo-Turkish war of 1787–91, was made major general in 1803, commanded a hussar regiment in the 1805–7 campaign, and in 1812 distinguished himself defending Bagration's flèches on the left wing at Borodino.

Duport, Louis (1781–1853): French ballet dancer who purified the classical style and was known for his multiple pirouettes and soaring leaps. He performed in Moscow and Petersburg from 1808 to 1812 along with the actress Mlle George.

Dürenstein: Now Dürnstein, a town in Austria where a battle was fought on 11 November 1805, midway between the battles of Ulm and Austerlitz, which pitted the French under General Mortier against the much larger forces of Kutuzov.

Duroc, Géraud Christophe Michel (1772–1813): Participated in Napoleon's Italian and Egyptian campaigns, was made duke of Frioul and grand marshal of the palace under the empire. A major general in 1805, he fought in all the French campaigns until he was killed at Markersdorf in May 1813. He is buried in the Invalides with Napoleon.

Durosnel, Count Antoine Jean Auguste (1771–1849): French general, fought in the campaigns in

Germany, Poland, Spain, and Austria, was made a count in 1808, and participated in the Russian campaign as adjutant general in charge of all French cavalry.

Eckmühl: A village in Bavaria where Napoleon defeated the Austrians in 1809, in honour of which he gave General Davout the title "duke of Eckmühl."

Elizaveta I (1709–61): Elizaveta Petrovna, daughter of Peter the Great, became empress of Russia in 1741, and died without an heir, leaving the throne to her nephew, Peter III.

Elizaveta Alexeevna (1779–1826): Born Louisa Maria Augusta von Baden, daughter of Karl Ludwig, prince of Baden, became Orthodox with the name of Elizaveta Alexeevna when she married Alexander I in 1793. In 1801 she became empress of Russia.

Enghien, Louis-Antoine-Henri de Bourbon-Condé, Duke of (1772–1804): The last male descendant of the princely house of Condé, emigrated in 1789, was falsely accused of taking part in a plot to assassinate Napoleon, who ordered him abducted and taken to the château de Vincennes, near Paris. Napoleon was informed of the falsity of the charge but still insisted on the duke's execution.

Ermolov, Alexei Petrovich (1777–1861): Russian general, served under Suvorov in Poland, distinguished himself during the French invasion at the battles of Valutino, Borodino, and Maloyaroslavets, after which Kutuzov made him army chief of staff. He was later responsible for the military government of the Caucasus and Georgia.

Eylau: Also known as Preussisch-Eylau, a town in north-east Prussia, now part of Russia (the name has been changed to Bagrationovsk in honour of the Russian general). It was the scene of a bloody and indecisive battle in 1807 between the French army and the mainly Russian forces commanded by General Bennigsen.

Fabvier, Baron Charles Nicolas (1782–1855): Began as an artillery officer, fought at the battle of Dürenstein and in Spain. At Borodino in 1812 he lost his right leg, but returned to service a few months later. Opposed to the restoration of the Bourbons, he went to England, then Spain, and in 1825 to Greece, where he played a key part in the Greek war of independence. He left Greece in 1830 and ended his days in France.

Ferdinand III (1769–1824): Archduke of Tuscany. Forced out by Napoleon, he was given the surrogate title of duke of the newly created state of Würzburg in 1805, but in 1814 returned to rule Tuscany until his death.

Fichte, Johann Gottlieb (1762–1814): German idealist philosopher in the period between Kant and Hegel, an advocate of civil liberty, who championed the French revolution and condemned Napoleon.

Figner, Alexander (1787–1813): A colourful figure from the war of 1812, who had served in the artillery during the second Russo-Turkish war. During the French occupation of Moscow, he disguised himself as a French soldier, slipped into the city, spent the days gathering intelligence, and performed acts of sabotage at night. Kutuzov used him in the same way, sending him into Tarutino in disguise, where he gathered information that made possible a surprise attack on the French there. He became one of the first partisan leaders, along with Davydov and Seslavin, and died while crossing the Elbe.

Filaret (1782–1867): Perhaps the most important figure of the Russian Orthodox Church in the mid-nineteenth century. Born Vassily Drozdov, he studied at the Trinity–St. Sergius Monastery and immediately afterwards was appointed a professor there. Deeply moved by the events of 1812, he spoke of the victory of Russia as a confirmation of her spiritual mission. In 1813 he delivered the funeral oration for Field Marshal Kutuzov. A prolific spiritual writer, he became a monk in 1817, and in 1826 metropolitan of Moscow.

Franz I (1768–1835): Emperor of Austria. Fought unsuccessfully against the armies of the French revolution and Napoleon, to whom he eventually had to give the hand of his daughter, Maria-Louisa. Rejoined the anti-French coalition in 1813.

Friant, Louis (1758–1829): French major general, fought in Italy under Bernadotte and in Egypt under Napoleon. Saw action at Austerlitz and Eylau in 1805–7, and was made count in 1808. In the Russian campaign he fought at Smolensk and Borodino. At Waterloo (18 June 1815) he commanded Napoleon's old guard.

Friedland: A town in north-west Prussia, near Königsberg (Kaliningrad), where, on 14 June 1807,

Napoleon's army fought a twenty-three-hour battle against the Russians under Bennigsen, which ended with a total victory for the French and led to the signing of the peace of Tilsit between Napoleon and Alexander.

Friedrich-Wilhelm III (1770–1840): King of Prussia. Unsuccessful adversary of Napoleon, his forces were crushed at the battle of Jena in 1806. He was excluded from the negotiations at Tilsit in July 1807, where half of his territory was divided between the French and the Russians.

Genlis, Stephanie Félicité du Crest de St-Albin, Countess of (1746–1830): French writer and educator. Became a lady-in-waiting in the Palais Royal and governess to the children of the Duke of Chartres. Wrote comedies and novels to support her theories of education. After her husband was guillotined in 1793, she lived abroad in Berlin and Hamburg, but in 1799 Napoleon allowed her to return to France and awarded her a pension. Her writings, of a moralistic tendency, were very popular in the Russia of Alexander I.

Gérard, François (1770–1837): Historical painter; his painting of the battle of Austerlitz hangs in the museum of Versailles.

Gérard, Maurice Etienne (1773–1852): Marshal of the empire. His early service was under Bernadotte, whose aide-de-camp he became in 1797. Saw action in Austria and in Spain. In the 1812 campaign, as brigadier and then major general, he fought at Smolensk and Borodino. During the French retreat, he was second under Marshal Ney at the crossing of the Berezina, commanding the rear guard.

Gervinus, Georg Gottfried (1805–71): German historian, professor of literature and history at Göttingen, author of numerous works, including the _History of the Nineteenth Century_ and a philosophical study, _The Principles of History._

Gibbon, Edward (1737–94): English historian. His classic work, _A History of the Decline and Fall of the Roman Empire,_ published in 1776–88, is marked by a strongly ironic style and a scorn of organized religion, especially Christianity.

Glinka, Sergei Nikolaevich (1774–1847): Elder brother of the composer Fyodor Nikolaevich Glinka, edited the _Russian Messenger_ from 1808 to 1820; minor poet and dramatist, author of a number of historical works, including _Notes of the Year 1812,_ which was one of Tolstoy's sources.

Golitsyn, Prince Alexander Nikolaevich (1773–1844): Descendant of an ancient family of the Russian nobility, conservative politician prominent in the later part of the reign of Alexander I, minister of education, procurator of the Holy Synod, and chairman of the State Council.

Heudelet de Bierre, Etienne (1770–1857): French general, commanded the vanguard under Delmas and Moreau, fought at Austerlitz, was made major general in 1805. Also fought at Jena and Eylau and later in Spain. During the 1812 campaign, he commanded the second division of reserves.

Hohenlohe-Ingelfingen, Friedrich-Ludwig, Prince of (1746–1818): Prussian major general, governor of Berlin, at one time the most popular soldier in the Prussian army. Largely as a result of internal dissensions, his army was virtually destroyed by Napoleon at Jena in 1806.

Izmail: Turkish fortress on the Danube which, during the Russo-Turkish wars, passed back and forth three times between Turks and Russians. Taken by assault in 1790 by the Russian army under Suvorov's command and with the participation of Kutuzov.

Jena: Town in eastern Germany, scene of a major battle between the French and the Prussians in 1806, in which Napoleon virtually destroyed the Prussian army led by Prince Hohenlohe.

Junot, Jean-Andoche (1771–1813): First met Napoleon at the siege of Toulon (1793), took part in the campaigns in Italy and Egypt, became major general and governor of Paris under the Consulat. Known for his sumptuous way of life. After some disputes with Napoleon, he was sent away as ambassador to Portugal. Rejoined the Grande Armée in 1808, fought in the Russian campaign, but became mentally unstable and was sent home to his father in Montbard (Burgundy), where he took his own life.

Kamensky, Count Mikhail Fyodorovich (1738–1809): Russian field marshal, fought in the first Russo-Turkish war (1768–74) alongside Suvorov, but had difficult relations with Catherine II and Paul I and was retired twice to his estate. Alexander I made him governor general of Petersburg, but then also dismissed him. He returned to the army for the campaign of 1806, which was his last.

Kamensky, Count Nikolai Mikhailovich (1778–1811): Younger son of M. F. Kamensky, took part in the Swedish war of 1808 with the rank of major general. In 1810 he was made commander in chief of the army in Moldavia, won some brilliant victories against the Turks, but fell gravely ill and died.

Kochubey, Viktor Pavlovich (1768–1834): Russian statesman of Ukrainian origin, close aide to Alexander I. Served as ambassador to London and Paris, then to Turkey; was minister of war in 1801–2, minister of the interior until 1812 and again from 1819 to 1825.

Kollowrath, Count Johann Karl von (1748–1816): Austrian field marshal, general commandant of Bavaria in 1803; fought in the 1809 campaign against Napoleon and was beaten in several battles, ending with Wagram.

Konovnitsyn, Count Pyotr Petrovich (1767–1822): Russian general. In 1810–11 commanded a division on the Baltic, in 1812 commanded the third infantry division, part of Barclay de Tolly's western army. Fought at Borodino, Tarutino, and Maloyaroslavets, and commanded the rear guard after Vyazma. Later served as minister of war.

Konstantin, Grand Duke (1779–1831): Konstantin Pavlovich Romanov, younger brother of Alexander I, commanded the imperial guard in the 1805 campaign and fought in the battle of Austerlitz, after which he returned to Petersburg.

Kurakin, Prince Alexei Borisovich (1752–1818): Russian statesman and diplomat; member of the State Council from its inception in 1810, ambassador to Vienna in 1806 and to Paris in 1808. In his dispatches, he repeatedly warned Alexander I of the impending war with France. Resigned as ambassador in April 1812.

Kutaisov, Alexander Ivanovich (1784–1812): Son of a Turkish prisoner, he was favoured by Paul I and rose quickly in the ranks, becoming a major general at the age of twenty-two. Fought at Eylau and Friedland in the Austrian campaign of 1805–7, and in 1812 commanded the artillery in Barclay de Tolly's western army. Killed in action at Borodino.

Kutuzov, Prince Mikhail Illarionovich (1745–1813): (Tolstoy spells his patronymic "Ilarionovich" and sometimes "Larionovich.") Russian field marshal, fought in Poland (1764–9) and against the Turks (1770–4), where he lost an eye. Major general, governor of the Crimea, he served under Suvorov in the Russo-Turkish war of 1787–92, was later made ambassador to Constantinople, governor general of Finland, and governor of Petersburg. Won the battle of Dürenstein against the French in 1805; opposed the battle of Austerlitz, but was overruled by the Austrians. Commander in chief of Russian forces in the Russo-Turkish wars of 1806–12, which ended in the treaty of Bucharest, very favourable to the Russians. Replaced Barclay de Tolly as commander in chief of the Russian army on 17 August 1812. Much criticized for retreating after Borodino and abandoning Moscow, he pursued his policy of non-confrontation throughout the French retreat to the Vistula. He was made prince of Smolensk in reward for his services.

Langeron, Gaspard Louis Andrault, Count of (1763–1831): Emigrated from France after the revolution, offered his services to Austria, and in 1790 entered the Russian army. Participated in the taking of Izmail. At Austerlitz commanded a division alongside Kutuzov, fought at the Berezina and in later battles during the European campaign.

Lannes, Jean (1769–1809): An apprentice tanner who joined the French republican volunteers, rose quickly in the ranks, and eventually became marshal of the empire, prince of Sievers, and duke of Montebello. Served in the Italian campaign, saved Napoleon from capture at Arcole, fought with distinction at Montebello and Marengo, took Saragossa in 1809, but was wounded at Essling and died of gangrene.

Larrey, Dominique (1766–1842): The outstanding surgeon of the Napoleonic era; introduced first aid and ambulances on the battlefield. Took part in all of Napoleon's campaigns from Egypt on, and in 1805 was made surgeon in chief of the French army.

Lauriston, Jacques Jean Alexandre Bernard Law de (1768–1828): Met Bonaparte when both were students at the École Militaire in Brienne; retired from service but was called back under the Consulat, fought at Marengo and in the Austrian campaign, also undertook diplomatic missions, and served throughout the Russian campaign. Grand-nephew of John Law, the notorious Scottish financier.

Lavater, Johann Caspar (1741–1801): Swiss Protestant theologian, poet, and philosopher, invented the theory of physiognomy, a system of determining a person's character by the distinguishing physical traits of the face and head.

Ledru des Essarts, François Roch (1766–1844): Fought in the early French republican campaigns in the Low Countries and Italy; brigadier general at Austerlitz and Eylau; major general in the Russian campaign, commanding a division under Ney. Fought at Borodino, Krasnoe, and during the entire retreat from Moscow to the Vistula.

Lemarrois, Jean Léonard François (1776–1836): Son of a Norman farmer, noticed by Napoleon at the siege of Toulon, became his aide-de-camp, and was witness at his marriage to Josephine. A major general at Austerlitz, appointed governor of Rome in 1809, he was left in charge of the camp at Boulogne during the Russian campaign.

Liechtenstein, Prince Johann von (1760–1836): Last of the princes of Liechtenstein to rule under the Holy Roman Empire. Field marshal and commander in chief of the Austrian army, he later led the peace negotiations with Napoleon, which were very fortunate for the French. Criticized, he resigned from the military in 1810. The Congress of Vienna declared the independence of his principality.

Ligne, Charles-Joseph, Prince of (1735–1814): General and writer, descendant of a princely family from Hainaut; served in the Austrian and Russian armies, was a friend of the Austrian emperor Joseph II, and journeyed to the Crimea with Catherine the Great in 1787.

Lodi: Town in northern Italy near Milan, scene of an important victory of Napoleon's forces over the Austrians in 1796.

Lopukhin, Pyotr Vassilievich (1753–1827): Russian statesman, governor of Yaroslavl and Vologda under Catherine the Great, minister of justice under Alexander I from 1803 to 1810, later president of the council of ministers.

Mack von Liebereich, Baron Karl Freiherr (1752–1828): Austrian general. Outmanoeuvred and surrounded by Napoleon's troops at Ulm on 20 October 1805, he surrendered without a fight along with 30,000 men. Napoleon allowed him to go free, but the Austrians eventually court-martialled him, stripped him of his rank, and sentenced him to twenty years in prison. Rehabilitated two years later.

Magnitsky, Mikhail Lavrentievich (1778–1855): Russian statesman, member of the State Council in 1812, collaborated with Speransky and was exiled along with him. He later reversed himself and made a career under the protection of the conservative ministers Arakcheev and Golitsyn.

Maloyaroslavets: Also written Maly Yaroslavets (Tolstoy uses both forms). Scene of a major battle on 24 October 1812, during the French retreat from Moscow. General Dokhturov, sent to intercept a foraging party, came upon the entire French army, quickly sent for reinforcements, and offered battle. At the end of the day, the town remained in French hands, but the strategic victory went to the Russians, since it forced Napoleon to retreat down the old Smolensk road.

Mamonov, Matvei Alexandrovich Dmitriev- (1790–1863): Son of one of Catherine the Great's favourites, a Mason, and later a leading Decembrist (a secret society of young aristocrats dedicated to the idea of constitutional monarchy). His regiment distinguished itself at the battles of Tarutino and Maloyaroslavets.

Marat, Jean-Paul (1743–93): French revolutionary politician, editor of L'Ami du peuple ("The Friend of the People"), deputy of the violent Montagnard party in the National Convention. He was assassinated by Charlotte Corday.

Marchand, Jean Gabriel (1765–1851): Made major general in 1805, fought at Jena and Friedland, saw four campaigns in Spain, and commanded a division at Borodino.

Marengo: Town in the Piedmont, in the north of Italy, scene of a battle on 14 June 1800 between the French and the Austrians. General Desaix, who led the French counter-attack, was killed, but the battle, which ended in a French victory and the withdrawal of Austrian forces from Italy, crowned the success of Napoleon's Italian campaign.

Maria Feodorovna (1759–1828): Born Sophia Maria Louisa of Württemberg, second wife of Paul I, mother of the emperors Alexander I and Nicholas I. On the assassination of her husband, she attempted to take the throne herself, as Catherine the Great had done before her, but gave way to her son and remained at court as dowager empress.

Metternich, Klemens Lothar Wenzel von (1773–1859): Austrian statesman and diplomat, ambassador to Berlin and, in 1806, to Paris; Austrian foreign minister in 1809. After the disastrous

Russian campaign of 1812, he tried unsuccessfully to persuade Napoleon to stop his wars, and then brought Austria into the anti-French alliance. Made count and prince by Franz I, he was the chief Austrian negotiator at the Congress of Vienna.

Michaud de Beauretour, Alexandre (1772–1841): Born in Nice, then part of the kingdom of Sardinia, he fought against the French revolutionary forces in southern France and northern Italy, joined the Russian army, became an imperial adjutant, and was much decorated for his services. After Borodino, Kutuzov sent him to Petersburg with news of the abandoning of Moscow. In 1815 Alexander I sent him to invite the king of Sardinia, Victor Emmanuel I, to return to his throne, for which the king rewarded Michaud with the title "Count of Beauretour," referring not to a place but to his own *beau retour* ("beautiful return") to his kingdom.

Mikhelson, Ivan Ivanovich (1755–1807): Russian cavalry general, took part in most of the major wars of the mid to late eighteenth century. Known as the "vanquisher of Pugachev" because of his final crushing of the popular revolt in the Volga region led by the impostor Emelyan Pugachev. In 1806 he was made commander in chief of the army in Moldavia.

Miloradovich, Mikhail Andreevich (1771–1825): Served under Suvorov in the Polish and Turkish wars, and against the French in Italy and Switzerland. In 1805, he served under Kutuzov at the battle of Austerlitz, where he defended the Pratzen heights. In 1812 he commanded the reserves at Borodino and the rear guard that delayed Napoleon's advance on Moscow. During the French retreat, he was victorious at the battle of Vyazma, and went on to the campaign in Europe. From 1818 to 1825, he was military governor of Petersburg, where he was killed while trying to quash the Decembrist uprising.

Montesquieu, Charles de Secondat, Baron (1689–1755): French philosopher and writer, author of *Lettres persanes* ("Persian Letters," 1721) and above all of *L'Esprit des lois* ("The Spirit of the Laws," 1748), in which he formulated important principles of the separation of powers that had great influence on later constitutional thinking.

Morand, Charles Antoine Louis Alexis (1771–1835): French general, participated in virtually all the campaigns of the republic and the empire, served with Soult at Austerlitz, where he led the assault on the Pratzen heights, and with Davout at Auerstädt, Eylau, and Wagram. Was made governor of Hamburg. In the Russian campaign, he fought at Smolensk, Borodino, and the Berezina; in 1815 he commanded part of the old guard at Waterloo.

Moreau, Jean Victor Marie (1763–1813): Joined the French republican volunteers in 1791, served in the Army of the North, was made commander in chief in 1795. Fought against Suvorov in Italy. Disputed with Bonaparte, later opposed him, and was banished to the United States. After the retreat from Russia and the destruction of the Grande Armée, he met with Alexander I through Bernadotte and advised him on the later war in Europe. Mortally wounded at the battle of Dresden in 1813.

Mortier, Édouard Adolphe Casimir Joseph (1768–1835): Served in the French republican Army of the North in 1792–3; was made major general in 1799 and marshal of the empire in 1804. Fought with distinction at Ulm, Dürenstein, and Friedland, and in 1808 was honoured by Napoleon with the title of duke of Treviso. Served in two Spanish campaigns, and commanded the young guard in the Russian campaign.

Mouton-Duvernet, Régis Barthélemy (1769–1816): Was a captain at the siege of Toulon, and later took part in all the wars of the revolution and the empire. Distinguished himself at Arcole; went to Spain as a colonel and came back as a major general. An intransigent opponent of the restoration of the Bourbons, he was eventually arrested and shot.

Mozhaisk: Town in Moscow province, on the Smolensk road, some seventy miles from the capital, where it commanded an important strategic position. The battle of Borodino took place seven miles from Mozhaisk.

Murat, Joachim (1767–1815): Became Napoleon's aide-de-camp in the Italian campaign; served as cavalry commander in the Egyptian campaign and was made major general. Instrumental in the coup d'état of the Consulat, he married Napoleon's sister Caroline in 1800. Under the empire, he commanded the cavalry and vanguard of the Grande Armée during the Austrian campaign, and led the campaign in Spain that ended with the taking of Madrid and the bestowing of the Spanish throne on Joseph Bonaparte. In reward Napoleon made Murat king of Naples, but their relations became strained (earlier he had opposed the execution of the duke of

Enghien). Took part in the Russian campaign, and during the retreat, when Napoleon went on ahead, was left in charge of the army, the remnants of which he led to Vilno and eventually into Poland. He then returned to Naples, where he entered into negotiations with the Austrians. Anxious to retain his kingdom, he was caught between several camps, and was finally taken by the Spanish and executed.

Muravyov-Karsky, Nikolai Nikolaevich (1794–1866): Took part in the war of 1812 and in the subsequent campaign abroad. Belonged to the circle of the Decembrists but was not prosecuted or punished.

Napoleon I (1769–1821): Born Napoleone Buonaparte, in Ajaccio, Corsica, he was educated at the École Militaire in Brienne, became captain of artillery in the revolutionary army, was made general in the Italian campaign in 1794, appointed head of the army in Italy in 1796, and returned to Paris in glory. There followed the Egyptian campaign of 1798–9, then the coup d'état of 18 Brumaire, which brought in the Consulat, with Napoleon as first consul and later consul for life. In 1804 he was accorded imperial dignity by the French senate. As emperor, he led the Grande Armée on campaigns in Spain, central Europe, and finally Russia, where, after so many successes, it was virtually annihilated. Obliged to abdicate at Fontainebleau in 1814, he was exiled to the island of Elba, but returned to Paris in 1815 for the so-called "Hundred Days." Definitively defeated at Waterloo on 18 June 1815 by coalition forces under the duke of Wellington, he spent his last days in exile on the island of St. Helena.

Nelson, Lord Horatio, First Viscount Nelson (1758–1805): English admiral of humble origins, famous for his part in the Napoleonic wars. On 21 October 1805, he won his last and most famous victory at Trafalgar, with twenty-seven ships against the thirty-three ships of the French admiral Villeneuve, but was killed in the battle.

Ney, Michel (1769–1815): Son of a Scottish cooper who had emigrated to the Saar, he became marshal of the empire, was named duke of Elchingen in 1808 and prince of the Moskova in 1812. One of the most able generals of Napoleon, who nicknamed him "the Bravest of the Brave." During the retreat from Moscow, he commanded the rear guard. Arrested by French restoration forces in August 1815 and condemned to death by firing squad, he refused to wear a blindfold and insisted on giving the order to fire himself.

Nostitz-Rieneck, Count Jan Nepomuk (1768–1840): Descendant of a noble Prague family; major general in the Austrian army. Tricked by Murat, he abandoned his advance post at Schöngraben in 1805, for which he was accused of high treason. Joined the Russian army in 1807.

Novosiltsev, Nikolai Nikolaievich (1761–1836): (Tolstoy first calls him Novosiltsov and, in French, Novosilzoff.) One of four members of a privy committee of advisers to the young emperor Alexander I, along with Czartoryski, Stroganov, and Kochubey, who urged him to make liberal reforms. He carried out several diplomatic missions in 1805–6, was president of the Petersburg Academy of Sciences from 1803 to 1810 and a member and then chairman of the State Council.

Ochakov: A fortress at the mouth of the Dnieper in the Ukraine. It was besieged for six months by the Russians in 1788, during the second Russo-Turkish war (1787–92), and finally taken by storm with great loss of life.

Oldenburg, Peter Friedrich Ludwig, Duke of (1755–1829): Lived in Russia and was married to Princess Elizabeth of Württemberg, sister of the Russian empress Maria Feodorovna. Fought in the second Russo-Turkish war and later served in government administration. In 1809 his son, Peter Friedrich Georg (1784–1812), was hastily married to Ekaterina Pavlovna (1788–1818), sister of Alexander I, to forestall Napoleon's courtship of her. In 1811, Napoleon seized the Oldenburg lands, but they were returned to the family after the battle of Leipzig in 1813.

Ordener, Michel (1755–1811): Entered the French army before the revolution, later served in the Army of the Rhine and fought in the Italian campaign. Was sent to Germany to arrest the duke of Enghien. Took part in the Austrian campaign, fought at Austerlitz, and was promoted to major general. Retired in October 1806.

Orlov-Chesmensky, Count Alexei Grigorievich (1735–1807): A favourite of Catherine the Great, younger brother of her lover Grigori Grigorievich (1734–83). The brothers took part in the murder of Catherine's husband, the emperor Peter III, and Alexei Grigorievich was rumoured to have struck the blow himself. He was famous for his lavish entertainment.

the 1812 war his Cossacks supported Bagration's army, fought at Borodino, and harried the French during the retreat.

Poniatowski, Jozef Antoni (1763–1813): Nephew of the last king of Poland, Stanislaw Poniatowski, he entered the Austrian military service in 1780, fought for Poland against the Russians in 1792, and joined Kosciuszko's insurrection in 1794, which ended in failure. In Napoleon's invasion of Russia, he commanded a 100,000-man Polish contingent which made up the fifth corps of the Grande Armée. Fought at Borodino, where his men stormed the Utitsa barrow. Made a marshal of the empire, he was killed defending the French rear at the battle of Leipzig.

Potemkin, Prince Grigori Alexandrovich (1739–91): Russian field marshal and statesman, the most important of Catherine the Great's lovers. Under his virtual leadership the boundaries of Russia were enlarged in the Ukraine and the Crimea, for the latter of which Catherine awarded him the title of prince of Tauride (the old name for the Crimea).

Pratzen heights: A key strategic high point on the battlefield of Austerlitz. Originally occupied by the French, who abandoned it in a simulation of fear, it was taken by the Russian-Austrian forces, who then swept down to attack the French left wing, allowing Marshal Soult to retake the heights and cut the allied troops in two, leading to their total defeat.

Prozorovsky, Alexander Alexandrovich (1732–1809): Russian field marshal under Catherine the Great, he retired to his estates, returned to become governor general of Moscow, and was then dismissed by Paul I. In 1808 he was recalled to service in the Turkish war, but asked to be replaced by Kutuzov. He died in the same year while crossing the Danube, and his body was transported and buried with honours in the Alexander Nevsky monastery in Petersburg.

Przebyszewski, Ignati Yakovlevich (1755–1810): Polish lieutenant general serving in the Russian army. At the battle of Austerlitz, he surrendered his column of Russian troops at the start of the action and was later court-martialled and broken to the ranks.

Pugachev, Emelyan Ivanovich (ca. 1740–75): Son of a Don Cossack leader. In 1773 he declared himself to be the emperor Peter III and organized a Cossack insurrection, which ignited the entire lower Volga region and was finally crushed in 1774 by General Mikhelson, with great loss of life.

Raevsky, Nikolai Nikolaevich (1771–1829): Russian general, became colonel when he was twenty, took part in the Polish and Turkish wars. Retired as major general for family reasons in 1801, but returned to duty in 1807 during the Austrian campaign, serving under Bagration. In 1812 he commanded the seventh infantry corps in Bagration's army, defended Smolensk for twenty-four hours against vastly superior forces, and at Borodino commanded the strategic position that came to be known as the Raevsky redoubt. Fought later at Maloyaroslavets and Krasnoe and in the European campaign.

Rapp, Jean (1771–1821): Served in the French republican Army of the Rhine, in 1796 became aide-de-camp to Dessaix, and took part in the campaign in Egypt. Followed Napoleon to Paris when the Consulat was declared. Fought in the Austrian campaigns and was made count of the empire in 1809. At Schönbrunn, on 12 October 1809, he prevented the young student Friedrich Staps from stabbing Napoleon. Unsuccessfully cautioned the emperor against invading Russia. Fought at Smolensk, was wounded four times at Borodino, nevertheless continued to fight at Maloyaroslavets, and supported Ney at the Berezina.

Rastophin (Rostopchin), Count Fyodor Vassilievich (1763–1826): Russian general and statesman, much favoured by Paul I, served as foreign minister, and was made count in 1799. In 1812 he was appointed governor general of Moscow, and was later blamed for the burning of the city in September of that year, the day after the French occupied it, but denied the charge. Fell into disgrace and moved abroad, where in 1823 he published a pamphlet in French justifying himself. Returned in 1825 to end his days in Petersburg.

Razumovsky, Prince Andrei Kirillovich (1752–1836): Son of Kirill Razumovsky, last hetman of the Ukraine, served as diplomat and for some years was Alexander's ambassador in Vienna, a crucial post during the Napoleonic era. Chief negotiator for Russia at the Congress of Vienna in 1814.

Repnin-Volkonsky, Prince Nikolai Grigorievich (1778–1845): Russian adjutant general and member of the State Council, governor of Saxony from 1813 to 1814, governor general of Little

Russia for eighteen years. Fought at Austerlitz, was gravely wounded and captured. On his recovery, Napoleon sent him to Alexander I with an offer to negotiate. Commanded a division in 1812 and fought later in the European campaign.

Rousseau, Jean-Jacques (1712–78): Born in Geneva, novelist, philosopher, and memoirist, his works were among the most widely read in the eighteenth century and his ideas had great influence on the development of social and educational theory in the Romantic period and later. Of major importance for Tolstoy.

Rumyantsev, Nikolai Petrovich (1754–1826): Russian statesman, served as minister of trade (1802–11) and chairman of the State Council (1810–12). As foreign minister, he advocated alliance with France. Suffered a stroke on learning of Napoleon's invasion in 1812; urged the dismissal of Kutuzov when he decided to abandon Moscow. Retired in 1814.

Saltykov, Prince Nikolai Ivanovich (1736–1816): Counsellor to Paul I before he assumed the throne and tutor to his sons, the future Alexander I and the grand duke Konstantin.

Savary, Anne Jean Marie René (1774–1833): Served in the early republican wars, and under Desaix in Egypt and at Marengo. Took part in the murder of the duke of Enghien. After the peace of Tilsit was sent to Petersburg as ambassador. Made duke of Rovigo in 1807, fought in Spain with Murat in 1808, and in 1810 took over the ministry of police, which he ran with inquisitorial vigour. After Waterloo, he accompanied Napoleon to England, but was not allowed to go with him to St. Helena.

Schelling, Friedrich Wilhelm Joseph von (1775–1854): German idealist philosopher midway between Fichte and Hegel, of a protean and unsystematic mind, wrote a *Naturphilosophie* admired as much for its poetry as for its thought.

Schöngraben: Scene of a battle on 14 November 1805, two weeks before Austerlitz, between the 45,000 troops of Murat and the 7,000 troops of Bagration's rear guard. Bagration's stiff defence of the position, followed by a skilful retreat, allowed Kutuzov time to join his main army with that of Buxhöwden. French historians refer to it as the battle of Hollabrunn, from the larger town nearby.

Schwarzenberg, Prince Karl Philipp (1771–1820): Austrian field marshal. Entered the cavalry in 1788, took part in the early battles against the French. In the 1805 campaign, at Ulm, when Mack was surrounded and chose to surrender, Schwarzenberg and his cavalry cut their way through the French lines. Sent as ambassador to Petersburg in 1808, he came back to fight at Wagram. In 1810 he went to Paris to negotiate Napoleon's marriage to Maria-Louisa of Austria. Reluctantly commanded an auxiliary corps under Napoleon in the Russian campaign. In 1813, when Austria decided to rejoin the anti-French coalition, he was made commander in chief of the army of Bohemia.

Semyonova, Nimfodora Semyonovna (1789–1876): Russian opera singer, made her début in 1807. Generally appreciated more for her acting than for her singing. The poets Pushkin, Griboedov, and Zhukovsky sought her company. She retired from the stage in the early 1830s.

Seslavin, Alexander Nikitich (1780–1858): A major general and partisan leader during the Napoleonic war. Fought in the Austrian campaigns. In 1812 distinguished himself at Borodino, and was instrumental in turning Napoleon's retreat from the Kaluga road to the Smolensk road at the battle of Maloyaroslavets. Later fought under Wittgenstein in the European campaign.

Shishkov, Alexander Semyonovich (1754–1841): Russian writer and statesman, a naval officer by training, retired in protest against the early liberal reforms of Alexander I. In 1811 he founded the Society of Lovers of the Russian Word, dedicated to preserving the old forms of Russian and purifying it of foreign influences, especially Gallicisms. In that same year, Alexander I, inspired by Shishkov's "Discourse on Love for One's Country," made him secretary of state. In 1813 he became president of the Russian Academy, in 1814 a member of the State Council, and later minister of education.

Sismondi, Jean Charles Léonard de (1773–1842): Swiss-born historian and economist of liberal leanings. His sixteen-volume *History of the Italian Republics in the Middle Ages*, published in 1817, brought him considerable fame.

Smolensk: Town on the Dnieper, on the road to Moscow, site of an important battle during the war of 1812 between the French under Bonaparte and the Russians under Bagration. The Russians fought a delaying action and then retreated; the town, a possible supply point for Napoleon, was virtually destroyed.

Sorbier, Jean Barthélemot de (1763–1827): Served in various parts of the French revolutionary army in the east of France; commanded three divisions of light artillery at Austerlitz, and later served in Spain. In 1808 Napoleon made him count of the empire; in 1811 he commanded the artillery of the imperial guard. Fought at Smolensk and Borodino during the 1812 campaign.

Soult, Nicolas Jean-de-Dieu (1769–1851): Served in the French republican Armies of the Rhine and the North; made major general in 1799. Fought in Switzerland under Masséna, whom he joined later in Italy, where he was taken prisoner at the siege of Genoa. In 1804 was made marshal of the empire. Fought at Austerlitz and Eylau, and was made duke of Dalmatia after the peace of Tilsit in 1807. Took part in all the campaigns in Spain and Portugal (1808–11), but in 1812 was defeated by Wellington at Salamanca.

Speransky, Mikhail Mikhailovich (1772–1839): Son of a village priest, educated at a Petersburg seminary, his intellectual abilities were quickly noticed, and he became secretary to Prince Kurakin. As adviser to the young Alexander I, he made plans for broad liberal reforms in Russia, with a code of law, a constitution, an assembly, and a state council, of which only the state council came into being (1810). From 1809 to 1812, Speransky was the most powerful man in Russia, but owing to the "French" tendencies of his reforms, he fell into disfavour and was accused of treason and exiled. His ideas continued to influence later Russian reformers.

Stein, Baron Heinrich Friedrich Karl von (1757–1831): German statesman who went into service in Prussia. After the peace of Tilsit (1807), which was disastrous for Prussia, Stein, who had been a severe critic of Prussian policy, was called by the king to serve with very broad powers and for a time became virtual dictator, but was forced to flee by Napoleon, who confiscated his lands. In 1812 Alexander I invited him to Petersburg, and after the French retreat, Stein urged the emperor to continue the war in Europe.

Stroganov, Count Pavel Alexandrovich (1774–1817): Russian general and statesman, one of the four members of the privy committee that advised Alexander I on liberal reform at the start of his reign. Commanded an infantry division during the war with Napoleon.

Sukhtelen, Pavel Pavlovich (1788–1833): Russian general. At the age of seventeen he took part in Depreradovich's famous cavalry charge at Austerlitz, was gravely wounded and taken prisoner. He went on to fight against Napoleon in 1807, and in 1811 was sent on a diplomatic mission to London. Became adjutant general in 1828.

Suvorov, Alexander Vassilievich (1729–1800): Known as "the general who never lost a battle," gained the highest distinctions in service to Catherine the Great, was dismissed by Paul I, then called back to fight against the French revolutionary forces in northern Italy, where he won a string of brilliant victories. Betrayed by the Austrians in Switzerland, he was forced to retreat over the Alps, which ironically became his most famous deed, and for the success of which he was promoted to generalissimo. He was promised a military triumph in Petersburg, but on his return in 1800, the emperor cancelled it and refused to see him. Suvorov died a few days later.

Talleyrand-Périgord, Charles-Maurice de (1754–1838): Bishop of Autun under the ancien régime, member of the Constituent Assembly (1791), became a constitutional bishop, then abandoned the Church altogether. Was minister of foreign relations under the Directoire, the Consulat, and the empire. Rallied to the Bourbons in 1814, and played a brilliant role at the Congress of Vienna (1814–15), where he was chief negotiator for France.

Tarutino: Scene of a battle on 6 October 1812 between Russian troops under Bennigsen and Miloradovich and Murat's 20,000-man corps. The Russians attacked by surprise and took the camp, many prisoners, and thirty-eight guns, but Murat's troops re-formed and returned fire, killing Bagovut among others, and eventually managed to retreat.

Thiers, Adolphe (1797–1877): French historian and liberal politician, author of *A History of the French Revolution* (1823–7) and *A History of the Consulate and the Empire* (1845–62). Thomas Carlyle said of his historical accuracy: "He is a brisk man, who will tell you much if you know nothing"—an opinion Tolstoy shared. He served in various capacities during the various governments of the time.

Tilsit: Two treaties were signed at Tilsit in 1807, after Napoleon's victory at Friedland, the first between Napoleon and Alexander I, on 7 July, on a raft in the middle of the Niemen; the second between Napoleon and Friedrich-Wilhelm III of Prussia, on 9 July, stripping Prussia of nearly half its territory.

Toll, Karl Fyodorovich von (1777–1842): Russian infantry general, fought in Switzerland under Suvorov, took part in the Austrian and Turkish campaigns (1805–9), in 1810 became part of the emperor's suite. Served as quartermaster general in the 1812 war, and as quartermaster general of imperial headquarters in the European campaign.

Tolstoy, Count Pyotr Alexandrovich (1769–1844): Entered the army in 1785, took part in the Russo-Swedish war of 1789–90, and served under Suvorov in Poland from 1792 to 1795 and later in the Italian and Swiss campaigns. In 1797 he was made adjutant general to the emperor Paul I. Ambassador to France from October 1807 to October 1808, he was recalled to Russia because of his criticisms of Napoleon and the treaty of Tilsit.

Tormasov, Count Alexander Petrovich (1752–1819): A major general during the Russo-Turkish war of 1787–92, fought in Poland in 1794, in 1804–11 was commander in chief in Georgia and the Caucasus, and was made a member of the State Council in 1811. In 1812 he commanded the third Russian army, in 1814 was appointed military governor of Moscow, and in 1816 was made a count.

Toulon: Port city in southern France, occupied by English and Spanish forces in 1793, besieged for four months by the French revolutionary army. Napoleon, as captain of artillery, first made his name there by placing his guns in such a way as to force the Royal Navy ships to withdraw, after which the resistance collapsed and the city was taken.

Tuchkov, Alexander Alexeevich (1777–1812): Youngest of the three Tuchkov brothers who fought in the Napoleonic wars. In 1812 he was a general in command of a brigade of the third infantry under his brother Pavel. At Borodino, in defence of Bagration's flèches, he seized a standard, led the Reval regiment in a bayonet attack under French canister shot, and was killed.

Ulm: A town in Württemberg where, on 16 October 1805, Napoleon won a great tactical victory by surrounding the forces of the Austrian general Mack, who surrendered with 30,000 men.

Uvarov, Fyodor Petrovich (1773–1824): Cavalry general; became close to Alexander I and accompanied him on his walks. Fought at Austerlitz, where he commanded a horse-guard regiment and covered the Russian retreat. Went with the emperor to Tilsit and Erfurt. Commanded the first cavalry corps in 1812, distinguished himself at Borodino, supported Miloradovich during the French retreat, and fought in the European campaign.

Vandamme, Dominique-Joseph René (1770–1830): Became a brigadier general at twenty-three, serving in the Army of the North. Fought in the Austrian campaign, commanded a division under Marshal Soult, led the assault on the Pratzen heights at Austerlitz, and took the village of Augesd. Quarrels with Napoleon's brother Jérôme kept him out of the 1812 campaign, but he returned to service in 1813.

Villeneuve, Pierre-Charles de (1763–1806): Joined the French navy in 1778, served in the West Indies, then accompanied Napoleon's expedition to Egypt. A rear admiral in 1796, his ship escaped destruction in the battle of the Nile against Admiral Nelson, but he was reprimanded for the defeat. In 1805 his fleet ran into Nelson's off Cape Trafalgar and was destroyed. Villeneuve committed suicide shortly afterwards.

Volkonsky, Prince Pyotr Mikhailovich (1776–1852): Participated in the plot to remove Paul I; became a close adviser to Alexander I. Was adjutant general in 1805, first in Buxhöwden's army, then in Kutuzov's, and fought at Austerlitz. Joined the emperor's suite in 1812, became army chief of staff, and from 1813 to 1823 was chief of the general staff with the rank of field marshal.

Voltaire, François-Marie Arouet, known as (1694–1778): French poet, dramatist, and philosopher. His *Lettres philosophiques* (1734), of a rationalist and antimetaphysical tendency, placed him in the forefront of the philosophical movement of his time, as did his "philosophical tales," the most famous of which is *Candide* (1759), his *Dictionnaire philosophique* (1764), and his contributions to the *Encyclopédie* of Diderot and d'Alembert.

Vyazma: Name of both a river and a town which was the scene of a battle on 3 November 1812, during the French retreat, in which the French rear guard was defeated by Miloradovich, who failed to destroy Davout's first corps, but initiated the disorder from which the French never recovered.

Vyazmitinov, Sergei Kuzmich (1744–1819): Fought in the first two Russo-Turkish wars, in 1796 became governor of Little Russia, in 1797 commander of the Peter and Paul fortress in Petersburg, but in 1799 was dismissed by Paul I. In 1801 he was reappointed governor of Little Russia, and in 1802 became the first Russian minister of defence. Was left in command of Petersburg when Alexander went to the front in 1805, and during the emperor's later absences. In 1811 he became a member of the State Council.

Weyrother, Franz Ritter von (1754–1807): Austrian general, chief of staff of the Austrian army in 1805, author of the allied battle plan for Austerlitz.

Wimpfen, Baron Maximilian von (1770–1854): Austrian general, took part in the Italian campaign against the French and fought at Arcole; in 1805 fought at Austerlitz under Liechtenstein. In 1813, when Austria joined the anti-French forces, fought at Leipzig and was made field marshal.

Wintzingerode, Ferdinand Ferdinandovich (1770–1818): Born in Saxony, entered the Austrian army in 1790, joined Suvorov in the Italian campaign of 1796, and was made adjutant to the grand duke Konstantin. In 1802 he became major general and adjutant to Alexander I. Took part in the Austrian campaign, and in 1809 rejoined the Austrian army. In 1812 he returned to the Russian army and later fought in the European campaign.

Wittgenstein, Prince Pyotr Khristianovich (1769–1843): Russian general of Prussian origin, fought at Austerlitz in 1805, at Friedland in 1807, and at the beginning of the war of 1812 was sent by Barclay de Tolly to command a mobile corps protecting the road to Petersburg. Later took part in the European campaign, and distinguished himself at the battle of Leipzig.

Wolzogen, Ludwig (1774–1845): Prussian general and military theoretician, entered Russian service in 1807 and was attached to general headquarters. He and Pfuel made up the plan for the 1812 campaign. Later accused of treason by the Russian military.

Württemberg, Alexander Friedrich, Duke of (1771–1833): Brother of the empress Maria Feodorovna. Entered Russian military service in 1800 as a cavalry general, took part in the 1812 war and the European campaigns of 1813–14.

Zubov, Prince Platon Alexandrovich (1767–1822): The last of Catherine the Great's lovers, he became enormously wealthy through her gifts, but was of a capricious and unstable nature. Ended his days in total seclusion on one of his many estates.

SUMMARY

VOLUME I

Part One

I–IV. Petersburg. A soirée at Anna Pavlovna Scherer's. Arrival of Prince Vassily Kuragin, his daughter Hélène, his son Ippolit, Princess Lise Bolkonsky, and Pierre Bezukhov, with other guests. Conversations about Napoleon and various society topics. Arrival of Prince Andrei Bolkonsky.

V–VI. Pierre goes to supper at Prince Andrei's and then to Anatole Kuragin's. The bet with Dolokhov.

VII–XI. Moscow. A name-day party at the Rostovs'. Anna Mikhailovna Drubetskoy and her son Boris. Natasha and Boris. Nikolai and Sonya.

XII–XIII. Anna Mikhailovna and Boris go to see the gravely ill Count Kirill Bezukhov. Prince Vassily and Pierre are there.

XIV. The countess Rostov and Anna Mikhailovna.

XV–XVII. Celebrations at the Rostovs'. Marya Dmitrievna Akhrosimov. The young Rostovs. "The Spring" and the "Daniel Cooper."

XVIII–XXI. Prince Vassily and Catiche at Count Bezukhov's. Anna Mikhailovna and Pierre arrive. The dispute over the inlaid portfolio.

XXII. At Bald Hills. The old prince. Marya and Julie exchange letters.

XXIII–XXIV. Prince Andrei brings the pregnant little princess to Bald Hills. The old prince's discourse on "Buonaparte."

XXV. Prince Andrei leaves for the army. Princess Marya gives him an icon. He parts from the little princess.

Part Two

I–II. Kutuzov reviews the troops at Braunau.

III. Prince Andrei in Kutuzov's headquarters. The unfortunate General Mack.

IV–V. Nikolai Rostov with Denisov. Telyanin and the stolen purse. Discussion and disapproval among the officers.

VI–VIII. Kutuzov falls back towards Vienna as the French advance. Crossing the Enns. Nikolai sees action for the first time.

IX–XII. Kutuzov sends Prince Andrei to the Austrian court in Brünn. Conversation with Bilibin. Morning with Bilibin, Ippolit Kuragin, and other diplomats. Prince Andrei is received by the emperor Franz. Bilibin's story of the bridge at Tabor.

XIII–XIV. Prince Andrei reports to Kutuzov. Bagration sent to Hollabrunn. Murat criticized by Napoleon.

XV–XVI. Prince Andrei reports to Bagration. Captain Tushin. Prince Andrei surveys the battlefield at Schöngraben. The action begins.

XVII–XX. The battle of Schöngraben. Nikolai is hurt. Persistence of Tushin's battery. Prince Andrei orders him to retreat.

XXI. The Russian forces withdraw. Tushin summoned before Bagration. Prince Andrei defends him.

Part Three

I–II. Prince Vassily and Pierre. Pierre well received at Anna Pavlovna's soirée. Hélène's name-day party. Pierre gets married.

III–V. Prince Vassily and Anatole visit the old prince Bolkonsky at Bald Hills. The courting of Princess Marya. Anatole and Mlle Bourienne in the conservatory.

VI. The Rostovs receive a letter from Nikolai.

VII. Nikolai in Kutuzov's camp at Olmütz. Visits Boris and Berg. Run-in with Prince Andrei.

VIII. Review of the Russian army by the emperors Alexander and Franz. Nikolai's enthusiasm.

IX. Boris visits Prince Andrei in Olmütz. They meet with Prince Dolgorukov.

X. Nikolai out of the action at Wischau. He sees the emperor Alexander again.

XI. The build-up to battle. Dolgorukov's views, Kutuzov's displeasure.

XII. The Russian-Austrian council of war. Weyrother's plan of battle. Kutuzov falls asleep. Prince Andrei debates with himself.

XIII. Rostov on the picket line with Bagration's army. Drowsy thoughts. Bagration and Dolgorukov disagree. Napoleon's orders to his army.

XIV–XIX. The battle of Austerlitz. Prince Andrei gravely wounded. Napoleon and the infinite sky.

VOLUME II

Part One

I. Nikolai brings Denisov home to Moscow on leave.

II. Count Ilya Andreich arranges a banquet for Bagration at the English Club.

III. The festivities begin. Bagration arrives.

IV. Pierre challenges Dolokhov to a duel.

V. The duel.

VI. Pierre's ruminations. He breaks with Hélène and leaves for Petersburg.

VII. At Bald Hills two months after Austerlitz. Prince Andrei presumed dead.

VIII–IX. The little princess goes into labour. Prince Andrei arrives. Lise dies giving birth to a son. Lise is buried and Prince Nikolai Andreevich is baptized.

X–XII. Dolokhov recovers in Moscow. The Rostovs come from the country for the winter season. Denisov and Dolokhov frequent the house. Courtships at Christmastime. The young people's ball at Iogel's.

XIII–XIV. Card playing at Dolokhov's. Nikolai loses heavily.

XV–XVI. Nikolai returns home. The party. Natasha sings. Nikolai's talk with his father. Denisov proposes to Natasha. Nikolai rejoins his regiment in Poland.

Part Two

I–II. Pierre meets the Mason Bazdeev.

III–IV. Pierre and Willarski. Pierre inducted into the Masons.

V. Pierre throws Prince Vassily out.

VI–VII. Soirée at Anna Pavlovna's after Prussian defeats at Jena and Auerstädt. Hélène befriends Boris Drubetskoy.

VIII–IX. Prince Andrei at Bald Hills. The baby's illness. Letters from the old prince and Bilibin.

Part Three

Part Four

Part Five

VOLUME III

Part One

Part Two

XXXIII–XXXIV. Napoleon during the battle. His generals ask for reinforcements. He reflects on the difference between this battle and all his previous ones.

XXXV. Kutuzov at the battle. Bagration wounded. Kutuzov shouts at Wolzogen. His certainty of victory.

XXXVI. Prince Andrei's regiment in reserve behind Semyonovskoe. Steady losses under artillery fire. Prince Andrei is wounded and taken to a dressing station.

XXXVII. Next to Prince Andrei a man has his leg amputated. Prince Andrei recognizes Anatole Kuragin. Pity and love.

XXXVIII. Napoleon looks at the bloody battlefield. A moment of insight. His later accounts of the battle.

XXXIX. Further reflections on the battle. Moral victory of the Russians.

Part Three

I. Achilles and the tortoise. The search for the laws of historical movement.

II. General reflections on the Russian retreat after Borodino and the role of the commander in chief.

III. Kutuzov and his generals on Poklonnaya Hill. Kutuzov's inner debate.

IV. The council of war in a peasant's cottage in Fili, viewed by the peasant's little daughter. Kutuzov's decision.

V. Thoughts on the abandoning and burning of Moscow. Rastopchin's role.

VI–VII. Hélène in Petersburg. Two suitors. Her conversion to Catholicism. The question of remarriage. Bilibin's views. She writes to Pierre.

VIII. Pierre after Borodino. Return to Mozhaisk with foot soldiers.

IX. Pierre's recollections and dreams at night in Mozhaisk. Return to Moscow.

X–XI. Pierre summoned to Rastopchin. The new poster. Vereshchagin and Klyucharev. Pierre's talk with Rastopchin. He disappears from home.

XII. The Rostovs in Moscow as the French approach. Late preparations for departure.

XIII. A convoy of wounded arrives. Natasha invites them to stay in their house.

XIV. The Rostovs packing. Another wounded man. He turns out to be Prince Andrei.

XV–XVII. Moscow's last day. The wounded ask to leave in some of the Rostovs' carts. A visit from Berg. Family conflict. Natasha insists that they unpack and give the carts to the wounded. Sonya discovers that Prince Andrei is in their train. They meet Pierre on their way out of Moscow.

XVIII. Pierre's recent days in Bazdeev's house. The mad Makar Alexeevich and the servant Gerasim. Pierre goes to buy a pistol.

XIX. The Russian troops leave Moscow. Napoleon on Poklonnaya Hill. *Le ridicule.*

XX. Moscow as an abandoned beehive.

XXI. Shops looted by departing Russian troops.

XXII. Mavra Kuzminishna helps a Rostov relative.

XXIII. Street scenes before the French arrive.

XXIV. Count Rastopchin in abandoned Moscow.

XXV. Count Rastopchin seeks a victim. He speaks to the mob. The killing of Vereshchagin. Rastopchin flees Moscow. His meeting with Kutuzov.

XXVI. The French enter Moscow. Moral collapse. Reflections on the burning of Moscow.

XXVII. Pierre at Bazdeev's. His plan to assassinate Napoleon. Indecision. Makar Alexeevich gets hold of the pistol. French officers come in.

XXVIII. Pierre saves the French captain's life. The captain befriends him.

XXIX. Pierre and Captain Ramballe talk over dinner. Pierre loses his resolve to kill Napoleon.

XXX. The glow of the first Moscow fires seen from Mytishchi, where the Rostovs have stopped.

XXXI. The Rostovs' reactions to the burning of Moscow. Natasha has learned that Prince Andrei is with them. While the family sleeps, she goes to him.

XXXII. Prince Andrei's inner state and thoughts in the days prior to seeing Natasha. Their meeting.

VOLUME IV

Part One

Part Two

Part Three

Part Four

EPILOGUE

Part One

I–IV. Seven years later. General thoughts on the war of 1812 and its historical representations. Chance and genius. Reasons for the movements of peoples. The role of great men.

V–VII. Marriage of Pierre and Natasha. Death of Count Ilya Andreich. Nikolai in straitened circumstances. Princess Marya comes to Moscow. Strained meeting with Nikolai. They marry and move to Bald Hills. Nikolai takes up estate management in earnest.

VIII–XVI. Life at Bald Hills. The feast of St. Nicholas in 1820. Pierre and Natasha visit Bald Hills. Gifts and children. Young Nikolai Bolkonsky listens to a political discussion between Pierre and Nikolai. Intimate conversation between Nikolai and Princess Marya. Her diary. Intimate conversation between Pierre and Natasha. Young Nikolai Bolkonsky's dream. Mucius Scaevola. Thoughts of Pierre and of his father.

Part Two

I–XII. Reflections on history and historians, greatness and power, freedom and necessity.

THE HISTORY OF VINTAGE

The famous American publisher Alfred A. Knopf (1892–1984) founded Vintage Books in the United States in 1954 as a paperback home for the authors published by his company. Vintage was launched in the United Kingdom in 1990 and works independently from the American imprint although both are part of the international publishing group, Random House.

Vintage in the United Kingdom was initially created to publish paperback editions of books acquired by the prestigious hardback imprints in the Random House Group such as Jonathan Cape, Chatto & Windus, Hutchinson and later William Heinemann, Secker & Warburg and The Harvill Press. There are many Booker and Nobel Prize-winning authors on the Vintage list and the imprint publishes a huge variety of fiction and non-fiction. Over the years Vintage has expanded and the list now includes both great authors of the past – who are published under the Vintage Classics imprint – as well as many of the most influential authors of the present.

For a full list of the books Vintage publishes, please visit our website
www.vintage-books.co.uk

For book details and other information about the classic authors we publish, please visit the Vintage Classics website
www.vintage-classics.info

www.vintage-classics.info